A STORM OF SWORDS

BY GEORGE R. R. MARTIN

A SONG OF ICE AND FIRE
Book One: *A Game of Thrones*
Book Two: *A Clash of Kings*
Book Three: *A Storm of Swords*
Book Four: *A Feast for Crows*
Book Five: *A Dance with Dragons*

Dying of the Light
Windhaven (with Lisa Tuttle)
Fevre Dream
The Armageddon Rag
Dead Man's Hand (with John J. Miller)

SHORT STORY COLLECTIONS
Dreamsongs, Volume I
Dreamsongs, Volume II
A Song of Lya and Other Stories
Songs of Stars and Shadows
Sandkings
Songs the Dead Men Sing
Nightflyers
Tuf Voyaging
Portraits of His Children
Quartet

EDITED BY GEORGE R. R. MARTIN
New Voices in Science Fiction, Volumes 1–4
The Science Fiction Weight-Loss Book
(with Isaac Asimov and Martin Harry Greenberg)
The John W. Campbell Awards, Volume 5
Night Visions 3
Wild Card I–XXI

A STORM
OF
SWORDS

BOOK THREE OF
A SONG OF ICE AND FIRE

GEORGE R. R. MARTIN

BANTAM BOOKS
NEW YORK

2011 Bantam Books Trade Paperback Edition

Copyright © 2000 by George R. R. Martin
Excerpt from *A Feast for Crows* copyright © 2005 by George R. R. Martin
All rights reserved.

Published in the United States by Bantam Books, an imprint of The Random House Publishing Group, a division of Random House, Inc., New York.

BANTAM BOOKS and the rooster colophon are registered trademarks of Random House, Inc.

Originally published in hardcover in the United States by Bantam Spectra, a division of Random House, Inc., in 2000.

Library of Congress Cataloging-in-Publication Data
Martin, George R. R.
A clash of kings : book three of A song of ice and fire / George R. R. Martin.
p. cm. — (A song of ice and fire, bk. 3)
ISBN 978-0-553-38170-2
eBook ISBN 978-0-553-89787-6
I. Title. II. Series: Martin, George R. R. Song of ice and fire, bk. 3.
PS3563.A7239S7 2000
813'.54—dc21   00-60827

Maps by James Sinclair
Heraldic crests by Virginia Norey

Printed in the United States of America

www.bantamdell.com

19 18 17

Design by James Sinclair

A NOTE ON CHRONOLOGY

A Song of Ice and Fire is told through the eyes of characters who are sometimes hundreds or even thousands of miles apart from one another. Some chapters cover a day, some only an hour; others might span a fortnight, a month, half a year. With such a structure, the narrative cannot be strictly sequential; sometimes important things are happening simultaneously, a thousand leagues apart.

In the case of the volume now in hand, the reader should realize that the opening chapters of *A Storm of Swords* do not follow the closing chapters of *A Clash of Kings* so much as overlap them. I open with a look at some of the things that were happening on the Fist of the First Men, at Riverrun, Harrenhal, and on the Trident while the Battle of the Blackwater was being fought at King's Landing, and during its aftermath . . .

George R.R. Martin

for Phyllis
who made me put the dragons in

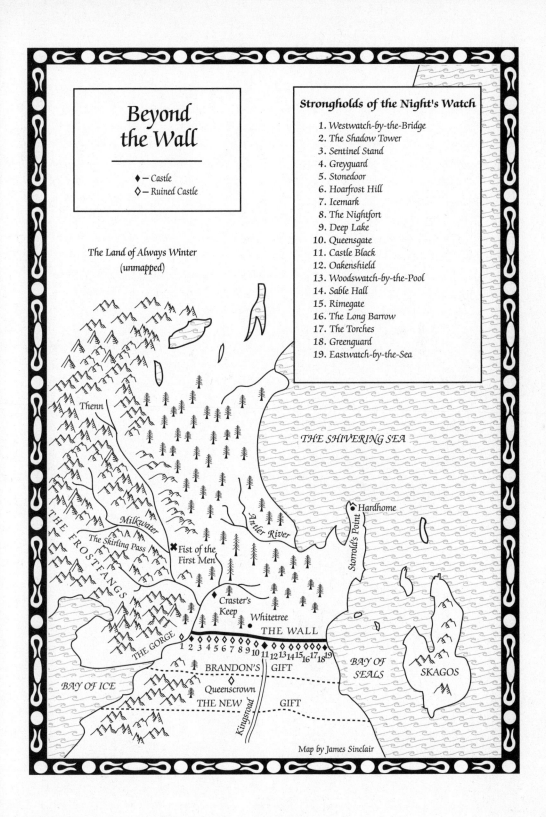

Beyond the Wall

◆ — Castle
◇ — Ruined Castle

The Land of Always Winter
(unmapped)

Strongholds of the Night's Watch

1. Westwatch-by-the-Bridge
2. The Shadow Tower
3. Sentinel Stand
4. Greyguard
5. Stonedoor
6. Hoarfrost Hill
7. Icemark
8. The Nightfort
9. Deep Lake
10. Queensgate
11. Castle Black
12. Oakenshield
13. Woodswatch-by-the-Pool
14. Sable Hall
15. Rimegate
16. The Long Barrow
17. The Torches
18. Greenguard
19. Eastwatch-by-the-Sea

THE SHIVERING SEA

Thenn

Milkwater

THE FROSTFANGS

The Skirling Pass

✖ Fist of the First Men

Antler River

Hardhome

Storrold's Point

◆ Craster's Keep

● Whitetree

THE WALL

THE GORGE

◆ ◇ ◇ ◇ ◇ ◇ ◇ ◇ ◆ ◇ ◇ ◇ ◇ ◇ ◇ ◆
1 2 3 4 5 6 7 8 9 10 11 12 13 14 15 16 17 18 19

BAY OF SEALS

SKAGOS

BRANDON'S GIFT

◇ Queenscrown

THE NEW GIFT

BAY OF ICE

Kingsroad

Map by James Sinclair

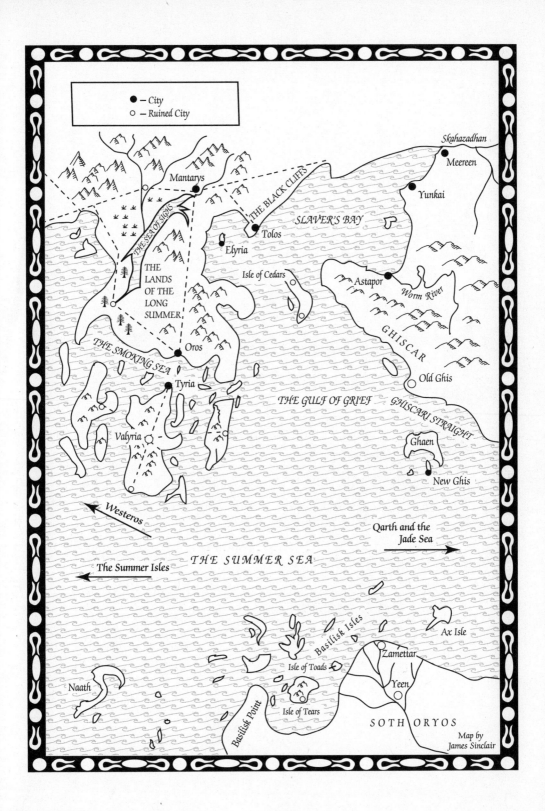

PROLOGUE

The day was grey and bitter cold, and the dogs would not take the scent.

The big black bitch had taken one sniff at the bear tracks, backed off, and skulked back to the pack with her tail between her legs. The dogs huddled together miserably on the riverbank as the wind snapped at them. Chett felt it too, biting through his layers of black wool and boiled leather. It was too bloody cold for man or beast, but here they were. His mouth twisted, and he could almost feel the boils that covered his cheeks and neck growing red and angry. *I should be safe back at the Wall, tending the bloody ravens and making fires for old Maester Aemon.* It was the bastard Jon Snow who had taken that from him, him and his fat friend Sam Tarly. It was their fault he was here, freezing his bloody balls off with a pack of hounds deep in the haunted forest.

"Seven hells." He gave the leashes a hard yank to get the dogs' attention. "*Track*, you bastards. That's a bear print. You want some meat or no? *Find!*" But the hounds only huddled closer, whining. Chett snapped his short lash above their heads, and the black bitch snarled at him. "Dog meat would taste as good as bear," he warned her, his breath frosting with every word.

Lark the Sisterman stood with his arms crossed over his chest and his hands tucked up into his armpits. He wore black wool gloves, but he was always complaining how his fingers were frozen. "It's too bloody cold to hunt," he said. "Bugger this bear, he's not worth freezing over."

"We can't go back emptyhand, Lark," rumbled Small Paul through the brown whiskers that covered most of his face. "The Lord Commander wouldn't like that." There was ice under the big man's squashed pug nose, where his snot had frozen. A huge hand in a thick fur glove clenched tight around the shaft of a spear.

"Bugger that Old Bear too," said the Sisterman, a thin man with sharp features and nervous eyes. "Mormont will be dead before daybreak, remember? Who cares what he likes?"

Small Paul blinked his black little eyes. Maybe he *had* forgotten, Chett thought; he was stupid enough to forget most anything. "Why do we have to kill the Old Bear? Why don't we just go off and let him be?"

"You think he'll let *us* be?" said Lark. "He'll hunt us down. You want to be hunted, you great muttonhead?"

"No," said Small Paul. "I don't want that. I don't."

"So you'll kill him?" said Lark.

"Yes." The huge man stamped the butt of his spear on the frozen riverbank. "I will. He shouldn't hunt us."

The Sisterman took his hands from his armpits and turned to Chett. "We need to kill *all* the officers, I say."

Chett was sick of hearing it. "We been over this. The Old Bear dies, and Blane from the Shadow Tower. Grubbs and Aethan as well, their ill luck for drawing the watch, Dywen and Bannen for their tracking, and Ser Piggy for the ravens. That's *all*. We kill them quiet, while they sleep. One scream and we're wormfood, every one of us." His boils were red with rage. "Just do your bit and see that your cousins do theirs. And Paul, try and remember, it's *third* watch, not second."

"Third watch," the big man said, through hair and frozen snot. "Me and Softfoot. I remember, Chett."

The moon would be black tonight, and they had jiggered the watches so as to have eight of their own standing sentry, with two more guarding the horses. It wasn't going to get much riper than that. Besides, the wildlings could be upon them any day now. Chett meant to be well away from here before that happened. He meant to live.

Three hundred sworn brothers of the Night's Watch had ridden north, two hundred from Castle Black and another hundred from the Shadow Tower. It was the biggest ranging in living memory, near a third of the Watch's strength. They meant to find Ben Stark, Ser Waymar Royce, and the other rangers who'd gone missing, and discover why the wildlings were leaving their villages. Well, they were no closer to Stark and Royce than when they'd left the Wall, but they'd learned where all the wildlings had gone – up into the icy heights of the godsforsaken Frostfangs. They could squat up there till the end of time and it wouldn't prick Chett's boils none.

But no. They were coming down. Down the Milkwater.

Chett raised his eyes and there it was. The river's stony banks were bearded by ice, its pale milky waters flowing endlessly down out of the Frostfangs. And now Mance Rayder and his wildlings were flowing down the same way. Thoren Smallwood had returned in a lather three days past. While he was telling the Old Bear what his scouts had seen, his man Kedge Whiteye told the rest of them. "They're still well up the foothills, but they're coming," Kedge said, warming his hands over the fire. "Harma the Dogshead has the van, the poxy bitch. Goady crept up on her camp and saw her plain by the fire. That fool Tumberjon wanted to pick her off with an arrow, but Smallwood had better sense."

Chett spat. "How many were there, could you tell?"

"Many and more. Twenty, thirty thousand, we didn't stay to count. Harma had five hundred in the van, every one ahorse."

The men around the fire exchanged uneasy looks. It was a rare thing to find even a dozen mounted wildlings, and *five hundred* . . .

"Smallwood sent Bannen and me wide around the van to catch a peek at the main body," Kedge went on. "There was no end of them. They're moving slow as a frozen river, four, five miles a day, but they don't look like they mean to go back to their villages neither. More'n half were women and children, and they were driving their animals before them, goats, sheep, even aurochs dragging sledges. They'd loaded up with bales of fur and sides of meat, cages of chickens, butter churns and spinning wheels, every damn thing they own. The mules and garrons was so heavy laden you'd think their backs would break. The women as well."

"And they follow the Milkwater?" Lark the Sisterman asked.

"I said so, didn't I?"

The Milkwater would take them past the Fist of the First Men, the ancient ringfort where the Night's Watch had made its camp. Any man with a thimble of sense could see that it was time to pull up stakes and fall back on the Wall. The Old Bear had strengthened the Fist with spikes and pits and caltrops, but against such a host all that was pointless. If they stayed here, they would be engulfed and overwhelmed.

And Thoren Smallwood wanted to *attack*. Sweet Donnel Hill was squire to Ser Mallador Locke, and the night before last Smallwood had come to Locke's tent. Ser Mallador had been of the same mind as old Ser Ottyn Wythers, urging a retreat on the Wall, but Smallwood wanted to convince him otherwise. "This King-beyond-the-Wall will never look for us so far north," Sweet Donnel reported him saying. "And this great host of his is a shambling horde, full of useless mouths who won't know what end of a sword to hold. One blow will take all the fight out of them and send them howling back to their hovels for another fifty years."

Three hundred against thirty thousand. Chett called that rank madness, and what was madder still was that Ser Mallador had been persuaded, and the two of them together were on the point of persuading the Old Bear. "If we wait too long, this chance may be lost, never to come again," Smallwood was saying to anyone who would listen. Against that, Ser Ottyn Wythers said, "We are the shield that guards the realms of men. You do not throw away your shield for no good purpose," but to that Thoren Smallwood said, "In a swordfight, a man's surest defense is the swift stroke that slays his foe, not cringing behind a shield."

Neither Smallwood nor Wythers had the command, though. Lord Mormont did, and Mormont was waiting for his other scouts, for Jarman Buckwell and the men who'd climbed the Giant's Stair, and for Qhorin Halfhand and Jon Snow, who'd gone to probe the Skirling Pass. Buckwell and the Halfhand were late in returning, though. *Dead, most like.* Chett pictured Jon Snow lying blue and frozen on some bleak mountaintop with a wildling spear up his bastard's arse. The thought made him smile. *I hope they killed his bloody wolf as well.*

"There's no bear here," he decided abruptly. "Just an old print, that's all. Back to the Fist." The dogs almost yanked him off his feet, as eager to get back as he was. Maybe they thought they were going to get fed. Chett had to laugh. He hadn't fed them for three days now, to turn them mean and hungry. Tonight, before slipping off into the dark, he'd turn them loose among the horse lines, after Sweet Donnel Hill and Clubfoot Karl cut the tethers. *They'll have snarling hounds and panicked horses all over the Fist, running through fires, jumping the ringwall, and trampling down tents.* With all the confusion, it might be hours before anyone noticed that fourteen brothers were missing.

Lark had wanted to bring in twice that number, but what could you expect from some stupid fishbreath Sisterman? Whisper a word in the wrong ear and before you knew it you'd be short a head. No, fourteen was a good number, enough to do what needed doing but not so many that they couldn't keep the secret. Chett had recruited most of them himself. Small Paul was one of his; the strongest man on the Wall, even if he was slower than a dead snail. He'd once broken a wildling's back with a hug. They had Dirk as well, named for his favorite weapon, and the little grey man the brothers called Softfoot, who'd raped a hundred women in his youth, and liked to boast how none had never seen nor heard him until he shoved it up inside them.

The plan was Chett's. He was the clever one; he'd been steward to old Maester Aemon for four good years before that bastard Jon Snow had done him out so his job could be handed to his fat pig of a friend. When he killed Sam Tarly tonight, he planned to whisper, "Give my love to Lord Snow," right in his ear before he sliced Ser Piggy's throat open to let the blood come bubbling out through all those layers of suet. Chett knew the ravens, so he wouldn't have no trouble there, no more than he would with Tarly. One touch of the knife and that craven would piss his pants and start blubbering for his life. *Let him beg, it won't do him no good.* After he opened his throat, he'd open the cages and shoo the birds away, so no messages reached the Wall. Softfoot and Small Paul would kill the Old Bear, Dirk would do Blane, and Lark and his cousins would silence Bannen and old Dywen, to keep them from sniffing after their trail. They'd been caching food for a fortnight, and Sweet Donnel and Clubfoot Karl would have the horses ready. With Mormont dead, command would pass to Ser Ottyn Wythers, an old done man, and failing. *He'll be running for the Wall before sundown, and he won't waste no men sending them after us neither.*

The dogs pulled at him as they made their way through the trees. Chett could see the Fist punching its way up through the green. The day was so dark that the Old Bear had the torches lit, a great circle of them burning all along the ringwall that crowned the top of the steep stony hill. The three of them waded across a brook. The water was icy cold, and patches of ice were spreading across its surface. "I'm going to make for the coast," Lark the Sisterman confided. "Me and my cousins. We'll build us a boat, sail back home to the Sisters."

And at home they'll know you for deserters and lop off your fool heads, thought Chett. There was no leaving the Night's Watch, once you said your words. Anywhere in the Seven Kingdoms, they'd take you and kill you.

Ollo Lophand now, he was talking about sailing back to Tyrosh, where he claimed men didn't lose their hands for a bit of honest thievery, nor get sent off to freeze their life away for being found in bed with some knight's wife. Chett had weighed going with him, but he didn't speak their wet girly tongue. And what could he do in Tyrosh? He had no trade to speak of, growing up in Hag's Mire. His father had spent his life grubbing in other men's fields and collecting leeches. He'd strip down bare but for a thick leather clout, and go wading in the murky waters. When he climbed out he'd be covered from nipple to ankle. Sometimes he made Chett help pull the leeches off. One had attached itself to his palm once, and he'd smashed it against a wall in revulsion. His father beat him bloody for that. The maesters bought the leeches at twelve-for-a-penny.

Lark could go home if he liked, and the damn Tyroshi too, but not Chett. If he never saw Hag's Mire again, it would be too bloody soon. He had liked the look of Craster's Keep, himself. Craster lived high as a lord there, so why shouldn't he do the same? That would be a laugh. Chett the leechman's son, a lord with a keep. His banner could be a dozen leeches on a field of pink. But why stop at lord? Maybe he should be a king. *Mance Rayder started out a crow. I could be a king same as him, and have me some wives.* Craster had nineteen, not even counting the young ones, the daughters he hadn't gotten around to bedding yet. Half them wives were as old and ugly as Craster, but that didn't matter. The old ones Chett could put to work cooking and cleaning for him, pulling carrots and slopping pigs, while the young ones warmed his bed and bore his children. Craster wouldn't object, not once Small Paul gave him a hug.

The only women Chett had ever known were the whores he'd bought in Mole's Town. When he'd been younger, the village girls took one look at his face, with its boils and its wen, and turned away sickened. The worst was that slattern Bessa. She'd spread her legs for every boy in Hag's Mire so he'd figured why not him too? He even spent a morning picking wildflowers when he heard she liked them, but she'd just laughed in his face and told him she'd crawl in a bed with his father's leeches before she'd crawl in one with him. She stopped laughing when he put his knife in her. That was sweet, the look on her face, so he pulled the knife out and put it in her again. When they caught him down near Sevenstreams, old Lord Walder Frey hadn't even bothered to come himself to do the judging. He'd sent one of his *bastards*, that Walder Rivers, and the next thing Chett had known he was walking to the Wall with that foul-smelling black devil Yoren. To pay for his one sweet moment, they took his whole life.

But now he meant to take it back, and Craster's women too. *That twisted old wildling has the right of it. If you want a woman to wife you take her, and none of this giving her flowers so that maybe she don't notice your bloody boils.* Chett didn't mean to make *that* mistake again.

It would work, he promised himself for the hundredth time. *So long as we get away clean.* Ser Ottyn would strike south for the Shadow Tower, the shortest way to the Wall. *He won't bother with us, not Wythers, all he'll want is to get back whole.* Thoren Smallwood now, he'd want to press on with the attack, but Ser Ottyn's caution ran too deep, and he was senior. *It won't matter anyhow. Once we're gone, Smallwood can attack anyone he likes. What do we care? If none of them ever returns to the Wall, no one will ever come looking for us, they'll think we died with the rest.* That was a new thought, and for a moment it tempted him. But they would need to kill Ser Ottyn and Ser Mallador Locke as well to give Smallwood the command, and both of them were well-attended day and night . . . no, the risk was too great.

"Chett," said Small Paul as they trudged along a stony game trail through sentinels and soldier pines, "what about the bird?"

"What bloody bird?" The last thing he needed now was some mutton-head going on about a bird.

"The Old Bear's raven," Small Paul said. "If we kill him, who's going to feed his bird?"

"Who bloody well cares? Kill the bird too if you like."

"I don't want to hurt no bird," the big man said. "But that's a talking bird. What if it tells what we did?"

Lark the Sisterman laughed. "Small Paul, thick as a castle wall," he mocked.

"You shut up with that," said Small Paul dangerously.

"Paul," said Chett, before the big man got too angry, "when they find the old man lying in a pool of blood with his throat slit, they won't need no bird to tell them someone killed him."

Small Paul chewed on that a moment. "That's true," he allowed. "Can I keep the bird, then? I like that bird."

"He's yours," said Chett, just to shut him up.

"We can always eat him if we get hungry," offered Lark.

Small Paul clouded up again. "Best not try and eat *my* bird, Lark. Best not."

Chett could hear voices drifting through the trees. "Close your bloody mouths, both of you. We're almost to the Fist."

They emerged near the west face of the hill, and walked around south where the slope was gentler. Near the edge of the forest a dozen men were taking archery practice. They had carved outlines on the trunks of trees, and were loosing shafts at them. "Look," said Lark. "A pig with a bow."

Sure enough, the nearest bowman was Ser Piggy himself, the fat boy who had stolen his place with Maester Aemon. Just the sight of Samwell Tarly filled him with anger. Stewarding for Maester Aemon had been as good a life as he'd ever known. The old blind man was undemanding, and Clydas had taken care of most of his wants anyway. Chett's duties were easy: cleaning the rookery, a few fires to build, a few meals to fetch . . . and Aemon never once hit him. *Thinks he can just walk in and shove me out, on account of being highborn and knowing how to read. Might be I'll ask him to read my knife before I open his throat with it.* "You go on," he told the others, "I want to watch this." The dogs were pulling, anxious to go with them, to the food they thought would be waiting at the top. Chett kicked the bitch with the toe of his boot, and that settled them down some.

He watched from the trees as the fat boy wrestled with a longbow as tall as he was, his red moon face screwed up with concentration. Three arrows stood in the ground before him. Tarly nocked and drew, held the draw a long moment as he tried to aim, and let fly. The shaft vanished into the greenery. Chett laughed loudly, a snort of sweet disgust.

"We'll never find that one, and I'll be blamed," announced Edd Tollett, the dour grey-haired squire everyone called Dolorous Edd. "Nothing ever goes missing that they don't look at me, ever since that time I lost my horse. As if that could be helped. He was white and it was snowing, what did they expect?"

"The wind took that one," said Grenn, another friend of Lord Snow's. "Try to hold the bow steady, Sam."

"It's heavy," the fat boy complained, but he pulled the second arrow all the same. This one went high, sailing through the branches ten feet above the target.

"I believe you knocked a leaf off that tree," said Dolorous Edd. "Fall is falling fast enough, there's no need to help it." He sighed. "And we all know what follows fall. Gods, but I am cold. Shoot the last arrow, Samwell, I believe my tongue is freezing to the roof of my mouth."

Ser Piggy lowered the bow, and Chett thought he was going to start bawling. "It's too hard."

"Notch, draw, and loose," said Grenn. "Go on."

Dutifully, the fat boy plucked his final arrow from the earth, notched it to his longbow, drew, and released. He did it quickly, without squinting along the shaft painstakingly as he had the first two times. The arrow struck the charcoal outline low in the chest and hung quivering. "I *hit* him." Ser Piggy sounded shocked. "Grenn, did you see? Edd, look, I hit him!"

"Put it between his ribs, I'd say," said Grenn.

"Did I kill him?" the fat boy wanted to know.

Tollett shrugged. "Might have punctured a lung, if he had a lung. Most trees don't, as a rule." He took the bow from Sam's hand. "I've seen worse shots, though. Aye, and made a few."

Ser Piggy was beaming. To look at him you'd think he'd actually *done* something. But when he saw Chett and the dogs, his smile curled up and died squeaking.

"You hit a tree," Chett said. "Let's see how you shoot when it's Mance Rayder's lads. They won't stand there with their arms out and their leaves rustling, oh no. They'll come right at you, screaming in your face, and I bet you'll piss those breeches. One o' them will plant his axe right between those little pig eyes. The last thing you'll hear will be the *thunk* it makes when it bites into your skull."

The fat boy was shaking. Dolorous Edd put a hand on his shoulder. "Brother," he said solemnly, "just because it happened that way for you doesn't mean Samwell will suffer the same."

"What are you talking about, Tollett?"

"The axe that split your skull. Is it true that half your wits leaked out on the ground and your dogs ate them?"

The big lout Grenn laughed, and even Samwell Tarly managed a weak little smile. Chett kicked the nearest dog, yanked on their leashes, and started up the hill. *Smile all you want, Ser Piggy. We'll see who laughs tonight.* He only wished he had time to kill Tollett as well. *Gloomy horsefaced fool, that's what he is.*

The climb was steep, even on this side of the Fist, which had the gentlest slope. Partway up the dogs started barking and pulling at him, figuring that they'd get fed soon. He gave them a taste of his boot instead, and a crack of the whip for the big ugly one that snapped at him. Once they were tied up, he went to report. "The prints were there like Giant said, but the dogs wouldn't track," he told Mormont in front of his big black tent. "Down by the river like that, could be old prints."

"A pity." Lord Commander Mormont had a bald head and a great shaggy grey beard, and sounded as tired as he looked. "We might all have been better for a bit of fresh meat." The raven on his shoulder bobbed its head and echoed, *"Meat. Meat. Meat."*

We could cook the bloody dogs, Chett thought, but he kept his mouth shut until the Old Bear sent him on his way. *And that's the last time I'll need to bow my head to that one,* he thought to himself with satisfaction. It seemed to him that it was growing even colder, which he would have sworn wasn't possible. The dogs huddled together miserably in the hard frozen mud, and Chett was half tempted to crawl in with them. Instead he wrapped a black wool scarf round the lower part of his face, leaving a slit for his mouth between the winds. It was warmer if he kept moving, he found, so he made a slow circuit of the perimeter with a wad of sourleaf, sharing a chew or two with the black brothers on guard and hearing what they had to say. None of the men on the day watch were part of his scheme; even so, he figured it was good to have some sense of what they were thinking.

Mostly what they were thinking was that it was bloody cold.

The wind was rising as the shadows lengthened. It made a high thin sound as it shivered through the stones of the ringwall. "I hate that sound," little Giant said. "It sounds like a babe in the brush, wailing away for milk."

When he finished the circuit and returned to the dogs, he found Lark waiting for him. "The officers are in the Old Bear's tent again, talking something fierce."

"That's what they do," said Chett. "They're highborn, all but Blane, they get drunk on words instead of wine."

Lark sidled closer. "Cheese-for-wits keeps going on about the bird," he warned, glancing about to make certain no one was close. "Now he's asking if we cached any seed for the damn thing."

"It's a raven," said Chett. "It eats corpses."

Lark grinned. "His, might be?"

Or yours. It seemed to Chett that they needed the big man more than they needed Lark. "Stop fretting about Small Paul. You do your part, he'll do his."

Twilight was creeping through the woods by the time he rid himself of the Sisterman and sat down to edge his sword. It was bloody hard work with his gloves on, but he wasn't about to take them off. Cold as it was, any fool that touched steel with a bare hand was going to lose a patch of skin.

The dogs whimpered when the sun went down. He gave them water and curses. "Half a night more, and you can find your own feast." By then he could smell supper.

Dywen was holding forth at the cookfire as Chett got his heel of hardbread and a bowl of bean and bacon soup from Hake the cook. "The wood's too silent," the old forester was saying. "No frogs near that river, no owls in the dark. I never heard no deader wood than this."

"Them teeth of yours sound pretty dead," said Hake.

Dywen clacked his wooden teeth. "No wolves neither. There was, before, but no more. Where'd they go, you figure?"

"Someplace warm," said Chett.

Of the dozen odd brothers who sat by the fire, four were his. He gave each one a hard squinty look as he ate, to see if any showed signs of breaking. Dirk seemed calm enough, sitting silent and sharpening his blade, the way he did every night. And Sweet Donnel Hill was all easy japes. He had white teeth and fat red lips and yellow locks that he wore in an artful tumble about his shoulders, and he claimed to be the bastard of some Lannister. Maybe he was at that. Chett had no use for pretty boys, nor for bastards neither, but Sweet Donnel seemed like to hold his own.

He was less certain about the forester the brothers called Sawwood, more for his snoring than for anything to do with trees. Just now he looked so restless he might never snore again. And Maslyn was worse. Chett could see sweat trickling down his face, despite the frigid wind. The beads of moisture sparkled in the firelight, like so many little wet jewels. Maslyn wasn't eating neither, only staring at his soup as if the smell of it was about to make him sick. *I'll need to watch that one*, Chett thought.

"Assemble!" The shout came suddenly, from a dozen throats, and quickly spread to every part of the hilltop camp. "Men of the Night's Watch! Assemble at the central fire!"

Frowning, Chett finished his soup and followed the rest.

The Old Bear stood before the fire with Smallwood, Locke, Wythers, and Blane ranged behind him in a row. Mormont wore a cloak of thick black fur, and his raven perched upon his shoulder, preening its black feathers. *This can't be good.* Chett squeezed between Brown Bernarr and some Shadow Tower men. When everyone was gathered, save for the watchers in the woods and the guards on the ringwall, Mormont cleared his throat and spat. The spittle was frozen before it hit the ground. "Brothers," he said, "men of the Night's Watch."

"*Men!*" his raven screamed. "*Men! Men!*"

"The wildlings are on the march, following the course of the Milkwater down out of the mountains. Thoren believes their van will be upon us ten days hence. Their most seasoned raiders will be with Harma Dogshead in that van. The rest will likely form a rearguard, or ride in close company with Mance Rayder himself. Elsewhere their fighters will be spread thin along the line of march. They have oxen, mules, horses . . . but few enough. Most will be afoot, and ill-armed and untrained. Such weapons as they carry are more like to be stone and bone than steel. They are burdened with women, children, herds of sheep and goats, and all their worldly goods besides. In short, though they are numerous, they are vulnerable . . . and *they do not know that we are here.* Or so we must pray."

They know, thought Chett. *You bloody old pus bag, they know, certain as sunrise. Qhorin Halfhand hasn't come back, has he? Nor Jarman Buckwell. If any of them got caught, you know damned well the wildlings will have wrung a song or two out of them by now.*

Smallwood stepped forward. "Mance Rayder means to break the Wall and bring red war to the Seven Kingdoms. Well, that's a game two can play. On the morrow we'll bring the war to him."

"We ride at dawn with all our strength," the Old Bear said as a murmur went through the assembly. "We will ride north, and loop around to the west. Harma's van will be well past the Fist by the time we turn. The foothills of the Frostfangs are full of narrow winding valleys made for ambush. Their line of march will stretch for many miles. We shall fall on them in several places at once, and make them swear we were three thousand, not three hundred."

"We'll hit hard and be away before their horsemen can form up to face us," Thoren Smallwood said. "If they pursue, we'll lead them a merry chase, then wheel and hit again farther down the column. We'll burn their wagons, scatter their herds, and slay as many as we can. Mance Rayder himself, if we find him. If they break and return to their hovels, we've won. If not, we'll harry them all the way to the Wall, and see to it that they leave a trail of corpses to mark their progress."

"*There are thousands,*" someone called from behind Chett.

"*We'll die.*" That was Maslyn's voice, green with fear.

"*Die,*" screamed Mormont's raven, flapping its black wings. "*Die, die, die.*"

"Many of us," the Old Bear said. "Mayhaps even all of us. But as another Lord Commander said a thousand years ago, that is why they dress us in black. Remember your words, brothers. For we are the swords in the darkness, the watchers on the walls . . ."

"The fire that burns against the cold." Ser Mallador Locke drew his longsword.

"The light that brings the dawn," others answered, and more swords were pulled from scabbards.

Then all of them were drawing, and it was near three hundred upraised swords and as many voices crying, *"The horn that wakes the sleepers! The shield that guards the realms of men!"* Chett had no choice but to join his voice to the others. The air was misty with their breath, and firelight glinted off the steel. He was pleased to see Lark and Softfoot and Sweet Donnel Hill joining in, as if they were as big fools as the rest. That was good. No sense to draw attention, when their hour was so close.

When the shouting died away, once more he heard the sound of the wind picking at the ringwall. The flames swirled and shivered, as if they too were cold, and in the sudden quiet the Old Bear's raven cawed loudly and once again said, *"Die."*

Clever bird, thought Chett as the officers dismissed them, warning everyone to get a good meal and a long rest tonight. Chett crawled under his furs near the dogs, his head full of things that could go wrong. What if that bloody oath gave one of his a change of heart? Or Small Paul forgot and tried to kill Mormont during the second watch in place of the third? Or Maslyn lost his courage, or someone turned informer, or . . .

He found himself listening to the night. The wind did sound like a wailing child, and from time to time he could hear men's voices, a horse's whinny, a log spitting in the fire. But nothing else. *So quiet.*

He could see Bessa's face floating before him. *It wasn't the knife I wanted to put in you*, he wanted to tell her. *I picked you flowers, wild roses and tansy and goldencups, it took me all morning.* His heart was thumping like a drum, so loud he feared it might wake the camp. Ice caked his beard all around his mouth. *Where did that come from, with Bessa?* Whenever he'd thought of her before, it had only been to remember the way she'd looked, dying. What was wrong with him? He could hardly breathe. Had he gone to sleep? He got to his knees, and something wet and cold touched his nose. Chett looked up.

Snow was falling.

He could feel tears freezing to his cheeks. *It isn't fair*, he wanted to scream. Snow would ruin everything he'd worked for, all his careful plans. It was a heavy fall, thick white flakes coming down all about him. How would they find their food caches in the snow, or the game trail they meant to follow east? *They won't need Dywen nor Bannen to hunt us down neither, not if we're tracking through fresh snow.* And snow hid the shape of the ground, especially by night. A horse could stumble over a root, break a leg on a stone. *We're done*, he realized. *Done before we began. We're lost.* There'd be no lord's life for the leechman's son, no keep to call his own, no wives nor crowns. Only a wildling's sword in his belly, and then an unmarked grave. *The snow's taken it all from me . . . the bloody snow . . .*

Snow had ruined him once before. Snow and his pet pig.

Chett got to his feet. His legs were stiff, and the falling snowflakes turned the distant torches to vague orange glows. He felt as though he were being attacked by a cloud of pale cold bugs. They settled on his shoulders, on his head, they flew at his nose and his eyes. Cursing, he brushed them off. *Samwell Tarly*, he remembered. *I can still deal with Ser Piggy.* He wrapped his scarf around his face, pulled up his hood, and went striding through the camp to where the coward slept.

The snow was falling so heavily that he got lost among the tents, but finally he spotted the snug little windbreak the fat boy had made for himself between a rock and the raven cages. Tarly was buried beneath a mound of black wool blankets and shaggy furs. The snow was drifting in to cover him. He looked like some kind of soft round mountain. Steel whispered on leather faint as hope as Chett eased his dagger from its sheath. One of the ravens *quork*ed. "Snow," another muttered, peering through the bars with black eyes. The first added a "Snow" of its own. He edged past them, placing each foot carefully. He would clap his left hand down over the fat boy's mouth to muffle his cries, and then . . .

Uuuuuuuhoooooooooo.

He stopped midstep, swallowing his curse as the sound of the horn shuddered through the camp, faint and far, yet unmistakable. *Not now. Gods be damned, not NOW!* The Old Bear had hidden far-eyes in a ring of trees around the Fist, to give warning of any approach. *Jarman Buckwell's back from the Giant's Stair*, Chett figured, *or Qhorin Halfhand from the Skirling Pass.* A single blast of the horn meant brothers returning. If it was the Halfhand, Jon Snow might be with him, alive.

Sam Tarly sat up puffy-eyed and stared at the snow in confusion. The ravens were cawing noisily, and Chett could hear his dogs baying. *Half the bloody camp's awake.* His gloved fingers clenched around the dagger's hilt as he waited for the sound to die away. But no sooner had it gone than it came again, louder and longer.

Uuuuuuuuuuuuhooooooooooooooooo.

"Gods," he heard Sam Tarly whimper. The fat boy lurched to his knees, his feet tangled in his cloak and blankets. He kicked them away and reached for a chainmail hauberk he'd hung on the rock nearby. As he slipped the huge tent of a garment down over his head and wriggled into it, he spied Chett standing there. "Was it two?" he asked. "I dreamed I heard two blasts . . ."

"No dream," said Chett. "Two blasts to call the Watch to arms. Two blasts for foes approaching. There's an axe out there with *Piggy* writ on it, fat boy. Two blasts means *wildlings*." The fear on that big moon face made him want to laugh. "Bugger them all to seven hells. Bloody Harma. Bloody Mance Rayder. Bloody Smallwood, he said they wouldn't be on us for another –"

Uuuuuuuuuuuuuuuuhooooooooooooooooooooooooooooo.

The sound went on and on and on, until it seemed it would never die. The ravens were flapping and screaming, flying about their cages and banging off the bars, and all about the camp the brothers of the Night's Watch were rising, donning their armor, buckling on swordbelts, reaching for battleaxes and bows. Samwell Tarly stood shaking, his face the same color as the snow that swirled down all around them. "Three," he squeaked to Chett, "that was three, I heard three. They never blow three. Not for hundreds and thousands of years. Three means –"

"– *Others*." Chett made a sound that was half a laugh and half a sob, and suddenly his smallclothes were wet, and he could feel the piss running down his leg, see steam rising off the front of his breeches.

JAIME

An east wind blew through his tangled hair, as soft and fragrant as Cersei's fingers. He could hear birds singing, and feel the river moving beneath the boat as the sweep of the oars sent them toward the pale pink dawn. After so long in darkness, the world was so sweet that Jaime Lannister felt dizzy. *I am alive, and drunk on sunlight.* A laugh burst from his lips, sudden as a quail flushed from cover.

"Quiet," the wench grumbled, scowling. Scowls suited her broad homely face better than a smile. Not that Jaime had ever seen her smiling. He amused himself by picturing her in one of Cersei's silken gowns in place of her studded leather jerkin. *As well dress a cow in silk as this one.*

But the cow could row. Beneath her roughspun brown breeches were calves like cords of wood, and the long muscles of her arms stretched and tightened with each stroke of the oars. Even after rowing half the night, she showed no signs of tiring, which was more than could be said for his cousin Ser Cleos, laboring on the other oar. *A big strong peasant wench to look at her, yet she speaks like one highborn and wears longsword and dagger. Ah, but can she use them?* Jaime meant to find out, as soon as he rid himself of these fetters.

He wore iron manacles on his wrists and a matching pair about his ankles, joined by a length of heavy chain no more than a foot long. "You'd think my word as a Lannister was not good enough," he'd japed as they bound him. He'd been very drunk by then, thanks to Catelyn Stark. Of their escape from Riverrun, he recalled only bits and pieces. There had been some trouble with the gaoler, but the big wench had overcome him.

After that they had climbed an endless stair, around and around. His legs were weak as grass, and he'd stumbled twice or thrice, until the wench lent him an arm to lean on. At some point he was bundled into a traveler's cloak and shoved into the bottom of a skiff. He remembered listening to Lady Catelyn command someone to raise the portcullis on the Water Gate. She was sending Ser Cleos Frey back to King's Landing with new terms for the queen, she'd declared in a tone that brooked no argument.

He must have drifted off then. The wine had made him sleepy, and it felt good to stretch, a luxury his chains had not permitted him in the cell. Jaime had long ago learned to snatch sleep in the saddle during a march. This was no harder. *Tyrion is going to laugh himself sick when he hears how I slept through my own escape.* He was awake now, though, and the fetters were irksome. "My lady," he called out, "if you'll strike off these chains, I'll spell you at those oars."

She scowled again, her face all horse teeth and glowering suspicion. "You'll wear your chains, Kingslayer."

"You figure to row all the way to King's Landing, wench?"

"You will call me Brienne. Not *wench*."

"My name is Ser Jaime. Not Kingslayer."

"Do you deny that you slew a king?"

"No. Do you deny your sex? If so, unlace those breeches and show me." He gave her an innocent smile. "I'd ask you to open your bodice, but from the look of you that wouldn't prove much."

Ser Cleos fretted. "Cousin, remember your courtesies."

The Lannister blood runs thin in this one. Cleos was his Aunt Genna's son by that dullard Emmon Frey, who had lived in terror of Lord Tywin Lannister since the day he wed his sister. When Lord Walder Frey had brought the Twins into the war on the side of Riverrun, Ser Emmon had chosen his wife's allegiance over his father's. *Casterly Rock got the worst of that bargain,* Jaime reflected. Ser Cleos looked like a weasel, fought like a goose, and had the courage of an especially brave ewe. Lady Stark had promised him release if he delivered her message to Tyrion, and Ser Cleos had solemnly vowed to do so.

They'd all done a deal of vowing back in that cell, Jaime most of all. That was Lady Catelyn's price for loosing him. She had laid the point of the big wench's sword against his heart and said, "Swear that you will never again take up arms against Stark nor Tully. Swear that you will compel your brother to honor his pledge to return my daughters safe and unharmed. Swear on your honor as a knight, on your honor as a Lannister, on your honor as a Sworn Brother of the Kingsguard. Swear it by your sister's life, and your father's, and your son's, by the old gods and the new, and I'll send you back to your sister. Refuse, and I will have your blood." He remembered the prick of the steel through his rags as she twisted the point of the sword.

I wonder what the High Septon would have to say about the sanctity of oaths sworn while dead drunk, chained to a wall, with a sword pressed to your chest? Not that Jaime was truly concerned about that fat fraud, or the gods he claimed to serve. He remembered the pail Lady Catelyn had kicked over in his cell. A strange woman, to trust her girls to a man with shit for honor. Though she was trusting him as little as she dared. *She is putting her hope in Tyrion, not in me.* "Perhaps she is not so stupid after all," he said aloud.

His captor took it wrong. "I am not stupid. Nor deaf."

He was gentle with her; mocking this one would be so easy there would be no sport to it. "I was speaking to myself, and not of you. It's an easy habit to slip into in a cell."

She frowned at him, pushing the oars forward, pulling them back, pushing them forward, saying nothing.

As glib of tongue as she is fair of face. "By your speech, I'd judge you nobly born."

"My father is Selwyn of Tarth, by the grace of the gods Lord of Evenfall." Even that was given grudgingly.

"Tarth," Jaime said. "A ghastly large rock in the narrow sea, as I recall. And Evenfall is sworn to Storm's End. How is it that you serve Robb of Winterfell?"

"It is Lady Catelyn I serve. And she commanded me to deliver you safe to your brother Tyrion at King's Landing, not to bandy words with you. Be silent."

"I've had a bellyful of silence, woman."

"Talk with Ser Cleos then. I have no words for monsters."

Jaime hooted. "Are there monsters hereabouts? Hiding beneath the water, perhaps? In that thick of willows? And me without my sword!"

"A man who would violate his own sister, murder his king, and fling an innocent child to his death deserves no other name."

Innocent? The wretched boy was spying on us. All Jaime had wanted was an hour alone with Cersei. Their journey north had been one long torment; seeing her every day, unable to touch her, knowing that Robert stumbled drunkenly into her bed every night in that great creaking wheelhouse. Tyrion had done his best to keep him in a good humor, but it had not been enough. "You will be courteous as concerns Cersei, wench," he warned her.

"My name is Brienne, not *wench*."

"What do you care what a monster calls you?"

"My name is Brienne," she repeated, dogged as a hound.

"Lady Brienne?" She looked so uncomfortable that Jaime sensed a weakness. "Or would *Ser* Brienne be more to your taste?" He laughed. "No, I fear not. You can trick out a milk cow in crupper, crinet, and chamfron, and bard her all in silk, but that doesn't mean you can ride her into battle."

"Cousin Jaime, please, you ought not speak so roughly." Under his cloak, Ser Cleos wore a surcoat quartered with the twin towers of House Frey and the golden lion of Lannister. "We have far to go, we should not quarrel amongst ourselves."

"When I quarrel I do it with a sword, coz. I was speaking to the lady. Tell me, wench, are all the women on Tarth as homely as you? I pity the men, if so. Perhaps they do not know what real women look like, living on a dreary mountain in the sea."

"Tarth is beautiful," the wench grunted between strokes. "The Sapphire Isle, it's called. Be quiet, monster, unless you mean to make me gag you."

"She's rude as well, isn't she, coz?" Jaime asked Ser Cleos. "Though she has steel in her spine, I'll grant you. Not many men dare name me monster to my face." *Though behind my back they speak freely enough, I have no doubt.*

Ser Cleos coughed nervously. "Lady Brienne had those lies from Catelyn Stark, no doubt. The Starks cannot hope to defeat you with swords, ser, so now they make war with poisoned words."

They did defeat me with swords, you chinless cretin. Jaime smiled knowingly. Men will read all sorts of things into a knowing smile, if you let them. *Has cousin Cleos truly swallowed this kettle of dung, or is he striving to ingratiate himself? What do we have here, an honest muttonhead or a lickspittle?*

Ser Cleos prattled blithely on. "Any man who'd believe that a Sworn Brother of the Kingsguard would harm a child does not know the meaning of honor."

Lickspittle. If truth be told, Jaime had come to rue heaving Brandon Stark out that window. Cersei had given him no end of grief afterward, when the boy refused to die. "He was *seven,* Jaime," she'd berated him. "Even if he understood what he saw, we should have been able to frighten him into silence."

"I didn't think you'd want –"

"You *never* think. If the boy should wake and tell his father what he saw –"

"If if if." He had pulled her into his lap. "If he wakes we'll say he was dreaming, we'll call him a liar, and should worse come to worst I'll kill Ned Stark."

"And then what do you imagine *Robert* will do?"

"Let Robert do as he pleases. I'll go to war with him if I must. The War for Cersei's Cunt, the singers will call it."

"Jaime, let go of me!" she raged, struggling to rise.

Instead he had kissed her. For a moment she resisted, but then her mouth opened under his. He remembered the taste of wine and cloves on her tongue. She gave a shudder. His hand went to her bodice and yanked, tearing the silk so her breasts spilled free, and for a time the Stark boy had been forgotten.

Had Cersei remembered him afterward and hired this man Lady Catelyn spoke of, to make sure the boy never woke? *If she wanted him dead she would have sent me. And it is not like her to chose a catspaw who would make such a royal botch of the killing.*

Downriver, the rising sun shimmered against the wind-whipped surface of the river. The south shore was red clay, smooth as any road. Smaller streams fed into the greater, and the rotting trunks of drowned trees clung to the banks. The north shore was wilder. High rocky bluffs rose twenty feet above them, crowned by stands of beech, oak, and chestnut. Jaime spied a watchtower on the heights ahead, growing taller with every stroke of the oars. Long before they were upon it, he knew that it stood abandoned, its weathered stones overgrown with climbing roses.

When the wind shifted, Ser Cleos helped the big wench run up the sail, a stiff triangle of striped red-and-blue canvas. Tully colors, sure to cause them grief if they encountered any Lannister forces on the river, but it was the only sail they had. Brienne took the rudder. Jaime threw out the leeboard, his chains rattling as he moved. After that, they made better speed, with wind and current both favoring their flight. "We could save a deal of traveling if you delivered me to my father instead of my brother," he pointed out.

"Lady Catelyn's daughters are in King's Landing. I will return with the girls or not at all."

Jaime turned to Ser Cleos. "Cousin, lend me your knife."

"No." The woman tensed. "I will not have you armed." Her voice was as unyielding as stone.

She fears me, even in irons. "Cleos, it seems I must ask you to shave me. Leave the beard, but take the hair off my head."

"You'd be shaved bald?" asked Cleos Frey.

"The realm knows Jaime Lannister as a beardless knight with long golden hair. A bald man with a filthy yellow beard may pass unnoticed. I'd sooner not be recognized while I'm in irons."

The dagger was not as sharp as it might have been. Cleos hacked away manfully, sawing and ripping his way through the mats and tossing the hair over the side. The golden curls floated on the surface of the water, gradually falling astern. As the tangles vanished, a louse went crawling down his neck. Jaime caught it and crushed it against his thumbnail. Ser Cleos picked others from his scalp and flicked them into the water. Jaime doused his head and made Ser Cleos whet the blade before he let him scrape away the last inch of yellow stubble. When that was done, they trimmed back his beard as well.

The reflection in the water was a man he did not know. Not only was he bald, but he looked as though he had aged five years in that dungeon; his face was thinner, with hollows under his eyes and lines he did not remember. *I don't look as much like Cersei this way. She'll hate that.*

By midday, Ser Cleos had fallen asleep. His snores sounded like ducks mating. Jaime stretched out to watch the world flow past; after the dark cell, every rock and tree was a wonder.

A few one-room shacks came and went, perched on tall poles that made them look like cranes. Of the folk who lived there they saw no sign. Birds flew overhead, or cried out from the trees along the shore, and Jaime glimpsed silvery fish knifing through the water. *Tully trout, there's a bad omen,* he thought, until he saw a worse – one of the floating logs they passed turned out to be a dead man, bloodless and swollen. His cloak was tangled in the roots of a fallen tree, its color unmistakably Lannister crimson. He wondered if the corpse had been someone he knew.

The forks of the Trident were the easiest way to move goods or men across the riverlands. In times of peace, they would have encountered fisherfolk in their skiffs, grain barges being poled downstream, merchants selling needles and bolts of cloth from floating shops, perhaps even a gaily painted mummer's boat with quilted sails of half a hundred colors, making its way upriver from village to village and castle to castle.

But the war had taken its toll. They sailed past villages, but saw no villagers. An empty net, slashed and torn and hanging from some trees, was the only sign of fisherfolk. A young girl watering her horse rode off as soon as she glimpsed their sail. Later they passed a dozen peasants digging in a field beneath the shell of a burnt towerhouse. The men gazed at them with dull eyes, and went back to their labors once they decided the skiff was no threat.

The Red Fork was wide and slow, a meandering river of loops and bends dotted with tiny wooded islets and frequently choked by sandbars and snags that lurked just below the water's surface. Brienne seemed to have a keen eye for the dangers, though, and always seemed to find the channel. When Jaime complimented her on her knowledge of the river, she looked at him suspiciously and said, "I do not know the river. Tarth is an island. I learned to manage oars and sail before I ever sat a horse."

Ser Cleos sat up and rubbed at his eyes. "Gods, my arms are sore. I hope the wind lasts." He sniffed at it. "I smell rain."

Jaime would welcome a good rain. The dungeons of Riverrun were not the cleanest place in the Seven Kingdoms. By now he must smell like an overripe cheese.

Cleos squinted downriver. "Smoke."

A thin grey finger crooked them on. It was rising from the south bank several miles on, twisting and curling. Below, Jaime made out the smouldering remains of a large building, and a live oak full of dead women.

The crows had scarcely started on their corpses. The thin ropes cut deeply into the soft flesh of their throats, and when the wind blew they twisted and swayed. "This was not chivalrously done," said Brienne when they were close enough to see it clearly. "No true knight would condone such wanton butchery."

"True knights see worse every time they ride to war, wench," said Jaime. "And *do* worse, yes."

Brienne turned the rudder toward the shore. "I'll leave no innocents to be food for crows."

"A heartless wench. Crows need to eat as well. Stay to the river and leave the dead alone, woman."

They landed upstream of where the great oak leaned out over the water. As Brienne lowered the sail, Jaime climbed out, clumsy in his chains. The Red Fork filled his boots and soaked through the ragged breeches. Laughing, he dropped to his knees, plunged his head under the water, and came up drenched and dripping. His hands were caked with dirt, and when he rubbed them clean in the current they seemed thinner and paler than he remembered. His legs were stiff as well, and unsteady when he put his weight upon them. *I was too bloody long in Hoster Tully's dungeon.*

Brienne and Cleos dragged the skiff onto the bank. The corpses hung above their heads, ripening in death like foul fruit. "One of us will need to cut them down," the wench said.

"I'll climb." Jaime waded ashore, clanking. "Just get these chains off."

The wench was staring up at one of the dead women. Jaime shuffled closer with small stutter steps, the only kind the foot-long chain permitted. When he saw the crude sign hung about the neck of the highest corpse, he smiled. *"They Lay With Lions,"* he read. "Oh, yes, woman, this was most *unchivalrously* done ... but by your side, not mine. I wonder who they were, these women?"

"Tavern wenches," said Ser Cleos Frey. "This was an inn, I remember it now. Some men of my escort spent the night here when we last returned to Riverrun." Nothing remained of the building but the stone foundation and a tangle of collapsed beams, charred black. Smoke still rose from the ashes.

Jaime left brothels and whores to his brother Tyrion; Cersei was the only woman he had ever wanted. "The girls pleasured some of my lord father's soldiers, it would seem. Perhaps served them food and drink.

That's how they earned their traitors' collars, with a kiss and a cup of ale." He glanced up and down the river, to make certain they were quite alone. "This is Bracken land. Lord Jonos might have ordered them killed. My father burned his castle, I fear he loves us not."

"It might be Marq Piper's work," said Ser Cleos. "Or that wisp o' the wood Beric Dondarrion, though I'd heard he kills only soldiers. Perhaps a band of Roose Bolton's northmen?"

"Bolton was defeated by my father on the Green Fork."

"But not broken," said Ser Cleos. "He came south again when Lord Tywin marched against the fords. The word at Riverrun was that he'd taken Harrenhal from Ser Amory Lorch."

Jaime liked the sound of that not at all. "Brienne," he said, granting her the courtesy of the name in the hopes that she might listen, "if Lord Bolton holds Harrenhal, both the Trident and the kingsroad are likely watched."

He thought he saw a touch of uncertainty in her big blue eyes. "You are under my protection. They'd need to kill me."

"I shouldn't think that would trouble them."

"I am as good a fighter as you," she said defensively. "I was one of King Renly's chosen seven. With his own hands, he cloaked me with the striped silk of the Rainbow Guard."

"The *Rainbow* Guard? You and six other girls, was it? A singer once said that all maids are fair in silk . . . but he never met you, did he?"

The woman turned red. "We have graves to dig." She went to climb the tree.

The lower limbs of the oak were big enough for her to stand upon once she'd gotten up the trunk. She walked amongst the leaves, dagger in hand, cutting down the corpses. Flies swarmed around the bodies as they fell, and the stench grew worse with each one she dropped. "This is a deal of trouble to take for whores," Ser Cleos complained. "What are we supposed to dig with? We have no spades, and I will not use my sword, I –"

Brienne gave a shout. She jumped down rather than climbing. "To the boat. Be quick. There's a sail."

They made what haste they could, though Jaime could hardly run, and had to be pulled back up into the skiff by his cousin. Brienne shoved off with an oar and raised sail hurriedly. "Ser Cleos, I'll need you to row as well."

He did as she bid. The skiff began to cut the water a bit faster; current, wind, and oars all worked for them. Jaime sat chained, peering upriver. Only the top of the other sail was visible. With the way the Red Fork looped, it looked to be across the fields, moving north behind a screen of trees while they moved south, but he knew that was deceptive. He lifted both hands to shade his eyes. "Mud red and watery blue," he announced.

Brienne's big mouth worked soundlessly, giving her the look of a cow chewing its cud. "Faster, ser."

The inn soon vanished behind them, and they lost sight of the top of the sail as well, but that meant nothing. Once the pursuers swung around the loop they would become visible again. "We can hope the noble Tullys will stop to bury the dead whores, I suppose." The prospect of returning to his cell did not appeal to Jaime. *Tyrion could think of something clever now, but all that occurs to me is to go at them with a sword.*

For the good part of an hour they played peek-and-seek with the pursuers, sweeping around bends and between small wooded isles. Just when they were starting to hope that somehow they might have left behind the pursuit, the distant sail became visible again. Ser Cleos paused in his stroke. "The Others take them." He wiped sweat from his brow.

"*Row!*" Brienne said.

"That is a river galley coming after us," Jaime announced after he'd watched for a while. With every stroke, it seemed to grow a little larger. "Nine oars on each side, which means eighteen men. More, if they crowded on fighters as well as rowers. And larger sails than ours. We cannot outrun her."

Ser Cleos froze at his oars. "Eighteen, you said?"

"Six for each of us. I'd want eight, but these bracelets hinder me somewhat." Jaime held up his wrists. "Unless the Lady Brienne would be so kind as to unshackle me?"

She ignored him, putting all her effort into her stroke.

"We had half a night's start on them," Jaime said. "They've been rowing since dawn, resting two oars at a time. They'll be exhausted. Just now the sight of our sail has given them a burst of strength, but that will not last. We ought to be able to kill a good many of them."

Ser Cleos gaped. "But . . . there are *eighteen*."

"At the least. More likely twenty or twenty-five."

His cousin groaned. "We can't hope to defeat eighteen."

"Did I say we could? The best we can hope for is to die with swords in our hands." He was perfectly sincere. Jaime Lannister had never been afraid of death.

Brienne broke off rowing. Sweat had stuck strands of her flax-colored hair to her forehead, and her grimace made her look homelier than ever. "You are under my protection," she said, her voice so thick with anger that it was almost a growl.

He had to laugh at such fierceness. *She's the Hound with teats*, he thought. *Or would be, if she had any teats to speak of.* "Then protect me, wench. Or free me to protect myself."

The galley was skimming downriver, a great wooden dragonfly. The water around her was churned white by the furious action of her oars. She was gaining visibly, the men on her deck crowding forward as she came on. Metal glinted in their hands, and Jaime could see bows as well. *Archers.* He hated archers.

At the prow of the onrushing galley stood a stocky man with a bald head, bushy grey eyebrows, and brawny arms. Over his mail he wore a soiled white surcoat with a weeping willow embroidered in pale green, but his cloak was fastened with a silver trout. *Riverrun's captain of guards.* In his day Ser Robin Ryger had been a notably tenacious fighter, but his day was done; he was of an age with Hoster Tully, and had grown old with his lord.

When the boats were fifty yards apart, Jaime cupped his hands around his mouth and shouted back over the water. *"Come to wish me godspeed, Ser Robin!"*

"Come to take you back, Kingslayer," Ser Robin Ryger bellowed. *"How is it that you've lost your golden hair?"*

"I hope to blind my enemies with the sheen off my head. It's worked well enough for you."

Ser Robin was unamused. The distance between skiff and galley had shrunk to forty yards. *"Throw your oars and your weapons into the river, and no one need be harmed."*

Ser Cleos twisted around. "Jaime, tell him we were freed by Lady Catelyn . . . an exchange of captives, lawful . . ."

Jaime told him, for all the good it did. *"Catelyn Stark does not rule in Riverrun,"* Ser Robin shouted back. Four archers crowded into position on either side of him, two standing and two kneeling. *"Cast your swords into the water."*

"I have no sword," he returned, *"but if I did, I'd stick it through your belly and hack the balls off those four cravens."*

A flight of arrows answered him. One thudded into the mast, two pierced the sail, and the fourth missed Jaime by a foot.

Another of the Red Fork's broad loops loomed before them. Brienne angled the skiff across the bend. The yard swung as they turned, their sail cracking as it filled with wind. Ahead a large island sat in midstream. The main channel flowed right. To the left a cutoff ran between the island and the high bluffs of the north shore. Brienne moved the tiller and the skiff sheared left, sail rippling. Jaime watched her eyes. *Pretty eyes,* he thought, *and calm.* He knew how to read a man's eyes. He knew what fear looked like. *She is determined, not desperate.*

Thirty yards behind, the galley was entering the bend. "Ser Cleos, take the tiller," the wench commanded. "Kingslayer, take an oar and keep us off the rocks."

"As my lady commands." An oar was not a sword, but the blade could break a man's face if well swung, and the shaft could be used to parry.

Ser Cleos shoved the oar into Jaime's hand and scrambled aft. They crossed the head of the island and turned sharply down the cutoff, sending a wash of water against the face of the bluff as the boat tilted. The island was densely wooded, a tangle of willows, oaks, and tall pines that cast deep shadows across the rushing water, hiding snags and the rotted trunks of drowned trees. To their left the bluff rose sheer and rocky, and at its foot the river foamed whitely around broken boulders and tumbles of rock fallen from the cliff face.

They passed from sunlight into shadow, hidden from the galley's view between the green wall of the trees and the stony grey-brown bluff. *A few moments' respite from the arrows*, Jaime thought, pushing them off a half-submerged boulder.

The skiff rocked. He heard a soft splash, and when he glanced around, Brienne was gone. A moment later he spied her again, pulling herself from the water at the base of the bluff. She waded through a shallow pool, scrambled over some rocks, and began to climb. Ser Cleos goggled, mouth open. *Fool*, thought Jaime. "Ignore the wench," he snapped at his cousin. "Steer."

They could see the sail moving behind the trees. The river galley came into full view at the top of the cutoff, twenty-five yards behind. Her bow swung hard as she came around, and a half-dozen arrows took flight, but all went well wide. The motion of the two boats was giving the archers difficulty, but Jaime knew they'd soon enough learn to compensate. Brienne was halfway up the cliff face, pulling herself from handhold to handhold. *Ryger's sure to see her, and once he does he'll have those bowmen bring her down.* Jaime decided to see if the old man's pride would make him stupid. *"Ser Robin,"* he shouted, *"hear me for a moment."*

Ser Robin raised a hand, and his archers lowered their bows. *"Say what you will, Kingslayer, but say it quickly."*

The skiff swung through a litter of broken stones as Jaime called out, *"I know a better way to settle this – single combat. You and I."*

"I was not born this morning, Lannister."

"No, but you're like to die this afternoon." Jaime raised his hands so the other could see the manacles. *"I'll fight you in chains. What could you fear?"*

"Not you, ser. If the choice were mine, I'd like nothing better, but I am commanded to bring you back alive if possible. Bowmen." He signaled them on. *"Notch. Draw. Loo –"*

The range was less than twenty yards. The archers could scarcely have missed, but as they pulled on their longbows a rain of pebbles cascaded down around them. Small stones rattled on their deck, bounced off their helms, and made splashes on both sides of the bow. Those who had wits enough to understand raised their eyes just as a boulder the size of a cow detached itself from the top of the bluff. Ser Robin shouted in dismay. The stone tumbled through the air, struck the face of the cliff, cracked in two, and smashed down on them. The larger piece snapped the mast, tore through the sail, sent two of the archers flying into the river, and crushed the leg of a rower as he bent over his oar. The rapidity with which the galley began to fill with water suggested that the smaller fragment had punched right through her hull. The oarsman's screams echoed off the bluff while the archers flailed wildly in the current. From the way they were splashing, neither man could swim. Jaime laughed.

By the time they emerged from the cutoff, the galley was foundering amongst pools, eddies, and snags, and Jaime Lannister had decided that the gods were good. Ser Robin and his thrice-damned archers would have a long wet walk back to Riverrun, and he was rid of the big homely wench as well. *I could not have planned it better myself. Once I'm free of these irons . . .*

Ser Cleos raised a shout. When Jaime looked up, Brienne was lumbering along the clifftop well ahead of them, having cut across a finger of land while they were following the bend in the river. She threw herself off the rock, and looked almost graceful as she folded into a dive. It would have been ungracious to hope that she would smash her head on a stone. Ser Cleos turned the skiff toward her. Thankfully, Jaime still had his oar. *One good swing when she comes paddling up and I'll be free of her.*

Instead he found himself stretching the oar out over the water. Brienne grabbed hold, and Jaime pulled her in. As he helped her into the skiff, water ran from her hair and dripped from her sodden clothing to pool on the deck. *She's even uglier wet. Who would have thought it possible?* "You're a bloody stupid wench," he told her. "We could have sailed on without you. I suppose you expect me to thank you?"

"I want none of your thanks, Kingslayer. I swore an oath to bring you safe to King's Landing."

"And you actually mean to keep it?" Jaime gave her his brightest smile. "Now there's a wonder."

CATELYN

Ser Desmond Grell had served House Tully all his life. He had been a squire when Catelyn was born, a knight when she learned to walk and ride and swim, master-at-arms by the day that she was wed. He had seen Lord Hoster's little Cat become a young woman, a great lord's lady, mother to a king. *And now he has seen me become a traitor as well.*

Her brother Edmure had named Ser Desmond castellan of Riverrun when he rode off to battle, so it fell to him to deal with her crime. To ease his discomfort he brought her father's steward with him, dour Utherydes Wayn. The two men stood and looked at her; Ser Desmond stout, red-faced, embarrassed, Utherydes grave, gaunt, melancholy. Each waited for the other to speak. *They have given their lives to my father's service, and I have repaid them with disgrace,* Catelyn thought wearily.

"Your sons," Ser Desmond said at last. "Maester Vyman told us. The poor lads. Terrible. Terrible. But . . ."

"We share your grief, my lady," said Utherydes Wayn. "All Riverrun mourns with you, but . . ."

"The news must have driven you mad," Ser Desmond broke in, "a madness of grief, a *mother's* madness, men will understand. You did not know . . ."

"I did," Catelyn said firmly. "I understood what I was doing and knew it was treasonous. If you fail to punish me, men will believe that we connived together to free Jaime Lannister. It was mine own act and mine alone, and I alone must answer for it. Put me in the Kingslayer's empty irons, and I will wear them proudly, if that is how it must be."

"Fetters?" The very word seemed to shock poor Ser Desmond. "For the king's mother, my lord's own daughter? Impossible."

"Mayhaps," said the steward Utherydes Wayn, "my lady would consent to be confined to her chambers until Ser Edmure returns. A time alone, to pray for her murdered sons?"

"Confined, aye," Ser Desmond said. "Confined to a tower cell, that would serve."

"If I am to be confined, let it be in my father's chambers, so I might comfort him in his last days."

Ser Desmond considered a moment. "Very well. You shall lack no comfort nor courtesy, but freedom of the castle is denied you. Visit the sept as you need, but elsewise remain in Lord Hoster's chambers until Lord Edmure returns."

"As you wish." Her brother was no lord while their father lived, but Catelyn did not correct him. "Set a guard on me if you must, but I give you my pledge that I shall attempt no escape."

Ser Desmond nodded, plainly glad to be done with his distasteful task, but sad-eyed Utherydes Wayn lingered a moment after the castellan took his leave. "It was a grave thing you did, my lady, but for naught. Ser Desmond has sent Ser Robin Ryger after them, to bring back the Kingslayer . . . or failing that, his head."

Catelyn had expected no less. *May the Warrior give strength to your sword arm, Brienne*, she prayed. She had done all she could; nothing remained but to hope.

Her things were moved into her father's bedchamber, dominated by the great canopied bed she had been born in, its pillars carved in the shapes of leaping trout. Her father himself had been moved half a turn down the stair, his sickbed placed to face the triangular balcony that opened off his solar, from whence he could see the rivers that he had always loved so well.

Lord Hoster was sleeping when Catelyn entered. She went out to the balcony and stood with one hand on the rough stone balustrade. Beyond the point of the castle the swift Tumblestone joined the placid Red Fork, and she could see a long way downriver. *If a striped sail comes from the east, it will be Ser Robin returning*. For the moment the surface of the waters was empty. She thanked the gods for that, and went back inside to sit with her father.

Catelyn could not say if Lord Hoster knew that she was there, or if her presence brought him any comfort, but it gave her solace to be with him. *What would you say if you knew my crime, Father?* she wondered. *Would you have done as I did, if it were Lysa and me in the hands of our enemies? Or would you condemn me too, and call it mother's madness?*

There was a smell of death about that room; a heavy smell, sweet and foul, clinging. It reminded her of the sons that she had lost, her sweet Bran and her little Rickon, slain at the hand of Theon Greyjoy, who had been Ned's ward. She still grieved for Ned, she would always grieve for Ned, but to have her babies taken as well . . . "It is a monstrous cruel thing to lose a child," she whispered softly, more to herself than to her father.

Lord Hoster's eyes opened. "*Tansy*," he husked in a voice thick with pain.

He does not know me. Catelyn had grown accustomed to him taking her for her mother or her sister Lysa, but Tansy was a name strange to her. "It's Catelyn," she said. "It's Cat, Father."

"Forgive me . . . the blood . . . oh, please . . . Tansy . . ."

Could there have been another woman in her father's life? Some village maiden he had wronged when he was young, perhaps? *Could he have found comfort in some serving wench's arms after Mother died?* It was a queer thought, unsettling. Suddenly she felt as though she had not known her father at all. "Who is Tansy, my lord? Do you want me to send for her, Father? Where would I find the woman? Does she still live?"

Lord Hoster groaned. "*Dead.*" His hand groped for hers. "You'll have others . . . sweet babes, and trueborn."

Others? Catelyn thought. *Has he forgotten that Ned is gone? Is he still talking to Tansy, or is it me now, or Lysa, or Mother?*

When he coughed, the sputum came up bloody. He clutched her fingers. ". . . be a good wife and the gods will bless you . . . sons . . . trueborn sons . . . *aaahhh*." The sudden spasm of pain made Lord Hoster's hand tighten. His nails dug into her hand, and he gave a muffled scream.

Maester Vyman came quickly, to mix another dose of milk of the poppy and help his lord swallow it down. Soon enough, Lord Hoster Tully had fallen back into a heavy sleep.

"He was asking after a woman," said Cat. "Tansy."

"Tansy?" The maester looked at her blankly.

"You know no one by that name? A serving girl, a woman from some nearby village? Perhaps someone from years past?" Catelyn had been gone from Riverrun for a very long time.

"No, my lady. I can make inquiries, if you like. Utherydes Wayn would surely know if any such person ever served at Riverrun. Tansy, did you say? The smallfolk often name their daughters after flowers and herbs." The maester looked thoughtful. "There was a widow, I recall, she used to come to the castle looking for old shoes in need of new soles. Her name was Tansy, now that I think on it. Or was it Pansy? Some such. But she has not come for many years . . ."

"Her name was Violet," said Catelyn, who remembered the old woman very well.

"Was it?" The maester looked apologetic. "My pardons, Lady Catelyn, but I may not stay. Ser Desmond has decreed that we are to speak to you only so far as our duties require."

"Then you must do as he commands." Catelyn could not blame Ser Desmond; she had given him small reason to trust her, and no doubt he feared that she might use the loyalty that many of the folk of Riverrun would still feel toward their lord's daughter to work some further mischief. *I am free of the war, at least,* she told herself, *if only for a little while.*

After the maester had gone, she donned a woolen cloak and stepped out onto the balcony once more. Sunlight shimmered on the rivers, gilding the surface of the waters as they rolled past the castle. Catelyn shaded her eyes against the glare, searching for a distant sail, dreading the sight of one. But there was nothing, and nothing meant that her hopes were still alive.

All that day she watched, and well into the night, until her legs ached from the standing. A raven came to the castle in late afternoon, flapping down on great black wings to the rookery. *Dark wings, dark words,* she thought, remembering the last bird that had come and the horror it had brought.

Maester Vyman returned at evenfall to minister to Lord Tully and bring Catelyn a modest supper of bread, cheese, and boiled beef with horseradish. "I spoke to Utherydes Wayn, my lady. He is quite certain that no woman by the name of Tansy has ever been at Riverrun during his service."

"There was a raven today, I saw. Has Jaime been taken again?" *Or slain, gods forbid?*

"No, my lady, we've had no word of the Kingslayer."

"Is it another battle, then? Is Edmure in difficulty? Or Robb? Please, be kind, put my fears at rest."

"My lady, I should not . . ." Vyman glanced about, as if to make certain no one else was in the room. "Lord Tywin has left the riverlands. All's quiet on the fords."

"Whence came the raven, then?"

"From the west," he answered, busying himself with Lord Hoster's bedclothes and avoiding her eyes.

"Was it news of Robb?"

He hesitated. "Yes, my lady."

"Something is wrong." She knew it from his manner. He was hiding something from her. "Tell me. Is it Robb? Is he hurt?" *Not dead, gods be good, please do not tell me that he is dead.*

"His Grace took a wound storming the Crag," Maester Vyman said, still evasive, "but writes that it is no cause for concern, and that he hopes to return soon."

"A wound? What sort of wound? How serious?"

"No cause for concern, he writes."

"All wounds concern me. Is he being cared for?"

"I am certain of it. The maester at the Crag will tend to him, I have no doubt."

"Where was he wounded?"

"My lady, I am commanded not to speak with you. I am sorry." Gathering up his potions, Vyman made a hurried exit, and once again Catelyn was left alone with her father. The milk of the poppy had done its work, and Lord Hoster was sunk in heavy sleep. A thin line of spittle ran down from one corner of his open mouth to dampen his pillow. Catelyn took a square of linen and wiped it away gently. When she touched him, Lord Hoster moaned. "Forgive me," he said, so softly she could scarcely hear the words. "Tansy . . . blood . . . the blood . . . gods be kind . . ."

His words disturbed her more than she could say, though she could make no sense of them. *Blood*, she thought. *Must it all come back to blood? Father, who was this woman, and what did you do to her that needs so much forgiveness?*

That night Catelyn slept fitfully, haunted by formless dreams of her children, the lost and the dead. Well before the break of day, she woke with her father's words echoing in her ears. *Sweet babes, and trueborn . . . why would he say that, unless . . . could he have fathered a bastard on this woman Tansy?* She could not believe it. Her brother Edmure, yes; it would not have surprised her to learn that Edmure had a dozen natural children. But not her father, not Lord Hoster Tully, never.

Could Tansy be some pet name he called Lysa, the way he called me Cat? Lord Hoster had mistaken her for her sister before. *You'll have others,* he said. *Sweet babes, and trueborn.* Lysa had miscarried five times, twice in the Eyrie, thrice at King's Landing . . . but never at Riverrun, where Lord Hoster would have been at hand to comfort her. *Never, unless . . . unless she was with child, that first time . . .*

She and her sister had been married on the same day, and left in their father's care when their new husbands had ridden off to rejoin Robert's rebellion. Afterward, when their moon blood did not come at the accustomed time, Lysa had gushed happily of the sons she was certain they carried. "Your son will be heir to Winterfell and mine to the Eyrie. Oh, they'll be the best of friends, like your Ned and Lord Robert. They'll be more brothers than cousins, truly, I just know it." *She was so happy.*

But Lysa's blood had come not long after, and all the joy had gone out of her. Catelyn had always thought that Lysa had simply been a little late, but if she *had* been with child . . .

She remembered the first time she gave her sister Robb to hold; small, red-faced, and squalling, but strong even then, full of life. No sooner had

Catelyn placed the babe in her sister's arms than Lysa's face dissolved into tears. Hurriedly she had thrust the baby back at Catelyn and fled.

If she had lost a child before, that might explain Father's words, and much else besides . . . Lysa's match with Lord Arryn had been hastily arranged, and Jon was an old man even then, older than their father. *An old man without an heir.* His first two wives had left him childless, his brother's son had been murdered with Brandon Stark in King's Landing, his gallant cousin had died in the Battle of the Bells. He needed a young wife if House Arryn was to continue . . . *a young wife known to be fertile.*

Catelyn rose, threw on a robe, and descended the steps to the darkened solar to stand over her father. A sense of helpless dread filled her. "Father," she said, "Father, I know what you did." She was no longer an innocent bride with a head full of dreams. She was a widow, a traitor, a grieving mother, and wise, wise in the ways of the world. "You made him take her," she whispered. "Lysa was the price Jon Arryn had to pay for the swords and spears of House Tully."

Small wonder her sister's marriage had been so loveless. The Arryns were proud, and prickly of their honor. Lord Jon might wed Lysa to bind the Tullys to the cause of the rebellion, and in hopes of a son, but it would have been hard for him to love a woman who came to his bed soiled and unwilling. He would have been kind, no doubt; dutiful, yes; but Lysa needed warmth.

The next day, as she broke her fast, Catelyn asked for quill and paper and began a letter to her sister in the Vale of Arryn. She told Lysa of Bran and Rickon, struggling with the words, but mostly she wrote of their father. *His thoughts are all of the wrong he did you, now that his time grows short. Maester Vyman says he dare not make the milk of the poppy any stronger. It is time for Father to lay down his sword and shield. It is time for him to rest. Yet he fights on grimly, will not yield. It is for your sake, I think. He needs your forgiveness. The war has made the road from the Eyrie to Riverrun dangerous to travel, I know, but surely a strong force of knights could see you safely through the Mountains of the Moon! A hundred men, or a thousand! And if you cannot come, will you not write him at least! A few words of love, so he might die in peace! Write what you will, and I shall read it to him, and ease his way.*

Even as she set the quill aside and asked for sealing wax, Catelyn sensed that the letter was like to be too little and too late. Maester Vyman did not believe Lord Hoster would linger long enough for a raven to reach the Eyrie and return. *Though he has said much the same before . . .* Tully men did not surrender easily, no matter the odds. After she entrusted the parchment to the maester's care, Catelyn went to the sept and lit a candle to the Father Above for her own father's sake, a second to the Crone, who had let the first raven into the world when she peered through the door of death, and a third to the Mother, for Lysa and all the children they had both lost.

Later that day, as she sat at Lord Hoster's bedside with a book, reading the same passage over and over, she heard the sound of loud voices and a trumpet's blare. *Ser Robin*, she thought at once, flinching. She went to the balcony, but there was nothing to be seen out on the rivers, but she could hear the voices more clearly from outside, the sound of many horses, the clink of armor, and here and there a cheer. Catelyn made her way up the winding stairs to the roof of the keep. *Ser Desmond did not forbid me the roof*, she told herself as she climbed.

The sounds were coming from the far side of the castle, by the main gate. A knot of men stood before the portcullis as it rose in jerks and starts, and in the fields beyond, outside the castle, were several hundred riders. When the wind blew, it lifted their banners, and she trembled in relief at the sight of the leaping trout of Riverrun. *Edmure*.

It was two hours before he saw fit to come to her. By then the castle rang to the sound of noisy reunions as men embraced the women and children they had left behind. Three ravens had risen from the rookery, black wings beating at the air as they took flight. Catelyn watched them from her father's balcony. She had washed her hair, changed her clothing, and prepared herself for her brother's reproaches ... but even so, the waiting was hard.

When at last she heard sounds outside her door, she sat and folded her hands in her lap. Dried red mud spattered Edmure's boots, greaves, and surcoat. To look at him, you would never know he had won his battle. He was thin and drawn, with pale cheeks, unkempt beard, and too-bright eyes.

"Edmure," Catelyn said, worried, "you look unwell. Has something happened? Have the Lannisters crossed the river?"

"I threw them back. Lord Tywin, Gregor Clegane, Addam Marbrand, I turned them away. Stannis, though ..." He grimaced.

"Stannis? What of Stannis?"

"He lost the battle at King's Landing," Edmure said unhappily. "His fleet was burned, his army routed."

A Lannister victory was ill tidings, but Catelyn could not share her brother's obvious dismay. She still had nightmares about the shadow she had seen slide across Renly's tent and the way the blood had come flowing out through the steel of his gorget. "Stannis was no more a friend than Lord Tywin."

"You do not understand. Highgarden has declared for Joffrey. Dorne as well. All the south." His mouth tightened. "And *you* see fit to loose the Kingslayer. You had no right."

"I had a mother's right." Her voice was calm, though the news about Highgarden was a savage blow to Robb's hopes. She could not think about that now, though.

"No right," Edmure repeated. "He was Robb's captive, your *king's* captive, and Robb charged me to keep him safe."

"Brienne will keep him safe. She swore it on her sword."

"That *woman?*"

"She will deliver Jaime to King's Landing, and bring Arya and Sansa back to us safely."

"Cersei will never give them up."

"Not Cersei. Tyrion. He swore it, in open court. And the Kingslayer swore it as well."

"Jaime's word is worthless. As for the Imp, it's said he took an axe in the head during the battle. He'll be dead before your Brienne reaches King's Landing, if she ever does."

"Dead?" *Could the gods truly be so merciless?* She had made Jaime swear a hundred oaths, but it was his brother's promise she had pinned her hopes on.

Edmure was blind to her distress. "Jaime was *my* charge, and I mean to have him back. I've sent ravens –"

"Ravens to whom? How many?"

"Three," he said, "so the message will be certain to reach Lord Bolton. By river or road, the way from Riverrun to King's Landing must needs take them close by Harrenhal."

"Harrenhal." The very word seemed to darken the room. Horror thickened her voice as she said, "Edmure, do you know what you have done?"

"Have no fear, I left your part out. I wrote that Jaime had escaped, and offered a thousand dragons for his recapture."

Worse and worse, Catelyn thought in despair. *My brother is a fool.* Unbidden, unwanted, tears filled her eyes. "If this was an escape," she said softly, "and not an exchange of hostages, why should the Lannisters give my daughters to Brienne?"

"It will never come to that. The Kingslayer will be returned to us, I have made certain of it."

"All you have made certain is that I shall never see my daughters again. Brienne might have gotten him to King's Landing safely . . . *so long as no one was hunting for them.* But now . . ." Catelyn could not go on. "Leave me, Edmure." She had no right to command him, here in the castle that would soon be his, yet her tone would brook no argument. "Leave me to Father and my grief, I have no more to say to you. Go. *Go.*" All she wanted was to lie down, to close her eyes and sleep, and pray no dreams would come.

ARYA

The sky was as black as the walls of Harrenhal behind them, and the rain fell soft and steady, muffling the sound of their horses' hooves and running down their faces.

They rode north, away from the lake, following a rutted farm road across the torn fields and into the woods and streams. Arya took the lead, kicking her stolen horse to a brisk heedless trot until the trees closed in around her. Hot Pie and Gendry followed as best they could. Wolves howled off in the distance, and she could hear Hot Pie's heavy breathing. No one spoke. From time to time Arya glanced over her shoulder, to make sure the two boys had not fallen too far behind, and to see if they were being pursued.

They would be, she knew. She had stolen three horses from the stables and a map and a dagger from Roose Bolton's own solar, and killed a guard on the postern gate, slitting his throat when he knelt to pick up the worn iron coin that Jaqen H'ghar had given her. Someone would find him lying dead in his own blood, and then the hue and cry would go up. They would wake Lord Bolton and search Harrenhal from crenel to cellar, and when they did they would find the map and the dagger missing, along with some swords from the armory, bread and cheese from the kitchens, a baker boy, a 'prentice smith, and a cupbearer called Nan . . . or Weasel, or Arry, depending on who you asked.

The Lord of the Dreadfort would not come after them himself. Roose Bolton would stay abed, his pasty flesh dotted with leeches, giving commands in his whispery soft voice. His man Walton might lead the hunt, the one they called Steelshanks for the greaves he always wore on his long legs. Or perhaps it would be slobbery Vargo Hoat and his sellswords, who named themselves the Brave Companions. Others called them Bloody Mummers (though never to their faces), and sometimes the Footmen, for Lord Vargo's habit of cutting off the hands and feet of men who displeased him.

If they catch us, he'll cut off our hands and feet, Arya thought, *and then Roose Bolton will peel the skin off us.* She was still dressed in her page's garb, and on the breast over her heart was sewn Lord Bolton's sigil, the flayed man of the Dreadfort.

Every time she looked back, she half expected to see a blaze of torches pouring out the distant gates of Harrenhal or rushing along the tops of its huge high walls, but there was nothing. Harrenhal slept on, until it was lost in darkness and hidden behind the trees.

When they crossed the first stream, Arya turned her horse aside and led them off the road, following the twisting course of the water for a quarter-mile before finally scrambling out and up a stony bank. If the hunters brought dogs, that might throw them off the scent, she hoped. They could not stay on the road. *There is death on the road,* she told herself, *death on all the roads.*

Gendry and Hot Pie did not question her choice. She had the map, after all, and Hot Pie seemed almost as terrified of her as of the men who might be coming after them. He had seen the guard she'd killed. *It's better if he's scared of me,* she told herself. *That way he'll do like I say, instead of something stupid.*

She should be more frightened herself, she knew. She was only ten, a skinny girl on a stolen horse with a dark forest ahead of her and men behind who would gladly cut off her feet. Yet somehow she felt calmer than she ever had in Harrenhal. The rain had washed the guard's blood off her fingers, she wore a sword across her back, wolves were prowling through the dark like lean grey shadows, and Arya Stark was unafraid. *Fear cuts deeper than swords,* she whispered under her breath, the words that Syrio Forel had taught her, and Jaqen's words too, *valar morghulis.*

The rain stopped and started again and stopped once more and started, but they had good cloaks to keep the water off. Arya kept them moving at a slow steady pace. It was too black beneath the trees to ride any faster; the boys were no horsemen, neither one, and the soft broken ground was treacherous with half-buried roots and hidden stones. They crossed another road, its deep ruts filled with runoff, but Arya shunned it. Up and down the rolling hills she took them, through brambles and briars and tangles of underbrush, along the bottoms of narrow gullies where branches heavy with wet leaves slapped at their faces as they passed.

Gendry's mare lost her footing in the mud once, going down hard on her hindquarters and spilling him from the saddle, but neither horse nor rider was hurt, and Gendry got that stubborn look on his face and mounted right up again. Not long after, they came upon three wolves devouring the corpse of a fawn. When Hot Pie's horse caught the scent, he shied and bolted. Two of the wolves fled as well, but the third raised his head and bared his teeth, prepared to defend his kill. "Back off," Arya told Gendry. "Slow, so you don't spook him." They edged their mounts away, until the wolf and his feast were no longer in sight. Only then did she swing about to ride after Hot Pie, who was clinging desperately to the saddle as he crashed through the trees.

Later they passed through a burned village, threading their way carefully between the shells of blackened hovels and past the bones of a dozen dead men hanging from a row of apple trees. When Hot Pie saw them he began to pray, a thin whispered plea for the Mother's mercy, repeated over and over. Arya looked up at the fleshless dead in their wet rotting clothes and said her own prayer. *Ser Gregor*, it went, *Dunsen, Polliver, Raff the Sweetling. The Tickler and the Hound. Ser Ilyn, Ser Meryn, King Joffrey, Queen Cersei.* She ended it with *valar morghulis*, touched Jaqen's coin where it nestled under her belt, and then reached up and plucked an apple from among the dead men as she rode beneath them. It was mushy and overripe, but she ate it worms and all.

That was the day without a dawn. Slowly the sky lightened around them, but they never saw the sun. Black turned to grey, and colors crept timidly back into the world. The soldier pines were dressed in somber greens, the broadleafs in russets and faded golds already beginning to brown. They stopped long enough to water the horses and eat a cold, quick breakfast, ripping apart a loaf of the bread that Hot Pie had stolen from the kitchens and passing chunks of hard yellow cheese from hand to hand.

"Do you know where we're going?" Gendry asked her.

"North," said Arya.

Hot Pie peered around uncertainly. "Which way is north?"

She used her cheese to point. "That way."

"But there's no sun. How do you know?"

"From the moss. See how it grows mostly on one side of the trees? That's south."

"What do we want with the north?" Gendry wanted to know.

"The Trident." Arya unrolled the stolen map to show them. "See? Once we reach the Trident, all we need to do is follow it upstream till we come to Riverrun, here." Her finger traced the path. "It's a long way, but we can't get lost so long as we keep to the river."

Hot Pie blinked at the map. "Which one is Riverrun?"

Riverrun was painted as a castle tower, in the fork between the flowing blue lines of two rivers, the Tumblestone and the Red Fork. "There." She touched it. "*Riverrun*, it reads."

"You can read writing?" he said to her, wonderingly, as if she'd said she could walk on water.

She nodded. "We'll be safe once we reach Riverrun."

"We will? Why?"

Because Riverrun is my grandfather's castle, and my brother Robb will be there, she wanted to say. She bit her lip and rolled up the map. "We just will. But only if we get there." She was the first one back in the saddle. It made her feel bad to hide the truth from Hot Pie, but she did not trust him with her secret. Gendry knew, but that was different. Gendry had his own secret, though even he didn't seem to know what it was.

That day Arya quickened their pace, keeping the horses to a trot as long as she dared, and sometimes spurring to a gallop when she spied a flat stretch of field before them. That was seldom enough, though; the ground was growing hillier as they went. The hills were not high, nor especially steep, but there seemed to be no end of them, and they soon grew tired of climbing up one and down the other, and found themselves following the lay of the land, along streambeds and through a maze of shallow wooded valleys where the trees made a solid canopy overhead.

From time to time she sent Hot Pie and Gendry on while she doubled back to try to confuse their trail, listening all the while for the first sign of pursuit. *Too slow*, she thought to herself, chewing her lip, *we're going too slow, they'll catch us for certain*. Once, from the crest of a ridge, she spied dark shapes crossing a stream in the valley behind them, and for half a heartbeat she feared that Roose Bolton's riders were on them, but when she looked again she realized they were only a pack of wolves. She cupped her hands around her mouth and howled down at them, "*Ahooooooooo, ahooooooooo.*" When the largest of the wolves lifted its head and howled back, the sound made Arya shiver.

By midday Hot Pie had begun to complain. His arse was sore, he told them, and the saddle was rubbing him raw inside his legs, and besides he had to get some sleep. "I'm so tired I'm going to fall off the horse."

Arya looked at Gendry. "If he falls off, who do you think will find him first, the wolves or the Mummers?"

"The wolves," said Gendry. "Better noses."

Hot Pie opened his mouth and closed it. He did not fall off his horse. The rain began again a short time later. They still had not seen so much as a glimpse of the sun. It was growing colder, and pale white mists were threading between the pines and blowing across the bare burned fields.

Gendry was having almost as bad a time of it as Hot Pie, though he was too stubborn to complain. He sat awkwardly in the saddle, a determined look on his face beneath his shaggy black hair, but Arya could tell he was no horseman. *I should have remembered*, she thought to herself. She had been riding as long as she could remember, ponies when she was little and later horses, but Gendry and Hot Pie were city-born, and in the city smallfolk walked. Yoren had given them mounts when he took them from King's Landing, but sitting on a donkey and plodding up the kingsroad behind a wagon was one thing. Guiding a hunting horse through wild woods and burned fields was something else.

She would make much better time on her own, Arya knew, but she could not leave them. They were her pack, her friends, the only living friends that remained to her, and if not for her they would still be safe at Harrenhal, Gendry sweating at his forge and Hot Pie in the kitchens. *If the Mummers catch us, I'll tell them that I'm Ned Stark's daughter and sister to the King in the North. I'll command them to take me to my brother, and to do no harm to Hot Pie and Gendry.* They might not believe her, though, and even if they did . . . Lord Bolton was her brother's bannerman, but he frightened her all the same. *I won't let them take us,* she vowed silently, reaching back over her shoulder to touch the hilt of the sword that Gendry had stolen for her. *I won't.*

Late that afternoon, they emerged from beneath the trees and found themselves on the banks of a river. Hot Pie gave a whoop of delight. "The *Trident*! Now all we have to do is go upstream, like you said. We're almost there!"

Arya chewed her lip. "I don't think this is the Trident." The river was swollen by the rain, but even so it couldn't be much more than thirty feet across. She remembered the Trident as being much wider. "It's too little to be the Trident," she told them, "and we didn't come far enough."

"Yes we did," Hot Pie insisted. "We rode all day, and hardly stopped at all. We must have come a long way."

"Let's have a look at that map again," said Gendry.

Arya dismounted, took out the map, unrolled it. The rain pattered against the sheepskin and ran off in rivulets. "We're someplace here, I think," she said, pointing, as the boys peered over her shoulders.

"But," said Hot Pie, "that's hardly any ways at all. See, Harrenhal's there by your finger, you're almost *touching* it. And we rode all day!"

"There's miles and miles before we reach the Trident," she said. "We won't be there for *days*. This must be some different river, one of these, see." She showed him some of the thinner blue lines the mapmaker had painted in, each with a name painted in fine script beneath it. "The Darry, the Greenapple, the Maiden . . . here, this one, the Little Willow, it might be that."

Hot Pie looked from the line to the river. "It doesn't look so little to me."

Gendry was frowning as well. "The one you're pointing at runs into that other one, see."

"The Big Willow," she read.

"The Big Willow, then. See, and the Big Willow runs into the Trident, so we could follow the one to the other, but we'd need to go downstream, not up. Only if this river *isn't* the Little Willow, if it's this other one here . . ."

"Rippledown Rill," Arya read.

"See, it loops around and flows down toward the lake, back to Harrenhal." He traced the line with a finger.

Hot Pie's eyes grew wide. "*No!* They'll kill us for sure."

"We have to know which river this is," declared Gendry, in his stubbornest voice. "We have to know."

"Well, we *don't*." The map might have names written beside the blue lines, but no one had written a name on the riverbank. "We won't go up *or* downstream," she decided, rolling up the map. "We'll cross and keep going north, like we were."

"Can horses swim?" asked Hot Pie. "It looks *deep*, Arry. What if there are snakes?"

"Are you sure we're going north?" asked Gendry. "All these hills . . . if we got turned around . . ."

"The moss on the trees –"

He pointed to a nearby tree. "That tree's got moss on three sides, and that next one has no moss at all. We could be lost, just riding around in a circle."

"We could be," said Arya, "but I'm going to cross the river anyway. You can come or you can stay here." She climbed back into the saddle, ignoring the both of them. If they didn't want to follow, they could find Riverrun on their own, though more likely the Mummers would just find them.

She had to ride a good half mile along the bank before she finally found a place where it looked as though it might be safe to cross, and even then her mare was reluctant to enter the water. The river, whatever its name, was running brown and fast, and the deep part in the middle came up past the horse's belly. Water filled her boots, but she pressed in her heels all the same and climbed out on the far bank. From behind she heard splashing, and a mare's nervous whinny. *They followed, then. Good.* She turned to watch as the boys struggled across and emerged dripping beside her. "It wasn't the Trident," she told them. "It *wasn't*."

The next river was shallower and easier to ford. That one wasn't the Trident either, and no one argued with her when she told them they would cross it.

Dusk was settling as they stopped to rest the horses once more and share another meal of bread and cheese. "I'm cold and wet," Hot Pie complained. "We're a long way from Harrenhal now, for sure. We could have us a fire –"

"*NO!*" Arya and Gendry both said, at the exact same instant. Hot Pie quailed a little. Arya gave Gendry a sideways look. *He said it with me, like Jon used to do, back in Winterfell.* She missed Jon Snow the most of all her brothers.

"Could we sleep at least?" Hot Pie asked. "I'm so tired, Arry, and my arse is sore. I think I've got blisters."

"You'll have more than that if you're caught," she said. "We've got to keep going. We've *got* to."

"But it's almost dark, and you can't even see the moon."

"Get back on your horse."

Plodding along at a slow walking pace as the light faded around them, Arya found her own exhaustion weighing heavy on her. She needed sleep as much as Hot Pie, but they dare not. If they slept, they might open their eyes to find Vargo Hoat standing over them with Shagwell the Fool and Faithful Urswyck and Rorge and Biter and Septon Utt and all his other monsters.

Yet after a while the motion of her horse became as soothing as the rocking of a cradle, and Arya found her eyes growing heavy. She let them close, just for an instant, then snapped them wide again. *I can't go to sleep,* she screamed at herself silently, *I can't, I can't.* She knuckled at her eye and rubbed it hard to keep it open, clutching the reins tightly and kicking her mount to a canter. But neither she nor the horse could sustain the pace, and it was only a few moments before they fell back to a walk again, and a few more until her eyes closed a second time. This time they did not open quite so quickly.

When they did, she found that her horse had come to a stop and was nibbling at a tuft of grass, while Gendry was shaking her arm. "You fell asleep," he told her.

"I was just resting my eyes."

"You were resting them a long while, then. Your horse was wandering in a circle, but it wasn't till she stopped that I realized you were sleeping. Hot Pie's just as bad, he rode into a tree limb and got knocked off, you should have heard him yell. Even *that* didn't wake you up. You need to stop and sleep."

"I can keep going as long as you can." She yawned.

"Liar," he said. "You keep going if you want to be stupid, but I'm stopping. I'll take the first watch. You sleep."

"What about Hot Pie?"

Gendry pointed. Hot Pie was already on the ground, curled up beneath his cloak on a bed of damp leaves and snoring softly. He had a big wedge of cheese in one fist, but it looked as though he had fallen asleep between bites.

It was no good arguing, Arya realized; Gendry had the right of it. *The Mummers will need to sleep too*, she told herself, hoping it was true. She was so weary it was a struggle even to get down from the saddle, but she remembered to hobble her horse before finding a place beneath a beech tree. The ground was hard and damp. She wondered how long it would be before she slept in a bed again, with hot food and a fire to warm her. The last thing she did before closing her eyes was unsheathe her sword and lay it down beside her. "Ser Gregor," she whispered, yawning. "Dunsen, Polliver, Raff the Sweetling. The Tickler and . . . the Tickler . . . the Hound . . ."

Her dreams were red and savage. The Mummers were in them, four at least, a pale Lyseni and a dark brutal axeman from Ib, the scarred Dothraki horse lord called Iggo and a Dornishman whose name she never knew. On and on they came, riding through the rain in rusting mail and wet leather, swords and axe clanking against their saddles. They thought they were hunting her, she knew with all the strange sharp certainty of dreams, but they were wrong. She was hunting them.

She was no little girl in the dream; she was a wolf, huge and powerful, and when she emerged from beneath the trees in front of them and bared her teeth in a low rumbling growl, she could smell the rank stench of fear from horse and man alike. The Lyseni's mount reared and screamed in terror, and the others shouted at one another in mantalk, but before they could act the other wolves came hurtling from the darkness and the rain, a great pack of them, gaunt and wet and silent.

The fight was short but bloody. The hairy man went down as he unslung his axe, the dark one died stringing an arrow, and the pale man from Lys tried to bolt. Her brothers and sisters ran him down, turning him again and again, coming at him from all sides, snapping at the legs of his horse and tearing the throat from the rider when he came crashing to the earth.

Only the belled man stood his ground. His horse kicked in the head of one of her sisters, and he cut another almost in half with his curved silvery claw as his hair tinkled softly.

Filled with rage, she leapt onto his back, knocking him head-first from his saddle. Her jaws locked on his arm as they fell, her teeth sinking through the leather and wool and soft flesh. When they landed she gave a savage jerk with her head and ripped the limb loose from his shoulder. Exulting, she shook it back and forth in her mouth, scattering the warm red droplets amidst the cold black rain.

TYRION

He woke to the creak of old iron hinges.

"Who?" he croaked. At least he had his voice back, raw and hoarse though it was. The fever was still on him, and Tyrion had no notion of the hour. How long had he slept this time? He was so weak, so damnably weak. "Who?" he called again, more loudly. Torchlight spilled through the open door, but within the chamber the only light came from the stub of a candle beside his bed.

When he saw a shape moving toward him, Tyrion shivered. Here in Maegor's Holdfast, every servant was in the queen's pay, so any visitor might be another of Cersei's catspaws, sent to finish the work Ser Mandon had begun.

Then the man stepped into the candlelight, got a good look at the dwarf's pale face, and chortled. "Cut yourself shaving, did you?"

Tyrion's fingers went to the great gash that ran from above one eye down to his jaw, across what remained of his nose. The proud flesh was still raw and warm to the touch. "With a fearful big razor, yes."

Bronn's coal-black hair was freshly washed and brushed straight back from the hard lines of his face, and he was dressed in high boots of soft, tooled leather, a wide belt studded with nuggets of silver, and a cloak of pale green silk. Across the dark grey wool of his doublet, a burning chain was embroidered diagonally in bright green thread.

"Where have you been?" Tyrion demanded of him. "I sent for you . . . it must have been a fortnight ago."

"Four days ago, more like," the sellsword said, "and I've been here twice, and found you dead to the world."

"Not dead. Though my sweet sister did try." Perhaps he should not have said that aloud, but Tyrion was past caring. Cersei was behind Ser Mandon's attempt to kill him, he knew that in his gut. "What's that ugly thing on your chest?"

Bronn grinned. "My knightly sigil. A flaming chain, green, on a smoke-grey field. By your lord father's command, I'm Ser Bronn of the Blackwater now, Imp. See you don't forget it."

Tyrion put his hands on the featherbed and squirmed back a few inches, against the pillows. "I was the one who promised you knighthood, remember?" He had liked that *"by your lord father's command"* not at all. Lord Tywin had wasted little time. Moving his son from the Tower of the Hand to claim it for himself was a message anyone could read, and this was another. "I lose half my nose and you gain a knighthood. The gods have a deal to answer for." His voice was sour. "Did my father dub you himself?"

"No. Them of us as survived the fight at the winch towers got ourselves dabbed by the High Septon and dubbed by the Kingsguard. Took half the bloody day, with only three of the White Swords left to do the honors."

"I knew Ser Mandon died in the battle." *Shoved into the river by Pod, half a heartbeat before the treacherous bastard could drive his sword through my heart.* "Who else was lost?"

"The Hound," said Bronn. "Not dead, only gone. The gold cloaks say he turned craven and you led a sortie in his place."

Not one of my better notions. Tyrion could feel the scar tissue pull tight when he frowned. He waved Bronn toward a chair. "My sister has mistaken me for a mushroom. She keeps me in the dark and feeds me shit. Pod's a good lad, but the knot in his tongue is the size of Casterly Rock, and I don't trust half of what he tells me. I sent him to bring Ser Jacelyn and he came back and told me he's dead."

"Him, and thousands more." Bronn sat.

"How?" Tyrion demanded, feeling that much sicker.

"During the battle. Your sister sent the Kettleblacks to fetch the king back to the Red Keep, the way I hear it. When the gold cloaks saw him leaving, half of them decided they'd leave with him. Ironhand put himself in their path and tried to order them back to the walls. They say Bywater was blistering them good and almost had 'em ready to turn when someone put an arrow through his neck. He didn't seem so fearsome then, so they dragged him off his horse and killed him."

Another debt to lay at Cersei's door. "My nephew," he said, "Joffrey. Was he in any danger?"

"No more'n some, and less than most."

"Had he suffered any harm? Taken a wound? Mussed his hair, stubbed his toe, cracked a nail?"

"Not as I heard."

"I warned Cersei what would happen. Who commands the gold cloaks now?"

"Your lord father's given them to one of his westermen, some knight named Addam Marbrand."

In most cases the gold cloaks would have resented having an outsider placed over them, but Ser Addam Marbrand was a shrewd choice. Like Jaime, he was the sort of man other men liked to follow. *I have lost the City Watch.* "I sent Pod looking for Shagga, but he's had no luck."

"The Stone Crows are still in the kingswood. Shagga seems to have taken a fancy to the place. Timett led the Burned Men home, with all the plunder they took from Stannis's camp after the fighting. Chella turned up with a dozen Black Ears at the River Gate one morning, but your father's red cloaks chased them off while the Kingslanders threw dung and cheered."

Ingrates. The Black Ears died for them. Whilst Tyrion lay drugged and dreaming, his own blood had pulled his claws out, one by one. "I want you to go to my sister. Her precious son made it through the battle unscathed, so Cersei has no more need of a hostage. She swore to free Alayaya once –"

"She did. Eight, nine days ago, after the whipping."

Tyrion shoved himself up higher, ignoring the sudden stab of pain through his shoulder. *"Whipping?"*

"They tied her to a post in the yard and scourged her, then shoved her out the gate naked and bloody."

She was learning to read, Tyrion thought, absurdly. Across his face the scar stretched tight, and for a moment it felt as though his head would burst with rage. Alayaya was a whore, true enough, but a sweeter, braver, more innocent girl he had seldom met. Tyrion had never touched her; she had been no more than a veil, to hide Shae. In his carelessness, he had never thought what the role might cost her. "I promised my sister I would treat Tommen as she treated Alayaya," he remembered aloud. He felt as though he might retch. "How can I scourge an eight-year-old boy?" *But if I don't, Cersei wins.*

"You don't have Tommen," Bronn said bluntly. "Once she learned that Ironhand was dead, the queen sent the Kettleblacks after him, and no one at Rosby had the balls to say them nay."

Another blow; yet a relief as well, he must admit it. He was fond of Tommen. "The Kettleblacks were supposed to be ours," he reminded Bronn with more than a touch of irritation.

"They were, so long as I could give them two of your pennies for every one they had from the queen, but now she's raised the stakes. Osney and Osfryd were made knights after the battle, same as me. Gods know what for, no one saw them do any fighting."

My hirelings betray me, my friends are scourged and shamed, and I lie here rotting, Tyrion thought. *I thought I won the bloody battle. Is this what triumph tastes like?* "Is it true that Stannis was put to rout by Renly's ghost?"

Bronn smiled thinly. "From the winch towers, all we saw was banners in the mud and men throwing down their spears to run, but there's hundreds in the pot shops and brothels who'll tell you how they saw Lord Renly kill this one or that one. Most of Stannis's host had been Renly's to start, and they went right back over at the sight of him in that shiny green armor."

After all his planning, after the sortie and the bridge of ships, after getting his face slashed in two, Tyrion had been eclipsed by a dead man. *If indeed Renly is dead.* Something else he would need to look into. "How did Stannis escape?"

"His Lyseni kept their galleys out in the bay, beyond your chain. When the battle turned bad, they put in along the bay shore and took off as many as they could. Men were killing each other to get aboard, toward the end."

"What of Robb Stark, what has he been doing?"

"There's some of his wolves burning their way down toward Dusken-dale. Your father's sending this Lord Tarly to sort them out. I'd half a mind to join him. It's said he's a good soldier, and openhanded with the plunder."

The thought of losing Bronn was the final straw. "No. Your place is here. You're the captain of the Hand's guard."

"You're not the Hand," Bronn reminded him sharply. "Your father is, and he's got his own bloody guard."

"What happened to all the men you hired for me?"

"Some died at the winch towers. That uncle of yours, Ser Kevan, he paid the rest of us and tossed us out."

"How good of him," Tyrion said acidly. "Does that mean you've lost your taste for gold?"

"Not bloody likely."

"Good," said Tyrion, "because as it happens, I still have need of you. What do you know of Ser Mandon Moore?"

Bronn laughed. "I know he's bloody well drowned."

"I owe him a great debt, but how to pay it?" He touched his face, feeling the scar. "I know precious little of the man, if truth be told."

"He had eyes like a fish and he wore a white cloak. What else do you need to know?"

"Everything," said Tyrion, "for a start." What he wanted was proof that Ser Mandon had been Cersei's, but he dare not say so aloud. In the Red Keep a man did best to hold his tongue. There were rats in the walls, and little birds who talked too much, and spiders. "Help me up," he said, struggling with the bedclothes. "It's time I paid a call on my father, and past time I let myself be seen again."

"Such a pretty sight," mocked Bronn.

"What's half a nose, on a face like mine? But speaking of pretty, is Margaery Tyrell in King's Landing yet?"

"No. She's coming, though, and the city's mad with love for her. The Tyrells have been carting food up from Highgarden and giving it away in her name. Hundreds of wayns each day. There's thousands of Tyrell men swaggering about with little golden roses sewn on their doublets, and not a one is buying his own wine. Wife, widow, or whore, the women are all giving up their virtue to every peach-fuzz boy with a gold rose on his teat."

They spit on me, and buy drinks for the Tyrells. Tyrion slid from the bed to the floor. His legs turned wobbly beneath him, the room spun, and he had to grasp Bronn's arm to keep from pitching headlong into the rushes. "*Pod!*" he shouted. "Podrick Payne! Where in the seven hells are you?" Pain gnawed at him like a toothless dog. Tyrion hated weakness, especially his own. It shamed him, and shame made him angry. "Pod, *get in here!*"

The boy came running. When he saw Tyrion standing and clutching Bronn's arm, he gaped at them. "My lord. You stood. Is that ... do you ... do you need wine? Dreamwine? Should I get the maester? He said you must stay. Abed, I mean."

"I have stayed abed too long. Bring me some clean garb."

"Garb?"

How the boy could be so clearheaded and resourceful in battle and so confused at all other times Tyrion could never comprehend. "Clothing," he repeated. "Tunic, doublet, breeches, hose. For me. To dress in. So I can leave this bloody cell."

It took all three of them to clothe him. Hideous though his face might be, the worst of his wounds was the one at the juncture of shoulder and arm, where his own mail had been driven back into his armpit by an arrow. Pus and blood still seeped from the discolored flesh whenever Maester Frenken changed his dressing, and any movement sent a stab of agony through him.

In the end, Tyrion settled for a pair of breeches and an oversized bed robe that hung loosely about his shoulders. Bronn yanked his boots onto his feet while Pod went in search of a stick for him to lean on. He drank a cup of dreamwine to fortify himself. The wine was sweetened with honey, with just enough of the poppy to make his wounds bearable for a time.

Even so, he was dizzy by the time he turned the latch, and the descent down the twisting stone steps made his legs tremble. He walked with the stick in one hand and the other on Pod's shoulder. A serving girl was coming up as they were going down. She stared at them with wide white eyes, as if she were looking at a ghost. *The dwarf has risen from the dead*, Tyrion thought. *And look, he's uglier than ever, run tell your friends.*

Maegor's Holdfast was the strongest place in the Red Keep, a castle within the castle, surrounded by a deep dry moat lined with spikes. The drawbridge was up for the night when they reached the door. Ser Meryn Trant stood before it in his pale armor and white cloak. "Lower the bridge," Tyrion commanded him.

"The queen's orders are to raise the bridge at night." Ser Meryn had always been Cersei's creature.

"The queen's asleep, and I have business with my father."

There was magic in the name of Lord Tywin Lannister. Grumbling, Ser Meryn Trant gave the command, and the drawbridge was lowered. A second Kingsguard knight stood sentry across the moat. Ser Osmund Kettleblack managed a smile when he saw Tyrion waddling toward him. "Feeling stronger, m'lord?"

"Much. When's the next battle? I can scarcely wait."

When Pod and he reached the serpentine steps, however, Tyrion could only gape at them in dismay. *I will never climb those by myself*, he confessed to himself. Swallowing his dignity, he asked Bronn to carry him, hoping against hope that at this hour there would be no one to see and smile, no one to tell the tale of the dwarf being carried up the steps like a babe in arms.

The outer ward was crowded with tents and pavilions, dozens of them. "Tyrell men," Podrick Payne explained as they threaded their way through a maze of silk and canvas. "Lord Rowan's too, and Lord Redwyne's. There wasn't room enough for all. In the castle, I mean. Some took rooms. Rooms in the city. In inns and all. They're here for the wedding. The king's wedding, King Joffrey's. Will you be strong enough to attend, my lord?"

"Ravening weasels could not keep me away." There was this to be said for weddings over battles, at least; it was less likely that someone would cut off your nose.

Lights still burned dimly behind shuttered windows in the Tower of the Hand. The men on the door wore the crimson cloaks and lion-crested helms of his father's household guard. Tyrion knew them both, and they admitted him on sight . . . though neither could bear to look long at his face, he noted.

Within, they came upon Ser Addam Marbrand, descending the turnpike stair in the ornate black breastplate and cloth-of-gold cloak of an officer in the City Watch. "My lord," he said, "how good to see you on your feet. I'd heard –"

" – rumors of a small grave being dug? Me too. Under the circumstances it seemed best to get up. I hear you're commander of the City Watch. Shall I offer congratulations or condolences?"

"Both, I fear." Ser Addam smiled. "Death and desertion have left me with some forty-four hundred. Only the gods and Littlefinger know how we are to go on paying wages for so many, but your sister forbids me to dismiss any."

Still anxious, Cersei? The battle's done, the gold cloaks won't help you now. "Do you come from my father?" he asked.

"Aye. I fear I did not leave him in the best of moods. Lord Tywin feels forty-four hundred guardsmen more than sufficient to find one lost squire, but your cousin Tyrek remains missing."

Tyrek was the son of his late Uncle Tygett, a boy of thirteen. He had vanished in the riot, not long after wedding the Lady Ermesande, a suckling babe who happened to be the last surviving heir of House Hayford. *And likely the first bride in the history of the Seven Kingdoms to be widowed before she was weaned.* "I couldn't find him either," confessed Tyrion.

"He's feeding worms," said Bronn with his usual tact. "Ironhand looked for him, and the eunuch rattled a nice fat purse. They had no more luck than we did. Give it up, ser."

Ser Addam gazed at the sellsword with distaste. "Lord Tywin is stubborn where his blood is concerned. He will have the lad, alive or dead, and I mean to oblige him." He looked back to Tyrion. "You will find your father in his solar."

My solar, thought Tyrion. "I believe I know the way."

The way was up more steps, but this time he climbed under his own power, with one hand on Pod's shoulder. Bronn opened the door for him. Lord Tywin Lannister was seated beneath the window, writing by the glow of an oil lamp. He raised his eyes at the sound of the latch. "Tyrion." Calmly, he laid his quill aside.

"I'm pleased you remember me, my lord." Tyrion released his grip on Pod, leaned his weight on the stick, and waddled closer. *Something is wrong,* he knew at once.

"Ser Bronn," Lord Tywin said, "Podrick. Perhaps you had best wait without until we are done."

The look Bronn gave the Hand was little less than insolent; nonetheless, he bowed and withdrew, with Pod on his heels. The heavy door swung shut behind them, and Tyrion Lannister was alone with his father. Even with the windows of the solar shuttered against the night, the chill in the room was palpable. *What sort of lies has Cersei been telling him?*

The Lord of Casterly Rock was as lean as a man twenty years younger, even handsome in his austere way. Stiff blond whiskers covered his cheeks, framing a stern face, a bald head, a hard mouth. About his throat he wore a chain of golden hands, the fingers of each clasping the wrist of the next. "That's a handsome chain," Tyrion said. *Though it looked better on me.*

Lord Tywin ignored the sally. "You had best be seated. Is it wise for you to be out of your sickbed?"

"I am sick of my sickbed." Tyrion knew how much his father despised weakness. He claimed the nearest chair. "Such pleasant chambers you have. Would you believe it, while I was dying, someone moved me to a dark little cell in Maegor's?"

"The Red Keep is overcrowded with wedding guests. Once they depart, we will find you more suitable accommodations."

"I rather liked *these* accommodations. Have you set a date for this great wedding?"

"Joffrey and Margaery shall marry on the first day of the new year, which as it happens is also the first day of the new century. The ceremony will herald the dawn of a new era."

A new Lannister era, thought Tyrion. "Oh, bother, I fear I've made other plans for that day."

"Did you come here just to complain of your bedchamber and make your lame japes? I have important letters to finish."

"*Important* letters. To be sure."

"Some battles are won with swords and spears, others with quills and ravens. Spare me these coy reproaches, Tyrion. I visited your sickbed as often as Maester Ballabar would allow it, when you seemed like to die." He steepled his fingers under his chin. "Why did you dismiss Ballabar?"

Tyrion shrugged. "Maester Frenken is not so determined to keep me insensate."

"Ballabar came to the city in Lord Redwyne's retinue. A gifted healer, it's said. It was kind of Cersei to ask him to look after you. She feared for your life."

Feared that I might keep it, you mean. "Doubtless that's why she's never once left my bedside."

"Don't be impertinent. Cersei has a royal wedding to plan, I am waging a war, and you have been out of danger for at least a fortnight." Lord Tywin studied his son's disfigured face, his pale green eyes unflinching. "Though the wound is ghastly enough, I'll grant you. What madness possessed you?"

"The foe was at the gates with a battering ram. If Jaime had led the sortie, you'd call it valor."

"Jaime would never be so foolish as to remove his helm in battle. I trust you killed the man who cut you?"

"Oh, the wretch is dead enough." Though it had been Podrick Payne who'd killed Ser Mandon, shoving him into the river to drown beneath the weight of his armor. "A dead enemy is a joy forever," Tyrion said blithely, though Ser Mandon was not his true enemy. The man had no reason to want him dead. *He was only a catspaw, and I believe I know the cat. She told him to make certain I did not survive the battle.* But without proof Lord Tywin would never listen to such a charge. "Why are you here in the city, Father?" he asked. "Shouldn't you be off fighting Lord Stannis or Robb Stark or someone?" *And the sooner the better.*

"Until Lord Redwyne brings his fleet up, we lack the ships to assail Dragonstone. It makes no matter. Stannis Baratheon's sun set on the Blackwater. As for Stark, the boy is still in the west, but a large force of northmen under Helman Tallhart and Robett Glover are descending toward Duskendale. I've sent Lord Tarly to meet them, while Ser Gregor drives up the kingsroad to cut off their retreat. Tallhart and Glover will be caught between them, with a third of Stark's strength."

"Duskendale?" There was nothing at Duskendale worth such a risk. Had the Young Wolf finally blundered?

"It's nothing you need trouble yourself with. Your face is pale as death, and there's blood seeping through your dressings. Say what you want and take yourself back to bed."

"What I want . . ." His throat felt raw and tight. What *did* he want? *More than you can ever give me, Father.* "Pod tells me that Littlefinger's been made Lord of Harrenhal."

"An empty title, so long as Roose Bolton holds the castle for Robb Stark, yet Lord Baelish was desirous of the honor. He did us good service in the matter of the Tyrell marriage. A Lannister pays his debts."

The Tyrell marriage had been Tyrion's notion, in point of fact, but it would seem churlish to try to claim that now. "That title may not be as empty as you think," he warned. "Littlefinger does nothing without good reason. But be that as it may. You said something about paying debts, I believe?"

"And you want your own reward, is that it? Very well. What is it you would have of me? Lands, castle, some office?"

"A little bloody gratitude would make a nice start."

Lord Tywin stared at him, unblinking. "Mummers and monkeys require applause. So did Aerys, for that matter. You did as you were commanded, and I am sure it was to the best of your ability. No one denies the part you played."

"The *part* I played?" What nostrils Tyrion had left must surely have flared. "I saved your bloody city, it seems to me."

"Most people seem to feel that it was my attack on Lord Stannis's flank that turned the tide of battle. Lords Tyrell, Rowan, Redwyne, and Tarly fought nobly as well, and I'm told it was your sister Cersei who set the pyromancers to making the wildfire that destroyed the Baratheon fleet."

"While all I did was get my nosehairs trimmed, is that it?" Tyrion could not keep the bitterness out of his voice.

"Your chain was a clever stroke, and crucial to our victory. Is that what you wanted to hear? I am told we have you to thank for our Dornish alliance as well. You may be pleased to learn that Myrcella has arrived safely at Sunspear. Ser Arys Oakheart writes that she has taken a great liking to Princess Arianne, and that Prince Trystane is enchanted with her. I mislike giving House Martell a hostage, but I suppose that could not be helped."

"We'll have our own hostage," Tyrion said. "A council seat was also part of the bargain. Unless Prince Doran brings an army when he comes to claim it, he'll be putting himself in our power."

"Would that a council seat were all Martell came to claim," Lord Tywin said. "You promised him vengeance as well."

"I promised him justice."

"Call it what you will. It still comes down to blood."

"Not an item in short supply, surely? I splashed through lakes of it during the battle." Tyrion saw no reason not to cut to the heart of the matter. "Or have you grown so fond of Gregor Clegane that you cannot bear to part with him?"

"Ser Gregor has his uses, as did his brother. Every lord has need of a beast from time to time . . . a lesson you seem to have learned, judging from Ser Bronn and those clansmen of yours."

Tyrion thought of Timett's burned eye, Shagga with his axe, Chella in her necklace of dried ears. And Bronn. Bronn most of all. "The woods are full of beasts," he reminded his father. "The alleyways as well."

"True. Perhaps other dogs would hunt as well. I shall think on it. If there is nothing else . . ."

"You have important letters, yes." Tyrion rose on unsteady legs, closed his eyes for an instant as a wave of dizziness washed over him, and took a shaky step toward the door. Later, he would reflect that he should have taken a second, and then a third. Instead he turned. "What do I want, you ask? I'll tell you what I want. I want what is mine by rights. I want Casterly Rock."

His father's mouth grew hard. "Your brother's birthright?"

"The knights of the Kingsguard are forbidden to marry, to father children, and to hold land, you know that as well as I. The day Jaime put on that white cloak, he gave up his claim to Casterly Rock, but never once have you acknowledged it. It's past time. I want you to stand up before the realm and proclaim that I am your son and your lawful heir."

Lord Tywin's eyes were a pale green flecked with gold, as luminous as they were merciless. "Casterly Rock," he declared in a flat cold dead tone. And then, "Never."

The word hung between them, huge, sharp, poisoned.

I knew the answer before I asked, Tyrion said. *Eighteen years since Jaime joined the Kingsguard, and I never once raised the issue. I must have known. I must always have known.* "Why?" he made himself ask, though he knew he would rue the question.

"You ask that? You, who killed your mother to come into the world? You are an ill-made, devious, disobedient, spiteful little creature full of envy, lust, and low cunning. Men's laws give you the right to bear my name and display my colors, since I cannot prove that you are not mine. To teach me humility, the gods have condemned me to watch you waddle about wearing that proud lion that was my father's sigil and his father's before him. But neither gods nor men shall ever compel me to let you turn Casterly Rock into your whorehouse."

"My *whorehouse!*" The dawn broke; Tyrion understood all at once where this bile had come from. He ground his teeth together and said, "Cersei told you about Alayaya."

"Is that her name? I confess, I cannot remember the names of all your whores. Who was the one you married as a boy?"

"Tysha." He spat out the answer, defiant.

"And that camp follower on the Green Fork?"

"Why do you care?" he asked, unwilling even to speak Shae's name in his presence.

"I don't. No more than I care if they live or die."

"It was *you* who had Yaya whipped." It was not a question.

"Your sister told me of your threats against my grandsons." Lord Tywin's voice was colder than ice. "Did she lie?"

Tyrion would not deny it. "I made threats, yes. To keep Alayaya safe. So the Kettleblacks would not misuse her."

"To save a whore's virtue, you threatened your own House, your own kin? Is that the way of it?"

"You were the one who taught me that a good threat is often more telling than a blow. Not that Joffrey hasn't tempted me sore a few hundred times. If you're so anxious to whip people, start with him. But Tommen . . . why would I harm Tommen? He's a good lad, and mine own blood."

"As was your mother." Lord Tywin rose abruptly, to tower over his dwarf son. "Go back to your bed, Tyrion, and speak to me no more of *your rights* to Casterly Rock. You shall have your reward, but it shall be one I deem appropriate to your service and station. And make no mistake – this was the last time I will suffer you to bring shame onto House Lannister. You are *done* with whores. The next one I find in your bed, I'll hang."

DAVOS

He watched the sail grow for a long time, trying to decide whether he would sooner live or die.

Dying would be easier, he knew. All he had to do was crawl inside his cave and let the ship pass by, and death would find him. For days now the fever had been burning through him, turning his bowels to brown water and making him shiver in his restless sleep. Each morning found him weaker. *It will not be much longer*, he had taken to telling himself.

If the fever did not kill him, thirst surely would. He had no fresh water here, but for the occasional rainfall that pooled in hollows on the rock. Only three days past (or had it been four? On his rock, it was hard to tell the days apart) his pools had been dry as old bone, and the sight of the bay rippling green and grey all around him had been almost more than he could bear. Once he began to drink seawater the end would come swiftly, he knew, but all the same he had almost taken that first swallow, so parched was his throat. A sudden squall had saved him. He had grown so feeble by then that it was all he could do to lie in the rain with his eyes closed and his mouth open, and let the water splash down on his cracked lips and swollen tongue. But afterward he felt a little stronger, and the island's pools and cracks and crevices once more had brimmed with life.

But that had been three days ago (or maybe four), and most of the water was gone now. Some had evaporated, and he had sucked up the rest. By the morrow he would be tasting the mud again, and licking the damp cold stones at the bottom of the depressions.

And if not thirst or fever, starvation would kill him. His island was no more than a barren spire jutting up out of the immensity of Blackwater Bay. When the tide was low, he could sometimes find tiny crabs along the stony strand where he had washed ashore after the battle. They nipped his fingers painfully before he smashed them apart on the rocks to suck the meat from their claws and the guts from their shells.

But the strand vanished whenever the tide came rushing in, and Davos had to scramble up the rock to keep from being swept out into the bay once more. The point of the spire was fifteen feet above the water at high tide, but when the bay grew rough the spray went even higher, so there was no way to keep dry, even in his cave (which was really no more than a hollow in the rock beneath an overhang). Nothing grew on the rock but lichen, and even the seabirds shunned the place. Now and again some gulls would land atop the spire and Davos would try to catch one, but they were too quick for him to get close. He took to flinging stones at them, but he was too weak to throw with much force, so even when his stones hit the gulls would only scream at him in annoyance and then take to the air.

There were other rocks visible from his refuge, distant stony spires taller than his own. The nearest stood a good forty feet above the water, he guessed, though it was hard to be sure at this distance. A cloud of gulls swirled about it constantly, and often Davos thought of crossing over to raid their nests. But the water was cold here, the currents strong and treacherous, and he knew he did not have the strength for such a swim. That would kill him as sure as drinking seawater.

Autumn in the narrow sea could often be wet and rainy, he remembered from years past. The days were not bad so long as the sun was shining, but the nights were growing colder and sometimes the wind would come gusting across the bay, driving a line of whitecaps before it, and before long Davos would be soaked and shivering. Fever and chills assaulted him in turn, and of late he had developed a persistent racking cough.

His cave was all the shelter he had, and that was little enough. Driftwood and bits of charred debris would wash up on the strand during low tide, but he had no way to strike a spark or start a fire. Once, in desperation, he had tried rubbing two pieces of driftwood against each other, but the wood was rotted, and his efforts earned him only blisters. His clothes were sodden as well, and he had lost one of his boots somewhere in the bay before he washed up here.

Thirst; hunger; exposure. They were his companions, with him every hour of every day, and in time he had come to think of them as his friends. Soon enough, one or the other of his friends would take pity on him and free him from this endless misery. Or perhaps he would simply walk into the water one day, and strike out for the shore that he knew lay somewhere to the north, beyond his sight. It was too far to swim, as weak as he was, but that did not matter. Davos had always been a sailor; he was meant to die at sea. *The gods beneath the waters have been waiting for me*, he told himself. *It's past time I went to them.*

But now there was a sail; only a speck on the horizon, but growing larger. *A ship where no ship should be.* He knew where his rock lay, more or less; it was one of a series of sea monts that rose from the floor of Blackwater Bay. The tallest of them jutted a hundred feet above the tide, and a dozen lesser monts stood thirty to sixty feet high. Sailors called them *spears of the merling king*, and knew that for every one that broke the surface, a dozen lurked treacherously just below it. Any captain with sense kept his course well away from them.

Davos watched the sail swell through pale red-rimmed eyes, and tried to hear the sound of the wind caught in the canvas. *She is coming this way.* Unless she changed course soon, she would pass within hailing distance of his meager refuge. It might mean life. If he wanted it. He was not sure he did.

Why should I live? he thought as tears blurred his vision. *Gods be good, why? My sons are dead, Dale and Allard, Maric and Matthos, perhaps Devan as well. How can a father outlive so many strong young sons? How would I go on? I am a hollow shell, the crab's died, there's nothing left inside. Don't they know that?*

They had sailed up the Blackwater Rush flying the fiery heart of the Lord of Light. Davos and *Black Betha* had been in the second line of battle, between Dale's *Wraith* and Allard on *Lady Marya*. Maric his third-born was oarmaster on *Fury*, at the center of the first line, while Matthos served as his father's second. Beneath the walls of the Red Keep Stannis Baratheon's galleys had joined in battle with the boy king Joffrey's smaller fleet, and for a few moments the river had rung to the thrum of bowstrings and the crash of iron rams shattering oars and hulls alike.

And then some vast beast had let out a roar, and green flames were all around them: wildfire, pyromancer's piss, the jade demon. Matthos had been standing at his elbow on the deck of *Black Betha* when the ship seemed to lift from the water. Davos found himself in the river, flailing as the current took him and spun him around and around. Upstream, the flames had ripped at the sky, fifty feet high. He had seen *Black Betha* afire, and *Fury*, and a dozen other ships, had seen burning men leaping into the water to drown. *Wraith* and *Lady Marya* were gone, sunk or shattered or vanished behind a veil of wildfire, and there was no time to look for them, because the mouth of the river was almost upon him, and across the mouth of the river the Lannisters had raised a great iron chain. From bank to bank there was nothing but burning ships and wildfire. The sight of it seemed to stop his heart for a moment, and he could still remember the sound of it, the crackle of flames, the hiss of steam, the shrieks of dying men, and the beat of that terrible heat against his face as the current swept him down toward hell.

All he needed to do was nothing. A few moments more, and he would be with his sons now, resting in the cool green mud on the bottom of the bay, with fish nibbling at his face.

Instead he sucked in a great gulp of air and dove, kicking for the bottom of the river. His only hope was to pass under the chain and the burning ships and the wildfire that floated on the surface of the water, to swim hard for the safety of the bay beyond. Davos had always been a strong swimmer, and he'd worn no steel that day, but for the helm he'd lost when he'd lost *Black Betha*. As he knifed through the green murk, he saw other men struggling beneath the water, pulled down to drown beneath the weight of plate and mail. Davos swam past them, kicking with all the strength left in his legs, giving himself up to the current, the water filling his eyes. Deeper he went, and deeper, and deeper still. With every stroke it grew harder to hold his breath. He remembered seeing the bottom, soft and dim, as a stream of bubbles burst from his lips. Something touched his leg . . . a snag or a fish or a drowning man, he could not tell.

He needed air by then, but he was afraid. Was he past the chain yet, was he out in the bay? If he came up under a ship he would drown, and if he surfaced amidst the floating patches of wildfire his first breath would sear his lungs to ash. He twisted in the water to look up, but there was nothing to see but green darkness and then he spun too far and suddenly he could no longer tell up from down. Panic took hold of him. His hands flailed against the bottom of the river and sent up a cloud of mud that blinded him. His chest was growing tighter by the instant. He clawed at the water, kicking, pushing himself, turning, his lungs screaming for air, kicking, kicking, lost now in the river murk, kicking, kicking, kicking until he could kick no longer. When he opened his mouth to scream, the water came rushing in, tasting of salt, and Davos Seaworth knew that he was drowning.

The next he knew the sun was up, and he lay upon a stony strand beneath a spire of naked stone, with the empty bay all around and a broken mast, a burned sail, and a swollen corpse beside him. The mast, the sail, and the dead man vanished with the next high tide, leaving Davos alone on his rock amidst the spears of the merling king.

His long years as a smuggler had made the waters around King's Landing more familiar to him than any home he'd ever had, and he knew his refuge was no more than a speck on the charts, in a place that honest sailors steered away from, not toward . . . though Davos himself had come by it once or twice in his smuggling days, the better to stay unseen. *When they find me dead here, if ever they do, perhaps they will name the rock for me,* he thought. *Onion Rock, they'll call it; it will be my tombstone and my legacy.* He deserved no more. *The Father protects his children,* the septons taught, but Davos had led his boys into the fire. Dale would never give his wife the child they had prayed for, and Allard, with his girl in Oldtown and his girl in King's Landing and his girl in Braavos, they would all be weeping soon. Matthos would never captain his own ship, as he'd dreamed. Maric would never have his knighthood.

How can I live when they are dead? So many brave knights and mighty lords have died, better men than me, and highborn. Crawl inside your cave, Davos. Crawl inside and shrink up small and the ship will go away, and no one will trouble you ever again. Sleep on your stone pillow, and let the gulls peck out your eyes while the crabs feast on your flesh. You've feasted on enough of them, you owe them. Hide, smuggler. Hide, and be quiet, and die.

The sail was almost on him. A few moments more, and the ship would be safely past, and he could die in peace.

His hand reached for his throat, fumbling for the small leather pouch he always wore about his neck. Inside he kept the bones of the four fingers his king had shortened for him, on the day he made Davos a knight. *My luck.* His shortened fingers patted at his chest, groping, finding nothing. The pouch was gone, and the fingerbones with them. Stannis could never understand why he'd kept the bones. "To remind me of my king's justice," he whispered through cracked lips. But now they were gone. *The fire took my luck as well as my sons.* In his dreams the river was still aflame and demons danced upon the waters with fiery whips in their hands, while men blackened and burned beneath the lash. "Mother, have mercy," Davos prayed. "Save me, gentle Mother, save us all. My luck is gone, and my sons." He was weeping freely now, salt tears streaming down his cheeks. "The fire took it all . . . the fire . . ."

Perhaps it was only wind blowing against the rock, or the sound of the sea on the shore, but for an instant Davos Seaworth heard her answer. "You called the fire," she whispered, her voice as faint as the sound of waves in a seashell, sad and soft. "You burned us . . . burned us . . . burrrrned ussssssss."

"It was *her!*" Davos cried. "Mother, don't forsake us. It was her who burned you, the red woman, Melisandre, *her!*" He could see her; the heart-shaped face, the red eyes, the long coppery hair, her red gowns moving like flames as she walked, a swirl of silk and satin. She had come from Asshai in the east, she had come to Dragonstone and won Selyse and her queen's men for her alien god, and then the king, Stannis Baratheon himself. He had gone so far as to put the fiery heart on his banners, the fiery heart of R'hllor, Lord of Light and God of Flame and Shadow. At Melisandre's urging, he had dragged the Seven from their sept at Dragonstone and burned them before the castle gates, and later he had burned the godswood at Storm's End as well, even the heart tree, a huge white weirwood with a solemn face.

"It was her work," Davos said again, more weakly. *Her work, and yours, onion knight. You rowed her into Storm's End in the black of night, so she might loose her shadow child. You are not guiltless, no. You rode beneath her banner and flew it from your mast. You watched the Seven burn at Dragonstone, and did nothing. She gave the Father's justice to the fire, and the Mother's mercy, and the wisdom of the Crone. Smith and Stranger, Maid and Warrior, she burnt them all to the glory of her cruel god, and you stood and held your tongue. Even when she killed old Maester Cressen, even then, you did nothing.*

The sail was a hundred yards away and moving fast across the bay. In a few more moments it would be past him, and dwindling.

Ser Davos Seaworth began to climb his rock.

He pulled himself up with trembling hands, his head swimming with fever. Twice his maimed fingers slipped on the damp stone and he almost fell, but somehow he managed to cling to his perch. If he fell he was dead, and he had to live. For a little while more, at least. There was something he had to do.

The top of the rock was too small to stand on safely, as weak as he was, so he crouched and waved his fleshless arms. "*Ship*," he screamed into the wind. "Ship, here, *here!*" From up here, he could see her more clearly; the lean striped hull, the bronze figurehead, the billowing sail. There was a name painted on her hull, but Davos had never learned to read. "*Ship*," he called again, "*help me, HELP ME!*"

A crewman on her forecastle saw him and pointed. He watched as other sailors moved to the gunwale to gape at him. A short while later the galley's sail came down, her oars slid out, and she swept around toward his refuge. She was too big to approach the rock closely, but thirty yards away she launched a small boat. Davos clung to his rock and watched it creep toward him. Four men were rowing, while a fifth sat in the prow. "You," the fifth man called out when they were only a few feet from his island, "you up on the rock. Who are you?"

A smuggler who rose above himself, thought Davos, *a fool who loved his king too much, and forgot his gods.* "I . . ." His throat was parched, and he had forgotten how to talk. The words felt strange on his tongue and sounded stranger in his ears. "I was in the battle. I was . . . a captain, a . . . a knight, I was a knight."

"Aye, ser," the man said, "and serving which king?"

The galley might be Joffrey's, he realized suddenly. If he spoke the wrong name now, she would abandon him to his fate. But no, her hull was striped. She was Lysene, she was Salladhor Saan's. The Mother sent her here, the Mother in her mercy. She had a task for him. *Stannis lives,* he knew then. *I have a king still. And sons, I have other sons, and a wife loyal and loving.* How could he have forgotten? The Mother was merciful indeed.

"Stannis," he shouted back at the Lyseni. "Gods be good, I serve King Stannis."

"Aye," said the man in the boat, "and so do we."

SANSA

The invitation seemed innocent enough, but every time Sansa read it her tummy tightened into a knot. *She's to be queen now, she's beautiful and rich and everyone loves her, why would she want to sup with a traitor's daughter?* It could be curiosity, she supposed; perhaps Margaery Tyrell wanted to get the measure of the rival she'd displaced. *Does she resent me, I wonder? Does she think I bear her ill will . . .*

Sansa had watched from the castle walls as Margaery Tyrell and her escort made their way up Aegon's High Hill. Joffrey had met his new bride-to-be at the King's Gate to welcome her to the city, and they rode side by side through cheering crowds, Joff glittering in gilded armor and the Tyrell girl splendid in green with a cloak of autumn flowers blowing from her shoulders. She was sixteen, brown-haired and brown-eyed, slender and beautiful. The people called out her name as she passed, held up their children for her blessing, and scattered flowers under the hooves of her horse. Her mother and grandmother followed close behind, riding in a tall wheelhouse whose sides were carved into the shape of a hundred twining roses, every one gilded and shining. The smallfolk cheered them as well.

The same smallfolk who pulled me from my horse and would have killed me, if not for the Hound. Sansa had done nothing to make the commons hate her, no more than Margaery Tyrell had done to win their love. *Does she want me to love her too?* She studied the invitation, which looked to be written in Margaery's own hand. *Does she want my blessing?* Sansa wondered if Joffrey knew of this supper. For all she knew, it might be his doing. That thought made her fearful. If Joff was behind the invitation, he would have some cruel jape planned to shame her in the older girl's eyes. Would he command his Kingsguard to strip her naked once again? The last time he had done that his uncle Tyrion had stopped him, but the Imp could not save her now.

No one can save me but my Florian. Ser Dontos had promised he would help her escape, but not until the night of Joffrey's wedding. The plans had been well laid, her dear devoted knight-turned-fool assured her; there was nothing to do until then but endure, and count the days.

And sup with my replacement . . .

Perhaps she was doing Margaery Tyrell an injustice. Perhaps the invitation was no more than a simple kindness, an act of courtesy. *It might be just a supper.* But this was the Red Keep, this was King's Landing, this was the court of King Joffrey Baratheon, the First of His Name, and if there was one thing that Sansa Stark had learned here, it was mistrust.

Even so, she must accept. She was nothing now, the discarded daughter of a traitor and disgraced sister of a rebel lord. She could scarcely refuse Joffrey's queen-to-be.

I wish the Hound were here. The night of the battle, Sandor Clegane had come to her chambers to take her from the city, but Sansa had refused. Sometimes she lay awake at night, wondering if she'd been wise. She had his stained white cloak hidden in a cedar chest beneath her summer silks. She could not say why she'd kept it. The Hound had turned craven, she heard it said; at the height of the battle, he got so drunk the Imp had to take his men. But Sansa understood. She knew the secret of his burned face. *It was only the fire he feared.* That night, the wildfire had set the river itself ablaze, and filled the very air with green flame. Even in the castle, Sansa had been afraid. Outside . . . she could scarcely imagine it.

Sighing, she got out quill and ink, and wrote Margaery Tyrell a gracious note of acceptance.

When the appointed night arrived, another of the Kingsguard came for her, a man as different from Sandor Clegane as . . . *well, as a flower from a dog.* The sight of Ser Loras Tyrell standing on her threshold made Sansa's heart beat a little faster. This was the first time she had been so close to him since he had returned to King's Landing, leading the vanguard of his father's host. For a moment she did not know what to say. "Ser Loras," she finally managed, "you . . . you look so lovely."

He gave her a puzzled smile. "My lady is too kind. And beautiful besides. My sister awaits you eagerly."

"I have so looked forward to our supper."

"As has Margaery, and my lady grandmother as well." He took her arm and led her toward the steps.

"Your grandmother?" Sansa was finding it hard to walk and talk and think all at the same time, with Ser Loras touching her arm. She could feel the warmth of his hand through the silk.

"Lady Olenna. She is to sup with you as well."

"Oh," said Sansa. *I am talking to him, and he's touching me, he's holding my arm and touching me.* "The Queen of Thorns, she's called. Isn't that right?"

"It is." Ser Loras laughed. *He has the warmest laugh,* she thought as he went on, "You'd best not use that name in her presence, though, or you're like to get pricked."

Sansa reddened. Any fool would have realized that no woman would be happy about being called "the Queen of Thorns." *Maybe I truly am as stupid as Cersei Lannister says.* Desperately she tried to think of something clever and charming to say to him, but her wits had deserted her. She almost told him how beautiful he was, until she remembered that she'd already done that.

He *was* beautiful, though. He seemed taller than he'd been when she'd first met him, but still so lithe and graceful, and Sansa had never seen another boy with such wonderful eyes. *He's no boy, though, he's a man grown, a knight of the Kingsguard.* She thought he looked even finer in white than in the greens and golds of House Tyrell. The only spot of color on him now was the brooch that clasped his cloak; the rose of Highgarden wrought in soft yellow gold, nestled in a bed of delicate green jade leaves.

Ser Balon Swann held the door of Maegor's for them to pass. He was all in white as well, though he did not wear it half so well as Ser Loras. Beyond the spiked moat, two dozen men were taking their practice with sword and shield. With the castle so crowded, the outer ward had been given over to guests to raise their tents and pavilions, leaving only the smaller inner yards for training. One of the Redwyne twins was being driven backward by Ser Tallad, with the eyes on his shield. Chunky Ser Kennos of Kayce, who chuffed and puffed every time he raised his longsword, seemed to be holding his own against Osney Kettleblack, but Osney's brother Ser Osfryd was savagely punishing the frog-faced squire Morros Slynt. Blunted swords or no, Slynt would have a rich crop of bruises by the morrow. It made Sansa wince just to watch. *They have scarcely finished burying the dead from the last battle, and already they are practicing for the next one.*

On the edge of the yard, a lone knight with a pair of golden roses on his shield was holding off three foes. Even as they watched, he caught one of them alongside the head, knocking him senseless. "Is that your brother?" Sansa asked.

"It is, my lady," said Ser Loras. "Garlan often trains against three men,

or even four. In battle it is seldom one against one, he says, so he likes
to be prepared."

"He must be very brave."

"He is a great knight," Ser Loras replied. "A better sword than me, in
truth, though I'm the better lance."

"I remember," said Sansa. "You ride wonderfully, ser."

"My lady is gracious to say so. When has she seen me ride?"

"At the Hand's tourney, don't you remember? You rode a white
courser, and your armor was a hundred different kinds of flowers. You
gave me a rose. A *red* rose. You threw white roses to the other girls that
day." It made her flush to speak of it. "You said no victory was half as
beautiful as me."

Ser Loras gave her a modest smile. "I spoke only a simple truth, that
any man with eyes could see."

He doesn't remember, Sansa realized, startled. *He is only being kind
to me, he doesn't remember me or the rose or any of it.* She had been so
certain that it meant something, that it meant *everything*. A *red* rose,
not a white. "It was after you unhorsed Ser Robar Royce," she said,
desperately.

He took his hand from her arm. "I slew Robar at Storm's End, my
lady." It was not a boast; he sounded sad.

Him, and another of King Renly's Rainbow Guard as well, yes. Sansa
had heard the women talking of it round the well, but for a moment
she'd forgotten. "That was when Lord Renly was killed, wasn't it? How
terrible for your poor sister."

"For Margaery?" His voice was tight. "To be sure. She was at
Bitterbridge, though. She did not see."

"Even so, when she heard . . ."

Ser Loras brushed the hilt of his sword lightly with his hand. Its grip
was white leather, its pommel a rose in alabaster. "Renly is dead. Robar
as well. What use to speak of them?"

The sharpness in his tone took her aback. "I . . . my lord, I . . . I did
not mean to give offense, ser."

"Nor could you, Lady Sansa," Ser Loras replied, but all the warmth
had gone from his voice. Nor did he take her arm again.

They ascended the serpentine steps in a deepening silence.

Oh, why did I have to mention Ser Robar? Sansa thought. *I've ruined
everything. He is angry with me now.* She tried to think of something
she might say to make amends, but all the words that came to her were
lame and weak. *Be quiet, or you will only make it worse*, she told herself.

Lord Mace Tyrell and his entourage had been housed behind the royal
sept, in the long slate-roofed keep that had been called the Maidenvault
since King Baelor the Blessed had confined his sisters therein, so the sight

of them might not tempt him into carnal thoughts. Outside its tall carved doors stood two guards in gilded halfhelms and green cloaks edged in gold satin, the golden rose of Highgarden sewn on their breasts. Both were seven-footers, wide of shoulder and narrow of waist, magnificently muscled. When Sansa got close enough to see their faces, she could not tell one from the other. They had the same strong jaws, the same deep blue eyes, the same thick red mustaches. "Who are they?" she asked Ser Loras, her discomfit forgotten for a moment.

"My grandmother's personal guard," he told her. "Their mother named them Erryk and Arryk, but Grandmother can't tell them apart, so she calls them Left and Right."

Left and Right opened the doors, and Margaery Tyrell herself emerged and swept down the short flight of steps to greet them. "Lady Sansa," she called, "I'm so pleased you came. Be welcome."

Sansa knelt at the feet of her future queen. "You do me great honor, Your Grace."

"Won't you call me Margaery? Please, rise. Loras, help the Lady Sansa to her feet. Might I call you Sansa?"

"If it please you." Ser Loras helped her up.

Margaery dismissed him with a sisterly kiss, and took Sansa by the hand. "Come, my grandmother awaits, and she is not the most patient of ladies."

A fire was crackling in the hearth, and sweet-swelling rushes had been scattered on the floor. Around the long trestle table a dozen women were seated.

Sansa recognized only Lord Tyrell's tall, dignified wife, Lady Alerie, whose long silvery braid was bound with jeweled rings. Margaery performed the other introductions. There were three Tyrell cousins, Megga and Alla and Elinor, all close to Sansa's age. Buxom Lady Janna was Lord Tyrell's sister, and wed to one of the green-apple Fossoways; dainty, bright-eyed Lady Leonette was a Fossoway as well, and wed to Ser Garlan. Septa Nysterica had a homely pox-scarred face but seemed jolly. Pale, elegant Lady Graceford was with child, and Lady Bulwer *was* a child, no more than eight. And "Merry" was what she was to call boisterous plump Meredyth Crane, but most definitely *not* Lady Merryweather, a sultry black-eyed Myrish beauty.

Last of all, Margaery brought her before the wizened white-haired doll of a woman at the head of the table. "I am honored to present my grandmother the Lady Olenna, widow to the late Luthor Tyrell, Lord of Highgarden, whose memory is a comfort to us all."

The old woman smelled of rosewater. *Why, she's just the littlest bit of a thing.* There was nothing the least bit thorny about her. "Kiss me, child," Lady Olenna said, tugging at Sansa's wrist with a soft spotted hand. "It is so kind of you to sup with me and my foolish flock of hens."

Dutifully, Sansa kissed the old woman on the cheek. "It is kind of you to have me, my lady."

"I knew your grandfather, Lord Rickard, though not well."

"He died before I was born."

"I am aware of that, child. It's said that your Tully grandfather is dying too. Lord Hoster, surely they told you? An old man, though not so old as me. Still, night falls for all of us in the end, and too soon for some. You would know that more than most, poor child. You've had your share of grief, I know. We are sorry for your losses."

Sansa glanced at Margaery. "I was saddened when I heard of Lord Renly's death, Your Grace. He was very gallant."

"You are kind to say so," answered Margaery.

Her grandmother snorted. "Gallant, yes, and charming, and very clean. He knew how to dress and he knew how to smile and he knew how to bathe, and somehow he got the notion that this made him fit to be king. The Baratheons have always had some queer notions, to be sure. It comes from their Targaryen blood, I should think." She sniffed. "They tried to marry me to a Targaryen once, but I soon put an end to that."

"Renly was brave and gentle, Grandmother," said Margaery. "Father liked him as well, and so did Loras."

"Loras is young," Lady Olenna said crisply, "and very good at knocking men off horses with a stick. That does not make him wise. As to your father, would that I'd been born a peasant woman with a big wooden spoon, I might have been able to beat some sense into his fat head."

"*Mother*," Lady Alerie scolded.

"Hush, Alerie, don't take that tone with me. And don't call me Mother. If I'd given birth to you, I'm sure I'd remember. I'm only to blame for your husband, the lord oaf of Highgarden."

"Grandmother," Margaery said, "mind your words, or what will Sansa think of us?"

"She might think we have some wits about us. One of us, at any rate." The old woman turned back to Sansa. "It's treason, I warned them, Robert has two sons, and Renly has an older brother, how can he *possibly* have any claim to that ugly iron chair? Tut-tut, says my son, don't you want your sweetling to be queen? You Starks were kings once, the Arryns and the Lannisters as well, and even the Baratheons through the female line, but the Tyrells were no more than stewards until Aegon the Dragon came along and cooked the rightful King of the Reach on the Field of Fire. If truth be told, even our claim to Highgarden is a bit dodgy, just as those dreadful Florents are always whining. 'What does it matter?' you ask, and of course it doesn't, except to oafs like my son. The thought that one day he may see his grandson with his arse on the Iron Throne makes

Mace puff up like . . . now, what do you call it? Margaery, you're clever, be a dear and tell your poor old half-daft grandmother the name of that queer fish from the Summer Isles that puffs up to ten times its own size when you poke it."

"They call them puff fish, Grandmother."

"Of course they do. Summer Islanders have no imagination. My son ought to take the puff fish for his sigil, if truth be told. He could put a crown on it, the way the Baratheons do their stag, mayhap that would make him happy. We should have stayed well out of all this bloody foolishness if you ask me, but once the cow's been milked there's no squirting the cream back up her udder. After Lord Puff Fish put that crown on Renly's head, we were into the pudding up to our knees, so here we are to see things through. And what do you say to that, Sansa?"

Sansa's mouth opened and closed. She felt very like a puff fish herself. "The Tyrells can trace their descent back to Garth Greenhand," was the best she could manage at short notice.

The Queen of Thorns snorted. "So can the Florents, the Rowans, the Oakhearts, and half the other noble houses of the south. Garth liked to plant his seed in fertile ground, they say. I shouldn't wonder that more than his hands were green."

"*Sansa*," Lady Alerie broke in, "you must be very hungry. Shall we have a bite of boar together, and some lemon cakes?"

"Lemon cakes are my favorite," Sansa admitted.

"So we have been told," declared Lady Olenna, who obviously had no intention of being hushed. "That Varys creature seemed to think we should be grateful for the information. I've never been quite sure what the *point* of a eunuch is, if truth be told. It seems to me they're only men with the useful bits cut off. Alerie, will you have them bring the food, or do you mean to starve me to death? Here, Sansa, sit here next to me, I'm much less boring than these others. I hope that you're fond of fools."

Sansa smoothed down her skirts and sat. "I think . . . fools, my lady? You mean . . . the sort in motley?"

"Feathers, in this case. What did you imagine I was speaking of? My son? Or these lovely ladies? No, don't blush, with your hair it makes you look like a pomegranate. All men are fools, if truth be told, but the ones in motley are more amusing than ones with crowns. Margaery, child, summon Butterbumps, let us see if we can't make Lady Sansa smile. The rest of you be seated, do I have to tell you everything? Sansa must think that my granddaughter is attended by a flock of sheep."

Butterbumps arrived before the food, dressed in a jester's suit of green and yellow feathers with a floppy coxcomb. An immense round fat man, as big as three Moon Boys, he came cartwheeling into the hall, vaulted onto the table, and laid a gigantic egg right in front of Sansa. "Break it, my lady," he commanded. When she did, a dozen yellow chicks escaped and began running in all directions. *"Catch them!"* Butterbumps exclaimed. Little Lady Bulwer snagged one and handed it to him, whereby he tilted back his head, popped it into his huge rubbery mouth, and seemed to swallow it whole. When he belched, tiny yellow feathers flew out his nose. Lady Bulwer began to wail in distress, but her tears turned into a sudden squeal of delight when the chick came squirming out of the sleeve of her gown and ran down her arm.

As the servants brought out a broth of leeks and mushrooms, Butterbumps began to juggle and Lady Olenna pushed herself forward to rest her elbows on the table. "Do you know my son, Sansa? Lord Puff Fish of Highgarden?"

"A great lord," Sansa answered politely.

"A great oaf," said the Queen of Thorns. "His father was an oaf as well. My husband, the late Lord Luthor. Oh, I loved him well enough, don't mistake me. A kind man, and not unskilled in the bedchamber, but an appalling oaf all the same. He managed to ride off a cliff whilst hawking. They say he was looking up at the sky and paying no mind to where his horse was taking him.

"And now my oaf son is doing the same, only he's riding a lion instead of a palfrey. It is easy to mount a lion and not so easy to get off, I warned him, but he only chuckles. Should you ever have a son, Sansa, beat him frequently so he learns to mind you. I only had the one boy and I hardly beat him at all, so now he pays more heed to Butterbumps than he does to me. A lion is not a lap cat, I told him, and he gives me a 'tut-tut-Mother.' There is entirely too much tut-tutting in this realm, if you ask me. All these kings would do a deal better if they would put down their swords and listen to their mothers."

Sansa realized that her mouth was open again. She filled it with a spoon of broth while Lady Alerie and the other women were giggling at the spectacle of Butterbumps bouncing oranges off his head, his elbows, and his ample rump.

"I want you to tell me the truth about this royal boy," said Lady Olenna abruptly. "This Joffrey."

Sansa's fingers tightened round her spoon. *The truth? I can't. Don't ask it, please, I can't.* "I . . . I . . . I . . ."

"You, yes. Who would know better? The lad seems kingly enough, I'll grant you. A bit full of himself, but that would be his Lannister blood. We have heard some troubling tales, however. Is there any truth to them? Has this boy mistreated you?"

Sansa glanced about nervously. Butterbumps popped a whole orange into his mouth, chewed and swallowed, slapped his cheek, and blew seeds out of his nose. The women giggled and laughed. Servants were coming and going, and the Maidenvault echoed to the clatter of spoons and plates. One of the chicks hopped back onto the table and ran through Lady Graceford's broth. No one seemed to be paying them any mind, but even so, she was frightened.

Lady Olenna was growing impatient. "Why are you gaping at Butterbumps? I asked a question, I expect an answer. Have the Lannisters stolen your tongue, child?"

Ser Dontos had warned her to speak freely only in the godswood. "Joff . . . King Joffrey, he's . . . His Grace is very fair and handsome, and . . . and as brave as a lion."

"Yes, all the Lannisters are lions, and when a Tyrell breaks wind it smells just like a rose," the old woman snapped. "But how *kind* is he? How clever? Has he a good heart, a gentle hand? Is he chivalrous as befits a king? Will he cherish Margaery and treat her tenderly, protect her honor as he would his own?"

"He will," Sansa lied. "He is very . . . very comely."

"You said that. You know, child, some say that you are as big a fool as Butterbumps here, and I am starting to believe them. *Comely!* I have taught my Margaery what comely is worth, I hope. Somewhat less than a mummer's fart. Aerion Brightfire was comely enough, but a monster all the same. The question is, what is Joffrey?" She reached to snag a passing servant. "I am not fond of leeks. Take this broth away, and bring me some cheese."

"The cheese will be served after the cakes, my lady."

"The cheese will be served when I want it served, and I want it served now." The old woman turned back to Sansa. "Are you frightened, child? No need for that, we're only women here. Tell me the truth, no harm will come to you."

"My father always told the truth." Sansa spoke quietly, but even so, it was hard to get the words out.

"Lord Eddard, yes, he had that reputation, but they named him traitor and took his head off even so." The old woman's eyes bore into her, sharp and bright as the points of swords.

"Joffrey," Sansa said. "Joffrey did that. He promised me he would be merciful, and cut my father's head off. He said *that* was mercy, and he took me up on the walls and made me look at it. The head. He wanted me to weep, but . . ." She stopped abruptly, and covered her mouth. *I've said too much, oh gods be good, they'll know, they'll hear, someone will tell on me.*

"Go on." It was Margaery who urged. Joffrey's own queen-to-be. Sansa did not know how much she had heard.

"I can't." *What if she tells him, what if she tells? He'll kill me for certain then, or give me to Ser Ilyn.* "I never meant . . . my father was a traitor, my brother as well, I have the traitor's blood, please, don't make me say more."

"Calm yourself, child," the Queen of Thorns commanded.

"She's terrified, Grandmother, just look at her."

The old woman called to Butterbumps. *"Fool!* Give us a song. A long one, I should think. 'The Bear and the Maiden Fair' will do nicely."

"It will!" the huge jester replied. "It will do nicely indeed! Shall I sing it standing on my head, my lady?"

"Will that make it sound better?"

"No."

"Stand on your feet, then. We wouldn't want your hat to fall off. As I recall, you never wash your hair."

"As my lady commands." Butterbumps bowed low, let loose of an enormous belch, then straightened, threw out his belly, and bellowed. *"A bear there was, a bear, a BEAR! All black and brown, and covered with hair . . ."*

Lady Olenna squirmed forward. "Even when I was a girl younger than you, it was well known that in the Red Keep the very walls have ears. Well, they will be the better for a song, and meanwhile we girls shall speak freely."

"But," Sansa said, "Varys . . . he *knows,* he always . . ."

"Sing louder!" the Queen of Thorns shouted at Butterbumps. "These old ears are almost deaf, you know. Are you whispering at me, you fat fool? I don't pay you for whispers. *Sing!"*

". . . THE BEAR!" thundered Butterbumps, his great deep voice echoing off the rafters. *"OH, COME, THEY SAID, OH COME TO THE FAIR! THE FAIR? SAID HE, BUT I'M A BEAR! ALL BLACK AND BROWN, AND COVERED WITH HAIR!"*

The wrinkled old lady smiled. "At Highgarden we have many spiders amongst the flowers. So long as they keep to themselves we let them spin their little webs, but if they get underfoot we step on them." She patted Sansa on the back of the hand. "Now, child, the truth. What sort of man is this Joffrey, who calls himself Baratheon but looks so very Lannister?"

"AND DOWN THE ROAD FROM HERE TO THERE. FROM HERE! TO THERE! THREE BOYS, A GOAT, AND A DANCING BEAR!"

Sansa felt as though her heart had lodged in her throat. The Queen of Thorns was so close she could smell the old woman's sour breath. Her gaunt thin fingers were pinching her wrist. To her other side, Margaery was listening as well. A shiver went through her. "A monster," she whispered, so tremulously she could scarcely hear her own voice. "Joffrey is a monster. He lied about the butcher's boy and made Father kill my wolf. When I displease him, he has the Kingsguard beat me. He's evil and cruel, my lady, it's so. And the queen as well."

Lady Olenna Tyrell and her granddaughter exchanged a look. "Ah," said the old woman, "that's a pity."

Oh, gods, thought Sansa, horrified. *If Margaery won't marry him, Joff will know that I'm to blame.* "Please," she blurted, "don't stop the wedding . . ."

"Have no fear, Lord Puff Fish is determined that Margaery shall be queen. And the word of a Tyrell is worth more than all the gold in Casterly Rock. At least it was in my day. Even so, we thank you for the truth, child."

"*. . . DANCED AND SPUN, ALL THE WAY TO THE FAIR! THE FAIR! THE FAIR!*" Butterbumps hopped and roared and stomped his feet.

"Sansa, would you like to visit Highgarden?" When Margaery Tyrell smiled, she looked very like her brother Loras. "All the autumn flowers are in bloom just now, and there are groves and fountains, shady court-yards, marble colonnades. My lord father always keeps singers at court, sweeter ones than Butters here, and pipers and fiddlers and harpers as well. We have the best horses, and pleasure boats to sail along the Mander. Do you hawk, Sansa?"

"A little," she admitted.

"*OH, SWEET SHE WAS, AND PURE, AND FAIR! THE MAID WITH HONEY IN HER HAIR!*"

"You will love Highgarden as I do, I know it." Margaery brushed back a loose strand of Sansa's hair. "Once you see it, you'll never want to leave. And perhaps you won't have to."

"*HER HAIR! HER HAIR! THE MAID WITH HONEY IN HER HAIR!*"

"Shush, child," the Queen of Thorns said sharply. "Sansa hasn't even told us that she would like to come for a visit."

"Oh, but I would," Sansa said. Highgarden sounded like the place she had always dreamed of, like the beautiful magical court she had once hoped to find at King's Landing.

"*. . . SMELLED THE SCENT ON THE SUMMER AIR. THE BEAR! THE BEAR! ALL BLACK AND BROWN AND COVERED WITH HAIR.*"

"But the queen," Sansa went on, "she won't let me go . . ."

"She will. Without Highgarden, the Lannisters have no hope of keeping Joffrey on his throne. If my son the lord oaf asks, she will have no choice but to grant his request."

"Will he?" asked Sansa. "Will he ask?"

Lady Olenna frowned. "I see no need to give him a choice. Of course, he has no hint of our true purpose."

"*HE SMELLED THE SCENT ON THE SUMMER AIR!*"

Sansa wrinkled her brow. "Our true purpose, my lady?"

"HE SNIFFED AND ROARED AND SMELLED IT THERE! HONEY ON THE SUMMER AIR!"

"To see you safely wed, child," the old woman said, as Butterbumps bellowed out the old, old song, "to my grandson."

Wed to Ser Loras, oh . . . Sansa's breath caught in her throat. She remembered Ser Loras in his sparkling sapphire armor, tossing her a rose. Ser Loras in white silk, so pure, innocent, beautiful. The dimples at the corner of his mouth when he smiled. The sweetness of his laugh, the warmth of his hand. She could only imagine what it would be like to pull up his tunic and caress the smooth skin underneath, to stand on her toes and kiss him, to run her fingers through those thick brown curls and drown in his deep brown eyes. A flush crept up her neck.

"OH, I'M A MAID, AND I'M PURE AND FAIR! I'LL NEVER DANCE WITH A HAIRY BEAR! A BEAR! A BEAR! I'LL NEVER DANCE WITH A HAIRY BEAR!"

"Would you like that, Sansa?" asked Margaery. "I've never had a sister, only brothers. Oh, please say yes, please say that you will consent to marry my brother."

The words came tumbling out of her. "Yes. I will. I would like that more than anything. To wed Ser Loras, to love him . . ."

"Loras?" Lady Olenna sounded annoyed. "Don't be foolish, child. Kingsguard never wed. Didn't they teach you anything in Winterfell? We were speaking of my grandson Willas. He is a bit old for you, to be sure, but a dear boy for all that. Not the least bit oafish, and heir to Highgarden besides."

Sansa felt dizzy; one instant her head was full of dreams of Loras, and the next they had all been snatched away. *Willas? Willas?* "I," she said stupidly. *Courtesy is a lady's armor. You must not offend them, be careful what you say.* "I do not know Ser Willas. I have never had the pleasure, my lady. Is he . . . is he as great a knight as his brothers?"

". . . LIFTED HER HIGH INTO THE AIR! THE BEAR! THE BEAR!"

"No," Margaery said. "He has never taken vows."

Her grandmother frowned. "Tell the girl the truth. The poor lad is crippled, and that's the way of it."

"He was hurt as a squire, riding in his first tourney," Margaery confided. "His horse fell and crushed his leg."

"That snake of a Dornishman was to blame, that Oberyn Martell. And his maester as well."

"I CALLED FOR A KNIGHT, BUT YOU'RE A BEAR! A BEAR! A BEAR! ALL BLACK AND BROWN AND COVERED WITH HAIR!"

"Willas has a bad leg but a good heart," said Margaery. "He used to read to me when I was a little girl, and draw me pictures of the stars. You will love him as much as we do, Sansa."

"SHE KICKED AND WAILED, THE MAID SO FAIR, BUT HE LICKED THE HONEY FROM HER HAIR. HER HAIR! HER HAIR! HE LICKED THE HONEY FROM HER HAIR!"

"When might I meet him?" asked Sansa, hesitantly.

"Soon," promised Margaery. "When you come to Highgarden, after Joffrey and I are wed. My grandmother will take you."

"I will," said the old woman, patting Sansa's hand and smiling a soft wrinkly smile. "I will indeed."

"THEN SHE SIGHED AND SQUEALED AND KICKED THE AIR! MY BEAR! SHE SANG. MY BEAR SO FAIR! AND OFF THEY WENT, FROM HERE TO THERE, THE BEAR, THE BEAR, AND THE MAIDEN FAIR." Butterbumps roared the last line, leapt into the air, and came down on both feet with a crash that shook the wine cups on the table. The women laughed and clapped.

"I thought that dreadful song would never end," said the Queen of Thorns. "But look, here comes my cheese."

JON

The world was grey darkness, smelling of pine and moss and cold. Pale mists rose from the black earth as the riders threaded their way through the scatter of stones and scraggly trees, down toward the welcoming fires strewn like jewels across the floor of the river valley below. There were more fires than Jon Snow could count, hundreds of fires, thousands, a second river of flickery lights along the banks of the icy white Milkwater. The fingers of his sword hand opened and closed.

They descended the ridge without banners or trumpets, the quiet broken only by the distant murmur of the river, the clop of hooves, and the clacking of Rattleshirt's bone armor. Somewhere above an eagle soared on great blue-grey wings, while below came men and dogs and horses and one white direwolf.

A stone bounced down the slope, disturbed by a passing hoof, and Jon saw Ghost turn his head at the sudden sound. He had followed the riders at a distance all day, as was his custom, but when the moon rose over the soldier pines he'd come bounding up, red eyes aglow. Rattleshirt's dogs greeted him with a chorus of snarls and growls and wild barking, as ever, but the direwolf paid them no mind. Six days ago, the largest hound had attacked him from behind as the wildlings camped for the night, but Ghost had turned and lunged, sending the dog fleeing with a bloody haunch. The rest of the pack maintained a healthy distance after that.

Jon Snow's garron whickered softly, but a touch and a soft word soon quieted the animal. Would that his own fears could be calmed so easily. He was all in black, the black of the Night's Watch, but the enemy rode before and behind. *Wildlings, and I am with them.* Ygritte wore the cloak of Qhorin Halfhand. Lenyl had his hauberk, the big spearwife Ragwyle his gloves, one of the bowmen his boots. Qhorin's helm had been won by the short homely man called Longspear Ryk, but it fit poorly on his narrow head, so he'd given that to Ygritte as well. And Rattleshirt had Qhorin's bones in his bag, along with the bloody head of Ebben, who set out with Jon to scout the Skirling Pass. *Dead, all dead but me, and I am dead to the world.*

Ygritte rode just behind him. In front was Longspear Ryk. The Lord of Bones had made the two of them his guards. "If the crow flies, I'll boil your bones as well," he warned them when they had set out, smiling through the crooked teeth of the giant's skull he wore for a helm.

Ygritte hooted at him. "*You* want to guard him? If you want us to do it, leave us be and we'll do it."

These are a free folk indeed, Jon saw. Rattleshirt might lead them, but none of them were shy in talking back to him.

The wildling leader fixed him with an unfriendly stare. "Might be you fooled these others, crow, but don't think you'll be fooling Mance. He'll take one look a' you and know you're false. And when he does, I'll make a cloak o' your wolf there, and open your soft boy's belly and sew a weasel up inside."

Jon's sword hand opened and closed, flexing the burned fingers beneath the glove, but Longspear Ryk only laughed. "And where would you find a weasel in the snow?"

That first night, after a long day ahorse, they made camp in a shallow stone bowl atop a nameless mountain, huddling close to the fire while the snow began to fall. Jon watched the flakes melt as they drifted over the flames. Despite his layers of wool and fur and leather, he'd felt cold to the bone. Ygritte sat beside him after she had eaten, her hood pulled up and her hands tucked into her sleeves for warmth. "When Mance hears how you did for Halfhand, he'll take you quick enough," she told him.

"Take me for what?"

The girl laughed scornfully. "For one o' us. D'ya think you're the first crow ever flew down off the Wall? In your hearts you all want to fly free."

"And when I'm free," he said slowly, "will I be free to go?"

"Sure you will." She had a warm smile, despite her crooked teeth. "And we'll be free to kill you. It's *dangerous* being free, but most come to like the taste o' it." She put her gloved hand on his leg, just above the knee. "You'll see."

I will, thought Jon. *I will see, and hear, and learn, and when I have I will carry the word back to the Wall.* The wildlings had taken him for an oathbreaker, but in his heart he was still a man of the Night's Watch, doing the last duty that Qhorin Halfhand had laid on him. *Before I killed him.*

At the bottom of the slope they came upon a little stream flowing down from the foothills to join the Milkwater. It looked all stones and glass, though they could hear the sound of water running beneath the frozen surface. Rattleshirt led them across, shattering the thin crust of ice.

Mance Rayder's outriders closed in as they emerged. Jon took their measure with a glance: eight riders, men and women both, clad in fur and boiled leather, with here and there a helm or bit of mail. They were armed with spears and fire-hardened lances, all but their leader, a fleshy blond man with watery eyes who bore a great curved scythe of sharpened steel. *The Weeper*, he knew at once. The black brothers told tales of this one. Like Rattleshirt and Harma Dogshead and Alfyn Crowkiller, he was a known raider.

"The Lord o' Bones," the Weeper said when he saw them. He eyed Jon and his wolf. "Who's this, then?"

"A crow come over," said Rattleshirt, who preferred to be called the Lord of Bones, for the clattering armor he wore. "He was afraid I'd take his bones as well as Halfhand's." He shook his sack of trophies at the other wildlings.

"He slew Qhorin Halfhand," said Longspear Ryk. "Him and that wolf o' his."

"And did for Orell too," said Rattleshirt.

"The lad's a warg, or close enough," put in Ragwyle, the big spearwife. "His wolf took a piece o' Halfhand's leg."

The Weeper's red rheumy eyes gave Jon another look. "Aye? Well, he has a wolfish cast to him, now as I look close. Bring him to Mance, might be he'll keep him." He wheeled his horse around and galloped off, his riders hard behind him.

The wind was blowing wet and heavy as they crossed the valley of the Milkwater and rode singlefile through the river camp. Ghost kept close to Jon, but the scent of him went before them like a herald, and soon there were wildling dogs all around them, growling and barking. Lenyl screamed at them to be quiet, but they paid him no heed. "They don't much care for that beast o' yours," Longspear Ryk said to Jon.

"They're dogs and he's a wolf," said Jon. "They know he's not their kind." *No more than I am yours.* But he had his duty to be mindful of, the task Qhorin Halfhand had laid upon him as they shared that final fire – to play the part of turncloak, and find whatever it was that the wildlings had been seeking in the bleak cold wilderness of the Frostfangs.

"Some *power*," Qhorin had named it to the Old Bear, but he had died before learning what it was, or whether Mance Rayder had found it with his digging.

There were cookfires all along the river, amongst wayns and carts and sleds. Many of the wildlings had thrown up tents, of hide and skin and felted wool. Others sheltered behind rocks in crude lean-tos, or slept beneath their wagons. At one fire Jon saw a man hardening the points of long wooden spears and tossing them in a pile. Elsewhere two bearded youths in boiled leather were sparring with staffs, leaping at each other over the flames, grunting each time one landed a blow. A dozen women sat nearby in a circle, fletching arrows.

Arrows for my brothers, Jon thought. *Arrows for my father's folk, for the people of Winterfell and Deepwood Motte and the Last Hearth. Arrows for the north.*

But not all he saw was warlike. He saw women dancing as well, and heard a baby crying, and a little boy ran in front of his garron, all bundled up in fur and breathless from play. Sheep and goats wandered freely, while oxen plodded along the riverbank in search of grass. The smell of roast mutton drifted from one cookfire, and at another he saw a boar turning on a wooden spit.

In an open space surrounded by tall green soldier pines, Rattleshirt dismounted. "We'll make camp here," he told Lenyl and Ragwyle and the others. "Feed the horses, then the dogs, then yourself. Ygritte, Longspear, bring the crow so Mance can have his look. We'll gut him after."

They walked the rest of the way, past more cookfires and more tents, with Ghost following at their heels. Jon had never seen so many wildlings. He wondered if anyone ever had. *The camp goes on forever,* he reflected, *but it's more a hundred camps than one, and each more vulnerable than the last.* Stretched out over long leagues, the wildlings had no defenses to speak of, no pits nor sharpened stakes, only small groups of outriders patrolling their perimeters. Each group or clan or village had simply stopped where they wanted, as soon as they saw others stopping or found a likely spot. *The free folk.* If his brothers were to catch them in such disarray, many of them would pay for that freedom with their life's blood. They had numbers, but the Night's Watch had discipline, and in battle discipline beats numbers nine times of every ten, his father had once told him.

There was no doubting which tent was the king's. It was thrice the size of the next largest he'd seen, and he could hear music drifting from within. Like many of the lesser tents it was made of sewn hides with the fur still on, but Mance Rayder's hides were the shaggy white pelts of snow bears. The peaked roof was crowned with a huge set of antlers from one of the giant elks that had once roamed freely throughout the Seven Kingdoms, in the times of the First Men.

Here at least they found defenders; two guards at the flap of the tent, leaning on tall spears with round leather shields strapped to their arms. When they caught sight of Ghost, one of them lowered his spearpoint and said, "That beast stays here."

"Ghost, stay," Jon commanded. The direwolf sat.

"Longspear, watch the beast." Rattleshirt yanked open the tent and gestured Jon and Ygritte inside.

The tent was hot and smoky. Baskets of burning peat stood in all four corners, filling the air with a dim reddish light. More skins carpeted the ground. Jon felt utterly alone as he stood there in his blacks, awaiting the pleasure of the turncloak who called himself King-beyond-the-Wall. When his eyes had adjusted to the smoky red gloom, he saw six people, none of whom paid him any mind. A dark young man and a pretty blonde woman were sharing a horn of mead. A pregnant woman stood over a brazier cooking a brace of hens, while a grey-haired man in a tattered cloak of black and red sat crosslegged on a pillow, playing a lute and singing:

> The Dornishman's wife was as fair as the sun,
>   and her kisses were warmer than spring.
> But the Dornishman's blade was made of black steel,
>   and its kiss was a terrible thing.

Jon knew the song, though it was strange to hear it here, in a shaggy hide tent beyond the Wall, ten thousand leagues from the red mountains and warm winds of Dorne.

Rattleshirt took off his yellowed helm as he waited for the song to end. Beneath his bone-and-leather armor he was a small man, and the face under the giant's skull was ordinary, with a knobby chin, thin mustache, and sallow, pinched cheeks. His eyes were close-set, one eyebrow creeping all the way across his forehead, dark hair thinning back from a sharp widow's peak.

> The Dornishman's wife would sing as she bathed,
>   in a voice that was sweet as a peach,
> But the Dornishman's blade had a song of its own,
>   and a bite sharp and cold as a leech.

Beside the brazier, a short but immensely broad man sat on a stool, eating a hen off a skewer. Hot grease was running down his chin and into his snow-white beard, but he smiled happily all the same. Thick gold bands graven with runes bound his massive arms, and he wore a heavy shirt of black ringmail that could only have come from a dead ranger. A few feet away, a taller, leaner man in a leather shirt sewn with bronze scales stood frowning over a map, a two-handed greatsword slung across his back in a leather sheath. He was straight as a spear, all long wiry muscle, clean-shaved, bald, with a strong straight nose and deepset grey eyes. He might even have been comely if he'd had ears, but he had lost both along the way, whether to frostbite or some enemy's knife Jon could not tell. Their lack made the man's head seem narrow and pointed.

Both the white-bearded man and the bald one were warriors, that was plain to Jon at a glance. *These two are more dangerous than Rattleshirt by far.* He wondered which was Mance Rayder.

As he lay on the ground with the darkness around,
* and the taste of his blood on his tongue,*
His brothers knelt by him and prayed him a prayer,
* and he smiled and he laughed and he sung,*
"Brothers, oh brothers, my days here are done,
* the Dornishman's taken my life,*
But what does it matter, for all men must die,
* and I've tasted the Dornishman's wife!"*

As the last strains of "The Dornishman's Wife" faded, the bald earless man glanced up from his map and scowled ferociously at Rattleshirt and Ygritte, with Jon between them. "What's this?" he said. "A crow?"

"The black bastard what gutted Orell," said Rattleshirt, "and a bloody warg as well."

"You were to kill them all."

"This one come over," explained Ygritte. "He slew Qhorin Halfhand with his own hand."

"This *boy?*" The earless man was angered by the news. "The Halfhand should have been mine. Do you have a name, crow?"

"Jon Snow, Your Grace." He wondered whether he was expected to bend the knee as well.

"Your Grace?" The earless man looked at the big white-bearded one. "You see. He takes me for a king."

The bearded man laughed so hard he sprayed bits of chicken everywhere. He rubbed the grease from his mouth with the back of a huge hand. "A blind boy, must be. Who ever heard of a king without ears? Why, his crown would fall straight down to his neck! Har!" He grinned at Jon, wiping his fingers clean on his breeches. "Close your beak, crow. Spin yourself around, might be you'd find who you're looking for."

Jon turned.

The singer rose to his feet. "I'm Mance Rayder," he said as he put aside the lute. "And you are Ned Stark's bastard, the Snow of Winterfell."

Stunned, Jon stood speechless for a moment, before he recovered enough to say, "How . . . how could you know . . ."

"That's a tale for later," said Mance Rayder. "How did you like the song, lad?"

"Well enough. I'd heard it before."

"*But what does it matter, for all men must die,*" the King-beyond-the-Wall said lightly, "*and I've tasted the Dornishman's wife.* Tell me, does my Lord of Bones speak truly? Did you slay my old friend the Halfhand?"

"I did." *Though it was his doing more than mine.*

"The Shadow Tower will never again seem as fearsome," the king said with sadness in his voice. "Qhorin was my enemy. But also my brother, once. So . . . shall I thank you for killing him, Jon Snow? Or curse you?" He gave Jon a mocking smile.

The King-beyond-the-Wall looked nothing like a king, nor even much a wildling. He was of middling height, slender, sharp-faced, with shrewd brown eyes and long brown hair that had gone mostly to grey. There was no crown on his head, no gold rings on his arms, no jewels at his throat, not even a gleam of silver. He wore wool and leather, and his only garment of note was his ragged black wool cloak, its long tears patched with faded red silk.

"You ought to thank me for killing your enemy," Jon said finally, "and curse me for killing your friend."

"*Har!*" boomed the white-bearded man. "Well answered!"

"Agreed." Mance Rayder beckoned Jon closer. "If you would join us, you'd best know us. The man you took for me is Styr, Magnar of Thenn. *Magnar* means 'lord' in the Old Tongue." The earless man stared at Jon coldly as Mance turned to the white-bearded one. "Our ferocious chicken-eater here is my loyal Tormund. The woman –"

Tormund rose to his feet. "Hold. You gave Styr his style, give me mine."

Mance Rayder laughed. "As you wish. Jon Snow, before you stands Tormund Giantsbane, Tall-talker, Horn-blower, and Breaker of Ice. And here also Tormund Thunderfist, Husband to Bears, the Mead-king of Ruddy Hall, Speaker to Gods and Father of Hosts."

"That sounds more like me," said Tormund. "Well met, Jon Snow. I am fond o' wargs, as it happens, though not o' Starks."

"The good woman at the brazier," Mance Rayder went on, "is Dalla." The pregnant woman smiled shyly. "Treat her like you would any queen, she is carrying my child." He turned to the last two. "This beauty is her sister Val. Young Jarl beside her is her latest pet."

"I am no man's pet," said Jarl, dark and fierce.

"And Val's no man," white-bearded Tormund snorted. "You ought to have noticed that by now, lad."

"So there you have us, Jon Snow," said Mance Rayder. "The King-beyond-the-Wall and his court, such as it is. And now some words from you, I think. Where did you come from?"

"Winterfell," he said, "by way of Castle Black."

"And what brings you up the Milkwater, so far from the fires of home?" He did not wait for Jon's answer, but looked at once to Rattleshirt. "How many were they?"

"Five. Three's dead and the boy's here. T'other went up a mountainside where no horse could follow."

Rayder's eyes met Jon's again. "Was it only the five of you? Or are more of your brothers skulking about?"

"We were four and the Halfhand. Qhorin was worth twenty common men."

The King-beyond-the-Wall smiled at that. "Some thought so. Still . . . a boy from Castle Black with rangers from the Shadow Tower? How did that come to be?"

Jon had his lie all ready. "The Lord Commander sent me to the Half-hand for seasoning, so he took me on his ranging."

Styr the Magnar frowned at that. "Ranging, you call it . . . why would crows come ranging up the Skirling Pass?"

"The villages were deserted," Jon said, truthfully. "It was as if all the free folk had vanished."

"Vanished, aye," said Mance Rayder. "And not just the free folk. Who told you where we were, Jon Snow?"

Tormund snorted. "It were Craster, or I'm a blushing maid. I told you, Mance, that creature needs to be shorter by a head."

The king gave the older man an irritated look. "Tormund, some day try thinking before you speak. I know it was Craster. I asked Jon to see if he would tell it true."

"Har." Tormund spat. "Well, I stepped in that!" He grinned at Jon. "See, lad, that's why he's king and I'm not. I can outdrink, outfight, and outsing him, and my member's thrice the size o' his, but Mance has cunning. He was raised a crow, you know, and the crow's a tricksy bird."

"I would speak with the lad alone, my Lord of Bones," Mance Rayder said to Rattleshirt. "Leave us, all of you."

"What, me as well?" said Tormund.

"No, you especially," said Mance.

"I eat in no hall where I'm not welcome." Tormund got to his feet. "Me and the hens are leaving." He snatched another chicken off the brazier, shoved it into a pocket sewn in the lining of his cloak, said "Har," and left licking his fingers. The others followed him out, all but the woman Dalla.

"Sit, if you like," Rayder said when they were gone. "Are you hungry? Tormund left us two birds at least."

"I would be pleased to eat, Your Grace. And thank you."

"Your Grace?" The king smiled. "That's not a style one often hears from the lips of free folk. I'm Mance to most, *The* Mance to some. Will you take a horn of mead?"

"Gladly," said Jon.

The king poured himself as Dalla cut the well-crisped hens apart and brought them each a half. Jon peeled off his gloves and ate with his fingers, sucking every morsel of meat off the bones.

"Tormund spoke truly," said Mance Rayder as he ripped apart a loaf of bread. "The black crow is a tricksy bird, that's so . . . but I was a crow when you were no bigger than the babe in Dalla's belly, Jon Snow. So take care not to play tricksy with me."

"As you say, Your – Mance."

The king laughed. "Your Mance! Why not? I promised you a tale before, of how I knew you. Have you puzzled it out yet?"

Jon shook his head. "Did Rattleshirt send word ahead?"

"By wing? We have no trained ravens. No, I knew your face. I've seen it before. Twice."

It made no sense at first, but as Jon turned it over in his mind, dawn broke. "When you were a brother of the Watch . . ."

"Very good! Yes, that was the first time. You were just a boy, and I was all in black, one of a dozen riding escort to old Lord Commander Qorgyle when he came down to see your father at Winterfell. I was walking the wall around the yard when I came on you and your brother Robb. It had snowed the night before, and the two of you had built a great mountain above the gate and were waiting for someone likely to pass underneath."

"I remember," said Jon with a startled laugh. A young black brother on the wallwalk, yes . . . "You swore not to tell."

"And kept my vow. That one, at least."

"We dumped the snow on Fat Tom. He was Father's slowest guardsman." Tom had chased them around the yard afterward, until all three were red as autumn apples. "But you said you saw me twice. When was the other time?"

"When King Robert came to Winterfell to make your father Hand," the King-beyond-the-Wall said lightly.

Jon's eyes widened in disbelief. "That can't be so."

"It was. When your father learned the king was coming, he sent word to his brother Benjen on the Wall, so he might come down for the feast. There is more commerce between the black brothers and the free folk than you know, and soon enough word came to my ears as well. It was too choice a chance to resist. Your uncle did not know me by sight, so I had no fear from that quarter, and I did not think your father was like to remember a young crow he'd met briefly years before. I wanted to see this Robert with my own eyes, king to king, and get the measure of your uncle Benjen as well. He was First Ranger by then, and the bane of all my people. So I saddled my fleetest horse, and rode."

"But," Jon objected, "the Wall . . ."

"The Wall can stop an army, but not a man alone. I took a lute and a bag of silver, scaled the ice near Long Barrow, walked a few leagues south of the New Gift, and bought a horse. All in all I made much better time than Robert, who was traveling with a ponderous great wheelhouse to keep his queen in comfort. A day south of Winterfell I came up on him and fell in with his company. Freeriders and hedge knights are always attaching themselves to royal processions, in hopes of finding service with the king, and my lute gained me easy acceptance." He laughed. "I know every bawdy song that's ever been made, north or south of the Wall. So there you are. The night your father feasted Robert, I sat in the back of his hall on a bench with the other freeriders, listening to Orland of Oldtown play the high harp and sing of dead kings beneath the sea. I betook of your lord father's meat and mead, had a look at Kingslayer and Imp . . . and made passing note of Lord Eddard's children and the wolf pups that ran at their heels."

"Bael the Bard," said Jon, remembering the tale that Ygritte had told him in the Frostfangs, the night he'd almost killed her.

"Would that I were. I will not deny that Bael's exploit inspired mine own . . . but I did not steal either of your sisters that I recall. Bael wrote his own songs, and lived them. I only sing the songs that better men have made. More mead?"

"No," said Jon. "If you had been discovered . . . taken . . ."

"Your father would have had my head off." The king gave a shrug. "Though once I had eaten at his board I was protected by guest right. The laws of hospitality are as old as the First Men, and sacred as a heart tree." He gestured at the board between them, the broken bread and chicken bones. "Here you are the guest, and safe from harm at my hands . . . this night, at least. So tell me truly, Jon Snow. Are you a craven who turned your cloak from fear, or is there another reason that brings you to my tent?"

Guest right or no, Jon Snow knew he walked on rotten ice here. One false step and he might plunge through, into water cold enough to stop his heart. *Weigh every word before you speak it*, he told himself. He took a long draught of mead to buy time for his answer. When he set the horn aside he said, "Tell me why you turned your cloak, and I'll tell you why I turned mine."

Mance Rayder smiled, as Jon had hoped he would. The king was plainly a man who liked the sound of his own voice. "You will have heard stories of my desertion, I have no doubt."

"Some say it was for a crown. Some say for a woman. Others that you had the wildling blood."

"The wildling blood is the blood of the First Men, the same blood that flows in the veins of the Starks. As to a crown, do you see one?"

"I see a woman." He glanced at Dalla.

Mance took her by the hand and pulled her close. "My lady is blameless. I met her on my return from your father's castle. The Halfhand was carved of old oak, but I am made of flesh, and I have a great fondness for the charms of women ... which makes me no different from three-quarters of the Watch. There are men still wearing black who have had ten times as many women as this poor king. You must guess again, Jon Snow."

Jon considered a moment. "The Halfhand said you had a passion for wildling music."

"I did. I do. That's closer to the mark, yes. But not a hit." Mance Rayder rose, unfastened the clasp that held his cloak, and swept it over the bench. "It was for this."

"A cloak?"

"The black wool cloak of a Sworn Brother of the Night's Watch," said the King-beyond-the-Wall. "One day on a ranging we brought down a fine big elk. We were skinning it when the smell of blood drew a shadow-cat out of its lair. I drove it off, but not before it shredded my cloak to ribbons. Do you see? Here, here, and here?" He chuckled. "It shredded my arm and back as well, and I bled worse than the elk. My brothers feared I might die before they got me back to Maester Mullin at the Shadow Tower, so they carried me to a wildling village where we knew an old wisewoman did some healing. She was dead, as it happened, but her daughter saw to me. Cleaned my wounds, sewed me up, and fed me porridge and potions until I was strong enough to ride again. And she sewed up the rents in my cloak as well, with some scarlet silk from Asshai that her grandmother had pulled from the wreck of a cog washed up on the Frozen Shore. It was the greatest treasure she had, and her gift to me." He swept the cloak back over his shoulders. "But at the Shadow Tower, I was given a new wool cloak from stores, black and black, and trimmed with black, to go with my black breeches and black boots, my black doublet and black mail. The new cloak had no frays nor rips nor tears ... and most of all, no red. The men of the Night's Watch dressed in *black*, Ser Denys Mallister reminded me sternly, as if I had forgotten. My old cloak was fit for burning now, he said.

"I left the next morning . . . for a place where a kiss was not a crime, and a man could wear any cloak he chose." He closed the clasp and sat back down again. "And you, Jon Snow?"

Jon took another swallow of mead. *There is only one tale that he might believe.* "You say you were at Winterfell, the night my father feasted King Robert."

"I did say it, for I was."

"Then you saw us all. Prince Joffrey and Prince Tommen, Princess Myrcella, my brothers Robb and Bran and Rickon, my sisters Arya and Sansa. You saw them walk the center aisle with every eye upon them and take their seats at the table just below the dais where the king and queen were seated."

"I remember."

"And did you see where I was seated, Mance?" He leaned forward. "Did you see where they put the bastard?"

Mance Rayder looked at Jon's face for a long moment. "I think we had best find you a new cloak," the king said, holding out his hand.

DAENERYS

Across the still blue water came the slow steady beat of drums and the soft swish of oars from the galleys. The great cog groaned in their wake, the heavy lines stretched taut between. *Balerion*'s sails hung limp, drooping forlorn from the masts. Yet even so, as she stood upon the forecastle watching her dragons chase each other across a cloudless blue sky, Daenerys Targaryen was as happy as she could ever remember being.

Her Dothraki called the sea *the poison water*, distrusting any liquid that their horses could not drink. On the day the three ships had lifted anchor at Qarth, you would have thought they were sailing to hell instead of Pentos. Her brave young bloodriders had stared off at the dwindling coastline with huge white eyes, each of the three determined to show no fear before the other two, while her handmaids Irri and Jhiqui clutched the rail desperately and retched over the side at every little swell. The rest of Dany's tiny *khalasar* remained below decks, preferring the company of their nervous horses to the terrifying landless world about the ships. When a sudden squall had enveloped them six days into the voyage, she heard them through the hatches; the horses kicking and screaming, the riders praying in thin quavery voices each time *Balerion* heaved or swayed.

No squall could frighten Dany, though. *Daenerys Stormborn*, she was called, for she had come howling into the world on distant Dragonstone as the greatest storm in the memory of Westeros howled outside, a storm so fierce that it ripped gargoyles from the castle walls and smashed her father's fleet to kindling.

The narrow sea was often stormy, and Dany had crossed it half a hundred times as a girl, running from one Free City to the next half a step ahead of the Usurper's hired knives. She loved the sea. She liked the sharp salty smell of the air, and the vastness of horizons bounded only by a vault of azure sky above. It made her feel small, but free as well. She liked the dolphins that sometimes swam along beside *Balerion*, slicing through the waves like silvery spears, and the flying fish they glimpsed now and again. She even liked the sailors, with all their songs and stories. Once on a voyage to Braavos, as she'd watched the crew wrestle down a great green sail in a rising gale, she had even thought how fine it would be to be a sailor. But when she told her brother, Viserys had twisted her hair until she cried. "You are blood of the dragon," he had screamed at her. "A *dragon*, not some smelly fish."

He was a fool about that, and so much else, Dany thought. *If he had been wiser and more patient, it would be him sailing west to take the throne that was his by rights*. Viserys had been stupid and vicious, she had come to realize, yet sometimes she missed him all the same. Not the cruel weak man he had become by the end, but the brother who had sometimes let her creep into his bed, the boy who told her tales of the Seven Kingdoms, and talked of how much better their lives would be once he claimed his crown.

The captain appeared at her elbow. "Would that this *Balerion* could soar as her namesake did, Your Grace," he said in bastard Valyrian heavily flavored with accents of Pentos. "Then we should not need to row, nor tow, nor pray for wind."

"Just so, Captain," she answered with a smile, pleased to have won the man over. Captain Groleo was an old Pentoshi like his master, Illyrio Mopatis, and he had been nervous as a maiden about carrying three dragons on his ship. Half a hundred buckets of seawater still hung from the gunwales, in case of fires. At first Groleo had wanted the dragons caged and Dany had consented to put his fears at ease, but their misery was so palpable that she soon changed her mind and insisted they be freed.

Even Captain Groleo was glad of that, now. There had been one small fire, easily extinguished; against that, *Balerion* suddenly seemed to have far fewer rats than she'd had before, when she sailed under the name *Saduleon*. And her crew, once as fearful as they were curious, had begun to take a queer fierce pride in "their" dragons. Every man of them, from captain to cook's boy, loved to watch the three fly . . . though none so much as Dany.

They are my children, she told herself, *and if the* maegi *spoke truly, they are the only children I am ever like to have.*

Viserion's scales were the color of fresh cream, his horns, wing bones, and spinal crest a dark gold that flashed bright as metal in the sun. Rhaegal was made of the green of summer and the bronze of fall. They soared above the ships in wide circles, higher and higher, each trying to climb above the other.

Dragons always preferred to attack from above, Dany had learned. Should either get between the other and the sun, he would fold his wings and dive screaming, and they would tumble from the sky locked together in a tangled scaly ball, jaws snapping and tails lashing. The first time they had done it, she feared that they meant to kill each other, but it was only sport. No sooner would they splash into the sea than they would break apart and rise again, shrieking and hissing, the salt water steaming off them as their wings clawed at the air. Drogon was aloft as well, though not in sight; he would be miles ahead, or miles behind, hunting.

He was always hungry, her Drogon. *Hungry and growing fast. Another year, or perhaps two, and he may be large enough to ride. Then I shall have no need of ships to cross the great salt sea.*

But that time was not yet come. Rhaegal and Viserion were the size of small dogs, Drogon only a little larger, and any dog would have outweighed them; they were all wings and neck and tail, lighter than they looked. And so Daenerys Targaryen must rely on wood and wind and canvas to bear her home.

The wood and the canvas had served her well enough so far, but the fickle wind had turned traitor. For six days and six nights they had been becalmed, and now a seventh day had come, and still no breath of air to fill their sails. Fortunately, two of the ships that Magister Illyrio had sent after her were trading galleys, with two hundred oars apiece and crews of strong-armed oarsmen to row them. But the great cog *Balerion* was a song of a different key; a ponderous broad-beamed sow of a ship with immense holds and huge sails, but helpless in a calm. *Vhagar* and *Meraxes* had let out lines to tow her, but it made for painfully slow going. All three ships were crowded, and heavily laden.

"I cannot see Drogon," said Ser Jorah Mormont as he joined her on the forecastle. "Is he lost again?"

"We are the ones who are lost, ser. Drogon has no taste for this wet creeping, no more than I do." Bolder than the other two, her black dragon had been the first to try his wings above the water, the first to flutter from ship to ship, the first to lose himself in a passing cloud . . . and the first to kill. The flying fish no sooner broke the surface of the water than they were enveloped in a lance of flame, snatched up, and swallowed. "How big will he grow?" Dany asked curiously. "Do you know?"

"In the Seven Kingdoms, there are tales of dragons who grew so huge that they could pluck giant krakens from the seas."

Dany laughed. "That would be a wondrous sight to see."

"It is only a tale, *Khaleesi*," said her exile knight. "They talk of wise old dragons living a thousand years as well."

"Well, how long *does* a dragon live?" She looked up as Viserion swooped low over the ship, his wings beating slowly and stirring the limp sails.

Ser Jorah shrugged. "A dragon's natural span of days is many times as long as a man's, or so the songs would have us believe . . . but the dragons the Seven Kingdoms knew best were those of House Targaryen. They were bred for war, and in war they died. It is no easy thing to slay a dragon, but it can be done."

The squire Whitebeard, standing by the figurehead with one lean hand curled about his tall hardwood staff, turned toward them and said, "Balerion the Black Dread was two hundred years old when he died during the reign of Jaehaerys the Conciliator. He was so large he could swallow an aurochs whole. A dragon never stops growing, Your Grace, so long as he has food and freedom." His name was Arstan, but Strong Belwas had named him Whitebeard for his pale whiskers, and most everyone called him that now. He was taller than Ser Jorah, though not so muscular; his eyes were a pale blue, his long beard as white as snow and as fine as silk.

"Freedom?" asked Dany, curious. "What do you mean?"

"In King's Landing, your ancestors raised an immense domed castle for their dragons. The Dragonpit, it is called. It still stands atop the Hill of Rhaenys, though all in ruins now. That was where the royal dragons dwelt in days of yore, and a cavernous dwelling it was, with iron doors so wide that thirty knights could ride through them abreast. Yet even so, it was noted that none of the pit dragons ever reached the size of their ancestors. The maesters say it was because of the walls around them, and the great dome above their heads."

"If walls could keep us small, peasants would all be tiny and kings as large as giants," said Ser Jorah. "I've seen huge men born in hovels, and dwarfs who dwelt in castles."

"Men are men," Whitebeard replied. "Dragons are dragons."

Ser Jorah snorted his disdain. "How profound." The exile knight had no love for the old man, he'd made that plain from the first. "What do you know of dragons, anyway?"

"Little enough, that's true. Yet I served for a time in King's Landing in the days when King Aerys sat the Iron Throne, and walked beneath the dragonskulls that looked down from the walls of his throne room."

"Viserys talked of those skulls," said Dany. "The Usurper took them down and hid them away. He could not bear them looking down on him upon his stolen throne." She beckoned Whitebeard closer. "Did you ever meet my royal father?" King Aerys II had died before his daughter was born.

"I had that great honor, Your Grace."

"Did you find him good and gentle?"

Whitebeard did his best to hide his feelings, but they were there, plain on his face. "His Grace was . . . often pleasant."

"Often?" Dany smiled. "But not always?"

"He could be very harsh to those he thought his enemies."

"A wise man never makes an enemy of a king," said Dany. "Did you know my brother Rhaegar as well?"

"It was said that no man ever knew Prince Rhaegar, truly. I had the privilege of seeing him in tourney, though, and often heard him play his harp with its silver strings."

Ser Jorah snorted. "Along with a thousand others at some harvest feast. Next you'll claim you squired for him."

"I make no such claim, ser. Myles Mooton was Prince Rhaegar's squire, and Richard Lonmouth after him. When they won their spurs, he knighted them himself, and they remained his close companions. Young Lord Connington was dear to the prince as well, but his oldest friend was Arthur Dayne."

"The Sword of the Morning!" said Dany, delighted. "Viserys used to talk about his wondrous white blade. He said Ser Arthur was the only knight in the realm who was our brother's peer."

Whitebeard bowed his head. "It is not my place to question the words of Prince Viserys."

"King," Dany corrected. "He was a king, though he never reigned. Viserys, the Third of His Name. But what do you mean?" His answer had not been one that she'd expected. "Ser Jorah named Rhaegar the last dragon once. He had to have been a peerless warrior to be called that, surely?"

"Your Grace," said Whitebeard, "the Prince of Dragonstone was a most puissant warrior, but . . ."

"Go on," she urged. "You may speak freely to me."

"As you command." The old man leaned upon his hardwood staff, his brow furrowed. "A warrior without peer . . . those are fine words, Your Grace, but words win no battles."

"Swords win battles," Ser Jorah said bluntly. "And Prince Rhaegar knew how to use one."

"He did, ser, but . . . I have seen a hundred tournaments and more wars than I would wish, and however strong or fast or skilled a knight may be, there are others who can match him. A man will win one tourney, and fall quickly in the next. A slick spot in the grass may mean defeat, or what you ate for supper the night before. A change in the wind may bring the gift of victory." He glanced at Ser Jorah. "Or a lady's favor knotted round an arm."

Mormont's face darkened. "Be careful what you say, old man."

Arstan had seen Ser Jorah fight at Lannisport, Dany knew, in the tourney Mormont had won with a lady's favor knotted round his arm. He had won the lady too; Lynesse of House Hightower, his second wife, highborn and beautiful . . . but she had ruined him, and abandoned him, and the memory of her was bitter to him now. "Be gentle, my knight." She put a hand on Jorah's arm. "Arstan had no wish to give offense, I'm certain."

"As you say, *Khaleesi*." Ser Jorah's voice was grudging.

Dany turned back to the squire. "I know little of Rhaegar. Only the tales Viserys told, and he was a little boy when our brother died. What was he truly like?"

The old man considered a moment. "Able. That above all. Determined, deliberate, dutiful, single-minded. There is a tale told of him . . . but doubtless Ser Jorah knows it as well."

"I would hear it from you."

"As you wish," said Whitebeard. "As a young boy, the Prince of Dragonstone was bookish to a fault. He was reading so early that men said Queen Rhaella must have swallowed some books and a candle whilst he was in her womb. Rhaegar took no interest in the play of other children. The maesters were awed by his wits, but his father's knights would jest sourly that Baelor the Blessed had been born again. Until one day Prince Rhaegar found something in his scrolls that changed him. No one knows what it might have been, only that the boy suddenly appeared early one morning in the yard as the knights were donning their steel. He walked up to Ser Willem Darry, the master-at-arms, and said, 'I will require sword and armor. It seems I must be a warrior.'"

"And he was!" said Dany, delighted.

"He was indeed." Whitebeard bowed. "My pardons, Your Grace. We speak of warriors, and I see that Strong Belwas has arisen. I must attend him."

Dany glanced aft. The eunuch was climbing through the hold amidships, nimble for all his size. Belwas was squat but broad, a good fifteen stone of fat and muscle, his great brown gut crisscrossed by faded white scars. He wore baggy pants, a yellow silk bellyband, and an absurdly tiny leather vest dotted with iron studs. "Strong Belwas is hungry!" he roared at everyone and no one in particular. "Strong Belwas will eat now!" Turning, he spied Arstan on the forecastle. "Whitebeard! You will bring food for Strong Belwas!"

"You may go," Dany told the squire. He bowed again, and moved off to tend the needs of the man he served.

Ser Jorah watched with a frown on his blunt honest face. Mormont was big and burly, strong of jaw and thick of shoulder. Not a handsome man by any means, but as true a friend as Dany had ever known. "You would be wise to take that old man's words well salted," he told her when Whitebeard was out of earshot.

"A queen must listen to all," she reminded him. "The highborn and the low, the strong and the weak, the noble and the venal. One voice may speak you false, but in many there is always truth to be found." She had read that in a book.

"Hear my voice then, Your Grace," the exile said. "This Arstan Whitebeard is playing you false. He is too old to be a squire, and too well spoken to be serving that oaf of a eunuch."

That does seem queer, Dany had to admit. Strong Belwas was an ex-slave, bred and trained in the fighting pits of Meereen. Magister Illyrio had sent him to guard her, or so Belwas claimed, and it was true that she needed guarding. The Usurper on his Iron Throne had offered land and lordship to any man who killed her. One attempt had been made already, with a cup of poisoned wine. The closer she came to Westeros, the more likely another attack became. Back in Qarth, the warlock Pyat Pree had sent a Sorrowful Man after her to avenge the Undying she'd burned in their House of Dust. Warlocks never forgot a wrong, it was said, and the Sorrowful Men never failed to kill. Most of the Dothraki would be against her as well. Khal Drogo's *kos* led *khalasars* of their own now, and none of them would hesitate to attack her own little band on sight, to slay and slave her people and drag Dany herself back to Vaes Dothrak to take her proper place among the withered crones of the *dosh khaleen*. She *hoped* that Xaro Xhoan Daxos was not an enemy, but the Qartheen merchant had coveted her dragons. And there was Quaithe of the Shadow, that strange woman in the red lacquer mask with all her cryptic counsel. Was she an enemy too, or only a dangerous friend? Dany could not say.

Ser Jorah saved me from the poisoner, and Arstan Whitebeard from the manticore. Perhaps Strong Belwas will save me from the next. He was huge enough, with arms like small trees and a great curved *arakh* so sharp he might have shaved with it, in the unlikely event of hair sprouting on those smooth brown cheeks. Yet he was childlike as well. *As a protector, he leaves much to be desired. Thankfully, I have Ser Jorah and my bloodriders. And my dragons, never forget.* In time, the dragons would be her most formidable guardians, just as they had been for Aegon the Conqueror and his sisters three hundred years ago. Just now, though, they brought her more danger than protection. In all the world there were but three living dragons, and those were hers; they were a wonder, and a terror, and beyond price.

She was pondering her next words when she felt a cool breath on the back of her neck, and a loose strand of her silver-gold hair stirred against her brow. Above, the canvas creaked and moved, and suddenly a great cry went up from all over *Balerion*. "Wind!" the sailors shouted. "The wind returns, the *wind!*"

Dany looked up to where the great cog's sails rippled and belled as the lines thrummed and tightened and sang the sweet song they had missed so for six long days. Captain Groleo rushed aft, shouting commands. The Pentoshi were scrambling up the masts, those that were not cheering. Even Strong Belwas let out a great bellow and did a little dance. "The gods are good!" Dany said. "You see, Jorah? We are on our way once more."

"Yes," he said, "but to what, my queen?"

All day the wind blew, steady from the east at first, and then in wild gusts. The sun set in a blaze of red. *I am still half a world from Westeros*, Dany reminded herself, *but every hour brings me closer*. She tried to imagine what it would feel like, when she first caught sight of the land she was born to rule. *It will be as fair a shore as I have ever seen, I know it. How could it be otherwise?*

But later that night, as *Balerion* plunged onward through the dark and Dany sat crosslegged on her bunk in the captain's cabin, feeding her dragons – "Even upon the sea," Groleo had said, so graciously, "queens take precedence over captains" – a sharp knock came upon the door.

Irri had been sleeping at the foot of her bunk (it was too narrow for three, and tonight was Jhiqui's turn to share the soft featherbed with her *khaleesi*), but the handmaid roused at the knock and went to the door. Dany pulled up a coverlet and tucked it in under her arms. She was naked, and had not expected a caller at this hour. "Come," she said when she saw Ser Jorah standing without, beneath a swaying lantern.

The exile knight ducked his head as he entered. "Your Grace. I am sorry to disturb your sleep."

"I was not sleeping, ser. Come and watch." She took a chunk of salt pork out of the bowl in her lap and held it up for her dragons to see. All three of them eyed it hungrily. Rhaegal spread green wings and stirred the air, and Viserion's neck swayed back and forth like a long pale snake's as he followed the movement of her hand. "Drogon," Dany said softly, "*dracarys*." And she tossed the pork in the air.

Drogon moved quicker than a striking cobra. Flame roared from his mouth, orange and scarlet and black, searing the meat before it began to fall. As his sharp black teeth snapped shut around it, Rhaegal's head darted close, as if to steal the prize from his brother's jaws, but Drogon swallowed and screamed, and the smaller green dragon could only *hiss* in frustration.

"Stop that, Rhaegal," Dany said in annoyance, giving his head a swat. "You had the last one. I'll have no greedy dragons." She smiled at Ser

Jorah. "I won't need to char their meat over a brazier any longer."

"So I see. *Dracarys!*"

All three dragons turned their heads at the sound of that word, and Viserion let loose with a blast of pale gold flame that made Ser Jorah take a hasty step backward. Dany giggled. "Be careful with that word, ser, or they're like to singe your beard off. It means 'dragonfire' in High Valyrian. I wanted to choose a command that no one was like to utter by chance."

Mormont nodded. "Your Grace," he said, "I wonder if I might have a few private words?"

"Of course. Irri, leave us for a bit." She put a hand on Jhiqui's bare shoulder and shook the other handmaid awake. "You as well, sweetling. Ser Jorah needs to talk to me."

"Yes, *Khaleesi.*" Jhiqui tumbled from the bunk, naked and yawning, her thick black hair tumbled about her head. She dressed quickly and left with Irri, closing the door behind them.

Dany gave the dragons the rest of the salt pork to squabble over, and patted the bed beside her. "Sit, good ser, and tell me what is troubling you."

"Three things." Ser Jorah sat. "Strong Belwas. This Arstan Whitebeard. And Illyrio Mopatis, who sent them."

Again? Dany pulled the coverlet higher and tugged one end over her shoulder. "And why is that?"

"The warlocks in Qarth told you that you would be betrayed three times," the exile knight reminded her, as Viserion and Rhaegal began to snap and claw at each other.

"Once for blood and once for gold and once for love." Dany was not like to forget. "Mirri Maz Duur was the first."

"Which means two traitors yet remain . . . and now these two appear. I find that troubling, yes. Never forget, Robert offered a lordship to the man who slays you."

Dany leaned forward and yanked Viserion's tail, to pull him off his green brother. Her blanket fell away from her chest as she moved. She grabbed it hastily and covered herself again. "The Usurper is dead," she said.

"But his son rules in his place." Ser Jorah lifted his gaze, and his dark eyes met her own. "A dutiful son pays his father's debts. Even blood debts."

"This boy Joffrey might want me dead . . . if he recalls that I'm alive. What has that to do with Belwas and Arstan Whitebeard? The old man does not even wear a sword. You've seen that."

"Aye. And I have seen how deftly he handles that staff of his. Recall how he killed that manticore in Qarth? It might as easily have been your throat he crushed."

"Might have been, but was not," she pointed out. "It was a stinging manticore meant to slay me. He saved my life."

"*Khaleesi*, has it occurred to you that Whitebeard and Belwas might have been in league with the assassin? It might all have been a ploy to win your trust."

Her sudden laughter made Drogon *hiss*, and sent Viserion flapping to his perch above the porthole. "The ploy worked well."

The exile knight did not return her smile. "These are Illyrio's ships, Illyrio's captains, Illyrio's sailors . . . and Strong Belwas and Arstan are his men as well, not yours."

"Magister Illyrio has protected me in the past. Strong Belwas says that he wept when he heard my brother was dead."

"Yes," said Mormont, "but did he weep for Viserys, or for the plans he had made with him?"

"His plans need not change. Magister Illyrio is a friend to House Targaryen, and wealthy . . ."

"He was not born wealthy. In the world as I have seen it, no man grows rich by kindness. The warlocks said the second treason would be for *gold*. What does Illyrio Mopatis love more than gold?"

"His skin." Across the cabin Drogon stirred restlessly, steam rising from his snout. "Mirri Maz Duur betrayed me. I burned her for it."

"Mirri Maz Duur was in your power. In Pentos, you shall be in Illyrio's power. It is not the same. I know the magister as well as you. He is a devious man, and clever –"

"I need clever men about me if I am to win the Iron Throne."

Ser Jorah snorted. "That wineseller who tried to poison you was a clever man as well. Clever men hatch ambitious schemes."

Dany drew her legs up beneath the blanket. "You will protect me. You, and my bloodriders."

"Four men? *Khaleesi*, you believe you know Illyrio Mopatis, very well. Yet you insist on surrounding yourself with men you do *not* know, like this puffed-up eunuch and the world's oldest squire. Take a lesson from Pyat Pree and Xaro Xhoan Daxos."

He means well, Dany reminded herself. *He does all he does for love.* "It seems to me that a queen who trusts no one is as foolish as a queen who trusts everyone. Every man I take into my service is a risk, I understand that, but how am I to win the Seven Kingdoms without such risks? Am I to conquer Westeros with one exile knight and three Dothraki bloodriders?"

His jaw set stubbornly. "Your path is dangerous, I will not deny that. But if you blindly trust in every liar and schemer who crosses it, you will end as your brothers did."

His obstinacy made her angry. *He treats me like some child.* "Strong

Belwas could not scheme his way to breakfast. And what lies has Arstan Whitebeard told me?"

"He is not what he pretends to be. He speaks to you more boldly than any squire would dare."

"He spoke frankly at my command. He knew my brother."

"A great many men knew your brother. Your Grace, in Westeros the Lord Commander of the Kingsguard sits on the small council, and serves the king with his wits as well as his steel. If I am the first of your Queensguard, I pray you, hear me out. I have a plan to put to you."

"What plan? Tell me."

"Illyrio Mopatis wants you back in Pentos, under his roof. Very well, go to him . . . but in your own time, and not alone. Let us see how loyal and obedient these new subjects of yours truly are. Command Groleo to change course for Slaver's Bay."

Dany was not certain she liked the sound of that at all. Everything she'd ever heard of the flesh marts in the great slave cities of Yunkai, Meereen, and Astapor was dire and frightening. "What is there for me in Slaver's Bay?"

"An army," said Ser Jorah. "If Strong Belwas is so much to your liking you can buy hundreds more like him out of the fighting pits of Meereen . . . but it is Astapor I'd set my sails for. In Astapor you can buy Unsullied."

"The slaves in the spiked bronze hats?" Dany had seen Unsullied guards in the Free Cities, posted at the gates of magisters, archons, and dynasts. "Why should I want Unsullied? They don't even ride horses, and most of them are fat."

"The Unsullied you may have seen in Pentos and Myr were household guards. That's soft service, and eunuchs tend to plumpness in any case. Food is the only vice allowed them. To judge all Unsullied by a few old household slaves is like judging all squires by Arstan Whitebeard, Your Grace. Do you know the tale of the Three Thousand of Qohor?"

"No." The coverlet slipped off Dany's shoulder, and she tugged it back into place.

"It was four hundred years ago or more, when the Dothraki first rode out of the east, sacking and burning every town and city in their path. The *khal* who led them was named Temmo. His *khalasar* was not so big as Drogo's, but it was big enough. Fifty thousand, at the least. Half of them braided warriors with bells ringing in their hair.

"The Qohorik knew he was coming. They strengthened their walls, doubled the size of their own guard, and hired two free companies besides, the Bright Banners and the Second Sons. And almost as an afterthought, they sent a man to Astapor to buy three thousand Unsullied. It was a long march back to Qohor, however, and as they approached they saw the smoke and dust and heard the distant din of battle.

"By the time the Unsullied reached the city the sun had set. Crows and wolves were feasting beneath the walls on what remained of the Qohorik heavy horse. The Bright Banners and Second Sons had fled, as sellswords are wont to do in the face of hopeless odds. With dark falling, the Dothraki had retired to their own camps to drink and dance and feast, but none doubted that they would return on the morrow to smash the city gates, storm the walls, and rape, loot, and slave as they pleased.

"But when dawn broke and Temmo and his bloodriders led their *khalasar* out of camp, they found three thousand Unsullied drawn up before the gates with the Black Goat standard flying over their heads. So small a force could easily have been flanked, but you know Dothraki. These were men on foot, and men on foot are fit only to be ridden down.

"The Dothraki charged. The Unsullied locked their shields, lowered their spears, and stood firm. Against twenty thousand screamers with bells in their hair, they stood firm.

"Eighteen times the Dothraki charged, and broke themselves on those shields and spears like waves on a rocky shore. Thrice Temmo sent his archers wheeling past and arrows fell like rain upon the Three Thousand, but the Unsullied merely lifted their shields above their heads until the squall had passed. In the end only six hundred of them remained . . . but more than twelve thousand Dothraki lay dead upon that field, including Khal Temmo, his bloodriders, his *kos*, and all his sons. On the morning of the fourth day, the new *khal* led the survivors past the city gates in a stately procession. One by one, each man cut off his braid and threw it down before the feet of the Three Thousand.

"Since that day, the city guard of Qohor has been made up solely of Unsullied, every one of whom carries a tall spear from which hangs a braid of human hair.

"*That* is what you will find in Astapor, Your Grace. Put ashore there, and continue on to Pentos overland. It will take longer, yes . . . but when you break bread with Magister Illyrio, you will have a thousand swords behind you, not just four."

There is wisdom in this, yes, Dany thought, *but* . . . "How am I to buy a thousand slave soldiers? All I have of value is the crown the Tourmaline Brotherhood gave me."

"Dragons will be as great a wonder in Astapor as they were in Qarth. It may be that the slavers will shower you with gifts, as the Qartheen did. If not . . . these ships carry more than your Dothraki and their horses. They took on trade goods at Qarth, I've been through the holds and seen for myself. Bolts of silk and bales of tiger skin, amber and jade carvings, saffron, myrrh . . . slaves are cheap, Your Grace. Tiger skins are costly."

"Those are *Illyrio*'s tiger skins," she objected.

"And Illyrio is a friend to House Targaryen."

"All the more reason not to steal his goods."

"What use are wealthy friends if they will not put their wealth at your disposal, my queen? If Magister Illyrio would deny you, he is only Xaro Xhoan Daxos with four chins. And if he is sincere in his devotion to your cause, he will not begrudge you three shiploads of trade goods. What better use for his tiger skins than to buy you the beginnings of an army?"

That's true. Dany felt a rising excitement. "There will be dangers on such a long march . . ."

"There are dangers at sea as well. Corsairs and pirates hunt the southern route, and north of Valyria the Smoking Sea is demon-haunted. The next storm could sink or scatter us, a kraken could pull us under . . . or we might find ourselves becalmed again, and die of thirst as we wait for the wind to rise. A march will have different dangers, my queen, but none greater."

"What if Captain Groleo refuses to change course, though? And Arstan, Strong Belwas, what will they do?"

Ser Jorah stood. "Perhaps it's time you found that out."

"Yes," she decided. "I'll do it!" Dany threw back the coverlets and hopped from the bunk. "I'll see the captain at once, command him to set course for Astapor." She bent over her chest, threw open the lid, and seized the first garment to hand, a pair of loose sandsilk trousers. "Hand me my medallion belt," she commanded Jorah as she pulled the sandsilk up over her hips. "And my vest – " she started to say, turning.

Ser Jorah slid his arms around her.

"Oh," was all Dany had time to say as he pulled her close and pressed his lips down on hers. He smelled of sweat and salt and leather, and the iron studs on his jerkin dug into her naked breasts as he crushed her hard against him. One hand held her by the shoulder while the other slid down her spine to the small of her back, and her mouth opened for his tongue, though she never told it to. *His beard is scratchy,* she thought, *but his mouth is sweet.* The Dothraki wore no beards, only long mustaches, and only Khal Drogo had ever kissed her before. *He should not be doing this. I am his queen, not his woman.*

It was a long kiss, though how long Dany could not have said. When it ended, Ser Jorah let go of her, and she took a quick step backward. "You . . . you should not have . . ."

"I should not have waited so long," he finished for her. "I should have kissed you in Qarth, in Vaes Tolorru. I should have kissed you in the red waste, every night and every day. You were made to be kissed, often and well." His eyes were on her breasts.

Dany covered them with her hands, before her nipples could betray her. "I . . . that was not fitting. I am your queen."

"My queen," he said, "and the bravest, sweetest, and most beautiful woman I have ever seen. Daenerys –"

"*Your Grace!*"

"Your Grace," he conceded, "*the dragon has three heads*, remember? You have wondered at that, ever since you heard it from the warlocks in the House of Dust. Well, here's your meaning: Balerion, Meraxes, and Vhagar, ridden by Aegon, Rhaenys, and Visenya. The three-headed dragon of House Targaryen – three dragons, and *three riders.*"

"Yes," said Dany, "but my brothers are dead."

"Rhaenys and Visenya were Aegon's wives as well as his sisters. You have no brothers, but you can take husbands. And I tell you truly, Daenerys, there is no man in all the world who will ever be half so true to you as me."

BRAN

The ridge slanted sharply from the earth, a long fold of stone and soil shaped like a claw. Trees clung to its lower slopes, pines and hawthorn and ash, but higher up the ground was bare, the ridgeline stark against the cloudy sky.

He could feel the high stone calling him. Up he went, loping easy at first, then faster and higher, his strong legs eating up the incline. Birds burst from the branches overhead as he raced by, clawing and flapping their way into the sky. He could hear the wind sighing up amongst the leaves, the squirrels chittering to one another, even the sound a pinecone made as it tumbled to the forest floor. The smells were a song around him, a song that filled the good green world.

Gravel flew from beneath his paws as he gained the last few feet to stand upon the crest. The sun hung above the tall pines huge and red, and below him the trees and hills went on and on as far as he could see or smell. A kite was circling far above, dark against the pink sky.

Prince. The man-sound came into his head suddenly, yet he could feel the rightness of it. *Prince of the green, prince of the wolfswood.* He was strong and swift and fierce, and all that lived in the good green world went in fear of him.

Far below, at the base of the woods, something moved amongst the trees. A flash of grey, quick-glimpsed and gone again, but it was enough to make his ears prick up. Down there beside a swift green brook, another form slipped by, running. *Wolves,* he knew. His little cousins, chasing down some prey. Now the prince could see more of them, shadows on fleet grey paws. *A pack.*

He had a pack as well, once. Five they had been, and a sixth who stood aside. Somewhere down inside him were the sounds the men had given them to tell one from the other, but it was not by their sounds he knew them. He remembered their scents, his brothers and his sisters. They all had smelled alike, had smelled of *pack*, but each was different too.

His angry brother with the hot green eyes was near, the prince felt, though he had not seen him for many hunts. Yet with every sun that set he grew more distant, and he had been the last. The others were far scattered, like leaves blown by the wild wind.

Sometimes he could sense them, though, as if they were still with him, only hidden from his sight by a boulder or a stand of trees. He could not smell them, nor hear their howls by night, yet he felt their presence at his back . . . all but the sister they had lost. His tail drooped when he remembered her. *Four now, not five. Four and one more, the white who has no voice.*

These woods belonged to them, the snowy slopes and stony hills, the great green pines and the golden leaf oaks, the rushing streams and blue lakes fringed with fingers of white frost. But his sister had left the wilds, to walk in the halls of man-rock where other hunters ruled, and once within those halls it was hard to find the path back out. The wolf prince remembered.

The wind shifted suddenly.

Deer, and fear, and blood. The scent of prey woke the hunger in him. The prince sniffed the air again, turning, and then he was off, bounding along the ridgetop with jaws half-parted. The far side of the ridge was steeper than the one he'd come up, but he flew surefoot over stones and roots and rotting leaves, down the slope and through the trees, long strides eating up the ground. The scent pulled him onward, ever faster.

The deer was down and dying when he reached her, ringed by eight of his small grey cousins. The heads of the pack had begun to feed, the male first and then his female, taking turns tearing flesh from the red underbelly of their prey. The others waited patiently, all but the tail, who paced in a wary circle a few strides from the rest, his own tail tucked low. He would eat the last of all, whatever his brothers left him.

The prince was downwind, so they did not sense him until he leapt up upon a fallen log six strides from where they fed. The tail saw him first, gave a piteous whine, and slunk away. His pack brothers turned at the sound and bared their teeth, snarling, all but the head male and female.

The direwolf answered the snarls with a low warning growl and showed them his own teeth. He was bigger than his cousins, twice the size of the scrawny tail, half again as large as the two pack heads. He leapt down into their midst, and three of them broke, melting away into the brush.

Another came at him, teeth snapping. He met the attack head on, caught the wolf's leg in his jaws when they met, and flung him aside yelping and limping.

And then there was only the head wolf to face, the great grey male with his bloody muzzle fresh from the prey's soft belly. There was white on his muzzle as well, to mark him as an old wolf, but when his mouth opened, red slaver ran from his teeth.

He has no fear, the prince thought, *no more than me*. It would be a good fight. They went for each other.

Long they fought, rolling together over roots and stones and fallen leaves and the scattered entrails of the prey, tearing at each other with tooth and claw, breaking apart, circling each round the other, and bolting in to fight again. The prince was larger, and much the stronger, but his cousin had a pack. The female prowled around them closely, snuffing and snarling, and would interpose herself whenever her mate broke off bloodied. From time to time the other wolves would dart in as well, to snap at a leg or an ear when the prince was turned the other way. One angered him so much that he whirled in a black fury and tore out the attacker's throat. After that the others kept their distance.

And as the last red light was filtering through green boughs and golden, the old wolf lay down weary in the dirt, and rolled over to expose his throat and belly. It was submission.

The prince sniffed at him and licked the blood from fur and torn flesh. When the old wolf gave a soft whimper, the direwolf turned away. He was very hungry now, and the prey was his.

"Hodor."

The sudden sound made him stop and snarl. The wolves regarded him with green and yellow eyes, bright with the last light of day. None of them had heard it. It was a queer wind that blew only in his ears. He buried his jaws in the deer's belly and tore off a mouthful of flesh.

"Hodor, hodor."

No, he thought. *No, I won't*. It was a boy's thought, not a direwolf's. The woods were darkening all about him, until only the shadows of the trees remained, and the glow of his cousins' eyes. And *through* those and behind those eyes, he saw a big man's grinning face, and a stone vault whose walls were spotted with niter. The rich warm taste of blood faded on his tongue. *No, don't, don't, I want to eat, I want to, I want . . .*

"Hodor, hodor, hodor, hodor, hodor," Hodor chanted as he shook him softly by the shoulders, back and forth and back and forth. He was trying to be gentle, he always tried, but Hodor was seven feet tall and stronger than he knew, and his huge hands rattled Bran's teeth together. *"NO!"* he shouted angrily. "Hodor, leave off, I'm here, I'm *here*."

Hodor stopped, looking abashed. "Hodor?"

The woods and wolves were gone. Bran was back again, down in the damp vault of some ancient watchtower that must have been abandoned thousands of years before. It wasn't much of a tower now. Even the tumbled stones were so overgrown with moss and ivy that you could hardly see them until you were right on top of them. "Tumbledown Tower", Bran had named the place; it was Meera who found the way down into the vault, however.

"You were gone too long." Jojen Reed was thirteen, only four years older than Bran. Jojen wasn't much bigger either, no more than two inches or maybe three, but he had a solemn way of talking that made him seem older and wiser than he really was. At Winterfell, Old Nan had dubbed him "little grandfather."

Bran frowned at him. "I wanted to eat."

"Meera will be back soon with supper."

"I'm sick of frogs." Meera was a frogeater from the Neck, so Bran couldn't really *blame* her for catching so many frogs, he supposed, but even so . . . "I wanted to eat the deer." For a moment he remembered the taste of it, the blood and the raw rich meat, and his mouth watered. *I won the fight for it. I won.*

"Did you mark the trees?"

Bran flushed. Jojen was always telling him to do things when he opened his third eye and put on Summer's skin. To claw the bark of a tree, to catch a rabbit and bring it back in his jaws uneaten, to push some rocks in a line. *Stupid things.* "I forgot," he said.

"You always forget."

It was true. He *meant* to do the things that Jojen asked, but once he was a wolf they never seemed important. There were always things to see and things to smell, a whole green world to hunt. And he could *run!* There was nothing better than running, unless it was running after prey. "I was a prince, Jojen," he told the older boy. "I was the prince of the woods."

"You are a prince," Jojen reminded him softly. "You remember, don't you? Tell me who you are."

"You *know.*" Jojen was his friend and his teacher, but sometimes Bran just wanted to hit him.

"I want you to say the words. Tell me who you are."

"Bran," he said sullenly. *Bran the Broken.* "Brandon Stark." *The cripple boy.* "The Prince of Winterfell." Of Winterfell burned and tumbled, its people scattered and slain. The glass gardens were smashed, and hot water gushed from the cracked walls to steam beneath the sun. *How can you be the prince of someplace you might never see again?*

"And who is Summer?" Jojen prompted.

"My direwolf." He smiled. "Prince of the green."

"Bran the boy and Summer the wolf. You are two, then?"

"Two," he sighed, "and one." He hated Jojen when he got stupid like this. *At Winterfell he wanted me to dream my wolf dreams, and now that I know how he's always calling me back.*

"Remember that, Bran. Remember *yourself*, or the wolf will consume you. When you join, it is not enough to run and hunt and howl in Summer's skin."

It is for me, Bran thought. He liked Summer's skin better than his own. *What good is it to be a skinchanger if you can't wear the skin you like?*

"Will you remember? And next time, mark the tree. Any tree, it doesn't matter, so long as you do it."

"I will. I'll remember. I could go back and do it now, if you like. I won't forget this time." *But I'll eat my deer first, and fight with those little wolves some more.*

Jojen shook his head. "No. Best stay, and eat. With your own mouth. A warg cannot live on what his beast consumes."

How would you know? Bran thought resentfully. *You've never been a warg, you don't know what it's like.*

Hodor jerked suddenly to his feet, almost hitting his head on the barrel-vaulted ceiling. "HODOR!" he shouted, rushing to the door. Meera pushed it open just before he reached it, and stepped through into their refuge. "Hodor, hodor," the huge stableboy said, grinning.

Meera Reed was sixteen, a woman grown, but she stood no higher than her brother. All the crannogmen were small, she told Bran once when he asked why she wasn't taller. Brown-haired, green-eyed, and flat as a boy, she walked with a supple grace that Bran could only watch and envy. Meera wore a long sharp dagger, but her favorite way to fight was with a slender three-pronged frog spear in one hand and a woven net in the other.

"Who's hungry?" she asked, holding up her catch: two small silvery trout and six fat green frogs.

"I am," said Bran. *But not for frogs.* Back at Winterfell before all the bad things had happened, the Walders used to say that eating frogs would turn your teeth green and make moss grow under your arms. He wondered if the Walders were dead. He hadn't seen their corpses at Winterfell . . . but there had been a *lot* of corpses, and they hadn't looked inside the buildings.

"We'll just have to feed you, then. Will you help me clean the catch, Bran?"

He nodded. It was hard to sulk with Meera. She was much more cheerful than her brother, and always seemed to know how to make him smile. Nothing ever scared her or made her angry. *Well, except Jojen, sometimes . . .* Jojen Reed could scare most anyone. He dressed all in green, his eyes were murky as moss, and he had green dreams. What Jojen dreamed came true. *Except he dreamed me dead, and I'm not.* Only he was, in a way.

Jojen sent Hodor out for wood and built them a small fire while Bran and Meera were cleaning the fish and frogs. They used Meera's helm for a cooking pot, chopping up the catch into little cubes and tossing in some water and some wild onions Hodor had found to make a froggy stew. It wasn't as good as deer, but it wasn't bad either, Bran decided as he ate. "Thank you, Meera," he said. "My lady."

"You are most welcome, Your Grace."

"Come the morrow," Jojen announced, "we had best move on."

Bran could see Meera tense. "Have you had a green dream?"

"No," he admitted.

"Why leave, then?" his sister demanded. "Tumbledown Tower's a good place for us. No villages near, the woods are full of game, there's fish and frogs in the streams and lakes . . . and who is ever going to find us here?"

"This is not the place we are meant to be."

"It is safe, though."

"It *seems* safe, I know," said Jojen, "but for how long? There was a battle at Winterfell, we saw the dead. Battles mean wars. If some army should take us unawares . . ."

"It might be Robb's army," said Bran. "Robb will come back from the south soon, I know he will. He'll come back with all his banners and chase the ironmen away."

"Your maester said naught of Robb when he lay dying," Jojen reminded him. "*Ironmen on the Stony Shore,* he said, and, *east, the Bastard of Bolton.* Moat Cailin and Deepwood Motte fallen, the heir to Cerwyn dead, and the castellan of Torrhen's Square. *War everywhere,* he said, *each man against his neighbor.*"

"We have plowed this field before," his sister said. "You want to make for the Wall, and your three-eyed crow. That's well and good, but the Wall is a very long way and Bran has no legs but Hodor. If we were mounted . . ."

"If we were eagles we might fly," said Jojen sharply, "but we have no wings, no more than we have horses."

"There are horses to be had," said Meera. "Even in the deep of the wolfswood there are foresters, crofters, hunters. Some will have horses."

"And if they do, should we steal them? Are we thieves? The last thing we need is men hunting us."

"We could buy them," she said. "Trade for them."

"Look at us, Meera. A crippled boy with a direwolf, a simpleminded giant, and two crannogmen a thousand leagues from the Neck. *We will be known.* And word will spread. So long as Bran remains dead, he is safe. Alive, he becomes prey for those who want him dead for good and true." Jojen went to the fire to prod the embers with a stick. "Somewhere to the north, the three-eyed crow awaits us. Bran has need of a teacher wiser than me."

"How, Jojen?" his sister asked. *"How?"*

"Afoot," he answered. "A step at a time."

"The road from Greywater to Winterfell went on forever, and we were mounted then. You want us to travel a longer road on foot, without even knowing where it ends. Beyond the Wall, you say. I haven't been there, no more than you, but I know that Beyond the Wall's a big place, Jojen. Are there many three-eyed crows, or only one? How do we find him?"

"Perhaps he will find us."

Before Meera could find a reply to that, they heard the sound; the distant howl of a wolf, drifting through the night. "Summer?" asked Jojen, listening.

"No." Bran knew the voice of his direwolf.

"Are you certain?" said the little grandfather.

"Certain." Summer had wandered far afield today, and would not be back till dawn. *Maybe Jojen dreams green, but he can't tell a wolf from a direwolf.* He wondered why they all listened to Jojen so much. He was not a prince like Bran, nor big and strong like Hodor, nor as good a hunter as Meera, yet somehow it was always Jojen telling them what to do. "We should steal horses like Meera wants," Bran said, "and ride to the Umbers up at Last Hearth." He thought a moment. "Or we could steal a boat and sail down the White Knife to White Harbor town. That fat Lord Manderly rules there, he was friendly at the harvest feast. He wanted to build ships. Maybe he built some, and we could sail to Riverrun and bring Robb home with all his army. Then it wouldn't matter who knew I was alive. Robb wouldn't let anyone hurt us."

"Hodor!" burped Hodor. "Hodor, hodor."

He was the only one who liked Bran's plan, though. Meera just smiled at him and Jojen frowned. They never listened to what he wanted, even though Bran was a Stark and a prince besides, and the Reeds of the Neck were Stark bannermen.

"Hoooodor," said Hodor, swaying. "Hooooooodor, hoooooodor, hoDOR, hoDOR, hoDOR." Sometimes he liked to do this, just saying his name different ways, over and over and over. Other times, he would stay so quiet you forgot he was there. There was never any knowing with Hodor. *"HODOR, HODOR, HODOR!"* he shouted.

He is not going to stop, Bran realized. "Hodor," he said, "why don't you go outside and train with your sword?"

The stableboy had forgotten about his sword, but now he remembered. "Hodor!" he burped. He went for his blade. They had three tomb swords taken from the crypts of Winterfell where Bran and his brother Rickon had hidden from Theon Greyjoy's ironmen. Bran claimed his uncle Brandon's sword, Meera the one she found upon the knees of his grandfather Lord Rickard. Hodor's blade was much older, a huge heavy piece of iron, dull from centuries of neglect and well spotted with rust. He could swing it for hours at a time. There was a rotted tree near the tumbled stones that he had hacked half to pieces.

Even when he went outside they could hear him through the walls, bellowing "HODOR!" as he cut and slashed at his tree. Thankfully the wolfswood was huge, and there was not like to be anyone else around to hear.

"Jojen, what did you mean about a teacher?" Bran asked. "*You're* my teacher. I know I never marked the tree, but I will the next time. My third eye is open like you wanted . . ."

"So wide open that I fear you may fall through it, and live all the rest of your days as a wolf of the woods."

"I won't, I promise."

"The boy promises. Will the wolf remember? You run with Summer, you hunt with him, kill with him . . . but you bend to his will more than him to yours."

"I just forget," Bran complained. "I'm only nine. I'll be better when I'm older. Even Florian the Fool and Prince Aemon the Dragonknight weren't great knights when they were *nine*."

"That is true," said Jojen, "and a wise thing to say, if the days were still growing longer . . . but they aren't. You are a summer child, I know. Tell me the words of House Stark."

"*Winter is coming.*" Just saying it made Bran feel cold.

Jojen gave a solemn nod. "I dreamed of a winged wolf bound to earth by chains of stone, and came to Winterfell to free him. The chains are off you now, yet still you do not fly."

"Then *you* teach me." Bran still feared the three-eyed crow who haunted his dreams sometimes, pecking endlessly at the skin between his eyes and telling him to fly. "You're a greenseer."

"No," said Jojen, "only a boy who dreams. The greenseers were more than that. They were wargs as well, as *you* are, and the greatest of them could wear the skins of *any* beast that flies or swims or crawls, and could look through the eyes of the weirwoods as well, and see the truth that lies beneath the world.

"The gods give many gifts, Bran. My sister is a hunter. It is given to her to run swiftly, and stand so still she seems to vanish. She has sharp ears, keen eyes, a steady hand with net and spear. She can breathe mud and fly through trees. I could not do these things, no more than you could. To me the gods gave the green dreams, and to you . . . you could be more than me, Bran. You are the winged wolf, and there is no saying how far and high you might fly . . . if you had someone to teach you. How can I help you master a gift I do not understand? We remember the First Men in the Neck, and the children of the forest who were their friends . . . but so much is forgotten, and so much we never knew."

Meera took Bran by the hand. "If we stay here, troubling no one, you'll be safe until the war ends. You will not learn, though, except what my brother can teach you, and you've heard what he says. If we leave this place to seek refuge at Last Hearth or beyond the Wall, we risk being taken. You are only a boy, I know, but you are our prince as well, our lord's son and our king's true heir. We have sworn you our faith by earth and water, bronze and iron, ice and fire. The risk is yours, Bran, as is the gift. The choice should be yours too, I think. We are your servants to command." She grinned. "At least in this."

"You mean," Bran said, "you'll do what *I* say? Truly?"

"Truly, my prince," the girl replied, "so consider well."

Bran tried to think it through, the way his father might have. The Greatjon's uncles Hother Whoresbane and Mors Crowfood were fierce men, but he thought they would be loyal. And the Karstarks, them too. Karhold was a strong castle, Father always said. *We would be safe with the Umbers or the Karstarks.*

Or they could go south to fat Lord Manderly. At Winterfell, he'd laughed a lot, and never seemed to look at Bran with so much pity as the other lords. Castle Cerwyn was closer than White Harbor, but Maester Luwin had said that Cley Cerwyn was dead. *The Umbers and the Karstarks and the Manderlys may all be dead as well*, he realized. As he would be, if he was caught by the ironmen or the Bastard of Bolton.

If they stayed here, hidden down beneath Tumbledown Tower, no one would find them. He would stay alive. *And crippled.*

Bran realized he was crying. *Stupid baby*, he thought at himself. No matter where he went, to Karhold or White Harbor or Greywater Watch, he'd be a cripple when he got there. He balled his hands into fists. "I want to fly," he told them. "Please. Take me to the crow."

DAVOS

When he came up on deck, the long point of Driftmark was dwindling behind them while Dragonstone rose from the sea ahead. A pale grey wisp of smoke blew from the top of the mountain to mark where the island lay. *Dragonmont is restless this morning*, Davos thought, *or else Melisandre is burning someone else.*

Melisandre had been much in his thoughts as *Shayala's Dance* made her way across Blackwater Bay and through the Gullet, tacking against perverse contrary winds. The great fire that burned atop the Sharp Point watchtower at the end of Massey's Hook reminded him of the ruby she wore at her throat, and when the world turned red at dawn and sunset the drifting clouds turned the same color as the silks and satins of her rustling gowns.

She would be waiting on Dragonstone as well, waiting in all her beauty and all her power, with her god and her shadows and his king. The red priestess had always seemed loyal to Stannis, until now. *She has broken him, as a man breaks a horse. She would ride him to power if she could, and for that she gave my sons to the fire. I will cut the living heart from her breast and see how it burns.* He touched the hilt of the fine long Lysene dirk that the captain had given him.

The captain had been very kind to him. His name was Khorane Sathmantes, a Lyseni like Salladhor Saan, whose ship this was. He had the pale blue eyes you often saw on Lys, set in a bony weatherworn face, but he had spent many years trading in the Seven Kingdoms. When he learned that the man he had plucked from the sea was the celebrated onion knight, he gave him the use of his own cabin and his own clothes, and a pair of new boots that almost fit. He insisted that Davos share his provisions as well, though that turned out badly. His stomach could not tolerate the snails and lampreys and other rich food Captain Khorane so relished, and after his first meal at the captain's table he spent the rest of the day with one end or the other dangling over the rail.

Dragonstone loomed larger with every stroke of the oars. Davos could see the shape of the mountain now, and on its side the great black citadel with its gargoyles and dragon towers. The bronze figurehead at the bow of *Shayala's Dance* sent up wings of salt spray as it cut the waves. He leaned his weight against the rail, grateful for its support. His ordeal had weakened him. If he stood too long his legs shook, and sometimes he fell prey to uncontrollable fits of coughing and brought up gobs of bloody phlegm. *It is nothing*, he told himself. *Surely the gods did not bring me safe through fire and sea only to kill me with a flux.*

As he listened to the pounding of the oarmaster's drum, the thrum of the sail, and the rhythmic swish and creak of the oars, he thought back to his younger days, when these same sounds woke dread in his heart on many a misty morn. They heralded the approach of old Ser Tristimun's sea watch, and the sea watch was death to smugglers when Aerys Targaryen sat the Iron Throne.

But that was another lifetime, he thought. *That was before the onion ship, before Storm's End, before Stannis shortened my fingers. That was before the war or the red comet, before I was a Seaworth or a knight. I was a different man in those days, before Lord Stannis raised me high.*

Captain Khorane had told him of the end of Stannis's hopes, on the night the river burned. The Lannisters had taken him from the flank, and his fickle bannermen had abandoned him by the hundreds in the hour of his greatest need. "King Renly's shade was seen as well," the captain said, "slaying right and left as he led the lion lord's van. It's said his green armor took a ghostly glow from the wildfire, and his antlers ran with golden flames."

Renly's shade. Davos wondered if his sons would return as shades as well. He had seen too many queer things on the sea to say that ghosts did not exist. "Did none keep faith?" he asked.

"Some few," the captain said. "The queen's kin, them in chief. We took off many who wore the fox-and-flowers, though many more were left ashore, with all manner of badges. Lord Florent is the King's Hand on Dragonstone now."

The mountain grew taller, crowned all in pale smoke. The sail sang, the drum beat, the oars pulled smoothly, and before very long the mouth of the harbor opened before them. *So empty,* Davos thought, remembering how it had been before, with the ships crowding every quay and rocking at anchor off the breakwater. He could see Salladhor Saan's flagship *Valyrian* moored at the quay where *Fury* and her sisters had once tied up. The ships on either side of her had striped Lysene hulls as well. In vain he looked for any sign of *Lady Marya* or *Wraith*.

They pulled down the sail as they entered the harbor, to dock on oars alone. The captain came to Davos as they were tying up. "My prince will wish to see you at once."

A fit of coughing seized Davos as he tried to answer. He clutched the rail for support and spat over the side. "The king," he wheezed. "I must go to the king." *For where the king is, I will find Melisandre.*

"No one goes to the king," Khorane Sathmantes replied firmly. "Salladhor Saan will tell you. Him first."

Davos was too weak to defy him. He could only nod.

Salladhor Saan was not aboard his *Valyrian*. They found him at another quay a quarter mile distant, down in the hold of a big-bellied Pentoshi cog named *Bountiful Harvest*, counting cargo with two eunuchs. One held a lantern, the other a wax tablet and stylus. "Thirty-seven, thirty-eight, thirty-nine," the old rogue was saying when Davos and the captain came down the hatch. Today he wore a wine-colored tunic and high boots of bleached white leather inlaid with silver scrollwork. Pulling the stopper from a jar, he sniffed, sneezed, and said, "A coarse grind, and of the second quality, my nose declares. The bill of lading is saying forty-three jars. Where have the others gotten to, I am wondering? These Pentoshi, do they think I am not counting?" When he saw Davos he stopped suddenly. "Is it pepper stinging my eyes, or tears? Is this the knight of the onions who stands before me? No, how can it be, my dear friend Davos died on the burning river, all agree. Why has he come to haunt me?"

"I am no ghost, Salla."

"What else? My onion knight was never so thin or so pale as you." Salladhor Saan threaded his way between the jars of spice and bolts of cloth that filled the hold of the merchanter, wrapped Davos in a fierce embrace, then kissed him once on each cheek and a third time on his forehead. "You are still warm, ser, and I feel your heart thumpety-thumping. Can it be true? The sea that swallowed you has spit you up again."

Davos was reminded of Patchface, Princess Shireen's lackwit fool. He had gone into the sea as well, and when he came out he was mad. *Am I mad as well?* He coughed into a gloved hand and said, "I swam beneath the chain and washed ashore on a spear of the merling king. I would have died there, if *Shayala's Dance* had not come upon me."

Salladhor Saan threw an arm around the captain's shoulders. "This was well done, Khorane. You will be having a fine reward, I am thinking. Meizo Mahr, be a good eunuch and take my friend Davos to the owner's cabin.

Fetch him some hot wine with cloves, I am misliking the sound of that cough. Squeeze some lime in it as well. And bring white cheese and a bowl of those cracked green olives we counted earlier! Davos, I will join you soon, once I have bespoken our good captain. You will be forgiving me, I know. Do not eat all the olives, or I must be cross with you!"

Davos let the elder of the two eunuchs escort him to a large and lavishly furnished cabin at the stern of the ship. The carpets were deep, the windows stained glass, and any of the great leather chairs would have seated three of Davos quite comfortably. The cheese and olives arrived shortly, and a cup of steaming hot red wine. He held it between his hands and sipped it gratefully. The warmth felt soothing as it spread through his chest.

Salladhor Saan appeared not long after. "You must be forgiving me for the wine, my friend. These Pentoshi would drink their own water if it were purple."

"It will help my chest," said Davos. "Hot wine is better than a compress, my mother used to say."

"You shall be needing compresses as well, I am thinking. Sitting on a spear all this long time, oh my. How are you finding that excellent chair? He has fat cheeks, does he not?"

"Who?" asked Davos, between sips of hot wine.

"Illyrio Mopatis. A whale with whiskers, I am telling you truly. These chairs were built to his measure, though he is seldom bestirring himself from Pentos to sit in them. A fat man always sits comfortably, I am thinking, for he takes his pillow with him wherever he goes."

"How is it you come by a Pentoshi ship?" asked Davos. "Have you gone pirate again, my lord?" He set his empty cup aside.

"Vile calumny. Who has suffered more from pirates than Salladhor Saan? I ask only what is due me. Much gold is owed, oh yes, but I am not without reason, so in place of coin I have taken a handsome parchment, very crisp. It bears the name and seal of Lord Alester Florent, the Hand of the King. I am made Lord of Blackwater Bay, and no vessel may be crossing my lordly waters without my lordly leave, no. And when these outlaws are trying to steal past me in the night to avoid my lawful duties and customs, why, they are no better than smugglers, so I am well within my rights to seize them." The old pirate laughed. "I cut off no man's fingers, though. What good are bits of fingers? The ships I am taking, the cargoes, a few ransoms, nothing unreasonable." He gave Davos a sharp look. "You are unwell, my friend. That cough . . . and so thin, I am seeing your bones through your skin. And yet I am not seeing your little bag of fingerbones . . ."

Old habit made Davos reach for the leather pouch that was no longer there. "I lost it in the river." *My luck.*

"The river was terrible," Salladhor Saan said solemnly. "Even from the bay, I was seeing, and shuddering."

Davos coughed, spat, and coughed again. "I saw *Black Betha* burning, and *Fury* as well," he finally managed, hoarsely. "Did none of our ships escape the fire?" Part of him still hoped.

"*Lord Steffon, Ragged Jenna, Swift Sword, Laughing Lord,* and some others were upstream of the pyromancers' pissing, yes. They did not burn, but with the chain raised, neither could they be flying. Some few were surrendering. Most rowed far up the Blackwater, away from the battling, and then were sunk by their crews so they would not be falling into Lannister hands. *Ragged Jenna* and *Laughing Lord* are still playing pirate on the river, I have heard, but who can say if it is so?"

"*Lady Marya?*" Davos asked. "*Wraith?*"

Salladhor Saan put a hand on Davos's forearm and gave a squeeze. "No. Of them, no. I am sorry, my friend. They were good men, your Dale and Allard. But this comfort I can give you – your young Devan was among those we took off at the end. The brave boy never once left the king's side, or so they say."

For a moment he felt almost dizzy, his relief was so palpable. He had been afraid to ask about Devan. "The Mother is merciful. I must go to him, Salla. I must see him."

"Yes," said Salladhor Saan. "And you will be wanting to sail to Cape Wrath, I know, to see your wife and your two little ones. You must be having a new ship, I am thinking."

"His Grace will give me a ship," said Davos.

The Lyseni shook his head. "Of ships, His Grace has none, and Salladhor Saan has many. The king's ships burned up on the river, but not mine. You shall have one, old friend. You will sail for me, yes? You will dance into Braavos and Myr and Volantis in the black of night, all unseen, and dance out again with silks and spices. We will be having fat purses, yes."

"You are kind, Salla, but my duty's to my king, not your purse. The war will go on. Stannis is still the rightful heir by all the laws of the Seven Kingdoms."

"All the laws are not helping when all the ships burn up, I am thinking. And your king, well, you will be finding him changed, I am fearing. Since the battle, he sees no one, but broods in his Stone Drum. Queen Selyse keeps court for him with her uncle the Lord Alester, who is naming himself the Hand. The king's seal she has given to this uncle, to fix to the letters he writes, even to my pretty parchment. But it is a little kingdom they are ruling, poor and rocky, yes. There is no gold, not even a little bit to pay faithful Salladhor Saan what is owed him, and only those knights that we took off at the end, and no ships but my little brave few."

A sudden racking cough bent Davos over. Salladhor Saan moved to help him, but he waved him off, and after a moment he recovered. "No one?" he wheezed. "What do you mean, he sees no one?" His voice sounded wet and thick, even in his own ears, and for a moment the cabin swam dizzily around him.

"No one but *her*," said Salladhor Saan, and Davos did not have to ask who he meant. "My friend, you tire yourself. It is a bed you are needing, not Salladhor Saan. A bed and many blankets, with a hot compress for your chest and more wine and cloves."

Davos shook his head. "I will be fine. Tell me, Salla, I must know. No one but Melisandre?"

The Lyseni gave him a long doubtful look, and continued reluctantly. "The guards keep all others away, even his queen and his little daughter. Servants bring meals that no one eats." He leaned forward and lowered his voice. "Queer talking I have heard, of hungry fires within the mountain, and how Stannis and the red woman go down together to watch the flames. There are shafts, they say, and secret stairs down into the mountain's heart, into hot places where only *she* may walk unburned. It is enough and more to give an old man such terrors that sometimes he can scarcely find the strength to eat."

Melisandre. Davos shivered. "The red woman did this to him," he said. "She sent the fire to consume us, to punish Stannis for setting her aside, to teach him that he could not hope to win without her sorceries."

The Lyseni chose a plump olive from the bowl between them. "You are not the first to be saying this, my friend. But if I am you, I am not saying it so loudly. Dragonstone crawls with these queen's men, oh yes, and they have sharp ears and sharper knives." He popped the olive into his mouth.

"I have a knife myself. Captain Khorane made me a gift of it." He pulled out the dirk and laid it on the table between them. "A knife to cut out Melisandre's heart. If she has one."

Salladhor Saan spit out an olive pit. "Davos, good Davos, you must not be saying such things, even in jest."

"No jest. I mean to kill her." *If she can be killed by mortal weapons.* Davos was not certain that she could. He had seen old Maester Cressen slip poison into her wine, with his own eyes he had seen it, but when they both drank from the poisoned cup it was the maester who died, not the red priestess. *A knife in the heart, though ... even demons can be killed by cold iron, the singers say.*

"These are dangerous talkings, my friend," Salladhor Saan warned him. "I am thinking you are still sick from the sea. The fever has cooked your wits, yes. Best you are taking to your bed for a long resting, until you are stronger."

Until my resolve weakens, you mean. Davos got to his feet. He did feel feverish and a little dizzy, but it did not matter. "You are a treacherous old rogue, Salladhor Saan, but a good friend all the same."

The Lyseni stroked his pointed silver beard. "So with this great friend you will be staying, yes?"

"No, I will be going." He coughed.

"Go? Look at you! You cough, you tremble, you are thin and weak. Where will you be going?"

"To the castle. My bed is there, and my son."

"And the red woman," Salladhor Saan said suspiciously. "She is in the castle also."

"Her too." Davos slid the dirk back into its sheath.

"You are an onion smuggler, what do you know of skulkings and stabbings? And you are ill, you cannot even hold the dirk. Do you know what will be happening to you, if you are caught? While we were burning on the river, the queen was burning traitors. *Servants of the dark*, she named them, poor men, and the red woman sang as the fires were lit."

Davos was unsurprised. *I knew,* he thought, *I knew before he told me.* "She took Lord Sunglass from the dungeons," he guessed, "and Hubard Rambton's sons."

"Just so, and burned them, as she will burn you. If you kill the red woman, they will burn you for revenge, and if you fail to kill her, they will burn you for the trying. She will sing and you will scream, and then you will die. And you have only just come back to life!"

"And this is why," said Davos. "To do this thing. To make an end of Melisandre of Asshai and all her works. Why else would the sea have spit me out? You know Blackwater Bay as well as I do, Salla. No sensible captain would ever take his ship through the spears of the merling king and risk ripping out his bottom. *Shayala's Dance* should never have come near me."

"A wind," insisted Salladhor Saan loudly, "an ill wind, is all. A wind drove her too far to the south."

"And who sent the wind? Salla, the Mother spoke to me."

The old Lyseni blinked at him. "Your mother is dead . . ."

"*The* Mother. She blessed me with seven sons, and yet I let them burn her. She spoke to me. We *called* the fire, she said. We called the shadows too. I rowed Melisandre into the bowels of Storm's End and watched her birth a horror." He saw it still in his nightmares, the gaunt black hands pushing against her thighs as it wriggled free of her swollen womb. "She killed Cressen and Lord Renly and a brave man named Cortnay Penrose, and she killed my sons as well. Now it is time someone killed her."

"*Someone,*" said Salladhor Saan. "Yes, just so, someone. But not you. You are weak as a child, and no warrior. Stay, I beg you, we will talk more and you will eat, and perhaps we will sail to Braavos and hire a Faceless Man to do this thing, yes? But you, no, you must sit and eat."

He is making this much harder, thought Davos wearily, *and it was perishingly hard to begin with*. "I have vengeance in my belly, Salla. It leaves no room for food. Let me go now. For our friendship, wish me luck and let me go."

Salladhor Saan pushed himself to his feet. "You are no true friend, I am thinking. When you are dead, who will be bringing your ashes and bones back to your lady wife and telling her that she has lost a husband and four sons? Only sad old Salladhor Saan. But so be it, brave ser knight, go rushing to your grave. I will gather your bones in a sack and give them to the sons you leave behind, to wear in little bags around their necks." He waved an angry hand, with rings on every finger. "Go, go, go, go, go."

Davos did not want to leave like this. "Salla –"

"*GO*. Or stay, better, but if you are going, go."

He went.

His walk up from the *Bountiful Harvest* to the gates of Dragonstone was long and lonely. The dockside streets where soldiers and sailors and smallfolk had thronged were empty and deserted. Where once he had stepped around squealing pigs and naked children, rats scurried. His legs felt like pudding beneath him, and thrice the coughing racked him so badly that he had to stop and rest. No one came to help him, nor even peered through a window to see what was the matter. The windows were shuttered, the doors barred, and more than half the houses displayed some mark of mourning. *Thousands sailed up the Blackwater Rush, and hundreds came back*, Davos reflected. *My sons did not die alone. May the Mother have mercy on them all.*

When he reached the castle gates, he found them shut as well. Davos pounded on the iron-studded wood with his fist. When there was no answer, he kicked at it, again and again. Finally a crossbowman appeared atop the barbican, peering down between two towering gargoyles. "Who goes there?"

He craned his head back and cupped his hands around his mouth. "Ser Davos Seaworth, to see His Grace."

"Are you drunk? Go away and stop that pounding."

Salladhor Saan had warned him. Davos tried a different tack. "Send for my son, then. Devan, the king's squire."

The guard frowned. "Who did you say you were?"

"Davos," he shouted. "The onion knight."

The head vanished, to return a moment later. "Be off with you. The onion knight died on the river. His ship burned."

"His ship burned," Davos agreed, "but he lived, and here he stands. Is Jate still captain of the gate?"

"Who?"

"Jate Blackberry. He knows me well enough."

"I never heard of him. Most like he's dead."

"Lord Chyttering, then."

"That one I know. He burned on the Blackwater."

"Hookface Will? Hal the Hog?"

"Dead and dead," the crossbowman said, but his face betrayed a sudden doubt. "You wait there." He vanished again.

Davos waited. *Gone, all gone,* he thought dully, remembering how fat Hal's white belly always showed beneath his grease-stained doublet, the long scar the fish hook had left across Will's face, the way Jate always doffed his cap at the women, be they five or fifty, highborn or low. *Drowned or burned, with my sons and a thousand others, gone to make a king in hell.*

Suddenly the crossbowman was back. "Go round to the sally port and they'll admit you."

Davos did as he was bid. The guards who ushered him inside were strangers to him. They carried spears, and on their breasts they wore the fox-and-flowers sigil of House Florent. They escorted him not to the Stone Drum, as he'd expected, but under the arch of the Dragon's Tail and down to Aegon's Garden. "Wait here," their sergeant told him.

"Does His Grace know that I've returned?" asked Davos.

"Bugger all if I know. Wait, I said." The man left, taking his spearmen with him.

Aegon's Garden had a pleasant piney smell to it, and tall dark trees rose on every side. There were wild roses as well, and towering thorny hedges, and a boggy spot where cranberries grew.

Why have they brought me here? Davos wondered.

Then he heard a faint ringing of bells, and a child's giggle, and suddenly the fool Patchface popped from the bushes, shambling along as fast as he could go with the Princess Shireen hot on his heels. "You come back now," she was shouting after him. "Patches, you come back."

When the fool saw Davos, he jerked to a sudden halt, the bells on his antlered tin helmet going *ting-a-ling, ting-a-ling.* Hopping from one foot to the other, he sang, *"Fool's blood, king's blood, blood on the maiden's thigh, but chains for the guests and chains for the bridegroom, aye aye aye."* Shireen almost caught him then, but at the last instant he hopped over a patch of bracken and vanished among the trees. The princess was right behind him. The sight of them made Davos smile.

He had turned to cough into his gloved hand when another small shape crashed out of the hedge and bowled right into him, knocking him off his feet.

The boy went down as well, but he was up again almost at once. "What are you doing here?" he demanded as he brushed himself off. Jet-black hair fell to his collar, and his eyes were a startling blue. "You shouldn't get in my way when I'm running."

"No," Davos agreed. "I shouldn't." Another fit of coughing seized him as he struggled to his knees.

"Are you unwell?" The boy took him by the arm and pulled him to his feet. "Should I summon the maester?"

Davos shook his head. "A cough. It will pass."

The boy took him at his word. "We were playing monsters and maidens," he explained. "I was the monster. It's a childish game but my cousin likes it. Do you have a name?"

"Ser Davos Seaworth."

The boy looked him up and down dubiously. "Are you certain? You don't look very knightly."

"I am the knight of the onions, my lord."

The blue eyes blinked. "The one with the black ship?"

"You know that tale?"

"You brought my uncle Stannis fish to eat before I was born, when Lord Tyrell had him under siege." The boy drew himself up tall. "I am Edric Storm," he announced. "King Robert's son."

"Of course you are." Davos had known that almost at once. The lad had the prominent ears of a Florent, but the hair, the eyes, the jaw, the cheekbones, those were all Baratheon.

"Did you know my father?" Edric Storm demanded.

"I saw him many a time while calling on your uncle at court, but we never spoke."

"My father taught me to fight," the boy said proudly. "He came to see me almost every year, and sometimes we trained together. On my last name day he sent me a warhammer just like his, only smaller. They made me leave it at Storm's End, though. Is it true my uncle Stannis cut off your fingers?"

"Only the last joint. I still have fingers, only shorter."

"Show me."

Davos peeled his glove off. The boy studied his hand carefully. "He did not shorten your thumb?"

"No." Davos coughed. "No, he left me that."

"He should not have chopped any of your fingers," the lad decided. "That was ill done."

"I was a smuggler."

"Yes, but you smuggled him fish and onions."

"Lord Stannis knighted me for the onions, and took my fingers for the smuggling." He pulled his glove back on.

"My father would not have chopped your fingers."

"As you say, my lord." *Robert was a different man than Stannis, true enough. The boy is like him. Aye, and like Renly as well.* That thought made him anxious.

The boy was about to say something more when they heard steps. Davos turned. Ser Axell Florent was coming down the garden path with a dozen guards in quilted jerkins. On their breasts they wore the fiery heart of the Lord of Light. *Queen's men,* Davos thought. A cough came on him suddenly.

Ser Axell was short and muscular, with a barrel chest, thick arms, bandy legs, and hair growing from his ears. The queen's uncle, he had served as castellan of Dragonstone for a decade, and had always treated Davos courteously, knowing he enjoyed the favor of Lord Stannis. But there was neither courtesy nor warmth in his tone as he said, "Ser Davos, and undrowned. How can that be?"

"Onions float, ser. Have you come to take me to the king?"

"I have come to take you to the dungeon." Ser Axell waved his men forward. "Seize him, and take his dirk. He means to use it on our lady."

JAIME

Jaime was the first to spy the inn. The main building hugged the
south shore where the river bent, its long low wings outstretched
along the water as if to embrace travelers sailing downstream. The
lower story was grey stone, the upper whitewashed wood, the roof slate.
He could see stables as well, and an arbor heavy with vines. "No smoke
from the chimneys," he pointed out as they approached. "Nor lights in
the windows."

"The inn was still open when last I passed this way," said Ser Cleos
Frey. "They brewed a fine ale. Perhaps there is still some to be had in
the cellars."

"There may be people," Brienne said. "Hiding. Or dead."

"Frightened of a few corpses, wench?" Jaime said.

She glared at him. "My name is –"

" – Brienne, yes. Wouldn't you like to sleep in a bed for a night, Brienne?
We'd be safer than on the open river, and it might be prudent to find
what's happened here."

She gave no answer, but after a moment she pushed at the tiller to
angle the skiff in toward the weathered wooden dock. Ser Cleos scrambled
to take down the sail. When they bumped softly against the pier, he
climbed out to tie them up. Jaime clambered after him, made awkward
by his chains.

At the end of the dock, a flaking shingle swung from an iron post,
painted with the likeness of a king upon his knees, his hands pressed
together in the gesture of fealty. Jaime took one look and laughed aloud.
"We could not have found a better inn."

"Is this some special place?" the wench asked, suspicious.

Ser Cleos answered. "This is the Inn of the Kneeling Man, my lady. It stands upon the very spot where the last King in the North knelt before Aegon the Conqueror to offer his submission. That's him on the sign, I suppose."

"Torrhen had brought his power south after the fall of the two kings on the Field of Fire," said Jaime, "but when he saw Aegon's dragon and the size of his host, he chose the path of wisdom and bent his frozen knees." He stopped at the sound of a horse's whinny. "Horses in the stable. One at least." *And one is all I need to put the wench behind me.* "Let's see who's home, shall we?" Without waiting for an answer, Jaime went clinking down the dock, put a shoulder to the door, shoved it open . . .

. . . and found himself eye to eye with a loaded crossbow. Standing behind it was a chunky boy of fifteen. "Lion, fish, or wolf?" the lad demanded.

"We were hoping for capon." Jaime heard his companions entering behind him. "The crossbow is a coward's weapon."

"It'll put a bolt through your heart all the same."

"Perhaps. But before you can wind it again my cousin here will spill your entrails on the floor."

"Don't be scaring the lad, now," Ser Cleos said.

"We mean no harm," the wench said. "And we have coin to pay for food and drink." She dug a silver piece from her pouch.

The boy looked suspiciously at the coin, and then at Jaime's manacles. "Why's this one in irons?"

"Killed some crossbowmen," said Jaime. "Do you have ale?"

"Yes." The boy lowered the crossbow an inch. "Undo your swordbelts and let them fall, and might be we'll feed you." He edged around to peer through the thick, diamond-shaped windowpanes and see if any more of them were outside. "That's a Tully sail."

"We come from Riverrun." Brienne undid the clasp on her belt and let it clatter to the floor. Ser Cleos followed suit.

A sallow man with a pocked doughy face stepped through the cellar door, holding a butcher's heavy cleaver. "Three, are you? We got horsemeat enough for three. The horse was old and tough, but the meat's still fresh."

"Is there bread?" asked Brienne.

"Hardbread and stale oatcakes."

Jaime grinned. "Now there's an honest innkeep. They'll all serve you stale bread and stringy meat, but most don't own up to it so freely."

"I'm no innkeep. I buried him out back, with his women."

"Did you kill them?"

"Would I tell you if I did?" The man spat. "Likely it were wolves' work, or maybe lions, what's the difference? The wife and I found them dead. The way we see it, the place is ours now."

"Where is this wife of yours?" Ser Cleos asked.

The man gave him a suspicious squint. "And why would you be wanting to know that? She's not here . . . no more'n you three will be, unless I like the taste of your silver."

Brienne tossed the coin to him. He caught it in the air, bit it, and tucked it away.

"She's got more," the boy with the crossbow announced.

"So she does. Boy, go down and find me some onions."

The lad raised the crossbow to his shoulder, gave them one last sullen look, and vanished into the cellar.

"Your son?" Ser Cleos asked.

"Just a boy the wife and me took in. We had two sons, but the lions killed one and the other died of the flux. The boy lost his mother to the Bloody Mummers. These days, a man needs someone to keep watch while he sleeps." He waved the cleaver at the tables. "Might as well sit."

The hearth was cold, but Jaime picked the chair nearest the ashes and stretched out his long legs under the table. The clink of his chains accompanied his every movement. *An irritating sound. Before this is done, I'll wrap these chains around the wench's throat, see how she likes them then.*

The man who wasn't an innkeep charred three huge horse steaks and fried the onions in bacon grease, which almost made up for the stale oatcakes. Jaime and Cleos drank ale, Brienne a cup of cider. The boy kept his distance, perching atop the cider barrel with his crossbow across his knees, cocked and loaded. The cook drew a tankard of ale and sat with them. "What news from Riverrun?" he asked Ser Cleos, taking him for their leader.

Ser Cleos glanced at Brienne before answering. "Lord Hoster is failing, but his son holds the fords of the Red Fork against the Lannisters. There have been battles."

"Battles everywhere. Where are you bound, ser?"

"King's Landing." Ser Cleos wiped grease off his lips.

Their host snorted. "Then you're three fools. Last I heard, King Stannis was outside the city walls. They say he has a hundred thousand men and a magic sword."

Jaime's hands wrapped around the chain that bound his wrists, and he twisted it taut, wishing for the strength to snap it in two. *Then I'd show Stannis where to sheathe his magic sword.*

"I'd stay well clear of that kingsroad, if I were you," the man went on. "It's worse than bad, I hear. Wolves and lions both, and bands of broken men preying on anyone they can catch."

"Vermin," declared Ser Cleos with contempt. "Such would never dare to trouble armed men."

"Begging your pardon, ser, but I see one armed man, traveling with a woman and a prisoner in chains."

Brienne gave the cook a dark look. *The wench does hate being reminded that she's a wench,* Jaime reflected, twisting at the chains again. The links were cold and hard against his flesh, the iron implacable. The manacles had chafed his wrists raw.

"I mean to follow the Trident to the sea," the wench told their host. "We'll find mounts at Maidenpool and ride by way of Duskendale and Rosby. That should keep us well away from the worst of the fighting."

Their host shook his head. "You'll never reach Maidenpool by river. Not thirty miles from here a couple boats burned and sank, and the channel's been silting up around them. There's a nest of outlaws there preying on anyone tries to come by, and more of the same downriver around the Skipping Stones and Red Deer Island. And the lightning lord's been seen in these parts as well. He crosses the river wherever he likes, riding this way and that way, never still."

"And who is this lightning lord?" demanded Ser Cleos Frey.

"Lord Beric, as it please you, ser. They call him that 'cause he strikes so sudden, like lightning from a clear sky. It's said he cannot die."

They all die when you shove a sword through them, Jaime thought. "Does Thoros of Myr still ride with him?"

"Aye. The red wizard. I've heard tell he has strange powers."

Well, he had the power to match Robert Baratheon drink for drink, and there were few enough who could say that. Jaime had once heard Thoros tell the king that he became a red priest because the robes hid the winestains so well. Robert had laughed so hard he'd spit ale all over Cersei's silken mantle. "Far be it from me to make objection," he said, "but perhaps the Trident is not our safest course."

"I'd say that's so," their cook agreed. "Even if you get past Red Deer Island and don't meet up with Lord Beric and the red wizard, there's still the ruby ford before you. Last I heard, it was the Leech Lord's wolves held the ford, but that was some time past. By now it could be lions again, or Lord Beric, or anyone."

"Or no one," Brienne suggested.

"If m'lady cares to wager her skin on that I won't stop her ... but if I was you, I'd leave this here river, cut overland. If you stay off the main roads and shelter under the trees of a night, hidden as it were ... well, I still wouldn't want to go with you, but you might stand a mummer's chance."

The big wench was looking doubtful. "We would need horses."

"There are horses here," Jaime pointed out. "I heard one in the stable."

"Aye, there are," said the innkeep, who wasn't an innkeep. "Three of them, as it happens, but they're not for sale."

Jaime had to laugh. "Of course not. But you'll show them to us anyway."

Brienne scowled, but the man who wasn't an innkeep met her eyes without blinking, and after a moment, reluctantly, she said, "Show me," and they all rose from the table.

The stables had not been mucked out in a long while, from the smell of them. Hundreds of fat black flies swarmed amongst the straw, buzzing from stall to stall and crawling over the mounds of horse dung that lay everywhere, but there were only the three horses to be seen. They made an unlikely trio; a lumbering brown plow horse, an ancient white gelding blind in one eye, and a knight's palfrey, dapple grey and spirited. "They're not for sale at any price," their alleged owner announced.

"How did you come by these horses?" Brienne wanted to know.

"The dray was stabled here when the wife and me come on the inn," the man said, "along with the one you just ate. The gelding come wandering up one night, and the boy caught the palfrey running free, still saddled and bridled. Here, I'll show you."

The saddle he showed them was decorated with silver inlay. The saddlecloth had originally been checkered pink and black, but now it was mostly brown. Jaime did not recognize the original colors, but he recognized bloodstains easily enough. "Well, her owner won't be coming to claim her anytime soon." He examined the palfrey's legs, counted the gelding's teeth. "Give him a gold piece for the grey, if he'll include the saddle," he advised Brienne. "A silver for the plow horse. He ought to pay us for taking the white off his hands."

"Don't speak discourteously of your horse, ser." The wench opened the purse Lady Catelyn had given her and took out three golden coins. "I will pay you a dragon for each."

He blinked and reached for the gold, then hesitated and drew his hand back. "I don't know. I can't ride no golden dragon if I need to get away. Nor eat one if I'm hungry."

"You can have our skiff as well," she said. "Sail up the river or down, as you like."

"Let me have a taste o' that gold." The man took one of the coins from her palm and bit it. "Hm. Real enough, I'd say. Three dragons *and* the skiff?"

"He's robbing you blind, wench," Jaime said amiably.

"I'll want provisions too," Brienne told their host, ignoring Jaime. "Whatever you have that you can spare."

"There's more oatcakes." The man scooped the other two dragons from her palm and jingled them in his fist, smiling at the sound they made. "Aye, and smoked salt fish, but that will cost you silver. My beds will be costing as well. You'll be wanting to stay the night."

"No," Brienne said at once.

The man frowned at her. "Woman, you don't want to go riding at night through strange country on horses you don't know. You're like to blunder into some bog or break your horse's leg."

"The moon will be bright tonight," Brienne said. "We'll have no trouble finding our way."

Their host chewed on that. "If you don't have the silver, might be some coppers would buy you them beds, and a coverlet or two to keep you warm. It's not like I'm turning travelers away, if you get my meaning."

"That sounds more than fair," said Ser Cleos.

"The coverlets is fresh washed, too. My wife saw to that before she had to go off. Not a flea to be found neither, you have my word on that." He jingled the coins again, smiling.

Ser Cleos was plainly tempted. "A proper bed would do us all good, my lady," he said to Brienne. "We'd make better time on the morrow once refreshed." He looked to his cousin for support.

"No, coz, the wench is right. We have promises to keep, and long leagues before us. We ought ride on."

"But," said Cleos, "you said yourself –"

"Then." *When I thought the inn deserted.* "Now I have a full belly, and a moonlight ride will be just the thing." He smiled for the wench. "But unless you mean to throw me over the back of that plow horse like a sack of flour, someone had best do something about these irons. It's difficult to ride with your ankles chained together."

Brienne frowned at the chain. The man who wasn't an innkeep rubbed his jaw. "There's a smithy round back of the stable."

"Show me," Brienne said.

"Yes," said Jaime, "and the sooner the better. There's far too much horse shit about here for my taste. I would hate to step in it." He gave the wench a sharp look, wondering if she was bright enough to take his meaning.

He hoped she might strike the irons off his wrists as well, but Brienne was still suspicious. She split the ankle chain in the center with a half-dozen sharp blows from the smith's hammer delivered to the blunt end of a steel chisel. When he suggested that she break the wrist chain as well, she ignored him.

"Six miles downriver you'll see a burned village," their host said as he was helping them saddle the horses and load their packs. This time he directed his counsel at Brienne. "The road splits there. If you turn south, you'll come on Ser Warren's stone towerhouse. Ser Warren went off and died, so I couldn't say who holds it now, but it's a place best shunned. You'd do better to follow the track through the woods, south by east."

"We shall," she answered. "You have my thanks."

More to the point, he has your gold. Jaime kept the thought to himself. He was tired of being disregarded by this huge ugly cow of a woman.

She took the plow horse for herself and assigned the palfrey to Ser Cleos. As threatened, Jaime drew the one-eyed gelding, which put an end to any thoughts he might have had of giving his horse a kick and leaving the wench in his dust.

The man and the boy came out to watch them leave. The man wished them luck and told them to come back in better times, while the lad stood silent, his crossbow under his arm. "Take up the spear or maul," Jaime told him, "they'll serve you better." The boy stared at him distrustfully. *So much for friendly advice.* He shrugged, turned his horse, and never looked back.

Ser Cleos was all complaints as they rode out, still in mourning for his lost featherbed. They rode east, along the bank of the moonlit river. The Red Fork was very broad here, but shallow, its banks all mud and reeds. Jaime's mount plodded along placidly, though the poor old thing had a tendency to want to drift off to the side of his good eye. It felt good to be mounted once more. He had not been on a horse since Robb Stark's archers had killed his destrier under him in the Whispering Wood.

When they reached the burned village, a choice of equally unpromising roads confronted them; narrow tracks, deeply rutted by the carts of farmers hauling their grain to the river. One wandered off toward the southeast and soon vanished amidst the trees they could see in the distance, while the other, straighter and stonier, arrowed due south. Brienne considered them briefly, and then swung her horse onto the southern road. Jaime was pleasantly surprised; it was the same choice he would have made.

"But this is the road the innkeep warned us against," Ser Cleos objected.

"He was no innkeep." She hunched gracelessly in the saddle, but seemed to have a sure seat nonetheless. "The man took too great an interest in our choice of route, and those woods ... such places are notorious haunts of outlaws. He may have been urging us into a trap."

"Clever wench." Jaime smiled at his cousin. "Our host has friends down that road, I would venture. The ones whose mounts gave that stable such a memorable aroma."

"He may have been lying about the river as well, to put us on these horses," the wench said, "but I could not take the risk. There will be soldiers at the ruby ford and the crossroads."

Well, she may be ugly but she's not entirely stupid. Jaime gave her a grudging smile.

The ruddy light from the upper windows of the stone towerhouse gave them warning of its presence a long way off, and Brienne led them off into the fields. Only when the stronghold was well to the rear did they angle back and find the road again.

Half the night passed before the wench allowed that it might be safe to stop. By then all three of them were drooping in their saddles. They sheltered in a small grove of oak and ash beside a sluggish stream. The wench would allow no fire, so they shared a midnight supper of stale oatcakes and salt fish. The night was strangely peaceful. The half-moon sat overhead in a black felt sky, surrounded by stars. Off in the distance, some wolves were howling. One of their horses whickered nervously. There was no other sound. *The war has not touched this place*, Jaime thought. He was glad to be here, glad to be alive, glad to be on his way back to Cersei.

"I'll take the first watch," Brienne told Ser Cleos, and Frey was soon snoring softly.

Jaime sat against the bole of an oak and wondered what Cersei and Tyrion were doing just now. "Do you have any siblings, my lady?" he asked.

Brienne squinted at him suspiciously. "No. I was my father's only s – child."

Jaime chuckled. "*Son*, you meant to say. Does he think of you as a son? You make a queer sort of daughter, to be sure."

Wordless, she turned away from him, her knuckles tight on her sword hilt. *What a wretched creature this one is.* She reminded him of Tyrion in some queer way, though at first blush two people could scarcely be any more dissimilar. Perhaps it was that thought of his brother that made him say, "I did not intend to give offense, Brienne. Forgive me."

"Your crimes are past forgiving, Kingslayer."

"That name again." Jaime twisted idly at his chains. "Why do I enrage you so? I've never done you harm that I know of."

"You've harmed others. Those you were sworn to protect. The weak, the innocent . . ."

". . . the king?" It always came back to Aerys. "Don't presume to judge what you do not understand, wench."

"My name is – "

"– Brienne, yes. Has anyone ever told you that you're as tedious as you are ugly?"

"You will not provoke me to anger, Kingslayer."

"Oh, I might, if I cared enough to try."

"Why did you take the oath?" she demanded. "Why don the white cloak if you meant to betray all it stood for?"

Why? What could he say that she might possibly understand? "I was a boy. Fifteen. It was a great honor for one so young."

"That is no answer," she said scornfully.

You would not like the truth. He had joined the Kingsguard for love, of course.

Their father had summoned Cersei to court when she was twelve, hoping to make her a royal marriage. He refused every offer for her hand, preferring to keep her with him in the Tower of the Hand while she grew older and more womanly and ever more beautiful. No doubt he was waiting for Prince Viserys to mature, or perhaps for Rhaegar's wife to die in childbed. Elia of Dorne was never the healthiest of women.

Jaime, meantime, had spent four years as squire to Ser Sumner Crakehall and earned his spurs against the Kingswood Brotherhood. But when he made a brief call at King's Landing on his way back to Casterly Rock, chiefly to see his sister, Cersei took him aside and whispered that Lord Tywin meant to marry him to Lysa Tully, had gone so far as to invite Lord Hoster to the city to discuss dower. But if Jaime took the white, he could be near her always. Old Ser Harlan Grandison had died in his sleep, as was only appropriate for one whose sigil was a sleeping lion. Aerys would want a young man to take his place, so why not a roaring lion in place of a sleepy one?

"Father will never consent," Jaime objected.

"The king won't ask him. And once it's done, Father can't object, not openly. Aerys had Ser Ilyn Payne's tongue torn out just for boasting that it was the Hand who truly ruled the Seven Kingdoms. The captain of the Hand's guard, and yet Father dared not try and stop it! He won't stop this, either."

"But," Jaime said, "there's Casterly Rock . . ."

"Is it a rock you want? Or me?"

He remembered that night as if it were yesterday. They spent it in an old inn on Eel Alley, well away from watchful eyes. Cersei had come to him dressed as a simple serving wench, which somehow excited him all the more. Jaime had never seen her more passionate. Every time he went to sleep, she woke him again. By morning Casterly Rock seemed a small price to pay to be near her always. He gave his consent, and Cersei promised to do the rest.

A moon's turn later, a royal raven arrived at Casterly Rock to inform him that he had been chosen for the Kingsguard. He was commanded to present himself to the king during the great tourney at Harrenhal to say his vows and don his cloak.

Jaime's investiture freed him from Lysa Tully. Elsewise, nothing went as planned. His father had never been more furious. He could not object openly – Cersei had judged that correctly – but he resigned the Handship on some thin pretext and returned to Casterly Rock, taking his daughter with him. Instead of being together, Cersei and Jaime just changed places, and he found himself alone at court, guarding a mad king while four lesser men took their turns dancing on knives in his father's ill-fitting shoes. So swiftly did the Hands rise and fall that Jaime remembered their heraldry better than their faces. The horn-of-plenty Hand and the dancing griffins Hand had both been exiled, the mace-and-dagger Hand dipped in wildfire and burned alive. Lord Rossart had been the last. His sigil had been a burning torch; an unfortunate choice, given the fate of his predecessor, but the alchemist had been elevated largely because he shared the king's passion for fire. *I ought to have drowned Rossart instead of gutting him.*

Brienne was still awaiting his answer. Jaime said, "You are not old enough to have known Aerys Targaryen . . ."

She would not hear it. "Aerys was mad and cruel, no one has ever denied that. He was still king, crowned and anointed. And you had sworn to protect him."

"I know what I swore."

"And what you did." She loomed above him, six feet of freckled, frowning, horse-toothed disapproval.

"Yes, and what *you* did as well. We're both kingslayers here, if what I've heard is true."

"I never harmed Renly. I'll kill the man who says I did."

"Best start with Cleos, then. And you'll have a deal of killing to do after that, the way he tells the tale."

"*Lies.* Lady Catelyn was there when His Grace was murdered, she saw. There was a shadow. The candles guttered and the air grew cold, and there was blood –"

"Oh, very good." Jaime laughed. "Your wits are quicker than mine, I confess it. When they found me standing over my dead king, I never thought to say, 'No, no, it wasn't me, it was a shadow, a terrible cold shadow.'" He laughed again. "Tell me true, one kingslayer to another – did the Starks pay you to slit his throat, or was it Stannis? Had Renly spurned you, was that the way of it? Or perhaps your moon's blood was on you. Never give a wench a sword when she's bleeding."

For a moment Jaime thought Brienne might strike him. *A step closer, and I'll snatch that dagger from her sheath and bury it up her womb.* He gathered a leg under him, ready to spring, but the wench did not move. "It is a rare and precious gift to be a knight," she said, "and even more so a knight of the Kingsguard. It is a gift given to few, a gift you scorned and soiled."

A gift you want desperately, wench, and can never have. "I earned my knighthood. Nothing was given to me. I won a tourney mêlée at thirteen, when I was yet a squire. At fifteen, I rode with Ser Arthur Dayne against the Kingswood Brotherhood, and he knighted me on the battlefield. It was that white cloak that soiled me, not the other way around. So spare me your envy. It was the gods who neglected to give you a cock, not me."

The look Brienne gave him then was full of loathing. *She would gladly hack me to pieces, but for her precious vow*, he reflected. *Good. I've had enough of feeble pieties and maidens' judgments.* The wench stalked off without saying a word. Jaime curled up beneath his cloak, hoping to dream of Cersei.

But when he closed his eyes, it was Aerys Targaryen he saw, pacing alone in his throne room, picking at his scabbed and bleeding hands. The fool was always cutting himself on the blades and barbs of the Iron Throne. Jaime had slipped in through the king's door, clad in his golden armor, sword in hand. *The golden armor, not the white, but no one ever remembers that. Would that I had taken off that damned cloak as well.*

When Aerys saw the blood on his blade, he demanded to know if it was Lord Tywin's. "I want him dead, the traitor. I want his head, you'll bring me his head, or you'll burn with all the rest. All the traitors. Rossart says they are *inside the walls!* He's gone to make them a warm welcome. Whose blood? *Whose?*"

"Rossart's," answered Jaime.

Those purple eyes grew huge then, and the royal mouth drooped open in shock. He lost control of his bowels, turned, and ran for the Iron Throne. Beneath the empty eyes of the skulls on the walls, Jaime hauled the last dragonking bodily off the steps, squealing like a pig and smelling like a privy. A single slash across his throat was all it took to end it. *So easy*, he remembered thinking. *A king should die harder than this.* Rossart at least had tried to make a fight of it, though if truth be told he fought like an alchemist. *Queer that they never ask who killed Rossart ... but of course, he was no one, lowborn, Hand for a fortnight, just another mad fancy of the Mad King.*

Ser Elys Westerling and Lord Crakehall and others of his father's knights burst into the hall in time to see the last of it, so there was no way for Jaime to vanish and let some braggart steal the praise or blame. It would be blame, he knew at once when he saw the way they looked at him ... though perhaps that was fear. Lannister or no, he was one of Aerys's seven.

"The castle is ours, ser, and the city," Roland Crakehall told him, which was half true. Targaryen loyalists were still dying on the serpentine steps and in the armory, Gregor Clegane and Amory Lorch were scaling the walls of Maegor's Holdfast, and Ned Stark was leading his northmen through the King's Gate even then, but Crakehall could not have known that. He had not seemed surprised to find Aerys slain; Jaime had been Lord Tywin's son long before he had been named to the Kingsguard.

"Tell them the Mad King is dead," he commanded. "Spare all those who yield and hold them captive."

"Shall I proclaim a new king as well?" Crakehall asked, and Jaime read the question plain: Shall it be your father, or Robert Baratheon, or do you mean to try to make a new dragonking? He thought for a moment of the boy Viserys, fled to Dragonstone, and of Rhaegar's infant son Aegon, still in Maegor's with his mother. *A new Targaryen king, and my father as Hand. How the wolves will howl, and the storm lord choke with rage.* For a moment he was tempted, until he glanced down again at the body on the floor, in its spreading pool of blood. *His blood is in both of them,* he thought. "Proclaim who you bloody well like," he told Crakehall. Then he climbed the Iron Throne and seated himself with his sword across his knees, to see who would come to claim the kingdom. As it happened, it had been Eddard Stark.

You had no right to judge me either, Stark.

In his dreams the dead came burning, gowned in swirling green flames. Jaime danced around them with a golden sword, but for every one he struck down two more arose to take his place.

Brienne woke him with a boot in the ribs. The world was still black, and it had begun to rain. They broke their fast on oatcakes, salt fish, and some blackberries that Ser Cleos had found, and were back in the saddle before the sun came up.

TYRION

The eunuch was humming tunelessly to himself as he came through
the door, dressed in flowing robes of peach-colored silk and smelling of lemons. When he saw Tyrion seated by the hearth, he
stopped and grew very still. "My lord Tyrion," came out in a squeak,
punctuated by a nervous giggle.

"So you *do* remember me? I had begun to wonder."

"It is so *very* good to see you looking so strong and well." Varys smiled
his slimiest smile. "Though I confess, I had not thought to find you in
mine own humble chambers."

"They are humble. Excessively so, in truth." Tyrion had waited until
Varys was summoned by his father before slipping in to pay him a visit.
The eunuch's apartments were sparse and small, three snug windowless
chambers under the north wall. "I'd hoped to discover bushel baskets of
juicy secrets to while away the waiting, but there's not a paper to be
found." He'd searched for hidden passages too, knowing the Spider must
have ways of coming and going unseen, but those had proved equally
elusive. "There was *water* in your flagon, gods have mercy," he went on,
"your sleeping cell is no wider than a coffin, and that bed . . . is it actually
made of stone, or does it only feel that way?"

Varys closed the door and barred it. "I am plagued with backaches, my
lord, and prefer to sleep upon a hard surface."

"I would have taken you for a featherbed man."

"I am full of surprises. Are you cross with me for abandoning you after
the battle?"

"It made me think of you as one of my family."

"It was not for want of love, my good lord. I have such a delicate disposition, and your scar is so dreadful to look upon . . ." He gave an exaggerated shudder. "Your poor nose . . ."

Tyrion rubbed irritably at the scab. "Perhaps I should have a new one made of gold. What sort of nose would you suggest, Varys? One like yours, to smell out secrets? Or should I tell the goldsmith that I want my father's nose?" He smiled. "My noble father labors so diligently that I scarce see him anymore. Tell me, is it true that he's restoring Grand Maester Pycelle to the small council?"

"It is, my lord."

"Do I have my sweet sister to thank for that?" Pycelle had been his sister's creature; Tyrion had stripped the man of office, beard, and dignity, and flung him down into a black cell.

"Not at all, my lord. Thank the archmaesters of Oldtown, those who wished to insist on Pycelle's restoration on the grounds that only the Conclave may make or unmake a Grand Maester."

Bloody fools, thought Tyrion. "I seem to recall that Maegor the Cruel's headsman unmade three with his axe."

"Quite true," Varys said. "And the second Aegon fed Grand Maester Gerardys to his dragon."

"Alas, I am quite dragonless. I suppose I could have dipped Pycelle in wildfire and set him ablaze. Would the Citadel have preferred that?"

"Well, it would have been more in keeping with tradition." The eunuch tittered. "Thankfully, wiser heads prevailed, and the Conclave accepted the fact of Pycelle's dismissal and set about choosing his successor. After giving due consideration to Maester Turquin the cordwainer's son and Maester Erreck the hedge knight's bastard, and thereby demonstrating to their own satisfaction that ability counts for more than birth in their order, the Conclave was on the verge of sending us Maester Gormon, a Tyrell of Highgarden. When I told your lord father, he acted at once."

The Conclave met in Oldtown behind closed doors, Tyrion knew; its deliberations were supposedly a secret. *So Varys has little birds in the Citadel too.* "I see. So my father decided to nip the rose before it bloomed." He had to chuckle. "Pycelle is a toad. But better a Lannister toad than a Tyrell toad, no?"

"Grand Maester Pycelle has always been a good friend to your House," Varys said sweetly. "Perhaps it will console you to learn that Ser Boros Blount is also being restored."

Cersei had stripped Ser Boros of his white cloak for failing to die in the defense of Prince Tommen when Bronn had seized the boy on the Rosby road. The man was no friend of Tyrion's, but after that he likely hated Cersei almost as much. *I suppose that's something.* "Blount is a blustering coward," he said amiably.

"Is he? Oh dear. Still, the knights of the Kingsguard *do* serve for life, traditionally. Perhaps Ser Boros will prove braver in future. He will no doubt remain very loyal."

"To my father," said Tyrion pointedly.

"While we are on the subject of the Kingsguard . . . I wonder, could this delightfully unexpected visit of yours happen to concern Ser Boros's fallen brother, the gallant Ser Mandon Moore?" The eunuch stroked a powdered cheek. "Your man Bronn seems most interested in him of late."

Bronn had turned up all he could on Ser Mandon, but no doubt Varys knew a deal more . . . should he choose to share it. "The man seems to have been quite friendless," Tyrion said carefully.

"Sadly," said Varys, "oh, sadly. You might find some kin if you turned over enough stones back in the Vale, but here . . . Lord Arryn brought him to King's Landing and Robert gave him his white cloak, but neither loved him much, I fear. Nor was he the sort the smallfolk cheer in tourneys, despite his undoubted prowess. Why, even his brothers of the Kingsguard never warmed to him. Ser Barristan was once heard to say that the man had no friend but his sword and no life but duty . . . but you know, I do not think Selmy meant it altogether as praise. Which is queer when you consider it, is it not? Those are the very qualities we seek in our Kingsguard, it could be said – men who live not for themselves, but for their king. By those lights, our brave Ser Mandon was the perfect white knight. And he died as a knight of the Kingsguard ought, with sword in hand, defending one of the king's own blood." The eunuch gave him a slimy smile and watched him sharply.

Trying to murder one of the king's own blood, you mean. Tyrion wondered if Varys knew rather more than he was saying. Nothing he'd just heard was new to him; Bronn had brought back much the same reports. He needed a link to Cersei, some sign that Ser Mandon had been his sister's catspaw. *What we want is not always what we get*, he reflected bitterly, which reminded him . . .

"It is not Ser Mandon who brings me here."

"To be sure." The eunuch crossed the room to his flagon of water. "May I serve you, my lord?" he asked as he filled a cup.

"Yes. But not with water." He folded his hands together. "I want you to bring me Shae."

Varys took a drink. "Is that wise, my lord? The dear sweet child. It would be such a shame if your father hanged her."

It did not surprise him that Varys knew. "No, it's not wise, it's bloody madness. I want to see her one last time, before I send her away. I cannot abide having her so close."

"I understand."

How could you! Tyrion had seen her only yesterday, climbing the serpentine steps with a pail of water. He had watched as a young knight had offered to carry the heavy pail. The way she had touched his arm and smiled for him had tied Tyrion's guts into knots. They passed within inches of each other, him descending and her climbing, so close that he could smell the clean fresh scent of her hair. "M'lord," she'd said to him, with a little curtsy, and he wanted to reach out and grab her and kiss her right there, but all he could do was nod stiffly and waddle on past. "I have seen her several times," he told Varys, "but I dare not speak to her. I suspect that all my movements are being watched."

"You are wise to suspect so, my good lord."

"Who?" He cocked his head.

"The Kettleblacks report frequently to your sweet sister."

"When I think of how much coin I paid those wretched . . . do you think there's any chance that more gold might win them away from Cersei?"

"There is always a chance, but I should not care to wager on the likelihood. They are knights now, all three, and your sister has promised them further advancement." A wicked little titter burst from the eunuch's lips. "And the eldest, Ser Osmund of the Kingsguard, dreams of certain other . . . favors . . . as well. You can match the queen coin for coin, I have no doubt, but she has a second purse that is quite inexhaustible."

Seven hells, thought Tyrion. "Are you suggesting that Cersei's fucking Osmund Kettleblack?"

"Oh, dear me, no, that would be dreadfully dangerous, don't you think? No, the queen only *hints* . . . perhaps on the morrow, or when the wedding's done . . . and then a smile, a whisper, a ribald jest . . . a breast brushing lightly against his sleeve as they pass . . . and yet it seems to serve. But what would a eunuch know of such things?" The tip of his tongue ran across his lower lip like a shy pink animal.

If I could somehow push them beyond sly fondling, arrange for Father to catch them abed together . . . Tyrion fingered the scab on his nose. He did not see how it could be done, but perhaps some plan would come to him later. "Are the Kettleblacks the only ones?"

"Would that were true, my lord. I fear there are many eyes upon you. You are . . . how shall we say? *Conspicuous!* And not well loved, it grieves me to tell you. Janos Slynt's sons would gladly inform on you to avenge their father, and our sweet Lord Petyr has friends in half the brothels of King's Landing. Should you be so unwise as to visit any of them, he will know at once, and your lord father soon thereafter."

It's even worse than I feared. "And my father? Who does he have spying on me?"

This time the eunuch laughed aloud. "Why, me, my lord."

Tyrion laughed as well. He was not so great a fool as to trust Varys any further than he had to – but the eunuch already knew enough about Shae to get her well and thoroughly hanged. "You will bring Shae to me through the walls, hidden from all these eyes. As you have done before."

Varys wrung his hands. "Oh, my lord, nothing would please me more, but . . . King Maegor wanted no rats in his own walls, if you take my meaning. He did require a means of secret egress, should he ever be trapped by his enemies, but that door does not connect with any other passages. I can steal your Shae away from Lady Lollys for a time, to be sure, but I have no way to bring her to your bedchamber without us being seen."

"Then bring her somewhere else."

"But where? There is no safe place."

"There is." Tyrion grinned. "Here. It's time to put that rock-hard bed of yours to better use, I think."

The eunuch's mouth opened. Then he giggled. "Lollys tires easily these days. She is great with child. I imagine she will be safely asleep by moonrise."

Tyrion hopped down from the chair. "Moonrise, then. See that you lay in some wine. And two clean cups."

Varys bowed. "It shall be as my lord commands."

The rest of the day seemed to creep by as slow as a worm in molasses. Tyrion climbed to the castle library and tried to distract himself with Beldecar's *History of the Rhoynish Wars*, but he could hardly see the elephants for imagining Shae's smile. Come the afternoon, he put the book aside and called for a bath. He scrubbed himself until the water grew cool, and then had Pod even out his whiskers. His beard was a trial to him; a tangle of yellow, white, and black hairs, patchy and coarse, it was seldom less than unsightly, but it did serve to conceal some of his face, and that was all to the good.

When he was as clean and pink and trimmed as he was like to get, Tyrion looked over his wardrobe, and chose a pair of tight satin breeches in Lannister crimson and his best doublet, the heavy black velvet with the lion's head studs. He would have donned his chain of golden hands as well, if his father hadn't stolen it while he lay dying. It was not until he was dressed that he realized the depths of his folly. *Seven hells, dwarf, did you lose all your sense along with your nose? Anyone who sees you is going to wonder why you've put on your court clothes to visit the eunuch.* Cursing, Tyrion stripped and dressed again, in simpler garb; black woolen breeches, an old white tunic, and a faded brown leather jerkin. *It doesn't matter*, he told himself as he waited for moonrise. *Whatever you wear, you're still a dwarf. You'll never be as tall as that knight on the steps, him with his long straight legs and hard stomach and wide manly shoulders.*

The moon was peeping over the castle wall when he told Podrick Payne that he was going to pay a call on Varys. "Will you be long, my lord?" the boy asked.

"Oh, I hope so."

With the Red Keep so crowded, Tyrion could not hope to go unnoticed. Ser Balon Swann stood guard on the door, and Ser Loras Tyrell on the drawbridge. He stopped to exchange pleasantries with both of them. It was strange to see the Knight of Flowers all in white when before he had always been as colorful as a rainbow. "How old are you, Ser Loras?" Tyrion asked him.

"Seventeen, my lord."

Seventeen, and beautiful, and already a legend. Half the girls in the Seven Kingdoms want to bed him, and all the boys want to be him. "If you will pardon my asking, ser – why would anyone choose to join the Kingsguard at seventeen?"

"Prince Aemon the Dragonknight took his vows at seventeen," Ser Loras said, "and your brother Jaime was younger still."

"I know their reasons. What are yours? The honor of serving beside such paragons as Meryn Trant and Boros Blount?" He gave the boy a mocking grin. "To guard the king's life, you surrender your own. You give up your lands and titles, give up hope of marriage, children . . ."

"House Tyrell continues through my brothers," Ser Loras said. "It is not necessary for a third son to wed, or breed."

"Not necessary, but some find it pleasant. What of love?"

"When the sun has set, no candle can replace it."

"Is that from a song?" Tyrion cocked his head, smiling. "Yes, you are seventeen, I see that now."

Ser Loras tensed. "Do you mock me?"

A prickly lad. "No. If I've given offense, forgive me. I had my own love once, and we had a song as well." *I loved a maid as fair as summer, with sunlight in her hair.* He bid Ser Loras a good evening and went on his way.

Near the kennels a group of men-at-arms were fighting a pair of dogs. Tyrion stopped long enough to see the smaller dog tear half the face off the larger one, and earned a few coarse laughs by observing that the loser now resembled Sandor Clegane. Then, hoping he had disarmed their suspicions, he proceeded to the north wall and down the short flight of steps to the eunuch's meager abode. The door opened as he was lifting his hand to knock.

"Varys?" Tyrion slipped inside. "Are you there?" A single candle lit the gloom, spicing the air with the scent of jasmine.

"My lord." A woman sidled into the light; plump, soft, matronly, with a round pink moon of a face and heavy dark curls. Tyrion recoiled. "Is something amiss?" she asked.

Varys, he realized with annoyance. "For one horrid moment I thought you'd brought me Lollys instead of Shae. Where is she?"

"Here, m'lord." She put her hands over his eyes from behind. "Can you guess what I'm wearing?"

"Nothing?"

"Oh, you're so *smart*," she pouted, snatching her hands away. "How did you know?"

"You're very beautiful in nothing."

"Am I?" she said. "Am I truly?"

"Oh yes."

"Then shouldn't you be fucking me instead of talking?"

"We need to rid ourselves of Lady Varys first. I am not the sort of dwarf who likes an audience."

"He's gone," Shae said.

Tyrion turned to look. It was true. The eunuch had vanished, skirts and all. *The hidden doors are here somewhere, they have to be.* That was as much as he had time to think, before Shae turned his head to kiss him. Her mouth was wet and hungry, and she did not even seem to see his scar, or the raw scab where his nose had been. Her skin was warm silk beneath his fingers. When his thumb brushed against her left nipple, it hardened at once. "Hurry," she urged, between kisses, as his fingers went to his laces, "oh, hurry, hurry, I want you in me, in me, in me." He did not even have time to undress properly. Shae pulled his cock out of his breeches, then pushed him down onto the floor and climbed atop him. She screamed as he pushed past her lips, and rode him wildly, moaning, "My giant, my giant, my giant," every time she slammed down on him. Tyrion was so eager that he exploded on the fifth stroke, but Shae did not seem to mind. She smiled wickedly when she felt him spurting, and leaned forward to kiss the sweat from his brow. "My giant of Lannister," she murmured. "Stay inside me, please. I like to feel you there."

So Tyrion did not move, except to put his arms around her. *It feels so good to hold her, and to be held*, he thought. *How can something this sweet be a crime worth hanging her for?* "Shae," he said, "sweetling, this must be our last time together. The danger is too great. If my lord father should find you . . ."

"I like your scar." She traced it with her finger. "It makes you look very fierce and strong."

He laughed. "Very ugly, you mean."

"M'lord will never be ugly in my eyes." She kissed the scab that covered the ragged stub of his nose.

"It's not my face that need concern you, it's my father –"

"He does not frighten me. Will m'lord give me back my jewels and silks now? I asked Varys if I could have them when you were hurt in the battle, but he wouldn't give them to me. What would have become of them if you'd died?"

"I didn't die. Here I am."

"I know." Shae wriggled atop him, smiling. "Just where you belong." Her mouth turned pouty. "But how long must I go on with Lollys, now that you're well?"

"Have you been listening?" Tyrion said. "You can stay with Lollys if you like, but it would be best if you left the city."

"I don't want to leave. You promised you'd move me into a manse again after the battle." Her cunt gave him a little squeeze, and he started to stiffen again inside her. "A Lannister always pays his debts, you said."

"Shae, gods be damned, stop that. *Listen* to me. You have to go away. The city's full of Tyrells just now, and I am closely watched. You don't understand the dangers."

"Can I come to the king's wedding feast? Lollys won't go. I told her no one's like to rape her in the king's own throne room, but she's so *stupid*." When Shae rolled off, his cock slid out of her with a soft wet sound. "Symon says there's to be a singers' tourney, and tumblers, even a fools' joust."

Tyrion had almost forgotten about Shae's thrice-damned singer. "How is it you spoke to Symon?"

"I told Lady Tanda about him, and she hired him to play for Lollys. The music calms her when the baby starts to kick. Symon says there's to be a dancing bear at the feast, and wines from the Arbor. I've never seen a bear dance."

"They do it worse than I do." It was the singer who concerned him, not the bear. One careless word in the wrong ear, and Shae would hang.

"Symon says there's to be seventy-seven courses and a hundred doves baked into a great pie," Shae gushed. "When the crust's opened, they'll all burst out and fly."

"After which they will roost in the rafters and rain down birdshit on the guests." Tyrion had suffered such wedding pies before. The doves liked to shit on *him* especially, or so he had always suspected.

"Couldn't I dress in my silks and velvets and go as a lady instead of a maidservant? No one would know I wasn't."

Everyone would know you weren't, thought Tyrion. "Lady Tanda might wonder where Lollys's bedmaid found so many jewels."

"There's to be a thousand guests, Symon says. She'd never even see me. I'd find a place in some dark corner below the salt, but whenever you got up to go to the privy I could slip out and meet you." She cupped his cock and stroked it gently. "I won't wear any smallclothes under my gown, so m'lord won't even need to unlace me." Her fingers teased him, up and down. "Or if he liked, I could do this for him." She took him in her mouth.

Tyrion was soon ready again. This time he lasted much longer. When he finished Shae crawled back up him and curled up naked under his arm. "You'll let me come, won't you?"

"Shae," he groaned, "it *is not safe.*"

For a time she said nothing at all. Tyrion tried to speak of other things, but he met a wall of sullen courtesy as icy and unyielding as the Wall he'd once walked in the north. *Gods be good*, he thought wearily as he watched the candle burn down and begin to gutter, *how could I let this happen again, after Tysha? Am I as great a fool as my father thinks?* Gladly would he have given her the promise she wanted, and gladly walked her back to his own bedchamber on his arm to let her dress in the silks and velvets she loved so much. Had the choice been his, she could have sat beside him at Joffrey's wedding feast, and danced with all the bears she liked. But he could not see her hang.

When the candle burned out, Tyrion disentangled himself and lit another. Then he made a round of the walls, tapping on each in turn, searching for the hidden door. Shae sat with her legs drawn up and her arms wrapped around them, watching him. Finally she said, "They're under the bed. The secret steps."

He looked at her, incredulous. "The bed? The bed is solid stone. It weighs half a ton."

"There's a place where Varys pushes, and it floats right up. I asked him how, and he said it was magic."

"Yes." Tyrion had to grin. "A counterweight spell."

Shae stood. "I should go back. Sometimes the baby kicks and Lollys wakes and calls for me."

"Varys should return shortly. He's probably listening to every word we say." Tyrion set the candle down. There was a wet spot on the front of his breeches, but in the darkness it ought to go unnoticed. He told Shae to dress and wait for the eunuch.

"I will," she promised. "You are my lion, aren't you? My giant of Lannister?"

"I am," he said. "And you're –"

"– your whore." She laid a finger to his lips. "I know. I'd be your lady, but I never can. Else you'd take me to the feast. It doesn't matter. I like being a whore for you, Tyrion. Just keep me, my lion, and keep me safe."

"I shall," he promised. *Fool, fool*, the voice inside him screamed. *Why did you say that? You came here to send her away!* Instead he kissed her once more.

The walk back seemed long and lonely. Podrick Payne was asleep in his trundle bed at the foot of Tyrion's, but he woke the boy. "Bronn," he said.

"Ser Bronn?" Pod rubbed the sleep from his eyes. "Oh. Should I get him? My lord?"

"Why no, I woke you up so we could have a little chat about the way he dresses," said Tyrion, but his sarcasm was wasted. Pod only gaped at him in confusion until he threw up his hands and said, "Yes, get him. Bring him. Now."

The lad dressed hurriedly and all but ran from the room. *Am I really so terrifying?* Tyrion wondered, as he changed into a bedrobe and poured himself some wine.

He was on his third cup and half the night was gone before Pod finally returned, with the sellsword knight in tow. "I hope the boy had a damn good reason dragging me out of Chataya's," Bronn said as he seated himself.

"*Chataya's?*" Tyrion said, annoyed.

"It's good to be a knight. No more looking for the cheaper brothels down the street." Bronn grinned. "Now it's Alayaya and Marei in the same featherbed, with Ser Bronn in the middle."

Tyrion had to bite back his annoyance. Bronn had as much right to bed Alayaya as any other man, but still . . . *I never touched her, much as I wanted to, but Bronn could not know that. He should have kept his cock out of her.* He dare not visit Chataya's himself. If he did, Cersei would see that his father heard of it, and 'Yaya would suffer more than a whipping. He'd sent the girl a necklace of silver and jade and a pair of matching bracelets by way of apology, but other than that . . .

This is fruitless. "There is a singer who calls himself Symon Silver Tongue," Tyrion said wearily, pushing his guilt aside. "He plays for Lady Tanda's daughter sometimes."

"What of him?"

Kill him, he might have said, but the man had done nothing but sing a few songs. *And fill Shae's sweet head with visions of doves and dancing bears.* "Find him," he said instead. "Find him before someone else does."

ARYA

She was grubbing for vegetables in a dead man's garden when she heard the singing.

Arya stiffened, still as stone, listening, the three stringy carrots in her hand suddenly forgotten. She thought of the Bloody Mummers and Roose Bolton's men, and a shiver of fear went down her back. *It's not fair, not when we finally found the Trident, not when we thought we were almost safe.*

Only why would the Mummers be singing?

The song came drifting up the river from somewhere beyond the little rise to the east. *"Off to Gulltown to see the fair maid, heigh-ho, heigh-ho . . ."*

Arya rose, carrots dangling from her hand. It sounded like the singer was coming up the river road. Over among the cabbages, Hot Pie had heard it too, to judge by the look on his face. Gendry had gone to sleep in the shade of the burned cottage, and was past hearing anything.

"I'll steal a sweet kiss with the point of my blade, heigh-ho, heigh-ho." She thought she heard a woodharp too, beneath the soft rush of the river.

"Do you hear?" Hot Pie asked in a hoarse whisper, as he hugged an armful of cabbages. "Someone's coming."

"Go wake Gendry," Arya told him. "Just shake him by the shoulder, don't make a lot of noise." Gendry was easy to wake, unlike Hot Pie, who needed to be kicked and shouted at.

"I'll make her my love and we'll rest in the shade, heigh-ho, heigh-ho." The song swelled louder with every word.

Hot Pie opened his arms. The cabbages fell to the ground with soft thumps. "We have to *hide*."

Where? The burned cottage and its overgrown garden stood hard beside the banks of the Trident. There were a few willows growing along the river's edge and reed beds in the muddy shallows beyond, but most of the ground hereabouts was painfully open. *I knew we should never have left the woods*, she thought. They'd been so hungry, though, and the garden had been too much a temptation. The bread and cheese they had stolen from Harrenhal had given out six days ago, back in the thick of the woods. "Take Gendry and the horses behind the cottage," she decided. There was part of one wall still standing, big enough, maybe, to conceal two boys and three horses. *If the horses don't whinny, and that singer doesn't come poking around the garden.*

"What about you?"

"I'll hide by the tree. He's probably alone. If he bothers me, I'll kill him. *Go!*"

Hot Pie went, and Arya dropped her carrots and drew the stolen sword from over her shoulder. She had strapped the sheath across her back; the longsword was made for a man grown, and it bumped against the ground when she wore it on her hip. *It's too heavy besides,* she thought, missing Needle the way she did every time she took this clumsy thing in her hand. But it was a sword and she could kill with it, that was enough.

Lightfoot, she moved to the big old willow that grew beside the bend in the road and went to one knee in the grass and mud, within the veil of trailing branches. *You old gods,* she prayed as the singer's voice grew louder, *you tree gods, hide me, and make him go past.* Then a horse whickered, and the song broke off suddenly. *He's heard,* she knew, *but maybe he's alone, or if he's not, maybe they'll be as scared of us as we are of them.*

"Did you hear that?" a man's voice said. "There's something behind that wall, I would say."

"Aye," replied a second voice, deeper. "What do you think it might be, Archer?"

Two, then. Arya bit her lip. She could not see them from where she knelt, on account of the willow. But she could hear.

"A bear." A third voice, or the first one again?

"A lot of meat on a bear," the deep voice said. "A lot of fat as well, in fall. Good to eat, if it's cooked up right."

"Could be a wolf. Maybe a lion."

"With four feet, you think? Or two?"

"Makes no matter. Does it?"

"Not so I know. Archer, what do you mean to do with all them arrows?"

"Drop a few shafts over the wall. Whatever's hiding back there will come out quick enough, watch and see."

"What if it's some honest man back there, though? Or some poor woman with a little babe at her breast?"

"An honest man would come out and show us his face. Only an outlaw would skulk and hide."

"Aye, that's so. Go on and loose your shafts, then."

Arya sprang to her feet. *"Don't!"* She showed them her sword. There were three, she saw. *Only three.* Syrio could fight more than three, and she had Hot Pie and Gendry to stand with her, maybe. *But they're boys, and these are men.*

They were men afoot, travel-stained and mud-specked. She knew the singer by the woodharp he cradled against his jerkin, as a mother might cradle a babe. A small man, fifty from the look of him, he had a big mouth, a sharp nose, and thinning brown hair. His faded greens were mended here and there with old leather patches, and he wore a brace of throwing knives on his hip and a woodman's axe slung across his back.

The man beside him stood a good foot taller, and had the look of a soldier. A longsword and dirk hung from his studded leather belt, rows of overlapping steel rings were sewn onto his shirt, and his head was covered by a black iron halfhelm shaped like a cone. He had bad teeth and a bushy brown beard, but it was his hooded yellow cloak that drew the eye. Thick and heavy, stained here with grass and there with blood, frayed along the bottom and patched with deerskin on the right shoulder, the greatcloak gave the big man the look of some huge yellow bird.

The last of the three was a youth as skinny as his longbow, if not quite as tall. Red-haired and freckled, he wore a studded brigantine, high boots, fingerless leather gloves, and a quiver on his back. His arrows were fletched with grey goose feathers, and six of them stood in the ground before him, like a little fence.

The three men looked at her, standing there in the road with her blade in hand. Then the singer idly plucked a string. "Boy," he said, "put up that sword now, unless you're wanting to be hurt. It's too big for you, lad, and besides, Anguy here could put three shafts through you before you could hope to reach us."

"He could not," Arya said, "and I'm a *girl*."

"So you are." The singer bowed. "My pardons."

"You go on down the road. Just walk right past here, and you keep on singing, so we'll know where you are. Go away and leave us be and I won't kill you."

The freckle-faced archer laughed. "Lem, she won't kill us, did you hear?"

"I heard," said Lem, the big soldier with the deep voice.

"Child," said the singer, "put up that sword, and we'll take you to a safe place and get some food in that belly. There are wolves in these parts, and lions, and worse things. No place for a little girl to be wandering alone."

"She's not alone." Gendry rode out from behind the cottage wall, and behind him Hot Pie, leading her horse. In his chainmail shirt with a sword in his hand, Gendry looked almost a man grown, and dangerous. Hot Pie looked like Hot Pie. "Do like she says, and leave us be," warned Gendry.

"Two and three," the singer counted, "and is that all of you? And horses too, lovely horses. Where did you steal them?"

"They're ours." Arya watched them carefully. The singer kept distracting her with his talk, but it was the archer who was the danger. *If he should pull an arrow from the ground . . .*

"Will you give us your names like honest men?" the singer asked the boys.

"I'm Hot Pie," Hot Pie said at once.

"Aye, and good for you." The man smiled. "It's not every day I meet a lad with such a tasty name. And what would your friends be called, Mutton Chop and Squab?"

Gendry scowled down from his saddle. "Why should I tell you my name? I haven't heard yours."

"Well, as to that, I'm Tom of Sevenstreams, but Tom Sevenstrings is what they call me, or Tom o' Sevens. This great lout with the brown teeth is Lem, short for Lemoncloak. It's yellow, you see, and Lem's a sour sort. And young fellow me lad over there is Anguy, or Archer as we like to call him."

"Now who are you?" demanded Lem, in the deep voice that Arya had heard through the branches of the willow.

She was not about to give up her true name as easy as that. "Squab, if you want," she said. "I don't care."

The big man laughed. "A squab with a sword," he said. "Now there's something you don't often see."

"I'm the Bull," said Gendry, taking his lead from Arya. She could not blame him for preferring Bull to Mutton Chop.

Tom Sevenstrings strummed his harp. "Hot Pie, Squab, and the Bull. Escaped from Lord Bolton's kitchen, did you?"

"How did you know?" Arya demanded, uneasy.

"You bear his sigil on your chest, little one."

She had forgotten that for an instant. Beneath her cloak, she still wore her fine page's doublet, with the flayed man of the Dreadfort sewn on her breast. "Don't call me little one!"

"Why not?" said Lem. "You're little enough."

"I'm bigger than I was. I'm not a *child*." Children didn't kill people, and she had.

"I can see that, Squab. You're none of you children, not if you were Bolton's."

"We never were." Hot Pie never knew when to keep quiet. "We were at Harrenhal before he came, that's all."

"So you're lion cubs, is that the way of it?" said Tom.

"Not that either. We're nobody's men. Whose men are you?"

Anguy the Archer said, "We're king's men."

Arya frowned. "Which king?"

"King Robert," said Lem, in his yellow cloak.

"That old drunk?" said Gendry scornfully. "He's dead, some boar killed him, everyone knows that."

"Aye, lad," said Tom Sevenstrings, "and more's the pity." He plucked a sad chord from his harp.

Arya didn't think they were king's men at all. They looked more like outlaws, all tattered and ragged. They didn't even have horses to ride. King's men would have had horses.

But Hot Pie piped up eagerly. "We're looking for Riverrun," he said. "How many days' ride is it, do you know?"

Arya could have killed him. "You be quiet, or I'll stuff rocks in your big stupid mouth."

"Riverrun is a long way upstream," said Tom. "A long hungry way. Might be you'd like a hot meal before you set out? There's an inn not far ahead kept by some friends of ours. We could share some ale and a bite of bread, instead of fighting one another."

"An inn?" The thought of hot food made Arya's belly rumble, but she didn't trust this Tom. Not everyone who spoke you friendly was really your friend. "It's near, you say?"

"Two miles upstream," said Tom. "A league at most."

Gendry looked as uncertain as she felt. "What do you mean, *friends?*" he asked warily.

"Friends. Have you forgotten what friends are?"

"Sharna is the innkeep's name," Tom put in. "She has a sharp tongue and a fierce eye, I'll grant you that, but her heart's a good one, and she's fond of little girls."

"I'm not a little girl," she said angrily. "Who else is there? You said *friends*."

"Sharna's husband, and an orphan boy they took in. They won't harm you. There's ale, if you think you're old enough. Fresh bread and maybe a bit of meat." Tom glanced toward the cottage. "And whatever you stole from Old Pate's garden besides."

"We never stole," said Arya.

"Are you Old Pate's daughter, then? A sister? A wife? Tell me no lies, Squab. I buried Old Pate myself, right there under that willow where you were hiding, and you don't have his look." He drew a sad sound from his harp. "We've buried many a good man this past year, but we've no wish to bury you, I swear it on my harp. Archer, show her."

The archer's hand moved quicker than Arya would have believed. His shaft went hissing past her head within an inch of her ear and buried itself in the trunk of the willow behind her. By then the bowman had a second arrow notched and drawn. She'd thought she understood what Syrio meant by *quick as a snake* and *smooth as summer silk*, but now she knew she hadn't. The arrow thrummed behind her like a bee. "You missed," she said.

"More fool you if you think so," said Anguy. "They go where I send them."

"That they do," agreed Lem Lemoncloak.

There were a dozen steps between the archer and the point of her sword. *We have no chance*, Arya realized, wishing she had a bow like his, and the skill to use it. Glumly, she lowered her heavy longsword till the point touched the ground. "We'll come see this inn," she conceded, trying to hide the doubt in her heart behind bold words. "You walk in front and we'll ride behind, so we can see what you're doing."

Tom Sevenstrings bowed deeply and said, "Before, behind, it makes no matter. Come along, lads, let's show them the way. Anguy, best pull up those arrows, we won't be needing them here."

Arya sheathed her sword and crossed the road to where her friends sat on their horses, keeping her distance from the three strangers. "Hot Pie, get those cabbages," she said as she vaulted into her saddle. "And the carrots too."

For once he did not argue. They set off as she had wanted, walking their horses slowly down the rutted road a dozen paces behind the three on foot. But before very long, somehow they were riding right on top of them. Tom Sevenstrings walked slowly, and liked to strum his woodharp as he went. "Do you know any songs?" he asked them. "I'd dearly love someone to sing with, that I would. Lem can't carry a tune, and our longbow lad only knows marcher ballads, every one of them a hundred verses long."

"We sing real songs in the marches," Anguy said mildly.

"Singing is *stupid*," said Arya. "Singing makes noise. We heard you a long way off. We could have killed you."

Tom's smile said he did not think so. "There are worse things than dying with a song on your lips."

"If there were wolves hereabouts, we'd know it," groused Lem. "Or lions. These are our woods."

"You never knew we were there," said Gendry.

"Now, lad, you shouldn't be so certain of that," said Tom. "Sometimes a man knows more than he says."

Hot Pie shifted his seat. "I know the song about the bear," he said. "Some of it, anyhow."

Tom ran his fingers down his strings. "Then let's hear it, pie boy." He threw back his head and sang, "*A bear there was, a bear, a bear! All black and brown, and covered with hair . . .*"

Hot Pie joined in lustily, even bouncing in his saddle a little on the rhymes. Arya stared at him in astonishment. He had a good voice and he sang well. *He never did anything well, except bake,* she thought to herself.

A small brook flowed into the Trident a little farther on. As they waded across, their singing flushed a duck from among the reeds. Anguy stopped where he stood, unslung his bow, notched an arrow, and brought it down. The bird fell in the shallows not far from the bank. Lem took off his yellow cloak and waded in knee-deep to retrieve it, complaining all the while. "Do you think Sharna might have lemons down in that cellar of hers?" said Anguy to Tom as they watched Lem splash around, cursing. "A Dornish girl once cooked me duck with lemons." He sounded wistful.

Tom and Hot Pie resumed their song on the other side of the brook, with the duck hanging from Lem's belt beneath his yellow cloak. Somehow the singing made the miles seem shorter. It was not very long at all until the inn appeared before them, rising from the riverbank where the Trident made a great bend to the north. Arya squinted at it suspiciously as they neared. It did not *look* like an outlaws' lair, she had to admit; it looked friendly, even homey, with its whitewashed upper story and slate roof and the smoke curling up lazy from its chimney. Stables and other outbuildings surrounded it, and there was an arbor in back, and apple trees, a small garden. The inn even had its own dock, thrusting out into the river, and . . .

"Gendry," she called, her voice low and urgent. "They have a boat. We could sail the rest of the way up to Riverrun. It would be faster than riding, I think."

He looked dubious. "Did you ever sail a boat?"

"You put up the sail," she said, "and the wind pushes it."

"What if the wind is blowing the wrong way?"

"Then there's oars to row."

"Against the current?" Gendry frowned. "Wouldn't that be slow? And what if the boat tips over and we fall into the water? It's not our boat anyway, it's the inn's."

We could take it. Arya chewed her lip and said nothing. They dismounted in front of stables. There were no other horses to be seen, but

Arya noticed fresh manure in many of the stalls. "One of us should watch the horses," she said, wary.

Tom overheard her. "There's no need for that, Squab. Come eat, they'll be safe enough."

"I'll stay," Gendry said, ignoring the singer. "You can come get me after you've had some food."

Nodding, Arya set off after Hot Pie and Lem. Her sword was still in its sheath across her back, and she kept a hand close to the hilt of the dagger she had stolen from Roose Bolton, in case she didn't like whatever they found within.

The painted sign above the door showed a picture of some old king on his knees. Inside was the common room, where a very tall ugly woman with a knobby chin stood with her hands on her hips, glaring. "Don't just stand there, boy," she snapped. "Or are you a girl? Either one, you're blocking my door. Get in or get out. Lem, what did I tell you about my floor? You're all mud."

"We shot a duck." Lem held it out like a peace banner.

The woman snatched it from his hand. "Anguy shot a duck, is what you're meaning. Get your boots off, are you deaf or just stupid?" She turned away. *"Husband!"* she called loudly. "Get up here, the lads are back. *Husband!"*

Up the cellar steps came a man in a stained apron, grumbling. He was a head shorter than the woman, with a lumpy face and loose yellowish skin that still showed the marks of some pox. "I'm here, woman, quit your bellowing. What is it now?"

"Hang this," she said, handing him the duck.

Anguy shuffled his feet. "We were thinking we might eat it, Sharna. With lemons. If you had some."

"Lemons. And where would we get lemons? Does this look like Dorne to you, you freckled fool? Why don't you hop out back to the lemon trees and pick us a bushel, and some nice olives and pomegranates too." She shook a finger at him. "Now, I suppose I could cook it with Lem's cloak, if you like, but not till it's hung for a few days. You'll eat rabbit, or you won't eat. Roast rabbit on a spit would be quickest, if you've got a hunger. Or might be you'd like it stewed, with ale and onions."

Arya could almost taste the rabbit. "We have no coin, but we brought some carrots and cabbages we could trade you."

"Did you now? And where would they be?"

"Hot Pie, give her the cabbages," Arya said, and he did, though he approached the old woman as gingerly as if she were Rorge or Biter or Vargo Hoat.

The woman gave the vegetables a close inspection, and the boy a closer one. "Where is this *hot pie?"*

"Here. Me. It's my name. And she's . . . ah . . . Squab."

"Not under my roof. I give my diners and my dishes different names, so as to tell them apart. *Husband!*"

Husband had stepped outside, but at her shout he hurried back. "The duck's hung. What is it now, woman?"

"Wash these vegetables," she commanded. "The rest of you, sit down while I start the rabbits. The boy will bring you drink." She looked down her long nose at Arya and Hot Pie. "I am not in the habit of serving ale to children, but the cider's run out, there's no cows for milk, and the river water tastes of war, with all the dead men drifting downstream. If I served you a cup of soup full of dead flies, would you drink it?"

"Arry would," said Hot Pie. "I mean, Squab."

"So would Lem," offered Anguy with a sly smile.

"Never you mind about Lem," Sharna said. "It's ale for all." She swept off toward the kitchen.

Anguy and Tom Sevenstrings took the table near the hearth while Lem was hanging his big yellow cloak on a peg. Hot Pie plopped down heavily on a bench at the table by the door, and Arya wedged herself in beside him.

Tom unslung his harp. "*A lonely inn on a forest road,*" he sang, slowly picking out a tune to go with the words. "*The innkeep's wife was plain as a toad.*"

"Shut up with that now or we won't be getting no rabbit," Lem warned him. "You know how she is."

Arya leaned close to Hot Pie. "Can you sail a boat?" she asked. Before he could answer, a thickset boy of fifteen or sixteen appeared with tankards of ale. Hot Pie took his reverently in both hands, and when he sipped he smiled wider than Arya had ever seen him smile. "Ale," he whispered, "and *rabbit.*"

"Well, here's to His Grace," Anguy the Archer called out cheerfully, lifting a toast. "Seven save the king!"

"All twelve o' them," Lem Lemoncloak muttered. He drank, and wiped the foam from his mouth with the back of his hand.

Husband came bustling in through the front door, with an apron full of washed vegetables. "There's strange horses in the stable," he announced, as if they hadn't known.

"Aye," said Tom, setting the woodharp aside, "and better horses than the three you gave away."

Husband dropped the vegetables on a table, annoyed. "I never gave them away. I *sold* them for a good price, and got us a skiff as well. Anyways, you lot were supposed to get them back."

I knew they were outlaws, Arya thought, listening. Her hand went under the table to touch the hilt of her dagger, and make sure it was still there. *If they try to rob us, they'll be sorry.*

"They never came our way," said Lem.

"Well, I sent them. You must have been drunk, or asleep."

"Us? Drunk?" Tom drank a long draught of ale. "Never."

"You could have taken them yourself," Lem told Husband.

"What, with only the boy here? I told you twice, the old woman was up to Lambswold helping that Fern birth her babe. And like as not it was one o' you planted the bastard in the poor girl's belly." He gave Tom a sour look. "You, I'd wager, with that harp o' yours, singing all them sad songs just to get poor Fern out of her smallclothes."

"If a song makes a maid want to slip off her clothes and feel the good warm sun kiss her skin, why, is that the singer's fault?" asked Tom. "And 'twas Anguy she fancied, besides. 'Can I touch your bow?' I heard her ask him. 'Ooohh, it feels so smooth and hard. Could I give it a little pull, do you think?'"

Husband snorted. "You and Anguy, makes no matter which. You're as much to blame as me for them horses. They was three, you know. What can one man do against three?"

"Three," said Lem scornfully, "but one a woman and t'other in chains, you said so yourself."

Husband made a face. "A *big* woman, dressed like a man. And the one in chains . . . I didn't fancy the look of his eyes."

Anguy smiled over his ale. "When I don't fancy a man's eyes, I put an arrow through one."

Arya remembered the shaft that had brushed by her ear. She wished she knew how to shoot arrows.

Husband was not impressed. "You be quiet when your elders are talking. Drink your ale and mind your tongue, or I'll have the old woman take a spoon to you."

"My elders talk too much, and I don't need you to tell me to drink my ale." He took a big swallow, to show that it was so.

Arya did the same. After days of drinking from brooks and puddles, and then the muddy Trident, the ale tasted as good as the little sips of wine her father used to allow her. A smell was drifting out from the kitchen that made her mouth water, but her thoughts were still full of that boat. *Sailing it will be harder than stealing it. If we wait until they're all asleep . . .*

The serving boy reappeared with big round loaves of bread. Arya broke off a chunk hungrily and tore into it. It was hard to chew, though, sort of thick and lumpy, and burned on the bottom.

Hot Pie made a face as soon as he tasted it. "That's bad bread," he said. "It's burned, and tough besides."

"It's better when there's stew to sop up," said Lem.

"No, it isn't," said Anguy, "but you're less like to break your teeth."

"You can eat it or go hungry," said Husband. "Do I look like some bloody baker? I'd like to see you make better."

"I could," said Hot Pie. "It's easy. You kneaded the dough too much, that's why it's so hard to chew." He took another sip of ale, and began talking lovingly of breads and pies and tarts, all the things he loved. Arya rolled her eyes.

Tom sat down across from her. "Squab," he said, "or Arry, or whatever your true name might be, this is for you." He placed a dirty scrap of parchment on the wooden tabletop between them.

She looked at it suspiciously. "What is it?"

"Three golden dragons. We need to buy those horses."

Arya looked at him warily. "They're *our* horses."

"Meaning you stole them yourselves, is that it? No shame in that, girl. War makes thieves of many honest folk." Tom tapped the folded parchment with his finger. "I'm paying you a handsome price. More than any horse is worth, if truth be told."

Hot Pie grabbed the parchment and unfolded it. "There's no gold," he complained loudly. "It's only writing."

"Aye," said Tom, "and I'm sorry for that. But after the war, we mean to make that good, you have my word as a king's man."

Arya pushed back from the table and got to her feet. "You're no king's men, you're robbers."

"If you'd ever met a true robber, you'd know they do not pay, not even in paper. It's not for us we take your horses, child, it's for the good of the realm, so we can get about more quickly and fight the fights that need fighting. The king's fights. Would you deny the king?"

They were all watching her; the Archer, big Lem, Husband with his sallow face and shifty eyes. Even Sharna, who stood in the door to the kitchen squinting. *They are going to take our horses no matter what I say*, she realized. *We'll need to walk to Riverrun, unless* . . . "We don't want paper." Arya slapped the parchment out of Hot Pie's hand. "You can have our horses for that boat outside. But only if you show us how to work it."

Tom Sevenstrings stared at her a moment, and then his wide homely mouth quirked into a rueful grin. He laughed aloud. Anguy joined in, and then they were all laughing, Lem Lemoncloak, Sharna and Husband, even the serving boy, who had stepped out from behind the casks with a crossbow under one arm. Arya wanted to scream at them, but instead she started to smile . . .

"*Riders!*" Gendry's shout was shrill with alarm. The door burst open and there he was. "*Soldiers*," he panted. "Coming down the·river road, a dozen of them."

Hot Pie leapt up, knocking over his tankard, but Tom and the others were unpertubed. "There's no cause for spilling good ale on my floor," said Sharna. "Sit back down and calm yourself, boy, there's rabbit coming. You too, girl. Whatever harm's been done you, it's over and it's done and you're with king's men now. We'll keep you safe as best we can."

Arya's only answer was to reach over her shoulder for her sword, but before she had it halfway drawn Lem grabbed her wrist. "We'll have no more of that, now." He twisted her arm until her hand opened. His fingers were hard with callus and fearsomely strong. *Again!* Arya thought. *It's happening again, like it happened in the village, with Chiswyck and Raff and the Mountain That Rides.* They were going to steal her sword and turn her back into a mouse. Her free hand closed around her tankard, and she swung it at Lem's face. The ale sloshed over the rim and splashed into his eyes, and she heard his nose break and saw the spurt of blood. When he roared his hands went to his face, and she was free. *"Run!"* she screamed, bolting.

But Lem was on her again at once, with his long legs that made one of his steps equal to three of hers. She twisted and kicked, but he yanked her off her feet effortlessly and held her dangling while the blood ran down his face.

"*Stop it*, you little fool," he shouted, shaking her back and forth. "Stop it now!" Gendry moved to help her, until Tom Sevenstrings stepped in front of him with a dagger.

By then it was too late to flee. She could hear horses outside, and the sound of men's voices. A moment later a man came swaggering through the open door, a Tyroshi even bigger than Lem with a great thick beard, bright green at the ends but growing out grey. Behind came a pair of crossbowmen helping a wounded man between them, and then others . . .

A more ragged band Arya had never seen, but there was nothing ragged about the swords, axes, and bows they carried. One or two gave her curious glances as they entered, but no one said a word. A one-eyed man in a rusty pothelm sniffed the air and grinned, while an archer with a head of stiff yellow hair was shouting for ale. After them came a spearman in a lion-crested helm, an older man with a limp, a Braavosi sellsword, a . . .

"Harwin?" Arya whispered. *It was!* Under the beard and the tangled hair was the face of Hullen's son, who used to lead her pony around the yard, ride at quintain with Jon and Robb, and drink too much on feast days. He was thinner, harder somehow, and at Winterfell he had never worn a beard, but it was him – her father's man. "*Harwin!*" Squirming, she threw herself forward, trying to wrench free of Lem's iron grip. "It's me," she shouted, "Harwin, it's me, don't you know me, don't you?" The tears came, and she found herself weeping like a baby, just like some stupid little girl. "Harwin, *it's me!*"

Harwin's eyes went from her face to the flayed man on her doublet. "How do you know me?" he said, frowning suspiciously. "The flayed man . . . who are you, some serving boy to Lord Leech?"

For a moment she did not know how to answer. She'd had so many names. Had she only dreamed Arya Stark? "I'm a girl," she sniffed. "I was Lord Bolton's cupbearer but he was going to leave me for the goat, so I ran off with Gendry and Hot Pie. You *have* to know me! You used to lead my pony, when I was little."

His eyes went wide. "Gods be good," he said in a choked voice. "Arya Underfoot? Lem, let go of her."

"She broke my nose." Lem dumped her unceremoniously to the floor. "Who in seven hells is she supposed to be?"

"The Hand's daughter." Harwin went to one knee before her. "Arya Stark, of Winterfell."

CATELYN

Robb, she knew, the moment she heard the kennels erupt.
Her son had returned to Riverrun, and Grey Wind with him.
Only the scent of the great grey direwolf could send the hounds
into such a frenzy of baying and barking. *He will come to me*, she knew.
Edmure had not returned after his first visit, preferring to spend his days
with Marq Piper and Patrek Mallister, listening to Rymund the Rhymer's
verses about the battle at the Stone Mill. *Robb is not Edmure, though.
Robb will see me.*

It had been raining for days now, a cold grey downpour that well suited
Catelyn's mood. Her father was growing weaker and more delirious with
every passing day, waking only to mutter, "Tansy," and beg forgiveness.
Edmure shunned her, and Ser Desmond Grell still denied her freedom of
the castle, however unhappy it seemed to make him. Only the return of
Ser Robin Ryger and his men, footweary and drenched to the bone, served
to lighten her spirits. They had walked back, it seemed. Somehow the
Kingslayer had contrived to sink their galley and escape, Maester Vyman
confided. Catelyn asked if she might speak with Ser Robin to learn more
of what had happened, but that was refused her.

Something else was wrong as well. On the day her brother returned,
a few hours after their argument, she had heard angry voices from the
yard below. When she climbed to the roof to see, there were knots of
men gathered across the castle beside the main gate. Horses were being
led from the stables, saddled and bridled, and there was shouting, though
Catelyn was too far away to make out the words. One of Robb's white
banners lay on the ground, and one of the knights turned his horse and

trampled over the direwolf as he spurred toward the gate. Several others did the same. *Those are men who fought with Edmure on the fords*, she thought. *What could have made them so angry? Has my brother slighted them somehow, given them some insult?* She thought she recognized Ser Perwyn Frey, who had traveled with her to Bitterbridge and Storm's End and back, and his bastard half brother Martyn Rivers as well, but from this vantage it was hard to be certain. Close to forty men poured out through the castle gates, to what end she did not know.

They did not come back. Nor would Maester Vyman tell her who they had been, where they had gone, or what had made them so angry. "I am here to see to your father, and only that, my lady," he said. "Your brother will soon be Lord of Riverrun. What he wishes you to know, he must tell you."

But now Robb was returned from the west, returned in triumph. *He will forgive me*, Catelyn told herself. *He must forgive me, he is my own son, and Arya and Sansa are as much his blood as mine. He will free me from these rooms and then I will know what has happened.*

By the time Ser Desmond came for her, she had bathed and dressed and combed out her auburn hair. "King Robb has returned from the west, my lady," the knight said, "and commands that you attend him in the Great Hall."

It was the moment she had dreamt of and dreaded. *Have I lost two sons, or three?* She would know soon enough.

The hall was crowded when they entered. Every eye was on the dais, but Catelyn knew their backs: Lady Mormont's patched ringmail, the Greatjon and his son looming above every other head in the hall, Lord Jason Mallister white-haired with his winged helm in the crook of his arm, Tytos Blackwood in his magnificent raven-feather cloak . . . *Half of them will want to hang me now. The other half may only turn their eyes away.* She had the uneasy feeling that someone was missing, too.

Robb stood on the dais. *He is a boy no longer*, she realized with a pang. *He is sixteen now, a man grown. Just look at him.* War had melted all the softness from his face and left him hard and lean. He had shaved his beard away, but his auburn hair fell uncut to his shoulders. The recent rains had rusted his mail and left brown stains on the white of his cloak and surcoat. Or perhaps the stains were blood. On his head was the sword crown they had fashioned him of bronze and iron. *He bears it more comfortably now. He bears it like a king.*

Edmure stood below the crowded dais, head bowed modestly as Robb praised his victory. ". . . fell at the Stone Mill shall never be forgotten. Small wonder Lord Tywin ran off to fight Stannis. He'd had his fill of northmen and rivermen both." That brought laughter and approving shouts, but Robb raised a hand for quiet. "Make no mistake, though. The

Lannisters will march again, and there will be other battles to win before the kingdom is secure."

The Greatjon roared out, *"King in the North!"* and thrust a mailed fist into the air. The river lords answered with a shout of *"King of the Trident!"* The hall grew thunderous with pounding fists and stamping feet.

Only a few noted Catelyn and Ser Desmond amidst the tumult, but they elbowed their fellows, and slowly a hush grew around her. She held her head high and ignored the eyes. *Let them think what they will. It is Robb's judgment that matters.*

The sight of Ser Brynden Tully's craggy face on the dais gave her comfort. A boy she did not know seemed to be acting as Robb's squire. Behind him stood a young knight in a sand-colored surcoat blazoned with seashells, and an older one who wore three black pepperpots on a saffron bend, across a field of green and silver stripes. Between them were a handsome older lady and a pretty maid who looked to be her daughter. There was another girl as well, near Sansa's age. The seashells were the sigil of some lesser house, Catelyn knew; the older man's she did not recognize. *Prisoners?* Why would Robb bring captives onto the dais?

Utherydes Wayn banged his staff on the floor as Ser Desmond escorted her forward. *If Robb looks at me as Edmure did, I do not know what I will do.* But it seemed to her that it was not anger she saw in her son's eyes, but something else . . . apprehension, perhaps? No, that made no sense. What should *he* fear? He was the Young Wolf, King of the Trident and the North.

Her uncle was the first to greet her. As black a fish as ever, Ser Brynden had no care for what others might think. He leapt off the dais and pulled Catelyn into his arms. When he said, "It is good to see you home, Cat," she had to struggle to keep her composure. "And you," she whispered.

"Mother."

Catelyn looked up at her tall kingly son. "Your Grace, I have prayed for your safe return. I had heard you were wounded."

"I took an arrow through the arm while storming the Crag," he said. "It's healed well, though. I had the best of care."

"The gods are good, then." Catelyn took a deep breath. *Say it. It cannot be avoided.* "They will have told you what I did. Did they tell you my reasons?"

"For the girls."

"I had five children. Now I have three."

"Aye, my lady." Lord Rickard Karstark pushed past the Greatjon, like some grim specter with his black mail and long ragged grey beard, his narrow face pinched and cold. "And I have one son, who once had three. You have robbed me of my vengeance."

Catelyn faced him calmly. "Lord Rickard, the Kingslayer's dying would not have bought life for your children. His living may buy life for mine."

The lord was unappeased. "Jaime Lannister has played you for a fool. You've bought a bag of empty words, no more. My Torrhen and my Eddard deserved better of you."

"Leave off, Karstark," rumbled the Greatjon, crossing his huge arms against his chest. "It was a mother's folly. Women are made that way."

"A mother's folly?" Lord Karstark rounded on Lord Umber. "I name it treason."

"*Enough.*" For just an instant Robb sounded more like Brandon than his father. "No man calls my lady of Winterfell a traitor in my hearing, Lord Rickard." When he turned to Catelyn, his voice softened. "If I could wish the Kingslayer back in chains I would. You freed him without my knowledge or consent . . . but what you did, I know you did for love. For Arya and Sansa, and out of grief for Bran and Rickon. Love's not always wise, I've learned. It can lead us to great folly, but we follow our hearts . . . wherever they take us. Don't we, Mother?"

Is that what I did? "If my heart led me into folly, I would gladly make whatever amends I can to Lord Karstark and yourself."

Lord Rickard's face was implacable. "Will your *amends* warm Torrhen and Eddard in the cold graves where the Kingslayer laid them?" He shouldered between the Greatjon and Maege Mormont and left the hall.

Robb made no move to detain him. "Forgive him, Mother."

"If you will forgive me."

"I have. I know what it is to love so greatly you can think of nothing else."

Catelyn bowed her head. "Thank you." *I have not lost this child, at least.*

"We must talk," Robb went on. "You and my uncles. Of this and . . . other things. Steward, call an end."

Utherydes Wayn slammed his staff on the floor and shouted the dismissal, and river lords and northerners alike moved toward the doors. It was only then that Catelyn realized what was amiss. *The wolf. The wolf is not here. Where is Grey Wind?* She knew the direwolf had returned with Robb, she had heard the dogs, but he was not in the hall, not at her son's side where he belonged.

Before she could think to question Robb, however, she found herself surrounded by a circle of well-wishers. Lady Mormont took her hand and said, "My lady, if Cersei Lannister held two of my daughters, I would have done the same." The Greatjon, no respecter of proprieties, lifted her off her feet and squeezed her arms with his huge hairy hands. "Your wolf pup mauled the Kingslayer once, he'll do it again if need be." Galbart Glover and Lord Jason Mallister were cooler, and Jonos Bracken almost icy, but their words were courteous enough. Her brother was the last to approach her. "I pray for your girls as well, Cat. I hope you do not doubt that."

"Of course not." She kissed him. "I love you for it."

When all the words were done, the Great Hall of Riverrun was empty save for Robb, the three Tullys, and the six strangers Catelyn could not place. She eyed them curiously. "My lady, sers, are you new to my son's cause?"

"New," said the younger knight, him of the seashells, "but fierce in our courage and firm in our loyalties, as I hope to prove to you, my lady."

Robb looked uncomfortable. "Mother," he said, "may I present the Lady Sybell, the wife of Lord Gawen Westerling of the Crag." The older woman came forward with solemn mien. "Her husband was one of those we took captive in the Whispering Wood."

Westerling, yes, Catelyn thought. *Their banner is six seashells, white on sand. A minor house sworn to the Lannisters.*

Robb beckoned the other strangers forward, each in turn. "Ser Rolph Spicer, Lady Sybell's brother. He was castellan at the Crag when we took it." The pepperpot knight inclined his head. A square-built man with a broken nose and a close-cropped grey beard, he looked doughty enough. "The children of Lord Gawen and Lady Sybell. Ser Raynald Westerling." The seashell knight smiled beneath a bushy mustache. Young, lean, rough-hewn, he had good teeth and a thick mop of chestnut hair. "Elenya." The little girl did a quick curtsy. "Rollam Westerling, my squire." The boy started to kneel, saw no one else was kneeling, and bowed instead.

"The honor is mine," Catelyn said. *Can Robb have won the Crag's allegiance?* If so, it was no wonder the Westerlings were with him. Casterly Rock did not suffer such betrayals gently. Not since Tywin Lannister had been old enough to go to war . . .

The maid came forward last, and very shy. Robb took her hand. "Mother," he said, "I have the great honor to present you the Lady Jeyne Westerling. Lord Gawen's elder daughter, and my . . . ah . . . my lady wife."

The first thought that flew across Catelyn's mind was, *No, that cannot be, you are only a child.*

The second was, *And besides, you have pledged another.*

The third was, *Mother have mercy, Robb, what have you done?*

Only then came her belated remembrance. *Follies done for love? He has bagged me neat as a hare in a snare. I seem to have already forgiven him.* Mixed with her annoyance was a rueful admiration; the scene had been staged with the cunning worthy of a master mummer . . . or a king. Catelyn saw no choice but to take Jeyne Westerling's hands. "I have a new daughter," she said, more stiffly than she'd intended. She kissed the terrified girl on both cheeks. "Be welcome to our hall and hearth."

"Thank you, my lady. I shall be a good and true wife to Robb, I swear. And as wise a queen as I can."

Queen. Yes, this pretty little girl is a queen, I must remember that. She *was* pretty, undeniably, with her chestnut curls and heart-shaped face, and that shy smile. Slender, but with good hips, Catelyn noted. *She should have no trouble bearing children, at least.*

Lady Sybell took a hand before any more was said. "We are honored to be joined to House Stark, my lady, but we are also very weary. We have come a long way in a short time. Perhaps we might retire to our chambers, so you may visit with your son?"

"That would be best." Robb kissed his Jeyne. "The steward will find you suitable accommodations."

"I'll take you to him," Ser Edmure Tully volunteered.

"You are most kind," said Lady Sybell.

"Must I go too?" asked the boy, Rollam. "I'm your squire."

Robb laughed. "But I'm not in need of squiring just now."

"Oh."

"His Grace has gotten along for sixteen years without you, Rollam," said Ser Raynald of the seashells. "He will survive a few hours more, I think." Taking his little brother firmly by the hand, he walked him from the hall.

"Your wife is lovely," Catelyn said when they were out of earshot, "and the Westerlings seem worthy ... though Lord Gawen is Tywin Lannister's sworn man, is he not?"

"Yes. Jason Mallister captured him in the Whispering Wood and has been holding him at Seagard for ransom. Of course I'll free him now, though he may not wish to join me. We wed without his consent, I fear, and this marriage puts him in dire peril. The Crag is not strong. For love of me, Jeyne may lose all."

"And you," she said softly, "have lost the Freys."

His wince told all. She understood the angry voices now, why Perwyn Frey and Martyn Rivers had left in such haste, trampling Robb's banner into the ground as they went.

"Dare I ask how many swords come with your bride, Robb?"

"Fifty. A dozen knights." His voice was glum, as well it might be. When the marriage contract had been made at the Twins, old Lord Walder Frey had sent Robb off with a thousand mounted knights and near three thousand foot. "Jeyne is bright as well as beautiful. And kind as well. She has a gentle heart."

It is swords you need, not gentle hearts. How could you do this, Robb? How could you be so heedless, so stupid? How could you be so ... so very ... young. Reproaches would not serve here, however. All she said was, "Tell me how this came to be."

"I took her castle and she took my heart." Robb smiled. "The Crag was weakly garrisoned, so we took it by storm one night. Black Walder and the Smalljon led scaling parties over the walls, while I broke the main gate with a ram. I took an arrow in the arm just before Ser Rolph yielded us the castle. It seemed nothing at first, but it festered. Jeyne had me taken to her own bed, and she nursed me until the fever passed. And she was with me when the Greatjon brought me the news of . . . of Winterfell. Bran and Rickon." He seemed to have trouble saying his brothers' names. "That night, she . . . she comforted me, Mother."

Catelyn did not need to be told what sort of comfort Jeyne Westerling had offered her son. "And you wed her the next day."

He looked her in the eyes, proud and miserable all at once. "It was the only honorable thing to do. She's gentle and sweet, Mother, she will make me a good wife."

"Perhaps. That will not appease Lord Frey."

"I know," her son said, stricken. "I've made a botch of everything but the battles, haven't I? I thought the battles would be the hard part, but . . . if I had listened to you and kept Theon as my hostage, I'd still rule the north, and Bran and Rickon would be alive and safe in Winterfell."

"Perhaps. Or not. Lord Balon might still have chanced war. The last time he reached for a crown, it cost him two sons. He might have thought it a bargain to lose only one this time." She touched his arm. "What happened with the Freys, after you wed?"

Robb shook his head. "With Ser Stevron, I might have been able to make amends, but Ser Ryman is dull-witted as a stone, and Black Walder . . . that one was not named for the color of his beard, I promise you. He went so far as to say that his sisters would not be loath to wed a widower. I would have killed him for that if Jeyne had not begged me to be merciful."

"You have done House Frey a grievous insult, Robb."

"I never meant to. Ser Stevron died for me, and Olyvar was as loyal a squire as any king could want. He asked to stay with me, but Ser Ryman took him with the rest. All their strength. The Greatjon urged me to attack them . . ."

"Fighting your own in the midst of your enemies?" she said. "It would have been the end of you."

"Yes. I thought perhaps we could arrange other matches for Lord Walder's daughters. Ser Wendel Manderly has offered to take one, and the Greatjon tells me his uncles wish to wed again. If Lord Walder will be reasonable –"

"He is *not* reasonable," said Catelyn. "He is proud, and prickly to a fault. You know that. He wanted to be grandfather to a king. You will not appease him with the offer of two hoary old brigands and the second son of the fattest man in the Seven Kingdoms. Not only have you broken your oath, but you've slighted the honor of the Twins by choosing a bride from a lesser house."

Robb bristled at that. "The Westerlings are better blood than the Freys. They're an ancient line, descended from the First Men. The Kings of the Rock sometimes wed Westerlings before the Conquest, and there was another Jeyne Westerling who was queen to King Maegor three hundred years ago."

"All of which will only salt Lord Walder's wounds. It has always rankled him that older houses look down on the Freys as upstarts. This insult is not the first he's borne, to hear him tell it. Jon Arryn was disinclined to foster his grandsons, and my father refused the offer of one of his daughters for Edmure." She inclined her head toward her brother as he rejoined them.

"Your Grace," Brynden Blackfish said, "perhaps we had best continue this in private."

"Yes." Robb sounded tired. "I would kill for a cup of wine. The audience chamber, I think."

As they started up the steps, Catelyn asked the question that had been troubling her since she entered the hall. "Robb, where is Grey Wind?"

"In the yard, with a haunch of mutton. I told the kennelmaster to see that he was fed."

"You always kept him with you before."

"A hall is no place for a wolf. He gets restless, you've seen. Growling and snapping. I should never have taken him into battle with me. He's killed too many men to fear them now. Jeyne's anxious around him, and he terrifies her mother."

And there's the heart of it, Catelyn thought. "He is part of you, Robb. To fear him is to fear you."

"I am not a wolf, no matter what they call me." Robb sounded cross. "Grey Wind killed a man at the Crag, another at Ashemark, and six or seven at Oxcross. If you had seen –"

"I saw Bran's wolf tear out a man's throat at Winterfell," she said sharply, "and loved him for it."

"That's different. The man at the Crag was a knight Jeyne had known all her life. You can't blame her for being afraid. Grey Wind doesn't like her uncle either. He bares his teeth every time Ser Rolph comes near him."

A chill went through her. "Send Ser Rolph away. At once."

"Where? Back to the Crag, so the Lannisters can mount his head on a spike? Jeyne loves him. He's her uncle, and a fair knight besides. I need more men like Rolph Spicer, not fewer. I am not going to banish him just because my wolf doesn't seem to like the way he smells."

"Robb." She stopped and held his arm. "I told you once to keep Theon Greyjoy close, and you did not listen. Listen now. *Send this man away.* I am not saying you must banish him. Find some task that requires a man of courage, some honorable duty, what it is matters not . . . but *do not keep him near you.*"

He frowned. "Should I have Grey Wind sniff all my knights? There might be others whose smell he mislikes."

"Any man Grey Wind mislikes is a man I do not want close to you. These wolves are more than wolves, Robb. You *must* know that. I think perhaps the gods sent them to us. Your father's gods, the old gods of the north. Five wolf pups, Robb, five for five Stark children."

"Six," said Robb. "There was a wolf for Jon as well. I found them, remember? I know how many there were and where they came from. I used to think the same as you, that the wolves were our guardians, our protectors, until . . ."

"Until?" she prompted.

Robb's mouth tightened. ". . . until they told me that Theon had murdered Bran and Rickon. Small good their wolves did them. I am no longer a boy, Mother. I'm a king, and I can protect myself." He sighed. "I will find some duty for Ser Rolph, some pretext to send him away. Not because of his smell, but to ease your mind. You have suffered enough."

Relieved, Catelyn kissed him lightly on the cheek before the others could come around the turn of the stair, and for a moment he was her boy again, and not her king.

Lord Hoster's private audience chamber was a small room above the Great Hall, better suited to intimate discussions. Robb took the high seat, removed his crown, and set it on the floor beside him as Catelyn rang for wine. Edmure was filling his uncle's ear with the whole story of the fight at the Stone Mill. It was only after the servants had come and gone that the Blackfish cleared his throat and said, "I think we've all heard sufficient of your boasting, Nephew."

Edmure was taken aback. "Boasting? What do you mean?"

"I mean," said the Blackfish, "that you owe His Grace your thanks for his forbearance. He played out that mummer's farce in the Great Hall so as not to shame you before your own people. Had it been me I would have flayed you for your stupidity rather than praising this folly of the fords."

"Good men died to defend those fords, Uncle." Edmure sounded outraged. "What, is no one to win victories but the Young Wolf? Did I steal some glory meant for you, Robb?"

"*Your Grace,*" Robb corrected, icy. "You took me for your king, Uncle. Or have you forgotten that as well?"

The Blackfish said, "You were commanded to hold Riverrun, Edmure, no more."

"I held Riverrun, *and* I bloodied Lord Tywin's nose –"

"So you did," said Robb. "But a bloody nose won't win the war, will it? Did you ever think to ask yourself why we remained in the west so long after Oxcross? You knew I did not have enough men to threaten Lannisport or Casterly Rock."

"Why ... there were other castles ... gold, cattle ..."

"You think we stayed for *plunder*?" Robb was incredulous. "Uncle, I wanted Lord Tywin to come west."

"We were all horsed," Ser Brynden said. "The Lannister host was mainly foot. We planned to run Lord Tywin a merry chase up and down the coast, then slip behind him to take up a strong defensive position athwart the gold road, at a place my scouts had found where the ground would have been greatly in our favor. If he had come at us there, he would have paid a grievous price. But if he did not attack, he would have been trapped in the west, a thousand leagues from where he needed to be. All the while we would have lived off his land, instead of him living off ours."

"Lord Stannis was about to fall upon King's Landing," Robb said. "He might have rid us of Joffrey, the queen, and the Imp in one red stroke. Then we might have been able to make a peace."

Edmure looked from uncle to nephew. "You never told me."

"I *told* you to hold Riverrun," said Robb. "What part of that command did you fail to comprehend?"

"When you stopped Lord Tywin on the Red Fork," said the Blackfish, "you delayed him just long enough for riders out of Bitterbridge to reach him with word of what was happening to the east. Lord Tywin turned his host at once, joined up with Matthis Rowan and Randyll Tarly near the headwaters of the Blackwater, and made a forced march to Tumbler's Falls, where he found Mace Tyrell and two of his sons waiting with a huge host and a fleet of barges. They floated down the river, disembarked half a day's ride from the city, and took Stannis in the rear."

Catelyn remembered King Renly's court, as she had seen it at Bitterbridge. A thousand golden roses streaming in the wind, Queen Margaery's shy smile and soft words, her brother the Knight of Flowers with the bloody linen around his temples. *If you had to fall into a woman's arms, my son, why couldn't they have been Margaery Tyrell's?* The wealth and power of Highgarden could have made all the difference in the fighting yet to come. *And perhaps Grey Wind would have liked the smell of her as well.*

Edmure looked ill. "I never meant ... *never*, Robb, you must let me make amends. I will lead the van in the next battle!"

For amends, Brother? Or for glory? Catelyn wondered.

"The next battle," Robb said. "Well, that will be soon enough. Once Joffrey is wed, the Lannisters will take the field against me once more, I don't doubt, and this time the Tyrells will march beside them. And I may need to fight the Freys as well, if Black Walder has his way . . ."

"So long as Theon Greyjoy sits in your father's seat with your brothers' blood on his hands, these other foes must wait," Catelyn told her son. "Your first duty is to defend your own people, win back Winterfell, and hang Theon in a crow's cage to die slowly. Or else put off that crown for good, Robb, for men will know that you are no true king at all."

From the way Robb looked at her, she could tell that it had been a long while since anyone had dared speak to him so bluntly. "When they told me Winterfell had fallen, I wanted to go north at once," he said, with a hint of defensiveness. "I wanted to free Bran and Rickon, but I thought . . . I never dreamed that Theon could harm them, truly. If I had . . ."

"It is too late for *ifs*, and too late for rescues," Catelyn said. "All that remains is vengeance."

"The last word we had from the north, Ser Rodrik had defeated a force of ironmen near Torrhen's Square, and was assembling a host at Castle Cerwyn to retake Winterfell," said Robb. "By now he may have done it. There has been no news for a long while. And what of the Trident, if I turn north? I can't ask the river lords to abandon their own people."

"No," said Catelyn. "Leave them to guard their own, and win back the north with northmen."

"How will you get the northmen to the north?" her brother Edmure asked. "The ironmen control the sunset sea. The Greyjoys hold Moat Cailin as well. No army has ever taken Moat Cailin from the south. Even to march against it is madness. We could be trapped on the causeway, with the ironborn before us and angry Freys at our backs."

"We must win back the Freys," said Robb. "With them, we still have some chance of success, however small. Without them, I see no hope. I am willing to give Lord Walder whatever he requires . . . apologies, honors, lands, gold . . . there must be *something* that would soothe his pride . . ."

"Not something," said Catelyn. "Some*one*."

JON

"**B**ig enough for you?" Snowflakes speckled Tormund's broad face, melting in his hair and beard.

The giants swayed slowly atop the mammoths as they rode past two by two. Jon's garron shied, frightened by such strangeness, but whether it was the mammoths or their riders that scared him it was hard to say. Even Ghost backed off a step, baring his teeth in a silent snarl. The direwolf was big, but the mammoths were a deal bigger, and there were many and more of them.

Jon took the horse in hand and held him still, so he could count the giants emerging from the blowing snow and pale mists that swirled along the Milkwater. He was well beyond fifty when Tormund said something and he lost the count. *There must be hundreds.* No matter how many went past, they just seemed to keep coming.

In Old Nan's stories, giants were outsized men who lived in colossal castles, fought with huge swords, and walked about in boots a boy could hide in. These were something else, more bearlike than human, and as wooly as the mammoths they rode. Seated, it was hard to say how big they truly were. *Ten feet tall maybe, or twelve,* Jon thought. *Maybe fourteen, but no taller.* Their sloping chests might have passed for those of men, but their arms hung down too far, and their lower torsos looked half again as wide as their upper. Their legs were shorter than their arms, but very thick, and they wore no boots at all; their feet were broad splayed things, hard and horny and black. Neckless, their huge heavy heads thrust forward from between their shoulder blades, and their faces were squashed and brutal. Rats' eyes no larger than beads were almost lost within folds of horny flesh, but they snuffled constantly, smelling as much as they saw.

They're not wearing skins, Jon realized. *That's hair.* Shaggy pelts covered their bodies, thick below the waist, sparser above. The stink that came off them was choking, but perhaps that was the mammoths. *And Joramun blew the Horn of Winter, and woke giants from the earth.* He looked for great swords ten feet long, but saw only clubs. Most were just the limbs of dead trees, some still trailing shattered branches. A few had stone balls lashed to the ends to make colossal mauls. *The song never says if the horn can put them back to sleep.*

One of the giants coming up on them looked older than the rest. His pelt was grey and streaked with white, and the mammoth he rode, larger than any of the others, was grey and white as well. Tormund shouted something up to him as he passed, harsh clanging words in a tongue that Jon did not comprehend. The giant's lips split apart to reveal a mouth full of huge square teeth, and he made a sound half belch and half rumble. After a moment Jon realized he was laughing. The mammoth turned its massive head to regard the two of them briefly, one huge tusk passing over the top of Jon's head as the beast lumbered by, leaving huge footprints in the soft mud and fresh snow along the river. The giant shouted down something in the same coarse tongue that Tormund had used.

"Was that their king?" asked Jon.

"Giants have no kings, no more'n mammoths do, nor snow bears, nor the great whales o' the grey sea. That was Mag Mar Tun Doh Weg. Mag the Mighty. You can kneel to him if you like, he won't mind. I know your kneeler's knees must be itching, for want of some king to bend to. Watch out he don't step on you, though. Giants have bad eyes, and might be he wouldn't see some little crow all the way down there by his feet."

"What did you say to him? Was that the Old Tongue?"

"Aye. I asked him if that was his father he was forking, they looked so much alike, except his father had a better smell."

"And what did he say to you?"

Tormund Thunderfist cracked a gap-toothed smile. "He asked me if that was my daughter riding there beside me, with her smooth pink cheeks." The wildling shook snow from his arm and turned his horse about. "It may be he never saw a man without a beard before. Come, we start back. Mance grows sore wroth when I'm not found in my accustomed place."

Jon wheeled and followed Tormund back toward the head of the column, his new cloak hanging heavy from his shoulders. It was made of unwashed sheepskins, worn fleece side in, as the wildlings suggested. It kept the snow off well enough, and at night it was good and warm, but he kept his black cloak as well, folded up beneath his saddle. "Is it true you killed a giant once?" he asked Tormund as they rode. Ghost loped silently beside them, leaving paw prints in the new-fallen snow.

"Now why would you doubt a mighty man like me? It was winter and I was half a boy, and stupid the way boys are. I went too far and my horse died and then a storm caught me. A *true* storm, not no little dusting such as this. Har! I knew I'd freeze to death before it broke. So I found me a sleeping giant, cut open her belly, and crawled up right inside her. Kept me warm enough, she did, but the stink near did for me. The worst thing was, she woke up when the spring come and took me for her babe. Suckled me for three whole moons before I could get away. Har! There's times I miss the taste o' giant's milk, though."

"If she nursed you, you couldn't have killed her."

"I never did, but see you don't go spreading that about. Tormund Giantsbane has a better ring to it than Tormund Giantsbabe, and that's the honest truth o' it."

"So how did you come by your other names?" Jon asked. "Mance called you the Horn-Blower, didn't he? Mead-king of Ruddy Hall, Husband to Bears, Father to Hosts?" It was the horn blowing he particularly wanted to hear about, but he dared not ask too plainly. *And Joramun blew the Horn of Winter, and woke giants from the earth.* Is that where they had come from, them and their mammoths? Had Mance Rayder found the Horn of Joramun, and given it to Tormund Thunderfist to blow?

"Are all crows so curious?" asked Tormund. "Well, here's a tale for you. It were another winter, colder even than the one I spent inside that giant, and snowing day and night, snowflakes as big as your head, not these little things. It snowed so hard the whole village was half buried. I was in me Ruddy Hall, with only a cask o' mead to keep me company and nothing to do but drink it. The more I drank the more I got to thinking about this woman lived close by, a fine strong woman with the biggest pair of teats you ever saw. She had a temper on her, that one, but oh, she could be warm too, and in the deep of winter a man needs his warmth.

"The more I drank the more I thought about her, and the more I thought the harder me member got, till I couldn't suffer it no more. Fool that I was, I bundled meself up in furs from head to heels, wrapped a winding wool around me face, and set off to find her. The snow was coming down so hard I got turned around once or twice, and the wind blew right through me and froze me bones, but finally I come on her, all bundled up like I was.

"The woman had a terrible temper, and she put up quite the fight when I laid hands on her. It was all I could do to carry her home and get her out o' them furs, but when I did, oh, she was hotter even than I remembered, and we had a fine old time, and then I went to sleep. Next morning when I woke the snow had stopped and the sun was shining, but I was in no fit state to enjoy it. All ripped and torn I was, and half me member bit right off, and there on me floor was a she-bear's pelt. And soon enough the free folk were telling tales o' this bald bear seen in the woods, with the queerest pair o' cubs behind her. Har!" He slapped a meaty thigh. "Would that I could find her again. She was fine to lay with, that bear. Never was a woman gave me such a fight, nor such strong sons neither."

"What could you do if you *did* find her?" Jon asked, smiling. "You said she bit your member off."

"Only half. And half me member is twice as long as any other man's." Tormund snorted. "Now as to you . . . is it true they cut your members off when they take you for the Wall?"

"No," Jon said, affronted.

"I think it must be true. Else why refuse Ygritte? She'd hardly give you any fight at all, seems to me. The girl wants you in her, that's plain enough to see."

Too bloody plain, thought Jon, *and it seems that half the column has seen it.* He studied the falling snow so Tormund might not see him redden. *I am a man of the Night's Watch*, he reminded himself. So why did he feel like some blushing maid?

He spent most of his days in Ygritte's company, and most nights as well. Mance Rayder had not been blind to Rattleshirt's mistrust of the "crow-come-over," so after he had given Jon his new sheepskin cloak he had suggested that he might want to ride with Tormund Giantsbane instead. Jon had happily agreed, and the very next day Ygritte and Longspear Ryk left Rattleshirt's band for Tormund's as well. "Free folk ride with who they want," the girl told him, "and we had a bellyful of Bag o' Bones."

Every night when they made camp, Ygritte threw her sleeping skins down beside his own, no matter if he was near the fire or well away from it. Once he woke to find her nestled against him, her arm across his chest. He lay listening to her breathe for a long time, trying to ignore the tension in his groin. Rangers often shared skins for warmth, but warmth was not all Ygritte wanted, he suspected. After that he had taken to using Ghost to keep her away. Old Nan used to tell stories about knights and their ladies who would sleep in a single bed with a blade between them for honor's sake, but he thought this must be the first time where a direwolf took the place of the sword.

Even then, Ygritte persisted. The day before last, Jon had made the mistake of wishing he had hot water for a bath. "Cold is better," she had said at once, "if you've got someone to warm you up after. The river's only part ice yet, go on."

Jon laughed. "You'd freeze me to death."

"Are all crows afraid of gooseprickles? A little ice won't kill you. I'll jump in with you t'prove it so."

"And ride the rest of the day with wet clothes frozen to our skins?" he objected.

"Jon Snow, you know nothing. You don't go in with clothes."

"I don't go in at all," he said firmly, just before he heard Tormund Thunderfist bellowing for him (he hadn't, but never mind).

The wildlings seemed to think Ygritte a great beauty because of her hair; red hair was rare among the free folk, and those who had it were said to be kissed by fire, which was supposed to be lucky. Lucky it might be, and red it certainly was, but Ygritte's hair was such a tangle that Jon was tempted to ask her if she only brushed it at the changing of the seasons.

At a lord's court the girl would never have been considered anything but common, he knew. She had a round peasant face, a pug nose, and slightly crooked teeth, and her eyes were too far apart. Jon had noticed all that the first time he'd seen her, when his dirk had been at her throat. Lately, though, he was noticing some other things. When she grinned, the crooked teeth didn't seem to matter. And maybe her eyes were too far apart, but they were a pretty blue-grey color, and lively as any eyes he knew. Sometimes she sang in a low husky voice that stirred him. And sometimes by the cookfire when she sat hugging her knees with the flames waking echoes in her red hair, and looked at him, just smiling . . . well, *that* stirred some things as well.

But he was a man of the Night's Watch, he had taken a vow. I shall take no wife, hold no lands, father no children. He had said the words before the weirwood, before his father's gods. He could not unsay them . . . no more than he could admit the reason for his reluctance to Tormund Thunderfist, Father to Bears.

"Do you mislike the girl?" Tormund asked him as they passed another twenty mammoths, these bearing wildlings in tall wooden towers instead of giants.

"No, but I . . ." *What can I say that he will believe?* "I am still too young to wed."

"Wed?" Tormund laughed. "Who spoke of wedding? In the south, must a man wed every girl he beds?"

Jon could feel himself turning red again. "She spoke for me when Rattleshirt would have killed me. I would not dishonor her."

"You are a free man now, and Ygritte is a free woman. What dishonor if you lay together?"

"I might get her with child."

"Aye, I'd hope so. A strong son or a lively laughing girl kissed by fire, and where's the harm in that?"

Words failed him for a moment. "The boy . . . the child would be a bastard."

"Are bastards weaker than other children? More sickly, more like to fail?"

"No, but –"

"You're bastard-born yourself. And if Ygritte does not want a child, she will go to some woods witch and drink a cup o' moon tea. You do not come into it, once the seed is planted."

"I will *not* father a bastard."

Tormund shook his shaggy head. "What fools you kneelers be. Why did you steal the girl if you don't want her?"

"*Steal?* I never . . ."

"You did," said Tormund. "You slew the two she was with and carried her off, what do you call it?"

"I took her prisoner."

"You made her yield to you."

"Yes, but . . . Tormund, I swear, I've never touched her."

"Are you *certain* they never cut your member off?" Tormund gave a shrug, as if to say he would never understand such madness. "Well, you are a free man now, but if you will not have the girl, best find yourself a she-bear. If a man does not use his member it grows smaller and smaller, until one day he wants to piss and cannot find it."

Jon had no answer for that. Small wonder that the Seven Kingdoms thought the free folk scarcely human. *They have no laws, no honor, not even simple decency. They steal endlessly from each other, breed like beasts, prefer rape to marriage, and fill the world with baseborn children.* Yet he was growing fond of Tormund Giantsbane, great bag of wind and lies though he was. Longspear as well. *And Ygritte . . . no, I will not think about Ygritte.*

Along with the Tormunds and the Longspears rode other sorts of wildlings, though; men like Rattleshirt and the Weeper who would as soon slit you as spit on you. There was Harma Dogshead, a squat keg of a woman with cheeks like slabs of white meat, who hated dogs and killed one every fortnight to make a fresh head for her banner; earless Styr, Magnar of Thenn, whose own people thought him more god than lord; Varamyr Sixskins, a small mouse of a man whose steed was a savage white snow bear that stood thirteen feet tall on its hind legs. And wherever the bear and Varamyr went, three wolves and a shadowcat came following. Jon had been in his presence only once, and once had been enough; the mere sight of the man had made him bristle, even as the fur on the back of Ghost's neck had bristled at the sight of the bear and that long black-and-white 'cat.

And there were folks fiercer even than Varamyr, from the northernmost reaches of the haunted forest, the hidden valleys of the Frostfangs, and even queerer places: the men of the Frozen Shore who rode in chariots made of walrus bones pulled along by packs of savage dogs, the terrible ice-river clans who were said to feast on human flesh, the cave dwellers with their faces dyed blue and purple and green. With his own eyes Jon had beheld the Hornfoot men trotting along in column on bare soles as hard as boiled leather. He had not seen any snarks or grumpkins, but for all he knew Tormund would be having some to supper.

Half the wildling host had lived all their lives without so much as a glimpse of the Wall, Jon judged, and most of those spoke no word of the Common Tongue. It did not matter. Mance Rayder spoke the Old Tongue, even sang in it, fingering his lute and filling the night with strange wild music.

Mance had spent years assembling this vast plodding host, talking to this clan mother and that magnar, winning one village with sweet words and another with a song and a third with the edge of his sword, making peace between Harma Dogshead and the Lord o' Bones, between the Hornfoots and the Nightrunners, between the walrus men of the Frozen Shore and the cannibal clans of the great ice rivers, hammering a hundred different daggers into one great spear, aimed at the heart of the Seven Kingdoms. He had no crown nor scepter, no robes of silk and velvet, but it was plain to Jon that Mance Rayder *was* a king in more than name.

Jon had joined the wildlings at Qhorin Halfhand's command. "Ride with them, eat with them, fight with them," the ranger had told him, the night before he died. "And *watch*." But all his watching had learned him little. The Halfhand had suspected that the wildlings had gone up into the bleak and barren Frostfangs in search of some weapon, some power, some fell sorcery with which to break the Wall . . . but if they had found any such, no one was boasting of it openly, or showing it to Jon. Nor had Mance Rayder confided any of his plans or strategies. Since that first night, he had hardly seen the man save at a distance.

I will kill him if I must. The prospect gave Jon no joy; there would be no honor in such a killing, and it would mean his own death as well. Yet he could not let the wildlings breach the Wall, to threaten Winterfell and the north, the barrowlands and the Rills, White Harbor and the Stony Shore, even the Neck. For eight thousand years the men of House Stark had lived and died to protect their people against such ravagers and reavers . . . and bastard-born or no, the same blood ran in his veins. *Bran and Rickon are still at Winterfell besides. Maester Luwin, Ser Rodrik, Old Nan, Farlen the kennelmaster, Mikken at his forge and Gage by his ovens . . . everyone I ever knew, everyone I ever loved.* If Jon must slay a man he half admired and almost liked to save them from the mercies of Rattleshirt and Harma Dogshead and the earless Magnar of Thenn, that was what he meant to do.

Still, he prayed his father's gods might spare him that bleak task. The host moved but slowly, burdened as it was by all the wildlings' herds and children and mean little treasures, and the snows had slowed its progress even more. Most of the column was out of the foothills now, oozing down along the west bank of the Milkwater like honey on a cold winter's morning, following the course of the river into the heart of the haunted forest.

And somewhere close ahead, Jon knew, the Fist of the First Men loomed above the trees, home to three hundred black brothers of the Night's Watch, armed, mounted, and waiting. The Old Bear had sent out other scouts besides the Halfhand, and surely Jarman Buckwell or Thoren Smallwood would have returned by now with word of what was coming down out of the mountains.

Mormont will not run, Jon thought. *He is too old and he has come too far. He will strike, and damn the numbers.* One day soon he would hear the sound of warhorns, and see a column of riders pounding down on them with black cloaks flapping and cold steel in their hands. Three hundred men could not hope to kill a hundred times their number, of course, but Jon did not think they would need to. *He need not slay a thousand, only one. Mance is all that keeps them together.*

The King-beyond-the-Wall was doing all he could, yet the wildlings remained hopelessly undisciplined, and that made them vulnerable. Here and there within the leagues-long snake that was their line of march were warriors as fierce as any in the Watch, but a good third of them were grouped at either end of the column, in Harma Dogshead's van and the savage rearguard with its giants, aurochs, and fire flingers. Another third rode with Mance himself near the center, guarding the wayns and sledges and dog carts that held the great bulk of the host's provisions and supplies, all that remained of the last summer harvest. The rest, divided into small bands under the likes of Rattleshirt, Jarl, Tormund Giantsbane, and the Weeper, served as outriders, foragers, and whips, galloping up and down the column endlessly to keep it moving in a more or less orderly fashion.

And even more telling, only one in a hundred wildlings was mounted. *The Old Bear will go through them like an axe through porridge.* And when that happened, Mance must give chase with his center, to try and blunt the threat. If he should fall in the fight that must follow, the Wall would be safe for another hundred years, Jon judged. *And if not . . .*

He flexed the burned fingers of his sword hand. Longclaw was slung to his saddle, the carved stone wolf's-head pommel and soft leather grip of the great bastard sword within easy reach.

The snow was falling heavily by the time they caught Tormund's band, several hours later. Ghost departed along the way, melting into the forest at the scent of prey. The direwolf would return when they made camp for the night, by dawn at the latest. However far he prowled, Ghost always came back . . . and so, it seemed, did Ygritte.

"So," the girl called when she saw him, "d'you believe us now, Jon Snow? Did you see the giants on their mammoths?"

"Har!" shouted Tormund, before Jon could reply. "The crow's in love! He means to marry one!"

"A giantess?" Longspear Ryk laughed.

"No, a *mammoth*!" Tormund bellowed. "Har!"

Ygritte trotted beside Jon as he slowed his garron to a walk. She claimed to be three years older than him, though she stood half a foot shorter; however old she might be, the girl was a tough little thing. Stonesnake had called her a "spearwife" when they'd captured her in the Skirling Pass. She wasn't wed and her weapon of choice was a short curved bow of horn and weirwood, but "spearwife" fit her all the same. She reminded him a little of his sister Arya, though Arya was younger and probably skinnier. It was hard to tell how plump or thin Ygritte might be, with all the furs and skins she wore.

"Do you know 'The Last of the Giants'?" Without waiting for an answer Ygritte said, "You need a deeper voice than mine to do it proper." Then she sang, "*Ooooooh, I am the last of the giants, my people are gone from the earth.*"

Tormund Giantsbane heard the words and grinned. "*The last of the great mountain giants, who ruled all the world at my birth,*" he bellowed back through the snow.

Longspear Ryk joined in, singing, "*Oh, the smallfolk have stolen my forests, they've stolen my rivers and hills.*"

"*And they've built a great wall through my valleys, and fished all the fish from my rills,*" Ygritte and Tormund sang back at him in turn, in suitably gigantic voices.

Tormund's sons Toregg and Dormund added their deep voices as well, then his daughter Munda and all the rest. Others began to bang their spears on leathern shields to keep rough time, until the whole war band was singing as they rode.

In stone halls they burn their great fires,
      in stone halls they forge their sharp spears.
Whilst I walk alone in the mountains,
      with no true companion but tears.
They hunt me with dogs in the daylight,
      they hunt me with torches by night.

For these men who are small can never stand tall,
  whilst giants still walk in the light.
Oooooooh, I am the LAST of the giants,
  so learn well the words of my song.
For when I am gone the singing will fade,
  and the silence shall last long and long.

There were tears on Ygritte's cheeks when the song ended.

"Why are you weeping?" Jon asked. "It was only a song. There are hundreds of giants, I've just seen them."

"Oh, hundreds," she said furiously. "You know nothing, Jon Snow. You – *JON!*"

Jon turned at the sudden sound of wings. Blue-grey feathers filled his eyes, as sharp talons buried themselves in his face. Red pain lanced through him sudden and fierce as pinions beat round his head. He saw the beak, but there was no time to get a hand up or reach for a weapon. Jon reeled backward, his foot lost the stirrup, his garron broke in panic, and then he was falling. And still the eagle clung to his face, its talons tearing at him as it flapped and shrieked and pecked. The world turned upside down in a chaos of feathers and horseflesh and blood, and then the ground came up to smash him.

The next he knew, he was on his face with the taste of mud and blood in his mouth and Ygritte kneeling over him protectively, a bone dagger in her hand. He could still hear wings, though the eagle was not in sight. Half his world was black. "My eye," he said in sudden panic, raising a hand to his face.

"It's only blood, Jon Snow. He missed the eye, just ripped your skin up some."

His face was throbbing. Tormund stood over them bellowing, he saw from his right eye as he rubbed blood from his left. Then there were hoofbeats, shouts, and the clacking of old dry bones.

"Bag o' Bones," roared Tormund, "call off your hellcrow!"

"There's your hellcrow!" Rattleshirt pointed at Jon. "Bleeding in the mud like a faithless dog!" The eagle came flapping down to land atop the broken giant's skull that served him for his helm. "I'm here for him."

"Come take him then," said Tormund, "but best come with sword in hand, for that's where you'll find mine. Might be I'll boil *your* bones, and use your skull to piss in. Har!"

"Once I prick you and let the air out, you'll shrink down smaller'n that girl. Stand aside, or Mance will hear o' this."

Ygritte stood. "What, is it *Mance* who wants him?"

"I said so, didn't I? Get him up on those black feet."

Tormund frowned down at Jon. "Best go, if it's the Mance who's want-ing you."

Ygritte helped pull him up. "He's bleeding like a butchered boar. Look what Orell did t' his sweet face."

Can a bird hate? Jon had slain the wildling Orell, but some part of the man remained within the eagle. The golden eyes looked out on him with cold malevolence. "I'll come," he said. The blood kept running down into his right eye, and his cheek was a blaze of pain. When he touched it his black gloves came away stained with red. "Let me catch my garron." It was not the horse he wanted so much as Ghost, but the direwolf was nowhere to be seen. *He could be leagues away by now, ripping out the throat of some elk.* Perhaps that was just as well.

The garron shied away from him when he approached, no doubt fright-ened by the blood on his face, but Jon calmed him with a few quiet words and finally got close enough to take the reins. As he swung back into the saddle his head whirled. *I will need to get this tended,* he thought, *but not just now. Let the King-beyond-the-Wall see what his eagle did to me.* His right hand opened and closed, and he reached down for Longclaw and slung the bastard sword over a shoulder before he wheeled to trot back to where the Lord of Bones and his band were waiting.

Ygritte was waiting too, sitting on her horse with a fierce look on her face. "I am coming too."

"Be gone." The bones of Rattleshirt's breastplate clattered together. "I was sent for the crow-come-down, none other."

"A free woman rides where she will," Ygritte said.

The wind was blowing snow into Jon's eyes. He could feel the blood freezing on his face. "Are we talking or riding?"

"Riding," said the Lord of Bones.

It was a grim gallop. They rode two miles down the column through swirling snows, then cut through a tangle of baggage wayns to splash across the Milkwater where it took a great loop toward the east. A crust of thin ice covered the river shallows; with every step their horses' hooves crashed through, until they reached the deeper water ten yards out. The snow seemed be falling even faster on the eastern bank, and the drifts were deeper too. *Even the wind is colder.* And night was falling too.

But even through the blowing snow, the shape of the great white hill that loomed above the trees was unmistakable. *The Fist of the First Men.* Jon heard the scream of the eagle overhead. A raven looked down from a soldier pine and *quork*ed as he went past. *Had the Old Bear made his attack?* Instead of the clash of steel and the thrum of arrows taking flight, Jon heard only the soft crunch of frozen crust beneath his garron's hooves.

In silence they circled round to the south slope, where the approach was easiest. It was there at the bottom that Jon saw the dead horse, sprawled at the base of the hill, half buried in the snow. Entrails spilled from the belly of the animal like frozen snakes, and one of its legs was gone. *Wolves,* was Jon's first thought, but that was wrong. Wolves eat their kill.

More garrons were strewn across the slope, legs twisted grotesquely, blind eyes staring in death. The wildlings crawled over them like flies, stripping them of saddles, bridles, packs, and armor, and hacking them apart with stone axes.

"Up," Rattleshirt told Jon. "Mance is up top."

Outside the ringwall they dismounted to squeeze through a crooked gap in the stones. The carcass of a shaggy brown garron was impaled upon the sharpened stakes the Old Bear had placed inside every entrance. *He was trying to get out, not in.* There was no sign of a rider.

Inside was more, and worse. Jon had never seen pink snow before. The wind gusted around him, pulling at his heavy sheepskin cloak. Ravens flapped from one dead horse to the next. *Are those wild ravens, or our own?* Jon could not tell. He wondered where poor Sam was now. And *what* he was.

A crust of frozen blood crunched beneath the heel of his boot. The wildlings were stripping the dead horses of every scrap of steel and leather, even prying the horseshoes off their hooves. A few were going through packs they'd turned up, looking for weapons and food. Jon passed one of Chett's dogs, or what remained of him, lying in a sludgy pool of half-frozen blood.

A few tents were still standing on the far side of the camp, and it was there they found Mance Rayder. Beneath his slashed cloak of black wool and red silk he wore black ringmail and shaggy fur breeches, and on his head was a great bronze-and-iron helm with raven wings at either temple. Jarl was with him, and Harma the Dogshead; Styr as well, and Varamyr Sixskins with his wolves and his shadowcat.

The look Mance gave Jon was grim and cold. "What happened to your face?"

Ygritte said, "Orell tried to take his eye out."

"It was him I asked. Has he lost his tongue? Perhaps he should, to spare us further lies."

Styr the Magnar drew a long knife. "The boy might see more clear with one eye, instead of two."

"Would you like to keep your eye, Jon?" asked the King-beyond-the-Wall. "If so, tell me how many they were. And try and speak the truth this time, Bastard of Winterfell."

Jon's throat was dry. "My lord . . . what . . ."

"I am not your lord," said Mance. "And the *what* is plain enough. Your brothers died. The question is, how many?"

Jon's face was throbbing, the snow kept coming down, and it was hard to think. *You must not balk, whatever is asked of you,* Qhorin had told him. The words stuck in his throat, but he made himself say, "There were three hundred of us."

"Us?" Mance said sharply.

"Them. Three hundred of them." *Whatever is asked, the Halfhand said. So why do I feel so craven?* "Two hundred from Castle Black, and one hundred from the Shadow Tower."

"There's a truer song than the one you sang in my tent." Mance looked to Harma Dogshead. "How many horses have we found?"

"More'n a hundred," that huge woman replied, "less than two. There's more dead to the east, under the snow, hard t' know how many." Behind her stood her banner bearer, holding a pole with a dog's head on it, fresh enough to still be leaking blood.

"You should never have lied to me, Jon Snow," said Mance.

"I . . . I know that." *What could he say?*

The wildling king studied his face. "Who had the command here? And tell me true. Was it Rykker? Smallwood? Not Wythers, he's too feeble. Whose tent was this?"

I have said too much. "You did not find his body?"

Harma snorted, her disdain frosting from her nostrils. "What fools these black crows be."

"The next time you answer me with a question, I will give you to my Lord of Bones," Mance Rayder promised Jon. He stepped closer. "Who led here?"

One more step, thought Jon. *Another foot.* He moved his hand closer to Longclaw's hilt. *If I hold my tongue . . .*

"Reach up for that bastard sword and I'll have your bastard head off before it clears the scabbard," said Mance. "I am fast losing patience with you, crow."

"Say it," Ygritte urged. "He's dead, whoever he was."

His frown cracked the blood on his cheek. *This is too hard,* Jon thought in despair. *How do I play the turncloak without becoming one?* Qhorin had not told him that. But the second step is always easier than the first. "The Old Bear."

"That old man?" Harma's tone said she did not believe it. "He came himself? Then who commands at Castle Black?"

"Bowen Marsh." This time Jon answered at once. *You must not balk, whatever is asked of you.*

Mance laughed. "If so, our war is won. Bowen knows a deal more about counting swords than he's ever known about using them."

"The Old Bear commanded," said Jon. "This place was high and strong, and he made it stronger. He dug pits and planted stakes, laid up food and water. He was ready for . . ."

"...me?" finished Mance Rayder. "Aye, he was. Had I been fool enough to storm this hill, I might have lost five men for every crow I slew and still counted myself lucky." His mouth grew hard. "But when the dead walk, walls and stakes and swords mean nothing. You cannot fight the dead, Jon Snow. No man knows that half so well as me." He gazed up at the darkening sky and said, "The crows may have helped us more than they know. I'd wondered why we'd suffered no attacks. But there's still a hundred leagues to go, and the cold is rising. Varamyr, send your wolves sniffing after the wights, I won't have them taking us unawares. My Lord of Bones, double all the patrols, and make certain every man has torch and flint. Styr, Jarl, you ride at first light."

"Mance," Rattleshirt said, "I want me some crow bones."

Ygritte stepped in front of Jon. "You can't kill a man for lying to protect them as was his brothers."

"They are still his brothers," declared Styr.

"They're *not*," insisted Ygritte. "He never killed me, like they told him. And he slew the Halfhand, we all saw."

Jon's breath misted the air. *If I lie to him, he'll know.* He looked Mance Rayder in the eyes, opened and closed his burned hand. "I wear the cloak you gave me, Your Grace."

"A sheepskin cloak!" said Ygritte. "And there's many a night we dance beneath it, too!"

Jarl laughed, and even Harma Dogshead smirked. "Is that the way of it, Jon Snow?" asked Mance Rayder, mildly. "Her and you?"

It was easy to lose your way beyond the Wall. Jon did not know that he could tell honor from shame anymore, or right from wrong. *Father forgive me.* "Yes," he said.

Mance nodded. "Good. You'll go with Jarl and Styr on the morrow, then. Both of you. Far be it from me to separate two hearts that beat as one."

"Go where?" said Jon.

"Over the Wall. It's past time you proved your faith with something more than words, Jon Snow."

The Magnar was not pleased. "What do I want with a crow?"

"He knows the Watch and he knows the Wall," said Mance, "and he knows Castle Black better than any raider ever could. You'll find a use for him, or you're a fool."

Styr scowled. "His heart may still be black."

"Then cut it out." Mance turned to Rattleshirt. "My Lord of Bones, keep the column moving at all costs. If we reach the Wall before Mormont, we've won."

"They'll move." Rattleshirt's voice was thick and angry.

Mance nodded, and walked away, Harma and Sixskins beside him.

Varamyr's wolves and shadowcat followed behind. Jon and Ygritte were left with Jarl, Rattleshirt, and the Magnar. The two older wildlings looked at Jon with ill-concealed rancor as Jarl said, "You heard, we ride at daybreak. Bring all the food you can, there'll be no time to hunt. And have your face seen to, crow. You look a bloody mess."

"I will," said Jon.

"You best not be lying, girl," Rattleshirt said to Ygritte, his eyes shiny behind the giant's skull.

Jon drew Longclaw. "Get away from us, unless you want what Qhorin got."

"You got no wolf to help you here, boy." Rattleshirt reached for his own sword.

"Sure o' that, are you?" Ygritte laughed.

Atop the stones of the ringwall, Ghost hunched with white fur bristling. He made no sound, but his dark red eyes spoke blood. The Lord of Bones moved his hand slowly away from his sword, backed off a step, and left them with a curse.

Ghost padded beside their garrons as Jon and Ygritte descended the Fist. It was not until they were halfway across the Milkwater that Jon felt safe enough to say, "I never asked you to lie for me."

"I never did," she said. "I left out part, is all."

"You said –"

"– that we fuck beneath your cloak many a night. I never said when we started, though." The smile she gave him was almost shy. "Find another place for Ghost to sleep tonight, Jon Snow. It's like Mance said. Deeds is truer than words."

SANSA

"A new gown?" she said, as wary as she was astonished.

"More lovely than any you have worn, my lady," the old woman promised. She measured Sansa's hips with a length of knotted string. "All silk and Myrish lace, with satin linings. You will be very beautiful. The queen herself has commanded it."

"Which queen?" Margaery was not yet Joff's queen, but she had been Renly's. Or did she mean the Queen of Thorns? Or . . .

"The Queen Regent, to be sure."

"Queen *Cersei?*"

"None other. She has honored me with her custom for many a year." The old woman laid her string along the inside of Sansa's leg. "Her Grace said to me that you are a woman now, and should not dress like a little girl. Hold out your arm."

Sansa lifted her arm. She needed a new gown, that was true. She had grown three inches in the past year, and most of her old wardrobe had been ruined by the smoke when she'd tried to burn her mattress on the day of her first flowering

"Your bosom will be as lovely as the queen's," the old woman said as she looped her string around Sansa's chest. "You should not hide it so."

The comment made her blush. Yet the last time she'd gone riding, she could not lace her jerkin all the way to the top, and the stableboy gaped at her as he helped her mount. Sometimes she caught grown men looking at her chest as well, and some of her tunics were so tight she could scarce breathe in them.

"What color will it be?" she asked the seamstress.

"Leave the colors to me, my lady. You will be pleased, I know you will. You shall have smallclothes and hose as well, kirtles and mantles and cloaks, and all else befitting a . . . a lovely young lady of noble birth."

"Will they be ready in time for the king's wedding?"

"Oh, sooner, much sooner, Her Grace insists. I have six seamstresses and twelve apprentice girls, and we have set all our other work aside for this. Many ladies will be cross with us, but it was the queen's command."

"Thank Her Grace kindly for her thoughtfulness," Sansa said politely. "She is too good to me."

"Her Grace is most generous," the seamstress agreed, as she gathered up her things and took her leave.

But why? Sansa wondered when she was alone. It made her uneasy. *I'll wager this gown is Margaery's doing somehow, or her grandmother's.*

Margaery's kindness had been unfailing, and her presence changed everything. Her ladies welcomed Sansa as well. It had been so long since she had enjoyed the company of other women, she had almost forgotten how pleasant it could be. Lady Leonette gave her lessons on the high harp, and Lady Janna shared all the choice gossip. Merry Crane always had an amusing story, and little Lady Bulwer reminded her of Arya, though not so fierce.

Closest to Sansa's own age were the cousins Elinor, Alla, and Megga, Tyrells from junior branches of the House. "Roses from lower on the bush," quipped Elinor, who was witty and willowy. Megga was round and loud, Alla shy and pretty, but Elinor ruled the three by right of womanhood; she was a maiden flowered, whereas Megga and Alla were mere girls.

The cousins took Sansa into their company as if they had known her all their lives. They spent long afternoons doing needlework and talking over lemon cakes and honeyed wine, played at tiles of an evening, sang together in the castle sept . . . and often one or two of them would be chosen to share Margaery's bed, where they would whisper half the night away. Alla had a lovely voice, and when coaxed would play the woodharp and sing songs of chivalry and lost loves. Megga couldn't sing, but she was mad to be kissed. She and Alla played a kissing game sometimes, she confessed, but it wasn't the same as kissing a man, much less a king. Sansa wondered what Megga would think about kissing the Hound, as she had. He'd come to her the night of the battle stinking of wine and blood. *He kissed me and threatened to kill me, and made me sing him a song.*

"King Joffrey has such beautiful lips," Megga gushed, oblivious, "oh, poor Sansa, how your heart must have broken when you lost him. Oh, how you must have wept!"

Joffrey made me weep more often than you know, she wanted to say, but Butterbumps was not on hand to drown out her voice, so she pressed her lips together and held her tongue.

As for Elinor, she was promised to a young squire, a son of Lord Ambrose; they would be wed as soon as he won his spurs. He had worn her favor in the Battle of the Blackwater, where he'd slain a Myrish crossbowman and a Mullendore man-at-arms. "Alyn said her favor made him fearless," said Megga. "He says he shouted her name for his battle cry, isn't that ever so gallant? Someday I want some champion to wear my favor, and kill a hundred men." Elinor told her to hush, but looked pleased all the same.

They are children, Sansa thought. *They are silly little girls, even Elinor. They've never seen a battle, they've never seen a man die, they know nothing.* Their dreams were full of songs and stories, the way hers had been before Joffrey cut her father's head off. Sansa pitied them. Sansa envied them.

Margaery was different, though. Sweet and gentle, yet there was a little of her grandmother in her, too. The day before last she'd taken Sansa hawking. It was the first time she had been outside the city since the battle. The dead had been burned or buried, but the Mud Gate was scarred and splintered where Lord Stannis's rams had battered it, and the hulls of smashed ships could be seen along both sides of the Blackwater, charred masts poking from the shallows like gaunt black fingers. The only traffic was the flat-bottomed ferry that took them across the river, and when they reached the kingswood they found a wilderness of ash and charcoal and dead trees. But the waterfowl teemed in the marshes along the bay, and Sansa's merlin brought down three ducks while Margaery's peregrine took a heron in full flight.

"Willas has the best birds in the Seven Kingdoms," Margaery said when the two of them were briefly alone. "He flies an eagle sometimes. You will see, Sansa." She took her by the hand and gave it a squeeze. "Sister."

Sister. Sansa had once dreamt of having a sister like Margaery; beautiful and gentle, with all the world's graces at her command. Arya had been entirely unsatisfactory as sisters went. *How can I let my sister marry Joffrey?* she thought, and suddenly her eyes were full of tears. "Margaery, please," she said, "you mustn't." It was hard to get the words out. "You *mustn't* marry him. He's not like he seems, he's not. He'll hurt you."

"I shouldn't think so." Margaery smiled confidently. "It's brave of you to warn me, but you need not fear. Joff's spoiled and vain and I don't doubt that he's as cruel as you say, but Father forced him to name Loras to his Kingsguard before he would agree to the match. I shall have the finest knight in the Seven Kingdoms protecting me night and day, as Prince Aemon protected Naerys. So our little lion had best behave, hadn't he?" She laughed, and said, "Come, sweet sister, let's race back to the river. It will drive our guards quite mad." And without waiting for an answer, she put her heels into her horse and flew.

She is so brave, Sansa thought, galloping after her ... and yet, her doubts still gnawed at her. Ser Loras was a great knight, all agreed. But Joffrey had other Kingsguard, and gold cloaks and red cloaks besides, and when he was older he would command armies of his own. Aegon the Unworthy had never harmed Queen Naerys, perhaps for fear of their brother the Dragonknight ... but when another of his Kingsguard fell in love with one of his mistresses, the king had taken both their heads.

Ser Loras is a Tyrell, Sansa reminded herself. *That other knight was only a Toyne. His brothers had no armies, no way to avenge him but with swords.* Yet the more she thought about it all, the more she wondered. *Joff might restrain himself for a few turns, perhaps as long as a year, but soon or late he will show his claws, and when he does ...* The realm might have a second Kingslayer, and there would be war *inside* the city, as the men of the lion and the men of the rose made the gutters run red.

Sansa was surprised that Margaery did not see it too. *She is older than me, she must be wiser. And her father, Lord Tyrell, he knows what he is doing, surely. I am just being silly.*

When she told Ser Dontos that she was going to Highgarden to marry Willas Tyrell, she thought he would be relieved and pleased for her. Instead he had grabbed her arm and said, "You *cannot!*" in a voice as thick with horror as with wine. "I tell you, these Tyrells are only Lannisters with flowers. I beg of you, forget this folly, give your Florian a kiss, and promise you'll go ahead as we have planned. The night of Joffrey's wedding, that's not so long, wear the silver hair net and do as I told you, and afterward we make our escape." He tried to plant a kiss on her cheek.

Sansa slipped from his grasp and stepped away from him. "I won't. I can't. Something would go wrong. When I *wanted* to escape you wouldn't take me, and now I don't need to."

Dontos stared at her stupidly. "But the arrangements are made, sweetling. The ship to take you home, the boat to take you to the ship, your Florian did it all for his sweet Jonquil."

"I am sorry for all the trouble I put you to," she said, "but I have no need of boats and ships now."

"But it's all to see you *safe*."

"I will be safe in Highgarden. Willas will keep me safe."

"But he does not know you," Dontos insisted, "and he will not love you. Jonquil, Jonquil, open your sweet eyes, these Tyrells care nothing for you. It's your *claim* they mean to wed."

"My claim?" She was lost for a moment.

"Sweetling," he told her, "you are heir to Winterfell." He grabbed her again, pleading that she must not do this thing, and Sansa wrenched free and left him swaying beneath the heart tree. She had not visited the godswood since.

But she had not forgotten his words, either. *The heir to Winterfell*, she would think as she lay abed at night. *It's your claim they mean to wed.* Sansa had grown up with three brothers. She never thought to have a claim, but with Bran and Rickon dead . . . *It doesn't matter, there's still Robb, he's a man grown now, and soon he'll wed and have a son. Anyway, Willas Tyrell will have Highgarden, what would he want with Winterfell?*

Sometimes she would whisper his name into her pillow just to hear the sound of it. "Willas, Willas, Willas." Willas was as good a name as Loras, she supposed. They even sounded the same, a little. What did it matter about his leg? Willas would be Lord of Highgarden and she would be his lady.

She pictured the two of them sitting together in a garden with puppies in their laps, or listening to a singer strum upon a lute while they floated down the Mander on a pleasure barge. *If I give him sons, he may come to love me.* She would name them Eddard and Brandon and Rickon, and raise them all to be as valiant as Ser Loras. *And to hate Lannisters, too.* In Sansa's dreams, her children looked just like the brothers she had lost. Sometimes there was even a girl who looked like Arya.

She could never hold a picture of Willas long in her head, though; her imaginings kept turning him back into Ser Loras, young and graceful and beautiful. *You must not think of him like that*, she told herself. *Or else he may see the disappointment in your eyes when you meet, and how could he marry you then, knowing it was his brother you loved?* Willas Tyrell was twice her age, she reminded herself constantly, and lame as well, and perhaps even plump and red-faced like his father. But comely or no, he might be the only champion she would ever have.

Once she dreamed it was still her marrying Joff, not Margaery, and on their wedding night he turned into the headsman Ilyn Payne. She woke trembling. She did not want Margaery to suffer as she had, but she dreaded the thought that the Tyrells might refuse to go ahead with the wedding. *I warned her, I did, I told her the truth of him.* Perhaps Margaery did not believe her. Joff always played the perfect knight with her, as once he had with Sansa. *She will see his true nature soon enough. After the wedding if not before.* Sansa decided that she would light a candle to the Mother Above the next time she visited the sept, and ask her to protect Margaery from Joffrey's cruelty. And perhaps a candle to the Warrior as well, for Loras.

She would wear her new gown for the ceremony at the Great Sept of Baelor, she decided as the seamstress took her last measurement. *That must be why Cersei is having it made for me, so I will not look shabby at the wedding.* She really ought to have a different gown for the feast afterward but she supposed one of her old ones would do. She did not want to risk getting food or wine on the new one. *I must take it with me to Highgarden.* She wanted to look beautiful for Willas Tyrell. *Even if Dontos was right, and it is Winterfell he wants and not me, he still may come to love me for myself.* Sansa hugged herself tightly, wondering how long it would be before the gown was ready. She could scarcely wait to wear it.

ARYA

The rains came and went, but there was more grey sky than blue, and all the streams were running high. On the morning of the third day, Arya noticed that the moss was growing mostly on the wrong side of the trees. "We're going the wrong way," she said to Gendry, as they rode past an especially mossy elm. "We're going south. See how the moss is growing on the trunk?"

He pushed thick black hair from eyes and said, "We're following the road, that's all. The road goes south here."

We've been going south all day, she wanted to tell him. *And yesterday too, when we were riding along that streambed.* But she hadn't been paying close attention yesterday, so she couldn't be certain. "I think we're lost," she said in a low voice. "We shouldn't have left the river. All we had to do was follow it."

"The river bends and loops," said Gendry. "This is just a shorter way, I bet. Some secret outlaw way. Lem and Tom and them have been living here for years."

That was true. Arya bit her lip. "But the moss . . ."

"The way it's raining, we'll have moss growing from our ears before long," Gendry complained.

"Only from our *south* ear," Arya declared stubbornly. There was no use trying to convince the Bull of anything. Still, he was the only true friend she had, now that Hot Pie had left them.

"Sharna says she needs me to bake bread," he'd told her, the day they rode. "Anyhow I'm tired of rain and saddlesores and being scared all the time. There's ale here, and rabbit to eat, and the bread will be better when I make it. You'll see, when you come back. You will come back, won't you? When the war's done?" He remembered who she was then, and added, "My lady," reddening.

Arya didn't know if the war would ever be done, but she had nodded. "I'm sorry I beat you that time," she said. Hot Pie was stupid and craven, but he'd been with her all the way from King's Landing and she'd gotten used to him. "I broke your nose."

"You broke Lem's too." Hot Pie grinned. "That was good."

"Lem didn't think so," Arya said glumly. Then it was time to go. When Hot Pie asked if he might kiss milady's hand, she punched his shoulder. "Don't call me that. You're Hot Pie, and I'm Arry."

"I'm not Hot Pie here. Sharna just calls me Boy. The same as she calls the other boy. It's going to be confusing."

She missed him more than she thought she would, but Harwin made up for it some. She had told him about his father Hullen, and how she'd found him dying by the stables in the Red Keep, the day she fled. "He always said he'd die in a stable," Harwin said, "but we all thought some bad-tempered stallion would be his death, not a pack of lions." Arya told of Yoren and their escape from King's Landing as well, and much that had happened since, but she left out the stableboy she'd stabbed with Needle, and the guard whose throat she'd cut to get out of Harrenhal. Telling Harwin would be almost like telling her father, and there were some things that she could not bear having her father know.

Nor did she speak of Jaqen H'ghar and the three deaths he'd owed and paid. The iron coin he'd given her Arya kept tucked away beneath her belt, but sometimes at night she would take it out and remember how his face had melted and changed when he ran his hand across it. "*Valar morghulis,*" she would say under her breath. "Ser Gregor, Dunsen, Polliver, Raff the Sweetling. The Tickler and the Hound. Ser Ilyn, Ser Meryn, Queen Cersei, King Joffrey."

Only six Winterfell men remained of the twenty her father had sent west with Beric Dondarrion, Harwin told her, and they were scattered. "It was a trap, milady. Lord Tywin sent his Mountain across the Red Fork with fire and sword, hoping to draw your lord father. He planned for Lord Eddard to come west himself to deal with Gregor Clegane. If he had he would have been killed, or taken prisoner and traded for the Imp, who was your lady mother's captive at the time. Only the Kingslayer never knew Lord Tywin's plan, and when he heard about his brother's capture he attacked your father in the streets of King's Landing."

"I remember," said Arya. "He killed Jory." Jory had always smiled at her, when he wasn't telling her to get from underfoot.

"He killed Jory," Harwin agreed, "and your father's leg was broken when his horse fell on him. So Lord Eddard *couldn't* go west. He sent Lord Beric instead, with twenty of his own men and twenty from Winterfell, me among them. There were others besides. Thoros and Ser Raymun Darry and their men, Ser Gladden Wylde, a lord named Lothar Mallery. But Gregor was waiting for us at the Mummer's Ford, with men concealed on both banks. As we crossed he fell upon us from front and rear.

"I saw the Mountain slay Raymun Darry with a single blow so terrible that it took Darry's arm off at the elbow and killed the horse beneath him too. Gladden Wylde died there with him, and Lord Mallery was ridden down and drowned. We had lions on every side, and I thought I was doomed with the rest, but Alyn shouted commands and restored order to our ranks, and those still ahorse rallied around Thoros and cut our way free. Six score we'd been that morning. By dark no more than two score were left, and Lord Beric was gravely wounded. Thoros drew a foot of lance from his chest that night, and poured boiling wine into the hole it left.

"Every man of us was certain his lordship would be dead by daybreak. But Thoros prayed with him all night beside the fire, and when dawn came, he was still alive, and stronger than he'd been. It was a fortnight before he could mount a horse, but his courage kept us strong. He told us that our war had not ended at the Mummer's Ford, but only begun there, and that every man of ours who'd fallen would be avenged tenfold.

"By then the fighting had passed by us. The Mountain's men were only the van of Lord Tywin's host. They crossed the Red Fork in strength and swept up into the riverlands, burning everything in their path. We were so few that all we could do was harry their rear, but we told each other that we'd join up with King Robert when he marched west to crush Lord Tywin's rebellion. Only then we heard that Robert was dead, and Lord Eddard as well, and Cersei Lannister's whelp had ascended the Iron Throne.

"That turned the whole world on its head. We'd been sent out by the King's Hand to deal with outlaws, you see, but now we *were* the outlaws, and Lord Tywin was the Hand of the King. There was some wanted to yield then, but Lord Beric wouldn't hear of it. We were still king's men, he said, and these were the king's people the lions were savaging. If we could not fight for Robert, we would fight for them, until every man of us was dead. And so we did, but as we fought something queer happened. For every man we lost, two showed up to take his place. A few were knights or squires, of gentle birth, but most were common men – fieldhands and fiddlers and innkeeps, servants and shoemakers, even two septons. Men of all sorts, and women too, children, dogs . . ."

"*Dogs?*" said Arya.

"Aye." Harwin grinned. "One of our lads keeps the meanest dogs you'd ever want to see."

"I wish I had a good mean dog," said Arya wistfully. "A lion-killing dog." She'd had a direwolf once, Nymeria, but she'd thrown rocks at her until she fled, to keep the queen from killing her. *Could a direwolf kill a lion?* she wondered.

It rained again that afternoon, and long into the evening. Thankfully the outlaws had secret friends all over, so they did not need to camp out in the open or seek shelter beneath some leaky bower, as she and Hot Pie and Gendry had done so often.

That night they sheltered in a burned, abandoned village. At least it *seemed* to be abandoned, until Jack-Be-Lucky blew two short blasts and two long ones on his hunting horn. Then all sorts of people came crawling out of the ruins and up from secret cellars. They had ale and dried apples and some stale barley bread, and the outlaws had a goose that Anguy had brought down on the ride, so supper that night was almost a feast.

Arya was sucking the last bit of meat off a wing when one of the villagers turned to Lem Lemoncloak and said, "There were men through here not two days past, looking for the Kingslayer."

Lem snorted. "They'd do better looking in Riverrun. Down in the deepest dungeons, where it's nice and damp." His nose looked like a squashed apple, red and raw and swollen, and his mood was foul.

"No," another villager said. "He's escaped."

The Kingslayer. Arya could feel the hair on the back of her neck prickling. She held her breath to listen.

"Could that be true?" Tom o' Sevens said.

"I'll not believe it," said the one-eyed man in the rusty pothelm. The other outlaws called him Jack-Be-Lucky, though losing an eye didn't seem very lucky to Arya. "I've had me a taste o' them dungeons. How could he escape?"

The villagers could only shrug at that. Greenbeard stroked his thick grey-and-green whiskers and said, "The wolves will drown in blood if the Kingslayer's loose again. Thoros must be told. The Lord of Light will show him Lannister in the flames."

"There's a fine fire burning here," said Anguy, smiling.

Greenbeard laughed, and cuffed the archer's ear. "Do I look a priest to you, Archer? When Pello of Tyrosh peers into the fire, the cinders singe his beard."

Lem cracked his knuckles and said, "Wouldn't Lord Beric love to capture Jaime Lannister, though . . ."

"Would he hang him, Lem?" one of the village women asked. "It'd be half a shame to hang a man as pretty as that one."

"A trial first!" said Anguy. "Lord Beric always gives them a trial, you know that." He smiled. "*Then* he hangs them."

There was laughter all around. Then Tom drew his fingers across the strings of his woodharp and broke into soft song.

> *The brothers of the Kingswood,*
> > *they were an outlaw band.*
> *The forest was their castle,*
> > *but they roamed across the land.*
> *No man's gold was safe from them,*
> > *nor any maiden's hand.*
> *Oh, the brothers of the Kingswood,*
> > *that fearsome outlaw band . . .*

Warm and dry in a corner between Gendry and Harwin, Arya listened to the singing for a time, then closed her eyes and drifted off to sleep. She dreamt of home; not Riverrun, but Winterfell. It was not a good dream, though. She was alone outside the castle, up to her knees in mud. She could see the grey walls ahead of her, but when she tried to reach the gates every step seemed harder than the one before, and the castle faded before her, until it looked more like smoke than granite. And there were wolves as well, gaunt grey shapes stalking through the trees all around her, their eyes shining. Whenever she looked at them, she remembered the taste of blood.

The next morning they left the road to cut across the fields. The wind was gusting, sending dry brown leaves swirling around the hooves of their horses, but for once it did not rain. When the sun came out from behind a cloud, it was so bright Arya had to pull her hood forward to keep it out of her eyes.

She reined up very suddenly. "We *are* going the wrong way!"

Gendry groaned. "What is it, moss again?"

"Look at the *sun*," she said. "We're going *south!*" Arya rummaged in her saddlebag for the map, so she could show them. "We should never have left the Trident. See." She unrolled the map on her leg. All of them were looking at her now. "See, there's Riverrun, between the rivers."

"As it happens," said Jack-Be-Lucky, "we know where Riverrun is. Every man o' us."

"You're not going to Riverrun," Lem told her bluntly.

I was almost there, Arya thought. *I should have let them take our horses. I could have walked the rest of the way.* She remembered her dream then, and bit her lip.

"Ah, don't look so hurt, child," said Tom Sevenstrings. "No harm will come to you, you have my word on that."

"The word of a *liar!*"

"No one lied," said Lem. "We made no promises. It's not for us to say what's to be done with you."

Lem was not the leader, though, no more than Tom; that was Greenbeard, the Tyroshi. Arya turned to face him. "Take me to Riverrun and you'll be rewarded," she said desperately.

"Little one," Greenbeard answered, "a peasant may skin a common squirrel for his pot, but if he finds a gold squirrel in his tree he takes it to his lord, or he will wish he did."

"I'm not a squirrel," Arya insisted.

"You are." Greenbeard laughed. "A little gold squirrel who's off to see the lightning lord, whether she wills it or not. He'll know what's to be done with you. I'll wager he sends you back to your lady mother, just as you wish."

Tom Sevenstrings nodded. "Aye, that's like Lord Beric. He'll do right by you, see if he don't."

Lord Beric Dondarrion. Arya remembered all she'd heard at Harrenhal, from the Lannisters and the Bloody Mummers alike. Lord Beric the wisp o' the wood. Lord Beric who'd been killed by Vargo Hoat and before that by Ser Amory Lorch, and twice by the Mountain That Rides. *If he won't send me home maybe I'll kill him too.* "Why do I have to see Lord Beric?" she asked quietly.

"We bring him all our highborn captives," said Anguy.

Captive. Arya took a breath to still her soul. *Calm as still water.* She glanced at the outlaws on their horses, and turned her horse's head. *Now, quick as a snake,* she thought, as she slammed her heels into the courser's flank. Right between Greenbeard and Jack-Be-Lucky she flew, and caught one glimpse of Gendry's startled face as his mare moved out of her way. And then she was in the open field, and running.

North or south, east or west, that made no matter now. She could find the way to Riverrun later, once she'd lost them. Arya leaned forward in the saddle and urged the horse to a gallop. Behind her the outlaws were cursing and shouting at her to come back. She shut her ears to the calls, but when she glanced back over her shoulder four of them were coming after her, Anguy and Harwin and Greenbeard racing side by side with Lem 'farther back, his big yellow cloak flapping behind him as he rode. "Swift as a deer," she told her mount. "Run, now, *run.*"

Arya dashed across brown weedy fields, through waist-high grass and piles of dry leaves that flurried and flew when her horse galloped past. There were woods to her left, she saw. *I can lose them there.* A dry ditch ran along one side of the field, but she leapt it without breaking stride, and plunged in among the stand of elm and yew and birch trees. A quick peek back showed Anguy and Harwin still hard on her heels. Greenbeard had fallen behind, though, and she could not see Lem at all. "Faster," she told her horse, "you can, you *can.*"

Between two elms she rode, and never paused to see which side the moss was growing on. She leapt a rotten log and swung wide around a monstrous deadfall, jagged with broken branches. Then up a gentle slope and down the other side, slowing and speeding up again, her horse's shoes striking sparks off the flintstones underfoot. At the top of the hill she glanced back. Harwin had pushed ahead of Anguy, but both were coming hard. Greenbeard had fallen further back and seemed to be flagging.

A stream barred her way. She splashed down into it, through water choked with wet brown leaves. Some clung to her horse's legs as they climbed the other side. The undergrowth was thicker here, the ground so full of roots and rocks that she had to slow, but she kept as good a pace as she dared. Another hill before her, this one steeper. Up she went, and down again. *How big are these woods?* she wondered. She had the faster horse, she knew that, she had stolen one of Roose Bolton's best from the stables at Harrenhal, but his speed was wasted here. *I need to find the fields again. I need to find a road.* Instead she found a game trail. It was narrow and uneven, but it was something. She raced along it, branches whipping at her face. One snagged her hood and yanked it back, and for half a heartbeat she feared they had caught her. A vixen burst from the brush as she passed, startled by the fury of her flight. The game trail brought her to another stream. Or was it the same one? Had she gotten turned around? There was no time to puzzle it out, she could hear their horses crashing through the trees behind her. Thorns scratched at her face like the cats she used to chase in King's Landing. Sparrows exploded from the branches of an alder. But the trees were thinning now, and suddenly she was out of them. Broad level fields stretched before her, all weeds and wild wheat, sodden and trampled. Arya kicked her horse back to a gallop. *Run,* she thought, *run for Riverrun, run for home.* Had she lost them? She took one quick look, and there was Harwin six yards back and gaining. *No,* she thought, *no, he can't, not him, it isn't fair.*

Both horses were lathered and flagging by the time he came up beside her, reached over, and grabbed her bridle. Arya was breathing hard herself then. She knew the fight was done. "You ride like a northman, milady," Harwin said when he'd drawn them to a halt. "Your aunt was the same. Lady Lyanna. But my father was master of horse, remember."

The look she gave him was full of hurt. "I thought you were my father's man."

"Lord Eddard's dead, milady. I belong to the lightning lord now, and to my brothers."

"What brothers?" Old Hullen had fathered no other sons that Arya could remember.

"Anguy, Lem, Tom o' Sevens, Jack and Greenbeard, all of them. We mean your brother Robb no ill, milady . . . but it's not him we fight for. He has an army all his own, and many a great lord to bend the knee. The smallfolk have only us." He gave her a searching look. "Can you understand what I am telling you?"

"Yes." That he was not Robb's man, she understood well enough. And that she was his captive. *I could have stayed with Hot Pie. We could have taken the little boat and sailed it up to Riverrun.* She had been better off as Squab. No one would take Squab captive, or Nan, or Weasel, or Arry the orphan boy. *I was a wolf,* she thought, *but now I'm just some stupid little lady again.*

"Will you ride back peaceful now," Harwin asked her, "or must I tie you up and throw you across your horse?"

"I'll ride peaceful," she said sullenly. *For now.*

SAMWELL

Sobbing, Sam took another step. *This is the last one, the very last, I can't go on, I can't.* But his feet moved again. One and then the other. They took a step, and then another, and he thought, *They're not my feet, they're someone else's, someone else is walking, it can't be me.*

When he looked down he could see them stumbling through the snow; shapeless things, and clumsy. His boots had been black, he seemed to remember, but the snow had caked around them, and now they were misshapen white balls. Like two clubfeet made of ice.

It would not stop, the snow. The drifts were up past his knees, and a crust covered his lower legs like a pair of white greaves. His steps were dragging, lurching. The heavy pack he carried made him look like some monstrous hunchback. And he was tired, so tired. *I can't go on. Mother have mercy, I can't.*

Every fourth or fifth step he had to reach down and tug up his swordbelt. He had lost the sword on the Fist, but the scabbard still weighed down the belt. He did have two knives; the dragonglass dagger Jon had given him and the steel one he cut his meat with. All that weight dragged heavy, and his belly was so big and round that if he forgot to tug the belt slipped right off and tangled round his ankles, no matter how tight he cinched it. He had tried belting it *above* his belly once, but then it came almost to his armpits. Grenn had laughed himself sick at the sight of it, and Dolorous Edd had said, "I knew a man once who wore his sword on a chain around his neck like that. One day he stumbled, and the hilt went up his nose."

Sam was stumbling himself. There were rocks beneath the snow, and the roots of trees, and sometimes deep holes in the frozen ground. Black Bernarr had stepped in one and broken his ankle three days past, or maybe four, or . . . he did not know how long it had been, truly. The Lord Commander had put Bernarr on a horse after that.

Sobbing, Sam took another step. It felt more like he was falling down than walking, falling endlessly but never hitting the ground, just falling forward and forward. *I have to stop, it hurts too much. I'm so cold and tired, I need to sleep, just a little sleep beside a fire, and a bite to eat that isn't frozen.*

But if he stopped he died. He knew that. They all knew that, the few who were left. They had been fifty when they fled the Fist, maybe more, but some had wandered off in the snow, a few wounded had bled to death . . . and sometimes Sam heard shouts behind him, from the rear guard, and once an *awful* scream. When he heard that he had run, twenty yards or thirty, as fast and as far as he could, his half-frozen feet kicking up the snow. He would be running still if his legs were stronger. *They are behind us, they are still behind us, they are taking us one by one.*

Sobbing, Sam took another step. He had been cold so long he was forgetting what it was like to feel warm. He wore three pairs of hose, two layers of smallclothes beneath a double lambswool tunic, and over that a thick quilted coat that padded him against the cold steel of his chainmail. Over the hauberk he had a loose surcoat, over *that* a triple-thick cloak with a bone button that fastened tight under his chins. Its hood flopped forward over his forehead. Heavy fur mitts covered his hands over thin wool-and-leather gloves, a scarf was wrapped snugly about the lower half of his face, and he had a tight-fitting fleece-lined cap to pull down over his ears beneath the hood. And still the cold was in him. His feet especially. He couldn't even feel them now, but only yesterday they had hurt so bad he could hardly bear to stand on them, let alone walk. Every step made him want to scream. Was that yesterday? He could not remember. He had not slept since the Fist, not once since the horn had blown. Unless it was while he was walking. Could a man walk while he was sleeping? Sam did not know, or else he had forgotten.

Sobbing, he took another step. The snow swirled down around him. Sometimes it fell from a white sky, and sometimes from a black, but that was all that remained of day and night. He wore it on his shoulders like a second cloak, and it piled up high atop the pack he carried and made it even heavier and harder to bear. The small of his back hurt abominably, as if someone had shoved a knife in there and was wiggling it back and forth with every step. His shoulders were in agony from the weight of the mail. He would have given most anything to take it off, but he was afraid to. Anyway he would have needed to remove his cloak and surcoat to get at it, and then the cold would have him.

If only I was stronger ... He wasn't, though, and it was no good wishing. Sam was weak, and fat, so very fat, he could hardly bear his own weight, the mail was much too much for him. It felt as though it was rubbing his shoulders raw, despite the layers of cloth and quilt between the steel and skin. The only thing he could do was cry, and when he cried the tears froze on his cheeks.

Sobbing, he took another step. The crust was broken where he set his feet, otherwise he did not think he could have moved at all. Off to the left and right, half-seen through the silent trees, torches turned to vague orange haloes in the falling snow. When he turned his head he could see them, slipping silent through the wood, bobbing up and down and back and forth. *The Old Bear's ring of fire,* he reminded himself, *and woe to him who leaves it.* As he walked, it seemed as if he were chasing the torches ahead of him, but they had legs as well, longer and stronger than his, so he could never catch them.

Yesterday he begged for them to let him be one of the torchbearers, even if it meant walking outside of the column with the darkness pressing close. He wanted the fire, dreamed of the fire. *If I had the fire, I would not be cold.* But someone reminded him that he'd *had* a torch at the start, but he'd dropped it in the snow and snuffed the fire out. Sam didn't remember dropping any torch, but he supposed it was true. He was too weak to hold his arm up for long. Was it Edd who reminded him about the torch, or Grenn? He couldn't remember that either. *Fat and weak and useless, even my wits are freezing now.* He took another step.

He had wrapped his scarf over his nose and mouth, but it was covered with snot now, and so stiff he feared it must be frozen to his face. Even breathing was hard, and the air was so cold it hurt to swallow it. "Mother have mercy," he muttered in a hushed husky voice beneath the frozen mask. "Mother have mercy, Mother have mercy, Mother have mercy." With each prayer he took another step, dragging his legs through the snow. "Mother have mercy, Mother have mercy, Mother have mercy."

His own mother was a thousand leagues south, safe with his sisters and his little brother Dickon in the keep at Horn Hill. *She can't hear me, no more than the Mother Above.* The Mother was merciful, all the septons agreed, but the Seven had no power beyond the Wall. This was where the old gods ruled, the nameless gods of the trees and the wolves and the snows. "Mercy," he whispered then, to whatever might be listening, old gods or new, or demons too, "oh, mercy, mercy me, mercy me."

Maslyn screamed for mercy. Why had he suddenly remembered that? It was nothing he wanted to remember. The man had stumbled backward, dropping his sword, pleading, yielding, even yanking off his thick black glove and thrusting it up before him as if it were a gauntlet. He was still shrieking for quarter as the wight lifted him in the air by the throat and near ripped the head off him. *The dead have no mercy left in them, and the Others . . . no, I mustn't think of that, don't think, don't remember, just walk, just walk, just walk.*

Sobbing, he took another step.

A root beneath the crust caught his toe, and Sam tripped and fell heavily to one knee, so hard he bit his tongue. He could taste the blood in his mouth, warmer than anything he had tasted since the Fist. *This is the end,* he thought. Now that he had fallen he could not seem to find the strength to rise again. He groped for a tree branch and clutched it tight, trying to pull himself back to his feet, but his stiff legs would not support him. The mail was too heavy, and he was too fat besides, and too weak, and too tired.

"Back on your feet, Piggy," someone growled as he went past, but Sam paid him no mind. *I'll just lie down in the snow and close my eyes.* It wouldn't be so bad, dying here. He couldn't possibly be any colder, and after a little while he wouldn't be able to feel the ache in his lower back or the terrible pain in his shoulders, no more than he could feel his feet. *I won't be the first to die, they can't say I was.* Hundreds had died on the Fist, they had died all around him, and more had died after, he'd seen them. Shivering, Sam released his grip on the tree and eased himself down in the snow. It was cold and wet, he knew, but he could scarcely feel it through all his clothing. He stared upward at the pale white sky as snowflakes drifted down upon his stomach and his chest and his eyelids. *The snow will cover me like a thick white blanket. It will be warm under the snow, and if they speak of me they'll have to say I died a man of the Night's Watch. I did. I did. I did my duty. No one can say I forswore myself. I'm fat and I'm weak and I'm craven, but I did my duty.*

The ravens had been his responsibility. That was why they had brought him along. He hadn't wanted to go, he'd told them so, he'd told them all what a big coward he was. But Maester Aemon was very old and blind besides, so they had to send Sam to tend to the ravens. The Lord Commander had given him his orders when they made their camp on the Fist. "You're no fighter. We both know that, boy. If it happens that we're attacked, don't go trying to prove otherwise, you'll just get in the way. You're to send a message. And don't come running to ask what the letter should say. Write it out yourself, and send one bird to Castle Black and another to the Shadow Tower." The Old Bear pointed a gloved finger right in Sam's face. "I don't care if you're so scared you foul your breeches, and I don't care if a thousand wildlings are coming over the walls howling for your blood, *you get those birds off,* or I swear I'll hunt you through all seven hells and make you damn sorry that you didn't." And Mormont's own raven had bobbed its head up and down and croaked, *"Sorry, sorry, sorry."*

Sam *was* sorry; sorry he hadn't been braver, or stronger, or good with

swords, that he hadn't been a better son to his father and a better brother
to Dickon and the girls. He was sorry to die too, but better men had died
on the Fist, good men and true, not squeaking fat boys like him. At least
he would not have the Old Bear hunting him through hell, though. *I got
the birds off. I did that right, at least.* He had written out the messages
ahead of time, short messages and simple, telling of an attack on the Fist
of the First Men, and then he had tucked them away safe in his parchment
pouch, hoping he would never need to send them.

When the horns blew Sam had been sleeping. He thought he was
dreaming them at first, but when he opened his eyes snow was falling
on the camp and the black brothers were all grabbing bows and spears
and running toward the ringwall. Chett was the only one nearby, Maester
Aemon's old steward with the face full of boils and the big wen on his
neck. Sam had never seen so much fear on a man's face as he saw on
Chett's when that third blast came moaning through the trees. "Help
me get the birds off," he pleaded, but the other steward had turned and
run off, dagger in hand. *He has the dogs to care for*, Sam remembered.
Probably the Lord Commander had given him some orders as well.

His fingers had been so stiff and clumsy in the gloves, and he was
shaking from fear and cold, but he found the parchment pouch and dug
out the messages he'd written. The ravens were shrieking furiously, and
when he opened the Castle Black cage one of them flew right in his face.
Two more escaped before Sam could catch one, and when he did it pecked
him through his glove, drawing blood. Yet somehow he held on long
enough to attach the little roll of parchment. The warhorn had fallen
silent by then, but the Fist rang with shouted commands and the clatter
of steel. "*Fly!*" Sam called as he tossed the raven into the air.

The birds in the Shadow Tower cage were screaming and fluttering
about so madly that he was afraid to open the door, but he made himself
do it anyway. This time he caught the first raven that tried to escape. A
moment later, it was clawing its way up through the falling snow, bearing
word of the attack.

His duty done, he finished dressing with clumsy, frightened fingers,
donning his cap and surcoat and hooded cloak and buckling on his swordbelt, buckling it real tight so it wouldn't fall down. Then he found his
pack and stuffed all his things inside, spare smallclothes and dry socks,
the dragonglass arrowheads and spearhead Jon had given him and the old
horn too, his parchments, inks, and quills, the maps he'd been drawing,
and a rock-hard garlic sausage he'd been saving since the Wall. He tied
it all up and shouldered the pack onto his back. *The Lord Commander
said I wasn't to rush to the ringwall*, he recalled, *but he said I shouldn't
come running to him either.* Sam took a deep breath and realized that
he did not know what to do next.

He remembered turning in a circle, lost, the fear growing inside him as it always did. There were dogs barking and horses trumpeting, but the snow muffled the sounds and made them seem far away. Sam could see nothing beyond three yards, not even the torches burning along the low stone wall that ringed the crown of the hill. *Could the torches have gone out?* That was too scary to think about. *The horn blew thrice long, three long blasts means Others.* The white walkers of the wood, the cold shadows, the monsters of the tales that made him squeak and tremble as a boy, riding their giant ice-spiders, hungry for blood . . .

Awkwardly he drew his sword, and plodded heavily through the snow holding it. A dog ran past barking, and he saw some of the men from the Shadow Tower, big bearded men with longaxes and eight-foot spears. He felt safer for their company, so he followed them to the wall. When he saw the torches still burning atop the ring of stones a shudder of relief went through him.

The black brothers stood with swords and spears in hand, watching the snow fall, waiting. Ser Mallador Locke went by on his horse, wearing a snow-speckled helm. Sam stood well back behind the others, looking for Grenn or Dolorous Edd. *If I have to die, let me die beside my friends,* he remembered thinking. But all the men around him were strangers, Shadow Tower men under the command of the ranger named Blane.

"Here they come," he heard a brother say.

"Notch," said Blane, and twenty black arrows were pulled from as many quivers, and notched to as many bowstrings.

"Gods be good, there's hundreds," a voice said softly.

"Draw," Blane said, and then, "hold." Sam could not see and did not want to see. The men of the Night's Watch stood behind their torches, waiting with arrows pulled back to their ears, as *something* came up that dark, slippery slope through the snow. "Hold," Blane said again, "hold, hold." And then, "Loose."

The arrows whispered as they flew.

A ragged cheer went up from the men along the ringwall, but it died quickly. "They're not stopping, m'lord," a man said to Blane, and another shouted, "*More!* Look there, coming from the trees," and yet another said, "Gods ha' mercy, they's crawling. They's almost here, *they's on us!*" Sam had been backing away by then, shaking like the last leaf on the tree when the wind kicks up, as much from cold as from fear. It had been very cold that night. *Even colder than now. The snow feels almost warm. I feel better now. A little rest was all I needed. Maybe in a little while I'll be strong enough to walk again. In a little while.*

A horse stepped past his head, a shaggy grey beast with snow in its mane and hooves crusted with ice. Sam watched it come and watched it go. Another appeared from out of the falling snow, with a man in black leading it. When he saw Sam in his path he cursed him and led the horse around. *I wish I had a horse*, he thought. *If I had a horse I could keep going. I could sit, and even sleep some in the saddle.* Most of their mounts had been lost at the Fist, though, and those that remained carried their food, their torches, and their wounded. Sam wasn't wounded. *Only fat and weak, and the greatest craven in the Seven Kingdoms.*

He was *such* a coward. Lord Randyll, his father, had always said so, and he had been right. Sam was his heir, but he had never been worthy, so his father had sent him away to the Wall. His little brother Dickon would inherit the Tarly lands and castle, and the greatsword Heartsbane that the lords of Horn Hill had borne so proudly for centuries. He wondered whether Dickon would shed a tear for his brother who died in the snow, somewhere off beyond the edge of the world. *Why should he? A coward's not worth weeping over.* He had heard his father tell his mother as much, half a hundred times. The Old Bear knew it too.

"Fire arrows," the Lord Commander roared that night on the Fist, when he appeared suddenly astride his horse, "give them flame." It was then he noticed Sam there quaking. *"Tarly!* Get out of here! Your place is with the ravens."

"I . . . I . . . I got the messages away."

"Good." On Mormont's shoulder his own raven echoed, *"Good, good."* The Lord Commander looked huge in fur and mail. Behind his black iron visor, his eyes were fierce. "You're in the way here. Go back to your cages. If I need to send another message, I don't want to have to find you first. See that the birds are ready." He did not wait for a response, but turned his horse and trotted around the ring, shouting, "Fire! Give them fire!"

Sam did not need to be told twice. He went back to the birds, as fast as his fat legs could carry him. *I should write the message ahead of time*, he thought, *so we can get the birds away as fast as need be.* It took him longer than it should have to light his little fire, to warm the frozen ink. He sat beside it on a rock with quill and parchment, and wrote his messages.

Attacked amidst snow and cold, but we've thrown them back with fire arrows, he wrote, as he heard Thoren Smallwood's voice ring out with a command of, "Notch, draw . . . loose." The flight of arrows made a sound as sweet as a mother's prayer. "Burn, you dead bastards, burn," Dywen sang out, cackling. The brothers cheered and cursed. *All safe*, he wrote. *We remain on the Fist of the First Men.* Sam hoped they were better archers than him.

He put that note aside and found another blank parchment. *Still fighting on the Fist, amidst heavy snow*, he wrote when someone shouted, "They're still coming." *Result uncertain.* "Spears," someone said. It might have been Ser Mallador, but Sam could not swear to it. *Wights attacked us on the Fist, in snow,* he wrote, *but we drove them off with fire.* He turned his head. Through the drifting snow, all he could see was the huge fire at the center of the camp, with mounted men moving restlessly around it. The reserve, he knew, ready to ride down anything that breached the ringwall. They had armed themselves with torches in place of swords, and were lighting them in the flames.

Wights all around us, he wrote, when he heard the shouts from the north face. *Coming up from north and south at once. Spears and swords don't stop them, only fire.* "Loose, loose, loose," a voice screamed in the night, and another shouted, "Bloody huge," and a third voice said, "A giant!" and a fourth insisted, "A bear, a *bear!*" A horse shrieked and the hounds began to bay, and there was so much shouting that Sam couldn't make out the voices anymore. He wrote faster, note after note. *Dead wildlings, and a giant, or maybe a bear, on us, all around.* He heard the crash of steel on wood, which could only mean one thing. *Wights over the ringwall. Fighting inside the camp.* A dozen mounted brothers pounded past him toward the east wall, burning brands streaming flames in each rider's hand. *Lord Commander Mormont is meeting them with fire. We've won. We're winning. We're holding our own. We're cutting our way free and retreating for the Wall. We're trapped on the Fist, hard pressed.*

One of the Shadow Tower men came staggering out of the darkness to fall at Sam's feet. He crawled within a foot of the fire before he died. *Lost,* Sam wrote, *the battle's lost. We're all lost.*

Why must he remember the fight at the Fist? He didn't want to remember. Not *that.* He tried to make himself remember his mother, or his little sister Talla, or that girl Gilly at Craster's Keep. Someone was shaking him by the shoulder. "Get up," a voice said. "Sam, you can't go to sleep here. Get up and keep walking."

I wasn't asleep, I was remembering. "Go away," he said, his words frosting in the cold air. "I'm well. I want to rest."

"Get up." Grenn's voice, harsh and husky. He loomed over Sam, his blacks crusty with snow. "There's no resting, the Old Bear said. You'll die."

"Grenn." He smiled. "No, truly, I'm good here. You just go on. I'll catch you after I've rested a bit longer."

"You won't." Grenn's thick brown beard was frozen all around his mouth. It made him look like some old man. "You'll freeze, or the Others will get you. Sam, *get up!*"

The night before they left the Wall, Pyp had teased Grenn the way he did, Sam remembered, smiling and saying how Grenn was a good choice for the ranging, since he was too stupid to be terrified. Grenn hotly denied it until he realized what he was saying. He was stocky and thick-necked and strong – Ser Alliser Thorne had called him "Aurochs," the same way he called Sam "Ser Piggy" and Jon "Lord Snow" – but he had always treated Sam nice enough. *That was only because of Jon, though. If it weren't for Jon, none of them would have liked me.* And now Jon was gone, lost in the Skirling Pass with Qhorin Halfhand, most likely dead. Sam would have cried for him, but those tears would only freeze as well, and he could scarcely keep his eyes open now.

A tall brother with a torch stopped beside them, and for a wonderful moment Sam felt the warmth on his face. "Leave him," the man said to Grenn. "If they can't walk, they're done. Save your strength for yourself, Grenn."

"He'll get up," Grenn replied. "He only needs a hand."

The man moved on, taking the blessed warmth with him. Grenn tried to pull Sam to his feet. "That hurts," he complained. "Stop it. Grenn, you're hurting my arm. Stop it."

"You're too bloody heavy." Grenn jammed his hands into Sam's armpits, gave a grunt, and hauled him upright. But the moment he let go, the fat boy sat back down in the snow. Grenn kicked him, a solid thump that cracked the crust of snow around his boot and sent it flying everywhere. "Get *up!*" He kicked him again. "Get up and walk. You have to walk."

Sam fell over sideways, curling up into a tight ball to protect himself from the kicks. He hardly felt them through all his wool and leather and mail, but even so, they hurt. *I thought Grenn was my friend. You shouldn't kick your friends. Why won't they let me be? I just need to rest, that's all, to rest and sleep some, and maybe die a little.*

"If you take the torch, I can take the fat boy."

Suddenly he was jerked up into the cold air, away from his sweet soft snow; he was floating. There was an arm under his knees, and another one under his back. Sam raised his head and blinked. A face loomed close, a broad brutal face with a flat nose and small dark eyes and a thicket of coarse brown beard. He had seen the face before, but it took him a moment to remember. *Paul. Small Paul.* Melting ice ran down into his eyes from the heat of the torch. "Can you carry him?" he heard Grenn ask.

"I carried a calf once was heavier than him. I carried him down to his mother so he could get a drink of milk."

Sam's head bobbed up and down with every step that Small Paul took. "Stop it," he muttered, "put me down, I'm not a baby. I'm a man of the Night's Watch." He sobbed. "Just let me die."

"Be quiet, Sam," said Grenn. "Save your strength. Think about your sisters and brother. Maester Aemon. Your favorite foods. Sing a song if you like."

"Aloud?"

"In your head."

Sam knew a hundred songs, but when he tried to think of one he couldn't. The words had all gone from his head. He sobbed again and said, "I don't know any songs, Grenn. I did know some, but now I don't."

"Yes you do," said Grenn. "How about 'The Bear and the Maiden Fair,' everybody knows that one. *A bear there was, a bear, a bear! All black and brown and covered with hair!*"

"No, not that one," Sam pleaded. The bear that had come up the Fist had no hair left on its rotted flesh. He didn't want to think about bears. "No songs. Please, Grenn."

"Think about your ravens, then."

"They were never mine." *They were the Lord Commander's ravens, the ravens of the Night's Watch.* "They belonged to Castle Black and the Shadow Tower."

Small Paul frowned. "Chett said I could have the Old Bear's raven, the one that talks. I saved food for it and everything." He shook his head. "I forgot, though. I left the food where I hid it." He plodded onward, pale white breath coming from his mouth with every step, then suddenly said, "Could I have one of your ravens? Just the one. I'd never let Lark eat it."

"They're gone," said Sam. "I'm sorry." *So sorry.* "They're flying back to the Wall now." He had set the birds free when he'd heard the warhorns sound once more, calling the Watch to horse. *Two short blasts and a long one, that was the call to mount up.* But there was no reason to mount, unless to abandon the Fist, and that meant the battle was lost. The fear bit him so strong then that it was all Sam could do to open the cages. Only as he watched the last raven flap up into the snowstorm did he realize that he had forgotten to send any of the messages he'd written.

"No," he'd squealed, "oh, no, oh, no." The snow fell and the horns blew; *ahooo ahooo ahoooooooooooooooooooooo*, they cried, *to horse, to horse, to horse.* Sam saw two ravens perched on a rock and ran after them, but the birds flapped off lazily through the swirling snow, in opposite directions. He chased one, his breath puffing out his nose in thick white clouds, stumbled, and found himself ten feet from the ringwall.

After that . . . he remembered the dead coming over the stones with arrows in their faces and through their throats. Some were all in ringmail and some were almost naked . . . wildlings, most of them, but a few wore faded blacks. He remembered one of the Shadow Tower men shoving his spear through a wight's pale soft belly and out his back, and how the thing staggered right up the shaft and reached out his black hands and twisted the brother's head around until blood came out his mouth. That was when his bladder let go the first time, he was almost sure.

He did not remember running, but he must have, because the next he knew he was near the fire half a camp away, with old Ser Ottyn Wythers and some archers. Ser Ottyn was on his knees in the snow, staring at the chaos around them, until a riderless horse came by and kicked him in the face. The archers paid him no mind. They were loosing fire arrows at shadows in the dark. Sam saw one wight hit, saw the flames engulf it, but there were a dozen more behind it, and a huge pale shape that must have been the bear, and soon enough the bowmen had no arrows.

And then Sam found himself on a horse. It wasn't his own horse, and he never recalled mounting up either. Maybe it was the horse that had smashed Ser Ottyn's face in. The horns were still blowing, so he kicked the horse and turned him toward the sound.

In the midst of carnage and chaos and blowing snow, he found Dolorous Edd sitting on his garron with a plain black banner on a spear. "Sam," Edd said when he saw him, "would you wake me, please? I am having this terrible nightmare."

More men were mounting up every moment. The warhorns called them back. *Ahooo ahooo ahoooooooooooooooooooooo.* "They're over the west wall, m'lord," Thoren Smallwood screamed at the Old Bear, as he fought to control his horse. "I'll send reserves . . ."

"*NO!*" Mormont had to bellow at the top of his lungs to be heard over the horns. "Call them back, we have to cut our way out." He stood in his stirrups, his black cloak snapping in the wind, the fire shining off his armor. "*Spearhead!*" he roared. "Form wedge, we ride. Down the south face, then east!"

"My lord, the south slope's crawling with them!"

"The others are too steep," Mormont said. "We have –"

His garron screamed and reared and almost threw him as the bear came staggering through the snow. Sam pissed himself all over again. *I didn't think I had any more left inside me.* The bear was dead, pale and rotting, its fur and skin all sloughed off and half its right arm burned to bone, yet still it came on. Only its eyes lived. *Bright blue, just as Jon said.* They shone like frozen stars. Thoren Smallwood charged, his longsword shining all orange and red from the light of the fire. His swing near took the bear's head off. And then the bear took his.

"*RIDE!*" the Lord Commander shouted, wheeling.

They were at the gallop by the time they reached the ring. Sam had always been too frightened to jump a horse before, but when the low stone wall loomed up before him he knew he had no choice. He kicked and closed his eyes and whimpered, and the garron took him over, somehow, *somehow*, the garron took him over. The rider to his right came crashing down in a tangle of steel and leather and screaming horseflesh, and then the wights were swarming over him and the wedge was closing up. They plunged down the hillside at a run, through clutching black hands and burning blue eyes and blowing snow. Horses stumbled and rolled, men were swept from their saddles, torches spun through the air, axes and swords hacked at dead flesh, and Samwell Tarly sobbed, clutching desperately to his horse with a strength he never knew he had.

He was in the middle of the flying spearhead with brothers on either side, and before and behind him as well. A dog ran with them for a ways, bounding down the snowy slope and in and out among the horses, but it could not keep up. The wights stood their ground and were ridden down and trampled underhoof. Even as they fell they clutched at swords and stirrups and the legs of passing horses. Sam saw one claw open a garron's belly with its right hand while it clung to the saddle with its left.

Suddenly the trees were all about them, and Sam was splashing through a frozen stream with the sounds of slaughter dwindling behind. He turned, breathless with relief . . . until a man in black leapt from the brush and yanked him out of the saddle. Who he was, Sam never saw; he was up in an instant, and galloping away the next. When he tried to run after the horse, his feet tangled in a root and he fell hard on his face and lay weeping like a baby until Dolorous Edd found him there.

That was his last coherent memory of the Fist of the First Men. Later, hours later, he stood shivering among the other survivors, half mounted and half afoot. They were miles from the Fist by then, though Sam did not remember how. Dywen had led down five packhorses, heavy laden with food and oil and torches, and three had made it this far. The Old Bear made them redistribute the loads, so the loss of any one horse and its provisions would not be such a catastrophe. He took garrons from the healthy men and gave them to the wounded, organized the walkers, and set torches to guard their flanks and rear. *All I need do is walk*, Sam told himself, as he took that first step toward home. But before an hour was gone he had begun to struggle, and to lag . . .

They were lagging now as well, he saw. He remembered Pyp saying once how Small Paul was the strongest man in the Watch. *He must be, to carry me.* Yet even so, the snow was growing deeper, the ground more treacherous, and Paul's strides had begun to shorten. More horsemen passed, wounded men who looked at Sam with dull incurious eyes. Some torch bearers went by as well. "You're falling behind," one told them. The next agreed. "No one's like to wait for you, Paul. Leave the pig for the dead men."

"He promised I could have a bird," Small Paul said, even though Sam hadn't, not truly. *They aren't mine to give.* "I want me a bird that talks, and eats corn from my hand."

"Bloody fool," the torch man said. Then he was gone.

It was a while after when Grenn stopped suddenly. "We're alone," he said in a hoarse voice. "I can't see the other torches. Was that the rear guard?"

Small Paul had no answer for him. The big man gave a grunt and sank to his knees. His arms trembled as he lay Sam gently in the snow. "I can't carry you no more. I would, but I can't." He shivered violently.

The wind sighed through the trees, driving a fine spray of snow into their faces. The cold was so bitter that Sam felt naked. He looked for the other torches, but they were gone, every one of them. There was only the one Grenn carried, the flames rising from it like pale orange silks. He could see through them, to the black beyond. *That torch will burn out soon*, he thought, *and we are all alone, without food or friends or fire.*

But that was wrong. They weren't alone at all.

The lower branches of the great green sentinel shed their burden of snow with a soft wet *plop*. Grenn spun, thrusting out his torch. "Who goes there?" A horse's head emerged from the darkness. Sam felt a moment's relief, until he saw the horse. Hoarfrost covered it like a sheen of frozen sweat, and a nest of stiff black entrails dragged from its open belly. On its back was a rider pale as ice. Sam made a whimpery sound deep in his throat. He was so scared he might have pissed himself all over again, but the cold was in him, a cold so savage that his bladder felt frozen solid. The Other slid gracefully from the saddle to stand upon the snow. Sword-slim it was, and milky white. Its armor rippled and shifted as it moved, and its feet did not break the crust of the new-fallen snow.

Small Paul unslung the long-hafted axe strapped across his back. "Why'd you hurt that horse? That was Mawney's horse."

Sam groped for the hilt of his sword, but the scabbard was empty. He had lost it on the Fist, he remembered too late.

"Get away!" Grenn took a step, thrusting the torch out before him. "*Away*, or you burn." He poked at it with the flames.

The Other's sword gleamed with a faint blue glow. It moved toward Grenn, lightning quick, slashing. When the ice blue blade brushed the flames, a screech stabbed Sam's ears sharp as a needle. The head of the torch tumbled sideways to vanish beneath a deep drift of snow, the fire snuffed out at once. And all Grenn held was a short wooden stick. He flung it at the Other, cursing, as Small Paul charged in with his axe.

The fear that filled Sam then was worse than any fear he had ever felt before, and Samwell Tarly knew every kind of fear. "Mother have mercy," he wept, forgetting the old gods in his terror. "Father protect me, oh oh . . ." His fingers found his dagger and he filled his hand with that.

The wights had been slow clumsy things, but the Other was light as snow on the wind. It slid away from Paul's axe, armor rippling, and its crystal sword twisted and spun and slipped between the iron rings of

Paul's mail, through leather and wool and bone and flesh. It came out his back with a *hissssssssssss* and Sam heard Paul say, "Oh," as he lost the axe. Impaled, his blood smoking around the sword, the big man tried to reach his killer with his hands and almost had before he fell. The weight of him tore the strange pale sword from the Other's grip.

Do it now. Stop crying and fight, you baby. Fight, craven. It was his father he heard, it was Alliser Thorne, it was his brother Dickon and the boy Rast. *Craven, craven, craven.* He giggled hysterically, wondering if they would make a wight of him, a huge fat white wight always tripping over its own dead feet. *Do it, Sam.* Was that Jon, now? Jon was dead. *You can do it, you can, just do it.* And then he was stumbling forward, falling more than running, really, closing his eyes and shoving the dagger blindly out before him with both hands. He heard a *crack*, like the sound ice makes when it breaks beneath a man's foot, and then a screech so shrill and sharp that he went staggering backward with his hands over his muffled ears, and fell hard on his arse.

When he opened his eyes the Other's armor was running down its legs in rivulets as pale blue blood hissed and steamed around the black dragonglass dagger in its throat. It reached down with two bone-white hands to pull out the knife, but where its fingers touched the obsidian they *smoked*.

Sam rolled onto his side, eyes wide as the Other shrank and puddled, dissolving away. In twenty heartbeats its flesh was gone, swirling away in a fine white mist. Beneath were bones like milkglass, pale and shiny, and they were melting too. Finally only the dragonglass dagger remained, wreathed in steam as if it were alive and sweating. Grenn bent to scoop it up and flung it down again at once. "Mother, that's *cold*."

"Obsidian." Sam struggled to his knees. "Dragonglass, they call it. Dragonglass. *Dragon* glass." He giggled, and cried, and doubled over to heave his courage out onto the snow.

Grenn pulled Sam to his feet, checked Small Paul for a pulse and closed his eyes, then snatched up the dagger again. This time he was able to hold it.

"You keep it," Sam said. "You're not craven like me."

"So craven you killed an Other." Grenn pointed with the knife. "Look there, through the trees. Pink light. Dawn, Sam. Dawn. That must be east. If we head that way, we should catch Mormont."

"If you say." Sam kicked his left foot against a tree, to knock off all the snow. Then the right. "I'll try." Grimacing, he took a step. "I'll try hard." And then another.

TYRION

Lord Tywin's chain of hands made a golden glitter against the deep wine velvet of his tunic. The Lords Tyrell, Redwyne, and Rowan gathered round him as he entered. He greeted each in turn, spoke a quiet word to Varys, kissed the High Septon's ring and Cersei's cheek, clasped the hand of Grand Maester Pycelle, and seated himself in the king's place at the head of the long table, between his daughter and his brother.

Tyrion had claimed Pycelle's old place at the foot, propped up by cushions so he could gaze down the length of the table. Dispossessed, Pycelle had moved up next to Cersei, about as far from the dwarf as he could get without claiming the king's seat. The Grand Maester was a shambling skeleton, leaning heavily on a twisted cane and shaking as he walked, a few white hairs sprouting from his long chicken's neck in place of his once-luxuriant white beard. Tyrion gazed at him without remorse.

The others had to scramble for seats: Lord Mace Tyrell, a heavy, robust man with curling brown hair and a spade-shaped beard well salted with white; Paxter Redwyne of the Arbor, stoop-shouldered and thin, his bald head fringed by tufts of orange hair; Mathis Rowan, Lord of Goldengrove, clean-shaven, stout, and sweating; the High Septon, a frail man with wispy white chin hair. *Too many strange faces,* Tyrion thought, *too many new players. The game changed while I lay rotting in my bed, and no one will tell me the rules.*

Oh, the lords had been courteous enough, though he could tell how uncomfortable it made them to look at him. "That chain of yours, that was cunning," Mace Tyrell had said in a jolly tone, and Lord Redwyne nodded and said, "Quite so, quite so, my lord of Highgarden speaks for all of us," and very cheerfully too.

Tell it to the people of this city, Tyrion thought bitterly. *Tell it to the bloody singers, with their songs of Renly's ghost.*

His uncle Kevan had been the warmest, going so far as to kiss his cheek and say, "Lancel has told me how brave you were, Tyrion. He speaks very highly of you."

He'd better, or I'll have a few things to say of him. He made himself smile and say, "My good cousin is too kind. His wound is healing, I trust?"

Ser Kevan frowned. "One day he seems stronger, the next . . . it is worrisome. Your sister often visits his sickbed, to lift his spirits and pray for him."

But is she praying that he lives, or dies? Cersei had made shameless use of their cousin, both in and out of bed; a little secret she no doubt hoped Lancel would carry to his grave now that Father was here and she no longer had need of him. *Would she go so far as to murder him, though?* To look at her today, you would never suspect Cersei was capable of such ruthlessness. She was all charm, flirting with Lord Tyrell as they spoke of Joffrey's wedding feast, complimenting Lord Redwyne on the valor of his twins, softening gruff Lord Rowan with jests and smiles, making pious noises at the High Septon. "Shall we begin with the wedding arrangements?" she asked as Lord Tywin took his seat.

"No," their father said. "With the war. Varys."

The eunuch smiled a silken smile. "I have such *delicious* tidings for you all, my lords. Yesterday at dawn our brave Lord Randyll caught Robett Glover outside Duskendale and trapped him against the sea. Losses were heavy on both sides, but in the end our loyal men prevailed. Ser Helman Tallhart is reported dead, with a thousand others. Robett Glover leads the survivors back toward Harrenhal in bloody disarray, little dreaming he will find valiant Ser Gregor and his stalwarts athwart his path."

"Gods be praised!" said Paxter Redwyne. "A great victory for King Joffrey!"

What did Joffrey have to do with it? thought Tyrion.

"And a terrible defeat for the north, certainly," observed Littlefinger, "yet one in which Robb Stark played no part. The Young Wolf remains unbeaten in the field."

"What do we know of Stark's plans and movements?" asked Mathis Rowan, ever blunt and to the point.

"He has run back to Riverrun with his plunder, abandoning the castles he took in the west," announced Lord Tywin. "Our cousin Ser Daven is reforming the remnants of his late father's army at Lannisport. When they are ready he shall join Ser Forley Prester at the Golden Tooth. As soon as the Stark boy starts north, Ser Forley and Ser Daven will descend on Riverrun."

"You are certain Lord Stark means to go north?" Lord Rowan asked. "Even with the ironmen at Moat Cailin?"

Mace Tyrell spoke up. "Is there anything as pointless as a king without a kingdom? No, it's plain, the boy must abandon the riverlands, join his forces to Roose Bolton's once more, and throw all his strength against Moat Cailin. That is what *I* would do."

Tyrion had to bite his tongue at that. Robb Stark had won more battles in a year than the Lord of Highgarden had in twenty. Tyrell's reputation rested on one indecisive victory over Robert Baratheon at Ashford, in a battle largely won by Lord Tarly's van before the main host had even arrived. The siege of Storm's End, where Mace Tyrell actually did hold the command, had dragged on a year to no result, and after the Trident was fought, the Lord of Highgarden had meekly dipped his banners to Eddard Stark.

"I ought to write Robb Stark a stern letter," Littlefinger was saying. "I understand his man Bolton is stabling goats in *my* high hall, it's really quite unconscionable."

Ser Kevan Lannister cleared his throat. "As regards the Starks . . . Balon Greyjoy, who now styles himself King of the Isles and the North, has written to us offering terms of alliance."

"He ought to be offering fealty," snapped Cersei. "By what right does he call himself king?"

"By right of conquest," Lord Tywin said. "King Balon has strangler's fingers round the Neck. Robb Stark's heirs are dead, Winterfell is fallen, and the ironmen hold Moat Cailin, Deepwood Motte, and most of the Stony Shore. King Balon's longships command the sunset sea, and are well placed to menace Lannisport, Fair Isle, and even Highgarden, should we provoke him."

"And if we accept this alliance?" inquired Lord Mathis Rowan. "What terms does he propose?"

"That we recognize his kingship and grant him everything north of the Neck."

Lord Redwyne laughed. "What is there north of the Neck that any sane man would want? If Greyjoy will trade swords and sails for stone and snow, I say do it, and count ourselves lucky."

"Truly," agreed Mace Tyrell. "That's what I would do. Let King Balon finish the northmen whilst we finish Stannis."

Lord Tywin's face gave no hint as to his feelings. "There is Lysa Arryn to deal with as well. Jon Arryn's widow, Hoster Tully's daughter, Catelyn Stark's sister . . . whose husband was conspiring with Stannis Baratheon at the time of his death."

"Oh," said Mace Tyrell cheerfully, "women have no stomach for war. Let her be, I say, she's not like to trouble us."

"I agree," said Redwyne. "The Lady Lysa took no part in the fighting, nor has she committed any overt acts of treason."

Tyrion stirred. "She did throw me in a cell and put me on trial for my life," he pointed out, with a certain amount of rancor. "Nor has she returned to King's Landing to swear fealty to Joff, as she was commanded. My lords, grant me the men, and I will sort out Lysa Arryn." He could think of nothing he would enjoy more, except perhaps strangling Cersei. Sometimes he still dreamed of the Eyrie's sky cells, and woke drenched in cold sweat.

Mace Tyrell's smile was jovial, but behind it Tyrion sensed contempt. "Perhaps you'd best leave the fighting to fighters," said the Lord of Highgarden. "Better men than you have lost great armies in the Mountains of the Moon, or shattered them against the Bloody Gate. We know your worth, my lord, no need to tempt fate."

Tyrion pushed off his cushions, bristling, but his father spoke before he could lash back. "I have other tasks in mind for Tyrion. I believe Lord Petyr may hold the key to the Eyrie."

"Oh, I do," said Littlefinger, "I have it here between my legs." There was mischief in his grey-green eyes. "My lords, with your leave, I propose to travel to the Vale and there woo and win Lady Lysa Arryn. Once I am her consort, I shall deliver you the Vale of Arryn without a drop of blood being spilled."

Lord Rowan looked doubtful. "Would Lady Lysa have you?"

"She's had me a few times before, Lord Mathis, and voiced no complaints."

"Bedding," said Cersei, "is not wedding. Even a cow like Lysa Arryn might be able to grasp the difference."

"To be sure. It would not have been fitting for a daughter of Riverrun to marry one so far below her." Littlefinger spread his hands. "Now, though . . . a match between the Lady of the Eyrie and the Lord of Harrenhal is not so unthinkable, is it?"

Tyrion noted the look that passed between Paxter Redwyne and Mace Tyrell. "It might serve," Lord Rowan said, "if you are certain that you can keep the woman loyal to the King's Grace."

"My lords," pronounced the High Septon, "autumn is upon us, and all men of good heart are weary of war. If Lord Baelish can bring the Vale back into the king's peace without more shedding of blood, the gods will surely bless him."

"But can he?" asked Lord Redwyne. "Jon Arryn's son is Lord of the Eyrie now. The Lord Robert."

"Only a boy," said Littlefinger. "I will see that he grows to be Joffrey's most loyal subject, and a fast friend to us all."

Tyrion studied the slender man with the pointed beard and irreverent grey-green eyes. *Lord of Harrenhal an empty honor! Bugger that, Father. Even if he never sets foot in the castle, the title makes this match possible, as he's known all along.*

"We have no lack of foes," said Ser Kevan Lannister. "If the Eyrie can be kept out of the war, all to the good. I am of a mind to see what Lord Petyr can accomplish."

Ser Kevan was his brother's vanguard in council, Tyrion knew from long experience; he never had a thought that Lord Tywin had not had first. *It has all been settled beforehand,* he concluded, *and this discussion's no more than show.*

The sheep were bleating their agreement, unaware of how neatly they'd been shorn, so it fell to Tyrion to object. "How will the crown pay its debts without Lord Petyr? He is our wizard of coin, and we have no one to replace him."

Littlefinger smiled. "My little friend is too kind. All I do is count coppers, as King Robert used to say. Any clever tradesman could do as well . . . and a Lannister, blessed with the golden touch of Casterly Rock, will no doubt far surpass me."

"A Lannister?" Tyrion had a bad feeling about this.

Lord Tywin's gold-flecked eyes met his son's mismatched ones. "You are admirably suited to the task, I believe."

"Indeed!" Ser Kevan said heartily. "I've no doubt you'll make a splendid master of coin, Tyrion."

Lord Tywin turned back to Littlefinger. "If Lysa Arryn will take you for a husband and return to the king's peace, we shall restore the Lord Robert to the honor of Warden of the East. How soon might you leave?"

"On the morrow, if the winds permit. There's a Braavosi galley standing out past the chain, taking on cargo by boat. The *Merling King*. I'll see her captain about a berth."

"You will miss the king's wedding," said Mace Tyrell.

Petyr Baelish gave a shrug. "Tides and brides wait on no man, my lord. Once the autumn storms begin the voyage will be much more hazardous. Drowning would definitely diminish my charms as a bridegroom."

Lord Tyrell chuckled. "True. Best you do not linger."

"May the gods speed you on your way," the High Septon said. "All King's Landing shall pray for your success."

Lord Redwyne pinched at his nose. "May we return to the matter of the Greyjoy alliance? In my view, there is much to be said for it. Greyjoy's longships will augment my own fleet and give us sufficient strength at sea to assault Dragonstone and end Stannis Baratheon's pretensions."

"King Balon's longships are occupied for the nonce," Lord Tywin said politely, "as are we. Greyjoy demands half the kingdom as the price of alliance, but what will he do to earn it? Fight the Starks? He is doing that already. Why should we pay for what he has given us for free? The best thing to do about our lord of Pyke is nothing, in my view. Granted enough time, a better option may well present itself. One that does not require the king to give up half his kingdom."

Tyrion watched his father closely. *There's something he's not saying.* He remembered those important letters Lord Tywin had been writing, the night Tyrion had demanded Casterly Rock. *What was it he said? Some battles are won with swords and spears, others with quills and ravens . . .* He wondered who the "better option" was, and what sort of price he was demanding.

"Perhaps we ought move on to the wedding," Ser Kevan said.

The High Septon spoke of the preparations being made at the Great Sept of Baelor, and Cersei detailed the plans she had been making for the feast. They would feed a thousand in the throne room, but many more outside in the yards. The outer and middle wards would be tented in silk, with tables of food and casks of ale for all those who could not be accommodated within the hall.

"Your Grace," said Grand Maester Pycelle, "in regard to the number of guests . . . we have had a raven from Sunspear. Three hundred Dornishmen are riding toward King's Landing as we speak, and hope to arrive before the wedding."

"How do they come?" asked Mace Tyrell gruffly. "They have not asked leave to cross *my* lands." His thick neck had turned a dark red, Tyrion noted. Dornishmen and Highgardeners had never had great love for one another; over the centuries, they had fought border wars beyond count, and raided back and forth across mountains and marches even when at peace. The enmity had waned a bit after Dorne had become part of the Seven Kingdoms . . . until the Dornish prince they called the Red Viper had crippled the young heir of Highgarden in a tourney. *This could be ticklish,* the dwarf thought, waiting to see how his father would handle it.

"Prince Doran comes at my son's invitation," Lord Tywin said calmly, "not only to join in our celebration, but to claim his seat on this council, and the justice Robert denied him for the murder of his sister Elia and her children."

Tyrion watched the faces of the Lords Tyrell, Redwyne, and Rowan, wondering if any of the three would be bold enough to say, "But Lord Tywin, wasn't it *you* who presented the bodies to Robert, all wrapped up in Lannister cloaks?" None of them did, but it was there on their faces all the same. *Redwyne does not give a fig,* he thought, *but Rowan looks fit to gag.*

"When the king is wed to your Margaery and Myrcella to Prince Trystane, we shall all be one great House," Ser Kevan reminded Mace Tyrell.

"The enmities of the past should remain there, would you not agree, my lord?"

"This is *my daughter's wedding –*"

"*–* and my grandson's," said Lord Tywin firmly. "No place for old quarrels, surely?"

"I have no quarrel with *Doran* Martell," insisted Lord Tyrell, though his tone was more than a little grudging. "If he wishes to cross the Reach in peace, he need only ask my leave."

Small chance of that, thought Tyrion. *He'll climb the Boneway, turn east near Summerhall, and come up the kingsroad.*

"Three hundred Dornishmen need not trouble our plans," said Cersei. "We can feed the men-at-arms in the yard, squeeze some extra benches into the throne room for the lordlings and highborn knights, and find Prince Doran a place of honor on the dais."

Not by me, was the message Tyrion saw in Mace Tyrell's eyes, but the Lord of Highgarden made no reply but a curt nod.

"Perhaps we can move to a more pleasant task," said Lord Tywin. "The fruits of victory await division."

"What could be sweeter?" said Littlefinger, who had already swallowed his own fruit, Harrenhal.

Each lord had his own demands; this castle and that village, tracts of lands, a small river, a forest, the wardship of certain minors left fatherless by the battle. Fortunately, these fruits were plentiful, and there were orphans and castles for all. Varys had lists. Forty-seven lesser lordlings and six hundred nineteen knights had lost their lives beneath the fiery heart of Stannis and his Lord of Light, along with several thousand common men-at-arms. Traitors all, their heirs were disinherited, their lands and castles granted to those who had proved more loyal.

Highgarden reaped the richest harvest. Tyrion eyed Mace Tyrell's broad belly and thought, *He has a prodigious appetite, this one.* Tyrell demanded the lands and castles of Lord Alester Florent, his own bannerman, who'd had the singular ill judgment to back first Renly and then Stannis. Lord Tywin was pleased to oblige. Brightwater Keep and all its lands and incomes were granted to Lord Tyrell's second son, Ser Garlan, transforming him into a great lord in the blink of an eye. His elder brother, of course, stood to inherit Highgarden itself.

Lesser tracts were granted to Lord Rowan, and set aside for Lord Tarly, Lady Oakheart, Lord Hightower, and other worthies not present. Lord Redwyne asked only for thirty years' remission of the taxes that Littlefinger and his wine factors had levied on certain of the Arbor's finest vintages. When that was granted, he pronounced himself well satisfied and suggested that they send for a cask of Arbor gold, to toast good King Joffrey and his wise and benevolent Hand. At that Cersei lost patience.

"It's swords Joff needs, not toasts," she snapped. "His realm is still plagued with would-be usurpers and self-styled kings."

"But not for long, I think," said Varys unctuously.

"A few more items remain, my lords." Ser Kevan consulted his papers. "Ser Addam has found some crystals from the High Septon's crown. It appears certain now that the thieves broke up the crystals and melted down the gold."

"Our Father Above knows their guilt and will sit in judgment on them all," the High Septon said piously.

"No doubt he will," said Lord Tywin. "All the same, you must be crowned at the king's wedding. Cersei, summon your goldsmiths, we must see to a replacement." He did not wait for her reply, but turned at once to Varys. "You have reports?"

The eunuch drew a parchment from his sleeve. "A kraken has been seen off the Fingers." He giggled. "Not a *Greyjoy*, mind you, a true kraken. It attacked an Ibbenese whaler and pulled it under. There is fighting on the Stepstones, and a new war between Tyrosh and Lys seems likely. Both hope to win Myr as ally. Sailors back from the Jade Sea report that a three-headed dragon has hatched in Qarth, and is the wonder of that city –"

"Dragons and krakens do not interest me, regardless of the number of their heads," said Lord Tywin. "Have your whisperers perchance found some trace of my brother's son?"

"Alas, our beloved Tyrek has quite vanished, the poor brave lad." Varys sounded close to tears.

"Tywin," Ser Kevan said, before Lord Tywin could vent his obvious displeasure, "some of the gold cloaks who deserted during the battle have drifted back to barracks, thinking to take up duty once again. Ser Addam wishes to know what to do with them."

"They might have endangered Joff with their cowardice," Cersei said at once. "I want them put to death."

Varys sighed. "They have surely earned death, Your Grace, none can deny it. And yet, perhaps we might be wiser to send them to the Night's Watch. We have had disturbing messages from the Wall of late. Of wildlings astir . . ."

"Wildlings, krakens, and dragons." Mace Tyrell chuckled. "Why, is there anyone *not* stirring?"

Lord Tywin ignored that. "The deserters serve us best as a lesson. Break their knees with hammers. They will not run again. Nor will any man who sees them begging in the streets." He glanced down the table to see if any of the other lords disagreed.

Tyrion remembered his own visit to the Wall, and the crabs he'd shared with old Lord Mormont and his officers. He remembered the Old Bear's fears as well. "Perhaps we might break the knees of a few to make our point. Those who killed Ser Jacelyn, say. The rest we can send to Marsh. The Watch is grievously under strength. If the Wall should fail . . ."

". . . the wildlings will flood the north," his father finished, "and the Starks and Greyjoys will have another enemy to contend with. They no longer wish to be subject to the Iron Throne, it would seem, so by what right do they look to the Iron Throne for aid? King Robb and King Balon both claim the north. Let *them* defend it, if they can. And if not, this Mance Rayder might even prove a useful ally." Lord Tywin looked to his brother. "Is there more?"

Ser Kevan shook his head. "We are done. My lords, His Grace King Joffrey would no doubt wish to thank you all for your wisdom and good counsel."

"I should like private words with my children," said Lord Tywin as the others rose to leave. "You as well, Kevan."

Obediently, the other councillors made their farewells, Varys the first to depart and Tyrell and Redwyne the last. When the chamber was empty but for the four Lannisters, Ser Kevan closed the door.

"*Master of coin!*" said Tyrion in a thin strained voice. "Whose notion was that, pray?"

"Lord Petyr's," his father said, "but it serves us well to have the treasury in the hands of a Lannister. You have asked for important work. Do you fear you might be incapable of the task?"

"No," said Tyrion, "I fear a trap. Littlefinger is subtle and ambitious. I do not trust him. Nor should you."

"He won Highgarden to our side . . ." Cersei began.

". . . and sold you Ned Stark, I know. He will sell us just as quick. A coin is as dangerous as a sword in the wrong hands."

His uncle Kevan looked at him oddly. "Not to us, surely. The gold of Casterly Rock . . ."

". . . is dug from the ground. Littlefinger's gold is made from thin air, with a snap of his fingers."

"A more useful skill than any of yours, sweet brother," purred Cersei, in a voice sweet with malice.

"Littlefinger is a liar —"

"— and black as well, said the raven of the crow."

Lord Tywin slammed his hand down on the table. "*Enough!* I will have no more of this unseemly squabbling. You are both Lannisters, and will comport yourselves as such."

Ser Kevan cleared his throat. "I would sooner have Petyr Baelish ruling the Eyrie than any of Lady Lysa's other suitors. Yohn Royce, Lyn Corbray, Horton Redfort . . . these are dangerous men, each in his own way. And proud. Littlefinger may be clever, but he has neither high birth nor skill at arms. The lords of the Vale will never accept such as their liege." He looked to his brother. When Lord Tywin nodded, he continued. "And there is this – Lord Petyr continues to demonstrate his loyalty. Only yesterday he brought us word of a Tyrell plot to spirit Sansa Stark off to Highgarden for a 'visit,' and there marry her to Lord Mace's eldest son, Willas."

"*Littlefinger* brought you word?" Tyrion leaned against the table. "Not our master of whisperers? How interesting."

Cersei looked at their uncle in disbelief. "Sansa is my hostage. She goes *nowhere* without my leave."

"Leave you must perforce grant, should Lord Tyrell ask," their father pointed out. "To refuse him would be tantamount to declaring that we did not trust him. He would take offense."

"Let him. What do we care?"

Bloody fool, thought Tyrion. "Sweet sister," he explained patiently, "offend Tyrell and you offend Redwyne, Tarly, Rowan, and Hightower as well, and perhaps start them wondering whether Robb Stark might not be more accommodating of their desires."

"I will not have the rose and the direwolf in bed together," declared Lord Tywin. "We must forestall him."

"How?" asked Cersei.

"By marriage. Yours, to begin with."

It came so suddenly that Cersei could only stare for a moment. Then her cheeks reddened as if she had been slapped. "No. Not again. I will not."

"Your Grace," said Ser Kevan, courteously, "you are a young woman, still fair and fertile. Surely you cannot wish to spend the rest of your days alone? And a new marriage would put to rest this talk of incest for good and all."

"So long as you remain unwed, you allow Stannis to spread his disgusting slander," Lord Tywin told his daughter. "You must have a new husband in your bed, to father children on you."

"Three children is quite sufficient. I am Queen of the Seven Kingdoms, not a brood mare! The Queen *Regent*!"

"You are my daughter, and will do as I command."

She stood. "I will not sit here and listen to this –"

"You will if you wish to have any voice in the choice of your next husband," Lord Tywin said calmly.

When she hesitated, then sat, Tyrion knew she was lost, despite her loud declaration of, "I will *not* marry again!"

"You will marry and you will breed. Every child you birth makes Stannis more a liar." Their father's eyes seemed to pin her to her chair. "Mace Tyrell, Paxter Redwyne, and Doran Martell are wed to younger women likely to outlive them. Balon Greyjoy's wife is elderly and failing, but such a match would commit us to an alliance with the Iron Islands, and I am still uncertain whether that would be our wisest course."

"No," Cersei said from between white lips. "No, no, no."

Tyrion could not quite suppress the grin that came to his lips at the thought of packing his sister off to Pyke. *Just when I was about to give up praying, some sweet god gives me this.*

Lord Tywin went on. "Oberyn Martell might suit, but the Tyrells would take that very ill. So we must look to the sons. I assume you do not object to wedding a man younger than yourself?"

"I object to wedding *any –*"

"I have considered the Redwyne twins, Theon Greyjoy, Quentyn Martell, and a number of others. But our alliance with Highgarden was the sword that broke Stannis. It should be tempered and made stronger. Ser Loras has taken the white and Ser Garlan is wed to one of the Fossoways, but there remains the eldest son, the boy they scheme to wed to Sansa Stark."

Willas Tyrell. Tyrion was taking a wicked pleasure in Cersei's helpless fury. "That would be the cripple," he said.

Their father chilled him with a look. "Willas is heir to Highgarden, and by all reports a mild and courtly young man, fond of reading books and looking at the stars. He has a passion for breeding animals as well, and owns the finest hounds, hawks, and horses in the Seven Kingdoms."

A perfect match, mused Tyrion. *Cersei also has a passion for breeding.* He pitied poor Willas Tyrell, and did not know whether he wanted to laugh at his sister or weep for her.

"The Tyrell heir would be my choice," Lord Tywin concluded, "but if you would prefer another, I will hear your reasons."

"That is so very kind of you, Father," Cersei said with icy courtesy. "It is such a difficult choice you give me. Who would I sooner take to bed, the old squid or the crippled dog boy? I shall need a few days to consider. Do I have your leave to go?"

You are the queen, Tyrion wanted to tell her. *He ought to be begging leave of you.*

"Go," their father said. "We shall talk again after you have composed yourself. Remember your duty."

Cersei swept stiffly from the room, her rage plain to see. *Yet in the end she will do as Father bid.* She had proved that with Robert. *Though there is Jaime to consider.* Their brother had been much younger when Cersei wed the first time; he might not acquiesce to a second marriage quite so easily. The unfortunate Willas Tyrell was like to contract a sudden fatal case of sword-through-bowels, which could rather sour the alliance between Highgarden and Casterly Rock. *I should say something, but what? Pardon me, Father, but it's our brother she wants to marry?*

"Tyrion."

He gave a resigned smile. "Do I hear the herald summoning me to the lists?"

"Your whoring is a weakness in you," Lord Tywin said without preamble, "but perhaps some share of the blame is mine. Since you stand no taller than a boy, I have found it easy to forget that you are in truth a man grown, with all of a man's baser needs. It is past time you were wed."

I was wed, or have you forgotten? Tyrion's mouth twisted, and the noise emerged that was half laugh and half snarl.

"Does the prospect of marriage amuse you?"

"Only imagining what a bugger-all handsome bridegroom I'll make." A wife might be the very thing he needed. If she brought him lands and a keep, it would give him a place in the world apart from Joffrey's court . . . and away from Cersei and their father.

On the other hand, there was Shae. *She will not like this, for all she swears that she is content to be my whore.*

That was scarcely a point to sway his father, however, so Tyrion squirmed higher in his seat and said, "You mean to wed me to Sansa Stark. But won't the Tyrells take the match as an affront, if they have designs on the girl?"

"Lord Tyrell will not broach the matter of the Stark girl until after Joffrey's wedding. If Sansa is wed before that, how can he take offense, when he gave us no hint of his intentions?"

"Quite so," said Ser Kevan, "and any lingering resentments should be soothed by the offer of Cersei for his Willas."

Tyrion rubbed at the raw stub of his nose. The scar tissue itched abominably sometimes. "His Grace the royal pustule has made Sansa's life a misery since the day her father died, and now that she is finally rid of Joffrey you propose to marry her to me. That seems singularly cruel. Even for you, Father."

"Why, do you plan to mistreat her?" His father sounded more curious than concerned. "The girl's happiness is not my purpose, nor should it be yours. Our alliances in the south may be as solid as Casterly Rock, but there remains the north to win, and the key to the north is Sansa Stark."

"She is no more than a child."

"Your sister swears she's flowered. If so, she is a woman, fit to be wed. You must needs take her maidenhead, so no man can say the marriage was not consummated. After that, if you prefer to wait a year or two before bedding her again, you would be within your rights as her husband."

Shae is all the woman I need just now, he thought, *and Sansa's a girl, no matter what you say.* "If your purpose here is to keep her from the

Tyrells, why not return her to her mother? Perhaps that would convince Robb Stark to bend the knee."

Lord Tywin's look was scornful. "Send her to Riverrun and her mother will match her with a Blackwood or a Mallister to shore up her son's alliances along the Trident. Send her north, and she will be wed to some Manderly or Umber before the moon turns. Yet she is no less dangerous here at court, as this business with the Tyrells should prove. She must marry a Lannister, and soon."

"The man who weds Sansa Stark can claim Winterfell in her name," his uncle Kevan put in. "Had that not occurred to you?"

"If you will not have the girl, we shall give her to one of your cousins," said his father. "Kevan, is Lancel strong enough to wed, do you think?"

Ser Kevan hesitated. "If we bring the girl to his bedside, he could say the words . . . but to consummate, no . . . I would suggest one of the twins, but the Starks hold them both at Riverrun. They have Genna's boy Tion as well, else he might serve."

Tyrion let them have their byplay; it was all for his benefit, he knew. *Sansa Stark*, he mused. Soft-spoken sweet-smelling Sansa, who loved silks, songs, chivalry and tall gallant knights with handsome faces. He felt as though he was back on the bridge of boats, the deck shifting beneath his feet.

"You asked me to reward you for your efforts in the battle," Lord Tywin reminded him forcefully. "This is a chance for you, Tyrion, the best you are ever likely to have." He drummed his fingers impatiently on the table. "I once hoped to marry your brother to Lysa Tully, but Aerys named Jaime to his Kingsguard before the arrangements were complete. When I suggested to Lord Hoster that Lysa might be wed to you instead, he replied that he wanted a whole man for his daughter."

So he wed her to Jon Arryn, who was old enough to be her grandfather. Tyrion was more inclined to be thankful than angry, considering what Lysa Arryn had become.

"When I offered you to Dorne I was told that the suggestion was an insult," Lord Tywin continued. "In later years I had similar answers from Yohn Royce and Leyton Hightower. I finally stooped so low as to suggest you might take the Florent girl Robert deflowered in his brother's wedding bed, but her father preferred to give her to one of his own household knights.

"If you will not have the Stark girl, I shall find you another wife. Somewhere in the realm there is doubtless some little lordling who'd gladly part with a daughter to win the friendship of Casterly Rock. Lady Tanda has offered Lollys . . ."

Tyrion gave a shudder of dismay. "I'd sooner cut it off and feed it to the goats."

"Then open your eyes. The Stark girl is young, nubile, tractable, of the highest birth, and still a maid. She is not uncomely. Why would you hesitate?"

Why indeed? "A quirk of mine. Strange to say, I would prefer a wife who wants me in her bed."

"If you think your whores want you in their bed, you are an even greater fool than I suspected," said Lord Tywin. "You disappoint me, Tyrion. I had hoped this match would please you."

"Yes, we all know how important my pleasure is to you, Father. But there's more to this. The key to the north, you say? The Greyjoys hold the north now, and King Balon has a daughter. Why Sansa Stark, and not her?" He looked into his father's cool green eyes with their bright flecks of gold.

Lord Tywin steepled his fingers beneath his chin. "Balon Greyjoy thinks in terms of plunder, not rule. Let him enjoy an autumn crown and suffer a northern winter. He will give his subjects no cause to love him. Come spring, the northmen will have had a bellyful of krakens. When you bring Eddard Stark's grandson home to claim his birthright, lords and little folk alike will rise as one to place him on the high seat of his ancestors. You *are* capable of getting a woman with child, I hope?"

"I believe I am," he said, bristling. "I confess, I cannot prove it. Though no one can say I have not tried. Why, I plant my little seeds just as often as I can . . ."

"In the gutters and the ditches," finished Lord Tywin, "and in common ground where only bastard weeds take root. It is past time you kept your own garden." He rose to his feet. "You shall never have Casterly Rock, I promise you. But wed Sansa Stark, and it is just possible that you might win Winterfell."

Tyrion Lannister, Lord Protector of Winterfell. The prospect gave him a queer chill. "Very good, Father," he said slowly, "but there's a big ugly roach in your rushes. Robb Stark is as *capable* as I am, presumably, and sworn to marry one of those fertile Freys. And once the Young Wolf sires a litter, any pups that Sansa births are heirs to nothing."

Lord Tywin was unconcerned. "Robb Stark will father no children on his fertile Frey, you have my word. There is a bit of news I have not yet seen fit to share with the council, though no doubt the good lords will hear it soon enough. The Young Wolf has taken Gawen Westerling's eldest daughter to wife."

For a moment Tyrion could not believe he'd heard his father right. "He broke his sworn word?" he said, incredulous. "He threw away the Freys for . . ." Words failed him.

"A maid of sixteen years, named Jeyne," said Ser Kevan. "Lord Gawen once suggested her to me for Willem or Martyn, but I had to refuse him.

Gawen is a good man, but his wife is Sybell Spicer. He should never have wed her. The Westerlings always did have more honor than sense. Lady Sybell's grandfather was a trader in saffron and pepper, almost as lowborn as that smuggler Stannis keeps. And the grandmother was some woman he'd brought back from the east. A frightening old crone, supposed to be a priestess. *Maegi*, they called her. No one could pronounce her real name. Half of Lannisport used to go to her for cures and love potions and the like." He shrugged. "She's long dead, to be sure. And Jeyne seemed a sweet child, I'll grant you, though I only saw her once. But with such doubtful blood . . ."

Having once married a whore, Tyrion could not entirely share his uncle's horror at the thought of wedding a girl whose great grandfather sold cloves. Even so . . . *A sweet child*, Ser Kevan had said, but many a poison was sweet as well. The Westerlings were old blood, but they had more pride than power. It would not surprise him to learn that Lady Sybell had brought more wealth to the marriage than her highborn husband. The Westerling mines had failed years ago, their best lands had been sold off or lost, and the Crag was more ruin than stronghold. *A romantic ruin, though, jutting up so brave above the sea.* "I am surprised," Tyrion had to confess. "I thought Robb Stark had better sense."

"He is a boy of sixteen," said Lord Tywin. "At that age, sense weighs for little, against lust and love and honor."

"He forswore himself, shamed an ally, betrayed a solemn promise. Where is the honor in that?"

Ser Kevan answered. "He chose the girl's honor over his own. Once he had deflowered her, he had no other course."

"It would have been kinder to leave her with a bastard in her belly," said Tyrion bluntly. The Westerlings stood to lose everything here; their lands, their castle, their very lives. *A Lannister always pays his debts.*

"Jeyne Westerling is her mother's daughter," said Lord Tywin, "and Robb Stark is his father's son."

This Westerling betrayal did not seem to have enraged his father as much as Tyrion would have expected. Lord Tywin did not suffer disloyalty in his vassals. He had extinguished the proud Reynes of Castamere and the ancient Tarbecks of Tarbeck Hall root and branch when he was still half a boy. The singers had even made a rather gloomy song of it. Some years later, when Lord Farman of Faircastle grew truculent, Lord Tywin sent an envoy bearing a lute instead of a letter. But once he'd heard "The Rains of Castamere" echoing through his hall, Lord Farman gave no further trouble. And if the song were not enough, the shattered castles of the Reynes and Tarbecks still stood as mute testimony to the fate that awaited those who chose to scorn the power of Casterly Rock. "The Crag is not so far from Tarbeck Hall and Castamere," Tyrion pointed out. "You'd think the Westerlings might have ridden past and seen the lesson there."

"Mayhaps they have," Lord Tywin said. "They are well aware of Castamere, I promise you."

"Could the Westerlings and Spicers be such great fools as to believe the wolf can defeat the lion?"

Every once in a very long while, Lord Tywin Lannister would actually threaten to smile; he never did, but the threat alone was terrible to behold. "The greatest fools are ofttimes more clever than the men who laugh at them," he said, and then, "You will marry Sansa Stark, Tyrion. And soon."

CATELYN

They carried the corpses in upon their shoulders and laid them beneath the dais. A silence fell across the torchlit hall, and in the quiet Catelyn could hear Grey Wind howling half a castle away. *He smells the blood,* she thought, *through stone walls and wooden doors, through night and rain, he still knows the scent of death and ruin.*

She stood at Robb's left hand beside the high seat, and for a moment felt almost as if she were looking down at her own dead, at Bran and Rickon. These boys had been much older, but death had shrunken them. Naked and wet, they seemed such little things, so still it was hard to remember them living.

The blond boy had been trying to grow a beard. Pale yellow peach fuzz covered his cheeks and jaw above the red ruin the knife had made of his throat. His long golden hair was still wet, as if he had been pulled from a bath. By the look of him, he had died peacefully, perhaps in sleep, but his brown-haired cousin had fought for life. His arms bore slashes where he'd tried to block the blades, and red still trickled slowly from the stab wounds that covered his chest and belly and back like so many tongueless mouths, though the rain had washed him almost clean.

Robb had donned his crown before coming to the hall, and the bronze shone darkly in the torchlight. Shadows hid his eyes as he looked upon the dead. *Does he see Bran and Rickon as well?* She might have wept, but there were no tears left in her. The dead boys were pale from long imprisonment, and both had been fair; against their smooth white skin, the blood was shockingly red, unbearable to look upon. *Will they lay Sansa down naked beneath the Iron Throne after they have killed her?*

Will her skin seem as white, her blood as red? From outside came the steady wash of rain and the restless howling of a wolf.

Her brother Edmure stood to Robb's right, one hand upon the back of his father's seat, his face still puffy from sleep. They had woken him as they had her, pounding on his door in the black of night to yank him rudely from his dreams. *Were they good dreams, brother? Do you dream of sunlight and laughter and a maiden's kisses? I pray you do.* Her own dreams were dark and laced with terrors.

Robb's captains and lords bannermen stood about the hall, some mailed and armed, others in various states of dishevelment and undress. Ser Raynald and his uncle Ser Rolph were among them, but Robb had seen fit to spare his queen this ugliness. *The Crag is not far from Casterly Rock,* Catelyn recalled. *Jeyne may well have played with these boys when all of them were children.*

She looked down again upon the corpses of the squires Tion Frey and Willem Lannister, and waited for her son to speak.

It seemed a very long time before Robb lifted his eyes from the bloody dead. "Smalljon," he said, "tell your father to bring them in." Wordless, Smalljon Umber turned to obey, his steps echoing in the great stone hall.

As the Greatjon marched his prisoners through the doors, Catelyn made note of how some other men stepped back to give them room, as if treason could somehow be passed by a touch, a glance, a cough. The captors and the captives looked much alike; big men, every one, with thick beards and long hair. Two of the Greatjon's men were wounded, and three of their prisoners. Only the fact that some had spears and others empty scabbards served to set them apart. All were clad in mail hauberks or shirts of sewn rings, with heavy boots and thick cloaks, some of wool and some of fur. *The north is hard and cold, and has no mercy,* Ned had told her when she first came to Winterfell a thousand years ago.

"Five," said Robb when the prisoners stood before him, wet and silent. "Is that all of them?"

"There were eight," rumbled the Greatjon. "We killed two taking them, and a third is dying now."

Robb studied the faces of the captives. "It required eight of you to kill two unarmed squires."

Edmure Tully spoke up. "They murdered two of my men as well, to get into the tower. Delp and Elwood."

"It was no murder, ser," said Lord Rickard Karstark, no more discomfited by the ropes about his wrists than by the blood that trickled down his face. "Any man who steps between a father and his vengeance asks for death."

His words rang against Catelyn's ears, harsh and cruel as the pounding of a war drum. Her throat was dry as bone. *I did this. These two boys died so my daughters might live.*

"I saw your sons die, that night in the Whispering Wood," Robb told Lord Karstark. "Tion Frey did not kill Torrhen. Willem Lannister did not slay Eddard. How then can you call this vengeance? This was folly, and bloody murder. Your sons died honorably on a battlefield, with swords in their hands."

"They *died*," said Rickard Karstark, yielding no inch of ground. "The Kingslayer cut them down. These two were of his ilk. Only blood can pay for blood."

"The blood of children?" Robb pointed at the corpses. "How old were they? Twelve, thirteen? *Squires*."

"Squires die in every battle."

"Die fighting, yes. Tion Frey and Willem Lannister gave up their swords in the Whispering Wood. They were captives, locked in a cell, asleep, unarmed . . . boys. *Look at them!*"

Lord Karstark looked instead at Catelyn. "Tell your mother to look at them," he said. "She slew them, as much as I."

Catelyn put a hand on the back of Robb's seat. The hall seemed to spin about her. She felt as though she might retch.

"My mother had naught to do with this," Robb said angrily. "This was your work. Your murder. Your *treason*."

"How can it be treason to kill Lannisters, when it is not treason to free them?" asked Karstark harshly. "Has Your Grace forgotten that we are at war with Casterly Rock? In war you kill your enemies. Didn't your father teach you that, boy?"

"*Boy?*" The Greatjon dealt Rickard Karstark a buffet with a mailed fist that sent the other lord to his knees.

"Leave him!" Robb's voice rang with command. Umber stepped back away from the captive.

Lord Karstark spit out a broken tooth. "Yes, Lord Umber, leave me to the king. He means to give me a scolding before he forgives me. That's how he deals with treason, our King in the North." He smiled a wet red smile. "Or should I call you the King Who Lost the North, Your Grace?"

The Greatjon snatched a spear from the man beside him and jerked it to his shoulder. "Let me spit him, sire. Let me open his belly so we can see the color of his guts."

The doors of the hall crashed open, and the Blackfish entered with water running from his cloak and helm. Tully men-at-arms followed him in, while outside lightning cracked across the sky and a hard black rain pounded against the stones of Riverrun. Ser Brynden removed his helm and went to one knee. "Your Grace," was all he said, but the grimness of his tone spoke volumes.

"I will hear Ser Brynden privily, in the audience chamber." Robb rose to his feet. "Greatjon, keep Lord Karstark here till I return, and hang the other seven."

The Greatjon lowered the spear. "Even the dead ones?"

"Yes. I will not have such fouling my lord uncle's rivers. Let them feed the crows."

One of the captives dropped to his knees. "Mercy, sire. I killed no one, I only stood at the door to watch for guards."

Robb considered that a moment. "Did you know what Lord Rickard intended? Did you see the knives drawn? Did you hear the shouts, the screams, the cries for mercy?"

"Aye, I did, but I took no part. I was only the watcher, I swear it . . ."

"Lord Umber," said Robb, "this one was only the watcher. Hang him last, so he may watch the others die. Mother, Uncle, with me, if you please." He turned away as the Greatjon's men closed upon the prisoners and drove them from the hall at spearpoint. Outside the thunder crashed and boomed, so loud it sounded as if the castle were coming down about their ears. *Is this the sound of a kingdom falling?* Catelyn wondered.

It was dark within the audience chamber, but at least the sound of the thunder was muffled by another thickness of wall. A servant entered with an oil lamp to light the fire, but Robb sent him away and kept the lamp. There were tables and chairs, but only Edmure sat, and he rose again when he realized that the others had remainded standing. Robb took off his crown and placed it on the table before him.

The Blackfish shut the door. "The Karstarks are gone."

"All?" Was it anger or despair that thickened Robb's voice like that? Even Catelyn was not certain.

"All the fighting men," Ser Brynden replied. "A few camp followers and serving men were left with their wounded. We questioned as many as we needed, to be certain of the truth. They started leaving at nightfall, stealing off in ones and twos at first, and then in larger groups. The wounded men and servants were told to keep the campfires lit so no one would know they'd gone, but once the rains began it didn't matter."

"Will they re-form, away from Riverrun?" asked Robb.

"No. They've scattered, hunting. Lord Karstark has sworn to give the hand of his maiden daughter to any man highborn or low who brings him the head of the Kingslayer."

Gods be good. Catelyn felt ill again.

"Near three hundred riders and twice as many mounts, melted away in the night." Robb rubbed his temples, where the crown had left its mark in the soft skin above his ears. "All the mounted strength of Karhold, lost."

Lost by me. By me, may the gods forgive me. Catelyn did not need to be a soldier to grasp the trap Robb was in. For the moment he held the riverlands, but his kingdom was surrounded by enemies to every side but east, where Lysa sat aloof on her mountaintop. Even the Trident was scarce secure so long as the Lord of the Crossing withheld his allegiance. *And now to lose the Karstarks as well . . .*

"No word of this must leave Riverrun," her brother Edmure said. "Lord Tywin would . . . the Lannisters pay their debts, they are always saying that. Mother have mercy, when he hears."

Sansa. Catelyn's nails dug into the soft flesh of her palms, so hard did she close her hand.

Robb gave Edmure a look that chilled. "Would you make me a liar as well as a murderer, Uncle?"

"We need speak no falsehood. Only say nothing. Bury the boys and hold our tongues till the war's done. Willem was son to Ser Kevan Lannister, and Lord Tywin's nephew. Tion was Lady Genna's, *and* a Frey. We must keep the news from the Twins as well, until . . ."

"Until we can bring the murdered dead back to life?" said Brynden Blackfish sharply. "The truth escaped with the Karstarks, Edmure. It is too late for such games."

"I owe their fathers truth," said Robb. "And justice. I owe them that as well." He gazed at his crown, the dark gleam of bronze, the circle of iron swords. "Lord Rickard defied me. Betrayed me. I have no choice but to condemn him. Gods know what the Karstark foot with Roose Bolton will do when they hear I've executed their liege for a traitor. Bolton must be warned."

"Lord Karstark's heir was at Harrenhal as well," Ser Brynden reminded him. "The eldest son, the one the Lannisters took captive on the Green Fork."

"Harrion. His name is Harrion." Robb laughed bitterly. "A king had best know the names of his enemies, don't you think?"

The Blackfish looked at him shrewdly. "You know that for a certainty? That this will make young Karstark your enemy?"

"What else would he be? I am about to kill his father, he's not like to thank me."

"He might. There are sons who hate their fathers, and in a stroke you will make him Lord of Karhold."

Robb shook his head. "Even if Harrion were that sort, he could never openly forgive his father's killer. His own men would turn on him. These are *northmen,* Uncle. The north remembers."

"Pardon him, then," urged Edmure Tully.

Robb stared at him in frank disbelief.

Under that gaze, Edmure's face reddened. "Spare his life, I mean. I don't like the taste of it any more than you, sire. He slew my men as well. Poor Delp had only just recovered from the wound Ser Jaime gave him. Karstark must be punished, certainly. Keep him in chains, I say."

"A hostage?" said Catelyn. *It might be best . . .*

"Yes, a hostage!" Her brother seized on her musing as agreement. "Tell the son that so long as he remains loyal, his father will not be harmed. Otherwise . . . we have no hope of the Freys now, not if I offered to marry *all* Lord Walder's daughters and carry his litter besides. If we should lose the Karstarks as well, what hope is there?"

"What hope . . ." Robb let out a breath, pushed his hair back from his eyes, and said, "We've had naught from Ser Rodrik in the north, no response from Walder Frey to our new offer, only silence from the Eyrie." He appealed to his mother. "Will your sister never answer us? How many times must I write her? I will not believe that *none* of the birds have reached her."

Her son wanted comfort, Catelyn realized; he wanted to hear that it would be all right. But her king needed truth. "The birds have reached her. Though she may tell you they did not, if it ever comes to that. Expect no help from that quarter, Robb.

"Lysa was never brave. When we were girls together, she would run and hide whenever she'd done something wrong. Perhaps she thought our lord father would forget to be wroth with her if he could not find her. It is no different now. She ran from King's Landing for fear, to the safest place she knows, and she sits on her mountain hoping everyone will forget her."

"The knights of the Vale could make all the difference in this war," said Robb, "but if she will not fight, so be it. I've asked only that she open the Bloody Gate for us, and provide ships at Gulltown to take us north. The high road would be hard, but not so hard as fighting our way up the Neck. If I could land at White Harbor I could flank Moat Cailin and drive the ironmen from the north in half a year."

"It will not happen, sire," said the Blackfish. "Cat is right. Lady Lysa is too fearful to admit an army to the Vale. *Any* army. The Bloody Gate will remain closed."

"The Others can take her, then," Robb cursed, in a fury of despair. "Bloody Rickard Karstark as well. And Theon Greyjoy, Walder Frey, Tywin Lannister, and all the rest of them. Gods be good, why would any man ever want to be king? When everyone was shouting *King in the North, King in the North*, I told myself . . . *swore* to myself . . . that I would be a good king, as honorable as Father, strong, just, loyal to my friends and brave when I faced my enemies . . . now I can't even tell one from the other. How did it all get so *confused?* Lord Rickard's fought at my side in half a dozen battles. His sons died for me in the Whispering

Wood. Tion Frey and Willem Lannister were my *enemies*. Yet now I have to kill my dead friends' father for their sakes." He looked at them all. "Will the Lannisters thank me for Lord Rickard's head? Will the Freys?"

"No," said Brynden Blackfish, blunt as ever.

"All the more reason to spare Lord Rickard's life and keep him hostage," Edmure urged.

Robb reached down with both hands, lifted the heavy bronze-and-iron crown, and set it back atop his head, and suddenly he was a king again. "Lord Rickard dies."

"But *why?*" said Edmure. "You said yourself –"

"I know what I said, Uncle. It does not change what I must do." The swords in his crown stood stark and black against his brow. "In battle I might have slain Tion and Willem myself, but this was no battle. They were asleep in their beds, naked and unarmed, in a cell where I put them. Rickard Karstark killed more than a Frey and a Lannister. *He killed my honor.* I shall deal with him at dawn."

When day broke, grey and chilly, the storm had diminished to a steady, soaking rain, yet even so the godswood was crowded. River lords and northmen, highborn and low, knights and sellswords and stableboys, they stood amongst the trees to see the end of the night's dark dance. Edmure had given commands, and a headsman's block had been set up before the heart tree. Rain and leaves fell all around them as the Greatjon's men led Lord Rickard Karstark through the press, hands still bound. His men already hung from Riverrun's high walls, slumping at the end of long ropes as the rain washed down their darkening faces.

Long Lew waited beside the block, but Robb took the poleaxe from his hand and ordered him to step aside. "This is my work," he said. "He dies at my word. He must die by my hand."

Lord Rickard Karstark dipped his head stiffly. "For that much, I thank you. But for naught else." He had dressed for death in a long black wool surcoat emblazoned with the white sunburst of his House. "The blood of the First Men flows in my veins as much as yours, boy. You would do well to remember that. I was named for your grandfather. I raised my banners against King Aerys for your father, and against King Joffrey for you. At Oxcross and the Whispering Wood and in the Battle of the Camps, I rode beside you, and I stood with Lord Eddard on the Trident. We are kin, Stark and Karstark."

"This kinship did not stop you from betraying me," Robb said. "And it will not save you now. Kneel, my lord."

Lord Rickard had spoken truly, Catelyn knew. The Karstarks traced their descent to Karlon Stark, a younger son of Winterfell who had put down a rebel lord a thousand years ago, and been granted lands for his valor. The castle he built had been named Karl's Hold, but that soon became Karhold, and over the centuries the Karhold Starks had become Karstarks.

"Old gods or new, it makes no matter," Lord Rickard told her son, "no man is so accursed as the kinslayer."

"Kneel, traitor," Robb said again. "Or must I have them force your head onto the block?"

Lord Karstark knelt. "The gods shall judge you, as you have judged me." He laid his head upon the block.

"Rickard Karstark, Lord of Karhold." Robb lifted the heavy axe with both hands. "Here in sight of gods and men, I judge you guilty of murder and high treason. In mine own name I condemn you. With mine own hand I take your life. Would you speak a final word?"

"Kill me, and be cursed. You are no king of mine."

The axe crashed down. Heavy and well-honed, it killed at a single blow, but it took three to sever the man's head from his body, and by the time it was done both living and dead were drenched in blood. Robb flung the poleaxe down in disgust, and turned wordless to the heart tree. He stood shaking with his hands half-clenched and the rain running down his cheeks. *Gods forgive him*, Catelyn prayed in silence. *He is only a boy, and he had no other choice.*

That was the last she saw of her son that day. The rain continued all through the morning, lashing the surface of the rivers and turning the godswood grass into mud and puddles. The Blackfish assembled a hundred men and rode out after Karstarks, but no one expected he would bring back many. "I only pray I do not need to hang them," he said as he departed. When he was gone, Catelyn retreated to her father's solar, to sit once more beside Lord Hoster's bed.

"It will not be much longer," Maester Vyman warned her, when he came that afternoon. "His last strength is going, though still he tries to fight."

"He was ever a fighter," she said. "A sweet stubborn man."

"Yes," the maester said, "but this battle he cannot win. It is time he lay down his sword and shield. Time to yield."

To yield, she thought, *to make a peace.* Was it her father the maester was speaking of, or her son?

At evenfall, Jeyne Westerling came to see her. The young queen entered the solar timidly. "Lady Catelyn, I do not mean to disturb you . . ."

"You are most welcome here, Your Grace." Catelyn had been sewing, but she put the needle aside now.

"Please. Call me Jeyne. I don't feel like a Grace."

"You are one, nonetheless. Please, come sit, Your Grace."

"Jeyne." She sat by the hearth and smoothed her skirt out anxiously.

"As you wish. How might I serve you, Jeyne?"

"It's Robb," the girl said. "He's so miserable, so . . . so angry and disconsolate. I don't know what to do."

"It is a hard thing to take a man's life."

"I know. I told him, he should use a headsman. When Lord Tywin sends a man to die, all he does is give the command. It's easier that way, don't you think?"

"Yes," said Catelyn, "but my lord husband taught his sons that killing should never be easy."

"Oh." Queen Jeyne wet her lips. "Robb has not eaten all day. I had Rollam bring him a nice supper, boar's ribs and stewed onions and ale, but he never touched a bite of it. He spent all morning writing a letter and told me not to disturb him, but when the letter was done he burned it. Now he is sitting and looking at maps. I asked him what he was looking for, but he never answered. I don't think he ever heard me. He wouldn't even change out of his clothes. They were damp all day, and bloody. I want to be a good wife to him, I do, but I don't know how to help. To cheer him, or comfort him. I don't know what he *needs*. Please, my lady, you're his mother, tell me what I should do."

Tell me what I should do. Catelyn might have asked the same, if her father had been well enough to ask. But Lord Hoster was gone, or near enough. Her Ned as well. *Bran and Rickon too, and Mother, and Brandon so long ago.* Only Robb remained to her, Robb and the fading hope of her daughters.

"Sometimes," Catelyn said slowly, "the best thing you can do is nothing. When I first came to Winterfell, I was hurt whenever Ned went to the godswood to sit beneath his heart tree. Part of his soul was in that tree, I knew, a part I would never share. Yet without that part, I soon realized, he would not have been Ned. Jeyne, child, you have wed the north, as I did . . . and in the north, the winters will come." She tried to smile. "Be patient. Be understanding. He loves you and he needs you, and he will come back to you soon enough. This very night, perhaps. Be there when he does. That is all I can tell you."

The young queen listened raptly. "I will," she said when Catelyn was done. "I'll be there." She got to her feet. "I should go back. He might have missed me. I'll see. But if he's still at his maps, I'll be patient."

"Do," said Catelyn, but when the girl was at the door, she thought of something else. "Jeyne," she called after, "there's one more thing Robb needs from you, though he may not know it yet himself. A king must have an heir."

The girl smiled at that. "My mother says the same. She makes a posset for me, herbs and milk and ale, to help make me fertile. I drink it every morning. I told Robb I'm sure to give him twins. An Eddard and a Brandon. He liked that, I think. We . . . we try most every day, my lady. Sometimes twice or more." The girl blushed very prettily. "I'll be with child soon, I promise. I pray to our Mother Above, every night."

"Very good. I will add my prayers as well. To the old gods *and* the new."

When the girl had gone, Catelyn turned back to her father and smoothed the thin white hair across his brow. "An Eddard and a Brandon," she sighed softly. "And perhaps in time a Hoster. Would you like that?" He did not answer, but she had never expected that he would. As the sound of the rain on the roof mingled with her father's breathing, she thought about Jeyne. The girl did seem to have a good heart, just as Robb had said. *And good hips, which might be more important.*

JAIME

Two days' ride to either side of the kingsroad, they passed through a wide swath of destruction, miles of blackened fields and orchards where the trunks of dead trees jutted into the air like archers' stakes. The bridges were burnt as well, and the streams swollen by autumn rains, so they had to range along the banks in search of fords. The nights were alive with howling of wolves, but they saw no people.

At Maidenpool, Lord Mooton's red salmon still flew above the castle on its hill, but the town walls were deserted, the gates smashed, half the homes and shops burned or plundered. They saw nothing living but a few feral dogs that went slinking away at the sound of their approach. The pool from which the town took its name, where legend said that Florian the Fool had first glimpsed Jonquil bathing with her sisters, was so choked with rotting corpses that the water had turned into a murky grey-green soup.

Jaime took one look and burst into song. "*Six maids there were in a spring-fed pool . . .*"

"What are you *doing?*" Brienne demanded.

"Singing. 'Six Maids in a Pool,' I'm sure you've heard it. And shy little maids they were, too. Rather like you. Though somewhat prettier, I'll warrant."

"Be quiet," the wench said, with a look that suggested she would love to leave him floating in the pool among the corpses.

"Please, Jaime," pleaded cousin Cleos. "Lord Mooton is sworn to Riverrun, we don't want to draw him out of his castle. And there may be other enemies hiding in the rubble . . ."

"Hers or ours? They are not the same, coz. I have a yen to see if the wench can use that sword she wears."

"If you won't be quiet, you leave me no choice but to gag you, Kingslayer."

"Unchain my hands and I'll play mute all the way to King's Landing. What could be fairer than that, wench?"

"*Brienne!* My name is *Brienne!*" Three crows went flapping into the air, startled at the sound.

"Care for a bath, Brienne?" He laughed. "You're a maiden and there's the pool. I'll wash your back." He used to scrub Cersei's back, when they were children together at Casterly Rock.

The wench turned her horse's head and trotted away. Jaime and Ser Cleos followed her out of the ashes of Maidenpool. A half mile on, green began to creep back into the world once more. Jaime was glad. The burned lands reminded him too much of Aerys.

"She's taking the Duskendale road," Ser Cleos muttered. "It would be safer to follow the coast."

"Safer but slower. I'm for Duskendale, coz. If truth be told, I'm bored with your company." *You may be half Lannister, but you're a far cry from my sister.*

He could never bear to be long apart from his twin. Even as children, they would creep into each other's beds and sleep with their arms entwined. *Even in the womb.* Long before his sister's flowering or the advent of his own manhood, they had seen mares and stallions in the fields and dogs and bitches in the kennels and played at doing the same. Once their mother's maid had caught them at it . . . he did not recall just what they had been doing, but whatever it was had horrified Lady Joanna. She'd sent the maid away, moved Jaime's bedchamber to the other side of Casterly Rock, set a guard outside Cersei's, and told them that they must *never* do that again or she would have no choice but to tell their lord father. They need not have feared, though. It was not long after that she died birthing Tyrion. Jaime barely remembered what his mother had looked like.

Perhaps Stannis Baratheon and the Starks had done him a kindness. They had spread their tale of incest all over the Seven Kingdoms, so there was nothing left to hide. *Why shouldn't I marry Cersei openly and share her bed every night? The dragons always married their sisters.* Septons, lords, and smallfolk had turned a blind eye to the Targaryens for hundreds of years, let them do the same for House Lannister. It would play havoc with Joffrey's claim to the crown, to be sure, but in the end it had been swords that had won the Iron Throne for Robert, and swords could keep Joffrey there as well, regardless of whose seed he was. *We could marry him to Myrcella, once we've sent Sansa Stark back to her mother. That*

*would show the realm that the Lannisters are above their laws, like
gods and Targaryens.*

Jaime had decided that he *would* return Sansa, and the younger girl as
well if she could be found. It was not like to win him back his lost honor,
but the notion of keeping faith when they all expected betrayal amused
him more than he could say.

They were riding past a trampled wheatfield and a low stone wall
when Jaime heard a soft *thrum* from behind, as if a dozen birds had taken
flight at once. "*Down!*" he shouted, throwing himself against the neck
of his horse. The gelding screamed and reared as an arrow took him in
the rump. Other shafts went hissing past. Jaime saw Ser Cleos lurch from
the saddle, twisting as his foot caught in the stirrup. His palfrey bolted,
and Frey was dragged past shouting, head bouncing against the ground.

Jaime's gelding lumbered off ponderously, blowing and snorting in
pain. He craned around to look for Brienne. She was still ahorse, an arrow
lodged in her back and another in her leg, but she seemed not to feel
them. He saw her pull her sword and wheel in a circle, searching for the
bowmen. "*Behind the wall,*" Jaime called, fighting to turn his half-blind
mount back toward the fight. The reins were tangled in his damned
chains, and the air was full of arrows again. "*At them!*" he shouted,
kicking to show her how it was done. The old sorry horse found a burst of
speed from somewhere. Suddenly they were racing across the wheatfield,
throwing up clouds of chaff. Jaime had just enough time to think, *The
wench had better follow before they realize they're being charged by an
unarmed man in chains.* Then he heard her coming hard behind. "Evenfall!" she shouted as her plow horse thundered by. She brandished her
longsword. "Tarth! Tarth!"

A few last arrows sped harmlessly past; then the bowmen broke and
ran, the way unsupported bowmen always broke and ran before the charge
of knights. Brienne reined up at the wall. By the time Jaime reached her,
they had all melted into the wood twenty yards away. "Lost your taste
for battle?"

"They were running."

"That's the best time to kill them."

She sheathed her sword. "Why did you charge?"

"Bowmen are fearless so long as they can hide behind walls and shoot
at you from afar, but if you come at them, they run. They know what
will happen when you reach them. You have an arrow in your back, you
know. And another in your leg. You ought to let me tend them."

"You?"

"Who else? The last I saw of cousin Cleos, his palfrey was using his
head to plow a furrow. Though I suppose we ought to find him. He *is* a
Lannister of sorts."

They found Cleos still tangled in his stirrup. He had an arrow through his right arm and a second in his chest, but it was the ground that had done for him. The top of his head was matted with blood and mushy to the touch, pieces of broken bone moving under the skin beneath the pressure of Jaime's hand.

Brienne knelt and held his hand. "He's still warm."

"He'll cool soon enough. I want his horse and his clothes. I'm weary of rags and fleas."

"He was your cousin." The wench was shocked.

"*Was*," Jaime agreed. "Have no fear, I am amply provisioned in cousins. I'll have his sword as well. You need someone to share the watches."

"You can stand a watch without weapons." She rose.

"Chained to a tree? Perhaps I could. Or perhaps I could make my own bargain with the next lot of outlaws and let them slit that thick neck of yours, wench."

"I will not arm you. And my name is –"

"– Brienne, I know. I'll swear an oath not to harm you, if that will ease your girlish fears."

"Your oaths are worthless. You swore an oath to Aerys."

"You haven't cooked anyone in their armor so far as I know. And we both want me safe and whole in King's Landing, don't we?" He squatted beside Cleos and began to undo his swordbelt.

"Step away from him. Now. Stop that."

Jaime was tired. Tired of her suspicions, tired of her insults, tired of her crooked teeth and her broad spotty face and that limp thin hair of hers. Ignoring her protests, he grasped the hilt of his cousin's longsword with both hands, held the corpse down with his foot, and pulled. As the blade slid from the scabbard, he was already pivoting, bringing the sword around and up in a swift deadly arc. Steel met steel with a ringing, bone-jarring *clang*. Somehow Brienne had gotten her own blade out in time. Jaime laughed. "Very good, wench."

"Give me the sword, Kingslayer."

"Oh, I will." He sprang to his feet and drove at her, the longsword alive in his hands. Brienne jumped back, parrying, but he followed, pressing the attack. No sooner did she turn one cut than the next was upon her. The swords kissed and sprang apart and kissed again. Jaime's blood was singing. This was what he was meant for; he never felt so alive as when he was fighting, with death balanced on every stroke. *And with my wrists chained together, the wench may even give me a contest for a time.* His chains forced him to use a two-handed grip, though of course the weight and reach were less than if the blade had been a true two-handed greatsword, but what did it matter? His cousin's sword was long enough to write an end to this Brienne of Tarth.

High, low, overhand, he rained down steel upon her. Left, right, backslash, swinging so hard that sparks flew when the swords came together, upswing, sideslash, overhand, always attacking, moving into her, step and slide, strike and step, step and strike, hacking, slashing, faster, faster, faster . . .

. . . until, breathless, he stepped back and let the point of the sword fall to the ground, giving her a moment of respite. "Not half bad," he acknowledged. "For a wench."

She took a slow deep breath, her eyes watching him warily. "I would not hurt you, Kingslayer."

"As if you could." He whirled the blade back up above his head and flew at her again, chains rattling.

Jaime could not have said how long he pressed the attack. It might have been minutes or it might have been hours; time slept when swords woke. He drove her away from his cousin's corpse, drove her across the road, drove her into the trees. She stumbled once on a root she never saw, and for a moment he thought she was done, but she went to one knee instead of falling, and never lost a beat. Her sword leapt up to block a downcut that would have opened her from shoulder to groin, and then she cut at *him*, again and again, fighting her way back to her feet stroke by stroke.

The dance went on. He pinned her against an oak, cursed as she slipped away, followed her through a shallow brook half-choked with fallen leaves. Steel rang, steel sang, steel screamed and sparked and scraped, and the woman started grunting like a sow at every crash, yet somehow he could not reach her. It was as if she had an iron cage around her that stopped every blow.

"Not bad at all," he said when he paused for a second to catch his breath, circling to her right.

"For a wench?"

"For a squire, say. A green one." He laughed a ragged, breathless laugh. "Come on, come on, my sweetling, the music's still playing. Might I have this dance, my lady?"

Grunting, she came at him, blade whirling, and suddenly it was Jaime struggling to keep steel from skin. One of her slashes raked across his brow, and blood ran down into his right eye. *The Others take her, and Riverrun as well!* His skills had gone to rust and rot in that bloody dungeon, and the chains were no great help either. His eye closed, his shoulders were going numb from the jarring they'd taken, and his wrists ached from the weight of chains, manacles, and sword. His longsword grew heavier with every blow, and Jaime knew he was not swinging it as quickly as he'd done earlier, nor raising it as high.

She is stronger than I am.

The realization chilled him. Robert had been stronger than him, to be sure. The White Bull Gerold Hightower as well, in his heyday, and Ser Arthur Dayne. Amongst the living, Greatjon Umber was stronger, Strongboar of Crakehall most likely, both Cleganes for a certainty. The Mountain's strength was like nothing human. It did not matter. With speed and skill, Jaime could beat them all. But this was a *woman*. A huge cow of a woman, to be sure, but even so . . . by rights, she should be the one wearing down.

Instead she forced him back into the brook again, shouting, "Yield! Throw down the sword!"

A slick stone turned under Jaime's foot. As he felt himself falling, he twisted the mischance into a diving lunge. His point scraped past her parry and bit into her upper thigh. A red flower blossomed, and Jaime had an instant to savor the sight of her blood before his knee slammed into a rock. The pain was blinding. Brienne splashed into him and kicked away his sword. *"YIELD!"*

Jaime drove his shoulder into her legs, bringing her down on top of him. They rolled, kicking and punching until finally she was sitting astride him. He managed to jerk her dagger from its sheath, but before he could plunge it into her belly she caught his wrist and slammed his hands back on a rock so hard he thought she'd wrenched an arm from its socket. Her other hand spread across his face. "Yield!" She shoved his head down, held it under, pulled it up. *"Yield!"* Jaime spit water into her face. A shove, a splash, and he was under again, kicking uselessly, fighting to breathe. Up again. *"Yield, or I'll drown you!"*

"And break your oath?" he snarled. "Like me?"

She let him go, and he went down with a splash.

And the woods rang with coarse laughter.

Brienne lurched to her feet. She was all mud and blood below the waist, her clothing askew, her face red. *She looks as if they caught us fucking instead of fighting.* Jaime crawled over the rocks to shallow water, wiping the blood from his eye with his chained hands. Armed men lined both sides of the brook. *Small wonder, we were making enough noise to wake a dragon.* "Well met, friends," he called to them amiably. "My pardons if I disturbed you. You caught me chastising my wife."

"Seemed to me she was doing the *chastising*." The man who spoke was thick and powerful, and the nasal bar of his iron halfhelm did not wholly conceal his lack of a nose.

These were not the outlaws who had killed Ser Cleos, Jaime realized suddenly. The scum of the earth surrounded them: swarthy Dornishmen and blond Lyseni, Dothraki with bells in their braids, hairy Ibbenese, coal-black Summer Islanders in feathered cloaks. He knew them. *The Brave Companions.*

Brienne found her voice. "I have a hundred stags –"

A cadaverous man in a tattered leather cloak said, "We'll take that for a start, m'lady."

"Then we'll have your cunt," said the noseless man. "It can't be as ugly as the rest of you."

"Turn her over and rape her arse, Rorge," urged a Dornish spearman with a red silk scarf wound about his helm. "That way you won't need to look at her."

"And rob her o' the pleasure o' looking at *me*?" noseless said, and the others laughed.

Ugly and stubborn though she might be, the wench deserved better than to be gang raped by such refuse as these. "Who commands here?" Jaime demanded loudly.

"I have that honor, Ser Jaime." The cadaver's eyes were rimmed in red, his hair thin and dry. Dark blue veins could be seen through the pallid skin of his hands and face. "Urswyck I am. Called Urswyck the Faithful."

"You know who I am?"

The sellsword inclined his head. "It takes more than a beard and a shaved head to deceive the Brave Companions."

The Bloody Mummers, you mean. Jaime had no more use for these than he did for Gregor Clegane or Amory Lorch. *Dogs*, his father called them all, and he used them like dogs, to hound his prey and put fear in their hearts. "If you know me, Urswyck, you know you'll have your reward. A Lannister always pays his debts. As for the wench, she's high-born, and worth a good ransom."

The other cocked his head. "Is it so? How fortunate."

There was something sly about the way Urswyck was smiling that Jaime did not like. "You heard me. Where's the goat?"

"A few hours distant. He will be pleased to see you, I have no doubt, but I would not call him a goat to his face. *Lord* Vargo grows prickly about his dignity."

Since when has that slobbering savage had dignity? "I'll be sure and remember that, when I see him. Lord of what, pray?"

"Harrenhal. It has been promised."

Harrenhal? Has my father taken leave of his senses? Jaime raised his hands. "I'll have these chains off."

Urswyck's chuckle was papery dry.

Something is very wrong here. Jaime gave no sign of his discomfiture, but only smiled. "Did I say something amusing?"

Noseless grinned. "You're the funniest thing I seen since Biter chewed that septa's teats off."

"You and your father lost too many battles," offered the Dornishman. "We had to trade our lion pelts for wolfskins."

Urswyck spread his hands. "What Timeon means to say is that the Brave Companions are no longer in the hire of House Lannister. We now serve Lord Bolton, and the King in the North."

Jaime gave him a cold, contemptuous smile. "And men say *I* have shit for honor?"

Urswyck was unhappy with that comment. At his signal, two of the Mummers grasped Jaime by the arms and Rorge drove a mailed fist into his stomach. As he doubled over grunting, he heard the wench protesting, "Stop, he's not to be harmed! Lady Catelyn sent us, an exchange of captives, he's under my protection . . ." Rorge hit him again, driving the air from his lungs. Brienne dove for her sword beneath the waters of the brook, but the Mummers were on her before she could lay hands on it. Strong as she was, it took four of them to beat her into submission.

By the end the wench's face was as swollen and bloody as Jaime's must have been, and they had knocked out two of her teeth. It did nothing to improve her appearance. Stumbling and bleeding, the two captives were dragged back through the woods to the horses, Brienne limping from the thigh wound he'd given her in the brook. Jaime felt sorry for her. She would lose her maidenhood tonight, he had no doubt. That noseless bastard would have her for a certainty, and some of the others would likely take a turn.

The Dornishman bound them back to back atop Brienne's plow horse while the other Mummers were stripping Cleos Frey to his skin to divvy up his possessions. Rorge won the bloodstained surcoat with its proud Lannister and Frey quarterings. The arrows had punched holes through lions and towers alike.

"I hope you're pleased, wench," Jaime whispered at Brienne. He coughed, and spat out a mouthful of blood. "If you'd armed me, we'd never have been taken." She made no answer. *There's a pig-stubborn bitch*, he thought. *But brave, yes.* He could not take that from her. "When we make camp for the night, you'll be raped, and more than once," he warned her. "You'd be wise not to resist. If you fight them, you'll lose more than a few teeth."

He felt Brienne's back stiffen against his. "Is that what *you* would do, if you were a woman?"

If I were a woman I'd be Cersei. "If I were a woman, I'd make them kill me. But I'm not." Jaime kicked their horse to a trot. "*Urswyck!* A word!"

The cadaverous sellsword in the ragged leather cloak reined up a moment, then fell in beside him. "What would you have of me, ser? And mind your tongue, or I'll chastise you again."

"Gold," said Jaime. "You do like gold?"

Urswyck studied him through reddened eyes. "It has its uses, I do confess."

Jaime gave Urswyck a knowing smile. "All the gold in Casterly Rock. Why let the goat enjoy it? Why not take us to King's Landing, and collect my ransom for yourself? Hers as well, if you like. Tarth is called the Sapphire Isle, a maiden told me once." The wench squirmed at that, but said nothing.

"Do you take me for a turncloak?"

"Certainly. What else?"

For half a heartbeat Urswyck considered the proposition. "King's Landing is a long way, and your father is there. Lord Tywin may resent us for selling Harrenhal to Lord Bolton."

He's cleverer than he looks. Jaime had been been looking forward to hanging the wretch while his pockets bulged with gold. "Leave me to deal with my father. I'll get you a royal pardon for any crimes you have committed. I'll get you a knighthood."

"Ser Urswyck," the man said, savoring the sound. "How proud my dear wife would be to hear it. If only I hadn't killed her." He sighed. "And what of brave Lord Vargo?"

"Shall I sing you a verse of 'The Rains of Castamere'? The goat won't be quite so brave when my father gets hold of him."

"And how will he do that? Are your father's arms so long that they can reach over the walls of Harrenhal and pluck us out?"

"If need be." King Harren's monstrous folly had fallen before, and it could fall again. "Are you such a fool as to think the goat can outfight the lion?"

Urswyck leaned over and slapped him lazily across the face. The sheer casual *insolence* of it was worse than the blow itself. *He does not fear me,* Jaime realized, with a chill. "I have heard enough, Kingslayer. I would have to be a great fool indeed to believe the promises of an oathbreaker like you." He kicked his horse and galloped smartly ahead.

Aerys, Jaime thought resentfully. *It always turns on Aerys.* He swayed with the motion of his horse, wishing for a sword. *Two swords would be even better. One for the wench and one for me. We'd die, but we'd take half of them down to hell with us.* "Why did you tell him Tarth was the Sapphire Isle?" Brienne whispered when Urswyck was out of earshot. "He's like to think my father's rich in gemstones . . ."

"You best pray he does."

"Is every word you say a lie, Kingslayer? Tarth is called the Sapphire Isle for the blue of its waters."

"Shout it a little louder, wench, I don't think Urswyck heard you. The sooner they know how little you're worth in ransom, the sooner the rapes begin. Every man here will mount you, but what do you care? Just close your eyes, open your legs, and pretend they're all Lord Renly."

Mercifully, that shut her mouth for a time.

The day was almost done by the time they found Vargo Hoat, sacking a small sept with another dozen of his Brave Companions. The leaded windows had been smashed, the carved wooden gods dragged out into the sunlight. The fattest Dothraki Jaime had ever seen was sitting on the Mother's chest when they rode up, prying out her chalcedony eyes with the point of his knife. Nearby, a skinny balding septon hung upside down from the limb of a spreading chestnut tree. Three of the Brave Companions were using his corpse for an archery butt. One of them must have been good; the dead man had arrows through both of his eyes.

When the sellswords spied Urswyck and the captives, a cry went up in half a dozen tongues. The goat was seated by a cookfire eating a half-cooked bird off a skewer, grease and blood running down his fingers into his long stringy beard. He wiped his hands on his tunic and rose. *"Kingthlayer,"* he slobbered. "You are my captifth."

"My lord, I am Brienne of Tarth," the wench called out. "Lady Catelyn Stark commanded me to deliver Ser Jaime to his brother at King's Landing."

The goat gave her a disinterested glance. "Thilence her."

"Hear me," Brienne entreated as Rorge cut the ropes that bound her to Jaime, "in the name of the King in the North, the king you serve, please, listen – "

Rorge dragged her off the horse and began to kick her. "See that you don't break any bones," Urswyck called out to him. "The horse-faced bitch is worth her weight in sapphires."

The Dornishman Timeon and a foul-smelling Ibbenese pulled Jaime down from the saddle and shoved him roughly toward the cookfire. It would not have been hard for him to have grasped one of their sword hilts as they manhandled him, but there were too many, and he was still in fetters. He might cut down one or two, but in the end he would die for it. Jaime was not ready to die just yet, and certainly not for the likes of Brienne of Tarth.

"Thith ith a thweet day," Vargo Hoat said. Around his neck hung a chain of linked coins, coins of every shape and size, cast and hammered, bearing the likenesses of kings, wizards, gods and demons, and all manner of fanciful beasts.

Coins from every land where he has fought, Jaime remembered. Greed was the key to this man. *If he was turned once, he can be turned again.* "Lord Vargo, you were foolish to leave my father's service, but it is not too late to make amends. He will pay well for me, you know it."

"Oh yeth," said Vargo Hoat. "Half the gold in Cathterly Rock, I thall have. But firth I mutht thend him a methage." He said something in his slithery goatish tongue.

Urswyck shoved him in the back, and a jester in green and pink motley kicked his legs out from under him. When he hit the ground one of the archers grabbed the chain between Jaime's wrists and used it to yank his arms out in front of him. The fat Dothraki put aside his knife to unsheathe a huge curved *arakh*, the wickedly sharp scythe-sword the horselords loved.

They mean to scare me. The fool hopped on Jaime's back, giggling, as the Dothraki swaggered toward him. *The goat wants me to piss my breeches and beg his mercy, but he'll never have that pleasure.* He was a Lannister of Casterly Rock, Lord Commander of the Kingsguard; no sellsword would make him scream.

Sunlight ran silver along the edge of the *arakh* as it came shivering down, almost too fast to see. And Jaime screamed.

ARYA

The small square keep was half a ruin, and so too the great grey knight who lived there. He was so old he did not understand their questions. No matter what was said to him, he would only smile and mutter, "I held the bridge against Ser Maynard. Red hair and a black temper, he had, but he could not move me. Six wounds I took before I killed him. Six!"

The maester who cared for him was a young man, thankfully. After the old knight had drifted to sleep in his chair, he took them aside and said, "I fear you seek a ghost. We had a bird, ages ago, half a year at least. The Lannisters caught Lord Beric near the Gods Eye. He was hanged."

"Aye, hanged he was, but Thoros cut him down before he died." Lem's broken nose was not so red or swollen as it had been, but it was healing crooked, giving his face a lopsided look. "His lordship's a hard man to kill, he is."

"And a hard man to find, it would seem," the maester said. "Have you asked the Lady of the Leaves?"

"We shall," said Greenbeard.

The next morning, as they crossed the little stone bridge behind the keep, Gendry wondered if this was the bridge the old man had fought over. No one knew. "Most like it is," said Jack-Be-Lucky. "Don't see no other bridges."

"You'd know for certain if there was a song," said Tom Sevenstrings. "One good song, and we'd know who Ser Maynard used to be and why he wanted to cross this bridge so bad. Poor old Lychester might be as far famed as the Dragonknight if he'd only had sense enough to keep a singer."

"Lord Lychester's sons died in Robert's Rebellion," grumbled Lem. "Some on one side, some on t'other. He's not been right in the head since. No bloody song's like to help any o' that."

"What did the maester mean, about asking the Lady of the Leaves?" Arya asked Anguy as they rode.

The archer smiled. "Wait and see."

Three days later, as they rode through a yellow wood, Jack-Be-Lucky unslung his horn and blew a signal, a different one than before. The sounds had scarcely died away when rope ladders unrolled from the limbs of trees. "Hobble the horses and up we go," said Tom, half singing the words. They climbed to a hidden village in the upper branches, a maze of rope walkways and little moss-covered houses concealed behind walls of red and gold, and were taken to the Lady of the Leaves, a stick-thin white-haired woman dressed in roughspun. "We cannot stay here much longer, with autumn on us," she told them. "A dozen wolves went down the Hayford road nine days past, hunting. If they'd chanced to look up they might have seen us."

"You've not seen Lord Beric?" asked Tom Sevenstrings.

"He's dead." The woman sounded sick. "The Mountain caught him, and drove a dagger through his eye. A begging brother told us. He had it from the lips of a man who saw it happen."

"That's an old stale tale, and false," said Lem. "The lightning lord's not so easy to kill. Ser Gregor might have put his eye out, but a man don't die o' that. Jack could tell you."

"Well, I never did," said one-eyed Jack-Be-Lucky. "My father got himself good and hanged by Lord Piper's bailiff, my brother Wat got sent to the Wall, and the Lannisters killed my other brothers. An eye, that's nothing."

"You swear he's not dead?" The woman clutched Lem's arm. "Bless you, Lem, that's the best tidings we've had in half a year. May the Warrior defend him, and the red priest too."

The next night they found shelter beneath the scorched shell of a sept, in a burned village called Sallydance. Only shards remained of its windows of leaded glass, and the aged septon who greeted them said the looters had even made off with the Mother's costly robes, the Crone's gilded lantern, and the silver crown the Father had worn. "They hacked the Maiden's breasts off too, though those were only wood," he told them. "And the eyes, the eyes were jet and lapis and mother-of-pearl, they pried them out with their knives. May the Mother have mercy on them all."

"Whose work was this?" said Lem Lemoncloak. "Mummers?"

"No," the old man said. "Northmen, they were. Savages who worship trees. They wanted the Kingslayer, they said."

Arya heard him, and chewed her lip. She could feel Gendry looking at her. It made her angry and ashamed.

There were a dozen men living in the vault beneath the sept, amongst cobwebs and roots and broken wine casks, but they had no word of Beric Dondarrion either. Not even their leader, who wore soot-blackened armor and a crude lightning bolt on his cloak. When Greenbeard saw Arya staring at him, he laughed and said, "The lightning lord is everywhere and nowhere, skinny squirrel."

"I'm not a squirrel," she said. "I'll almost be a woman soon. I'll be one-and-ten."

"Best watch out I don't marry you, then!" He tried to tickle her under the chin, but Arya slapped his stupid hand away.

Lem and Gendry played tiles with their hosts that night, while Tom Sevenstrings sang a silly song about Big Belly Ben and the High Septon's goose. Anguy let Arya try his longbow, but no matter how hard she bit her lip she could not draw it. "You need a lighter bow, milady," the freckled bowman said. "If there's seasoned wood at Riverrun, might be I'll make you one."

Tom overheard him, and broke off his song. "You're a young fool, Archer. If we go to Riverrun it will only be to collect her ransom, won't be no time for you to sit about making bows. Be thankful if you get out with your hide. Lord Hoster was hanging outlaws before you were shaving. And that son of his . . . a man who hates music can't be trusted, I always say."

"It's not music he hates," said Lem. "It's you, fool."

"Well, he has no cause. The wench was willing to make a man of him, is it my fault he drank too much to do the deed?"

Lem snorted through his broken nose. "Was it you who made a song of it, or some other bloody arse in love with his own voice?"

"I only sang it the once," Tom complained. "And who's to say the song was about him? 'Twas a song about a fish."

"A floppy fish," said Anguy, laughing.

Arya didn't care what Tom's stupid songs were about. She turned to Harwin. "What did he mean about ransom?"

"We have sore need of horses, milady. Armor as well. Swords, shields, spears. All the things coin can buy. Aye, and seed for planting. Winter is coming, remember?" He touched her under the chin. "You will not be the first highborn captive we've ransomed. Nor the last, I'd hope."

That much was true, Arya knew. Knights were captured and ransomed all the time, and sometimes women were too. *But what if Robb won't pay their price?* She wasn't a famous knight, and kings were supposed to put the realm before their sisters. And her lady mother, what would she say? Would she still want her back, after all the things she'd done? Arya chewed her lip and wondered.

The next day they rode to a place called High Heart, a hill so lofty that from atop it Arya felt as though she could see half the world. Around its brow stood a ring of huge pale stumps, all that remained of a circle of once-mighty weirwoods. Arya and Gendry walked around the hill to count them. There were thirty-one, some so wide that she could have used them for a bed.

High Heart had been sacred to the children of the forest, Tom Sevenstrings told her, and some of their magic lingered here still. "No harm can ever come to those as sleep here," the singer said. Arya thought that must be true; the hill was so high and the surrounding lands so flat that no enemy could approach unseen.

The smallfolk hereabouts shunned the place, Tom told her; it was said to be haunted by the ghosts of the children of the forest who had died here when the Andal king named Erreg the Kinslayer had cut down their grove. Arya knew about the children of the forest, and about the Andals too, but ghosts did not frighten her. She used to hide in the crypts of Winterfell when she was little, and play games of come-into-my-castle and monsters and maidens amongst the stone kings on their thrones.

Yet even so, the hair on the back of her neck stood up that night. She had been asleep, but the storm woke her. The wind pulled the coverlet right off her and sent it swirling into the bushes. When she went after it she heard voices.

Beside the embers of their campfire, she saw Tom, Lem, and Greenbeard talking to a tiny little woman, a foot shorter than Arya and older than Old Nan, all stooped and wrinkled and leaning on a gnarled black cane. Her white hair was so long it came almost to the ground. When the wind gusted it blew about her head in a fine cloud. Her flesh was whiter, the color of milk, and it seemed to Arya that her eyes were red, though it was hard to tell from the bushes. "The old gods stir and will not let me sleep," she heard the woman say. "I dreamt I saw a shadow with a burning heart butchering a golden stag, aye. I dreamt of a man without a face, waiting on a bridge that swayed and swung. On his shoulder perched a drowned crow with seaweed hanging from his wings. I dreamt of a roaring river and a woman that was a fish. Dead she drifted, with red tears on her cheeks, but when her eyes did open, *oh*, I woke from terror. All this I dreamt, and more. Do you have gifts for me, to pay me for my dreams?"

"Dreams," grumbled Lem Lemoncloak, "what good are dreams? Fish women and drowned crows. I had a dream myself last night. I was kissing this tavern wench I used to know. Are you going to pay me for that, old woman?"

"The wench is dead," the woman hissed. "Only worms may kiss her now." And then to Tom Sevenstrings she said, "I'll have my song or I'll have you gone."

So the singer played for her, so soft and sad that Arya only heard snatches of the words, though the tune was half-familiar. *Sansa would know it, I bet.* Her sister had known all the songs, and she could even play a little, and sing so sweetly. *All I could ever do was shout the words.*

The next morning the little white woman was nowhere to be seen. As they saddled their horses, Arya asked Tom Sevenstrings if the children of the forest still dwelled on High Heart. The singer chuckled. "Saw her, did you?"

"Was she a ghost?"

"Do ghosts complain of how their joints creak? No, she's only an old dwarf woman. A queer one, though, and evil-eyed. But she knows things she has no business knowing, and sometimes she'll tell you if she likes the look of you."

"Did she like the looks of *you?*" Arya asked doubtfully.

The singer laughed. "The sound of me, at least. She always makes me sing the same bloody song, though. Not a bad song, mind you, but I know others just as good." He shook his head. "What matters is, we have the scent now. You'll soon be seeing Thoros and the lightning lord, I'll wager."

"If you're their men, why do they hide from you?"

Tom Sevenstrings rolled his eyes at that, but Harwin gave her an answer. "I wouldn't call it hiding, milady, but it's true, Lord Beric moves about a lot, and seldom lets on what his plans are. That way no one can betray him. By now there must be hundreds of us sworn to him, maybe thousands, but it wouldn't do for us all to trail along behind him. We'd eat the country bare, or get butchered in a battle by some bigger host. The way we're scattered in little bands, we can strike in a dozen places at once, and be off somewhere else before they know. And when one of us is caught and put to the question, well, we can't tell them where to find Lord Beric no matter what they do to us." He hesitated. "You know what it means, to be put to the question?"

Arya nodded. "Tickling, they called it. Polliver and Raff and all." She told them about the village by the Gods Eye where she and Gendry had been caught, and the questions that the Tickler had asked. "Is there gold hidden in the village?" he would always begin. "Silver, gems? Is there food? Where is Lord Beric? Which of you village folk helped him? Where did he go? How many men did he have with him? How many knights? How many bowmen? How many were horsed? How are they armed? How many wounded? Where did they go, did you say?" Just thinking of it, she could hear the shrieks again, and smell the stench of blood and shit and burning flesh. "He always asked the same questions," she told the outlaws solemnly, "but he changed the tickling every day."

"No child should be made to suffer that," Harwin said when she was done. "The Mountain lost half his men at the Stone Mill, we hear. Might be this Tickler's floating down the Red Fork even now, with fish biting at his face. If not, well, it's one more crime they'll answer for. I've heard his lordship say this war began when the Hand sent him out to bring the king's justice to Gregor Clegane, and that's how he means for it to end." He gave her shoulder a reassuring pat. "You best mount up, milady. It's a long day's ride to Acorn Hall, but at the end of it we'll have a roof above our heads and a hot supper in our bellies."

It *was* a long day's ride, but as dusk was settling they forded a brook and came up on Acorn Hall, with its stone curtain walls and great oaken keep. Its master was away fighting in the retinue of *his* master, Lord Vance, the castle gates closed and barred in his absence. But his lady wife was an old friend of Tom Sevenstrings, and Anguy said they'd once been lovers. Anguy often rode beside her; he was closer to her in age than any of them but Gendry, and he told her droll tales of the Dornish Marches. He never fooled her, though. *He's not my friend. He's only staying close to watch me and make sure I don't ride off again.* Well, Arya could watch as well. Syrio Forel had taught her how.

Lady Smallwood welcomed the outlaws kindly enough, though she gave them a tongue lashing for dragging a young girl through the war. She became even more wroth when Lem let slip that Arya was highborn. "Who dressed the poor child in those Bolton rags?" she demanded of them. "That badge . . . there's many a man who would hang her in half a heartbeat for wearing a flayed man on her breast." Arya promptly found herself marched upstairs, forced into a tub, and doused with scalding hot water. Lady Smallwood's maidservants scrubbed her so hard it felt like they were flaying her themselves. They even dumped in some stinky-sweet stuff that smelled like flowers.

And afterward, they insisted she dress herself in girl's things, brown woolen stockings and a light linen shift, and over that a light green gown with acorns embroidered all over the bodice in brown thread, and more acorns bordering the hem. "My great-aunt is a septa at a motherhouse in Oldtown," Lady Smallwood said as the women laced the gown up Arya's back. "I sent my daughter there when the war began. She'll have outgrown these things by the time she returns, no doubt. Are you fond of dancing, child? My Carellen's a lovely dancer. She sings beautifully as well. What do you like to do?"

She scuffed a toe amongst the rushes. "Needlework."

"Very restful, isn't it?"

"Well," said Arya, "not the way I do it."

"No? I have always found it so. The gods give each of us our little gifts and talents, and it is meant for us to use them, my aunt always says. Any act can be a prayer, if done as well as we are able. Isn't that a lovely thought? Remember that the next time you do your needlework. Do you work at it every day?"

"I did till I lost Needle. My new one's not as good."

"In times like these, we all must make do as best we can." Lady Smallwood fussed at the bodice of the gown. "Now you look a proper young lady."

I'm not a lady, Arya wanted to tell her, *I'm a wolf.*

"I do not know who you are, child," the woman said, "and it may be that's for the best. Someone important, I fear." She smoothed down Arya's collar. "In times like these, it is better to be insignificant. Would that I could keep you here with me. That would not be safe, though. I have walls, but too few men to hold them." She sighed.

Supper was being served in the hall by the time Arya was all washed and combed and dressed. Gendry took one look and laughed so hard that wine came out his nose, until Harwin gave him a *thwack* alongside his ear. The meal was plain but filling; mutton and mushrooms, brown bread, pease pudding, and baked apples with yellow cheese. When the food had been cleared and the servants sent away, Greenbeard lowered his voice to ask if her ladyship had word of the lightning lord.

"Word?" She smiled. "They were here not a fortnight past. Them and a dozen more, driving sheep. I could scarcely believe my eyes. Thoros gave me three as thanks. You've eaten one tonight."

"Thoros herding sheep?" Anguy laughed aloud.

"I grant you it was an odd sight, but Thoros claimed that as a priest he knew how to tend a flock."

"Aye, and shear them too," chuckled Lem Lemoncloak.

"Someone could make a rare fine song of that." Tom plucked a string on his woodharp.

Lady Smallwood gave him a withering look. "Someone who doesn't rhyme *carry on* with *Dondarrion*, perhaps. Or play 'Oh, Lay My Sweet Lass Down in the Grass' to every milkmaid in the shire and leave two of them with big bellies."

"It was 'Let Me Drink Your Beauty,'" said Tom defensively, "and milkmaids are always glad to hear it. As was a certain highborn lady I do recall. I play to please."

Her nostrils flared. "The riverlands are full of maids you've pleased, all drinking tansy tea. You'd think a man as old as you would know to spill his seed on their bellies. Men will be calling you Tom Sevensons before much longer."

"As it happens," said Tom, "I passed seven many years ago. And fine boys they are too, with voices sweet as nightingales." Plainly he did not care for the subject.

"Did his lordship say where he was bound, milady?" asked Harwin.

"Lord Beric never shares his plans, but there's hunger down near Stoney Sept and the Threepenny Wood. I should look for him there." She took a sip of wine. "You'd best know, I've had less pleasant callers as well. A pack of wolves came howling around my gates, thinking I might have Jaime Lannister in here."

Tom stopped his plucking. "Then it's true, the Kingslayer is loose again?"

Lady Smallwood gave him a scornful look. "I hardly think they'd be hunting him if he was chained up under Riverrun."

"What did m'lady tell them?" asked Jack-Be-Lucky.

"Why, that I had Ser Jaime naked in my bed, but I'd left him much too exhausted to come down. One of them had the effrontery to call me a liar, so we saw them off with a few quarrels. I believe they made for Blackbottom Bend."

Arya squirmed restlessly in her seat. "What northmen was it, who came looking after the Kingslayer?"

Lady Smallwood seemed surprised that she'd spoken. "They did not give their names, child, but they wore black, with the badge of a white sun on the breast."

A white sun on black was the sigil of Lord Karstark, Arya thought. *Those were Robb's men.* She wondered if they were still close. If she could give the outlaws the slip and find them, maybe they would take her to her mother at Riverrun . . .

"Did they say how Lannister came to escape?" Lem asked.

"They did," said Lady Smallwood. "Not that I believe a word of it. They claimed that Lady Catelyn set him free."

That startled Tom so badly he snapped a string. "Go on with you," he said. "That's madness."

It's not true, thought Arya. *It couldn't be true.*

"I thought the same," said Lady Smallwood.

That was when Harwin remembered Arya. "Such talk is not for your ears, milady."

"No, I want to hear."

The outlaws were adamant. "Go on with you, skinny squirrel," said Greenbeard. "Be a good little lady and go play in the yard while we talk, now."

Arya stalked away angry, and would have slammed the door if it hadn't been so heavy. Darkness had settled over Acorn Hall. A few torches burned along the walls, but that was all. The gates of the little castle were closed and barred. She had promised Harwin that she would not try and run away again, she knew, but that was before they started telling lies about her mother.

"Arya?" Gendry had followed her out. "Lady Smallwood said there's a smithy. Want to have a look?"

"If you want." She had nothing else to do.

"This Thoros," Gendry said as they walked past the kennels, "is he the same Thoros who lived in the castle at King's Landing? A red priest, fat, with a shaved head?"

"I think so." Arya had never spoken to Thoros at King's Landing that she could recall, but she knew who he was. He and Jalabhar Xho had been the most colorful figures at Robert's court, and Thoros was a great friend of the king as well.

"He won't remember me, but he used to come to our forge." The Smallwood forge had not been used in some time, though the smith had hung his tools neatly on the wall. Gendry lit a candle and set it on the anvil while he took down a pair of tongs. "My master always scolded him about his flaming swords. It was no way to treat good steel, he'd say, but this Thoros never used good steel. He'd just dip some cheap sword in wildfire and set it alight. It was only an alchemist's trick, my master said, but it scared the horses and some of the greener knights."

She screwed up her face, trying to remember if her father had ever talked about Thoros. "He isn't very priestly, is he?"

"No," Gendry admitted. "Master Mott said Thoros could outdrink even King Robert. They were pease in a pod, he told me, both gluttons and sots."

"You shouldn't call the king a sot." Maybe King Robert had drunk a lot, but he'd been her father's friend.

"I was talking about Thoros." Gendry reached out with the tongs as if to pinch her face, but Arya swatted them away. "He liked feasts and tourneys, that was why King Robert was so fond of him. And this Thoros was brave. When the walls of Pyke crashed down, he was the first through the breach. He fought with one of his flaming swords, setting ironmen afire with every slash."

"I wish I had a flaming sword." Arya could think of lots of people she'd like to set on fire.

"It's only a trick, I told you. The wildfire ruins the steel. My master sold Thoros a new sword after every tourney. Every time they would have a fight about the price." Gendry hung the tongs back up and took down the heavy hammer. "Master Mott said it was time I made my first longsword. He gave me a sweet piece of steel, and I knew just how I wanted to shape the blade. Only Yoren came, and took me away for the Night's Watch."

"You can still make swords if you want," said Arya. "You can make them for my brother Robb when we get to Riverrun."

"Riverrun." Gendry put the hammer down and looked at her. "You look different now. Like a proper little girl."

"I look like an oak tree, with all these stupid acorns."

"Nice, though. A nice oak tree." He stepped closer, and *sniffed* at her. "You even smell nice for a change."

"You don't. You *stink*." Arya shoved him back against the anvil and made to run, but Gendry caught her arm. She stuck a foot between his legs and tripped him, but he yanked her down with him, and they rolled across the floor of the smithy. He was very strong, but she was quicker. Every time he tried to hold her still she wriggled free and punched him. Gendry only laughed at the blows, which made her mad. He finally caught both her wrists in one hand and started to tickle her with the other, so Arya slammed her knee between his legs, and wrenched free. Both of them were covered in dirt, and one sleeve was torn on her stupid acorn dress. "I bet I don't look so nice *now*," she shouted.

Tom was singing when they returned to the hall.

> *My featherbed is deep and soft,*
> > *and there I'll lay you down,*
> *I'll dress you all in yellow silk,*
> > *and on your head a crown.*
> *For you shall be my lady love,*
> > *and I shall be your lord.*
> *I'll always keep you warm and safe,*
> > *and guard you with my sword.*

Harwin took one look at them and burst out laughing, and Anguy smiled one of his stupid freckly smiles and said, "Are we *certain* this one is a highborn lady?" But Lem Lemoncloak gave Gendry a clout alongside the head. "You want to fight, fight with me! She's a girl, and half your age! You keep your hands off o' her, you hear me?"

"I started it," said Arya. "Gendry was just talking."

"Leave the boy, Lem," said Harwin. "Arya did start it, I have no doubt. She was much the same at Winterfell."

Tom winked at her as he sang:

> *And how she smiled and how she laughed,*
> > *the maiden of the tree.*
> *She spun away and said to him,*
> > *no featherbed for me.*
> *I'll wear a gown of golden leaves,*
> > *and bind my hair with grass,*
> *But you can be my forest love,*
> > *and me your forest lass.*

"I have no gowns of leaves," said Lady Smallwood with a small fond smile, "but Carellen left some other dresses that might serve. Come, child, let us go upstairs and see what we can find."

It was even worse than before; Lady Smallwood insisted that Arya take *another* bath, and cut and comb her hair besides; the dress she put her in this time was sort of lilac-colored, and decorated with little baby pearls. The only good thing about it was that it was so delicate that no one could expect her to ride in it. So the next morning as they broke their fast, Lady Smallwood gave her breeches, belt, and tunic to wear, and a brown doeskin jerkin dotted with iron studs. "They were my son's things," she said. "He died when he was seven."

"I'm sorry, my lady." Arya suddenly felt bad for her, and ashamed. "I'm sorry I tore the acorn dress too. It was pretty."

"Yes, child. And so are you. Be brave."

DAENERYS

I n the center of the Plaza of Pride stood a red brick fountain whose
waters smelled of brimstone, and in the center of the fountain a
monstrous harpy made of hammered bronze. Twenty feet tall she
reared. She had a woman's face, with gilded hair, ivory eyes, and pointed
ivory teeth. Water gushed yellow from her heavy breasts. But in place of
arms she had the wings of a bat or a dragon, her legs were the legs of an
eagle, and behind she wore a scorpion's curled and venomous tail.

The harpy of Ghis, Dany thought. Old Ghis had fallen five thousand
years ago, if she remembered true; its legions shattered by the might of
young Valyria, its brick walls pulled down, its streets and buildings turned
to ash and cinder by dragonflame, its very fields sown with salt, sulfur,
and skulls. The gods of Ghis were dead, and so too its people; these
Astapori were mongrels, Ser Jorah said. Even the Ghiscari tongue was
largely forgotten; the slave cities spoke the High Valyrian of their conquerors, or what they had made of it.

Yet the symbol of the Old Empire still endured here, though this bronze
monster had a heavy chain dangling from her talons, an open manacle
at either end. *The harpy of Ghis had a thunderbolt in her claws. This is
the harpy of Astapor.*

"Tell the Westerosi whore to lower her eyes," the slaver Kraznys mo
Nakloz complained to the slave girl who spoke for him. "I deal in meat,
not metal. The bronze is not for sale. Tell her to look at the soldiers.
Even the dim purple eyes of a sunset savage can see how magnificent
my creatures are, surely."

Kraznys's High Valyrian was twisted and thickened by the characteristic growl of Ghis, and flavored here and there with words of slaver argot. Dany understood him well enough, but she smiled and looked blankly at the slave girl, as if wondering what he might have said.

"The Good Master Kraznys asks, are they not magnificent?" The girl spoke the Common Tongue well, for one who had never been to Westeros. No older than ten, she had the round flat face, dusky skin, and golden eyes of Naath. *The Peaceful People*, her folk were called. All agreed that they made the best slaves.

"They might be adequate to my needs," Dany answered. It had been Ser Jorah's suggestion that she speak only Dothraki and the Common Tongue while in Astapor. *My bear is more clever than he looks.* "Tell me of their training."

"The Westerosi woman is pleased with them, but speaks no praise, to keep the price down," the translator told her master. "She wishes to know how they were trained."

Kraznys mo Nakloz bobbed his head. He smelled as if he'd bathed in raspberries, this slaver, and his jutting red-black beard glistened with oil. *He has larger breasts than I do*, Dany reflected. She could see them through the thin sea-green silk of the gold-fringed *tokar* he wound about his body and over one shoulder. His left hand held the *tokar* in place as he walked, while his right clasped a short leather whip. "Are all Westerosi pigs so ignorant?" he complained. "All the world knows that the Unsullied are masters of spear and shield and shortsword." He gave Dany a broad smile. "Tell her what she would know, slave, and be quick about it. The day is hot."

That much at least is no lie. A matched pair of slave girls stood behind them, holding a striped silk awning over their heads, but even in the shade Dany felt light-headed, and Kraznys was perspiring freely. The Plaza of Pride had been baking in the sun since dawn. Even through the thickness of her sandals, she could feel the warmth of the red bricks underfoot. Waves of heat rose off them shimmering to make the stepped pyramids of Astapor around the plaza seem half a dream.

If the Unsullied felt the heat, however, they gave no hint of it. *They could be made of brick themselves, the way they stand there.* A thousand had been marched out of their barracks for her inspection; drawn up in ten ranks of one hundred before the fountain and its great bronze harpy, they stood stiffly at attention, their stony eyes fixed straight ahead. They wore nought but white linen clouts knotted about their loins, and conical bronze helms topped with a sharpened spike a foot tall. Kraznys had commanded them to lay down their spears and shields, and doff their swordbelts and quilted tunics, so the Queen of Westeros might better inspect the lean hardness of their bodies.

"They are chosen young, for size and speed and strength," the slave told her. "They begin their training at five. Every day they train from dawn to dusk, until they have mastered the shortsword, the shield, and the three spears. The training is most rigorous, Your Grace. Only one boy in three survives it. This is well known. Among the Unsullied it is said that on the day they win their spiked cap, the worst is done with, for no duty that will ever fall to them could be as hard as their training."

Kraznys mo Nakloz supposedly spoke no word of the Common Tongue, but he bobbed his head as he listened, and from time to time gave the slave girl a poke with the end of his lash. "Tell her that these have been standing here for a day and a night, with no food nor water. Tell her that they will stand until they drop if I should command it, and when nine hundred and ninety-nine have collapsed to die upon the bricks, the last will stand there still, and never move until his own death claims him. Such is their courage. Tell her that."

"I call that madness, not courage," said Arstan Whitebeard, when the solemn little scribe was done. He tapped the end of his hardwood staff against the bricks, *tap tap*, as if to tell his displeasure. The old man had not wanted to sail to Astapor; nor did he favor buying this slave army. A queen should hear all sides before reaching a decision. That was why Dany had brought him with her to the Plaza of Pride, not to keep her safe. Her bloodriders would do that well enough. Ser Jorah Mormont she had left aboard *Balerion* to guard her people and her dragons. Much against her inclination, she had locked the dragons belowdecks. It was too dangerous to let them fly freely over the city; the world was all too full of men who would gladly kill them for no better reason than to name themselves *dragonslayer*.

"What did the smelly old man say?" the slaver demanded of his translator. When she told him, he smiled and said, "Inform the savages that we call this *obedience*. Others may be stronger or quicker or larger than the Unsullied. Some few may even equal their skill with sword and spear and shield. But nowhere between the seas will you ever find any more obedient."

"Sheep are obedient," said Arstan when the words had been translated. He had some Valyrian as well, though not so much as Dany, but like her he was feigning ignorance.

Kraznys mo Nakloz showed his big white teeth when that was rendered back to him. "A word from me and these sheep would spill his stinking old bowels on the bricks," he said, "but do not say that. Tell them that these creatures are more dogs than sheep. Do they eat dogs or horse in these Seven Kingdoms?"

"They prefer pigs and cows, your worship."

"Beef. Pfag. Food for unwashed savages."

Ignoring them all, Dany walked slowly down the line of slave soldiers.

The girls followed close behind with the silk awning, to keep her in the shade, but the thousand men before her enjoyed no such protection. More than half had the copper skins and almond eyes of Dothraki and Lhazerene, but she saw men of the Free Cities in the ranks as well, along with pale Qartheen, ebon-faced Summer Islanders, and others whose origins she could not guess. And some had skins of the same amber hue as Kraznys mo Nakloz, and the bristly red-black hair that marked the ancient folk of Ghis, who named themselves the harpy's sons. *They sell even their own kind.* It should not have surprised her. The Dothraki did the same, when *khalasar* met *khalasar* in the sea of grass.

Some of the soldiers were tall and some were short. They ranged in age from fourteen to twenty, she judged. Their cheeks were smooth, and their eyes all the same, be they black or brown or blue or grey or amber. *They are like one man,* Dany thought, until she remembered that they were no men at all. The Unsullied were eunuchs, every one of them. "Why do you cut them?" she asked Kraznys through the slave girl. "Whole men are stronger than eunuchs, I have always heard."

"A eunuch who is cut young will never have the brute strength of one of your Westerosi knights, this is true," said Kraznys mo Nakloz when the question was put to him. "A bull is strong as well, but bulls die every day in the fighting pits. A girl of nine killed one not three days past in Jothiel's Pit. The Unsullied have something better than strength, tell her. They have discipline. We fight in the fashion of the Old Empire, yes. They are the lockstep legions of Old Ghis come again, absolutely obedient, absolutely loyal, and utterly without fear."

Dany listened patiently to the translation.

"Even the bravest men fear death and maiming," Arstan said when the girl was done.

Kraznys smiled again when he heard that. "Tell the old man that he smells of piss, and needs a stick to hold him up."

"Truly, your worship?"

He poked her with his lash. "No, not truly, are you a girl or a goat, to ask such folly? Say that Unsullied are not men. Say that death means nothing to them, and maiming less than nothing." He stopped before a thickset man who had the look of Lhazar about him and brought his whip up sharply, laying a line of blood across one copper cheek. The eunuch blinked, and stood there, bleeding. "Would you like another?" asked Kraznys.

"If it please your worship."

It was hard to pretend not to understand. Dany laid a hand on Kraznys's arm before he could raise the whip again. "Tell the Good Master that I see how strong his Unsullied are, and how bravely they suffer pain."

Kraznys chuckled when he heard her words in Valyrian. "Tell this ignorant whore of a westerner that courage has nothing to do with it."

"The Good Master says that was not courage, Your Grace."

"Tell her to open those slut's eyes of hers."

"He begs you attend this carefully, Your Grace."

Kraznys moved to the next eunuch in line, a towering youth with the blue eyes and flaxen hair of Lys. "Your sword," he said. The eunuch knelt, unsheathed the blade, and offered it up hilt first. It was a short-sword, made more for stabbing than for slashing, but the edge looked razor-sharp. "Stand," Kraznys commanded.

"Your worship." The eunuch stood, and Kraznys mo Nakloz slid the sword slowly up his torso, leaving a thin red line across his belly and between his ribs. Then he jabbed the swordpoint in beneath a wide pink nipple and began to work it back and forth.

"What is he doing?" Dany demanded of the girl, as the blood ran down the man's chest.

"Tell the cow to stop her bleating," said Kraznys, without waiting for the translation. "This will do him no great harm. Men have no need of nipples, eunuchs even less so." The nipple hung by a thread of skin. He slashed, and sent it tumbling to the bricks, leaving behind a round red eye copiously weeping blood. The eunuch did not move, until Kraznys offered him back his sword, hilt first. "Here, I'm done with you."

"This one is pleased to have served you."

Kraznys turned back to Dany. "They feel no pain, you see."

"How can that be?" she demanded through the scribe.

"*The wine of courage,*" was the answer he gave her. "It is no true wine at all, but made from deadly nightshade, bloodfly larva, black lotus root, and many secret things. They drink it with every meal from the day they are cut, and with each passing year feel less and less. It makes them fearless in battle. Nor can they be tortured. Tell the savage her secrets are safe with the Unsullied. She may set them to guard her councils and even her bedchamber, and never a worry as to what they might overhear.

"In Yunkai and Meereen, eunuchs are often made by removing a boy's testicles, but leaving the penis. Such a creature is infertile, yet often still capable of erection. Only trouble can come of this. We remove the penis as well, leaving nothing. The Unsullied are the purest creatures on the earth." He gave Dany and Arstan another of his broad white smiles. "I have heard that in the Sunset Kingdoms men take solemn vows to keep chaste and father no children, but live only for their duty. Is it not so?"

"It is," Arstan said, when the question was put. "There are many such orders. The maesters of the Citadel, the septons and septas who serve the Seven, the silent sisters of the dead, the Kingsguard and the Night's Watch . . ."

"Poor things," growled the slaver, after the translation. "Men were not made to live thus. Their days are a torment of temptation, any fool must see, and no doubt most succumb to their baser selves. Not so our Unsullied. They are wed to their swords in a way that your Sworn Brothers cannot hope to match. No woman can ever tempt them, nor any man."

His girl conveyed the essence of his speech, more politely. "There are other ways to tempt men, besides the flesh," Arstan Whitebeard objected, when she was done.

"Men, yes, but not Unsullied. Plunder interests them no more than rape. They own nothing but their weapons. We do not even permit them names."

"No names?" Dany frowned at the little scribe. "Can that be what the Good Master said? They have no names?"

"It is so, Your Grace."

Kraznys stopped in front of a Ghiscari who might have been his taller fitter brother, and flicked his lash at a small bronze disk on the swordbelt at his feet. "There is his name. Ask the whore of Westeros whether she can read Ghiscari glyphs." When Dany admitted that she could not, the slaver turned to the Unsullied. "What is your name?" he demanded.

"This one's name is Red Flea, your worship."

The girl repeated their exchange in the Common Tongue.

"And yesterday, what was it?"

"Black Rat, your worship."

"The day before?"

"Brown Flea, your worship."

"Before that?"

"This one does not recall, your worship. Blue Toad, perhaps. Or Blue Worm."

"Tell her all their names are such," Kraznys commanded the girl. "It reminds them that by themselves they are vermin. The name disks are thrown in an empty cask at duty's end, and each dawn plucked up again at random."

"More madness," said Arstan, when he heard. "How can any man possibly remember a new name every day?"

"Those who cannot are culled in training, along with those who cannot run all day in full pack, scale a mountain in the black of night, walk across a bed of coals, or slay an infant."

Dany's mouth surely twisted at that. *Did he see, or is he blind as well as cruel?* She turned away quickly, trying to keep her face a mask until she heard the translation. Only then did she allow herself to say, "Whose infants do they slay?"

"To win his spiked cap, an Unsullied must go to the slave marts with a silver mark, find some wailing newborn, and kill it before its mother's eyes. In this way, we make certain that there is no weakness left in them."

She was feeling faint. *The heat*, she tried to tell herself. "You take a babe from its mother's arms, kill it as she watches, and pay for her pain with a silver coin?"

When the translation was made for him, Kraznys mo Nakloz laughed aloud. "What a soft mewling fool this one is. Tell the whore of Westeros that the mark is for the child's owner, not the mother. The Unsullied are not permitted to steal." He tapped his whip against his leg. "Tell her that few ever fail that test. The dogs are harder for them, it must be said. We give each boy a puppy on the day that he is cut. At the end of the first year, he is required to strangle it. Any who cannot are killed, and fed to the surviving dogs. It makes for a good strong lesson, we find."

Arstan Whitebeard tapped the end of his staff on the bricks as he listened to that. *Tap tap tap.* Slow and steady. *Tap tap tap.* Dany saw him turn his eyes away, as if he could not bear to look at Kraznys any longer.

"The Good Master has said that these eunuchs cannot be tempted with coin or flesh," Dany told the girl, "but if some enemy of mine should offer them *freedom* for betraying me . . ."

"They would kill him out of hand and bring her his head, tell her that," the slaver answered. "Other slaves may steal and hoard up silver in hopes of buying freedom, but an Unsullied would not take it if the little mare offered it as a gift. They have no life outside their duty. They are *soldiers*, and that is all."

"It is soldiers I need," Dany admitted.

"Tell her it is well she came to Astapor, then. Ask her how large an army she wishes to buy."

"How many Unsullied do you have to sell?"

"Eight thousand fully trained and available at present. We sell them only by the unit, she should know. By the thousand or the century. Once we sold by the ten, as household guards, but that proved unsound. Ten is too few. They mingle with other slaves, even freemen, and forget who and what they are." Kraznys waited for that to be rendered in the Common Tongue, and then continued. "This beggar queen must understand, such wonders do not come cheaply. In Yunkai and Meereen, slave swordsmen can be had for less than the price of their swords, but Unsullied are the finest foot in all the world, and each represents many years of training. Tell her they are like Valyrian steel, folded over and over and hammered for years on end, until they are stronger and more resilient than any metal on earth."

"I know of Valyrian steel," said Dany. "Ask the Good Master if the Unsullied have their own officers."

"You must set your own officers over them. We train them to obey, not to think. If it is wits she wants, let her buy scribes."

"And their gear?"

"Sword, shield, spear, sandals, and quilted tunic are included," said Kraznys. "And the spiked caps, to be sure. They will wear such armor as you wish, but you must provide it."

Dany could think of no other questions. She looked at Arstan. "You have lived long in the world, Whitebeard. Now that you have seen them, what do you say?"

"I say *no*, Your Grace," the old man answered at once.

"Why?" she asked. "Speak freely." Dany thought she knew what he would say, but she wanted the slave girl to hear, so Kraznys mo Nakloz might hear later.

"My queen," said Arstan, "there have been no slaves in the Seven Kingdoms for thousands of years. The old gods and the new alike hold slavery to be an abomination. Evil. If you should land in Westeros at the head of a slave army, many good men will oppose you for no other reason than that. You will do great harm to your cause, and to the honor of your House."

"Yet I must have some army," Dany said. "The boy Joffrey will not give me the Iron Throne for asking politely."

"When the day comes that you raise your banners, half of Westeros will be with you," Whitebeard promised. "Your brother Rhaegar is still remembered, with great love."

"And my father?" Dany said.

The old man hesitated before saying, "King Aerys is also remembered. He gave the realm many years of peace. Your Grace, you have no need of slaves. Magister Illyrio can keep you safe while your dragons grow, and send secret envoys across the narrow sea on your behalf, to sound out the high lords for your cause."

"Those same high lords who abandoned my father to the Kingslayer and bent the knee to Robert the Usurper?"

"Even those who bent their knees may yearn in their hearts for the return of the dragons."

"*May*," said Dany. That was such a slippery word, *may*. In any language. She turned back to Kraznys mo Nakloz and his slave girl. "I must consider carefully."

The slaver shrugged. "Tell her to consider quickly. There are many other buyers. Only three days past I showed these same Unsullied to a corsair king who hopes to buy them all."

"The corsair wanted only a hundred, your worship," Dany heard the slave girl say.

He poked her with the end of the whip. "Corsairs are all liars. He'll buy them all. Tell her that, girl."

Dany knew she would take more than a hundred, if she took any at all. "Remind your Good Master of who I am. Remind him that I am Daenerys Stormborn, Mother of Dragons, the Unburnt, trueborn queen of the Seven Kingdoms of Westeros. My blood is the blood of Aegon the Conqueror, and of old Valyria before him."

Yet her words did not move the plump perfumed slaver, even when rendered in his own ugly tongue. "Old Ghis ruled an empire when the Valyrians were still fucking sheep," he growled at the poor little scribe, "and we are the sons of the harpy." He gave a shrug. "My tongue is wasted wagging at women. East or west, it makes no matter, they cannot decide until they have been pampered and flattered and stuffed with sweetmeats. Well, if this is my fate, so be it. Tell the whore that if she requires a guide to our sweet city, Kraznys mo Nakloz will gladly serve her . . . and service her as well, if she is more woman than she looks."

"Good Master Kraznys would be most pleased to show you Astapor while you ponder, Your Grace," the translator said.

"I will feed her jellied dog brains, and a fine rich stew of red octopus and unborn puppy." He wiped his lips.

"Many delicious dishes can be had here, he says."

"Tell her how pretty the pyramids are at night," the slaver growled. "Tell her I will lick honey off her breasts, or allow her to lick honey off mine if she prefers."

"Astapor is most beautiful at dusk, Your Grace," said the slave girl. "The Good Masters light silk lanterns on every terrace, so all the pyramids glow with colored lights. Pleasure barges ply the Worm, playing soft music and calling at the little islands for food and wine and other delights."

"Ask her if she wishes to view our fighting pits," Kraznys added. "Douquor's Pit has a fine folly scheduled for the evening. A bear and three small boys. One boy will be rolled in honey, one in blood, and one in rotting fish, and she may wager on which the bear will eat first."

Tap tap tap, Dany heard. Arstan Whitebeard's face was still, but his staff beat out his rage. *Tap tap tap*. She made herself smile. "I have my own bear on *Balerion*," she told the translator, "and he may well eat me if I do not return to him."

"See," said Kraznys when her words were translated. "It is not the woman who decides, it is this man she runs to. As ever!"

"Thank the Good Master for his patient kindness," Dany said, "and tell him that I will think on all I learned here." She gave her arm to Arstan Whitebeard, to lead her back across the plaza to her litter. Aggo and Jhogo fell in to either side of them, walking with the bowlegged swagger all the horselords affected when forced to dismount and stride the earth like common mortals.

Dany climbed into her litter frowning, and beckoned Arstan to climb in beside her. A man as old as him should not be walking in such heat. She did not close the curtains as they got under way. With the sun beating down so fiercely on this city of red brick, every stray breeze was to be cherished, even if it did come with a swirl of fine red dust. *Besides, I need to see.*

Astapor was a queer city, even to the eyes of one who had walked within the House of Dust and bathed in the Womb of the World beneath the Mother of Mountains. All the streets were made of the same red brick that had paved the plaza. So too were the stepped pyramids, the deep-dug fighting pits with their rings of descending seats, the sulfurous fountains and gloomy wine caves, and the ancient walls that encircled them. *So many bricks*, she thought, *and so old and crumbling.* Their fine red dust was everywhere, dancing down the gutters at each gust of wind. Small wonder so many Astapori women veiled their faces; the brick dust stung the eyes worse than sand.

"Make way!" Jhogo shouted as he rode before her litter. "Make way for the Mother of Dragons!" But when he uncoiled the great silver-handled whip that Dany had given him, and made to crack it in the air, she leaned out and told him nay. "Not in this place, blood of my blood," she said, in his own tongue. "These bricks have heard too much of the sound of whips."

The streets had been largely deserted when they had set out from the port that morning, and scarcely seemed more crowded now. An elephant lumbered past with a latticework litter on its back. A naked boy with peeling skin sat in a dry brick gutter, picking his nose and staring sullenly at some ants in the street. He lifted his head at the sound of hooves, and gaped as a column of mounted guards trotted by in a cloud of red dust and brittle laughter. The copper disks sewn to their cloaks of yellow silk glittered like so many suns, but their tunics were embroidered linen, and below the waist they wore sandals and pleated linen skirts. Bareheaded, each man had teased and oiled and twisted his stiff red-black hair into some fantastic shape, horns and wings and blades and even grasping hands, so they looked like some troupe of demons escaped from the seventh hell. The naked boy watched them for a bit, along with Dany, but soon enough they were gone, and he went back to his ants, and a knuckle up his nose.

An old city, this, she reflected, *but not so populous as it was in its glory, nor near so crowded as Qarth or Pentos or Lys.*

Her litter came to a sudden halt at the cross street, to allow a coffle of slaves to shuffle across her path, urged along by the crack of an over-seer's lash. These were no Unsullied, Dany noted, but a more common sort of men, with pale brown skins and black hair. There were women among them, but no children. All were naked. Two Astapori rode behind them on white asses, a man in a red silk *tokar* and a veiled woman in sheer blue linen decorated with flakes of lapis lazuli. In her red-black hair she wore an ivory comb. The man laughed as he whispered to her, paying no more mind to Dany than to his slaves, nor the overseer with his twisted five-thonged lash, a squat broad Dothraki who had the harpy and chains tattooed proudly across his muscular chest.

"Bricks and blood built Astapor," Whitebeard murmured at her side, "and bricks and blood her people."

"What is that?" Dany asked him, curious.

"An old rhyme a maester taught me, when I was a boy. I never knew how true it was. The bricks of Astapor are red with the blood of the slaves who make them."

"I can well believe that," said Dany.

"Then leave this place before your heart turns to brick as well. Sail this very night, on the evening tide."

Would that I could, thought Dany. "When I leave Astapor it must be with an army, Ser Jorah says."

"Ser Jorah was a slaver himself, Your Grace," the old man reminded her. "There are sellswords in Pentos and Myr and Tyrosh you can hire. A man who kills for coin has no honor, but at least they are no slaves. Find your army there, I beg you."

"My brother visited Pentos, Myr, Braavos, near all the Free Cities. The magisters and archons fed him wine and promises, but his soul was starved to death. A man cannot sup from the beggar's bowl all his life and stay a man. I had my taste in Qarth, that was enough. I will not come to Pentos bowl in hand."

"Better to come a beggar than a slaver," Arstan said.

"There speaks one who has been neither." Dany's nostrils flared. "Do you know what it is like to be *sold*, squire? I do. My brother sold me to Khal Drogo for the promise of a golden crown. Well, Drogo crowned him in gold, though not as he had wished, and I . . . my sun-and-stars made a queen of me, but if he had been a different man, it might have been much otherwise. Do you think I have forgotten how it felt to be afraid?"

Whitebeard bowed his head. "Your Grace, I did not mean to give offense."

"Only lies offend me, never honest counsel." Dany patted Arstan's spotted hand to reassure him. "I have a dragon's temper, that's all. You must not let it frighten you."

"I shall try and remember." Whitebeard smiled.

He has a good face, and great strength to him, Dany thought. She could not understand why Ser Jorah mistrusted the old man so. *Could he be jealous that I have found another man to talk to?* Unbidden, her thoughts went back to the night on *Balerion* when the exile knight had kissed her. *He should never have done that. He is thrice my age, and of too low a birth for me, and I never gave him leave. No true knight would ever kiss a queen without her leave.* She had taken care never to be alone with Ser Jorah after that, keeping her handmaids with her aboard ship, and sometimes her bloodriders. *He wants to kiss me again, I see it in his eyes.*

What Dany wanted she could not begin to say, but Jorah's kiss had woken something in her, something that been sleeping since Khal Drogo died. Lying abed in her narrow bunk, she found herself wondering how it would be to have a man squeezed in beside her in place of her handmaid, and the thought was more exciting than it should have been. Sometimes she would close her eyes and dream of him, but it was never Jorah Mormont she dreamed of; her lover was always younger and more comely, though his face remained a shifting shadow.

Once, so tormented she could not sleep, Dany slid a hand down between her legs, and gasped when she felt how wet she was. Scarce daring to breathe, she moved her fingers back and forth between her lower lips, slowly so as not to wake Irri beside her, until she found one sweet spot and lingered there, touching herself lightly, timidly at first and then faster. Still, the relief she wanted seemed to recede before her, until her dragons stirred, and one screamed out across the cabin, and Irri woke and saw what she was doing.

Dany knew her face was flushed, but in the darkness Irri surely could not tell. Wordless, the handmaid put a hand on her breast, then bent to take a nipple in her mouth. Her other hand drifted down across the soft curve of belly, through the mound of fine silvery-gold hair, and went to work between Dany's thighs. It was no more than a few moments until her legs twisted and her breasts heaved and her whole body shuddered. She screamed then. Or perhaps that was Drogon. Irri never said a thing, only curled back up and went back to sleep the instant the thing was done.

The next day, it all seemed a dream. And what did Ser Jorah have to do with it, if anything? *It is Drogo I want, my sun-and-stars,* Dany reminded herself. *Not Irri, and not Ser Jorah, only Drogo.* Drogo was dead, though. She'd thought these feelings had died with him there in the red waste, but one treacherous kiss had somehow brought them back to life. *He should never have kissed me. He presumed too much, and I permitted it. It must never happen again.* She set her mouth grimly and gave her head a shake, and the bell in her braid chimed softly.

Closer to the bay, the city presented a fairer face. The great brick pyramids lined the shore, the largest four hundred feet high. All manner of trees and vines and flowers grew on their broad terraces, and the winds that swirled around them smelled green and fragrant. Another gigantic harpy stood atop the gate, this one made of baked red clay and crumbling visibly, with no more than a stub of her scorpion's tail remaining. The chain she grasped in her clay claws was old iron, rotten with rust. It was cooler down by the water, though. The lapping of the waves against the rotting pilings made a curiously soothing sound.

Aggo helped Dany down from her litter. Strong Belwas was seated on a massive piling, eating a great haunch of brown roasted meat. "Dog," he said happily when he saw Dany. "Good dog in Astapor, little queen. Eat?" He offered it with a greasy grin.

"That is kind of you, Belwas, but no." Dany had eaten dog in other places, at other times, but just now all she could think of was the Unsullied and their stupid puppies. She swept past the huge eunuch and up the plank onto the deck of *Balerion*.

Ser Jorah Mormont stood waiting for her. "Your Grace," he said, bowing his head. "The slavers have come and gone. Three of them, with a dozen scribes and as many slaves to lift and fetch. They crawled over every foot of our holds and made note of all we had." He walked her aft. "How many men do they have for sale?"

"None." Was it Mormont she was angry with, or this city with its sullen heat, its stinks and sweats and crumbling bricks? "They sell eunuchs, not men. Eunuchs made of brick, like the rest of Astapor. Shall I buy eight thousand brick eunuchs with dead eyes that never move, who kill suckling babes for the sake of a spiked hat and strangle their own dogs? They don't even have names. So don't call them *men*, ser."

"*Khaleesi*," he said, taken aback by her fury, "the Unsullied are chosen as boys, and trained—"

"I have heard all I care to of their *training*." Dany could feel tears welling in her eyes, sudden and unwanted. Her hand flashed up and cracked Ser Jorah hard across the face. It was either that, or cry.

Mormont touched the cheek she'd slapped. "If I have displeased my queen—"

"You *have*. You've displeased me greatly, ser. If you were my true knight, you would never have brought me to this vile sty." *If you were my true knight, you would never have kissed me, or looked at my breasts the way you did, or . . .*

"As Your Grace commands. I shall tell Captain Groleo to make ready to sail on the evening tide, for some sty less vile."

"No," said Dany. Groleo watched them from the forecastle, and his crew was watching too. Whitebeard, her bloodriders, Jhiqui, every one had stopped what they were doing at the sound of the slap. "I want to sail *now*, not on the tide, I want to sail far and fast and never look back. But I can't, can I? There are eight thousand brick eunuchs for sale, and

I must find some way to buy them." And with that she left him, and went below.

Behind the carved wooden door of the captain's cabin, her dragons were restless. Drogon raised his head and screamed, pale smoke venting from his nostrils, and Viserion flapped at her and tried to perch on her shoulder, as he had when he was smaller. "No," Dany said, trying to shrug him off gently. "You're too big for that now, sweetling." But the dragon coiled his white and gold tail around one arm and dug black claws into the fabric of her sleeve, clinging tightly. Helpless, she sank into Groleo's great leather chair, giggling.

"They have been wild while you were gone, *Khaleesi*," Irri told her. "Viserion clawed splinters from the door, do you see? And Drogon made to escape when the slaver men came to see them. When I grabbed his tail to hold him back, he turned and bit me." She showed Dany the marks of his teeth on her hand.

"Did any of them try to burn their way free?" That was the thing that frightened Dany the most.

"No, *Khaleesi*. Drogon breathed his fire, but in the empty air. The slaver men feared to come near him."

She kissed Irri's hand where Drogon had bitten it. "I'm sorry he hurt you. Dragons are not meant to be locked up in a small ship's cabin."

"Dragons are like horses in this," Irri said. "And riders, too. The horses scream below, *Khaleesi*, and kick at the wooden walls. I hear them. And Jhiqui says the old women and the little ones scream too, when you are not here. They do not like this water cart. They do not like the black salt sea."

"I know," Dany said. "I do, I know."

"My *khaleesi* is sad?"

"Yes," Dany admitted. *Sad and lost.*

"Should I pleasure the *khaleesi*?"

Dany stepped away from her. "No. Irri, you do not need to do that. What happened that night, when you woke . . . you're no bed slave, I freed you, remember? You . . ."

"I am handmaid to the Mother of Dragons," the girl said. "It is great honor to please my *khaleesi*."

"I don't want that," she insisted. "I don't." She turned away sharply. "Leave me now. I want to be alone. To think."

Dusk had begun to settle over the waters of Slaver's Bay before Dany returned to the deck. She stood by the rail and looked out over Astapor. *From here it looks almost beautiful*, she thought. The stars were coming out above, and the silk lanterns below, just as Kraznys's translator had promised. The brick pyramids were all glimmery with light. *But it is dark below, in the streets and plazas and fighting pits. And it is darkest*

of all in the barracks, where some little boy is feeding scraps to the
puppy they gave him when they took away his manhood.

There was a soft step behind her. *"Khaleesi."* His voice. "Might I speak
frankly?"

Dany did not turn. She could not bear to look at him just now. If she
did, she might well slap him again. Or cry. Or kiss him. And never know
which was right and which was wrong and which was madness. "Say
what you will, ser."

"When Aegon the Dragon stepped ashore in Westeros, the kings of
Vale and Rock and Reach did not rush to hand him their crowns. If you
mean to sit his Iron Throne, you must win it as he did, with steel and
dragonfire. And that will mean blood on your hands before the thing is
done."

Blood and fire, thought Dany. The words of House Targaryen. She had
known them all her life. "The blood of my enemies I will shed gladly.
The blood of innocents is another matter. Eight thousand Unsullied they
would offer me. Eight thousand dead babes. Eight thousand strangled
dogs."

"Your Grace," said Jorah Mormont, "I saw King's Landing after the
Sack. Babes were butchered that day as well, and old men, and children
at play. More women were raped than you can count. There is a savage
beast in every man, and when you hand that man a sword or spear and
send him forth to war, the beast stirs. The scent of blood is all it takes
to wake him. Yet I have never heard of these Unsullied raping, nor putting
a city to the sword, nor even plundering, save at the express command
of those who lead them. Brick they may be, as you say, but if you buy
them henceforth the only dogs they'll kill are those *you* want dead. And
you do have some dogs you want dead, as I recall."

The Usurper's dogs. "Yes." Dany gazed off at the soft colored lights
and let the cool salt breeze caress her. "You speak of sacking cities.
Answer me this, ser – why have the Dothraki never sacked *this* city?"
She pointed. "Look at the walls. You can see where they've begun to
crumble. There, and there. Do you see any guards on those towers? I
don't. Are they hiding, ser? I saw these sons of the harpy today, all their
proud highborn warriors. They dressed in linen skirts, and the fiercest
thing about them was their hair. Even a modest *khalasar* could crack
this Astapor like a nut and spill out the rotted meat inside. So tell me,
why is that ugly harpy not sitting beside the godsway in Vaes Dothrak
among the other stolen gods?"

"You have a dragon's eye, *Khaleesi*, that's plain to see."

"I wanted an answer, not a compliment."

"There are two reasons. Astapor's brave defenders are so much chaff,
it's true. Old names and fat purses who dress up as Ghiscari scourges to

pretend they still rule a vast empire. Every one is a high officer. On feastdays they fight mock wars in the pits to demonstrate what brilliant commanders they are, but it's the eunuchs who do the dying. All the same, any enemy wanting to sack Astapor would have to know that they'd be facing Unsullied. The slavers would turn out the whole garrison in the city's defense. The Dothraki have not ridden against Unsullied since they left their braids at the gates of Qohor."

"And the second reason?" Dany asked.

"Who would attack Astapor?" Ser Jorah asked. "Meereen and Yunkai are rivals but not enemies, the Doom destroyed Valyria, the folk of the eastern hinterlands are all Ghiscari, and beyond the hills lies Lhazar. The Lamb Men, as your Dothraki call them, a notably unwarlike people."

"Yes," she agreed, "but *north* of the slave cities is the Dothraki sea, and two dozen mighty *khals* who like nothing more than sacking cities and carrying off their people into slavery."

"Carrying them off *where?* What good are slaves once you've killed the slavers? Valyria is no more, Qarth lies beyond the red waste, and the Nine Free Cities are thousands of leagues to the west. And you may be sure the sons of the harpy give lavishly to every passing *khal*, just as the magisters do in Pentos and Norvos and Myr. They know that if they feast the horselords and give them gifts, they will soon ride on. It's cheaper than fighting, and a deal more certain."

Cheaper than fighting, Dany thought. *Yes, it might be.* If only it could be that easy for her. How pleasant it would be to sail to King's Landing with her dragons, and pay the boy Joffrey a chest of gold to make him go away.

"*Khaleesi?*" Ser Jorah prompted, when she had been silent for a long time. He touched her elbow lightly.

Dany shrugged him off. "Viserys would have bought as many Unsullied as he had the coin for. But you once said I was like Rhaegar . . ."

"I remember, Daenerys."

"*Your Grace,*" she corrected. "Prince Rhaegar led free men into battle, not slaves. Whitebeard said he dubbed his squires himself, and made many other knights as well."

"There was no higher honor than to receive your knighthood from the Prince of Dragonstone."

"Tell me, then – when he touched a man on the shoulder with his sword, what did he say? 'Go forth and kill the weak'? Or 'Go forth and defend them'? At the Trident, those brave men Viserys spoke of who died beneath our dragon banners – did they give their lives because they *believed* in Rhaegar's cause, or because they had been bought and paid for?" Dany turned to Mormont, crossed her arms, and waited for an answer.

"My queen," the big man said slowly, "all you say is true. But Rhaegar lost on the Trident. He lost the battle, he lost the war, he lost the kingdom, and he lost his life. His blood swirled downriver with the rubies from his breastplate, and Robert the Usurper rode over his corpse to steal the Iron Throne. Rhaegar fought valiantly, Rhaegar fought nobly, Rhaegar fought honorably. And Rhaegar *died*."

BRAN

No roads ran through the twisted mountain valleys where they walked now. Between the grey stone peaks lay still blue lakes, long and deep and narrow, and the green gloom of endless piney woods. The russet and gold of autumn leaves grew less common when they left the wolfswood to climb amongst the old flint hills, and vanished by the time those hills had turned to mountains. Giant grey-green sentinels loomed above them now, and spruce and fir and soldier pines in endless profusion. The undergrowth was sparse beneath them, the forest floor carpeted in dark green needles.

When they lost their way, as happened once or twice, they need only wait for a clear cold night when the clouds did not intrude, and look up in the sky for the Ice Dragon. The blue star in the dragon's eye pointed the way north, as Osha told him once. Thinking of Osha made Bran wonder where she was. He pictured her safe in White Harbor with Rickon and Shaggydog, eating eels and fish and hot crab pie with fat Lord Manderly. Or maybe they were warming themselves at the Last Hearth before the Greatjon's fires. But Bran's life had turned into endless chilly days on Hodor's back, riding his basket up and down the slopes of mountains.

"Up and down," Meera would sigh sometimes as they walked, "then down and up. Then up and down again. I hate these stupid mountains of yours, Prince Bran."

"Yesterday you said you loved them."

"Oh, I do. My lord father told me about mountains, but I never saw one till now. I love them more than I can say."

Bran made a face at her. "But you just said you hated them."

"Why can't it be both?" Meera reached up to pinch his nose.

"Because they're *different*," he insisted. "Like night and day, or ice and fire."

"If ice can burn," said Jojen in his solemn voice, "then love and hate can mate. Mountain or marsh, it makes no matter. The land is one."

"One," his sister agreed, "but over wrinkled."

The high glens seldom did them the courtesy of running north and south, so often they found themselves going long leagues in the wrong direction, and sometimes they were forced to double back the way they'd come. "If we took the kingsroad we could be at the Wall by now," Bran would remind the Reeds. He wanted to find the three-eyed crow, so he could learn to fly. Half a hundred times he said it if he said it once, until Meera started teasing by saying it along with him.

"If we took the kingsroad we wouldn't be so hungry either," he started saying then. Down in the hills they'd had no lack of food. Meera was a fine huntress, and even better at taking fish from streams with her three-pronged frog spear. Bran liked to watch her, admiring her quickness, the way she sent the spear lancing down and pulled it back with a silvery trout wriggling on the end of it. And they had Summer hunting for them as well. The direwolf vanished most every night as the sun went down, but he was always back again before dawn, most often with something in his jaws, a squirrel or a hare.

But here in the mountains, the streams were smaller and more icy, and the game scarcer. Meera still hunted and fished when she could, but it was harder, and some nights even Summer found no prey. Often they went to sleep with empty bellies.

But Jojen remained stubbornly determined to stay well away from roads. "Where you find roads you find travelers," he said in that way he had, "and travelers have eyes to see, and mouths to spread tales of the crippled boy, his giant, and the wolf that walks beside them." No one could get as stubborn as Jojen, so they struggled on through the wild, and every day climbed a little higher, and moved a little farther north.

Some days it rained, some days were windy, and once they were caught in a sleet storm so fierce that even Hodor bellowed in dismay. On the clear days, it often seemed as if they were the only living things in all the world. "Does no one live up here?" Meera Reed asked once, as they made their way around a granite upthrust as large as Winterfell.

"There's people," Bran told her. "The Umbers are mostly east of the kingsroad, but they graze their sheep in the high meadows in summer. There are Wulls west of the mountains along the Bay of Ice, Harclays back behind us in the hills, and Knotts and Liddles and Norreys and even some Flints up here in the high places." His father's mother's mother had been a Flint of the mountains. Old Nan once said that it was her blood in him that made Bran such a fool for climbing before his fall. She had died years and years and years before he was born, though, even before his father had been born.

"Wull?" said Meera. "Jojen, wasn't there a Wull who rode with Father during the war?"

"Theo Wull." Jojen was breathing hard from the climb. "Buckets, they used to call him."

"That's their sigil," said Bran. "Three brown buckets on a blue field, with a border of white and grey checks. Lord Wull came to Winterfell once, to do his fealty and talk with Father, and he had the buckets on his shield. He's no true lord, though. Well, he is, but they call him just *the Wull*, and there's the Knott and the Norrey and the Liddle too. At Winterfell we called them lords, but their own folk don't."

Jojen Reed stopped to catch his breath. "Do you think these mountain folk know we're here?"

"They know." Bran had seen them watching; not with his own eyes, but with Summer's sharper ones, that missed so little. "They won't bother us so long as we don't try and make off with their goats or horses."

Nor did they. Only once did they encounter any of the mountain people, when a sudden burst of freezing rain sent them looking for shelter. Summer found it for them, sniffing out a shallow cave behind the grey-green branches of a towering sentinel tree, but when Hodor ducked beneath the stony overhang, Bran saw the orange glow of fire farther back and realized they were not alone. "Come in and warm yourselves," a man's voice called out. "There's stone enough to keep the rain off all our heads."

He offered them oatcakes and blood sausage and a swallow of ale from a skin he carried, but never his name; nor did he ask theirs. Bran figured him for a Liddle. The clasp that fastened his squirrelskin cloak was gold and bronze and wrought in the shape of a pinecone, and the Liddles bore pinecones on the white half of their green-and-white shields.

"Is it far to the Wall?" Bran asked him as they waited for the rain to stop.

"Not so far as the raven flies," said the Liddle, if that was who he was. "Farther, for them as lacks wings."

Bran started, "I'd bet we'd be there if . . ."

". . . we took the kingsroad," Meera finished with him.

The Liddle took out a knife and whittled at a stick. "When there was a Stark in Winterfell, a maiden girl could walk the kingsroad in her name-day gown and still go unmolested, and travelers could find fire, bread, and salt at many an inn and holdfast. But the nights are colder now, and doors are closed. There's squids in the wolfswood, and flayed men ride the kingsroad asking after strangers."

The Reeds exchanged a look. "Flayed men?" said Jojen.

"The Bastard's boys, aye. He was dead, but now he's not. And paying good silver for wolfskins, a man hears, and maybe gold for word of certain other walking dead." He looked at Bran when he said that, and at Summer stretched out beside him. "As to that Wall," the man went on, "it's not a place that I'd be going. The Old Bear took the Watch into the haunted woods, and all that come back was his ravens, with hardly a message between them. *Dark wings, dark words*, me mother used to say, but when the birds fly silent, seems to me that's even darker." He poked at the fire with his stick. "It was different when there was a Stark in Winterfell. But the old wolf's dead and young one's gone south to play the game of thrones, and all that's left us is the ghosts."

"The wolves will come again," said Jojen solemnly.

"And how would you be knowing, boy?"

"I dreamed it."

"Some nights I dream of me mother that I buried nine years past," the man said, "but when I wake, she's not come back to us."

"There are dreams and dreams, my lord."

"Hodor," said Hodor.

They spent that night together, for the rain did not let up till well past dark, and only Summer seemed to want to leave the cave. When the fire had burned down to embers, Bran let him go. The direwolf did not feel the damp as people did, and the night was calling him. Moonlight painted the wet woods in shades of silver and turned the grey peaks white. Owls hooted through the dark and flew silently between the pines, while pale goats moved along the mountainsides. Bran closed his eyes and gave himself up to the wolf dream, to the smells and sounds of midnight.

When they woke the next morning, the fire had gone out and the Liddle was gone, but he'd left a sausage for them, and a dozen oatcakes folded up neatly in a green and white cloth. Some of the cakes had pinenuts baked in them and some had blackberries. Bran ate one of each, and still did not know which sort he liked the best. One day there would be Starks in Winterfell again, he told himself, and then he'd send for the Liddles and pay them back a hundredfold for every nut and berry.

The trail they followed was a little easier that day, and by noon the sun came breaking through the clouds. Bran sat in his basket up on Hodor's back and felt almost content. He dozed off once, lulled to sleep by the smooth swing of the big stableboy's stride and the soft humming sound he made sometimes when he walked. Meera woke him up with a light touch on his arm. "Look," she said, pointing at the sky with her frog spear, "an eagle."

Bran lifted his head and saw it, its grey wings spread and still as it floated on the wind. He followed it with his eyes as it circled higher, wondering what it would be like to soar about the world so effortless. *Better than climbing, even.* He tried to reach the eagle, to leave his stupid crippled body and rise into the sky to join it, the way he joined with Summer. *The greenseers could do it. I should be able to do it too.* He tried and tried, until the eagle vanished in the golden haze of the afternoon. "It's gone," he said, disappointed.

"We'll see others," said Meera. "They live up here."

"I suppose."

"Hodor," said Hodor.

"Hodor," Bran agreed.

Jojen kicked a pinecone. "Hodor likes it when you say his name, I think."

"Hodor's not his true name," Bran explained. "It's just some word he says. His real name is Walder, Old Nan told me. She was his grandmother's grandmother or something." Talking about Old Nan made him sad. "Do you think the ironmen killed her?" They hadn't seen her body at Winterfell. He didn't remember seeing any women dead, now that he thought back. "She never hurt no one, not even Theon. She just told stories. Theon wouldn't hurt someone like that. Would he?"

"Some people hurt others just because they can," said Jojen.

"And it wasn't Theon who did the killing at Winterfell," said Meera. "Too many of the dead were ironmen." She shifted her frog spear to her other hand. "Remember Old Nan's stories, Bran. Remember the way she told them, the sound of her voice. So long as you do that, part of her will always be alive in you."

"I'll remember," he promised. They climbed without speaking for a long time, following a crooked game trail over the high saddle between two stony peaks. Scrawny soldier pines clung to the slopes around them. Far ahead Bran could see the icy glitter of a stream where it tumbled down a mountainside. He found himself listening to Jojen's breathing and the crunch of pine needles under Hodor's feet. "Do you know any stories?" he asked the Reeds all of a sudden.

Meera laughed. "Oh, a few."

"A few," her brother admitted.

"Hodor," said Hodor, humming.

"You could tell one," said Bran. "While we walked. Hodor likes stories about knights. I do, too."

"There are no knights in the Neck," said Jojen.

"Above the water," his sister corrected. "The bogs are full of dead ones, though."

"That's true," said Jojen. "Andals and ironmen, Freys and other fools, all those proud warriors who set out to conquer Greywater. Not one of them could find it. They ride into the Neck, but not back out. And sooner or later they blunder into the bogs and sink beneath the weight of all that steel and drown there in their armor."

The thought of drowned knights under the water gave Bran the shivers. He didn't object, though; he *liked* the shivers.

"There was one knight," said Meera, "in the year of the false spring. The Knight of the Laughing Tree, they called him. He might have been a crannogman, that one."

"Or not." Jojen's face was dappled with green shadows. "Prince Bran has heard that tale a hundred times, I'm sure."

"No," said Bran. "I haven't. And if I have it doesn't matter. Sometimes Old Nan would tell the same story she'd told before, but we never minded, if it was a good story. Old stories are like old friends, she used to say. You have to visit them from time to time."

"That's true." Meera walked with her shield on her back, pushing an occasional branch out of the way with her frog spear. Just when Bran began to think that she wasn't going to tell the story after all, she began, "Once there was a curious lad who lived in the Neck. He was small like all crannogmen, but brave and smart and strong as well. He grew up hunting and fishing and climbing trees, and learned all the magics of my people."

Bran was almost certain he had never heard this story. "Did he have green dreams like Jojen?"

"No," said Meera, "but he could breathe mud and run on leaves, and change earth to water and water to earth with no more than a whispered word. He could talk to trees and weave words and make castles appear and disappear."

"I wish I could," Bran said plaintively. "When does he meet the tree knight?"

Meera made a face at him. "Sooner if a certain prince would be quiet."

"I was just asking."

"The lad knew the magics of the crannogs," she continued, "but he wanted more. Our people seldom travel far from home, you know. We're a small folk, and our ways seem queer to some, so the big people do not always treat us kindly. But this lad was bolder than most, and one day when he had grown to manhood he decided he would leave the crannogs and visit the Isle of Faces."

"No one visits the Isle of Faces," objected Bran. "That's where the green men live."

"It was the green men he meant to find. So he donned a shirt sewn with bronze scales, like mine, took up a leathern shield and a three-pronged spear, like mine, and paddled a little skin boat down the Green Fork."

Bran closed his eyes to try and see the man in his little skin boat. In his head, the crannogman looked like Jojen, only older and stronger and dressed like Meera.

"He passed beneath the Twins by night so the Freys would not attack him, and when he reached the Trident he climbed from the river and put his boat on his head and began to walk. It took him many a day, but finally he reached the Gods Eye, threw his boat in the lake, and paddled out to the Isle of Faces."

"Did he meet the green men?"

"Yes," said Meera, "but that's another story, and not for me to tell. My prince asked for knights."

"Green men are good too."

"They are," she agreed, but said no more about them. "All that winter the crannogman stayed on the isle, but when the spring broke he heard the wide world calling and knew the time had come to leave. His skin boat was just where he'd left it, so he said his farewells and paddled off toward shore. He rowed and rowed, and finally saw the distant towers of a castle rising beside the lake. The towers reached ever higher as he neared shore, until he realized that this must be the greatest castle in all the world."

"Harrenhal!" Bran knew at once. "It was Harrenhal!"

Meera smiled. "Was it? Beneath its walls he saw tents of many colors, bright banners cracking in the wind, and knights in mail and plate on barded horses. He smelled roasting meats, and heard the sound of laughter and the blare of heralds' trumpets. A great tourney was about to commence, and champions from all over the land had come to contest it. The king himself was there, with his son the dragon prince. The White Swords had come, to welcome a new brother to their ranks. The storm lord was on hand, and the rose lord as well. The great lion of the rock had quarreled with the king and stayed away, but many of his bannermen and knights attended all the same. The crannogman had never seen such pageantry, and knew he might never see the like again. Part of him wanted nothing so much as to be part of it."

Bran knew that feeling well enough. When he'd been little, all he had ever dreamed of was being a knight. But that had been before he fell and lost his legs.

"The daughter of the great castle reigned as queen of love and beauty when the tourney opened. Five champions had sworn to defend her crown; her four brothers of Harrenhal, and her famous uncle, a white knight of the Kingsguard."

"Was she a fair maid?"

"She was," said Meera, hopping over a stone, "but there were others fairer still. One was the wife of the dragon prince, who'd brought a dozen lady companions to attend her. The knights all begged them for favors to tie about their lances."

"This isn't going to be one of those *love* stories, is it?" Bran asked suspiciously. "Hodor doesn't like those so much."

"Hodor," said Hodor agreeably.

"He likes the stories where the knights fight monsters."

"Sometimes the knights are the monsters, Bran. The little crannogman was walking across the field, enjoying the warm spring day and harming none, when he was set upon by three squires. They were none older than fifteen, yet even so they were bigger than him, all three. This was *their* world, as they saw it, and he had no right to be there. They snatched away his spear and knocked him to the ground, cursing him for a frogeater."

"Were they Walders?" It sounded like something Little Walder Frey might have done.

"None offered a name, but he marked their faces well so he could revenge himself upon them later. They shoved him down every time he tried to rise, and kicked him when he curled up on the ground. But then they heard a roar. 'That's my father's man you're kicking,' howled the she-wolf."

"A wolf on four legs, or two?"

"Two," said Meera. "The she-wolf laid into the squires with a tourney sword, scattering them all. The crannogman was bruised and bloodied, so she took him back to her lair to clean his cuts and bind them up with linen. There he met her pack brothers: the wild wolf who led them, the quiet wolf beside him, and the pup who was youngest of the four.

"That evening there was to be a feast in Harrenhal, to mark the opening of the tourney, and the she-wolf insisted that the lad attend. He was of high birth, with as much a right to a place on the bench as any other man. She was not easy to refuse, this wolf maid, so he let the young pup find him garb suitable to a king's feast, and went up to the great castle.

"Under Harren's roof he ate and drank with the wolves, and many of their sworn swords besides, barrowdown men and moose and bears and mermen. The dragon prince sang a song so sad it made the wolf maid sniffle, but when her pup brother teased her for crying she poured wine over his head. A black brother spoke, asking the knights to join the Night's Watch. The storm lord drank down the knight of skulls and kisses in a wine-cup war. The crannogman saw a maid with laughing purple eyes dance with a white sword, a red snake, and the lord of griffins, and lastly with the quiet wolf . . . but only after the wild wolf spoke to her on behalf of a brother too shy to leave his bench.

"Amidst all this merriment, the little crannogman spied the three squires who'd attacked him. One served a pitchfork knight, one a porcupine, while the last attended a knight with two towers on his surcoat, a sigil all crannogmen know well."

"The Freys," said Bran. "The Freys of the Crossing."

"Then, as now," she agreed. "The wolf maid saw them too, and pointed them out to her brothers. 'I could find you a horse, and some armor that might fit,' the pup offered. The little crannogman thanked him, but gave no answer. His heart was torn. Crannogmen are smaller than most, but just as proud. The lad was no knight, no more than any of his people. We sit a boat more often than a horse, and our hands are made for oars, not lances. Much as he wished to have his vengeance, he feared he would only make a fool of himself and shame his people. The quiet wolf had offered the little crannogman a place in his tent that night, but before he slept he knelt on the lakeshore, looking across the water to where the Isle of Faces would be, and said a prayer to the old gods of north and Neck . . ."

"You never heard this tale from your father?" asked Jojen.

"It was Old Nan who told the stories. Meera, go on, you can't stop there."

Hodor must have felt the same. "Hodor," he said, and then, "Hodor hodor hodor hodor."

"Well," said Meera, "if you would hear the rest . . ."

"Yes. *Tell* it."

"Five days of jousting were planned," she said. "There was a great seven-sided mêlée as well, and archery and axe-throwing, a horse race and tourney of singers . . ."

"Never mind about all that." Bran squirmed impatiently in his basket on Hodor's back. "Tell about the jousting."

"As my prince commands. The daughter of the castle was the queen of love and beauty, with four brothers and an uncle to defend her, but all four sons of Harrenhal were defeated on the first day. Their conquerors reigned briefly as champions, until they were vanquished in turn. As it happened, the end of the first day saw the porcupine knight win a place among the champions, and on the morning of the second day the pitchfork knight and the knight of the two towers were victorious as well. But late on the afternoon of that second day, as the shadows grew long, a mystery knight appeared in the lists."

Bran nodded sagely. Mystery knights would oft appear at tourneys, with helms concealing their faces, and shields that were either blank or bore some strange device. Sometimes they were famous champions in disguise. The Dragonknight once won a tourney as the Knight of Tears, so he could name his sister the queen of love and beauty in place of the king's mistress. And Barristan the Bold twice donned a mystery knight's armor, the first time when he was only ten. "It was the little crannogman, I bet."

"No one knew," said Meera, "but the mystery knight was short of stature, and clad in ill-fitting armor made up of bits and pieces. The device upon his shield was a heart tree of the old gods, a white weirwood with a laughing red face."

"Maybe he came from the Isle of Faces," said Bran. "Was he green?" In Old Nan's stories, the guardians had dark green skin and leaves instead of hair. Sometimes they had antlers too, but Bran didn't see how the mystery knight could have worn a helm if he had antlers. "I bet the old gods sent him."

"Perhaps they did. The mystery knight dipped his lance before the king and rode to the end of the lists, where the five champions had their pavilions. You know the three he challenged."

"The porcupine knight, the pitchfork knight, and the knight of the twin towers." Bran had heard enough stories to know *that*. "He was the little crannogman, I told you."

"Whoever he was, the old gods gave strength to his arm. The porcupine knight fell first, then the pitchfork knight, and lastly the knight of the two towers. None were well loved, so the common folk cheered lustily for the Knight of the Laughing Tree, as the new champion soon was called. When his fallen foes sought to ransom horse and armor, the Knight of the Laughing Tree spoke in a booming voice through his helm, saying, '*Teach your squire honor, that shall be ransom enough.*' Once the defeated knights chastised their squires sharply, their horses and armor were returned. And so the little crannogman's prayer was answered . . . by the green men, or the old gods, or the children of the forest, who can say?"

It was a good story, Bran decided after thinking about it a moment or two. "Then what happened? Did the Knight of the Laughing Tree win the tourney and marry a princess?"

"No," said Meera. "That night at the great castle, the storm lord and the knight of skulls and kisses each swore they would unmask him, and the king himself urged men to challenge him, declaring that the face behind that helm was no friend of his. But the next morning, when the heralds blew their trumpets and the king took his seat, only two champions appeared. The Knight of the Laughing Tree had vanished. The king was wroth, and even sent his son the dragon prince to seek the man, but all they ever found was his painted shield, hanging abandoned in a tree. It was the dragon prince who won that tourney in the end."

"Oh." Bran thought about the tale awhile. "That was a good story. But it should have been the three bad knights who hurt him, not their squires. Then the little crannogman could have killed them all. The part about the ransoms was stupid. And the mystery knight should win the tourney, defeating every challenger, and name the wolf maid the queen of love and beauty."

"She was," said Meera, "but that's a sadder story."

"Are you certain you never heard this tale before, Bran?" asked Jojen. "Your lord father never told it to you?"

Bran shook his head. The day was growing old by then, and long shadows were creeping down the mountainsides to send black fingers through the pines. *If the little crannogman could visit the Isle of Faces, maybe I could too.* All the tales agreed that the green men had strange magic powers. Maybe they could help him walk again, even turn him into a knight. *They turned the little crannogman into a knight, even if it was only for a day*, he thought. *A day would be enough.*

DAVOS

T he cell was warmer than any cell had a right to be.

It was dark, yes. Flickering orange light fell through the ancient iron bars from the torch in the sconce on the wall outside, but the back half of the cell remained drenched in gloom. It was dank as well, as might be expected on an isle such as Dragonstone, where the sea was never far. And there were rats, as many as any dungeon could expect to have and a few more besides.

But Davos could not complain of chill. The smooth stony passages beneath the great mass of Dragonstone were always warm, and Davos had often heard it said they grew warmer the farther down one went. He was well below the castle, he judged, and the wall of his cell often felt warm to his touch when he pressed a palm against it. Perhaps the old tales were true, and Dragonstone was built with the stones of hell.

He was sick when they first brought him here. The cough that had plagued him since the battle grew worse, and a fever took hold of him as well. His lips broke with blood blisters, and the warmth of the cell did not stop his shivering. *I will not linger long*, he remembered thinking. *I will die soon, here in the dark.*

Davos soon found that he was wrong about that, as about so much else. Dimly he remembered gentle hands and a firm voice, and young Maester Pylos looking down on him. He was given hot garlic broth to drink, and milk of the poppy to take away his aches and shivers. The poppy made him sleep and while he slept they leeched him to drain off the bad blood. Or so he surmised, by the leech marks on his arms when he woke. Before very long the coughing stopped, the blisters vanished, and his broth had chunks of whitefish in it, and carrots and onions as well. And one day he realized that he felt stronger than he had since *Black Betha* shattered beneath him and flung him in the river.

He had two gaolers to tend him. One was broad and squat, with thick shoulders and huge strong hands. He wore a leather brigantine dotted with iron studs, and once a day brought Davos a bowl of oaten porridge. Sometimes he sweetened it with honey or poured in a bit of milk. The other gaoler was older, stooped and sallow, with greasy unwashed hair and pebbled skin. He wore a doublet of white velvet with a ring of stars worked upon the breast in golden thread. It fit him badly, being both too short and too loose, and was soiled and torn besides. He would bring Davos plates of meat and mash, or fish stew, and once even half a lamprey pie. The lamprey was so rich he could not keep it down, but even so, it was a rare treat for a prisoner in a dungeon.

Neither sun nor moon shone in the dungeons; no windows pierced the thick stone walls. The only way to tell day from night was by his gaolers. Neither man would speak to him, though he knew they were no mutes; sometimes he heard them exchange a few brusque words as the watch was changing. They would not even tell him their names, so he gave them names of his own. The short strong one he called Porridge, the stooped sallow one Lamprey, for the pie. He marked the passage of days by the meals they brought, and by the changing of the torches in the sconce outside his cell.

A man grows lonely in the dark, and hungers for the sound of a human voice. Davos would talk to the gaolers whenever they came to his cell, whether to bring him food or change his slops pail. He knew they would be deaf to pleas for freedom or mercy; instead he asked them questions, hoping perhaps one day one might answer. "What news of the war?" he asked, and "Is the king well?" He asked after his son Devan, and the Princess Shireen, and Salladhor Saan. "What is the weather like?" he asked, and "Have the autumn storms begun yet? Do ships still sail the narrow sea?"

It made no matter what he asked; they never answered, though sometimes Porridge gave him a look, and for half a heartbeat Davos would think that he was about to speak. With Lamprey there was not even that much. *I am not a man to him,* Davos thought, *only a stone that eats and shits and speaks.* He decided after a while that he liked Porridge much the better. Porridge at least seemed to know he was alive, and there was a queer sort of kindness to the man. Davos suspected that he fed the rats; that was why there were so many. Once he thought he heard the gaoler talking to them as if they were children, but perhaps he'd only dreamed that.

They do not mean to let me die, he realized. *They are keeping me alive, for some purpose of their own.* He did not like to think what that might be. Lord Sunglass had been confined in the cells beneath Dragonstone for a time, as had Ser Hubard Rambton's sons; all of them had ended on the pyre. *I should have given myself to the sea,* Davos thought as he sat staring at the torch beyond the bars. *Or let the sail pass me by, to perish on my rock. I would sooner feed crabs than flames.*

Then one night as he was finishing his supper, Davos felt a queer flush come over him. He glanced up through the bars, and there she stood in shimmering scarlet with her great ruby at her throat, her red eyes gleaming as bright as the torch that bathed her. "Melisandre," he said, with a calm he did not feel.

"Onion Knight," she replied, just as calmly, as if the two of them had met on a stair or in the yard, and were exchanging polite greetings. "Are you well?"

"Better than I was."

"Do you lack for anything?"

"My king. My son. I lack for them." He pushed the bowl aside and stood. "Have you come to burn me?"

Her strange red eyes studied him through the bars. "This is a bad place, is it not? A dark place, and foul. The good sun does not shine here, nor the bright moon." She lifted a hand toward the torch in the wall sconce. "This is all that stands between you and the darkness, Onion Knight. This little fire, this gift of R'hllor. Shall I put it out?"

"No." He moved toward the bars. "Please." He did not think he could bear that, to be left alone in utter blackness with no one but the rats for company.

The red woman's lips curved upward in a smile. "So you have come to love the fire, it would seem."

"I need the torch." His hands opened and closed. *I will not beg her. I will not.*

"I am like this torch, Ser Davos. We are both instruments of R'hllor. We were made for a single purpose – to keep the darkness at bay. Do you believe that?"

"No." Perhaps he should have lied, and told her what she wanted to hear, but Davos was too accustomed to speaking truth. "You are the mother of darkness. I saw that under Storm's End, when you gave birth before my eyes."

"Is the brave Ser Onions so frightened of a passing shadow? Take heart, then. Shadows only live when given birth by light, and the king's fires burn so low I dare not draw off any more to make another son. It might well kill him." Melisandre moved closer. "With another man, though . . . a man whose flames still burn hot and high . . . if you truly wish to serve your king's cause, come to my chamber one night. I could give you pleasure such as you have never known, and with your life-fire I could make . . ."

". . . a horror." Davos retreated from her. "I want no part of you, my lady. Or your god. May the Seven protect me."

Melisandre sighed. "They did not protect Guncer Sunglass. He prayed thrice each day, and bore seven seven-pointed stars upon his shield, but when R'hllor reached out his hand his prayers turned to screams, and he burned. Why cling to these false gods?"

"I have worshiped them all my life."

"All your life, Davos Seaworth? As well say *it was so yesterday*." She shook her head sadly. "You have never feared to speak the truth to kings, why do you lie to yourself? Open your eyes, ser knight."

"What is it you would have me see?"

"The way the world is made. The truth is all around you, plain to behold. The night is dark and full of terrors, the day bright and beautiful and full of hope. One is black, the other white. There is ice and there is fire. Hate and love. Bitter and sweet. Male and female. Pain and pleasure. Winter and summer. Evil and good." She took a step toward him. "*Death and life*. Everywhere, opposites. Everywhere, the war."

"The war?" asked Davos.

"The war," she affirmed. "*There are two*, Onion Knight. Not seven, not one, not a hundred or a thousand. *Two!* Do you think I crossed half the world to put yet another vain king on yet another empty throne? The war has been waged since time began, and before it is done, all men must choose where they will stand. On one side is R'hllor, the Lord of Light, the Heart of Fire, the God of Flame and Shadow. Against him stands the Great Other whose name may not be spoken, the Lord of Darkness, the Soul of Ice, the God of Night and Terror. Ours is not a choice between Baratheon and Lannister, between Greyjoy and Stark. It is death we choose, or life. Darkness, or light." She clasped the bars of his cell with her slender white hands. The great ruby at her throat seemed to pulse with its own radiance. "So tell me, Ser Davos Seaworth, and tell me truly – does your heart burn with the shining light of R'hllor? Or is it black and cold and full of worms?" She reached through the bars and laid three fingers upon his breast, as if to feel the truth of him through flesh and wool and leather.

"My heart," Davos said slowly, "is full of doubts."

Melisandre sighed. "Ahhhh, Davos. The good knight is honest to the last, even in his day of darkness. It is well you did not lie to me. I would have known. The Other's servants oft hide black hearts in gaudy light, so R'hllor gives his priests the power to see through falsehoods." She stepped lightly away from the cell. "Why did you mean to kill me?"

"I will tell you," said Davos, "if you will tell me who betrayed me."

It could only have been Salladhor Saan, and yet even now he prayed it was not so.

The red woman laughed. "No one betrayed you, onion knight. I saw your purpose in my flames."

The flames. "If you can see the future in these flames, how is it that we burned upon the Blackwater? You gave my sons to the fire . . . my sons, my ship, my men, all burning . . ."

Melisandre shook her head. "You wrong me, onion knight. Those were no fires of mine. Had I been with you, your battle would have had a different ending. But His Grace was surrounded by unbelievers, and his pride proved stronger than his faith. His punishment was grievous, but he has learned from his mistake."

Were my sons no more than a lesson for a king, then? Davos felt his mouth tighten.

"It is night in your Seven Kingdoms now," the red woman went on, "but soon the sun will rise again. The war continues, Davos Seaworth, and some will soon learn that even an ember in the ashes can still ignite a great blaze. The old maester looked at Stannis and saw only a man. You see a king. You are both wrong. He is the Lord's chosen, the warrior of fire. I have seen him leading the fight against the dark, I have seen it in the flames. The flames do not lie, else you would not be here. It is written in prophecy as well. When the red star bleeds and the darkness gathers, Azor Ahai shall be born again amidst smoke and salt to wake dragons out of stone. The bleeding star has come and gone, and Dragonstone is the place of smoke and salt. Stannis Baratheon is Azor Ahai reborn!" Her red eyes blazed like twin fires, and seemed to stare deep into his soul. "You do not believe me. You doubt the truth of R'hllor even now . . . yet have served him all the same, and will serve him again. I shall leave you here to think on all that I have told you. And because R'hllor is the source of all good, I shall leave the torch as well."

With a smile and swirl of scarlet skirts, she was gone. Only her scent lingered after. That, and the torch. Davos lowered himself to the floor of the cell and wrapped his arms about his knees. The shifting torchlight washed over him. Once Melisandre's footsteps faded away, the only sound was the scrabbling of rats. *Ice and fire,* he thought. *Black and white. Dark and light.* Davos could not deny the power of her god. He had seen the shadow crawling from Melisandre's womb, and the priestess knew things she had no way of knowing. *She saw my purpose in her flames.* It was good to learn that Salla had not sold him, but the thought of the red woman spying out his secrets with her fires disquieted him more than he could say. *And what did she mean when she said that I had served her god and would serve him again?* He did not like that either.

He lifted his eyes to stare up at the torch. He looked for a long time, never blinking, watching the flames shift and shimmer. He tried to see beyond them, to peer through the fiery curtain and glimpse whatever lived back there . . . but there was nothing, only fire, and after a time his eyes began to water.

God-blind and tired, Davos curled up on the straw and gave himself to sleep.

Three days later – well, Porridge had come thrice, and Lamprey twice – Davos heard voices outside his cell. He sat up at once, his back to the stone wall, listening to the sounds of struggle. This was new, a change in his unchanging world. The noise was coming from the left, where the steps led up to daylight. He could hear a man's voice, pleading and shouting.

"*. . . madness!*" the man was saying as he came into view, dragged along between two guardsmen with fiery hearts on their breasts. Porridge went before them, jangling a ring of keys, and Ser Axell Florent walked behind. "Axell," the prisoner said desperately, "for the love you bear me, *unhand me!* You cannot do this, I'm no traitor." He was an older man, tall and slender, with silvery grey hair, a pointed beard, and a long elegant face twisted in fear. "Where is Selyse, where is the queen? I demand to see her. The Others take you all! *Release me!*"

The guards paid no mind to his outcries. "Here?" Porridge asked in front of the cell. Davos got to his feet. For an instant he considered trying to rush them when the door was opened, but that was madness. There were too many, the guards wore swords, and Porridge was strong as a bull.

Ser Axell gave the gaoler a curt nod. "Let the traitors enjoy each other's company."

"*I am no traitor!*" screeched the prisoner as Porridge was unlocking the door. Though he was plainly dressed, in grey wool doublet and black breeches, his speech marked him as highborn. *His birth will not serve him here*, thought Davos.

Porridge swung the bars wide, Ser Axell gave a nod, and the guards flung their charge in headlong. The man stumbled and might have fallen, but Davos caught him. At once he wrenched away and staggered back toward the door, only to have it slammed in his pale, pampered face. "*No*," he shouted. "*Nooooo.*" All the strength suddenly left his legs, and he slid slowly to the floor, clutching at the iron bars. Ser Axell, Porridge, and the guards had already turned to leave. "You cannot do this," the prisoner shouted at their retreating backs. "*I am the King's Hand!*"

It was then that Davos knew him. "You are Alester Florent."

The man turned his head. "Who . . . ?"

"Ser Davos Seaworth."

Lord Alester blinked. "Seaworth . . . the onion knight. You tried to murder Melisandre."

Davos did not deny it. "At Storm's End you wore red-gold armor, with inlaid lapis flowers on your breastplate." He reached down a hand to help the other man to his feet.

Lord Alester brushed the filthy straw from his clothing. "I . . . I must apologize for my appearance, ser. My chests were lost when the Lannisters overran our camp. I escaped with no more than the mail on my back and the rings on my fingers."

He still wears those rings, noted Davos, who had lacked even all of his fingers.

"No doubt some cook's boy or groom is prancing around King's Landing just now in my slashed velvet doublet and jeweled cloak," Lord Alester went on, oblivious. "But war has its horrors, as all men know. No doubt you suffered your own losses."

"My ship," said Davos. "All my men. Four of my sons."

"May the . . . may the Lord of Light lead them through the darkness to a better world," the other man said.

May the Father judge them justly, and the Mother grant them mercy, Davos thought, but he kept his prayer to himself. The Seven had no place on Dragonstone now.

"My own son is safe at Brightwater," the lord went on, "but I lost a nephew on the *Fury.* Ser Imry, my brother Ryam's son."

It had been Ser Imry Florent who led them blindly up the Blackwater Rush with all oars pulling, paying no heed to the small stone towers at the mouth of the river. Davos was not like to forget him. "My son Maric was your nephew's oarmaster." He remembered his last sight of *Fury,* engulfed in wildfire. "Has there been any word of survivors?"

"The *Fury* burned and sank with all hands," his lordship said. "Your son and my nephew were lost, with countless other good men. The war itself was lost that day, ser."

This man is defeated. Davos remembered Melisandre's talk of embers in the ashes igniting great blazes. *Small wonder he ended here.* "His Grace will never yield, my lord."

"Folly, that's folly." Lord Alester sat on the floor again, as if the effort of standing for a moment had been too much for him. "Stannis Baratheon will never sit the Iron Throne. Is it treason to say the truth? A bitter truth, but no less true for that. His fleet is gone, save for the Lyseni, and Salladhor Saan will flee at the first sight of a Lannister sail. Most of the lords who supported Stannis have gone over to Joffrey or died . . ."

"Even the lords of the narrow sea? The lords sworn to Dragonstone?"

Lord Alester waved his hand feebly. "Lord Celtigar was captured and bent the knee. Monford Velaryon died with his ship, the red woman burned Sunglass, and Lord Bar Emmon is fifteen, fat, and feeble. Those are your lords of the narrow sea. Only the strength of House Florent is left to Stannis, against all the might of Highgarden, Sunspear, and Casterly Rock, and now most of the storm lords as well. The best hope that remains is to try and salvage something with a peace. That is all I meant to do. Gods be good, how can they call it *treason?*"

Davos stood frowning. "My lord, what did you do?"

"Not treason. Never treason. I love His Grace as much as any man. My own niece is his queen, and I remained loyal to him when wiser men fled. I am his *Hand*, the Hand of the King, how can I be a traitor? I only meant to save our lives, and . . . honor . . . yes." He licked his lips. "I penned a letter. Salladhor Saan swore that he had a man who could get it to King's Landing, to Lord Tywin. His lordship is a . . . a man of reason, and my terms . . . the terms were fair . . . more than fair."

"What terms were these, my lord?"

"It is filthy here," Lord Alester said suddenly. "And that odor . . . what is that odor?"

"The pail," said Davos, gesturing. "We have no privy here. What terms?"

His lordship stared at the pail in horror. "That Lord Stannis give up his claim to the Iron Throne and retract all he said of Joffrey's bastardy, on the condition that he be accepted back into the king's peace and confirmed as Lord of Dragonstone and Storm's End. I vowed to do the same, for the return of Brightwater Keep and all our lands. I thought . . . Lord Tywin would see the sense in my proposal. He still has the Starks to deal with, and the ironmen as well. I offered to seal the bargain by wedding Shireen to Joffrey's brother Tommen." He shook his head. "The terms . . . they are as good as we are ever like to get. Even you can see that, surely?"

"Yes," said Davos, "even me." Unless Stannis should father a son, such a marriage would mean that Dragonstone and Storm's End would one day pass to Tommen, which would doubtless please Lord Tywin. Meanwhile, the Lannisters would have Shireen as hostage to make certain Stannis raised no new rebellions. "And what did His Grace say when you proposed these terms to him?"

"He is always with the red woman, and . . . he is not in his right mind, I fear. This talk of a stone dragon . . . madness, I tell you, sheer madness. Did we learn nothing from Aerion Brightfire, from the nine mages, from the alchemists? Did we learn nothing from *Summerhall?* No good has ever come from these dreams of dragons, I told Axell as much. My way was better. Surer. And Stannis gave me his seal, he gave me leave to rule. The Hand speaks with the king's voice."

"Not in this." Davos was no courtier, and he did not even try to blunt his words. "It is not in Stannis to yield, so long as he knows his claim is just. No more than he can unsay his words against Joffrey, when he believes them true. As for the marriage, Tommen was born of the same incest as Joffrey, and His Grace would sooner see Shireen dead than wed to such."

A vein throbbed in Florent's forehead. *"He has no choice."*

"You are wrong, my lord. He can choose to die a king."

"And us with him? Is that what you desire, Onion Knight?"

"No. But I am the king's man, and I will make no peace without his leave."

Lord Alester stared at him helplessly for a long moment, and then began to weep.

JON

The last night fell black and moonless, but for once the sky was clear. "I am going up the hill to look for Ghost," he told the Thenns at the cave mouth, and they grunted and let him pass.

So many stars, he thought as he trudged up the slope through pines and firs and ash. Maester Luwin had taught him his stars as a boy in Winterfell; he had learned the names of the twelve houses of heaven and the rulers of each; he could find the seven wanderers sacred to the Faith; he was old friends with the Ice Dragon, the Shadowcat, the Moonmaid, and the Sword of the Morning. All those he shared with Ygritte, but not some of the others. *We look up at the same stars, and see such different things.* The King's Crown was the Cradle, to hear her tell it; the Stallion was the Horned Lord; the red wanderer that septons preached was sacred to their Smith up here was called the Thief. And when the Thief was in the Moonmaid, that was a propitious time for a man to steal a woman, Ygritte insisted. "Like the night you stole me. The Thief was bright that night."

"I never meant to steal you," he said. "I never knew you were a girl until my knife was at your throat."

"If you kill a man, and never mean t', he's just as dead," Ygritte said stubbornly. Jon had never met anyone so stubborn, except maybe for his little sister Arya. *Is she still my sister?* he wondered. *Was she ever?* He had never truly been a Stark, only Lord Eddard's motherless bastard, with no more place at Winterfell than Theon Greyjoy. And even that he'd lost. When a man of the Night's Watch said his words, he put aside his old family and joined a new one, but Jon Snow had lost those brothers too.

He found Ghost atop the hill, as he thought he might. The white wolf never howled, yet something drew him to the heights all the same, and he would squat there on his hindquarters, hot breath rising in a white mist as his red eyes drank the stars.

"Do you have names for them as well?" Jon asked, as he went to one knee beside the direwolf and scratched the thick white fur on his neck. "The Hare? The Doe? The She-Wolf?" Ghost licked his face, his rough wet tongue rasping against the scabs where the eagle's talons had ripped Jon's cheek. *The bird marked both of us*, he thought. "Ghost," he said quietly, "on the morrow we go over. There's no steps here, no cage-and-crane, no way for me to get you to the other side. We have to part. Do you understand?"

In the dark, the direwolf's red eyes looked black. He nuzzled at Jon's neck, silent as ever, his breath a hot mist. The wildlings called Jon Snow a warg, but if so he was a poor one. He did not know how to put on a wolf skin, the way Orell had with his eagle before he'd died. Once Jon had dreamed that he was Ghost, looking down upon the valley of the Milkwater where Mance Rayder had gathered his people, and that dream had turned out to be true. But he was not dreaming now, and that left him only words.

"You cannot come with me," Jon said, cupping the wolf's head in his hands and looking deep into those eyes. "You have to go to Castle Black. Do you understand? *Castle Black.* Can you find it? The way home? Just follow the ice, east and east, into the sun, and you'll find it. They will know you at Castle Black, and maybe your coming will warn them." He had thought of writing out a warning for Ghost to carry, but he had no ink, no parchment, not even a writing quill, and the risk of discovery was too great. "I will meet you again at Castle Black, but you have to get there by yourself. We must each hunt alone for a time. *Alone.*"

The direwolf twisted free of Jon's grasp, his ears pricked up. And suddenly he was bounding away. He loped through a tangle of brush, leapt a deadfall, and raced down the hillside, a pale streak among the trees. *Off to Castle Black?* Jon wondered. *Or off after a hare?* He wished he knew. He feared he might prove just as poor a warg as a sworn brother and a spy.

A wind sighed through the trees, rich with the smell of pine needles, tugging at his faded blacks. Jon could see the Wall looming high and dark to the south, a great shadow blocking out the stars. The rough hilly ground made him think they must be somewhere between the Shadow Tower and Castle Black, and likely closer to the former. For days they had been wending their way south between deep lakes that stretched like long thin fingers along the floors of narrow valleys, while flint ridges and pine-clad hills jostled against one another to either side. Such ground made for slow riding, but offered easy concealment for those wishing to approach the Wall unseen.

For wildling raiders, he thought. *Like us. Like me.*

Beyond that Wall lay the Seven Kingdoms, and everything he had sworn to protect. He had said the words, had pledged his life and honor, and by rights he should be up there standing sentry. He should be raising a horn to his lips to rouse the Night's Watch to arms. He had no horn, though. It would not be hard to steal one from the wildlings, he suspected, but what would that accomplish? Even if he blew it, there was no one to hear. The Wall was a hundred leagues long and the Watch sadly dwindled. All but three of the strongholds had been abandoned; there might not be a brother within forty miles of here, but for Jon. If he was a brother still . . .

I should have tried to kill Mance Rayder on the Fist, even if it meant my life. That was what Qhorin Halfhand would have done. But Jon had hesitated, and the chance passed. The next day he had ridden off with Styr the Magnar, Jarl, and more than a hundred picked Thenns and raiders. He told himself that he was only biding his time, that when the moment came he would slip away and ride for Castle Black. The moment never came. They rested most nights in empty wildling villages, and Styr always set a dozen of his Thenns to guard the horses. Jarl watched him suspiciously. And Ygritte was never far, day or night.

Two hearts that beat as one. Mance Rayder's mocking words rang bitter in his head. Jon had seldom felt so confused. *I have no choice*, he'd told himself the first time, when she slipped beneath his sleeping skins. *If I refuse her, she will know me for a turncloak. I am playing the part the Halfhand told me to play.*

His body had played the part eagerly enough. His lips on hers, his hand sliding under her doeskin shirt to find a breast, his manhood stiffening when she rubbed her mound against it through their clothes. *My vows*, he'd thought, remembering the weirwood grove where he had said them, the nine great white trees in a circle, the carved red faces watching, listening. But her fingers were undoing his laces and her tongue was in his mouth and her hand slipped inside his smallclothes and brought him out, and he could not see the weirwoods anymore, only her. She bit his neck and he nuzzled hers, burying his nose in her thick red hair. *Lucky*, he thought, *she is lucky, fire-kissed*. "Isn't that good?" she whispered as she guided him inside her. She was sopping wet down there, and no maiden, that was plain, but Jon did not care. His vows, her maidenhood, none of it mattered, only the heat of her, the mouth on his, the finger that pinched at his nipple. "Isn't that sweet?" she said again. "Not so fast, oh, slow, yes, like that. There now, there now, yes, sweet, sweet. You know nothing, Jon Snow, but I can show you. Harder now. Yessss."

A part, he tried to remind himself afterward. *I am playing a part. I had to do it once, to prove I'd abandoned my vows. I had to make her trust me.* It need never happen again. He was still a man of the Night's Watch, and a son of Eddard Stark. He had done what needed to be done, proved what needed to be proven.

The proving had been so sweet, though, and Ygritte had gone to sleep beside him with her head against his chest, and that was sweet as well, dangerously sweet. He thought of the weirwoods again, and the words he'd said before them. *It was only once, and it had to be. Even my father stumbled once, when he forgot his marriage vows and sired a bastard.* Jon vowed to himself that it would be the same with him. *It will never happen again.*

It happened twice more that night, and again in the morning, when she woke to find him hard. The wildlings were stirring by then, and several could not help but notice what was going on beneath the pile of furs. Jarl told them to be quick about it, before he had to throw a pail of water over them. *Like a pair of rutting dogs*, Jon thought afterward. Was that what he'd become? *I am a man of the Night's Watch*, a small voice inside insisted, but every night it seemed a little fainter, and when Ygritte kissed his ears or bit his neck, he could not hear it at all. *Was this how it was for my father?* he wondered. *Was he as weak as I am, when he dishonored himself in my mother's bed?*

Something was coming up the hill behind him, he realized suddenly. For half a heartbeat he thought it might be Ghost come back, but the direwolf never made so much noise. Jon drew Longclaw in a single smooth motion, but it was only one of the Thenns, a broad man in a bronze helm. "Snow," the intruder said. "Come. Magnar wants." The men of Thenn spoke the Old Tongue, and most had only a few words of the Common.

Jon did not much care what the Magnar wanted, but there was no use arguing with someone who could scarcely understand him, so he followed the man back down the hill.

The mouth of the cave was a cleft in the rock barely wide enough for a horse, half concealed behind a soldier pine. It opened to the north, so the glows of the fires within would not be visible from the Wall. Even if by some mischance a patrol should happen to pass atop the Wall tonight, they would see nothing but hills and pines and the icy sheen of starlight on a half-frozen lake. Mance Rayder had planned his thrust well.

Within the rock, the passage descended twenty feet before it opened out onto a space as large as Winterfell's Great Hall. Cookfires burned amongst the columns, their smoke rising to blacken the stony ceiling. The horses had been hobbled along one wall, beside a shallow pool. A sinkhole in the center of the floor opened on what might have been an even greater cavern below, though the darkness made it hard to tell. Jon could hear the soft rushing sound of an underground stream somewhere below as well.

Jarl was with the Magnar; Mance had given them the joint command. Styr was none too pleased by that, Jon had noted early on. Mance Rayder had called the dark youth a "pet" of Val, who was sister to Dalla, his own queen, which made Jarl a sort of good brother once removed to the King-beyond-the-Wall. The Magnar plainly resented sharing his authority. He had brought a hundred Thenns, five times as many men as Jarl, and often acted as if he had the sole command. But it would be the younger man who got them over the ice, Jon knew. Though he could not have been older than twenty, Jarl had been raiding for eight years, and had gone over the Wall a dozen times with the likes of Alfyn Crowkiller and the Weeper, and more recently with his own band.

The Magnar was direct. "Jarl has warned me of crows, patrolling on high. Tell me all you know of these patrols."

Tell me, Jon noted, not *tell us*, though Jarl stood right beside him. He would have liked nothing better than to refuse the brusque demand, but he knew Styr would put him to death at the slightest disloyalty, and Ygritte as well, for the crime of being his. "There are four men in each patrol, two rangers and two builders," he said. "The builders are supposed to make note of cracks, melting, and other structural problems, while the rangers look for signs of foes. They ride mules."

"Mules?" The earless man frowned. "Mules are slow."

"Slow, but more surefooted on the ice. The patrols often ride atop the Wall, and aside from Castle Black, the paths up there have not been graveled for long years. The mules are bred at Eastwatch, and specially trained to their duty."

"They *often* ride atop the Wall? Not always?"

"No. One patrol in four follows the base instead, to search for cracks in the foundation ice or signs of tunneling."

The Magnar nodded. "Even in far Thenn we know the tale of Arson Iceaxe and his tunnel."

Jon knew the tale as well. Arson Iceaxe had been halfway through the Wall when his tunnel was found by rangers from the Nightfort. They did not trouble to disturb him at his digging, only sealed the way behind with ice and stone and snow. Dolorous Edd used to say that if you pressed your ear flat to the Wall, you could still hear Arson chipping away with his axe.

"When do these patrols go out? How often?"

Jon shrugged. "It changes. I've heard that Lord Commander Qorgyle used to send them out every third day from Castle Black to Eastwatch-by-the-Sea, and every second day from Castle Black to the Shadow Tower. The Watch had more men in his day, though. Lord Commander Mormont prefers to vary the number of patrols and the days of their departure, to make it more difficult for anyone to know their comings and goings. And sometimes the Old Bear will even send a larger force to one of the abandoned castles for a fortnight or a moon's turn." His uncle had originated that tactic, Jon knew. Anything to make the enemy unsure.

"Is Stonedoor manned at present?" asked Jarl. "Greyguard?"

So we're between those two, are we? Jon kept his face carefully blank. "Only Eastwatch, Castle Black, and the Shadow Tower were manned when I left the Wall. I can't speak to what Bowen Marsh or Ser Denys might have done since."

"How many crows remain within the castles?" asked Styr.

"Five hundred at Castle Black. Two hundred at Shadow Tower, perhaps three hundred at Eastwatch." Jon added three hundred men to the count. *If only it were that easy . . .*

Jarl was not fooled, however. "He's lying," he told Styr. "Or else including those they lost on the Fist."

"Crow," the Magnar warned, "do not take me for Mance Rayder. If you lie to me, I will have your tongue."

"I'm no crow, and won't be called a liar." Jon flexed the fingers of his sword hand.

The Magnar of Thenn studied Jon with his chilly grey eyes. "We shall learn their numbers soon enough," he said after a moment. "Go. I will send for you if I have further questions."

Jon bowed his head stiffly, and went. *If all the wildlings were like Styr, it would be easier to betray them.* The Thenns were not like other free folk, though. The Magnar claimed to be the last of the First Men, and ruled with an iron hand. His little land of Thenn was a high mountain valley hidden amongst the northernmost peaks of the Frostfangs, surrounded by cave dwellers, Hornfoot men, giants, and the cannibal clans of the ice rivers. Ygritte said the Thenns were savage fighters, and that their Magnar was a god to them. Jon could believe that. Unlike Jarl and Harma and Rattleshirt, Styr commanded absolute obedience from his men, and that discipline was no doubt part of why Mance had chosen him to go over the Wall.

He walked past the Thenns, sitting atop their rounded bronze helms about their cookfires. *Where did Ygritte get herself to?* He found her gear and his together, but no sign of the girl herself. "She took a torch and went off that way," Grigg the Goat told him, pointing toward the back of the cavern.

Jon followed his finger, and found himself in a dim back room wandering through a maze of columns and stalactites. *She can't be here*, he was thinking, when he heard her laugh. He turned toward the sound, but within ten paces he was in a dead end, facing a blank wall of rose and white flowstone. Baffled, he made his way back the way he'd come, and then he saw it: a dark hole under an outthrust of wet stone. He knelt, listened, heard the faint sound of water. "Ygritte?"

"In here," her voice came back, echoing faintly.

Jon had to crawl a dozen paces before the cave opened up around him. When he stood again, it took his eyes a moment to adjust. Ygritte had brought a torch, but there was no other light. She stood beside a little waterfall that fell from a cleft in the rock down into a wide dark pool. The orange and yellow flames shone against the pale green water.

"What are you doing here?" he asked her.

"I heard water. I wanted t'see how deep the cave went." She pointed with the torch. "There's a passage goes down further. I followed it a hundred paces before I turned back."

"A dead end?"

"You know nothing, Jon Snow. It went on and on and on. There are hundreds o' caves in these hills, and down deep they all connect. There's even a way under your Wall. Gorne's Way."

"Gorne," said Jon. "Gorne was King-beyond-the-Wall."

"Aye," said Ygritte. "Together with his brother Gendel, three thousand years ago. They led a host o' free folk through the caves, and the Watch was none the wiser. But when they come out, the wolves o' Winterfell fell upon them."

"There was a battle," Jon recalled. "Gorne slew the King in the North, but his son picked up his banner and took the crown from his head, and cut down Gorne in turn."

"And the sound o' swords woke the crows in their castles, and they rode out all in black to take the free folk in the rear."

"Yes. Gendel had the king to the south, the Umbers to the east, and the Watch to the north of him. He died as well."

"You know nothing, Jon Snow. Gendel did not die. He cut his way free, through the crows, and led his people back north with the wolves howling at their heels. Only Gendel did not know the caves as Gorne had, and took a wrong turn." She swept the torch back and forth, so the shadows jumped and moved. "Deeper he went, and deeper, and when he tried t' turn back the ways that seemed familiar ended in stone rather than sky. Soon his torches began t' fail, one by one, till finally there was naught but dark. Gendel's folk were never seen again, but on a still night you can hear their children's children's children sobbing under the hills, still looking for the way back up. Listen? Do you hear them?"

All Jon could hear was the falling water and the faint crackle of flames. "This way under the Wall was lost as well?"

"Some have searched for it. Them that go too deep find Gendel's children, and Gendel's children are always hungry." Smiling, she set the torch carefully in a notch of rock, and came toward him. "There's naught to eat in the dark but flesh," she whispered, biting at his neck.

Jon nuzzled her hair and filled his nose with the smell of her. "You sound like Old Nan, telling Bran a monster story."

Ygritte punched his shoulder. "An old woman, am I?"

"You're older than me."

"Aye, and wiser. You know nothing, Jon Snow." She pushed away from him, and shrugged out of her rabbitskin vest.

"What are you doing?"

"Showing you how old I am." She unlaced her doeskin shirt, tossed it aside, pulled her three woolen undershirts up over her head all at once. "I want you should see me."

"We shouldn't –"

"We *should*." Her breasts bounced as she stood on one leg to pull one boot, then hopped onto her other foot to attend to the other. Her nipples were wide pink circles. "You as well," Ygritte said as she yanked down her sheepskin breeches. "If you want to look you have to show. You know nothing, Jon Snow."

"I know I want you," he heard himself say, all his vows and all his honor forgotten. She stood before him naked as her name day, and he was as hard as the rock around them. He had been in her half a hundred times by now, but always beneath the furs, with others all around them. He had never seen how beautiful she was. Her legs were skinny but well muscled, the hair at the juncture of her thighs a brighter red than that on her head. *Does that make it even luckier?* He pulled her close. "I love the smell of you," he said. "I love your red hair. I love your mouth, and the way you kiss me. I love your smile. I love your teats." He kissed them, one and then the other. "I love your skinny legs, and what's between them." He knelt to kiss her there, lightly on her mound at first, but Ygritte moved her legs apart a little, and he saw the pink inside and kissed that as well, and tasted her. She gave a little gasp. "If you love me all so much, why are you still dressed?" she whispered. "You know nothing, Jon Snow. *Noth – oh. Oh. OHHH.*"

Afterward, she was almost shy, or as shy as Ygritte ever got. "That thing you did," she said, when they lay together on their piled clothes. "With your . . . mouth." She hesitated. "Is that . . . is it what lords do to their ladies, down in the south?"

"I don't think so." No one had ever told Jon just what lords did with their ladies. "I only . . . wanted to kiss you there, that's all. You seemed to like it."

"Aye. I . . . I liked it some. No one taught you such?"

"There's been no one," he confessed. "Only you."

"A maid," she teased. "You were a maid."

He gave her closest nipple a playful pinch. "I was a man of the Night's Watch." *Was*, he heard himself say. What was he now? He did not want to look at that. "Were you a maid?"

Ygritte pushed herself onto an elbow. "I am nineteen, and a spearwife, and kissed by fire. How could I be maiden?"

"Who was he?"

"A boy at a feast, five years past. He'd come trading with his brothers, and he had hair like mine, kissed by fire, so I thought he would be lucky. But he was weak. When he came back t' try and steal me, Longspear broke his arm and ran him off, and he never tried again, not once."

"It wasn't Longspear, then?" Jon was relieved. He liked Longspear, with his homely face and friendly ways.

She punched him. "That's vile. Would you bed your sister?"

"Longspear's not your brother."

"He's of my village. You know nothing, Jon Snow. A true man steals a woman from afar, t' strengthen the clan. Women who bed brothers or fathers or clan kin offend the gods, and are cursed with weak and sickly children. Even monsters."

"Craster weds his daughters," Jon pointed out.

She punched him again. "Craster's more your kind than ours. His father was a crow who stole a woman out of Whitetree village, but after he had her he flew back t' his Wall. She went t' Castle Black once t' show the crow his son, but the brothers blew their horns and run her off. Craster's blood is black, and he bears a heavy curse." She ran her fingers lightly across his stomach. "I feared you'd do the same once. Fly back to the Wall. You never knew what t' do after you stole me."

Jon sat up. "Ygritte, I never stole you."

"Aye, you did. You jumped down the mountain and killed Orell, and afore I could get my axe you had a knife at my throat. I thought you'd have me then, or kill me, or maybe both, but you never did. And when I told you the tale o' Bael the Bard and how he plucked the rose o' Winterfell, I thought you'd know to pluck me then for certain, but you didn't. You know *nothing*, Jon Snow." She gave him a shy smile. "You might be learning some, though."

The light was shifting all about her, Jon noticed suddenly. He looked around. "We had best go up. The torch is almost done."

"Is the crow afeared o' Gendel's children?" she said, with a grin. "It's only a little way up, and I'm not done with you, Jon Snow." She pushed him back down on the clothes and straddled him. "Would you . . ." She hesitated.

"What?" he prompted, as the torch began to gutter.

"Do it again?" Ygritte blurted. "With your mouth? The lord's kiss? And I . . . I could see if you liked it any."

By the time the torch burned out, Jon Snow no longer cared.

His guilt came back afterward, but weaker than before. *If this is so wrong*, he wondered, *why did the gods make it feel so good?*

The grotto was pitch-dark by the time they finished. The only light was the dim glow of the passage back up to the larger cavern, where a score of fires burned. They were soon fumbling and bumping into each other as they tried to dress in the dark. Ygritte stumbled into the pool and screeched at the cold of the water. When Jon laughed, she pulled him in too. They wrestled and splashed in the dark, and then she was in his arms again, and it turned out they were not finished after all.

"Jon Snow," she told him, when he'd spent his seed inside her, "don't move now, sweet. I like the feel of you in there, I do. Let's not go back t' Styr and Jarl. Let's go down inside, and join up with Gendel's children. I don't ever want t' leave this cave, Jon Snow. Not ever."

DAENERYS

"**A** ll?" The slave girl sounded wary. "Your Grace, did this one's worthless ears mishear you?"

Cool green light filtered down through the diamond-shaped panes of colored glass set in the sloping triangular walls, and a breeze was blowing gently through the terrace doors, carrying the scents of fruit and flowers from the garden beyond. "Your ears heard true," said Dany. "I want to buy them all. Tell the Good Masters, if you will."

She had chosen a Qartheen gown today. The deep violet silk brought out the purple of her eyes. The cut of it bared her left breast. While the Good Masters of Astapor conferred among themselves in low voices, Dany sipped tart persimmon wine from a tall silver flute. She could not quite make out all that they were saying, but she could hear the greed.

Each of the eight brokers was attended by two or three body slaves . . . though one Grazdan, the eldest, had six. So as not to seem a beggar, Dany had brought her own attendants; Irri and Jhiqui in their sandsilk trousers and painted vests, old Whitebeard and mighty Belwas, her bloodriders. Ser Jorah stood behind her sweltering in his green surcoat with the black bear of Mormont embroidered upon it. The smell of his sweat was an earthy answer to the sweet perfumes that drenched the Astapori.

"All," growled Kraznys mo Nakloz, who smelled of peaches today. The slave girl repeated the word in the Common Tongue of Westeros. "Of thousands, there are eight. Is this what she means by *all*? There are also six centuries, who shall be part of a ninth thousand when complete. Would she have them too?"

"I would," said Dany when the question was put to her. "The eight thousands, the six centuries . . . and the ones still in training as well. The ones who have not earned the spikes."

Kraznys turned back to his fellows. Once again they conferred among themselves. The translator had told Dany their names, but it was hard to keep them straight. Four of the men seemed to be named Grazdan, presumably after Grazdan the Great who had founded Old Ghis in the dawn of days. They all looked alike; thick fleshy men with amber skin, broad noses, dark eyes. Their wiry hair was black, or a dark red, or that queer mixture of red and black that was peculiar to Ghiscari. All wrapped themselves in *tokars*, a garment permitted only to freeborn men of Astapor.

It was the fringe on the *tokar* that proclaimed a man's status, Dany had been told by Captain Groleo. In this cool green room atop the pyramid, two of the slavers wore *tokars* fringed in silver, five had gold fringes, and one, the oldest Grazdan, displayed a fringe of fat white pearls that clacked together softly when he shifted in his seat or moved an arm.

"We cannot sell half-trained boys," one of the silver-fringe Grazdans was saying to the others.

"We can, if her gold is good," said a fatter man whose fringe was gold.

"They are not Unsullied. They have not killed their sucklings. If they fail in the field, they will shame us. And even if we cut five thousand raw boys tomorrow, it would be ten years before they are fit for sale. What would we tell the next buyer who comes seeking Unsullied?"

"We will tell him that he must wait," said the fat man. "Gold in my purse is better than gold in my future."

Dany let them argue, sipping the tart persimmon wine and trying to keep her face blank and ignorant. *I will have them all, no matter the price*, she told herself. The city had a hundred slave traders, but the eight before her were the greatest. When selling bed slaves, fieldhands, scribes, craftsmen, and tutors, these men were rivals, but their ancestors had allied one with the other for the purpose of making and selling the Unsullied. *Brick and blood built Astapor, and brick and blood her people.*

It was Kraznys who finally announced their decision. "Tell her that the eight thousands she shall have, if her gold proves sufficient. And the six centuries, if she wishes. Tell her to come back in a year, and we will sell her another two thousand."

"In a year I shall be in Westeros," said Dany when she had heard the translation. "My need is *now*. The Unsullied are well trained, but even so, many will fall in battle. I shall need the boys as replacements to take up the swords they drop." She put her wine aside and leaned toward the slave girl. "Tell the Good Masters that I will want even the little ones who still have their puppies. Tell them that I will pay as much for the boy they cut yesterday as for an Unsullied in a spiked helm."

The girl told them. The answer was still no.

Dany frowned in annoyance. "Very well. Tell them I will pay double, so long as I get them all."

"Double?" The fat one in the gold fringe all but drooled.

"This little whore is a fool, truly," said Khaznys mo Nakloz. "Ask her for triple, I say. She is desperate enough to pay. Ask for ten times the price of every slave, yes."

The tall Grazdan with the spiked beard spoke in the Common Tongue, though not so well as the slave girl. "Your Grace," he growled, "Westeros is being wealthy, yes, but you are not being queen now. Perhaps will never being queen. Even Unsullied may be losing battles to savage steel knights of Seven Kingdoms. I am reminding, the Good Masters of Astapor are not selling flesh for promisings. Are you having gold and trading goods sufficient to be paying for all these eunuchs you are wanting?"

"You know the answer to that better than I, Good Master," Dany replied. "Your men have gone through my ships and tallied every bead of amber and jar of saffron. How much do I have?"

"Sufficient to be buying one of thousands," the Good Master said, with a contemptuous smile. "Yet you are paying double, you are saying. Five centuries, then, is all you buy."

"Your pretty crown might buy another century," said the fat one in Valyrian. "Your crown of the three dragons."

Dany waited for his words to be translated. "My crown is not for sale." When Viserys sold their mother's crown, the last joy had gone from him, leaving only rage. "Nor will I enslave my people, nor sell their goods and horses. But my ships you can have. The great cog *Balerion* and the galleys *Vhagar* and *Meraxes*." She had warned Groleo and the other captains it might come to this, though they had protested the necessity of it furiously. "Three good ships should be worth more than a few paltry eunuchs."

The fat Grazdan turned to the others. They conferred in low voices once again. "Two of the thousands," the one with the spiked beard said when he turned back. "It is too much, but the Good Masters are being generous and your need is being great."

Two thousand would never serve for what she meant to do. *I must have them all.* Dany knew what she must do now, though the taste of it was so bitter that even the persimmon wine could not cleanse it from her month. She had considered long and hard and found no other way. *It is my only choice.* "Give me all," she said, "and you may have a dragon."

There was the sound of indrawn breath from Jhiqui beside her. Kraznys smiled at his fellows. "Did I not tell you? Anything, she would give us."

Whitebeard stared in shocked disbelief. His hand trembled where it grasped the staff. *"No."* He went to one knee before her. "Your Grace, I beg you, win your throne with dragons, not slaves. You must not do this thing – "

"You must not presume to instruct me. Ser Jorah, remove Whitebeard from my presence."

Mormont seized the old man roughly by an elbow, yanked him back to his feet, and marched him out onto the terrace.

"Tell the Good Masters I regret this interruption," said Dany to the slave girl. "Tell them I await their answer."

She knew the answer, though; she could see it in the glitter of their eyes and the smiles they tried so hard to hide. Astapor had thousands of eunuchs, and even more slave boys waiting to be cut, but there were only three living dragons in all the great wide world. *And the Ghiscari lust for dragons.* How could they not? Five times had Old Ghis contended with Valyria when the world was young, and five times gone down to bleak defeat. For the Freehold had dragons, and the Empire had none.

The oldest Grazdan stirred in his seat, and his pearls clacked together softly. "A dragon of our choice," he said in a thin, hard voice. "The black one is largest and healthiest."

"His name is Drogon." She nodded.

"All your goods, save your crown and your queenly raiment, which we will allow you to keep. The three ships. And Drogon."

"Done," she said, in the Common Tongue.

"Done," the old Grazdan answered in his thick Valyrian.

The others echoed that old man of the pearl fringe. "Done," the slave girl translated, "and done, and done, eight times done."

"The Unsullied will learn your savage tongue quick enough," added Kraznys mo Nakloz, when all the arrangements had been made, "but until such time you will need a slave to speak to them. Take this one as our gift to you, a token of a bargain well struck."

"I shall," said Dany.

The slave girl rendered his words to her, and hers to him. If she had feelings about being given for a token, she took care not to let them show.

Arstan Whitebeard held his tongue as well, when Dany swept by him on the terrace. He followed her down the steps in silence, but she could hear his hardwood staff *tap tap*ping on the red bricks as they went. She did not blame him for his fury. It was a wretched thing she did. *The Mother of Dragons has sold her strongest child.* Even the thought made her ill.

Yet down in the Plaza of Pride, standing on the hot red bricks between the slavers' pyramid and the barracks of the eunuchs, Dany turned on the old man. "Whitebeard," she said, "I want your counsel, and you should never fear to speak your mind with me ... when we are alone. But *never* question me in front of strangers. Is that understood?"

"Yes, Your Grace," he said unhappily.

"I am not a child," she told him. "I am a queen."

"Yet even queens can err. The Astapori have cheated you, Your Grace. A dragon is worth more than any army. Aegon proved that three hundred years ago, upon the Field of Fire."

"I know what Aegon proved. I mean to prove a few things of my own." Dany turned away from him, to the slave girl standing meekly beside her litter. "Do you have a name, or must you draw a new one every day from some barrel?"

"That is only for Unsullied," the girl said. Then she realized the question had been asked in High Valyrian. Her eyes went wide. "Oh."

"Your name is Oh?"

"No. Your Grace, forgive this one her outburst. Your slave's name is Missandei, but ..."

"Missandei is no longer a slave. I free you, from this instant. Come ride with me in the litter, I wish to talk." Rakharo helped them in, and Dany drew the curtains shut against the dust and heat. "If you stay with me you will serve as one of my handmaids," she said as they set off. "I shall keep you by my side to speak for me as you spoke for Kraznys. But you may leave my service whenever you choose, if you have father or mother you would sooner return to."

"This one will stay," the girl said. "This one ... I ... there is no place for me to go. This ... I will serve you, gladly."

"I can give you freedom, but not safety," Dany warned. "I have a world to cross and wars to fight. You may go hungry. You may grow sick. You may be killed."

"*Valar morghulis*," said Missandei, in High Valyrian.

"All men must die," Dany agreed, "but not for a long while, we may pray." She leaned back on the pillows and took the girl's hand. "Are these Unsullied truly fearless?"

"Yes, Your Grace."

"You serve me now. Is it true they feel no pain?"

"The wine of courage kills such feelings. By the time they slay their sucklings, they have been drinking it for years."

"And they are obedient?"

"Obedience is all they know. If you told them not to breathe, they would find that easier than not to obey."

Dany nodded. "And when I am done with them?"

"Your Grace?"

"When I have won my war and claimed the throne that was my father's, my knights will sheathe their swords and return to their keeps, to their wives and children and mothers . . . to their *lives*. But these eunuchs have no lives. What am I to do with eight thousand eunuchs when there are no more battles to be fought?"

"The Unsullied make fine guards and excellent watchmen, Your Grace," said Missandei. "And it is never hard to find a buyer for such fine well-blooded troops."

"Men are not bought and sold in Westeros, they tell me."

"With all respect, Your Grace, Unsullied are not men."

"If I did resell them, how would I know they could not be used against me?" Dany asked pointedly. "Would they do that? Fight *against* me, even do me harm?"

"If their master commanded. They do not question, Your Grace. All the questions have been culled from them. They obey." She looked troubled. "When you are . . . when you are done with them . . . Your Grace might command them to fall upon their swords."

"And even that, they would do?"

"Yes." Missandei's voice had grown soft. "Your Grace."

Dany squeezed her hand. "You would sooner I did not ask it of them, though. Why is that? Why do you care?"

"This one does not . . . I . . . Your Grace . . ."

"Tell me."

The girl lowered her eyes. "Three of them were my brothers once, Your Grace."

Then I hope your brothers are as brave and clever as you. Dany leaned back into her pillow, and let the litter bear her onward, back to *Balerion* one last time to set her world in order. *And back to Drogon.* Her mouth set grimly.

It was a long, dark, windy night that followed. Dany fed her dragons as she always did, but found she had no appetite herself. She cried awhile, alone in her cabin, then dried her tears long enough for yet another argument with Groleo. "Magister Illyrio is not here," she finally had to tell him, "and if he was, he could not sway me either. I need the Unsullied more than I need these ships, and I will hear no more about it."

The anger burned the grief and fear from her, for a few hours at the least. Afterward she called her bloodriders to her cabin, with Ser Jorah. They were the only ones she truly trusted.

She meant to sleep afterward, to be well rested for the morrow, but an hour of restless tossing in the stuffy confines of the cabin soon convinced her that was hopeless. Outside her door she found Aggo fitting anew string to his bow by the light of a swinging oil lamp. Rakharo sat crosslegged on the deck beside him, sharpening his *arakh* with a whetstone. Dany told them both to keep on with what they were doing, and went up on deck for a taste of the cool night air. The crew left her alone as they went about their business, but Ser Jorah soon joined her by the rail. *He is never far,* Dany thought. *He knows my moods too well.*

"*Khaleesi.* You ought to be asleep. Tomorrow will be hot and hard, I promise you. You'll need your strength."

"Do you remember Eroeh?" she asked him.

"The Lhazareen girl?"

"They were raping her, but I stopped them and took her under my protection. Only when my sun-and-stars was dead Mago took her back, used her again, and killed her. Aggo said it was her fate."

"I remember," Ser Jorah said.

"I was alone for a long time, Jorah. All alone but for my brother. I was such a small scared thing. Viserys should have protected me, but instead he hurt me and scared me worse. He shouldn't have done that. He wasn't just my brother, he was my *king.* Why do the gods make kings and queens, if not to protect the ones who can't protect themselves?"

"Some kings make themselves. Robert did."

"He was no true king," Dany said scornfully. "He did no justice. Justice . . . that's what kings are *for.*"

Ser Jorah had no answer. He only smiled, and touched her hair, so lightly. It was enough.

That night she dreamt that she was Rhaegar, riding to the Trident. But she was mounted on a dragon, not a horse. When she saw the Usurper's rebel host across the river they were armored all in ice, but she bathed them in dragonfire and they melted away like dew and turned the Trident into a torrent. Some small part of her knew that she was dreaming, but another part exulted. *This is how it was meant to be. The other was a nightmare, and I have only now awakened.*

She woke suddenly in the darkness of her cabin, still flush with triumph. *Balerion* seemed to wake with her, and she heard the faint creak of wood, water lapping against the hull, a footfall on the deck above her head. And something else.

Someone was in the cabin with her.

"Irri? Jhiqui? Where are you?" Her handmaids did not respond. It was too black to see, but she could hear them breathing. "Jorah, is that you?"

"They sleep," a woman said. "They all sleep." The voice was very close. "Even dragons must sleep."

She is standing over me. "Who's there?" Dany peered into the darkness. She thought she could see a shadow, the faintest outline of a shape. "What do you want of me?"

"Remember. To go north, you must journey south. To reach the west, you must go east. To go forward you must go back, and to touch the light you must pass beneath the shadow."

"*Quaithe?*" Dany sprung from the bed and threw open the door. Pale yellow lantern light flooded the cabin, and Irri and Jhiqui sat up sleepily. *"Khaleesi?"* murmured Jhiqui, rubbing her eyes. Viserion woke and opened his jaws, and a puff of flame brightened even the darkest corners. There was no sign of a woman in a red lacquer mask. *"Khaleesi,* are you unwell?" asked Jhiqui.

"A dream." Dany shook her head. "I dreamed a dream, no more. Go back to sleep. All of us, go back to sleep." Yet try as she might, sleep would not come again.

If I look back I am lost, Dany told herself the next morning as she entered Astapor through the harbor gates. She dared not remind herself how small and insignificant her following truly was, or she would lose all courage. Today she rode her silver, clad in horsehair pants and painted leather vest, a bronze medallion belt about her waist and two more crossed between her breasts. Irri and Jhiqui had braided her hair and hung it with a tiny silver bell whose chime sang of the Undying of Qarth, burned in their Palace of Dust.

The red brick streets of Astapor were almost crowded this morning. Slaves and servants lined the ways, while the slavers and their women donned their *tokars* to look down from their stepped pyramids. *They are not so different from Qartheen after all,* she thought. *They want a glimpse of dragons to tell their children of, and their children's children.* It made her wonder how many of them would ever have children.

Aggo went before her with his great Dothraki bow. Strong Belwas walked to the right of her mare, the girl Missandei to her left. Ser Jorah Mormont was behind in mail and surcoat, glowering at anyone who came too near. Rakharo and Jhogo protected the litter. Dany had commanded that the top be removed, so her three dragons might be chained to the platform. Irri and Jhiqui rode with them, to try and keep them calm. Yet Viserion's tail lashed back and forth, and smoke rose angry from his nostrils. Rhaegal could sense something wrong as well. Thrice he tried to take wing, only to be pulled down by the heavy chain in Jhiqui's hand. Drogon coiled into a ball, wings and tail tucked tight. Only his eyes remained to tell that he was not asleep.

The rest of her people followed: Groleo and the other captains and their crews, and the eighty-three Dothraki who remained to her of the hundred thousand who had once ridden in Drogo's *khalasar.* She put the oldest and weakest on the inside of the column, with the nursing women and those with child, and the little girls, and the boys too young to braid their hair. The rest – her warriors, such as they were – rode outside and moved their dismal herd along, the hundred-odd gaunt horses that had survived both red waste and black salt sea.

I ought to have a banner sewn, she thought as she led her tattered band up along Astapor's meandering river. She closed her eyes to imagine how it would look: all flowing black silk, and on it the red three-headed dragon of Targaryen, breathing golden flames. *A banner such as Rhaegar might have borne.* The river's banks were strangely tranquil. The Worm, the Astapori called the stream. It was wide and slow and crooked, dotted with tiny wooded islands. She glimpsed children playing on one of them, darting amongst elegant marble statues. On another island two lovers kissed in the shade of tall green trees, with no more shame than Dothraki at a wedding. Without clothing, she could not tell if they were slave or free.

The Plaza of Pride with its great bronze harpy was too small to hold all the Unsullied she had bought. Instead they had been assembled in the Plaza of Punishment, fronting on Astapor's main gate, so they might be marched directly from the city once Daenerys had taken them in hand. There were no bronze statues here; only a wooden platform where rebellious slaves were racked, and flayed, and hanged. "The Good Masters place them so they will be the first thing a new slave sees upon entering the city," Missandei told her as they came to the plaza.

At first glimpse, Dany thought their skin was striped like the zorses of the Jogos Nhai. Then she rode her silver nearer and saw the raw red flesh beneath the crawling black stripes. *Flies. Flies and maggots.* The rebellious slaves had been peeled like a man might peel an apple, in a long curling strip. One man had an arm black with flies from fingers to elbow, and red and white beneath. Dany reined in beneath him. "What did this one do?"

"He raised a hand against his owner."

Her stomach roiling, Dany wheeled her silver about and trotted toward the center of the plaza, and the army she had bought so dear. Rank on rank on rank they stood, her stone halfmen with their hearts of brick; eight thousand and six hundred in the spiked bronze caps of fully trained Unsullied, and five thousand odd behind them, bareheaded, yet armed with spears and shortswords. The ones farthest to the back were only boys, she saw, but they stood as straight and still as all the rest.

Kraznys mo Nakloz and his fellows were all there to greet her. Other well-born Astapori stood in knots behind them, sipping wine from silver flutes as slaves circulated among them with trays of olives and cherries and figs. The elder Grazdan sat in a sedan chair supported by four huge copper-skinned slaves. Half a dozen mounted lancers rode along the edges of the plaza, keeping back the crowds who had come to watch. The sun flashed blinding bright off the polished copper disks sewn to their cloaks, but she could not help but notice how nervous their horses seemed. *They fear the dragons. And well they might.*

Kraznys had a slave help her from her saddle. His own hands were full; one clutched his *tokar*, while the other held an ornate whip. "Here they are." He looked at Missandei. "Tell her they are hers ... if she can pay."

"She can," the girl said.

Ser Jorah barked a command, and the trade goods were brought forward. Six bales of tiger skins, three hundred bolts of fine silk. Jars of saffron, jars of myrrh, jars of pepper and curry and cardamom, an onyx mask, twelve jade monkeys, casks of ink in red and black and green, a box of rare black amethysts, a box of pearls, a cask of pitted olives stuffed with maggots, a dozen casks of pickled cave fish, a great brass gong and a hammer to beat it with, seventeen ivory eyes, and a huge chest full of books written in tongues that Dany could not read. And more, and more, and more. Her people stacked it all before the slavers.

While the payment was being made, Kraznys mo Nakloz favored her with a few final words on the handling of her troops. "They are green as yet," he said through Missandei. "Tell the whore of Westeros she would be wise to blood them early. There are many small cities between here and there, cities ripe for sacking. Whatever plunder she takes will be hers alone. Unsullied have no lust for gold or gems. And should she take captives, a few guards will suffice to march them back to Astapor. We'll buy the healthy ones, and for a good price. And who knows? In ten years, some of the boys she sends us may be Unsullied in their turn. Thus all shall prosper."

Finally there were no more trade goods to add to the pile. Her Dothraki mounted their horses once more, and Dany said, "This was all we could carry. The rest awaits you on the ships, a great quantity of amber and wine and black rice. And you have the ships themselves. So all that remains is ..."

"... the dragon," finished the Grazdan with the spiked beard, who spoke the Common Tongue so thickly.

"And here he waits." Ser Jorah and Belwas walked beside her to the litter, where Drogon and his brothers lay basking in the sun. Jhiqui unfastened one end of the chain, and handed it down to her. When she gave a yank, the black dragon raised his head, hissing, and unfolded wings of night and scarlet. Kraznys mo Nakloz smiled broadly as their shadow fell across him.

Dany handed the slaver the end of Drogon's chain. In return he presented her with the whip. The handle was black dragonbone, elaborately carved and inlaid with gold. Nine long thin leather lashes trailed from it, each one tipped by a gilded claw. The gold pommel was a woman's head, with pointed ivory teeth. "The harpy's fingers," Kraznys named the scourge.

Dany turned the whip in her hand. *Such a light thing, to bear such weight.* "Is it done, then? Do they belong to me?"

"It is done," he agreed, giving the chain a sharp pull to bring Drogon down from the litter.

Dany mounted her silver. She could feel her heart thumping in her chest. She felt desperately afraid. *Was this what my brother would have done?* She wondered if Prince Rhaegar had been this anxious when he saw the Usurper's host formed up across the Trident with all their banners floating on the wind.

She stood in her stirrups and raised the harpy's fingers above her head for all the Unsullied to see. *"IT IS DONE!"* she cried at the top of her lungs. *"YOU ARE MINE!"* She gave the mare her heels and galloped along the first rank, holding the fingers high. *"YOU ARE THE DRAGON'S NOW! YOU'RE BOUGHT AND PAID FOR! IT IS DONE! IT IS DONE!"*

She glimpsed old Grazdan turn his grey head sharply. *He hears me speak Valyrian.* The other slavers were not listening. They crowded around Kraznys and the dragon, shouting advice. Though the Astapori yanked and tugged, Drogon would not budge off the litter. Smoke rose grey from his open jaws, and his long neck curled and straightened as he snapped at the slaver's face.

It is time to cross the Trident, Dany thought, as she wheeled and rode her silver back. Her bloodriders moved in close around her. "You are in difficulty," she observed.

"He will not come," Kraznys said.

"There is a reason. A dragon is no slave." And Dany swept the lash down as hard as she could across the slaver's face. Kraznys screamed and staggered back, the blood running red down his cheeks into his perfumed beard. The harpy's fingers had torn his features half to pieces with one slash, but she did not pause to contemplate the ruin. "Drogon," she sang out loudly, sweetly, all her fear forgotten. *"Dracarys."*

The black dragon spread his wings and roared.

A lance of swirling dark flame took Kraznys full in the face. His eyes melted and ran down his cheeks, and the oil in his hair and beard burst so fiercely into fire that for an instant the slaver wore a burning crown twice as tall as his head. The sudden stench of charred meat overwhelmed even his perfume, and his wail seemed to drown all other sound.

Then the Plaza of Punishment blew apart into blood and chaos. The Good Masters were shrieking, stumbling, shoving one another aside and tripping over the fringes of their *tokars* in their haste. Drogon flew almost lazily at Kraznys, black wings beating. As he gave the slaver another taste of fire, Irri and Jhiqui unchained Viserion and Rhaegal, and suddenly there were three dragons in the air. When Dany turned to look, a third of Astapor's proud demon-horned warriors were fighting to stay atop their terrified mounts, and another third were fleeing in a bright blaze of shiny copper. One man kept his saddle long enough to draw a sword, but Jhogo's whip coiled about his neck and cut off his shout. Another lost a hand to Rakharo's *arakh* and rode off reeling and spurting blood. Aggo sat calmly notching arrows to his bowstring and sending them at *tokars*. Silver, gold, or plain, he cared nothing for the fringe. Strong Belwas had his *arakh* out as well, and he spun it as he charged.

"*Spears!*" Dany heard one Astapori shout. It was Grazdan, old Grazdan in his tokar heavy with pearls. "*Unsullied!* Defend us, stop them, defend your masters! Spears! Swords!"

When Rakharo put an arrow through his mouth, the slaves holding his sedan chair broke and ran, dumping him unceremoniously on the ground. The old man crawled to the first rank of eunuchs, his blood pooling on the bricks. The Unsullied did not so much as look down to watch him die. Rank on rank on rank, they stood.

And did not move. *The gods have heard my prayer.*

"*Unsullied!*" Dany galloped before them, her silver-gold braid flying behind her, her bell chiming with every stride. "Slay the Good Masters, slay the soldiers, slay every man who wears a *tokar* or holds a whip, but harm no child under twelve, and strike the chains off every slave you see." She raised the harpy's fingers in the air . . . and then she flung the scourge aside. "Freedom!" she sang out. "*Dracarys! Dracarys!*"

"*Dracarys!*" they shouted back, the sweetest word she'd ever heard. "*Dracarys! Dracarys!*" And all around them slavers ran and sobbed and begged and died, and the dusty air was filled with spears and fire.

SANSA

On the morning her new gown was to be ready, the serving girls filled Sansa's tub with steaming hot water and scrubbed her head to toe until she glowed pink. Cersei's own bedmaid trimmed her nails and brushed and curled her auburn hair so it fell down her back in soft ringlets. She brought a dozen of the queen's favorite scents as well. Sansa chose a sharp sweet fragrance with a hint of lemon in it under the smell of flowers. The maid dabbed some on her finger and touched Sansa behind each ear, and under her chin, and then lightly on her nipples.

Cersei herself arrived with the seamstress, and watched as they dressed Sansa in her new clothes. The smallclothes were all silk, but the gown itself was ivory samite and cloth-of-silver, and lined with silvery satin. The points of the long dagged sleeves almost touched the ground when she lowered her arms. And it was a woman's gown, not a little girl's, there was no doubt of that. The bodice was slashed in front almost to her belly, the deep vee covered over with a panel of ornate Myrish lace in dove-grey. The skirts were long and full, the waist so tight that Sansa had to hold her breath as they laced her into it. They brought her new shoes as well, slippers of soft grey doeskin that hugged her feet like lovers. "You are very beautiful, my lady," the seamstress said when she was dressed.

"I am, aren't I?" Sansa giggled, and spun, her skirts swirling around her. "Oh, I *am*." She could not wait for Willas to see her like this. *He will love me, he will, he must . . . he will forget Winterfell when he sees me, I'll see that he does.*

Queen Cersei studied her critically. "A few gems, I think. The moonstones Joffrey gave her."

"At once, Your Grace," her maid replied.

When the moonstones hung from Sansa's ears and about her neck, the queen nodded. "Yes. The gods have been kind to you, Sansa. You are a lovely girl. It seems almost obscene to squander such sweet innocence on that gargoyle."

"What gargoyle?" Sansa did not understand. Did she mean Willas? *How could she know?* No one knew, but her and Margaery and the Queen of Thorns . . . oh, and Dontos, but he didn't count.

Cersei Lannister ignored the question. "The cloak," she commanded, and the women brought it out: a long cloak of white velvet heavy with pearls. A fierce direwolf was embroidered upon it in silver thread. Sansa looked at it with sudden dread. "Your father's colors," said Cersei, as they fastened it about her neck with a slender silver chain.

A maiden's cloak. Sansa's hand went to her throat. She would have torn the thing away if she had dared.

"You're prettier with your mouth closed, Sansa," Cersei told her. "Come along now, the septon is waiting. And the wedding guests as well."

"No," Sansa blurted. "*No.*"

"Yes. You are a ward of the crown. The king stands in your father's place, since your brother is an attainted traitor. That means he has every right to dispose of your hand. You are to marry my brother Tyrion."

My claim, she thought, sickened. Dontos the Fool was not so foolish after all; he had seen the truth of it. Sansa backed away from the queen. "I won't." *I'm to marry Willas, I'm to be the lady of Highgarden, please . . .*

"I understand your reluctance. Cry if you must. In your place, I would likely rip my hair out. He's a loathsome little imp, no doubt of it, but marry him you shall."

"You can't make me."

"Of course we can. You may come along quietly and say your vows as befits a lady, or you may struggle and scream and make a spectacle for the stableboys to titter over, but you will end up wedded and bedded all the same." The queen opened the door. Ser Meryn Trant and Ser Osmund Kettleblack were waiting without, in the white scale armor of the Kingsguard. "Escort Lady Sansa to the sept," she told them. "Carry her if you must, but try not to tear the gown, it was very costly."

Sansa tried to run, but Cersei's handmaid caught her before she'd gone a yard. Ser Meryn Trant gave her a look that made her cringe, but Kettleblack touched her almost gently and said, "Do as you're told, sweetling, it won't be so bad. Wolves are supposed to be brave, aren't they?"

Brave. Sansa took a deep breath. *I am a Stark, yes, I can be brave.* They were all looking at her, the way they had looked at her that day in the yard when Ser Boros Blount had torn her clothes off. It had been the

Imp who saved her from a beating that day, the same man who was waiting for her now. *He is not so bad as the rest of them,* she told herself. "I'll go."

Cersei smiled. "I knew you would."

Afterward, she could not remember leaving the room or descending the steps or crossing the yard. It seemed to take all her attention just to put one foot down in front of the other. Ser Meryn and Ser Osmund walked beside her, in cloaks as pale as her own, lacking only the pearls and the direwolf that had been her father's. Joffrey himself was waiting for her on the steps of the castle sept. The king was resplendent in crimson and gold, his crown on his head. "I'm your father today," he announced.

"You're not," she flared. "You'll never be."

His face darkened. "I am. I'm your father, and I can marry you to whoever I like. To *anyone.* You'll marry the pig boy if I say so, and bed down with him in the sty." His green eyes glittered with amusement. "Or maybe I should give you to Ilyn Payne, would you like him better?"

Her heart lurched. "Please, Your Grace," she begged. "If you ever loved me even a little bit, don't make me marry your –"

"– uncle?" Tyrion Lannister stepped through the doors of the sept. "Your Grace," he said to Joffrey. "Grant me a moment alone with Lady Sansa, if you would be so kind?"

The king was about to refuse, but his mother gave him a sharp look. They drew off a few feet.

Tyrion wore a doublet of black velvet covered with golden scrollwork, thigh-high boots that added three inches to his height, a chain of rubies and lions' heads. But the gash across his face was raw and red, and his nose was a hideous scab. "You are very beautiful, Sansa," he told her.

"It is good of you to say so, my lord." She did not know what else to say. *Should I tell him he is handsome? He'll think me a fool or a liar.* She lowered her gaze and held her tongue.

"My lady, this is no way to bring you to your wedding. I am sorry for that. And for making this so sudden, and so secret. My lord father felt it necessary, for reasons of state. Else I would have come to you sooner, as I wished." He waddled closer. "You did not ask for this marriage, I know. No more than I did. If I had refused you, however, they would have wed you to my cousin Lancel. Perhaps you would prefer that. He is nearer your age, and fairer to look upon. If that is your wish, say so, and I will end this farce."

I don't want any Lannister, she wanted to say. *I want Willas, I want Highgarden and the puppies and the barge, and sons named Eddard and Bran and Rickon.* But then she remembered what Dontos had told her in the godswood. *Tyrell or Lannister, it makes no matter, it's not me they want, only my claim.* "You are kind, my lord," she said, defeated. "I am a ward of the throne and my duty is to marry as the king commands."

He studied her with his mismatched eyes. "I know I am not the sort of husband young girls dream of, Sansa," he said softly, "but neither am I Joffrey."

"No," she said. "You were kind to me. I remember."

Tyrion offered her a thick, blunt-fingered hand. "Come, then. Let us do our duty."

So she put her hand in his, and he led her to the marriage altar, where the septon waited between the Mother and the Father to join their lives together. She saw Dontos in his fool's motley, looking at her with big round eyes. Ser Balon Swann and Ser Boros Blount were there in Kingsguard white, but not Ser Loras. *None of the Tyrells are here,* she realized suddenly. But there were other witnesses aplenty; the eunuch Varys, Ser Addam Marbrand, Lord Philip Foote, Ser Bronn, Jalabhar Xho, a dozen others. Lord Gyles was coughing, Lady Ermesande was at the breast, and Lady Tanda's pregnant daughter was sobbing for no apparent reason. *Let her sob,* Sansa thought. *Perhaps I shall do the same before this day is done.*

The ceremony passed as in a dream. Sansa did all that was required of her. There were prayers and vows and singing, and tall candles burning, a hundred dancing lights that the tears in her eyes transformed into a thousand. Thankfully no one seemed to notice that she was crying as she stood there, wrapped in her father's colors; or if they did, they pretended not to. In what seemed no time at all, they came to the changing of the cloaks.

As father of the realm, Joffrey took the place of Lord Eddard Stark. Sansa stood stiff as a lance as his hands came over her shoulders to fumble with the clasp of her cloak. One of them brushed her breast and lingered to give it a little squeeze. Then the clasp opened, and Joff swept her maiden's cloak away with a kingly flourish and a grin.

His uncle's part went less well. The bride's cloak he held was huge and heavy, crimson velvet richly worked with lions and bordered with gold satin and rubies. No one had thought to bring a stool, however, and Tyrion stood a foot and a half shorter than his bride. As he moved behind her, Sansa felt a sharp tug on her skirt. *He wants me to kneel,* she realized, blushing. She was mortified. It was not supposed to be this way. She had dreamed of her wedding a thousand times, and always she had pictured how her betrothed would stand behind her tall and strong, sweep the cloak of his protection over her shoulders, and tenderly kiss her cheek as he leaned forward to fasten the clasp.

She felt another tug at her skirt, more insistent. *I won't. Why should I spare his feelings, when no one cares about mine?*

The dwarf tugged at her a third time. Stubbornly she pressed her lips together and pretended not to notice. Someone behind them tittered. *The queen*, she thought, but it didn't matter. They were all laughing by then, Joffrey the loudest. "Dontos, down on your hands and knees," the king commanded. "My uncle needs a boost to climb his bride."

And so it was that her lord husband cloaked her in the colors of House Lannister whilst standing on the back of a fool.

When Sansa turned, the little man was gazing up at her, his mouth tight, his face as red as her cloak. Suddenly she was ashamed of her stubbornness. She smoothed her skirts and knelt in front of him, so their heads were on the same level. "With this kiss I pledge my love, and take you for my lord and husband."

"With this kiss I pledge my love," the dwarf replied hoarsely, "and take you for my lady and wife." He leaned forward, and their lips touched briefly.

He is so ugly, Sansa thought when his face was close to hers. *He is even uglier than the Hound.*

The septon raised his crystal high, so the rainbow light fell down upon them. "Here in the sight of gods and men," he said, "I do solemnly proclaim Tyrion of House Lannister and Sansa of House Stark to be man and wife, one flesh, one heart, one soul, now and forever, and cursed be the one who comes between them."

She had to bite her lip to keep from sobbing.

The wedding feast was held in the Small Hall. There were perhaps fifty guests; Lannister retainers and allies for the most part, joining those who had been at the wedding. And here Sansa found the Tyrells. Margaery gave her such a sad look, and when the Queen of Thorns tottered in between Left and Right, she never looked at her at all. Elinor, Alla, and Megga seemed determined not to know her. *My friends*, Sansa thought bitterly.

Her husband drank heavily and ate but little. He listened whenever someone rose to make a toast and sometimes nodded a curt acknowledgment, but otherwise his face might have been made of stone. The feast seemed to go on forever, though Sansa tasted none of the food. She wanted it to be done, and yet she dreaded its end. For after the feast would come the bedding. The men would carry her up to her wedding bed, undressing her on the way and making rude jokes about the fate that awaited her between the sheets, while the women did Tyrion the same honors. Only after they had been bundled naked into bed would they be left alone, and even then the guests would stand outside the bridal chamber, shouting ribald suggestions through the door. The bedding had seemed wonderfully wicked and exciting when Sansa was a girl, but now that the moment was upon her she felt only dread. She did not think she could bear for them to rip off her clothes, and she was certain she would burst into tears at the first randy jape.

When the musicians began to play, she timidly laid her hand on Tyrion's and said, "My lord, should we lead the dance?"

His mouth twisted. "I think we have already given them sufficent amusement for one day, don't you?"

"As you say, my lord." She pulled her hand back.

Joffrey and Margaery led in their place. *How can a monster dance so beautifully?* Sansa wondered. She had often daydreamed of how she would dance at her wedding, with every eye upon her and her handsome lord. In her dreams they had all been smiling. *Not even my husband is smiling.*

Other guests soon joined the king and his betrothed on the floor. Elinor danced with her young squire, and Megga with Prince Tommen. Lady Merryweather, the Myrish beauty with the black hair and the big dark eyes, spun so provocatively that every man in the hall was soon watching her. Lord and Lady Tyrell moved more sedately. Ser Kevan Lannister begged the honor of Lady Janna Fossoway, Lord Tyrell's sister. Merry Crane took the floor with the exile prince Jalabhar Xho, gorgeous in his feathered finery. Cersei Lannister partnered first Lord Redwyne, then Lord Rowan, and finally her own father, who danced with smooth unsmiling grace.

Sansa sat with her hands in her lap, watching how the queen moved and laughed and tossed her blonde curls. *She charms them all*, she thought dully. *How I hate her.* She looked away, to where Moon Boy danced with Dontos.

"Lady Sansa." Ser Garlan Tyrell stood beside the dais. "Would you honor me? If your lord consents?"

The Imp's mismatched eyes narrowed. "My lady can dance with whomever she pleases."

Perhaps she ought to have remained beside her husband, but she wanted to dance so badly . . . and Ser Garlan was brother to Margaery, to Willas, to her Knight of Flowers. "I see why they name you Garlan the Gallant, ser," she said, as she took his hand.

"My lady is gracious to say so. My brother Willas gave me that name, as it happens. To protect me."

"To protect you?" She gave him a puzzled look.

Ser Garlan laughed. "I was a plump little boy, I fear, and we do have an uncle called Garth the Gross. So Willas struck first, though not before threatening me with Garlan the Greensick, Garlan the Galling, and Garlan the Gargoyle."

It was so sweet and silly that Sansa had to laugh, despite everything. Afterward she was absurdly grateful. Somehow the laughter made her hopeful again, if only for a little while. Smiling, she let the music take her, losing herself in the steps, in the sound of flute and pipes and harp, in the rhythm of the drum ... and from time to time in Ser Garlan's arms, when the dance brought them together. "My lady wife is most concerned for you," he said quietly, one such time.

"Lady Leonette is too sweet. Tell her I am well."

"A bride at her wedding should be more than *well*." His voice was not unkind. "You seemed close to tears."

"Tears of joy, ser."

"Your eyes give the lie to your tongue." Ser Garlan turned her, drew her close to his side. "My lady, I have seen how you look at my brother. Loras is valiant and handsome, and we all love him dearly ... but your Imp will make a better husband. He is a bigger man than he seems, I think."

The music spun them apart before Sansa could think of a reply. It was Mace Tyrell opposite her, red-faced and sweaty, and then Lord Merryweather, and then Prince Tommen. "I want to be married too," said the plump little princeling, who was all of nine. "I'm taller than my uncle!"

"I know you are," said Sansa, before the partners changed again. Ser Kevan told her she was beautiful, Jalabhar Xho said something she did not understand in the Summer Tongue, and Lord Redwyne wished her many fat children and long years of joy. And then the dance brought her face-to-face with Joffrey.

Sansa stiffened as his hand touched hers, but the king tightened his grip and drew her closer. "You shouldn't look so sad. My uncle is an ugly little thing, but you'll still have me."

"You're to marry Margaery!"

"A king can have other women. Whores. My father did. One of the Aegons did too. The third one, or the fourth. He had lots of whores and lots of bastards." As they whirled to the music, Joff gave her a moist kiss. "My uncle will bring you to my bed whenever I command it."

Sansa shook her head. "He won't."

"He will, or I'll have his head. That King Aegon, he had any woman he wanted, whether they were married or no."

Thankfully, it was time to change again. Her legs had turned to wood, though, and Lord Rowan, Ser Tallad, and Elinor's squire all must have thought her a very clumsy dancer. And then she was back with Ser Garlan once more, and soon, blessedly, the dance was over.

Her relief was short-lived. No sooner had the music died than she heard Joffrey say, "It's time to bed them! Let's get the clothes off her, and have a look at what the she-wolf's got to give my uncle!" Other men took up the cry, loudly.

Her dwarf husband lifted his eyes slowly from his wine cup. "I'll have no bedding."

Joffrey seized Sansa's arm. "You will if I command it."

The Imp slammed his dagger down in the table, where it stood quivering. "Then you'll service your own bride with a wooden prick. I'll geld you, I swear it."

A shocked silence fell. Sansa pulled away from Joffrey, but he had a grip on her, and her sleeve ripped. No one even seemed to hear. Queen Cersei turned to her father. "Did you hear him?"

Lord Tywin rose from his seat. "I believe we can dispense with the bedding. Tyrion, I am certain you did not mean to threaten the king's royal person."

Sansa saw a spasm of rage pass across her husband's face. "I misspoke," he said. "It was a bad jape, sire."

"You threatened to *geld* me!" Joffrey said shrilly.

"I did, Your Grace," said Tyrion, "but only because I envied your royal manhood. Mine own is so small and stunted." His face twisted into a leer. "And if you take my tongue, you will leave me no way at all to pleasure this sweet wife you gave me."

Laughter burst from the lips of Ser Osmund Kettleblack. Someone else sniggered. But Joff did not laugh, nor Lord Tywin. "Your Grace," he said, "my son is drunk, you can see that."

"I am," the Imp confessed, "but not so drunk that I cannot attend to my own bedding." He hopped down from the dais and grabbed Sansa roughly. "Come, wife, time to smash your portcullis. I want to play come-into-the-castle."

Red-faced, Sansa went with him from the Small Hall. *What choice do I have?* Tyrion waddled when he walked, especially when he walked as quickly as he did now. The gods were merciful, and neither Joffrey nor any of the others moved to follow.

For their wedding night, they had been granted the use of an airy bedchamber high in the Tower of the Hand. Tyrion kicked the door shut behind them. "There is a flagon of good Arbor gold on the sideboard, Sansa. Will you be so kind as to pour me a cup?"

"Is that wise, my lord?"

"Nothing was ever wiser. I am not truly drunk, you see. But I mean to be."

Sansa filled a goblet for each of them. *It will be easier if I am drunk as well.* She sat on the edge of the great curtained bed and drained half her cup in three long swallows. No doubt it was very fine wine, but she was too nervous to taste it. It made her head swim. "Would you have me undress, my lord?"

"Tyrion." He cocked his head. "My name is Tyrion, Sansa."

"Tyrion. My lord. Should I take off my gown, or do you want to undress me?" She took another swallow of wine.

The Imp turned away from her. "The first time I wed, there was us and a drunken septon, and some pigs to bear witness. We ate one of our witnesses at our wedding feast. Tysha fed me crackling and I licked the grease off her fingers, and we were laughing when we fell into bed."

"You were wed before? I . . . I had forgotten."

"You did not forget. You never knew."

"Who was she, my lord?" Sansa was curious despite herself.

"Lady Tysha." His mouth twisted. "Of House Silverfist. Their arms have one gold coin and a hundred silver, upon a bloody sheet. Ours was a very short marriage . . . as befits a very short man, I suppose."

Sansa stared down at her hands and said nothing.

"How old are you, Sansa?" asked Tyrion, after a moment.

"Thirteen," she said, "when the moon turns."

"Gods have mercy." The dwarf took another swallow of wine. "Well, talk won't make you older. Shall we get on with this, my lady? If it please you?"

"It will please me to please my lord husband."

That seemed to anger him. "You hide behind courtesy as if it were a castle wall."

"Courtesy is a lady's armor," Sansa said. Her septa had always told her that.

"I am your husband. You can take off your armor now."

"And my clothing?"

"That too." He waved his wine cup at her. "My lord father has commanded me to consummate this marriage."

Her hands trembled as she began fumbling at her clothes. She had ten thumbs instead of fingers, and all of them were broken. Yet somehow she managed the laces and buttons, and her cloak and gown and girdle and undersilk slid to the floor, until finally she was stepping out of her smallclothes. Gooseprickles covered her arms and legs. She kept her eyes on the floor, too shy to look at him, but when she was done she glanced up and found him staring. There was hunger in his green eye, it seemed to her, and fury in the black. Sansa did not know which scared her more.

"You're a child," he said.

She covered her breasts with her hands. "I've flowered."

"A child," he repeated, "but I want you. Does that frighten you, Sansa?"

"Yes."

"Me as well. I know I am ugly –"

"No, my –"

He pushed himself to his feet. "Don't lie, Sansa. I am malformed, scarred, and small, but . . ." she could see him groping ". . . abed, when the candles are blown out, I am made no worse than other men. In the dark, I am the Knight of Flowers." He took a draught of wine. "I am generous. Loyal to those who are loyal to me. I've proven I'm no craven. And I am cleverer than most, surely wits count for something. I can even be kind. Kindness is not a habit with us Lannisters, I fear, but I know I have some somewhere. I could be . . . I could be good to you."

He is as frightened as I am, Sansa realized. Perhaps that should have made her feel more kindly toward him, but it did not. All she felt was pity, and pity was death to desire. He was looking at her, waiting for her to say something, but all her words had withered. She could only stand there trembling.

When he finally realized that she had no answer for him, Tyrion Lannister drained the last of his wine. "I understand," he said bitterly. "Get in the bed, Sansa. We need to do our duty."

She climbed onto the featherbed, conscious of his stare. A scented beeswax candle burned on the bedside table and rose petals had been strewn between the sheets. She had started to pull up a blanket to cover herself when she heard him say, "No."

The cold made her shiver, but she obeyed. Her eyes closed, and she waited. After a moment she heard the sound of her husband pulling off his boots, and the rustle of clothing as he undressed himself. When he hopped up on the bed and put his hand on her breast, Sansa could not help but shudder. She lay with her eyes closed, every muscle tense, dreading what might come next. Would he touch her again? Kiss her? Should she open her legs for him now? She did not know what was expected of her.

"Sansa." The hand was gone. "Open your eyes."

She had promised to obey; she opened her eyes. He was sitting by her feet, naked. Where his legs joined, his man's staff poked up stiff and hard from a thicket of coarse yellow hair, but it was the only thing about him that was straight.

"My lady," Tyrion said, "you are lovely, make no mistake, but . . . I cannot do this. My father be damned. We will wait. The turn of a moon, a year, a season, however long it takes. Until you have come to know me better, and perhaps to trust me a little." His smile might have been meant to be reassuring, but without a nose it only made him look more grotesque and sinister.

Look at him, Sansa told herself, *look at your husband, at all of him, Septa Mordane said all men are beautiful, find his beauty, try.* She stared at the stunted legs, the swollen brutish brow, the green eye and the black one, the raw stump of his nose and crooked pink scar, the coarse tangle of black and gold hair that passed for his beard. Even his manhood was ugly, thick and veined, with a bulbous purple head. *This is not right, this is not fair, how have I sinned that the gods would do this to me, how?*

"On my honor as a Lannister," the Imp said, "I will not touch you until you want me to."

It took all the courage that was in her to look in those mismatched eyes and say, "And if I never want you to, my lord?"

His mouth jerked as if she had slapped him. "Never?"

Her neck was so tight she could scarcely nod.

"Why," he said, "that is why the gods made whores for imps like me." He closed his short blunt fingers into a fist, and climbed down off the bed.

ARYA

Stoney Sept was the biggest town Arya had seen since King's Landing, and Harwin said her father had won a famous battle here.

"The Mad King's men had been hunting Robert, trying to catch him before he could rejoin your father," he told her as they rode toward the gate. "He was wounded, being tended by some friends, when Lord Connington the Hand took the town with a mighty force and started searching house by house. Before they could find him, though, Lord Eddard and your grandfather came down on the town and stormed the walls. Lord Connington fought back fierce. They battled in the streets and alleys, even on the rooftops, and all the septons rang their bells so the smallfolk would know to lock their doors. Robert came out of hiding to join the fight when the bells began to ring. He slew six men that day, they say. One was Myles Mooton, a famous knight who'd been Prince Rhaegar's squire. He would have slain the Hand too, but the battle never brought them together. Connington wounded your grandfather Tully sore, though, and killed Ser Denys Arryn, the darling of the Vale. But when he saw the day was lost, he flew off as fast as the griffins on his shield. The Battle of the Bells, they called it after. Robert always said your father won it, not him."

More recent battles had been fought here as well, Arya thought from the look of the place. The town gates were made of raw new wood; outside the walls a pile of charred planks remained to tell what had happened to the old ones.

Stoney Sept was closed up tight, but when the captain of the gate saw who they were, he opened a sally port for them. "How you fixed for food?" Tom asked as they entered.

"Not so bad as we were. The Huntsman brought in a flock o' sheep, and there's been some trading across the Blackwater. The harvest wasn't burned south o' the river. Course, there's plenty want to take what we got. Wolves one day, Mummers the next. Them that's not looking for food are looking for plunder, or women to rape, and them that's not out for gold or wenches are looking for the bloody Kingslayer. Talk is, he slipped right through Lord Edmure's fingers."

"*Lord* Edmure?" Lem frowned. "Is Lord Hoster dead, then?"

"Dead or dying. Think Lannister might be making for the Blackwater? It's the quickest way to King's Landing, the Huntsman swears." The captain did not wait for an answer. "He took his dogs out for a sniff round. If Ser Jaime's hereabouts, they'll find him. I've seen them dogs rip bears apart. Think they'll like the taste of lion blood?"

"A chewed-up corpse's no good to no one," said Lem. "The Huntsman bloody well knows that, too."

"When the westermen came through they raped the Huntsman's wife and sister, put his crops to the torch, ate half his sheep, and killed the other half for spite. Killed six dogs too, and threw the carcasses down his well. A chewed-up corpse would be plenty good enough for him, I'd say. Me as well."

"He'd best not," said Lem. "That's all I got to say. He'd best not, and you're a bloody fool."

Arya rode between Harwin and Anguy as the outlaws moved down the streets where her father once had fought. She could see the sept on its hill, and below it a stout strong holdfast of grey stone that looked much too small for such a big town. But every third house they passed was a blackened shell, and she saw no people. "Are all the townfolk dead?"

"Only shy." Anguy pointed out two bowmen on a roof, and some boys with sooty faces crouched in the rubble of an alehouse. Farther on, a baker threw open a shuttered window and shouted down to Lem. The sound of his voice brought more people out of hiding, and Stoney Sept slowly seemed to come to life around them.

In the market square at the town's heart stood a fountain in the shape of a leaping trout, spouting water into a shallow pool. Women were filling pails and flagons there. A few feet away, a dozen iron cages hung from creaking wooden posts. *Crow cages*, Arya knew. The crows were mostly outside the cages, splashing in the water or perched atop the bars; inside were men. Lem reined up scowling. "What's this, now?"

"Justice," answered a woman at the fountain.

"What, did you run short o' hempen rope?"

"Was this done at Ser Wilbert's decree?" asked Tom.

A man laughed bitterly. "The lions killed Ser Wilbert a year ago. His sons are all off with the Young Wolf, getting fat in the west. You think they give a damn for the likes of us? It was the Mad Huntsman caught these wolves."

Wolves. Arya went cold. *Robb's men, and my father's.* She felt drawn toward the cages. The bars allowed so little room that prisoners could neither sit nor turn; they stood naked, exposed to sun and wind and rain. The first three cages held dead men. Carrion crows had eaten out their eyes, yet the empty sockets seemed to follow her. The fourth man in the row stirred as she passed. Around his mouth his ragged beard was thick with blood and flies. They exploded when he spoke, buzzing around his head. *"Water."* The word was a croak. "Please . . . water . . ."

The man in the next cage opened his eyes at the sound. "Here," he said. "Here, me." An old man, he was; his beard was grey and his scalp was bald and mottled brown with age.

There was another dead man beyond the old one, a big red-bearded man with a rotting grey bandage covering his left ear and part of his temple. But the worst thing was between his legs, where nothing remained but a crusted brown hole crawling with maggots. Farther down was a fat man. The crow cage was so cruelly narrow it was hard to see how they'd ever gotten him inside. The iron dug painfully into his belly, squeezing bulges out between the bars. Long days baking in the sun had burned him a painful red from head to heel. When he shifted his weight, his cage creaked and swayed, and Arya could see pale white stripes where the bars had shielded his flesh from the sun.

"Whose men were you?" she asked them.

At the sound of her voice, the fat man opened his eyes. The skin around them was so red they looked like boiled eggs floating in a dish of blood. "Water . . . a drink . . ."

"Whose?" she said again.

"Pay them no mind, boy," the townsman told her. "They're none o' your concern. Ride on by."

"What did they do?" she asked him.

"They put eight people to the sword at Tumbler's Falls," he said. "They wanted the Kingslayer, but he wasn't there so they did some rape and murder." He jerked a thumb toward the corpse with maggots where his manhood ought to be. "That one there did the raping. Now move along."

"A swallow," the fat one called down. "Ha' mercy, boy, a swallow." The old one slid an arm up to grasp the bars. The motion made his cage swing violently. "Water," gasped the one with the flies in his beard.

She looked at their filthy hair and scraggly beards and reddened eyes, at their dry, cracked, bleeding lips. *Wolves*, she thought again. *Like me.* Was this her pack? *How could they be Robb's men?* She wanted to hit them. She wanted to hurt them. She wanted to cry. They all seemed to be looking at her, the living and the dead alike. The old man had squeezed three fingers out between the bars. "Water," he said, "water."

Arya swung down from her horse. *They can't hurt me, they're dying.* She took her cup from her bedroll and went to the fountain. "What do you think you're doing, boy?" the townsman snapped. "They're no concern o' yours." She raised the cup to the fish's mouth. The water splashed across her fingers and down her sleeve, but Arya did not move until the cup was brimming over. When she turned back toward the cages, the townsman moved to stop her. "You get away from them, boy –"

"She's a girl," said Harwin. "Leave her be."

"Aye," said Lem. "Lord Beric don't hold with caging men to die of thirst. Why don't you hang them decent?"

"There was nothing decent 'bout them things they did at Tumbler's Falls," the townsman growled right back at him.

The bars were too narrow to pass a cup through, but Harwin and Gendry offered her a leg up. She planted a foot in Harwin's cupped hands, vaulted onto Gendry's shoulders, and grabbed the bars on top of the cage. The fat man turned his face up and pressed his cheek to the iron, and Arya poured the water over him. He sucked at it eagerly and let it run down over his head and cheeks and hands, and then he licked the dampness off the bars. He would have licked Arya's fingers if she hadn't snatched them back. By the time she served the other two the same, a crowd had gathered to watch her. "The Mad Huntsman will hear of this," a man threatened. "He won't like it. No, he won't."

"He'll like this even less, then." Anguy strung his longbow, slid an arrow from his quiver, nocked, drew, loosed. The fat man shuddered as the shaft drove up between his chins, but the cage would not let him fall. Two more arrows ended the other two northmen. The only sound in the market square was the splash of falling water and the buzzing of flies.

Valar morghulis, Arya thought.

On the east side of the market square stood a modest inn with white-washed walls and broken windows. Half its roof had burnt off recently, but the hole had been patched over. Above the door hung a wooden shingle painted as a peach, with a big bite taken out of it. They dismounted at the stables sitting catty-corner, and Greenbeard bellowed for grooms.

The buxom red-haired innkeep howled with pleasure at the sight of them, then promptly set to tweaking them. "Greenbeard, is it? Or Greybeard? Mother take mercy, when did you get so old? Lem, is that you?

Still wearing the same ratty cloak, are you? I know why you never wash it, I do. You're afraid all the piss will wash out and we'll see you're really a knight o' the Kingsguard! And Tom o' Sevens, you randy old goat! You come to see that son o' yours? Well, you're too late, he's off riding with that bloody Huntsman. And don't tell me he's not yours!"

"He hasn't got my voice," Tom protested weakly.

"He's got your nose, though. Aye, and t'other parts as well, to hear the girls talk." She spied Gendry then, and pinched him on the cheek. "Look at this fine young ox. Wait till Alyce sees those arms. Oh, and he blushes like a maid, too. Well, Alyce will fix that for you, boy, see if she don't."

Arya had never seen Gendry turn so red. "Tansy, you leave the Bull alone, he's a good lad," said Tom Sevenstrings. "All we need from you is safe beds for a night."

"Speak for yourself, singer." Anguy slid his arm around a strapping young serving girl as freckly as he was.

"Beds we got," said red-haired Tansy. "There's never been no lack o' beds at the Peach. But you'll all climb in a tub first. Last time you lot stayed under my roof you left your fleas behind." She poked Greenbeard in the chest. "And yours was green, too. You want food?"

"If you can spare it, we won't say no," Tom conceded.

"Now when did you ever say no to anything, Tom?" the woman hooted. "I'll roast some mutton for your friends, and an old dry rat for you. It's more than you deserve, but if you gargle me a song or three, might be I'll weaken. I always pity the afflicted. Come on, come on. Cass, Lanna, put some kettles on. Jyzene, help me get the clothes off them, we'll need to boil those too."

She made good on all her threats. Arya tried to tell them that she'd been bathed *twice* at Acorn Hall, not a fortnight past, but the red-haired woman was having none of it. Two serving wenches carried her up the stairs bodily, arguing about whether she was a girl or a boy. The one called Helly won, so the other had to fetch the hot water and scrub Arya's back with a stiff bristly brush that almost took her skin off. Then they stole all the clothes that Lady Smallwood had given her and dressed her up like one of Sansa's dolls in linen and lace. But at least when they were done she got to go down and eat.

As she sat in the common room in her stupid girl clothes, Arya remembered what Syrio Forel had told her, the trick of looking and seeing what was there. When she looked, she saw more serving wenches than any inn could want, and most of them young and comely. And come evenfall, lots of men started coming and going at the Peach. They did not linger long in the common room, not even when Tom took out his woodharp and began to sing "Six Maids in a Pool." The wooden steps were old and steep, and creaked something fierce whenever one of the men took a girl upstairs. "I bet this is a brothel," she whispered to Gendry.

"You don't even know what a brothel is."

"I do so," she insisted. "It's like an inn, with girls."

He was turning red again. "What are you doing here, then?" he demanded. "A brothel's no fit place for no bloody highborn lady, everybody knows that."

One of the girls sat down on the bench beside him. "Who's a highborn lady? The little skinny one?" She looked at Arya and laughed. "I'm a king's daughter myself."

Arya knew she was being mocked. "You are not."

"Well, I might be." When the girl shrugged, her gown slipped off one shoulder. "They say King Robert fucked my mother when he hid here, back before the battle. Not that he didn't have all the other girls too, but Leslyn says he liked my ma the best."

The girl *did* have hair like the old king's, Arya thought; a great thick mop of it, as black as coal. *That doesn't mean anything, though. Gendry has the same kind of hair too. Lots of people have black hair.*

"I'm named Bella," the girl told Gendry. "For the battle. I bet I could ring *your* bell, too. You want to?"

"No," he said gruffly.

"I bet you do." She ran a hand along his arm. "I don't cost nothing to friends of Thoros and the lightning lord."

"*No*, I said." Gendry rose abruptly and stalked away from the table out into the night.

Bella turned to Arya. "Don't he like girls?"

Arya shrugged. "He's just stupid. He likes to polish helmets and beat on swords with hammers."

"Oh." Bella tugged her gown back over her shoulder and went to talk with Jack-Be-Lucky. Before long she was sitting in his lap, giggling and drinking wine from his cup. Greenbeard had two girls, one on each knee. Anguy had vanished with his freckle-faced wench, and Lem was gone as well. Tom Sevenstrings sat by the fire, singing, "The Maids that Bloom in Spring." Arya sipped at the cup of watered wine the red-haired woman had allowed her, listening. Across the square the dead men were rotting in their crow cages, but inside the Peach everyone was jolly. Except it seemed to her that some of them were laughing too hard, somehow.

It would have been a good time to sneak away and steal a horse, but Arya couldn't see how that would help her. She could only ride as far as the city gates. *That captain would never let me pass, and if he did, Harwin would come after me, or that Huntsman with his dogs.* She wished she had her map, so she could see how far Stoney Sept was from Riverrun.

By the time her cup was empty, Arya was yawning. Gendry hadn't come back. Tom Sevenstrings was singing "Two Hearts that Beat as One," and kissing a different girl at the end of every verse. In the corner by the window Lem and Harwin sat talking to red-haired Tansy in low voices. ". . . spent the night in Jaime's cell," she heard the woman say. "Her and this other wench, the one who slew Renly. All three o' them together, and come the morn Lady Catelyn cut him loose for love." She gave a throaty chuckle.

It's not true, Arya thought. *She never would.* She felt sad and angry and lonely, all at once.

An old man sat down beside her. "Well, aren't you a pretty little peach?" His breath smelled near as foul as the dead men in the cages, and his little pig eyes were crawling up and down her. "Does my sweet peach have a name?"

For half a heartbeat she forgot who she was supposed to be. She wasn't any peach, but she couldn't be Arya Stark either, not here with some smelly drunk she did not know. "I'm . . ."

"She's my sister." Gendry put a heavy hand on the old man's shoulder, and squeezed. "Leave her be."

The man turned, spoiling for a quarrel, but when he saw Gendry's size he thought better of it. "Your sister, is she? What kind of brother are you? I'd never bring no sister of mine to the Peach, that I wouldn't." He got up from the bench and moved off muttering, in search of a new friend.

"Why did you say that?" Arya hopped to her feet. "You're not my brother."

"That's right," he said angrily. "I'm too bloody lowborn to be kin to m'lady high."

Arya was taken aback by the fury in his voice. "That's not the way I meant it."

"Yes it is." He sat down on the bench, cradling a cup of wine between his hands. "Go away. I want to drink this wine in peace. Then maybe I'll go find that black-haired girl and ring her bell for her."

"But . . ."

"I said, *go away.* M'lady."

Arya whirled and left him there. *A stupid bullheaded bastard boy, that's all he is.* He could ring all the bells he wanted, it was nothing to her.

Their sleeping room was at the top of the stairs, under the eaves. Maybe the Peach had no lack of beds, but there was only one to spare for the likes of them. It was a *big* bed, though. It filled the whole room, just about, and the musty straw-stuffed mattress looked large enough for all of them. Just now, though, she had it to herself. Her real clothes were hanging from a peg on the wall, between Gendry's stuff and Lem's. Arya took off the linen and lace, pulled her tunic over her head, climbed up into the bed, and burrowed under the blankets. "Queen Cersei," she whispered into the pillow. "King Joffrey, Ser Ilyn, Ser Meryn. Dunsen, Raff, and Polliver. The Tickler, the Hound, and Ser Gregor the Mountain." She liked to mix up the order of the names sometimes. It helped her remember who they were and what they'd done. *Maybe some of them are dead*, she thought. *Maybe they're in iron cages someplace, and the crows are picking out their eyes.*

Sleep came as quick as she closed her eyes. She dreamed of wolves that night, stalking through a wet wood with the smell of rain and rot and blood thick in the air. Only they were good smells in the dream, and Arya knew she had nothing to fear. She was strong and swift and fierce, and her pack was all around her, her brothers and her sisters. They ran down a frightened horse together, tore its throat out, and feasted. And when the moon broke through the clouds, she threw back her head and *howled*.

But when the day came, she woke to the barking of dogs.

Arya sat up yawning. Gendry was stirring on her left and Lem Lemoncloak snoring loudly to her right, but the baying outside all but drowned him out. *There must be half a hundred dogs out there.* She crawled from under the blankets and hopped over Lem, Tom, and Jack-Be-Lucky to the window. When she opened the shutters wide, wind and wet and cold all came flooding in together. The day was grey and overcast. Down below, in the square, the dogs were barking, running in circles, growling and howling. There was a pack of them, great black mastiffs and lean wolfhounds and black-and-white sheepdogs and kinds Arya did not know, shaggy brindled beasts with long yellow teeth. Between the inn and the fountain, a dozen riders sat astride their horses, watching the townsmen open the fat man's cage and tug his arm until his swollen corpse spilled out onto the ground. The dogs were at him at once, tearing chunks of flesh off his bones.

Arya heard one of the riders laugh. "Here's your new castle, you bloody Lannister bastard," he said. "A little snug for the likes o' you, but we'll squeeze you in, never fret." Beside him a prisoner sat sullen, with coils of hempen rope tight around his wrists. Some of the townsmen were throwing dung at him, but he never flinched. "You'll *rot* in them cages," his captor was shouting. "The crows will be picking out your eyes while we're spending all that good Lannister gold o' yours! And when them crows are done, we'll send what's left o' you to your bloody brother. Though I doubt he'll know you."

The noise had woken half the Peach. Gendry squeezed into the window beside Arya, and Tom stepped up behind them naked as his name day. "What's all that bloody shouting?" Lem complained from bed. "A man's trying to get some bloody sleep."

"Where's Greenbeard?" Tom asked him.

"Abed with Tansy," Lem said. "Why?"

"Best find him. Archer too. The Mad Huntsman's come back, with another man for the cages."

"Lannister," said Arya. "I heard him say *Lannister*."

"Have they caught the Kingslayer?" Gendry wanted to know.

Down in the square, a thrown stone caught the captive on the cheek, turning his head. *Not the Kingslayer*, Arya thought, when she saw his face. The gods had heard her prayers after all.

JON

Ghost was gone when the wildlings led their horses from the cave. *Did he understand about Castle Black?* Jon took a breath of the crisp morning air and allowed himself to hope. The eastern sky was pink near the horizon and pale grey higher up. The Sword of the Morning still hung in the south, the bright white star in its hilt blazing like a diamond in the dawn, but the blacks and greys of the darkling forest were turning once again to greens and golds, reds and russets. And above the soldier pines and oaks and ash and sentinels stood the Wall, the ice pale and glimmering beneath the dust and dirt that pocked its surface.

The Magnar sent a dozen men riding west and a dozen more east, to climb the highest hills they could find and watch for any sign of rangers in the wood or riders on the high ice. The Thenns carried bronze-banded warhorns to give warning should the Watch be sighted. The other wildlings fell in behind Jarl, Jon and Ygritte with the rest. This was to be the young raider's hour of glory.

The Wall was often said to stand seven hundred feet high, but Jarl had found a place where it was both higher and lower. Before them, the ice rose sheer from out of the trees like some immense cliff, crowned by wind-carved battlements that loomed at least eight hundred feet high, perhaps nine hundred in spots. But that was deceptive, Jon realized as they drew closer. Brandon the Builder had laid his huge foundation blocks along the heights wherever feasible, and hereabouts the hills rose wild and rugged.

He had once heard his uncle Benjen say that the Wall was a sword east of Castle Black, but a snake to the west. It was true. Sweeping in over one huge humped hill, the ice dipped down into a valley, climbed the knife edge of a long granite ridgeline for a league or more, ran along a jagged crest, dipped again into a valley deeper still, and then rose higher and higher, leaping from hill to hill as far as the eye could see, into the mountainous west.

Jarl had chosen to assault the stretch of ice along the ridge. Here, though the top of the Wall loomed eight hundred feet above the forest floor, a good third of that height was earth and stone rather than ice; the slope was too steep for their horses, almost as difficult a scramble as the Fist of the First Men, but still vastly easier to ascend than the sheer vertical face of the Wall itself. And the ridge was densely wooded as well, offering easy concealment. Once brothers in black had gone out every day with axes to cut back the encroaching trees, but those days were long past, and here the forest grew right up to the ice.

The day promised to be damp and cold, and damper and colder by the Wall, beneath those tons of ice. The closer they got, the more the Thenns held back. *They have never seen the Wall before, not even the Magnar,* Jon realized. *It frightens them.* In the Seven Kingdoms it was said that the Wall marked the end of the world. *That is true for them as well.* It was all in where you stood.

And where do I stand? Jon did not know. To stay with Ygritte, he would need to become a wildling heart and soul. If he abandoned her to return to his duty, the Magnar might cut her heart out. And if he took her with him . . . assuming she would go, which was far from certain . . . well, he could scarcely bring her back to Castle Black to live among the brothers. A deserter and a wildling could expect no welcome anywhere in the Seven Kingdoms. *We could go look for Gendel's children, I suppose. Though they'd be more like to eat us than to take us in.*

The Wall did not awe Jarl's raiders, Jon saw. *They have done this before, every man of them.* Jarl called out names when they dismounted beneath the ridge, and eleven gathered round him. All were young. The oldest could not have been more than five-and-twenty, and two of the ten were younger than Jon. Every one was lean and hard, though; they had a look of sinewy strength that reminded him of Stonesnake, the brother the Halfhand had sent off afoot when Rattleshirt was hunting them.

In the very shadow of the Wall the wildlings made ready, winding thick coils of hempen rope around one shoulder and down across their chests, and lacing on queer boots of supple doeskin. The boots had spikes jutting from the toes; iron, for Jarl and two others, bronze for some, but most often jagged bone. Small stone-headed hammers hung from one hip, a leathern bag of stakes from the other. Their ice axes were antlers with

sharpened tines, bound to wooden hafts with strips of hide. The eleven
climbers sorted themselves into three teams of four; Jarl himself made
the twelfth man. "Mance promises swords for every man of the first
team to reach the top," he told them, his breath misting in the cold air.
"Southron swords of castle-forged steel. And your name in the song he'll
make of this, that too. What more could a free man ask? *Up*, and the
Others take the hindmost!"

The Others take them all, thought Jon, as he watched them scramble
up the steep slope of the ridge and vanish beneath the trees. It would not
be the first time wildlings had scaled the Wall, not even the hundred and
first. The patrols stumbled on climbers two or three times a year, and
rangers sometimes came on the broken corpses of those who had fallen.
Along the east coast the raiders most often built boats to slip across the
Bay of Seals. In the west they would descend into the black depths of
the Gorge to make their way around the Shadow Tower. But in between
the only way to defeat the Wall was to go over it, and many a raider
had. *Fewer come back, though*, he thought with a certain grim pride.
Climbers must of necessity leave their mounts behind, and many
younger, greener raiders began by taking the first horses they found. Then
a hue and cry would go up, ravens would fly, and as often as not the
Night's Watch would hunt them down and hang them before they could
get back with their plunder and stolen women. Jarl would not make that
mistake, Jon knew, but he wondered about Styr. *The Magnar is a ruler,
not a raider. He may not know how the game is played.*

"There they are," Ygritte said, and Jon glanced up to see the first
climber emerge above the treetops. It was Jarl. He had found a sentinel
tree that leaned against the Wall, and led his men up the trunk to get a
quicker start. *The wood should never have been allowed to creep so
close. They're three hundred feet up, and they haven't touched the ice
itself yet.*

He watched the wildling move carefully from wood to Wall, hacking
out a handhold with short sharp blows of his ice axe, then swinging over.
The rope around his waist tied him to the second man in line, still edging
up the tree. Step by slow step, Jarl moved higher, kicking out toeholds
with his spiked boots when there were no natural ones to be found. When
he was ten feet above the sentinel, he stopped upon a narrow icy ledge,
slung his axe from his belt, took out his hammer, and drove an iron stake
into a cleft. The second man moved onto the Wall behind him while the
third was scrambling to the top of the tree.

The other two teams had no happily placed trees to give them a leg
up, and before long the Thenns were wondering whether they had gotten
lost climbing the ridge. Jarl's party were all on the Wall and eighty feet
up before the leading climbers from the other groups came into view.

The teams were spaced a good twenty yards apart. Jarl's four were in the center. To the right of them was a team headed up by Grigg the Goat, whose long blond braid made him easy to spot from below. To the left a very thin man named Errok led the climbers.

"So slow," the Magnar complained loudly, as he watched them edge their way upward. "Has he forgotten the crows? He should climb faster, afore we are discovered."

Jon had to hold his tongue. He remembered the Skirling Pass all too well, and the moonlight climb he'd made with Stonesnake. He had swallowed his heart a half-dozen times that night, and by the end his arms and legs had been aching and his fingers were half frozen. *And that was stone, not ice.* Stone was solid. Ice was treacherous stuff at the best of times, and on a day like this, when the Wall was weeping, the warmth of a climber's hand might be enough to melt it. The huge blocks could be frozen rock-hard inside, but their outer surface would be slick, with runnels of water trickling down, and patches of rotten ice where the air had gotten in. *Whatever else the wildlings are, they're brave.*

All the same, Jon found himself hoping that Styr's fears proved well founded. *If the gods are good, a patrol will chance by and put an end to this.* "No wall can keep you safe," his father had told him once, as they walked the walls of Winterfell. "A wall is only as strong as the men who defend it." The wildlings might have a hundred and twenty men, but four defenders would be enough to see them off, with a few well-placed arrows and perhaps a pail of stones.

No defenders appeared, however; not four, not even one. The sun climbed the sky and the wildlings climbed the Wall. Jarl's four remained well ahead till noon, when they hit a pitch of bad ice. Jarl had looped his rope around a wind-carved pinnace and was using it to support his weight when the whole jagged thing suddenly crumbled and came crashing down, and him with it. Chunks of ice as big as a man's head bombarded the three below, but they clung to the handholds and the stakes held, and Jarl jerked to a sudden halt at the end of the rope.

By the time his team had recovered from that mischance, Grigg the Goat had almost drawn even with them. Errok's four remained well behind. The face where they were climbing looked smooth and unpitted, covered with a sheet of icemelt that glistened wetly where the sun brushed it. Grigg's section was darker to the eye, with more obvious features; long horizontal ledges where a block had been imperfectly positioned atop the block below, cracks and crevices, even chimneys along the vertical joins, where wind and water had eaten holes large enough for a man to hide in.

Jarl soon had his men edging upward again. His four and Grigg's moved almost side by side, with Errok's fifty feet below. Deerhorn axes chopped and hacked, sending showers of glittery shards cascading down onto the trees. Stone hammers pounded stakes deep into the ice to serve as anchors for the ropes; the iron stakes ran out before they were halfway up, and after that the climbers used horn and sharpened bone. And the men kicked, driving the spikes on their boots against the hard unyielding ice again and again and again and again to make one foothold. *Their legs must be numb,* Jon thought by the fourth hour. *How long can they keep on with that?* He watched as restless as the Magnar, listening for the distant moan of a Thenn warhorn. But the horns stayed silent, and there was no sign of the Night's Watch.

By the sixth hour, Jarl had moved ahead of Grigg the Goat again, and his men were widening the gap. "The Mance's pet must want a sword," the Magnar said, shading his eyes. The sun was high in the sky, and the upper third of the Wall was a crystalline blue from below, reflecting so brilliantly that it hurt the eyes to look on it. Jarl's four and Grigg's were all but lost in the glare, though Errok's team was still in shadow. Instead of moving upward they were edging their way sideways at about five hundred feet, making for a chimney. Jon was watching them inch along when he heard the sound – a sudden *crack* that seemed to roll along the ice, followed by a shout of alarm. And then the air was full of shards and shrieks and falling men, as a sheet of ice a foot thick and fifty feet square broke off from the Wall and came tumbling, crumbling, rumbling, sweeping all before it. Even down at the foot of the ridge, some chunks came spinning through the trees and rolling down the slope. Jon grabbed Ygritte and pulled her down to shield her, and one of the Thenns was struck in the face by a chunk that broke his nose.

And when they looked up Jarl and his team were gone. Men, ropes, stakes, all gone; nothing remained above six hundred feet. There was a wound in the Wall where the climbers had clung half a heartbeat before, the ice within as smooth and white as polished marble and shining in the sun. Far far below there was a faint red smear where someone had smashed against a frozen pinnace.

The Wall defends itself, Jon thought as he pulled Ygritte back to her feet.

They found Jarl in a tree, impaled upon a splintered branch and still roped to the three men who lay broken beneath him. One was still alive, but his legs and spine were shattered, and most of his ribs as well. "Mercy," he said when they came upon him. One of the Thenns smashed his head in with a big stone mace. The Magnar gave orders, and his men began to gather fuel for a pyre.

The dead were burning when Grigg the Goat reached the top of the Wall. By the time Errok's four had joined them, nothing remained of Jarl and his team but bone and ash.

The sun had begun to sink by then, so the climbers wasted little time. They unwound the long coils of hemp they'd had looped around their chests, tied them all together, and tossed down one end. The thought of trying to climb five hundred feet up that rope filled Jon with dread, but Mance had planned better than that. The raiders Jarl had left below uncasked a huge ladder, with rungs of woven hemp as thick as a man's arm, and tied it to the climbers' rope. Errok and Grigg and their men grunted and heaved, pulled it up, staked it to the top, then lowered the rope again to haul up a second ladder. There were five altogether.

When all of them were in place, the Magnar shouted a brusque command in the Old Tongue, and five of his Thenns started up together. Even with the ladders, it was no easy climb. Ygritte watched them struggle for a while. "I hate this Wall," she said in a low angry voice. "Can you feel how *cold* it is?"

"It's made of ice," Jon pointed out.

"You know nothing, Jon Snow. This wall is made o' blood."

Nor had it drunk its fill. By sunset, two of the Thenns had fallen from the ladder to their deaths, but they were the last. It was near midnight before Jon reached the top. The stars were out again, and Ygritte was trembling from the climb. "I almost fell," she said, with tears in her eyes. "Twice. Thrice. The Wall was trying t' shake me off, I could feel it." One of the tears broke free and trickled slowly down her cheek.

"The worst is behind us." Jon tried to sound confident. "Don't be frightened." He tried to put an arm around her.

Ygritte slammed the heel of her hand into his chest, so hard it stung even through his layers of wool, mail, and boiled leather. "I wasn't *frightened*. You know nothing, Jon Snow."

"Why are you crying, then?"

"Not for fear!" She kicked savagely at the ice beneath her with a heel, chopping out a chunk. "I'm crying because we never found the Horn of Winter. We opened half a hundred graves and let all those shades loose in the world, and never found the Horn of Joramun to bring this cold thing down!"

JAIME

His hand burned.

Still, *still*, long after they had snuffed out the torch they'd used to sear his bloody stump, days after, he could still feel the fire lancing up his arm, and his fingers twisting in the flames, the fingers he no longer had.

He had taken wounds before, but never like this. He had never known there could be such pain. Sometimes, unbidden, old prayers bubbled from his lips, prayers he learned as a child and never thought of since, prayers he had first prayed with Cersei kneeling beside him in the sept at Casterly Rock. Sometimes he even wept, until he heard the Mummers laughing. Then he made his eyes go dry and his heart go dead, and prayed for his fever to burn away his tears. *Now I know how Tyrion has felt, all those times they laughed at him.*

After the second time he fell from the saddle, they bound him tight to Brienne of Tarth and made them share a horse again. One day, instead of back to front, they bound them face-to-face. "The lovers," Shagwell sighed loudly, "and what a lovely sight they are. 'Twould be cruel to separate the good knight and his lady." Then he laughed that high shrill laugh of his, and said, "Ah, but which one is the knight and which one is the lady?"

If I had my hand, you'd learn that soon enough, Jaime thought. His arms ached and his legs were numb from the ropes, but after a while none of that mattered. His world shrunk to the throb of agony that was his phantom hand, and Brienne pressed against him. *She's warm, at least,* he consoled himself, though the wench's breath was as foul as his own.

His hand was always between them. Urswyck had hung it about his neck on a cord, so it dangled down against his chest, slapping Brienne's breasts as Jaime slipped in and out of consciousness. His right eye was swollen shut, the wound inflamed where Brienne had cut him during their fight, but it was his hand that hurt the most. Blood and pus seeped from his stump, and the missing hand throbbed every time the horse took a step.

His throat was so raw that he could not eat, but he drank wine when they gave it to him, and water when that was all they offered. Once they handed him a cup and he quaffed it straight away, trembling, and the Brave Companions burst into laughter so loud and harsh it hurt his ears. "That's horse piss you're drinking, Kingslayer," Rorge told him. Jaime was so thirsty he drank it anyway, but afterward he retched it all back up. They made Brienne wash the vomit out of his beard, just as they made her clean him up when he soiled himself in the saddle.

One damp cold morning when he was feeling slightly stronger, a madness took hold of him and he reached for the Dornishman's sword with his left hand and wrenched it clumsily from its scabbard. *Let them kill me,* he thought, *so long as I die fighting, a blade in hand.* But it was no good. Shagwell came hopping from leg to leg, dancing nimbly aside when Jaime slashed at him. Unbalanced, he staggered forward, hacking wildly at the fool, but Shagwell spun and ducked and darted until all the Mummers were laughing at Jaime's futile efforts to land a blow. When he tripped over a rock and stumbled to his knees, the fool leapt in and planted a wet kiss atop his head.

Rorge finally flung him aside and kicked the sword from Jaime's feeble fingers as he tried to bring it up. "That wath amuthing, Kingthlayer," said Vargo Hoat, "but if you try it again, I thall take your other hand, or perhapth a foot."

Jaime lay on his back afterward, staring at the night sky, trying not to feel the pain that snaked up his right arm every time he moved it. The night was strangely beautiful. The moon was a graceful crescent, and it seemed as though he had never seen so many stars. The King's Crown was at the zenith, and he could see the Stallion rearing, and there the Swan. The Moonmaid, shy as ever, was half-hidden behind a pine tree. *How can such a night be beautiful?* he asked himself. *Why would the stars want to look down on such as me?*

"Jaime," Brienne whispered, so faintly he thought he was dreaming it. "Jaime, what are you doing?"

"Dying," he whispered back.

"No," she said, "no, you must live."

He wanted to laugh. "Stop telling me what do, wench. I'll die if it pleases me."

"Are you so craven?"

The word shocked him. He was Jaime Lannister, a knight of the Kings-guard, he was the Kingslayer. No man had ever called him craven. Other things they called him, yes; oathbreaker, liar, murderer. They said he was cruel, treacherous, reckless. But never craven. "What else can I do, but die?"

"Live," she said, "live, and fight, and take revenge." But she spoke too loudly. Rorge heard her voice, if not her words, and came over to kick her, shouting at her to hold her bloody tongue if she wanted to keep it.

Craven, Jaime thought, as Brienne fought to stifle her moans. *Can it be? They took my sword hand. Was that all I was, a sword hand? Gods be good, is it true?*

The wench had the right of it. He could not die. Cersei was waiting for him. She would have need of him. And Tyrion, his little brother, who loved him for a lie. And his enemies were waiting too; the Young Wolf who had beaten him in the Whispering Wood and killed his men around him, Edmure Tully who had kept him in darkness and chains, these Brave Companions.

When morning came, he made himself eat. They fed him a mush of oats, horse food, but he forced down every spoon. He ate again at evenfall, and the next day. *Live,* he told himself harshly, when the mush was like to gag him, *live for Cersei, live for Tyrion. Live for vengeance. A Lannister always pays his debts.* His missing hand throbbed and burned and stank. *When I reach King's Landing I'll have a new hand forged, a golden hand, and one day I'll use it to rip out Vargo Hoat's throat.*

The days and the nights blurred together in a haze of pain. He would sleep in the saddle, pressed against Brienne, his nose full of the stink of his rotting hand, and then at night he would lie awake on the hard ground, caught in a waking nightmare. Weak as he was, they always bound him to a tree. It gave him some cold consolation to know that they feared him that much, even now.

Brienne was always bound beside him. She lay there in her bonds like a big dead cow, saying not a word. *The wench has built a fortress inside herself. They will rape her soon enough, but behind her walls they cannot touch her.* But Jaime's walls were gone. They had taken his hand, they had taken his *sword hand*, and without it he was nothing. The other was no good to him. Since the time he could walk, his left arm had been his shield arm, no more. It was his right hand that made him a knight; his right arm that made him a man.

One day, he heard Urswyck say something about Harrenhal, and remembered that was to be their destination. That made him laugh aloud, and *that* made Timeon slash his face with a long thin whip. The cut bled, but beside his hand he scarcely felt it. "Why did you laugh?" the wench asked him that night, in a whisper.

"Harrenhal was where they gave me the white cloak," he whispered back. "Whent's great tourney. He wanted to show us all his big castle and his fine sons. I wanted to show them too. I was only fifteen, but no one could have beaten me that day. Aerys never let me joust." He laughed again. "He sent me away. But now I'm coming back."

They heard the laugh. That night it was Jaime who got the kicks and punches. He hardly felt them either, until Rorge slammed a boot into his stump, and then he fainted.

It was the next night when they finally came, three of the worst; Shagwell, noseless Rorge, and the fat Dothraki Zollo, the one who'd cut his hand off. Zollo and Rorge were arguing about who would go first as they approached; there seemed to be no question but that the fool would be going last. Shagwell suggested that they should both go first, and take her front and rear. Zollo and Rorge liked that notion, only then they began to fight about who would get the front and who the rear.

They will leave her a cripple too, but inside, where it does not show. "Wench," he whispered as Zollo and Rorge were cursing one another, "let them have the meat, and you go far away. It will be over quicker, and they'll get less pleasure from it."

"They'll get no pleasure from what I'll give them," she whispered back, defiant.

Stupid stubborn brave bitch. She was going to get herself good and killed, he knew it. *And what do I care if she does? If she hadn't been so pigheaded, I'd still have a hand.* Yet he heard himself whisper, "Let them do it, and go away inside." That was what he'd done, when the Starks had died before him, Lord Rickard cooking in his armor while his son Brandon strangled himself trying to save him. "Think of Renly, if you loved him. Think of Tarth, mountains and seas, pools, waterfalls, whatever you have on your Sapphire Isle, think . . ."

But Rorge had won the argument by then. "You're the ugliest woman I ever seen," he told Brienne, "but don't think I can't make you uglier. You want a nose like mine? Fight me, and you'll get one. And two eyes, that's too many. One scream out o' you, and I'll pop one out and make you eat it, and then I'll pull your fucking teeth out one by one."

"Oh, do it, Rorge," pleaded Shagwell. "Without her teeth, she'll look just like my dear old mother." He cackled. "And I *always* wanted to fuck my dear old mother up the arse."

Jaime chuckled. "There's a funny fool. I have a riddle for you, Shagwell. Why do you care if she screams? Oh, wait, I know." He shouted, "*SAPPH-IRES,*" as loudly as he could.

Cursing, Rorge kicked at his stump again. Jaime howled. *I never knew there was such agony in the world,* was the last thing he remembered thinking. It was hard to say how long he was gone, but when the pain spit him out, Urswyck was there, and Vargo Hoat himself. "Thee'th not to be touched," the goat screamed, spraying spittle all over Zollo. "Thee hath to be a maid, you foolth! Thee'th worth a bag of thapphireth!" And from then on, every night Hoat put guards on them, to protect them from his own.

Two nights passed in silence before the wench finally found the courage to whisper, "Jaime? Why did you shout out?"

"Why did I shout *'sapphires,'* you mean? Use your wits, wench. Would this lot have cared if I shouted *'rape'?*"

"You did not need to shout at all."

"You're hard enough to look at *with* a nose. Besides, I wanted to make the goat say 'thapphireth.'" He chuckled. "A good thing for you I'm such a liar. An honorable man would have told the truth about the Sapphire Isle."

"All the same," she said. "I thank you, ser."

His hand was throbbing again. He ground his teeth and said, "A Lannister pays his debts. That was for the river, and those rocks you dropped on Robin Ryger."

The goat wanted to make a show of parading him in, so Jaime was made to dismount a mile from the gates of Harrenhal. A rope was looped around his waist, a second around Brienne's wrists; the ends were tied to the pommel of Vargo Hoat's saddle. They stumbled along side by side behind the Qohorik's striped zorse.

Jaime's rage kept him walking. The linen that covered the stump was grey and stinking with pus. His phantom fingers screamed with every step. *I am stronger than they know,* he told himself. *I am still a Lannister. I am still a knight of the Kingsguard.* He would reach Harrenhal, and then King's Landing. He would live. *And I will pay this debt with interest.*

As they approached the clifflike walls of Black Harren's monstrous castle, Brienne squeezed his arm. "Lord Bolton holds this castle. The Boltons are bannermen to the Starks."

"The Boltons skin their enemies." Jaime remembered that much about the northman. Tyrion would have known all there was to know about the Lord of the Dreadfort, but Tyrion was a thousand leagues away, with Cersei. *I cannot die while Cersei lives,* he told himself. *We will die together as we were born together.*

The castleton outside the walls had been burned to ash and blackened stone, and many men and horses had recently encamped beside the lakeshore, where Lord Whent had staged his great tourney in the year of the false spring. A bitter smile touched Jaime's lips as they crossed that torn ground. Someone had dug a privy trench in the very spot where he'd once knelt before the king to say his vows. *I never dreamed how quick the sweet would turn to sour. Aerys would not even let me savor that one night. He honored me, and then he spat on me.*

"The banners," Brienne observed. "Flayed man and twin towers, see. King Robb's sworn men. There, above the gatehouse, grey on white. They fly the direwolf."

Jaime twisted his head upward for a look. "That's your bloody wolf, true enough," he granted her. "And those are heads to either side of it."

Soldiers, servants, and camp followers gathered to hoot at them. A spotted bitch followed them through the camps barking and growling until one of the Lyseni impaled her on a lance and galloped to the front of the column. "I am bearing Kingslayer's banner," he shouted, shaking the dead dog above Jaime's head.

The walls of Harrenhal were so thick that passing beneath them was like passing through a stone tunnel. Vargo Hoat had sent two of his Dothraki ahead to inform Lord Bolton of their coming, so the outer ward was full of the curious. They gave way as Jaime staggered past, the rope around his waist jerking and pulling at him whenever he slowed. "I give you the *Kingthlayer*," Vargo Hoat proclaimed in that thick slobbery voice of his. A spear jabbed at the small of Jaime's back, sending him sprawling.

Instinct made him put out his hands to stop his fall. When his stump smashed against the ground the pain was blinding, yet somehow he managed to fight his way back to one knee. Before him, a flight of broad stone steps led up to the entrance of one of Harrenhal's colossal round towers. Five knights and a northman stood looking down on him; the one pale-eyed in wool and fur, the five fierce in mail and plate, with the twin towers sigil on their surcoats. "A fury of Freys," Jaime declared. "Ser Danwell, Ser Aenys, Ser Hosteen." He knew Lord Walder's sons by sight; his aunt had married one, after all. "You have my condolences."

"For what, ser?" Ser Danwell Frey asked.

"Your brother's son, Ser Cleos," said Jaime. "He was with us until outlaws filled him full of arrows. Urswyck and this lot took his goods and left him for the wolves."

"*My lords!*" Brienne wrenched herself free and pushed forward. "I saw your banners. Hear me for your oath!"

"Who speaks?" demanded Ser Aenys Frey.

"Lannither'th wet nurth."

"I am Brienne of Tarth, daughter to Lord Selwyn the Evenstar, and sworn to House Stark even as you are."

Ser Aenys spit at her feet. "That's for your oaths. We trusted the word of Robb Stark, and he repaid our faith with betrayal."

Now this is interesting. Jaime twisted to see how Brienne might take the accusation, but the wench was as singleminded as a mule with a bit between his teeth. "I know of no betrayal." She chafed at the ropes around her wrists. "Lady Catelyn commanded me to deliver Lannister to his brother at King's Landing –"

"She was trying to drown him when we found them," said Urswyck the Faithful.

She reddened. "In anger I forgot myself, but I would never have killed him. If he dies the Lannisters will put my lady's daughters to the sword."

Ser Aenys was unmoved. "Why should that trouble us?"

"Ransom him back to Riverrun," urged Ser Danwell.

"Casterly Rock has more gold," one brother objected.

"Kill him!" said another. "His head for Ned Stark's!"

Shagwell the Fool somersaulted to the foot of the steps in his grey and pink motley and began to sing. *"There once was a lion who danced with a bear, oh my, oh my . . ."*

"Thilenth, fool." Vargo Hoat cuffed the man. "The Kingthlayer ith not for the bear. He ith mine."

"He is no one's should he die." Roose Bolton spoke so softly that men quieted to hear him. "And pray recall, my lord, you are not master of Harrenhal till I march north."

Fever made Jaime as fearless as he was lightheaded. "Can this be the Lord of the Dreadfort? When last I heard, my father had sent you scampering off with your tail betwixt your legs. When did you stop running, my lord?"

Bolton's silence was a hundred times more threatening than Vargo Hoat's slobbering malevolence. Pale as morning mist, his eyes concealed more than they told. Jaime misliked those eyes. They reminded him of the day at King's Landing when Ned Stark had found him seated on the Iron Throne. The Lord of the Dreadfort finally pursed his lips and said, "You have lost a hand."

"No," said Jaime, "I have it here, hanging round my neck."

Roose Bolton reached down, snapped the cord, and flung the hand at Hoat. "Take this away. The sight of it offends me."

"I will thend it to hith lord father. I will tell him he muth pay one hundred thouthand dragonth, or we thall return the Kingthlayer to him pieth by pieth. And when we hath hith gold, we thall deliver Ther Jaime to Karthark, and collect a maiden too!" A roar of laughter went up from the Brave Companions.

"A fine plan," said Roose Bolton, the same way he might say, "A fine wine," to a dinner companion, "though Lord Karstark will not be giving you his daughter. King Robb has shortened him by a head, for treason and murder. As to Lord Tywin, he remains at King's Landing, and there he will stay till the new year, when his grandson takes for bride a daughter of Highgarden."

"Winterfell," said Brienne. "You mean Winterfell. King Joffrey is betrothed to Sansa Stark."

"No longer. The Battle of the Blackwater changed all. The rose and the lion joined there, to shatter Stannis Baratheon's host and burn his fleet to ashes."

I warned you, Urswyck, Jaime thought, *and you, goat. When you bet against the lions, you lose more than your purse.* "Is there word of my sister?" he asked.

"She is well. As is your . . . nephew." Bolton paused before he said *nephew,* a pause that said *I know.* "Your brother also lives, though he took a wound in the battle." He beckoned to a dour northman in a studded brigantine. "Escort Ser Jaime to Qyburn. And unbind this woman's hands." As the rope between Brienne's wrists was slashed in two, he said, "Pray forgive us, my lady. In such troubled times it is hard to know friend from foe."

Brienne rubbed inside her wrist where the hemp had scraped her skin bloody. "My lord, these men tried to rape me."

"Did they?" Lord Bolton turned his pale eyes on Vargo Hoat. "I am displeased. By that, and this of Ser Jaime's hand."

There were five northmen and as many Freys in the yard for every Brave Companion. The goat might not be as clever as some, but he could count that high at least. He held his tongue.

"They took my sword," Brienne said, "my armor . . ."

"You shall have no need of armor here, my lady," Lord Bolton told her. "In Harrenhal, you are under my protection. Amabel, find suitable rooms for the Lady Brienne. Walton, you will see to Ser Jaime at once." He did not wait for an answer, but turned and climbed the steps, his fur-trimmed cloak swirling behind. Jaime had only enough time to exchange a quick look with Brienne before they were marched away, separately.

In the maester's chambers beneath the rookery, a grey-haired, fatherly man named Qyburn sucked in his breath when he cut away the linen from the stump of Jaime's hand.

"That bad? Will I die?"

Qyburn pushed at the wound with a finger, and wrinkled his nose at the gush of pus. "No. Though in a few more days . . ." He sliced away Jaime's sleeve. "The corruption has spread. See how tender the flesh is? I must cut it all away. The safest course would be to take the arm off."

"Then *you'll* die," Jaime promised. "Clean the stump and sew it up. I'll take my chances."

Qyburn frowned. "I can leave you the upper arm, make the cut at your elbow, but . . ."

"Take any part of my arm, and you'd best chop off the other one as well, or I'll strangle you with it afterward."

Qyburn looked in his eyes. Whatever he saw there gave him pause. "Very well. I will cut away the rotten flesh, no more. Try to burn out the corruption with boiling wine and a poultice of nettle, mustard seed, and bread mold. Mayhaps that will suffice. It is on your head. You will want milk of the poppy – "

"No." Jaime dare not let himself be put to sleep; he might be short an arm when he woke, no matter what the man said.

Qyburn was taken aback. "There will be pain."

"I'll scream."

"A great deal of pain."

"I'll scream very loudly."

"Will you take some wine at least?"

"Does the High Septon ever pray?"

"Of that I am not certain. I shall bring the wine. Lie back, I must needs strap down your arm."

With a bowl and a sharp blade, Qyburn cleaned the stump while Jaime gulped down strongwine, spilling it all over himself in the process. His left hand did not seem to know how to find his mouth, but there was something to be said for that. The smell of wine in his sodden beard helped disguise the stench of pus.

Nothing helped when the time came to pare away the rotten flesh. Jaime did scream then, and pounded his table with his good fist, over and over and over again. He screamed again when Qyburn poured boiling wine over what remained of his stump. Despite all his vows and all his fears, he lost consciousness for a time. When he woke, the maester was sewing at his arm with needle and catgut. "I left a flap of skin to fold back over your wrist."

"You have done this before," muttered Jaime, weakly. He could taste blood in his mouth where he'd bitten his tongue.

"No man who serves with Vargo Hoat is a stranger to stumps. He makes them wherever he goes."

Qyburn did not look a monster, Jaime thought. He was spare and soft-spoken, with warm brown eyes. "How does a maester come to ride with the Brave Companions?"

"The Citadel took my chain." Qyburn put away his needle. "I should do something about that wound above your eye as well. The flesh is badly inflamed."

Jaime closed his eyes and let the wine and Qyburn do their work. "Tell me of the battle." As keeper of Harrenhal's ravens, Qyburn would have been the first to hear the news.

"Lord Stannis was caught between your father and the fire. It's said the Imp set the river itself aflame."

Jaime saw green flames reaching up into the sky higher than the tallest towers, as burning men screamed in the streets. *I have dreamed this dream before.* It was almost funny, but there was no one to share the joke.

"Open your eye." Qyburn soaked a cloth in warm water and dabbed at the crust of dried blood. The eyelid was swollen, but Jaime found he could force it open halfway. Qyburn's face loomed above. "How did you come by this one?" the maester asked.

"A wench's gift."

"Rough wooing, my lord?"

"This wench is bigger than me and uglier than you. You'd best see to her as well. She's still limping on the leg I pricked when we fought."

"I will ask after her. What is this woman to you?"

"My protector." Jaime had to laugh, no matter how it hurt.

"I'll grind some herbs you can mix with wine to bring down your fever. Come back on the morrow and I'll put a leech on your eye to drain the bad blood."

"A leech. Lovely."

"Lord Bolton is very fond of leeches," Qyburn said primly.

"Yes," said Jaime. "He would be."

TYRION

Nothing remained beyond the King's Gate but mud and ashes and bits of burned bone, yet already there were people living in the shadow of the city walls, and others selling fish from barrows and barrels. Tyrion felt their eyes on him as he rode past; chilly eyes, angry and unsympathetic. No one dared speak to him, or try to bar his way; not with Bronn beside him in oiled black mail. *If I were alone, though, they would pull me down and smash my face in with a cobble-stone, as they did for Preston Greenfield.*

"They come back quicker than the rats," he complained. "We burned them out once, you'd think they'd take that as a lesson."

"Give me a few dozen gold cloaks and I'll kill them all," said Bronn. "Once they're dead they don't come back."

"No, but others come in their places. Leave them be ... but if they start throwing up hovels against the wall again, pull them down at once. The war's not done yet, no matter what these fools may think." He spied the Mud Gate up ahead. "I have seen enough for now. We'll return on the morrow with the guild masters to go over their plans." He sighed. *Well, I burned most of this, I suppose it's only just that I rebuild it.*

That task was to have been his uncle's, but solid, steady, tireless Ser Kevan Lannister had not been himself since the raven had come from Riverrun with word of his son's murder. Willem's twin Martyn had been taken captive by Robb Stark as well, and their elder brother Lancel was still abed, beset by an ulcerating wound that would not heal. With one son dead and two more in mortal danger, Ser Kevan was consumed by grief and fear. Lord Tywin had always relied on his brother, but now he had no choice but to turn again to his dwarf son.

The cost of rebuilding was going to be ruinous, but there was no help for that. King's Landing was the realm's principal harbor, rivaled only by Oldtown. The river had to be reopened, and the sooner the better. *And where am I going to find the bloody coin?* It was almost enough to make him miss Littlefinger, who had sailed north a fortnight past. *While he beds Lysa Arryn and rules the Vale beside her, I get to clean up the mess he left behind him.* Though at least his father was giving him significant work to do. *He won't name me heir to Casterly Rock, but he'll make use of me wherever he can,* Tyrion thought, as a captain of gold cloaks waved them through the Mud Gate.

The Three Whores still dominated the market square inside the gate, but they stood idle now, and the boulders and barrels of pitch had all been trundled away. There were children climbing the towering wooden structures, swarming up like monkeys in roughspun to perch on the throwing arms and hoot at each other.

"Remind me to tell Ser Addam to post some gold cloaks here," Tyrion told Bronn as they rode between two of the trebuchets. "Some fool boy's like to fall off and break his back." There was a shout from above, and a clod of manure exploded on the ground a foot in front of them. Tyrion's mare reared and almost threw him. "On second thoughts," he said when he had the horse in hand, "let the poxy brats splatter on the cobbles like overripe melons."

He was in a black mood, and not just because a few street urchins wanted to pelt him with dung. His marriage was a daily agony. Sansa Stark remained a maiden, and half the castle seemed to know it. When they had saddled up this morning, he'd heard two of the stableboys sniggering behind his back. He could almost imagine that the horses were sniggering as well. He'd risked his skin to avoid the bedding ritual, hoping to preserve the privacy of his bedchamber, but that hope had been dashed quick enough. Either Sansa had been stupid enough to confide in one of her bedmaids, every one of whom was a spy for Cersei, or Varys and his little birds were to blame.

What difference did it make? They were laughing at him all the same. The only person in the Red Keep who didn't seem to find his marriage a source of amusement was his lady wife.

Sansa's misery was deepening every day. Tyrion would gladly have broken through her courtesy to give her what solace he might, but it was no good. No words would ever make him fair in her eyes. *Or any less a Lannister.* This was the wife they had given him, for all the rest of his life, and she hated him.

And their nights together in the great bed were another source of torment. He could no longer bear to sleep naked, as had been his custom. His wife was too well trained ever to say an unkind word, but the revulsion in her eyes whenever she looked on his body was more than he could bear. Tyrion had commanded Sansa to wear a sleeping shift as well. *I want her*, he realized. *I want Winterfell, yes, but I want her as well, child or woman or whatever she is. I want to comfort her. I want to hear her laugh. I want her to come to me willingly, to bring me her joys and her sorrows and her lust.* His mouth twisted in a bitter smile. *Yes, and I want to be tall as Jaime and as strong as Ser Gregor the Mountain too, for all the bloody good it does.*

Unbidden, his thoughts went to Shae. Tyrion had not wanted her to hear the news from any lips but his own, so he had commanded Varys to bring her to him the night before his wedding. They met again in the eunuch's chambers, and when Shae began to undo the laces of his jerkin, he'd caught her by the wrist and pushed her away. "Wait," he said, "there is something you must hear. On the morrow I am to be wed . . ."

". . . to Sansa Stark. I know."

He was speechless for an instant. Even *Sansa* did not know, not then. "How could you know? Did Varys tell you?"

"Some page was telling Ser Tallad about it when I took Lollys to the sept. He had it from this serving girl who heard Ser Kevan talking to your father." She wriggled free of his grasp and pulled her dress up over her head. As ever, she was naked underneath. "I don't care. She's only a little girl. You'll give her a big belly and come back to me."

Some part of him had hoped for less indifference. *Had hoped*, he jeered bitterly, *but now you know better, dwarf. Shae is all the love you're ever like to have.*

Muddy Way was crowded, but soldiers and townfolk alike made way for the Imp and his escort. Hollow-eyed children swarmed underfoot, some looking up in silent appeal whilst others begged noisily. Tyrion pulled a big fistful of coppers from his purse and tossed them in the air, and the children went running for them, shoving and shouting. The lucky ones might be able to buy a heel of stale bread tonight. He had never seen markets so crowded, and for all the food the Tyrells were bringing in, prices remained shockingly high. Six coppers for a melon, a silver stag for a bushel of corn, a dragon for a side of beef or six skinny piglets. Yet there seemed no lack of buyers. Gaunt men and haggard women crowded around every wagon and stall, while others even more ragged looked on sullenly from the mouths of alleys.

"This way," Bronn said, when they reached the foot of the Hook. "If you still mean to . . . ?"

"I do." The riverfront had made a convenient excuse, but Tyrion had another purpose today. It was not a task he relished, but it must be done.

They turned away from Aegon's High Hill, into the maze of smaller streets that clustered around the foot of Visenya's. Bronn led the way. Once or twice Tyrion glanced back over his shoulder to see if they were being followed, but there was nothing to be seen except the usual rabble: a carter beating his horse, an old woman throwing nightsoil from her window, two little boys fighting with sticks, three gold cloaks escorting a captive . . . they all looked innocent, but any one of them could be his undoing. Varys had informers everywhere.

They turned at a corner, and again at the next, and rode slowly through a crowd of women at a well. Bronn led him along a curving wynd, through an alley, under a broken archway. They cut through the rubble where a house had burned and walked their horses up a shallow flight of stone steps. The buildings were close and poor. Bronn halted at the mouth of a crooked alley, too narrow for two to ride abreast. "There's two jags and then a dead end. The sink is in the cellar of the last building."

Tyrion swung down off his horse. "See that no one enters or leaves till I return. This won't take long." His hand went into his cloak, to make certain the gold was still there in the hidden pocket. Thirty dragons. *A bloody fortune, for a man like him.* He waddled up the alley quickly, anxious to be done with this.

The wine sink was a dismal place, dark and damp, walls pale with niter, the ceiling so low that Bronn would have had to duck to keep from hitting his head on the beams. Tyrion Lannister had no such problem. At this hour, the front room was empty but for a dead-eyed woman who sat on a stool behind a rough plank bar. She handed him a cup of sour wine and said, "In the back."

The back room was even darker. A flickering candle burned on a low table, beside a flagon of wine. The man behind it scarce looked a danger; a short man – though all men were tall to Tyrion – with thinning brown hair, pink cheeks, and a little pot pushing at the bone buttons of his doeskin jerkin. In his soft hands he held a twelve-stringed woodharp more deadly than a longsword.

Tyrion sat across from him. "Symon Silver Tongue."

The man inclined his head. He was bald on top. "My lord Hand," he said.

"You mistake me. My father is the King's Hand. I am no longer even a finger, I fear."

"You shall rise again, I am sure. A man like you. My sweet lady Shae tells me you are newly wed. Would that you had sent for me earlier. I should have been honored to sing at your feast."

"The last thing my wife needs is more songs," said Tyrion. "As for Shae, we both know she is no lady, and I would thank you never to speak her name aloud."

"As the Hand commands," Symon said.

The last time Tyrion had seen the man, a sharp word had been enough to set him sweating, but it seemed the singer had found some courage somewhere. *Most like in that flagon.* Or perhaps Tyrion himself was to blame for this new boldness. *I threatened him, but nothing ever came of the threat, so now he believes me toothless.* He sighed. "I am told you are a very gifted singer."

"You are most kind to say so, my lord."

Tyrion gave him a smile. "I think it is time you brought your music to the Free Cities. They are great lovers of song in Braavos and Pentos and Lys, and generous with those who please them." He took a sip of wine. It was foul stuff, but strong. "A tour of all nine cities would be best. You wouldn't want to deny anyone the joy of hearing you sing. A year in each should suffice." He reached inside his cloak, to where the gold was hidden. "With the port closed, you will need to go to Duskendale to take ship, but my man Bronn will find a horse for you, and I would be honored if you would let me pay your passage . . ."

"But my lord," the man objected, "you have never heard me sing. Pray listen a moment." His fingers moved deftly over the strings of the woodharp, and soft music filled the cellar. Symon began to sing.

> He rode through the streets of the city,
> > down from his hill on high,
> O'er the wynds and the steps and the cobbles,
> > he rode to a woman's sigh.
> For she was, his secret treasure,
> > she was his shame and his bliss.
> And a chain and a keep are nothing,
> > compared to a woman's kiss.

"There's more," the man said as he broke off. "Oh, a good deal more. The refrain is especially nice, I think. *For hands of gold are always cold, but a woman's hands are warm . . .*"

"Enough." Tyrion slid his fingers from his cloak, empty. "That's not a song I would care to hear again. Ever."

"No?" Symon Silver Tongue put his harp aside and took a sip of wine. "A pity. Still, each man has his song, as my old master used to say when he was teaching me to play. Others might like my tune better. The queen, perhaps. Or your lord father."

Tyrion rubbed the scar over his nose, and said, "My father has no time for singers, and my sister is not as generous as one might think. A wise man could earn more from silence than from song." He could not put it much plainer than that.

Symon seemed to take his meaning quick enough. "You will find my price modest, my lord."

"That's good to know." This would not be a matter of thirty golden dragons, Tyrion feared. "Tell me."

"At King Joffrey's wedding feast," the man said, "there is to be a tournament of singers."

"And jugglers, and jesters, and dancing bears."

"Only one dancing bear, my lord," said Symon, who had plainly attended Cersei's arrangements with far more interest than Tyrion had, "but seven singers. Galyeon of Cuy, Bethany Fair-fingers, Aemon Costayne, Alaric of Eysen, Hamish the Harper, Collio Quaynis, and Orland of Oldtown will compete for a gilded lute with silver strings . . . yet unaccountably, no invitation has been forthcoming for one who is master of them all."

"Let me guess. Symon Silver Tongue?"

Symon smiled modestly. "I am prepared to prove the truth of my boast before king and court. Hamish is old, and oft forgets what he is singing. And Collio, with that absurd Tyroshi accent! If you understand one word in three, count yourself fortunate."

"My sweet sister has arranged the feast. Even if I could secure you this invitation, it might look queer. Seven kingdoms, seven vows, seven challenges, seventy-seven dishes . . . but *eight* singers? What would the High Septon think?"

"You did not strike me as a pious man, my lord."

"Piety is not the point. Certain forms must be observed."

Symon took a sip of wine. "Still . . . a singer's life is not without peril. We ply our trade in alehouses and wine sinks, before unruly drunkards. If one of your sister's seven should suffer some mishap, I hope you might consider me to fill his place." He smiled slyly, inordinately pleased with himself.

"Six singers would be as unfortunate as eight, to be sure. I will inquire after the health of Cersei's seven. If any of them should be indisposed, my man Bronn will find you."

"Very good, my lord." Symon might have left it at that, but flushed with triumph, he added, "I *shall* sing the night of King Joffrey's wedding. Should it happen that I am called to court, why, I will want to offer the king my very best compositions, songs I have sung a thousand times that are certain to please. If I should find myself singing in some dreary winesink, though . . . well, that would be an apt occasion to try my new song. *For hands of gold are always cold, but a woman's hands are warm.*"

"That will not be necessary," said Tyrion. "You have my word as a Lannister, Bronn will call upon you soon."

"Very *good*, my lord." The balding kettle-bellied singer took up his woodharp again.

Bronn was waiting with the horses at the mouth of the alley. He helped Tyrion into his saddle. "When do I take the man to Duskendale?"

"You don't." Tyrion turned his horse. "Give him three days, then inform him that Hamish the Harper has broken his arm. Tell him that his clothes will never serve for court, so he must be fitted for new garb at once. He'll come with you quick enough." He grimaced. "You may want his tongue, I understand it's made of silver. The rest of him should never be found."

Bronn grinned. "There's a pot shop I know in Flea Bottom makes a savory bowl of brown. All kinds of meat in it, I hear."

"Make certain I never eat there." Tyrion spurred to a trot. He wanted a bath, and the hotter the better.

Even that modest pleasure was denied him, however; no sooner had he returned to his chambers than Podrick Payne informed him that he had been summoned to the Tower of the Hand. "His lordship wants to see you. The Hand. Lord Tywin."

"I recall who the Hand is, Pod," Tyrion said. "I lost my nose, not my wits."

Bronn laughed. "Don't bite the boy's head off now."

"Why not? He never uses it." Tyrion wondered what he'd done now. *Or more like, what I have failed to do.* A summons from Lord Tywin always had teeth; his father never sent for him just to share a meal or a cup of wine, that was for certain.

As he entered his lord father's solar a few moments later, he heard a voice saying, ". . . cherrywood for the scabbards, bound in red leather and ornamented with a row of lion's-head studs in pure gold. Perhaps with garnets for the eyes . . ."

"Rubies," Lord Tywin said. "Garnets lack the fire."

Tyrion cleared his throat. "My lord. You sent for me?"

His father glanced up. "I did. Come have a look at this." A bundle of oilcloth lay on the table between them, and Lord Tywin had a longsword in his hand. "A wedding gift for Joffrey," he told Tyrion. The light streaming through the diamond-shaped panes of glass made the blade shimmer black and red as Lord Tywin turned it to inspect the edge, while the pommel and crossguard flamed gold. "With this fool's jabber of Stannis and his magic sword, it seemed to me that we had best give Joffrey something extraordinary as well. A king should bear a kingly weapon."

"That's much too much sword for Joff," Tyrion said.

"He will grow into it. Here, feel the weight of it." He offered the weapon hilt first.

The sword was much lighter than he had expected. As he turned it in his hand he saw why. Only one metal could be beaten so thin and still have strength enough to fight with, and there was no mistaking those ripples, the mark of steel that has been folded back on itself many thousands of times. "Valyrian steel?"

"Yes," Lord Tywin said, in a tone of deep satisfaction.

At long last, Father! Valyrian steel blades were scarce and costly, yet thousands remained in the world, perhaps two hundred in the Seven Kingdoms alone. It had always irked his father that none belonged to House Lannister. The old Kings of the Rock had owned such a weapon, but the greatsword Brightroar had been lost when the second King Tommen carried it back to Valyria on his fool's quest. He had never returned; nor had Uncle Gery, the youngest and most reckless of his father's brothers, who had gone seeking after the lost sword some eight years past.

Thrice at least Lord Tywin had offered to buy Valyrian longswords from impoverished lesser houses, but his advances had always been firmly rebuffed. The little lordlings would gladly part with their daughters should a Lannister come asking, but they cherished their old family swords.

Tyrion wondered where the metal for this one had come from. A few master armorers could rework old Valyrian steel, but the secrets of its making had been lost when the Doom came to old Valyria. "The colors are strange," he commented as he turned the blade in the sunlight. Most Valyrian steel was a grey so dark it looked almost black, as was true here as well. But blended into the folds was a red as deep as the grey. The two colors lapped over one another without ever touching, each ripple distinct, like waves of night and blood upon some steely shore. "How did you get this patterning? I've never seen anything like it."

"Nor I, my lord," said the armorer. "I confess, these colors were not what I intended, and I do not know that I could duplicate them. Your lord father had asked for the crimson of your House, and it was that color I set out to infuse into the metal. But Valyrian steel is stubborn. These old swords remember, it is said, and they do not change easily. I worked half a hundred spells and brightened the red time and time again, but always the color would darken, as if the blade was drinking the sun from it. And some folds would not take the red at all, as you can see. If my lords of Lannister are displeased, I will of course try again, as many times as you should require, but –"

"No need," Lord Tywin said. "This will serve."

"A crimson sword might flash prettily in the sun, but if truth be told I like these colors better," said Tyrion. "They have an ominous beauty . . . and they make this blade unique. There is no other sword like it in all the world, I should think."

"There is one." The armorer bent over the table and unfolded the bundle of oilcloth, to reveal a second longsword.

Tyrion put down Joffrey's sword and took up the other. If not twins, the two were at least close cousins. This one was thicker and heavier, a half-inch wider and three inches longer, but they shared the same fine clean lines and the same distinctive color, the ripples of blood and night. Three fullers, deeply incised, ran down the second blade from hilt to point; the king's sword had only two. Joff's hilt was a good deal more ornate, the arms of its crossguard done as lions' paws with ruby claws unsheathed, but both swords had grips of finely tooled red leather and gold lions' heads for pommels.

"Magnificent." Even in hands as unskilled as Tyrion's, the blade felt alive. "I have never felt better balance."

"It is meant for my son."

No need to ask which son. Tyrion placed Jaime's sword back on the table beside Joffrey's, wondering if Robb Stark would let his brother live long enough to wield it. *Our father must surely think so, else why have this blade forged?*

"You have done good work, Master Mott," Lord Tywin told the armorer. "My steward will see to your payment. And remember, rubies for the scabbards."

"I shall, my lord. You are most generous." The man folded the swords up in the oilcloth, tucked the bundle under one arm, and went to his knee. "It is an honor to serve the King's Hand. I shall deliver the swords the day before the wedding."

"See that you do."

When the guards had seen the armorer out, Tyrion clambered up onto a chair. "So . . . a sword for Joff, a sword for Jaime, and not even a dagger for the dwarf. Is that the way of it, Father?"

"The steel was sufficient for two blades, not three. If you have need of a dagger, take one from the armory. Robert left a hundred when he died. Gerion gave him a gilded dagger with an ivory grip and a sapphire pommel for a wedding gift, and half the envoys who came to court tried to curry favor by presenting His Grace with jewel-encrusted knives and silver inlay swords."

Tyrion smiled. "They'd have pleased him more if they'd presented him with their daughters."

"No doubt. The only blade he ever used was the hunting knife he had from Jon Arryn, when he was a boy." Lord Tywin waved a hand, dismissing King Robert and all his knives. "What did you find at the riverfront?"

"Mud," said Tyrion, "and a few dead things no one's bothered to bury. Before we can open the port again, the Blackwater's going to have to be dredged, the sunken ships broken up or raised. Three-quarters of the quays need repair, and some may have to be torn down and rebuilt. The entire fish market is gone, and both the River Gate and the King's Gate are splintered from the battering Stannis gave them and should be replaced. I shudder to think of the cost." *If you do shit gold, Father, find a privy and get busy*, he wanted to say, but he knew better.

"You will find whatever gold is required."

"Will I? Where? The treasury is empty, I've told you that. We're not done paying the alchemists for all that wildfire, or the smiths for my chain, and Cersei's pledged the crown to pay half the costs of Joff's wedding – seventy-seven bloody courses, a thousand guests, a pie full of doves, singers, jugglers . . ."

"Extravagance has its uses. We must demonstrate the power and wealth of Casterly Rock for all the realm to see."

"Then perhaps Casterly Rock should pay."

"Why? I have seen Littlefinger's accounts. Crown incomes are ten times higher than they were under Aerys."

"As are the crown's expenses. Robert was as generous with his coin as he was with his cock. Littlefinger borrowed heavily. From you, amongst others. Yes, the incomes are considerable, but they are barely sufficient to cover the usury on Littlefinger's loans. Will you forgive the throne's debt to House Lannister?"

"Don't be absurd."

"Then perhaps seven courses would suffice. Three hundred guests instead of a thousand. I understand that a marriage can be just as binding *without* a dancing bear."

"The Tyrells would think us niggardly. I will have the wedding *and* the waterfront. If you cannot pay for them, say so, and I shall find a master of coin who can."

The disgrace of being dismissed after so short a time was not something Tyrion cared to suffer. "I will find your money."

"You will," his father promised, "and while you are about it, see if you can find your wife's bed as well."

So the talk has reached even him. "I have, thank you. It's that piece of furniture between the window and the hearth, with the velvet canopy and the mattress stuffed with goose down."

"I am pleased you know of it. Now perhaps you ought to try and know the woman who shares it with you."

Woman? Child, you mean. "Has a spider been whispering in your ear, or do I have my sweet sister to thank?" Considering the things that went on beneath Cersei's blankets, you would think she'd have the decency to keep her nose out of his. "Tell me, why is it that all of Sansa's maids are women in Cersei's service? I am sick of being spied upon in my own chambers."

"If you mislike your wife's servants, dismiss them and hire ones more to your liking. That is your right. It is your wife's maidenhood that concerns me, not her maids. This . . . delicacy puzzles me. You seem to have no difficulty bedding whores. Is the Stark girl made differently?"

"Why do you take so much bloody interest in where I put my cock?" Tyrion demanded. "Sansa is too young."

"She is old enough to be Lady of Winterfell once her brother is dead. Claim her maidenhood and you will be one step closer to claiming the north. Get her with child, and the prize is all but won. Do I need to remind you that a marriage that has not been consummated can be set aside?"

"By the High Septon or a Council of Faith. Our present High Septon is a trained seal who barks prettily on command. Moon Boy is more like to annul my marriage than he is."

"Perhaps I should have married Sansa Stark to Moon Boy. He might have known what to do with her."

Tyrion's hands clenched on the arms of his chair. "I have heard all I mean to hear on the subject of my wife's maidenhead. But so long as we are discussing marriage, why is it that I hear nothing of my sister's impending nuptials? As I recall – "

Lord Tywin cut him off. "Mace Tyrell has refused my offer to marry Cersei to his heir Willas."

"*Refused* our sweet Cersei?" That put Tyrion in a *much* better mood.

"When I first broached the match to him, Lord Tyrell seemed well enough disposed," his father said. "A day later, all was changed. The old woman's work. She hectors her son unmercifully. Varys claims she told him that your sister was too old and too *used* for this precious one-legged grandson of hers."

"Cersei must have loved that." He laughed.

Lord Tywin gave him a chilly look. "She does not know. Nor will she. It is better for all of us if the offer was never made. See that you remember that, Tyrion. *The offer was never made.*"

"What offer?" Tyrion rather suspected that Lord Tyrell might come to regret this rebuff.

"Your sister *will* be wed. The question is, to whom? I have several thoughts – " Before he could get to them, there was a rap at the door and a guardsman stuck in his head to announce Grand Maester Pycelle. "He may enter," said Lord Tywin.

Pycelle tottered in on a cane, and stopped long enough to give Tyrion a look that would curdle milk. His once-magnificent white beard, which someone had unaccountably shaved off, was growing back sparse and wispy, leaving him with unsightly pink wattles to dangle beneath his neck. "My lord Hand," the old man said, bowing as deeply as he could without falling, "there has been another bird from Castle Black. Mayhaps we could consult privily?"

"There's no need for that." Lord Tywin waved Grand Maester Pycelle to a seat. "Tyrion may stay."

Oooooh, may I? He rubbed his nose, and waited.

Pycelle cleared his throat, which involved a deal of coughing and hawking. "The letter is from the same Bowen Marsh who sent the last. The castellan. He writes that Lord Mormont has sent word of wildlings moving south in vast numbers."

"The lands beyond the Wall cannot support vast numbers," said Lord Tywin firmly. "This warning is not new."

"This last is, my lord. Mormont sent a bird from the haunted forest, to report that he was under attack. More ravens have returned since, but none with letters. This Bowen Marsh fears Lord Mormont slain, with all his strength."

Tyrion had rather liked old Jeor Mormont, with his gruff manner and talking bird. "Is this certain?" he asked.

"It is not," Pycelle admitted, "but none of Mormont's men have returned as yet. Marsh fears the wildlings have killed them, and that the Wall itself may be attacked next." He fumbled in his robe and found the paper. "Here is his letter, my lord, a plea to all five kings. He wants men, as many men as we can send him."

"Five kings?" His father was annoyed. "There is one king in Westeros. Those fools in black might try and remember that if they wish His Grace to heed them. When you reply, tell him that Renly is dead and the others are traitors and pretenders."

"No doubt they will be glad to learn it. The Wall is a world apart, and news oft reaches them late." Pycelle bobbed his head up and down. "What shall I tell Marsh concerning the men he begs for? Shall we convene the council . . ."

"There is no need. The Night's Watch is a pack of thieves, killers, and baseborn churls, but it occurs to me that they *could* prove otherwise, given proper discipline. If Mormont is indeed dead, the black brothers must choose a new Lord Commander."

Pycelle gave Tyrion a sly glance. "An excellent thought, my lord. I know the very man. Janos Slynt."

Tyrion liked that notion not at all. "The black brothers choose their own commander," he reminded them. "Lord Slynt is new to the Wall. I know, I sent him there. Why should they pick *him* over a dozen more senior men?"

"Because," his father said, in a tone that suggested Tyrion was quite the simpleton, "if they do not vote as they are told, their Wall will melt before it sees another man."

Yes, that would work. Tyrion hitched forward. "Janos Slynt is the wrong man, Father. We'd do better with the commander of the Shadow Tower. Or Eastwatch-by-the-Sea."

"The commander of the Shadow Tower is a Mallister of Seagard. Eastwatch is held by an ironman." Neither would serve his purposes, Lord Tywin's tone said clear enough.

"Janos Slynt is a butcher's son," Tyrion reminded his father forcefully. "You yourself told me –"

"I recall what I told you. Castle Black is not Harrenhal, however. The Night's Watch is not the king's council. There is a tool for every task, and a task for every tool."

Tyrion's anger flashed. "Lord Janos is a hollow suit of armor who will sell himself to the highest bidder."

"I count that a point in his favor. Who is like to bid higher than us?" He turned to Pycelle. "Send a raven. Write that King Joffrey was deeply saddened to hear of Lord Commander Mormont's death, but regrets that he can spare no men just now, whilst so many rebels and usurpers remain in the field. Suggest that matters might be quite different once the throne is secure . . . provided the king has full confidence in the leadership of the Watch. In closing, ask Marsh to pass along His Grace's fondest regards to his faithful friend and servant, Lord Janos Slynt."

"Yes, my lord." Pycelle bobbed his withered head once more. "I shall write as the Hand commands. With great pleasure."

I should have trimmed his head, not his beard, Tyrion reflected. *And Slynt should have gone for a swim with his dear friend Allar Deem.* At least he had not made the same foolish mistake with Symon Silver Tongue. *See there, Father!* he wanted to shout. *See how fast I learn my lessons!*

SAMWELL

Up in the loft a woman was giving birth noisily, while below a man lay dying by the fire. Samwell Tarly could not say which frightened him more.

They'd covered poor Bannen with a pile of furs and stoked the fire high, yet all he could say was, "I'm cold. Please. I'm so cold." Sam was trying to feed him onion broth, but he could not swallow. The broth dribbled over his lips and down his chin as fast as Sam could spoon it in.

"That one's dead." Craster eyed the man with indifference as he worried at a sausage. "Be kinder to stick a knife in his chest than that spoon down his throat, you ask me."

"I don't recall as we did." Giant was no more than five feet tall – his true name was Bedwyck – but a fierce little man for all that. "Slayer, did you ask Craster for his counsel?"

Sam cringed at the name, but shook his head. He filled another spoon, brought it to Bannen's mouth, and tried to ease it between his lips.

"Food and fire," Giant was saying, "that was all we asked of you. And you grudge us the food."

"Be glad I didn't grudge you fire too." Craster was a thick man made thicker by the ragged smelly sheepskins he wore day and night. He had a broad flat nose, a mouth that drooped to one side, and a missing ear. And though his matted hair and tangled beard might be grey going white, his hard knuckly hands still looked strong enough to hurt. "I fed you what I could, but you crows are always hungry. I'm a godly man, else I would have chased you off. You think I need the likes of him, dying on my floor? You think I need all your mouths, little man?" The wildling spat. "Crows. When did a black bird ever bring good to a man's hall, I ask you? Never. Never."

More broth ran from the corner of Bannen's mouth. Sam dabbed it away with a corner of his sleeve. The ranger's eyes were open but unseeing. "I'm cold," he said again, so faintly. A maester might have known how to save him, but they had no maester. Kedge Whiteye had taken Bannen's mangled foot off nine days past, in a gout of pus and blood that made Sam sick, but it was too little, too late. "I'm so cold," the pale lips repeated.

About the hall, a ragged score of black brothers squatted on the floor or sat on rough-hewn benches, drinking cups of the same thin onion broth and gnawing on chunks of hardbread. A couple were wounded worse than Bannen, to look at them. Fornio had been delirious for days, and Ser Byam's shoulder was oozing a foul yellow pus. When they'd left Castle Black, Brown Bernarr had been carrying bags of Myrish fire, mustard salve, ground garlic, tansy, poppy, kingscopper, and other healing herbs. Even sweetsleep, which gave the gift of painless death. But Brown Bernarr had died on the Fist and no one had thought to search for Maester Aemon's medicines. Hake had known some herblore as well, being a cook, but Hake was also lost. So it was left to the surviving stewards to do what they could for the wounded, which was little enough. *At least they are dry here, with a fire to warm them. They need more food, though.*

They all needed more food. The men had been grumbling for days. Clubfoot Karl kept saying how Craster had to have a hidden larder, and Garth of Oldtown had begun to echo him, when he was out of the Lord Commander's hearing. Sam had thought of begging for something more nourishing for the wounded men at least, but he did not have the courage. Craster's eyes were cold and mean, and whenever the wildling looked his way his hands twitched a little, as if they wanted to curl up into fists. *Does he know I spoke to Gilly, the last time we were here?* he wondered. *Did she tell him I said we'd take her? Did he beat it out of her?*

"I'm cold," said Bannen. "Please. I'm cold."

For all the heat and smoke in Craster's hall, Sam felt cold himself. *And tired, so tired.* He needed sleep, but whenever he closed his eyes he dreamed of blowing snow and dead men shambling toward him with black hands and bright blue eyes.

Up in the loft, Gilly let out a shuddering sob that echoed down the long low windowless hall. "Push," he heard one of Craster's older wives tell her. "Harder. *Harder.* Scream if it helps." She did, so loud it made Sam wince.

Craster turned his head to glare. "I've had a bellyful o' that shrieking," he shouted up. "Give her a rag to bite down on, or I'll come up there and give her a taste o' my hand."

He would too, Sam knew. Craster had nineteen wives, but none who'd dare interfere once he started up that ladder. No more than the black brothers had two nights past, when he was beating one of the younger girls. There had been mutterings, to be sure. "He's killing her," Garth of Greenaway had said, and Clubfoot Karl laughed and said, "If he don't want the little sweetmeat he could give her to me." Black Bernarr cursed in a low angry voice, and Alan of Rosby got up and went outside so he wouldn't have to hear. "His roof, his rule," the ranger Ronnel Harclay had reminded them. "Craster's a friend to the Watch."

A friend, thought Sam, as he listened to Gilly's muffled shrieks. Craster was a brutal man who ruled his wives and daughters with an iron hand, but his keep was a refuge all the same. "Frozen crows," Craster sneered when they straggled in, those few who had survived the snow, the wights, and the bitter cold. "And not so big a flock as went north, neither." Yet he had given them space on his floor, a roof to keep the snow off, a fire to dry them out, and his wives had brought them cups of hot wine to put some warmth in their bellies. "Bloody crows," he called them, but he'd fed them too, meager though the fare might be.

We are guests, Sam reminded himself. *Gilly is his. His daughter, his wife. His roof, his rule.*

The first time he'd seen Craster's Keep, Gilly had come begging for help, and Sam had lent her his black cloak to conceal her belly when she went to find Jon Snow. *Knights are supposed to defend women and children.* Only a few of the black brothers were knights, but even so . . . *We all say the words*, Sam thought. *I am the shield that guards the realms of men.* A woman was a woman, even a wildling woman. *We should help her. We should.* It was her child Gilly feared for; she was frightened that it might be a boy. Craster raised up his daughters to be his wives, but there were neither men nor boys to be seen about his compound. Gilly had told Jon that Craster gave his sons to the gods. *If the gods are good, they will send her a daughter*, Sam prayed.

Up in the loft, Gilly choked back a scream. "That's it," a woman said. "Another push, now. Oh, I see his head."

Hers, Sam thought miserably. *Her head, hers.*

"Cold," said Bannen, weakly. "Please. I'm so cold." Sam put the bowl and spoon aside, tossed another fur across the dying man, put another stick on the fire. Gilly gave a shriek, and began to pant. Craster gnawed on his hard black sausage. He had sausages for himself and his wives, he said, but none for the Watch. "Women," he complained. "The way they wail . . . I had me a fat sow once birthed a litter of eight with no more'n a grunt." Chewing, he turned his head to squint contemptuously at Sam. "She was near as fat as you, boy. Slayer." He laughed.

It was more than Sam could stand. He stumbled away from the firepit, stepping awkwardly over and around the men sleeping and squatting and dying upon the hard-packed earthen floor. The smoke and screams and moans were making him feel faint. Bending his head, he pushed through the hanging deerhide flaps that served Craster for a door and stepped out into the afternoon.

The day was cloudy, but still bright enough to blind him after the gloom of the hall. Some patches of snow weighed down the limbs of surrounding trees and blanketed the gold and russet hills, but fewer than there had been. The storm had passed on, and the days at Craster's Keep had been . . . well, not warm perhaps, but not so bitter cold. Sam could hear the soft *drip-drip-drip* of water melting off the icicles that bearded the edge of the thick sod roof. He took a deep shuddering breath and looked around.

To the west Ollo Lophand and Tim Stone were moving through the horselines, feeding and watering the remaining garrons.

Downwind, other brothers were skinning and butchering the animals deemed too weak to go on. Spearmen and archers walked sentry behind the earthen dikes that were Craster's only defense against whatever hid in the wood beyond, while a dozen firepits sent up thick fingers of blue-grey smoke. Sam could hear the distant echoes of axes at work in the forest, where a work detail was harvesting enough wood to keep the blazes burning all through the night. Nights were the bad time. When it got dark. And *cold*.

There had been no attacks while they had been at Craster's, neither wights nor Others. Nor would there be, Craster said. "A godly man got no cause to fear such. I said as much to that Mance Rayder once, when he come sniffing round. He never listened, no more'n you crows with your swords and your bloody fires. That won't help you none when the white cold comes. Only the gods will help you then. You best get right with the gods."

Gilly had spoken of the white cold as well, and she'd told them what sort of offerings Craster made to his gods. Sam had wanted to kill him when he heard. *There are no laws beyond the Wall,* he reminded himself, *and Craster's a friend to the Watch.*

A ragged shout went up from behind the daub-and-wattle hall. Sam went to take a look. The ground beneath his feet was a slush of melting snow and soft mud that Dolorous Edd insisted was made of Craster's shit. It was thicker than shit, though; it sucked at Sam's boots so hard he felt one pull loose.

Back of a vegetable garden and empty sheepfold, a dozen black brothers were loosing arrows at a butt they'd built of hay and straw. The slender blond steward they called Sweet Donnel had laid a shaft just off the bull's eye at fifty yards. "Best that, old man," he said.

"Aye. I will." Ulmer, stooped and grey-bearded and loose of skin and limb, stepped to the mark and pulled an arrow from the quiver at his waist. In his youth he had been an outlaw, a member of the infamous Kingswood Brotherhood. He claimed he'd once put an arrow through the hand of the White Bull of the Kingsguard to steal a kiss from the lips of a Dornish princess. He had stolen her jewels too, and a chest of golden dragons, but it was the kiss he liked to boast of in his cups.

He notched and drew, all smooth as summer silk, then let fly. His shaft struck the butt an inch inside of Donnel Hill's. "Will that do, lad?" he asked, stepping back.

"Well enough," said the younger man, grudgingly. "The crosswind helped you. It blew more strongly when I loosed."

"You ought to have allowed for it, then. You have a good eye and a steady hand, but you'll need a deal more to best a man of the kingswood. Fletcher Dick it was who showed me how to bend the bow, and no finer archer ever lived. Have I told you about old Dick, now?"

"Only three hundred times." Every man at Castle Black had heard Ulmer's tales of the great outlaw band of yore; of Simon Toyne and the Smiling Knight, Oswyn Longneck the Thrice-Hanged, Wenda the White Fawn, Fletcher Dick, Big Belly Ben, and all the rest. Searching for escape, Sweet Donnel looked about and spied Sam standing in the muck. "*Slayer*," he called. "Come, show us how you slew the Other." He held out the tall yew longbow.

Sam turned red. "It wasn't an arrow, it was a dagger, dragonglass . . ." He knew what would happen if he took the bow. He would miss the butt and send the arrow sailing over the dike off into the trees. Then he'd hear the laughter.

"No matter," said Alan of Rosby, another fine bowman. "We're all keen to see the Slayer shoot. Aren't we, lads?"

He could not face them; the mocking smiles, the mean little jests, the contempt in their eyes. Sam turned to go back the way he'd come, but his right foot sank deep in the muck, and when he tried to pull it out his boot came off. He had to kneel to wrench it free, laughter ringing in his ears. Despite all his socks, the snowmelt had soaked through to his toes by the time he made his escape. *Useless*, he thought miserably. *My father saw me true. I have no right to be alive when so many brave men are dead.*

Grenn was tending the firepit south of the compound gate, stripped to the waist as he split logs. His face was red with exertion, the sweat steaming off his skin. But he grinned as Sam came chuffing up. "The Others get your boot, Slayer?"

Him too! "It was the mud. Please don't call me that."

"Why not?" Grenn sounded honestly puzzled. "It's a good name, and you came by it fairly."

Pyp always teased Grenn about being thick as a castle wall, so Sam explained patiently. "It's just a different way of calling me a coward," he said, standing on his left leg and wriggling back into his muddy boot. "They're mocking me, the same way they mock Bedwyck by calling him 'Giant.'"

"He's not a giant, though," said Grenn, "and Paul was never small. Well, maybe when he was a babe at the breast, but not after. You *did* slay the Other, though, so it's not the same."

"I just . . . I never . . . I was *scared!*"

"No more than me. It's only Pyp who says I'm too dumb to be frightened. I get as frightened as anyone." Grenn bent to scoop up a split log, and tossed it into the fire. "I used to be scared of Jon, whenever I had to fight him. He was so quick, and he fought like he meant to kill me." The green damp wood sat in the flames, smoking before it took fire. "I never said, though. Sometimes I think everyone is just pretending to be brave, and none of us really are. Maybe pretending is how you *get* brave, I don't know. Let them call you Slayer, who cares?"

"You never liked Ser Alliser to call you Aurochs."

"He was saying I was big and stupid." Grenn scratched at his beard. "If Pyp wanted to call me Aurochs, though, he could. Or you, or Jon. An aurochs is a fierce strong beast, so that's not so bad, and I *am* big, and getting bigger. Wouldn't you rather be Sam the Slayer than Ser Piggy?"

"Why can't I just be Samwell Tarly?" He sat down heavily on a wet log that Grenn had yet to split. "It was the dragonglass that slew it. Not me, the dragonglass."

He had told them. He had told them all. Some of them didn't believe him, he knew. Dirk had shown Sam his dirk and said, "I got iron, what do I want with glass?" Black Bernarr and the three Garths made it plain that they doubted his whole story, and Rolley of Sisterton came right out and said, "More like you stabbed some rustling bushes and it turned out to be Small Paul taking a shit, so you came up with a lie."

But Dywen listened, and Dolorous Edd, and they made Sam and Grenn tell the Lord Commander. Mormont frowned all through the tale and asked pointed questions, but he was too cautious a man to shun any possible advantage. He asked Sam for all the dragonglass in his pack, though that was little enough. Whenever Sam thought of the cache Jon had found buried beneath the Fist, it made him want to cry. There'd been dagger blades and spearheads, and two or three hundred arrowheads at least. Jon had made daggers for himself, Sam, and Lord Commander

Mormont, and he'd given Sam a spearhead, an old broken horn, and some arrowheads. Grenn had taken a handful of arrowheads as well, but that was all.

So now all they had was Mormont's dagger and the one Sam had given Grenn, plus nineteen arrows and a tall hardwood spear with a black dragonglass head. The sentries passed the spear along from watch to watch, while Mormont had divided the arrows among his best bowmen. Muttering Bill, Garth Greyfeather, Ronnel Harclay, Sweet Donnel Hill, and Alan of Rosby had three apiece, and Ulmer had four. But even if they made every shaft tell, they'd soon be down to fire arrows like all the rest. They had loosed hundreds of fire arrows on the Fist, yet still the wights kept coming.

It will not be enough, Sam thought. Craster's sloping palisades of mud and melting snow would hardly slow the wights, who'd climbed the much steeper slopes of the Fist to swarm over the ringwall. And instead of three hundred brothers drawn up in disciplined ranks to meet them, the wights would find forty-one ragged survivors, nine too badly hurt to fight. Forty-four had come straggling into Craster's out of the storm, out of the sixty-odd who'd cut their way free of the Fist, but three of those had died of their wounds, and Bannen would soon make four.

"Do you think the wights are gone?" Sam asked Grenn. "Why don't they come finish us?"

"They only come when it's cold."

"Yes," said Sam, "but is it the cold that brings the wights, or the wights that bring the cold?"

"Who cares?" Grenn's axe sent wood chips flying. "They come together, that's what matters. Hey, now that we know that dragonglass kills them, maybe they won't come at all. Maybe they're frightened of *us* now!"

Sam wished he could believe that, but it seemed to him that when you were dead, fear had no more meaning than pain or love or duty. He wrapped his hands around his legs, sweating under his layers of wool and leather and fur. The dragonglass dagger had melted the pale thing in the woods, true . . . but Grenn was talking like it would do the same to the wights. *We don't know that,* he thought. *We don't know anything, really. I wish Jon was here.* He liked Grenn, but he couldn't talk to him the same way. *Jon wouldn't call me Slayer, I know. And I could talk to him about Gilly's baby.* Jon had ridden off with Qhorin Halfhand, though, and they'd had no word of him since. *He had a dragonglass dagger too, but did he think to use it? Is he lying dead and frozen in some ravine . . . or worse, is he dead and walking?*

He could not understand why the gods would want to take Jon Snow and Bannen and leave him, craven and clumsy as he was. He *should* have died on the Fist, where he'd pissed himself three times and lost his sword besides. And he *would* have died in the woods if Small Paul had not come along to carry him. *I wish it was all a dream. Then I could wake up.* How fine that would be, to wake back on the Fist of the First Men with all his brothers still around him, even Jon and Ghost. Or even better, to wake in Castle Black behind the Wall and go to the common room for a bowl of Three-Finger Hobb's thick cream of wheat, with a big spoon of butter melting in the middle and a dollop of honey besides. Just the thought of it made his empty stomach rumble.

"*Snow.*"

Sam glanced up at the sound. Lord Commander Mormont's raven was circling the fire, beating the air with wide black wings.

"*Snow,*" the bird cawed. "*Snow, snow.*"

Wherever the raven went, Mormont soon followed. The Lord Commander emerged from beneath the trees, mounted on his garron between old Dywen and the fox-faced ranger Ronnel Harclay, who'd been raised to Thoren Smallwood's place. The spearmen at the gate shouted a challenge, and the Old Bear returned a gruff, "Who in seven hells do you *think* goes there? Did the Others take your eyes?" He rode between the gateposts, one bearing a ram's skull and the other the skull of a bear, then reined up, raised a fist, and whistled. The raven came flapping down at his call.

"My lord," Sam heard Ronnel Harclay say, "we have only twenty-two mounts, and I doubt half will reach the Wall."

"I know that," Mormont grumbled. "We must go all the same. Craster's made that plain." He glanced to the west, where a bank of dark clouds hid the sun. "The gods gave us a respite, but for how long?" Mormont swung down from the saddle, jolting his raven back into the air. He saw Sam then, and bellowed, "*Tarly!*"

"Me?" Sam got awkwardly to his feet.

"*Me?*" The raven landed on the old man's head. "*Me?*"

"Is your name Tarly? Do you have a brother hereabouts? Yes, you. Close your mouth and come with me."

"With you?" The words tumbled out in a squeak.

Lord Commander Mormont gave him a withering look. "You are a man of the Night's Watch. Try not to soil your smallclothes every time I look at you. Come, I said." His boots made squishing sounds in the mud, and Sam had to hurry to keep up. "I've been thinking about this dragonglass of yours."

"It's not *mine,*" Sam said.

"Jon Snow's dragonglass, then. If dragonglass daggers are what we need, why do we have only two of them? Every man on the Wall should be armed with one the day he says his words."

"We never knew . . ."

"We *never knew!* But we must have known once. The Night's Watch has forgotten its true purpose, Tarly. You don't build a wall seven hundred feet high to keep savages in skins from stealing women. The Wall was made *to guard the realms of men* ... and not against other men, which is all the wildlings are when you come right down to it. Too many years, Tarly, too many hundreds and thousands of years. We lost sight of the true enemy. And now he's here, but we don't know how to fight him. Is dragonglass made by dragons, as the smallfolk like to say?"

"The m-maesters think not," Sam stammered. "The maesters say it comes from the fires of the earth. They call it obsidian."

Mormont snorted. "They can call it lemon pie for all I care. If it kills as you claim, I want more of it."

Sam stumbled. "Jon found more, on the Fist. Hundreds of arrowheads, spearheads as well . . ."

"So you said. Small good it does us there. To reach the Fist again we'd need to be armed with the weapons we won't have until we reach the bloody Fist. And there are still the wildlings to deal with. We need to find dragonglass someplace else."

Sam had almost forgotten about the wildlings, so much had happened since. "The children of the forest used dragonglass blades," he said. "They'd know where to find obsidian."

"The children of the forest are all dead," said Mormont. "The First Men killed half of them with bronze blades, and the Andals finished the job with iron. Why a glass dagger should –"

The Old Bear broke off as Craster emerged from between the deerhide flaps of his door. The wildling smiled, revealing a mouth of brown rotten teeth. "I have a son."

"*Son,*" cawed Mormont's raven. "*Son, son, son.*"

The Lord Commander's face was stiff. "I'm glad for you."

"Are you, now? Me, I'll be glad when you and yours are gone. Past time, I'm thinking."

"As soon as our wounded are strong enough . . ."

"They're strong as they're like to get, old crow, and both of us know it. Them that's dying, you know them too, cut their bloody throats and be done with it. Or leave them, if you don't have the stomach, and I'll sort them out myself."

Lord Commander Mormont bristled. "Thoren Smallwood claimed you were a friend to the Watch –"

"Aye," said Craster. "I gave you all I could spare, but winter's coming on, and now the girl's stuck me with another squalling mouth to feed."

"We could take him," someone squeaked.

Craster's head turned. His eyes narrowed. He spat on Sam's foot. "What did you say, Slayer?"

Sam opened and closed his mouth. "I . . . I . . . I only meant . . . if you didn't want him . . . his mouth to feed . . . with winter coming on, we . . . we could take him, and . . ."

"My son. My blood. You think I'd give him to you crows?"

"I only thought . . ." *You have no sons, you expose them, Gilly said as much, you leave them in the woods, that's why you have only wives here, and daughters who grow up to be wives.*

"Be quiet, Sam," said Lord Commander Mormont. "You've said enough. Too much. Inside."

"M-my lord –"

"*Inside!*"

Red-faced, Sam pushed through the deerhides, back into the gloom of the hall. Mormont followed. "How great a fool are you?" the old man said within, his voice choked and angry. "Even if Craster gave us the child, he'd be dead before we reached the Wall. We need a newborn babe to care for near as much as we need more snow. Do you have milk to feed him in those big teats of yours? Or did you mean to take the mother too?"

"She wants to come," Sam said. "She begged me . . ."

Mormont raised a hand. "I will hear no more of this, Tarly. You've been told and *told* to stay well away from Craster's wives."

"She's his daughter," Sam said feebly.

"Go see to Bannen. Now. Before you make me wroth."

"Yes, my lord." Sam hurried off quivering.

But when he reached the fire, it was only to find Giant pulling a fur cloak up over Bannen's head. "He said he was cold," the small man said. "I hope he's gone someplace warm, I do."

"His wound . . ." said Sam.

"Bugger his wound." Dirk prodded the corpse with his foot. "His *foot* was hurt. I knew a man back in my village lost a foot. He lived to nine-and-forty."

"The cold," said Sam. "He was never warm."

"He was never *fed*," said Dirk. "Not proper. That bastard Craster starved him dead."

Sam looked around anxiously, but Craster had not returned to the hall. If he had, things might have grown ugly. The wildling hated bastards, though the rangers said he was baseborn himself, fathered on a wildling woman by some long-dead crow.

"Craster's got his own to feed," said Giant. "All these women. He's given us what he can."

"Don't you bloody believe it. The day we leave, he'll tap a keg o' mead and sit down to feast on ham and honey. And *laugh* at us, out starving in the snow. He's a bloody wildling, is all he is. There's none o' them friends of the Watch." He kicked at Bannen's corpse. "Ask him if you don't believe me."

They burned the ranger's corpse at sunset, in the fire that Grenn had been feeding earlier that day. Tim Stone and Garth of Oldtown carried out the naked corpse and swung him twice between them before heaving him into the flames. The surviving brothers divided up his clothes, his weapons, his armor, and everything else he owned. At Castle Black, the Night's Watch buried its dead with all due ceremony. They were not at Castle Black, though. *And bones do not come back as wights.*

"His name was Bannen," Lord Commander Mormont said, as the flames took him. "He was a brave man, a good ranger. He came to us from . . . where did he come from?"

"Down White Harbor way," someone called out.

Mormont nodded. "He came to us from White Harbor, and never failed in his duty. He kept his vows as best he could, rode far, fought fiercely. We shall never see his like again."

"*And now his watch is ended,*" the black brothers said, in solemn chant.

"And now his watch is ended," Mormont echoed.

"*Ended,*" cried his raven. "*Ended.*"

Sam was red-eyed and sick from the smoke. When he looked at the fire, he thought he saw Bannen sitting up, his hands coiling into fists as if to fight off the flames that were consuming him, but it was only for an instant, before the swirling smoke hid all. The worst thing was the *smell*, though. If it had been a foul unpleasant smell he might have stood it, but his burning brother smelled so much like roast pork that Sam's mouth began to water, and that was so horrible that as soon as the bird squawked "*Ended*" he ran behind the hall to throw up in the ditch.

He was there on his knees in the mud when Dolorous Edd came up. "Digging for worms, Sam? Or are you just sick?"

"Sick," said Sam weakly, wiping his mouth with the back of his hand. "The smell . . ."

"Never knew Bannen could smell so good." Edd's tone was as morose as ever. "I had half a mind to carve a slice off him. If we had some applesauce, I might have done it. Pork's always best with applesauce, I find." Edd undid his laces and pulled out his cock. "You best not die, Sam, or I fear I might succumb. There's bound to be more crackling on you than Bannen ever had, and I never could resist a bit of crackling." He sighed as his piss arced out, yellow and steaming. "We ride at first light, did you hear? Sun or snow, the Old Bear tells me."

Sun or snow. Sam glanced up anxiously at the sky. "Snow?" he squeaked. "We . . . ride? All of us?"

"Well, no, some will need to walk." He shook himself. "Dywen now, he says we need to learn to ride dead horses, like the Others do. He claims it would save on feed. How much could a dead horse eat?" Edd laced himself back up. "Can't say I fancy the notion. Once they figure a way to work a dead horse, we'll be next. Likely I'll be the first too. 'Edd,' they'll say, 'dying's no excuse for lying down no more, so get on up and take this spear, you've got the watch tonight.' Well, I shouldn't be so gloomy. Might be I'll die before they work it out."

Might be we'll all die, and sooner than we'd like, Sam thought, as he climbed awkwardly to his feet.

When Craster learned that his unwanted guests would be departing on the morrow, the wildling became almost amiable, or as close to amiable as Craster ever got. "Past time," he said, "you don't belong here, I told you that. All the same, I'll see you off proper, with a feast. Well, a feed. My wives can roast them horses you slaughtered, and I'll find some beer and bread." He smiled his brown smile. "Nothing better than beer and horsemeat. If you can't ride 'em, eat 'em, that's what I say."

His wives and daughters dragged out the benches and the long log tables, and cooked and served as well. Except for Gilly, Sam could hardly tell the women apart. Some were old and some were young and some were only girls, but a lot of them were Craster's daughters as well as his wives, and they all looked sort of alike. As they went about their work, they spoke in soft voices to each other, but never to the men in black.

Craster owned but one chair. He sat in it, clad in a sleeveless sheepskin jerkin. His thick arms were covered with white hair, and about one wrist was a twisted ring of gold. Lord Commander Mormont took the place at the top of the bench to his right, while the brothers crowded in knee to knee; a dozen remained outside to guard the gate and tend the fires.

Sam found a place between Grenn and Orphan Oss, his stomach rumbling. The charred horsemeat dripped with grease as Craster's wives turned the spits above the firepit, and the smell of it set his mouth to watering again, but that reminded him of Bannen. Hungry as he was, Sam knew he would retch if he so much as tried a bite. How could they eat the poor faithful garrons who had carried them so far? When Craster's wives brought onions, he seized one eagerly. One side was black with rot, but he cut that part off with his dagger and ate the good half raw. There was bread as well, but only two loaves. When Ulmer asked for more, the woman only shook her head. That was when the trouble started.

"Two loaves?" Clubfoot Karl complained from down the bench. "How stupid are you women? We need more bread than this!"

Lord Commander Mormont gave him a hard look. "Take what you're given, and be thankful. Would you sooner be out in the storm eating snow?"

"We'll be there soon enough." Clubfoot Karl did not flinch from the Old Bear's wrath. "I'd sooner eat what Craster's hiding, my lord."

Craster narrowed his eyes. "I gave you crows enough. I got me women to feed."

Dirk speared a chunk of horsemeat. "Aye. So you admit you got a secret larder. How else to make it through a winter?"

"I'm a godly man . . ." Craster started.

"You're a niggardly man," said Karl, "and a liar."

"Hams," Garth of Oldtown said, in a reverent voice. "There were pigs, last time we come. I bet he's got hams hid someplace. Smoked and salted hams, and bacon too."

"Sausage," said Dirk. "Them long black ones, they're like rocks, they keep for years. I bet he's got a hundred hanging in some cellar."

"Oats," suggested Ollo Lophand. "Corn. Barley."

"Corn," said Mormont's raven, with a flap of the wings. "Corn, corn, corn, corn, corn."

"Enough," said Lord Commander Mormont over the bird's raucous calls. "Be quiet, all of you. This is folly."

"Apples," said Garth of Greenaway. "Barrels and barrels of crisp autumn apples. There are apple trees out there, I saw 'em."

"Dried berries. Cabbages. Pine nuts."

"Corn. Corn. Corn."

"Salt mutton. There's a sheepfold. He's got casks and casks of mutton laid by, you know he does."

Craster looked fit to spit them all by then. Lord Commander Mormont rose. "Silence. I'll hear no more such talk."

"Then stuff bread in your ears, old man." Clubfoot Karl pushed back from the table. "Or did you swallow your bloody crumb already?"

Sam saw the Old Bear's face go red. "Have you forgotten who I am? Sit, eat, and be silent. That is a command."

No one spoke. No one moved. All eyes were on the Lord Commander and the big clubfooted ranger, as the two of them stared at each other across the table. It seemed to Sam that Karl broke first, and was about to sit, though sullenly . . .

. . . but Craster stood, and his axe was in his hand. The big black steel axe that Mormont had given him as a guest gift. "No," he growled. "You'll not sit. No one who calls me niggard will sleep beneath my roof nor eat at my board. Out with you, cripple. And you and you and you." He jabbed the head of the axe toward Dirk and Garth and Garth in turn. "Go sleep in the cold with empty bellies, the lot o' you, or . . ."

"Bloody *bastard!*" Sam heard one of the Garths curse. He never saw which one.

"*Who calls me bastard?*" Craster roared, sweeping platter and meat and wine cups from the table with his left hand while lifting the axe with his right.

"It's no more than all men know," Karl answered.

Craster moved quicker than Sam would have believed possible, vaulting across the table with axe in hand. A woman screamed, Garth Greenaway and Orphan Oss drew knives, Karl stumbled back and tripped over Ser Byam lying wounded on the floor. One instant Craster was coming after him spitting curses. The next he was spitting blood. Dirk had grabbed him by the hair, yanked his head back, and opened his throat ear to ear with one long slash. Then he gave him a rough shove, and the wildling fell forward, crashing face first across Ser Byam. Byam screamed in agony as Craster drowned in his own blood, the axe slipping from his fingers. Two of Craster's wives were wailing, a third cursed, a fourth flew at Sweet Donnel and tried to scratch his eyes out. He knocked her to the floor. The Lord Commander stood over Craster's corpse, dark with anger. "The gods will curse us," he cried. "There is no crime so foul as for a guest to bring murder into a man's hall. By all the laws of the hearth, we –"

"There are no laws beyond the Wall, old man. Remember?" Dirk grabbed one of Craster's wives by the arm, and shoved the point of his bloody dirk up under her chin. "Show us where he keeps the food, or you'll get the same as he did, woman."

"Unhand her." Mormont took a step. "I'll have your head for this, you –"

Garth of Greenaway blocked his path, and Ollo Lophand yanked him back. They both had blades in hand. "Hold your tongue," Ollo warned. Instead the Lord Commander grabbed for his dagger. Ollo had only one hand, but that was quick. He twisted free of the old man's grasp, shoved the knife into Mormont's belly, and yanked it out again, all red. And then the world went mad.

Later, much later, Sam found himself sitting crosslegged on the floor, with Mormont's head in his lap. He did not remember how they'd gotten there, or much of anything else that had happened after the Old Bear was stabbed. Garth of Greenaway had killed Garth of Oldtown, he recalled, but not why. Rolley of Sisterton had fallen from the loft and broken his neck after climbing the ladder to have a taste of Craster's wives. Grenn . . .

Grenn had shouted and slapped him, and then he'd run away with Giant and Dolorous Edd and some others. Craster still sprawled across Ser Byam, but the wounded knight no longer moaned. Four men in black sat on the bench eating chunks of burned horsemeat while Ollo coupled with a weeping woman on the table.

"Tarly." When he tried to speak, the blood dribbled from the Old Bear's mouth down into his beard. "Tarly, go. *Go.*"

"Where, my lord?" His voice was flat and lifeless. *I am not afraid.* It was a queer feeling. "There's no place to go."

"The Wall. Make for the Wall. Now."

"*Now,*" squawked the raven. "*Now. Now.*" The bird walked up the old man's arm to his chest, and plucked a hair from his beard.

"You must. Must tell them."

"Tell them what, my lord?" Sam asked politely.

"All. The Fist. The wildlings. Dragonglass. This. *All.*" His breathing was very shallow now, his voice a whisper. "Tell my son. Jorah. Tell him, take the black. My wish. Dying wish."

"*Wish?*" The raven cocked its head, beady black eyes shining. "*Corn?*" the bird asked.

"No corn," said Mormont feebly. "Tell Jorah. Forgive him. My son. Please. Go."

"It's too far," said Sam. "I'll never reach the Wall, my lord." He was so very tired. All he wanted was to sleep, to sleep and sleep and never wake, and he knew that if he just stayed here soon enough Dirk or Ollo Lophand or Clubfoot Karl would get angry with him and grant his wish, just to see him die. "I'd sooner stay with you. See, I'm not frightened anymore. Of you, or . . . of anything."

"You should be," said a woman's voice.

Three of Craster's wives were standing over them. Two were haggard old women he did not know, but Gilly was between them, all bundled up in skins and cradling a bundle of brown and white fur that must have held her baby. "We're not supposed to talk to Craster's wives," Sam told them. "We have orders."

"That's done now," said the old woman on the right.

"The blackest crows are down in the cellar, gorging," said the old woman on the left, "or up in the loft with the young ones. They'll be back soon, though. Best you be gone when they do. The horses run off, but Dyah's caught two."

"You said you'd help me," Gilly reminded him.

"I said Jon would help you. Jon's brave, and he's a good fighter, but I think he's dead now. I'm a craven. And fat. Look how fat I am. Besides, Lord Mormont's hurt. Can't you see? I couldn't leave the Lord Commander."

"Child," said the other old woman, "that old crow's gone before you. Look."

Mormont's head was still in his lap, but his eyes were open and staring and his lips no longer moved. The raven cocked its head and squawked, then looked up at Sam. "*Corn?*"

"No corn. He has no corn." Sam closed the Old Bear's eyes and tried to think of a prayer, but all that came to mind was, "Mother have mercy. Mother have mercy. Mother have mercy."

"Your mother can't help you none," said the old woman on the left. "That dead old man can't neither. You take his sword and you take that big warm fur cloak o' his and you take his horse if you can find him. And you go."

"The girl don't lie," the old woman on the right said. "She's my girl, and I beat the lying out of her early on. You said you'd help her. Do what Ferny says, boy. Take the girl and be quick about it."

"*Quick,*" the raven said. "*Quick quick quick.*"

"Where?" asked Sam, puzzled. "Where should I take her?"

"Someplace warm," the two old women said as one.

Gilly was crying. "Me and the babe. Please. I'll be your wife, like I was Craster's. Please, ser crow. He's a boy, just like Nella said he'd be. If you don't take him, *they* will."

"They?" said Sam, and the raven cocked its black head and echoed, "*They. They. They.*"

"The boy's brothers," said the old woman on the left. "Craster's sons. The white cold's rising out there, crow. I can feel it in my bones. These poor old bones don't lie. They'll be here soon, the sons."

ARYA

Her eyes had grown accustomed to blackness. When Harwin pulled the hood off her head, the ruddy glare inside the hollow hill made Arya blink like some stupid owl.

A huge firepit had been dug in the center of the earthen floor, and its flames rose swirling and crackling toward the smoke-stained ceiling. The walls were equal parts stone and soil, with huge white roots twisting through them like a thousand slow pale snakes. People were emerging from between those roots as she watched; edging out from the shadows for a look at the captives, stepping from the mouths of pitch-black tunnels, popping out of crannies and crevices on all sides. In one place on the far side of the fire, the roots formed a kind of stairway up to a hollow in the earth where a man sat almost lost in the tangle of weirwood.

Lem unhooded Gendry. "What is this place?" he asked.

"An old place, deep and secret. A refuge where neither wolves nor lions come prowling."

Neither wolves nor lions. Arya's skin prickled. She remembered the dream she'd had, and the taste of blood when she tore the man's arm from his shoulder.

Big as the fire was, the cave was bigger; it was hard to tell where it began and where it ended. The tunnel mouths might have been two feet deep or gone on two miles. Arya saw men and women and little children, all of them watching her warily.

Greenbeard said, "Here's the wizard, skinny squirrel. You'll get your answers now." He pointed toward the fire, where Tom Sevenstrings stood talking to a tall thin man with oddments of old armor buckled on over his ratty pink robes. *That can't be Thoros of Myr.* Arya remembered the red priest as fat, with a smooth face and a shiny bald head. This man had a droopy face and a full head of shaggy grey hair. Something Tom said made him look at her, and Arya thought he was about to come over to her. Only then the Mad Huntsman appeared, shoving his captive down into the light, and she and Gendry were forgotten.

The Huntsman had turned out to be a stocky man in patched tan leathers, balding and weak-chinned and quarrelsome. At Stoney Sept she had thought that Lem and Greenbeard might be torn to pieces when they faced him at the crow cages to claim his captive for the lightning lord. The hounds had been all around them, sniffing and snarling. But Tom o' Sevens soothed them with his playing, Tansy marched across the square with her apron full of bones and fatty mutton, and Lem pointed out Anguy in the brothel window, standing with an arrow notched. The Mad Huntsman had cursed them all for lickspittles, but finally he had agreed to take his prize to Lord Beric for judgment.

They had bound his wrists with hempen rope, strung a noose around his neck, and pulled a sack down over his head, but even so there was danger in the man. Arya could feel it across the cave. Thoros – if that *was* Thoros – met captor and captive halfway to the fire. "How did you take him?" the priest asked.

"The dogs caught the scent. He was sleeping off a drunk under a willow tree, if you believe it."

"Betrayed by his own kind." Thoros turned to the prisoner and yanked his hood off. "Welcome to our humble hall, dog. It is not so grand as Robert's throne room, but the company is better."

The shifting flames painted Sandor Clegane's burned face with orange shadows, so he looked even more terrible than he did in daylight. When he pulled at the rope that bound his wrists, flakes of dry blood fell off. The Hound's mouth twitched. "I know you," he said to Thoros.

"You did. In mêlées, you'd curse my flaming sword, though thrice I overthrew you with it."

"Thoros of Myr. You used to shave your head."

"To betoken a humble heart, but in truth my heart was vain. Besides, I lost my razor in the woods." The priest slapped his belly. "I am less than I was, but more. A year in the wild will melt the flesh off a man. Would that I could find a tailor to take in my skin. I might look young again, and pretty maids would shower me with kisses."

"Only the blind ones, priest."

The outlaws hooted, none so loud as Thoros. "Just so. Yet I am not the false priest you knew. The Lord of Light has woken in my heart. Many powers long asleep are waking, and there are forces moving in the land. I have seen them in my flames."

The Hound was unimpressed. "Bugger your flames. And you as well." He looked around at the others. "You keep queer company for a holy man."

"These are my brothers," Thoros said simply.

Lem Lemoncloak pushed forward. He and Greenbeard were the only men there tall enough to look the Hound in the eye. "Be careful how you bark, dog. We hold your life in our hands."

"Best wipe the shit off your fingers, then." The Hound laughed. "How long have you been hiding in this hole?"

Anguy the Archer bristled at the suggestion of cowardice. "Ask the goat if we've hidden, Hound. Ask your brother. Ask the lord of leeches. We've bloodied them all."

"You lot? Don't make me laugh. You look more swineherds than soldiers."

"Some of us was swineherds," said a short man Arya did not know. "And some was tanners or singers or masons. But that was before the war come."

"When we left King's Landing we were men of Winterfell and men of Darry and men of Blackhaven, Mallery men and Wylde men. We were knights and squires and men-at-arms, lords and commoners, bound together only by our purpose." The voice came from the man seated amongst the weirwood roots halfway up the wall. "Six score of us set out to bring the king's justice to your brother." The speaker was descending the tangle of steps toward the floor. "Six score brave men and true, led by a fool in a starry cloak." A scarecrow of a man, he wore a ragged black cloak speckled with stars and an iron breastplate dinted by a hundred battles. A thicket of red-gold hair hid most of his face, save for a bald spot above his left ear where his head had been smashed in. "More than eighty of our company are dead now, but others have taken up the swords that fell from their hands." When he reached the floor, the outlaws moved aside to let him pass. One of his eyes was gone, Arya saw, the flesh about the socket scarred and puckered, and he had a dark black ring all around his neck. "With their help, we fight on as best we can, for Robert and the realm."

"Robert?" rasped Sandor Clegane, incredulous.

"Ned Stark sent us out," said pothelmed Jack-Be-Lucky, "but he was sitting the Iron Throne when he gave us our commands, so we were never truly his men, but Robert's."

"Robert is the king of the worms now. Is that why you're down in the earth, to keep his court for him?"

"The king is dead," the scarecrow knight admitted, "but we are still king's men, though the royal banner we bore was lost at the Mummer's Ford when your brother's butchers fell upon us." He touched his breast with a fist. "Robert is slain, but his realm remains. And we defend her."

"*Her?*" The Hound snorted. "Is she your mother, Dondarrion? Or your whore?"

Dondarrion? Beric Dondarrion had been handsome; Sansa's friend Jeyne had fallen in love with him. Even Jeyne Poole was not so blind as to think this man was fair. Yet when Arya looked at him again, she saw it; the remains of a forked purple lightning bolt on the cracked enamel of his breastplate.

"Rocks and trees and rivers, that's what your realm is made of," the Hound was saying. "Do the rocks need defending? Robert wouldn't have thought so. If he couldn't fuck it, fight it, or drink it, it bored him, and so would you . . . you *brave companions*."

Outrage swept the hollow hill. "Call us that name again, dog, and you'll swallow that tongue." Lem drew his longsword.

The Hound stared at the blade with contempt. "Here's a brave man, baring steel on a bound captive. Untie me, why don't you? We'll see how brave you are then." He glanced at the Mad Huntsman behind him. "How about you? Or did you leave all your courage in your kennels?"

"No, but I should have left you in a crow cage." The Huntsman drew a knife. "I might still."

The Hound laughed in his face.

"We are brothers here," Thoros of Myr declared. "Holy brothers, sworn to the realm, to our god, and to each other."

"The brotherhood without banners." Tom Sevenstrings plucked a string. "The knights of the hollow hill."

"*Knights?*" Clegane made the word a sneer. "Dondarrion's a knight, but the rest of you are the sorriest lot of outlaws and broken men I've ever seen. I shit better men than you."

"Any knight can make a knight," said the scarecrow that was Beric Dondarrion, "and every man you see before you has felt a sword upon his shoulder. We are the forgotten fellowship."

"Send me on my way and I'll forget you too," Clegane rasped. "But if you mean to murder me, then bloody well get on with it. You took my sword, my horse, and my gold, so take my life and be done with it . . . but spare me this pious bleating."

"You will die soon enough, dog," promised Thoros, "but it shan't be murder, only justice."

"Aye," said the Mad Huntsman, "and a kinder fate than you deserve for all your kind have done. Lions, you call yourselves. At Sherrer and the Mummer's Ford, girls of six and seven years were raped, and babes still on the breast were cut in two while their mothers watched. No lion ever killed so cruel."

"I was not at Sherrer, nor the Mummer's Ford," the Hound told him. "Lay your dead children at some other door."

Thoros answered him. "Do you deny that House Clegane was built upon dead children? I saw them lay Prince Aegon and Princess Rhaenys before the Iron Throne. By rights your arms should bear two bloody infants in place of those ugly dogs."

The Hound's mouth twitched. "Do you take me for my brother? Is being born Clegane a crime?"

"Murder is a crime."

"Who did I murder?"

"Lord Lothar Mallery and Ser Gladden Wylde," said Harwin.

"My brothers Lister and Lennocks," declared Jack-Be-Lucky.

"Goodman Beck and Mudge the miller's son, from Donnelwood," an old woman called from the shadows.

"Merriman's widow, who loved so sweet," added Greenbeard.

"Them septons at Sludgy Pond."

"Ser Andrey Charlton. His squire Lucas Roote. Every man, woman, and child in Fieldstone and Mousedown Mill."

"Lord and Lady Deddings, that was so rich."

Tom Sevenstrings took up the count. "Alyn of Winterfell, Joth Quick-bow, Little Matt and his sister Randa, Anvil Ryn. Ser Ormond. Ser Dudley. Pate of Mory, Pate of Lancewood, Old Pate, and Pate of Shermer's Grove. Blind Wyl the Whittler. Goodwife Maerie. Maerie the Whore. Becca the Baker. Ser Raymun Darry, Lord Darry, young Lord Darry. The Bastard of Bracken. Fletcher Will. Harsley. Goodwife Nolla –"

"Enough." The Hound's face was tight with anger. "You're making noise. These names mean nothing. Who were they?"

"People," said Lord Beric. "People great and small, young and old. Good people and bad people, who died on the points of Lannister spears or saw their bellies opened by Lannister swords."

"It wasn't my sword in their bellies. Any man who says it was is a bloody liar."

"You serve the Lannisters of Casterly Rock," said Thoros.

"Once. Me and thousands more. Is each of us guilty of the crimes of the others?" Clegane spat. "Might be you are knights after all. You lie like knights, maybe you murder like knights."

Lem and Jack-Be-Lucky began to shout at him, but Dondarrion raised a hand for silence. "Say what you mean, Clegane."

"A knight's a sword with a horse. The rest, the vows and the sacred oils and the lady's favors, they're silk ribbons tied round the sword. Maybe the sword's prettier with ribbons hanging off it, but it will kill you just as dead. Well, bugger your ribbons, and shove your swords up your arses. I'm the same as you. The only difference is, I don't lie about what I am.

So kill me, but don't call me a murderer while you stand there telling each other that your shit don't stink. *You hear me?*"

Arya squirted past Greenbeard so fast he never saw her. "You *are* a murderer!" she screamed. "You killed *Mycah*, don't say you never did. You *murdered* him!"

The Hound stared at her with no flicker of recognition. "And who was this Mycah, boy?"

"I'm not a boy! But Mycah was. He was a butcher's boy and you *killed* him. Jory said you cut him near in half, and he never even had a sword." She could feel them looking at her now, the women and the children and the men who called themselves the knights of the hollow hill. "Who's this now?" someone asked.

The Hound answered. "*Seven hells.* The little sister. The brat who tossed Joff's pretty sword in the river." He gave a bark of laughter. "Don't you know you're dead?"

"No, *you're* dead," she threw back at him.

Harwin took her arm to draw her back as Lord Beric said, "The girl has named you a murderer. Do you deny killing this butcher's boy, Mycah?"

The big man shrugged. "I was Joffrey's sworn shield. The butcher's boy attacked a prince of the blood."

"That's a *lie!*" Arya squirmed in Harwin's grip. "It was *me.* I hit Joffrey and threw Lion's Paw in the river. Mycah just ran away, like I told him."

"Did you see the boy attack Prince Joffrey?" Lord Beric Dondarrion asked the Hound.

"I heard it from the royal lips. It's not my place to question princes." Clegane jerked his hands toward Arya. "This one's own sister told the same tale when she stood before your precious Robert."

"Sansa's just a liar," Arya said, furious at her sister all over again. "It wasn't like she said. It *wasn't.*"

Thoros drew Lord Beric aside. The two men stood talking in low whispers while Arya seethed. *They have to kill him. I prayed for him to die, hundreds and hundreds of times.*

Beric Dondarrion turned back to the Hound. "You stand accused of murder, but no one here knows the truth or falsehood of the charge, so it is not for us to judge you. Only the Lord of Light may do that now. I sentence you to trial by battle."

The Hound frowned suspiciously, as if he did not trust his ears. "Are you a fool or a madman?"

"Neither. I am a just lord. Prove your innocence with a blade, and you shall be free to go."

"No," Arya cried, before Harwin covered her mouth. *No, they can't, he'll go free.* The Hound was deadly with a sword, everyone knew that. *He'll laugh at them,* she thought.

And so he did, a long rasping laugh that echoed off the cave walls, a laugh choking with contempt. "So who will it be?" He looked at Lem Lemoncloak. "The brave man in the piss-yellow cloak? No? How about you, Huntsman? You've kicked dogs before, try me." He saw Greenbeard. "You're big enough, Tyrosh, step forward. Or do you mean to make the little girl fight me herself?" He laughed again. "Come on, who wants to die?"

"It's me you'll face," said Lord Beric Dondarrion.

Arya remembered all the tales. *He can't be killed,* she thought, hoping against hope. The Mad Huntsman sliced apart the ropes that bound Sandor Clegane's hands together. "I'll need sword and armor." The Hound rubbed a torn wrist.

"Your sword you shall have," declared Lord Beric, "but your innocence must be your armor."

Clegane's mouth twitched. "My innocence against your breastplate, is that the way of it?"

"Ned, help me remove my breastplate."

Arya got goosebumps when Lord Beric said her father's name, but this Ned was only a boy, a fair-haired squire no more than ten or twelve. He stepped up quickly to undo the clasps that fastened the battered steel about the Marcher lord. The quilting beneath was rotten with age and sweat, and fell away when the metal was pulled loose. Gendry sucked in his breath. "Mother have mercy."

Lord Beric's ribs were outlined starkly beneath his skin. A puckered crater scarred his breast just above his left nipple, and when he turned to call for sword and shield, Arya saw a matching scar upon his back. *The lance went through him.* The Hound had seen it too. *Is he scared?* Arya wanted him to be scared before he died, as scared as Mycah must have been.

Ned fetched Lord Beric his swordbelt and a long black surcoat. It was meant to be worn over armor, so it draped his body loosely, but across it crackled the forked purple lightning of his House. He unsheathed his sword and gave the belt back to his squire.

Thoros brought the Hound his swordbelt. "Does a dog have honor?" the priest asked. "Lest you think to cut your way free of here, or seize some child for a hostage . . . Anguy, Dennet, Kyle, feather him at the first sign of treachery." Only when the three bowmen had notched their shafts did Thoros hand Clegane the belt.

The Hound ripped the sword free and threw away the scabbard. The Mad Huntsman gave him his oaken shield, all studded with iron and painted yellow, the three black dogs of Clegane emblazoned upon it. The boy Ned helped Lord Beric with his own shield, so hacked and battered that the purple lightning and the scatter of stars upon it had almost been obliterated.

But when the Hound made to step toward his foe, Thoros of Myr stopped him. "First we pray." He turned toward the fire and lifted his arms. "Lord of Light, look down upon us."

All around the cave, the brotherhood without banners lifted their own voices in response. *"Lord of Light, defend us."*

"Lord of Light, protect us in the darkness."

"Lord of Light, shine your face upon us."

"Light your flame among us, R'hllor," said the red priest. "Show us the truth or falseness of this man. Strike him down if he is guilty, and give strength to his sword if he is true. Lord of Light, give us wisdom."

"For the night is dark," the others chanted, Harwin and Anguy loud as all the rest, *"and full of terrors."*

"This cave is dark too," said the Hound, "but I'm the terror here. I hope your god's a sweet one, Dondarrion. You're going to meet him shortly."

Unsmiling, Lord Beric laid the edge of his longsword against the palm of his left hand, and drew it slowly down. Blood ran dark from the gash he made, and washed over the steel.

And then the sword took fire.

Arya heard Gendry whisper a prayer.

"Burn in seven hells," the Hound cursed. "You, and Thoros too." He threw a glance at the red priest. "When I'm done with him you'll be next, Myr."

"Every word you say proclaims your guilt, dog," answered Thoros, while Lem and Greenbeard and Jack-Be-Lucky shouted threats and curses. Lord Beric himself waited silent, calm as still water, his shield on his left arm and his sword burning in his right hand. *Kill him,* Arya thought, *please, you have to kill him.* Lit from below, his face was a death mask, his missing eye a red and angry wound. The sword was aflame from point to crossguard, but Dondarrion seemed not to feel the heat. He stood so still he might have been carved of stone.

But when the Hound charged him, he moved fast enough.

The flaming sword leapt up to meet the cold one, long streamers of fire trailing in its wake like the ribbons the Hound had spoken of. Steel rang on steel. No sooner was his first slash blocked than Clegane made another, but this time Lord Beric's shield got in the way, and wood chips flew from the force of the blow. Hard and fast the cuts came, from low and high, from right and left, and each one Dondarrion blocked. The flames swirled about his sword and left red and yellow ghosts to mark its passage. Each move Lord Beric made fanned them and made them burn the brighter, until it seemed as though the lightning lord stood within a cage of fire. "Is it wildfire?" Arya asked Gendry.

"No. This is different. This is . . ."

". . . magic?" she finished as the Hound edged back. Now it was Lord

Beric attacking, filling the air with ropes of fire, driving the bigger man back on his heels. Clegane caught one blow high on his shield, and a painted dog lost a head. He countercut, and Dondarrion interposed his own shield and launched a fiery backslash. The outlaw brotherhood shouted on their leader. *"He's yours!"* Arya heard, and *"At him! At him! At him!"* The Hound parried a cut at his head, grimacing as the heat of the flames beat against his face. He grunted and cursed and reeled away.

Lord Beric gave him no respite. Hard on the big man's heels he followed, his arm never still. The swords clashed and sprang apart and clashed again, splinters flew from the lightning shield while swirling flames kissed the dogs once, and twice, and thrice. The Hound moved to his right, but Dondarrion blocked him with a quick sidestep and drove him back the other way . . . toward the sullen red blaze of the firepit. Clegane gave ground until he felt the heat at his back. A quick glance over his shoulder showed him what was behind him, and almost cost him his head when Lord Beric attacked anew.

Arya could see the whites of Sandor Clegane's eyes as he bulled his way forward again. Three steps up and two back, a move to the left that Lord Beric blocked, two more forward and one back, *clang* and *clang*, and the big oaken shields took blow after blow after blow. The Hound's lank dark hair was plastered to his brow in a sheen of sweat. *Wine sweat,* Arya thought, remembering that he'd been taken drunk. She thought she could see the beginnings of fear wake in his eyes. *He's going to lose,* she told herself, exulting, as Lord Beric's flaming sword whirled and slashed. In one wild flurry, the lightning lord took back all the ground the Hound had gained, sending Clegane staggering to the very edge of the firepit once more. *He is, he is, he's going to die.* She stood on her toes for a better look.

"Bloody bastard!" the Hound screamed as he felt the fire licking against the back of his thighs. He charged, swinging the heavy sword harder and harder, trying to smash the smaller man down with brute force, to break blade or shield or arm. But the flames of Dondarrion's parries snapped at his eyes, and when the Hound jerked away from them, his foot went out from under him and he staggered to one knee. At once Lord Beric closed, his downcut screaming through the air trailing pennons of fire. Panting from exertion, Clegane jerked his shield up over his head just in time, and the cave rang with the loud *crack* of splintering oak.

"His shield is afire," Gendry said in a hushed voice. Arya saw it in the same instant. The flames had spread across the chipped yellow paint, and the three black dogs were engulfed.

Sandor Clegane had fought his way back to his feet with a reckless counterattack. Not until Lord Beric retreated a pace did the Hound seem to realize that the fire that roared so near his face was his own shield,

burning. With a shout of revulsion, he hacked down savagely on the
broken oak, completing its destruction. The shield shattered, one piece
of it spinning away, still afire, while the other clung stubbornly to his
forearm. His efforts to free himself only fanned the flames. His sleeve
caught, and now his whole left arm was ablaze. *"Finish him!"* Greenbeard
urged Lord Beric, and other voices took up the chant of *"Guilty!"* Arya
shouted with the rest. *"Guilty, guilty, kill him, guilty!"*

Smooth as summer silk, Lord Beric slid close to make an end of the
man before him. The Hound gave a rasping scream, raised his sword in
both hands and brought it crashing down with all his strength. Lord Beric
blocked the cut easily . . .

"Noooooo," Arya shrieked.

. . . but the burning sword snapped in two, and the Hound's cold steel
plowed into Lord Beric's flesh where his shoulder joined his neck and
clove him clean down to the breastbone. The blood came rushing out in
a hot black gush.

Sandor Clegane jerked backward, still burning. He ripped the remnants
of his shield off and flung them away with a curse, then rolled in the
dirt to smother the fire running along his arm.

Lord Beric's knees folded slowly, as if for prayer. When his mouth
opened only blood came out. The Hound's sword was still in him as he
toppled face forward. The dirt drank his blood. Beneath the hollow hill
there was no sound but the soft crackling of flames and the whimper the
Hound made when he tried to rise. Arya could only think of Mycah and
all the stupid prayers she'd prayed for the Hound to die. *If there were
gods, why didn't Lord Beric win?* She *knew* the Hound was guilty.

"Please," Sandor Clegane rasped, cradling his arm. "I'm burned. Help
me. Someone. Help me." He was crying. *"Please."*

Arya looked at him in astonishment. *He's crying like a little baby,*
she thought.

"Melly, see to his burns," said Thoros. "Lem, Jack, help me with Lord
Beric. Ned, you'd best come too." The red priest wrenched the Hound's
sword from the body of his fallen lord and thrust the point of it down in
the blood-soaked earth. Lem slid his big hands under Dondarrion's arms,
while Jack-Be-Lucky took his feet. They carried him around the firepit,
into the darkness of one of the tunnels. Thoros and the boy Ned followed
after.

The Mad Huntsman spat. "I say we take him back to Stoney Sept and
put him in a crow cage."

"Yes," Arya said. "He murdered Mycah. He *did*."

"Such an angry squirrel," murmured Greenbeard.

Harwin sighed. "R'hllor has judged him innocent."

"Who's *Rulore?*" She couldn't even say it.

"The Lord of Light. Thoros has taught us –"

She didn't care what Thoros had taught them. She yanked Greenbeard's dagger from its sheath and spun away before he could catch her. Gendry made a grab for her as well, but she had always been too fast for Gendry.

Tom Sevenstrings and some woman were helping the Hound to his feet. The sight of his arm shocked her speechless. There was a strip of pink where the leather strap had clung, but above and below the flesh was cracked and red and bleeding from elbow to wrist. When his eyes met hers, his mouth twitched. "You want me dead that bad? Then do it, wolf girl. Shove it in. It's cleaner than fire." Clegane tried to stand, but as he moved a piece of burned flesh sloughed right off his arm, and his knees went out from under him. Tom caught him by his good arm and held him up.

His arm, Arya thought, and *his face*. But he was the Hound. He deserved to burn in a fiery hell. The knife felt heavy in her hand. She gripped it tighter. "You killed Mycah," she said once more, daring him to deny it. "Tell them. You did. You *did*."

"I did." His whole face twisted. "I rode him down and cut him in half, and laughed. I watched them beat your sister bloody too, watched them cut your father's head off."

Lem grabbed her wrist and twisted, wrenching the dagger away. She kicked at him, but he would not give it back. "You go to hell, Hound," she screamed at Sandor Clegane in helpless empty-handed rage. "*You just go to hell!*"

"He has," said a voice scarce stronger than a whisper.

When Arya turned, Lord Beric Dondarrion was standing behind her, his bloody hand clutching Thoros by the shoulder.

CATELYN

*L*et the kings of winter have their cold crypt under the earth, Catelyn thought. The Tullys drew their strength from the river, and it was to the river they returned when their lives had run their course.

They laid Lord Hoster in a slender wooden boat, clad in shining silver armor, plate-and-mail. His cloak was spread beneath him, rippling blue and red. His surcoat was divided blue-and-red as well. A trout, scaled in silver and bronze, crowned the crest of the greathelm they placed beside his head. On his chest they placed a painted wooden sword, his fingers curled about its hilt. Mail gauntlets hid his wasted hands, and made him look almost strong again. His massive oak-and-iron shield was set by his left side, his hunting horn to his right. The rest of the boat was filled with driftwood and kindling and scraps of parchment, and stones to make it heavy in the water. His banner flew from the prow, the leaping trout of Riverrun.

Seven were chosen to push the funereal boat to the water, in honor of the seven faces of god. Robb was one, Lord Hoster's liege lord. With him were the Lords Bracken, Blackwood, Vance, and Mallister, Ser Marq Piper . . . and Lame Lothar Frey, who had come down from the Twins with the answer they had awaited. Forty soldiers rode in his escort, commanded by Walder Rivers, the eldest of Lord Walder's bastard brood, a stern, grey-haired man with a formidable reputation as a warrior. Their arrival, coming within hours of Lord Hoster's passing, had sent Edmure into a rage. "Walder Frey should be flayed and quartered!" he'd shouted. "He sends a cripple and a bastard to treat with us, tell me there is no insult meant by that."

"I have no doubt that Lord Walder chose his envoys with care," she replied. "It was a peevish thing to do, a petty sort of revenge, but remember who we are dealing with. The Late Lord Frey, Father used to call him. The man is ill-tempered, envious, and above all *prideful*."

Blessedly, her son had shown better sense than her brother. Robb had greeted the Freys with every courtesy, found barracks space for the escort, and quietly asked Ser Desmond Grell to stand aside so Lothar might have the honor of helping to send Lord Hoster on his last voyage. *He has learned a rough wisdom beyond his years, my son.* House Frey might have abandoned the King in the North, but the Lord of the Crossing remained the most powerful of Riverrun's bannermen, and Lothar was here in his stead.

The seven launched Lord Hoster from the water stair, wading down the steps as the portcullis was winched upward. Lothar Frey, a soft-bodied portly man, was breathing heavily as they shoved the boat out into the current. Jason Mallister and Tytos Blackwood, at the prow, stood chest deep in the river to guide it on its way.

Catelyn watched from the battlements, waiting and watching as she had waited and watched so many times before. Beneath her, the swift wild Tumblestone plunged like a spear into the side of the broad Red Fork, its blue-white current churning the muddy red-brown flow of the greater river. A morning mist hung over the water, as thin as gossamer and the wisps of memory.

Bran and Rickon will be waiting for him, Catelyn thought sadly, *as once I used to wait.*

The slim boat drifted out from under the red stone arch of the Water Gate, picking up speed as it was caught in the headlong rush of the Tumblestone and pushed out into the tumult where the waters met. As the boat emerged from beneath the high sheltering walls of the castle, its square sail filled with wind, and Catelyn saw sunlight flashing on her father's helm. Lord Hoster Tully's rudder held true, and he sailed serenely down the center of the channel, into the rising sun.

"Now," her uncle urged. Beside him, her brother Edmure – *Lord Edmure* now in truth, and how long would that take to grow used to? – nocked an arrow to his bowstring. His squire held a brand to its point. Edmure waited until the flame caught, then lifted the great bow, drew the string to his ear, and let fly. With a deep *thrum*, the arrow sped upward. Catelyn followed its flight with her eyes and heart, until it plunged into the water with a soft *hiss*, well astern of Lord Hoster's boat.

Edmure cursed softly. "The wind," he said, pulling a second arrow. "Again." The brand kissed the oil-soaked rag behind the arrowhead, the flames went licking up, Edmure lifted, pulled, and released. High and far the arrow flew. Too far. It vanished in the river a dozen yards beyond the boat, its fire winking out in an instant. A flush was creeping up Edmure's neck, red as his beard. "Once more," he commanded, taking a third arrow from the quiver. *He is as tight as his bowstring*, Catelyn thought.

Ser Brynden must have seen the same thing. "Let me, my lord," he offered.

"I can do it," Edmure insisted. He let them light the arrow, jerked the bow up, took a deep breath, drew back the arrow. For a long moment he seemed to hesitate while the fire crept up the shaft, crackling. Finally he released. The arrow flashed up and up, and finally curved down again, falling, falling . . . and hissing past the billowing sail.

A narrow miss, no more than a handspan, and yet a miss. "The Others take it!" her brother swore. The boat was almost out of range, drifting in and out among the river mists. Wordless, Edmure thrust the bow at his uncle.

"Swiftly," Ser Brynden said. He nocked an arrow, held it steady for the brand, drew and released before Catelyn was quite sure that the fire had caught . . . but as the shot rose, she saw the flames trailing through the air, a pale orange pennon. The boat had vanished in the mists. Falling, the flaming arrow was swallowed up as well . . . but only for a heartbeat. Then, sudden as hope, they saw the red bloom flower. The sails took fire, and the fog glowed pink and orange. For a moment Catelyn saw the outline of the boat clearly, wreathed in leaping flames.

Watch for me, little cat, she could hear him whisper.

Catelyn reached out blindly, groping for her brother's hand, but Edmure had moved away, to stand alone on the highest point of the battlements. Her uncle Brynden took her hand instead, twining his strong fingers through hers. Together they watched the little fire grow smaller as the burning boat receded in the distance.

And then it was gone . . . drifting downriver still, perhaps, or broken up and sinking. The weight of his armor would carry Lord Hoster down to rest in the soft mud of the riverbed, in the watery halls where the Tullys held eternal court, with schools of fish their last attendants.

No sooner had the burning boat vanished from their sight than Edmure walked off. Catelyn would have liked to embrace him, if only for a moment; to sit for an hour or a night or the turn of a moon to speak of the dead and mourn. Yet she knew as well as he that this was not the time; he was Lord of Riverrun now, and his knights were falling in around him, murmuring condolences and promises of fealty, walling him off from something as small as a sister's grief. Edmure listened, hearing none of the words.

"It is no disgrace to miss your shot," her uncle told her quietly. "Edmure should hear that. The day my own lord father went downriver, Hoster missed as well."

"With his first shaft." Catelyn had been too young to remember, but Lord Hoster had often told the tale. "His second found the sail." She sighed. Edmure was not as strong as he seemed. Their father's death had been a mercy when it came at last, but even so her brother had taken it hard.

Last night in his cups he had broken down and wept, full of regrets for things undone and words unsaid. He ought never to have ridden off to fight his battle on the fords, he told her tearfully; he should have stayed at their father's bedside. "I should have been with him, as you were," he said. "Did he speak of me at the end? Tell me true, Cat. Did he ask for me?"

Lord Hoster's last word had been *"Tansy,"* but Catelyn could not bring herself to tell him that. "He whispered your name," she lied, and her brother had nodded gratefully and kissed her hand. *If he had not tried to drown his grief and guilt, he might have been able to bend a bow,* she thought to herself, sighing, but that was something else she dare not say.

The Blackfish escorted her down from the battlements to where Robb stood among his bannermen, his young queen at his side. When he saw her, her son took her silently in his arms.

"Lord Hoster looked as noble as a king, my lady," murmured Jeyne. "Would that I had been given the chance to know him."

"And I to know him better," added Robb.

"He would have wished that too," said Catelyn. "There were too many leagues between Riverrun and Winterfell." *And too many mountains and rivers and armies between Riverrun and the Eyrie, it would seem.* Lysa had made no reply to her letter.

And from King's Landing came only silence as well. By now she had hoped that Brienne and Ser Cleos would have reached the city with their captive. It might even be that Brienne was on her way back, and the girls with her. *Ser Cleos swore he would make the Imp send a raven once the trade was made. He swore it!* Ravens did not always win through. Some bowman could have brought the bird down and roasted him for supper. The letter that would have set her heart at ease might even now be lying by the ashes of some campfire beside a pile of raven bones.

Others were waiting to offer Robb their consolations, so Catelyn stood aside patiently while Lord Jason Mallister, the Greatjon, and Ser Rolph Spicer spoke to him each in turn. But when Lothar Frey approached, she gave his sleeve a tug. Robb turned, and waited to hear what Lothar would say.

"Your Grace." A plump man in his middle thirties, Lothar Frey had close-set eyes, a pointed beard, and dark hair that fell to his shoulders in ringlets. A leg twisted at birth had earned him the name *Lame Lothar*. He had served as his father's steward for the past dozen years. "We are loath to intrude upon your grief, but perhaps you might grant us audience tonight?"

"It would be my pleasure," said Robb. "It was never my wish to sow enmity between us."

"Nor mine to be the cause of it," said Queen Jeyne.

Lothar Frey smiled. "I understand, as does my lord father. He instructed me to say that he was young once, and well remembers what it is like to lose one's heart to beauty."

Catelyn doubted very much that Lord Walder had said any such thing, or that he had ever lost his heart to beauty. The Lord of the Crossing had outlived seven wives and was now wed to his eighth, but he spoke of them only as bedwarmers and brood mares. Still, the words were fairly spoken, and she could scarce object to the compliment. Nor did Robb. "Your father is most gracious," he said. "I shall look forward to our talk."

Lothar bowed, kissed the queen's hand, and withdrew. By then a dozen others had gathered for a word. Robb spoke with them each, giving a thanks here, a smile there, as needed. Only when the last of them was done did he turn back to Catelyn. "There is something we must speak of. Will you walk with me?"

"As you command, Your Grace."

"That wasn't a command, Mother."

"It will be my pleasure, then." Her son had treated her kindly enough since returning to Riverrun, yet he seldom sought her out. If he was more comfortable with his young queen, she could scarcely blame him. *Jeyne makes him smile, and I have nothing to share with him but grief.* He seemed to enjoy the company of his bride's brothers, as well; young Rollam his squire and Ser Raynald his standard-bearer. *They are standing in the boots of those he's lost,* Catelyn realized when she watched them together. *Rollam has taken Bran's place, and Raynald is part Theon and part Jon Snow.* Only with the Westerlings did she see Robb smile, or hear him laugh like the boy he was. To the others he was always the King in the North, head bowed beneath the weight of the crown even when his brows were bare.

Robb kissed his wife gently, promised to see her in their chambers, and went off with his lady mother. His steps led them toward the godswood. "Lothar seemed amiable, that's a hopeful sign. We need the Freys."

"That does not mean we shall have them."

He nodded, and there was glumness to his face and a slope to his shoulders that made her heart go out to him. *The crown is crushing him,* she thought. *He wants so much to be a good king, to be brave and honorable and clever, but the weight is too much for a boy to bear.* Robb was doing all he could, yet still the blows kept falling, one after the other, relentless. When they brought him word of the battle at Duskendale, where Lord Randyll Tarly had shattered Robett Glover and Ser Helman Tallhart, he might have been expected to rage. Instead he'd stared in dumb disbelief and said, "Duskendale, on the narrow sea? Why would they go to Duskendale?" He'd shook his head, bewildered. "A third of my foot, lost for *Duskendale?*"

"The ironmen have my castle and now the Lannisters hold my brother," Galbart Glover said, in a voice thick with despair. Robett Glover had survived the battle, but had been captured near the kingsroad not long after.

"Not for long," her son promised. "I will offer them Martyn Lannister in exchange. Lord Tywin will have to accept, for his brother's sake." Martyn was Ser Kevan's son, a twin to the Willem that Lord Karstark had butchered. Those murders still haunted her son, Catelyn knew. He had tripled the guard around Martyn, but still feared for his safety.

"I should have traded the Kingslayer for Sansa when you first urged it," Robb said as they walked the gallery. "If I'd offered to wed her to the Knight of Flowers, the Tyrells might be ours instead of Joffrey's. I should have thought of that."

"Your mind was on your battles, and rightly so. Even a king cannot think of everything."

"Battles," muttered Robb as he led her out beneath the trees. "I have won every battle, yet somehow I'm losing the war." He looked up, as if the answer might be written on the sky. "The ironmen hold Winterfell, and Moat Cailin too. Father's dead, and Bran and Rickon, maybe Arya. And now your father too."

She could not let him despair. She knew the taste of that draught too well herself. "My father has been dying for a long time. You could not have changed that. You have made mistakes, Robb, but what king has not? Ned would have been proud of you."

"Mother, there is something you must know."

Catelyn's heart skipped a beat. *This is something he hates. Something he dreads to tell me.* All she could think of was Brienne and her mission. "Is it the Kingslayer?"

"No. It's Sansa."

She's dead, Catelyn thought at once. *Brienne failed, Jaime is dead, and Cersei has killed my sweet girl in retribution.* For a moment she could barely speak. "Is . . . is she gone, Robb?"

"Gone?" He looked startled. "Dead? Oh, Mother, no, not that, they haven't harmed her, not that way, only . . . a bird came last night, but I couldn't bring myself to tell you, not until your father was sent to his rest." Robb took her hand. "They married her to Tyrion Lannister."

Catelyn's fingers clutched at his. "The Imp."

"Yes."

"He swore to trade her for his brother," she said numbly. "Sansa and Arya both. We would have them back if we returned his precious Jaime, he swore it before the whole court. How could he marry her, after saying that in sight of gods and men?"

"He's the Kingslayer's brother. Oathbreaking runs in their blood." Robb's fingers brushed the pommel of his sword. "If I could I'd take his ugly head off. Sansa would be a widow then, and free. There's no other way that I can see. They made her speak the vows before a septon and don a crimson cloak."

Catelyn remembered the twisted little man she had seized at the crossroads inn and carried all the way to the Eyrie. "I should have let Lysa push him out her Moon Door. My poor sweet Sansa . . . why would anyone do this to her?"

"For Winterfell," Robb said at once. "With Bran and Rickon dead, Sansa is my heir. If anything should happen to me . . ."

She clutched tight at his hand. "Nothing will happen to you. *Nothing.* I could not stand it. They took Ned, and your sweet brothers. Sansa is married, Arya is lost, my father's dead . . . if anything befell you, I would go mad, Robb. You are all I have left. You are all the *north* has left."

"I am not dead yet, Mother."

Suddenly Catelyn was full of dread. "Wars need not be fought until the last drop of blood." Even she could hear the desperation in her voice. "You would not be the first king to bend the knee, nor even the first Stark."

His mouth tightened. "No. Never."

"There is no shame in it. Balon Greyjoy bent the knee to Robert when his rebellion failed. Torrhen Stark bent the knee to Aegon the Conqueror rather than see his army face the fires."

"Did Aegon kill King Torrhen's father?" He pulled his hand from hers. "Never, I said."

He is playing the boy now, not the king. "The Lannisters do not need the north. They will require homage and hostages, no more . . . and the Imp will keep Sansa no matter what we do, so they have their hostage. The ironmen will prove a more implacable enemy, I promise you. To have any hope of holding the north, the Greyjoys must leave no single sprig of House Stark alive to dispute their right. Theon's murdered Bran and Rickon, so now all they need do is kill you . . . *and* Jeyne, yes. Do you think Lord Balon can afford to let her live to bear you heirs?"

Robb's face was cold. "Is that why you freed the Kingslayer? To make a peace with the Lannisters?"

"I freed Jaime for Sansa's sake . . . and Arya's, if she still lives. You know that. But if I nurtured some hope of buying peace as well, was that so ill?"

"Yes," he said. "The Lannisters killed my father."

"Do you think I have forgotten that?"

"I don't know. Have you?"

Catelyn had never struck her children in anger, but she almost struck Robb then. It was an effort to remind herself how frightened and alone he must feel. "You are King in the North, the choice is yours. I only ask that you think on what I've said. The singers make much of kings who die valiantly in battle, but your life is worth more than a song. To me at least, who gave it to you." She lowered her head. "Do I have your leave to go?"

"Yes." He turned away and drew his sword. What he meant to do with it, she could not say. There was no enemy there, no one to fight. Only her and him, amongst tall trees and fallen leaves. *There are fights no sword can win*, Catelyn wanted to tell him, but she feared the king was deaf to such words.

Hours later, she was sewing in her bedchamber when young Rollam Westerling came running with the summons to supper. *Good*, Catelyn thought, relieved. She had not been certain that her son would want her there, after their quarrel. "A dutiful squire," she said to Rollam gravely. *Bran would have been the same.*

If Robb seemed cool at table and Edmure surly, Lame Lothar made up for them both. He was the model of courtesy, reminiscing warmly about Lord Hoster, offering Catelyn gentle condolences on the loss of Bran and Rickon, praising Edmure for the victory at Stone Mill, and thanking Robb for the "swift sure justice" he had meted out to Rickard Karstark. Lothar's bastard brother Walder Rivers was another matter; a harsh sour man with old Lord Walder's suspicious face, he spoke but seldom and devoted most of his attention to the meat and mead that was set before him.

When all the empty words were said, the queen and the other Westerlings excused themselves, the remains of the meal were cleared away, and Lothar Frey cleared his throat. "Before we turn to the business that brings us here, there is another matter," he said solemnly. "A grave matter, I fear. I had hoped it would not fall to me to bring you these tidings, but it seems I must. My lord father has had a letter from his grandsons."

Catelyn had been so lost in grief for her own that she had almost forgotten the two Freys she had agreed to foster. *No more*, she thought. *Mother have mercy, how many more blows can we bear?* Somehow she knew the next words she heard would plunge yet another blade into her heart. "The grandsons at Winterfell?" she made herself ask. "My wards?"

"Walder and Walder, yes. But they are presently at the Dreadfort, my lady. I grieve to tell you this, but there has been a battle. Winterfell is burned."

"*Burned?*" Robb's voice was incredulous.

"Your northern lords tried to retake it from the ironmen. When Theon Greyjoy saw that his prize was lost, he put the castle to the torch."

"We have heard naught of any battle," said Ser Brynden.

"My nephews are young, I grant you, but they were there. Big Walder wrote the letter, though his cousin signed as well. It was a bloody bit of business, by their account. Your castellan was slain. Ser Rodrik, was that his name?"

"Ser Rodrik Cassel," said Catelyn numbly. *That dear brave loyal old soul.* She could almost see him, tugging on his fierce white whiskers. "What of our other people?"

"The ironmen put many of them to the sword, I fear."

Wordless with rage, Robb slammed a fist down on the table and turned his face away, so the Freys would not see his tears.

But his mother saw them. *The world grows a little darker every day.* Catelyn's thoughts went to Ser Rodrik's little daughter Beth, to tireless Maester Luwin and cheerful Septon Chayle, Mikken at the forge, Farlen and Palla in the kennels, Old Nan and simple Hodor. Her heart was sick. "Please, not *all.*"

"No," said Lame Lothar. "The women and children hid, my nephews Walder and Walder among them. With Winterfell in ruins, the survivors were carried back to the Dreadfort by this son of Lord Bolton's."

"Bolton's *son?*" Robb's voice was strained.

Walder Rivers spoke up. "A bastard son, I believe."

"Not Ramsay Snow? Does Lord Roose have another bastard?" Robb scowled. "This Ramsay was a monster and a murderer, and he died a coward. Or so I was told."

"I cannot speak to that. There is much confusion in any war. Many false reports. All I can tell you is that my nephews claim it was this bastard son of Bolton's who saved the women of Winterfell, and the little ones. They are safe at the Dreadfort now, all those who remain."

"Theon," Robb said suddenly. "What happened to Theon Greyjoy? Was he slain?"

Lame Lothar spread his hands. "That I cannot say, Your Grace. Walder and Walder made no mention of his fate. Perhaps Lord Bolton might know, if he has had word from this son of his."

Ser Brynden said, "We will be certain to ask him."

"You are all distraught, I see. I am sorry to have brought you such fresh grief. Perhaps we should adjourn until the morrow. Our business can wait until you have composed yourselves . . ."

"No," said Robb, "I want the matter settled."

Her brother Edmure nodded. "Me as well. Do you have an answer to our offer, my lord?"

"I do." Lothar smiled. "My lord father bids me tell Your Grace that he will agree to this new marriage alliance between our houses and renew his fealty to the King in the North, upon the condition that the King's Grace apologize for the insult done to House Frey, in his royal person, face to face."

An apology was a small enough price to pay, but Catelyn misliked this petty condition of Lord Walder's at once.

"I am pleased," Robb said cautiously. "It was never my wish to cause this rift between us, Lothar. The Freys have fought valiantly for my cause. I would have them at my side once more."

"You are too kind, Your Grace. As you accept these terms, I am then instructed to offer Lord Tully the hand of my sister, the Lady Roslin, a maid of sixteen years. Roslin is my lord father's youngest daughter by Lady Bethany of House Rosby, his sixth wife. She has a gentle nature and a gift for music."

Edmure shifted in his seat. "Might not it be better if I first met –"

"You'll meet when you're wed," said Walder Rivers curtly. "Unless Lord Tully feels a need to count her teeth first?"

Edmure kept his temper. "I will take your word so far as her teeth are concerned, but it would be pleasant if I might gaze upon her face before I espoused her."

"You must accept her now, my lord," said Walder Rivers. "Else my father's offer is withdrawn."

Lame Lothar spread his hands. "My brother has a soldier's bluntness, but what he says is true. It is my lord father's wish that this marriage take place at once."

"*At once?*" Edmure sounded so unhappy that Catelyn had the unworthy thought that perhaps he had been entertaining notions of breaking the betrothal after the fighting was done.

"Has Lord Walder forgotten that we are fighting a war?" Brynden Blackfish asked sharply.

"Scarcely," said Lothar. "That is why he insists that the marriage take place now, ser. Men die in war, even men who are young and strong. What would become of our alliance should Lord Edmure fall before he took Roslin to bride? And there is my father's age to consider as well. He is past ninety and not like to see the end of this struggle. It would put his noble heart at peace if he could see his dear Roslin safely wed before the gods take him, so he might die with the knowledge that the girl had a strong husband to cherish and protect her."

We all want Lord Walder to die happy. Catelyn was growing less and less comfortable with this arrangement. "My brother has just lost his own father. He needs time to mourn."

"Roslin is a cheerful girl," said Lothar. "She may be the very thing Lord Edmure needs to help him through his grief."

"And my grandfather has come to mislike lengthy betrothals," the bastard Walder Rivers added. "I cannot imagine why."

Robb gave him a chilly look. "I take your meaning, Rivers. Pray excuse us."

"As Your Grace commands." Lame Lothar rose, and his bastard brother helped him hobble from the room.

Edmure was seething. "They're as much as saying that my promise is worthless. Why should I let that old weasel choose my bride? Lord Walder has other daughters besides this Roslin. Granddaughters as well. I should be offered the same choice you were. I'm his liege lord, he should be overjoyed that I'm willing to wed *any* of them."

"He is a proud man, and we've wounded him," said Catelyn.

"The Others take his pride! I will not be shamed in my own hall. My answer is no."

Robb gave him a weary look. "I will not command you. Not in this. But if you refuse, Lord Frey will take it for another slight, and any hope of putting this arights will be gone."

"You cannot know that," Edmure insisted. "Frey has wanted me for one of his daughters since the day I was born. He will not let a chance like this slip between those grasping fingers of his. When Lothar brings him our answer, he'll come wheedling back and accept a betrothal . . . and to a daughter of *my* choosing."

"Perhaps, in time," said Brynden Blackfish. "But can we wait, while Lothar rides back and forth with offers and counters?"

Robb's hands curled into fists. "I *must* get back to the north. My brothers dead, Winterfell burned, my smallfolk put to the sword . . . the gods only know what this bastard of Bolton's is about, or whether Theon is still alive and on the loose. I can't sit here waiting for a wedding that might or might not happen."

"It *must* happen," said Catelyn, though not gladly. "I have no more wish to suffer Walder Frey's insults and complaints than you do, Brother, but I see little choice here. Without this wedding, Robb's cause is lost. Edmure, we must accept."

"*We* must accept?" he echoed peevishly. "I don't see you offering to become the ninth Lady Frey, Cat."

"The eighth Lady Frey is still alive and well, so far as I know," she replied. *Thankfully.* Otherwise it might well have come to that, knowing Lord Walder.

The Blackfish said, "I am the last man in the Seven Kingdoms to tell anyone who they must wed, Nephew. Nonetheless, you *did* say something of making amends for your Battle of the Fords."

"I had in mind a different sort of amends. Single combat with the Kingslayer. Seven years of penance as a begging brother. Swimming the sunset sea with my legs tied." When he saw that no one was smiling, Edmure threw up his hands. "The Others take you all! Very well, I'll wed the wench. As *amends*."

DAVOS

Lord Alester looked up sharply. "Voices," he said. "Do you hear, Davos? Someone is coming for us."

"Lamprey," said Davos. "It's time for our supper, or near enough." Last night Lamprey had brought them half a beef-and-bacon pie, and a flagon of mead as well. Just the thought of it made his belly start to rumble.

"No, there's more than one."

He's right. Davos heard two voices at least, and footsteps, growing louder. He got to his feet and moved to the bars.

Lord Alester brushed the straw from his clothes. "The king has sent for me. Or the queen, yes, Selyse would never let me rot here, her own blood."

Outside the cell, Lamprey appeared with a ring of keys in hand. Ser Axell Florent and four guardsmen followed close behind him. They waited beneath the torch while Lamprey searched for the correct key.

"Axell," Lord Alester said. "Gods be good. Is it the king who sends for me, or the queen?"

"No one has sent for you, traitor," Ser Axell said.

Lord Alester recoiled as if he'd been slapped. "No, I swear to you, I committed no treason. Why won't you listen? If His Grace would only let me explain – "

Lamprey thrust a great iron key into the lock, turned it, and pulled open the cell. The rusted hinges screamed in protest. "You," he said to Davos. "Come."

"Where?" Davos looked to Ser Axell. "Tell me true, ser, do you mean to burn me?"

"You are sent for. Can you walk?"

"I can walk." Davos stepped from the cell. Lord Alester gave a cry of dismay as Lamprey slammed the door shut once more.

"Take the torch," Ser Axell commanded the gaoler. "Leave the traitor to the darkness."

"No," his brother said. "Axell, please, don't take the light . . . gods have mercy . . ."

"Gods? There is only R'hllor, and the Other." Ser Axell gestured sharply, and one of his guardsmen pulled the torch from its sconce and led the way to the stair.

"Are you taking me to Melisandre?" Davos asked.

"She will be there," Ser Axell said. "She is never far from the king. But it is His Grace himself who asked for you."

Davos lifted his hand to his chest, where once his luck had hung in a leather bag on a thong. *Gone now*, he remembered, *and the ends of four fingers as well*. But his hands were still long enough to wrap about a woman's throat, he thought, especially a slender throat like hers.

Up they went, climbing the turnpike stair in single file. The walls were rough dark stone, cool to the touch. The light of the torches went before them, and their shadows marched beside them on the walls. At the third turn they passed an iron gate that opened on blackness, and another at the fifth turn. Davos guessed that they were near the surface by then, perhaps even above it. The next door they came to was made of wood, but still they climbed. Now the walls were broken by arrow slits, but no shafts of sunlight pried their way through the thickness of the stone. It was night outside.

His legs were aching by the time Ser Axell thrust open a heavy door and gestured him through. Beyond, a high stone bridge arched over emptiness to the massive central tower called the Stone Drum. A sea wind blew restlessly through the arches that supported the roof, and Davos could smell the salt water as they crossed. He took a deep breath, filling his lungs with the clean cold air. *Wind and water, give me strength*, he prayed. A huge nightfire burned in the yard below, to keep the terrors of the dark at bay, and the queen's men were gathered around it, singing praises to their new red god.

They were in the center of the bridge when Ser Axell stopped suddenly. He made a brusque gesture with his hand, and his men moved out of earshot. "Were it my choice, I would burn you with my brother Alester," he told Davos. "You are both traitors."

"Say what you will. I would never betray King Stannis."

"You would. You will. I see it in your face. And I have seen it in the flames as well. R'hllor has blessed me with that gift. Like Lady Melisandre, he shows me the future in the fire. Stannis Baratheon *will* sit the

Iron Throne. I have seen it. And I know what must be done. His Grace must make me his Hand, in place of my traitor brother. And you will tell him so."

Will I? Davos said nothing.

"The queen has urged my appointment," Ser Axell went on. "Even your old friend from Lys, the pirate Saan, he says the same. We have made a plan together, him and me. Yet His Grace does not act. The defeat gnaws inside him, a black worm in his soul. It is up to us who love him to show him what to do. If you are as devoted to his cause as you claim, smuggler, you will join your voice to ours. Tell him that I am the only Hand he needs. Tell him, and when we sail I shall see that you have a new ship."

A ship. Davos studied the other man's face. Ser Axell had big Florent ears, much like the queen's. Coarse hair grew from them, as from his nostrils; more sprouted in tufts and patches beneath his double chin. His nose was broad, his brow beetled, his eyes close-set and hostile. *He would sooner give me a pyre than a ship, he said as much, but if I do him this favor . . .*

"If you think to betray me," Ser Axell said, "pray remember that I have been castellan of Dragonstone a good long time. The garrison is mine. Perhaps I cannot burn you without the king's consent, but who is to say you might not suffer a fall." He laid a meaty hand on the back of Davos's neck and shoved him bodily against the waist-high side of the bridge, then shoved a little harder to force his face out over the yard. "Do you hear me?"

"I hear," said Davos. *And you dare name me traitor?*

Ser Axell released him. "Good." He smiled. "His Grace awaits. Best we do not keep him."

At the very top of Stone Drum, within the great round room called the Chamber of the Painted Table, they found Stannis Baratheon standing behind the artifact that gave the hall its name, a massive slab of wood carved and painted in the shape of Westeros as it had been in the time of Aegon the Conqueror. An iron brazier stood beside the king, its coals glowing a ruddy orange. Four tall pointed windows looked out to north, south, east, and west. Beyond was the night and the starry sky. Davos could hear the wind moving, and fainter, the sounds of the sea.

"Your Grace," Ser Axell said, "as it please you, I have brought the onion knight."

"So I see." Stannis wore a grey wool tunic, a dark red mantle, and a plain black leather belt from which his sword and dagger hung. A red-gold crown with flame-shaped points encircled his brows. The look of him was a shock. He seemed ten years older than the man that Davos had left at Storm's End when he set sail for the Blackwater and the battle that would be their undoing. The king's close-cropped beard was spiderwebbed with grey hairs, and he had dropped two stone or more of weight. He had never been a fleshy man, but now the bones moved beneath his skin like spears, fighting to cut free. Even his crown seemed too large for his head. His eyes were blue pits lost in deep hollows, and the shape of a skull could be seen beneath his face.

Yet when he saw Davos, a faint smile brushed his lips. "So the sea has returned me my knight of the fish and onions."

"It did, Your Grace." *Does he know that he had me in his dungeon?* Davos went to one knee.

"Rise, Ser Davos," Stannis commanded. "I have missed you, ser. I have need of good counsel, and you never gave me less. So tell me true – what is the penalty for treason?"

The word hung in the air. *A frightful word*, thought Davos. Was he being asked to condemn his cellmate? Or himself, perchance? *Kings know the penalty for treason better than any man.* "Treason?" he finally managed, weakly.

"What else would you call it, to deny your king and seek to steal his rightful throne. I ask you again – what is the penalty for treason under the law?"

Davos had no choice but to answer. "Death," he said. "The penalty is death, Your Grace."

"It has always been so. I am *not* . . . I am not a cruel man, Ser Davos. You know me. Have known me long. This is not my decree. It has always been so, since Aegon's day and before. Daemon Blackfyre, the brothers Toyne, the Vulture King, Grand Maester Hareth . . . traitors have always paid with their lives . . . even Rhaenyra Targaryen. She was daughter to one king and mother to two more, yet she died a traitor's death for trying to usurp her brother's crown. It is law. *Law*, Davos. Not cruelty."

"Yes, Your Grace." *He does not speak of me.* Davos felt a moment's pity for his cellmate down in the dark. He knew he should keep silent, but he was tired and sick of heart, and he heard himself say, "Sire, Lord Florent meant no treason."

"Do smugglers have another name for it? I made him Hand, and he would have sold my rights for a bowl of pease porridge. He would even have given them Shireen. Mine only child, he would have wed to a bastard born of incest." The king's voice was thick with anger. "My brother had a gift for inspiring loyalty. Even in his foes. At Summerhall he won three battles in a single day, and brought Lords Grandison and Cafferen back to Storm's End as prisoners. He hung their banners in the hall as trophies. Cafferen's white fawns were spotted with blood and Grandison's sleeping lion was torn near in two. Yet they would sit beneath those banners of a night, drinking and feasting with Robert. He even took them hunting.

'These men meant to deliver you to Aerys to be burned,' I told him after I saw them throwing axes in the yard. 'You should not be putting axes in their hands.' Robert only laughed. I would have thrown Grandison and Cafferen into a dungeon, but he turned them into friends. Lord Cafferen died at Ashford Castle, cut down by Randyll Tarly whilst fighting *for* Robert. Lord Grandison was wounded on the Trident and died of it a year after. My brother made them love him, but it would seem that I inspire only betrayal. Even in mine own blood and kin. Brother, grandfather, cousins, good uncle . . .''

"Your Grace," said Ser Axell, "I beg you, give me the chance to prove to you that not all Florents are so feeble."

"Ser Axell would have me resume the war," King Stannis told Davos. "The Lannisters think I am done and beaten, and my sworn lords have forsaken me, near every one. Even Lord Estermont, my own mother's father, has bent his knee to Joffrey. The few loyal men who remain to me are losing heart. They waste their days drinking and gambling, and lick their wounds like beaten curs."

"Battle will set their hearts ablaze once more, Your Grace," Ser Axell said. "Defeat is a disease, and victory is the cure."

"Victory." The king's mouth twisted. "There are victories and victories, ser. But tell your plan to Ser Davos. I would hear his views on what you propose."

Ser Axell turned to Davos, with a look on his face much like the look that proud Lord Belgrave must have worn, the day King Baelor the Blessed had commanded him to wash the beggar's ulcerous feet. Nonetheless, he obeyed.

The plan Ser Axell had devised with Salladhor Saan was simple. A few hours' sail from Dragonstone lay Claw Isle, ancient sea-girt seat of House Celtigar. Lord Ardrian Celtigar had fought beneath the fiery heart on the Blackwater, but once taken, he had wasted no time in going over to Joffrey. He remained in King's Landing even now. "Too frightened of His Grace's wrath to come near Dragonstone, no doubt," Ser Axell declared. "And wisely so. The man has betrayed his rightful king."

Ser Axell proposed to use Salladhor Saan's fleet and the men who had escaped the Blackwater – Stannis still had some fifteen hundred on Dragonstone, more than half of them Florents – to exact retribution for Lord Celtigar's defection. Claw Isle was but lightly garrisoned, its castle reputedly stuffed with Myrish carpets, Volantene glass, gold and silver plate, jeweled cups, magnificent hawks, an axe of Valyrian steel, a horn that could summon monsters from the deep, chests of rubies, and more wines than a man could drink in a hundred years. Though Celtigar had shown the world a niggardly face, he had never stinted on his own comforts. "Put his castle to the torch and his people to the sword, I say," Ser

Axell concluded. "Leave Claw Isle a desolation of ash and bone, fit only for carrion crows, so the realm might see the fate of those who bed with Lannisters."

Stannis listened to Ser Axell's recitation in silence, grinding his jaw slowly from side to side. When it was done, he said, "It could be done, I believe. The risk is small. Joffrey has no strength at sea until Lord Redwyne sets sail from the Arbor. The plunder might serve to keep that Lysene pirate Salladhor Saan loyal for a time. By itself Claw Isle is worthless, but its fall would serve notice to Lord Tywin that my cause is not yet done." The king turned back to Davos. "Speak truly, ser. What do you make of Ser Axell's proposal?"

Speak truly, ser. Davos remembered the dark cell he had shared with Lord Alester, remembered Lamprey and Porridge. He thought of the promises that Ser Axell had made on the bridge above the yard. *A ship or a shove, what shall it be?* But this was Stannis asking. "Your Grace," he said slowly, "I make it folly . . . aye, and cowardice."

"*Cowardice?*" Ser Axell all but shouted. "No man calls me craven before my king!"

"Silence," Stannis commanded. "Ser Davos, speak on, I would hear your reasons."

Davos turned to face Ser Axell. "You say we ought show the realm we are not done. Strike a blow. Make war, aye . . . but on what enemy? You will find no Lannisters on Claw Isle."

"We will find *traitors*," said Ser Axell, "though it may be I could find some closer to home. Even in this very room."

Davos ignored the jibe. "I don't doubt Lord Celtigar bent the knee to the boy Joffrey. He is an old done man, who wants no more than to end his days in his castle, drinking his fine wine out of his jeweled cups." He turned back to Stannis. "Yet he came when you called, sire. Came, with his ships and swords. He stood by you at Storm's End when Lord Renly came down on us, and his ships sailed up the Blackwater. His men fought for you, killed for you, *burned* for you. Claw Isle is weakly held, yes. Held by women and children and old men. And why is that? Because their husbands and sons and fathers died on the Blackwater, that's why. Died at their oars, or with swords in their hands, fighting beneath our banners. Yet Ser Axell proposes we swoop down on the homes they left behind, to rape their widows and put their children to the sword. These smallfolk are no traitors . . ."

"They *are*," insisted Ser Axell. "Not all of Celtigar's men were slain on the Blackwater. Hundreds were taken with their lord, and bent the knee when he did."

"*When he did*," Davos repeated. "They were his men. His sworn men. What choice were they given?"

"Every man has choices. They might have refused to kneel. Some did, and died for it. Yet they died true men, and loyal."

"Some men are stronger than others." It was a feeble answer, and Davos knew it. Stannis Baratheon was a man of iron will who neither understood nor forgave weakness in others. *I am losing*, he thought, despairing.

"It is every man's duty to remain loyal to his rightful king, even if the lord he serves proves false," Stannis declared in a tone that brooked no argument.

A desperate folly took hold of Davos, a recklessness akin to madness. "As you remained loyal to King Aerys when your brother raised his banners?" he blurted.

Shocked silence followed, until Ser Axell cried, *"Treason!"* and snatched his dagger from its sheath. "Your Grace, he speaks his infamy to your face!"

Davos could hear Stannis grinding his teeth. A vein bulged, blue and swollen, in the king's brow. Their eyes met. "Put up your knife, Ser Axell. And leave us."

"As it please Your Grace –"

"It would please me for you to leave," said Stannis. "Take yourself from my presence, and send me Melisandre."

"As you command." Ser Axell slid the knife away, bowed, and hurried toward the door. His boots rang against the floor, angry.

"You have always presumed on my forbearance," Stannis warned Davos when they were alone. "I can shorten your tongue as easy as I did your fingers, smuggler."

"I am your man, Your Grace. So it is your tongue, to do with as you please."

"It is," he said, calmer. "And I would have it speak the truth. Though the truth is a bitter draught at times. *Aerys!* If you only knew ... that was a hard choosing. My blood or my liege. My brother or my king." He grimaced. "Have you ever seen the Iron Throne? The barbs along the back, the ribbons of twisted steel, the jagged ends of swords and knives all tangled up and melted? It is not a *comfortable* seat, ser. Aerys cut himself so often men took to calling him King Scab, and Maegor the Cruel was murdered in that chair. *By* that chair, to hear some tell it. It is not a seat where a man can rest at ease. Ofttimes I wonder why my brothers wanted it so desperately." ·

"Why would *you* want it, then?" Davos asked him.

"It is not a question of wanting. The throne is mine, as Robert's heir. That is law. After me, it must pass to my daughter, unless Selyse should finally give me a son." He ran three fingers lightly down the table, over the layers of smooth hard varnish, dark with age. "I *am* king. Wants do not enter into it. I have a duty to my daughter. To the realm. Even to Robert. He loved me but little, I know, yet he was my brother. The Lannister woman gave him horns and made a motley fool of him. She may have murdered him as well, as she murdered Jon Arryn and Ned Stark. For such crimes there must be justice. Starting with Cersei and her abominations. But only starting. I mean to scour that court clean. As Robert should have done, after the Trident. Ser Barristan once told me that the rot in King Aerys's reign began with Varys. The eunuch should never have been pardoned. No more than the Kingslayer. At the least, Robert should have stripped the white cloak from Jaime and sent him to the Wall, as Lord Stark urged. He listened to Jon Arryn instead. I was still at Storm's End, under siege and unconsulted." He turned abruptly, to give Davos a hard shrewd look. "The truth, now. Why did you wish to murder Lady Melisandre?"

So he does know. Davos could not lie to him. "Four of my sons burned on the Blackwater. She gave them to the flames."

"You wrong her. Those fires were no work of hers. Curse the Imp, curse the pyromancers, curse that fool of Florent who sailed my fleet into the jaws of a trap. Or curse me for my stubborn pride, for sending her away when I needed her most. But not Melisandre. She remains my faithful servant."

"Maester Cressen was your faithful servant. She slew him, as she killed Ser Cortnay Penrose and your brother Renly."

"Now you sound a fool," the king complained. "She *saw* Renly's end in the flames, yes, but she had no more part in it than I did. The priestess was with me. Your Devan would tell you so. Ask him, if you doubt me. She would have spared Renly if she could. It was Melisandre who urged me to meet with him, and give him one last chance to amend his treason. And it was Melisandre who told me to send for you when Ser Axell wished to give you to R'hllor." He smiled thinly. "Does that surprise you?"

"Yes. She knows I am no friend to her or her red god."

"But you are a friend to me. She knows that as well." He beckoned Davos closer. "The boy is sick. Maester Pylos has been leeching him."

"The boy?" His thoughts went to his Devan, the king's squire. "My son, sire?"

"Devan? A good boy. He has much of you in him. It is Robert's bastard who is sick, the boy we took at Storm's End."

Edric Storm. "I spoke with him in Aegon's Garden."

"As she wished. As she saw." Stannis sighed. "Did the boy charm you? He has that gift. He got it from his father, with the blood. He knows he is a king's son, but chooses to forget that he is bastard-born. And he worships Robert, as Renly did when he was young. My royal brother

played the fond father on his visits to Storm's End, and there were gifts
... swords and ponies and fur-trimmed cloaks. The eunuch's work, every
one. The boy would write the Red Keep full of thanks, and Robert would
laugh and ask Varys what he'd sent this year. Renly was no better. He
left the boy's upbringing to castellans and maesters, and every one fell
victim to his charm. Penrose chose to die rather than give him up." The
king ground his teeth together. "It still angers me. How could he think
I would hurt the boy? I chose Robert, did I not? When that hard day
came. I chose blood over honor."

He does not use the boy's name. That made Davos very uneasy. "I
hope young Edric will recover soon."

Stannis waved a hand, dismissing his concern. "It is a chill, no more.
He coughs, he shivers, he has a fever. Maester Pylos will soon set him
right. By himself the boy is nought, you understand, but in his veins
flows my brother's blood. There is power in a king's blood, she says."

Davos did not have to ask who *she* was.

Stannis touched the Painted Table. "Look at it, onion knight. My
realm, by rights. My Westeros." He swept a hand across it. "This talk of
Seven Kingdoms is a folly. Aegon saw that three hundred years ago when
he stood where we are standing. They painted this table at his command.
Rivers and bays they painted, hills and mountains, castles and cities and
market towns, lakes and swamps and forests ... but no borders. *It is all
one.* One realm, for one king to rule alone."

"One king," agreed Davos. "One king means peace."

"I shall bring justice to Westeros. A thing Ser Axell understands as
little as he does war. Claw Isle would gain me naught ... and it was evil,
just as you said. Celtigar must pay the traitor's price himself, in his own
person. And when I come into my kingdom, he shall. Every man shall
reap what he has sown, from the highest lord to the lowest gutter rat.
And some will lose more than the tips off their fingers, I promise you.
They have made my kingdom bleed, and I do not forget that." King
Stannis turned from the table. "On your knees, Onion Knight."

"Your Grace?"

"For your onions and fish, I made you a knight once. For this, I am of
a mind to raise you to lord."

This? Davos was lost. "I am content to be your knight, Your Grace. I
would not know how to begin being lordly."

"Good. To be lordly is to be false. I have learned that lesson hard.
Now, *kneel.* Your king commands."

Davos knelt, and Stannis drew his longsword. *Lightbringer,* Melisandre
had named it; the red sword of heroes, drawn from the fires where the seven
gods were consumed. The room seemed to grow brighter as the blade slid
from its scabbard. The steel had a glow to it; now orange, now yellow, now

red. The air shimmered around it, and no jewel had ever sparkled so brilliantly. But when Stannis touched it to Davos's shoulder, it felt no different than any other longsword. "Ser Davos of House Seaworth," the king said, "are you my true and honest liege man, now and forever?"

"I am, Your Grace."

"And do you swear to serve me loyally all your days, to give me honest counsel and swift obedience, to defend my rights and my realm against all foes in battles great and small, to protect my people and punish my enemies?"

"I do, Your Grace."

"Then rise again, Davos Seaworth, and rise as Lord of the Rainwood, Admiral of the Narrow Sea, and Hand of the King."

For a moment Davos was too stunned to move. *I woke this morning in his dungeon.* "Your Grace, you cannot ... I am no fit man to be a King's Hand."

"There is no man fitter." Stannis sheathed Lightbringer, gave Davos his hand, and pulled him to his feet.

"I am lowborn," Davos reminded him. "An upjumped smuggler. Your lords will never obey me."

"Then we will make new lords."

"But ... I cannot read ... nor write ..."

"Maester Pylos can read for you. As to writing, my last Hand wrote the head off his shoulders. All I ask of you are the things you've always given me. Honesty. Loyalty. Service."

"Surely there is someone better ... some great lord ..."

Stannis snorted. "Bar Emmon, that boy? My faithless grandfather? Celtigar has abandoned me, the new Velaryon is six years old, and the new Sunglass sailed for Volantis after I burned his brother." He made an angry gesture. "A few good men remain, it's true. Ser Gilbert Farring holds Storm's End for me still, with two hundred loyal men. Lord Morrigen, the Bastard of Nightsong, young Chyttering, my cousin Andrew ... but I trust none of them as I trust you, my lord of Rainwood. You will be my Hand. It is you I want beside me for the battle."

Another battle will be the end of all of us, thought Davos. *Lord Alester saw that much true enough.* "Your Grace asked for honest counsel. In honesty then ... we lack the strength for another battle against the Lannisters."

"It is the great battle His Grace is speaking of," said a woman's voice, rich with the accents of the east. Melisandre stood at the door in her red silks and shimmering satins, holding a covered silver dish in her hands. "These little wars are no more than a scuffle of children before what is to come. The one whose name may not be spoken is marshaling his power, Davos Seaworth, a power fell and evil and strong beyond measure.

Soon comes the cold, and the night that never ends." She placed the silver dish on the Painted Table. "Unless true men find the courage to fight it. Men whose hearts are fire."

Stannis stared at the silver dish. "She has shown it to me, Lord Davos. In the flames."

"*You* saw it, sire?" It was not like Stannis Baratheon to lie about such a thing.

"With mine own eyes. After the battle, when I was lost to despair, the Lady Melisandre bid me gaze into the hearthfire. The chimney was drawing strongly, and bits of ash were rising from the fire. I stared at them, feeling half a fool, but she bid me look deeper, and . . . the ashes were white, rising in the updraft, yet all at once it seemed as if they were falling. *Snow,* I thought. Then the sparks in the air seemed to circle, to become a ring of torches, and I was looking *through* the fire down on some high hill in a forest. The cinders had become men in black behind the torches, and there were shapes moving through the snow. For all the heat of the fire, I felt a cold so terrible I shivered, and when I did the sight was gone, the fire but a fire once again. But what I saw was real, I'd stake my kingdom on it."

"And have," said Melisandre.

The conviction in the king's voice frightened Davos to the core. "A hill in a forest . . . shapes in the snow . . . I don't . . ."

"It means that the battle is begun," said Melisandre. "The sand is running through the glass more quickly now, and man's hour on earth is almost done. We must act boldly, or all hope is lost. Westeros must unite beneath her one true king, the prince that was promised, Lord of Dragonstone and chosen of R'hllor."

"R'hllor chooses queerly, then." The king grimaced, as if he'd tasted something foul. "Why me, and not my brothers? Renly and his peach. In my dreams I see the juice running from his mouth, the blood from his throat. If he had done his duty by his brother, we would have smashed Lord Tywin. A victory even Robert could be proud of. Robert . . ." His teeth ground side to side. "He is in my dreams as well. Laughing. Drinking. Boasting. Those were the things he was best at. Those, and fighting. I never bested him at anything. The Lord of Light should have made Robert his champion. Why me?"

"Because you are a righteous man," said Melisandre.

"A righteous man." Stannis touched the covered silver platter with a finger. "With leeches."

"Yes," said Melisandre, "but I must tell you once more, this is not the way."

"You swore it would work." The king looked angry.

"It will . . . and it will not."

"Which?"

"Both."

"Speak sense to me, woman."

"When the fires speak more plainly, so shall I. There is truth in the flames, but it is not always easy to see." The great ruby at her throat drank fire from the glow of the brazier. "Give me the boy, Your Grace. It is the surer way. The better way. Give me the boy and I shall wake the stone dragon."

"I have told you, no."

"He is only one baseborn boy, against all the boys of Westeros, and all the girls as well. Against all the children that might ever be born, in all the kingdoms of the world."

"The boy is innocent."

"The boy defiled your marriage bed, else you would surely have sons of your own. He shamed you."

"*Robert* did that. Not the boy. My daughter has grown fond of him. And he is mine own blood."

"Your brother's blood," Melisandre said. "A king's blood. Only a king's blood can wake the stone dragon."

Stannis ground his teeth. "I'll hear no more of this. The dragons are done. The Targaryens tried to bring them back half a dozen times. And made fools of themselves, or corpses. Patchface is the only fool we need on this godsforsaken rock. You have the leeches. Do your work."

Melisandre bowed her head stiffly, and said, "As my king commands." Reaching up her left sleeve with her right hand, she flung a handful of powder into the brazier. The coals roared. As pale flames writhed atop them, the red woman retrieved the silver dish and brought it to the king. Davos watched her lift the lid. Beneath were three large black leeches, fat with blood.

The boy's blood, Davos knew. *A king's blood.*

Stannis stretched forth a hand, and his fingers closed around one of the leeches.

"Say the name," Melisandre commanded.

The leech was twisting in the king's grip, trying to attach itself to one of his fingers. "The usurper," he said. "Joffrey Baratheon." When he tossed the leech into the fire, it curled up like an autumn leaf amidst the coals, and burned.

Stannis grasped the second. "The usurper," he declared, louder this time. "Balon Greyjoy." He flipped it lightly onto the brazier, and its flesh split and cracked. The blood burst from it, hissing and smoking.

The last was in the king's hand. This one he studied a moment as it writhed between his fingers. "The usurper," he said at last. "Robb Stark." And he threw it on the flames.

JAIME

Harrenhal's bathhouse was a dim, steamy, low-ceilinged room filled with great stone tubs. When they led Jaime in, they found Brienne seated in one of them, scrubbing her arm almost angrily.

"Not so hard, wench," he called. "You'll scrub the skin off." She dropped her brush and covered her teats with hands as big as Gregor Clegane's. The pointy little buds she was so intent on hiding would have looked more natural on some ten-year-old than they did on her thick muscular chest.

"What are you doing here?" she demanded.

"Lord Bolton insists I sup with him, but he neglected to invite my fleas." Jaime tugged at his guard with his left hand. "Help me out of these stinking rags." One-handed, he could not so much as unlace his breeches. The man obeyed grudgingly, but he obeyed. "Now leave us," Jaime said when his clothes lay in a pile on the wet stone floor. "My lady of Tarth doesn't want the likes of you scum gaping at her teats." He pointed his stump at the hatchet-faced woman attending Brienne. "You too. Wait without. There's only the one door, and the wench is too big to try and shinny up a chimney."

The habit of obedience went deep. The woman followed his guard out, leaving the bathhouse to the two of them. The tubs were large enough to hold six or seven, after the fashion of the Free Cities, so Jaime climbed in with the wench, awkward and slow. Both his eyes were open, though the right remained somewhat swollen, despite Qyburn's leeches. Jaime felt a hundred and nine years old, which was a deal better than he had been feeling when he came to Harrenhal.

Brienne shrunk away from him. "There are other tubs."

"This one suits me well enough." Gingerly, he immersed himself up to the chin in the steaming water. "Have no fear, wench. Your thighs are purple and green, and I'm not interested in what you've got between them." He had to rest his right arm on the rim, since Qyburn had warned him to keep the linen dry. He could feel the tension drain from his legs, but his head spun. "If I faint, pull me out. No Lannister has ever drowned in his bath and I don't mean to be the first."

"Why should I care how you die?"

"You swore a solemn vow." He smiled as a red flush crept up the thick white column of her neck. She turned her back to him. "Still the shy maiden? What is it that you think I haven't seen?" He groped for the brush she had dropped, caught it with his fingers, and began to scrub himself desultorily. Even that was difficult, awkward. *My left hand is good for nothing.*

Still, the water darkened as the caked dirt dissolved off his skin. The wench kept her back to him, the muscles in her great shoulders hunched and hard.

"Does the sight of my stump distress you so?" Jaime asked. "You ought to be pleased. I've lost the hand I killed the king with. The hand that flung the Stark boy from that tower. The hand I'd slide between my sister's thighs to make her wet." He thrust his stump at her face. "No wonder Renly died, with you guarding him."

She jerked to her feet as if he'd struck her, sending a wash of hot water across the tub. Jaime caught a glimpse of the thick blonde bush at the juncture of her thighs as she climbed out. She was much hairier than his sister. Absurdly, he felt his cock stir beneath the bathwater. *Now I know I have been too long away from Cersei.* He averted his eyes, troubled by his body's response. "That was unworthy," he mumbled. "I'm a maimed man, and bitter. Forgive me, wench. You protected me as well as any man could have, and better than most."

She wrapped her nakedness in a towel. "Do you mock me?"

That pricked him back to anger. "Are you as thick as a castle wall? That was an apology. I am tired of fighting with you. What say we make a truce?"

"Truces are built on trust. Would you have me trust –"

"The Kingslayer, yes. The oathbreaker who murdered poor sad Aerys Targaryen." Jaime snorted. "It's not Aerys I rue, it's Robert. 'I hear they've named you Kingslayer,' he said to me at his coronation feast. 'Just don't think to make it a habit.' And he laughed. Why is it that no one names Robert oathbreaker? He tore the realm apart, yet *I* am the one with shit for honor."

"Robert did all he did for love." Water ran down Brienne's legs and pooled beneath her feet.

"Robert did all he did for pride, a cunt, and a pretty face." He made a fist . . . or would have, if he'd had a hand. Pain lanced up his arm, cruel as laughter.

"He rode to save the realm," she insisted.

To save the realm. "Did you know that my brother set the Blackwater Rush afire? Wildfire will burn on water. Aerys would have bathed in it if he'd dared. The Targaryens were all mad for fire." Jaime felt light-headed. *It is the heat in here, the poison in my blood, the last of my fever. I am not myself.* He eased himself down until the water reached his chin. "Soiled my white cloak . . . I wore my gold armor that day, but . . ."

"Gold armor?" Her voice sounded far off, faint.

He floated in heat, in memory. "After dancing griffins lost the Battle of the Bells, Aerys exiled him." *Why am I telling this absurd ugly child?* "He had finally realized that Robert was no mere outlaw lord to be crushed at whim, but the greatest threat House Targaryen had faced since Daemon Blackfyre. The king reminded Lewyn Martell gracelessly that he held Elia and sent him to take command of the ten thousand Dornishmen coming up the kingsroad. Jon Darry and Barristan Selmy rode to Stoney Sept to rally what they could of griffins' men, and Prince Rhaegar returned from the south and persuaded his father to swallow his pride and summon my father. But no raven returned from Casterly Rock, and that made the king even more afraid. He saw traitors everywhere, and Varys was always there to point out any he might have missed. So His Grace commanded his alchemists to place caches of wildfire all over King's Landing. Beneath Baelor's Sept and the hovels of Flea Bottom, under stables and store-houses, at all seven gates, even in the cellars of the Red Keep itself.

"Everything was done in the utmost secrecy by a handful of master pyromancers. They did not even trust their own acolytes to help. The queen's eyes had been closed for years, and Rhaegar was busy marshaling an army. But Aerys's new mace-and-dagger Hand was not utterly stupid, and with Rossart, Belis, and Garigus coming and going night and day, he became suspicious. Chelsted, that was his name, Lord Chelsted." It had come back to him suddenly, with the telling. "I'd thought the man craven, but the day he confronted Aerys he found some courage somewhere. He did all he could to dissuade him. He reasoned, he jested, he threatened, and finally he begged. When that failed he took off his chain of office and flung it down on the floor. Aerys burnt him alive for that, and hung his chain about the neck of Rossart, his favorite pyromancer. The man who had cooked Lord Rickard Stark in his own armor. And all the time, I stood by the foot of the Iron Throne in my white plate, still as a corpse, guarding my liege and all his sweet secrets.

"My Sworn Brothers were all away, you see, but Aerys liked to keep me close. I was my father's son, so he did not trust me. He wanted me where Varys could watch me, day and night. So I heard it all." He remembered how Rossart's eyes would shine when he unrolled his maps to show where *the substance* must be placed. Garigus and Belis were the same. "Rhaegar met Robert on the Trident, and you know what happened there. When the word reached court, Aerys packed the queen off to Dragonstone with Prince Viserys. Princess Elia would have gone as well, but he forbade it. Somehow he had gotten it in his head that Prince Lewyn must have betrayed Rhaegar on the Trident, but he thought he could keep Dorne loyal so long as he kept Elia and Aegon by his side. *The traitors want my city,* I heard him tell Rossart, *but I'll give them naught but ashes. Let Robert be king over charred bones and cooked meat.* The Targaryens never bury their dead, they burn them. Aerys meant to have the greatest funeral pyre of them all. Though if truth be told, I do not believe he truly expected to die. Like Aerion Brightfire before him, Aerys thought the fire would transform him . . . that he would rise again, reborn as a dragon, and turn all his enemies to ash.

"Ned Stark was racing south with Robert's van, but my father's forces reached the city first. Pycelle convinced the king that his Warden of the West had come to defend him, so he opened the gates. The one time he *should* have heeded Varys, and he ignored him. My father had held back from the war, brooding on all the wrongs Aerys had done him and determined that House Lannister should be on the winning side. The Trident decided him.

"It fell to me to hold the Red Keep, but I knew we were lost. I sent to Aerys asking his leave to make terms. My man came back with a royal command. *'Bring me your father's head, if you are no traitor.'* Aerys would have no yielding. Lord Rossart was with him, my messenger said. I knew what *that* meant.

"When I came on Rossart, he was dressed as a common man-at-arms, hurrying to a postern gate. I slew him first. Then I slew Aerys, before he could find someone else to carry his message to the pyromancers. Days later, I hunted down the others and slew them as well. Belis offered me gold, and Garigus wept for mercy. Well, a sword's more merciful than fire, but I don't think Garigus much appreciated the kindness I showed him."

The water had grown cool. When Jaime opened his eyes, he found himself staring at the stump of his sword hand. *The hand that made me Kingslayer.* The goat had robbed him of his glory and his shame, both at once. *Leaving what? Who am I now?*

The wench looked ridiculous, clutching her towel to her meager teats with her thick white legs sticking out beneath. "Has my tale turned you speechless? Come, curse me or kiss me or call me a liar. *Something.*"

"If this is true, how is it no one knows?"

"The knights of the Kingsguard are sworn to keep the king's secrets. Would you have me break my oath?" Jaime laughed. "Do you think the noble Lord of Winterfell wanted to hear my feeble explanations? Such an *honorable* man. He only had to look at me to judge me guilty." Jaime lurched to his feet, the water running cold down his chest. "By what right does the wolf judge the lion? *By what right!*" A violent shiver took him, and he smashed his stump against the rim of the tub as he tried to climb out.

Pain shuddered through him . . . and suddenly the bathhouse was spinning. Brienne caught him before he could fall. Her arm was all gooseflesh, clammy and chilled, but she was strong, and gentler than he would have thought. *Gentler than Cersei*, he thought as she helped him from the tub, his legs wobbly as a limp cock. "*Guards!*" he heard the wench shout. "The Kingslayer!"

Jaime, he thought, *my name is Jaime.*

The next he knew, he was lying on the damp floor with the guards and the wench and Qyburn all standing over him looking concerned. Brienne was naked, but she seemed to have forgotten that for the moment. "The heat of the tubs will do it," Maester Qyburn was telling them. *No, he's not a maester, they took his chain.* "There's still poison in his blood as well, and he's malnourished. What have you been feeding him?"

"Worms and piss and grey vomit," offered Jaime.

"Hardbread and water and oat porridge," insisted the guard. "He don't hardly eat it, though. What should we do with him?"

"Scrub him and dress him and carry him to Kingspyre, if need be," Qyburn said. "Lord Bolton insists he will sup with him tonight. The time is growing short."

"Bring me clean garb for him," Brienne said, "I'll see that he's washed and dressed."

The others were all too glad to give her the task. They lifted him to his feet and sat him on a stone bench by the wall. Brienne went away to retrieve her towel, and returned with a stiff brush to finish scrubbing him. One of the guards gave her a razor to trim his beard. Qyburn returned with roughspun smallclothes, clean black woolen breeches, a loose green tunic, and a leather jerkin that laced up the front. Jaime was feeling less dizzy by then, though no less clumsy. With the wench's help he managed to dress himself. "Now all I need is a silver looking glass."

The Bloody Maester had brought fresh clothing for Brienne as well; a stained pink satin gown and a linen undertunic. "I am sorry, my lady. These were the only women's garments in Harrenhal large enough to fit you."

It was obvious at once that the gown had been cut for someone with slimmer arms, shorter legs, and much fuller breasts. The fine Myrish lace did little to conceal the bruising that mottled Brienne's skin. All in all, the garb made the wench look ludicrous. *She has thicker shoulders than I do, and a bigger neck,* Jaime thought. *Small wonder she prefers to dress in mail.* Pink was not a kind color for her either. A dozen cruel japes leaped into his head, but for once he kept them there. Best not to make her angry; he was no match for her one-handed.

Qyburn had brought a flask as well. "What is it?" Jaime demanded when the chainless maester pressed him to drink.

"Licorice steeped in vinegar, with honey and cloves. It will give you some strength and clear your head."

"Bring me the potion that grows new hands," said Jaime. "That's the one I want."

"Drink it," Brienne said, unsmiling, and he did.

It was half an hour before he felt strong enough to stand. After the dim wet warmth of the bathhouse, the air outside was a slap across the face. "M'lord will be looking for him by now," a guard told Qyburn. "Her too. Do I need to carry him?"

"I can still walk. Brienne, give me your arm."

Clutching her, Jaime let them herd him across the yard to a vast draughty hall, larger even than the throne room in King's Landing. Huge hearths lined the walls, one every ten feet or so, more than he could count, but no fires had been lit, so the chill between the walls went bone-deep. A dozen spearmen in fur cloaks guarded the doors and the steps that led up to the two galleries above. And in the center of that immense emptiness, at a trestle table surrounded by what seemed like acres of smooth slate floor, the Lord of the Dreadfort waited, attended only by a cupbearer.

"My lord," said Brienne, when they stood before him.

Roose Bolton's eyes were paler than stone, darker than milk, and his voice was spider soft. "I am pleased that you are strong enough to attend me, ser. My lady, do be seated." He gestured at the spread of cheese, bread, cold meat, and fruit that covered the table. "Will you drink red or white? Of indifferent vintage, I fear. Ser Amory drained Lady Whent's cellars nearly dry."

"I trust you killed him for it." Jaime slid into the offered seat quickly, so Bolton could not see how weak he was. "White is for Starks. I'll drink red like a good Lannister."

"I would prefer water," said Brienne.

"Elmar, the red for Ser Jaime, water for the Lady Brienne, and hippocras for myself." Bolton waved a hand at their escort, dismissing them, and the men beat a silent retreat.

Habit made Jaime reach for his wine with his right hand. His stump rocked the goblet, spattering his clean linen bandages with bright red spots and forcing him to catch the cup with his left hand before it fell, but Bolton pretended not to notice his clumsiness. The northman helped himself to a prune and ate it with small sharp bites. "Do try these, Ser Jaime. They are most sweet, and help move the bowels as well. Lord Vargo took them from an inn before he burnt it."

"My bowels move fine, that goat's no lord, and your prunes don't interest me half so much as your intentions."

"Regarding you?" A faint smile touched Roose Bolton's lips. "You are a perilous prize, ser. You sow dissension wherever you go. Even here, in my happy house of Harrenhal." His voice was a whisker above a whisper. "And in Riverrun as well, it seems. Do you know, Edmure Tully has offered a thousand golden dragons for your recapture?"

Is that all? "My sister will pay ten times as much."

"Will she?" That smile again, there for an instant, gone as quick. "Ten thousand dragons is a formidable sum. Of course, there is Lord Karstark's offer to consider as well. He promises the hand of his daughter to the man who brings him your head."

"Leave it to your goat to get it backward," said Jaime.

Bolton gave a soft chuckle. "Harrion Karstark was captive here when we took the castle, did you know? I gave him all the Karhold men still with me and sent him off with Glover. I do hope nothing ill befell him at Duskendale . . . else Alys Karstark would be all that remains of Lord Rickard's progeny." He chose another prune. "Fortunately for you, I have no need of a wife. I wed the Lady Walda Frey whilst I was at the Twins."

"Fair Walda?" Awkwardly, Jaime tried to hold the bread with his stump while tearing it with his left hand.

"Fat Walda. My lord of Frey offered me my bride's weight in silver for a dowry, so I chose accordingly. Elmar, break off some bread for Ser Jaime."

The boy tore a fist-sized chunk off one end of the loaf and handed it to Jaime. Brienne tore her own bread. "Lord Bolton," she asked, "it's said you mean to give Harrenhal to Vargo Hoat."

"That was his price," Lord Bolton said. "The Lannisters are not the only men who pay their debts. I must take my leave soon in any case. Edmure Tully is to wed the Lady Roslin Frey at the Twins, and my king commands my attendance."

"*Edmure* weds?" said Jaime. "Not Robb Stark?"

"His Grace King Robb is wed." Bolton spit a prune pit into his hand and put it aside. "To a Westerling of the Crag. I am told her name is Jeyne. No doubt you know her, ser. Her father is your father's bannerman."

"My father has a good many bannermen, and most of them have daughters." Jaime groped one-handed for his goblet, trying to recall this Jeyne. The Westerlings were an old house, with more pride than power.

"This cannot be true," Brienne said stubbornly. "King Robb was sworn to wed a Frey. He would never break faith, he –"

"His Grace is a boy of sixteen," said Roose Bolton mildly. "And I would thank you not to question my word, my lady."

Jaime felt almost sorry for Robb Stark. *He won the war on the battle-field and lost it in a bedchamber, poor fool.* "How does Lord Walder relish dining on trout in place of wolf?" he asked.

"Oh, trout makes for a tasty supper." Bolton lifted a pale finger toward his cupbearer. "Though my poor Elmar is bereft. He was to wed Arya Stark, but my good father of Frey had no choice but to break the betrothal when King Robb betrayed him."

"Is there word of Arya Stark?" Brienne leaned forward. "Lady Catelyn had feared that . . . is the girl still alive?"

"Oh, yes," said the Lord of the Dreadfort.

"You have certain knowledge of that, my lord?"

Roose Bolton shrugged. "Arya Stark was lost for a time, it was true, but now she has been found. I mean to see her returned safely to the north."

"Her and her sister both," said Brienne. "Tyrion Lannister has promised us both girls for his brother."

That seemed to amuse the Lord of the Dreadfort. "My lady, has no one told you? Lannisters lie."

"Is that a slight on the honor of my House?" Jaime picked up the cheese knife with his good hand. "A rounded point, and dull," he said, sliding his thumb along the edge of the blade, "but it will go through your eye all the same." Sweat beaded his brow. He could only hope he did not look as feeble as he felt.

Lord Bolton's little smile paid another visit to his lips. "You speak boldly for a man who needs help to break his bread. My guards are all around us, I remind you."

"All around us, and half a league away." Jaime glanced down the vast length of the hall. "By the time they reach us, you'll be as dead as Aerys."

" 'Tis scarcely chivalrous to threaten your host over his own cheese and olives," the Lord of the Dreadfort scolded. "In the north, we hold the laws of hospitality sacred still."

"I'm a captive here, not a guest. Your goat cut off my hand. If you think some prunes will make me overlook that, you're bloody well mistaken."

That took Roose Bolton aback. "Perhaps I am. Perhaps I ought to make a wedding gift of you to Edmure Tully . . . or strike your head off, as your sister did for Eddard Stark."

"I would not advise it. Casterly Rock has a long memory."

"A thousand leagues of mountain, sea, and bog lie between my walls and your rock. Lannister enmity means little to Bolton."

"Lannister friendship could mean much." Jaime thought he knew the game they were playing now. *But does the wench know as well?* He dare not look to see.

"I am not certain you are the sort of friends a wise man would want." Roose Bolton beckoned to the boy. "Elmar, carve our guests a slice off the roast."

Brienne was served first, but made no move to eat. "My lord," she said, "Ser Jaime is to be exchanged for Lady Catelyn's daughters. You must free us to continue on our way."

"The raven that came from Riverrun told of an escape, not an exchange. And if you helped this captive slip his bonds, you are guilty of treason, my lady."

The big wench rose to her feet. "I serve Lady Stark."

"And I the King in the North. Or the King Who Lost the North, as some now call him. Who never wished to trade Ser Jaime back to the Lannisters."

"Sit down and eat, Brienne," Jaime urged, as Elmar placed a slice of roast before him, dark and bloody. "If Bolton meant to kill us, he wouldn't be wasting his precious prunes on us, at such peril to his bowels." He stared at the meat and realized there was no way to cut it, one-handed. *I am worth less than a girl now,* he thought. *The goat's evened the trade, though I doubt Lady Catelyn will thank him when Cersei returns her whelps in like condition.* The thought made him grimace. *I will get the blame for that as well, I'll wager.*

Roose Bolton cut his meat methodically, the blood running across his plate. "Lady Brienne, will you sit if I tell you that I hope to send Ser Jaime on, just as you and Lady Stark desire?"

"I . . . you'd send us on?" The wench sounded wary, but she sat. "That is good, my lord."

"It is. However, Lord Vargo has created me one small . . . difficulty." He turned his pale eyes on Jaime. "Do you know why Hoat cut off your hand?"

"He enjoys cutting off hands." The linen that covered Jaime's stump was spotted with blood and wine. "He enjoys cutting off feet as well. He doesn't seem to need a reason."

"Nonetheless, he had one. Hoat is more cunning than he appears. No man commands a company such as the Brave Companions for long unless he has some wits about him." Bolton stabbed a chunk of meat with the point of his dagger, put it in his mouth, chewed thoughtfully, swallowed. "Lord Vargo abandoned House Lannister because I offered him Harrenhal, a reward a thousand times greater than any he could hope to have from Lord Tywin. As a stranger to Westeros, he did not know the prize was poisoned."

"The curse of Harren the Black?" mocked Jaime.

"The curse of Tywin Lannister." Bolton held out his goblet and Elmar refilled it silently. "Our goat should have consulted the Tarbecks or the Reynes. They might have warned him how your lord father deals with betrayal."

"There are no Tarbecks or Reynes," said Jaime.

"My point precisely. Lord Vargo doubtless hoped that Lord Stannis would triumph at King's Landing, and thence confirm him in his possession of this castle in gratitude for his small part in the downfall of House Lannister." He gave a dry chuckle. "He knows little of Stannis Baratheon either, I fear. That one might have given him Harrenhal for his service . . . but he would have given him a noose for his crimes as well."

"A noose is kinder than what he'll get from my father."

"By now he has come to the same realization. With Stannis broken and Renly dead, only a Stark victory can save him from Lord Tywin's vengeance, but the chances of that grow perishingly slim."

"King Robb has won every battle," Brienne said stoutly, as stubbornly loyal of speech as she was of deed.

"Won every battle, while losing the Freys, the Karstarks, Winterfell, and the north. A pity the wolf is so young. Boys of sixteen always believe they are immortal and invincible. An older man would bend the knee, I'd think. After a war there is always a peace, and with peace there are pardons . . . for the Robb Starks, at least. Not for the likes of Vargo Hoat." Bolton gave him a small smile. "Both sides have made use of him, but neither will shed a tear at his passing. The Brave Companions did not fight in the Battle of the Blackwater, yet they died there all the same."

"You'll forgive me if I don't mourn?"

"You have no pity for our wretched doomed goat? Ah, but the gods must . . . else why deliver *you* into his hands?" Bolton chewed another chunk of meat. "Karhold is smaller and meaner than Harrenhal, but it lies well beyond the reach of the lion's claws. Once wed to Alys Karstark, Hoat might be a lord in truth. If he could collect some gold from your father so much the better, but he would have delivered you to Lord Rickard no matter how much Lord Tywin paid. His price would be the maid, and safe refuge.

"But to sell you he must keep you, and the riverlands are full of those who would gladly steal you away. Glover and Tallhart were broken at Duskendale, but remnants of their host are still abroad, with the Mountain slaughtering the stragglers. A thousand Karstarks prowl the lands south and east of Riverrun, hunting you. Elsewhere are Darry men left lordless and lawless, packs of four-footed wolves, and the lightning lord's outlaw bands. Dondarrion would gladly hang you and the goat together from the same tree." The Lord of the Dreadfort sopped up some of the blood with a chunk of bread. "Harrenhal was the only place Lord Vargo could hope to hold you safe, but here his Brave Companions are much outnumbered by my own men, and by Ser Aenys and his Freys. No doubt he feared I might return you to Ser Edmure at Riverrun . . . or worse, send you on to your father.

"By maiming you, he meant to remove your sword as a threat, gain himself a grisly token to send to your father, and diminish your value to me. For he is my man, as I am King Robb's man. Thus his crime is mine, or may seem so in your father's eyes. And therein lies my . . . small difficulty." He gazed at Jaime, his pale eyes unblinking, expectant, chill.

I see. "You want me to absolve you of blame. To tell my father that this stump is no work of yours." Jaime laughed. "My lord, send me to Cersei, and I'll sing as sweet a song as you could want, of how gently you treated me." Any other answer, he knew, and Bolton would give him back to the goat. "Had I a hand, I'd write it out. How I was maimed by the sellsword my own father brought to Westeros, and saved by the noble Lord Bolton."

"I will trust to your word, ser."

There's something I don't often hear. "How soon might we be permitted to leave? And how do you mean to get me past all these wolves and brigands and Karstarks?"

"You will leave when Qyburn says you are strong enough, with a strong escort of picked men under the command of my captain, Walton. Steelshanks, he is called. A soldier of iron loyalty. Walton will see you safe and whole to King's Landing."

"Provided Lady Catelyn's daughters are delivered safe and whole as well," said the wench. "My lord, your man Walton's protection is welcome, but the girls are *my* charge."

The Lord of the Dreadfort gave her an uninterested glance. "The girls need not concern you any further, my lady. The Lady Sansa is the dwarf's wife, only the gods can part them now."

"His wife?" Brienne said, appalled. "The Imp? But . . . he swore, before the whole court, in sight of gods and men . . ."

She is such an innocent. Jaime was almost as surprised, if truth be told, but he hid it better. *Sansa Stark, that ought to put a smile on Tyrion's face.* He remembered how happy his brother had been with his little crofter's daughter . . . for a fortnight.

"What the Imp did or did nor swear scarcely matters now," said Lord Bolton. "Least of all to you." The wench looked almost wounded. Perhaps she finally felt the steel jaws of the trap when Roose Bolton beckoned to his guards. "Ser Jaime will continue on to King's Landing. I said nothing about you, I fear. It would be unconscionable of me to deprive Lord Vargo of both his prizes." The Lord of the Dreadfort reached out to pick another prune. "Were I you, my lady, I should worry less about Starks and rather more about sapphires."

TYRION

A horse whickered impatiently behind him, from amidst the ranks of gold cloaks drawn up across the road. Tyrion could hear Lord Gyles coughing as well. He had not asked for Gyles, no more than he'd asked for Ser Addam or Jalabhar Xho or any of the rest, but his lord father felt Doran Martell might take it ill if only a dwarf came out to escort him across the Blackwater.

Joffrey should have met the Dornishmen himself, he reflected as he sat waiting, *but he would have mucked it up, no doubt*. Of late the king had been repeating little jests about the Dornish that he'd picked up from Mace Tyrell's men-at-arms. *How many Dornishmen does it take to shoe a horse? Nine. One to do the shoeing, and eight to lift the horse up.* Somehow Tyrion did not think Doran Martell would find that amusing.

He could see their banners flying as the riders emerged from the green of the living wood in a long dusty column. From here to the river, only bare black trees remained, a legacy of his battle. *Too many banners*, he thought sourly, as he watched the ashes kick up under the hooves of the approaching horses, as they had beneath the hooves of the Tyrell van as it smashed Stannis in the flank. *Martell's brought half the lords of Dorne, by the look of it.* He tried to think of some good that might come of that, and failed. "How many banners do you count?" he asked Bronn.

The sellsword knight shaded his eyes. "Eight . . . no, nine."

Tyrion turned in his saddle. "Pod, come up here. Describe the arms you see, and tell me which houses they represent."

Podrick Payne edged his gelding closer. He was carrying the royal standard, Joffrey's great stag-and-lion, and struggling with its weight.

Bronn bore Tyrion's own banner, the lion of Lannister gold on crimson.

He's getting taller, Tyrion realized as Pod stood in his stirrups for a better look. *He'll soon tower over me like all the rest.* The lad had been making a diligent study of Dornish heraldry, at Tyrion's command, but as ever he was nervous. "I can't see. The wind is flapping them."

"Bronn, tell the boy what you see."

Bronn looked very much the knight today, in his new doublet and cloak, the flaming chain across his chest. "A red sun on orange," he called, "with a spear through its back."

"Martell," Podrick Payne said at once, visibly relieved. "House Martell of Sunspear, my lord. The Prince of Dorne."

"My horse would have known that one," said Tyrion dryly. "Give him another, Bronn."

"There's a purple flag with yellow balls."

"Lemons?" Pod said hopefully. "A purple field strewn with lemons? For House Dalt? Of, of Lemonwood."

"Might be. Next's a big black bird on yellow. Something pink or white in its claws, hard to say with the banner flapping."

"The vulture of Blackmont grasps a baby in its talons," said Pod. "House Blackmont of Blackmont, ser."

Bronn laughed. "Reading books again? Books will ruin your sword eye, boy. I see a skull too. A black banner."

"The crowned skull of House Manwoody, bone and gold on black." Pod sounded more confident with every correct answer. "The Manwoodys of Kingsgrave."

"Three black spiders?"

"They're scorpions, ser. House Qorgyle of Sandstone, three scorpions black on red."

"Red and yellow, a jagged line between."

"The flames of Hellholt. House Uller."

Tyrion was impressed. *The boy's not half stupid, once he gets his tongue untied.* "Go on, Pod," he urged. "If you get them all, I'll make you a gift."

"A pie with red and black slices," said Bronn. "There's a gold hand in the middle."

"House Allyrion of Godsgrace."

"A red chicken eating a snake, looks like."

"The Gargalens of Salt Shore. A cockatrice. Ser. Pardon. Not a chicken. Red, with a black snake in its beak."

"Very good!" exclaimed Tyrion. "One more, lad."

Bronn scanned the ranks of the approaching Dornishmen. "The last's a golden feather on green checks."

"A golden quill, ser. Jordayne of the Tor."

Tyrion laughed. "Nine, and well done. I could not have named them all myself." That was a lie, but it would give the boy some pride, and that he badly needed.

Martell brings some formidable companions, it would seem. Not one of the houses Pod had named was small or insignificant. Nine of the greatest lords of Dorne were coming up the kingsroad, them or their heirs, and somehow Tyrion did not think they had come all this way just to see the dancing bear. There was a message here. *And not one I like.* He wondered if it had been a mistake to ship Myrcella down to Sunspear.

"My lord," Pod said, a little timidly, "there's no litter."

Tyrion turned his head sharply. The boy was right.

"Doran Martell always travels in a litter," the boy said. "A carved litter with silk hangings, and suns on the drapes."

Tyrion had heard the same talk. Prince Doran was past fifty, and gouty. *He may have wanted to make faster time*, he told himself. *He may have feared his litter would make too tempting a target for brigands, or that it would prove too cumbersome in the high passes of the Boneway. Perhaps his gout is better.*

So why did he have such a bad feeling about this?

This waiting was intolerable. "Banners forward," he snapped. "We'll meet them." He kicked his horse. Bronn and Pod followed, one to either side. When the Dornishmen saw them coming, they spurred their own mounts, banners rippling as they rode. From their ornate saddles were slung the round metal shields they favored, and many carried bundles of short throwing spears, or the double-curved Dornish bows they used so well from horseback.

There were three sorts of Dornishmen, the first King Daeron had observed. There were the salty Dornishmen who lived along the coasts, the sandy Dornishmen of the deserts and long river valleys, and the stony Dornishmen who made their fastnesses in the passes and heights of the Red Mountains. The salty Dornishmen had the most Rhoynish blood, the stony Dornishmen the least.

All three sorts seemed well represented in Doran's retinue. The salty Dornishmen were lithe and dark, with smooth olive skin and long black hair streaming in the wind. The sandy Dornishmen were even darker, their faces burned brown by the hot Dornish sun. They wound long bright scarfs around their helms to ward off sunstroke. The stony Dornishmen were biggest and fairest, sons of the Andals and the First Men, brown-haired or blond, with faces that freckled or burned in the sun instead of browning.

The lords wore silk and satin robes with jeweled belts and flowing sleeves. Their armor was heavily enameled and inlaid with burnished copper, shining silver, and soft red gold. They came astride red horses and golden ones and a few as pale as snow, all slim and swift, with long necks and narrow beautiful heads. The fabled sand steeds of Dorne were smaller than proper warhorses and could not bear such weight of armor, but it was said that they could run for a day and night and another day, and never tire.

The Dornish leader forked a stallion black as sin with a mane and tail the color of fire. He sat his saddle as if he'd been born there, tall, slim, graceful. A cloak of pale red silk fluttered from his shoulders, and his shirt was armored with overlapping rows of copper disks that glittered like a thousand bright new pennies as he rode. His high gilded helm displayed a copper sun on its brow, and the round shield slung behind him bore the sun-and-spear of House Martell on its polished metal surface.

A Martell sun, but ten years too young, Tyrion thought as he reined up, *too fit as well, and far too fierce.* He knew what he must deal with by then. *How many Dornishmen does it take to start a war?* he asked himself. *Only one.* Yet he had no choice but to smile. "Well met, my lords. We had word of your approach, and His Grace King Joffrey bid me ride out to welcome you in his name. My lord father the King's Hand sends his greetings as well." He feigned an amiable confusion. "Which of you is Prince Doran?"

"My brother's health requires he remain at Sunspear." The princeling removed his helm. Beneath, his face was lined and saturnine, with thin arched brows above large eyes as black and shiny as pools of coal oil. Only a few streaks of silver marred the lustrous black hair that receded from his brow in a widow's peak as sharply pointed as his nose. *A salty Dornishmen for certain.* "Prince Doran has sent me to join King Joffrey's council in his stead, as it please His Grace."

"His Grace will be most honored to have the counsel of a warrior as renowned as Prince Oberyn of Dorne," said Tyrion, thinking, *This will mean blood in the gutters.* "And your noble companions are most welcome as well."

"Permit me to acquaint you with them, my lord of Lannister. Ser Deziel Dalt, of Lemonwood. Lord Tremond Gargalen. Lord Harmen Uller and his brother Ser Ulwyck. Ser Ryon Allyrion and his natural son Ser Daemon Sand, the Bastard of Godsgrace. Lord Dagos Manwoody, his brother Ser Myles, his sons Mors and Dickon. Ser Arron Qorgyle. And never let it be thought that I would neglect the ladies. Myria Jordayne, heir to the Tor. Lady Larra Blackmont, her daughter Jynessa, her son Perros." He raised a slender hand toward a black-haired woman to the rear, beckoning her forward. "And this is Ellaria Sand, mine own paramour."

Tyrion swallowed a groan. *His paramour, and bastard-born, Cersei*

will pitch a holy fit if he wants her at the wedding. If she consigned the
woman to some dark corner below the salt, his sister would risk the Red
Viper's wrath. Seat her beside him at the high table, and every other lady
on the dais was like to take offense. *Did Prince Doran mean to provoke
a quarrel?*

Prince Oberyn wheeled his horse about to face his fellow Dornishmen.
"Ellaria, lords and ladies, sers, see how well King Joffrey loves us. His
Grace has been so kind as to send his own Uncle Imp to bring us to his
court."

Bronn snorted back laughter, and Tyrion perforce must feign amusement as well. "Not alone, my lords. That would be too enormous a task
for a little man like me." His own party had come up on them, so it was
his turn to name the names. "Let me present Ser Flement Brax, heir to
Hornvale. Lord Gyles of Rosby. Ser Addam Marbrand, Lord Commander
of the City Watch. Jalabhar Xho, Prince of the Red Flower Vale. Ser Harys
Swyft, my uncle Kevan's good father by marriage. Ser Merlon Crakehall.
Ser Philip Foote and Ser Bronn of the Blackwater, two heroes of our recent
battle against the rebel Stannis Baratheon. And mine own squire, young
Podrick of House Payne." The names had a nice ringing sound as Tyrion
reeled them off, but the bearers were nowise near as distinguished nor
formidable a company as those who accompanied Prince Oberyn, as both
of them knew full well.

"My lord of Lannister," said Lady Blackmont, "we have come a long
dusty way, and rest and refreshment would be most welcome. Might we
continue on to the city?"

"At once, my lady." Tyrion turned his horse's head, and called to Ser
Addam Marbrand. The mounted gold cloaks who formed the greatest part
of his honor guard turned their horses crisply at Ser Addam's command,
and the column set off for the river and King's Landing beyond.

Oberyn Nymeros Martell, Tyrion muttered under his breath as he fell
in beside the man. *The Red Viper of Dorne. And what in the seven hells
am I supposed to do with him?*

He knew the man only by reputation, to be sure . . . but the reputation
was fearsome. When he was no more than sixteen, Prince Oberyn had
been found abed with the paramour of old Lord Yronwood, a huge man
of fierce repute and short temper. A duel ensued, though in view of the
prince's youth and high birth, it was only to first blood. Both men took
cuts, and honor was satisfied. Yet Prince Oberyn soon recovered, while
Lord Yronwood's wounds festered and killed him. Afterward men whispered that Oberyn had fought with a poisoned sword, and ever thereafter
friends and foes alike called him the Red Viper.

That was many years ago, to be sure. The boy of sixteen was a man
past forty now, and his legend had grown a deal darker. He had traveled

in the Free Cities, learning the poisoner's trade and perhaps arts darker
still, if rumors could be believed. He had studied at the Citadel, going so
far as to forge six links of a maester's chain before he grew bored. He had
soldiered in the Disputed Lands across the narrow sea, riding with the
Second Sons for a time before forming his own company. His tourneys,
his battles, his duels, his horses, his carnality ... it was said that he
bedded men and women both, and had begotten bastard girls all over
Dorne. The *sand snakes*, men called his daughters. So far as Tyrion had
heard, Prince Oberyn had never fathered a son.

And of course, he had crippled the heir to Highgarden.

*There is no man in the Seven Kingdoms who will be less welcome at a
Tyrell wedding*, thought Tyrion. To send Prince Oberyn to King's Landing
while the city still hosted Lord Mace Tyrell, two of his sons, and thousands of their men-at-arms was a provocation as dangerous as Prince
Oberyn himself. *A wrong word, an ill-timed jest, a look, that's all it will
take, and our noble allies will be at one another's throats.*

"We have met before," the Dornish prince said lightly to Tyrion as
they rode side by side along the kingsroad, past ashen fields and the
skeletons of trees. "I would not expect you to remember, though. You
were even smaller than you are now."

There was a mocking edge to his voice that Tyrion misliked, but he
was not about to let the Dornishman provoke him. "When was this, my
lord?" he asked in tones of polite interest.

"Oh, many and many a year ago, when my mother ruled in Dorne and
your lord father was Hand to a different king."

Not so different as you might think, reflected Tyrion.

"It was when I visited Casterly Rock with my mother, her consort,
and my sister Elia. I was, oh, fourteen, fifteen, thereabouts, Elia a year
older. Your brother and sister were eight or nine, as I recall, and you had
just been born."

A queer time to come visiting. His mother had died giving him birth,
so the Martells would have found the Rock deep in mourning. His father
especially. Lord Tywin seldom spoke of his wife, but Tyrion had heard
his uncles talk of the love between them. In those days, his father had
been Aerys's Hand, and many people said that Lord Tywin Lannister
ruled the Seven Kingdoms, but Lady Joanna ruled Lord Tywin. "He was
not the same man after she died, Imp," his Uncle Gery told him once.
"The best part of him died with her." Gerion had been the youngest of
Lord Tytos Lannister's four sons, and the uncle Tyrion liked best.

But he was gone now, lost beyond the seas, and Tyrion himself had
put Lady Joanna in her grave. "Did you find Casterly Rock to your liking,
my lord?"

"Scarcely. Your father ignored us the whole time we were there, after commanding Ser Kevan to see to our entertainment. The cell they gave me had a featherbed to sleep in and Myrish carpets on the floor, but it was dark and windowless, much like a dungeon when you come down to it, as I told Elia at the time. Your skies were too grey, your wines too sweet, your women too chaste, your food too bland . . . and you yourself were the greatest disappointment of all."

"I had just been born. What did you expect of me?"

"*Enormity*," the black-haired prince replied. "You were small, but far-famed. We were in Oldtown at your birth, and all the city talked of was the monster that had been born to the King's Hand, and what such an omen might foretell for the realm."

"Famine, plague, and war, no doubt." Tyrion gave a sour smile. "It's always famine, plague, and war. Oh, and winter, and the long night that never ends."

"All that," said Prince Oberyn, "and your father's fall as well. Lord Tywin had made himself greater than King Aerys, I heard one begging brother preach, but only a god is meant to stand above a king. You were his curse, a punishment sent by the gods to teach him that he was no better than any other man."

"I try, but he refuses to learn." Tyrion gave a sigh. "But do go on, I pray you. I love a good tale."

"And well you might, since you were said to have one, a stiff curly tail like a swine's. Your head was monstrous huge, we heard, half again the size of your body, and you had been born with thick black hair and a beard besides, an evil eye, and lion's claws. Your teeth were so long you could not close your mouth, and between your legs were a girl's privates as well as a boy's."

"Life would be much simpler if men could fuck themselves, don't you agree? And I can think of a few times when claws and teeth might have proved useful. Even so, I begin to see the nature of your complaint."

Bronn gave out with a chuckle, but Oberyn only smiled. "We might never have seen you at all but for your sweet sister. You were never seen at table or hall, though sometimes at night we could hear a baby howling down in the depths of the Rock. You did have a monstrous great voice, I must grant you that. You would wail for hours, and nothing would quiet you but a woman's teat."

"Still true, as it happens."

This time Prince Oberyn did laugh. "A taste we share. Lord Gargalen once told me he hoped to die with a sword in his hand, to which I replied that I would sooner go with a breast in mine."

Tyrion had to grin. "You were speaking of my sister?"

"Cersei promised Elia to show you to us. The day before we were to sail, whilst my mother and your father were closeted together, she and

Jaime took us down to your nursery. Your wet nurse tried to send us off, but your sister was having none of that. 'He's mine,' she said, 'and you're just a milk cow, you can't tell me what to do. Be quiet or I'll have my father cut your tongue out. A cow doesn't need a tongue, only udders.'"

"Her Grace learned charm at an early age," said Tyrion, amused by the notion of his sister claiming him as hers. *She's never been in any rush to claim me since, the gods know.*

"Cersei even undid your swaddling clothes to give us a better look," the Dornish prince continued. "You did have one evil eye, and some black fuzz on your scalp. Perhaps your head was larger than most . . . but there was no tail, no beard, neither teeth nor claws, and nothing between your legs but a tiny pink cock. After all the wonderful whispers, Lord Tywin's Doom turned out to be just a hideous red infant with stunted legs. Elia even made the noise that young girls make at the sight of infants, I'm sure you've heard it. The same noise they make over cute kittens and playful puppies. I believe she wanted to nurse you herself, ugly as you were. When I commented that you seemed a poor sort of monster, your sister said, 'He killed my mother,' and twisted your little cock so hard I thought she was like to pull it off. You shrieked, but it was only when your brother Jaime said, 'Leave him be, you're hurting him,' that Cersei let go of you. 'It doesn't matter,' she told us. 'Everyone says he's like to die soon. He shouldn't even have lived this long.'"

The sun was shining bright above them, and the day was pleasantly warm for autumn, but Tyrion Lannister went cold all over when he heard that. *My sweet sister.* He scratched at the scar of his nose and gave the Dornishman a taste of his "evil eye." *Now why would he tell such a tale? Is he testing me, or simply twisting my cock as Cersei did, so he can hear me scream?* "Be sure and tell that story to my father. It will delight him as much as it did me. The part about my tail, especially. I did have one, but he had it lopped off."

Prince Oberyn had a chuckle. "You've grown more amusing since last we met."

"Yes, but I *meant* to grow taller."

"While we are speaking of amusement, I heard a curious tale from Lord Buckler's steward. He claimed that you had put a tax on women's privy purses."

"It is a tax on whoring," said Tyrion, irritated all over again. *And it was my bloody father's notion.* "Only a penny for each, ah . . . act. The King's Hand felt it might help improve the morals of the city." *And pay for Joffrey's wedding besides.* Needless to say, as master of coin, Tyrion had gotten all the blame for it. Bronn said they were calling it the dwarf's penny in the streets. "Spread your legs for the Halfman, now," they were shouting in the brothels and wine sinks, if the sellsword could be believed.

"I will make certain to keep my pouch full of pennies. Even a prince must pay his taxes."

"Why should you need to go whoring?" He glanced back to where Ellaria Sand rode among the other women. "Did you tire of your paramour on the road?"

"Never. We share too much." Prince Oberyn shrugged. "We have never shared a beautiful blonde woman, however, and Ellaria is curious. Do you know of such a creature?"

"I am a man wedded." *Though not yet bedded.* "I no longer frequent whores." *Unless I want to see them hanged.*

Oberyn abruptly changed the subject. "It's said there are to be seventy-seven dishes served at the king's wedding feast."

"Are you hungry, my prince?"

"I have hungered for a long time. Though not for food. Pray tell me, when will the *justice* be served?"

"Justice." *Yes, that is why he's here, I should have seen that at once.* "You were close to your sister?"

"As children Elia and I were inseparable, much like your own brother and sister."

Gods, I hope not. "Wars and weddings have kept us well occupied, Prince Oberyn. I fear no one has yet had the time to look into murders sixteen years stale, dreadful as they were. We shall, of course, just as soon as we may. Any help that Dorne might be able to provide to restore the king's peace would only hasten the beginning of my lord father's inquiry –"

"Dwarf," said the Red Viper, in a tone grown markedly less cordial, "spare me your Lannister lies. Is it sheep you take us for, or fools? My brother is not a bloodthirsty man, but neither has he been asleep for sixteen years. Jon Arryn came to Sunspear the year after Robert took the throne, and you can be sure that he was questioned closely. Him, and a hundred more. I did not come for some mummer's show of an *inquiry*. I came for justice for Elia and her children, and I will have it. Starting with this lummox Gregor Clegane ... but not, I think, ending there. Before he dies, the Enormity That Rides will tell me whence came his orders, please assure your lord father of that." He smiled. "An old septon once claimed I was living proof of the goodness of the gods. Do you know why that is, Imp?"

"No," Tyrion admitted warily.

"Why, if the gods were cruel, they would have made me my mother's firstborn, and Doran her third. I *am* a bloodthirsty man, you see. And it is me you must contend with now, not my patient, prudent, and gouty brother."

Tyrion could see the sun shining on the Blackwater Rush half a mile ahead, and on the walls and towers and hills of King's Landing beyond.

He glanced over his shoulder, at the glittering column following them up the kingsroad. "You speak like a man with a great host at his back," he said, "yet all I see are three hundred. Do you spy that city there, north of the river?"

"The midden heap you call King's Landing?"

"That's the very one."

"Not only do I see it, I believe I smell it now."

"Then take a good sniff, my lord. Fill up your nose. Half a million people stink more than three hundred, you'll find. Do you smell the gold cloaks? There are near five thousand of them. My father's own sworn swords must account for another twenty thousand. And then there are the roses. Roses smell so sweet, don't they? Especially when there are so *many* of them. Fifty, sixty, seventy thousand roses, in the city or camped outside it, I can't really say how many are left, but there's more than I care to count, anyway."

Martell gave a shrug. "In Dorne of old before we married Daeron, it was said that all flowers bow before the sun. Should the roses seek to hinder me I'll gladly trample them underfoot."

"As you trampled Willas Tyrell?"

The Dornishman did not react as expected. "I had a letter from Willas not half a year past. We share an interest in fine horseflesh. He has never borne me any ill will for what happened in the lists. I struck his breast-plate clean, but his foot caught in a stirrup as he fell and his horse came down on top of him. I sent a maester to him afterward, but it was all he could do to save the boy's leg. The knee was far past mending. If any were to blame, it was his fool of a father. Willas Tyrell was green as his surcoat and had no business riding in such company. The Fat Flower thrust him into tourneys at too tender an age, just as he did with the other two. He wanted another Leo Longthorn, and made himself a cripple."

"There are those who say Ser Loras is better than Leo Longthorn ever was," said Tyrion.

"Renly's little rose? I doubt that."

"Doubt it all you wish," said Tyrion, "but Ser Loras has defeated many good knights, including my brother Jaime."

"By *defeated*, you mean *unhorsed*, in tourney. Tell me who he's slain in battle if you mean to frighten me."

"Ser Robar Royce and Ser Emmon Cuy, for two. And men say he performed prodigious feats of valor on the Blackwater, fighting beside Lord Renly's ghost."

"So these same men who saw the prodigious feats saw the ghost as well, yes?" The Dornishman laughed lightly.

Tyrion gave him a long look. "Chataya's on the Street of Silk has several girls who might suit your needs. Dancy has hair the color of honey. Marei's is pale white-gold. I would advise you to keep one or the other by your side at all times, my lord."

"At all times?" Prince Oberyn lifted a thin black eyebrow. "And why is that, my good Imp?"

"You want to die with a breast in hand, you said." Tyrion cantered on ahead to where the ferry barges waited on the south bank of the Blackwater. He had suffered all he meant to suffer of what passed for Dornish wit. *Father should have sent Joffrey after all. He could have asked Prince Oberyn if he knew how a Dornishman differed from a cowflop.* That made him grin despite himself. He would have to make a point of being on hand when the Red Viper was presented to the king.

ARYA

The man on the roof was the first to die. He was crouched down by the chimney two hundred yards away, no more than a vague shadow in the predawn gloom, but as the sky began to lighten he stirred, stretched, and stood. Anguy's arrow took him in the chest. He tumbled bonelessly down the steep slate pitch, and fell in front of the septry door.

The Mummers had posted two guards there, but their torch left them night blind, and the outlaws had crept in close. Kyle and Notch let fly together. One man went down with an arrow through his throat, the other through his belly. The second man dropped the torch, and the flames licked up at him. He screamed as his clothes took fire, and that was the end of stealth. Thoros gave a shout, and the outlaws attacked in earnest.

Arya watched from atop her horse, on the crest of the wooded ridge that overlooked the septry, mill, brewhouse, and stables and the desolation of weeds, burnt trees, and mud that surrounded them. The trees were mostly bare now, and the few withered brown leaves that still clung to the branches did little to obstruct her view. Lord Beric had left Beardless Dick and Mudge to guard them. Arya hated being left behind like she was some stupid *child*, but at least Gendry had been kept back as well. She knew better than to try and argue. This was battle, and in battle you had to obey.

The eastern horizon glowed gold and pink, and overhead a half moon peeked out through low scuttling clouds. The wind blew cold, and Arya could hear the rush of water and the creak of the mill's great wooden waterwheel. There was a smell of rain in the dawn air, but no drops were falling yet. Flaming arrows flew through the morning mists, trailing pale ribbons of fire, and thudded into the wooden walls of the septry. A few smashed through shuttered windows, and soon enough thin tendrils of smoke were rising between the broken shutters.

Two Mummers came bursting from the septry side by side, axes in their hands. Anguy and the other archers were waiting. One axeman died at once. The other managed to duck, so the shaft ripped through his shoulder. He staggered on, till two more arrows found him, so quickly it was hard to say which had struck first. The long shafts punched through his breastplate as if it had been made of silk instead of steel. He fell heavily. Anguy had arrows tipped with bodkins as well as broadheads. A bodkin could pierce even heavy plate. *I'm going to learn to shoot a bow*, Arya thought. She loved swordfighting, but she could see how arrows were good too.

Flames were creeping up the west wall of the septry, and thick smoke poured through a broken window. A Myrish crossbowman poked his head out a different window, got off a bolt, and ducked down to rewind. She could hear fighting from the stables as well, shouts well mingled with the screams of horses and the clang of steel. *Kill them all*, she thought fiercely. She bit her lip so hard she tasted blood. *Kill every single one.*

The crossbowman appeared again, but no sooner had he loosed than three arrows hissed past his head. One rattled off his helm. He vanished, bow and all. Arya could see flames in several of the second-story windows. Between the smoke and the morning mists, the air was a haze of blowing black and white. Anguy and the other bowmen were creeping closer, the better to find targets.

Then the septry erupted, the Mummers boiling out like angry ants. Two Ibbenese rushed through the door with shaggy brown shields held high before them, and behind them came a Dothraki with a great curved *arakh* and bells in his braid, and behind him three Volantene sellswords covered with fierce tattoos. Others were climbing out windows and leaping to the ground. Arya saw a man take an arrow through the chest with one leg across a windowsill, and heard his scream as he fell. The smoke was thickening. Quarrels and arrows sped back and forth. Watty fell with a grunt, his bow slipping from his hand. Kyle was trying to nock another shaft to his string when a man in black mail flung a spear through his belly. She heard Lord Beric shout. From out of the ditches and trees the rest of his band came pouring, steel in hand. Arya saw Lem's bright yellow cloak flapping behind him as he rode down the man who'd killed Kyle. Thoros and Lord Beric were everywhere, their swords swirling fire. The red priest hacked at a hide shield until it flew to pieces, while his horse kicked the man in the face. A Dothraki screamed and charged the lightning lord, and the flaming sword leapt out to meet his *arakh*. The blades kissed and spun and kissed again. Then the Dothraki's hair was ablaze, and a moment later he was dead. She spied Ned too, fighting at the lightning lord's side. *It's not fair, he's only a little older than me, they should have let me fight.*

The battle did not last very long. The Brave Companions still on their feet soon died, or threw down their swords. Two of the Dothraki managed to regain their horses and flee, but only because Lord Beric let them go. "Let them carry the word back to Harrenhal," he said, with flaming sword in hand. "It will give the Leech Lord and his goat a few more sleepless nights."

Jack-Be-Lucky, Harwin, and Merrit o' Moontown braved the burning septry to search for captives. They emerged from the smoke and flames a few moments later with eight brown brothers, one so weak that Merrit had to carry him across a shoulder. There was a septon with them as well, round-shouldered and balding, but he wore black chainmail over his grey robes. "Found him hiding under the cellar steps," said Jack, coughing.

Thoros smiled to see him. "You are Utt."

"*Septon* Utt. A man of god."

"What god would want the likes o' you?" growled Lem.

"I have sinned," the septon wailed. "I know, I know. Forgive me, Father. Oh, grievously have I sinned."

Arya remembered Septon Utt from her time at Harrenhal. Shagwell the Fool said he always wept and prayed for forgiveness after he'd killed his latest boy. Sometimes he even made the other Mummers scourge him. They all thought that was very funny.

Lord Beric slammed his sword into its scabbard, quenching the flames. "Give the dying the gift of mercy and bind the others hand and foot for trial," he commanded, and it was done.

The trials went swiftly. Various of the outlaws came forward to tell of things the Brave Companions had done; towns and villages sacked, crops burned, women raped and murdered, men maimed and tortured. A few spoke of the boys that Septon Utt had carried off. The septon wept and prayed through it all. "I am a weak reed," he told Lord Beric. "I pray to the Warrior for strength, but the gods made me weak. Have mercy on my weakness. The boys, the sweet boys ... I never mean to hurt them ..."

Septon Utt soon dangled beneath a tall elm, swinging slowly by the neck, as naked as his name day. The other Brave Companions followed one by one. A few fought, kicking and struggling as the noose was tightened round their throats. One of the crossbowmen kept shouting, "I soldier, I soldier," in a thick Myrish accent. Another offered to lead his captors to gold; a third told them what a good outlaw he would make. Each was stripped and bound and hanged in turn. Tom Sevenstrings played a dirge for them on his woodharp, and Thoros implored the Lord of Light to roast their souls until the end of time.

A mummer tree, Arya thought as she watched them dangle, their pale skins painted a sullen red by the flames of the burning septry. Already the crows were coming, appearing out of nowhere. She heard them croaking and cackling at one another, and wondered what they were saying. Arya had not feared Septon Utt as much as she did Rorge and Biter and some of the others still at Harrenhal, but she was glad that he was dead all the same. *They should have hanged the Hound too, or chopped his head off.* Instead, to her disgust, the outlaws had treated Sandor Clegane's burned arm, restored his sword and horse and armor, and set him free a few miles from the hollow hill. All they'd taken was his gold.

The septry soon collapsed in a roar of smoke and flame, its walls no longer able to support the weight of its heavy slate roof. The eight brown brothers watched with resignation. They were all that remained, explained the eldest, who wore a small iron hammer on a thong about his neck to signify his devotion to the Smith. "Before the war we were four-and-forty, and this was a prosperous place. We had a dozen milk cows and a bull, a hundred beehives, a vineyard and an apple arbor. But when the lions came through they took all our wine and milk and honey, slaughtered the cows, and put our vineyard to the torch. After that . . . I have lost count of our visitors. This false septon was only the latest. There was one monster . . . we gave him all our silver, but he was certain we were hiding gold, so his men killed us one by one to make Elder Brother talk."

"How did the eight of you survive?" asked Anguy the Archer.

"I am ashamed," the old man said. "It was me. When it came my turn to die, I told them where our gold was hidden."

"Brother," said Thoros of Myr, "the only shame was not telling them at once."

The outlaws sheltered that night in the brewhouse beside the little river. Their hosts had a cache of food hidden beneath the floor of the stables, so they shared a simple supper; oaten bread, onions, and a watery cabbage soup tasting faintly of garlic. Arya found a slice of carrot floating in her bowl, and counted herself lucky. The brothers never asked the outlaws for names. *They know*, Arya thought. How could they not? Lord Beric wore the lightning bolt on breastplate, shield, and cloak, and Thoros his red robes, or what remained of them. One brother, a young novice, was bold enough to tell the red priest not to pray to his false god so long as he was under their roof. "Bugger that," said Lem Lemoncloak. "He's our god too, and you owe us for your bloody lives. And what's false about him? Might be your Smith can mend a broken sword, but can he heal a broken man?"

"Enough, Lem," Lord Beric commanded. "Beneath their roof we will honor their rules."

"The sun will not cease to shine if we miss a prayer or two," Thoros agreed mildly. "I am one who would know."

Lord Beric himself did not eat. Arya had never seen him eat, though from time to time he took a cup of wine. He did not seem to sleep, either. His good eye would often close, as if from weariness, but when you spoke to him it would flick open again at once. The Marcher lord was still clad in his ratty black cloak and dented breastplate with its chipped enamel lightning. He even slept in that breastplate. The dull black steel hid the terrible wound the Hound had given him, the same way his thick woolen scarf concealed the dark ring about his throat. But nothing hid his broken head, all caved in at the temple, or the raw red pit that was his missing eye, or the shape of the skull beneath his face.

Arya looked at him warily, remembering all the tales told of him in Harrenhal. Lord Beric seemed to sense her fear. He turned his head, and beckoned her closer. "Do I frighten you, child?"

"No." She chewed her lip. "Only . . . well . . . I thought the Hound had killed you, but . . ."

"A wound," said Lem Lemoncloak. "A grievous wound, aye, but Thoros healed it. There's never been no better healer."

Lord Beric gazed at Lem with a queer look in his good eye and no look at all in the other, only scars and dried blood. "No better healer," he agreed wearily. "Lem, past time to change the watch, I'd think. See to it, if you'd be so good."

"Aye, m'lord." Lem's big yellow cloak swirled behind him as he strode out into the windy night.

"Even brave men blind themselves sometimes, when they are afraid to see," Lord Beric said when Lem was gone. "Thoros, how many times have you brought me back now?"

The red priest bowed his head. "It is R'hllor who brings you back, my lord. The Lord of Light. I am only his instrument."

"How many times?" Lord Beric insisted.

"Six," Thoros said reluctantly. "And each time is harder. You have grown reckless, my lord. Is death so very sweet?"

"Sweet? No, my friend. Not sweet."

"Then do not court it so. Lord Tywin leads from the rear. Lord Stannis as well. You would be wise to do the same. A seventh death might mean the end of both of us."

Lord Beric touched the spot above his left ear where his temple was caved in. "Here is where Ser Burton Crakehall broke helm and head with a blow of his mace." He unwound his scarf, exposing the black bruise that encircled his neck. "Here the mark the manticore made at Rushing Falls. He seized a poor beekeeper and his wife, thinking they were mine, and let it be known far and wide that he would hang them both unless I gave myself up to him. When I did he hanged them anyway, and me on the gibbet between them." He lifted a finger to the raw red pit of his eye. "Here is where the Mountain thrust his dirk through my visor." A weary smile brushed his lips. "That's thrice I have died at the hands of House Clegane. You would think that I might have learned . . ."

It was a jest, Arya knew, but Thoros did not laugh. He put a hand on Lord Beric's shoulder. "Best not to dwell on it."

"Can I dwell on what I scarce remember? I held a castle on the Marches once, and there was a woman I was pledged to marry, but I could not find that castle today, nor tell you the color of that woman's hair. Who knighted me, old friend? What were my favorite foods? It all fades. Sometimes I think I was born on the bloody grass in that grove of ash, with the taste of fire in my mouth and a hole in my chest. Are you my mother, Thoros?"

Arya stared at the Myrish priest, all shaggy hair and pink rags and bits of old armor. Grey stubble covered his cheeks and the sagging skin beneath his chin. He did not look much like the wizards in Old Nan's stories, but even so . . .

"Could you bring back a man without a head?" Arya asked. "Just the once, not six times. Could you?"

"I have no magic, child. Only prayers. That first time, his lordship had a hole right through him and blood in his mouth, I knew there was no hope. So when his poor torn chest stopped moving, I gave him the good god's own kiss to send him on his way. I filled my mouth with fire and breathed the flames inside him, down his throat to lungs and heart and soul. The *last kiss* it is called, and many a time I saw the old priests bestow it on the Lord's servants as they died. I had given it a time or two myself, as all priests must. But never before had I felt a dead man shudder as the fire filled him, nor seen his eyes come open. It was not me who raised him, my lady. It was the Lord. R'hllor is not done with him yet. Life is warmth, and warmth is fire, and fire is God's and God's alone."

Arya felt tears well in her eyes. Thoros used a lot of words, but all they meant was *no*, that much she understood.

"Your father was a good man," Lord Beric said. "Harwin has told me much of him. For his sake, I would gladly forgo your ransom, but we need the gold too desperately."

She chewed her lip. *That's true, I guess.* He had given the Hound's gold to Greenbeard and the Huntsman to buy provisions south of the Mander, she knew. "The last harvest burned, this one is drowning, and winter will soon be on us," she had heard him say when he sent them off. "The smallfolk need grain and seed, and we need blades and horses. Too many of my men ride rounseys, drays, and mules against foes mounted on coursers and destriers."

Arya didn't know how much Robb would pay for her, though. He was a king now, not the boy she'd left at Winterfell with snow melting in his hair. And if he knew the things she'd done, the stableboy and the guard at Harrenhal and all ... "What if my brother doesn't want to ransom me?"

"Why would you think that?" asked Lord Beric.

"Well," Arya said, "my hair's messy and my nails are dirty and my feet are all hard." Robb wouldn't care about that, probably, but her mother would. Lady Catelyn always wanted her to be like Sansa, to sing and dance and sew and mind her courtesies. Just thinking of it made Arya try to comb her hair with her fingers, but it was all tangles and mats, and all she did was tear some out. "I ruined that gown that Lady Small-wood gave me, and I don't sew so good." She chewed her lip. "I don't sew *very well*, I mean. Septa Mordane used to say I had a blacksmith's hands."

Gendry hooted. "Those soft little things?" he called out. "You couldn't even hold a hammer."

"I could if I wanted!" she snapped at him.

Thoros chuckled. "Your brother will pay, child. Have no fear on that count."

"Yes, but what if he *won't*?" she insisted.

Lord Beric sighed. "Then I will send you to Lady Smallwood for a time, or perhaps to mine own castle of Blackhaven. But that will not be necessary, I'm certain. I do not have the power to give you back your father, no more than Thoros does, but I can at least see that you are returned safely to your mother's arms."

"Do you *swear*?" she asked him. Yoren had promised to take her home too, only he'd gotten killed instead.

"On my honor as a knight," the lightning lord said solemnly.

It was raining when Lem returned to the brewhouse, muttering curses as water ran off his yellow cloak to puddle on the floor. Anguy and Jack-Be-Lucky sat by the door rolling dice, but no matter which game they played one-eyed Jack had no luck at all. Tom Sevenstrings replaced a string on his woodharp, and sang "The Mother's Tears," "When Wil-lum's Wife Was Wet," "Lord Harte Rode Out on a Rainy Day," and then "The Rains of Castamere."

And who are you, the proud lord said,
   that I must bow so low?
Only a cat of a different coat,
   that's all the truth I know.
In a coat of gold or a coat of red,
   a lion still has claws,
And mine are long and sharp, my lord,
   as long and sharp as yours.
And so he spoke, and so he spoke,
   that lord of Castamere,
But now the rains weep o'er his hall,
   with no one there to hear.
Yes now the rains weep o'er his hall,
   and not a soul to hear.

Finally Tom ran out of rain songs and put away his harp. Then there was only the sound of the rain itself beating down on the slate roof of the brewhouse. The dice game ended, and Arya stood on one leg and then the other listening to Merrit complain about his horse throwing a shoe.

"I could shoe him for you," said Gendry, all of a sudden. "I was only a 'prentice, but my master said my hand was made to hold a hammer. I can shoe horses, close up rents in mail, and beat the dents from plate. I bet I could make swords too."

"What are you saying, lad?" asked Harwin.

"I'll smith for you." Gendry went to one knee before Lord Beric. "If you'll have me, m'lord, I could be of use. I've made tools and knives and once I made a helmet that wasn't so bad. One of the Mountain's men stole it from me when we was taken."

Arya bit her lip. *He means to leave me too.*

"You would do better serving Lord Tully at Riverrun," said Lord Beric. "I cannot pay for your work."

"No one ever did. I want a forge, and food to eat, some place I can sleep. That's enough, m'lord."

"A smith can find a welcome most anywhere. A skilled armorer even more so. Why would you choose to stay with us?"

Arya watched Gendry screw up his stupid face, thinking. "At the hollow hill, what you said about being King Robert's men, and brothers, I liked that. I liked that you gave the Hound a trial. Lord Bolton just hanged folk or took off their heads, and Lord Tywin and Ser Amory were the same. I'd sooner smith for you."

"We got plenty of mail needs mending, m'lord," Jack reminded Lord Beric. "Most we took off the dead, and there's holes where the death came through."

"You must be a lackwit, boy," said Lem. "We're *outlaws*. Lowborn scum, most of us, excepting his lordship. Don't think it'll be like Tom's fool songs neither. You won't be stealing no kisses from a princess, nor riding in no tourneys in stolen armor. You join us, you'll end with your neck in a noose, or your head mounted up above some castle gate."

"It's no more than they'd do for you," said Gendry.

"Aye, that's so," said Jack-Be-Lucky cheerfully. "The crows await us all. M'lord, the boy seems brave enough, and we do have need of what he brings us. Take him, says Jack."

"And quick," suggested Harwin, chuckling, "before the fever passes and he comes back to his senses."

A wan smile crossed Lord Beric's lips. "Thoros, my sword."

This time the lightning lord did not set the blade afire, but merely laid it light on Gendry's shoulder. "Gendry, do you swear before the eyes of gods and men to defend those who cannot defend themselves, to protect all women and children, to obey your captains, your liege lord, and your king, to fight bravely when needed and do such other tasks as are laid upon you, however hard or humble or dangerous they may be?"

"I do, m'lord."

The marcher lord moved the sword from the right shoulder to the left, and said, "Arise Ser Gendry, knight of the hollow hill, and be welcome to our brotherhood."

From the door came rough, rasping laughter.

The rain was running off him. His burned arm was wrapped in leaves and linen and bound tight against his chest by a crude rope sling, but the older burns that marked his face glistened black and slick in the glow of their little fire. "Making more knights, Dondarrion?" the intruder said in a growl. "I ought to kill you all over again for that."

Lord Beric faced him coolly. "I'd hoped we'd seen the last of you, Clegane. How did you come to find us?"

"It wasn't hard. You made enough bloody smoke to be seen in Oldtown."

"What's become of the sentries I posted?"

Clegane's mouth twitched. "Those two blind men? Might be I killed them both. What would you do if I had?"

Anguy strung his bow. Notch was doing the same. "Do you wish to die so very much, Sandor?" asked Thoros. "You must be mad or drunk to follow us here."

"Drunk on rain? You didn't leave me enough gold to buy a cup of wine, you whoresons."

Anguy drew an arrow. "We're outlaws. Outlaws steal. It's in the songs, if you ask nice Tom may sing you one. Be thankful we didn't kill you."

"Come try it, Archer. I'll take that quiver off you and shove those arrows up your freckly little arse."

Anguy raised his longbow, but Lord Beric lifted a hand before he could loose. "Why did you come here, Clegane?"

"To get back what's mine."

"Your gold?"

"What else? It wasn't for the pleasure of looking at your face, Dondarrion, I'll tell you that. You're uglier than me now. And a robber knight besides, it seems."

"I gave you a note for your gold," Lord Beric said calmly. "A promise to pay, when the war's done."

"I wiped my arse with your paper. I want the gold."

"We don't have it. I sent it south with Greenbeard and the Huntsman, to buy grain and seed across the Mander."

"To feed all them whose crops you burned," said Gendry.

"Is that the tale, now?" Sandor Clegane laughed again. "As it happens, that's just what I meant to do with it. Feed a bunch of ugly peasants and their poxy whelps."

"You're lying," said Gendry.

"The boy has a mouth on him, I see. Why believe them and not me? Couldn't be my face, could it?" Clegane glanced at Arya. "You going to make her a knight too, Dondarrion? The first eight-year-old girl knight?"

"I'm *twelve*," Arya lied loudly, "and I could be a knight if I wanted. I could have killed you too, only Lem took my knife." Remembering that still made her angry.

"Complain to Lem, not me. Then tuck your tail between your legs and run. Do you know what dogs do to wolves?"

"Next time I *will* kill you. I'll kill your brother too!"

"No." His dark eyes narrowed. "That you won't." He turned back to Lord Beric. "Say, make my horse a knight. He never shits in the hall and doesn't kick more than most, he deserves to be knighted. Unless you meant to steal him too."

"Best climb on that horse and go," warned Lem.

"I'll go with my gold. Your own god said I'm guiltless –"

"The Lord of Light gave you back your life," declared Thoros of Myr. "He did not proclaim you Baelor the Blessed come again." The red priest unsheathed his sword, and Arya saw that Jack and Merrit had drawn as well. Lord Beric still held the blade he'd used to dub Gendry. *Maybe this time they'll kill him.*

The Hound's mouth gave another twitch. "You're no more than common thieves."

Lem glowered. "Your lion friends ride into some village, take all the food and every coin they find, and call it *foraging*. The wolves as well, so why not us? No one robbed you, dog. You just been good and *foraged*."

Sandor Clegane looked at their faces, every one, as if he were trying to commit them all to memory. Then he walked back out into the darkness and the pouring rain from whence he'd come, with never another word. The outlaws waited, wondering . . .

"I best go see what he did to our sentries." Harwin took a wary look out the door before he left, to make certain the Hound was not lurking just outside.

"How'd that bloody bastard get all that gold anyhow?" Lem Lemoncloak said, to break the tension.

Anguy shrugged. "He won the Hand's tourney. In King's Landing." The bowman grinned. "I won a fair fortune myself, but then I met Dancy, Jayde, and Alayaya. They taught me what roast swan tastes like, and how to bathe in Arbor wine."

"Pissed it all away, did you?" laughed Harwin.

"Not *all*. I bought these boots, and this excellent dagger."

"You ought t'have bought some land and made one o' them roast swan girls an honest woman," said Jack-Be-Lucky. "Raised yourself a crop o' turnips and a crop o' sons."

"Warrior defend me! What a waste that would have been, to turn my gold to turnips."

"I like turnips," said Jack, aggrieved. "I could do with some mashed turnips right now."

Thoros of Myr paid no heed to the banter. "The Hound has lost more than a few bags of coin," he mused. "He has lost his master and kennel as well. He cannot go back to the Lannisters, the Young Wolf would never have him, nor would his brother be like to welcome him. That gold was all he had left, it seems to me."

"Bloody hell," said Watty the Miller. "He'll come murder us in our sleep for sure, then."

"No." Lord Beric had sheathed his sword. "Sandor Clegane would kill us all gladly, but not in our sleep. Anguy, on the morrow, take the rear with Beardless Dick. If you see Clegane still sniffing after us, kill his horse."

"That's a good horse," Anguy protested.

"Aye," said Lem. "It's the bloody rider we should be killing. We could use that horse."

"I'm with Lem," Notch said. "Let me feather the dog a few times, discourage him some."

Lord Beric shook his head. "Clegane won his life beneath the hollow hill. I will not rob him of it."

"My lord is wise," Thoros told the others. "Brothers, a trial by battle is a holy thing. You heard me ask R'hllor to take a hand, and you saw his fiery finger snap Lord Beric's sword, just as he was about to make an end of it. The Lord of Light is not yet done with Joffrey's Hound, it would seem."

Harwin soon returned to the brewhouse. "Puddingfoot was sound asleep, but unharmed."

"Wait till I get hold of him," said Lem. "I'll cut him a new bunghole. He could have gotten every one of us killed."

No one rested very comfortably that night, knowing that Sandor Clegane was out there in the dark, somewhere close. Arya curled up near the fire, warm and snug, yet sleep would not come. She took out the coin that Jaqen H'ghar had given her and curled her fingers around it as she lay beneath her cloak. It made her feel strong to hold it, remembering how she'd been the ghost in Harrenhal. She could kill with a whisper then.

Jaqen was gone, though. He'd left her. *Hot Pie left me too, and now Gendry is leaving.* Lommy had died, Yoren had died, Syrio Forel had died, even her father had died, and Jaqen had given her a stupid iron penny and vanished. "*Valar morghulis,*" she whispered softly, tightening her fist so the hard edges of the coin dug into her palm. "Ser Gregor, Dunsen, Polliver, Raff the Sweetling. The Tickler and the Hound. Ser Ilyn, Ser Meryn, King Joffrey, Queen Cersei." Arya tried to imagine how they would look when they were dead, but it was hard to bring their faces to mind. The Hound she could see, and his brother the Mountain, and she would never forget Joffrey's face, or his mother's . . . but Raff and Dunsen and Polliver were all fading, and even the Tickler, whose looks had been so commonplace.

Sleep took her at last, but in the black of night Arya woke again, tingling. The fire had burned down to embers. Mudge stood by the door, and another guard was pacing outside. The rain had stopped, and she could hear wolves howling. *So close,* she thought, *and so many.* They sounded as if they were all around the stable, dozens of them, maybe hundreds. *I hope they eat the Hound.* She remembered what he'd said, about wolves and dogs.

Come morning, Septon Utt still swung beneath the tree, but the brown brothers were out in the rain with spades, digging shallow graves for the other dead. Lord Beric thanked them for the night's lodging and the meal, and gave them a bag of silver stags to help rebuild. Harwin, Likely Luke, and Watty the Miller went out scouting, but neither wolves nor hounds were found.

As Arya was cinching her saddle girth, Gendry came up to say that he was sorry. She put a foot in the stirrup and swung up into her saddle, so she could look down on him instead of up. *You could have made swords at Riverrun for my brother,* she thought, but what she said was, "If you want to be some stupid outlaw knight and get hanged, why should I care? I'll be at Riverrun, ransomed, with my brother."

There was no rain that day, thankfully, and for once they made good time.

BRAN

The tower stood upon an island, its twin reflected on the still blue waters. When the wind blew, ripples moved across the surface of the lake, chasing one another like boys at play. Oak trees grew thick along the lakeshore, a dense stand of them with a litter of fallen acorns on the ground beneath. Beyond them was the village, or what remained of it.

It was the first village they had seen since leaving the foothills. Meera had scouted ahead to make certain there was no one lurking amongst the ruins. Sliding in and amongst oaks and apple trees with her net and spear in hand, she startled three red deer and sent them bounding away through the brush. Summer saw the flash of motion and was after them at once. Bran watched the direwolf lope off, and for a moment wanted nothing so much as to slip his skin and run with him, but Meera was waving for them to come ahead. Reluctantly, he turned away from Summer and urged Hodor on, into the village. Jojen walked with them.

The ground from here to the Wall was grasslands, Bran knew; fallow fields and low rolling hills, high meadows and lowland bogs. It would be much easier going than the mountains behind, but so much open space made Meera uneasy. "I feel naked," she confessed. "There's no place to hide."

"Who holds this land?" Jojen asked Bran.

"The Night's Watch," he answered. "This is the Gift. The New Gift, and north of that Brandon's Gift." Maester Luwin had taught him the history. "Brandon the Builder gave all the land south of the Wall to the black brothers, to a distance of twenty-five leagues. For their . . . for their *sustenance and support."* He was proud that he still remembered that part. "Some maesters say it was some other Brandon, not the Builder, but it's still Brandon's Gift. Thousands of years later, Good Queen Alysanne visited the Wall on her dragon Silverwing, and she thought the Night's Watch was so brave that she had the Old King double the size of their lands, to fifty leagues. So that was the New Gift." He waved a hand. "Here. All this."

No one had lived in the village for long years, Bran could see. All the houses were falling down. Even the inn. It had never been *much* of an inn, to look at it, but now all that remained was a stone chimney and two cracked walls, set amongst a dozen apple trees. One was growing up through the common room, where a layer of wet brown leaves and rotting apples carpeted the floor. The air was thick with the smell of them, a cloying cidery scent that was almost overwhelming. Meera stabbed a few apples with her frog spear, trying to find some still good enough to eat, but they were all too brown and wormy.

It was a peaceful spot, still and tranquil and lovely to behold, but Bran thought there was something sad about an empty inn, and Hodor seemed to feel it too. "Hodor?" he said in a confused sort of way. "Hodor? Hodor?"

"This is good land." Jojen picked up a handful of dirt, rubbing it between his fingers. "A village, an inn, a stout holdfast in the lake, all these apple trees ... but where are the people, Bran? Why would they leave such a place?"

"They were afraid of the wildlings," said Bran. "Wildlings come over the Wall or through the mountains, to raid and steal and carry off women. If they catch you, they make your skull into a cup to drink blood, Old Nan used to say. The Night's Watch isn't so strong as it was in Brandon's day or Queen Alysanne's, so more get through. The places nearest the Wall got raided so much the smallfolk moved south, into the mountains or onto the Umber lands east of the kingsroad. The Greatjon's people get raided too, but not so much as the people who used to live in the Gift."

Jojen Reed turned his head slowly, listening to music only he could hear. "We need to shelter here. There's a storm coming. A bad one."

Bran looked up at the sky. It had been a beautiful crisp clear autumn day, sunny and almost warm, but there were dark clouds off to the west now, that was true, and the wind seemed to be picking up. "There's no roof on the inn and only the two walls," he pointed out. "We should go out to the holdfast."

"Hodor," said Hodor. Maybe he agreed.

"We have no boat, Bran." Meera poked through the leaves idly with her frog spear.

"There's a causeway. A stone causeway, hidden under the water. We could walk out." *They* could, anyway; he would have to ride on Hodor's back, but at least he'd stay dry that way.

The Reeds exchanged a look. "How do you know that?" asked Jojen. "Have you been here before, my prince?"

"No. Old Nan told me. The holdfast has a golden crown, see?" He pointed across the lake. You could see patches of flaking gold paint up around the crenellations. "Queen Alysanne slept there, so they painted the merlons gold in her honor."

"A causeway?" Jojen studied the lake. "You are certain?"

"Certain," said Bran.

Meera found the foot of it easily enough, once she knew to look; a stone pathway three feet wide, leading right out into the lake. She took them out step by careful step, probing ahead with her frog spear. They could see where the path emerged again, climbing from the water onto the island and turning into a short flight of stone steps that led to the holdfast door.

Path, steps, and door were in a straight line, which made you think the causeway ran straight, but that wasn't so. Under the lake it zigged and zagged, going a third of a way around the island before jagging back. The turns were treacherous, and the long path meant that anyone approaching would be exposed to arrow fire from the tower for a long time. The hidden stones were slimy and slippery too; twice Hodor almost lost his footing and shouted *"HODOR!"* in alarm before regaining his balance. The second time scared Bran badly. If Hodor fell into the lake with him in his basket, he could well drown, especially if the huge stableboy panicked and forgot that Bran was there, the way he did sometimes. *Maybe we should have stayed at the inn, under the apple tree*, he thought, but by then it was too late.

Thankfully there was no third time, and the water never got up past Hodor's waist, though the Reeds were in it up to their chests. And before long they were on the island, climbing the steps to the holdfast. The door was still stout, though its heavy oak planks had warped over the years and it could no longer be closed completely. Meera shoved it open all the way, the rusted iron hinges screaming. The lintel was low. "Duck down, Hodor," Bran said, and he did, but not enough to keep Bran from hitting his head. "That hurt," he complained.

"Hodor," said Hodor, straightening.

They found themselves in a gloomy strongroom, barely large enough to hold the four of them. Steps built into the inner wall of the tower curved away upward to their left, downward to their right, behind iron grates. Bran looked up and saw another grate just above his head. *A murder hole.* He was glad there was no one up there now to pour boiling oil down on them.

The grates were locked, but the iron bars were red with rust. Hodor grabbed hold of the lefthand door and gave it a pull, grunting with effort. Nothing happened. He tried pushing with no more success. He shook the bars, kicked, shoved against them and rattled them and punched the hinges with a huge hand until the air was filled with flakes of rust, but the iron door would not budge. The one down to the undervault was no more accommodating. "No way in," said Meera, shrugging.

The murder hole was just above Bran's head, as he sat in his basket on Hodor's back. He reached up and grabbed the bars to give them a try. When he pulled down the grating came out of the ceiling in a cascade of rust and crumbling stone. "*HODOR!*" Hodor shouted. The heavy iron grate gave Bran another bang in the head, and crashed down near Jojen's fect when he shoved it off of him. Meera laughed. "Look at that, my prince," she said, "you're stronger than Hodor." Bran blushed.

With the grate gone, Hodor was able to boost Meera and Jojen up through the gaping murder hole. The crannogmen took Bran by the arms and drew him up after them. Getting Hodor inside was the hard part. He was too heavy for the Reeds to lift the way they'd lifted Bran. Finally Bran told him to go look for some big rocks. The island had no lack of those, and Hodor was able to pile them high enough to grab the crumbling edges of the hole and climb through. "Hodor," he panted happily, grinning at all of them.

They found themselves in a maze of small cells, dark and empty, but Meera explored until she found the way back to the steps. The higher they climbed, the better the light; on the third story the thick outer wall was pierced by arrow slits, the fourth had actual windows, and the fifth and highest was one big round chamber with arched doors on three sides opening onto small stone balconies. On the fourth side was a privy chamber perched above a sewer chute that dropped straight down into the lake.

By the time they reached the roof the sky was completely overcast, and the clouds to the west were black. The wind was blowing so strong it lifted up Bran's cloak and made it flap and snap. "Hodor," Hodor said at the noise.

Meera spun in a circle. "I feel almost a giant, standing high above the world."

"There are trees in the Neck that stand twice as tall as this," her brother reminded her.

"Aye, but they have other trees around them just as high," said Meera. "The world presses close in the Neck, and the sky is so much smaller. Here ... feel that wind, Brother? And look how large the world has grown."

It was true, you could see a long ways from up here. To the south the foothills rose, with the mountains grey and green beyond them. The rolling plains of the New Gift stretched away to all the other directions, as far as the eye could see. "I was hoping we could see the Wall from here," said Bran, disappointed. "That was stupid, we must still be fifty leagues away." Just speaking of it made him feel tired, and cold as well. "Jojen, what will we do when we reach the Wall? My uncle always said how big it was. Seven hundred feet high, and so thick at the base that the gates are more like tunnels through the ice. How are we going to get past to find the three-eyed crow?"

"There are abandoned castles along the Wall, I've heard," Jojen answered. "Fortresses built by the Night's Watch but now left empty. One of them may give us our way through."

The ghost castles, Old Nan had called them. Maester Luwin had once made Bran learn the names of every one of the forts along the Wall. That had been hard; there were nineteen of them all told, though no more than seventeen had ever been manned at any one time. At the feast in honor of King Robert's visit to Winterfell, Bran had recited the names for his uncle Benjen, east to west and then west to east. Benjen Stark had laughed and said, "You know them better than I do, Bran. Perhaps you should be First Ranger. I'll stay here in your place." That was before Bran fell, though. Before he was broken. By the time he'd woken crippled from his sleep, his uncle had gone back to Castle Black.

"My uncle said the gates were sealed with ice and stone whenever a castle had to be abandoned," said Bran.

"Then we'll have to open them again," said Meera.

That made him uneasy. "We shouldn't do that. Bad things might come through from the other side. We should just go to Castle Black and tell the Lord Commander to let us pass."

"Your Grace," said Jojen, "we must avoid Castle Black, just as we avoided the kingsroad. There are hundreds of men there."

"Men of the Night's Watch," said Bran. "They say vows, to take no part in wars and stuff."

"Aye," said Jojen, "but one man willing to forswear himself would be enough to sell your secret to the ironmen or the Bastard of Bolton. And we cannot be certain that the Watch would agree to let us pass. They might decide to hold us or send us back."

"But my father was a friend of the Night's Watch, and my uncle is First Ranger. He might know where the three-eyed crow lives. And Jon's at Castle Black too." Bran had been hoping to see Jon again, and their uncle too. The last black brothers to visit Winterfell said that Benjen Stark had vanished on a ranging, but surely he would have made his way back by *now*. "I bet the Watch would even give us horses," he went on.

"Quiet." Jojen shaded his eyes with a hand and gazed off toward the setting sun. "Look. There's something . . . a rider, I think. Do you see him?"

Bran shaded his eyes as well, and even so he had to squint. He saw nothing at first, till some movement made him turn. At first he thought it might be Summer, but no. *A man on a horse.* He was too far away to see much else.

"Hodor?" Hodor had put a hand over his eyes as well, only he was looking the wrong way. "Hodor?"

"He is in no haste," said Meera, "but he's making for this village, it seems to me."

"We had best go inside, before we're seen," said Jojen.

"Summer's near the village," Bran objected.

"Summer will be fine," Meera promised. "It's only one man on a tired horse."

A few fat wet drops began to patter against the stone as they retreated to the floor below. That was well timed; the rain began to fall in earnest a short time later. Even through the thick walls they could hear it lashing against the surface of the lake. They sat on the floor in the round empty room, amidst gathering gloom. The north-facing balcony looked out toward the abandoned village. Meera crept out on her belly to peer across the lake and see what had become of the horseman. "He's taken shelter in the ruins of the inn," she told them when she came back. "It looks as though he's making a fire in the hearth."

"I wish we could have a fire," Bran said. "I'm cold. There's broken furniture down the stairs, I saw it. We could have Hodor chop it up and get warm."

Hodor liked that idea. "Hodor," he said hopefully.

Jojen shook his head. "Fire means smoke. Smoke from this tower could be seen a long way off."

"If there were anyone to see," his sister argued.

"There's a man in the village."

"One man."

"One man would be enough to betray Bran to his enemies, if he's the wrong man. We still have half a duck from yesterday. We should eat and rest. Come morning the man will go on his way, and we will do the same."

Jojen had his way; he always did. Meera divided the duck between the four of them. She'd caught it in her net the day before, as it tried to rise from the marsh where she'd surprised it. It wasn't as tasty cold as it had been hot and crisp from the spit, but at least they did not go hungry. Bran and Meera shared the breast while Jojen ate the thigh. Hodor devoured the wing and leg, muttering "Hodor" and licking the grease off his fingers after every bite. It was Bran's turn to tell a story, so he told them about another Brandon Stark, the one called Brandon the Shipwright, who had sailed off beyond the Sunset Sea.

Dusk was settling by the time duck and tale were done, and the rain still fell. Bran wondered how far Summer had roamed and whether he had caught one of the deer.

Grey gloom filled the tower, and slowly changed to darkness. Hodor grew restless and walked awhile, striding round and round the walls and stopping to peer into the privy on every circuit, as if he had forgotten what was in there. Jojen stood by the north balcony, hidden by the shadows, looking out at the night and the rain. Somewhere to the north a lightning bolt crackled across the sky, brightening the inside of the tower for an instant. Hodor jumped and made a frightened noise. Bran counted to eight, waiting for the thunder. When it came, Hodor shouted, *"Hodor!"*

I hope Summer isn't scared too, Bran thought. The dogs in Winterfell's kennels had always been spooked by thunderstorms, just like Hodor. *I should go see, to calm him . . .*

The lightning flashed again, and this time the thunder came at six. "Hodor!" Hodor yelled again. "HODOR! HODOR!" He snatched up his sword, as if to fight the storm.

Jojen said, "Be quiet, Hodor. Bran, tell him not to shout. Can you get the sword away from him, Meera?"

"I can try."

"Hodor, *hush,*" said Bran. "Be quiet now. No more stupid hodoring. Sit down."

"Hodor?" He gave the longsword to Meera meekly enough, but his face was a mask of confusion.

Jojen turned back to the darkness, and they all heard him suck in his breath. "What is it?" Meera asked.

"Men in the village."

"The man we saw before?"

"Other men. Armed. I saw an axe, and spears as well." Jojen had never sounded so much like the boy he was. "I saw them when the lightning flashed, moving under the trees."

"How many?"

"Many and more. Too many to count."

"Mounted?"

"No."

"Hodor." Hodor sounded frightened. "Hodor. Hodor."

Bran felt a little scared himself, though he didn't want to say so in front of Meera. "What if they come out here?"

"They won't." She sat down beside him. "Why should they?"

"For shelter." Jojen's voice was grim. "Unless the storm lets up. Meera, could you go down and bar the door?"

"I couldn't even close it. The wood's too warped. They won't get past those iron gates, though."

"They might. They could break the lock, or the hinges. Or climb up through the murder hole as we did."

Lightning slashed the sky, and Hodor whimpered. Then a clap of thunder rolled across the lake. "HODOR!" he roared, clapping his hands over his ears and stumbling in a circle through the darkness. "HODOR! HODOR! HODOR!"

"*NO!*" Bran shouted back. "NO HODORING!"

It did no good. "HOOOODOR!" moaned Hodor. Meera tried to catch him and calm him, but he was too strong. He flung her aside with no more than a shrug. "HOOOOOODOOOOOOOR!" the stableboy screamed as lightning filled the sky again, and even Jojen was shouting now, shouting at Bran and Meera to shut him up.

"Be *quiet!*" Bran said in a shrill scared voice, reaching up uselessly for Hodor's leg as he crashed past, reaching, *reaching*.

Hodor staggered, and closed his mouth. He shook his head slowly from side to side, sank back to the floor, and sat crosslegged. When the thunder boomed, he scarcely seemed to hear it. The four of them sat in the dark tower, scarce daring to breathe.

"Bran, what did you do?" Meera whispered.

"Nothing." Bran shook his head. "I don't know." But he did. *I reached for him, the way I reach for Summer.* He had *been* Hodor for half a heartbeat. It scared him.

"Something is happening across the lake," said Jojen. "I thought I saw a man pointing at the tower."

I won't be afraid. He was the Prince of Winterfell, Eddard Stark's son, almost a man grown and a warg too, not some little baby boy like Rickon. *Summer would not be afraid.* "Most like they're just some Umbers," he said. "Or they could be Knotts or Norreys or Flints come down from the mountains, or even brothers from the Night's Watch. Were they wearing black cloaks, Jojen?"

"By night all cloaks are black, Your Grace. And the flash came and went too fast for me to tell what they were wearing."

Meera was wary. "If they were black brothers, they'd be mounted, wouldn't they?"

Bran had thought of something else. "It doesn't matter," he said confidently. "They couldn't get out to us even if they wanted. Not unless they had a boat, or knew about the causeway."

"The causeway!" Meera mussed Bran's hair and kissed him on the forehead. "Our sweet prince! He's right, Jojen, they won't know about the causeway. Even if they did they could never find the way across at night in the rain."

"The night will end, though. If they stay till morning . . ." Jojen left the rest unsaid. After a few moments he said, "They are feeding the fire the first man started." Lightning crashed through the sky, and light filled the tower and etched them all in shadow. Hodor rocked back and forth, humming.

Bran could feel Summer's fear in that bright instant. He closed two eyes and opened a third, and his boy's skin slipped off him like a cloak as he left the tower behind . . .

. . . and found himself out in the rain, his belly full of deer, cringing in the brush as the sky broke and boomed above him. The smell of rotten apples and wet leaves almost drowned the scent of man, but it was there. He heard the clink and slither of hardskin, saw men moving under the trees. A man with a stick blundered by, a skin pulled up over his head to make him blind and deaf. The wolf went wide around him, behind a dripping thornbush and beneath the bare branches of an apple tree. He could hear them talking, and there beneath the scents of rain and leaves and horse came the sharp red stench of fear . . .

JON

The ground was littered with pine needles and blown leaves, a carpet of green and brown still damp from the recent rains. It squished beneath their feet. Huge bare oaks, tall sentinels, and hosts of soldier pines stood all around them. On a hill above them was another roundtower, ancient and empty, thick green moss crawling up its side almost to the summit. "Who built that, all of stone like that?" Ygritte asked him. "Some king?"

"No. Just the men who used to live here."

"What happened to them?"

"They died or went away." Brandon's Gift had been farmed for thousands of years, but as the Watch dwindled there were fewer hands to plow the fields, tend the bees, and plant the orchards, so the wild had reclaimed many a field and hall. In the New Gift there had been villages and holdfasts whose taxes, rendered in goods and labor, helped feed and clothe the black brothers. But those were largely gone as well.

"They were fools to leave such a castle," said Ygritte.

"It's only a towerhouse. Some little lordling lived there once, with his family and a few sworn men. When raiders came he would light a beacon from the roof. Winterfell has towers three times the size of that."

She looked as if she thought he was making that up. "How could men build so high, with no giants to lift the stones?"

In legend, Brandon the Builder *had* used giants to help raise Winterfell, but Jon did not want to confuse the issue. "Men can build a lot higher than this. In Oldtown there's a tower taller than the Wall." He could tell she did not believe him. *If I could show her Winterfell ... give her a flower from the glass gardens, feast her in the Great Hall, and show her the stone kings on their thrones. We could bathe in the hot pools, and love beneath the heart tree while the old gods watched over us.*

The dream was sweet . . . but Winterfell would never be his to show. It belonged to his brother, the King in the North. He was a Snow, not a Stark. *Bastard, oathbreaker, and turncloak . . .*

"Might be after we could come back here, and live in that tower," she said. "Would you want that, Jon Snow? After?"

After. The word was a spear thrust. *After the war. After the conquest. After the wildlings break the Wall . . .*

His lord father had once talked about raising new lords and settling them in the abandoned holdfasts as a shield against wildlings. The plan would have required the Watch to yield back a large part of the Gift, but his uncle Benjen believed the Lord Commander could be won around, so long as the new lordlings paid taxes to Castle Black rather than Winterfell. "It is a dream for spring, though," Lord Eddard had said. "Even the promise of land will not lure men north with a winter coming on."

If winter had come and gone more quickly and spring had followed in its turn, I might have been chosen to hold one of these towers in my father's name. Lord Eddard was dead, however, his brother Benjen lost; the shield they dreamt together would never be forged. "This land belongs to the Watch," Jon said.

Her nostrils flared. "No one lives here."

"Your raiders drove them off."

"They were cowards, then. If they wanted the land they should have stayed and fought."

"Maybe they were tired of fighting. Tired of barring their doors every night and wondering if Rattleshirt or someone like him would break them down to carry off their wives. Tired of having their harvests stolen, and any valuables they might have. It's easier to move beyond the reach of raiders." *But if the Wall should fail, all the north will lie within the reach of raiders.*

"You know nothing, Jon Snow. Daughters are taken, not wives. *You're* the ones who steal. You took the whole world, and built the Wall t' keep the free folk out."

"Did we?" Sometimes Jon forgot how wild she was, and then she would remind him. "How did that happen?"

"The gods made the earth for all men t' share. Only when the kings come with their crowns and steel swords, they claimed it was all theirs. *My trees,* they said, *you can't eat them apples. My stream, you can't fish here. My wood, you're not t' hunt. My earth, my water, my castle, my daughter, keep your hands away or I'll chop 'em off, but maybe if you kneel t' me I'll let you have a sniff.* You call us thieves, but at least a thief has t' be brave and clever and quick. A kneeler only has t' kneel."

"Harma and the Bag of Bones don't come raiding for fish and apples. They steal swords and axes. Spices, silks, and furs. They grab every coin and ring and jeweled cup they can find, casks of wine in summer and casks of beef in winter, and they take women in any season and carry them off beyond the Wall."

"And what if they do? I'd sooner be stolen by a strong man than be given t' some weakling by my father."

"You say that, but how can you know? What if you were stolen by someone you hated?"

"He'd have t' be quick and cunning and brave t' steal *me*. So his sons would be strong and smart as well. Why would I hate such a man as that?"

"Maybe he never washes, so he smells as rank as a bear."

"Then I'd push him in a stream or throw a bucket o' water on him. Anyhow, men shouldn't smell sweet like flowers."

"What's wrong with flowers?"

"Nothing, for a bee. For bed I want one o' these." Ygritte made to grab the front of his breeches.

Jon caught her wrist. "What if the man who stole you drank too much?" he insisted. "What if he was brutal or cruel?" He tightened his grip to make a point. "What if he was stronger than you, and liked to beat you bloody?"

"I'd cut his throat while he slept. You know nothing, Jon Snow." Ygritte twisted like an eel and wrenched away from him.

I know one thing. I know that you are wildling to the bone. It was easy to forget that sometimes, when they were laughing together, or kissing. But then one of them would say something, or do something, and he would suddenly be reminded of the wall between their worlds.

"A man can own a woman or a man can own a knife," Ygritte told him, "but no man can own both. Every little girl learns that from her mother." She raised her chin defiantly and gave her thick red hair a shake. "And men can't own the land no more'n they can own the sea or the sky. You kneelers think you do, but Mance is going t' show you different."

It was a fine brave boast, but it rang hollow. Jon glanced back to make certain the Magnar was not in earshot. Errok, Big Boil, and Hempen Dan were walking a few yards behind them, but paying no attention. Big Boil was complaining of his arse. "Ygritte," he said in a low voice, "Mance cannot win this war."

"He can!" she insisted. "You know nothing, Jon Snow. You have never seen the free folk fight!"

Wildlings fought like heroes or demons, depending on who you talked to, but it came down to the same thing in the end. *They fight with reckless courage, every man out for glory.* "I don't doubt that you're all very brave, but when it comes to battle, discipline beats valor every time. In the end Mance will fail as all the Kings-beyond-the-Wall have failed before him. And when he does, you'll die. All of you."

Ygritte had looked so angry he thought she was about to strike him. "All of *us*," she said. "You too. You're no crow now, Jon Snow. I swore you weren't, so you better not be." She pushed him back against the trunk of a tree and kissed him, full on the lips right there in the midst of the ragged column. Jon heard Grigg the Goat urging her on. Someone else laughed. He kissed her back despite all that. When they finally broke apart, Ygritte was flushed. "You're mine," she whispered. "Mine, as I'm yours. And if we die, we die. All men must die, Jon Snow. But first we'll live."

"Yes." His voice was thick. "First we'll live."

She grinned at that, showing Jon the crooked teeth that he had somehow come to love. *Wildling to the bone*, he thought again, with a sick sad feeling in the pit of his stomach. He flexed the fingers of his sword hand, and wondered what Ygritte would do if she knew his heart. Would she betray him if he sat her down and told her that he was still Ned Stark's son and a man of the Night's Watch? He hoped not, but he dare not take that risk. Too many lives depended on his somehow reaching Castle Black before the Magnar . . . assuming he found a chance to escape the wildlings.

They had descended the south face of the Wall at Greyguard, abandoned for two hundred years. A section of the huge stone steps had collapsed a century before, but even so the descent was a good deal easier than the climb. From there Styr marched them deep into the Gift, to avoid the Watch's customary patrols. Grigg the Goat led them past the few inhabited villages that remained in these lands. Aside from a few scattered roundtowers poking the sky like stone fingers, they saw no sign of man. Through cold wet hills and windy plains they marched, unwatched, unseen.

You must not balk, whatever is asked of you, the Halfhand had said. *Ride with them, eat with them, fight with them, for as long as it takes.* He'd ridden many leagues and walked for more, had shared their bread and salt, and Ygritte's blankets as well, but still they did not trust him. Day and night the Thenns watched him, alert for any signs of betrayal. He could not get away, and soon it would be too late.

Fight with them, Qhorin had said, before he surrendered his own life to Longclaw . . . but it had not come to that, till now. *Once I shed a brother's blood I am lost. I cross the Wall for good then, and there is no crossing back.*

After each day's march the Magnar summoned him to ask shrewd sharp questions about Castle Black, its garrison and defenses. Jon lied where he dared and feigned ignorance a few times, but Grigg the Goat and Errok listened as well, and they knew enough to make Jon careful. Too blatant a lie would betray him.

But the truth was terrible. Castle Black had no defenses, but for the Wall itself. It lacked even wooden palisades or earthen dikes. The "castle" was nothing more than a cluster of towers and keeps, two-thirds of them falling into ruin. As for the garrison, the Old Bear had taken two hundred on his ranging. Had any returned? Jon could not know. Perhaps four hundred remained at the castle, but most of those were builders or stewards, not rangers.

The Thenns were hardened warriors, and more disciplined than the common run of wildling; no doubt that was why Mance had chosen them. The defenders of Castle Black would include blind Maester Aemon and his half-blind steward Clydas, one-armed Donal Noye, drunken Septon Cellador, Deaf Dick Follard, Three-Finger Hobb the cook, old Ser Wynton Stout, as well as Halder and Toad and Pyp and Albett and the rest of the boys who'd trained with Jon. And commanding them would be red-faced Bowen Marsh, the plump Lord Steward who had been made castellan in Lord Mormont's absence. Dolorous Edd sometimes called Marsh "the Old Pomegranate," which fit him just as well as "the Old Bear" fit Mormont. "He's the man you want in front when the foes are in the field," Edd would say in his usual dour voice. "He'll count them right up for you. A regular demon for counting, that one."

If the Magnar takes Castle Black unawares, it will be red slaughter, boys butchered in their beds before they know they are under attack. Jon had to warn them, but how? He was never sent out to forage or hunt, nor allowed to stand a watch alone. And he feared for Ygritte as well. He could not take her, but if he left her, would the Magnar make her answer for his treachery? *Two hearts that beat as one . . .*

They shared the same sleeping skins every night, and he went to sleep with her head against his chest and her red hair tickling his chin. The smell of her had become a part of him. Her crooked teeth, the feel of her breast when he cupped it in his hand, the taste of her mouth . . . they were his joy and his despair. Many a night he lay with Ygritte warm beside him, wondering if his lord father had felt this confused about his mother, whoever she had been. *Ygritte set the trap and Mance Rayder pushed me into it.*

Every day he spent among the wildlings made what he had to do that much harder. He was going to have to find some way to betray these men, and when he did they would die. He did not want their friendship, any more than he wanted Ygritte's love. And yet . . . the Thenns spoke the Old Tongue and seldom talked to Jon at all, but it was different with

Jarl's raiders, the men who'd climbed the Wall. Jon was coming to know them despite himself: gaunt, quiet Errok and gregarious Grigg the Goat, the boys Quort and Bodger, Hempen Dan the ropemaker. The worst of the lot was Del, a horsefaced youth near Jon's own age, who would talk dreamily of this wildling girl he meant to steal. "She's lucky, like your Ygritte. She's kissed by fire."

Jon had to bite his tongue. He didn't want to know about Del's girl or Bodger's mother, the place by the sea that Henk the Helm came from, how Grigg yearned to visit the green men on the Isle of Faces, or the time a moose had chased Toefinger up a tree. He didn't want to hear about the boil on Big Boil's arse, how much ale Stone Thumbs could drink, or how Quort's little brother had begged him not to go with Jarl. Quort could not have been older than fourteen, though he'd already stolen himself a wife and had a child on the way. "Might be he'll be born in some castle," the boy boasted. "Born in a castle like a lord!" He was very taken with the "castles" they'd seen, by which he meant watchtowers.

Jon wondered where Ghost was now. Had he gone to Castle Black, or was he was running with some wolfpack in the woods? He had no sense of the direwolf, not even in his dreams. It made him feel as if part of himself had been cut off. Even with Ygritte sleeping beside him, he felt alone. He did not want to die alone.

By that afternoon the trees had begun to thin, and they marched east over gently rolling plains. Grass rose waist high around them, and stands of wild wheat swayed gently when the wind came gusting, but for the most part the day was warm and bright. Toward sunset, however, clouds began to threaten in the west. They soon engulfed the orange sun, and Lenn foretold a bad storm coming. His mother was a woods witch, so all the raiders agreed he had a gift for foretelling the weather. "There's a village close," Grigg the Goat told the Magnar. "Two miles, three. We could shelter there." Styr agreed at once.

It was well past dark and the storm was raging by the time they reached the place. The village sat beside a lake, and had been so long abandoned that most of the houses had collapsed. Even the small timber inn that must once have been a welcome sight for travelers stood half-fallen and roofless. *We will find scant shelter here,* Jon thought gloomily. Whenever the lightning flashed he could see a stone roundtower rising from an island out in the lake, but without boats they had no way to reach it.

Errok and Del had crept ahead to scout the ruins, but Del was back almost at once. Styr halted the column and sent a dozen of his Thenns trotting forward, spears in hand. By then Jon had seen it too: the glimmer of a fire, reddening the chimney of the inn. *We are not alone.* Dread coiled inside him like a snake. He heard a horse neigh, and then shouts. *Ride with them, eat with them, fight with them,* Qhorin had said.

But the fighting was done. "There's only one of them," Errok said when he came back. "An old man with a horse."

The Magnar shouted commands in the Old Tongue and a score of his Thenns spread out to establish a perimeter around the village, whilst others went prowling through the houses to make certain no one else was hiding amongst the weeds and tumbled stones. The rest crowded into the roofless inn, jostling each other to get closer to the hearth. The broken branches the old man had been burning seemed to generate more smoke than heat, but any warmth was welcome on such a wild rainy night. Two of the Thenns had thrown the man to the ground and were going through his things. Another held his horse, while three more looted his saddlebags.

Jon walked away. A rotten apple squished beneath his heel. *Styr will kill him.* The Magnar had said as much at Greyguard; any kneelers they met were to be put to death at once, to make certain they could not raise the alarm. *Ride with them, eat with them, fight with them.* Did that mean he must stand mute and helpless while they slit an old man's throat?

Near the edge of the village, Jon came face-to-face with one of the guards Styr had posted. The Thenn growled something in the Old Tongue and pointed his spear back toward the inn. *Get back where you belong,* Jon guessed. *But where is that?*

He walked towards the water, and discovered an almost dry spot beneath the leaning daub-and-wattle wall of a tumbledown cottage that had mostly tumbled down. That was where Ygritte found him sitting, staring off across the rain-whipped lake. "I know this place," he told her when she sat beside him. "That tower . . . look at the top of it the next time the lightning flashes, and tell me what you see."

"Aye, if you like," she said, and then, "Some o' the Thenns are saying they heard noises out there. Shouting, they say."

"Thunder."

"They say shouting. Might be it's ghosts."

The holdfast did have a grim haunted look, standing there black against the storm on its rocky island with the rain lashing at the lake all around it. "We could go out and take a look," he suggested. "I doubt we could get much wetter than we are."

"Swimming? In the storm?" She laughed at the notion. "Is this a trick t' get the clothes off me, Jon Snow?"

"Do I need a trick for that now?" he teased. "Or is that you can't swim a stroke?" Jon was a strong swimmer himself, having learned the art as a boy in Winterfell's great moat.

Ygritte punched his arm. "You know nothing, Jon Snow. I'm half a fish, I'll have you know."

"Half fish, half goat, half horse . . . there's too many halves to you, Ygritte." He shook his head. "We wouldn't need to swim, if this is the place I think. We could walk."

She pulled back and gave him a look. "Walk on water? What southron sorcery is that?"

"No sorc –" he began, as a huge bolt of lightning stabbed down from the sky and touched the surface of the lake. For half a heartbeat the world was noonday bright. The clap of thunder was so loud that Ygritte gasped and covered her ears.

"Did you look?" Jon asked, as the sound rolled away and the night turned black again. "Did you see?"

"Yellow," she said. "Is that what you meant? Some o' them standing stones on top were yellow."

"We call them merlons. They were painted gold a long time ago. This is Queenscrown."

Across the lake, the tower was black again, a dim shape dimly seen. "A queen lived there?" asked Ygritte.

"A queen stayed there for a night." Old Nan had told him the story, but Maester Luwin had confirmed most of it. "Alysanne, the wife of King Jaehaerys the Conciliator. He's called the Old King because he reigned so long, but he was young when he first came to the Iron Throne. In those days, it was his wont to travel all over the realm. When he came to Winterfell, he brought his queen, six dragons, and half his court. The king had matters to discuss with his Warden of the North, and Alysanne grew bored, so she mounted her dragon Silverwing and flew north to see the Wall. This village was one of the places where she stopped. Afterward the smallfolk painted the top of their holdfast to look like the golden crown she'd worn when she spent the night among them."

"I have never seen a dragon."

"No one has. The last dragons died a hundred years ago or more. But this was before that."

"Queen Alysanne, you say?"

"Good Queen Alysanne, they called her later. One of the castles on the Wall was named for her as well. Queensgate. Before her visit they called it Snowgate."

"If she was so good, she should have torn that Wall down."

No, he thought. *The Wall protects the realm. From the Others . . . and from you and your kind as well, sweetling.* "I had another friend who dreamed of dragons. A dwarf. He told me –"

"*JON SNOW!*" One of the Thenns loomed above them, frowning. "Magnar wants." Jon thought it might have been the same man who'd found him outside the cave, the night before they climbed the Wall, but he could not be sure. He got to his feet. Ygritte came with him, which always made Styr frown, but whenever he tried to dismiss her she would remind him that she was a free woman, not a kneeler. She came and went as she pleased.

They found the Magnar standing beneath the tree that grew through the floor of the common room. His captive knelt before the hearth, encircled by wooden spears and bronze swords. He watched Jon approach, but did not speak. The rain was running down the walls and pattering against the last few leaves that still clung to the tree, while smoke swirled thick from the fire.

"He must die," Styr the Magnar said. "Do it, crow."

The old man said no word. He only looked at Jon, standing amongst the wildlings. Amidst the rain and smoke, lit only by the fire, he could not have seen that Jon was all in black, but for his sheepskin cloak. *Or could he?*

Jon drew Longclaw from its sheath. Rain washed the steel, and the firelight traced a sullen orange line along the edge. *Such a small fire, to cost a man his life.* He remembered what Qhorin Halfhand had said when they spied the fire in the Skirling Pass. *Fire is life up here*, he told them, *but it can be death as well.* That was high in the Frostfangs, though, in the lawless wild beyond the Wall. This was the Gift, protected by the Night's Watch and the power of Winterfell. A man should have been free to build a fire here, without dying for it.

"Why do you hesitate?" Styr said. "Kill him, and be done."

Even then the captive did not speak. "Mercy," he might have said, or "You have taken my horse, my coin, my food, let me keep my life," or "No, please, I have done you no harm." He might have said a thousand things, or wept, or called upon his gods. No words would save him now, though. Perhaps he knew that. So he held his tongue, and looked at Jon in accusation and appeal.

You must not balk, whatever is asked of you. Ride with them, eat with them, fight with them . . . But this old man had offered no resistance. He had been unlucky, that was all. Who he was, where he came from, where he meant to go on his sorry sway-backed horse . . . none of it mattered.

He is an old man, Jon told himself. *Fifty, maybe even sixty. He lived a longer life than most. The Thenns will kill him anyway, nothing I can say or do will save him.* Longclaw seemed heavier than lead in his hand, too heavy to lift. The man kept staring at him, with eyes as big and black as wells. *I will fall into those eyes and drown.* The Magnar was looking at him too, and he could almost taste the mistrust. *The man is dead. What matter if it is my hand that slays him?* One cut would do it, quick and clean. Longclaw was forged of Valyrian steel. *Like Ice.* Jon remembered another killing; the deserter on his knees, his head rolling, the brightness of blood on snow . . . his father's sword, his father's words, his father's face . . .

"Do it, Jon Snow," Ygritte urged. "You must. T' prove you are no crow, but one o' the free folk."

"An old man sitting by a fire?"

"Orell was sitting by a fire too. You killed him quick enough." The look she gave him then was hard. "You meant t' kill me too, till you saw I was a woman. And I was asleep."

"That was different. You were soldiers . . . sentries."

"Aye, and you crows didn't want t' be seen. No more'n we do, now. It's just the same. Kill him."

He turned his back on the man. "No."

The Magnar moved closer, tall, cold, and dangerous. "I say yes. I command here."

"You command Thenns," Jon told him, "not free folk."

"I see no free folk. I see a crow and a crow wife."

"I'm no crow wife!" Ygritte snatched her knife from its sheath. Three quick strides, and she yanked the old man's head back by the hair and opened his throat from ear to ear. Even in death, the man did not cry out. "You know *nothing*, Jon Snow!" she shouted at him, and flung the bloody blade at his feet.

The Magnar said something in the Old Tongue. He might have been telling the Thenns to kill Jon where he stood, but he would never know the truth of that. Lightning crashed down from the sky, a searing blue-white bolt that touched the top of the tower in the lake. They could smell the fury of it, and when the thunder came it seemed to shake the night.

And death leapt down amongst them.

The lightning flash left Jon night-blind, but he glimpsed the hurtling shadow half a heartbeat before he heard the shriek. The first Thenn died as the old man had, blood gushing from his torn throat. Then the light was gone and the shape was spinning away, snarling, and another man went down in the dark. There were curses, shouts, howls of pain. Jon saw Big Boil stumble backward and knock down three men behind him. *Ghost*, he thought for one mad instant. *Ghost leapt the Wall.* Then the lightning turned the night to day, and he saw the wolf standing on Del's chest, blood running black from his jaws. *Grey. He's grey.*

Darkness descended with the thunderclap. The Thenns were jabbing with their spears as the wolf darted between them. The old man's mare reared, maddened by the smell of slaughter, and lashed out with her hooves. Longclaw was still in his hand. All at once Jon Snow knew he would never get a better chance.

He cut down the first man as he turned toward the wolf, shoved past a second, slashed at a third. Through the madness he heard someone call his name, but whether it was Ygritte or the Magnar he could not say. The Thenn fighting to control the horse never saw him. Longclaw was feather-light. He swung at the back of the man's calf, and felt the steel bite down to the bone. When the wildling fell the mare bolted, but somehow Jon managed to grab her mane with his off hand and vault himself onto her back. A hand closed round his ankle, and he hacked down and saw Bodger's face dissolve in a welter of blood. The horse reared, lashing out. One hoof caught a Thenn in the temple, with a *crunch*.

And then they were running. Jon made no effort to guide the horse. It was all he could do to stay on her as they plunged through mud and rain and thunder. Wet grass whipped at his face and a spear flew past his ear. *If the horse stumbles and breaks a leg, they will run me down and kill me*, he thought, but the old gods were with him and the horse did not stumble. Lightning shivered through the black dome of sky, and thunder rolled across the plains. The shouts dwindled and died behind him.

Long hours later, the rain stopped. Jon found himself alone in a sea of tall black grass. There was a deep throbbing ache in his right thigh. When he looked down, he was surprised to see an arrow jutting out the back of it. *When did that happen?* He grabbed hold of the shaft and gave it a tug, but the arrowhead was sunk deep in the meat of his leg, and the pain when he pulled on it was excruciating. He tried to think back on the madness at the inn, but all he could remember was the beast, gaunt and grey and terrible. *It was too large to be a common wolf. A direwolf, then. It had to be.* He had never seen an animal move so fast. *Like a grey wind . . .* Could Robb have returned to the north?

Jon shook his head. He had no answers. It was too hard to think . . . about the wolf, the old man, Ygritte, any of it . . .

Clumsily, he slid down off the mare's back. His wounded leg buckled under him, and he had to swallow a scream. *This is going to be agony.* The arrow had to come out, though, and nothing good could come of waiting. Jon curled his hand around the fletching, took a deep breath, and shoved the arrow forward. He grunted, then cursed. It hurt so much he had to stop. *I am bleeding like a butchered pig*, he thought, but there was nothing to be done for it until the arrow was out. He grimaced and tried again . . . and soon stopped again, trembling. *Once more.* This time he screamed, but when he was done the arrowhead was poking through the front of his thigh. Jon pushed back his bloody breeches to get a better grip, grimaced, and slowly drew the shaft through his leg. How he got through that without fainting he never knew.

He lay on the ground afterward, clutching his prize and bleeding quietly, too weak to move. After a while, he realized that if he did not *make* himself move he was like to bleed to death. Jon crawled to the shallow stream where the mare was drinking, washed his thigh in the cold water, and bound it tight with a strip of cloth torn from his cloak. He washed the arrow too, turning it in his hands. Was the fletching grey, or white? Ygritte fletched her arrows with pale grey goose feathers. *Did she loose a shaft at me as I fled?* Jon could not blame her for that. He wondered if she'd been aiming for him or the horse. If the mare had gone down, he would have been doomed. "A lucky thing my leg got in the way," he muttered.

He rested for a while to let the horse graze. She did not wander far. That was good. Hobbled with a bad leg, he could never have caught her. It was all he could do to force himself back to his feet and climb onto her back. *How did I ever mount her before, without saddle or stirrups, and a sword in one hand?* That was another question he could not answer.

Thunder rumbled softly in the distance, but above him the clouds were breaking up. Jon searched the sky until he found the Ice Dragon, then turned the mare north for the Wall and Castle Black. The throb of pain in his thigh muscle made him wince as he put his heels into the old man's horse. *I am going home,* he told himself. But if that was true, why did he feel so hollow?

He rode till dawn, while the stars stared down like eyes.

DAENERYS

Her Dothraki scouts had told her how it was, but Dany wanted to see for herself. Ser Jorah Mormont rode with her through a birchwood forest and up a slanting sandstone ridge. "Near enough," he warned her at the crest.

Dany reined in her mare and looked across the fields, to where the Yunkish host lay athwart her path. Whitebeard had been teaching her how best to count the numbers of a foe. "Five thousand," she said after a moment.

"I'd say so." Ser Jorah pointed. "Those are sellswords on the flanks. Lances and mounted bowmen, with swords and axes for the close work. The Second Sons on the left wing, the Stormcrows to the right. About five hundred men apiece. See the banners?"

Yunkai's harpy grasped a whip and iron collar in her talons instead of a length of chain. But the sellswords flew their own standards beneath those of the city they served: on the right four crows between crossed thunderbolts, on the left a broken sword. "The Yunkai'i hold the center themselves," Dany noted. Their officers looked indistinguishable from Astapor's at a distance; tall bright helms and cloaks sewn with flashing copper disks. "Are those slave soldiers they lead?"

"In large part. But not the equal of Unsullied. Yunkai is known for training bed slaves, not warriors."

"What say you? Can we defeat this army?"

"Easily," Ser Jorah said.

"But not bloodlessly." Blood aplenty had soaked into the bricks of Astapor the day that city fell, though little of it belonged to her or hers.

"We might win a battle here, but at such cost we cannot take the city."

"That is ever a risk, *Khaleesi*. Astapor was complacent and vulnerable. Yunkai is forewarned."

Dany considered. The slaver host seemed small compared to her own numbers, but the sellswords were ahorse. She'd ridden too long with Dothraki not to have a healthy respect for what mounted warriors could do to foot. *The Unsullied could withstand their charge, but my freedmen will be slaughtered.* "The slavers like to talk," she said. "Send word that I will hear them this evening in my tent. And invite the captains of the sellsword companies to call on me as well. But not together. The Stormcrows at midday, the Second Sons two hours later."

"As you wish," Ser Jorah said. "But if they do not come –"

"They'll come. They will be curious to see the dragons and hear what I might have to say, and the clever ones will see it for a chance to gauge my strength." She wheeled her silver mare about. "I'll await them in my pavilion."

Slate skies and brisk winds saw Dany back to her host. The deep ditch that would encircle her camp was already half dug, and the woods were full of Unsullied lopping branches off birch trees to sharpen into stakes. The eunuchs could not sleep in an unfortified camp, or so Grey Worm insisted. He was there watching the work. Dany halted a moment to speak with him. "Yunkai has girded up her loins for battle."

"This is good, Your Grace. These ones thirst for blood."

When she had commanded the Unsullied to choose officers from amongst themselves, Grey Worm had been their overwhelming choice for the highest rank. Dany had put Ser Jorah over him to train him for command, and the exile knight said that so far the young eunuch was hard but fair, quick to learn, tireless, and utterly unrelenting in his attention to detail.

"The Wise Masters have assembled a slave army to meet us."

"A slave in Yunkai learns the way of seven sighs and the sixteen seats of pleasure, Your Grace. The Unsullied learn the way of the three spears. Your Grey Worm hopes to show you."

One of the first things Dany had done after the fall of Astapor was abolish the custom of giving the Unsullied new slave names every day. Most of those born free had returned to their birth names; those who still remembered them, at least. Others had called themselves after heroes or gods, and sometimes weapons, gems, and even flowers, which resulted in soldiers with some very peculiar names, to Dany's ears. Grey Worm had remained Grey Worm. When she asked him why, he said, "It is a lucky name. The name this one was born to was accursed. That was the name he had when he was taken for a slave. But Grey Worm is the name this one drew the day Daenerys Stormborn set him free."

"If battle is joined, let Grey Worm show wisdom as well as valor," Dany told him. "Spare any slave who runs or throws down his weapon. The fewer slain, the more remain to join us after."

"This one will remember."

"I know he will. Be at my tent by midday. I want you there with my other officers when I treat with the sellsword captains." Dany spurred her silver on to camp.

Within the perimeter the Unsullied had established, the tents were going up in orderly rows, with her own tall golden pavilion at the center. A second encampment lay close beyond her own; five times the size, sprawling and chaotic, this second camp had no ditches, no tents, no sentries, no horselines. Those who had horses or mules slept beside them, for fear they might be stolen. Goats, sheep, and half-starved dogs wandered freely amongst hordes of women, children, and old men. Dany had left Astapor in the hands of a council of former slaves led by a healer, a scholar, and a priest. Wise men all, she thought, and just. Yet even so, tens of thousands preferred to follow her to Yunkai, rather than remain behind in Astapor. *I gave them the city, and most of them were too frightened to take it.*

The raggle-taggle host of freedmen dwarfed her own, but they were more burden than benefit. Perhaps one in a hundred had a donkey, a camel, or an ox; most carried weapons looted from some slaver's armory, but only one in ten was strong enough to fight, and none was trained. They ate the land bare as they passed, like locusts in sandals. Yet Dany could not bring herself to abandon them as Ser Jorah and her bloodriders urged. *I told them they were free. I cannot tell them now they are not free to join me.* She gazed at the smoke rising from their cookfires and swallowed a sigh. She might have the best footsoldiers in the world, but she also had the worst.

Arstan Whitebeard stood outside the entrance of her tent, while Strong Belwas sat crosslegged on the grass nearby, eating a bowl of figs. On the march, the duty of guarding her fell upon their shoulders. She had made Jhogo, Aggo, and Rakharo her *kos* as well as her bloodriders, and just now she needed them more to command her Dothraki than to protect her person. Her *khalasar* was tiny, some thirty-odd mounted warriors, and most of them braidless boys and bentback old men. Yet they were all the horse she had, and she dared not go without them. The Unsullied might be the finest infantry in all the world, as Ser Jorah claimed, but she needed scouts and outriders as well.

"Yunkai will have war," Dany told Whitebeard inside the pavilion. Irri and Jhiqui had covered the floor with carpets while Missandei lit a stick of incense to sweeten the dusty air. Drogon and Rhaegal were asleep atop some cushions, curled about each other, but Viserion perched on the edge of her empty bath. "Missandei, what language will these Yunkai'i speak, Valyrian?"

"Yes, Your Grace," the child said. "A different dialect than Astapor's, yet close enough to understand. The slavers name themselves the Wise Masters."

"Wise?" Dany sat crosslegged on a cushion, and Viserion spread his white-and-gold wings and flapped to her side. "We shall see how wise they are," she said as she scratched the dragon's scaly head behind the horns.

Ser Jorah Mormont returned an hour later, accompanied by three captains of the Stormcrows. They wore black feathers on their polished helms, and claimed to be all equal in honor and authority. Dany studied them as Irri and Jhiqui poured the wine. Prendahl na Ghezn was a thickset Ghiscari with a broad face and dark hair going grey; Sallor the Bald had a twisting scar across his pale Qartheen cheek; and Daario Naharis was flamboyant even for a Tyroshi. His beard was cut into three prongs and dyed blue, the same color as his eyes and the curly hair that fell to his collar. His pointed mustachios were painted gold. His clothes were all shades of yellow; a foam of Myrish lace the color of butter spilled from his collar and cuffs, his doublet was sewn with brass medallions in the shape of dandelions, and ornamental goldwork crawled up his high leather boots to his thighs. Gloves of soft yellow suede were tucked into a belt of gilded rings, and his fingernails were enameled blue.

But it was Prendahl na Ghezn who spoke for the sellswords. "You would do well to take your rabble elsewhere," he said. "You took Astapor by treachery, but Yunkai shall not fall so easily."

"Five hundred of your Stormcrows against ten thousand of my Unsullied," said Dany. "I am only a young girl and do not understand the ways of war, yet these odds seem poor to me."

"The Stormcrows do not stand alone," said Prendahl.

"Stormcrows do not stand at all. They fly, at the first sign of thunder. Perhaps you should be flying now. I have heard that sellswords are notoriously unfaithful. What will it avail you to be staunch, when the Second Sons change sides?"

"That will not happen," Prendahl insisted, unmoved. "And if it did, it would not matter. The Second Sons are nothing. We fight beside the stalwart men of Yunkai."

"You fight beside bed-boys armed with spears." When she turned her head, the twin bells in her braid rang softly. "Once battle is joined, do not think to ask for quarter. Join me now, however, and you shall keep the gold the Yunkai'i paid you and claim a share of the plunder besides, with greater rewards later when I come into my kingdom. Fight for the Wise Masters, and your wages will be death. Do you imagine that Yunkai will open its gates when my Unsullied are butchering you beneath the walls?"

"Woman, you bray like an ass, and make no more sense."

"*Woman?*" She chuckled. "Is that meant to insult me? I would return the slap, if I took you for a man." Dany met his stare. "I am Daenerys Stormborn of House Targaryen, the Unburnt, Mother of Dragons, *khaleesi* to Drogo's riders, and queen of the Seven Kingdoms of Westeros."

"What you are," said Prendahl na Ghezn, "is a horselord's whore. When we break you, I will breed you to my stallion."

Strong Belwas drew his *arakh*. "Strong Belwas will give his ugly tongue to the little queen, if she likes."

"No, Belwas. I have given these men my safe conduct." She smiled. "Tell me this – are the Stormcrows slave or free?"

"We are a brotherhood of free men," Sallor declared.

"Good." Dany stood. "Go back and tell your brothers what I said, then. It may be that some of them would sooner sup on gold and glory than on death. I shall want your answer on the morrow."

The Stormcrow captains rose in unison. "Our answer is no," said Prendahl na Ghezn. His fellows followed him out of the tent . . . but Daario Naharis glanced back as he left, and inclined his head in polite farewell.

Two hours later the commander of the Second Sons arrived alone. He proved to be a towering Braavosi with pale green eyes and a bushy red-gold beard that reached nearly to his belt. His name was Mero, but he called himself the Titan's Bastard.

Mero tossed down his wine straightaway, wiped his mouth with the back of his hand, and leered at Dany. "I believe I fucked your twin sister in a pleasure house back home. Or was it you?"

"I think not. I would remember a man of such magnificence, I have no doubt."

"Yes, that is so. No woman has ever forgotten the Titan's Bastard." The Braavosi held out his cup to Jhiqui. "What say you take those clothes off and come sit on my lap? If you please me, I might bring the Second Sons over to your side."

"If you bring the Second Sons over to my side, I might not have you gelded."

The big man laughed. "Little girl, another woman once tried to geld me with her teeth. She has no teeth now, but my sword is as long and thick as ever. Shall I take it out and show you?"

"No need. After my eunuchs cut it off, I can examine it at my leisure." Dany took a sip of wine. "It is true that I am only a young girl, and do not know the ways of war. Explain to me how you propose to defeat ten thousand Unsullied with your five hundred. Innocent as I am, these odds seem poor to me."

"The Second Sons have faced worse odds and won."

"The Second Sons have faced worse odds and run. At Qohor, when the Three Thousand made their stand. Or do you deny it?"

"That was many and more years ago, before the Second Sons were led by the Titan's Bastard."

"So it is from you they get their courage?" Dany turned to Ser Jorah. "When the battle is joined, kill this one first."

The exile knight smiled. "Gladly, Your Grace."

"Of course," she said to Mero, "you could run again. We will not stop you. Take your Yunkish gold and go."

"Had you ever seen the Titan of Braavos, foolish girl, you would know that it has no tail to turn."

"Then stay, and fight for me."

"You are worth fighting for, it is true," the Braavosi said, "and I would gladly let you kiss my sword, if I were free. But I have taken Yunkai's coin and pledged my holy word."

"Coins can be returned," she said. "I will pay you as much and more. I have other cities to conquer, and a whole kingdom awaiting me half a world away. Serve me faithfully, and the Second Sons need never seek hire again."

The Braavosi tugged on his thick red beard. "As much and more, and perhaps a kiss besides, eh? Or more than a kiss? For a man as magnificent as me?"

"Perhaps."

"I will like the taste of your tongue, I think."

She could sense Ser Jorah's anger. *My black bear does not like this talk of kissing.* "Think on what I've said tonight. Can I have your answer on the morrow?"

"You can." The Titan's Bastard grinned. "Can I have a flagon of this fine wine to take back to my captains?"

"You may have a tun. It is from the cellars of the Good Masters of Astapor, and I have wagons full of it."

"Then give me a wagon. A token of your good regard."

"You have a big thirst."

"I am big all over. And I have many brothers. The Titan's Bastard does not drink alone, *Khaleesi.*"

"A wagon it is, if you promise to drink to my health."

"Done!" he boomed. "And done, and done! Three toasts we'll drink you, and bring you an answer when the sun comes up."

But when Mero was gone, Arstan Whitebeard said, "That one has an evil reputation, even in Westeros. Do not be misled by his manner, Your

Grace. He will drink three toasts to your health tonight, and rape you on the morrow."

"The old man's right for once," Ser Jorah said. "The Second Sons are an old company, and not without valor, but under Mero they've turned near as bad as the Brave Companions. The man is as dangerous to his employers as to his foes. That's why you find him out here. None of the Free Cities will hire him any longer."

"It is not his reputation that I want, it's his five hundred horse. What of the Stormcrows, is there any hope there?"

"No," Ser Jorah said bluntly. "That Prendahl is Ghiscari by blood. Likely he had kin in Astapor."

"A pity. Well, perhaps we will not need to fight. Let us wait and hear what the Yunkai'i have to say."

The envoys from Yunkai arrived as the sun was going down; fifty men on magnificent black horses and one on a great white camel. Their helms were twice as tall as their heads, so as not to crush the bizarre twists and towers and shapes of their oiled hair beneath. They dyed their linen skirts and tunics a deep yellow, and sewed copper disks to their cloaks.

The man on the white camel named himself Grazdan mo Eraz. Lean and hard, he had a white smile such as Kraznys had worn until Drogon burned off his face. His hair was drawn up in a unicorn's horn that jutted from his brow, and his *tokar* was fringed with golden Myrish lace. "Ancient and glorious is Yunkai, the queen of cities," he said when Dany welcomed him to her tent. "Our walls are strong, our nobles proud and fierce, our common folk without fear. Ours is the blood of ancient Ghis, whose empire was old when Valyria was yet a squalling child. You were wise to sit and speak, *Khaleesi*. You shall find no easy conquest here."

"Good. My Unsullied will relish a bit of a fight." She looked to Grey Worm, who nodded.

Grazdan shrugged expansively. "If blood is what you wish, let it flow. I am told you have freed your eunuchs. Freedom means as much to an Unsullied as a hat to a haddock." He smiled at Grey Worm, but the eunuch might have been made of stone. "Those who survive we shall enslave again, and use to retake Astapor from the rabble. We can make a slave of you as well, do not doubt it. There are pleasure houses in Lys and Tyrosh where men would pay handsomely to bed the last Targaryen."

"It is good to see you know who I am," said Dany mildly.

"I pride myself on my knowledge of the savage senseless west." Grazdan spread his hands, a gesture of conciliation. "And yet, why should we speak thus harshly to one another? It is true that you committed savageries in Astapor, but we Yunkai'i are a most forgiving people. Your quarrel is not with us, Your Grace. Why squander your strength against our mighty walls when you will need every man to regain your father's throne in far Westeros? Yunkai wishes you only well in that endeavor. And to prove the truth of that, I have brought you a gift." He clapped his hands, and two of his escort came forward bearing a heavy cedar chest bound in bronze and gold. They set it at her feet. "Fifty thousand golden marks," Grazdan said smoothly. "Yours, as a gesture of friendship from the Wise Masters of Yunkai. Gold given freely is better than plunder bought with blood, surely? So I say to you, Daenerys Targaryen, take this chest, and go."

Dany pushed open the lid of the chest with a small slippered foot. It was full of gold coins, just as the envoy said. She grabbed a handful and let them run through her fingers. They shone brightly as they tumbled and fell; new minted, most of them, stamped with a stepped pyramid on one face and the harpy of Ghis on the other. "Very pretty. I wonder how many chests like this I shall find when I take your city?"

He chuckled. "None, for that you shall never do."

"I have a gift for you as well." She slammed the chest shut. "Three days. On the morning of the third day, send out your slaves. All of them. Every man, woman, and child shall be given a weapon, and as much food, clothing, coin, and goods as he or she can carry. These they shall be allowed to choose freely from among their masters' possessions, as payment for their years of servitude. When all the slaves have departed, you will open your gates and allow my Unsullied to enter and search your city, to make certain none remain in bondage. If you do this, Yunkai will not be burned or plundered, and none of your people shall be molested. The Wise Masters will have the peace they desire, and will have proved themselves wise indeed. What say you?"

"I say, you are mad."

"Am I?" Dany shrugged, and said, "*Dracarys*."

The dragons answered. Rhaegal *hiss*ed and smoked, Viserion snapped, and Drogon spat swirling red-black flame. It touched the drape of Grazdan's *tokar*, and the silk caught in half a heartbeat. Golden marks spilled across the carpets as the envoy stumbled over the chest, shouting curses and beating at his arm until Whitebeard flung a flagon of water over him to douse the flames. "You swore I should have safe conduct!" the Yunkish envoy wailed.

"Do all the Yunkai'i whine so over a singed *tokar*? I shall buy you a new one . . . if you deliver up your slaves within three days. Elsewise, Drogon shall give you a warmer kiss." She wrinkled her nose. "You've soiled yourself. Take your gold and go, and see that the Wise Masters hear my message."

Grazdan mo Eraz pointed a finger. "You shall rue this arrogance, whore. These little lizards will not keep you safe, I promise you. We will fill the air with arrows if they come within a league of Yunkai. Do you think it is so hard to kill a dragon?"

"Harder than to kill a slaver. Three days, Grazdan. Tell them. By the end of the third day, I will be in Yunkai, whether you open your gates for me or no."

Full dark had fallen by the time the Yunkai'i departed from her camp. It promised to be a gloomy night; moonless, starless, with a chill wet wind blowing from the west. *A fine black night*, thought Dany. The fires burned all around her, small orange stars strewn across hill and field. "Ser Jorah," she said, "summon my bloodriders." Dany seated herself on a mound of cushions to await them, her dragons all about her. When they were assembled, she said, "An hour past midnight should be time enough."

"Yes, *Khaleesi*," said Rakharo. "Time for what?"

"To mount our attack."

Ser Jorah Mormont scowled. "You told the sellswords –"

"– that I wanted their answers on the morrow. I made no promises about tonight. The Stormcrows will be arguing about my offer. The Second Sons will be drunk on the wine I gave Mero. And the Yunkai'i believe they have three days. We will take them under cover of this darkness."

"They will have scouts watching for us."

"And in the dark, they will see hundreds of campfires burning," said Dany. "If they see anything at all."

"*Khaleesi*," said Jhogo, "I will deal with these scouts. They are no riders, only slavers on horses."

"Just so," she agreed. "I think we should attack from three sides. Grey Worm, your Unsullied shall strike at them from right and left, while my *ko*s lead my horse in wedge for a thrust through their center. Slave soldiers will never stand before mounted Dothraki." She smiled. "To be sure, I am only a young girl and know little of war. What do you think, my lords?"

"I think you are Rhaegar Targaryen's sister," Ser Jorah said with a rueful half smile.

"Aye," said Arstan Whitebeard, "and a queen as well."

It took an hour to work out all the details. *Now begins the most dangerous time*, Dany thought as her captains departed to their commands. She could only pray that the gloom of the night would hide her preparations from the foe.

Near midnight, she got a scare when Ser Jorah bulled his way past Strong Belwas. "The Unsullied caught one of the sellswords trying to sneak into the camp."

"A spy?" That frightened her. If they'd caught one, how many others might have gotten away?

"He claims to come bearing gifts. It's the yellow fool with the blue hair."

Daario Naharis. "That one. I'll hear him, then."

When the exile knight delivered him, she asked herself whether two men had ever been so different. The Tyroshi was fair where Ser Jorah was swarthy; lithe where the knight was brawny; graced with flowing locks where the other was balding, yet smooth-skinned where Mormont was hairy. And her knight dressed plainly while this other made a peacock look drab, though he had thrown a heavy black cloak over his bright yellow finery for this visit. He carried a heavy canvas sack slung over one shoulder.

"*Khaleesi,*" he cried, "I bring gifts and glad tidings. The Stormcrows are yours." A golden tooth gleamed in his mouth when he smiled. "And so is Daario Naharis!"

Dany was dubious. If this Tyroshi had come to spy, this declaration might be no more than a desperate plot to save his head. "What do Prendahl na Ghezn and Sallor say of this?"

"Little." Daario upended the sack, and the heads of Sallor the Bald and Prendahl na Ghezn spilled out upon her carpets. "My gifts to the dragon queen."

Viserion sniffed the blood leaking from Prendahl's neck, and let loose a gout of flame that took the dead man full in the face, blackening and blistering his bloodless cheeks. Drogon and Rhaegal stirred at the smell of roasted meat.

"You did this?" Dany asked queasily.

"None other." If her dragons discomfited Daario Naharis, he hid it well. For all the mind he paid them, they might have been three kittens playing with a mouse.

"Why?"

"Because you are so beautiful." His hands were large and strong, and there was something in his hard blue eyes and great curving nose that suggested the fierceness of some splendid bird of prey. "Prendahl talked too much and said too little." His garb, rich as it was, had seen hard wear; salt stains patterned his boots, the enamel of his nails was chipped, his lace was soiled by sweat, and she could see where the end of his cloak was fraying. "And Sallor picked his nose as if his snot was gold." He stood with his hands crossed at the wrists, his palms resting on the pommels of his blades; a curving Dothraki *arakh* on his left hip, a Myrish stiletto on his right. Their hilts were a matched pair of golden women, naked and wanton.

"Are you skilled in the use of those handsome blades?" Dany asked him.

"Prendahl and Sallor would tell you so, if dead men could talk. I count no day as lived unless I have loved a woman, slain a foeman, and eaten a fine meal . . . and the days that I have lived are as numberless as the stars in the sky. I make of slaughter a thing of beauty, and many a tumbler and fire dancer has wept to the gods that they might be half so quick, a quarter so graceful. I would tell you the names of all the men I have slain, but before I could finish your dragons would grow large as castles, the walls of Yunkai would crumble into yellow dust, and winter would come and go and come again."

Dany laughed. She liked the swagger she saw in this Daario Naharis. "Draw your sword and swear it to my service."

In a blink, Daario's *arakh* was free of its sheath. His submission was as outrageous as the rest of him, a great swoop that brought his face down to her toes. "My sword is yours. My life is yours. My love is yours. My blood, my body, my songs, you own them all. I live and die at your command, fair queen."

"Then live," Dany said, "and fight for me tonight."

"That would not be wise, my queen." Ser Jorah gave Daario a cold, hard stare. "Keep this one here under guard until the battle's fought and won."

She considered a moment, then shook her head. "If he can give us the Stormcrows, surprise is certain."

"And if he betrays you, surprise is lost."

Dany looked down at the sellsword again. He gave her such a smile that she flushed and turned away. "He won't."

"How can you know that?"

She pointed to the lumps of blackened flesh the dragons were consuming, bite by bloody bite. "I would call that proof of his sincerity. Daario Naharis, have your Stormcrows ready to strike the Yunkish rear when my attack begins. Can you get back safely?"

"If they stop me, I will say I have been scouting, and saw nothing." The Tyroshi rose to his feet, bowed, and swept out.

Ser Jorah Mormont lingered. "Your Grace," he said, too bluntly, "that was a mistake. We know nothing of this man –"

"We know that he is a great fighter."

"A great talker, you mean."

"He brings us the Stormcrows." *And he has blue eyes.*

"Five hundred sellswords of uncertain loyalty."

"All loyalties are uncertain in such times as these," Dany reminded him. *And I shall be betrayed twice more, once for gold and once for love.*

"Daenerys, I am thrice your age," Ser Jorah said. "I have seen how false men are. Very few are worthy of trust, and Daario Naharis is not one of them. Even his beard wears false colors."

That angered her. "Whilst you have an honest beard, is that what you are telling me? You are the only man I should ever trust?"

He stiffened. "I did not say that."

"You say it every day. Pyat Pree's a liar, Xaro's a schemer, Belwas a braggart, Arstan an assassin . . . do you think I'm still some virgin girl, that I cannot hear the words behind the words?"

"Your Grace –"

She bulled over him. "You have been a better friend to me than any I have known, a better brother than Viserys ever was. You are the first of my Queensguard, the commander of my army, my most valued counselor, my good right hand. I honor and respect and cherish you – but I do not desire you, Jorah Mormont, and I am weary of your trying to push every other man in the world away from me, so I must needs rely on you and you alone. It will not serve, and it will not make me love you any better."

Mormont had flushed red when she first began, but by the time Dany was done his face was pale again. He stood still as stone. "If my queen commands," he said, curt and cold.

Dany was warm enough for both of them. "She does," she said. "She *commands*. Now go see to your Unsullied, ser. You have a battle to fight and win."

When he was gone, Dany threw herself down on her pillows beside her dragons. She had not meant to be so sharp with Ser Jorah, but his endless suspicion had finally woken her dragon.

He will forgive me, she told herself. *I am his liege.* Dany found herself wondering whether he was right about Daario. She felt very lonely all of a sudden. Mirri Maz Duur had promised that she would never bear a living child. *House Targaryen will end with me.* That made her sad. "You must be my children," she told the dragons, "my three fierce children. Arstan says dragons live longer than men, so you will go on after I am dead."

Drogon looped his neck around to nip at her hand. His teeth were very sharp, but he never broke her skin when they played like this. Dany laughed, and rolled him back and forth until he roared, his tail lashing like a whip. *It is longer than it was*, she saw, *and tomorrow it will be longer still. They grow quickly now, and when they are grown I shall have my wings.* Mounted on a dragon, she could lead her own men into battle, as she had in Astapor, but as yet they were still too small to bear her weight.

A stillness settled over her camp when midnight came and went. Dany remained in her pavilion with her maids, while Arstan Whitebeard and Strong Belwas kept the guard. *The waiting is the hardest part.* To sit in her tent with idle hands while her battle was being fought without her made Dany feel half a child again.

The hours crept by on turtle feet. Even after Jhiqui rubbed the knots from her shoulders, Dany was too restless for sleep. Missandei offered to sing her a lullaby of the Peaceful People, but Dany shook her head. "Bring me Arstan," she said.

When the old man came, she was curled up inside her *hrakkar* pelt, whose musty smell still reminded her of Drogo. "I cannot sleep when men are dying for me, Whitebeard," she said. "Tell me more of my brother Rhaegar, if you would. I liked the tale you told me on the ship, of how he decided that he must be a warrior."

"Your Grace is kind to say so."

"Viserys said that our brother won many tourneys."

Arstan bowed his white head respectfully. "It is not meet for me to deny His Grace's words . . ."

"But?" said Dany sharply. "Tell me. I command it."

"Prince Rhaegar's prowess was unquestioned, but he seldom entered the lists. He never loved the song of swords the way that Robert did, or Jaime Lannister. It was something he had to do, a task the world had set him. He did it well, for he did everything well. That was his nature. But he took no joy in it. Men said that he loved his harp much better than his lance."

"He won *some* tourneys, surely," said Dany, disappointed.

"When he was young, His Grace rode brilliantly in a tourney at Storm's End, defeating Lord Steffon Baratheon, Lord Jason Mallister, the Red Viper of Dorne, and a mystery knight who proved to be the infamous Simon Toyne, chief of the kingswood outlaws. He broke twelve lances against Ser Arthur Dayne that day."

"Was he the champion, then?"

"No, Your Grace. That honor went to another knight of the Kingsguard, who unhorsed Prince Rhaegar in the final tilt."

Dany did not want to hear about Rhaegar being unhorsed. "But what tourneys did my brother *win*?"

"Your Grace." The old man hesitated. "He won the greatest tourney of them all."

"Which was that?" Dany demanded.

"The tourney Lord Whent staged at Harrenhal beside the Gods Eye, in the year of the false spring. A notable event. Besides the jousting, there was a mêlée in the old style fought between seven teams of knights, as well as archery and axe-throwing, a horse race, a tournament of singers, a mummer show, and many feasts and frolics. Lord Whent was as open handed as he was rich. The lavish purses he proclaimed drew hundreds of challengers. Even your royal father came to Harrenhal, when he had not left the Red Keep for long years. The greatest lords and mightiest champions of the Seven Kingdoms rode in that tourney, and the Prince of Dragonstone bested them all."

"But that was the tourney when he crowned Lyanna Stark as queen of love and beauty!" said Dany. "Princess Elia was there, his wife, and yet my brother gave the crown to the Stark girl, and later stole her away from her betrothed. How could he do that? Did the Dornish woman treat him so ill?"

"It is not for such as me to say what might have been in your brother's heart, Your Grace. The Princess Elia was a good and gracious lady, though her health was ever delicate."

Dany pulled the lion pelt tighter about her shoulders. "Viserys said once that it was my fault, for being born too late." She had denied it hotly, she remembered, going so far as to tell Viserys that it was his fault for not being born a girl. He beat her cruelly for that insolence. "If I had been born more timely, he said, Rhaegar would have married me instead of Elia, and it would all have come out different. If Rhaegar had been happy in his wife, he would not have needed the Stark girl."

"Perhaps so, Your Grace." Whitebeard paused a moment. "But I am not certain it was in Rhaegar to be happy."

"You make him sound so sour," Dany protested.

"Not sour, no, but . . . there was a melancholy to Prince Rhaegar, a sense . . ." The old man hesitated again.

"Say it," she urged. "A sense . . . ?"

". . . of doom. He was born in grief, my queen, and that shadow hung over him all his days."

Viserys had spoken of Rhaegar's birth only once. Perhaps the tale saddened him too much. "It was the shadow of Summerhall that haunted him, was it not?"

"Yes. And yet Summerhall was the place the prince loved best. He would go there from time to time, with only his harp for company. Even the knights of the Kingsguard did not attend him there. He liked to sleep in the ruined hall, beneath the moon and stars, and whenever he came back he would bring a song. When you heard him play his high harp with the silver strings and sing of twilights and tears and the death of kings, you could not but feel that he was singing of himself and those he loved."

"What of the Usurper? Did he play sad songs as well?"

Arstan chuckled. "Robert? Robert liked songs that made him laugh, the bawdier the better. He only sang when he was drunk, and then it was like to be 'A Cask of Ale' or 'Fifty-Four Tuns' or 'The Bear and the Maiden Fair.' Robert was much –"

As one, her dragons lifted their heads and roared.

"Horses!" Dany leapt to her feet, clutching the lion pelt. Outside, she heard Strong Belwas bellow something, and then other voices, and the sounds of many horses. "Irri, go see who . . ."

The tent flap pushed open, and Ser Jorah Mormont entered. He was dusty, and spattered with blood, but otherwise none the worse for battle. The exile knight went to one knee before Dany and said, "Your Grace, I bring you victory. The Stormcrows turned their cloaks, the slaves broke, and the Second Sons were too drunk to fight, just as you said. Two hundred dead, Yunkai'i for the most part. Their slaves threw down their spears and ran, and their sellswords yielded. We have several thousand captives."

"Our own losses?"

"A dozen. If that many."

Only then did she allow herself to smile. "Rise, my good brave bear. Was Grazdan taken? Or the Titan's Bastard?"

"Grazdan went to Yunkai to deliver your terms." Ser Jorah got to his feet. "Mero fled, once he realized the Stormcrows had turned. I have men hunting him. He shouldn't escape us long."

"Very well," Dany said. "Sellsword or slave, spare all those who will pledge me their faith. If enough of the Second Sons will join us, keep the company intact."

The next day they marched the last three leagues to Yunkai. The city was built of yellow bricks instead of red; elsewise it was Astapor all over again, with the same crumbling walls and high stepped pyramids, and a great harpy mounted above its gates. The wall and towers swarmed with crossbowmen and slingers. Ser Jorah and Grey Worm deployed her men, Irri and Jhiqui raised her pavilion, and Dany sat down to wait.

On the morning of the third day, the city gates swung open and a line of slaves began to emerge. Dany mounted her silver to greet them. As they passed, little Missandei told them that they owed their freedom to Daenerys Stormborn, the Unburnt, Queen of the Seven Kingdoms of Westeros and Mother of Dragons.

"*Mhysa!*" a brown-skinned man shouted out at her. He had a child on his shoulder, a little girl, and she screamed the same word in her thin voice. "*Mhysa! Mhysa!*"

Dany looked at Missandei. "What are they shouting?"

"It is Ghiscari, the old pure tongue. It means 'Mother.'"

Dany felt a lightness in her chest. *I will never bear a living child*, she remembered. Her hand trembled as she raised it. Perhaps she smiled. She must have, because the man grinned and shouted again, and others took up the cry. "*Mhysa!*" they called. "*Mhysa! MHYSA!*" They were all smiling at her, reaching for her, kneeling before her. "*Maela*," some called her, while others cried "*Aelalla*" or "*Qathei*" or "*Tato*," but whatever the tongue it all meant the same thing. *Mother. They are calling me Mother.*

The chant grew, spread, swelled. It swelled so loud that it frightened her horse, and the mare backed and shook her head and lashed her silver-grey tail. It swelled until it seemed to shake the yellow walls of Yunkai. More slaves were streaming from the gates every moment, and as they came they took up the call. They were running toward her now, pushing, stumbling, wanting to touch her hand, to stroke her horse's mane, to kiss her feet. Her poor bloodriders could not keep them all away, and even Strong Belwas grunted and growled in dismay.

Ser Jorah urged her to go, but Dany remembered a dream she had dreamed in the House of the Undying. "They will not hurt me," she told him. "They are my children, Jorah." She laughed, put her heels into her horse, and rode to them, the bells in her hair ringing sweet victory. She trotted, then cantered, then broke into a gallop, her braid streaming behind. The freed slaves parted before her. "Mother," they called from a hundred throats, a thousand, ten thousand. "Mother," they sang, their fingers brushing her legs as she flew by. "Mother, Mother, Mother!"

ARYA

When Arya saw the shape of a great hill looming in the distance, golden in the afternoon sun, she knew it at once. They had come all the way back to High Heart.

By sunset they were at the top, making camp where no harm could come to them. Arya walked around the circle of weirwood stumps with Lord Beric's squire Ned, and they stood on top of one watching the last light fade in the west. From up here she could see a storm raging to the north, but High Heart stood *above* the rain. It wasn't above the wind, though; the gusts were blowing so strongly that it felt like someone was behind her, yanking on her cloak. Only when she turned, no one was there.

Ghosts, she remembered. *High Heart is haunted.*

They built a great fire atop the hill, and Thoros of Myr sat crosslegged beside it, gazing deep into the flames as if there was nothing else in all the world.

"What is he doing?" Arya asked Ned.

"Sometimes he sees things in the flames," the squire told her. "The past. The future. Things happening far away."

Arya squinted at the fire to see if she could see what the red priest was seeing, but it only made her eyes water and before long she turned away. Gendry was watching the red priest as well. "Can you truly see the future there?" he asked suddenly.

Thoros turned from the fire, sighing. "Not here. Not now. But some days, yes, the Lord of Light grants me visions."

Gendry looked dubious. "My master said you were a sot and a fraud, as bad a priest as there ever was."

"That was unkind." Thoros chuckled. "True, but unkind. Who was this master of yours? Did I know you, boy?"

"I was 'prenticed to the master armorer Tobho Mott, on the Street of Steel. You used to buy your swords from him."

"Just so. He charged me twice what they were worth, then scolded me for setting them afire." Thoros laughed. "Your master had it right. I was no very holy priest. I was born youngest of eight, so my father gave me over to the Red Temple, but it was not the path I would have chosen. I prayed the prayers and I spoke the spells, but I would also lead raids on the kitchens, and from time to time they found girls in my bed. Such wicked girls, I never knew how they got there.

"I had a gift for tongues, though. And when I gazed into the flames, well, from time to time I saw things. Even so, I was more bother than I was worth, so they sent me finally to King's Landing to bring the Lord's light to seven-besotted Westeros. King Aerys so loved fire it was thought he might make a convert. Alas, his pyromancers knew better tricks than I did.

"King Robert was fond of me, though. The first time I rode into a mêlée with a flaming sword, Kevan Lannister's horse reared and threw him and His Grace laughed so hard I thought he might rupture." The red priest smiled at the memory. "It was no way to treat a blade, though, your master had the right of that too."

"Fire consumes." Lord Beric stood behind them, and there was something in his voice that silenced Thoros at once. "It *consumes*, and when it is done there is nothing left. *Nothing.*"

"Beric. Sweet friend." The priest touched the lightning lord on the forearm. "What are you saying?"

"Nothing I have not said before. Six times, Thoros? Six times is too many." He turned away abruptly.

That night the wind was howling almost like a wolf and there were some real wolves off to the west giving it lessons. Notch, Anguy, and Merrit o' Moontown had the watch. Ned, Gendry, and many of the others were fast asleep when Arya spied the small pale shape creeping behind the horses, thin white hair flying wild as she leaned upon a gnarled cane. The woman could not have been more than three feet tall. The firelight made her eyes gleam as red as the eyes of Jon's wolf. *He was a ghost too.* Arya stole closer, and knelt to watch.

Thoros and Lem were with Lord Beric when the dwarf woman sat down uninvited by the fire. She squinted at them with eyes like hot coals. "The Ember and the Lemon come to honor me again, and His Grace the Lord of Corpses."

"An ill-omened name. I have asked you not to use it."

"Aye, you have. But the stink of death is fresh on you, my lord." She

had but a single tooth remaining. "Give me wine or I will go. My bones
are old. My joints ache when the winds do blow, and up here the winds
are always blowing."

"A silver stag for your dreams, my lady," Lord Beric said, with solemn
courtesy. "Another if you have news for us."

"I cannot eat a silver stag, nor ride one. A skin of wine for my dreams,
and for my news a kiss from the great oaf in the yellow cloak." The little
woman cackled. "Aye, a sloppy kiss, a bit of tongue. It has been too
long, too long. His mouth will taste of lemons, and mine of bones. I am
too old."

"Aye," Lem complained. "Too old for wine and kisses. All you'll get
from me is the flat of my sword, crone."

"My hair comes out in handfuls and no one has kissed me for a thousand years. It is hard to be so old. Well, I will have a song then. A song
from Tom o' Sevens, for my news."

"You will have your song from Tom," Lord Beric promised. He gave
her the wineskin himself.

The dwarf woman drank deep, the wine running down her chin. When
she lowered the skin, she wiped her mouth with the back of a wrinkled
hand and said, "Sour wine for sour tidings, what could be more fitting?
The king is dead, is that sour enough for you?"

Arya's heart caught in her throat.

"*Which* bloody king is dead, crone?" Lem demanded.

"The wet one. The kraken king, m'lords. I dreamt him dead and he
died, and the iron squids now turn on one another. Oh, and Lord Hoster
Tully's died too, but you know that, don't you? In the hall of kings, the
goat sits alone and fevered as the great dog descends on him." The old
woman took another long gulp of wine, squeezing the skin as she raised
it to her lips.

The great dog. Did she mean the Hound? Or maybe his brother, the
Mountain That Rides? Arya was not certain. They bore the same arms,
three black dogs on a yellow field. Half the men whose deaths she prayed
for belonged to Ser Gregor Clegane; Polliver, Dunsen, Raff the Sweetling,
the Tickler, and Ser Gregor himself. *Maybe Lord Beric will hang
them all.*

"I dreamt a wolf howling in the rain, but no one heard his grief," the
dwarf woman was saying. "I dreamt such a clangor I thought my head
might burst, drums and horns and pipes and screams, but the saddest
sound was the little bells. I dreamt of a maid at a feast with purple
serpents in her hair, venom dripping from their fangs. And later I dreamt
that maid again, slaying a savage giant in a castle built of snow." She
turned her head sharply and smiled through the gloom, right at Arya.
"You cannot hide from me, child. Come closer, now."

Cold fingers walked down Arya's neck. *Fear cuts deeper than swords*, she reminded herself. She stood and approached the fire warily, light on the balls of her feet, poised to flee.

The dwarf woman studied her with dim red eyes. "I see you," she whispered. "I see you, wolf child. Blood child. I thought it was the lord who smelled of death . . ." She began to sob, her little body shaking. "You are cruel to come to my hill, cruel. I gorged on grief at Summerhall, I need none of yours. Begone from here, dark heart. *Begone!*"

There was such fear in her voice that Arya took a step backward, wondering if the woman was mad. "Don't frighten the child," Thoros protested. "There's no harm in her."

Lem Lemoncloak's finger went to his broken nose. "Don't be so bloody sure of that."

"She will leave on the morrow, with us," Lord Beric assured the little woman. "We're taking her to Riverrun, to her mother."

"Nay," said the dwarf. "You're not. The black fish holds the rivers now. If it's the mother you want, seek her at the Twins. For there's to be a *wedding*." She cackled again. "Look in your fires, pink priest, and you will see. Not now, though, not here, you'll see nothing here. This place belongs to the old gods still . . . they linger here as I do, shrunken and feeble but not yet dead. Nor do they love the flames. For the oak recalls the acorn, the acorn dreams the oak, the stump lives in them both. And they remember when the First Men came with fire in their fists." She drank the last of the wine in four long swallows, flung the skin aside, and pointed her stick at Lord Beric. "I'll have my payment now. I'll have the song you promised me."

And so Lem woke Tom Sevenstrings beneath his furs, and brought him yawning to the fireside with his woodharp in hand. "The same song as before?" he asked.

"Oh, aye. My Jenny's song. Is there another?"

And so he sang, and the dwarf woman closed her eyes and rocked slowly back and forth, murmuring the words and crying. Thoros took Arya firmly by the hand and drew her aside. "Let her savor her song in peace," he said. "It is all she has left."

I wasn't going to hurt her, Arya thought. "What did she mean about the Twins? My mother's at Riverrun, isn't she?"

"She was." The red priest rubbed beneath his chin. "A wedding, she said. We shall see. Whenever she is, Lord Beric will find her, though."

Not long after, the sky opened. Lightning cracked and thunder rolled across the hills, and the rain fell in blinding sheets. The dwarf woman vanished as suddenly as she had appeared, while the outlaws gathered branches and threw up crude shelters.

It rained all through that night, and come morning Ned, Lem, and

Watty the Miller awoke with chills. Watty could not keep his breakfast down, and young Ned was feverish and shivering by turns, with skin clammy to the touch. There was an abandoned village half a day's ride to the north, Notch told Lord Beric; they'd find better shelter there, a place to wait out the worst of the rains. So they dragged themselves back into the saddles and urged their horses down the great hill.

The rains did not let up. They rode through woods and fields, fording swollen streams where the rushing water came up to the bellies of their horses. Arya pulled up the hood of her cloak and hunched down, sodden and shivering but determined not to falter. Merrit and Mudge were soon coughing as bad as Watty, and poor Ned seemed to grow more miserable with every mile. "When I wear my helm, the rain beats against the steel and gives me headaches," he complained. "But when I take it off, my hair gets soaked and sticks to my face and in my mouth."

"You have a knife," Gendry suggested. "If your hair annoys you so much, shave your bloody head."

He doesn't like Ned. The squire seemed nice enough to Arya; maybe a little shy, but good-natured. She had always heard that Dornishmen were small and swarthy, with black hair and small black eyes, but Ned had big blue eyes, so dark that they looked almost purple. And his hair was a pale blond, more ash than honey.

"How long have you been Lord Beric's squire?" she asked, to take his mind from his misery.

"He took me for his page when he espoused my aunt." He coughed. "I was seven, but when I turned ten he raised me to squire. I won a prize once, riding at rings."

"I never learned the lance, but I could beat you with a sword," said Arya. "Have you killed anyone?"

That seemed to startle him. "I'm only twelve."

I killed a boy when I was eight, Arya almost said, but she thought she'd better not. "You've been in battles, though."

"Yes." He did not sound very proud of it. "I was at the Mummer's Ford. When Lord Beric fell into the river, I dragged him up onto the bank so he wouldn't drown and stood over him with my sword. I never had to fight, though. He had a broken lance sticking out of him, so no one bothered us. When we regrouped, Green Gergen helped pull his lordship back onto a horse."

Arya was remembering the stableboy at King's Landing. After him there'd been that guard whose throat she cut at Harrenhal, and Ser Amory's men at that holdfast by the lake. She didn't know if Weese and Chiswyck counted, or the ones who'd died on account of the weasel soup . . . all of a sudden, she felt very sad. "My father was called Ned too," she said.

"I know. I saw him at the Hand's tourney. I wanted to go up and speak with him, but I couldn't think what to say." Ned shivered beneath his cloak, a sodden length of pale purple. "Were you at the tourney? I saw your sister there. Ser Loras Tyrell gave her a rose."

"She told me." It all seemed so long ago. "Her friend Jeyne Poole fell in love with your Lord Beric."

"He's promised to my aunt." Ned looked uncomfortable. "That was before, though. Before he . . ."

. . . *died?* she thought, as Ned's voice trailed off into an awkward silence. Their horses' hooves made sucking sounds as they pulled free of the mud.

"My lady?" Ned said at last. "You have a baseborn brother . . . Jon Snow?"

"He's with the Night's Watch on the Wall." *Maybe I should go to the Wall instead of Riverrun. Jon wouldn't care who I killed or whether I brushed my hair . . .* "Jon looks like me, even though he's bastard-born. He used to muss my hair and call me 'little sister.'" Arya missed Jon most of all. Just saying his name made her sad. "How do you know about Jon?"

"He is my milk brother."

"Brother?" Arya did not understand. "But you're from Dorne. How could you and Jon be blood?"

"*Milk* brothers. Not blood. My lady mother had no milk when I was little, so Wylla had to nurse me."

Arya was lost. "Who's Wylla?"

"Jon Snow's mother. He never told you? She's served us for years and years. Since before I was born."

"Jon never knew his mother. Not even her name." Arya gave Ned a wary look. "You know her? Truly?" *Is he making mock of me?* "If you lie I'll punch your face."

"Wylla was my wetnurse," he repeated solemnly. "I swear it on the honor of my House."

"You have a House?" That was stupid; he was a squire, of course he had a House. "Who *are* you?"

"My lady?" Ned looked embarrassed. "I'm Edric Dayne, the . . . the Lord of Starfall."

Behind them, Gendry groaned. "Lords and ladies," he proclaimed in a disgusted tone. Arya plucked a withered crabapple off a passing branch and whipped it at him, bouncing it off his thick bull head. "Ow," he said. "That hurt." He felt the skin above his eye. "What kind of lady throws crabapples at people?"

"The bad kind," said Arya, suddenly contrite. She turned back to Ned. "I'm sorry I didn't know who you were. My lord."

"The fault is mine, my lady." He was very polite.

Jon has a mother. Wylla, her name is Wylla. She would need to remember so she could tell him, the next time she saw him. She wondered if he would still call her "little sister." *I'm not so little anymore. He'd have to call me something else.* Maybe once she got to Riverrun she could write Jon a letter and tell him what Ned Dayne had said. "There was an Arthur Dayne," she remembered. "The one they called the Sword of the Morning."

"My father was Ser Arthur's elder brother. Lady Ashara was my aunt. I never knew her, though. She threw herself into the sea from atop the Palestone Sword before I was born."

"Why would she do that?" said Arya, startled.

Ned looked wary. Maybe he was afraid that she was going to throw something at him. "Your lord father never spoke of her?" he said. "The Lady Ashara Dayne, of Starfall?"

"No. Did he know her?"

"Before Robert was king. She met your father and his brothers at Harrenhal, during the year of the false spring."

"Oh." Arya did not know what else to say. "Why did she jump in the sea, though?"

"Her heart was broken."

Sansa would have sighed and shed a tear for true love, but Arya just thought it was stupid. She couldn't say that to Ned, though, not about his own aunt. "Did someone break it?"

He hesitated. "Perhaps it's not my place . . ."

"Tell me."

He looked at her uncomfortably. "My aunt Allyria says Lady Ashara and your father fell in love at Harrenhal –"

"That's not so. He loved my lady mother."

"I'm sure he did, my lady, but –"

"She was the *only* one he loved."

"He must have found that bastard under a cabbage leaf, then," Gendry said behind them.

Arya wished she had another crabapple to bounce off his face. "My father had *honor*," she said angrily. "And we weren't talking to *you* anyway. Why don't you go back to Stoney Sept and ring that girl's stupid bells?"

Gendry ignored that. "At least your father *raised* his bastard, not like mine. I don't even know my father's name. Some smelly drunk, I'd wager, like the others my mother dragged home from the alehouse. Whenever she got mad at me, she'd say, 'If your father was here, he'd beat you bloody.' That's all I know of him." He spat. "Well, if he was here now, might be I'd beat *him* bloody. But he's dead, I figure, and your father's dead too, so what does it matter who he lay with?"

It mattered to Arya, though she could not have said why. Ned was trying to apologize for upsetting her, but she did not want to hear it. She pressed her heels into her horse and left them both. Anguy the Archer was riding a few yards ahead. When she caught up with him, she said, "Dornishmen lie, don't they?"

"They're famous for it." The bowman grinned. "Of course, they say the same of us marchers, so there you are. What's the trouble now? Ned's a good lad . . ."

"He's just a stupid liar." Arya left the trail, leapt a rotten log and splashed across a streambed, ignoring the shouts of the outlaws behind her. *They just want to tell me more lies.* She thought about trying to get away from them, but there were too many and they knew these lands too well. What was the use of running if they caught you?

It was Harwin who rode up beside her, in the end. "Where do you think you're going, milady? You shouldn't run off. There are wolves in these woods, and worse things."

"I'm not afraid," she said. "That boy Ned said . . ."

"Aye, he told me. Lady Ashara Dayne. It's an old tale, that one. I heard it once at Winterfell, when I was no older than you are now." He took hold of her bridle firmly and turned her horse around. "I doubt there's any truth to it. But if there is, what of it? When Ned met this Dornish lady, his brother Brandon was still alive, and it was him betrothed to Lady Catelyn, so there's no stain on your father's honor. There's nought like a tourney to make the blood run hot, so maybe some words were whispered in a tent of a night, who can say? Words or kisses, maybe more, but where's the harm in that? Spring had come, or so they thought, and neither one of them was pledged."

"She killed herself, though," said Arya uncertainly. "Ned says she jumped from a tower into the sea."

"So she did," Harwin admitted, as he led her back, "but that was for grief, I'd wager. She'd lost a brother, the Sword of the Morning." He shook his head. "Let it lie, my lady. They're dead, all of them. Let it lie . . . and please, when we come to Riverrun, say naught of this to your mother."

The village was just where Notch had promised it would be. They took shelter in a grey stone stable. Only half a roof remained, but that was half a roof more than any other building in the village. *It's not a village, it's only black stones and old bones.* "Did the Lannisters kill the people who lived here?" Arya asked as she helped Anguy dry the horses.

"No." He pointed. "Look at how thick the moss grows on the stones. No one's moved them for a long time. And there's a tree growing out of the wall there, see? This place was put to the torch a long time ago."

"Who did it, then?" asked Gendry.

"Hoster Tully." Notch was a stooped thin grey-haired man, born in these parts. "This was Lord Goodbrook's village. When Riverrun declared for Robert, Goodbrook stayed loyal to the king, so Lord Tully came down on him with fire and sword. After the Trident, Goodbrook's son made his peace with Robert and Lord Hoster, but that didn't help the dead none."

A silence fell. Gendry gave Arya a queer look, then turned away to brush his horse. Outside the rain came down and down. "I say we need a fire," Thoros declared. "The night is dark and full of terrors. And wet too, eh? Too very wet."

Jack-Be-Lucky hacked some dry wood from a stall, while Notch and Merrit gathered straw for kindling. Thoros himself struck the spark, and Lem fanned the flames with his big yellow cloak until they roared and swirled. Soon it grew almost hot inside the stable. Thoros sat before it crosslegged, devouring the flames with his eyes just as he had atop High Heart. Arya watched him closely, and once his lips moved, and she thought she heard him mutter, "Riverrun." Lem paced back and forth, coughing, a long shadow matching him stride for stride, while Tom o' Sevens pulled off his boots and rubbed his feet. "I must be mad, to be going back to Riverrun," the singer complained. "The Tullys have never been lucky for old Tom. It was that Lysa sent me up the high road, when the moon men took my gold and my horse and all my clothes as well. There's knights in the Vale still telling how I came walking up to the Bloody Gate with only my harp to keep me modest. They made me sing 'The Name Day Boy' and 'The King Without Courage' before they opened that gate. My only solace was that three of them died laughing. I haven't been back to the Eyrie since, and I won't sing 'The King Without Courage' either, not for all the gold in Casterly –"

"*Lannisters*," Thoros said. "Roaring red and gold." He lurched to his feet and went to Lord Beric. Lem and Tom wasted no time joining them. Arya could not make out what they were saying, but the singer kept glancing at her, and one time Lem got so angry he pounded a fist against the wall. That was when Lord Beric gestured for her to come closer. It was the last thing she wanted to do, but Harwin put a hand in the small of her back and pushed her forward. She took two steps and hesitated, full of dread. "My lord." She waited to hear what Lord Beric would say.

"Tell her," the lightning lord commanded Thoros.

The red priest squatted down beside her. "My lady," he said, "the Lord granted me a view of Riverrun. An island in a sea of fire, it seemed. The flames were leaping lions with long crimson claws. And how they roared! A sea of Lannisters, my lady. Riverrun will soon come under attack."

Arya felt as though he'd punched her in the belly. "*No!*"

"Sweetling," said Thoros, "the flames do not lie. Sometimes I read them wrongly, blind fool that I am. But not this time, I think. The Lannisters will soon have Riverrun under siege."

"Robb will beat them." Arya got a stubborn look. "He'll beat them like he did before."

"Your brother may be gone," said Thoros. "Your mother as well. I did not see them in the flames. This wedding the old one spoke of, a wedding on the Twins . . . she has her own ways of knowing things, that one. The weirwoods whisper in her ear when she sleeps. If she says your mother is gone to the Twins . . ."

Arya turned on Tom and Lem. "If you hadn't caught me, I would have *been* there. I would have been *home*."

Lord Beric paid no heed to her outburst. "My lady," he said with weary courtesy, "would you know your grandfather's brother by sight? Ser Brynden Tully, called the Blackfish? Would he know you, perchance?"

Arya shook her head miserably. She had heard her mother speak of Ser Brynden Blackfish, but if she had ever met him herself it had been when she was too little to remember.

"Small chance the Blackfish will pay good coin for a girl he doesn't know," said Tom. "Those Tullys are a sour, suspicious lot, he's like to think we're selling him false goods."

"We'll convince him," Lem Lemoncloak insisted. "*She* will, or Harwin. Riverrun is closest. I say we take her there, get the gold, and be bloody well done with her."

"And if the lions catch us inside the castle?" said Tom. "They'd like nothing better than to hang his lordship in a cage from the top of Casterly Rock."

"I do not mean to be taken," said Lord Beric. A final word hung unspoken in the air. *Alive.* They all heard it, even Arya, though it never passed his lips. "Still, we dare not go blindly here. I want to know where the armies are, the wolves and lions both. Sharna will know something, and Lord Vance's maester will know more. Acorn Hall's not far. Lady Smallwood will shelter us for a time while we send scouts ahead to learn . . ."

His words beat at her ears like the pounding of a drum, and suddenly it was more than Arya could stand. She wanted Riverrun, not Acorn Hall; she wanted her mother and her brother Robb, not Lady Smallwood or some uncle she never knew. Whirling, she broke for the door, and when Harwin tried to grab her arm she spun away from him quick as a snake.

Outside the stables the rain was still falling, and distant lightning flashed in the west. Arya ran as fast as she could. She did not know where she was going, only that she wanted to be alone, away from all the voices, away from their hollow words and broken promises. *All I wanted was to go to Riverrun.* It was her own fault, for taking Gendry and Hot Pie with her when she left Harrenhal. She would have been better alone. If she had been alone, the outlaws would never have caught her, and she'd be with Robb and her mother by now. *They were never my pack. If they had been, they wouldn't leave me.* She splashed through a puddle of muddy water. Someone was shouting her name, Harwin probably, or Gendry, but the thunder drowned them out as it rolled across the hills, half a heartbeat behind the lightning. *The lightning lord,* she thought angrily. Maybe he couldn't die, but he could lie.

Somewhere off to her left a horse whinnied. Arya couldn't have gone more than fifty yards from the stables, yet already she was soaked to the bone. She ducked around the corner of one of the tumbledown houses, hoping the mossy walls would keep the rain off, and almost bowled right into one of the sentries. A mailed hand closed hard around her arm.

"You're *hurting* me," she said, twisting in his grasp. "Let *go,* I was going to go back, I . . ."

"Back?" Sandor Clegane's laughter was iron scraping over stone. "Bugger that, wolf girl. You're *mine.*" He needed only one hand to yank her off her feet and drag her kicking toward his waiting horse. The cold rain lashed them both and washed away her shouts, and all that Arya could think of was the question he had asked her. *Do you know what dogs do to wolves?*

JAIME

Though his fever lingered stubbornly, the stump was healing clean, and Qyburn said his arm was no longer in danger. Jaime was anxious to be gone, to put Harrenhal, the Bloody Mummers, and Brienne of Tarth all behind him. A real woman waited for him in the Red Keep.

"I am sending Qyburn with you, to look after you on the way to King's Landing," Roose Bolton said on the morn of their departure. "He has a fond hope that your father will force the Citadel to give him back his chain, in gratitude."

"We all have fond hopes. If he grows me back a hand, my father will make him Grand Maester."

Steelshanks Walton commanded Jaime's escort; blunt, brusque, brutal, at heart a simple soldier. Jaime had served with his sort all his life. Men like Walton would kill at their lord's command, rape when their blood was up after battle, and plunder wherever they could, but once the war was done they would go back to their homes, trade their spears for hoes, wed their neighbors' daughters, and raise a pack of squalling children. Such men obeyed without question, but the deep malignant cruelty of the Brave Companions was not a part of their nature.

Both parties left Harrenhal the same morning, beneath a cold grey sky that promised rain. Ser Aenys Frey had marched three days before, striking northeast for the kingsroad. Bolton meant to follow him. "The Trident is in flood," he told Jaime. "Even at the ruby ford, the crossing will be difficult. You will give my warm regards to your father?"

"So long as you give mine to Robb Stark."

"That I shall."

Some Brave Companions had gathered in the yard to watch them leave. Jaime trotted over to where they stood. "Zollo. How kind of you to see me off. Pyg. Timeon. Will you miss me? No last jest to share, Shagwell? To lighten my way down the road? And Rorge, did you come to kiss me goodbye?"

"Bugger off, cripple," said Rorge.

"If you insist. Rest assured, though, I will be back. A Lannister always pays his debts." Jaime wheeled his horse around and rejoined Steelshanks Walton and his two hundred.

Lord Bolton had accoutred him as a knight, preferring to ignore the missing hand that made such warlike garb a travesty. Jaime rode with sword and dagger on his belt, shield and helm hung from his saddle, chainmail under a dark brown surcoat. He was not such a fool as to show the lion of Lannister on his arms, though, nor the plain white blazon that was his right as a Sworn Brother of the Kingsguard. He found an old shield in the armory, battered and splintered, the chipped paint still showing most of the great black bat of House Lothston upon a field of silver and gold. The Lothstons held Harrenhal before the Whents and had been a powerful family in their day, but they had died out ages ago, so no one was likely to object to him bearing their arms. He would be no one's cousin, no one's enemy, no one's sworn sword . . . in sum, no one.

They left through Harrenhal's smaller eastern gate, and took their leave of Roose Bolton and his host six miles farther on, turning south to follow along the lake road for a time. Walton meant to avoid the kingsroad as long as he could, preferring the farmer's tracks and game trails near the Gods Eye.

"The kingsroad would be faster." Jaime was anxious to return to Cersei as quickly as he could. If they made haste, he might even arrive in time for Joffrey's wedding.

"I want no trouble," said Steelshanks. "Gods know who we'd meet along that kingsroad."

"No one you need fear, surely? You have two hundred men."

"Aye. But others might have more. M'lord said to bring you safe to your lord father, and that's what I mean to do."

I have come this way before, Jaime reflected a few miles further on, when they passed a deserted mill beside the lake. Weeds now grew where once the miller's daughter had smiled shyly at him, and the miller himself had shouted out, "The tourney's back the other way, ser." *As if I had not known.*

King Aerys made a great show of Jaime's investiture. He said his vows before the king's pavilion, kneeling on the green grass in white armor while half the realm looked on. When Ser Gerold Hightower raised him up and put the white cloak about his shoulders, a roar went up that Jaime still remembered, all these years later. But that very night Aerys had turned sour, declaring that he had no need of *seven* Kingsguard here at Harrenhal. Jaime was commanded to return to King's Landing to guard the queen and little Prince Viserys, who'd remained behind. Even when the White Bull offered to take that duty himself, so Jaime might compete in Lord Whent's tourney, Aerys had refused. "He'll win no glory here," the king had said. "He's mine now, not Tywin's. He'll serve as I see fit. I am the king. I rule, and he'll obey."

That was the first time that Jaime understood. It was not his skill with sword and lance that had won him his white cloak, nor any feats of valor he'd performed against the Kingswood Brotherhood. Aerys had chosen him to spite his father, to rob Lord Tywin of his heir.

Even now, all these years later, the thought was bitter. And that day, as he'd ridden south in his new white cloak to guard an empty castle, it had been almost too much to stomach. He would have ripped the cloak off then and there if he could have, but it was too late. He had said the words whilst half the realm looked on, and a Kingsguard served for life.

Qyburn fell in beside him. "Is your hand troubling you?"

"The lack of my hand is troubling me." The mornings were the hardest. In his dreams Jaime was a whole man, and each dawn he would lie half-awake and feel his fingers move. *It was a nightmare*, some part of him would whisper, refusing to believe even now, *only a nightmare*. But then he would open his eyes.

"I understand you had a visitor last night," said Qyburn. "I trust that you enjoyed her?"

Jaime gave him a cool look. "She did not say who sent her."

The maester smiled modestly. "Your fever was largely gone, and I thought you might enjoy a bit of exercise. Pia is quite skilled, would you not agree? And so . . . willing."

She had been that, certainly. She had slipped in his door and out of her clothes so quickly that Jaime had thought he was still dreaming.

It hadn't been until the woman slid in under his blankets and put his good hand on her breast that he roused. *She was a pretty little thing, too.* "I was a slip of a girl when you came for Lord Whent's tourney and the king gave you your cloak," she confessed. "You were so handsome all in white, and everyone said what a brave knight you were. Sometimes when I'm with some man, I close my eyes and pretend it's you on top of me, with your smooth skin and gold curls. I never truly thought I'd have you, though."

Sending her away had not been easy after that, but Jaime had done it all the same. *I have a woman*, he reminded himself. "Do you send girls to everyone you leech?" he asked Qyburn.

"More often Lord Vargo sends them to me. He likes me to examine them, before . . . well, suffice it to say that once he loved unwisely, and he has no wish to do so again. But have no fear, Pia is quite healthy. As is your maid of Tarth."

Jaime gave him a sharp look. "Brienne?"

"Yes. A strong girl, that one. And her maidenhead is still intact. As of last night, at least." Qyburn gave a chuckle.

"He sent you to examine her?"

"To be sure. He is . . . fastidious, shall we say?"

"Does this concern the ransom?" Jaime asked. "Does her father require proof she is still maiden?"

"You have not heard?" Qyburn gave a shrug. "We had a bird from Lord Selwyn. In answer to mine. The Evenstar offers three hundred dragons for his daughter's safe return. I had told Lord Vargo there were no sapphires on Tarth, but he will not listen. He is convinced the Evenstar intends to cheat him."

"Three hundred dragons is a fair ransom for a knight. The goat should take what he can get."

"The goat is Lord of Harrenhal, and the Lord of Harrenhal does not haggle."

The news irritated him, though he supposed he should have seen it coming. *The lie spared you awhile, wench. Be grateful for that much.* "If her maidenhead's as hard as the rest of her, the goat will break his cock off trying to get in," he jested. Brienne was tough enough to survive a few rapes, Jaime judged, though if she resisted too vigorously Vargo Hoat might start lopping off her hands and feet. *And if he does, why should I care? I might still have a hand if she had let me have my cousin's sword without getting stupid.* He had almost taken off her leg himself with that first stroke of his, but after that she had given him more than he wanted. *Hoat may not know how freakish strong she is. He had best be careful, or she'll snap that skinny neck of his, and wouldn't that be sweet?*

Qyburn's companionship was wearing on him. Jaime trotted toward the head of the column. A round little tick of a northman name of Nage went before Steelshanks with the peace banner; a rainbow-striped flag with seven long tails, on a staff topped by a seven-pointed star. "Shouldn't you northmen have a different sort of peace banner?" he asked Walton. "What are the Seven to you?"

"Southron gods," the man said, "but it's a southron peace we need, to get you safe to your father."

My father. Jaime wondered whether Lord Tywin had received the goat's demand for ransom, with or without his rotted hand. *What is a swordsman worth without his sword hand? Half the gold in Casterly Rock?*

Three hundred dragons? Or nothing? His father had never been unduly swayed by sentiment. Tywin Lannister's own father Lord Tytos had once imprisoned an unruly bannerman, Lord Tarbeck. The redoubtable Lady Tarbeck responded by capturing three Lannisters, including young Stafford, whose sister was betrothed to cousin Tywin. "Send back my lord and love, or these three shall answer for any harm that comes him," she had written to Casterly Rock. Young Tywin suggested his father oblige by sending back Lord Tarbeck in three pieces. Lord Tytos was a gentler sort of lion, however, so Lady Tarbeck won a few more years for her muttonheaded lord, and Stafford wed and bred and blundered on till Oxcross. But Tywin Lannister endured, eternal as Casterly Rock. *And now you have a cripple for a son as well as a dwarf, my lord. How you will hate that . . .*

The road led them through a burned village. It must have been a year or more since the place had been put to torch. The hovels stood blackened and roofless, but weeds were growing waist high in all the surrounding fields. Steelshanks called a halt to allow them to water the horses. *I know this place too*, Jaime thought as he waited by the well. There had been a small inn where only a few foundation stones and a chimney now stood, and he had gone in for a cup of ale. A dark-eyed serving wench brought him cheese and apples, but the innkeep had refused his coin. "It's an honor to have a knight of the Kingsguard under my roof, ser," the man had said. "It's a tale I'll tell my grandchildren." Jaime looked at the chimney poking out of the weeds and wondered whether he had ever gotten those grandchildren. *Did he tell them the Kingslayer once drank his ale and ate his cheese and apples, or was he ashamed to admit he fed the likes of me?* Not that he would ever know; whoever burned the inn had likely killed the grandchildren as well.

He could feel his phantom fingers clench. When Steelshanks said that perhaps they should have a fire and a bit of food, Jaime shook his head. "I mislike this place. We'll ride on."

By evenfall they had left the lake to follow a rutted track through a wood of oak and elm. Jaime's stump was throbbing dully when Steelshanks decided to make camp. Qyburn had brought a skin of dreamwine, thankfully. While Walton set the watches, Jaime stretched out near the fire and propped a rolled-up bearskin against a stump as a pillow for his head. The wench would have told him he had to eat before he slept, to keep his strength up, but he was more tired than hungry. He closed his eyes, and hoped to dream of Cersei. The fever dreams were all so vivid . . .

Naked and alone he stood, surrounded by enemies, with stone walls all around him pressing close. *The Rock*, he knew. He could feel the immense weight of it above his head. He was home. He was home and whole.

He held his right hand up and flexed his fingers to feel the strength in them. It felt as good as sex. As good as swordplay. *Four fingers and a thumb.* He had dreamed that he was maimed, but it wasn't so. Relief made him dizzy. *My hand, my good hand.* Nothing could hurt him so long as he was whole.

Around him stood a dozen tall dark figures in cowled robes that hid their faces. In their hands were spears. "Who are you?" he demanded of them. "What business do you have in Casterly Rock?"

They gave no answer, only prodded him with the points of their spears. He had no choice but to descend. Down a twisting passageway he went, narrow steps carved from the living rock, down and down. *I must go up,* he told himself. *Up, not down. Why am I going down?* Below the earth his doom awaited, he knew with the certainty of dream; something dark and terrible lurked there, something that wanted him. Jaime tried to halt, but their spears prodded him on. *If only I had my sword, nothing could harm me.*

The steps ended abruptly on echoing darkness. Jaime had the sense of vast space before him. He jerked to a halt, teetering on the edge of nothingness. A spearpoint jabbed at the small of the back, shoving him into the abyss. He shouted, but the fall was short. He landed on his hands and knees, upon soft sand and shallow water. There were watery caverns deep below Casterly Rock, but this one was strange to him. "What place is this?"

"Your place." The voice echoed; it was a hundred voices, a thousand, the voices of all the Lannisters since Lann the Clever, who'd lived at the dawn of days. But most of all it was his father's voice, and beside Lord Tywin stood his sister, pale and beautiful, a torch burning in her hand. Joffrey was there as well, the son they'd made together, and behind them a dozen more dark shapes with golden hair.

"Sister, why has Father brought us here?"

"Us? This is your place, Brother. This is your darkness." Her torch was the only light in the cavern. Her torch was the only light in the world. She turned to go.

"Stay with me," Jaime pleaded. "Don't leave me here alone." But they were leaving. *"Don't leave me in the dark!"* Something terrible lived down here. "Give me a sword, at least."

"I gave you a sword," Lord Tywin said.

It was at his feet. Jaime groped under the water until his hand closed upon the hilt. *Nothing can hurt me so long as I have a sword.* As he raised the sword a finger of pale flame flickered at the point and crept up along the edge, stopping a hand's breath from the hilt. The fire took on the color of the steel itself so it burned with a silvery-blue light, and the gloom pulled back. Crouching, listening, Jaime moved in a circle,

ready for anything that might come out of the darkness. The water flowed
into his boots, ankle deep and bitterly cold. *Beware the water*, he told
himself. *There may be creatures living in it, hidden deeps . . .*

From behind came a great splash. Jaime whirled toward the sound . . .
but the faint light revealed only Brienne of Tarth, her hands bound in
heavy chains. "I swore to keep you safe," the wench said stubbornly. "I
swore an oath." Naked, she raised her hands to Jaime. "Ser. Please. If
you would be so good."

The steel links parted like silk. "A sword," Brienne begged, and there
it was, scabbard, belt, and all. She buckled it around her thick waist. The
light was so dim that Jaime could scarcely see her, though they stood a
scant few feet apart. *In this light she could almost be a beauty*, he
thought. *In this light she could almost be a knight.* Brienne's sword took
flame as well, burning silvery blue. The darkness retreated a little more.

"The flames will burn so long as you live," he heard Cersei call. "When
they die, so must you."

"*Sister!*" he shouted. "Stay with me. *Stay!*" There was no reply but
the soft sound of retreating footsteps.

Brienne moved her longsword back and forth, watching the silvery
flames shift and shimmer. Beneath her feet, a reflection of the burning
blade shone on the surface of the flat black water. She was as tall and
strong as he remembered, yet it seemed to Jaime that she had more of a
woman's shape now.

"Do they keep a bear down here?" Brienne was moving, slow and wary,
sword to hand; step, turn, and listen. Each step made a little splash. "A
cave lion? Direwolves? Some bear? Tell me, Jaime. What lives here? What
lives in the darkness?"

"Doom." *No bear*, he knew. *No lion.* "Only doom."

In the cool silvery-blue light of the swords, the big wench looked pale
and fierce. "I mislike this place."

"I'm not fond of it myself." Their blades made a little island of light,
but all around them stretched a sea of darkness, unending. "My feet
are wet."

"We could go back the way they brought us. If you climbed on my
shoulders you'd have no trouble reaching that tunnel mouth."

Then I could follow Cersei. He could feel himself growing hard at the
thought, and turned away so Brienne would not see.

"Listen." She put a hand on his shoulder, and he trembled at the
sudden touch. *She's warm.* "Something comes." Brienne lifted her sword
to point off to his left. "There."

He peered into the gloom until he saw it too. Something was moving
through the darkness, he could not quite make it out . . .

"A man on a horse. No, two. Two riders, side by side."

"Down here, beneath the Rock?" It made no sense. Yet there came two riders on pale horses, men and mounts both armored. The destriers emerged from the blackness at a slow walk. *They make no sound*, Jaime realized. *No splashing, no clink of mail nor clop of hoof.* He remembered Eddard Stark, riding the length of Aerys's throne room wrapped in silence. Only his eyes had spoken; a lord's eyes, cold and grey and full of judgment.

"Is it you, Stark?" Jaime called. "Come ahead. I never feared you living, I do not fear you dead."

Brienne touched his arm. "There are more."

He saw them too. They were armored all in snow, it seemed to him, and ribbons of mist swirled back from their shoulders. The visors of their helms were closed, but Jaime Lannister did not need to look upon their faces to know them.

Five had been his brothers. Oswell Whent and Jon Darry. Lewyn Martell, a prince of Dorne. The White Bull, Gerold Hightower. Ser Arthur Dayne, Sword of the Morning. And beside them, crowned in mist and grief with his long hair streaming behind him, rode Rhaegar Targaryen, Prince of Dragonstone and rightful heir to the Iron Throne.

"You don't frighten me," he called, turning as they split to either side of him. He did not know which way to face. "I will fight you one by one or all together. But who is there for the wench to duel? She gets cross when you leave her out."

"I swore an oath to keep him safe," she said to Rhaegar's shade. "I swore a holy oath."

"We all swore oaths," said Ser Arthur Dayne, so sadly.

The shades dismounted from their ghostly horses. When they drew their longswords, it made not a sound. "He was going to burn the city," Jaime said. "To leave Robert only ashes."

"He was your king," said Darry.

"You swore to keep him safe," said Whent.

"And the children, them as well," said Prince Lewyn.

Prince Rhaegar burned with a cold light, now white, now red, now dark. "I left my wife and children in your hands."

"I never thought he'd hurt them." Jaime's sword was burning less brightly now. "I was with the king . . ."

"Killing the king," said Ser Arthur.

"Cutting his throat," said Prince Lewyn.

"The king you had sworn to die for," said the White Bull.

The fires that ran along the blade were guttering out, and Jaime remembered what Cersei had said. *No.* Terror closed a hand about his throat. Then his sword went dark, and only Brienne's burned, as the ghosts came rushing in.

"No," he said, "no, no, no. *Noooooooooo!*"

Heart pounding, he jerked awake, and found himself in starry darkness amidst a grove of trees. He could taste bile in his mouth, and he was shivering with sweat, hot and cold at once. When he looked down for his sword hand, his wrist ended in leather and linen, wrapped snug around an ugly stump. He felt sudden tears well up in his eyes. *I felt it, I felt the strength in my fingers, and the rough leather of the sword's grip. My hand . . .*

"My lord." Qyburn knelt beside him, his fatherly face all crinkly with concern. "What is it? I heard you cry out."

Steelshanks Walton stood above them, tall and dour. "What is it? Why did you scream?"

"A dream . . . only a dream." Jaime stared at the camp around him, lost for a moment. "I was in the dark, but I had my hand back." He looked at the stump and felt sick all over again. *There's no place like that beneath the Rock,* he thought. His stomach was sour and empty, and his head was pounding where he'd pillowed it against the stump.

Qyburn felt his brow. "You still have a touch of fever."

"A fever dream." Jaime reached up. "Help me." Steelshanks took him by his good hand and pulled him to his feet.

"Another cup of dreamwine?" asked Qyburn.

"No. I've dreamt enough this night." He wondered how long it was till dawn. Somehow he knew that if he closed his eyes, he would be back in that dark wet place again.

"Milk of the poppy, then? And something for your fever? You are still weak, my lord. You need to sleep. To rest."

That is the last thing I mean to do. The moonlight glimmered pale upon the stump where Jaime had rested his head. The moss covered it so thickly he had not noticed before, but now he saw that the wood was white. It made him think of Winterfell, and Ned Stark's heart tree. *It was not him,* he thought. *It was never him.* But the stump was dead and so was Stark and so were all the others, Prince Rhaegar and Ser Arthur and the children. *And Aerys. Aerys is most dead of all.* "Do you believe in ghosts, Maester?" he asked Qyburn.

The man's face grew strange. "Once, at the Citadel, I came into an empty room and saw an empty chair. Yet I knew a woman had been there, only a moment before. The cushion was dented where she'd sat, the cloth was still warm, and her scent lingered in the air. If we leave our smells behind us when we leave a room, surely something of our souls must remain when we leave this life?" Qyburn spread his hands. "The archmaesters did not like my thinking, though. Well, Marwyn did, but he was the only one."

Jaime ran his fingers through his hair. "Walton," he said, "saddle the horses. I want to go back."

"Back?" Steelshanks regarded him dubiously.

He thinks I've gone mad. And perhaps I have. "I left something at Harrenhal."

"Lord Vargo holds it now. Him and his Bloody Mummers."

"You have twice the men he does."

"If I don't serve you up to your father as commanded, Lord Bolton will have my hide. We press on to King's Landing."

Once Jaime might have countered with a smile and a threat, but one-handed cripples do not inspire much fear. He wondered what his brother would do. *Tyrion would find a way.* "Lannisters lie, Steelshanks. Didn't Lord Bolton tell you that?"

The man frowned suspiciously. "What if he did?"

"Unless you take me back to Harrenhal, the song I sing my father may not be one the Lord of the Dreadfort would wish to hear. I might even say it was Bolton ordered my hand cut off, and Steelshanks Walton who swung the blade."

Walton gaped at him. "That isn't so."

"No, but who will my father believe?" Jaime made himself smile, the way he used to smile when nothing in the world could frighten him. "It will be so much easier if we just go back. We'd be on our way again soon enough, and I'd sing such a sweet song in King's Landing you'll never believe your ears. You'd get the girl, and a nice fat purse of gold as thanks."

"Gold?" Walton liked that well enough. "How much gold?"

I have him. "Why, how much would you want?"

And by the time the sun came up, they were halfway back to Harrenhal.

Jaime pushed his horse much harder than he had the day before, and Steelshanks and the northmen were forced to match his pace. Even so, it was midday before they reached the castle on the lake. Beneath a darkening sky that threatened rain, the immense walls and five great towers stood black and ominous. *It looks so dead.* The walls were empty, the gates closed and barred. But high above the barbican, a single banner hung limp. *The black goat of Qohor,* he knew. Jaime cupped his hands to shout. "You in there! Open your gates, or I'll kick them down!"

It was not until Qyburn and Steelshanks added their voices that a head finally appeared on the battlements above them. He goggled down at them, then vanished. A short time later, they heard the portcullis being drawn upward. The gates swung open, and Jaime Lannister spurred his horse through the walls, scarcely glancing at the murder holes as he passed beneath them. He had been worried that the goat might not admit them, but it seemed as if the Brave Companions still thought of them as allies. *Fools.*

The outer ward was deserted; only the long slate-roofed stables showed any signs of life, and it was not horses that interested Jaime just then. He reined up and looked about. He could hear sounds from somewhere behind the Tower of Ghosts, and men shouting in half a dozen tongues. Steelshanks and Qyburn rode up on either side. "Get what you came back for, and we'll be gone again," said Walton. "I want no trouble with the Mummers."

"Tell your men to keep their hands on their sword hilts, and the Mummers will want no trouble with you. Two to one, remember?" Jaime's head jerked round at the sound of a distant roar, faint but ferocious. It echoed off the walls of Harrenhal, and the laughter swelled up like the sea. All of a sudden, he knew what was happening. *Have we come too late?* His stomach did a lurch, and he slammed his spurs into his horse, galloping across the outer ward, beneath an arched stone bridge, around the Wailing Tower, and through the Flowstone Yard.

They had her in the bear pit.

King Harren the Black had wished to do even his bear-baiting in lavish style. The pit was ten yards across and five yards deep, walled in stone, floored with sand, and encircled by six tiers of marble benches. The Brave Companions filled only a quarter of the seats, Jaime saw as he swung down clumsily from his horse. The sellswords were so fixed on the spectacle beneath that only those across the pit noticed their arrival.

Brienne wore the same ill-fitting gown she'd worn to supper with Roose Bolton. No shield, no breastplate, no chainmail, not even boiled leather, only pink satin and Myrish lace. Maybe the goat thought she was more amusing when dressed as a woman. Half her gown was hanging off in tatters, and her left arm dripped blood where the bear had raked her.

At least they gave her a sword. The wench held it one-handed, moving sideways, trying to put some distance between her and the bear. *That's no good, the ring's too small.* She needed to attack, to make a quick end to it. Good steel was a match for any bear. But the wench seemed afraid to close. The Mummers showered her with insults and obscene suggestions.

"This is none of our concern," Steelshanks warned Jaime. "Lord Bolton said the wench was theirs, to do with as they liked."

"Her name's Brienne." Jaime descended the steps, past a dozen startled sellswords. Vargo Hoat had taken the lord's box in the lowest tier. "Lord Vargo," he called over the shouts.

The Qohorik almost spilt his wine. *"Kingthlayer?"* The left side of his face was bandaged clumsily, the linen over his ear spotted with blood.

"Pull her out of there."

"Thay out of thith, Kingthlayer, unleth you'd like another thump."

He waved a wine cup. "Your thee-mooth bit oth my ear. Thmall wonder her father will not ranthom thuch a freak."

A roar turned Jaime back around. The bear was eight feet tall. *Gregor Clegane with a pelt,* he thought, *though likely smarter.* The beast did not have the reach the Mountain had with that monster greatsword of his, though.

Bellowing in fury, the bear showed a mouth full of great yellow teeth, then fell back to all fours and went straight at Brienne. *There's your chance,* Jaime thought. *Strike! Now!*

Instead, she poked out ineffectually with the point of her blade. The bear recoiled, then came on, rumbling. Brienne slid to her left and poked again at the bear's face. This time he lifted a paw to swat the sword aside.

He's wary, Jaime realized. *He's gone up against other men. He knows swords and spears can hurt him. But that won't keep him off her long.* "Kill him!" he shouted, but his voice was lost amongst all the other shouts. If Brienne heard, she gave no sign. She moved around the pit, keeping the wall at her back. *Too close. If the bear pins her by the wall . . .*

The beast turned clumsily, too far and too fast. Quick as a cat, Brienne changed direction. *There's the wench I remember.* She leapt in to land a cut across the bear's back. Roaring, the beast went up on his hind legs again. Brienne scrambled back away. *Where's the blood?* Then suddenly he understood. Jaime rounded on Hoat. "You gave her a tourney sword."

The goat brayed laughter, spraying him with wine and spittle. "Of courth."

"*I'll* pay her bloody ransom. Gold, sapphires, whatever you want. Pull her out of there."

"You want her? Go get her."

So he did.

He put his good hand on the marble rail and vaulted over, rolling as he hit the sand. The bear turned at the *thump,* sniffing, watching this new intruder warily. Jaime scrambled to one knee. *Well, what in seven hells do I do now?* He filled his fist with sand. "Kingslayer?" he heard Brienne say, astonished.

"Jaime." He uncoiled, flinging the sand at the bear's face. The bear mauled the air and roared like blazes.

"What are you *doing* here?"

"Something stupid. Get behind me." He circled toward her, putting himself between Brienne and the bear.

"*You* get behind. I have the sword."

"A sword with no point and no edge. *Get behind me!*" He saw something half-buried in the sand, and snatched it up with his good hand. It proved to be a human jawbone, with some greenish flesh still clinging to it, crawling with maggots. *Charming,* he thought, wondering whose face he held. The bear was edging closer, so Jaime whipped his arm around and flung bone, meat, and maggots at the beast's head. He missed by a good yard. *I ought to lop my left hand off as well, for all the good it does me.*

Brienne tried to dart around, but he kicked her legs out from under her. She fell in the sand, clutching the useless sword. Jaime straddled her, and the bear came charging.

There was a deep *twang*, and a feathered shaft sprouted suddenly beneath the beast's left eye. Blood and slaver ran from his open mouth, and another bolt took him in the leg. The bear roared, reared. He saw Jaime and Brienne again and lumbered toward them. More crossbows fired, the quarrels ripping through fur and flesh. At such short range, the bowmen could hardly miss. The shafts hit as hard as maces, but the bear took another step. *The poor dumb brave brute.* When the beast swiped at him, he danced aside, shouting, kicking sand. The bear turned to follow his tormentor, and took another two quarrels in the back. He gave one last rumbling growl, settled back onto his haunches, stretched out on the bloodstained sand, and died.

Brienne got back to her knees, clutching the sword and breathing short ragged breaths. Steelshanks's archers were winding their crossbows and reloading while the Bloody Mummers shouted curses and threats at them. Rorge and Three Toes had swords out, Jaime saw, and Zollo was uncoiling his whip.

"You thlew my bear!" Vargo Hoat shrieked.

"And I'll serve you the same if you give me trouble," Steelshanks threw back. "We're taking the wench."

"Her name is Brienne," Jaime said. "Brienne, the maid of Tarth. You *are* still maiden, I hope?"

Her broad homely face turned red. "Yes."

"Oh, good," Jaime said. "I only rescue maidens." To Hoat he said, "You'll have your ransom. For both of us. A Lannister pays his debts. Now fetch some ropes and get us out of here."

"Bugger that," Rorge growled. "Kill them, Hoat. Or you'll bloody well wish you had!"

The Qohorik hesitated. Half his men were drunk, the northmen stone sober, and there were twice as many. Some of the crossbowmen had reloaded by now. "Pull them out," Hoat said, and then, to Jaime, "I hath chothen to be merthiful. Tell your lord father."

"I will, my lord." *Not that it will do you any good.*

Not until they were half a league from Harrenhal and out of range of archers on the walls did Steelshanks Walton let his anger show. "Are you *mad*, Kingslayer? Did you mean to die? No man can fight a bear with his bare hands!"

"One bare hand and one bare stump," Jaime corrected. "But I hoped you'd kill the beast before the beast killed me. Elsewise, Lord Bolton would have peeled you like an orange, no?"

Steelshanks cursed him roundly for a fool of Lannister, spurred his horse, and galloped away up the column.

"Ser Jaime?" Even in soiled pink satin and torn lace, Brienne looked more like a man in a gown than a proper woman. "I am grateful, but . . . you were well away. Why come back?"

A dozen quips came to mind, each crueler than the one before, but Jaime only shrugged. "I dreamed of you," he said.

CATELYN

Robb bid farewell to his young queen thrice. Once in the godswood before the heart tree, in sight of gods and men. The second time beneath the portcullis, where Jeyne sent him forth with a long embrace and a longer kiss. And finally an hour beyond the Tumblestone, when the girl came galloping up on a well-lathered horse to plead with her young king to take her along.

Robb was touched by that, Catelyn saw, but abashed as well. The day was damp and grey, a drizzle had begun to fall, and the last thing he wanted was to call a halt to his march so he could stand in the wet and console a tearful young wife in front of half his army. *He speaks her gently*, she thought as she watched them together, *but there is anger underneath*.

All the time the king and queen were talking, Grey Wind prowled around them, stopping only to shake the water from his coat and bare his teeth at the rain. When at last Robb gave Jeyne one final kiss, dispatched a dozen men to take her back to Riverrun, and mounted his horse once more, the direwolf raced off ahead as swift as an arrow loosed from a longbow.

"Queen Jeyne has a loving heart, I see," said Lame Lothar Frey to Catelyn. "Not unlike my own sisters. Why, I would wager a guess that even now Roslin is dancing round the Twins chanting 'Lady *Tully*, Lady *Tully*, Lady *Roslin* Tully.' By the morrow she'll be holding swatches of Riverrun red-and-blue to her cheek to picture how she'll look in her bride's cloak." He turned in the saddle to smile at Edmure. "But you are strangely quiet, Lord Tully. How do *you* feel, I wonder?"

"Much as I did at the Stone Mill just before the warhorns sounded," Edmure said, only half in jest.

Lothar gave a good-natured laugh. "Let us pray your marriage ends as happily, my lord."

And may the gods protect us if it does not. Catelyn pressed her heels into her horse, leaving her brother and Lame Lothar to each other's company.

It had been her who had insisted that Jeyne remain at Riverrun, when Robb would sooner have kept her by his side. Lord Walder might well construe the queen's absence from the wedding as another slight, yet her presence would have been a different sort of insult, salt in the old man's wound. "Walder Frey has a sharp tongue and a long memory," she had warned her son. "I do not doubt that you are strong enough to suffer an old man's rebukes as the price of his allegiance, but you have too much of your father in you to sit there while he insults Jeyne to her face."

Robb could not deny the sense of that. *Yet all the same, he resents me for it*, Catelyn thought wearily. *He misses Jeyne already, and some part of him blames me for her absence, though he knows it was good counsel.*

Of the six Westerlings who had come with her son from the Crag, only one remained by his side; Ser Raynald, Jeyne's brother, the royal banner-bearer. Robb had dispatched Jeyne's uncle Rolph Spicer to deliver young Martyn Lannister to the Golden Tooth the very day he received Lord Tywin's assent to the exchange of captives. It was deftly done. Her son was relieved of his fear for Martyn's safety, Galbart Glover was relieved to hear that his brother Robett had been put on a ship at Dusken-dale, Ser Rolph had important and honorable employment . . . and Grey Wind was at the king's side once more. *Where he belongs.*

Lady Westerling had remained at Riverrun with her children; Jeyne, her little sister Eleyna, and young Rollam, Robb's squire, who complained bitterly about being left. Yet that was wise as well. Olyvar Frey had squired for Robb previously, and would doubtless be present for his sister's wedding; to parade his replacement before him would be as unwise as it was unkind. As for Ser Raynald, he was a cheerful young knight who swore that no insult of Walder Frey's could possibly provoke him. *And let us pray that insults are all we need to contend with.*

Catelyn had her fears on that score, though. Her lord father had never trusted Walder Frey after the Trident, and she was ever mindful of that. Queen Jeyne would be safest behind the high, strong walls of Riverrun, with the Blackfish to protect her. Robb had even created him a new title, Warden of the Southern Marches. Ser Brynden would hold the Trident if any man could.

All the same, Catelyn would miss her uncle's craggy face, and Robb would miss his counsel. Ser Brynden had played a part in every victory her son had won. Galbart Glover had taken command of the scouts and outriders in his place; a good man, loyal and steady, but without the Blackfish's brilliance.

Behind Glover's screen of scouts, Robb's line of march stretched several miles. The Greatjon led the van. Catelyn traveled in the main column, surrounded by plodding warhorses with steelclad men on their backs. Next came the baggage train, a procession of wayns laden with food, fodder, camp supplies, wedding gifts, and the wounded too weak to walk, under the watchful eye of Ser Wendel Manderly and his White Harbor knights. Herds of sheep and goats and scrawny cattle trailed behind, and then a little tail of footsore camp followers. Even farther back was Robin Flint and the rearguard. There was no enemy in back of them for hundreds of leagues, but Robb would take no chances.

Thirty-five hundred they were, thirty-five hundred who had been blooded in the Whispering Wood, who had reddened their swords at the Battle of the Camps, at Oxcross, Ashemark, and the Crag, and all through the gold-rich hills of the Lannister west. Aside from her brother Edmure's modest retinue of friends, the lords of the Trident had remained to hold the riverlands while the king retook the north. Ahead awaited Edmure's bride and Robb's next battle . . . *and for me, two dead sons, an empty bed, and a castle full of ghosts.* It was a cheerless prospect. *Brienne, where are you? Bring my girls back to me, Brienne. Bring them back safe.*

The drizzle that had sent them off turned into a soft steady rain by midday, and continued well past nightfall. The next day the northmen never saw the sun at all, but rode beneath leaden skies with their hoods pulled up to keep the water from their eyes. It was a heavy rain, turning roads to mud and fields to quagmires, swelling the rivers and stripping the trees of their leaves. The constant patter made idle chatter more bother than it was worth, so men spoke only when they had something to say, and that was seldom enough.

"We are stronger than we seem, my lady," Lady Maege Mormont said as they rode. Catelyn had grown fond of Lady Maege and her eldest daughter, Dacey; they were more understanding than most in the matter of Jaime Lannister, she had found. The daughter was tall and lean, the mother short and stout, but they dressed alike in mail and leather, with the black bear of House Mormont on shield and surcoat. By Catelyn's lights, that was queer garb for a lady, yet Dacey and Lady Maege seemed more comfortable, both as warriors and as women, than ever the girl from Tarth had been.

"I have fought beside the Young Wolf in every battle," Dacey Mormont said cheerfully. "He has not lost one yet."

No, but he has lost everything else, Catelyn thought, but it would not do to say it aloud. The northmen did not lack for courage, but they were far from home, with little enough to sustain them but for their faith in their young king. That faith must be protected, at all costs. *I must be stronger,* she told herself. *I must be strong for Robb. If I despair, my grief will consume me.* Everything would turn on this marriage. If Edmure and Roslin were happy in one another, if the Late Lord Frey could be appeased and his power once more wedded to Robb's . . . *Even then, what chance will we have, caught between Lannister and Greyjoy?* It was a question Catelyn dared not dwell on, though Robb dwelt on little else. She saw how he studied his maps whenever they made camp, searching for some plan that might win back the north.

Her brother Edmure had other cares. "You don't suppose *all* Lord Walder's daughters look like him, do you?" he wondered, as he sat in his tall striped pavilion with Catelyn and his friends.

"With so many different mothers, a few of the maids are bound to turn up comely," said Ser Marq Piper, "but why should the old wretch give you a pretty one?"

"No reason at all," said Edmure in a glum tone.

It was more than Catelyn could stand. "Cersei Lannister is comely," she said sharply. "You'd be wiser to pray that Roslin is strong and healthy, with a good head and a loyal heart." And with that she left them.

Edmure did not take that well. The next day he avoided her entirely on the march, preferring the company of Marq Piper, Lymond Goodbrook, Patrek Mallister, and the young Vances. *They do not scold him, except in jest,* Catelyn told herself when they raced by her that afternoon with nary a word. *I have always been too hard with Edmure, and now grief sharpens my every word.* She regretted her rebuke. There was rain enough falling from the sky without her making more. And was it really such a terrible thing, to want a pretty wife? She remembered her own childish disappointment, the first time she had laid eyes on Eddard Stark. She had pictured him as a younger version of his brother Brandon, but that was wrong. Ned was shorter and plainer of face, and so somber. He spoke courteously enough, but beneath the words she sensed a coolness that was all at odds with Brandon, whose mirths had been as wild as his rages. Even when he took her maidenhood, their love had more of duty to it than of passion. *We made Robb that night, though; we made a king together. And after the war, at Winterfell, I had love enough for any woman, once I found the good sweet heart beneath Ned's solemn face. There is no reason Edmure should not find the same, with his Roslin.*

As the gods would have it, their route took them through the Whispering Wood where Robb had won his first great victory. They followed the course of the twisting stream on the floor of that pinched narrow valley, much as Jaime Lannister's men had done that fateful night. *It was warmer then*, Catelyn remembered, *the trees were still green, and the stream did not overflow its banks.* Fallen leaves choked the flow now and lay in sodden snarls among the rocks and roots, and the trees that had once hidden Robb's army had exchanged their green raiment for leaves of dull gold spotted with brown, and a red that reminded her of rust and dry blood. Only the spruce and the soldier pines still showed green, thrusting up at the belly of the clouds like tall dark spears.

More than the trees have died since then, she reflected. On the night of the Whispering Wood, Ned was still alive in his cell beneath Aegon's High Hill, Bran and Rickon were safe behind the walls of Winterfell. *And Theon Greyjoy fought at Robb's side, and boasted of how he had almost crossed swords with the Kingslayer. Would that he had. If Theon had died in place of Lord Karstark's sons, how much ill would have been undone?*

As they passed through the battleground, Catelyn glimpsed signs of the carnage that had been; an overturned helm filling with rain, a splintered lance, the bones of a horse. Stone cairns had been raised over some of the men who had fallen here, but scavengers had already been at them. Amidst the tumbles of rock, she spied brightly colored cloth and bits of shiny metal. Once she saw a face peering out at her, the shape of the skull beginning to emerge from beneath the melting brown flesh.

It made her wonder where Ned had come to rest. The silent sisters had taken his bones north, escorted by Hallis Mollen and a small honor guard. Had Ned ever reached Winterfell, to be interred beside his brother Brandon in the dark crypts beneath the castle? Or did the door slam shut at Moat Cailin before Hal and the sisters could pass?

Thirty-five hundred riders wound their way along the valley floor through the heart of the Whispering Wood, but Catelyn Stark had seldom felt lonelier. Every league she crossed took her farther from Riverrun, and she found herself wondering whether she would ever see the castle again. Or was it lost to her forever, like so much else?

Five days later, their scouts rode back to warn them that the rising waters had washed out the wooden bridge at Fairmarket. Galbart Glover and two of his bolder men had tried swimming their mounts across the turbulent Blue Fork at Ramsford. Two of the horses had been swept under and drowned, and one of the riders; Glover himself managed to cling to a rock until they could pull him in. "The river hasn't run this high since spring," Edmure said. "And if this rain keeps falling, it will go higher yet."

"There's a bridge further upstream, near Oldstones," remembered Catelyn, who had often crossed these lands with her father. "It's older and smaller, but if it still stands –"

"It's gone, my lady," Galbart Glover said. "Washed away even before the one at Fairmarket."

Robb looked to Catelyn. "Is there another bridge?"

"No. And the fords will be impassable." She tried to remember. "If we cannot cross the Blue Fork, we'll have to go around it, through Sevenstreams and Hag's Mire."

"Bogs and bad roads, or none at all," warned Edmure. "The going will be slow, but we'll get there, I suppose."

"Lord Walder will wait, I'm sure," said Robb. "Lothar sent him a bird from Riverrun, he knows we are coming."

"Yes, but the man is prickly, and suspicious by nature," said Catelyn. "He may take this delay as a deliberate insult."

"Very well, I'll beg his pardon for our tardiness as well. A sorry king I'll be, apologizing with every second breath." Robb made a wry face. "I hope Bolton got across the Trident before the rains began. The kingsroad runs straight north, he'll have an easy march. Even afoot, he should reach the Twins before us."

"And when you've joined his men to yours and seen my brother married, what then?" Catelyn asked him.

"North." Robb scratched Grey Wind behind an ear.

"By the causeway? Against Moat Cailin?"

He gave her an enigmatic smile. "That's one way to go," he said, and she knew from his tone that he would say no more. *A wise king keeps his own counsel*, she reminded herself.

They reached Oldstones after eight more days of steady rain, and made their camp upon the hill overlooking the Blue Fork, within a ruined stronghold of the ancient river kings. Its foundations remained amongst the weeds to show where the walls and keeps had stood, but the local smallfolk had long ago made off with most of the stones to raise their barns and septs and holdfasts. Yet in the center of what once would have been the castle's yard, a great carved sepulcher still rested, half hidden in waist-high brown grass amongst a stand of ash.

The lid of the sepulcher had been carved into a likeness of the man whose bones lay beneath, but the rain and the wind had done their work. The king had worn a beard, they could see, but otherwise his face was smooth and featureless, with only vague suggestions of a mouth, a nose, eyes, and the crown about the temples. His hands folded over the shaft of a stone warhammer that lay upon his chest. Once the warhammer would have been carved with runes that told its name and history, but all that the centuries had worn away. The stone itself was cracked and crumbling at the corners, discolored here and there by spreading white splotches of lichen, while wild roses crept up over the king's feet almost to his chest.

It was there that Catelyn found Robb, standing somber in the gathering dusk with only Grey Wind beside him. The rain had stopped for once, and he was bareheaded. "Does this castle have a name?" he asked quietly, when she came up to him.

"Oldstones, all the smallfolk called it when I was a girl, but no doubt it had some other name when it was still a hall of kings." She had camped here once with her father, on their way to Seagard. *Petyr was with us too . . .*

"There's a song," he remembered. "'Jenny of Oldstones, with the flowers in her hair.'"

"We're all just songs in the end. If we are lucky." She had played at being Jenny that day, had even wound flowers in her hair. And Petyr had pretended to be her Prince of Dragonflies. Catelyn could not have been more than twelve, Petyr just a boy.

Robb studied the sepulcher. "Whose grave is this?"

"Here lies Tristifer, the Fourth of His Name, King of the Rivers and the Hills." Her father had told her his story once. "He ruled from the Trident to the Neck, thousands of years before Jenny and her prince, in the days when the kingdoms of the First Men were falling one after the other before the onslaught of the Andals. The Hammer of Justice, they called him. He fought a hundred battles and won nine-and-ninety, or so the singers say, and when he raised this castle it was the strongest in Westeros." She put a hand on her son's shoulder. "He died in his hundredth battle, when seven Andal kings joined forces against him. The fifth Tristifer was not his equal, and soon the kingdom was lost, and then the castle, and last of all the line. With Tristifer the Fifth died House Mudd, that had ruled the riverlands for a thousand years before the Andals came."

"His heir failed him." Robb ran a hand over the rough weathered stone. "I had hoped to leave Jeyne with child . . . we tried often enough, but I'm not certain . . ."

"It does not always happen the first time." *Though it did with you.* "Nor even the hundredth. You are very young."

"Young, and a king," he said. "A king must have an heir. If I should die in my next battle, the kingdom must not die with me. By law Sansa is next in line of succession, so Winterfell and the north would pass to her." His mouth tightened. "To her, and her lord husband. Tyrion Lannister. I cannot allow that. I *will* not allow that. That dwarf must never have the north."

"No," Catelyn agreed. "You must name another heir, until such time as Jeyne gives you a son." She considered a moment. "Your father's father had no siblings, but his father had a sister who married a younger son of Lord Raymar Royce, of the junior branch. They had three daughters, all of whom wed Vale lordlings. A Waynwood and a Corbray, for certain. The youngest . . . it might have been a Templeton, but . . ."

"Mother." There was a sharpness in Robb's tone. "You forget. My father had four sons."

She had not forgotten; she had not wanted to look at it, yet there it was. "A Snow is not a Stark."

"Jon's more a Stark than some lordlings from the Vale who have never so much as set eyes on Winterfell."

"Jon is a brother of the Night's Watch, sworn to take no wife and hold no lands. Those who take the black serve for life."

"So do the knights of the Kingsguard. That did not stop the Lannisters from stripping the white cloaks from Ser Barristan Selmy and Ser Boros Blount when they had no more use for them. If I send the Watch a hundred men in Jon's place, I'll wager they find some way to release him from his vows."

He is set on this. Catelyn knew how stubborn her son could be. "A bastard cannot inherit."

"Not unless he's legitimized by a royal decree," said Robb. "There is more precedent for that than for releasing a Sworn Brother from his oath."

"Precedent," she said bitterly. "Yes, Aegon the Fourth legitimized all his bastards on his deathbed. And how much pain, grief, war, and murder grew from that? I know you trust Jon. But can you trust his sons? Or *their* sons? The Blackfyre pretenders troubled the Targaryens for five generations, until Barristan the Bold slew the last of them on the Stepstones. If you make Jon legitimate, there is no way to turn him bastard again. Should he wed and breed, any sons you may have by Jeyne will never be safe."

"Jon would never harm a son of mine."

"No more than Theon Greyjoy would harm Bran or Rickon?"

Grey Wind leapt up atop King Tristifer's crypt, his teeth bared. Robb's own face was cold. "That is as cruel as it is unfair. Jon is no Theon."

"So you pray. Have you considered your sisters? What of *their* rights? I agree that the north must not be permitted to pass to the Imp, but what of Arya? By law, she comes after Sansa . . . your own sister, trueborn . . ."

". . . and *dead*. No one has seen or heard of Arya since they cut Father's head off. Why do you lie to yourself? Arya's gone, the same as Bran and Rickon, and they'll kill Sansa too once the dwarf gets a child from her. Jon is the only brother that remains to me. Should I die without issue, I want him to succeed me as King in the North. I had hoped you would support my choice."

"I cannot," she said. "In all else, Robb. In everything. But not in this . . . this folly. Do not ask it."

"I don't have to. I'm the king." Robb turned and walked off, Grey Wind bounding down from the tomb and loping after him.

What have I done? Catelyn thought wearily, as she stood alone by Tristifer's stone sepulcher. *First I anger Edmure, and now Robb, but all I have done is speak the truth. Are men so fragile they cannot bear to hear it?* She might have wept then, had not the sky begun to do it for her. It was all she could do to walk back to her tent, and sit there in the silence.

In the days that followed, Robb was everywhere and anywhere; riding at the head of the van with the Greatjon, scouting with Grey Wind, racing back to Robin Flint and the rearguard. Men said proudly that the Young Wolf was the first to rise each dawn and the last to sleep at night, but Catelyn wondered whether he was sleeping at all. *He grows as lean and hungry as his direwolf.*

"My lady," Maege Mormont said to her one morning as they rode through a steady rain, "you seem so somber. Is aught amiss?"

My lord husband is dead, as is my father. Two of my sons have been murdered, my daughter has been given to a faithless dwarf to bear his vile children, my other daughter is vanished and likely dead, and my last son and my only brother are both angry with me. What could possibly be amiss? That was more truth than Lady Maege would wish to hear, however. "This is an evil rain," she said instead. "We have suffered much, and there is more peril and more grief ahead. We need to face it boldly, with horns blowing and banners flying bravely. But this rain beats us down. The banners hang limp and sodden, and the men huddle under their cloaks and scarcely speak to one another. Only an evil rain would chill our hearts when most we need them to burn hot."

Dacey Mormont looked up at the sky. "I would sooner have water raining down on me than arrows."

Catelyn smiled despite herself. "You are braver than I am, I fear. Are all your Bear Island women such warriors?"

"She-bears, aye," said Lady Maege. "We have needed to be. In olden days the ironmen would come raiding in their longboats, or wildlings from the Frozen Shore. The men would be off fishing, like as not. The wives they left behind had to defend themselves and their children, or else be carried off."

"There's a carving on our gate," said Dacey. "A woman in a bearskin, with a child in one arm suckling at her breast. In the other hand she holds a battleaxe. She's no proper lady, that one, but I always loved her."

"My nephew Jorah brought home a proper lady once," said Lady Maege. "He won her in a tourney. How she hated that carving."

"Aye, and all the rest," said Dacey. "She had hair like spun gold, that Lynesse. Skin like cream. But her soft hands were never made for axes."

"Nor her teats for giving suck," her mother said bluntly.

Catelyn knew of whom they spoke; Jorah Mormont had brought his second wife to Winterfell for feasts, and once they had guested for a fortnight. She remembered how young the Lady Lynesse had been, how fair, and how unhappy. One night, after several cups of wine, she had confessed to Catelyn that the north was no place for a Hightower of Oldtown. "There was a Tully of Riverrun who felt the same once," she had answered gently, trying to console, "but in time she found much here she could love."

All lost now, she reflected. *Winterfell and Ned, Bran and Rickon, Sansa, Arya, all gone. Only Robb remains.* Had there been too much of Lynesse Hightower in her after all, and too little of the Starks? *Would that I had known how to wield an axe, perhaps I might have been able to protect them better.*

Day followed day, and still the rain kept falling. All the way up the Blue Fork they rode, past Sevenstreams where the river unraveled into a confusion of rills and brooks, then through Hag's Mire, where glistening green pools waited to swallow the unwary and the soft ground sucked at the hooves of their horses like a hungry babe at its mother's breast. The going was worse than slow. Half the wayns had to be abandoned to the muck, their loads distributed amongst mules and draft horses.

Lord Jason Mallister caught up with them amidst the bogs of Hag's Mire. There was more than an hour of daylight remaining when he rode up with his column, but Robb called a halt at once, and Ser Raynald Westerling came to escort Catelyn to the king's tent. She found her son seated beside a brazier, a map across his lap. Grey Wind slept at his feet. The Greatjon was with him, along with Galbart Glover, Maege Mormont, Edmure, and a man that Catelyn did not know, a fleshy balding man with a cringing look to him. *No lordling, this one*, she knew the moment she laid eyes on the stranger. *Not even a warrior.*

Jason Mallister rose to offer Catelyn his seat. His hair had almost as much white in it as brown, but the Lord of Seagard was still a handsome man; tall and lean, with a chiseled clean-shaven face, high cheekbones, and fierce blue-grey eyes. "Lady Stark, it is ever a pleasure. I bring good tidings, I hope."

"We are in sore need of some, my lord." She sat, listening to the rain patter down noisily against the canvas overhead.

Robb waited for Ser Raynald to close the tent flap. "The gods have heard our prayers, my lords. Lord Jason has brought us the captain of the *Myraham*, a merchanter out of Oldtown. Captain, tell them what you told me."

"Aye, Your Grace." He licked his thick lips nervously. "My last port of call afore Seagard, that was Lordsport on Pyke. The ironmen kept me there more'n half a year, they did. King Balon's command. Only, well, the long and the short of it is, he's dead."

"Balon Greyjoy?" Catelyn's heart skipped a beat. "You are telling us that Balon Greyjoy is dead?"

The shabby little captain nodded. "You know how Pyke's built on a headland, and part on rocks and islands off the shore, with bridges between? The way I heard it in Lordsport, there was a blow coming in from the west, rain and thunder, and old King Balon was crossing one of them bridges when the wind got hold of it and just tore the thing to pieces. He washed up two days later, all bloated and broken. Crabs ate his eyes, I hear."

The Greatjon laughed. "King crabs, I hope, to sup upon such royal jelly, eh?"

The captain bobbed his head. "Aye, but that's not all of it, no!" He leaned forward. "The *brother's* back."

"Victarion?" asked Galbart Glover, surprised.

"Euron. Crow's Eye, they call him, as black a pirate as ever raised a sail. He's been gone for years, but Lord Balon was no sooner cold than there he was, sailing into Lordsport in his *Silence*. Black sails and a red hull, and crewed by mutes. He'd been to Asshai and back, I heard. Wherever he was, though, he's home now, and he marched right into Pyke and sat his arse in the Seastone Chair, and drowned Lord Botley in a cask of seawater when he objected. That was when I ran back to *Myraham* and slipped anchor, hoping I could get away whilst things were confused. And so I did, and here I am."

"Captain," said Robb when the man was done, "you have my thanks, and you will not go unrewarded. Lord Jason will take you back to your ship when we are done. Pray wait outside."

"That I will, Your Grace. That I will."

No sooner had he left the king's pavilion than the Greatjon began to laugh, but Robb silenced him with a look. "Euron Greyjoy is no man's notion of a king, if half of what Theon said of him was true. Theon is the rightful heir, unless he's dead . . . but Victarion commands the Iron Fleet. I can't believe he would remain at Moat Cailin while Euron Crow's Eye holds the Seastone Chair. He *has* to go back."

"There's a daughter as well," Galbart Glover reminded him. "The one who holds Deepwood Motte, and Robett's wife and child."

"If she stays at Deepwood Motte that's *all* she can hope to hold," said Robb. "What's true for the brothers is even more true for her. She will need to sail home to oust Euron and press her own claim." Her son turned to Lord Jason Mallister. "You have a fleet at Seagard?"

"A fleet, Your Grace? Half a dozen longships and two war galleys. Enough to defend my own shores against raiders, but I could not hope to meet the Iron Fleet in battle."

"Nor would I ask it of you. The ironborn will be setting sail toward Pyke, I expect. Theon told me how his people think. Every captain a king on his own deck. They will all want a voice in the succession. My lord, I need two of your longships to sail around the Cape of Eagles and up the Neck to Greywater Watch."

Lord Jason hesitated. "A dozen streams drain the wetwood, all shallow, silty, and uncharted. I would not even call them rivers. The channels are ever drifting and changing. There are endless sandbars, deadfalls, and tangles of rotting trees. And Greywater Watch *moves*. How are my ships to find it?"

"Go upriver flying my banner. The crannogmen will find you. I want two ships to double the chances of my message reaching Howland Reed. Lady Maege shall go on one, Galbart on the second." He turned to the two he'd named. "You'll carry letters for those lords of mine who remain in the north, but all the commands within will be false, in case you have the misfortune to be taken. If that happens, you must tell them that you were sailing for the north. Back to Bear Island, or for the Stony Shore." He tapped a finger on the map. "Moat Cailin is the key. Lord Balon knew that, which is why he sent his brother Victarion there with the hard heart of the Greyjoy strength."

"Succession squabbles or no, the ironborn are not such fools as to abandon Moat Cailin," said Lady Maege.

"No," Robb admitted. "Victarion will leave the best part of his garrison, I'd guess. Every man he takes will be one less man we need to fight, however. And he *will* take many of his captains, count on that. The leaders. He will need such men to speak for him if he hopes to sit the Seastone Chair."

"You cannot mean to attack up the causeway, Your Grace," said Galbart Glover. "The approaches are too narrow. There is no way to deploy. No one has ever taken the Moat."

"From the south," said Robb. "But if we can attack from the north and west simultaneously, and take the ironmen in the rear while they are beating off what they think is my main thrust up the causeway, then we have a chance. Once I link up with Lord Bolton and the Freys, I will have more than twelve thousand men. I mean to divide them into three battles and start up the causeway a half-day apart. If the Greyjoys have eyes south of the Neck, they will see my whole strength rushing headlong at Moat Cailin.

"Roose Bolton will have the rearguard, while I command the center. Greatjon, you shall lead the van against Moat Cailin. Your attack must

be so fierce that the ironborn have no leisure to wonder if anyone is
creeping down on them from the north."

The Greatjon chuckled. "Your creepers best come fast, or my men will
swarm those walls and win the Moat before you show your face. I'll make
a gift of it to you when you come dawdling up."

"That's a gift I should be glad to have," said Robb.

Edmure was frowning. "You talk of attacking the ironmen in the rear,
sire, but how do you mean to get north of them?"

"There are ways through the Neck that are not on any map, Uncle.
Ways known only to the crannogmen – narrow trails between the bogs,
and wet roads through the reeds that only boats can follow." He turned
to his two messengers. "Tell Howland Reed that he is to send guides to
me, two days after I have started up the causeway. To the *center* battle,
where my own standard flies. Three hosts will leave the Twins, but only
two will reach Moat Cailin. Mine own battle will melt away into the
Neck, to reemerge on the Fever. If we move swiftly once my uncle's wed,
we can all be in position by year's end. We will fall upon the Moat from
three sides on the first day of the new century, as the ironmen are waking
with hammers beating at their heads from the mead they'll quaff the
night before."

"I like this plan," said the Greatjon. "I like it well."

Galbart Glover rubbed his mouth. "There are risks. If the crannogmen
should fail you . . ."

"We will be no worse than before. But they will not fail. My father
knew the worth of Howland Reed." Robb rolled up the map, and only
then looked at Catelyn. "Mother."

She tensed. "Do you have some part in this for me?"

"Your part is to stay safe. Our journey through the Neck will be dangerous, and naught but battle awaits us in the north. But Lord Mallister has
kindly offered to keep you safe at Seagard until the war is done. You will
be comfortable there, I know."

*Is this my punishment for opposing him about Jon Snow? Or for being
a woman, and worse, a mother?* It took her a moment to realize that
they were all watching her. They had *known*, she realized. Catelyn should
not have been surprised. She had won no friends by freeing the Kingslayer,
and more than once she had heard the Greatjon say that women had no
place on a battlefield.

Her anger must have blazed across her face, because Galbart Glover
spoke up before she said a word. "My lady, His Grace is wise. It's best
you do not come with us."

"Seagard will be brightened by your presence, Lady Catelyn," said Lord
Jason Mallister.

"You would make me a prisoner," she said.

"An honored guest," Lord Jason insisted.

Catelyn turned to her son. "I mean no offense to Lord Jason," she said stiffly, "but if I cannot continue on with you, I would sooner return to Riverrun."

"I left my wife at Riverrun. I want my mother elsewhere. If you keep all your treasures in one purse, you only make it easier for those who would rob you. After the wedding, you shall go to Seagard, that is my royal command." Robb stood, and as quick as that, her fate was settled. He picked up a sheet of parchment. "One more matter. Lord Balon has left chaos in his wake, we hope. I would not do the same. Yet I have no son as yet, my brothers Bran and Rickon are dead, and my sister is wed to a Lannister. I've thought long and hard about who might follow me. I command you now as my true and loyal lords to fix your seals to this document as witnesses to my decision."

A king indeed, Catelyn thought, defeated. She could only hope that the trap he'd planned for Moat Cailin worked as well as the one in which he'd just caught her.

SAMWELL

hitetree, Sam thought. *Please, let this be Whitetree.* He remembered Whitetree. Whitetree was on the maps he'd drawn, on their way north. If this village was Whitetree, he knew where they were. *Please, it has to be.* He wanted that so badly that he forgot his feet for a little bit, he forgot the ache in his calves and his lower back and the stiff frozen fingers he could scarcely feel. He even forgot about Lord Mormont and Craster and the wights and the Others. *Whitetree*, Sam prayed, to any god that might be listening.

All wildling villages looked much alike, though. A huge weirwood grew in the center of this one . . . but a white tree did not mean Whitetree, necessarily. Hadn't the weirwood at Whitetree been bigger than this one? Maybe he was remembering it wrong. The face carved into the bone pale trunk was long and sad; red tears of dried sap leaked from its eyes. *Was that how it looked when we came north?* Sam couldn't recall.

Around the tree stood a handful of one-room hovels with sod roofs, a longhall built of logs and grown over with moss, a stone well, a sheepfold . . . but no sheep, nor any people. The wildlings had gone to join Mance Rayder in the Frostfangs, taking all they owned except their houses. Sam was thankful for that. Night was coming on, and it would be good to sleep beneath a roof for once. He was so tired. It seemed as though he had been walking half his life. His boots were falling to pieces, and all the blisters on his feet had burst and turned to callus, but now he had new blisters *under* the callus, and his toes were getting frostbitten.

But it was either walk or die, Sam knew. Gilly was still weak from childbirth and carrying the babe besides; she needed the horse more than he did. The second horse had died on them three days out from Craster's Keep. It was a wonder she lasted that long, poor half-starved thing. Sam's weight had probably done for her. They might have tried riding double, but he was afraid the same thing would happen again. *It's better that I walk.*

Sam left Gilly in the longhall to make a fire while he poked his head into the hovels. She was better at making fires; he could never seem to get the kindling to catch, and the last time he'd tried to strike a spark off flint and steel he managed to cut himself on his knife. Gilly bound up the gash for him, but his hand was stiff and sore, even clumsier than it had been before. He knew he should wash the wound and change the binding, but he was afraid to look at it. Besides, it was so cold that he hated taking off his gloves.

Sam did not know what he hoped to find in the empty houses. Maybe the wildlings had left some food behind. He had to take a look. Jon had searched the huts at Whitetree, on their way north. Inside one hovel Sam heard a rustling of rats from a dark corner, but otherwise there was nothing in any of them but old straw, old smells, and some ashes beneath the smoke hole.

He turned back to the weirwood and studied the carved face a moment. *It is not the face we saw,* he admitted to himself. *The tree's not half as big as the one at Whitetree.* The red eyes wept blood, and he didn't remember that either. Clumsily, Sam sank to his knees. "Old gods, hear my prayer. The Seven were my father's gods but I said my words to you when I joined the Watch. Help us now. I fear we might be lost. We're hungry too, and so cold. I don't know what gods I believe in now, but . . . please, if you're there, help us. Gilly has a little son." That was all that he could think to say. The dusk was deepening, the leaves of the weirwood rustling softly, waving like a thousand blood-red hands. Whether Jon's gods had heard him or not he could not say.

By the time he returned to the longhall, Gilly had the fire going. She sat close to it with her furs opened, the babe at her breast. *He's as hungry as we are,* Sam thought. The old women had smuggled out food for them from Craster's, but they had eaten most of it by now. Sam had been a hopeless hunter even at Horn Hill, where game was plentiful and he had hounds and huntsmen to help him; here in this endless empty forest, the chances of him catching anything were remote. His efforts at fishing the lakes and half-frozen streams had been dismal failures as well.

"How much longer, Sam?" Gilly asked. "Is it far, still?"

"Not so far. Not so far as it was." Sam shrugged out of his pack, eased himself awkwardly to the floor, and tried to cross his legs. His back ached so abominably from the walking that he would have liked to lean up against one of the carved wooden pillars that supported the roof, but the fire was in the center of the hall beneath the smoke hole and he craved warmth even more than comfort. "Another few days should see us there."

Sam had his maps, but if this wasn't Whitetree then they weren't going to be much use. *We went too far east to get around that lake*, he fretted, *or maybe too far west when I tried to double back.* He was coming to hate lakes and rivers. Up here there was never a ferry or bridge, which meant walking all the way around the lakes and searching for places to ford the rivers. It was easier to follow a game trail than to struggle through the brush, easier to circle a ridge instead of climbing it. *If Bannen or Dywen were with us we'd be at Castle Black by now, warming our feet in the common room.* Bannen was dead, though, and Dywen gone with Grenn and Dolorous Edd and the others.

The Wall is three hundred miles long and seven hundred feet high, Sam reminded himself. If they kept going south, they *had* to find it, sooner or later. And he was certain that they had been going south. By day he took directions from the sun, and on clear nights they could follow the Ice Dragon's tail, though they hadn't traveled much by night since the second horse had died. Even when the moon was full it was too dark beneath the trees, and it would have been so easy for Sam or the last garron to break a leg. *We have to be well south by now, we have to be.*

What he wasn't so certain of was how far east or west they might have strayed. They would reach the Wall, yes . . . in a day or a fortnight, it couldn't be farther than that, surely, surely . . . but *where?* It was the gate at Castle Black they needed to find; the only way through the Wall for a hundred leagues.

"Is the Wall as big as Craster used to say?" Gilly asked.

"Bigger." Sam tried to sound cheerful. "So big you can't even see the castles hidden behind it. But they're there, you'll see. The Wall is all ice, but the castles are stone and wood. There are tall towers and deep vaults and a huge longhall with a great fire burning in the hearth, day and night. It's so hot in there, Gilly, you'll hardly believe it."

"Could I stand by the fire? Me and the boy? Not for a long time, just till we're good and warm?"

"You can stand by the fire as long as you like. You'll have food and drink, too. Hot mulled wine and a bowl of venison stewed with onions, and Hobb's bread right out of the oven, so hot it will burn your fingers." Sam peeled a glove off to wriggle his own fingers near the flames, and soon regretted it. They had been numb with cold, but as feeling returned they hurt so much he almost cried. "Sometimes one of the brothers will sing," he said, to take his mind off the pain. "Dareon sang best, but they sent him to Eastwatch. There's still Halder, though. And Toad. His real name is Todder, but he looks like a toad, so we call him that. He likes to sing, but he has an awful voice."

"Do you sing?" Gilly rearranged her furs, and she moved the babe from one breast to the other.

Sam blushed. "I . . . I know some songs. When I was little I liked to sing. I danced too, but my lord father never liked me to. He said if I wanted to prance around I should do it in the yard with a sword in my hand."

"Could you sing some southron song? For the babe?"

"If you like." Sam thought for a moment. "There's a song our septon used to sing to me and my sisters, when we were little and it was time for us to go to sleep. 'The Song of the Seven,' it's called." He cleared his throat and softly sang:

The Father's face is stern and strong,
  he sits and judges right from wrong.
He weighs our lives, the short and long,
  and loves the little children.

The Mother gives the gift of life,
  and watches over every wife.
Her gentle smile ends all strife,
  and she loves her little children.

The Warrior stands before the foe,
  protecting us where e'er we go.
With sword and shield and spear and bow,
  he guards the little children.

The Crone is very wise and old,
  and sees our fates as they unfold.
She lifts her lamp of shining gold,
  to lead the little children.

The Smith, he labors day and night,
  to put the world of men to right.
With hammer, plow, and fire bright,
  he builds for little children.

The Maiden dances through the sky,
  she lives in every lover's sigh,
Her smiles teach the birds to fly,
  and give dreams to little children.

The Seven Gods who made us all,
  are listening if we should call.
So close your eyes, you shall not fall,
  they see you, little children,

Just close your eyes, you shall not fall,
they see you, little children.

Sam remembered the last time he'd sung the song with his mother, to lull baby Dickon to sleep. His father had heard their voices and come barging in, angry. "I will have no more of that," Lord Randyll told his wife harshly. "You ruined one boy with those soft septon's songs, do you mean to do the same to this babe?" Then he looked at Sam and said, "Go sing to your sisters, if you must sing. I don't want you near my son."

Gilly's babe had gone to sleep. He was such a tiny thing, and so quiet that Sam feared for him. He didn't even have a name. He had asked Gilly about that, but she said it was bad luck to name a child before he was two. So many of them died.

She tucked her nipple back inside her furs. "That was pretty, Sam. You sing good."

"You should hear Dareon. His voice is sweet as mead."

"We drank the sweetest mead the day Craster made me a wife. It was summer then, and not so cold." Gilly gave him a puzzled look. "Did you only sing of six gods? Craster always told us you southrons had seven."

"Seven," he agreed, "but no one sings of the Stranger." The Stranger's face was the face of death. Even talking of him made Sam uncomfortable. "We should eat something. A bite or two."

Nothing was left but a few black sausages, as hard as wood. Sam sawed off a few thin slices for each of them. The effort made his wrist ache, but he was hungry enough to persist. If you chewed the slices long enough they softened up, and tasted good. Craster's wives seasoned them with garlic.

After they had finished, Sam begged her pardon and went out to relieve himself and look after the horse. A biting wind was blowing from the north, and the leaves in the trees rattled at him as he passed. He had to break the thin scum of ice on top of the stream so the horse could get a drink. *I had better bring her inside.* He did not want to wake up at break of day to find that their horse had frozen to death during the night. *Gilly would keep going even if that happened.* The girl was very brave, not like him. He wished he knew what he was going to do with her back at Castle Black. She kept saying how she'd be his wife if he wanted, but black brothers didn't keep wives; besides, he was a Tarly of Horn Hill, he could never wed a wildling. *I'll have to think of something. So long as we reach the Wall alive, the rest doesn't matter, it doesn't matter one little bit.*

Leading the horse to the longhall was simple enough. Getting her through the door was not, but Sam persisted. Gilly was already dozing by the time he got the garron inside. He hobbled the horse in a corner, fed some fresh wood to the fire, took off his heavy cloak, and wriggled down under the furs beside the wildling woman. His cloak was big enough to cover all three of them and keep in the warmth of their bodies.

Gilly smelled of milk and garlic and musty old fur, but he was used to that by now. They were good smells, so far as Sam was concerned. He liked sleeping next to her. It made him remember times long past, when he had shared a huge bed at Horn Hill with two of his sisters. That had ended when Lord Randyll decided it was making him soft as a girl. *Sleeping alone in my own cold cell never made me any harder or braver, though.* He wondered what his father would say if he could see him now. *I killed one of the Others, my lord,* he imagined saying. *I stabbed him with an obsidian dagger, and my Sworn Brothers call me Sam the Slayer now.* But even in his fancies, Lord Randyll only scowled, disbelieving.

His dreams were strange that night. He was back at Horn Hill, at the castle, but his father was not there. It was Sam's castle now. Jon Snow was with him. Lord Mormont too, the Old Bear, and Grenn and Dolorous Edd and Pyp and Toad and all his other brothers from the Watch, but they wore bright colors instead of black. Sam sat at the high table and feasted them all, cutting thick slices off a roast with his father's greatsword Heartsbane. There were sweet cakes to eat and honeyed wine to drink, there was singing and dancing, and everyone was warm. When the feast was done he went up to sleep; not to the lord's bedchamber where his mother and father lived but to the room he had once shared with his sisters. Only instead of his sisters it was Gilly waiting in the huge soft bed, wearing nothing but a big shaggy fur, milk leaking from her breasts.

He woke suddenly, in cold and dread.

The fire had burned down to smouldering red embers. The air itself seemed frozen, it was so cold. In the corner the garron was whinnying and kicking the logs with her hind legs. Gilly sat beside the fire, hugging her babe. Sam sat up groggy, his breath puffing pale from his open mouth. The longhall was dark with shadows, black and blacker. The hair on his arms was standing up.

It's nothing, he told himself. *I'm cold, that's all.*

Then, by the door, one of the shadows moved. A big one.

This is still a dream, Sam prayed. *Oh, make it that I'm still asleep, make it a nightmare. He's dead, he's dead, I saw him die.* "He's come for the babe," Gilly wept. "He smells him. A babe fresh-born stinks o' life. He's come for the life."

The huge dark shape stooped under the lintel, into the hall, and shambled toward them. In the dim light of the fire, the shadow became Small Paul.

"Go away," Sam croaked. "We don't want you here."

Paul's hands were coal, his face was milk, his eyes shone a bitter blue. Hoarfrost whitened his beard, and on one shoulder hunched a raven, pecking at his cheek, eating the dead white flesh. Sam's bladder let go, and he felt the warmth running down his legs. "Gilly, calm the horse and lead her out. You do that."

"You –" she started.

"I have the knife. The dragonglass dagger." He fumbled it out as he got to his feet. He'd given the first knife to Grenn, but thankfully he'd remembered to take Lord Mormont's dagger before fleeing Craster's Keep. He clutched it tight, moving away from the fire, away from Gilly and the babe. "Paul?" He meant to sound brave, but it came out in a squeak. "Small Paul. Do you know me? I'm Sam, fat Sam, Sam the Scared, you saved me in the woods. You carried me when I couldn't walk another step. No one else could have done that, but you did." Sam backed away, knife in hand, sniveling. *I am such a coward.* "Don't hurt us, Paul. Please. Why would you want to hurt us?"

Gilly scrabbled backward across the hard dirt floor. The wight turned his head to look at her, but Sam shouted *"NO!"* and he turned back. The raven on his shoulder ripped a strip of flesh from his pale ruined cheek. Sam held the dagger before him, breathing like a blacksmith's bellows. Across the longhall, Gilly reached the garron. *Gods give me courage,* Sam prayed. *For once, give me a little courage. Just long enough for her to get away.*

Small Paul moved toward him. Sam backed off until he came up against a rough log wall. He clutched the dagger with both hands to hold it steady. The wight did not seem to fear the dragonglass. Perhaps he did not know what it was. He moved slowly, but Small Paul had never been quick even when he'd been alive. Behind him, Gilly murmured to calm the garron and tried to urge it toward the door. But the horse must have caught a whiff of the wight's queer cold scent. Suddenly she balked, rearing, her hooves lashing at the frosty air. Paul swung toward the sound, and seemed to lose all interest in Sam.

There was no time to think or pray or be afraid. Samwell Tarly threw himself forward and plunged the dagger down into Small Paul's back. Half-turned, the wight never saw him coming. The raven gave a shriek and took to the air. "You're dead!" Sam screamed as he stabbed. "You're dead, you're dead." He stabbed and screamed, again and again, tearing huge rents in Paul's heavy black cloak. Shards of dragonglass flew everywhere as the blade shattered on the iron mail beneath the wool.

Sam's wail made a white mist in the black air. He dropped the useless hilt and took a hasty step backwards as Small Paul twisted around. Before he could get out his other knife, the steel knife that every brother carried, the wight's black hands locked beneath his chins. Paul's fingers were so cold they seemed to burn. They burrowed deep into the soft flesh of Sam's throat. *Run, Gilly, run*, he wanted to scream, but when he opened his mouth only a choking sound emerged.

His fumbling fingers finally found the dagger, but when he slammed it up into the wight's belly the point skidded off the iron links, and the blade went spinning from Sam's hand. Small Paul's fingers tightened inexorably, and began to twist. *He's going to rip my head off*, Sam thought in despair. His throat felt frozen, his lungs on fire. He punched and pulled at the wight's wrists, to no avail. He kicked Paul between the legs, uselessly. The world shrank to two blue stars, a terrible crushing pain, and a cold so fierce that his tears froze over his eyes. Sam squirmed and pulled, desperate . . . and then he lurched forward.

Small Paul was big and powerful, but Sam still outweighed him, and the wights were clumsy, he had seen that on the Fist. The sudden shift sent Paul staggering back a step, and the living man and the dead one went crashing down together. The impact knocked one hand from Sam's throat, and he was able to suck in a quick breath of air before the icy black fingers returned. The taste of blood filled his mouth. He twisted his neck around, looking for his knife, and saw a dull orange glow. *The fire!* Only ember and ashes remained, but still . . . he could not breathe, or think . . . Sam wrenched himself sideways, pulling Paul with him . . . his arms flailed against the dirt floor, groping, reaching, scattering the ashes, until at last they found something hot . . . a chunk of charred wood, smouldering red and orange within the black . . . his fingers closed around it, and he smashed it into Paul's mouth, so hard he felt teeth shatter.

Yet even so the wight's grip did not loosen. Sam's last thoughts were for the mother who had loved him and the father he had failed. The longhall was spinning around him when he saw the wisp of smoke rising from between Paul's broken teeth. Then the dead man's face burst into flame, and the hands were gone.

Sam sucked in air, and rolled feebly away. The wight was burning, hoarfrost dripping from his beard as the flesh beneath blackened. Sam heard the raven shriek, but Paul himself made no sound. When his mouth opened, only flames came out. And his eyes . . . *It's gone, the blue glow is gone.*

He crept to the door. The air was so cold that it hurt to breathe, but such a fine sweet hurt. He ducked from the longhall. "Gilly?" he called. "Gilly, I killed it. Gil –"

She stood with her back against the weirwood, the boy in her arms. The wights were all around her. There were a dozen of them, a score, more . . . some had been wildlings once, and still wore skins and hides . . . but more had been his brothers. Sam saw Lark the Sisterman, Softfoot,

Ryles. The wen on Chett's neck was black, his boils covered with a thin
film of ice. And that one looked like Hake, though it was hard to know
for certain with half his head missing. They had torn the poor garron
apart, and were pulling out her entrails with dripping red hands. Pale
steam rose from her belly.

Sam made a whimpery sound. "It's not fair . . ."

"*Fair.*" The raven landed on his shoulder. "*Fair, far, fear.*" It flapped
its wings, and screamed along with Gilly. The wights were almost on
her. He heard the dark red leaves of the weirwood rustling, whispering
to one another in a tongue he did not know. The starlight itself seemed
to stir, and all around them the trees groaned and creaked. Sam Tarly
turned the color of curdled milk, and his eyes went wide as plates. *Ravens!*
They were in the weirwood, hundreds of them, thousands, perched on
the bone-white branches, peering between the leaves. He saw their beaks
open as they screamed, saw them spread their black wings. Shrieking,
flapping, they descended on the wights in angry clouds. They swarmed
round Chett's face and pecked at his blue eyes, they covered the Sisterman
like flies, they plucked gobbets from inside Hake's shattered head. There
were so many that when Sam looked up, he could not see the moon.

"*Go,*" said the bird on his shoulder. "*Go, go, go.*"

Sam ran, puffs of frost exploding from his mouth. All around him the
wights flailed at the black wings and sharp beaks that assailed them,
falling in an eerie silence with never a grunt nor cry. But the ravens
ignored Sam. He took Gilly by the hand and pulled her away from the
weirwood. "We have to go."

"But where?" Gilly hurried after him, holding her baby. "They killed
our horse, how will we . . ."

"*Brother!*" The shout cut through the night, through the shrieks of a
thousand ravens. Beneath the trees, a man muffled head to heels in
mottled blacks and greys sat astride an elk. "*Here,*" the rider called. A
hood shadowed his face.

He's wearing blacks. Sam urged Gilly toward him. The elk was huge,
a great elk, ten feet tall at the shoulder, with a rack of antlers near as
wide. The creature sank to his knees to let them mount. "Here," the
rider said, reaching down with a gloved hand to pull Gilly up behind
him. Then it was Sam's turn. "My thanks," he puffed. Only when he
grasped the offered hand did he realize that the rider wore no glove. His
hand was black and cold, with fingers hard as stone.

ARYA

When they reached the top of the ridge and saw the river, Sandor Clegane reined up hard and cursed.

The rain was falling from a black iron sky, pricking the green and brown torrent with ten thousand swords. *It must be a mile across*, Arya thought. The tops of half a hundred trees poked up out the swirling waters, their limbs clutching for the sky like the arms of drowning men. Thick mats of sodden leaves choked the shoreline, and farther out in the channel she glimpsed something pale and swollen, a deer or perhaps a dead horse, moving swiftly downstream. There was a sound too, a low rumble at the edge of hearing, like the sound a dog makes just before he growls.

Arya squirmed in the saddle and felt the links of the Hound's mail digging into her back. His arms encircled her; on the left, the burned arm, he'd donned a steel vambrace for protection, but she'd seen him change the dressings, and the flesh beneath was still raw and seeping. If the burns pained him, though, Sandor Clegane gave no hint of it.

"Is this the Blackwater Rush?" They had ridden so far in rain and darkness, through trackless woods and nameless villages, that Arya had lost all sense of where they were.

"It's a river we need to cross, that's all you need to know." Clegane would answer her from time to time, but he had warned her not to talk back. He had given her a lot of warnings that first day. "The next time you hit me, I'll tie your hands behind your back," he'd said. "The next time you try and run off, I'll bind your feet together. Scream or shout or bite me again, and I'll gag you. We can ride double, or I can throw you across the back of the horse trussed up like a sow for slaughter. Your choice."

She had chosen to ride, but the first time they made camp she'd waited until she thought he was asleep, and found a big jagged rock to smash his ugly head in. *Quiet as a shadow*, she told herself as she crept toward him, but that wasn't quiet enough. The Hound hadn't been asleep after all. Or maybe he'd woken. Whichever it was, his eyes opened, his mouth twitched, and he took the rock away from her as if she were a baby. The best she could do was kick him. "I'll give you that one," he said, when he flung the rock into the bushes. "But if you're stupid enough to try again, I'll hurt you."

"Why don't you just *kill* me like you did Mycah?" Arya had screamed at him. She was still defiant then, more angry than scared.

He answered by grabbing the front of her tunic and yanking her within an inch of his burned face. "The next time you say that name I'll beat you so bad you'll *wish* I killed you."

After that, he rolled her in his horse blanket every night when he went to sleep, and tied ropes around her top and bottom so she was bound up as tight as a babe in swaddling clothes.

It has to be the Blackwater, Arya decided as she watched the rain lash the river. The Hound was Joffrey's dog; he was taking her back to the Red Keep, to hand to Joffrey and the queen. She wished that the sun would come out, so she could tell which way they were going. The more she looked at the moss on the trees the more confused she got. *The Blackwater wasn't so wide at King's Landing, but that was before the rains.*

"The fords will all be gone," Sandor Clegane said, "and I wouldn't care to try and swim over neither."

There's no way across, she thought. *Lord Beric will catch us for sure.* Clegane had pushed his big black stallion hard, doubling back thrice to throw off pursuit, once even riding half a mile up the center of a swollen stream ... but Arya still expected to see the outlaws every time she looked back. She had tried to help them by scratching her name on the trunks of trees when she went in the bushes to make water, but the fourth time she did it he caught her, and that was the end of that. *It doesn't matter*, Arya told herself, *Thoros will find me in his flames.* Only he hadn't. Not yet, anyway, and once they crossed the river ...

"Harroway town shouldn't be far," the Hound said. "Where Lord Roote stables Old King Andahar's two-headed water horse. Maybe we'll ride across."

Arya had never heard of Old King Andahar. She'd never seen a horse with two heads either, especially not one who could run on water, but she knew better than to ask. She held her tongue and sat stiff as the Hound turned the stallion's head and trotted along the ridgeline, following the river downstream. At least the rain was at their backs this way. She'd had enough of it stinging her eyes half-blind and washing down her cheeks like she was crying. *Wolves never cry*, she reminded herself again.

It could not have been much past noon, but the sky was dark as dusk. They had not seen the sun in more days than she could count. Arya was soaked to the bone, saddle-sore, sniffling, and achy. She had a fever too, and sometimes shivered uncontrollably, but when she'd told the Hound that she was sick he'd only snarled at her. "Wipe your nose and shut your mouth," he told her. Half the time he slept in the saddle now, trusting his stallion to follow whatever rutted farm track or game trail they were on. The horse was a heavy courser, almost as big as a destrier but much faster. *Stranger*, the Hound called him. Arya had tried to steal him once, when Clegane was taking a piss against a tree, thinking she could ride off before he could catch her. Stranger had almost bitten her face off. He was gentle as an old gelding with his master, but otherwise he had a temper as black as he was. She had never known a horse so quick to bite or kick.

They rode beside the river for hours, splashing across two muddy vassal streams before they reached the place that Sandor Clegane had spoken of. "Lord Harroway's Town," he said, and then, when he saw it, "*Seven hells!*" The town was drowned and desolate. The rising waters had over-flowed the riverbanks. All that remained of Harroway town was the upper story of a daub-and-wattle inn, the seven-sided dome of a sunken sept, two-thirds of a stone roundtower, some moldy thatch roofs, and a forest of chimneys.

But there was smoke coming from the tower, Arya saw, and below one arched window a wide flat-bottomed boat was chained up tight. The boat had a dozen oarlocks and a pair of great carved wooden horse heads mounted fore and aft. *The two-headed horse*, she realized. There was a wooden house with a sod roof right in the middle of the deck, and when the Hound cupped his hands around his mouth and shouted two men came spilling out. A third appeared in the window of the roundtower, clutching a loaded crossbow. "*What do you want?*" he shouted across the swirling brown waters.

"*Take us over*," the Hound shouted back.

The men in the boat conferred with one another. One of them, a grizzled grey-haired man with thick arms and a bent back, stepped to the rail. "*It will cost you.*"

"*Then I'll pay.*"

With what? Arya wondered. The outlaws had taken Clegane's gold, but maybe Lord Beric had left him some silver and copper. A ferry ride shouldn't cost more than a few coppers . . .

The ferrymen were talking again. Finally the bent-backed one turned away and gave a shout. Six more men appeared, pulling up hoods to keep the rain off their heads. Still more squirmed out the holdfast window and leapt down onto the deck. Half of them looked enough like the bent-backed man to be his kin. Some of them undid the chains and took up long poles, while the others slid heavy wide-bladed oars through the locks. The ferry swung about and began to creep slowly toward the shallows, oars stroking smoothly on either side. Sandor Clegane rode down the hill to meet it.

When the aft end of the boat slammed into the hillside, the ferrymen opened a wide door beneath the carved horse's head, and extended a heavy oaken plank. Stranger balked at the water's edge, but the Hound put his heels into the courser's flank and urged him up the gangway. The bent-backed man was waiting for them on deck. "Wet enough for you, ser?" he asked, smiling.

The Hound's mouth gave a twitch. "I need your boat, not your bloody wit." He dismounted, and pulled Arya down beside him. One of the boatmen reached for Stranger's bridle. "I wouldn't," Clegane said, as the horse kicked. The man leapt back, slipped on the rain-slick deck, and crashed onto his arse, cursing.

The ferryman with the bent back wasn't smiling any longer. "We can get you across," he said sourly. "It will cost you a gold piece. Another for the horse. A third for the boy."

"Three dragons?" Clegane gave a bark of laughter. "For three dragons I should own the bloody ferry."

"Last year, might be you could. But with this river, I'll need extra hands on the poles and oars just to see we don't get swept a hundred miles out to sea. Here's your choice. Three dragons, or you teach that hellhorse how to walk on water."

"I like an honest brigand. Have it your way. Three dragons . . . when you put us ashore safe on the north bank."

"I'll have them now, or we don't go." The man thrust out a thick, callused hand, palm up.

Clegane rattled his longsword to loosen the blade in the scabbard. "Here's *your* choice. Gold on the north bank, or steel on the south."

The ferryman looked up at the Hound's face. Arya could tell that he didn't like what he saw there. He had a dozen men behind him, strong men with oars and hardwood poles in their hands, but none of them were rushing forward to help him. Together they could overwhelm Sandor Clegane, though he'd likely kill three or four of them before they took him down. "How do I know you're good for it?" the bent-backed man asked, after a moment.

He's not, she wanted to shout. Instead she bit her lip.

"Knight's honor," the Hound said, unsmiling.

He's not even a knight. She did not say that either.

"That will do." The ferryman spat. "Come on then, we can have you across before dark. Tie the horse up, I don't want him spooking when we're under way. There's a brazier in the cabin if you and your son want to get warm."

"*I'm not his stupid son!*" said Arya furiously. That was even worse than being taken for a boy. She was so angry that she might have told them who she *really* was, only Sandor Clegane grabbed her by the back of the collar and hoisted her one-handed off the deck. "How many times do I need to tell you to *shut your bloody mouth?*" He shook her so hard her teeth rattled, then let her fall. "Get in there and get dry, like the man said."

Arya did as she was told. The big iron brazier was glowing red, filling the room with a sullen suffocating heat. It felt pleasant to stand beside it, to warm her hands and dry off a little bit, but as soon as she felt the deck move under her feet she slipped back out through the forward door.

The two-headed horse eased slowly through the shallows, picking its way between the chimneys and rooftops of drowned Harroway. A dozen men labored at the oars while four more used the long poles to push off whenever they came too close to a rock, a tree, or a sunken house. The bent-backed man had the rudder. Rain pattered against the smooth planks of the deck and splashed off the tall carved horseheads fore and aft. Arya was getting soaked again, but she didn't care. She wanted to see. The man with the crossbow still stood in the window of the roundtower, she saw. His eyes followed her as the ferry slid by underneath. She wondered if he was this Lord Roote that the Hound had mentioned. *He doesn't look much like a lord.* But then, she didn't look much like a lady either.

Once they were beyond the town and out in the river proper, the current grew much stronger. Through the grey haze of rain Arya could make out a tall stone pillar on the far shore that surely marked the ferry landing, but no sooner had she seen it than she realized that they were being pushed away from it, downstream. The oarsmen were rowing more vigorously now, fighting the rage of the river. Leaves and broken branches swirled past as fast as if they'd been fired from a scorpion. The men with the poles leaned out and shoved away anything that came too close. It was windier out here, too. Whenever she turned to look upstream, Arya got a face full of blowing rain. Stranger was screaming and kicking as the deck moved underfoot.

If I jumped over the side, the river would wash me away before the Hound even knew that I was gone. She looked back over a shoulder, and saw Sandor Clegane struggling with his frightened horse, trying to calm him. She would never have a better chance to get away from him. *I might drown, though.* Jon used to say that she swam like a fish, but even a fish might have trouble in this river. Still, drowning might be better than

King's Landing. She thought about Joffrey and crept up to the prow. The river was murky brown with mud and lashed by rain, looking more like soup than water. Arya wondered how cold it would be. *I couldn't get much wetter than I am now.* She put a hand on the rail.

But a sudden shout snapped her head about before she could leap. The ferrymen were rushing forward, poles in hand. For a moment she did not understand what was happening. Then she saw it: an uprooted tree, huge and dark, coming straight at them. A tangle of roots and limbs poked up out of the water as it came, like the reaching arms of a great kraken. The oarsmen were backing water frantically, trying to avoid a collision that could capsize them or stove their hull in. The old man had wrenched the rudder about, and the horse at the prow was swinging downstream, but too slowly. Glistening brown and black, the tree rushed toward them like a battering ram.

It could not have been more than ten feet from their prow when two of the boatmen somehow caught it with their long poles. One snapped, and the long splintering *craaaack* made it sound as if the ferry were breaking up beneath them. But the second man managed to give the trunk a hard shove, just enough to deflect it away from them. The tree swept past the ferry with inches to spare, its branches scrabbling like claws against the horsehead. Only just when it seemed as if they were clear, one of the monster's upper limbs dealt them a glancing thump. The ferry seemed to shudder, and Arya slipped, landing painfully on one knee. The man with the broken pole was not so lucky. She heard him shout as he stumbled over the side. Then the raging brown water closed over him, and he was gone in the time it took Arya to climb back to her feet. One of the other boatmen snatched up a coil of rope, but there was no one to throw it to.

Maybe he'll wash up someplace downstream, Arya tried to tell herself, but the thought had a hollow ring. She had lost all desire to go swimming. When Sandor Clegane shouted at her to get back inside before he beat her bloody, she went meekly. The ferry was fighting to turn back on course by then, against a river that wanted nothing more than to carry it down to the sea.

When they finally came ashore, it was a good two miles downriver of their usual landing. The boat slammed into the bank so hard that another pole snapped, and Arya almost lost her feet again. Sandor Clegane lifted her onto Stranger's back as if she weighed no more than a doll. The boatmen stared at them with dull, exhausted eyes, all but the bent-backed man, who held his hand out. "Six dragons," he demanded. "Three for the passage, and three for the man I lost."

Sandor Clegane rummaged in his pouch and shoved a crumpled wad of parchment into the boatman's palm. "There. Take ten."

"Ten?" The ferryman was confused. "What's this, now?"

"A dead man's note, good for nine thousand dragons or nearabouts."
The Hound swung up into the saddle behind Arya, and smiled down
unpleasantly. "Ten of it is yours. I'll be back for the rest one day, so see
you don't go spending it."

The man squinted down at the parchment. "Writing. What good's
writing? You promised gold. Knight's honor, you said."

"Knights have no bloody honor. Time you learned that, old man."
The Hound gave Stranger the spur and galloped off through the rain. The
ferrymen threw curses at their backs, and one or two threw stones.
Clegane ignored rocks and words alike, and before long they were lost in
the gloom of the trees, the river a dwindling roar behind them. "The
ferry won't cross back till morning," he said, "and that lot won't be
taking paper promises from the next fools to come along. If your friends
are chasing us, they're going to need to be bloody strong swimmers."

Arya huddled down and held her tongue. *Valar morghulis*, she thought
sullenly. *Ser Ilyn, Ser Meryn, King Joffrey, Queen Cersei. Dunsen, Polliver, Raff the Sweetling, Ser Gregor and the Tickler. And the Hound,
the Hound, the Hound.*

By the time the rain stopped and the clouds broke, she was shivering
and sneezing so badly that Clegane called a halt for the night, and even
tried to make a fire. The wood they gathered proved too wet, though.
Nothing he tried was enough to make the spark catch. Finally he kicked
it all apart in disgust. "Seven bloody hells," he swore. "I hate fires."

They sat on damp rocks beneath an oak tree, listening to the slow
patter of water dripping from the leaves as they ate a cold supper of
hardbread, moldy cheese, and smoked sausage. The Hound sliced the
meat with his dagger, and narrowed his eyes when he caught Arya looking
at the knife. "Don't even think about it."

"I wasn't," she lied.

He snorted to show what he thought of *that*, but he gave her a thick
slice of sausage. Arya worried it with her teeth, watching him all the
while. "I never beat your sister," the Hound said. "But I'll beat you if
you make me. Stop trying to think up ways to kill me. None of it will
do you a bit of good."

She had nothing to say to that. She gnawed on the sausage and stared
at him coldly. *Hard as stone*, she thought.

"At least you look at my face. I'll give you that, you little she-wolf.
How do you like it?"

"I don't. It's all burned and ugly."

Clegane offered her a chunk of cheese on the point of his dagger.
"You're a little fool. What good would it do you if you *did* get away?
You'd just get caught by someone worse."

"I would *not*," she insisted. "There is no one worse."

"You never knew my brother. Gregor once killed a man for snoring. His own man." When he grinned, the burned side of his face pulled tight, twisting his mouth in a queer unpleasant way. He had no lips on that side, and only the stump of an ear.

"I did so know your brother." Maybe the Mountain *was* worse, now that Arya thought about it. "Him and Dunsen and Polliver, and Raff the Sweetling and the Tickler."

The Hound seemed surprised. "And how would Ned Stark's precious little daughter come to know the likes of them? Gregor never brings his pet rats to court."

"I know them from the village." She ate the cheese, and reached for a hunk of hardbread. "The village by the lake where they caught Gendry, me, and Hot Pie. They caught Lommy Greenhands too, but Raff the Sweetling killed him because his leg was hurt."

Clegane's mouth twitched. "Caught you? My brother *caught* you?" That made him laugh, a sour sound, part rumble and part snarl. "Gregor never knew what he had, did he? He couldn't have, or he would have dragged you back kicking and screaming to King's Landing and dumped you in Cersei's lap. Oh, that's bloody sweet. I'll be sure and tell him that, before I cut his heart out."

It wasn't the first time he had talked of killing the Mountain. "But he's your brother," Arya said dubiously.

"Didn't you ever have a brother you wanted to kill?" He laughed again. "Or maybe a sister?" He must have seen something in her face then, for he leaned closer. "Sansa. That's it, isn't it? The wolf bitch wants to kill the pretty bird."

"No," Arya spat back at him. "I'd like to kill *you*."

"Because I hacked your little friend in two? I've killed a lot more than him, I promise you. You think that makes me some monster. Well, maybe it does, but I saved your sister's life too. The day the mob pulled her off her horse, I cut through them and brought her back to the castle, else she would have gotten what Lollys Stokeworth got. And she sang for me. You didn't know that, did you? Your sister sang me a sweet little song."

"You're lying," she said at once.

"You don't know half as much as you think you do. The *Blackwater?* Where in seven hells do you think we are? Where do you think we're going?"

The scorn in his voice made her hesitate. "Back to King's Landing," she said. "You're bringing me to Joffrey and the queen." That was wrong, she realized all of a sudden, just from the way he asked the questions. But she had to say *something*.

"Stupid blind little wolf bitch." His voice was rough and hard as an iron rasp. "Bugger Joffrey, bugger the queen, and bugger that twisted little gargoyle she calls a brother. I'm done with their city, done with their Kingsguard, done with Lannisters. What's a dog to do with lions, I ask you?" He reached for his waterskin, took a long pull. As he wiped his mouth, he offered the skin to Arya and said, "The river was the Trident, girl. The *Trident*, not the Blackwater. Make the map in your head, if you can. On the morrow we should reach the kingsroad. We'll make good time after that, straight up to the Twins. It's going to be me who hands you over to that mother of yours. Not the noble lightning lord or that flaming fraud of a priest, the monster." He grinned at the look on her face. "You think your outlaw friends are the only ones can smell a ransom? Dondarrion took my gold, so I took you. You're worth twice what they stole from me, I'd say. Maybe even more if I sold you back to the Lannisters like you fear, but I won't. Even a dog gets tired of being kicked. If this Young Wolf has the wits the gods gave a toad, he'll make me a lordling and beg me to enter his service. He *needs* me, though he may not know it yet. Maybe I'll even kill Gregor for him, he'd like that."

"He'll never take you," she spat back. "Not *you*."

"Then I'll take as much gold as I can carry, laugh in his face, and ride off. If he doesn't take me, he'd be wise to kill me, but he won't. Too much his father's son, from what I hear. Fine with me. Either way I win. And so do you, she-wolf. So stop whimpering and snapping at me, I'm sick of it. Keep your mouth shut and do as I tell you, and maybe we'll even be in time for your uncle's bloody wedding."

JON

The mare was blown, but Jon could not let up on her. He had to reach the Wall before the Magnar. He would have slept in the saddle if he'd had one; lacking that, it was hard enough to stay ahorse while awake. His wounded leg grew ever more painful. He dare not rest long enough to let it heal. Instead he ripped it open anew each time he mounted up.

When he crested a rise and saw the brown rutted kingsroad before him wending its way north through hill and plain, he patted the mare's neck and said, "Now all we need do is follow the road, girl. Soon the Wall." His leg had gone as stiff as wood by then, and fever had made him so light-headed that twice he found himself riding in the wrong direction.

Soon the Wall. He pictured his friends drinking mulled wine in the common hall. Hobb would be with his kettles, Donal Noye at his forge, Maester Aemon in his rooms beneath the rookery. *And the Old Bear? Sam, Grenn, Dolorous Edd, Dywen with his wooden teeth . . .* Jon could only pray that some had escaped the Fist.

Ygritte was much in his thoughts as well. He remembered the smell of her hair, the warmth of her body . . . and the look on her face as she slit the old man's throat. *You were wrong to love her*, a voice whispered. *You were wrong to leave her*, a different voice insisted. He wondered if his father had been torn the same way, when he'd left Jon's mother to return to Lady Catelyn. *He was pledged to Lady Stark, and I am pledged to the Night's Watch.*

He almost rode through Mole's Town, so feverish that he did not know where he was. Most of the village was hidden underground, only a handful of small hovels to be seen by the light of the waning moon. The brothel was a shed no bigger than a privy, its red lantern creaking in the wind, a bloodshot eye peering through the blackness. Jon dismounted at the adjoining stable, half-stumbling from the mare's back as he shouted two boys awake. "I need a fresh mount, with saddle and bridle," he told them, in a tone that brooked no argument. They brought him that; a skin of wine as well, and half a loaf of brown bread. "Wake the village," he told them. "Warn them. There are wildlings south of the Wall. Gather your goods and make for Castle Black." He pulled himself onto the black gelding they'd given him, gritting his teeth at the pain in his leg, and rode hard for the north.

As the stars began to fade in the eastern sky, the Wall appeared before him, rising above the trees and the morning mists. Moonlight glimmered pale against the ice. He urged the gelding on, following the muddy slick road until he saw the stone towers and timbered halls of Castle Black huddled like broken toys beneath the great cliff of ice. By then the Wall glowed pink and purple with the first light of dawn.

No sentries challenged him as he rode past the outbuildings. No one came forth to bar his way. Castle Black seemed as much a ruin as Greyguard. Brown brittle weeds grew between cracks in the stones of the courtyards. Old snow covered the roof of the Flint Barracks and lay in drifts against the north side of Hardin's Tower, where Jon used to sleep before being made the Old Bear's steward. Fingers of soot streaked the Lord Commander's Tower where the smoke had boiled from the windows. Mormont had moved to the King's Tower after the fire, but Jon saw no lights there either. From the ground he could not tell if there were sentries walking the Wall seven hundred feet above, but he saw no one on the huge switchback stair that climbed the south face of the ice like some great wooden thunderbolt.

There was smoke rising from the chimney of the armory, though; only a wisp, almost invisible against the grey northern sky, but it was enough. Jon dismounted and limped toward it. Warmth poured out the open door like the hot breath of summer. Within, one-armed Donal Noye was working his bellows at the fire. He looked up at the noise. "Jon Snow?"

"None else." Despite fever, exhaustion, his leg, the Magnar, the old man, Ygritte, Mance, despite it all, Jon smiled. It was good to be back, good to see Noye with his big belly and pinned-up sleeve, his jaw bristling with black stubble.

The smith released his grip on the bellows. "Your face . . ."

He had almost forgotten about his face. "A skinchanger tried to rip out my eye."

Noye frowned. "Scarred or smooth, it's a face I thought I'd seen the last of. We heard you'd gone over to Mance Rayder."

Jon grasped the door to stay upright. "Who told you that?"

"Jarman Buckwell. He returned a fortnight past. His scouts claim they saw you with their own eyes, riding along beside the wildling column and wearing a sheepskin cloak." Noye eyed him. "I see the last part's true."

"It's all true," Jon confessed. "As far as it goes."

"Should I be pulling down a sword to gut you, then?"

"No. I was acting on orders. Qhorin Halfhand's last command. Noye, where is the garrison?"

"Defending the Wall against your wildling friends."

"Yes, but *where?*"

"Everywhere. Harma Dogshead was seen at Woodswatch-by-the-Pool, Rattleshirt at Long Barrow, the Weeper near Icemark. All along the Wall . . . they're here, they're there, they're climbing near Queensgate, they're hacking at the gates of Greyguard, they're massing against Eastwatch . . . but one glimpse of a black cloak and they're gone. Next day they're somewhere else."

Jon swallowed a groan. "Feints. Mance wants us to spread ourselves thin, don't you see?" *And Bowen Marsh has obliged him.* "The gate is here. The attack is here."

Noye crossed the room. "Your leg is drenched in blood."

Jon looked down dully. It was true. His wound had opened again. "An arrow wound . . ."

"A wildling arrow." It was not a question. Noye had only one arm, but that was thick with muscle. He slid it under Jon's to help support him. "You're white as milk, and burning hot besides. I'm taking you to Aemon."

"There's no time. There are wildlings *south* of the Wall, coming up from Queenscrown to open the gate."

"How many?" Noye half-carried Jon out the door.

"A hundred and twenty, and well armed for wildlings. Bronze armor, some bits of steel. How many men are left here?"

"Forty odd," said Donal Noye. "The crippled and infirm, and some green boys still in training."

"If Marsh is gone, who did he name as castellan?"

The armorer laughed. "Ser Wynton, gods preserve him. Last knight in the castle and all. The thing is, Stout seems to have forgotten and no one's been rushing to remind him. I suppose I'm as much a commander as we have now. The meanest of the cripples."

That was for the good, at least. The one-armed armorer was hard headed, tough, and well seasoned in war. Ser Wynton Stout, on the other hand . . . well, he had been a good man once, everyone agreed, but he had been eighty years a ranger, and both strength and wits were gone. Once he'd fallen asleep at supper and almost drowned in a bowl of pea soup.

"Where's your wolf?" Noye asked as they crossed the yard.

"Ghost. I had to leave him when I climbed the Wall. I'd hoped he'd make his way back here."

"I'm sorry, lad. There's been no sign of him." They limped up to the maester's door, in the long wooden keep beneath the rookery. The armorer gave it a kick. "*Clydas!*"

After a moment a stooped, round-shouldered little man in black peered out. His small pink eyes widened at the sight of Jon. "Lay the lad down, I'll fetch the maester."

A fire was burning in the hearth, and the room was almost stuffy. The warmth made Jon sleepy. As soon as Noye eased him down onto his back, he closed his eyes to stop the world from spinning. He could hear the ravens *quork*ing and complaining in the rookery above. "*Snow,*" one bird was saying. "*Snow, snow, snow.*" That was Sam's doing, Jon remembered. Had Samwell Tarly made it home safely, he wondered, or only the birds?

Maester Aemon was not long in coming. He moved slowly, one spotted hand on Clydas's arm as he shuffled forward with small careful steps. Around his thin neck his chain hung heavy, gold and silver links glinting amongst iron, lead, tin, and other base metals. "Jon Snow," he said, "you must tell me all you've seen and done when you are stronger. Donal, put a kettle of wine on the fire, and my irons as well. I will want them red-hot. Clydas, I shall need that good sharp knife of yours." The maester was more than a hundred years old; shrunken, frail, hairless, and quite blind. But if his milky eyes saw nothing, his wits were still as sharp as they had ever been.

"There are wildlings coming," Jon told him, as Clydas ran a blade up the leg of his breeches, slicing the heavy black cloth, crusty with old blood and sodden with new. "From the south. We climbed the Wall . . ."

Maester Aemon gave Jon's crude bandage a sniff when Clydas cut it away. "We?"

"I was with them. Qhorin Halfhand commanded me to join them." Jon winced as the maester's finger explored his wound, poking and prodding. "The Magnar of Thenn – *aaaaah*, that hurts." He clenched his teeth. "Where is the Old Bear?"

"Jon . . . it grieves me to say, but Lord Commander Mormont was murdered at Craster's Keep, at the hands of his Sworn Brothers."

"Bro . . . *our own men!*" Aemon's words hurt a hundred times worse than his fingers. Jon remembered the Old Bear as last he'd seen him, standing before his tent with his raven on his arm croaking for corn. *Mormont gone!* He had feared it ever since he'd seen the aftermath of battle on the Fist, yet it was no less a blow. "Who was it? Who turned on him?"

"Garth of Oldtown, Ollo Lophand, Dirk . . . thieves, cowards and killers, the lot of them. We should have seen it coming. The Watch is not what it was. Too few honest men to keep the rogues in line." Donal Noye turned the maester's blades in the fire. "A dozen true men made it back. Dolorous Edd, Giant, your friend the Aurochs. We had the tale from them."

Only a dozen? Two hundred men had left Castle Black with Lord Commander Mormont, two hundred of the Watch's best. "Does this mean Marsh is Lord Commander, then?" The Old Pomegranate was amiable, and a diligent First Steward, but he was woefully ill-suited to face a wildling host.

"For the nonce, until we can hold a choosing," said Maester Aemon. "Clydas, bring me the flask."

A choosing. With Qhorin Halfhand and Ser Jaremy Rykker both dead and Ben Stark still missing, who was there? Not Bowen Marsh or Ser Wynton Stout, that was certain. Had Thoren Smallwood survived the Fist, or Ser Ottyn Wythers? *No, it will be Cotter Pyke or Ser Denys Mallister. Which, though?* The commanders at the Shadow Tower and Eastwatch were good men, but very different; Ser Denys courtly and cautious, as chivalrous as he was elderly, Pyke younger, bastard-born, rough-tongued, and bold to a fault. Worse, the two men despised each other. The Old Bear had always kept them far apart, at opposite ends of the Wall. The Mallisters had a bone-deep mistrust of the ironborn, Jon knew.

A stab of pain reminded him of his own woes. The maester squeezed his hand. "Clydas is bringing milk of the poppy."

Jon tried to rise. "I don't need –"

"You do," Aemon said firmly. "This will hurt."

Donal Noye crossed the room and shoved Jon back onto his back. "Be still, or I'll tie you down." Even with only one arm, the smith handled him as if he were a child. Clydas returned with a green flask and a rounded stone cup. Maester Aemon poured it full. "Drink this."

Jon had bitten his lip in his struggles. He could taste blood mingled with the thick, chalky potion. It was all he could do not to retch it back up.

Clydas brought a basin of warm water, and Maester Aemon washed the pus and blood from his wound. Gentle as he was, even the lightest touch made Jon want to scream. "The Magnar's men are disciplined, and they have bronze armor," he told them. Talking helped keep his mind off his leg.

"The Magnar's a lord on Skagos," Noye said. "There were Skagossons at Eastwatch when I first came to the Wall, I remember hearing them talk of him."

"Jon was using the word in its older sense, I think," Maester Aemon said, "not as a family name but as a title. It derives from the Old Tongue."

"It means lord," Jon agreed. "Styr is the Magnar of some place called Thenn, in the far north of the Frostfangs. He has a hundred of his own men, and a score of raiders who know the Gift almost as well as we do. Mance never found the horn, though, that's something. The Horn of Winter, that's what he was digging for up along the Milkwater."

Maester Aemon paused, washcloth in hand. "The Horn of Winter is an ancient legend. Does the King-beyond-the-Wall truly believe that such a thing exists?"

"They all do," said Jon. "Ygritte said they opened a hundred graves . . . graves of kings and heroes, all over the valley of the Milkwater, but they never . . ."

"Who is *Ygritte*?" Donal Noye asked pointedly.

"A woman of the free folk." How could he explain Ygritte to them? *She's warm and smart and funny and she can kiss a man or slit his throat.* "She's with Styr, but she's not . . . she's young, only a girl, in truth, wild, but she . . ." *She killed an old man for building a fire.* His tongue felt thick and clumsy. The milk of the poppy was clouding his wits. "I broke my vows with her. I never meant to, but . . ." *It was wrong. Wrong to love her, wrong to leave her . . .* "I wasn't strong enough. The Halfhand commanded me, ride with them, watch, I must not balk, I . . ." His head felt as if it were packed with wet wool.

Maester Aemon sniffed Jon's wound again. Then he put the bloody cloth back in the basin and said, "Donal, the hot knife, if you please. I shall need you to hold him still."

I will not scream, Jon told himself when he saw the blade glowing red hot. But he broke that vow as well. Donal Noye held him down, while Clydas helped guide the maester's hand. Jon did not move, except to pound his fist against the table, again and again and again. The pain was so huge he felt small and weak and helpless inside it, a child whimpering in the dark. *Ygritte*, he thought, when the stench of burning flesh was in his nose and his own shriek echoing in her ears. *Ygritte, I had to.* For half a heartbeat the agony started to ebb. But then the iron touched him once again, and he fainted.

When his eyelids fluttered open, he was wrapped in thick wool and floating. He could not seem to move, but that did not matter. For a time he dreamed that Ygritte was with him, tending him with gentle hands. Finally he closed his eyes and slept.

The next waking was not so gentle. The room was dark, but under the blankets the pain was back, a throbbing in his leg that turned into a hot knife at the least motion. Jon learned that the hard way when he tried to see if he still had a leg. Gasping, he swallowed a scream and made another fist.

"Jon?" A candle appeared, and a well-remembered face was looking down on him, big ears and all. "You shouldn't move."

"Pyp?" Jon reached up, and the other boy clasped his hand and gave it a squeeze. "I thought you'd gone . . ."

". . . with the Old Pomegranate? No, he thinks I'm too small and green. Grenn's here too."

"I'm here too." Grenn stepped to the other side of the bed. "I fell asleep."

Jon's throat was dry. "Water," he gasped. Grenn brought it, and held it to his lips. "I saw the Fist," he said, after a long swallow. "The blood, and the dead horses . . . Noye said a dozen made it back . . . who?"

"Dywen did. Giant, Dolorous Edd, Sweet Donnel Hill, Ulmer, Left Hand Lew, Garth Greyfeather. Four or five more. Me."

"Sam?"

Grenn looked away. "He killed one of the Others, Jon. I saw it. He stabbed him with that dragonglass knife you made him, and we started calling him Sam the Slayer. He hated that."

Sam the Slayer. Jon could hardly imagine a less likely warrior than Sam Tarly. "What happened to him?"

"We left him." Grenn sounded miserable. "I shook him and screamed at him, even slapped his face. Giant tried to drag him to his feet, but he was too heavy. Remember in training how he'd curl up on the ground and lie there whimpering? At Craster's he wouldn't even whimper. Dirk and Ollo were tearing up the walls looking for food, Garth and Garth were fighting, some of the others were raping Craster's wives. Dolorous Edd figured Dirk's bunch would kill all the loyal men to keep us from telling what they'd done, and they had us two to one. We left Sam with the Old Bear. He wouldn't *move*, Jon."

You were his brother, he almost said. *How could you leave him amongst wildlings and murderers?*

"He might still be alive," said Pyp. "He might surprise us all and come riding up tomorrow."

"With Mance Rayder's head, aye." Grenn was trying to sound cheerful, Jon could tell. "Sam the Slayer!"

Jon tried to sit again. It was as much a mistake as the first time. He cried out, cursing.

"Grenn, go wake Maester Aemon," said Pyp. "Tell him Jon needs more milk of the poppy."

Yes, Jon thought. "No," he said. "The Magnar . . ."

"We know," said Pyp. "The sentries on the Wall have been told to keep one eye on the south, and Donal Noye dispatched some men to

Weatherback Ridge to watch the kingsroad. Maester Aemon's sent birds
to Eastwatch and the Shadow Tower too."

Maester Aemon shuffled to the bedside, one hand on Grenn's shoulder.
"Jon, be gentle with yourself. It is good that you have woken, but you
must give yourself time to heal. We drowned the wound with boiling
wine, and closed you up with a poultice of nettle, mustard seed and
moldy bread, but unless you rest . . ."

"I can't." Jon fought through the pain to sit. "Mance will be here
soon . . . thousands of men, giants, mammoths . . . has word been sent to
Winterfell? To the king?" Sweat dripped off his brow. He closed his eyes
a moment.

Grenn gave Pyp a strange look. "He doesn't know."

"Jon," said Maester Aemon, "much and more happened while you
were away, and little of it good. Balon Greyjoy has crowned himself again
and sent his longships against the north. Kings sprout like weeds at every
hand and we have sent appeals to all of them, yet none will come. They
have more pressing uses for their swords, and we are far off and forgotten.
And Winterfell . . . Jon, be strong . . . Winterfell is no more . . ."

"No more?" Jon stared at Aemon's white eyes and wrinkled face. "My
brothers are at Winterfell. Bran and Rickon . . ."

The maester touched his brow. "I am so very sorry, Jon. Your brothers
died at the command of Theon Greyjoy, after he took Winterfell in his
father's name. When your father's bannermen threatened to retake it, he
put the castle to the torch."

"Your brothers were avenged," Grenn said. "Bolton's son killed all the
ironmen, and it's said he's flaying Theon Greyjoy inch by inch for what
he did."

"I'm sorry, Jon." Pyp squeezed his shoulder. "We are all."

Jon had never liked Theon Greyjoy, but he had been their father's
ward. Another spasm of pain twisted up his leg, and the next he knew
he was flat on his back again. "There's some mistake," he insisted. "At
Queenscrown I saw a direwolf, a *grey* direwolf . . . grey . . . *it knew me.*"
If Bran was dead, could some part of him live on in his wolf, as Orell
lived within his eagle?

"Drink this." Grenn held a cup to his lips. Jon drank. His head was
full of wolves and eagles, the sound of his brothers' laughter. The faces
above him began to blur and fade. *They can't be dead. Theon would
never do that. And Winterfell . . . grey granite, oak and iron, crows wheeling around the towers, steam rising off the hot pools in the godswood,
the stone kings sitting on their thrones . . . how could Winterfell be gone?*

When the dreams took him, he found himself back home once more,
splashing in the hot pools beneath a huge white weirwood that had his
father's face. Ygritte was with him, laughing at him, shedding her skins

till she was naked as her name day, trying to kiss him, but he couldn't, not with his father watching. He was the blood of Winterfell, a man of the Night's Watch. *I will not father a bastard*, he told her. *I will not. I will not.* "You know nothing, Jon Snow," she whispered, her skin dissolving in the hot water, the flesh beneath sloughing off her bones until only skull and skeleton remained, and the pool bubbled thick and red.

CATELYN

They heard the Green Fork before they saw it, an endless susurrus, like the growl of some great beast. The river was a boiling torrent, half again as wide as it had been last year, when Robb had divided his army here and vowed to take a Frey to bride as the price of his crossing. *He needed Lord Walder and his bridge then, and he needs them even more now.* Catelyn's heart was full of misgivings as she watched the murky green waters swirl past. *There is no way we will ford this, nor swim across, and it could be a moon's turn before these waters fall again.*

As they neared the Twins, Robb donned his crown and summoned Catelyn and Edmure to ride beside him. Ser Raynald Westerling bore his banner, the direwolf of Stark on its ice-white field.

The gatehouse towers emerged from the rain like ghosts, hazy grey apparitions that grew more solid the closer they rode. The Frey stronghold was not one castle but two; mirror images in wet stone standing on opposite sides of the water, linked by a great arched bridge. From the center of its span rose the Water Tower, the river running straight and swift below. Channels had been cut from the banks, to form moats that made each twin an island. The rains had turned the moats to shallow lakes.

Across the turbulent waters, Catelyn could see several thousand men encamped around the eastern castle, their banners hanging like so many drowned cats from the lances outside their tents. The rain made it impossible to distinguish colors and devices. Most were grey, it seemed to her, though beneath such skies the whole world seemed grey.

"Tread lightly here, Robb," she cautioned her son. "Lord Walder has a thin skin and a sharp tongue, and some of these sons of his will doubtless take after their father. You must not let yourself be provoked."

"I know the Freys, Mother. I know how much I wronged them, and how much I *need* them. I shall be as sweet as a septon."

Catelyn shifted her seat uncomfortably. "If we are offered refreshment when we arrive, on no account refuse. Take what is offered, and eat and drink where all can see. If nothing is offered, ask for bread and cheese and a cup of wine."

"I'm more wet than hungry . . ."

"Robb, *listen to me.* Once you have eaten of his bread and salt, you have the guest right, and the laws of hospitality protect you beneath his roof."

Robb looked more amused than afraid. "I have an army to protect me, Mother, I don't need to trust in bread and salt. But if it pleases Lord Walder to serve me stewed crow smothered in maggots, I'll eat it and ask for a second bowl."

Four Freys rode out from the western gatehouse, wrapped in heavy cloaks of thick grey wool. Catelyn recognized Ser Ryman, son of the late Ser Stevron, Lord Walder's firstborn. With his father dead, Ryman was heir to the Twins. The face she saw beneath his hood was fleshy, broad, and stupid. The other three were likely his own sons, Lord Walder's great grandsons.

Edmure confirmed as much. "Edwyn is eldest, the pale slender man with the constipated look. The wiry one with the beard is Black Walder, a nasty bit of business. Petyr is on the bay, the lad with the unfortunate face. Petyr Pimple, his brothers call him. Only a year or two older than Robb, but Lord Walder married him off at ten to a woman thrice his age. Gods, I hope Roslin doesn't take after *him*."

They halted to let their hosts come to them. Robb's banner drooped on its staff, and the steady sound of rainfall mingled with the rush of the swollen Green Fork on their right. Grey Wind edged forward, tail stiff, watching through slitted eyes of dark gold. When the Freys were a half-dozen yards away Catelyn heard him growl, a deep rumble that seemed almost one with rush of the river. Robb looked startled. "Grey Wind, to me. To *me!*"

Instead the direwolf leapt forward, snarling.

Ser Ryman's palfrey shied off with a whinny of fear, and Petyr Pimple's reared and threw him. Only Black Walder kept his mount in hand. He reached for the hilt of his sword. *"No!"* Robb was shouting. "Grey Wind, here. *Here.*" Catelyn spurred between the direwolf and the horses. Mud spattered from the hooves of her mare as she cut in front of Grey Wind. The wolf veered away, and only then seemed to hear Robb calling.

"Is this how a Stark makes amends?" Black Walder shouted, with naked steel in hand. "A poor greeting I call it, to set your wolf upon us. Is this why you've come?"

Ser Ryman had dismounted to help Petyr Pimple back to his feet. The lad was muddy, but unhurt.

"I've come to make my apology for the wrong I did your House, and to see my uncle wed." Robb swung down from the saddle. "Petyr, take my horse. Yours is almost back to the stable."

Petyr looked to his father and said, "I can ride behind one of my brothers."

The Freys made no sign of obeisance. "You come late," Ser Ryman declared.

"The rains delayed us," said Robb. "I sent a bird."

"I do not see the woman."

By *the woman* Ser Ryman meant Jeyne Westerling, all knew. Lady Catelyn smiled apologetically. "Queen Jeyne was weary after so much travel, sers. No doubt she will be pleased to visit when times are more settled."

"My grandfather will be displeased." Though Black Walder had sheathed his sword, his tone was no friendlier. "I've told him much of the lady, and he wished to behold her with his own eyes."

Edwyn cleared his throat. "We have chambers prepared for you in the Water Tower, Your Grace," he told Robb with careful courtesy, "as well as for Lord Tully and Lady Stark. Your lords bannermen are also welcome to shelter under our roof and partake of the wedding feast."

"And my men?" asked Robb.

"My lord grandfather regrets that he cannot feed nor house so large a host. We have been sore pressed to find fodder and provender for our own levies. Nonetheless, your men shall not be neglected. If they will cross and set up their camp beside our own, we will bring out enough casks of wine and ale for all to drink the health of Lord Edmure and his bride. We have thrown up three great feast tents on the far bank, to provide them with some shelter from the rains."

"Your lord father is most kind. My men will thank him. They have had a long wet ride."

Edmure Tully edged his horse forward. "When shall I meet my betrothed?"

"She waits for you within," promised Edwyn Frey. "You will forgive her if she seems shy, I know. She has been awaiting this day most anxiously, poor maid. But perhaps we might continue this out of the rain?"

"Truly." Ser Ryman mounted up again, pulling Petyr Pimple up behind him. "If you would follow me, my father awaits." He turned the palfrey's head back toward the Twins.

Edmure fell in beside Catelyn. "The Late Lord Frey might have seen fit to welcome us in person," he complained. "I am his liege lord as well as his son-to-be, and Robb's his king."

"When you are one-and-ninety, Brother, see how eager *you* are to go riding in the rain." Yet she wondered if that was the whole truth of it. Lord Walder normally went about in a covered litter, which would have kept the worst of the rain off him. *A deliberate slight?* If so, it might be the first of many yet to come.

There was more trouble at the gatehouse. Grey Wind balked in the middle of the drawbridge, shook the rain off, and howled at the portcullis. Robb whistled impatiently. "Grey Wind. What is it? Grey Wind, with me." But the direwolf only bared his teeth. *He does not like this place*, Catelyn thought. Robb had to squat and speak softly to the wolf before he would consent to pass beneath the portcullis. By then Lame Lothar and Walder Rivers had come up. "It's the sound of the water he fears," Rivers said. "Beasts know to avoid the river in flood."

"A dry kennel and a leg of mutton will see him right again," said Lothar cheerfully. "Shall I summon our master of hounds?"

"He's a direwolf, not a dog," said Robb, "and dangerous to men he does not trust. Ser Raynald, stay with him. I won't take him into Lord Walder's hall like this."

Deftly done, Catelyn decided. *Robb keeps the Westerling out of Lord Walder's sight as well.*

Gout and brittle bones had taken their toll of old Walder Frey. They found him propped up in his high seat with a cushion beneath him and an ermine robe across his lap. His chair was black oak, its back carved into the semblance of two stout towers joined by an arched bridge, so massive that its embrace turned the old man into a grotesque child. There was something of the vulture about Lord Walder, and rather more of the weasel. His bald head, spotted with age, thrust out from his scrawny shoulders on a long pink neck. Loose skin dangled beneath his receding chin, his eyes were runny and clouded, and his toothless mouth moved constantly, sucking at the empty air as a babe sucks at his mother's breast.

The eighth Lady Frey stood beside Lord Walder's high seat. At his feet sat a somewhat younger version of himself, a stooped thin man of fifty whose costly garb of blue wool and grey satin was strangely accented by a crown and collar ornamented with tiny brass bells. The likeness between him and his lord was striking, save for their eyes; Lord Frey's small, dim, and suspicious, the other's large, amiable, and vacant. Catelyn recalled that one of Lord Walder's brood had fathered a halfwit long years ago. During past visits, the Lord of the Crossing had always taken care to hide this one away. *Did he always wear a fool's crown, or is that meant as mockery of Robb?* It was a question she dare not ask.

Frey sons, daughters, children, grandchildren, husbands, wives, and servants crowded the rest of the hall. But it was the old man who spoke. "You will forgive me if I do not kneel, I know. My legs no longer work as they did, though that which hangs between 'em serves well enough, *heh*." His mouth split in a toothless smile as he eyed Robb's crown. "Some would say it's a poor king who crowns himself with bronze, Your Grace."

"Bronze and iron are stronger than gold and silver," Robb answered. "The old Kings of Winter wore such a sword-crown."

"Small good it did them when the dragons came. *Heh*." That *heh* seemed to please the lackwit, who bobbed his head from side to side, jingling crown and collar. "Sire," Lord Walder said, "forgive my Aegon the noise. He has less wits than a crannogman, and he's never met a king before. One of Stevron's boys. We call him Jinglebell."

"Ser Stevron mentioned him, my lord." Robb smiled at the lackwit. "Well met, Aegon. Your father was a brave man."

Jinglebell jingled his bells. A thin line of spit ran from one corner of his mouth when he smiled.

"Save your royal breath. You'd do as well talking to a chamberpot." Lord Walder shifted his gaze to the others. "Well, Lady Catelyn, I see you have returned to us. And young Ser Edmure, the victor of the Stone Mill. Lord Tully now, I'll need to remember that. You're the fifth Lord Tully I've known. I outlived the other four, *heh*. Your bride's about here somewhere. I suppose you want a look at her."

"I would, my lord."

"Then you'll have it. But clothed. She's a modest girl, and a maid. You won't see her naked till the bedding." Lord Walder cackled. "*Heh*. Soon enough, soon enough." He craned his head about. "Benfrey, go fetch your sister. Be quick about it, Lord Tully's come all the way from Riverrun." A young knight in a quartered surcoat bowed and took his leave, and the old man turned back to Robb. "And where's *your* bride, Your Grace? The fair Queen Jeyne. A Westerling of the Crag, I'm told, *heh*."

"I left her at Riverrun, my lord. She was too weary for more travel, as we told Ser Ryman."

"That makes me grievous sad. I wanted to behold her with mine own weak eyes. We all did, *heh*. Isn't that so, my lady?"

Pale wispy Lady Frey seemed startled that she would be called upon to speak. "Y-yes, my lord. We all so wanted to pay homage to Queen Jeyne. She must be fair to look on."

"She is most fair, my lady." There was an icy stillness in Robb's voice that reminded Catelyn of his father.

The old man either did not hear it or refused to pay it any heed. "Fairer than my own get, *heh*? Elsewise how could her face and form have made the King's Grace forget his solemn promise."

Robb suffered the rebuke with dignity. "No words can set that right, I know, but I have come to make my apologies for the wrong I did your House, and to beg for your forgiveness, my lord."

"Apologies, *heh*. Yes, you vowed to make one, I recall. I'm old, but I don't forget such things. Not like some kings, it seems. The young remember nothing when they see a pretty face and a nice firm pair of teats, isn't that so? I was the same. Some might say I still am, *heh heh*. They'd be wrong, though, wrong as you were. But now you're here to make amends. It was my girls you spurned, though. Mayhaps it's them should hear you beg for pardon, Your Grace. My maiden girls. Here, have a look at them." When he waggled his fingers, a flurry of femininity left their places by the walls to line up beneath the dais. Jinglebell started to rise as well, his bells ringing merrily, but Lady Frey grabbed the lackwit's sleeve and tugged him back down.

Lord Walder named the names. "My daughter Arwyn," he said of a girl of fourteen. "Shirei, my youngest trueborn daughter. Ami and Marianne are granddaughters. I married Ami to Ser Pate of Sevenstreams, but the Mountain killed the oaf so I got her back. That's a Cersei, but we call her Little Bee, her mother's a Beesbury. More granddaughters. One's a Walda, and the others . . . well, they have names, whatever they are . . ."

"I'm Merry, Lord Grandfather," one girl said.

"You're noisy, that's for certain. Next to Noisy is my daughter Tyta. Then another Walda. Alyx, Marissa . . . are you Marissa? I thought you were. She's not always bald. The maester shaved her hair off, but he swears it will soon grow back. The twins are Serra and Sarra." He squinted down at one of the younger girls. "*Heh*, are you another Walda?"

The girl could not have been more than four. "I'm Ser Aemon Rivers's Walda, lord great grandfather." She curtsied.

"How long have you been talking? Not that you're like to have anything sensible to say, your father never did. He's a bastard's son besides, *heh*. Go away, I wanted only Freys up here. The King in the North has no interest in base stock." Lord Walder glanced to Robb, as Jinglebell bobbed his head and chimed. "There they are, all maidens. Well, and one widow, but there's some who like a woman broken in. You might have had any one of them."

"It would have been an impossible choice, my lord," said Robb with careful courtesy. "They're all too lovely."

Lord Walder snorted. "And they say *my* eyes are bad. Some will do well enough, I suppose. Others . . . well, it makes no matter. They weren't good enough for the King in the North, *heh*. Now what is it you have to say?"

"My ladies." Robb looked desperately uncomfortable, but he had known this moment must come, and he faced it without flinching. "All men should keep their word, kings most of all. I was pledged to marry one of you and I broke that vow. The fault is not in you. What I did was not done to slight you, but because I loved another. No words can set it right, I know, yet I come before you to ask forgiveness, that the Freys of the Crossing and the Starks of Winterfell may once again be friends."

The smaller girls fidgeted anxiously. Their older sisters waited for Lord Walder on his black oak throne. Jinglebell rocked back and forth, bells chiming on collar and crown.

"Good," the Lord of the Crossing said. "That was very good, Your Grace. 'No words can set it right,' *heh*. Well said, well said. At the wedding feast I hope you will not refuse to dance with my daughters. It would please an old man's heart, *heh*." He bobbed his wrinkled pink head up and down, in much the same way his lackwit grandson did, though Lord Walder wore no bells. "And here she is, Lord Edmure. My daughter Roslin, my most precious little blossom, *heh*."

Ser Benfrey led her into the hall. They looked enough alike to be full siblings. Judging from their age, both were children of the sixth Lady Frey; a Rosby, Catelyn seemed to recall.

Roslin was small for her years, her skin as white as if she had just risen from a milk bath. Her face was comely, with a small chin, delicate nose, and big brown eyes. Thick chestnut hair fell in loose waves to a waist so tiny that Edmure would be able to put his hands around it. Beneath the lacy bodice of her pale blue gown, her breasts looked small but shapely.

"Your Grace." The girl went to her knees. "Lord Edmure, I hope I am not a disappointment to you."

Far from it, thought Catelyn. Her brother's face had lit up at the sight of her. "You are a delight to me, my lady," Edmure said. "And ever will be, I know."

Roslin had a small gap between two of her front teeth that made her shy with her smiles, but the flaw was almost endearing. *Pretty enough*, Catelyn thought, *but so small, and she comes of Rosby stock*. The Rosbys had never been robust. She much preferred the frames of some of the older girls in the hall; daughters or granddaughters, she could not be sure. They had a Crakehall look about them, and Lord Walder's third wife had been of that House. *Wide hips to bear children, big breasts to nurse them, strong arms to carry them. The Crakehalls have always been a big-boned family, and strong.*

"My lord is kind," the Lady Roslin said to Edmure.

"My lady is beautiful." Edmure took her hand and drew her to her feet. "But why are you crying?"

"For joy," Roslin said. "I weep for joy, my lord."

"*Enough,*" Lord Walder broke in. "You may weep and whisper after you're wed, *heh.* Benfrey, see your sister back to her chambers, she has a wedding to prepare for. And a bedding, *heh,* the sweetest part. For all, for all." His mouth moved in and out. "We'll have music, such sweet music, and wine, *heh,* the red will run, and we'll put some wrongs aright. But now you're weary, and wet as well, dripping on my floor. There's fires waiting for you, and hot mulled wine, and baths if you want 'em. Lothar, show our guests to their quarters."

"I need to see my men across the river, my lord," Robb said.

"They shan't get lost," Lord Walder complained. "They've crossed before, haven't they? When you came down from the north. You wanted crossing and I gave it to you, and you never said mayhaps, *heh.* But suit yourself. Lead each man across by the hand if you like, it's naught to me."

"*My lord!*" Catelyn had almost forgotten. "Some food would be most welcome. We have ridden many leagues in the rain."

Walder Frey's mouth moved in and out. "Food, *heh.* A loaf of bread, a bite of cheese, mayhaps a sausage."

"Some wine to wash it down," Robb said. "And salt."

"Bread and salt. *Heh.* Of course, of course." The old man clapped his hands together, and servants came into the hall, bearing flagons of wine and trays of bread, cheese, and butter. Lord Walder took a cup of red himself, and raised it high with a spotted hand. "My guests," he said. "My honored guests. Be welcome beneath my roof, and at my table."

"We thank you for your hospitality, my lord," Robb replied. Edmure echoed him, along with the Greatjon, Ser Marq Piper, and the others. They drank his wine and ate his bread and butter. Catelyn tasted the wine and nibbled at some bread, and felt much the better for it. *Now we should be safe,* she thought.

Knowing how petty the old man could be, she had expected their rooms to be bleak and cheerless. But the Freys had made more than ample provision for them, it seemed. The bridal chamber was large and richly appointed, dominated by a great featherbed with corner posts carved in the likeness of castle towers. Its draperies were Tully red and blue, a nice courtesy. Sweet-smelling carpets covered a plank floor, and a tall shuttered window opened to the south. Catelyn's own room was smaller, but handsomely furnished and comfortable, with a fire burning in the hearth. Lame Lothar assured them that Robb would have an entire suite, as befit a king. "If there is anything you require, you need only tell one of the guards." He bowed and withdrew, limping heavily as he made his way down the curving steps.

"We should post our own guards," Catelyn told her brother. She would rest easier with Stark and Tully men outside her door. The audience with

Lord Walder had not been as painful as she feared, yet all the same she would be glad to be done with this. *A few more days, and Robb will be off to battle, and me to a comfortable captivity at Seagard.* Lord Jason would show her every courtesy, she had no doubt, but the prospect still depressed her.

She could hear the sounds of horses below as the long column of mounted men wound their way across the bridge from castle to castle. The stones rumbled to the passage of heavy-laden wayns. Catelyn went to the window and gazed out, to watch Robb's host emerge from the eastern twin. "The rain seems to be lessening."

"Now that we're inside." Edmure stood before the fire, letting the warmth wash over him. "What did you make of Roslin?"

Too small and delicate. Childbirth will go hard on her. But her brother seemed well pleased with the girl, so all she said was, "Sweet."

"I believe she liked me. Why was she crying?"

"She's a maid on the eve of her wedding. A few tears are to be expected." Lysa had wept lakes the morning of their own wedding, though she had managed to be dry-eyed and radiant when Jon Arryn swept his cream-and-blue cloak about her shoulders.

"She's prettier than I dared hope." Edmure raised a hand before she could speak. "I know there are more important things, spare me the sermon, septa. Even so . . . did you see some of those other maids Frey trotted out? The one with the twitch? Was that the shaking sickness? And those twins had more craters and eruptions on their faces than Petyr Pimple. When I saw that lot, I knew Roslin would be bald and one-eyed, with Jinglebell's wits and Black Walder's temper. But she seems gentle as well as fair." He looked perplexed. "Why would the old weasel refuse to let me choose unless he meant to foist off someone hideous?"

"Your fondness for a pretty face is well known," Catelyn reminded him. "Perhaps Lord Walder actually wants you to be happy with your bride." *Or more like, he did not want you balking over a boil and upsetting all his plans.* "Or it may be that Roslin is the old man's favorite. The Lord of Riverrun is a much better match than most of his daughters can hope for."

"True." Her brother still seemed uncertain, however. "Is it possible the girl is barren?"

"Lord Walder wants his grandson to inherit Riverrun. How would it serve him to give you a barren wife?"

"It rids him of a daughter no one else would take."

"Small good that will do him. Walder Frey is a peevish man, not a stupid one."

"Still . . . it *is* possible?"

"Yes," Catelyn conceded, reluctantly. "There are illnesses a girl can have in childhood that leave her unable to conceive. There's no reason to believe that Lady Roslin was so afflicted, though." She looked round the room. "The Freys have received us more kindly than I had anticipated, if truth be told."

Edmure laughed. "A few barbed words and some unseemly gloating. From him that's courtesy. I expected the old weasel to piss in our wine and make us praise the vintage."

The jest left Catelyn strangely disquieted. "If you will excuse me, I should change from these wet clothes.

"As you wish." Edmure yawned. "I may nap an hour."

She retreated to her own room. The chest of clothes she'd brought from Riverrun had been carried up and laid at the foot of the bed. After she'd undressed and hung her wet clothing by the fire, she donned a warm wool dress of Tully red and blue, washed and brushed her hair and let it dry, and went in search of Freys.

Lord Walder's black oak throne was empty when she entered the hall, but some of his sons were drinking by the fire. Lame Lothar rose clumsily when he saw her. "Lady Catelyn, I thought you would be resting. How may I be of service?"

"Are these your brothers?" she asked.

"Brothers, half-brothers, good brothers, and nephews. Raymund and I shared a mother. Lord Lucias Vypren is my half-sister Lythene's husband, and Ser Damon is their son. My half-brother Ser Hosteen I believe you know. And this is Ser Leslyn Haigh and his sons, Ser Harys and Ser Donnel."

"Well met, sers. Is Ser Perwyn about? He helped escort me to Storm's End and back, when Robb sent me to speak with Lord Renly. I was looking forward to seeing him again."

"Perwyn is away," Lame Lothar said. "I shall give him your regards. I know he will regret having missed you."

"Surely he will return in time for Lady Roslin's wedding?"

"He had hoped to," said Lame Lothar, "but with this rain . . . you saw how the rivers ran, my lady."

"I did indeed," said Catelyn. "I wonder if you would be so good as to direct me to your maester?"

"Are you unwell, my lady?" asked Ser Hosteen, a powerful man with a square strong jaw.

"A woman's complaint. Nothing to concern you, ser."

Lothar, ever gracious, escorted her from the hall, up some steps, and across a covered bridge to another stair. "You should find Maester Brenett in the turret on the top, my lady."

Catelyn half expected that the maester would be yet another son of Walder Frey's, but Brenett did not have the look. He was a great fat man, bald and double-chinned and none too clean, to judge from the raven droppings that stained the sleeves of his robes, yet he seemed amiable enough. When she told him of Edmure's concerns about Lady Roslin's fertility, he chuckled. "Your lord brother need have no fear, Lady Catelyn. She's small, I'll grant you, and narrow in the hips, but her mother was the same, and Lady Bethany gave Lord Walder a child every year."

"How many lived past infancy?" she asked bluntly.

"Five." He ticked them off on fingers plump as sausages. "Ser Perwyn. Ser Benfrey. Maester Willamen, who took his vows last year and now serves Lord Hunter in the Vale. Olyvar, who squired for your son. And Lady Roslin, the youngest. Four boys to one girl. Lord Edmure will have more sons than he knows what to do with."

"I am sure that will please him." So the girl was like to be fertile as well as fair of face. *That should put Edmure's mind at ease.* Lord Walder had left her brother no cause for complaint, so far as she could see.

Catelyn did not return to her own room after leaving the maester; instead she went to Robb. She found Robin Flint and Ser Wendel Manderly with him, along with the Greatjon and his son, who was still called the Smalljon though he threatened to overtop his father. They were all damp. Another man, still wetter, stood before the fire in a pale pink cloak trimmed with white fur. "Lord Bolton," she said.

"Lady Catelyn," he replied, his voice faint, "it is a pleasure to look on you again, even in such trying times."

"You are kind to say so." Catelyn could feel gloom in the room. Even the Greatjon seemed somber and subdued. She looked at their grim faces and said, "What's happened?"

"Lannisters on the Trident," said Ser Wendel unhappily. "My brother is taken again."

"And Lord Bolton has brought us further word of Winterfell," Robb added. "Ser Rodrik was not the only good man to die. Cley Cerwyn and Leobald Tallhart were slain as well."

"Cley Cerwyn was only a boy," she said, saddened. "Is this true, then? All dead, and Winterfell gone?"

Bolton's pale eyes met her own. "The ironmen burned both castle and winter town. Some of your people were taken back to the Dreadfort by my son, Ramsay."

"Your bastard was accused of grievous crimes," Catelyn reminded him sharply. "Of murder, rape, and worse."

"Yes," Roose Bolton said. "His blood is tainted, that cannot be denied. Yet he is a good fighter, as cunning as he is fearless. When the ironmen cut down Ser Rodrik, and Leobald Tallhart soon after, it fell to Ramsay to lead the battle, and he did. He swears that he shall not sheathe his sword so long as a single Greyjoy remains in the north. Perhaps such

service might atone in some small measure for whatever crimes his bastard blood has led him to commit." He shrugged. "Or not. When the war
is done, His Grace must weigh and judge. By then I hope to have a
trueborn son by Lady Walda."

This is a cold man, Catelyn realized, not for the first time.

"Did Ramsay mention Theon Greyjoy?" Robb demanded. "Was he
slain as well, or did he flee?"

Roose Bolton removed a ragged strip of leather from the pouch at his
belt. "My son sent this with his letter."

Ser Wendel turned his fat face away. Robin Flint and Smalljon Umber
exchanged a look, and the Greatjon snorted like a bull. "Is that . . . skin?"
said Robb.

"The skin from the little finger of Theon Greyjoy's left hand. My son
is cruel, I confess it. And yet . . . what is a little skin, against the lives
of two young princes? You were their mother, my lady. May I offer you
this . . . small token of revenge?"

Part of Catelyn wanted to clutch the grisly trophy to her heart, but
she made herself resist. "Put it away. Please."

"Flaying Theon will not bring my brothers back," Robb said. "I want
his head, not his skin."

"He is Balon Greyjoy's only living son," Lord Bolton said softly, as if
they had forgotten, "and now rightful King of the Iron Islands. A captive
king has great value as a hostage."

"Hostage?" The word raised Catelyn's hackles. Hostages were oft
exchanged. "Lord Bolton, I hope you are not suggesting that we *free* the
man who killed my sons."

"Whoever wins the Seastone Chair will want Theon Greyjoy dead,"
Bolton pointed out. "Even in chains, he has a better claim than any of
his uncles. Hold him, I say, and demand concessions from the ironborn
as the price of his execution."

Robb considered that reluctantly, but in the end he nodded. "Yes. Very
well. Keep him alive, then. For the present. Hold him secure at the
Dreadfort till we've retaken the north."

Catelyn turned back to Roose Bolton. "Ser Wendel said something of
Lannisters on the Trident?"

"He did, my lady. I blame myself. I delayed too long before leaving
Harrenhal. Aenys Frey departed several days before me and crossed the
Trident at the ruby ford, though not without difficulty. But by the time
we came up the river was a torrent. I had no choice but to ferry my men
across in small boats, of which we had too few. Two-thirds of my strength
was on the north side when the Lannisters attacked those still waiting
to cross. Norrey, Locke, and Burley men chiefly, with Ser Wylis Manderly
and his White Harbor knights as rear guard. I was on the wrong side of

the Trident, powerless to help them. Ser Wylis rallied our men as best he could, but Gregor Clegane attacked with heavy horse and drove them into the river. As many drowned as were cut down. More fled, and the rest were taken captive."

Gregor Clegane was always ill news, Catelyn reflected. Would Robb need to march south again to deal with him? Or was the Mountain coming here? "Is Clegane across the river, then?"

"No." Bolton's voice was soft, but certain. "I left six hundred men at the ford. Spearmen from the rills, the mountains, and the White Knife, a hundred Hornwood longbows, some freeriders and hedge knights, and a strong force of Stout and Cerwyn men to stiffen them. Ronnel Stout and Ser Kyle Condon have the command. Ser Kyle was the late Lord Cerwyn's right hand, as I'm sure you know, my lady. Lions swim no better than wolves. So long as the river runs high, Ser Gregor will not cross."

"The last thing we need is the Mountain at our backs when we start up the causeway," said Robb. "You did well, my lord."

"Your Grace is too kind. I suffered grievous losses on the Green Fork, and Glover and Tallhart worse at Duskendale."

"*Duskendale.*" Robb made the word a curse. "Robett Glover will answer for that when I see him, I promise you."

"A folly," Lord Bolton agreed, "but Glover was heedless after he learned that Deepwood Motte had fallen. Grief and fear will do that to a man."

Duskendale was done and cold; it was the battles still to come that worried Catelyn. "How many men have you brought my son?" she asked Roose Bolton pointedly.

His queer colorless eyes studied her face a moment before he answered. "Some five hundred horse and three thousand foot, my lady. Dreadfort men, in chief, and some from Karhold. With the loyalty of the Karstarks so doubtful now, I thought it best to keep them close. I regret there are not more."

"It should be enough," said Robb. "You will have command of my rear guard, Lord Bolton. I mean to start for the Neck as soon as my uncle has been wedded and bedded. We're going home."

ARYA

The outriders came on them an hour from the Green Fork, as the wayn was slogging down a muddy road.

"Keep your head down and your mouth shut," the Hound warned her as the three spurred toward them; a knight and two squires, lightly armored and mounted on fast palfreys. Clegane cracked his whip at the team, a pair of old drays that had known better days. The wayn was creaking and swaying, its two huge wooden wheels squeezing mud up out of the deep ruts in the road with every turn. Stranger followed, tied to the wagon.

The big bad-tempered courser wore neither armor, barding, nor harness, and the Hound himself was garbed in splotchy green roughspun and a soot-grey mantle with a hood that swallowed his head. So long as he kept his eyes down you could not see his face, only the whites of his eyes peering out. He looked like some down-at-heels farmer. A *big* farmer, though. And under the roughspun was boiled leather and oiled mail, Arya knew. She looked like a farmer's son, or maybe a swineherd. And behind them were four squat casks of salt pork and one of pickled pigs' feet.

The riders split and circled them for a look before they came up close. Clegane drew the wayn to a halt and waited patiently on their pleasure. The knight bore spear and sword while his squires carried longbows. The badges on their jerkins were smaller versions of the sigil sewn on their master's surcoat; a black pitchfork on a golden bar sinister, upon a russet field. Arya had thought of revealing herself to the first outriders they encountered, but she had always pictured grey-cloaked men with the direwolf on their breasts. She might have risked it even if they'd worn the Umber giant or the Glover fist, but she did not know this pitchfork knight or whom he served. The closest thing to a pitchfork she had ever seen at Winterfell was the trident in the hand of Lord Manderly's merman.

"You have business at the Twins?" the knight asked.

"Salt pork for the wedding feast, if it please you, ser." The Hound mumbled his reply, his eyes down, his face hidden.

"Salt pork never pleases me." The pitchfork knight gave Clegane only the most cursory glance, and paid no attention at all to Arya, but he looked long and hard at Stranger. The stallion was no plow horse, that was plain at a glance. One of the squires almost wound up in the mud when the big black courser bit at his own mount. "How did you come by this beast?" the pitchfork knight demanded.

"M'lady told me to bring him, ser," Clegane said humbly. "He's a wedding gift for young Lord Tully."

"What lady? Who is it you serve?"

"Old Lady Whent, ser."

"Does she think she can buy Harrenhal back with a horse?" the knight asked. "Gods, is there any fool like an old fool?" Yet he waved them down the road. "Go on with you, then."

"Aye, m'lord." The Hound snapped his whip again, and the old drays resumed their weary trek. The wheels had settled deep into the mud during the halt, and it took several moments for the team to pull them free again. By then the outriders were riding off. Clegane gave them one last look and snorted. "Ser Donnel Haigh," he said. "I've taken more horses off him than I can count. Armor as well. Once I near killed him in a mêlée."

"How come he didn't know you, then?" Arya asked.

"Because knights are fools, and it would have been beneath him to look twice at some poxy peasant." He gave the horses a lick with the whip. "Keep your eyes down and your tone respectful and say *ser* a lot, and most knights will never see you. They pay more mind to horses than to smallfolk. He might have known Stranger if he'd ever seen me ride him."

He would have known your face, though. Arya had no doubt of that. Sandor Clegane's burns would not be easy to forget, once you saw them. He couldn't hide the scars behind a helm, either; not so long as the helm was made in the shape of a snarling dog.

That was why they'd needed the wayn and the pickled pigs' feet. "I'm not going to be dragged before your brother in chains," the Hound had told her, "and I'd just as soon not have to cut through his men to get to him. So we play a little game."

A farmer chance-met on the kingsroad had provided them with wayn, horses, garb, and casks, though not willingly. The Hound had taken them at swordpoint. When the farmer cursed him for a robber, he said, "No, a forager. Be grateful you get to keep your smallclothes. Now take those boots off. Or I'll take your legs off. Your choice." The farmer was as big as Clegane, but all the same he chose to give up his boots and keep his legs.

Evenfall found them still trudging toward the Green Fork and Lord Frey's twin castles. *I am almost there*, Arya thought. She knew she ought to be excited, but her belly was all knotted up tight. Maybe that was just the fever she'd been fighting, but maybe not. Last night she'd had a bad dream, a *terrible* dream. She couldn't remember what she'd dreamed of now, but the feeling had lingered all day. If anything, it had only gotten stronger. *Fear cuts deeper than swords.* She had to be strong now, the way her father told her. There was nothing between her and her mother but a castle gate, a river, and an army ... but it was *Robb's* army, so there was no real danger there. Was there?

Roose Bolton was one of them, though. The Leech Lord, as the outlaws called him. That made her uneasy. She had fled Harrenhal to get away from Bolton as much as from the Bloody Mummers, and she'd had to cut the throat of one of his guards to escape. Did he know she'd done that? Or did he blame Gendry or Hot Pie? Would he have told her mother? What would he do if he saw her? *He probably won't even know me.* She looked more like a drowned rat than a lord's cupbearer these days. A drowned *boy* rat. The Hound had hacked handfuls of her hair off only two days past. He was an even worse barber than Yoren, and he'd left her half bald on one side. *Robb won't know me either, I bet. Or even Mother.* She had been a little girl the last time she saw them, the day Lord Eddard Stark left Winterfell.

They heard the music before they saw the castle; the distant rattle of drums, the brazen blare of horns, the thin skirling of pipes faint beneath the growl of the river and the sound of the rain beating on their heads. "We've missed the wedding," the Hound said, "but it sounds as though the feast is still going. I'll be rid of you soon."

No, I'll be rid of you, Arya thought.

The road had been running mostly northwest, but now it turned due west between an apple orchard and a field of drowned corn beaten down by the rain. They passed the last of the apple trees and crested a rise, and the castles, river, and camps all appeared at once. There were hundreds of horses and thousands of men, most of them milling about the three huge feast tents that stood side by side facing the castle gates, like three great canvas longhalls. Robb had made his camp well back from the walls, on higher, drier ground, but the Green Fork had overflown its bank and even claimed a few carelessly placed tents.

The music from the castles was louder here. The sound of the drums and horns rolled across the camp. The musicians in the nearer castle were playing a different song than the ones in the castle on the far bank, though, so it sounded more like a battle than a song. "They're not very good," Arya observed.

The Hound made a sound that might have been a laugh. "There's old deaf women in Lannisport complaining of the din, I'll warrant. I'd heard Walder Frey's eyes were failing, but no one mentioned his bloody ears."

Arya found herself wishing it were day. If the sun was out and the wind was blowing, she would have been able to see the banners better. She would have looked for the direwolf of Stark, or maybe the Cerwyn battleaxe or the Glover fist. But in the gloom of night all the colors looked grey. The rain had dwindled down to a fine drizzle, almost a mist, but an earlier downpour had left the banners wet as dishrags, sodden and unreadable.

A hedge of wagons and carts had been drawn up along the perimeter to make a crude wooden wall against any attack. That was where the guards stopped them. The lantern their sergeant carried shed enough light for Arya to see that his cloak was a pale pink, spotted with red teardrops. The men under him had the Leech Lord's badge sewn over their hearts, the flayed man of the Dreadfort. Sandor Clegane gave them the same tale he'd used on the outriders, but the Bolton sergeant was a harder sort of nut than Ser Donnel Haigh had been. "Salt pork's no fit meat for a lord's wedding feast," he said scornfully.

"Got pickled pigs' feet too, ser."

"Not for the feast, you don't. The feast's half done. And I'm a northman, not some milksuck southron knight."

"I was told to see the steward, or the cook . . ."

"Castle's closed. The lordlings are not to be disturbed." The sergeant considered a moment. "You can unload by the feast tents, there." He pointed with a mailed hand. "Ale makes a man hungry, and old Frey won't miss a few pigs' feet. He don't have the teeth for such anyhow. Ask for Sedgekins, he'll know what's to be done with you." He barked a command, and his men rolled one of the wagons aside for them to enter.

The Hound's whip spurred the team toward the tents. No one seemed to pay them any mind. They splashed past rows of brightly colored pavilions, their walls of wet silk lit up like magic lanterns by lamps and braziers inside; pink and gold and green they glimmered, striped and fretty and chequy, emblazoned with birds and beasts, chevrons and stars, wheels and weapons. Arya spotted a yellow tent with six acorns on its panels, three over two over one. *Lord Smallwood*, she knew, remembering Acorn Hall so far away, and the lady who'd said she was pretty.

But for every shimmering silk pavilion there were two dozen of felt

or canvas, opaque and dark. There were barracks tents too, big enough
to shelter two score footsoldiers, though even those were dwarfed by the
three great feast tents. The drinking had been going on for hours, it
seemed. Arya heard shouted toasts and the clash of cups, mixed in with
all the usual camp sounds, horses whinnying and dogs barking, wagons
rumbling through the dark, laughter and curses, the clank and clatter of
steel and wood. The music grew still louder as they approached the castle,
but under that was a deeper, darker sound: the river, the swollen Green
Fork, growling like a lion in its den.

Arya twisted and turned, trying to look everywhere at once, hoping
for a glimpse of a direwolf badge, for a tent done up in grey and white,
for a face she knew from Winterfell. All she saw were strangers. She
stared at a man relieving himself in the reeds, but he wasn't Alebelly.
She saw a half-dressed girl burst from a tent laughing, but the tent was
pale blue, not grey like she'd thought at first, and the man who went
running after her wore a treecat on his doublet, not a wolf. Beneath a
tree, four archers were slipping waxed strings over the notches of their
longbows, but they were not her father's archers. A maester crossed
their path, but he was too young and thin to be Maester Luwin. Arya
gazed up at the Twins, their high tower windows glowing softly wherever
a light was burning. Through the haze of rain, the castles looked spooky
and mysterious, like something from one of Old Nan's tales, but they
weren't Winterfell.

The press was thickest at the feast tents. The wide flaps were tied
back, and men were pushing in and out with drinking horns and tankards
in their hands, some with camp followers. Arya glanced inside as the
Hound drove past the first of the three, and saw hundreds of men crowding
the benches and jostling around the casks of mead and ale and wine.
There was hardly room to move inside, but none of them seemed to
mind. At least they were warm and dry. Cold wet Arya envied them.
Some were even singing. The fine misty rain was steaming all around
the door from the heat escaping from inside. "Here's to Lord Edmure and
Lady Roslin," she heard a voice shout. They all drank, and someone
yelled, "Here's to the Young Wolf and Queen Jeyne."

Who is Queen Jeyne? Arya wondered briefly. The only queen she knew
was Cersei.

Firepits had been dug outside the feast tents, sheltered beneath rude
canopies of woven wood and hides that kept the rain out, so long as it
fell straight down. The wind was blowing off the river, though, so the
drizzle came in anyway, enough to make the fires hiss and swirl. Serving
men were turning joints of meat on spits above the flames. The smells
made Arya's mouth water. "Shouldn't we stop?" she asked Sandor
Clegane. "There's northmen in the tents." She knew them by their

beards, by their faces, by their cloaks of bearskin and sealskin, by their half-heard toasts and the songs they sang; Karstarks and Umbers and men of the mountain clans. "I bet there are Winterfell men too." Her father's men, the Young Wolf's men, the direwolves of Stark.

"Your brother will be in the castle," he said. "Your mother too. You want them or not?"

"Yes," she said. "What about Sedgekins?" The sergeant had told them to ask for Sedgekins.

"Sedgekins can bugger himself with a hot poker." Clegane shook out his whip, and sent it hissing through the soft rain to bite at a horse's flank. "It's your bloody brother I want."

CATELYN

The drums were pounding, pounding, pounding, and her head with them. Pipes wailed and flutes trilled from the musicians' gallery at the foot of the hall; fiddles screeched, horns blew, the skins skirled a lively tune, but the drumming drove them all. The sounds echoed off the rafters, whilst the guests ate, drank, and shouted at one another below. *Walder Frey must be deaf as a stone to call this music.* Catelyn sipped a cup of wine and watched Jinglebell prance to the sounds of "Alysanne." At least she thought it was meant to be "Alysanne." With these players, it might as easily have been "The Bear and the Maiden Fair."

Outside the rain still fell, but within the Twins the air was thick and hot. A fire roared in the hearth and rows of torches burned smokily from iron sconces on the walls. Yet most of the heat came off the bodies of the wedding guests, jammed in so thick along the benches that every man who tried to lift his cup poked his neighbor in the ribs.

Even on the dais they were closer than Catelyn would have liked. She had been placed between Ser Ryman Frey and Roose Bolton, and had gotten a good noseful of both. Ser Ryman drank as if Westeros was about to run short of wine, and sweated it all out under his arms. He had bathed in lemonwater, she judged, but no lemon could mask so much sour sweat. Roose Bolton had a sweeter smell to him, yet no more pleasant. He sipped hippocras in preference to wine or mead, and ate but little.

Catelyn could not fault him for his lack of appetite. The wedding feast began with a thin leek soup, followed by a salad of green beans, onions, and beets, river pike poached in almond milk, mounds of mashed turnips that were cold before they reached the table, jellied calves' brains, and a leche of stringy beef. It was poor fare to set before a king, and the calves' brains turned Catelyn's stomach. Yet Robb ate it uncomplaining, and her brother was too caught up with his bride to pay much attention.

You would never guess Edmure complained of Roslin all the way from Riverrun to the Twins. Husband and wife ate from a single plate, drank from a single cup, and exchanged chaste kisses between sips. Most of the dishes Edmure waved away. She could not blame him for that. She remembered little of the food served at her own wedding feast. *Did I even taste it? Or spend the whole time gazing at Ned's face, wondering who he was?*

Poor Roslin's smile had a fixed quality to it, as if someone had sewn it onto her face. *Well, she is a maid wedded, but the bedding's yet to come. No doubt she's as terrified as I was.* Robb was seated between Alyx Frey and Fair Walda, two of the more nubile Frey maidens. "At the wedding feast I hope you will not refuse to dance with my daughters," Walder Frey had said. "It would please an old man's heart." His heart should be well pleased, then; Robb had done his duty like a king. He had danced with each of the girls, with Edmure's bride and the eighth Lady Frey, with the widow Ami and Roose Bolton's wife Fat Walda, with the pimply twins Serra and Sarra, even with Shirei, Lord Walder's youngest, who must have been all of six. Catelyn wondered whether the Lord of the Crossing would be satisfied, or if he would find cause for complaint in all the other daughters and granddaughters who had not had a turn with the king. "Your sisters dance very well," she said to Ser Ryman Frey, trying to be pleasant.

"They're aunts and cousins." Ser Ryman drank a swallow of wine, the sweat trickling down his cheek into his beard.

A sour man, and in his cups, Catelyn thought. The Late Lord Frey might be niggardly when it came to feeding his guests, but he did not stint on the drink. The ale, wine, and mead were flowing as fast as the river outside. The Greatjon was already roaring drunk. Lord Walder's son Merrett was matching him cup for cup, but Ser Whalen Frey had passed out trying to keep up with the two of them. Catelyn would sooner Lord Umber had seen fit to stay sober, but telling the Greatjon not to drink was like telling him not to breathe for a few hours.

Smalljon Umber and Robin Flint sat near Robb, to the other side of Fair Walda and Alyx, respectively. Neither of them was drinking; along with Patrek Mallister and Dacey Mormont, they were her son's guards this evening. A wedding feast was not a battle, but there were always dangers when men were in their cups, and a king should never be unguarded. Catelyn was glad of that, and even more glad of the swordbelts hanging on pegs along the walls. *No man needs a longsword to deal with jellied calves' brains.*

"Everyone thought my lord would choose Fair Walda," Lady Walda Bolton told Ser Wendel, shouting to be heard above the music. Fat Walda was a round pink butterball of a girl with watery blue eyes, limp yellow hair, and a huge bosom, yet her voice was a fluttering squeak. It was hard to picture her in the Dreadfort in her pink lace and cape of vair. "My lord grandfather offered Roose his bride's weight in silver as a dowry, though, so my lord of Bolton picked *me*." The girl's chins jiggled when she laughed. "I weigh six stone more than Fair Walda, but that was the first time I was glad of it. I'm Lady Bolton now and my cousin's still a maid, and she'll be *nineteen* soon, poor thing."

The Lord of the Dreadfort paid the chatter no mind, Catelyn saw. Sometimes he tasted a bite of this, a spoon of that, tearing bread from the loaf with short strong fingers, but the meal could not distract him. Bolton had made a toast to Lord Walder's grandsons when the wedding feast began, pointedly mentioning that Walder and Walder were in the care of his bastard son. From the way the old man had squinted at him, his mouth sucking at the air, Catelyn knew he had heard the unspoken threat.

Was there ever a wedding less joyful? she wondered, until she remembered her poor Sansa and her marriage to the Imp. *Mother take mercy on her. She has a gentle soul.* The heat and smoke and noise were making her sick. The musicians in the gallery might be numerous and loud, but they were not especially gifted. Catelyn took another swallow of wine and allowed a page to refill her cup. *A few more hours, and the worst will be over.* By this hour tomorrow Robb would be off to another battle, this time with the ironmen at Moat Cailin. Strange, how that prospect seemed almost a relief. *He will win his battle. He wins all his battles, and the ironborn are without a king. Besides, Ned taught him well.* The drums were pounding. Jinglebell hopped past her once again, but the music was so loud she could scarcely hear his bells.

Above the din came a sudden snarling as two dogs fell upon each other over a scrap of meat. They rolled across the floor, snapping and biting, as a howl of mirth went up. Someone doused them with a flagon of ale and they broke apart. One limped toward the dais. Lord Walder's toothless mouth opened in a bark of laughter as the dripping wet dog shook ale and hair all over three of his grandsons.

The sight of the dogs made Catelyn wish once more for Grey Wind, but Robb's direwolf was nowhere to be seen. Lord Walder had refused to allow him in the hall. "Your wild beast has a taste for human flesh, I hear, *heh*," the old man had said. "Rips out throats, yes. I'll have no such creature at my Roslin's feast, amongst women and little ones, all my sweet innocents."

"Grey Wind is no danger to them, my lord," Robb protested. "Not so long as I am there."

"You were there at my gates, were you not? When the wolf attacked the grandsons I sent to greet you? I heard all about that, don't think I didn't, *heh*."

"No harm was done –"

"No harm, the king says? No harm? Petyr fell from his horse, *fell*. I lost a wife the same way, falling." His mouth worked in and out. "Or was she just some strumpet? Bastard Walder's mother, yes, now I recall. She fell off her horse and cracked her head. What would Your Grace do if Petyr had broken his neck, *heh*? Give me another apology in place of a grandson? No, no, no. Might be you're king, I won't say you're not, the King in the North, *heh*, but under my roof, my rule. Have your wolf or have your wedding, sire. You'll not have both."

Catelyn could tell that her son was furious, but he yielded with as much courtesy as he could summon. *If it pleases Lord Walder to serve me stewed crow smothered in maggots,* he'd told her, *I'll eat it and ask for a second bowl.* And so he had.

The Greatjon had drunk another of Lord Walder's brood under the table, Petyr Pimple this time. *The lad has a third his capacity, what did he expect?* Lord Umber wiped his mouth, stood, and began to sing. *"A bear there was, a bear, a BEAR! All black and brown and covered with hair!"* His voice was not at all bad, though somewhat thick from drink. Unfortunately the fiddlers and drummers and flutists up above were playing "Flowers of Spring," which suited the words of "The Bear and the Maiden Fair" as well as snails might suit a bowl of porridge. Even poor Jinglebell covered his ears at the cacophony.

Roose Bolton murmured some words too soft to hear and went off in search of a privy. The cramped hall was in a constant uproar of guests and servants coming and going. A second feast, for knights and lords of somewhat lesser rank, was roaring along in the other castle, she knew. Lord Walder had exiled his baseborn children and their offspring to that side of the river, so that Robb's northmen had taken to referring to it as "the bastard feast." Some guests were no doubt stealing off to see if the bastards were having a better time than they were. Some might even be venturing as far as the camps. The Freys had provided wagons of wine, ale, and mead, so the common soldiers could drink to the wedding of Riverrun and the Twins.

Robb sat down in Bolton's vacant place. "A few more hours and this farce is done, Mother," he said in a low voice, as the Greatjon sang of the maid with honey in her hair. "Black Walder's been mild as a lamb for once. And Uncle Edmure seems well content in his bride." He leaned across her. "Ser Ryman?"

Ser Ryman Frey blinked and said, "Sire. Yes?"

"I'd hoped to ask Olyvar to squire for me when we march north," said Robb, "but I do not see him here. Would he be at the other feast?"

"Olyvar?" Ser Ryman shook his head. "No. Not Olyvar. Gone . . . gone from the castles. Duty."

"I see." Robb's tone suggested otherwise. When Ser Ryman offered nothing more, the king got to his feet again. "Would you care for a dance, Mother?"

"Thank you, but no." A dance was the last thing she needed, the way her head was throbbing. "No doubt one of Lord Walder's daughters would be pleased to partner you."

"Oh, no doubt." His smile was resigned.

The musicians were playing "Iron Lances" by then, while the Greatjon sang "The Lusty Lad." *Someone should acquaint them with each other, it might improve the harmony.* Catelyn turned back to Ser Ryman. "I had heard that one of your cousins was a singer."

"Alesander. Symond's son. Alyx is his sister." He raised a cup toward where she danced with Robin Flint.

"Will Alesander be playing for us tonight?"

Ser Ryman squinted at her. "Not him. He's away." He wiped sweat from his brow and lurched to his feet. "Pardons, my lady. Pardons." Catelyn watched him stagger toward the door.

Edmure was kissing Roslin and squeezing her hand. Elsewhere in the hall, Ser Marq Piper and Ser Danwell Frey played a drinking game, Lame Lothar said something amusing to Ser Hosteen, one of the younger Freys juggled three daggers for a group of giggly girls, and Jinglebell sat on the floor sucking wine off his fingers. The servers were bringing out huge silver platters piled high with cuts of juicy pink lamb, the most appetizing dish they'd seen all evening. And Robb was leading Dacey Mormont in a dance.

When she wore a dress in place of a hauberk, Lady Maege's eldest daughter was quite pretty; tall and willowy, with a shy smile that made her long face light up. It was pleasant to see that she could be as graceful on the dance floor as in the training yard. Catelyn wondered if Lady Maege had reached the Neck as yet. She had taken her other daughters with her, but as one of Robb's battle companions Dacey had chosen to remain by his side. *He has Ned's gift for inspiring loyalty.* Olyvar Frey had been devoted to her son as well. Hadn't Robb said that Olyvar wanted to remain with him even *after* he'd married Jeyne?

Seated betwixt his black oak towers, the Lord of the Crossing clapped his spotted hands together. The noise they made was so faint that even those on the dais scarce heard it, but Ser Aenys and Ser Hosteen saw and began to pound their cups on the table. Lame Lothar joined them, then Marq Piper and Ser Danwell and Ser Raymund. Half the guests were soon pounding. Finally even the mob of musicians in the gallery took note. The piping, drumming, and fiddling trailed off into quiet.

"Your Grace," Lord Walder called out to Robb, "the septon has prayed his prayers, some words have been said, and Lord Edmure's wrapped my sweetling in a fish cloak, but they are not yet man and wife. A sword needs a sheath, *heh*, and a wedding needs a bedding. What does my sire say? Is it meet that we should bed them?"

A score or more of Walder Frey's sons and grandsons began to bang their cups again, shouting, "To bed! To bed! *To bed with them!*" Roslin had gone white. Catelyn wondered whether it was the prospect of losing her maidenhead that frightened the girl, or the bedding itself. With so many siblings, she was not like to be a stranger to the custom, but it was different when you were the one being bedded. On Catelyn's own wedding night, Jory Cassell had torn her gown in his haste to get her out of it, and drunken Desmond Grell kept apologizing for every bawdy joke, only to make another. When Lord Dustin had beheld her naked, he'd told Ned that her breasts were enough to make him wish he'd never been weaned. *Poor man*, she thought. He had ridden south with Ned, never to return. Catelyn wondered how many of the men here tonight would be dead before the year was done. *Too many, I fear.*

Robb raised a hand. "If you think the time is meet, Lord Walder, by all means let us bed them."

A roar of approval greeted his pronouncement. Up in the gallery the musicians took up their pipes and horns and fiddles again, and began to play "The Queen Took Off Her Sandal, the King Took Off His Crown." Jinglebell hopped from foot to foot, his own crown ringing. "I hear Tully men have trout between their legs instead of cocks," Alyx Frey called out boldly. "Does it take a worm to make them rise?" To which Ser Marq Piper threw back, "*I* hear that Frey women have two gates in place of one!" and Alyx said, "Aye, but both are closed and barred to little things like you!" A gust of laughter followed, until Patrek Mallister climbed up onto a table to propose a toast to Edmure's one-eyed fish. "And a mighty pike it is!" he proclaimed. "Nay, I'll wager it's a minnow," Fat Walda Bolton shouted out from Catelyn's side. Then the general cry of *"Bed them! Bed them!"* went up again.

The guests swarmed the dais, the drunkest in the forefront as ever. The men and boys surrounded Roslin and lifted her into the air whilst the maids and mothers in the hall pulled Edmure to his feet and began tugging at his clothing. He was laughing and shouting bawdy jokes back at them, though the music was too loud for Catelyn to hear. She heard the Greatjon, though. "Give this little bride to me," he bellowed as he shoved through the other men and threw Roslin over one shoulder. "Look at this little thing! No meat on her at all!"

Catelyn felt sorry for the girl. Most brides tried to return the banter, or at least pretended to enjoy it, but Roslin was stiff with terror, clutching the Greatjon as if she feared he might drop her. *She's crying too*, Catelyn realized as she watched Ser Marq Piper pull off one of the bride's shoes. *I hope Edmure is gentle with the poor child.* Jolly, bawdy music still poured down from the gallery; the queen was taking off her kirtle now, and the king his tunic.

She knew she should join the throng of women round her brother, but she would only ruin their fun. The last thing she felt just now was bawdy. Edmure would forgive her absence, she did not doubt; much jollier to be stripped and bedded by a score of lusty, laughing Freys than by a sour, stricken sister.

As man and maid were carried from the hall, a trail of clothing behind them, Catelyn saw that Robb had also remained. Walder Frey was prickly enough to see some insult to his daughter in that. *He should join in Roslin's bedding, but is it my place to tell him so?* She tensed, until she saw that others had stayed as well. Petyr Pimple and Ser Whalen Frey slept on, their heads on the table. Merrett Frey poured himself another cup of wine, while Jinglebell wandered about stealing bites off the plates of those who'd left. Ser Wendel Manderly was lustily attacking a leg of lamb. And of course Lord Walder was far too feeble to leave his seat without help. *He will expect Robb to go, though.* She could almost hear the old man asking why His Grace did not want to see his daughter naked. The drums were pounding again, pounding and pounding and pounding.

Dacey Mormont, who seemed to be the only woman left in the hall besides Catelyn, stepped up behind Edwyn Frey, and touched him lightly on the arm as she said something in his ear. Edwyn wrenched himself away from her with unseemly violence. "No," he said, too loudly. "I'm done with dancing for the nonce." Dacey paled and turned away. Catelyn got slowly to her feet. *What just happened there?* Doubt gripped her heart, where an instant before had been only weariness. *It is nothing,* she tried to tell herself, *you are seeing grumkins in the woodpile, you are become an old silly woman sick with grief and fear.* But something must have shown on her face. Even Ser Wendel Manderly took note. "Is something amiss?" he asked, the leg of lamb in his hands.

She did not answer him. Instead she went after Edwyn Frey. The players in the gallery had finally gotten both king and queen down to their name-day suits. With scarcely a moment's respite, they began to play a very different sort of song. No one sang the words, but Catelyn knew "The Rains of Castamere" when she heard it. Edwyn was hurrying toward a door. She hurried faster, driven by the music. Six quick strides and she caught him. *And who are you, the proud lord said, that I must bow so low?* She grabbed Edwyn by the arm to turn him and went cold all over when she felt the iron rings beneath his silken sleeve.

Catelyn slapped him so hard she broke his lip. *Olyvar*, she thought, *and Perwyn, Alesander, all absent. And Roslin wept . . .*

Edwyn Frey shoved her aside. The music drowned all other sound, echoing off the walls as if the stones themselves were playing. Robb gave Edwyn an angry look and moved to block his way . . . and staggered suddenly as a quarrel sprouted from his side, just beneath the shoulder. If he screamed then, the sound was swallowed by the pipes and horns and fiddles. Catelyn saw a second bolt pierce his leg, saw him fall. Up in the gallery, half the musicians had crossbows in their hands instead of drums or lutes. She ran toward her son, until something punched in the small of the back and the hard stone floor came up to slap her. *"Robb!"* she screamed. She saw Smalljon Umber wrestle a table off its trestles. Crossbow bolts thudded into the wood, one two three, as he flung it down on top of his king. Robin Flint was ringed by Freys, their daggers rising and falling. Ser Wendel Manderly rose ponderously to his feet, holding his leg of lamb. A quarrel went in his open mouth and came out the back of his neck. Ser Wendel crashed forward, knocking the table off its trestles and sending cups, flagons, trenchers, platters, turnips, beets, and wine bouncing, spilling, and sliding across the floor.

Catelyn's back was on fire. *I have to reach him.* The Smalljon bludgeoned Ser Raymund Frey across the face with a leg of mutton. But when he reached for his swordbelt a crossbow bolt drove him to his knees. *In a coat of gold or a coat of red, a lion still has claws.* She saw Lucas Blackwood cut down by Ser Hosteen Frey. One of the Vances was hamstrung by Black Walder as he was wrestling with Ser Harys Haigh. *And mine are long and sharp, my lord, as long and sharp as yours.* The crossbows took Donnel Locke, Owen Norrey, and half a dozen more. Young Ser Benfrey had seized Dacey Mormont by the arm, but Catelyn saw her grab up a flagon of wine with her other hand, smash it full in his face, and run for the door. It flew open before she reached it. Ser Ryman Frey pushed into the hall, clad in steel from helm to heel. A dozen Frey men-at-arms packed the door behind him. They were armed with heavy longaxes.

"Mercy!" Catelyn cried, but horns and drums and the clash of steel smothered her plea. Ser Ryman buried the head of his axe in Dacey's stomach. By then men were pouring in the other doors as well, mailed men in shaggy fur cloaks with steel in their hands. *Northmen!* She took them for rescue for half a heartbeat, till one of them struck the Smalljon's head off with two huge blows of his axe. Hope blew out like a candle in a storm.

In the midst of slaughter, the Lord of the Crossing sat on his carved oaken throne, watching greedily.

There was a dagger on the floor a few feet away. Perhaps it had skittered there when the Smalljon knocked the table off its trestles, or perhaps it had fallen from the hand of some dying man. Catelyn crawled toward it. Her limbs were leaden, and the taste of blood was in her mouth. *I will kill Walder Frey*, she told herself. Jinglebell was closer to the knife, hiding under a table, but he only cringed away as she snatched up the blade. *I will kill the old man, I can do that much at least.*

Then the tabletop that the Smalljon had flung over Robb shifted, and her son struggled to his knees. He had an arrow in his side, a second in his leg, a third through his chest. Lord Walder raised a hand, and the music stopped, all but one drum. Catelyn heard the crash of distant battle, and closer the wild howling of a wolf. *Grey Wind*, she remembered too late. "Heh," Lord Walder cackled at Robb, "the King in the North arises. Seems we killed some of your men, Your Grace. Oh, but I'll make you an *apology*, that will mend them all again, *heh*."

Catelyn grabbed a handful of Jinglebell Frey's long grey hair and dragged him out of his hiding place. "Lord Walder!" she shouted. "*LORD WALDER!*" The drum beat slow and sonorous, *doom boom doom*. "Enough," said Catelyn. "*Enough*, I say. You have repaid betrayal with betrayal, let it end." When she pressed her dagger to Jinglebell's throat, the memory of Bran's sickroom came back to her, with the feel of steel at her own throat. The drum went *boom doom boom doom boom doom*. "Please," she said. "He is my son. My first son, and my last. Let him go. Let him go and I swear we will forget this . . . forget all you've done here. I swear it by the old gods and new, we . . . we will take no vengeance . . ."

Lord Walder peered at her in mistrust. "Only a fool would believe such blather. D'you take me for a fool, my lady?"

"I take you for a father. Keep me for a hostage, Edmure as well if you haven't killed him. But let Robb go."

"No." Robb's voice was whisper faint. "Mother, no . . ."

"Yes. Robb, get up. Get up and walk out, please, *please*. Save yourself . . . if not for me, for Jeyne."

"Jeyne?" Robb grabbed the edge of the table and forced himself to stand. "Mother," he said, "Grey Wind . . ."

"Go to him. Now. Robb, *walk out of here.*"

Lord Walder snorted. "And why would I let him do that?"

She pressed the blade deeper into Jinglebell's throat. The lackwit rolled his eyes at her in mute appeal. A foul stench assailed her nose, but she paid it no more mind than she did the sullen ceaseless pounding of that drum, *boom doom boom doom boom doom*. Ser Ryman and Black Walder were circling round her back, but Catelyn did not care. They could do as they wished with her; imprison her, rape her, kill her, it made no matter. She had lived too long, and Ned was waiting. It was Robb she feared for.

"On my honor as a Tully," she told Lord Walder, "on my honor as a Stark, I will trade your boy's life for Robb's. A son for a son." Her hand shook so badly she was ringing Jinglebell's head.

Boom, the drum sounded, *boom doom boom doom*. The old man's lips went in and out. The knife trembled in Catelyn's hand, slippery with sweat. "A son for a son, *heh*," he repeated. "But that's a grandson . . . and he never was much use."

A man in dark armor and a pale pink cloak spotted with blood stepped up to Robb. "Jaime Lannister sends his regards." He thrust his longsword through her son's heart, and twisted.

Robb had broken his word, but Catelyn kept hers. She tugged hard on Aegon's hair and sawed at his neck until the blade grated on bone. Blood ran hot over her fingers. His little bells were ringing, ringing, ringing, and the drum went *boom doom boom*.

Finally someone took the knife away from her. The tears burned like vinegar as they ran down her cheeks. Ten fierce ravens were raking her face with sharp talons and tearing off strips of flesh, leaving deep furrows that ran red with blood. She could taste it on her lips.

It hurts so much, she thought. *Our children, Ned, all our sweet babes. Rickon, Bran, Arya, Sansa, Robb . . . Robb . . . please, Ned, please, make it stop, make it stop hurting . . .* The white tears and the red ones ran together until her face was torn and tattered, the face that Ned had loved. Catelyn Stark raised her hands and watched the blood run down her long fingers, over her wrists, beneath the sleeves of her gown. Slow red worms crawled along her arms and under her clothes. *It tickles*. That made her laugh until she screamed. "Mad," someone said, "she's lost her wits," and someone else said, "Make an end," and a hand grabbed her scalp just as she'd done with Jinglebell, and she thought, *No, don't, don't cut my hair, Ned loves my hair*. Then the steel was at her throat, and its bite was red and cold.

ARYA

The feast tents were behind them now. They squished over wet clay and torn grass, out of the light and back into the gloom. Ahead loomed the castle gatehouse. She could see torches moving on the walls, their flames dancing and blowing in the wind. The light shone dully against the wet mail and helms. More torches were moving on the dark stone bridge that joined the Twins, a column of them streaming from the west bank to the east.

"The castle's not closed," Arya said suddenly. The sergeant had said it would be, but he was wrong. The portcullis was being drawn upward even as she watched, and the drawbridge had already been lowered to span the swollen moat. She had been afraid that Lord Frey's guardsmen would refuse to let them in. For half a heartbeat she chewed her lip, too anxious to smile.

The Hound reined up so suddenly that she almost fell off the wayn. "Seven bloody buggering hells," Arya heard him curse, as their left wheel began to sink in soft mud. The wayn tilted slowly. "Get *down*," Clegane roared at her, slamming the heel of his hand into her shoulder to knock her sideways. She landed light, the way Syrio had taught her, and bounced up at once with a face full of mud. "*Why did you do that?*" she screamed. The Hound had leapt down as well. He tore the seat off the front of the wayn and reached in for the swordbelt he'd hidden beneath it.

It was only then that she heard the riders pouring out the castle gate in a river of steel and fire, the thunder of their destriers crossing the drawbridge almost lost beneath the drumming from the castles. Men and mounts wore plate armor, and one in every ten carried a torch. The rest had axes, longaxes with spiked heads and heavy bone-crushing armor-smashing blades.

Somewhere far off she heard a wolf howling. It wasn't very loud compared to the camp noise and the music and the low ominous growl of the river running wild, but she heard it all the same. Only maybe it wasn't her ears that heard it. The sound shivered through Arya like a knife, sharp with rage and grief. More and more riders were emerging from the castle, a column four wide with no end to it, knights and squires and freeriders, torches and longaxes. And there was noise coming from behind as well.

When Arya looked around, she saw that there were only two of the huge feast tents where once there had been three. The one in the middle had collapsed. For a moment she did not understand what she was seeing. Then the flames went licking up from the fallen tent, and now the other two were collapsing, heavy oiled cloth settling down on the men beneath. A flight of fire arrows streaked through the air. The second tent took fire, and then the third. The screams grew so loud she could hear words through the music. Dark shapes moved in front of the flames, the steel of their armor shining orange from afar.

A battle, Arya knew. *It's a battle. And the riders . . .*

She had no more time to watch the tents then. With the river overflowing its banks, the dark swirling waters at the end of the drawbridge reached as high as a horse's belly, but the riders splashed through them all the same, spurred on by the music. For once the same song was coming from both castles. *I know this song*, Arya realized suddenly. Tom o' Sevens had sung it for them, that rainy night the outlaws had sheltered in the brewhouse with the brothers. *And who are you, the proud lord said, that I must bow so low?*

The Frey riders were struggling through the mud and reeds, but some of them had seen the wayn. She watched as three riders left the main column, pounding through the shallows. *Only a cat of a different coat, that's all the truth I know.*

Clegane cut Stranger loose with a single slash of his sword and leapt onto his back. The courser knew what was wanted of him. He pricked up his ears and wheeled toward the charging destriers. *In a coat of gold or a coat of red, a lion still has claws. And mine are long and sharp, my lord, as long and sharp as yours.* Arya had prayed a hundred hundred times for the Hound to die, but now . . . there was a rock in her hand, slimy with mud, and she didn't even remember picking it up. *Who do I throw it at?*

She jumped at the clash of metal as Clegane turned aside the first longaxe. While he was engaged with the first man, the second circled behind him and aimed a blow for the small of his back. Stranger was wheeling, so the Hound took only a glancing blow, enough to rip a great gash in his baggy peasant's blouse and expose the mail below. *He is one against three.* Arya still clutched her rock. *They're sure to kill him.* She thought of Mycah, the butcher's boy who had been her friend so briefly.

Then she saw the third rider coming her way. Arya moved behind the wayn. *Fear cuts deeper than swords.* She could hear drums and warhorns and pipes, stallions trumpeting, the shriek of steel on steel, but all the sounds seemed so far away. There was only the oncoming horseman and the longaxe in his hand. He wore a surcoat over his armor and she saw the two towers that marked him for a Frey. She did not understand. Her uncle was marrying Lord Frey's daughter, the Freys were her brother's friends. *"Don't!"* she screamed as he rode around the wayn, but he paid no mind.

When he charged Arya threw the rock, the way she'd once thrown a crabapple at Gendry. She'd gotten Gendry right between the eyes, but this time her aim was off, and the stone caromed sideways off his temple. It was enough to break his charge, but no more. She retreated, darting across the muddy ground on the balls of her feet, putting the wayn between them once more. The knight followed at a trot, only darkness behind his eyeslit. She hadn't even dented his helm. They went round once, twice, a third time. The knight cursed her. *"You can't run for –"*

The axehead caught him square in the back of the head, crashing through his helm and the skull beneath and sending him flying face first from his saddle. Behind him was the Hound, still mounted on Stranger. *How did you get an axe?* she almost asked, before she saw. One of the other Freys was trapped beneath his dying horse, drowning in a foot of water. The third man was sprawled on his back, unmoving. He hadn't worn a gorget, and a foot of broken sword jutted from beneath his chin.

"Get my helm," Clegane growled at her.

It was stuffed at the bottom of a sack of dried apples, in the back of the wayn behind the pickled pigs' feet. Arya upended the sack and tossed it to him. He snatched it one-handed from the air and lowered it over his head, and where the man had sat only a steel dog remained, snarling at the fires.

"My brother . . ."

"Dead," he shouted back at her. "Do you think they'd slaughter his men and leave him alive?" He turned his head back toward the camp. "Look. *Look*, damn you."

The camp had become a battlefield. *No, a butcher's den.* The flames from the feasting tents reached halfway up the sky. Some of the barracks tents were burning too, and half a hundred silk pavilions. Everywhere swords were singing. *And now the rains weep o'er his hall, with not a soul to hear.* She saw two knights ride down a running man. A wooden barrel came crashing onto one of the burning tents and burst apart, and the flames leapt twice as high. *A catapult*, she knew. The castle was flinging oil or pitch or something.

"Come with me." Sandor Clegane reached down a hand. "We have to get away from here, and now." Stranger tossed his head impatiently, his nostrils flaring at the scent of blood. The song was done. There was only one solitary drum, its slow monotonous beats echoing across the river like the pounding of some monstrous heart. The black sky wept, the river grumbled, men cursed and died. Arya had mud in her teeth and her face was wet. *Rain. It's only rain. That's all it is.* "We're *here*," she shouted. Her voice sounded thin and scared, a little girl's voice. "Robb's just in the castle, and my mother. The gate's even open." There were no more Freys riding out. *I came so far.* "We have to go get my *mother*."

"Stupid little bitch." Fires glinted off the snout of his helm, and made the steel teeth shine. "You go in there, you won't come out. Maybe Frey will let you kiss your mother's corpse."

"Maybe we can *save* her . . ."

"Maybe you can. I'm not done living yet." He rode toward her, crowding her back toward the wayn. "Stay or go, she-wolf. Live or die. Your –"

Arya spun away from him and darted for the gate. The portcullis was coming down, but slowly. *I have to run faster.* The mud slowed her, though, and then the water. *Run fast as a wolf.* The drawbridge had begun to lift, the water running off it in a sheet, the mud falling in heavy clots. *Faster.* She heard loud splashing and looked back to see Stranger pounding after her, sending up gouts of water with every stride. She saw the longaxe too, still wet with blood and brains. And Arya ran. Not for her brother now, not even for her mother, but for herself. She ran faster than she had ever run before, her head down and her feet churning up the river, she ran from him as Mycah must have run.

His axe took her in the back of the head.

TYRION

They supped alone, as they did so often.

"The pease are overcooked," his wife ventured once.

"No matter," he said. "So is the mutton."

It was a jest, but Sansa took it for criticism. "I am sorry, my lord."

"Why? Some cook should be sorry. Not you. The pease are not your province, Sansa."

"I . . . I am sorry that my lord husband is displeased."

"Any displeasure I'm feeling has naught to do with pease. I have Joffrey and my sister to displease me, and my lord father, and three hundred bloody Dornishmen." He had settled Prince Oberyn and his lords in a cornerfort facing the city, as far from the Tyrells as he could put them without evicting them from the Red Keep entirely. It was not nearly far enough. Already there had been a brawl in a Flea Bottom pot-shop that left one Tyrell man-at-arms dead and two of Lord Gargalen's scalded, and an ugly confrontation in the yard when Mace Tyrell's wizened little mother called Ellaria Sand "the serpent's whore." Every time he chanced to see Oberyn Martell the prince asked when the justice would be served. Overcooked pease were the least of Tyrion's troubles, but he saw no point in burdening his young wife with any of that. Sansa had enough griefs of her own.

"The pease suffice," he told her curtly. "They are green and round, what more can one expect of pease? Here, I'll have another serving, if it please my lady." He beckoned, and Podrick Payne spooned so many pease onto his plate that Tyrion lost sight of his mutton. *That was stupid*, he told himself. *Now I have to eat them all, or she'll be sorry all over again.*

The supper ended in a strained silence, as so many of their suppers did. Afterward, as Pod was removing the cups and platters, Sansa asked Tyrion for leave to visit the godswood.

"As you wish." He had become accustomed to his wife's nightly devotions. She prayed at the royal sept as well, and often lit candles to Mother, Maid, and Crone. Tyrion found all this piety excessive, if truth be told, but in her place he might want the help of the gods as well. "I confess, I know little of the old gods," he said, trying to be pleasant. "Perhaps someday you might enlighten me. I could even accompany you."

"No," Sansa said at once. "You . . . you are kind to offer, but . . . there are no *devotions*, my lord. No priests or songs or candles. Only trees, and silent prayer. You would be bored."

"No doubt you're right." *She knows me better than I thought.* "Though the sound of rustling leaves might be a pleasant change from some septon droning on about the seven aspects of grace." Tyrion waved her off. "I won't intrude. Dress warmly, my lady, the wind is brisk out there." He was tempted to ask what she prayed for, but Sansa was so dutiful she might actually tell him, and he didn't think he wanted to know.

He went back to work after she left, trying to track some golden dragons through the labyrinth of Littlefinger's ledgers. Petyr Baelish had not believed in letting gold sit about and grow dusty, that was for certain, but the more Tyrion tried to make sense of his accounts the more his head hurt. It was all very well to talk of breeding dragons instead of locking them up in the treasury, but some of these ventures smelled worse than week-old fish. *I wouldn't have been so quick to let Joffrey fling the Antler Men over the walls if I'd known how many of the bloody bastards had taken loans from the crown.* He would have to send Bronn to find their heirs, but he feared that would prove as fruitful as trying to squeeze silver from a silverfish.

When the summons from his lord father arrived, it was the first time Tyrion could ever recall being pleased to see Ser Boros Blount. He closed the ledgers gratefully, blew out the oil lamp, tied a cloak around his shoulders, and waddled across the castle to the Tower of the Hand. The wind *was* brisk, just as he'd warned Sansa, and there was a smell of rain in the air. Perhaps when Lord Tywin was done with him he should go to the godswood and fetch her home before she got soaked.

But all that went straight out of his head when he entered the Hand's solar to find Cersei, Ser Kevan, and Grand Maester Pycelle gathered about Lord Tywin and the king. Joffrey was almost bouncing, and Cersei was savoring a smug little smile, though Lord Tywin looked as grim as ever. *I wonder if he could smile even if he wanted to.* "What's happened?" Tyrion asked.

His father offered him a roll of parchment. Someone had flattened it, but it still wanted to curl. *"Roslin caught a fine fat trout,"* the message read. *"Her brothers gave her a pair of wolf pelts for her wedding."* Tyrion turned it over to inspect the broken seal. The wax was silvery-grey, and pressed into it were the twin towers of House Frey. "Does the Lord of the Crossing imagine he's being poetic? Or is this meant to confound us?" Tyrion snorted. "The trout would be Edmure Tully, the pelts . . ."

"He's *dead!*" Joffrey sounded so proud and happy you might have thought he'd skinned Robb Stark himself.

First Greyjoy and now Stark. Tyrion thought of his child wife, praying in the godswood even now. *Praying to her father's gods to bring her brother victory and keep her mother safe, no doubt.* The old gods paid no more heed to prayer than the new ones, it would seem. Perhaps he should take comfort in that. "Kings are falling like leaves this autumn," he said. "It would seem our little war is winning itself."

"Wars do not win themselves, Tyrion," Cersei said with poisonous sweetness. "Our lord father won this war."

"Nothing is won so long as we have enemies in the field," Lord Tywin warned them.

"The river lords are no fools," the queen argued. "Without the northmen they cannot hope to stand against the combined power of Highgarden, Casterly Rock, and Dorne. Surely they will choose submission rather than destruction."

"Most," agreed Lord Tywin. "Riverrun remains, but so long as Walder Frey holds Edmure Tully hostage, the Blackfish dare not mount a threat. Jason Mallister and Tytos Blackwood will fight on for honor's sake, but the Freys can keep the Mallisters penned up at Seagard, and with the right inducement Jonos Bracken can be persuaded to change his allegiance and attack the Blackwoods. In the end they will bend the knee, yes. I mean to offer generous terms. Any castle that yields to us will be spared, save one."

"Harrenhal?" said Tyrion, who knew his sire.

"The realm is best rid of these Brave Companions. I have commanded Ser Gregor to put the castle to the sword."

Gregor Clegane. It appeared as if his lord father meant to mine the Mountain for every last nugget of ore before turning him over to Dornish justice. The Brave Companions would end as heads on spikes, and Littlefinger would stroll into Harrenhal without so much as a spot of blood on those fine clothes of his. He wondered if Petyr Baelish had reached the Vale yet. *If the gods are good, he ran into a storm at sea and sank.* But when had the gods ever been especially good?

"They should all be put to the sword," Joffrey declared suddenly. "The Mallisters and Blackwoods and Brackens . . . all of them. They're traitors.

I want them killed, Grandfather. I won't have any *generous terms*." The king turned to Grand Maester Pycelle. "And I want Robb Stark's head too. Write to Lord Frey and tell him. The king commands. I'm going to have it served to Sansa at my wedding feast."

"Sire," Ser Kevan said, in a shocked voice, "the lady is now your aunt by marriage."

"A jest." Cersei smiled. "Joff did not mean it."

"Yes I did," Joffrey insisted. "He was a traitor, and I want his stupid head. I'm going to make Sansa kiss it."

"*No.*" Tyrion's voice was hoarse. "Sansa is no longer yours to torment. Understand that, monster."

Joffrey sneered. "You're the monster, Uncle."

"Am I?" Tyrion cocked his head. "Perhaps you should speak more softly to me, then. Monsters are dangerous beasts, and just now kings seem to be dying like flies."

"I could have your tongue out for saying that," the boy king said, reddening. "I'm the king."

Cersei put a protective hand on her son's shoulder. "Let the dwarf make all the threats he likes, Joff. I want my lord father and my uncle to see what he is."

Lord Tywin ignored that; it was Joffrey he addressed. "Aerys also felt the need to remind men that he was king. And he was passing fond of ripping tongues out as well. You could ask Ser Ilyn Payne about that, though you'll get no reply."

"Ser Ilyn never dared provoke Aerys the way your Imp provokes Joff," said Cersei. "You heard him. 'Monster,' he said. To the King's Grace. And he threatened him . . ."

"Be quiet, Cersei. Joffrey, when your enemies defy you, you must serve them steel and fire. When they go to their knees, however, you must help them back to their feet. Elsewise no man will ever bend the knee to you. And any man who must say 'I am the king' is no true king at all. Aerys never understood that, but you will. When I've won your war for you, we will restore the king's peace and the king's justice. The only head that need concern you is Margaery Tyrell's maidenhead."

Joffrey had that sullen, sulky look he got. Cersei had him firmly by the shoulder, but perhaps she should have had him by the throat. The boy surprised them all. Instead of scuttling safely back under his rock, Joff drew himself up defiantly and said, "You talk about Aerys, Grandfather, but you were scared of him."

Oh, my, hasn't this gotten interesting? Tyrion thought.

Lord Tywin studied his grandchild in silence, gold flecks shining in his pale green eyes. "Joffrey, apologize to your grandfather," said Cersei.

He wrenched free of her. "Why should I? Everyone knows it's true. My father won all the battles. He killed Prince Rhaegar and took the crown, while *your* father was hiding under Casterly Rock." The boy gave his grandfather a defiant look. "A *strong* king acts boldly, he doesn't just talk."

"Thank you for that wisdom, Your Grace," Lord Tywin said, with a courtesy so cold it was like to freeze their ears off. "Ser Kevan, I can see the king is tired. Please see him safely back to his bedchamber. Pycelle, perhaps some gentle potion to help His Grace sleep restfully?"

"Dreamwine, my lord?"

"I don't want any dreamwine," Joffrey insisted.

Lord Tywin would have paid more heed to a mouse squeaking in the corner. "Dreamwine will serve. Cersei, Tyrion, remain."

Ser Kevan took Joffrey firmly by the arm and marched him out the door, where two of the Kingsguard were waiting. Grand Maester Pycelle scurried after them as fast as his shaky old legs could take him. Tyrion remained where he was.

"Father, I am sorry," Cersei said, when the door was shut. "Joff has always been willful, I did warn you . . ."

"There is a long league's worth of difference between willful and stupid. 'A strong king acts boldly?' Who told him that?"

"Not me, I promise you," said Cersei. "Most like it was something he heard Robert say . . ."

"The part about you hiding under Casterly Rock does sound like Robert." Tyrion didn't want Lord Tywin forgetting that bit.

"Yes, I recall now," Cersei said, "Robert *often* told Joff that a king must be bold."

"And what were *you* telling him, pray? I did not fight a war to seat Robert the Second on the Iron Throne. You gave me to understand the boy cared nothing for his father."

"Why would he? Robert ignored him. He would have *beat* him if I'd allowed it. That brute you made me marry once hit the boy so hard he knocked out two of his baby teeth, over some mischief with a cat. I told him I'd kill him in his sleep if he ever did it again, and he never did, but sometimes he would say things . . ."

"It appears things needed to be said." Lord Tywin waved two fingers at her, a brusque dismissal. "Go."

She went, seething.

"Not Robert the Second," Tyrion said. "Aerys the Third."

"The boy is thirteen. There is time yet." Lord Tywin paced to the window. That was unlike him; he was more upset than he wished to show. "He requires a sharp lesson."

Tyrion had gotten his own sharp lesson at thirteen. He felt almost sorry for his nephew. On the other hand, no one deserved it more. "Enough of Joffrey," he said. "Wars are won with quills and ravens, wasn't that what you said? I must congratulate you. How long have you and Walder Frey been plotting this?"

"I mislike that word," Lord Tywin said stiffly.

"And I mislike being left in the dark."

"There was no reason to tell you. You had no part in this."

"Was Cersei told?" Tyrion demanded to know.

"No one was told, save those who had a part to play. And they were only told as much as they needed to know. You ought to know that there is no other way to keep a secret – here, especially. My object was to rid us of a dangerous enemy as cheaply as I could, not to indulge your curiosity or make your sister feel important." He closed the shutters, frowning. "You have a certain cunning, Tyrion, but the plain truth is *you talk too much*. That loose tongue of yours will be your undoing."

"You should have let Joff tear it out," suggested Tyrion.

"You would do well not to tempt me," Lord Tywin said. "I'll hear no more of this. I have been considering how best to appease Oberyn Martell and his entourage."

"Oh? Is this something I'm allowed to know, or should I leave so you can discuss it with yourself?"

His father ignored the sally. "Prince Oberyn's presence here is unfortunate. His brother is a cautious man, a *reasoned* man, subtle, deliberate, even indolent to a degree. He is a man who weighs the consequences of every word and every action. But Oberyn has always been half-mad."

"Is it true he tried to raise Dorne for Viserys?"

"No one speaks of it, but yes. Ravens flew and riders rode, with what secret messages I never knew. Jon Arryn sailed to Sunspear to return Prince Lewyn's bones, sat down with Prince Doran, and ended all the talk of war. But Robert never went to Dorne thereafter, and Prince Oberyn seldom left it."

"Well, he's here now, with half the nobility of Dorne in his tail, and he grows more impatient every day," said Tyrion. "Perhaps I should show him the brothels of King's Landing, that might distract him. A tool for every task, isn't that how it works? My tool is yours, Father. Never let it be said that House Lannister blew its trumpets and I did not respond."

Lord Tywin's mouth tightened. "Very droll. Shall I have them sew you a suit of motley, and a little hat with bells on it?"

"If I wear it, do I have leave to say anything I want about His Grace King Joffrey?"

Lord Tywin seated himself again and said, "I was made to suffer my father's follies. I will not suffer yours. Enough."

"Very well, as you ask so pleasantly. The Red Viper is *not* going to be pleasant, I fear . . . nor will he content himself with Ser Gregor's head alone."

"All the more reason not to give it to him."

"*Not* to . . . ?" Tyrion was shocked. "I thought we were agreed that the woods were full of beasts."

"Lesser beasts." Lord Tywin's fingers laced together under his chin. "Ser Gregor has served us well. No other knight in the realm inspires such terror in our enemies."

"Oberyn *knows* that Gregor was the one who . . ."

"He knows nothing. He has heard tales. Stable gossip and kitchen calumnies. He has no crumb of proof. Ser Gregor is certainly not about to confess to him. I mean to keep him well away for so long as the Dornishmen are in King's Landing."

"And when Oberyn demands the justice he's come for?"

"I will tell him that Ser Amory Lorch killed Elia and her children," Lord Tywin said calmly. "So will you, if he asks."

"Ser Amory Lorch is dead," Tyrion said flatly.

"Precisely. Vargo Hoat had Ser Amory torn apart by a bear after the fall of Harrenhal. That ought to be sufficiently grisly to appease even Oberyn Martell."

"You may call that justice . . ."

"It *is* justice. It was Ser Amory who brought me the girl's body, if you must know. He found her hiding under her father's bed, as if she believed Rhaegar could still protect her. Princess Elia and the babe were in the nursery a floor below."

"Well, it's a tale, and Ser Amory's not like to deny it. What will you tell Oberyn when he asks who gave Lorch his orders?"

"Ser Amory acted on his own in the hope of winning favor from the new king. Robert's hatred for Rhaegar was scarcely a secret."

It might serve, Tyrion had to concede, *but the snake will not be happy.* "Far be it from me to question your cunning, Father, but in your place I do believe I'd have let Robert Baratheon bloody his own hands."

Lord Tywin stared at him as if he had lost his wits. "You deserve that motley, then. We had come late to Robert's cause. It was necessary to demonstrate our loyalty. When I laid those bodies before the throne, no man could doubt that we had forsaken House Targaryen forever. And Robert's relief was palpable. As stupid as he was, even he knew that Rhaegar's children had to die if his throne was ever to be secure. Yet he saw himself as a hero, and heroes do not kill children." His father shrugged. "I grant you, it was done too brutally. Elia need not have been harmed at all, that was sheer folly. By herself she was nothing."

"Then why did the Mountain kill her?"

"Because I did not tell him to spare her. I doubt I mentioned her at all. I had more pressing concerns. Ned Stark's van was rushing south from the Trident, and I feared it might come to swords between us. And it was in Aerys to murder Jaime, with no more cause than spite. That was the thing I feared most. That, and what Jaime himself might do." He closed a fist. "Nor did I yet grasp what I had in Gregor Clegane, only that he was huge and terrible in battle. The rape ... even you will not accuse me of giving *that* command, I would hope. Ser Amory was almost as bestial with Rhaenys. I asked him afterward why it had required half a hundred thrusts to kill a girl of ... two? Three? He said she'd kicked him and would not stop screaming. If Lorch had half the wits the gods gave a turnip, he would have calmed her with a few sweet words and used a soft silk pillow." His mouth twisted in distaste. "The blood was in him."

But not in you, Father. There is no blood in Tywin Lannister. "Was it a soft silk pillow that slew Robb Stark?"

"It was to be an arrow, at Edmure Tully's wedding feast. The boy was too wary in the field. He kept his men in good order, and surrounded himself with outriders and bodyguards."

"So Lord Walder slew him under his own roof, at his own table?" Tyrion made a fist. "What of Lady Catelyn?"

"Slain as well, I'd say. *A pair of wolfskins.* Frey had intended to keep her captive, but perhaps something went awry."

"So much for guest right."

"The blood is on Walder Frey's hands, not mine."

"Walder Frey is a peevish old man who lives to fondle his young wife and brood over all the slights he's suffered. I have no doubt he hatched this ugly chicken, but he would never have dared such a thing without a promise of protection."

"I suppose you would have spared the boy and told Lord Frey you had no need of his allegiance? That would have driven the old fool right back into Stark's arms and won you another year of war. Explain to me why it is more noble to kill ten thousand men in battle than a dozen at dinner." When Tyrion had no reply to that, his father continued. "The price was cheap by any measure. The crown shall grant Riverrun to Ser Emmon Frey once the Blackfish yields. Lancel and Daven must marry Frey girls, Joy is to wed one of Lord Walder's natural sons when she's old enough, and Roose Bolton becomes Warden of the North and takes home Arya Stark."

"*Arya* Stark?" Tyrion cocked his head. "And Bolton? I might have known Frey would not have the stomach to act alone. But Arya ... Varys and Ser Jacelyn searched for her for more than half a year. Arya Stark is surely dead."

"So was Renly, until the Blackwater."

"What does that mean?"

"Perhaps Littlefinger succeeded where you and Varys failed. Lord

Bolton will wed the girl to his bastard son. We shall allow the Dreadfort to fight the ironborn for a few years, and see if he can bring Stark's other bannermen to heel. Come spring, all of them should be at the end of their strength and ready to bend the knee. The north will go to your son by Sansa Stark . . . if you ever find enough manhood in you to breed one. Lest you forget, it is not only Joffrey who must needs take a maidenhead."

I had not forgotten, though I'd hoped you had. "And when do you imagine Sansa will be at her most fertile?" Tyrion asked his father in tones that dripped acid. "Before or after I tell her how we murdered her mother and her brother?"

DAVOS

For a moment it seemed as though the king had not heard. Stannis showed no pleasure at the news, no anger, no disbelief, not even relief. He stared at his Painted Table with teeth clenched hard. "You are certain?" he asked.

"I am not seeing the body, no, Your Kingliness," said Salladhor Saan. "Yet in the city, the lions prance and dance. *The Red Wedding*, the smallfolk are calling it. They swear Lord Frey had the boy's head hacked off, sewed the head of his direwolf in its place, and nailed a crown about his ears. His lady mother was slain as well, and thrown naked in the river."

At a wedding, thought Davos. *As he sat at his slayer's board, a guest beneath his roof. These Freys are cursed.* He could smell the burning blood again, and hear the leech hissing and spitting on the brazier's hot coals.

"It was the Lord's wrath that slew him," Ser Axell Florent declared. "It was the hand of R'hllor!"

"*Praise the Lord of Light!*" sang out Queen Selyse, a pinched thin hard woman with large ears and a hairy upper lip.

"Is the hand of R'hllor spotted and palsied?" asked Stannis. "This sounds more Walder Frey's handiwork than any god's."

"R'hllor chooses such instruments as he requires." The ruby at Melisandre's throat shone redly. "His ways are mysterious, but no man may withstand his fiery will."

"*No man may withstand him!*" the queen cried.

"Be quiet, woman. You are not at a nightfire now." Stannis considered the Painted Table. "The wolf leaves no heirs, the kraken too many. The lions will devour them unless . . . Saan, I will require your fastest ships to carry envoys to the Iron Islands and White Harbor. I shall offer pardons." The way he snapped his teeth showed how little he liked that word. "Full pardons, for all those who repent of treason and swear fealty to their rightful king. They must see . . ."

"They will not." Melisandre's voice was soft. "I am sorry, Your Grace. This is not an end. More false kings will soon rise to take up the crowns of those who've died."

"More?" Stannis looked as though he would gladly have throttled her. "More usurpers? *More* traitors?"

"I have seen it in the flames."

Queen Selyse went to the king's side. "The Lord of Light sent Melisandre to guide you to your glory. Heed her, I beg you. R'hllor's holy flames do not lie."

"There are lies and lies, woman. Even when these flames speak truly, they are full of tricks, it seems to me."

"An ant who hears the words of a king may not comprehend what he is saying," Melisandre said, "and all men are ants before the fiery face of god. If sometimes I have mistaken a warning for a prophecy or a prophecy for a warning, the fault lies in the reader, not the book. But this I know for a certainty – envoys and pardons will not serve you now, no more than leeches. You must show the realm a sign. A sign that proves your power!"

"Power?" The king snorted. "I have thirteen hundred men on Dragonstone, another three hundred at Storm's End." His hand swept over the Painted Table. "The rest of Westeros is in the hands of my foes. I have no fleet but Salladhor Saan's. No coin to hire sellswords. No prospect of plunder or glory to lure freeriders to my cause."

"Lord husband," said Queen Selyse, "you have more men than Aegon did three hundred years ago. All you lack are dragons."

The look Stannis gave her was dark. "Nine mages crossed the sea to hatch Aegon the Third's cache of eggs. Baelor the Blessed prayed over his for half a year. Aegon the Fourth built dragons of wood and iron. Aerion Brightflame drank wildfire to transform himself. The mages failed, King Baelor's prayers went unanswered, the wooden dragons burned, and Prince Aerion died screaming."

Queen Selyse was adamant. "None of these was the chosen of R'hllor. No red comet blazed across the heavens to herald their coming. None wielded Lightbringer, the red sword of heroes. And none of them paid the price. Lady Melisandre will tell you, my lord. Only death can pay for life."

"The boy?" The king almost spat the words.

"The boy," agreed the queen.

"The boy," Ser Axell echoed.

"I was sick unto death of this wretched boy before he was even born," the king complained. "His very name is a roaring in my ears and a dark cloud upon my soul."

"Give the boy to me and you need never hear his name spoken again," Melisandre promised.

No, but you'll hear him screaming when she burns him. Davos held his tongue. It was wiser not to speak until the king commanded it.

"Give me the boy for R'hllor," the red woman said, "and the ancient prophecy shall be fulfilled. Your dragon shall awaken and spread his stony wings. The kingdom shall be yours."

Ser Axell went to one knee. "On bended knee I beg you, sire. Wake the stone dragon and let the traitors tremble. Like Aegon you begin as Lord of Dragonstone. Like Aegon you shall conquer. Let the false and the fickle feel your flames."

"Your own wife begs as well, lord husband." Queen Selyse went down on both knees before the king, hands clasped as if in prayer. "Robert and Delena defiled our bed and laid a curse upon our union. This boy is the foul fruit of their fornications. Lift his shadow from my womb and I will bear you many trueborn sons, I know it." She threw her arms around his legs. "He is only one boy, born of your brother's lust and my cousin's shame."

"He is mine own blood. Stop clutching me, woman." King Stannis put a hand on her shoulder, awkwardly untangling himself from her grasp. "Perhaps Robert did curse our marriage bed. He swore to me that he never meant to shame me, that he was drunk and never knew which bedchamber he entered that night. But does it matter? The boy was not at fault, whatever the truth."

Melisandre put her hand on the king's arm. "The Lord of Light cherishes the innocent. There is no sacrifice more precious. From his king's blood and his untainted fire, a dragon shall be born."

Stannis did not pull away from Melisandre's touch as he had from his queen's. The red woman was all Selyse was not; young, full-bodied, and strangely beautiful, with her heart-shaped face, coppery hair, and unearthly red eyes. "It would be a wondrous thing to see stone come to life," he admitted, grudging. "And to mount a dragon . . . I remember the first time my father took me to court, Robert had to hold my hand. I could not have been older than four, which would have made him five or six. We agreed afterward that the king had been as noble as the dragons were fearsome." Stannis snorted. "Years later, our father told us that Aerys had cut himself on the throne that morning, so his Hand had taken his place. It was Tywin Lannister who'd so impressed us." His fingers touched the surface of the table, tracing a path lightly across the varnished hills. "Robert took the skulls down when he donned the crown, but he could not bear to have them destroyed. Dragon wings over Westeros . . . there would be such a . . ."

"*Your Grace!*" Davos edged forward. "Might I speak?"

Stannis closed his mouth so hard his teeth snapped. "My lord of the Rainwood. Why do you think I made you Hand, if not to speak?" The king waved a hand. "Say what you will."

Warrior, make me brave. "I know little of dragons and less of gods . . . but the queen spoke of curses. No man is as cursed as the kinslayer, in the eyes of gods and men."

"There are no gods save R'hllor and the Other, whose name must not be spoken." Melisandre's mouth made a hard red line. "And small men curse what they cannot understand."

"I am a small man," Davos admitted, "so tell me why you need this boy Edric Storm to wake your great stone dragon, my lady." He was determined to say the boy's name as often as he could.

"Only death can pay for life, my lord. A great gift requires a great sacrifice."

"Where is the greatness in a baseborn child?"

"He has kings' blood in his veins. You have seen what even a little of that blood could do –"

"I saw you burn some leeches."

"And two false kings are dead."

"Robb Stark was murdered by Lord Walder of the Crossing, and we have heard that Balon Greyjoy fell from a bridge. Who did your leeches kill?"

"Do you doubt the power of R'hllor?"

No. Davos remembered too well the living shadow that had squirmed from out her womb that night beneath Storm's End, its black hands pressing at her thighs. *I must go carefully here, or some shadow may come seeking me as well.* "Even an onion smuggler knows two onions from three. You are short a king, my lady."

Stannis gave a snort of laughter. "He has you there, my lady. Two is not three."

"To be sure, Your Grace. One king might die by chance, even two . . . but three? If Joffrey should die in the midst of all his power, surrounded by his armies and his Kingsguard, would not that show the power of the Lord at work?"

"It might." The king spoke as if he grudged each word.

"Or not." Davos did his best to hide his fear.

"Joffrey *shall* die," Queen Selyse declared, serene in her confidence.

"It may be that he is dead already," Ser Axell added.

Stannis looked at them with annoyance. "Are you trained crows, to croak at me in turns? Enough."

"Husband, hear me –" the queen entreated.

"Why? Two is not three. Kings can count as well as smugglers. You may go." Stannis turned his back on them.

Melisandre helped the queen to her feet. Selyse swept stiffly from the chamber, the red woman trailing behind. Ser Axell lingered long enough to give Davos one last look. *An ugly look on an ugly face*, he thought as he met the stare.

After the others had gone, Davos cleared his throat. The king looked up. "Why are you still here?"

"Sire, about Edric Storm . . ."

Stannis made a sharp gesture. "Spare me."

Davos persisted. "Your daughter takes her lessons with him, and plays with him every day in Aegon's Garden."

"I know that."

"Her heart would break if anything ill should –"

"I know that as well."

"If you would only see him –"

"I have seen him. He looks like Robert. Aye, and worships him. Shall I tell him how often his beloved father ever gave him a thought? My brother liked the making of children well enough, but after birth they were a bother."

"He asks after you every day, he –"

"You are making me angry, Davos. I will hear no more of this bastard boy."

"His name is Edric Storm, sire."

"I know his name. Was there ever a name so apt? It proclaims his bastardy, his high birth, and the turmoil he brings with him. Edric Storm. There, I have said it. Are you satisfied, my lord Hand?"

"Edric –" he started.

"– is *one boy!* He may be the best boy who ever drew breath and it would not matter. My duty is to the realm." His hand swept across the Painted Table. "How many boys dwell in Westeros? How many girls? How many men, how many women? The darkness will devour them all, she says. The night that never ends. She talks of prophecies . . . a hero reborn in the sea, living dragons hatched from dead stone . . . she speaks of *signs* and swears they point to me. I never asked for this, no more than I asked to be king. Yet dare I disregard her?" He ground his teeth. "We do not choose our destinies. Yet we must . . . we must do our duty, no? Great or small, *we must do our duty.* Melisandre swears that she has seen me in her flames, facing the dark with Lightbringer raised on high. *Lightbringer!*" Stannis gave a derisive snort. "It glimmers prettily,

I'll grant you, but on the Blackwater this magic sword served me no better than any common steel. A dragon would have turned that battle. Aegon once stood here as I do, looking down on this table. Do you think we would name him Aegon the Conqueror today if he had not had *dragons?*"

"Your Grace," said Davos, "the cost . . ."

"*I know the cost!* Last night, gazing into that hearth, I saw things in the flames as well. I saw a king, a crown of fire on his brows, burning . . . *burning*, Davos. His own crown consumed his flesh and turned him into ash. Do you think I need Melisandre to tell me what that means? Or *you?*" The king moved, so his shadow fell upon King's Landing. "If Joffrey should die . . . what is the life of one bastard boy against a kingdom?"

"Everything," said Davos, softly.

Stannis looked at him, jaw clenched. "Go," the king said at last, "before you talk yourself back into the dungeon."

Sometimes the storm winds blow so strong a man has no choice but to furl his sails. "Aye, Your Grace." Davos bowed, but Stannis had seemingly forgotten him already.

It was chilly in the yard when he left the Stone Drum. A wind blew briskly from the east, making the banners snap and flap noisily along the walls. Davos could smell salt in the air. *The sea.* He loved that smell. It made him want to walk a deck again, to raise his canvas and sail off south to Marya and his two small ones. He thought of them most every day now, and even more at night. Part of him wanted nothing so much as to take Devan and go home. *I cannot. Not yet. I am a lord now, and the King's Hand, I must not fail him.*

He raised his eyes to gaze up at the walls. In place of merlons, a thousand grotesques and gargoyles looked down on him, each different from all the others; wyverns, griffins, demons, manticores, minotaurs, basilisks, hellhounds, cockatrices, and a thousand queerer creatures sprouted from the castle's battlements as if they'd grown there. And the dragons were everywhere. The Great Hall was a dragon lying on its belly. Men entered through its open mouth. The kitchens were a dragon curled up in a ball, with the smoke and steam of the ovens vented through its nostrils. The towers were dragons hunched above the walls or poised for flight; the Windwyrm seemed to scream defiance, while Sea Dragon Tower gazed serenely out across the waves. Smaller dragons framed the gates. Dragon claws emerged from walls to grasp at torches, great stone wings enfolded the smith and armory, and tails formed arches, bridges, and exterior stairs.

Davos had often heard it said that the wizards of Valyria did not cut and chisel as common masons did, but worked stone with fire and magic as a potter might work clay. But now he wondered. *What if they were real dragons, somehow turned to stone?*

"If the red woman brings them to life, the castle will come crashing down, I am thinking. What kind of dragons are full of rooms and stairs and furniture? And windows. And chimneys. And privy shafts."

Davos turned to find Salladhor Saan beside him. "Does this mean you have forgiven my treachery, Salla?"

The old pirate wagged a finger at him. "Forgiving, yes. Forgetting, no. All that good gold on Claw Isle that might have been mine, it makes me old and tired to think of it. When I die impoverished, my wives and concubines will curse you, Onion Lord. Lord Celtigar had many fine wines that now I am not tasting, a sea eagle he had trained to fly from the wrist, and a magic horn to summon krakens from the deep. Very useful such a horn would be, to pull down Tyroshi and other vexing creatures. But do I have this horn to blow? No, because the king made my old friend his Hand." He slipped his arm through Davos's and said, "The queen's men love you not, old friend. I am hearing that a certain Hand has been making friends of his own. This is true, yes?"

You hear too much, you old pirate. A smuggler had best know men as well as tides, or he would not live to smuggle long. The queen's men might remain fervent followers of the Lord of Light, but the lesser folk of Dragonstone were drifting back to the gods they'd known all their lives. They said Stannis was ensorceled, that Melisandre had turned him away from the Seven to bow before some demon out of shadow, and . . . worst sin of all . . . that she and her god had failed him. And there were knights and lordlings who felt the same. Davos had sought them out, choosing them with the same care with which he'd once picked his crews. Ser Gerald Gower fought stoutly on the Blackwater, but afterward had been heard to say that R'hllor must be a feeble god to let his followers be chased off by a dwarf and a dead man. Ser Andrew Estermont was the king's cousin, and had served as his squire years ago. The Bastard of Nightsong had commanded the rearguard that allowed Stannis to reach the safety of Salladhor Saan's galleys, but he worshiped the Warrior with a faith as fierce as he was. *King's men, not queen's men.* But it would not do to boast of them.

"A certain Lysene pirate once told me that a good smuggler stays out of sight," Davos replied carefully. "Black sails, muffled oars, and a crew that knows how to hold their tongues."

The Lyseni laughed. "A crew with no tongues is even better. Big strong mutes who cannot read or write." But then he grew more somber. "But I am glad to know that someone watches your back, old friend. Will the king give the boy to the red priestess, do you think? One little dragon could end this great big war."

Old habit made him reach for his luck, but his fingerbones no longer hung about his neck, and he found nothing. "He will not do it," said Davos. "He could not harm his own blood."

"Lord Renly will be glad to hear this."

"Renly was a traitor in arms. Edric Storm is innocent of any crime. His Grace is a just man."

Salla shrugged. "We shall be seeing. Or you shall. For myself, I am returning to sea. Even now, rascally smugglers may be sailing across the Blackwater Bay, hoping to avoid paying their lord's lawful duties." He slapped Davos on the back. "Take care. You with your mute friends. You are grown so very great now, yet the higher a man climbs the farther he has to fall."

Davos reflected on those words as he climbed the steps of Sea Dragon Tower to the maester's chambers below the rookery. He did not need Salla to tell him that he had risen too high. *I cannot read, I cannot write, the lords despise me, I know nothing of ruling, how can I be the King's Hand? I belong on the deck of a ship, not in a castle tower.*

He had said as much to Maester Pylos. "You are a notable captain," the maester replied. "A captain rules his ship, does he not? He must navigate treacherous waters, set his sails to catch the rising wind, know when a storm is coming and how best to weather it. This is much the same."

Pylos meant it kindly, but his assurances rang hollow. "It is not at all the same!" Davos had protested. "A kingdom's not a ship . . . and a good thing, or this kingdom would be sinking. I know wood and rope and water, yes, but how will that serve me now? Where do I find the wind to blow King Stannis to his throne?"

The maester laughed at that. "And there you have it, my lord. Words are wind, you know, and you've blown mine away with your good sense. His Grace knows what he has in you, I think."

"Onions," said Davos glumly. "That is what he has in me. The King's Hand should be a highborn lord, someone wise and learned, a battle commander or a great knight . . ."

"Ser Ryam Redwyne was the greatest knight of his day, and one of the worst Hands ever to serve a king. Septon Murmison's prayers worked miracles, but as Hand he soon had the whole realm praying for his death. Lord Butterwell was renowned for wit, Myles Smallwood for courage, Ser Otto Hightower for learning, yet they failed as Hands, every one. As for birth, the dragonkings oft chose Hands from amongst their own blood, with results as various as Baelor Breakspear and Maegor the Cruel. Against this, you have Septon Barth, the blacksmith's son the Old King plucked from the Red Keep's library, who gave the realm forty years of peace and plenty." Pylos smiled. "Read your history, Lord Davos, and you will see that your doubts are groundless."

"How can I read history, when I cannot read?"

"Any man can read, my lord," said Maester Pylos. "There is no magic needed, nor high birth. I am teaching the art to your son, at the king's command. Let me teach you as well."

It was a kindly offer, and not one that Davos could refuse. And so every day he repaired to the maester's chambers high atop Sea Dragon Tower, to frown over scrolls and parchments and great leather tomes and try to puzzle out a few more words. His efforts often gave him headaches, and made him feel as big a fool as Patchface besides. His son Devan was not yet twelve, yet he was well ahead of his father, and for Princess Shireen and Edric Storm reading seemed as natural as breathing. When it came to books, Davos was more a child than any of them. Yet he persisted. He was the King's Hand now, and a King's Hand should read.

The narrow twisting steps of Sea Dragon Tower had been a sore trial to Maester Cressen after he broke his hip. Davos still found himself missing the old man. He thought Stannis must as well. Pylos seemed clever and diligent and well-meaning, but he was so young, and the king did not confide in him as he had in Cressen. The old man had been with Stannis so long . . . *Until he ran afoul of Melisandre, and died for it.*

At the top of the steps Davos heard a soft jingle of bells that could only herald Patchface. The princess's fool was waiting outside the maester's door for her like a faithful hound. Dough-soft and slump-shouldered, his broad face tattooed in a motley pattern of red and green squares, Patchface wore a helm made of a rack of deer antlers strapped to a tin bucket. A dozen bells hung from the tines and rang when he moved . . . which meant constantly, since the fool seldom stood still. He jingled and jangled his way everywhere he went; small wonder that Pylos had exiled him from Shireen's lessons. "Under the sea the old fish eat the young fish," the fool muttered at Davos. He bobbed his head, and his bells clanged and chimed and sang. "I know, I know, oh oh oh."

"Up here the young fish teach the old fish," said Davos, who never felt so ancient as when he sat down to try and read. It might have been different if aged Maester Cressen had been the one teaching him, but Pylos was young enough to be his son.

He found the maester seated at his long wooden table covered with books and scrolls, across from the three children. Princess Shireen sat between the two boys. Even now Davos could take great pleasure in the sight of his own blood keeping company with a princess and a king's bastard. *Devan will be a lord now, not merely a knight. The Lord of the Rainwood.* Davos took more pride in that than in wearing the title himself. *He reads too. He reads and he writes, as if he had been born to it.* Pylos had naught but praise for his diligence, and the master-at-arms said Devan was showing promise with sword and lance as well. *And he is a godly lad, too.* "My brothers have ascended to the Hall of Light, to sit beside the Lord," Devan had said when his father told him how his four elder brothers had died. "I will pray for them at the nightfires, and for you as well, Father, so you might walk in the Light of the Lord till the end of your days."

"Good morrow to you, Father," the boy greeted him. *He looks so much like Dale did at his age,* Davos thought. His eldest had never dressed so fine as Devan in his squire's raiment, to be sure, but they shared the same square plain face, the same forthright brown eyes, the same thin brown flyaway hair. Devan's cheeks and chin were dusted with blond hair, a fuzz that would have shamed a proper peach, though the boy was fiercely proud of his "beard." *Just as Dale was proud of his, once.* Devan was the oldest of the three children at the table.

Yet Edric Storm was three inches taller and broader in the chest and shoulders. He was his father's son in that; nor did he ever miss a morning's work with sword and shield. Those old enough to have known Robert and Renly as children said that the bastard boy had more of their look than Stannis had ever shared; the coal-black hair, the deep blue eyes, the mouth, the jaw, the cheekbones. Only his ears reminded you that his mother had been a Florent.

"Yes, good morrow, my lord," Edric echoed. The boy could be fierce and proud, but the maesters and castellans and masters-at-arms who'd raised him had schooled him well in courtesy. "Do you come from my uncle? How fares His Grace?"

"Well," Davos lied. If truth be told, the king had a haggard, haunted look about him, but he saw no need to burden the boy with his fears. "I hope I have not disturbed your lesson."

"We had just finished, my lord," Maester Pylos said.

"We were reading about King Daeron the First." Princess Shireen was a sad, sweet, gentle child, far from pretty. Stannis had given her his square jaw and Selyse her Florent ears, and the gods in their cruel wisdom had seen fit to compound her homeliness by afflicting her with greyscale in the cradle. The disease had left one cheek and half her neck grey and cracked and hard, though it had spared both her life and her sight. "He went to war and conquered Dorne. The Young Dragon, they called him."

"He worshiped false gods," said Devan, "but he was a great king otherwise, and very brave in battle."

"He was," agreed Edric Storm, "but my father was braver. The Young Dragon never won three battles in a day."

The princess looked at him wide-eyed. "Did Uncle Robert win three battles in a day?"

The bastard nodded. "It was when he'd first come home to call his banners. Lords Grandison, Cafferen, and Fell planned to join their strength at Summerhall and march on Storm's End, but he learned their plans from an informer and rode at once with all his knights and squires. As the plotters came up on Summerhall one by one, he defeated each of them in turn before they could join up with the others. He slew Lord Fell in single combat and captured his son Silveraxe."

Devan looked to Pylos. "Is that how it happened?"

"I *said* so, didn't I?" Edric Storm said before the maester could reply. "He smashed all three of them, and fought so bravely that Lord Grandison and Lord Cafferen became his men afterward, and Silveraxe too. No one ever beat my father."

"Edric, you ought not boast," Maester Pylos said. "King Robert suffered defeats like any other man. Lord Tyrell bested him at Ashford, and he lost many a tourney tilt as well."

"He won more than he lost, though. And he killed Prince Rhaegar on the Trident."

"That he did," the maester agreed. "But now I must give my attention to Lord Davos, who has waited so patiently. We will read more of King Daeron's *Conquest of Dorne* on the morrow."

Princess Shireen and the boys said their farewells courteously. When they had taken their leaves, Maester Pylos moved closer to Davos. "My lord, perhaps you would like to try a bit of *Conquest of Dorne* as well?" He slid the slender leather-bound book across the table. "King Daeron wrote with an elegant simplicity, and his history is rich with blood, battle, and bravery. Your son is quite engrossed."

"My son is not quite twelve. I am the King's Hand. Give me another letter, if you would."

"As you wish, my lord." Maester Pylos rummaged about his table, unrolling and then discarding various scraps of parchment. "There are no new letters. Perhaps an old one . . ."

Davos enjoyed a good story as well as any man, but Stannis had not named him Hand for his enjoyment, he felt. His first duty was to help his king rule, and for that he must needs understand the words the ravens brought. The best way to learn a thing was to do it, he had found; sails or scrolls, it made no matter.

"This might serve our purpose." Pylos passed him a letter.

Davos flattened down the little square of crinkled parchment and squinted at the tiny crabbed letters. Reading was hard on the eyes, that much he had learned early. Sometimes he wondered if the Citadel offered a champion's purse to the maester who wrote the smallest hand. Pylos had laughed at the notion, but . . .

"To the . . . five kings," read Davos, hesitating briefly over *five*, which he did not often see written out. "The king . . . be . . . the king . . . beware?"

"*Beyond*," the maester corrected.

Davos grimaced. "The King beyond the Wall comes . . . comes *south*. He leads a . . . a . . . fast . . ."

"Vast."

". . . a *vast* host of wil . . . wild . . . wildlings. Lord M . . . Mmmor . . . Mormont sent a . . . raven from the . . . ha . . . ha . . ."

"Haunted. The *haunted forest*." Pylos underlined the words with the point of his finger.

". . . the haunted forest. He is . . . *under* a . . . attack?"

"Yes."

Pleased, he plowed onward. "Oth . . . other birds have come since, with no words. We . . . fear . . . Mormont slain with all . . . with all his . . . stench . . . no, *strength*. We fear Mormont slain with all his strength . . ." Davos suddenly realized just what he was reading. He turned the letter over, and saw that the wax that had sealed it had been black. "This is from the Night's Watch. Maester, has King Stannis seen this letter?"

"I brought it to Lord Alester when it first arrived. He was the Hand then. I believed he discussed it with the queen. When I asked him if he wished to send a reply, he told me not to be a fool. 'His Grace lacks the men to fight his own battles, he has none to waste on wildlings,' he said to me."

That was true enough. And this talk of five kings would certainly have angered Stannis. "Only a starving man begs bread from a beggar," he muttered.

"Pardon, my lord?"

"Something my wife said once." Davos drummed his shortened fingers against the tabletop. The first time he had seen the Wall he had been younger than Devan, serving aboard the *Cobblecat* under Roro Uhoris, a Tyroshi known up and down the narrow sea as the Blind Bastard, though he was neither blind nor baseborn. Roro had sailed past Skagos into the Shivering Sea, visiting a hundred little coves that had never seen a trading ship before. He brought steel; swords, axes, helms, good chainmail hauberks, to trade for furs, ivory, amber, and obsidian. When the *Cobblecat* turned back south her holds were stuffed, but in the Bay of Seals three black galleys came out to herd her into Eastwatch. They lost their cargo and the Bastard lost his head, for the crime of trading weapons to the wildlings.

Davos had traded at Eastwatch in his smuggling days. The black brothers made hard enemies but good customers, for a ship with the right cargo. But while he might have taken their coin, he had never forgotten how the Blind Bastard's head had rolled across the *Cobblecat*'s deck. "I met some wildlings when I was a boy," he told Maester Pylos. "They were fair thieves but bad hagglers. One made off with our cabin girl. All in all, they seemed men like any other men, some fair, some foul."

"Men are men," Maester Pylos agreed. "Shall we return to our reading, my lord Hand?"

I am the Hand of the King, yes. Stannis might be the King of Westeros in name, but in truth he was the King of the Painted Table. He held Dragonstone and Storm's End, and had an ever-more-uneasy alliance with Salladhor Saan, but that was all. How could the Watch have looked to him for help? *They may not know how weak he is, how lost his cause.* "King Stannis never saw this letter, you are quite certain? Nor Melisandre?"

"No. Should I bring it to them? Even now?"

"No," Davos said at once. "You did your duty when you brought it to Lord Alester." *If Melisandre knew of this letter . . .* What was it she had said? *One whose name may not be spoken is marshaling his power, Davos Seaworth. Soon comes the cold, and the night that never ends . . .* And Stannis had seen a vision in the flames, a ring of torches in the snow with terror all around.

"My lord, are you unwell?" asked Pylos.

I am frightened, Maester, he might have said. Davos was remembering a tale Salladhor Saan had told him, of how Azor Ahai tempered Lightbringer by thrusting it through the heart of the wife he loved. *He slew his wife to fight the dark. If Stannis is Azor Ahai come again, does that mean Edric Storm must play the part of Nissa Nissa?* "I was thinking, Maester. My pardons." *What harm if some wildling king conquers the north?* It was not as though Stannis *held* the north. His Grace could scarcely be expected to defend people who refused to acknowledge him as king. "Give me another letter," he said abruptly. "This one is too . . ."

". . . difficult?" suggested Pylos.

Soon comes the cold, whispered Melisandre, *and the night that never ends.* "Troubling," said Davos. "Too . . . troubling. A different letter, please."

JON

They woke to the smoke of Mole's Town burning.

Atop the King's Tower, Jon Snow leaned on the padded crutch that Maester Aemon had given him and watched the grey plume rise. Styr had lost all hope of taking Castle Black unawares when Jon escaped him, yet even so, he need not have warned of his approach so bluntly. *You may kill us*, he reflected, *but no one will be butchered in their beds. That much I did, at least.*

His leg still hurt like blazes when he put his weight on it. He'd needed Clydas to help him don his fresh-washed blacks and lace up his boots that morning, and by the time they were done he'd wanted to drown himself in the milk of the poppy. Instead he had settled for half a cup of dreamwine, a chew of willow bark, and the crutch. The beacon was burning on Weatherback Ridge, and the Night's Watch had need of every man.

"I can fight," he insisted when they tried to stop him.

"Your leg's healed, is it?" Noye snorted. "You won't mind me giving it a little kick, then?"

"I'd sooner you didn't. It's stiff, but I can hobble around well enough, and stand and fight if you have need of me."

"I have need of every man who knows which end of the spear to stab into the wildlings."

"The pointy end." Jon had told his little sister something like that once, he remembered.

Noye rubbed the bristle on his chin. "Might be you'll do. We'll put you on a tower with a longbow, but if you bloody well fall off don't come crying to me."

He could see the kingsroad wending its way south through stony brown fields and over windswept hills. The Magnar would be coming up that road before the day was done, his Thenns marching behind him with axes and spears in their hands and their bronze-and-leather shields on their backs. *Grigg the Goat, Quort, Big Boil, and the rest will be coming as well. And Ygritte.* The wildlings had never been his friends, he had not *allowed* them to be his friends, but her . . .

He could feel the throb of pain where her arrow had gone through the meat and muscle of his thigh. He remembered the old man's eyes too, and the black blood rushing from his throat as the storm cracked overhead. But he remembered the grotto best of all, the look of her naked in the torchlight, the taste of her mouth when it opened under his. *Ygritte, stay away. Go south and raid, go hide in one of those roundtowers you liked so well. You'll find nothing here but death.*

Across the yard, one of the bowmen on the roof of the old Flint Barracks had unlaced his breeches and was pissing through a crenel. *Mully*, he knew from the man's greasy orange hair. Men in black cloaks were visible on other roofs and tower tops as well, though nine of every ten happened to be made of straw. "The scarecrow sentinels," Donal Noye called them. *Only we're the crows,* Jon mused, *and most of us were scared enough.*

Whatever you called them, the straw soldiers had been Maester Aemon's notion. They had more breeches and jerkins and tunics in the storerooms than they'd had men to fill them, so why not stuff some with straw, drape a cloak around their shoulders, and set them to standing watches? Noye had placed them on every tower and in half the windows. Some were even clutching spears, or had crossbows cocked under their arms. The hope was that the Thenns would see them from afar and decide that Castle Black was too well defended to attack.

Jon had six scarecrows sharing the roof of the King's Tower with him, along with two actual breathing brothers. Deaf Dick Follard sat in a crenel, methodically cleaning and oiling the mechanism of his crossbow to make sure the wheel turned smoothly, while the Oldtown boy wandered restlessly around the parapets, fussing with the clothes on straw men. *Maybe he thinks they will fight better if they're posed just right. Or maybe this waiting is fraying his nerves the way it's fraying mine.*

The boy claimed to be eighteen, older than Jon, but he was green as summer grass for all that. Satin, they called him, even in the wool and mail and boiled leather of the Night's Watch; the name he'd gotten in the brothel where he'd been born and raised. He was pretty as a girl with his dark eyes, soft skin, and raven's ringlets. Half a year at Castle Black had toughened up his hands, however, and Noye said he was passable with a crossbow. Whether he had the courage to face what was coming, though . . .

Jon used the crutch to limp across the tower top. The King's Tower was not the castle's tallest – the high, slim, crumbling Lance held that honor, though Othell Yarwyck had been heard to say it might topple any day. Nor was the King's Tower strongest – the Tower of Guards beside the kingsroad would be a tougher nut to crack. But it was tall enough, strong enough, and well placed beside the Wall, overlooking the gate and the foot of the wooden stair.

The first time he had seen Castle Black with his own eyes, Jon had wondered why anyone would be so foolish as to build a castle without walls. How could it be defended?

"It can't," his uncle told him. "That is the point. The Night's Watch is pledged to take no part in the quarrels of the realm. Yet over the centuries certain Lords Commander, more proud than wise, forgot their vows and near destroyed us all with their ambitions. Lord Commander Runcel Hightower tried to bequeathe the Watch to his bastard son. Lord Commander Rodrik Flint thought to make himself King-beyond-the-Wall. Tristan Mudd, Mad Marq Rankenfell, Robin Hill . . . did you know that six hundred years ago, the commanders at Snowgate and the Night-fort went to war *against each other?* And when the Lord Commander tried to stop them, they joined forces to murder him? The Stark in Win-terfell had to take a hand . . . and both their heads. Which he did easily, because *their strongholds were not defensible.* The Night's Watch had nine hundred and ninety-six Lords Commander before Jeor Mormont, most of them men of courage and honor . . . but we have had cowards and fools as well, our tyrants and our madmen. We survive because the lords and kings of the Seven Kingdoms know that we pose no threat to them, no matter *who* should lead us. Our only foes are to the north, and to the north we have the Wall."

Only now those foes have gotten past the Wall to come up from the south, Jon reflected, *and the lords and kings of the Seven Kingdoms have forgotten us. We are caught between the hammer and the anvil.* Without a wall Castle Black could not be held; Donal Noye knew that as well as any. "The castle does them no good," the armorer told his little garrison. "Kitchens, common hall, stables, even the towers . . . let them take it all. We'll empty the armory and move what stores we can to the top of the Wall, and make our stand around the gate."

So Castle Black had a wall of sorts at last, a crescent-shaped barricade ten feet high made of stores; casks of nails and barrels of salt mutton, crates, bales of black broadcloth, stacked logs, sawn timbers, fire-hardened stakes, and sacks and sacks of grain. The crude rampart enclosed the two things most worth defending; the gate to the north, and the foot of the great wooden switchback stair that clawed and climbed its way up the face of the Wall like a drunken thunderbolt, supported by wooden beams as big as tree trunks driven deep into the ice.

The last few moles were still making the long climb, Jon saw, urged on by his brothers. Grenn was carrying a little boy in his arms, while Pyp, two flights below, let an old man lean upon his shoulder. The oldest villagers still waited below for the cage to make its way back down to them. He saw a mother pulling along two children, one on either hand, as an older boy ran past her up the steps. Two hundred feet above them, Sky Blue Su and Lady Meliana (who was no lady, all her friends agreed) stood on a landing, looking south. They had a better view of the smoke than he did, no doubt. Jon wondered about the villagers who had chosen not to flee. There were always a few, too stubborn or too stupid or too brave to run, a few who preferred to fight or hide or bend the knee. Maybe the Thenns would spare them.

The thing to do would be to take the attack to them, he thought. *With fifty rangers well mounted, we could cut them apart on the road.* They did not have fifty rangers, though, nor half as many horses. The garrison had not returned, and there was no way to know just where they were, or even whether the riders that Noye had sent out had reached them.

We are the garrison, Jon told himself, *and look at us.* The brothers Bowen Marsh had left behind were old men, cripples, and green boys, just as Donal Noye had warned him. He could see some wrestling barrels up the steps, others on the barricade; stout old Kegs, as slow as ever, Spare Boot hopping along briskly on his carved wooden leg, half-mad Easy who fancied himself Florian the Fool reborn, Dornish Dilly, Red Alyn of the Rosewood, Young Henly (well past fifty), Old Henly (well past seventy), Hairy Hal, Spotted Pate of Maidenpool. A couple of them saw Jon looking down from atop the King's Tower and waved up at him. Others turned away. *They still think me a turncloak.* That was a bitter draft to drink, but Jon could not blame them. He was a bastard, after all. Everyone knew that bastards were wanton and treacherous by nature, having been born of lust and deceit. And he had made as many enemies as friends at Castle Black ... Rast, for one. Jon had once threatened to have Ghost rip his throat out unless he stopped tormenting Samwell Tarly, and Rast did not forget things like that. He was raking dry leaves into piles under the stairs just now, but every so often he stopped long enough to give Jon a nasty look.

"No," Donal Noye roared at three of the Mole's Town men, down below. "The pitch goes to the hoist, the oil up the steps, crossbow bolts to the fourth, fifth, and sixth landings, spears to first and second. Stack the lard under the stair, yes, there, behind the planks. The casks of meat are for the barricade. *Now*, you poxy plow pushers, *NOW!*"

He has a lord's voice, Jon thought. His father had always said that in battle a captain's lungs were as important as his sword arm. "It does not matter how brave or brilliant a man is, if his commands cannot be heard," Lord Eddard told his sons, so Robb and he used to climb the towers of Winterfell to shout at each other across the yard. Donal Noye could have drowned out both of them. The moles all went in terror of him, and rightfully so, since he was always threatening to rip their heads off.

Three-quarters of the village had taken Jon's warning to heart and come to Castle Black for refuge. Noye had decreed that every man still spry enough to hold a spear or swing an axe would help defend the barricade, else they could damn well go home and take their chances with the Thenns. He had emptied the armory to put good steel in their hands; big double-bladed axes, razor-sharp daggers, longswords, maces, spiked morningstars. Clad in studded leather jerkins and mail hauberks, with greaves for their legs and gorgets to keep their heads on their shoulders, a few of them even looked like soldiers. *In a bad light. If you squint.*

Noye had put the women and children to work as well. Those too young to fight would carry water and tend the fires, the Mole's Town midwife would assist Clydas and Maester Aemon with any wounded, and Three-Finger Hobb suddenly had more spit boys, kettle stirrers, and onion choppers than he knew what to do with. Two of the whores had even offered to fight, and had shown enough skill with the crossbow to be given a place on the steps forty feet up.

"It's cold." Satin stood with his hands tucked into his armpits under his cloak. His cheeks were bright red.

Jon made himself smile. "The Frostfangs are cold. This is a brisk autumn day."

"I hope I never see the Frostfangs then. I knew a girl in Oldtown who liked to ice her wine. That's the best place for ice, I think. In wine." Satin glanced south, frowned. "You think the scarecrow sentinels scared them off, my lord?"

"We can hope." It was possible, Jon supposed . . . but more likely the wildlings had simply paused for a bit of rape and plunder in Mole's Town. Or maybe Styr was waiting for nightfall, to move up under cover of darkness.

Midday came and went, with still no sign of Thenns on the kingsroad. Jon heard footsteps inside the tower, though, and Owen the Oaf popped up out of the trapdoor, red-faced from the climb. He had a basket of buns under one arm, a wheel of cheese under the other, a bag of onions dangling from one hand. "Hobb said to feed you, in case you're stuck up here awhile."

That, or for our last meal. "Thank him for us, Owen."

Dick Follard was deaf as a stone, but his nose worked well enough.

The buns were still warm from the oven when he went digging in the basket and plucked one out. He found a crock of butter as well, and spread some with his dagger. "Raisins," he announced happily. "Nuts, too." His speech was thick, but easy enough to understand once you got used to it.

"You can have mine too," said Satin. "I'm not hungry."

"Eat," Jon told him. "There's no knowing when you'll have another chance." He took two buns himself. The nuts were pine nuts, and besides the raisins there were bits of dried apple.

"Will the wildlings come today, Lord Snow?" Owen asked.

"You'll know if they do," said Jon. "Listen for the horns."

"Two. Two is for wildlings." Owen was tall, towheaded, and amiable, a tireless worker and surprisingly deft when it came to working wood and fixing catapults and the like, but as he'd gladly tell you, his mother had dropped him on his head when he was a baby, and half his wits had leaked out through his ear.

"You remember where to go?" Jon asked him.

"I'm to go to the stairs, Donal Noye says. I'm to go up to the third landing and shoot my crossbow down at the wildlings if they try to climb over the barrier. The *third* landing, one two three." His head bobbed up and down. "If the wildlings attack, the king will come and help us, won't he? He's a mighty warrior, King Robert. He's sure to come. Maester Aemon sent him a bird."

There was no use telling him that Robert Baratheon was dead. He would forget it, as he'd forgotten it before. "Maester Aemon sent him a bird," Jon agreed. That seemed to make Owen happy.

Maester Aemon had sent a lot of birds . . . not to one king, but to four. *Wildlings at the gate,* the message ran. *The realm in danger. Send all the help you can to Castle Black.* Even as far as Oldtown and the Citadel the ravens flew, and to half a hundred mighty lords in their castles. The northern lords offered their best hope, so to them Aemon had sent two birds. To the Umbers and the Boltons, to Castle Cerwyn and Torrhen's Square, Karhold and Deepwood Motte, to Bear Island, Oldcastle, Widow's Watch, White Harbor, Barrowton, and the Rills, to the mountain fastnesses of the Liddles, the Burleys, the Norreys, the Harclays, and the Wulls, the black birds brought their plea. *Wildlings at the gate. The north in danger. Come with all your strength.*

Well, ravens might have wings, but lords and kings do not. If help was coming, it would not come today.

As morning turned to afternoon, the smoke of Mole's Town blew away and the southern sky was clear again. *No clouds,* thought Jon. That was good. Rain or snow could doom them all.

Clydas and Maester Aemon rode the winch cage up to safety at the top of the Wall, and most of the Mole's Town wives as well. Men in black cloaks paced restlessly on the tower tops and shouted back and forth across the courtyards. Septon Cellador led the men on the barricade in a prayer, beseeching the Warrior to give them strength. Deaf Dick Follard curled up beneath his cloak and went to sleep. Satin walked a hundred leagues in circles, round and round the crenellations. The Wall wept and the sun crept across a hard blue sky. Near evenfall, Owen the Oaf returned with a loaf of black bread and a pail of Hobb's best mutton, cooked in a thick broth of ale and onions. Even Dick woke up for that. They ate every bit of it, using chunks of bread to wipe the bottom of the pail. By the time they were done the sun was low in the west, the shadows sharp and black throughout the castle. "Light the fire," Jon told Satin, "and fill the kettle with oil."

He went downstairs himself to bar the door, to try and work some of the stiffness from his leg. That was a mistake, and Jon soon knew it, but he clutched the crutch and saw it through all the same. The door to the King's Tower was oak studded with iron. It might delay the Thenns, but it would not stop them if they wanted to come in. Jon slammed the bar down in its notches, paid a visit to the privy – it might well be his last chance – and hobbled back up to the roof, grimacing at the pain.

The west had gone the color of a blood bruise, but the sky above was cobalt blue, deepening to purple, and the stars were coming out. Jon sat between two merlons with only a scarecrow for company and watched the Stallion gallop up the sky. Or was it the Horned Lord? He wondered where Ghost was now. He wondered about Ygritte as well, and told himself that way lay madness.

They came in the night, of course. *Like thieves*, Jon thought. *Like murderers.*

Satin pissed himself when the horns blew, but Jon pretended not to notice. "Go shake Dick by the shoulder," he told the Oldtown boy, "else he's liable to sleep through the fight."

"I'm frightened." Satin's face was a ghastly white.

"So are they." Jon leaned his crutch up against a merlon and took up his longbow, bending the smooth thick Dornish yew to slip a bowstring through the notches. "Don't waste a quarrel unless you know you have a good clean shot," he said when Satin returned from waking Dick. "We have an ample supply up here, but *ample* doesn't mean inexhaustible. And step behind a merlon to reload, don't try and hide in back of a scarecrow. They're made of straw, an arrow will punch through them." He did not bother telling Dick Follard anything. Dick could read your lips if there was enough light and he gave a damn what you were saying, but he knew it all already.

The three of them took up positions on three sides of the round tower.

Jon hung a quiver from his belt and pulled an arrow. The shaft was black, the fletching grey. As he notched it to his string, he remembered something that Theon Greyjoy had once said after a hunt. "The boar can keep his tusks and the bear his claws," he had declared, smiling that way he did. "There's nothing half so mortal as a grey goose feather."

Jon had never been half the hunter that Theon was, but he was no stranger to the longbow either. There were dark shapes slipping around the armory, backs against the stone, but he could not see them well enough to waste an arrow. He heard distant shouts, and saw the archers on the Tower of Guards loosing shafts at the ground. That was too far off to concern Jon. But when he glimpsed three shadows detach themselves from the old stables fifty yards away, he stepped up to the crenel, raised his bow, and drew. They were running, so he led them, waiting, waiting . . .

The arrow made a soft *hiss* as it left his string. A moment later there was a grunt, and suddenly only two shadows were loping across the yard. They ran all the faster, but Jon had already pulled a second arrow from his quiver. This time he hurried the shot too much, and missed. The wildlings were gone by the time he nocked again. He searched for another target, and found four, rushing around the empty shell of the Lord Commander's Keep. The moonlight glimmered off their spears and axes, and the gruesome devices on their round leathern shields; skulls and bones, serpents, bear claws, twisted demonic faces. *Free folk*, he knew. The Thenns carried shields of black boiled leather with bronze rims and bosses, but theirs were plain and unadorned. These were the lighter wicker shields of raiders.

Jon pulled the goose feather back to his ear, aimed, and loosed the arrow, then nocked and drew and loosed again. The first shaft pierced the bearclaw shield, the second one a throat. The wildling screamed as he went down. He heard the deep *thrum* of Deaf Dick's crossbow to his left, and Satin's a moment later. "I got one!" the boy cried hoarsely. "I got one in the chest."

"Get another," Jon called.

He did not have to search for targets now; only choose them. He dropped a wildling archer as he was fitting an arrow to his string, then sent a shaft toward the axeman hacking at the door of Hardin's Tower. That time he missed, but the arrow quivering in the oak made the wildling reconsider. It was only as he was running off that Jon recognized Big Boil. Half a heartbeat later, old Mully put an arrow through his leg from the roof of the Flint Barracks, and he crawled off bleeding. *That will stop him bitching about his boil*, Jon thought.

When his quiver was empty, he went to get another, and moved to a different crenel, side by side with Deaf Dick Follard. Jon got off three arrows for every bolt Deaf Dick discharged, but that was the advantage of the longbow. The crossbow penetrated better, some insisted, but it was slow and cumbersome to reload. He could hear the wildlings shouting to each other, and somewhere to the west a warhorn blew. The world was moonlight and shadow, and time became an endless round of notch and draw and loose. A wildling arrow ripped through the throat of the straw sentinel beside him, but Jon Snow scarcely noticed. *Give me one clean shot at the Magnar of Thenn*, he prayed to his father's gods. The Magnar at least was a foe that he could hate. *Give me Styr.*

His fingers were growing stiff and his thumb was bleeding, but still Jon notched and drew and loosed. A gout of flame caught his eye, and he turned to see door of the common hall afirc. It was only a few moments before the whole great timbered hall was burning. Three-Finger Hobb and his Mole's Town helpers were safe atop the Wall, he knew, but it felt like a punch in the belly all the same. "*JON,*" Deaf Dick yelled in his thick voice, "*the armory.*" They were on the roof, he saw. One had a torch. Dick hopped up on the crenel for a better shot, jerked his crossbow to his shoulder, and sent a quarrel thrumming toward the torch man. He missed.

The archer down below him didn't.

Follard never made a sound, only toppled forward headlong over the parapet. It was a hundred feet to the yard below. Jon heard the thump as he was peering round a straw soldier, trying to see where the arrow had come from. Not ten feet from Deaf Dick's body, he glimpsed a leather shield, a ragged cloak, a mop of thick red hair. *Kissed by fire*, he thought, *lucky*. He brought his bow up, but his fingers would not part, and she was gone as suddenly as she'd appeared. He swiveled, cursing, and loosed a shaft at the men on the armory roof instead, but he missed them as well.

By then the east stables were afire too, black smoke and wisps of burning hay pouring from the stalls. When the roof collapsed, a flames rose up roaring, so loud they almost drowned out the warhorns of the Thenns. Fifty of them were pounding up the kingsroad in tight column, their shields held up above their heads. Others were swarming through the vegetable garden, across the flagstone yard, around the old dry well. Three had hacked their way through the doors of Maester Aemon's apartments in the timber keep below the rookery, and a desperate fight was going on atop the Silent Tower, longswords against bronze axes. None of that mattered. *The dance has moved on*, he thought.

Jon hobbled across to Satin and grabbed him by the shoulder. "With me," he shouted. Together they moved to the north parapet, where the King's Tower looked down on the gate and Donal Noye's makeshift wall of logs and barrels and sacks of corn. The Thenns were there before them.

They wore halfhelms, and had thin bronze disks sewn to their long leather shirts. Many wielded bronze axes, though a few were chipped stone. More had short stabbing spears with leaf-shaped heads that gleamed redly in the light from the burning stables. They were screaming in the Old Tongue as they stormed the barricade, jabbing with their spears, swinging their bronze axes, spilling corn and blood with equal abandon while crossbow quarrels and arrows rained down on them from the archers that Donal Noye had posted on the stair.

"What do we *do*?" Satin shouted.

"We kill them," Jon shouted back, a black arrow in his hand.

No archer could have asked for an easier shot. The Thenns had their backs to the King's Tower as they charged the crescent, clambering over bags and barrels to reach the men in black. Both Jon and Satin chanced to choose the same target. He had just reached the top of the barricade when an arrow sprouted from his neck and a quarrel between his shoulder blades. Half a heartbeat later a longsword took him in the belly and he fell back onto the man behind him. Jon reached down to his quiver and found it empty again. Satin was winding back his crossbow. He left him to it and went for more arrows, but he hadn't taken more than three steps before the trap slammed open three feet in front of him. *Bloody hell, I never even heard the door break.*

There was no time to think or plan or shout for help. Jon dropped his bow, reached back over his shoulder, ripped Longclaw from its sheath, and buried the blade in the middle of the first head to pop out of the tower. Bronze was no match for Valyrian steel. The blow sheared right through the Thenn's helm and deep into his skull, and he went crashing back down where he'd come from. There were more behind him, Jon knew from the shouting. He fell back and called to Satin. The next man to make the climb got a quarrel through his cheek. He vanished too. "The oil," Jon said. Satin nodded. Together they snatched up the thick quilted pads they'd left beside the fire, lifted the heavy kettle of boiling oil, and dumped it down the hole on the Thenns below. The shrieks were as bad as anything he had ever heard, and Satin looked as though he was going to be sick. Jon kicked the trapdoor shut, set the heavy iron kettle on top of it, and gave the boy with the pretty face a hard shake. "Retch later," Jon yelled. "*Come.*"

They had only been gone from the parapets for a few moments, but everything below had changed. A dozen black brothers and a few Mole's Town men still stood atop the crates and barrels, but the wildlings were swarming over all along the crescent, pushing them back. Jon saw one shove his spear up through Rast's belly so hard he lifted him into the air. Young Henly was dead and Old Henly was dying, surrounded by foes. He could see Easy spinning and slashing, laughing like a loon, his cloak flapping as he leapt from cask to cask. A bronze axe caught him just below the knee and the laughter turned into a bubbling shriek.

"They're breaking," Satin said.

"No," said Jon, "they're broken."

It happened quickly. One mole fled and then another, and suddenly all the villagers were throwing down their weapons and abandoning the barricade. The brothers were too few to hold alone. Jon watched them try and form a line to fall back in order, but the Thenns washed over them with spear and axe, and then they were fleeing too. Dornish Dilly slipped and went down on his face, and a wildling planted a spear between his shoulder blades. Kegs, slow and short of breath, had almost reached the bottom step when a Thenn caught the end of his cloak and yanked him around . . . but a crossbow quarrel dropped the man before his axe could fall. "*Got* him," Satin crowed, as Kegs staggered to the stair and began to crawl up the steps on hands and knees.

The gate is lost. Donal Noye had closed and chained it, but it was there for the taking, the iron bars glimmering red with reflected firelight, the cold black tunnel behind. No one had fallen back to defend it; the only safety was on top of the Wall, seven hundred feet up the crooked wooden stairs.

"What gods do you pray to?" Jon asked Satin.

"The Seven," the boy from Oldtown said.

"Pray, then," Jon told him. "Pray to your new gods, and I'll pray to my old ones." It all turned here.

With the confusion at the trapdoor, Jon had forgotten to fill his quiver. He limped back across the roof and did that now, and picked up his bow as well. The kettle had not moved from where he'd left it, so it seemed as though they were safe enough for the nonce. *The dance has moved on, and we're watching from the gallery*, he thought as he hobbled back. Satin was loosing quarrels at the wildlings on the steps, then ducking down behind a merlon to cock the crossbow. *He may be pretty, but he's quick.*

The real battle was on the steps. Noye had put spearmen on the two lowest landings, but the headlong flight of the villagers had panicked them and they had joined the flight, racing up toward the third landing with the Thenns killing anyone who fell behind. The archers and crossbowmen on the higher landings were trying to drop shafts over their heads. Jon nocked an arrow, drew, and loosed, and was pleased when one of the wildlings went rolling down the steps. The heat of the fires was making the Wall weep, and the flames danced and shimmered against the ice. The steps shook to the footsteps of men running for their lives.

Again Jon notched and drew and loosed, but there was only one of him and one of Satin, and a good sixty or seventy Thenns pounding up the stairs, killing as they went, drunk on victory. On the fourth landing, three brothers in black cloaks stood shoulder to shoulder with longswords in their hands, and battle was joined again, briefly. But there were only three and soon enough the wildling tide washed over them, and their blood dripped down the steps. "A man is never so vulnerable in battle as when he flees," Lord Eddard had told Jon once. "A running man is like a wounded animal to a soldier. It gets his bloodlust up." The archers on the fifth landing fled before the battle even reached them. It was a rout, a red rout.

"Fetch the torches," Jon told Satin. There were four of them stacked beside the fire, their heads wrapped in oily rags. There were a dozen fire arrows too. The Oldtown boy thrust one torch into the fire until it was blazing brightly, and brought the rest back under his arm, unlit. He looked frightened again, as well he might. Jon was frightened too.

It was then that he saw Styr. The Magnar was climbing up the barricade, over the gutted corn sacks and smashed barrels and the bodies of friends and foe alike. His bronze scale armor gleamed darkly in the firelight. Styr had taken off his helm to survey the scene of his triumph, and the bald earless whoreson was smiling. In his hand was a long weirwood spear with an ornate bronze head. When he saw the gate, he pointed the spear at it and barked something in the Old Tongue to the half-dozen Thenns around him. *Too late*, Jon thought. *You should have led your men over the barricade, you might have been able to save a few.*

Up above, a warhorn sounded, long and low. Not from the top of the Wall, but from the ninth landing, some two hundred feet up, where Donal Noye was standing.

Jon notched a fire arrow to his bowstring, and Satin lit it from the torch. He stepped to the parapet, drew, aimed, loosed. Ribbons of flame trailed behind as the shaft sped downward and thudded into its target, crackling.

Not Styr. The steps. Or more precisely, the casks and kegs and sacks that Donal Noye had piled up *beneath* the steps, as high as the first landing; the barrels of lard and lamp oil, the bags of leaves and oily rags, the split logs, bark, and wood shavings. "Again," said Jon, and, "Again," and, "Again." Other longbowmen were firing too, from every tower top in range, some sending their arrows up in high arcs to drop before the Wall. When Jon ran out of fire arrows, he and Satin began to light the torches and fling them from the crenels.

Up above another fire was blooming. The old wooden steps had drunk up oil like a sponge, and Donal Noye had drenched them from the ninth landing all the way down to the seventh. Jon could only hope that most of their own people had staggered up to safety before Noye threw the torches. The black brothers at least had known the plan, but the villagers had not.

Wind and fire did the rest. All Jon had to do was watch. With flames below and flames above, the wildlings had nowhere to go. Some continued upward, and died. Some went downward, and died. Some stayed where they were. They died as well. Many leapt from the steps before they burned, and died from the fall. Twenty-odd Thenns were still huddled together between the fires when the ice cracked from the heat, and the whole lower third of the stair broke off, along with several tons of ice. That was the last that Jon Snow saw of Styr, the Magnar of Thenn. *The Wall defends itself*, he thought.

Jon asked Satin to help him down to the yard. His wounded leg hurt so badly that he could hardly walk, even with the crutch. "Bring the torch," he told the boy from Oldtown. "I need to look for someone." It had been mostly Thenns on the steps. Surely some of the free folk had escaped. Mance's people, not the Magnar's. She might have been one. So they climbed down past the bodies of the men who'd tried the trapdoor, and Jon wandered through the dark with his crutch under one arm, and the other around the shoulders of a boy who'd been a whore in Oldtown.

The stables and the common hall had burned down to smoking cinders by then, but the fire still raged along the wall, climbing step by step and landing by landing. From time to time they'd hear a groan and then a *craaaack*, and another chunk would come crashing off the Wall. The air was full of ash and ice crystals.

He found Quort dead, and Stone Thumbs dying. He found some dead and dying Thenns he had never truly known. He found Big Boil, weak from all the blood he'd lost but still alive.

He found Ygritte sprawled across a patch of old snow beneath the Lord Commander's Tower, with an arrow between her breasts. The ice crystals had settled over her face, and in the moonlight it looked as though she wore a glittering silver mask.

The arrow was black, Jon saw, but it was fletched with white duck feathers. *Not mine*, he told himself, *not one of mine*. But he felt as if it were.

When he knelt in the snow beside her, her eyes opened. "Jon Snow," she said, very softly. It sounded as though the arrow had found a lung. "Is *this* a proper castle now? Not just a tower?"

"It is." Jon took her hand.

"Good," she whispered. "I wanted t' see one proper castle, before . . . before I . . ."

"You'll see a hundred castles," he promised her. "The battle's done. Maester Aemon will see to you." He touched her hair. "You're kissed by fire, remember? Lucky. It will take more than an arrow to kill you.

Aemon will draw it out and patch you up, and we'll get you some milk of the poppy for the pain."

She just smiled at that. "D'you remember that cave? We should have stayed in that cave. I told you so."

"We'll go back to the cave," he said. "You're not going to die, Ygritte. You're not."

"Oh." Ygritte cupped his cheek with her hand. "You know nothing, Jon Snow," she sighed, dying.

BRAN

"It is only another empty castle," Meera Reed said as she gazed across
the desolation of rubble, ruins, and weeds.

No, thought Bran, *it is the Nightfort, and this is the end of the
world.* In the mountains, all he could think of was reaching the Wall and
finding the three-eyed crow, but now that they were here he was filled
with fears. The dream he'd had . . . the dream *Summer* had had . . . *No,
I mustn't think about that dream.* He had not even told the Reeds,
though Meera at least seemed to sense that something was wrong. If he
never talked of it maybe he could forget he ever dreamed it, and then it
wouldn't have happened and Robb and Grey Wind would still be . . .

"Hodor." Hodor shifted his weight, and Bran with it. He was tired.
They had been walking for hours. *At least he's not afraid.* Bran was
scared of this place, and almost as scared of admitting it to the Reeds.
*I'm a prince of the north, a Stark of Winterfell, almost a man grown, I
have to be as brave as Robb.*

Jojen gazed up at him with his dark green eyes. "There's nothing here
to hurt us, Your Grace."

Bran wasn't so certain. The Nightfort had figured in some of Old Nan's
scariest stories. It was here that Night's King had reigned, before his
name was wiped from the memory of man. This was where the Rat
Cook had served the Andal king his prince-and-bacon pie, where the
seventy-nine sentinels stood their watch, where brave young Danny Flint
had been raped and murdered. This was the castle where King Sherrit
had called down his curse on the Andals of old, where the 'prentice
boys had faced the thing that came in the night, where blind Symeon

Star-Eyes had seen the hellhounds fighting. Mad Axe had once walked these yards and climbed these towers, butchering his brothers in the dark.

All that had happened hundreds and thousands of years ago, to be sure, and some maybe never happened at all. Maester Luwin always said that Old Nan's stories shouldn't be swallowed whole. But once his uncle came to see Father, and Bran asked about the Nightfort. Benjen Stark never said the tales were true, but he never said they weren't; he only shrugged and said, "We left the Nightfort two hundred years ago," as if that was an answer.

Bran forced himself to look around. The morning was cold but bright, the sun shining down from a hard blue sky, but he did not like the *noises*. The wind made a nervous whistling sound as it shivered through the broken towers, the keeps groaned and settled, and he could hear rats scrabbling under the floor of the great hall. *The Rat Cook's children running from their father.* The yards were small forests where spindly trees rubbed their bare branches together and dead leaves scuttled like roaches across patches of old snow. There were trees growing where the stables had been, and a twisted white weirwood pushing up through the gaping hole in the roof of the domed kitchen. Even Summer was not at ease here. Bran slipped inside his skin, just for an instant, to get the smell of the place. He did not like that either.

And there was no way through.

Bran had told them there wouldn't be. He had told them and *told* them, but Jojen Reed had insisted on seeing for himself. He had had a green dream, he said, and his green dreams did not lie. *They don't open any gates either*, thought Bran.

The gate the Nightfort guarded had been sealed since the day the black brothers had loaded up their mules and garrons and departed for Deep Lake; its iron portcullis lowered, the chains that raised it carried off, the tunnel packed with stone and rubble all frozen together until they were as impenetrable as the Wall itself. "We should have followed Jon," Bran said when he saw it. He thought of his bastard brother often, since the night that Summer had watched him ride off through the storm. "We should have found the kingsroad and gone to Castle Black."

"We dare not, my prince," Jojen said. "I've told you why."

"But there are *wildlings*. They killed some man and they wanted to kill Jon too. Jojen, there were a *hundred* of them."

"So you said. We are four. You helped your brother, if that was him in truth, but it almost cost you Summer."

"I know," said Bran miserably. The direwolf had killed three of them, maybe more, but there had been too many. When they formed a tight ring around the tall earless man, he had tried to slip away through the rain, but one of their arrows had come flashing after him, and the sudden stab of pain had driven Bran out of the wolf's skin and back into his own. After the storm finally died, they had huddled in the dark without a fire, talking in whispers if they talked at all, listening to Hodor's heavy breathing and wondering if the wildlings might try and cross the lake in the morning. Bran had reached out for Summer time and time again, but the pain he found drove him back, the way a red-hot kettle makes you pull your hand back even when you mean to grab it. Only Hodor slept that night, muttering "Hodor, hodor," as he tossed and turned. Bran was terrified that Summer was off dying in the darkness. *Please, you old gods*, he prayed, *you took Winterfell, and my father, and my legs, please don't take Summer too. And watch over Jon Snow too, and make the wildlings go away.*

No weirwoods grew on that stony island in the lake, yet somehow the old gods must have heard. The wildlings took their sweet time about departing the next morning, stripping the bodies of their dead and the old man they'd killed, even pulling a few fish from the lake, and there was a scary moment when three of them found the causeway and started to walk out ... but the path turned and they didn't, and two of them nearly drowned before the others pulled them out. The tall bald man yelled at them, his words echoing across the water in some tongue that even Jojen did not know, and a little while later they gathered up their shields and spears and marched off north by east, the same way Jon had gone. Bran wanted to leave too, to look for Summer, but the Reeds said no. "We will stay another night," said Jojen, "put some leagues between us and the wildlings. You don't want to meet them again, do you?" Late that afternoon Summer returned from wherever he'd been hiding, dragging his back leg. He ate parts of the bodies in the inn, driving off the crows, then swam out to the island. Meera had drawn the broken arrow from his leg and rubbed the wound with the juice of some plants she found growing around the base of the tower. The direwolf was still limping, but a little less each day, it seemed to Bran. The gods had heard.

"Maybe we should try another castle," Meera said to her brother. "Maybe we could get through the gate somewhere else. I could go scout if you wanted, I'd make better time by myself."

Bran shook his head. "If you go east there's Deep Lake, then Queensgate. West is Icemark. But they'll be the same, only smaller. All the gates are sealed except the ones at Castle Black, Eastwatch, and the Shadow Tower."

Hodor said, "Hodor," to that, and the Reeds exchanged a look. "At least I should climb to the top of the Wall," Meera decided. "Maybe I'll see something up there."

"What could you hope to see?" Jojen asked.

"*Something*," said Meera, and for once she was adamant.

It should be me. Bran raised his head to look up at the Wall, and imagined himself climbing inch by inch, squirming his fingers into cracks in the ice and kicking footholds with his toes. That made him smile in spite of everything, the dreams and the wildlings and Jon and *everything.* He had climbed the walls of Winterfell when he was little, and all the towers too, but none of them had been so high, and they were only stone. The Wall could *look* like stone, all grey and pitted, but then the clouds would break and the sun would hit it differently, and all at once it would transform, and stand there white and blue and glittering. It was the end of the world, Old Nan always said. On the other side were monsters and giants and ghouls, but they could not pass so long as the Wall stood strong. *I want to stand on top with Meera,* Bran thought. *I want to stand on top and see.*

But he was a broken boy with useless legs, so all he could do was watch from below as Meera went up in his stead.

She wasn't really *climbing*, the way he used to climb. She was only walking up some steps that the Night's Watch had hewn hundreds and thousands of years ago. He remembered Maester Luwin saying the Night-fort was the only castle where the steps had been cut from the ice of the Wall itself. Or maybe it had been Uncle Benjen. The newer castles had wooden steps, or stone ones, or long ramps of earth and gravel. *Ice is too treacherous.* It was his uncle who'd told him that. He said that the outer surface of the Wall wept icy tears sometimes, though the core inside stayed frozen hard as rock. The steps must have melted and refrozen a thousand times since the last black brothers left the castle, and every time they did they shrunk a little and got smoother and rounder and more treacherous.

And smaller. *It's almost like the Wall was swallowing them back into itself.* Meera Reed was very surefooted, but even so she was going slowly, moving from nub to nub. In two places where the steps were hardly there at all she got down on all fours. *It will be worse when she comes down,* Bran thought, watching. Even so, he wished it was him up there. When she reached the top, crawling up the icy knobs that were all that remained of the highest steps, Meera vanished from his sight.

"When will she come down?" Bran asked Jojen.

"When she is ready. She will want to have a good look . . . at the Wall and what's beyond. We should do the same down here."

"Hodor?" said Hodor, doubtfully.

"We might find something," Jojen insisted.

Or something might find us. Bran couldn't say it, though; he did not want Jojen to think he was craven.

So they went exploring, Jojen Reed leading, Bran in his basket on Hodor's back, Summer padding by their side. Once the direwolf bolted through a dark door and returned a moment later with a grey rat between his teeth. *The Rat Cook*, Bran thought, but it was the wrong color, and only as big as a cat. The Rat Cook was white, and almost as huge as a sow . . .

There were a lot of dark doors in the Nightfort, and a lot of rats. Bran could hear them scurrying through the vaults and cellars, and the maze of pitch-black tunnels that connected them. Jojen wanted to go poking around down there, but Hodor said *"Hodor"* to that, and Bran said "No." There were worse things than rats down in the dark beneath the Nightfort.

"This seems an old place," Jojen said as they walked down a gallery where the sunlight fell in dusty shafts through empty windows.

"Twice as old as Castle Black," Bran said, remembering. "It was the first castle on the Wall, and the largest." But it had also been the first abandoned, all the way back in the time of the Old King. Even then it had been three-quarters empty and too costly to maintain. Good Queen Alysanne had suggested that the Watch replace it with a smaller, newer castle at a spot only seven miles east, where the Wall curved along the shore of a beautiful green lake. Deep Lake had been paid for by the queen's jewels and built by the men the Old King had sent north, and the black brothers had abandoned the Nightfort to the rats.

That was two centuries past, though. Now Deep Lake stood as empty as the castle it had replaced, and the Nightfort . . .

"There are ghosts here," Bran said. Hodor had heard all the stories before, but Jojen might not have. *"Old* ghosts, from before the Old King, even before Aegon the Dragon, seventy-nine deserters who went south to be outlaws. One was Lord Ryswell's youngest son, so when they reached the barrowlands they sought shelter at his castle, but Lord Ryswell took them captive and returned them to the Nightfort. The Lord Commander had holes hewn in the top of the Wall and he put the deserters in them and sealed them up alive in the ice. They have spears and horns and they all face north. The seventy-nine sentinels, they're called. They left their posts in life, so in death their watch goes on forever. Years later, when Lord Ryswell was old and dying, he had himself carried to the Nightfort so he could take the black and stand beside his son. He'd sent him back to the Wall for honor's sake, but he loved him still, so he came to share his watch."

They spent half the day poking through the castle. Some of the towers had fallen down and others looked unsafe, but they climbed the bell tower (the bells were gone) and the rookery (the birds were gone). Beneath the brewhouse they found a vault of huge oaken casks that boomed hollowly when Hodor knocked on them. They found a library (the shelves and bins had collapsed, the books were gone, and rats were everywhere).

They found a dank and dim-lit dungeon with cells enough to hold five hundred captives, but when Bran grabbed hold of one of the rusted bars it broke off in his hand. Only one crumbling wall remained of the great hall, the bathhouse seemed to be sinking into the ground, and a huge thornbush had conquered the practice yard outside the armory where black brothers had once labored with spear and shield and sword. The armory and the forge still stood, however, though cobwebs, rats, and dust had taken the places of blades, bellows, and anvil. Sometimes Summer would hear sounds that Bran seemed deaf to, or bare his teeth at nothing, the fur on the back of his neck bristling . . . but the Rat Cook never put in an appearance, nor the seventy-nine sentinels, nor Mad Axe. Bran was much relieved. *Maybe it is only a ruined empty castle.*

By the time Meera returned, the sun was only a sword's breath above the western hills. "What did you see?" her brother Jojen asked her.

"I saw the haunted forest," she said in a wistful tone. "Hills rising wild as far as the eye can see, covered with trees that no axe has ever touched. I saw the sunlight glinting off a lake, and clouds sweeping in from the west. I saw patches of old snow, and icicles long as pikes. I even saw an eagle circling. I think he saw me too. I waved at him."

"Did you see a way down?" asked Jojen.

She shook her head. "No. It's a sheer drop, and the ice is so smooth . . . I might be able to make the descent if I had a good rope and an axe to chop out handholds, but . . ."

". . . but not us," Jojen finished.

"No," his sister agreed. "Are you sure this is the place you saw in your dream? Maybe we have the wrong castle."

"No. This is the castle. There is a gate here."

Yes, thought Bran, *but it's blocked by stone and ice.*

As the sun began to set the shadows of the towers lengthened and the wind blew harder, sending gusts of dry dead leaves rattling through the yards. The gathering gloom put Bran in mind of another of Old Nan's stories, the tale of Night's King. He had been the thirteenth man to lead the Night's Watch, she said; a warrior who knew no fear. "And that was the fault in him," she would add, "for all men must know fear." A woman was his downfall; a woman glimpsed from atop the Wall, with skin as white as the moon and eyes like blue stars. Fearing nothing, he chased her and caught her and loved her, though her skin was cold as ice, and when he gave his seed to her he gave his soul as well.

He brought her back to the Nightfort and proclaimed her a queen and himself her king, and with strange sorceries he bound his Sworn Brothers to his will. For thirteen years they had ruled, Night's King and his corpse queen, till finally the Stark of Winterfell and Joramun of the wildlings had joined to free the Watch from bondage. After his fall, when it was found he had been sacrificing to the Others, all records of Night's King had been destroyed, his very name forbidden.

"Some say he was a Bolton," Old Nan would always end. "Some say a Magnar out of Skagos, some say Umber, Flint, or Norrey. Some would have you think he was a Woodfoot, from them who ruled Bear Island before the ironmen came. He never was. He was a Stark, the brother of the man who brought him down." She always pinched Bran on the nose then, he would never forget it. "He was a Stark of Winterfell, and who can say? Mayhaps his name was *Brandon.* Mayhaps he slept in this very bed in this very room."

No, Bran thought, *but he walked in this castle, where we'll sleep tonight.* He did not like that notion very much at all. Night's King was only a man by light of day, Old Nan would always say, but the night was his to rule. *And it's getting dark.*

The Reeds decided that they would sleep in the kitchens, a stone octagon with a broken dome. It looked to offer better shelter than most of the other buildings, even though a crooked weirwood had burst up through the slate floor beside the huge central well, stretching slantwise toward the hole in the roof, its bone-white branches reaching for the sun. It was a queer kind of tree, skinnier than any other weirwood that Bran had ever seen and faceless as well, but it made him feel as if the old gods were with him here, at least.

That was the only thing he liked about the kitchens, though. The roof was mostly there, so they'd be dry if it rained again, but he didn't think they would ever get *warm* here. You could feel the cold seeping up through the slate floor. Bran did not like the shadows either, or the huge brick ovens that surrounded them like open mouths, or the rusted meat hooks, or the scars and stains he saw in the butcher's block along one wall. *That was where the Rat Cook chopped the prince to pieces,* he knew, *and he baked the pie in one of these ovens.*

The well was the thing he liked the least, though. It was a good twelve feet across, all stone, with *steps* built into its side, circling down and down into darkness. The walls were damp and covered with niter, but none of them could see the water at the bottom, not even Meera with her sharp hunter's eyes. "Maybe it doesn't have a bottom," Bran said uncertainly.

Hodor peered over the knee-high lip of the well and said, "*HODOR!*" The word echoed down the well, "Hodorhodorhodorhodor," fainter and fainter, "hodorhodorhodorhodor," until it was less than a whisper. Hodor looked startled. Then he laughed, and bent to scoop a broken piece of slate off the floor.

"Hodor, *don't!*" said Bran, but too late. Hodor tossed the slate over the edge. "You shouldn't have done that. You don't know what's down there. You might have hurt something, or . . . or woken something up."

Hodor looked at him innocently. "Hodor?"

Far, far, far below, they heard the sound as the stone found water. It wasn't a *splash*, not truly. It was more a *gulp*, as if whatever was below had opened a quivering gelid mouth to swallow Hodor's stone. Faint echoes traveled up the well, and for a moment Bran thought he heard something moving, thrashing about in the water. "Maybe we shouldn't stay here," he said uneasily.

"By the well?" asked Meera. "Or in the Nightfort?"

"Yes," said Bran.

She laughed, and sent Hodor out to gather wood. Summer 'went too. It was almost dark by then, and the direwolf wanted to hunt.

Hodor returned alone with both arms full of deadwood and broken branches. Jojen Reed took his flint and knife and set about lighting a fire while Meera boned the fish she'd caught at the last stream they'd crossed. Bran wondered how many years had passed since there had last been a supper cooked in the kitchens of the Nightfort. He wondered who had cooked it too, though maybe it was better not to know.

When the flames were blazing nicely Meera put the fish on. *At least it's not a meat pie.* The Rat Cook had cooked the son of the Andal king in a big pie with onions, carrots, mushrooms, lots of pepper and salt, a rasher of bacon, and a dark red Dornish wine. Then he served him to his father, who praised the taste and had a second slice. Afterward the gods transformed the cook into a monstrous white rat who could only eat his own young. He had roamed the Nightfort ever since, devouring his children, but still his hunger was not sated. "It was not for murder that the gods cursed him," Old Nan said, "nor for serving the Andal king his son in a pie. A man has a right to vengeance. But he slew a *guest* beneath his roof, and that the gods cannot forgive."

"We should sleep," Jojen said solemnly, after they were full. The fire was burning low. He stirred it with a stick. "Perhaps I'll have another green dream to show us the way."

Hodor was already curled up and snoring lightly. From time to time he thrashed beneath his cloak, and whimpered something that might have been "Hodor." Bran wriggled closer to the fire. The warmth felt good, and the soft crackling of flames soothed him, but sleep would not come. Outside the wind was sending armies of dead leaves marching across the courtyards to scratch faintly at the doors and windows. The sounds made him think of Old Nan's stories. He could almost hear the ghostly sentinels calling to each other atop the Wall and winding their ghostly warhorns. Pale moonlight slanted down through the hole in the dome, painting the branches of the weirwood as they strained up toward the roof. It looked as if the tree was trying to catch the moon and drag it down into the well. *Old gods,* Bran prayed, *if you hear me, don't send a dream tonight. Or if you do, make it a good dream.* The gods made no answer.

Bran made himself close his eyes. Maybe he even slept some, or maybe he was just drowsing, floating the way you do when you are half awake and half asleep, trying not to think about Mad Axe or the Rat Cook or the thing that came in the night.

Then he heard the noise.

His eyes opened. *What was that?* He held his breath. *Did I dream it? Was I having a stupid nightmare?* He didn't want to wake Meera and Jojen for a bad dream, but ... *there* ... a soft scuffling sound, far off ... *Leaves, it's leaves rattling off the walls outside and rustling together ... or the wind, it could be the wind ...* The sound wasn't coming from outside, though. Bran felt the hairs on his arm start to rise. *The sound's inside, it's in here with us, and it's getting louder.* He pushed himself up onto an elbow, listening. There *was* wind, and blowing leaves as well, but this was something else. *Footsteps.* Someone was coming this way. Some*thing* was coming this way.

It wasn't the sentinels, he knew. The sentinels never left the Wall. But there might be other ghosts in the Nightfort, ones even more terrible. He remembered what Old Nan had said of Mad Axe, how he took his boots off and prowled the castle halls barefoot in the dark, with never a sound to tell you where he was except for the drops of blood that fell from his axe and his elbows and the end of his wet red beard. Or maybe it wasn't Mad Axe at all, maybe it was the thing that came in the night. The 'prentice boys all saw it, Old Nan said, but afterward when they told their Lord Commander every description had been different. *And three died within the year, and the fourth went mad, and a hundred years later when the thing had come again, the 'prentice boys were seen shambling along behind it, all in chains.*

That was only a story, though. He was just scaring himself. There was no thing that comes in the night, Maester Luwin had said so. If there had ever been such a thing, it was gone from the world now, like giants and dragons. *It's nothing,* Bran thought.

But the sounds were louder now.

It's coming from the well, he realized. That made him even more afraid. Something was coming up from under the ground, coming up out of the dark. *Hodor woke it up. He woke it up with that stupid piece of slate, and now it's coming.* It was hard to hear over Hodor's snores and the thumping of his own heart. Was that the sound blood made dripping from an axe? Or was it the faint, far-off rattling of ghostly chains? Bran listened harder. *Footsteps.* It was definitely footsteps, each one a little louder than the one before. He couldn't tell how many, though. The well made the sounds echo. He didn't hear any dripping, or chains either, but there *was* something else . . . a high thin whimpering sound, like someone in pain, and heavy muffled breathing. But the footsteps were loudest. The footsteps were coming closer.

Bran was too frightened to shout. The fire had burned down to a few faint embers and his friends were all asleep. He almost slipped his skin and reached out for his wolf, but Summer might be miles away. He couldn't leave his friends helpless in the dark to face whatever was coming up out of the well. *I told them not to come here*, he thought miserably. *I told them there were ghosts. I told them that we should go to Castle Black.*

The footfalls sounded heavy to Bran, slow, ponderous, scraping against the stone. *It must be huge.* Mad Axe had been a big man in Old Nan's story, and the thing that came in the night had been monstrous. Back in Winterfell, Sansa had told him that the demons of the dark couldn't touch him if he hid beneath his blanket. He almost did that now, before he remembered that he was a prince, and almost a man grown.

Bran wriggled across the floor, dragging his dead legs behind him until he could reach out and touch Meera on the foot. She woke at once. He had never known anyone to wake as quick as Meera Reed, or to be so alert so fast. Bran pressed a finger to his mouth so she'd know not to speak. She heard the sound at once, he could see that on her face; the echoing footfalls, the faint whimpering, the heavy breathing.

Meera rose to her feet without a word and reclaimed her weapons. With her three-pronged frog spear in her right hand and the folds of her net dangling from her left, she slipped barefoot toward the well. Jojen dozed on, oblivious, while Hodor muttered and thrashed in restless sleep. She kept to the shadows as she moved, stepped around the shaft of moonlight as quiet as a cat. Bran was watching her all the while, and even he could barely see the faint sheen of her spear. *I can't let her fight the thing alone*, he thought. Summer was far away, but . . .

. . . he slipped his skin, and reached for Hodor.

It was not like sliding into Summer. That was so easy now that Bran hardly thought about it. This was harder, like trying to pull a left boot on your right foot. It fit all wrong, and the boot was *scared* too, the boot didn't know what was happening, the boot was pushing the foot away. He tasted vomit in the back of *Hodor's* throat, and that was almost enough to make him flee. Instead he squirmed and shoved, sat up, gathered his legs under him – his huge strong legs – and rose. *I'm standing.* He took a step. *I'm walking.* It was such a strange feeling that he almost fell. He could see himself on the cold stone floor, a little broken thing, but he wasn't broken now. He grabbed Hodor's longsword. The breathing was as loud as a blacksmith's bellows.

From the well came a wail, a piercing *creech* that went through him like a knife. A huge black shape heaved itself up into the darkness and lurched toward the moonlight, and the fear rose up in Bran so thick that before he could even *think* of drawing Hodor's sword the way he'd meant to, he found himself back on the floor again with Hodor roaring *"Hodor hodor HODOR,"* the way he had in the lake tower whenever the lightning flashed. But the thing that came in the night was screaming too, and thrashing wildly in the folds of Meera's net. Bran saw her spear dart out of the darkness to snap at it, and the thing staggered and fell, struggling with the net. The wailing was still coming from the well, even louder now. On the floor the black thing flopped and fought, screeching, *"No, no, don't, please, DON'T . . ."*

Meera stood over him, the moonlight shining silver off the prongs of her frog spear. "Who are you?" she demanded.

"I'm *SAM*," the black thing sobbed. "Sam, Sam, I'm Sam, let me *out*, you *stabbed* me . . ." He rolled through the puddle of moonlight, flailing and flopping in the tangles of Meera's net. Hodor was still shouting, "Hodor hodor hodor."

It was Jojen who fed the sticks to the fire and blew on them until the flames leapt up crackling. Then there was light, and Bran saw the pale thin-faced girl by the lip of the well, all bundled up in furs and skins beneath an enormous black cloak, trying to shush the screaming baby in her arms. The thing on the floor was pushing an arm through the net to reach his knife, but the loops wouldn't let him. He wasn't any monster beast, or even Mad Axe drenched in gore; only a big fat man dressed up in black wool, black fur, black leather, and black mail. "He's a black brother," said Bran. "Meera, he's from the Night's Watch."

"Hodor?" Hodor squatted down on his haunches to peer at the man in the net. "Hodor," he said again, hooting.

"The Night's Watch, yes." The fat man was still breathing like a bellows. "I'm a brother of the Watch." He had one cord under his chins, forcing his head up, and others digging deep into his cheeks. "I'm a crow, please. Let me out of this."

Bran was suddenly uncertain. "Are you the three-eyed crow?" *He can't be the three-eyed crow.*

"I don't think so." The fat man rolled his eyes, but there were only two of them. "I'm only Sam. Samwell Tarly. Let me *out*, it's hurting me." He began to struggle again.

Meera made a disgusted sound. "Stop flopping around. If you tear my net I'll throw you back down the well. Just lie still and I'll untangle you."

"Who are you?" Jojen asked the girl with the baby.

"Gilly," she said. "For the gillyflower. He's Sam. We never meant to scare you." She rocked her baby and murmured at it, and finally it stopped crying.

Meera was untangling the fat brother. Jojen went to the well and peered down. "Where did you come from?"

"From Craster's," the girl said. "Are you the one?"

Jojen turned to look at her. "The one?"

"He said that Sam wasn't the one," she explained. "There was someone else, he said. The one he was sent to find."

"Who said?" Bran demanded.

"Coldhands," Gilly answered softly.

Meera peeled back one end of her net, and the fat man managed to sit up. He was shaking, Bran saw, and still struggling to catch his breath. "He said there would be people," he huffed. "People in the castle. I didn't know you'd be right at the top of the steps, though. I didn't know you'd throw a net on me or stab me in the stomach." He touched his belly with a black-gloved hand. "Am I bleeding? I can't see."

"It was just a poke to get you off your feet," said Meera. "Here, let me have a look." She went to one knee, and felt around his navel. "You're wearing *mail*. I never got near your skin."

"Well, it hurt all the same," Sam complained.

"Are you *really* a brother of the Night's Watch?" Bran asked.

The fat man's chins jiggled when he nodded. His skin looked pale and saggy. "Only a steward. I took care of Lord Mormont's ravens." For a moment he looked like he was going to cry. "I lost them at the Fist, though. It was my fault. I got us lost too. I couldn't even find the Wall. It's a hundred leagues long and seven hundred feet high and *I couldn't find it!*"

"Well, you've found it now," said Meera. "Lift your rump off the ground, I want my net back."

"How did you get through the Wall?" Jojen demanded as Sam struggled to his feet. "Does the well lead to an underground river, is that where you came from? You're not even wet . . ."

"There's a gate," said fat Sam. "A hidden gate, as old as the Wall itself. *The Black Gate*, he called it."

The Reeds exchanged a look. "We'll find this gate at the bottom of the well?" asked Jojen.

Sam shook his head. "*You* won't. I have to take you."

"Why?" Meera demanded. "If there's a gate . . ."

"You won't find it. If you did it wouldn't open. Not for you. It's the *Black* Gate." Sam plucked at the faded black wool of his sleeve. "Only a man of the Night's Watch can open it, he said. A Sworn Brother who has said his words."

"*He* said." Jojen frowned. "This . . . Coldhands?"

"That wasn't his true name," said Gilly, rocking. "We only called him that, Sam and me. His hands were cold as ice, but he saved us from the dead men, him and his ravens, and he brought us here on his elk."

"His elk?" said Bran, wonderstruck.

"His elk?" said Meera, startled.

"His *ravens?*" said Jojen.

"Hodor?" said Hodor.

"Was he green?" Bran wanted to know. "Did he have antlers?"

The fat man was confused. "The elk?"

"*Coldhands*," said Bran impatiently. "The green men ride on elks, Old Nan used to say. Sometimes they have antlers too."

"He wasn't a green man. He wore blacks, like a brother of the Watch, but he was pale as a wight, with hands so cold that at first I was afraid. The wights have blue eyes, though, and they don't have tongues, or they've forgotten how to use them." The fat man turned to Jojen. "He'll be waiting. We should go. Do you have anything warmer to wear? The Black Gate is cold, and the other side of the Wall is even colder. You –"

"Why didn't he come with you?" Meera gestured toward Gilly and her babe. "*They* came with you, why not him? Why didn't you bring him through this Black Gate too?"

"He . . . he can't."

"Why not?"

"The Wall. The Wall is more than just ice and stone, he said. There are spells woven into it . . . old ones, and strong. He cannot pass beyond the Wall."

It grew very quiet in the castle kitchen then. Bran could hear the soft crackle of the flames, the wind stirring the leaves in the night, the creak of the skinny weirwood reaching for the moon. *Beyond the gates the monsters live, and the giants and the ghouls,* he remembered Old Nan saying, *but they cannot pass so long as the Wall stands strong. So go to sleep, my little Brandon, my baby boy. You needn't fear. There are no monsters here.*

"I am not the one you were told to bring," Jojen Reed told fat Sam in his stained and baggy blacks. "*He* is."

"Oh." Sam looked down at him uncertainly. It might have been just then that he realized Bran was crippled. "I don't . . . I'm not strong enough to carry you, I . . ."

"Hodor can carry me." Bran pointed at his basket. "I ride in that, up on his back."

Sam was staring at him. "You're Jon Snow's brother. The one who fell . . ."

"No," said Jojen. "That boy is dead."

"Don't tell," Bran warned. "Please."

Sam looked confused for a moment, but finally he said, "I . . . I can keep a secret. Gilly too." When he looked at her, the girl nodded. "Jon

. . . Jon was *my* brother too. He was the best friend I ever had, but he went off with Qhorin Halfhand to scout the Frostfangs and never came back. We were waiting for him on the Fist when . . . when . . ."

"Jon's here," Bran said. "Summer saw him. He was with some wildlings, but they killed a man and Jon took his horse and escaped. I bet he went to Castle Black."

Sam turned big eyes on Meera. "You're certain it was Jon? You saw him?"

"I'm Meera," Meera said with a smile. "Summer is . . ."

A shadow detached itself from the broken dome above and leapt down through the moonlight. Even with his injured leg, the wolf landed as light and quiet as a snowfall. The girl Gilly made a frightened sound and clutched her babe so hard against her that it began to cry again.

"He won't hurt you," Bran said. "*That*'s Summer."

"Jon said you all had wolves." Sam pulled off a glove. "I know Ghost." He held out a shaky hand, the fingers white and soft and fat as little sausages. Summer padded closer, sniffed them, and gave the hand a lick.

That was when Bran made up his mind. "We'll go with you."

"All of you?" Sam seemed surprised by that.

Meera ruffled Bran's hair. "He's our prince."

Summer circled the well, sniffing. He paused by the top step and looked back at Bran. *He wants to go.*

"Will Gilly be safe if I leave her here till I come back?" Sam asked them.

"She should be," said Meera. "She's welcome to our fire."

Jojen said, "The castle is empty."

Gilly looked around. "Craster used to tell us tales of castles, but I never knew they'd be so big."

It's only the kitchens. Bran wondered what she'd think when she saw Winterfell, if she ever did.

It took them a few minutes to gather their things and hoist Bran into his wicker seat on Hodor's back. By the time they were ready to go, Gilly sat nursing her babe by the fire. "You'll come back for me," she said to Sam.

"As soon as I can," he promised, "then we'll go somewhere warm." When he heard that, part of Bran wondered what he was doing. *Will I ever go someplace warm again?*

"I'll go first, I know the way." Sam hesitated at the top. "There's just so many *steps*," he sighed, before he started down. Jojen followed, then Summer, then Hodor with Bran riding on his back. Meera took the rear, with her spear and net in hand.

It was a long way down. The top of the well was bathed in moonlight, but it grew smaller and dimmer every time they went around. Their footsteps echoed off the damp stones, and the water sounds grew louder. "Should we have brought torches?" Jojen asked.

"Your eyes will adjust," said Sam. "Keep one hand on the wall and you won't fall."

The well grew darker and colder with every turn. When Bran finally lifted his head around to look back up the shaft, the top of the well was no bigger than a half-moon. *"Hodor,"* Hodor whispered, *"Hodorhodorho-dorhodorhodorhodor,"* the well whispered back. The water sounds were close, but when Bran peered down he saw only blackness.

A turn or two later Sam stopped suddenly. He was a quarter of the way around the well from Bran and Hodor and six feet farther down, yet Bran could barely see him. He could see the door, though. *The Black Gate*, Sam had called it, but it wasn't black at all.

It was white weirwood, and there was a face on it.

A glow came from the wood, like milk and moonlight, so faint it scarcely seemed to touch anything beyond the door itself, not even Sam standing right before it. The face was old and pale, wrinkled and shrunken. *It looks dead.* Its mouth was closed, and its eyes; its cheeks were sunken, its brow withered, its chin sagging. *If a man could live for a thousand years and never die but just grow older, his face might come to look like that.*

The door opened its eyes.

They were white too, and blind. "Who are you?" the door asked, and the well whispered, *"Who-who-who-who-who-who-who."*

"I am the sword in the darkness," Samwell Tarly said. "I am the watcher on the walls. I am the fire that burns against the cold, the light that brings the dawn, the horn that wakes the sleepers. I am the shield that guards the realms of men."

"Then pass," the door said. Its lips opened, wide and wider and wider still, until nothing at all remained but a great gaping mouth in a ring of wrinkles. Sam stepped aside and waved Jojen through ahead of him. Summer followed, sniffing as he went, and then it was Bran's turn. Hodor ducked, but not low enough. The door's upper lip brushed softly against the top of Bran's head, and a drop of water fell on him and ran slowly down his nose. It was strangely warm, and salty as a tear.

DAENERYS

Meereen was as large as Astapor and Yunkai combined. Like her sister cities she was built of brick, but where Astapor had been red and Yunkai yellow, Meereen was made with bricks of many colors. Her walls were higher than Yunkai's and in better repair, studded with bastions and anchored by great defensive towers at every angle. Behind them, huge against the sky, could be seen the top of the Great Pyramid, a monstrous thing eight hundred feet tall with a towering bronze harpy at its top.

"The harpy is a craven thing," Daario Naharis said when he saw it. "She has a woman's heart and a chicken's legs. Small wonder her sons hide behind their walls."

But the hero did not hide. He rode out the city gates, armored in scales of copper and jet and mounted upon a white charger whose striped pink-and-white barding matched the silk cloak flowing from the hero's shoulders. The lance he bore was fourteen feet long, swirled in pink and white, and his hair was shaped and teased and lacquered into two great curling ram's horns. Back and forth he rode beneath the walls of multi-colored bricks, challenging the besiegers to send a champion forth to meet him in single combat.

Her bloodriders were in such a fever to go meet him that they almost came to blows. "Blood of my blood," Dany told them, "your place is here by me. This man is a buzzing fly, no more. Ignore him, he will soon be gone." Aggo, Jhogo, and Rakharo were brave warriors, but they were young, and too valuable to risk. They kept her *khalasar* together, and were her best scouts too.

"That was wisely done," Ser Jorah said as they watched from the front of her pavilion. "Let the fool ride back and forth and shout until his horse goes lame. He does us no harm."

"He does," Arstan Whitebeard insisted. "Wars are not won with swords and spears alone, ser. Two hosts of equal strength may come together, but one will break and run whilst the other stands. This hero builds courage in the hearts of his own men and plants the seeds of doubt in ours."

Ser Jorah snorted. "And if our champion were to lose, what sort of seed would that plant?"

"A man who fears battle wins no victories, ser."

"We're not speaking of battle. Meereen's gates will not open if that fool falls. Why risk a life for naught?"

"For honor, I would say."

"I have heard enough." Dany did not need their squabbling on top of all the other troubles that plagued her. Meereen posed dangers far more serious than one pink-and-white hero shouting insults, and she could not let herself be distracted. Her host numbered more than eighty thousand after Yunkai, but fewer than a quarter of them were soldiers. The rest ... well, Ser Jorah called them mouths with feet, and soon they would be starving.

The Great Masters of Meereen had withdrawn before Dany's advance, harvesting all they could and burning what they could not harvest. Scorched fields and poisoned wells had greeted her at every hand. Worst of all, they had nailed a slave child up on every milepost along the coast road from Yunkai, nailed them up still living with their entrails hanging out and one arm always outstretched to point the way to Meereen. Leading her van, Daario had given orders for the children to be taken down before Dany had to see them, but she had countermanded him as soon as she was told. "I *will* see them," she said. "I will see every one, and count them, and look upon their faces. And I will remember."

By the time they came to Meereen sitting on the salt coast beside her river, the count stood at one hundred and sixty-three. *I will have this city*, Dany pledged to herself once more.

The pink-and-white hero taunted the besiegers for an hour, mocking their manhood, mothers, wives, and gods. Meereen's defenders cheered him on from the city walls. "His name is Oznak zo Pahl," Brown Ben Plumm told her when he arrived for the war council. He was the new commander of the Second Sons, chosen by a vote of his fellow sellswords. "I was bodyguard to his uncle once, before I joined the Second Sons. The Great Masters, what a ripe lot o' maggots. The women weren't so bad, though it was worth your life to look at the wrong one the wrong way. I knew a man, Scarb, this Oznak cut his liver out. Claimed to be defending a lady's honor, he did, said Scarb had raped her with his eyes. How do you rape a wench with *eyes*, I ask you? But his uncle is the richest man in Meereen and his father commands the city guard, so I had to run like a rat before he killed me too."

They watched Oznak zo Pahl dismount his white charger, undo his robes, pull out his manhood, and direct a stream of urine in the general direction of the olive grove where Dany's gold pavilion stood among the burnt trees. He was still pissing when Daario Naharis rode up, *arakh* in hand. "Shall I cut that off for you and stuff it down his mouth, Your Grace?" His tooth shone gold amidst the blue of his forked beard.

"It's his city I want, not his meager manhood." She was growing angry, however. *If I ignore this any longer, my own people will think me weak.* Yet who could she send? She needed Daario as much as she did her bloodriders. Without the flamboyant Tyroshi, she had no hold on the Stormcrows, many of whom had been followers of Prendahl na Ghezn and Sallor the Bald.

High on the walls of Meereen, the jeers had grown louder, and now hundreds of the defenders were taking their lead from the hero and pissing down through the ramparts to show their contempt for the besiegers. *They are pissing on slaves, to show how little they fear us,* she thought. *They would never dare such a thing if it were a Dothraki khalasar outside their gates.*

"This challenge must be met," Arstan said again.

"It will be." Dany said, as the hero tucked his penis away again. "Tell Strong Belwas I have need of him."

They found the huge brown eunuch sitting in the shade of her pavilion, eating a sausage. He finished it in three bites, wiped his greasy hands clean on his trousers, and sent Arstan Whitebeard to fetch him his steel. The aged squire honed Belwas's *arakh* every evening and rubbed it down with bright red oil.

When Whitebeard brought the sword, Strong Belwas squinted down the edge, grunted, slid the blade back into its leather sheath, and tied the swordbelt about his vast waist. Arstan had brought his shield as well: a round steel disk no larger than a pie plate, which the eunuch grasped with his off hand rather than strapping to his forearm in the manner of Westeros. "Find liver and onions, Whitebeard," Belwas said. "Not for now, for after. Killing makes Strong Belwas hungry." He did not wait for a reply, but lumbered from the olive grove toward Oznak zo Pahl.

"Why that one, *Khaleesi?*" Rakharo demanded of her. "He is fat and stupid."

"Strong Belwas was a slave here in the fighting pits. If this highborn Oznak should fall to such the Great Masters will be shamed, while if he wins . . . well, it is a poor victory for one so noble, one that Meereen can take no pride in." And unlike Ser Jorah, Daario, Brown Ben, and her three bloodriders, the eunuch did not lead troops, plan battles, or give her counsel. *He does nothing but eat and boast and bellow at Arstan.* Belwas was the man she could most easily spare. And it was time she learned what sort of protector Magister Illyrio had sent her.

A thrum of excitement went through the siege lines when Belwas was seen plodding toward the city, and from the walls and towers of Meereen came shouts and jeers. Oznak zo Pahl mounted up again, and waited, his striped lance held upright. The charger tossed his head impatiently and pawed the sandy earth. As massive as he was, the eunuch looked small beside the hero on his horse.

"A chivalrous man would dismount," said Arstan.

Oznak zo Pahl lowered his lance and charged.

Belwas stopped with legs spread wide. In one hand was his small round shield, in the other the curved *arakh* that Arstan tended with such care. His great brown stomach and sagging chest were bare above the yellow silk sash knotted about his waist, and he wore no armor but his studded leather vest, so absurdly small that it did not even cover his nipples. "We should have given him chainmail," Dany said, suddenly anxious.

"Mail would only slow him," said Ser Jorah. "They wear no armor in the fighting pits. It's blood the crowds come to see."

Dust flew from the hooves of the white charger. Oznak thundered toward Strong Belwas, his striped cloak streaming from his shoulders. The whole city of Meereen seemed to be screaming him on. The besiegers' cheers seemed few and thin by comparison; her Unsullied stood in silent ranks, watching with stone faces. Belwas might have been made of stone as well. He stood in the horse's path, his vest stretched tight across his broad back. Oznak's lance was leveled at the center of his chest. Its bright steel point winked in the sunlight. *He's going to be impaled*, she thought . . . as the eunuch spun sideways. And quick as the blink of an eye the horseman was beyond him, wheeling, raising the lance. Belwas made no move to strike at him. The Meereenese on the walls screamed even louder. "What is he doing?" Dany demanded.

"Giving the mob a show," Ser Jorah said.

Oznak brought the horse around Belwas in a wide circle, then dug in with his spurs and charged again. Again Belwas waited, then spun and knocked the point of the lance aside. She could hear the eunuch's booming laughter echoing across the plain as the hero went past him. "The lance is too long," Ser Jorah said. "All Belwas needs do is avoid the point. Instead of trying to spit him so prettily, the fool should ride right over him."

Oznak zo Pahl charged a third time, and now Dany could see plainly that he was riding *past* Belwas, the way a Westerosi knight might ride

at an opponent in a tilt, rather than *at* him, like a Dothraki riding down
a foe. The flat level ground allowed the charger to get up a good speed, but
it also made it easy for the eunuch to dodge the cumbersome fourteen-foot
lance.

Meereen's pink-and-white hero tried to anticipate this time, and swung
his lance sideways at the last second to catch Strong Belwas when he
dodged. But the eunuch had anticipated too, and this time he dropped
down instead of spinning sideways. The lance passed harmlessly over his
head. And suddenly Belwas was rolling, and bringing the razor-sharp
arakh around in a silver arc. They heard the charger scream as the blade
bit into his legs, and then the horse was falling, the hero tumbling from
the saddle.

A sudden silence swept along the brick parapets of Meereen. Now it
was Dany's people who were screaming and cheering.

Oznak leapt clear of his horse and managed to draw his sword before
Strong Belwas was on him. Steel sang against steel, too fast and furious
for Dany to follow the blows. It could not have been a dozen heartbeats
before Belwas's chest was awash in blood from a slice below his breasts,
and Oznak zo Pahl had an *arakh* planted right between his ram's horns.
The eunuch wrenched the blade loose and parted the hero's head from
his body with three savage blows to the neck. He held it up high for the
Meereenese to see, then flung it toward the city gates and let it bounce
and roll across the sand.

"So much for the hero of Meereen," said Daario, laughing.

"A victory without meaning," Ser Jorah cautioned. "We will not win
Meereen by killing its defenders one at a time."

"No," Dany agreed, "but I'm pleased we killed this one."

The defenders on the walls began firing their crossbows at Belwas, but
the bolts fell short or skittered harmlessly along the ground. The eunuch
turned his back on the steel-tipped rain, lowered his trousers, squatted,
and shat in the direction of the city. He wiped himself with Oznak's
striped cloak, and paused long enough to loot the hero's corpse and put
the dying horse out of his agony before trudging back to the olive grove.

The besiegers gave him a raucous welcome as soon as he reached the
camp. Her Dothraki hooted and screamed, and the Unsullied sent up a
great clangor by banging their spears against their shields. "Well done,"
Ser Jorah told him, and Brown Ben tossed the eunuch a ripe plum and
said, "A sweet fruit for a sweet fight." Even her Dothraki handmaids had
words of praise. "We would braid your hair and hang a bell in it, Strong
Belwas," said Jhiqui, "but you have no hair to braid."

"Strong Belwas needs no tinkly bells." The eunuch ate Brown Ben's
plum in four big bites and tossed aside the stone. "Strong Belwas needs
liver and onions."

"You shall have it," said Dany. "Strong Belwas is hurt." His stomach was red with the blood sheeting down from the meaty gash beneath his breasts.

"It is nothing. I let each man cut me once, before I kill him." He slapped his bloody belly. "Count the cuts and you will know how many Strong Belwas has slain."

But Dany had lost Khal Drogo to a similar wound, and she was not willing to let it go untreated. She sent Missandei to find a certain Yunkish freedman renowned for his skill in the healing arts. Belwas howled and complained, but Dany scolded him and called him a big bald baby until he let the healer stanch the wound with vinegar, sew it shut, and bind his chest with strips of linen soaked in fire wine. Only then did she lead her captains and commanders inside her pavilion for their council.

"I must have this city," she told them, sitting crosslegged on a pile of cushions, her dragons all about her. Irri and Jhiqui poured wine. "Her granaries are full to bursting. There are figs and dates and olives growing on the terraces of her pyramids, and casks of salt fish and smoked meat buried in her cellars."

"And fat chests of gold, silver, and gemstones as well," Daario reminded them. "Let us not forget the gemstones."

"I've had a look at the landward walls, and I see no point of weakness," said Ser Jorah Mormont. "Given time, we might be able to mine beneath a tower and make a breach, but what do we eat while we're digging? Our stores are all but exhausted."

"No weakness in the *landward* walls?" said Dany. Meereen stood on a jut of sand and stone where the slow brown Skahazadhan flowed into Slaver's Bay. The city's north wall ran along the riverbank, its west along the bay shore. "Does that mean we might attack from the river or the sea?"

"With three ships? We'll want to have Captain Groleo take a good look at the wall along the river, but unless it's crumbling that's just a wetter way to die."

"What if we were to build siege towers? My brother Viserys told tales of such, I know they can be made."

"From wood, Your Grace," Ser Jorah said. "The slavers have burnt every tree within twenty leagues of here. Without wood, we have no trebuchets to smash the walls, no ladders to go over them, no siege towers, no turtles, and no rams. We can storm the gates with axes, to be sure, but . . ."

"Did you see them bronze heads above the gates?" asked Brown Ben Plumm. "Rows of harpy heads with open mouths? The Meereenese can squirt boiling oil out them mouths, and cook your axemen where they stand."

Daario Naharis gave Grey Worm a smile. "Perhaps the Unsullied should wield the axes. Boiling oil feels like no more than a warm bath to you, I have heard."

"This is false." Grey Worm did not return the smile. "These ones do not feel burns as men do, yet such oil blinds and kills. The Unsullied do not fear to die, though. Give these ones rams, and we will batter down these gates or die in the attempt."

"You would die," said Brown Ben. At Yunkai, when he took command of the Second Sons, he claimed to be the veteran of a hundred battles. "Though I will not say I fought bravely in all of them. There are old sellswords and bold sellswords, but no old bold sellswords." She saw that it was true.

Dany sighed. "I will not throw away Unsullied lives, Grey Worm. Perhaps we can starve the city out."

Ser Jorah looked unhappy. "We'll starve long before they do, Your Grace. There's no food here, nor fodder for our mules and horses. I do not like this river water either. Meereen shits into the Skahazadhan but draws its drinking water from deep wells. Already we've had reports of sickness in the camps, fever and brownleg and three cases of the bloody flux. There will be more if we remain. The slaves are weak from the march."

"Freedmen," Dany corrected. "They are slaves no longer."

"Slave or free, they are hungry and they'll soon be sick. The city is better provisioned than we are, and can be resupplied by water. Your three ships are not enough to deny them access to both the river and the sea."

"Then what do you advise, Ser Jorah?"

"You will not like it."

"I would hear it all the same."

"As you wish. I say, let this city be. You cannot free every slave in the world, *Khaleesi*. Your war is in Westeros."

"I have not forgotten Westeros." Dany dreamt of it some nights, this fabled land that she had never seen. "If I let Meereen's old brick walls defeat me so easily, though, how will I ever take the great stone castles of Westeros?"

"As Aegon did," Ser Jorah said, "with fire. By the time we reach the Seven Kingdoms, your dragons will be grown. And we will have siege towers and trebuchets as well, all the things we lack here . . . but the way across the Lands of the Long Summer is long and grueling, and there are dangers we cannot know. You stopped at Astapor to buy an army, not to start a war. Save your spears and swords for the Seven Kingdoms, my queen. Leave Meereen to the Meereenese and march west for Pentos."

"Defeated?" said Dany, bristling.

"When cowards hide behind great walls, it is they who are defeated, *Khaleesi*," Ko Jhogo said.

Her other bloodriders concurred. "Blood of my blood," said Rakharo, "when cowards hide and burn the food and fodder, great *khals* must seek for braver foes. This is known."

"It is known," Jhiqui agreed, as she poured.

"Not to me." Dany set great store by Ser Jorah's counsel, but to leave Meereen untouched was more than she could stomach. She could not forget the children on their posts, the birds tearing at their entrails, their skinny arms pointing up the coast road. "Ser Jorah, you say we have no food left. If I march west, how can I feed my freedmen?"

"You can't. I am sorry, *Khaleesi*. They must feed themselves or starve. Many and more will die along the march, yes. That will be hard, but there is no way to save them. We need to put this scorched earth well behind us."

Dany had left a trail of corpses behind her when she crossed the red waste. It was a sight she never meant to see again. "No," she said. "I will not march my people off to die." *My children.* "There must be *some* way into this city."

"I know a way." Brown Ben Plumm stroked his speckled grey-and-white beard. "Sewers."

"Sewers? What do you mean?"

"Great brick sewers empty into the Skahazadhan, carrying the city's wastes. They might be a way in, for a few. That was how I escaped Meereen, after Scarb lost his head." Brown Ben made a face. "The smell has never left me. I dream of it some nights."

Ser Jorah looked dubious. "Easier to go out than in, it would seem to me. These sewers empty into the river, you say? That would mean the mouths are right below the walls."

"And closed with iron grates," Brown Ben admitted, "though some have rusted through, else I would have drowned in shit. Once inside, it is a long foul climb in pitch-dark through a maze of brick where a man could lose himself forever. The filth is never lower than waist high, and can rise over your head from the stains I saw on the walls. There's *things* down there too. Biggest rats you ever saw, and worse things. Nasty."

Daario Naharis laughed. "As nasty as you, when you came crawling out? If any man were fool enough to try this, every slaver in Meereen would smell them the moment they emerged."

Brown Ben shrugged. "Her Grace asked if there was a way in, so I told her . . . but Ben Plumm isn't going down in them sewers again, not for all the gold in the Seven Kingdoms. If there's others want to try it, though, they're welcome."

Aggo, Jhogo, and Grey Worm all tried to speak at once, but Dany raised her hand for silence. "These sewers do not sound promising." Grey Worm would lead his Unsullied down the sewers if she commanded it, she knew; her bloodriders would do no less. But none of them was suited to the task. The Dothraki were horsemen, and the strength of the Unsullied was their discipline on the battlefield. *Can I send men to die in the dark on such a slender hope?* "I must think on this some more. Return to your duties."

Her captains bowed and left her with her handmaids and her dragons. But as Brown Ben was leaving, Viserion spread his pale white wings and flapped lazily at his head. One of the wings buffeted the sellsword in his face. The white dragon landed awkwardly with one foot on the man's head and one on his shoulder, shrieked, and flew off again. "He likes you, Ben," said Dany.

"And well he might." Brown Ben laughed. "I have me a drop of the dragon blood myself, you know."

"You?" Dany was startled. Plumm was a creature of the free companies, an amiable mongrel. He had a broad brown face with a broken nose and a head of nappy grey hair, and his Dothraki mother had bequeathed him large, dark, almond-shaped eyes. He claimed to be part Braavosi, part Summer Islander, part Ibbenese, part Qohorik, part Dothraki, part Dornish, and part Westerosi, but this was the first she had heard of Targaryen blood. She gave him a searching look and said, "How could that be?"

"Well," said Brown Ben, "there was some old Plumm in the Sunset Kingdoms who wed a dragon princess. My grandmama told me the tale. He lived in King Aegon's day."

"Which King Aegon?" Dany asked. "Five Aegons have ruled in Westeros." Her brother's son would have been the sixth, but the Usurper's men had dashed his head against a wall.

"Five, were there? Well, that's a confusion. I could not give you a number, my queen. This old Plumm was a lord, though, must have been a famous fellow in his day, the talk of all the land. The thing was, begging your royal pardon, he had himself a cock six foot long."

The three bells in Dany's braid tinkled when she laughed. "You mean inches, I think."

"Feet," Brown Ben said firmly. "If it was inches, who'd want to talk about it, now? Your Grace."

Dany giggled like a little girl. "Did your grandmother claim she'd actually seen this prodigy?"

"That the old crone never did. She was half-Ibbenese and half-Qohorik, never been to Westeros, my grandfather must have told her. Some Dothraki killed him before I was born."

"And where did your grandfather's knowledge come from?"

"One of them tales told at the teat, I'd guess." Brown Ben shrugged. "That's all I know about Aegon the Unnumbered or old Lord Plumm's mighty manhood, I fear. I best see to my Sons."

"Go do that," Dany told him.

When Brown Ben left, she lay back on her cushions. "If you were grown," she told Drogon, scratching him between the horns, "I'd fly you over the walls and melt that harpy down to slag." But it would be years before her dragons were large enough to ride. *And when they are, who shall ride them? The dragon has three heads, but I have only one.* She thought of Daario. *If ever there was a man who could rape a woman with his eyes . . .*

To be sure, she was just as guilty. Dany found herself stealing looks at the Tyroshi when her captains came to council, and sometimes at night she remembered the way his gold tooth glittered when he smiled. That, and his eyes. *His bright blue eyes.* On the road from Yunkai, Daario had brought her a flower or a sprig of some plant every evening when he made his report . . . to help her learn the land, he said. Waspwillow, dusky roses, wild mint, lady's lace, daggerleaf, broom, prickly ben, harpy's gold . . . *He tried to spare me the sight of the dead children too.* He should not have done that, but he meant it kindly. And Daario Naharis made her laugh, which Ser Jorah never did.

Dany tried to imagine what it would be like if she allowed Daario to kiss her, the way Jorah had kissed her on the ship. The thought was exciting and disturbing, both at once. *It is too great a risk.* The Tyroshi sellsword was not a good man, no one needed to tell her that. Under the smiles and the jests he was dangerous, even cruel. Sallor and Prendahl had woken one morning as his partners; that very night he'd given her their heads. *Khal Drogo could be cruel as well, and there was never a man more dangerous.* She had come to love him all the same. *Could I love Daario? What would it mean, if I took him into my bed? Would that make him one of the heads of the dragon?* Ser Jorah would be angry, she knew, but he was the one who'd said she had to take two husbands. *Perhaps I should marry them both and be done with it.*

But these were foolish thoughts. She had a city to take, and dreaming of kisses and some sellsword's bright blue eyes would not help her breach the walls of Meereen. *I am the blood of the dragon*, Dany reminded herself. Her thoughts were spinning in circles, like a rat chasing its tail. Suddenly she could not stand the close confines of the pavilion another moment. *I want to feel the wind on my face, and smell the sea.* "Missandei," she called, "have my silver saddled. Your own mount as well."

The little scribe bowed. "As Your Grace commands. Shall I summon your bloodriders to guard you?"

"We'll take Arstan. I do not mean to leave the camps." She had no enemies among her children. And the old squire would not talk too much as Belwas would, or look at her like Daario.

The grove of burnt olive trees in which she'd raised her pavilion stood beside the sea, between the Dothraki camp and that of the Unsullied. When the horses had been saddled, Dany and her companions set out along the shoreline, away from the city. Even so, she could feel Meereen at her back, mocking her. When she looked over one shoulder, there it stood, the afternoon sun blazing off the bronze harpy atop the Great Pyramid. Inside Meereen the slavers would soon be reclining in their fringed *tokar*s to feast on lamb and olives, unborn puppies, honeyed dormice and other such delicacies, whilst outside her children went hungry. A sudden wild anger filled her. *I will bring you down*, she swore.

As they rode past the stakes and pits that surrounded the eunuch encampment, Dany could hear Grey Worm and his sergeants running one company through a series of drills with shield, shortsword, and heavy spear. Another company was bathing in the sea, clad only in white linen breechclouts. The eunuchs were very clean, she had noticed. Some of her sellswords smelled as if they had not washed or changed their clothes since her father lost the Iron Throne, but the Unsullied bathed each evening, even if they'd marched all day. When no water was available they cleansed themselves with sand, the Dothraki way.

The eunuchs knelt as she passed, raising clenched fists to their breasts. Dany returned the salute. The tide was coming in, and the surf foamed about the feet of her silver. She could see her ships standing out to sea. *Balerion* floated nearest; the great cog once known as *Saduleon*, her sails furled. Further out were the galleys *Meraxes* and *Vhagar*, formerly *Joso's Prank* and *Summer Sun*. They were Magister Illyrio's ships, in truth, not hers at all, and yet she had given them new names with hardly a thought. Dragon names, and more; in old Valyria before the Doom, Balerion, Meraxes, and Vhagar had been gods.

South of the ordered realm of stakes, pits, drills, and bathing eunuchs lay the encampments of her freedmen, a far noisier and more chaotic place. Dany had armed the former slaves as best she could with weapons from Astapor and Yunkai, and Ser Jorah had organized the fighting men into four strong companies, yet she saw no one drilling here. They passed a driftwood fire where a hundred people had gathered to roast the carcass of a horse. She could smell the meat and hear the fat sizzling as the spit boys turned, but the sight only made her frown.

Children ran behind their horses, skipping and laughing. Instead of salutes, voices called to her on every side in a babble of tongues. Some of the freedmen greeted her as "Mother," while others begged for boons or favors. Some prayed for strange gods to bless her, and some asked her to bless them instead. She smiled at them, turning right and left, touching their hands when they raised them, letting those who knelt reach up to touch her stirrup or her leg. Many of the freedmen believed there was good fortune in her touch. *If it helps give them courage, let them touch me*, she thought. *There are hard trials yet ahead . . .*

Dany had stopped to speak to a pregnant woman who wanted the Mother of Dragons to name her baby when someone reached up and grabbed her left wrist. Turning, she glimpsed a tall ragged man with a shaved head and a sunburnt face. "Not so hard," she started to say, but before she could finish he'd yanked her bodily from the saddle. The ground came up and knocked the breath from her, as her silver whinnied and backed away. Stunned, Dany rolled to her side and pushed herself onto one elbow . . .

. . . and then she saw the sword.

"There's the treacherous sow," he said. "I knew you'd come to get your feet kissed one day." His head was bald as a melon, his nose red and peeling, but she knew that voice and those pale green eyes. "I'm going to start by cutting off your teats." Dany was dimly aware of Missandei shouting for help. A freedman edged forward, but only a step. One quick slash, and he was on his knees, blood running down his face. Mero wiped his sword on his breeches. "Who's next?"

"I am." Arstan Whitebeard leapt from his horse and stood over her, the salt wind riffling through his snowy hair, both hands on his tall hardwood staff.

"Grandfather," Mero said, "run off before I break your stick in two and bugger you with –"

The old man feinted with one end of the staff, pulled it back, and whipped the other end about faster than Dany would have believed. The Titan's Bastard staggered back into the surf, spitting blood and broken teeth from the ruin of his mouth. Whitebeard put Dany behind him. Mero slashed at his face. The old man jerked back, cat-quick. The staff thumped Mero's ribs, sending him reeling. Arstan splashed sideways, parried a looping cut, danced away from a second, checked a third mid-swing. The moves were so fast she could hardly follow. Missandei was pulling Dany to her feet when she heard a *crack*. She thought Arstan's staff had snapped until she saw the jagged bone jutting from Mero's calf. As he fell, the Titan's Bastard twisted and lunged, sending his point straight at the old man's chest. Whitebeard swept the blade aside almost contemptuously and smashed the other end of his staff against the big man's temple. Mero went sprawling, blood bubbling from his mouth as the waves washed over him. A moment later the freedmen washed over him too, knives and stones and angry fists rising and falling in a frenzy.

Dany turned away, sickened. She was more frightened now than when it had been happening. *He would have killed me.*

"Your Grace." Arstan knelt. "I am an old man, and shamed. He should never have gotten close enough to seize you. I was lax. I did not know him without his beard and hair."

"No more than I did." Dany took a deep breath to stop her shaking. *Enemies everywhere.* "Take me back to my tent. Please."

By the time Mormont arrived, she was huddled in her lion pelt, drinking a cup of spice wine. "I had a look at the river wall," Ser Jorah started. "It's a few feet higher than the others, and just as strong. And the Meereenese have a dozen fire hulks tied up beneath the ramparts –"

She cut him off. "You might have warned me that the Titan's Bastard had escaped."

He frowned. "I saw no need to frighten you, Your Grace. I have offered a reward for his head –"

"Pay it to Whitebeard. Mero has been with us all the way from Yunkai. He shaved his beard off and lost himself amongst the freedmen, waiting for a chance for vengeance. Arstan killed him."

Ser Jorah gave the old man a long look. "A squire with a stick slew Mero of Braavos, is that the way of it?"

"A stick," Dany confirmed, "but no longer a squire. Ser Jorah, it's my wish that Arstan be knighted."

"*No.*"

The loud refusal was surprise enough. Stranger still, it came from both men at once.

Ser Jorah drew his sword. "The Titan's Bastard was a nasty piece of work. And good at killing. Who are you, old man?"

"A better knight than you, ser," Arstan said coldly.

Knight? Dany was confused. "You said you were a squire."

"I was, Your Grace." He dropped to one knee. "I squired for Lord Swann in my youth, and at Magister Illyrio's behest I have served Strong Belwas as well. But during the years between, I was a knight in Westeros. I have told you no lies, my queen. Yet there are truths I have withheld, and for that and all my other sins I can only beg your forgiveness."

"What truths have you withheld?" Dany did not like this. "You will tell me. Now."

He bowed his head. "At Qarth, when you asked my name, I said I was called Arstan. That much was true. Many men had called me by that name while Belwas and I were making our way east to find you. But it is not my true name."

She was more confused than angry. *He has played me false, just as Jorah warned me, yet he saved my life just now.*

Ser Jorah flushed red. "Mero shaved his beard, but you grew one, didn't you? No wonder you looked so bloody familiar . . ."

"You know him?" Dany asked the exile knight, lost.

"I saw him perhaps a dozen times . . . from afar most often, standing with his brothers or riding in some tourney. But every man in the Seven Kingdoms knew Barristan the Bold." He laid the point of his sword against the old man's neck. "*Khaleesi*, before you kneels Ser Barristan Selmy, Lord Commander of the Kingsguard, who betrayed your House to serve the Usurper Robert Baratheon."

The old knight did not so much as blink. "The crow calls the raven black, and *you* speak of betrayal."

"Why are you here?" Dany demanded of him. "If Robert sent you to kill me, why did you save my life?" *He served the Usurper. He betrayed Rhaegar's memory, and abandoned Viserys to live and die in exile. Yet if he wanted me dead, he need only have stood aside . . .* "I want the *whole* truth now, on your honor as a knight. Are you the Usurper's man, or mine?"

"Yours, if you will have me." Ser Barristan had tears in his eyes. "I took Robert's pardon, aye. I served him in Kingsguard and council. Served with the Kingslayer and others near as bad, who soiled the white cloak I wore. Nothing will excuse that. I might be serving in King's Landing still if the vile boy upon the Iron Throne had not cast me aside, it shames me to admit. But when he took the cloak that the White Bull had draped about my shoulders, and sent men to kill me that selfsame day, it was as though he'd ripped a caul off my eyes. That was when I knew I must find my true king, and die in his service –"

"I can grant that wish," Ser Jorah said darkly.

"Quiet," said Dany. "I'll hear him out."

"It may be that I must die a traitor's death," Ser Barristan said. "If so, I should not die alone. Before I took Robert's pardon I fought against him on the Trident. You were on the other side of that battle, Mormont, were you not?" He did not wait for an answer. "Your Grace, I am sorry I misled you. It was the only way to keep the Lannisters from learning that I had joined you. You are watched, as your brother was. Lord Varys reported every move Viserys made, for years. Whilst I sat on the small council, I heard a hundred such reports. And since the day you wed Khal Drogo, there has been an informer by your side selling your secrets, trading whispers to the Spider for gold and promises."

He cannot mean . . . "You are mistaken." Dany looked at Jorah Mormont. "Tell him he's mistaken. There's no informer. Ser Jorah, tell him. We crossed the Dothraki sea together, and the red waste . . ." Her heart fluttered like a bird in a trap. "Tell him, Jorah. Tell him how he got it wrong."

"The Others take you, Selmy." Ser Jorah flung his longsword to the carpet. *"Khaleesi,* it was only at the start, before I came to know you . . . before I came to love . . ."

"Do not say that word!" She backed away from him. *"How could you!* What did the Usurper promise you? Gold, was it gold?" The Undying had said she would be betrayed twice more, once for gold and once for love. "Tell me what you were promised?"

"Varys said . . . I might go home." He bowed his head.

I was going to take you home! Her dragons sensed her fury. Viserion roared, and smoke rose grey from his snout. Drogon beat the air with black wings, and Rhaegal twisted his head back and belched flame. *I should say the word and burn the two of them.* Was there no one she could trust, no one to keep her safe? "Are all the knights of Westeros so false as you two? Get out, before my dragons roast you both. What does roast liar smell like? As foul as Brown Ben's sewers? *Go!"*

Ser Barristan rose stiff and slow. For the first time, he looked his age. "Where shall we go, Your Grace?"

"To hell, to serve King Robert." Dany felt hot tears on her cheeks. Drogon screamed, lashing his tail back and forth. "The Others can have you both." *Go, go away forever, both of you, the next time I see your faces I'll have your traitors' heads off.* She could not say the words, though. *They betrayed me. But they saved me. But they lied.* "You go . . ." *My bear, my fierce strong bear, what will I do without him! And the old man, my brother's friend.* "You go . . . go . . ." *Where!*

And then she knew.

TYRION

Tyrion dressed himself in darkness, listening to his wife's soft breathing from the bed they shared. *She dreams*, he thought, when Sansa murmured something softly – a name, perhaps, though it was too faint to say – and turned onto her side. As man and wife they shared a marriage bed, but that was all. *Even her tears she hoards to herself.*

He had expected anguish and anger when he told her of her brother's death, but Sansa's face had remained so still that for a moment he feared she had not understood. It was only later, with a heavy oaken door between them, that he heard her sobbing. Tyrion had considered going to her then, to offer what comfort he could. *No*, he had to remind himself, *she will not look for solace from a Lannister.* The most he could do was to shield her from the uglier details of the Red Wedding as they came down from the Twins. Sansa did not need to hear how her brother's body had been hacked and mutilated, he decided; nor how her mother's corpse had been dumped naked into the Green Fork in a savage mockery of House Tully's funeral customs. The last thing the girl needed was more fodder for her nightmares.

It was not enough, though. He had wrapped his cloak around her shoulders and sworn to protect her, but that was as cruel a jape as the crown the Freys had placed atop the head of Robb Stark's direwolf after they'd sewn it onto his headless corpse. Sansa knew that as well. The way she looked at him, her stiffness when she climbed into their bed . . . when he was with her, never for an instant could he forget who he was, or *what* he was. No more than she did. She still went nightly to the godswood to pray, and Tyrion wondered if she were praying for his death. She had lost her home, her place in the world, and everyone she had ever loved or trusted. *Winter is coming*, warned the Stark words, and truly it had come for them with a vengeance. *But it is high summer for House Lannister. So why am I so bloody cold?*

He pulled on his boots, fastened his cloak with a lion's head brooch, and slipped out into the torchlit hall. There was this much to be said for his marriage; it had allowed him to escape Maegor's Holdfast. Now that he had a wife and household, his lord father had agreed that more suitable accommodations were required, and Lord Gyles had found himself abruptly dispossessed of his spacious apartments atop the Kitchen Keep. And splendid apartments they were too, with a large bedchamber and adequate solar, a bath and dressing room for his wife, and small adjoining chambers for Pod and Sansa's maids. Even Bronn's cell by the stair had a window of sorts. *Well, more an arrow slit, but it lets in light.* The castle's main kitchen was just across the courtyard, true, but Tyrion found those sounds and smells infinitely preferable to sharing Maegor's with his sister. The less he had to see of Cersei the happier he was like to be.

Tyrion could hear Brella's snoring as he passed her cell. Shae complained of that, but it seemed a small enough price to pay. Varys had suggested the woman to him; in former days, she had run Lord Renly's household in the city, which had given her a deal of practice at being blind, deaf, and mute.

Lighting a taper, he made his way back to the servants' steps and descended. The floors below his own were still, and he heard no footsteps but his own. Down he went, to the ground floor and beyond, to emerge in a gloomy cellar with a vaulted stone ceiling. Much of the castle was connected underground, and the Kitchen Keep was no exception. Tyrion waddled along a long dark passageway until he found the door he wanted, and pushed through.

Within, the dragon skulls were waiting, and so was Shae. "I thought m'lord had forgotten me." Her dress was draped over a black tooth near as tall as she was, and she stood within the dragon's jaws, nude. *Balerion*, he thought. Or was it Vhagar? One dragon skull looked much like another.

Just the sight of her made him hard. "Come out of there."

"I won't." She smiled her wickedest smile. "M'lord will pluck me from the dragon's jaws, I know." But when he waddled closer she leaned forward and blew out the taper.

"Shae . . ." He reached, but she spun and slipped free.

"You have to catch me." Her voice came from his left. "M'lord must have played monsters and maidens when he was little."

"Are you calling me a monster?"

"No more than I'm a maiden." She was behind him, her steps soft against the floor. "You need to catch me all the same."

He did, finally, but only because she let herself be caught. By the time she slipped into his arms, he was flushed and out of breath from stumbling into dragon skulls. All that was forgotten in an instant when he felt her small breasts pressed against his face in the dark, her stiff little nipples brushing lightly over his lips and the scar where his nose had been. Tyrion pulled her down onto the floor. "My giant," she breathed as he entered her. "My giant's come to save me."

After, as they lay entwined amongst the dragon skulls, he rested his head against her, inhaling the smooth clean smell of her hair. "We should go back," he said reluctantly. "It must be near dawn. Sansa will be waking."

"You should give her dreamwine," Shae said, "like Lady Tanda does with Lollys. A cup before she goes to sleep, and we could fuck in bed beside her without her waking." She giggled. "Maybe we should, some night. Would m'lord like that?" Her hand found his shoulder, and began to knead the muscles there. "Your neck is hard as stone. What troubles you?"

Tyrion could not see his fingers in front of his face, but he ticked his woes off on them all the same. "My wife. My sister. My nephew. My father. The Tyrells." He had to move to his other hand. "Varys. Pycelle. Littlefinger. The Red Viper of Dorne." He had come to his last finger. "The face that stares back out of the water when I wash."

Shae kissed his maimed scarred nose. "A brave face. A kind and good face. I wish I could see it now."

All the sweet innocence of the world was in her voice. *Innocence! Fool, she's a whore, all she knows of men is the bit between their legs. Fool, fool.* "Better you than me." Tyrion sat. "We have a long day before us, both of us. You shouldn't have blown out that taper. How are we to find our clothing?"

She laughed. "Maybe we'll have to go naked."

And if we're seen, my lord father will hang you. Hiring Shae as one of Sansa's maids had given him an excuse to be seen talking with her, but Tyrion did not delude himself that they were safe. Varys had warned him. "I gave Shae a false history, but it was meant for Lollys and Lady Tanda. Your sister is of a more suspicious mind. If she should ask me what I know . . ."

"You will tell her some clever lie."

"No. I will tell her that the girl is a common camp follower that you acquired before the battle on the Green Fork and brought to King's Landing against your lord father's express command. I will not lie to the queen."

"You have lied to her before. Shall I tell her that?"

The eunuch sighed. "That cuts more deeply than a knife, my lord. I have served you loyally, but I must also serve your sister when I can. How long do you think she would let me live if I were of no further use to her whatsoever? I have no fierce sellsword to protect me, no valiant brother to avenge me, only some little birds who whisper in my ear. With those whisperings I must buy my life anew each day."

"Pardon me if I do not weep for you."

"I shall, but you must pardon me if I do not weep for Shae. I confess, I do not understand what there is in her to make a clever man like you act such a fool."

"You might, if you were not a eunuch."

"Is that the way of it? A man may have wits, or a bit of meat between his legs, but not both?" Varys tittered. "Perhaps I should be grateful I was cut, then."

The Spider was right. Tyrion groped through the dragon-haunted darkness for his smallclothes, feeling wretched. The risk he was taking left him tight as a drumhead, and there was guilt as well. *The Others can take my guilt,* he thought as he slipped his tunic over his head. *Why should I be guilty? My wife wants no part of me, and most especially not the part that seems to want her.* Perhaps he ought to *tell* her about Shae. It was not as though he was the first man ever to keep a concubine. Sansa's own oh-so-honorable father had given her a bastard brother. For all he knew, his wife might be thrilled to learn that he was fucking Shae, so long as it spared her his unwelcome touch.

No, I dare not. Vows or no, his wife could not be trusted. She might be maiden between the legs, but she was hardly innocent of betrayal; she had once spilled her own father's plans to Cersei. And girls her age were not known for keeping secrets.

The only safe course was to rid himself of Shae. *I might send her to Chataya,* Tyrion reflected, reluctantly. In Chataya's brothel, Shae would have all the silks and gems she could wish for, and the gentlest highborn patrons. It would be a better life by far than the one she had been living when he'd found her.

Or, if she was tired of earning her bread on her back, he might arrange a marriage for her. *Bronn, perhaps?* The sellsword had never balked at eating off his master's plate, and he was a knight now, a better match than she could elsewise hope for. *Or Ser Tallad?* Tyrion had noticed that one gazing wistfully at Shae more than once. *Why not? He's tall, strong, not hard to look upon, every inch the gifted young knight.* Of course, Tallad knew Shae only as a pretty young lady's maid in service at the castle. *If he wed her and then learned she was a whore . . .*

"M'lord, where are you? Did the dragons eat you up?"

"No. Here." He groped at a dragon skull. "I have found a shoe, but I believe it's yours."

"M'lord sounds very solemn. Have I displeased you?"

"No," he said, too curtly. "You always please me." *And therein is our danger.* He might dream of sending her away at times like this, but that never lasted long. Tyrion saw her dimly through the gloom, pulling a woolen sock up a slender leg. *I can see.* A vague light was leaking through the row of long narrow windows set high in the cellar wall. The skulls of the Targaryen dragons were emerging from the darkness around them, black amidst grey. "Day comes too soon." *A new day. A new year. A new century. I survived the Green Fork and the Blackwater, I can bloody well survive King Joffrey's wedding.*

Shae snatched her dress down off the dragon's tooth and slipped it over her head. "I'll go up first. Brella will want help with the bathwater." She bent over to give him one last kiss, upon the brow. "My giant of Lannister. I love you so."

And I love you as well, sweetling. A whore she might well be, but she deserved better than what he had to give her. *I will wed her to Ser Tallad. He seems a decent man. And tall . . .*

SANSA

That was such a sweet dream, Sansa thought drowsily. She had been back in Winterfell, running through the godswood with her Lady. Her father had been there, and her brothers, all of them warm and safe. *If only dreaming could make it so . . .*

She threw back the coverlets. *I must be brave.* Her torments would soon be ended, one way or the other. *If Lady was here, I would not be afraid.* Lady was dead, though; Robb, Bran, Rickon, Arya, her father, her mother, even Septa Mordane. *All of them are dead but me.* She was alone in the world now.

Her lord husband was not beside her, but she was used to that. Tyrion was a bad sleeper and often rose before the dawn. Usually she found him in the solar, hunched beside a candle, lost in some old scroll or leatherbound book. Sometimes the smell of the morning bread from the ovens took him to the kitchens, and sometimes he would climb up to the roof garden or wander all alone down Traitor's Walk.

She threw back the shutters and shivered as gooseprickles rose along her arms. There were clouds massing in the eastern sky, pierced by shafts of sunlight. *They look like two huge castles afloat in the morning sky.* Sansa could see their walls of tumbled stone, their mighty keeps and barbicans. Wispy banners swirled from atop their towers and reached for the fast-fading stars. The sun was coming up behind them, and she watched them go from black to grey to a thousand shades of rose and gold and crimson. Soon the wind mushed them together, and there was only one castle where there had been two.

She heard the door open as her maids brought the hot water for her bath. They were both new to her service; Tyrion said the women who'd tended to her previously had all been Cersei's spies, just as Sansa had always suspected. "Come see," she told them. "There's a castle in the sky."

They came to have a look. "It's made of gold." Shae had short dark hair and bold eyes. She did all that was asked of her, but sometimes she gave Sansa the most insolent looks. "A castle all of gold, there's a sight I'd like to see."

"A castle, is it?" Brella had to squint. "That tower's tumbling over, looks like. It's all ruins, that is."

Sansa did not want to hear about falling towers and ruined castles. She closed the shutters and said, "We are expected at the queen's breakfast. Is my lord husband in the solar?"

"No, m'lady," said Brella. "I have not seen him."

"Might be he went to see his father," Shae declared. "Might be the King's Hand had need of his counsel."

Brella gave a sniff. "Lady Sansa, you'll be wanting to get into the tub before the water gets too cool."

Sansa let Shae pull her shift up over her head and climbed into the big wooden tub. She was tempted to ask for a cup of wine, to calm her nerves. The wedding was to be at midday in the Great Sept of Baelor across the city. And come evenfall the feast would be held in the throne room; a thousand guests and seventy-seven courses, with singers and jugglers and mummers. But first came breakfast in the Queen's Ballroom, for the Lannisters and the Tyrell men – the Tyrell women would be breaking their fast with Margaery – and a hundred odd knights and lordlings. *They have made me a Lannister*, Sansa thought bitterly.

Brella sent Shae to fetch more hot water while she washed Sansa's back. "You are trembling, m'lady."

"The water is not hot enough," Sansa lied.

Her maids were dressing her when Tyrion appeared, Podrick Payne in tow. "You look lovely, Sansa." He turned to his squire. "Pod, be so good as to pour me a cup of wine."

"There will be wine at the breakfast, my lord," Sansa said.

"There's wine here. You don't expect me to face my sister sober, surely? It's a new century, my lady. The three hundredth year since Aegon's Conquest." The dwarf took a cup of red from Podrick and raised it high. "To Aegon. What a fortunate fellow. Two sisters, two wives, and three big dragons, what more could a man ask for?" He wiped his mouth with the back of his hand.

The Imp's clothing was soiled and unkempt, Sansa noticed; it looked as though he'd slept in it. "Will you be changing into fresh garb, my lord? Your new doublet is very handsome."

"The *doublet* is handsome, yes." Tyrion put the cup aside. "Come, Pod, let us see if we can find some garments to make me look less dwarfish. I would not want to shame my lady wife."

When the Imp returned a short time later, he was presentable enough, and even a little taller. Podrick Payne had changed as well, and looked almost a proper squire for once, although a rather large red pimple in the fold beside his nose spoiled the effect of his splendid purple, white, and gold raiment. *He is such a timid boy.* Sansa had been wary of Tyrion's squire at first; he was a Payne, cousin to Ser Ilyn Payne who had taken her father's head off. However, she'd soon come to realize that Pod was as frightened of her as she was of his cousin. Whenever she spoke to him, he turned the most alarming shade of red.

"Are purple, gold, and white the colors of House Payne, Podrick?" she asked him politely.

"No. I mean, yes." He blushed. "The colors. Our arms are purple and white chequy, my lady. With gold coins. In the checks. Purple and white. Both." He studied her feet.

"There's a tale behind those coins," said Tyrion. "No doubt Pod will confide it to your toes one day. Just now we are expected at the Queen's Ballroom, however. Shall we?"

Sansa was tempted to beg off. *I could tell him that my tummy was upset, or that my moon's blood had come.* She wanted nothing more than to crawl back in bed and pull the drapes. *I must be brave, like Robb,* she told herself, as she took her lord husband stiffly by the arm.

In the Queen's Ballroom they broke their fast on honeycakes baked with blackberries and nuts, gammon steaks, bacon, fingerfish crisped in breadcrumbs, autumn pears, and a Dornish dish of onions, cheese, and chopped eggs cooked up with fiery peppers. "Nothing like a hearty breakfast to whet one's appetite for the seventy-seven-course feast to follow," Tyrion commented as their plates were filled. There were flagons of milk and flagons of mead and flagons of a light sweet golden wine to wash it down. Musicians strolled among the tables, piping and fluting and fiddling, while Ser Dontos galloped about on his broomstick horse and Moon Boy made farting sounds with his cheeks and sang rude songs about the guests.

Tyrion scarce touched his food, Sansa noticed, though he drank several cups of the wine. For herself, she tried a little of the Dornish eggs, but the peppers burned her mouth. Otherwise she only nibbled at the fruit and fish and honeycakes. Every time Joffrey looked at her, her tummy got so fluttery that she felt as though she'd swallowed a bat.

When the food had been cleared away, the queen solemnly presented Joff with the wife's cloak that he would drape over Margaery's shoulders. "It is the cloak I donned when Robert took me for his queen, the same cloak my mother Lady Joanna wore when wed to my lord father." Sansa thought it looked threadbare, if truth be told, but perhaps because it was so used.

Then it was time for gifts. It was traditional in the Reach to give presents to bride and groom on the morning of their wedding; on the morrow they would receive more presents as a couple, but today's tokens were for their separate persons.

From Jalabhar Xho, Joffrey received a great bow of golden wood and quiver of long arrows fletched with green and scarlet feathers; from Lady Tanda a pair of supple riding boots; from Ser Kevan a magnificent red leather jousting saddle; a red gold brooch wrought in the shape of a scorpion from the Dornishman, Prince Oberyn; silver spurs from Ser Addam Marbrand; a red silk tourney pavilion from Lord Mathis Rowan. Lord Paxter Redwyne brought forth a beautiful wooden model of the war galley of two hundred oars being built even now on the Arbor. "If it please Your Grace, she will be called *King Joffrey's Valor*," he said, and Joff allowed that he was very pleased indeed. "I will make it my flagship when I sail to Dragonstone to kill my traitor uncle Stannis," he said.

He plays the gracious king today. Joffrey could be gallant when it suited him, Sansa knew, but it seemed to suit him less and less. Indeed, all his courtesy vanished at once when Tyrion presented him with their own gift: a huge old book called *Lives of Four Kings*, bound in leather and gorgeously illuminated. The king leafed through it with no interest. "And what is this, Uncle?"

A book. Sansa wondered if Joffrey moved those fat wormy lips of his when he read.

"Grand Maester Kaeth's history of the reigns of Daeron the Young Dragon, Baelor the Blessed, Aegon the Unworthy, and Daeron the Good," her small husband answered.

"A book every king should read, Your Grace," said Ser Kevan.

"My father had no time for books." Joffrey shoved the tome across the table. "If you read less, Uncle Imp, perhaps Lady Sansa would have a baby in her belly by now." He laughed . . . and when the king laughs, the court laughs with him. "Don't be sad, Sansa, once I've gotten Queen Margaery with child I'll visit your bedchamber and show my little uncle how it's done."

Sansa reddened. She glanced nervously at Tyrion, afraid of what he might say. This could turn as nasty as the bedding had at their own feast. But for once the dwarf filled his mouth with wine instead of words.

Lord Mace Tyrell came forward to present his gift: a golden chalice three feet tall, with two ornate curved handles and seven faces glittering with gemstones. "Seven faces for Your Grace's seven kingdoms," the bride's father explained. He showed them how each face bore the sigil of one of the great houses: ruby lion, emerald rose, onyx stag, silver trout, blue jade falcon, opal sun, and pearl direwolf.

"A splendid cup," said Joffrey, "but we'll need to chip the wolf off and put a squid in its place, I think."

Sansa pretended that she had not heard.

"Margaery and I shall drink deep at the feast, good father." Joffrey lifted the chalice above his head, for everyone to admire.

"The damned thing's as tall as I am," Tyrion muttered in a low voice. "Half a chalice and Joff will be falling down drunk."

Good, she thought. *Perhaps he'll break his neck.*

Lord Tywin waited until last to present the king with his own gift: a longsword. Its scabbard was made of cherrywood, gold, and oiled red leather, studded with golden lions' heads. The lions had ruby eyes, she saw. The ballroom fell silent as Joffrey unsheathed the blade and thrust the sword above his head. Red and black ripples in the steel shimmered in the morning light.

"Magnificent," declared Mathis Rowan.

"A sword to sing of, sire," said Lord Redwyne.

"A *king's* sword," said Ser Kevan Lannister.

King Joffrey looked as if he wanted to kill someone right then and there, he was so excited. He slashed at the air and laughed. "A great sword must have a great name, my lords! What shall I call it?"

Sansa remembered Lion's Tooth, the sword Arya had flung into the Trident, and Hearteater, the one he'd made her kiss before the battle. She wondered if he'd want Margaery to kiss this one.

The guests were shouting out names for the new blade. Joff dismissed a dozen before he heard one he liked. *"Widow's Wail!"* he cried. "Yes! It shall make many a widow, too!" He slashed again. "And when I face my uncle Stannis it will break his magic sword clean in two." Joff tried a downcut, forcing Ser Balon Swann to take a hasty step backward. Laughter rang through the hall at the look on Ser Balon's face.

"Have a care, Your Grace," Ser Addam Marbrand warned the king. "Valyrian steel is perilously sharp."

"I remember." Joffrey brought Widow's Wail down in a savage two-handed slice, onto the book that Tyrion had given him. The heavy leather cover parted at a stroke. "Sharp! I told you, I am no stranger to Valyrian steel." It took him half a dozen further cuts to hack the thick tome apart, and the boy was breathless by the time he was done. Sansa could feel her husband struggling with his fury as Ser Osmund Kettleblack shouted, "I pray you never turn that wicked edge on me, sire."

"See that you never give me cause, ser." Joffrey flicked a chunk of *Lives of Four Kings* off the table at swordpoint, then slid Widow's Wail back into its scabbard.

"Your Grace," Ser Garlan Tyrell said. "Perhaps you did not know. In all of Westeros there were but four copies of that book illuminated in Kaeth's own hand."

"Now there are three." Joffrey undid his old swordbelt to don his new one. "You and Lady Sansa owe me a better present, Uncle Imp. This one is all chopped to pieces."

Tyrion was staring at his nephew with his mismatched eyes. "Perhaps a knife, sire. To match your sword. A dagger of the same fine Valyrian steel . . . with a dragonbone hilt, say?"

Joff gave him a sharp look. "You . . . yes, a dagger to match my sword, good." He nodded. "A . . . a gold hilt with rubies in it. Dragonbone is too plain."

"As you wish, Your Grace." Tyrion drank another cup of wine. He might have been all alone in his solar for all the attention he paid Sansa. But when the time came to leave for the wedding, he took her by the hand.

As they were crossing the yard, Prince Oberyn of Dorne fell in beside them, his black-haired paramour on his arm. Sansa glanced at the woman curiously. She was baseborn and unwed, and had borne two bastard daughters for the prince, but she did not fear to look even the queen in the eye. Shae had told her that this Ellaria worshiped some Lysene love goddess. "She was almost a whore when he found her, m'lady," her maid confided, "and now she's near a princess." Sansa had never been this close to the Dornishwoman before. *She is not truly beautiful*, she thought, *but something about her draws the eye.*

"I once had the great good fortune to see the Citadel's copy of *Lives of Four Kings*," Prince Oberyn was telling her lord husband. "The illuminations were wondrous to behold, but Kaeth was too kind by half to King Viserys."

Tyrion gave him a sharp look. "Too kind? He scants Viserys shamefully, in my view. It should have been *Lives of Five Kings*."

The prince laughed. "Viserys hardly reigned a fortnight."

"He reigned more than a year," said Tyrion.

Oberyn gave a shrug. "A year or a fortnight, what does it matter? He poisoned his own nephew to gain the throne and then did nothing once he had it."

"Baelor starved himself to death, fasting," said Tyrion. "His uncle served him loyally as Hand, as he had served the Young Dragon before him. Viserys might only have reigned a year, but he ruled for fifteen, while Daeron warred and Baelor prayed." He made a sour face. "And if he did remove his nephew, can you blame him? Someone had to save the realm from Baelor's follies."

Sansa was shocked. "But Baelor the Blessed was a great king. He walked the Boneway barefoot to make peace with Dorne, and rescued the

Dragonknight from a snakepit. The vipers refused to strike him because he was so pure and holy."

Prince Oberyn smiled. "If you were a viper, my lady, would you want to bite a bloodless stick like Baelor the Blessed? I'd sooner save my fangs for someone juicier . . ."

"My prince is playing with you, Lady Sansa," said the woman Ellaria Sand. "The septons and singers like to say that the snakes did not bite Baelor, but the truth is very different. He was bitten half a hundred times, and should have died from it."

"If he had, Viserys would have reigned a dozen years," said Tyrion, "and the Seven Kingdoms might have been better served. Some believe Baelor was deranged by all that venom."

"Yes," said Prince Oberyn, "but I've seen no snakes in this Red Keep of yours. So how do you account for Joffrey?"

"I prefer not to." Tyrion inclined his head stiffly. "If you will excuse us. Our litter awaits." The dwarf helped Sansa up inside and clambered awkwardly after her. "Close the curtains, my lady, if you'd be so good."

"Must we, my lord?" Sansa did not want to be shut behind the curtains. "The day is so lovely."

"The good people of King's Landing are like to throw dung at the litter if they see me inside it. Do us both a kindness, my lady. Close the curtains."

She did as he bid her. They sat for a time, as the air grew warm and stuffy around them. "I was sorry about your book, my lord," she made herself say.

"It was Joffrey's book. He might have learned a thing or two if he'd read it." He sounded distracted. "I should have known better. I should have seen . . . a good many things."

"Perhaps the dagger will please him more."

When the dwarf grimaced, his scar tightened and twisted. "The boy's earned himself a dagger, wouldn't you say?" Thankfully Tyrion did not wait for her reply. "Joff quarreled with your brother Robb at Winterfell. Tell me, was there ill feeling between Bran and His Grace as well?"

"Bran?" The question confused her. "Before he fell, you mean?" She had to try and think back. It was all so long ago. "Bran was a sweet boy. Everyone loved him. He and Tommen fought with wooden swords, I remember, but just for play."

Tyrion lapsed back into moody silence. Sansa heard the distant clank of chains from outside; the portcullis was being drawn up. A moment later there was a shout, and their litter swayed into motion. Deprived of the passing scenery, she chose to stare at her folded hands, uncomfortably aware of her husand's mismatched eyes. *Why is he looking at me that way?*

"You loved your brothers, much as I love Jaime."

Is this some Lannister trap to make me speak treason? "My brothers were traitors, and they've gone to traitors' graves. It is treason to love a traitor."

Her little husband snorted. "Robb rose in arms against his rightful king. By law, that made him a traitor. The others died too young to know what treason was." He rubbed his nose. "Sansa, do you know what happened to Bran at Winterfell?"

"Bran fell. He was always climbing things, and finally he fell. We always feared he would. And Theon Greyjoy killed him, but that was later."

"Theon Greyjoy." Tyrion sighed. "Your lady mother once accused me . . . well, I will not burden you with the ugly details. She accused me falsely. I never harmed your brother Bran. And I mean no harm to you."

What does he want me to say? "That is good to know, my lord." He wanted something from her, but Sansa did not know what it was. *He looks like a starving child, but I have no food to give him. Why won't he leave me be?*

Tyrion rubbed at his scarred, scabby nose yet again, an ugly habit that drew the eye to his ugly face. "You have never asked me how Robb died, or your lady mother."

"I . . . would sooner not know. It would give me bad dreams."

"Then I will say no more."

"That . . . that's kind of you."

"Oh, yes," said Tyrion. "I am the very soul of kindness. And I know about bad dreams."

TYRION

The new crown that his father had given the Faith stood twice as tall as the one the mob had smashed, a glory of crystal and spun gold. Rainbow light flashed and shimmered every time the High Septon moved his head, but Tyrion had to wonder how the man could bear the weight. And even he had to concede that Joffrey and Margaery made a regal couple, as they stood side-by-side between the towering gilded statues of the Father and the Mother.

The bride was lovely in ivory silk and Myrish lace, her skirts decorated with floral patterns picked out in seed pearls. As Renly's widow, she might have worn the Baratheon colors, gold and black, yet she came to them a Tyrell, in a maiden's cloak made of a hundred cloth-of-gold roses sewn to green velvet. He wondered if she really was a maiden. *Not that Joffrey is like to know the difference.*

The king looked near as splendid as his bride, in his doublet of dusky rose, beneath a cloak of deep crimson velvet blazoned with his stag and lion. The crown rested easily on his curls, gold on gold. *I saved that bloody crown for him.* Tyrion shifted his weight uncomfortably from one foot to the other. He could not stand still. *Too much wine.* He should have thought to relieve himself before they set out from the Red Keep. The sleepless night he'd spent with Shae was making itself felt too, but most of all he wanted to strangle his bloody royal nephew.

I am no stranger to Valyrian steel, the boy had boasted. The septons were always going on about how the Father Above judges us all. *If the Father would be so good as to topple over and crush Joff like a dung beetle, I might even believe it.*

He ought to have seen it long ago. Jaime would never send another man to do his killing, and Cersei was too cunning to use a knife that could be traced back to her, but Joff, arrogant vicious stupid little wretch that he was . . .

He remembered a cold morning when he'd climbed down the steep exterior steps from Winterfell's library to find Prince Joffrey jesting with the Hound about killing wolves. *Send a dog to kill a wolf*, he said. Even Joffrey was not so foolish as to command Sandor Clegane to slay a son of Eddard Stark, however; the Hound would have gone to Cersei. Instead the boy found his catspaw among the unsavory lot of freeriders, merchants, and camp followers who'd attached themselves to the king's party as they made their way north. *Some poxy lackwit willing to risk his life for a prince's favor and a little coin.* Tyrion wondered whose idea it had been to wait until Robert left Winterfell before opening Bran's throat. *Joff's, most like. No doubt he thought it was the height of cunning.*

The prince's own dagger had a jeweled pommel and inlaid goldwork on the blade, Tyrion seemed to recall. At least Joff had not been stupid enough to use that. Instead he went poking among his father's weapons. Robert Baratheon was a man of careless generosity, and would have given his son any dagger he wanted . . . but Tyrion guessed that the boy had just taken it. Robert had come to Winterfell with a long tail of knights and retainers, a huge wheelhouse, and a baggage train. No doubt some diligent servant had made certain that the king's weapons went with him, in case he should desire any of them.

The blade Joff chose was nice and plain. No goldwork, no jewels in the hilt, no silver inlay on the blade. King Robert never wore it, had likely forgotten he owned it. Yet the Valyrian steel was deadly sharp . . . sharp enough to slice through skin, flesh, and muscle in one quick stroke. *I am no stranger to Valyrian steel.* But he had been, hadn't he? Else he would never have been so foolish as to pick Littlefinger's knife.

The *why* of it still eluded him. *Simple cruelty, perhaps?* His nephew had that in abundance. It was all Tyrion could do not to retch up all the wine he'd drunk, piss in his breeches, or both. He squirmed uncomfortably. He ought to have held his tongue at breakfast. *The boy knows I know now. My big mouth will be the death of me, I swear it.*

The seven vows were made, the seven blessings invoked, and the seven promises exchanged. When the wedding song had been sung and the challenge had gone unanswered, it was time for the exchange of cloaks. Tyrion shifted his weight from one stunted leg to the other, trying to see between his father and his uncle Kevan. *If the gods are just, Joff will make a hash of this.* He made certain not to look at Sansa, lest his bitterness show in his eyes. *You might have knelt, damn you. Would it have been so bloody hard to bend those stiff Stark knees of yours and let me keep a little dignity?*

Mace Tyrell removed his daughter's maiden cloak tenderly, while Joffrey accepted the folded bride's cloak from his brother Tommen and shook it out with a flourish. The boy king was as tall at thirteen as his bride was at sixteen; he would not require a fool's back to climb upon. He draped Margaery in the crimson-and-gold and leaned close to fasten it at her throat. And that easily she passed from her father's protection to her husband's. *But who will protect her from Joff?* Tyrion glanced at the Knight of Flowers, standing with the other Kingsguard. *You had best keep your sword well honed, Ser Loras.*

"With this kiss I pledge my love!" Joffrey declared in ringing tones. When Margaery echoed the words he pulled her close and kissed her long and deep. Rainbow lights danced once more about the High Septon's crown as he solemnly declared Joffrey of the Houses Baratheon and Lannister and Margaery of House Tyrell to be one flesh, one heart, one soul.

Good, that's done with. Now let's get back to the bloody castle so I can have a piss.

Ser Loras and Ser Meryn led the procession from the sept in their white scale armor and snowy cloaks. Then came Prince Tommen, scattering rose petals from a basket before the king and queen. After the royal couple followed Queen Cersei and Lord Tyrell, then the bride's mother arm-in-arm with Lord Tywin. The Queen of Thorns tottered after them with one hand on Ser Kevan Lannister's arm and the other on her cane, her twin guardsmen close behind her in case she fell. Next came Ser Garlan Tyrell and his lady wife, and finally it was their turn.

"My lady." Tyrion offered Sansa his arm. She took it dutifully, but he could feel her stiffness as they walked up the aisle together. She never once looked down at him.

He heard them cheering outside even before he reached the doors. The mob loved Margaery so much they were even willing to love Joffrey again. She had belonged to Renly, the handsome young prince who had loved them so well he had come back from beyond the grave to save them. And the bounty of Highgarden had come with her, flowing up the roseroad from the south. The fools didn't seem to remember that it had been Mace Tyrell who *closed* the roseroad to begin with, and made the bloody famine.

They stepped out into the crisp autumn air. "I feared we'd never escape," Tyrion quipped.

Sansa had no choice but to look at him then. "I . . . yes, my lord. As you say." She looked sad. "It was such a beautiful ceremony, though."

As ours was not. "It was long, I'll say that much. I need to return to the castle for a good piss." Tyrion rubbed the stump of his nose. "Would that I'd contrived some mission to take me out of the city. Littlefinger was the clever one."

Joffrey and Margaery stood surrounded by Kingsguard atop the steps that fronted on the broad marble plaza. Ser Addam and his gold cloaks held back the crowd, while the statue of King Baelor the Blessed gazed down on them benevolently. Tyrion had no choice but to queue up with the rest to offer congratulations. He kissed Margaery's fingers and wished her every happiness. Thankfully, there were others behind them waiting their turn, so they did not need to linger long.

Their litter had been sitting in the sun, and it was very warm inside the curtains. As they lurched into motion, Tyrion reclined on an elbow while Sansa sat staring at her hands. *She is just as comely as the Tyrell girl.* Her hair was a rich autumn auburn, her eyes a deep Tully blue. Grief had given her a haunted, vulnerable look; if anything, it had only made her more beautiful. He wanted to reach her, to break through the armor of her courtesy. Was that what made him speak? Or just the need to distract himself from the fullness in his bladder?

"I had been thinking that when the roads are safe again, we might journey to Casterly Rock." *Far from Joffrey and my sister.* The more he thought about what Joff had done to *Lives of Four Kings,* the more it troubled him. *There was a message there, oh yes.* "It would please me to show you the Golden Gallery and the Lion's Mouth, and the Hall of Heroes where Jaime and I played as boys. You can hear thunder from below where the sea comes in . . ."

She raised her head slowly. He knew what she was seeing; the swollen brutish brow, the raw stump of his nose, his crooked pink scar and mismatched eyes. Her own eyes were big and blue and empty. "I shall go wherever my lord husband wishes."

"I had hoped it might please you, my lady."

"It will please me to please my lord."

His mouth tightened. *What a pathetic little man you are. Did you think babbling about the Lion's Mouth would make her smile? When have you ever made a woman smile but with gold?* "No, it was a foolish notion. Only a Lannister can love the Rock."

"Yes, my lord. As you wish."

Tyrion could hear the commons shouting out King Joffrey's name. *In three years that cruel boy will be a man, ruling in his own right . . . and every dwarf with half his wits will be a long way from King's Landing.* Oldtown, perhaps. Or even the Free Cities. He had always had a yen to see the Titan of Braavos. *Perhaps that would please Sansa.* Gently, he spoke of Braavos, and met a wall of sullen courtesy as icy and unyielding as the Wall he had walked once in the north. It made him weary. Then and now.

They passed the rest of the journey in silence. After a while, Tyrion found himself hoping that Sansa would say something, anything, the merest word, but she never spoke. When the litter halted in the castle yard, he let one of the grooms help her down. "We will be expected at the feast an hour hence, my lady. I will join you shortly." He walked off stiff-legged. Across the yard, he could hear Margaery's breathless laugh as Joffrey swept her from the saddle. *The boy will be as tall and strong as Jaime one day*, he thought, *and I'll still be a dwarf beneath his feet. And one day he's like to make me even shorter . . .*

He found a privy and sighed gratefully as he relieved himself of the morning's wine. There were times when a piss felt near as good as a woman, and this was one. He wished he could relieve himself of his doubts and guilts half as easily.

Podrick Payne was waiting outside his chambers. "I laid out your new doublet. Not here. On your bed. In the bedchamber."

"Yes, that's where we keep the bed." Sansa would be in there, dressing for the feast. *Shae as well.* "Wine, Pod."

Tyrion drank it in his window seat, brooding over the chaos of the kitchens below. The sun had not yet touched the top of the castle wall, but he could smell breads baking and meats roasting. The guests would soon be pouring into the throne room, full of anticipation; this would be an evening of song and splendor, designed not only to unite Highgarden and Casterly Rock but to trumpet their power and wealth as a lesson to any who might still think to oppose Joffrey's rule.

But who would be mad enough to contest Joffrey's rule now, after what had befallen Stannis Baratheon and Robb Stark? There was still fighting in the riverlands, but everywhere the coils were tightening. Ser Gregor Clegane had crossed the Trident and seized the ruby ford, then captured Harrenhal almost effortlessly. Seagard had yielded to Black Walder Frey, Lord Randyll Tarly held Maidenpool, Duskendale, and the kingsroad. In the west, Ser Daven Lannister had linked up with Ser Forley Prester at the Golden Tooth for a march on Riverrun. Ser Ryman Frey was leading two thousand spears down from the Twins to join them. And Paxter Redwyne claimed his fleet would soon set sail from the Arbor, to begin the long voyage around Dorne and through the Stepstones. Stannis's Lyseni pirates would be outnumbered ten to one. The struggle that the maesters were calling the War of the Five Kings was all but at an end. Mace Tyrell had been heard complaining that Lord Tywin had left no victories for him.

"My lord?" Pod was at his side. "Will you be changing? I laid out the doublet. On your bed. For the feast."

"Feast?" said Tyrion sourly. "What feast?"

"The wedding feast." Pod missed the sarcasm, of course. "King Joffrey and Lady Margaery. Queen Margaery, I mean."

Tyrion resolved to get very, very drunk tonight. "Very well, young Podrick, let us go make me festive."

Shae was helping Sansa with her hair when they entered the bed-chamber. *Joy and grief,* he thought when he beheld them there together. *Laughter and tears.* Sansa wore a gown of silvery satin trimmed in vair, with dagged sleeves that almost touched the floor, lined in soft purple felt. Shae had arranged her hair artfully in a delicate silver net winking with dark purple gemstones. Tyrion had never seen her look more lovely, yet she wore sorrow on those long satin sleeves. "Lady Sansa," he told her, "you shall be the most beautiful woman in the hall tonight."

"My lord is too kind."

"My lady," said Shae wistfully. "Couldn't I come serve at table? I so want to see the pigeons fly out of the pie."

Sansa looked at her uncertainly. "The queen has chosen all the servers."

"And the hall will be too crowded." Tyrion had to bite back his annoyance. "There will be musicians strolling all through the castle, though, and tables in the outer ward with food and drink for all." He inspected his new doublet, crimson velvet with padded shoulders and puffed sleeves slashed to show the black satin underlining. *A handsome garment. All it wants is a handsome man to wear it.* "Come, Pod, help me into this."

He had another cup of wine as he dressed, then took his wife by the arm and escorted her from the Kitchen Keep to join the river of silk, satin, and velvet flowing toward the throne room. Some guests had gone inside to find their places on the benches. Others were milling in front of the doors, enjoying the unseasonable warmth of the afternoon. Tyrion led Sansa around the yard, to perform the necessary courtesies.

She is good at this, he thought, as he watched her tell Lord Gyles that his cough was sounding better, compliment Elinor Tyrell on her gown, and question Jalabhar Xho about wedding customs in the Summer Isles. His cousin Ser Lancel had been brought down by Ser Kevan, the first time he'd left his sickbed since the battle. *He looks ghastly.* Lancel's hair had turned white and brittle, and he was thin as a stick. Without his father beside him holding him up, he would surely have collapsed. Yet when Sansa praised his valor and said how good it was to see him getting strong again, both Lancel and Ser Kevan beamed. *She would have made Joffrey a good queen and a better wife if he'd had the sense to love her.* He wondered if his nephew was capable of loving anyone.

"You do look quite exquisite, child," Lady Olenna Tyrell told Sansa when she tottered up to them in a cloth-of-gold gown that must have weighed more than she did. "The wind has been at your hair, though." The little old woman reached up and fussed at the loose strands, tucking them back into place and straightening Sansa's hair net. "I was very sorry to hear about your losses," she said as she tugged and fiddled. "Your brother was a terrible traitor, I know, but if we start killing men at weddings they'll be even more frightened of marriage than they are presently. There, that's better." Lady Olenna smiled. "I am pleased to say I shall be leaving for Highgarden the day after next. I have had quite enough of this smelly city, thank you. Perhaps you would like to accompany me for a little visit, whilst the men are off having their war? I shall miss my Margaery so dreadfully, and all her lovely ladies. Your company would be such sweet solace."

"You are too kind, my lady," said Sansa, "but my place is with my lord husband."

Lady Olenna gave Tyrion a wrinkled, toothless smile. "Oh? Forgive a silly old woman, my lord, I did not mean to steal your lovely wife. I assumed you would be off leading a Lannister host against some wicked foe."

"A host of dragons and stags. The master of coin must remain at court to see that all the armies are paid for."

"To be sure. Dragons and stags, that's very clever. And dwarf's pennies as well. I have heard of these dwarf's pennies. No doubt collecting those is *such* a dreadful chore."

"I leave the collecting to others, my lady."

"Oh, do you? I would have thought you might want to tend to it yourself. We can't have the crown being cheated of its dwarf's pennies, now. Can we?"

"Gods forbid." Tyrion was beginning to wonder whether Lord Luthor Tyrell had ridden off that cliff intentionally. "If you will excuse us, Lady Olenna, it is time we were in our places."

"Myself as well. Seventy-seven courses, I daresay. Don't you find that a bit *excessive*, my lord? I shan't eat more than three or four bites myself, but you and I are very little, aren't we?" She patted Sansa's hair again and said, "Well, off with you, child, and try to be merrier. Now where have my guardsmen gone? Left, Right, where are you? Come help me to the dais."

Although evenfall was still an hour away, the throne room was already a blaze of light, with torches burning in every sconce. The guests stood along the tables as heralds called out the names and titles of the lords and ladies making their entrance. Pages in the royal livery escorted them down the broad central aisle. The gallery above was packed with musicians; drummers and pipers and fiddlers, strings and horns and skins.

Tyrion clutched Sansa's arm and made the walk with a heavy waddling stride. He could feel their eyes on him, picking at the fresh new scar that had left him even uglier than he had been before. *Let them look*, he thought as he hopped up onto his seat. *Let them stare and whisper until they've had their fill, I will not hide myself for their sake.* The Queen of Thorns followed them in, shuffling along with tiny little steps. Tyrion wondered which of them looked more absurd, him with Sansa or the wizened little woman between her seven-foot-tall twin guardsmen.

Joffrey and Margaery rode into the throne room on matched white chargers. Pages ran before them, scattering rose petals under their hooves. The king and queen had changed for the feast as well. Joffrey wore striped black-and-crimson breeches and a cloth-of-gold doublet with black satin sleeves and onyx studs. Margaery had exchanged the demure gown that she had worn in the sept for one much more revealing, a confection in pale green samite with a tight-laced bodice that bared her shoulders and the tops of her small breasts. Unbound, her soft brown hair tumbled over her white shoulders and down her back almost to her waist. Around her brows was a slim golden crown. Her smile was shy and sweet. *A lovely girl*, thought Tyrion, *and a kinder fate than my nephew deserves.*

The Kingsguard escorted them onto the dais, to the seats of honor beneath the shadow of the Iron Throne, draped for the occasion in long silk streamers of Baratheon gold, Lannister crimson, and Tyrell green. Cersei embraced Margaery and kissed her cheeks. Lord Tywin did the same, and then Lancel and Ser Kevan. Joffrey received loving kisses from the bride's father and his two new brothers, Loras and Garlan. No one seemed in any great rush to kiss Tyrion. When the king and queen had taken their seats, the High Septon rose to lead a prayer. *At least he does not drone as badly as the last one*, Tyrion consoled himself.

He and Sansa had been seated far to the king's right, beside Ser Garlan Tyrell and his wife, the Lady Leonette. A dozen others sat closer to Joffrey, which a pricklier man might have taken for a slight, given that he had been the King's Hand only a short time past. Tyrion would have been glad if there had been a hundred.

"Let the cups be filled!" Joffrey proclaimed, when the gods had been given their due. His cupbearer poured a whole flagon of dark Arbor red into the golden wedding chalice that Lord Tyrell had given him that morning. The king had to use both hands to lift it. *"To my wife the queen!"*

"Margaery!" the hall shouted back at him. *"Margaery! Margaery! To the queen!"* A thousand cups rang together, and the wedding feast was well and truly begun. Tyrion Lannister drank with the rest, emptying his cup on that first toast and signaling for it to be refilled as soon as he was seated again.

The first dish was a creamy soup of mushrooms and buttered snails, served in gilded bowls. Tyrion had scarcely touched the breakfast, and the wine had already gone to his head, so the food was welcome. He finished quickly. *One done, seventy-six to come. Seventy-seven dishes, while there are still starving children in this city, and men who would kill for a radish. They might not love the Tyrells half so well if they could see us now.*

Sansa tasted a spoonful of soup and pushed the bowl away. "Not to your liking, my lady?" Tyrion asked.

"There's to be so much, my lord. I have a little tummy." She fiddled nervously with her hair and looked down the table to where Joffrey sat with his Tyrell queen.

Does she wish it were her in Margaery's place? Tyrion frowned. *Even a child should have better sense.* He turned away, wanting distraction, but everywhere he looked were women, fair-fine beautiful happy women who belonged to other men. Margaery, of course, smiling sweetly as she and Joffrey shared a drink from the great seven-sided wedding chalice. Her mother Lady Alerie, silver-haired and handsome, still proud beside Mace Tyrell. The queen's three young cousins, bright as birds. Lord Merryweather's dark-haired Myrish wife with her big black sultry eyes. Ellaria Sand among the Dornishmen (Cersei had placed them at their own table, just below the dais in a place of high honor but as far from the Tyrells as the width of the hall would allow), laughing at something the Red Viper had told her.

And there was one woman, sitting almost at the foot of the third table on the left . . . the wife of one of the Fossoways, he thought, and heavy with his child. Her delicate beauty was in no way diminished by her belly, nor was her pleasure in the food and frolics. Tyrion watched as her husband fed her morsels off his plate. They drank from the same cup, and would kiss often and unpredictably. Whenever they did, his hand would gently rest upon her stomach, a tender and protective gesture.

He wondered what Sansa would do if he leaned over and kissed her right now. *Flinch away, most likely.* Or be brave and suffer through it, as was her duty. *She is nothing if not dutiful, this wife of mine.* If he told her that he wished to have her maidenhead tonight, she would suffer that dutifully as well, and weep no more than she had to.

He called for more wine. By the time he got it, the second course was being served, a pastry coffyn filled with pork, pine nuts, and eggs. Sansa ate no more than a bite of hers, as the heralds were summoning the first of the seven singers.

Grey-bearded Hamish the Harper announced that he would perform "for the ears of gods and men, a song ne'er heard before in all the Seven Kingdoms." He called it "Lord Renly's Ride."

His fingers moved across the strings of the high harp, filling the throne room with sweet sound. *"From his throne of bones the Lord of Death looked down on the murdered lord,"* Hamish began, and went on to tell how Renly, repenting his attempt to usurp his nephew's crown, had defied the Lord of Death himself and crossed back to the land of the living to defend the realm against his brother.

And for this poor Symon wound up in a bowl of brown, Tyrion mused. Queen Margaery was teary-eyed by the end, when the shade of brave Lord Renly flew to Highgarden to steal one last look at his true love's face. "Renly Baratheon never repented of anything in his life," the Imp told Sansa, "but if I'm any judge, Hamish just won himself a gilded lute."

The Harper also gave them several more familiar songs. "A Rose of Gold" was for the Tyrells, no doubt, as "The Rains of Castamere" was meant to flatter his father. "Maiden, Mother, and Crone" delighted the High Septon, and "My Lady Wife" pleased all the little girls with romance in their hearts, and no doubt some little boys as well. Tyrion listened with half a ear, as he sampled sweetcorn fritters and hot oatbread baked with bits of date, apple, and orange, and gnawed on the rib of a wild boar.

Thereafter dishes and diversions succeeded one another in a staggering profusion, buoyed along upon a flood of wine and ale. Hamish left them, his place taken by a smallish elderly bear who danced clumsily to pipe and drum while the wedding guests ate trout cooked in a crust of crushed almonds. Moon Boy mounted his stilts and strode around the tables in pursuit of Lord Tyrell's ludicrously fat fool Butterbumps, and the lords and ladies sampled roast herons and cheese-and-onion pies. A troupe of Pentoshi tumblers performed cartwheels and handstands, balanced platters on their bare feet, and stood upon each other's shoulders to form a pyramid. Their feats were accompanied by crabs boiled in fiery eastern spices, trenchers filled with chunks of chopped mutton stewed in almond milk with carrots, raisins, and onions, and fish tarts fresh from the ovens, served so hot they burned the fingers.

Then the heralds summoned another singer; Collio Quaynis of Tyrosh, who had a vermilion beard and an accent as ludicrous as Symon had promised. Collio began with his version of "The Dance of the Dragons," which was more properly a song for two singers, male and female. Tyrion suffered through it with a double helping of honey-ginger partridge and several cups of wine. A haunting ballad of two dying lovers amidst the Doom of Valyria might have pleased the hall more if Collio had not sung it in High Valyrian, which most of the guests could not speak. But "Bessa the Barmaid" won them back with its ribald lyrics. Peacocks were served in their plumage, roasted whole and stuffed with dates, while Collio summoned a drummer, bowed low before Lord Tywin, and launched into "The Rains of Castamere."

If I have to hear seven versions of that, I may go down to Flea Bottom and apologize to the stew. Tyrion turned to his wife. "So which did you prefer?"

Sansa blinked at him. "My lord?"

"The singers. Which did you prefer?"

"I . . . I'm sorry, my lord. I was not listening."

She was not eating, either. "Sansa, is aught amiss?" He spoke without thinking, and instantly felt the fool. *All her kin are slaughtered and she's wed to me, and I wonder what's amiss.*

"No, my lord." She looked away from him, and feigned an unconvincing interest in Moon Boy pelting Ser Dontos with dates.

Four master pyromancers conjured up beasts of living flame to tear at each other with fiery claws whilst the serving men ladeled out bowls of blandissory, a mixture of beef broth and boiled wine sweetened with honey and dotted with blanched almonds and chunks of capon. Then came some strolling pipers and clever dogs and sword swallowers, with buttered pease, chopped nuts, and slivers of swan poached in a sauce of saffron and peaches. ("Not swan again," Tyrion muttered, remembering his supper with his sister on the eve of battle.) A juggler kept a half-dozen swords and axes whirling through the air as skewers of blood sausage were brought sizzling to the tables, a juxtaposition that Tyrion thought passing clever, though not perhaps in the best of taste.

The heralds blew their trumpets. "To sing for the golden lute," one cried, "we give you Galyeon of Cuy."

Galyeon was a big barrel-chested man with a black beard, a bald head, and a thunderous voice that filled every corner of the throne room. He brought no fewer than six musicians to play for him. "Noble lords and ladies fair, I sing but one song for you this night," he announced. "It is the song of the Blackwater, and how a realm was saved." The drummer began a slow ominous beat.

"The dark lord brooded high in his tower," Galyeon began, *"in a castle as black as the night."*

"Black was his hair and black was his soul," the musicians chanted in unison. A flute came in.

"He feasted on bloodlust and envy, and filled his cup full up with spite," sang Galyeon. *"My brother once ruled seven kingdoms, he said to his harridan wife. I'll take what was his and make it all mine. Let his son feel the point of my knife."*

"A brave young boy with hair of gold," his players chanted, as a woodharp and a fiddle began to play.

"If I am ever Hand again, the first thing I'll do is hang all the singers," said Tyrion, too loudly.

Lady Leonette laughed lightly beside him, and Ser Garlan leaned over to say, "A valiant deed unsung is no less valiant."

"The dark lord assembled his legions, they gathered around him like crows. And thirsty for blood they boarded their ships . . ."

". . . and cut off poor Tyrion's nose," Tyrion finished.

Lady Leonette giggled. "Perhaps you should be a singer, my lord. You rhyme as well as this Galyeon."

"No, my lady," Ser Garlan said. "My lord of Lannister was made to do great deeds, not to sing of them. But for his chain and his wildfire, the foe would have been across the river. And if Tyrion's wildlings had not slain most of Lord Stannis's scouts, we would never have been able to take him unawares."

His words made Tyrion feel absurdly grateful, and helped to mollify him as Galyeon sang endless verses about the valor of the boy king and his mother, the golden queen.

"She never did that," Sansa blurted out suddenly.

"Never believe anything you hear in a song, my lady." Tyrion summoned a serving man to refill their wine cups.

Soon it was full night outside the tall windows, and still Galyeon sang on. His song had seventy-seven verses, though it seemed more like a thousand. *One for every guest in the hall.* Tyrion drank his way through the last twenty or so, to help resist the urge to stuff mushrooms in his ears. By the time the singer had taken his bows, some of the guests were drunk enough to begin providing unintentional entertainments of their own. Grand Maester Pycelle fell asleep while dancers from the Summer Isles swirled and spun in robes made of bright feathers and smoky silk. Roundels of elk stuffed with ripe blue cheese were being brought out when one of Lord Rowan's knights stabbed a Dornishman. The gold cloaks dragged them both away, one to a cell to rot and the other to get sewn up by Maester Ballabar.

Tyrion was toying with a leche of brawn, spiced with cinnamon, cloves, sugar, and almond milk, when King Joffrey lurched suddenly to his feet. "*Bring on my royal jousters!*" he shouted in a voice thick with wine, clapping his hands together.

My nephew is drunker than I am, Tyrion thought as the gold cloaks opened the great doors at the end of the hall. From where he sat, he could only see the tops of two striped lances as a pair of riders entered side by side. A wave of laughter followed them down the center aisle toward the king. *They must be riding ponies*, he concluded . . . until they came into full view.

The jousters were a pair of dwarfs. One was mounted on an ugly grey dog, long of leg and heavy of jaw. The other rode an immense spotted sow. Painted wooden armor clattered and clacked as the little knights bounced up and down in their saddles. Their shields were bigger than they were, and they wrestled manfully with their lances as they clomped along, swaying this way and that and eliciting gusts of mirth. One knight was all in gold, with a black stag painted on his shield; the other wore grey and white, and bore a wolf device. Their mounts were barded likewise.

Tyrion glanced along the dais at all the laughing faces. Joffrey was red and breathless, Tommen was hooting and hopping up and down in his seat, Cersei was chuckling politely, and even Lord Tywin looked mildly amused. Of all those at the high table, only Sansa Stark was not smiling. He could have loved her for that, but if truth be told the Stark girl's eyes were far away, as if she had not even seen the ludicrous riders loping toward her.

The dwarfs are not to blame, Tyrion decided. *When they are done, I shall compliment them and give them a fat purse of silver. And come the morrow, I will find whoever planned this little diversion and arrange for a different sort of thanks.*

When the dwarfs reined up beneath the dais to salute the king, the wolf knight dropped his shield. As he leaned over to grab for it, the stag knight lost control of his heavy lance and slammed him across the back. The wolf knight fell off his pig, and his lance tumbled over and boinked his foe on the head. They both wound up on the floor in a great tangle. When they rose, both tried to mount the dog. Much shouting and shoving followed. Finally they regained their saddles, only mounted on each other's steed, holding the wrong shield and facing backward.

It took some time to sort that out, but in the end they spurred to opposite ends of the hall, and wheeled about for the tilt. As the lords and ladies guffawed and giggled, the little men came together with a crash and a clatter, and the wolf knight's lance struck the helm of the stag knight and knocked his head clean off. It spun through the air spattering blood to land in the lap of Lord Gyles. The headless dwarf careened around the tables, flailing his arms. Dogs barked, women shrieked, and Moon Boy made a great show of swaying perilously back and forth on his stilts, until Lord Gyles pulled a dripping red melon out of the shattered helm, at which point the stag knight poked his face up out of his armor, and another storm of laughter rocked the hall. The knights waited for it to die, circled around each other trading colorful insults, and were about to separate for another joust when the dog threw its rider to the floor and mounted the sow. The huge pig squealed in distress, while the wedding guests squealed with laughter, especially when the stag knight leapt onto the wolf knight, let down his wooden breeches, and started to pump away frantically at the other's nether portions.

"I yield, I yield," the dwarf on the bottom screamed. "Good ser, put up your sword!"

"I would, I would, if you'll stop moving the sheath!" the dwarf on the top replied, to the merriment of all.

Joffrey was snorting wine from both nostrils. Gasping, he lurched to his feet, almost knocking over his tall two-handed chalice. "A champion," he shouted. "We have a champion!" The hall began to quiet when it was seen that the king was speaking. The dwarfs untangled, no doubt anticipating the royal thanks. "Not a *true* champion, though," said Joff. "A true champion defeats *all* challengers." The king climbed up on the table. "Who else will challenge our tiny champion?" With a gleeful smile, he turned toward Tyrion. "*Uncle!* You'll defend the honor of my realm, won't you? You can ride the pig!"

The laughter crashed over him like a wave. Tyrion Lannister did not remember rising, nor climbing on his chair, but he found himself standing on the table. The hall was a torchlit blur of leering faces. He twisted his face into the most hideous mockery of a smile the Seven Kingdoms had ever seen. "Your Grace," he called, "I'll ride the pig . . . but only if you ride the dog!"

Joff scowled, confused. "Me? I'm no dwarf. Why me?"

Stepped right into the cut, Joff. "Why, you're the only man in the hall that I'm certain of defeating!"

He could not have said which was sweeter; the instant of shocked silence, the gale of laughter that followed, or the look of blind rage on his nephew's face. The dwarf hopped back to the floor well satisfied, and by the time he looked back Ser Osmund and Ser Meryn were helping Joff climb down as well. When he noticed Cersei glaring at him, Tyrion blew her a kiss.

It was a relief when the musicians began to play. The tiny jousters led dog and sow from the hall, the guests returned to their trenchers of brawn, and Tyrion called for another cup of wine. But suddenly he felt Ser Garlan's hand on his sleeve. "My lord, beware," the knight warned. "The king."

Tyrion turned in his seat. Joffrey was almost upon him, red-faced and staggering, wine slopping over the rim of the great golden wedding chalice he carried in both hands. "Your Grace," was all he had time to say before the king upended the chalice over his head. The wine washed down over his face in a red torrent. It drenched his hair, stung his eyes, burned in his wound, ran down his cheeks, and soaked the velvet of his new doublet. "How do you like that, Imp?" Joffrey mocked.

Tyrion's eyes were on fire. He dabbed at his face with the back of a sleeve and tried to blink the world back into clarity. "That was ill done, Your Grace," he heard Ser Garlan say quietly.

"Not at all, Ser Garlan." Tyrion dare not let this grow any uglier than it was, not here, with half the realm looking on. "Not every king would think to honor a humble subject by serving him from his own royal chalice. A pity the wine spilled."

"It didn't *spill*," said Joffrey, too graceless to take the retreat Tyrion offered him. "And I wasn't *serving* you, either."

Queen Margaery appeared suddenly at Joffrey's elbow. "My sweet king," the Tyrell girl entreated, "come, return to your place, there's another singer waiting."

"Alaric of Eysen," said Lady Olenna Tyrell, leaning on her cane and taking no more notice of the wine-soaked dwarf than her granddaughter had done. "I do so hope he plays us 'The Rains of Castamere.' It has been an hour, I've forgotten how it goes."

"Ser Addam has a toast he wants to make as well," said Margaery. "Your Grace, please."

"I have no wine," Joffrey declared. "How can I drink a toast if I have no wine? Uncle Imp, you can serve me. Since you won't joust you'll be my cupbearer."

"I would be most honored."

"*It's not meant to be an honor!*" Joffrey screamed. "Bend down and pick up my chalice." Tyrion did as he was bid, but as he reached for the handle Joff kicked the chalice through his legs. "Pick it *up!* Are you as clumsy as you are ugly?" He had to crawl under the table to find the thing. "Good, now fill it with wine." He claimed a flagon from a serving girl and filled the goblet three-quarters full. "No, on your knees, dwarf." Kneeling, Tyrion raised up the heavy cup, wondering if he was about to get a second bath. But Joffrey took the wedding chalice one-handed, drank deep, and set it on the table. "You can get up now, Uncle."

His legs cramped as he tried to rise, and almost spilled him again. Tyrion had to grab hold of a chair to steady himself. Ser Garlan lent him a hand. Joffrey laughed, and Cersei as well. Then others. He could not see who, but he heard them.

"Your Grace." Lord Tywin's voice was impeccably correct. "They are bringing in the pie. Your sword is needed."

"The pie?" Joffrey took his queen by the hand. "Come, my lady, it's the pie."

The guests stood, shouting and applauding and smashing their wine cups together as the great pie made its slow way down the length of the hall, wheeled along by a half-dozen beaming cooks. Two yards across it was, crusty and golden brown, and they could hear squeaks and thumpings coming from inside it.

Tyrion pulled himself back into his chair. All he needed now was for a dove to shit on him and his day would be complete. The wine had soaked through his doublet and smallclothes, and he could feel the wetness against his skin. He ought to change, but no one was permitted to leave the feast until the time came for the bedding ceremony. That was still a good twenty or thirty dishes off, he judged.

King Joffrey and his queen met the pie below the dais. As Joff drew his sword, Margaery laid a hand on his arm to restrain him. "Widow's Wail was not meant for slicing pies."

"True." Joffrey lifted his voice. "Ser Ilyn, your sword!"

From the shadows at the back of the hall, Ser Ilyn Payne appeared. *The specter at the feast,* thought Tyrion as he watched the King's Justice stride forward, gaunt and grim. He had been too young to have known Ser Ilyn before he'd lost his tongue. *He would have been a different man in those days, but now the silence is as much a part of him as those hollow eyes, that rusty chainmail shirt, and the greatsword on his back.*

Ser Ilyn bowed before the king and queen, reached back over his shoulder, and drew forth six feet of ornate silver bright with runes. He knelt to offer the huge blade to Joffrey, hilt first; points of red fire winked from ruby eyes on the pommel, a chunk of dragonglass carved in the shape of a grinning skull.

Sansa stirred in her seat. "What sword is that?"

Tyrion's eyes still stung from the wine. He blinked and looked again. Ser Ilyn's greatsword was as long and wide as Ice, but it was too silvery-bright; Valyrian steel had a darkness to it, a smokiness in its soul. Sansa clutched his arm. "What has Ser Ilyn done with my father's sword?"

I should have sent Ice back to Robb Stark, Tyrion thought. He glanced at his father, but Lord Tywin was watching the king.

Joffrey and Margaery joined hands to lift the greatsword and swung it down together in a silvery arc. When the piecrust broke, the doves burst forth in a swirl of white feathers, scattering in every direction, flapping for the windows and the rafters. A roar of delight went up from the benches, and the fiddlers and pipers in the gallery began to play a sprightly tune. Joff took his bride in his arms, and whirled her around merrily.

A serving man placed a slice of hot pigeon pie in front of Tyrion and covered it with a spoon of lemon cream. The pigeons were well and truly cooked in *this* pie, but he found them no more appetizing than the white ones fluttering about the hall. Sansa was not eating either. "You're deathly pale, my lady," Tyrion said. "You need a breath of cool air, and I need a fresh doublet." He stood and offered her his hand. "Come."

But before they could make their retreat, Joffrey was back. "Uncle, where are you going? You're my cupbearer, remember?"

"I need to change into fresh garb, Your Grace. May I have your leave?"

"No. I like the look of you this way. Serve me my wine."

The king's chalice was on the table where he'd left it. Tyrion had to climb back onto his chair to reach it. Joff yanked it from his hands and drank long and deep, his throat working as the wine ran purple down his chin. "My lord," Margaery said, "we should return to our places. Lord Buckler wants to toast us."

"My uncle hasn't eaten his pigeon pie." Holding the chalice one-handed, Joff jammed his other into Tyrion's pie. "It's ill luck not to eat the pie," he scolded as he filled his mouth with hot spiced pigeon. "See, it's good." Spitting out flakes of crust, he coughed and helped himself to another fistful. "Dry, though. Needs washing down." Joff took a swallow of wine and coughed again, more violently. "I want to see, *kof*, see you ride that, *kof kof*, pig, Uncle. I want . . ." His words broke up in a fit of coughing.

Margaery looked at him with concern. "Your Grace?"

"It's, *kof*, the pie, noth – *kof*, pie." Joff took another drink, or tried to, but all the wine came spewing back out when another spate of coughing doubled him over. His face was turning red. "I, *kof*, I can't, *kof kof kof kof* . . ." The chalice slipped from his hand and dark red wine went running across the dais.

"He's choking," Queen Margaery gasped.

Her grandmother moved to her side. "Help the poor boy!" the Queen of Thorns screeched, in a voice ten times her size. "*Dolts!* Will you all stand about gaping? *Help* your king!"

Ser Garlan shoved Tyrion aside and began to pound Joffrey on the back. Ser Osmund Kettleblack ripped open the king's collar. A fearful high thin sound emerged from the boy's throat, the sound of a man trying to suck a river through a reed; then it stopped, and that was more terrible still. "Turn him over!" Mace Tyrell bellowed at everyone and no one. "Turn him over, shake him by his heels!" A different voice was calling, "Water, give him some *water!*" The High Septon began to pray loudly. Grand Maester Pycelle shouted for someone to help him back to his chambers, to fetch his potions. Joffrey began to claw at his throat, his nails tearing bloody gouges in the flesh. Beneath the skin, the muscles stood out hard as stone. Prince Tommen was screaming and crying.

He is going to die, Tyrion realized. He felt curiously calm, though pandemonium raged all about him. They were pounding Joff on the back again, but his face was only growing darker. Dogs were barking, children were wailing, men were shouting useless advice at each other. Half the wedding guests were on their feet, some shoving at each other for a better view, others rushing for the doors in their haste to get away.

Ser Meryn pried the king's mouth open to jam a spoon down his throat. As he did, the boy's eyes met Tyrion's. *He has Jaime's eyes.* Only he had never seen Jaime look so scared. *The boy's only thirteen.* Joffrey was making a dry clacking noise, trying to speak. His eyes bulged white with terror, and he lifted a hand . . . reaching for his uncle, or pointing . . . *Is he begging my forgiveness, or does he think I can save him?* "Noooo," Cersei wailed, "Father help him, someone help him, my son, my *son* . . ."

Tyrion found himself thinking of Robb Stark. *My own wedding is looking much better in hindsight.* He looked to see how Sansa was taking this, but there was so much confusion in the hall that he could not find her. But his eyes fell on the wedding chalice, forgotten on the floor. He went and scooped it up. There was still a half-inch of deep purple wine in the bottom of it. Tyrion considered it a moment, then poured it on the floor.

Margaery Tyrell was weeping in her grandmother's arms as the old lady said, "Be brave, be brave." Most of the musicians had fled, but one last flutist in the gallery was blowing a dirge. In the rear of the throne room scuffling had broken out around the doors, and the guests were trampling on each other. Ser Addam's gold cloaks moved in to restore order. Guests were rushing headlong out into the night, some weeping, some stumbling and retching, others white with fear. It occurred to Tyrion belatedly that it might be wise to leave himself.

When he heard Cersei's scream, he knew that it was over.

I should leave. Now. Instead he waddled toward her.

His sister sat in a puddle of wine, cradling her son's body. Her gown was torn and stained, her face white as chalk. A thin black dog crept up beside her, sniffing at Joffrey's corpse. "The boy is gone, Cersei," Lord Tywin said. He put his gloved hand on his daughter's shoulder as one of his guardsmen shooed away the dog. "Unhand him now. Let him go." She did not hear. It took two Kingsguard to pry loose her fingers, so the body of King Joffrey Baratheon could slide limp and lifeless to the floor.

The High Septon knelt beside him. "Father Above, judge our good King Joffrey justly," he intoned, beginning the prayer for the dead. Margaery Tyrell began to sob, and Tyrion heard her mother Lady Alerie saying, "He choked, sweetling. He choked on the pie. It was naught to do with you. He choked. We all saw."

"He did not choke." Cersei's voice was sharp as Ser Ilyn's sword. "My son was poisoned." She looked to the white knights standing helplessly around her. "Kingsguard, do your duty."

"My lady?" said Ser Loras Tyrell, uncertain.

"Arrest my brother," she commanded him. "He did this, the dwarf. Him and his little wife. They killed my son. Your king. *Take them!* Take them both!"

SANSA

F ar across the city, a bell began to toll.

Sansa felt as though she were in a dream. "Joffrey is dead," she told the trees, to see if that would wake her.

He had not been dead when she left the throne room. He had been on his knees, though, clawing at his throat, tearing at his own skin as he fought to breathe. The sight of it had been too terrible to watch, and she had turned and fled, sobbing. Lady Tanda had been fleeing as well. "You have a good heart, my lady," she said to Sansa. "Not every maid would weep so for a man who set her aside and wed her to a dwarf."

A good heart. I have a good heart. Hysterical laughter rose up her gullet, but Sansa choked it back down. The bells were ringing, slow and mournful. Ringing, ringing, ringing. They had rung for King Robert the same way. Joffrey was dead, he was dead, he was dead, dead, dead. Why was she crying, when she wanted to dance? Were they tears of joy?

She found her clothes where she had hidden them, the night before last. With no maids to help her, it took her longer than it should have to undo the laces of her gown. Her hands were strangely clumsy, though she was not as frightened as she ought to have been. "The gods are cruel to take him so young and handsome, at his own wedding feast," Lady Tanda had said to her.

The gods are just, thought Sansa. Robb had died at a wedding feast as well. It was Robb she wept for. *Him and Margaery.* Poor Margaery, twice wed and twice widowed. Sansa slid her arm from a sleeve, pushed down the gown, and wriggled out of it. She balled it up and shoved it into the bole of an oak, shook out the clothing she had hidden there. *Dress warmly*, Ser Dontos had told her, *and dress dark*. She had no blacks, so she chose a dress of thick brown wool. The bodice was decorated with freshwater pearls, though. *The cloak will cover them*. The cloak was a deep green, with a large hood. She slipped the dress over her head, and donned the cloak, though she left the hood down for the moment. There were shoes as well, simple and sturdy, with flat heels and square toes. *The gods heard my prayer*, she thought. She felt so numb and dreamy. *My skin has turned to porcelain, to ivory, to steel.* Her hands moved stiffly, awkwardly, as if they had never let down her hair before. For a moment she wished Shae was there, to help her with the net.

When she pulled it free, her long auburn hair cascaded down her back and across her shoulders. The web of spun silver hung from her fingers, the fine metal glimmering softly, the stones black in the moonlight. *Black amethysts from Asshai.* One of them was missing. Sansa lifted the net for a closer look. There was a dark smudge in the silver socket where the stone had fallen out.

A sudden terror filled her. Her heart hammered against her ribs, and for an instant she held her breath. *Why am I so scared, it's only an amethyst, a black amethyst from Asshai, no more than that. It must have been loose in the setting, that's all. It was loose and it fell out, and now it's lying somewhere in the throne room, or in the yard, unless . . .*

Ser Dontos had said the hair net was magic, that it would take her home. He told her she must wear it tonight at Joffrey's wedding feast. The silver wire stretched tight across her knuckles. Her thumb rubbed back and forth against the hole where the stone had been. She tried to stop, but her fingers were not her own. Her thumb was drawn to the hole as the tongue is drawn to a missing tooth. *What kind of magic?* The king was dead, the cruel king who had been her gallant prince a thousand years ago. If Dontos had lied about the hair net, had he lied about the rest as well? *What if he never comes? What if there is no ship, no boat on the river, no escape?* What would happen to her then?

She heard a faint rustle of leaves, and stuffed the silver hair net down deep in the pocket of her cloak. "Who's there?" she cried. "Who is it?" The godswood was dim and dark, and the bells were ringing Joff into his grave.

"Me." He staggered out from under the trees, reeling drunk. He caught her arm to steady himself. "Sweet Jonquil, I've come. Your Florian has come, don't be afraid."

Sansa pulled away from his touch. "You said I must wear the hair net. The silver net with . . . what sort of stones are those?"

"Amethysts. Black amethysts from Asshai, my lady."

"They're no amethysts. Are they? *Are they?* You lied."

"Black amethysts," he swore. "There was magic in them."

"There was *murder* in them!"

"Softly, my lady, softly. No murder. He choked on his pigeon pie." Dontos chortled. "Oh, tasty tasty pie. Silver and stones, that's all it was, silver and stone and magic."

The bells were tolling, and the wind was making a noise like *he* had made as he tried to suck a breath of air. "You poisoned him. You did. You took a stone from my hair . . ."

"Hush, you'll be the death of us. I did nothing. Come, we must away, they'll search for you. Your husband's been arrested."

"Tyrion?" she said, shocked.

"Do you have another husband? The Imp, the dwarf uncle, she thinks he did it." He grabbed her hand and pulled at her. "This way, we must away, quickly now, have no fear."

Sansa followed unresisting. *I could never abide the weeping of women,* Joff once said, but his mother was the only woman weeping now. In Old Nan's stories the grumkins crafted magic things that could make a wish come true. *Did I wish him dead?* she wondered, before she remembered that she was too old to believe in grumkins. "*Tyrion* poisoned him?" Her dwarf husband had hated his nephew, she knew. Could he truly have killed him? *Did he know about my hair net, about the black amethysts? He brought Joff wine.* How could you make someone choke by putting an amethyst in their wine? *If Tyrion did it, they will think I was part of it as well,* she realized with a start of fear. How not? They were man and wife, and Joff had killed her father and mocked her with her brother's death. *One flesh, one heart, one soul.*

"Be quiet now, my sweetling," said Dontos. "Outside the godswood, we must make no sound. Pull up your hood and hide your face." Sansa nodded, and did as he said.

He was so drunk that sometimes Sansa had to lend him her arm to keep him from falling. The bells were ringing out across the city, more and more of them joining in. She kept her head down and stayed in the shadows, close behind Dontos. While descending the serpentine steps he stumbled to his knees and retched. *My poor Florian,* she thought, as he wiped his mouth with a floppy sleeve. *Dress dark,* he'd said, yet under his brown hooded cloak he was wearing his old surcoat; red and pink horizontal stripes beneath a black chief bearing three gold crowns, the arms of House Hollard. "Why are you wearing your surcoat? Joff decreed it was death if you were caught dressed as a knight again, he . . . oh . . ." Nothing Joff had decreed mattered any longer.

"I wanted to be a knight. For this, at least." Dontos lurched back to his feet and took her arm. "Come. Be quiet now, no questions."

They continued down the serpentine and across a small sunken courtyard. Ser Dontos shoved open a heavy door and lit a taper. They were inside a long gallery. Along the walls stood empty suits of armor, dark and dusty, their helms crested with rows of scales that continued down their backs. As they hurried past, the taper's light made the shadows of each scale stretch and twist. *The hollow knights are turning into dragons*, she thought.

One more stair took them to an oaken door banded with iron. "Be strong now, my Jonquil, you are almost there." When Dontos lifted the bar and pulled open the door, Sansa felt a cold breeze on her face. She passed through twelve feet of wall, and then she was outside the castle, standing at the top of the cliff. Below was the river, above the sky, and one was as black as the other.

"We must climb down," Ser Dontos said. "At the bottom, a man is waiting to row us out to the ship."

"I'll fall." Bran had fallen, and he had loved to climb.

"No you won't. There's a sort of ladder, a secret ladder, carved into the stone. Here, you can feel it, my lady." He got down on his knees with her and made her lean over the edge of the cliff, groping with her fingers until she found the handhold cut into the face of the bluff. "Almost as good as rungs."

Even so, it was a long way down. "I *can't*."

"You must."

"Isn't there another way?"

"This is the way. It won't be so hard for a strong young girl like you. Hold on tight and never look down and you'll be at the bottom in no time at all." His eyes were shiny. "Your poor Florian is fat and old and drunk, I'm the one should be afraid. I used to fall off my horse, don't you remember? That was how we began. I was drunk and fell off my horse and Joffrey wanted my fool head, but you saved me. You *saved* me, sweetling."

He's weeping, she realized. "And now you have saved me."

"Only if you go. If not, I have killed us both."

It was him, she thought. *He killed Joffrey.* She had to go, for him as much as for herself. "You go first, ser." If he *did* fall, she did not want him falling down on her head and knocking both of them off the cliff.

"As you wish, my lady." He gave her a sloppy kiss and swung his legs clumsily over the precipice, kicking about until he found a foothold. "Let me get down a bit, and come after. You will come now? You must swear it."

"I'll come," she promised.

Ser Dontos disappeared. She could hear him huffing and puffing as he began the descent. Sansa listened to the tolling of the bell, counting each ring. At ten, gingerly, she eased herself over the edge of the cliff, poking with her toes until they found a place to rest. The castle walls loomed large above her, and for a moment she wanted nothing so much as to pull herself up and run back to her warm rooms in the Kitchen Keep. *Be brave*, she told herself. *Be brave, like a lady in a song.*

Sansa dared not look down. She kept her eyes on the face of the cliff, making certain of each step before reaching for the next. The stone was rough and cold. Sometimes she could feel her fingers slipping, and the handholds were not as evenly spaced as she would have liked. The bells would not stop ringing. Before she was halfway down her arms were trembling and she knew that she was going to fall. *One more step*, she told herself, *one more step*. She had to keep moving. If she stopped, she would never start again, and dawn would find her still clinging to the cliff, frozen in fear. *One more step, and one more step.*

The ground took her by surprise. She stumbled and fell, her heart pounding. When she rolled onto her back and stared up at from where she had come, her head swam dizzily and her fingers clawed at the dirt. *I did it. I did it, I didn't fall, I made the climb and now I'm going home.*

Ser Dontos pulled her back onto her feet. "This way. Quiet now, quiet, quiet." He stayed close to the shadows that lay black and thick beneath the cliffs. Thankfully they did not have to go far. Fifty yards downriver, a man sat in a small skiff, half-hidden by the remains of a great galley that had gone aground there and burned. Dontos limped up to him, puffing. "Oswell?"

"No names," the man said. "In the boat." He sat hunched over his oars, an old man, tall and gangling, with long white hair and a great hooked nose, with eyes shaded by a cowl. "Get in, be quick about it," he muttered. "We need to be away."

When both of them were safe aboard, the cowled man slid the blades into the water and put his back into the oars, rowing them out toward the channel. Behind them the bells were still tolling the boy king's death. They had the dark river all to themselves.

With slow, steady, rhythmic strokes, they threaded their way downstream, sliding above the sunken galleys, past broken masts, burned hulls, and torn sails. The oarlocks had been muffled, so they moved almost soundlessly. A mist was rising over the water. Sansa saw the embattled ramparts of one of the Imp's winch towers looming above, but the great chain had been lowered, and they rowed unimpeded past the spot where a thousand men had burned. The shore fell away, the fog grew thicker, the sound of the bells began to fade. Finally even the lights were gone, lost somewhere behind them. They were out in Blackwater Bay, and the world shrank to dark water, blowing mist, and their silent companion stooped over the oars. "How far must we go?" she asked.

"No talk." The oarsman was old, but stronger than he looked, and his voice was fierce. There was something oddly familiar about his face, though Sansa could not say what it was.

"Not far." Ser Dontos took her hand in his own and rubbed it gently. "Your friend is near, waiting for you."

"*No talk!*" the oarsman growled again. "Sound carries over water, Ser Fool."

Abashed, Sansa bit her lip and huddled down in silence. The rest was rowing, rowing, rowing.

The eastern sky was vague with the first hint of dawn when Sansa finally saw a ghostly shape in the darkness ahead; a trading galley, her sails furled, moving slowly on a single bank of oars. As they drew closer, she saw the ship's figurehead, a merman with a golden crown blowing on a great sea-shell horn. She heard a voice cry out, and the galley swung slowly about.

As they came alongside, the galley dropped a rope ladder over the rail. The rower shipped the oars and helped Sansa to her feet. "Up now. Go on, girl, I got you." Sansa thanked him for his kindness, but received no answer but a grunt. It was much easier going up the rope ladder than it had been coming down the cliff. The oarsman Oswell followed close behind her, while Ser Dontos remained in the boat.

Two sailors were waiting by the rail to help her onto the deck. Sansa was trembling. "She's cold," she heard someone say. He took off his cloak and put it around her shoulders. "There, is that better, my lady? Rest easy, the worst is past and done."

She knew the voice. *But he's in the Vale,* she thought. Ser Lothor Brune stood beside him with a torch.

"Lord Petyr," Dontos called from the boat. "I must needs row back, before they think to look for me."

Petyr Baelish put a hand on the rail. "But first you'll want your payment. Ten thousand dragons, was it?"

"Ten thousand." Dontos rubbed his mouth with the back of his hand. "As you promised, my lord."

"Ser Lothor, the reward."

Lothor Brune dipped his torch. Three men stepped to the gunwale, raised crossbows, fired. One bolt took Dontos in the chest as he looked up, punching through the left crown on his surcoat. The others ripped into throat and belly. It happened so quickly neither Dontos nor Sansa had time to cry out. When it was done, Lothor Brune tossed the torch down on top of the corpse. The little boat was blazing fiercely as the galley moved away.

"You *killed* him." Clutching the rail, Sansa turned away and retched. Had she escaped the Lannisters to tumble into worse?

"My lady," Littlefinger murmured, "your grief is wasted on such a man as that. He was a sot, and no man's friend."

"But he *saved* me."

"He sold you for a promise of ten thousand dragons. Your disappearance will make them suspect you in Joffrey's death. The gold cloaks will hunt, and the eunuch will jingle his purse. Dontos . . . well, you heard him. He sold you for gold, and when he'd drunk it up he would have sold you again. A bag of dragons buys a man's silence for a while, but a well-placed quarrel buys it forever." He smiled sadly. "All he did he did at my behest. I dared not befriend you openly. When I heard how you saved his life at Joff's tourney, I knew he would be the perfect catspaw."

Sansa felt sick. "He said he was my Florian."

"Do you perchance recall what I said to you that day your father sat the Iron Throne?"

The moment came back to her vividly. "You told me that life was not a song. That I would learn that one day, to my sorrow." She felt tears in her eyes, but whether she wept for Ser Dontos Hollard, for Joff, for Tyrion, or for herself, Sansa could not say. "Is it *all* lies, forever and ever, everyone and everything?"

"Almost everyone. Save you and I, of course." He smiled. "*Come to the godswood tonight if you want to go home.*"

"The note . . . it was you?"

"It had to be the godswood. No other place in the Red Keep is safe from the eunuch's little birds . . . or little rats, as I call them. There are trees in the godswood instead of walls. Sky above instead of ceiling. Roots and dirt and rock in place of floor. The rats have no place to scurry. Rats need to hide, lest men skewer them with swords." Lord Petyr took her arm. "Let me show you to your cabin. You have had a long and trying day, I know. You must be weary."

Already the little boat was no more than a swirl of smoke and fire behind them, almost lost in the immensity of the dawn sea. There was no going back; her only road was forward. "Very weary," she admitted.

As he led her below, he said, "Tell me of the feast. The queen took such pains. The singers, the jugglers, the dancing bear . . . did your little lord husband enjoy my jousting dwarfs?"

"Yours?"

"I had to send to Braavos for them and hide them away in a brothel until the wedding. The expense was exceeded only by the bother. It is surprisingly difficult to hide a dwarf, and Joffrey . . . you can lead a king to water, but with Joff one had to splash it about before he realized he could drink it. When I told him about my little surprise, His Grace said, 'Why would I want some ugly dwarfs at my feast? I hate dwarfs.' I had to take him by the shoulder and whisper, 'Not as much as your uncle will.'"

The deck rocked beneath her feet, and Sansa felt as if the world itself had grown unsteady. "They think Tyrion poisoned Joffrey. Ser Dontos said they seized him."

Littlefinger smiled. "Widowhood will become you, Sansa."

The thought made her tummy flutter. She might never need to share a bed with Tyrion again. That *was* what she'd wanted . . . wasn't it?

The cabin was low and cramped, but a featherbed had been laid upon the narrow sleeping shelf to make it more comfortable, and thick furs piled atop it. "It will be snug, I know, but you shouldn't be too uncomfortable." Littlefinger pointed out a cedar chest under the porthole. "You'll find fresh garb within. Dresses, smallclothes, warm stockings, a cloak. Wool and linen only, I fear. Unworthy of a maid so beautiful, but they'll serve to keep you dry and clean until we can find you something finer."

He had this all prepared for me. "My lord, I . . . I do not understand . . . Joffrey gave you Harrenhal, made you Lord Paramount of the Trident . . . why . . ."

"Why should I wish him dead?" Littlefinger shrugged. "I had no motive. Besides, I am a thousand leagues away in the Vale. Always keep your foes confused. If they are never certain who you are or what you want, they cannot know what you are like to do next. Sometimes the best way to baffle them is to make moves that have no purpose, or even seem to work against you. Remember that, Sansa, when you come to play the game."

"What . . . what game?"

"The only game. The game of thrones." He brushed back a strand of her hair. "You are old enough to know that your mother and I were more than friends. There was a time when Cat was all I wanted in this world. I dared to dream of the life we might make and the children she would give me . . . but she was a daughter of Riverrun, and Hoster Tully. *Family, Duty, Honor,* Sansa. *Family, Duty, Honor* meant I could never have her hand. But she gave me something finer, a gift a woman can give but once. How could I turn my back upon her daughter? In a better world, you might have been mine, not Eddard Stark's. My loyal loving daughter . . . Put Joffrey from your mind, sweetling. Dontos, Tyrion, all of them. They will never trouble you again. You are safe now, that's all that matters. You are safe with me, and sailing home."

JAIME

*T*he king is dead, they told him, never knowing that Joffrey was his son as well as his sovereign.

"The Imp opened his throat with a dagger," a costermonger declared at the roadside inn where they spent the night. "He drank his blood from a big gold chalice." The man did not recognize the bearded one-handed knight with the big bat on his shield, no more than any of them, so he said things he might otherwise have swallowed, had he known who was listening.

"It was poison did the deed," the innkeep insisted. "The boy's face turned black as a plum."

"May the Father judge him justly," murmured a septon.

"The dwarf's wife did the murder with him," swore an archer in Lord Rowan's livery. "Afterward, she vanished from the hall in a puff of brimstone, and a ghostly direwolf was seen prowling the Red Keep, blood dripping from his jaws."

Jaime sat silent through it all, letting the words wash over him, a horn of ale forgotten in his one good hand. *Joffrey. My blood. My firstborn. My son.* He tried to bring the boy's face to mind, but his features kept turning into Cersei's. *She will be in mourning, her hair in disarray and her eyes red from crying, her mouth trembling as she tries to speak. She will cry again when she sees me, though she'll fight the tears.* His sister seldom wept but when she was with him. She could not stand for others to think her weak. Only to her twin did she show her wounds. *She will look to me for comfort and revenge.*

They rode hard the next day, at Jaime's insistence. His son was dead, and his sister needed him.

When he saw the city before him, its watchtowers dark against the gathering dusk, Jaime Lannister cantered up to Steelshanks Walton, behind Nage with the peace banner.

"What's that awful stink?" the northman complained.

Death, thought Jaime, but he said, "Smoke, sweat, and shit. King's Landing, in short. If you have a good nose you can smell the treachery too. You've never smelled a city before?"

"I smelled White Harbor. It never stank like this."

"White Harbor is to King's Landing as my brother Tyrion is to Ser Gregor Clegane."

Nage led them up a low hill, the seven-tailed peace banner lifting and turning in the wind, the polished seven-pointed star shining bright upon its staff. He would see Cersei soon, and Tyrion, and their father. *Could my brother truly have killed the boy?* Jaime found that hard to believe.

He was curiously calm. Men were supposed to go mad with grief when their children died, he knew. They were supposed to tear their hair out by the roots, to curse the gods and swear red vengeance. So why was it that he felt so little? *The boy lived and died believing Robert Baratheon his sire.*

Jaime had seen him born, that was true, though more for Cersei than the child. But he had never held him. "How would it look?" his sister warned him when the women finally left them. "Bad enough Joff looks like you without you mooning over him." Jaime yielded with hardly a fight. The boy had been a squalling pink thing who demanded too much of Cersei's time, Cersei's love, and Cersei's breasts. Robert was welcome to him.

And now he's dead. He pictured Joff lying still and cold with a face black from poison, and still felt nothing. Perhaps he *was* the monster they claimed. If the Father Above came down to offer him back his son or his hand, Jaime knew which he would choose. He had a second son, after all, and seed enough for many more. *If Cersei wants another child I'll give her one ... and this time I'll hold him, and the Others take those who do not like it.* Robert was rotting in his grave, and Jaime was sick of lies.

He turned abruptly and galloped back to find Brienne. *Gods know why I bother. She is the least companionable creature I've ever had the misfortune to meet.* The wench rode well behind and a few feet off to the side, as if to proclaim that she was no part of them. They had found men's garb for her along the way; a tunic here, a mantle there, a pair of breeches and a cowled cloak, even an old iron breastplate. She looked more comfortable dressed as a man, but nothing would ever make her look handsome. *Nor happy.* Once out of Harrenhal, her usual pighead stubbornness had soon reasserted itself. "I want my arms and armor back," she had insisted. "Oh, by all means, let us have you back in steel," Jaime replied. "A helm, especially. We'll all be happier if you keep your mouth shut and your visor down."

That much Brienne could do, but her sullen silences soon began to fray his good humor almost as much as Qyburn's endless attempts to be ingratiating. *I never thought I would find myself missing the company of Cleos Frey, gods help me.* He was beginning to wish he had left her for the bear after all.

"King's Landing," Jaime announced when he found her. "Our journey's done, my lady. You've kept your vow, and delivered me to King's Landing. All but a few fingers and a hand."

Brienne's eyes were listless. "That was only half my vow. I told Lady Catelyn I would bring her back her daughters. Or Sansa, at the least. And now . . ."

She never met Robb Stark, yet her grief for him runs deeper than mine for Joff. Or perhaps it was Lady Catelyn she mourned. They had been at Brindlewood when they had *that* news, from a red-faced tub of a knight named Ser Bertram Beesbury, whose arms were three beehives on a field striped black and yellow. A troop of Lord Piper's men had passed through Brindlewood only yesterday, Beesbury told them, rushing to King's Landing beneath a peace banner of their own. "With the Young Wolf dead Piper saw no point to fighting on. His son is captive at the Twins." Brienne gaped like a cow about to choke on her cud, so it fell to Jaime to draw out the tale of the Red Wedding.

"Every great lord has unruly bannermen who envy him his place," he told her afterward. "My father had the Reynes and Tarbecks, the Tyrells have the Florents, Hoster Tully had Walder Frey. Only strength keeps such men in their place. The moment they smell weakness . . . during the Age of Heroes, the Boltons used to flay the Starks and wear their skins as cloaks." She looked so miserable that Jaime almost found himself wanting to comfort her.

Since that day Brienne had been like one half-dead. Even calling her "wench" failed to provoke any response. *The strength is gone from her.* The woman had dropped a rock on Robin Ryger, battled a bear with a tourney sword, bitten off Vargo Hoat's ear, and fought Jaime to exhaustion . . . but she was broken now, done. "I'll speak to my father about returning you to Tarth, if it please you," he told her. "Or if you would rather stay, I could perchance find some place for you at court."

"As a lady companion to the queen?" she said dully.

Jaime remembered the sight of her in that pink satin gown, and tried not to imagine what his sister might say of such a companion. "Perhaps a post with the City Watch . . ."

"I will not serve with oathbreakers and murderers."

Then why did you ever bother putting on a sword? he might have said, but he bit back the words. "As you will, Brienne." One-handed, he wheeled his horse about and left her.

The Gate of the Gods was open when they reached it, but two dozen wayns were lined up along the roadside, loaded with casks of cider, barrels of apples, bales of hay, and some of the biggest pumpkins Jaime had ever seen. Almost every wagon had its guards; men-at-arms wearing the badges of small lordlings, sellswords in mail and boiled leather, sometimes only a pink-cheeked farmer's son clutching a homemade spear with a fire-hardened point. Jaime smiled at them all as he trotted past. At the gate, the gold cloaks were collecting coin from each driver before waving the wagons through. "What's this?" Steelshanks demanded.

"They got to pay for the right to sell inside the city. By command of the King's Hand and the master of coin."

Jaime looked at the long line of wayns, carts, and laden horses. "Yet they still line up to pay?"

"There's good coin to be made here now that the fighting's done," the miller in the nearest wagon told them cheerfully. "It's the Lannisters hold the city now, old Lord Tywin of the Rock. They say he shits silver."

"Gold," Jaime corrected dryly. "And Littlefinger mints the stuff from goldenrod, I vow."

"The Imp is master of coin now," said the captain of the gate. "Or was, till they arrested him for murdering the king." The man looked the northmen over suspiciously. "Who are you lot?"

"Lord Bolton's men, come to see the King's Hand."

The captain glanced at Nage with his peace banner. "Come to bend the knee, you mean. You're not the first. Go straight up to the castle, and see you make no trouble." He waved them through and turned back to the wagons.

If King's Landing mourned its dead boy king, Jaime would never have known it. On the Street of Seeds a begging brother in threadbare robes was praying loudly for Joffrey's soul, but the passersby paid him no more heed than they would a loose shutter banging in the wind. Elsewhere milled the usual crowds; gold cloaks in their black mail, bakers' boys selling tarts and breads and hot pies, whores leaning out of windows with their bodices half unlaced, gutters redolent of nightsoil. They passed five men trying to drag a dead horse from the mouth of an alley, and elsewhere a juggler spinning knives through the air to delight a throng of drunken Tyrell soldiers and small children.

Riding down familiar streets with two hundred northmen, a chainless maester, and an ugly freak of a woman at his side, Jaime found he scarcely drew a second look. He did not know whether he ought to be amused or annoyed. "They do not know me," he said to Steelshanks as they rode through Cobbler's Square.

"Your face is changed, and your arms as well," the northman said, "and they have a new Kingslayer now."

The gates to the Red Keep were open, but a dozen gold cloaks armed with pikes barred the way. They lowered their points as Steelshanks came trotting up, but Jaime recognized the white knight commanding them. "Ser Meryn."

Ser Meryn Trant's droopy eyes went wide. "Ser Jaime?"

"How nice to be remembered. Move these men aside."

It had been a long time since anyone had leapt to obey him quite so fast. Jaime had forgotten how well he liked it.

They found two more Kingsguard in the outer ward, two who had not worn white cloaks when Jaime last served here. *How like Cersei to name me Lord Commander and then choose my colleagues without consulting me.* "Someone has given me two new brothers, I see," he said as he dismounted.

"We have that honor, ser." The Knight of Flowers shone so fine and pure in his white scales and silk that Jaime felt a tattered and tawdry thing by contrast.

Jaime turned to Meryn Trant. "Ser, you've been remiss in teaching our new brothers their duties."

"What duties?" said Meryn Trant defensively.

"Keeping the king alive. How many monarchs have you lost since I left the city? Two, is it?"

Then Ser Balon saw the stump. *"Your hand..."*

Jaime made himself smile. "I fight with my left now. It makes for more of a contest. Where will I find my lord father?"

"In the solar with Lord Tyrell and Prince Oberyn."

Mace Tyrell and the Red Viper breaking bread together? Strange and stranger. "Is the queen with them as well?"

"No, my lord," Ser Balon answered. "You'll find her in the sept, praying over King Joff – "

"You!"

The last of the northmen had dismounted, Jaime saw, and now Loras Tyrell had seen Brienne.

"Ser Loras." She stood stupidly, holding her bridle.

Loras Tyrell strode toward her. "Why?" he said. "You will tell me why. He treated you kindly, gave you a rainbow cloak. Why would you kill him?"

"I never did. I would have died for him."

"You will." Ser Loras drew his longsword.

"It was not me."

"Emmon Cuy swore it was, with his dying breath."

"He was outside the tent, he never saw –"

"There was no one *in* the tent but you and Lady Stark. Do you claim that old woman could cut through hardened steel?"

"There was a *shadow*. I know how mad it sounds, but . . . I was helping Renly into his armor, and the candles blew out and there was blood everywhere. It was Stannis, Lady Catelyn said. His . . . his shadow. I had no part in it, on my honor . . ."

"You have no honor. Draw your sword. I won't have it said that I slew you while your hand was empty."

Jaime stepped between them. "Put the sword away, ser."

Ser Loras edged around him. "Are you a craven as well as a killer, Brienne? Is that why you ran, with his blood on your hands? *Draw your sword, woman!*"

"Best hope she doesn't." Jaime blocked his path again. "Or it's like to be your corpse we carry out. The wench is as strong as Gregor Clegane, though not so pretty."

"This is no concern of yours." Ser Loras shoved him aside.

Jaime grabbed the boy with his good hand and yanked him around. "I am the *Lord Commander of the Kingsguard*, you arrogant pup. *Your* commander, so long as you wear that white cloak. Now *sheathe your bloody sword*, or I'll take it from you and shove it up some place even Renly never found."

The boy hesitated half a heartbeat, long enough for Ser Balon Swann to say, "Do as the Lord Commander says, Loras." Some of the gold cloaks drew their steel then, and that made some Dreadfort men do the same. *Splendid,* thought Jaime, *no sooner do I climb down off my horse than we have a bloodbath in the yard.*

Ser Loras Tyrell slammed his sword back into its sheath.

"That wasn't so difficult, was it?"

"I want her arrested." Ser Loras pointed. "Lady Brienne, I charge you with the murder of Lord Renly Baratheon."

"For what it's worth," said Jaime, "the wench does have honor. More than I have seen from you. And it may even be she's telling it true. I'll grant you, she's not what you'd call clever, but even my horse could come up with a better lie, if it was a lie she meant to tell. As you insist, however . . . Ser Balon, escort Lady Brienne to a tower cell and hold her there under guard. And find some suitable quarters for Steelshanks and his men, until such time as my father can see them."

"Yes, my lord."

Brienne's big blue eyes were full of hurt as Balon Swann and a dozen gold cloaks led her away. *You ought to be blowing me kisses, wench,* he wanted to tell her. Why must they misunderstand every bloody thing he did? *Aerys. It all grows from Aerys.* Jaime turned his back on the wench and strode across the yard.

Another knight in white armor was guarding the doors of the royal sept; a tall man with a black beard, broad shoulders, and a hooked nose. When he saw Jaime he gave a sour smile and said, "And where do you think you're going?"

"Into the sept." Jaime lifted his stump to point. "That one right there. I mean to see the queen."

"Her Grace is in mourning. And why would she be wanting to see the likes of you?"

Because I'm her lover, and the father of her murdered son, he wanted to say. "Who in seven hells are you?"

"A knight of the Kingsguard, and you'd best learn some respect, cripple, or I'll have that other hand and leave you to suck up your porridge of a morning."

"I am the queen's brother, ser."

The white knight thought that funny. "Escaped, have you? And grown a bit as well, m'lord?"

"Her *other* brother, dolt. And the Lord Commander of the Kingsguard. Now stand aside, or you'll wish you had."

The dolt took a long look this time. "Is it . . . Ser Jaime." He straightened. "My pardons, milord. I did not know you. I have the honor to be Ser Osmund Kettleblack."

Where's the honor in that? "I want some time alone with my sister. See that no one else enters the sept, ser. If we're disturbed, I'll have your bloody head."

"Aye, ser. As you say." Ser Osmund opened the door.

Cersei was kneeling before the altar of the Mother. Joffrey's bier had been laid out beneath the Stranger, who led the newly dead to the other world. The smell of incense hung heavy in the air, and a hundred candles burned, sending up a hundred prayers. *Joff's like to need every one of them, too.*

His sister looked over her shoulder. "Who?" she said, then, "Jaime?" She rose, her eyes brimming with tears. "Is it truly you?" She did not come to him, however. *She has never come to me,* he thought. *She has always waited, letting me come to her. She gives, but I must ask.* "You should have come sooner," she murmured, when he took her in his arms. "Why couldn't you have come sooner, to keep him safe? My boy . . ."

Our boy. "I came as fast I could." He broke from the embrace, and stepped back a pace. "It's war out there, Sister."

"You look so thin. And your hair, your golden hair . . ."

"The hair will grow back." Jaime lifted his stump. *She needs to see.* "This won't."

Her eyes went wide. "The Starks . . ."

"No. This was Vargo Hoat's work."

The name meant nothing to her. "Who?"

"The Goat of Harrenhal. For a little while."

Cersei turned to gaze at Joffrey's bier. They had dressed the dead king in gilded armor, eerily similar to Jaime's own. The visor of the helm was closed, but the candles reflected softly off the gold, so the boy shimmered bright and brave in death. The candlelight woke fires in the rubies that decorated the bodice of Cersei's mourning dress as well. Her hair fell to her shoulders, undressed and unkempt. "He killed him, Jaime. Just as he'd warned me. One day when I thought myself safe and happy he would turn my joy to ashes in my mouth, he said."

"Tyrion said that?" Jaime had not wanted to believe it. Kinslaying was worse than kingslaying, in the eyes of gods and men. *He knew the boy was mine. I loved Tyrion. I was good to him.* Well, but for that one time . . . but the Imp did not know the truth of that. *Or did he?* "Why would he kill Joff?"

"For a whore." She clutched his good hand and held it tight in hers. "He *told* me he was going to do it. Joff knew. As he was dying, he *pointed* at his murderer. At our twisted little monster of a brother." She kissed Jaime's fingers. "You'll kill him for me, won't you? You'll avenge our son."

Jaime pulled away. "He is still my brother." He shoved his stump at her face, in case she failed to see it. "And I am in no fit state to be killing anyone."

"You have another hand, don't you? I am not asking you to best the Hound in battle. Tyrion is a *dwarf*, locked in a cell. The guards would stand aside for *you*."

The thought turned his stomach. "I must know more of this. Of how it happened."

"You shall," Cersei promised. "There's to be a trial. When you hear all he did, you'll want him dead as much as I do." She touched his face. "I was lost without you, Jaime. I was afraid the Starks would send me your head. I could not have borne that." She kissed him. A light kiss, the merest brush of her lips on his, but he could feel her tremble as he slid his arms around her. "I am not whole without you."

There was no tenderness in the kiss he returned to her, only hunger. Her mouth opened for his tongue. "No," she said weakly when his lips moved down her neck, "not here. The septons . . ."

"The Others can take the septons." He kissed her again, kissed her silent, kissed her until she moaned. Then he knocked the candles aside and lifted her up onto the Mother's altar, pushing up her skirts and the silken shift beneath. She pounded on his chest with feeble fists, murmuring about the risk, the danger, about their father, about the septons, about the wrath of gods. He never heard her. He undid his breeches and climbed up and pushed her bare white legs apart. One hand slid up her thigh and underneath her smallclothes. When he tore them away, he saw that her moon's blood was on her, but it made no difference.

"Hurry," she was whispering now, "quickly, *quickly*, now, do it now, do me now. Jaime Jaime Jaime." Her hands helped guide him. "Yes," Cersei said as he thrust, "my brother, sweet brother, yes, like that, yes, I have you, you're home now, you're home now, you're *home*." She kissed his ear and stroked his short bristly hair. Jaime lost himself in her flesh. He could feel Cersei's heart beating in time with his own, and the wetness of blood and seed where they were joined.

But no sooner were they done than the queen said, "Let me up. If we are discovered like this . . ."

Reluctantly he rolled away and helped her off the altar. The pale marble was smeared with blood. Jaime wiped it clean with his sleeve, then bent to pick up the candles he had knocked over. Fortunately they had all gone out when they fell. *If the sept had caught fire I might never have noticed.*

"This was folly." Cersei pulled her gown straight. "With Father in the castle . . . Jaime, we must be careful."

"I am sick of being careful. The Targaryens wed brother to sister, why shouldn't we do the same? Marry me, Cersei. Stand up before the realm and say it's me you want. We'll have our own wedding feast, and make another son in place of Joffrey."

She drew back. "That's not funny."

"Do you hear me chuckling?"

"Did you leave your wits at Riverrun?" Her voice had an edge to it. "Tommen's throne derives from Robert, you know that."

"He'll have Casterly Rock, isn't that enough? Let Father sit the throne. All I want is you." He made to touch her cheek. Old habits die hard, and it was his right arm he lifted.

Cersei recoiled from his stump. "*Don't* . . . don't talk like this. You're scaring me, Jaime. Don't be *stupid*. One wrong word and you'll cost us everything. What did they do to you?"

"They cut off my hand."

"No, it's more, you're *changed*." She backed off a step. "We'll talk later. On the morrow. I have Sansa Stark's maids in a tower cell, I need to question them . . . you should go to Father."

"I crossed a thousand leagues to come to you, and lost the best part of me along the way. Don't tell me to leave."

"*Leave me*," she repeated, turning away.

Jaime laced up his breeches and did as she commanded. Weary as he was, he could not seek a bed. By now his lord father knew that he was back in the city.

The Tower of the Hand was guarded by Lannister household guards, who knew him at once. "The gods are good, to give you back to us, ser," one said, as he held the door.

"The gods had no part in it. Catelyn Stark gave me back. Her, and the Lord of the Dreadfort."

He climbed the stairs and pushed into the solar unannounced, to find his father sitting by the fire. Lord Tywin was alone, for which Jaime was thankful. He had no desire to flaunt his maimed hand for Mace Tyrell or the Red Viper just now, much less the two of them together.

"Jaime," Lord Tywin said, as if they'd last seen each other at breakfast. "Lord Bolton led me to expect you earlier. I had hoped you'd be here for the wedding."

"I was delayed." Jaime closed the door softly. "My sister outdid herself, I'm told. Seventy-seven courses and a regicide, never a wedding like it. How long have you known I was free?"

"The eunuch told me a few days after your escape. I sent men into the riverlands to look for you. Gregor Clegane, Samwell Spicer, the brothers Plumm. Varys put out the word as well, but quietly. We agreed that the fewer people who knew you were free, the fewer would be hunting you."

"Did Varys mention this?" He moved closer to the fire, to let his father see.

Lord Tywin pushed himself out of his chair, breath hissing between his teeth. "*Who did this?* If Lady Catelyn thinks –"

"Lady Catelyn held a sword to my throat and made me swear to return her daughters. This was your goat's work. Vargo Hoat, the Lord of Harrenhal!"

Lord Tywin looked away, disgusted. "No longer. Ser Gregor's taken the castle. The sellswords deserted their erstwhile captain almost to a man, and some of Lady Whent's old people opened a postern gate. Clegane found Hoat sitting alone in the Hall of a Hundred Hearths, half-mad with pain and fever from a wound that festered. His ear, I'm told."

Jaime had to laugh. *Too sweet! His ear!* He could scarcely wait to tell Brienne, though the wench wouldn't find it half so funny as he did. "Is he dead yet?"

"Soon. They have taken off his hands and feet, but Clegane seems amused by the way the Qohorik slobbers."

Jaime's smile curdled. "What about his Brave Companions?"

"The few who stayed at Harrenhal are dead. The others scattered. They'll make for ports, I'll warrant, or try and lose themselves in the woods." His eyes went back to Jaime's stump, and his mouth grew taut with fury. "We'll have their heads. Every one. Can you use a sword with your left hand?"

I can hardly dress myself in the morning. Jaime held up the hand in question for his father's inspection. "Four fingers, a thumb, much like the other. Why shouldn't it work as well?"

"Good." His father sat. "That is good. I have a gift for you. For your return. After Varys told me . . ."

"Unless it's a new hand, let it wait." Jaime took the chair across from him. "How did Joffrey die?"

"Poison. It was meant to appear as though he choked on a morsel of food, but I had his throat slit open and the maesters could find no obstruction."

"Cersei claims that Tyrion did it."

"Your brother served the king the poisoned wine, with a thousand people looking on."

"That was rather foolish of him."

"I have taken Tyrion's squire into custody. His wife's maids as well. We shall see if they have anything to tell us. Ser Addam's gold cloaks are searching for the Stark girl, and Varys has offered a reward. The king's justice will be done."

The king's justice. "You would execute your own son?"

"He stands accused of regicide and kinslaying. If he is innocent, he has nothing to fear. First we must needs consider the evidence for and against him."

Evidence. In this city of liars, Jaime knew what sort of evidence would be found. "Renly died strangely as well, when Stannis needed him to."

"Lord Renly was murdered by one of his own guards, some woman from Tarth."

"That woman from Tarth is the reason I'm here. I tossed her into a cell to appease Ser Loras, but I'll believe in Renly's ghost before I believe she did him any harm. But Stannis – "

"It was poison that killed Joffrey, not sorcery." Lord Tywin glanced at Jaime's stump again. "You cannot serve in the Kingsguard without a sword hand – "

"I can," he interrupted. "And I will. There's precedent. I'll look in the White Book and find it, if you like. Crippled or whole, a knight of the Kingsguard serves for life."

"Cersei ended that when she replaced Ser Barristan on grounds of age. A suitable gift to the Faith will persuade the High Septon to release you from your vows. Your sister was foolish to dismiss Selmy, admittedly, but now that she has opened the gates – "

"– someone needs to close them again." Jaime stood. "I am tired of having highborn women kicking pails of shit at me, Father. No one ever asked me if I wanted to be Lord Commander of the Kingsguard, but it seems I am. I have a duty – "

"You do." Lord Tywin rose as well. "A duty to House Lannister. You are the heir to Casterly Rock. That is where you should be. Tommen should accompany you, as your ward and squire. The Rock is where he'll learn to be a Lannister, and I want him away from his mother. I mean to find a new husband for Cersei. Oberyn Martell perhaps, once I convince Lord Tyrell that the match does not threaten Highgarden. And it is past time you were wed. The Tyrells are now insisting that Margaery be wed to Tommen, but if I were to offer you instead –"

"*NO!*" Jaime had heard all that he could stand. No, *more* than he could stand. He was sick of it, sick of lords and lies, sick of his father, his sister, sick of the whole bloody business. "No. No. No. No. No. How many times must I say *no* before you'll hear it? *Oberyn Martell?* The man's infamous, and not just for poisoning his sword. He has more bastards than Robert, and beds with boys as well. And if you think for one misbegotten moment that I would wed Joffrey's widow . . ."

"Lord Tyrell swears the girl's still maiden."

"She can die a maiden as far as I'm concerned. *I don't want her, and I don't want your Rock!*"

"You are my son –"

"I am a knight of the Kingsguard. The *Lord Commander* of the Kingsguard! And that's *all* I mean to be!"

Firelight gleamed golden in the stiff whiskers that framed Lord Tywin's face. A vein pulsed in his neck, but he did not speak. And did not speak. And did not speak.

The strained silence went on until it was more than Jaime could endure. "Father . . ." he began.

"You are not my son." Lord Tywin turned his face away. "You say you are the Lord Commander of the Kingsguard, and only that. Very well, ser. Go do your duty."

DAVOS

Their voices rose like cinders, swirling up into purple evening sky. "Lead us from the darkness, O my Lord. Fill our hearts with fire, so we may walk your shining path."

The nightfire burned against the gathering dark, a great bright beast whose shifting orange light threw shadows twenty feet tall across the yard. All along the walls of Dragonstone the army of gargoyles and grotesques seemed to stir and shift.

Davos looked down from an arched window in the gallery above. He watched Melisandre lift her arms, as if to embrace the shivering flames. "R'hllor," she sang in a voice loud and clear, "you are the light in our eyes, the fire in our hearts, the heat in our loins. Yours is the sun that warms our days, yours the stars that guard us in the dark of night."

"Lord of Light, defend us. The night is dark and full of terrors." Queen Selyse led the responses, her pinched face full of fervor. King Stannis stood beside her, jaw clenched hard, the points of his red-gold crown shimmering whenever he moved his head. *He is with them, but not of them,* Davos thought. Princess Shireen was between them, the mottled grey patches on her face and neck almost black in the firelight.

"Lord of Light, protect us," the queen sang. The king did not respond with the others. He was staring into the flames. Davos wondered what he saw there. *Another vision of the war to come? Or something closer to home?*

"R'hllor who gave us breath, we thank you," sang Melisandre. "R'hllor who gave us day, we thank you."

"We thank you for the sun that warms us," Queen Selyse and the

other worshipers replied. *"We thank you for the stars that watch us. We thank you for our hearths and for our torches, that keep the savage dark at bay."* There were fewer voices saying the responses than there had been the night before, it seemed to Davos; fewer faces flushed with orange light about the fire. But would there be fewer still on the morrow . . . or more?

The voice of Ser Axell Florent rang loud as a trumpet. He stood barrel-chested and bandy-legged, the firelight washing his face like a monstrous orange tongue. Davos wondered if Ser Axell would thank him, after. The work they did tonight might well make him the King's Hand, as he dreamed.

Melisandre cried, "We thank you for Stannis, by your grace our king. We thank you for the pure white fire of his goodness, for the red sword of justice in his hand, for the love he bears his leal people. Guide him and defend him, R'hllor, and grant him strength to smite his foes."

"Grant him strength," answered Queen Selyse, Ser Axell, Devan, and the rest. *"Grant him courage. Grant him wisdom."*

When he was a boy, the septons had taught Davos to pray to the Crone for wisdom, to the Warrior for courage, to the Smith for strength. But it was the Mother he prayed to now, to keep his sweet son Devan safe from the red woman's demon god.

"Lord Davos? We'd best be about it." Ser Andrew touched his elbow gently. "My lord?"

The title still rang queer in his ears, yet Davos turned away from the window. "Aye. It's time." Stannis, Melisandre, and the queen's men would be at their prayers an hour or more. The red priests lit their fires every day at sunset, to thank R'hllor for the day just ending, and beg him to send his sun back on the morrow to banish the gathering darkness. *A smuggler must know the tides and when to seize them.* That was all he was at the end of the day; Davos the smuggler. His maimed hand rose to his throat for his luck, and found nothing. He snatched it down and walked a bit more quickly.

His companions kept pace, matching their strides to his own. The Bastard of Nightsong had a pox-ravaged face and an air of tattered chivalry; Ser Gerald Gower was broad, bluff, and blond; Ser Andrew Estermont stood a head taller, with a spade-shaped beard and shaggy brown eyebrows. They were all good men in their own ways, Davos thought. *And they will all be dead men soon, if this night's work goes badly.*

"Fire is a living thing," the red woman told him, when he asked her to teach him how to see the future in the flames. "It is always moving, always changing . . . like a book whose letters dance and shift even as you try to read them. It takes years of training to see the shapes beyond the flames, and more years still to learn to tell the shapes of what will be from what may be or what was. Even then it comes hard, *hard*. You do not understand that, you men of the sunset lands." Davos asked her then how it was that Ser Axell had learned the trick of it so quickly, but to that she only smiled enigmatically and said, "Any cat may stare into a fire and see red mice at play."

He had not lied to his king's men, about that or any of it. "The red woman may see what we intend," he warned them.

"We should start by killing her, then," urged Lewys the Fishwife. "I know a place where we could waylay her, four of us with sharp swords . . ."

"You'd doom us all," said Davos. "Maester Cressen tried to kill her, and she knew at once. From her flames, I'd guess. It seems to me that she is very quick to sense any threat to her own person, but surely she cannot see *everything*. If we ignore her, perhaps we might escape her notice."

"There is no honor in hiding and sneaking," objected Ser Triston of Tally Hill, who had been a Sunglass man before Lord Guncer went to Melisandre's fires.

"Is it so honorable to burn?" Davos asked him. "You saw Lord Sunglass die. Is that what you want? I don't need men of honor now. I need *smugglers*. Are you with me, or no?"

They were. Gods be good, they were.

Maester Pylos was leading Edric Storm through his sums when Davos pushed open the door. Ser Andrew was close behind him; the others had been left to guard the steps and cellar door. The maester broke off. "That will be enough for now, Edric."

The boy was puzzled by the intrusion. "Lord Davos, Ser Andrew. We were doing sums."

Ser Andrew smiled. "I hated sums when I was your age, coz."

"I don't mind them so much. I like history best, though. It's full of tales."

"Edric," said Maester Pylos, "run and get your cloak now. You're to go with Lord Davos."

"I am?" Edric got to his feet. "Where are we going?" His mouth set stubbornly. "I won't go pray to the Lord of Light. I am a Warrior's man, like my father."

"We know," Davos said. "Come, lad, we must not dawdle."

Edric donned a thick hooded cloak of undyed wool. Maester Pylos helped him fasten it, and pulled the hood up to shadow his face. "Are you coming with us, Maester?" the boy asked.

"No." Pylos touched the chain of many metals he wore about his neck. "My place is here on Dragonstone. Go with Lord Davos now, and do as he says. He is the King's Hand, remember. What did I tell you about the King's Hand?"

"The Hand speaks with the king's voice."

The young maester smiled. "That's so. Go now."

Davos had been uncertain of Pylos. Perhaps he resented him for taking old Cressen's place. But now he could only admire the man's courage. *This could mean his life as well.*

Outside the maester's chambers, Ser Gerald Gower waited by the steps. Edric Storm looked at him curiously. As they made their descent he asked, "Where are we going, Lord Davos?"

"To the water. A ship awaits you."

The boy stopped suddenly. "A ship?"

"One of Salladhor Saan's. Salla is a good friend of mine."

"I shall go with you, Cousin," Ser Andrew assured him. "There's nothing to be frightened of."

"I am not *frightened,*" Edric said indignantly. "Only . . . is Shireen coming too?"

"No," said Davos. "The princess must remain here with her father and mother."

"I have to see her then," Edric explained. "To say my farewells. Otherwise she'll be sad."

Not so sad as if she sees you burn. "There is no time," Davos said. "I will tell the princess that you were thinking of her. And you can write her, when you get to where you're going."

The boy frowned. "Are you sure I must go? Why would my uncle send me from Dragonstone? Did I displease him? I never meant to." He got that stubborn look again. "I want to see my uncle. I want to see King Stannis."

Ser Andrew and Ser Gerald exchanged a look. "There's no time for that, Cousin," Ser Andrew said.

"I want to see him!" Edric insisted, louder.

"He does not want to see you." Davos had to say something, to get the boy moving. "I am his Hand, I speak with his voice. Must I go to the king and tell him that you would not do as you were told? Do you know how angry that will make him? Have you ever seen your uncle angry?" He pulled off his glove and showed the boy the four fingers that Stannis had shortened. "I have."

It was all lies; there had been no anger in Stannis Baratheon when he cut the ends off his onion knight's fingers, only an iron sense of justice. But Edric Storm had not been born then, and could not know that. And the threat had the desired effect. "He should not have done that," the boy said, but he let Davos take him by the hand and draw him down the steps.

The Bastard of Nightsong joined them at the cellar door. They walked quickly, across a shadowed yard and down some steps, under the stone tail of a frozen dragon. Lewys the Fishwife and Omer Blackberry waited at the postern gate, two guards bound and trussed at their feet. "The boat?" Davos asked them.

"It's there," Lewys said. "Four oarsmen. The galley is anchored just past the point. *Mad Prendos.*"

Davos chuckled. *A ship named after a madman. Yes, that's fitting.* Salla had a streak of the pirate's black humor.

He went to one knee before Edric Storm. "I must leave you now," he said. "There's a boat waiting, to row you out to a galley. Then it's off across the sea. You are Robert's son so I know you will be brave, no matter what happens."

"I will. Only . . ." The boy hesitated.

"Think of this as an adventure, my lord." Davos tried to sound hale and cheerful. "It's the start of your life's great adventure. May the Warrior defend you."

"And may the Father judge you justly, Lord Davos." The boy went with his cousin Ser Andrew out the postern gate. The others followed, all but the Bastard of Nightsong. *May the Father judge me justly,* Davos thought ruefully. But it was the king's judgment that concerned him now.

"These two?" asked Ser Rolland of the guards, when he had closed and barred the gate.

"Drag them into a cellar," said Davos. "You can cut them free when Edric's safely under way."

The Bastard gave a curt nod. There were no more words to say; the easy part was done. Davos pulled his glove on, wishing he had not lost his luck. He had been a better man and a braver one with that bag of bones around his neck. He ran his shortened fingers through thinning brown hair, and wondered if it needed to be cut. He must look presentable when he stood before the king.

Dragonstone had never seemed so dark and fearsome. He walked slowly, his footsteps echoing off black walls and dragons. *Stone dragons who will never wake, I pray.* The Stone Drum loomed huge ahead of him. The guards at the door uncrossed their spears as he approached. *Not for the onion knight, but for the King's Hand.* Davos was the Hand going in, at least. He wondered what he would be coming out. *If I ever do . . .*

The steps seemed longer and steeper than before, or perhaps it was just that he was tired. *The Mother never made me for tasks like this.* He had risen too high and too fast, and up here on the mountain the air was too thin for him to breathe. As a boy he'd dreamed of riches, but that was long ago. Later, grown, all he had wanted was a few acres of good land, a hall to grow old in, a better life for his sons. The Blind Bastard used to tell him that a clever smuggler did not overreach, nor draw too much attention to himself. *A few acres, a timbered roof, a "ser" before my name, I should have been content.* If he survived this night, he would take Devan and sail home to Cape Wrath and his gentle Marya. *We will grieve together for our dead sons, raise the living ones to be good men, and speak no more of kings.*

The Chamber of the Painted Table was dark and empty when Davos entered; the king would still be at the nightfire, with Melisandre and the queen's men. He knelt and made a fire in the hearth, to drive the chill from the round chamber and chase the shadows back into their corners. Then he went around the room to each window in turn, opening the heavy velvet curtains and unlatching the wooden shutters. The wind came in, strong with the smell of salt and sea, and pulled at his plain brown cloak.

At the north window, he leaned against the sill for a breath of the cold night air, hoping to catch a glimpse of *Mad Prendos* raising sail, but the sea seemed black and empty as far as the eye could see. *Is she gone already?* He could only pray that she was, and the boy with her. A half moon was sliding in and out amongst thin high clouds, and Davos could see familiar stars. There was the Galley, sailing west; there the Crone's Lantern, four bright stars that enclosed a golden haze. The clouds hid most of the Ice Dragon, all but the bright blue eye that marked due north. *The sky is full of smugglers' stars.* They were old friends, those stars; Davos hoped that meant good luck.

But when he lowered his gaze from the sky to the castle ramparts, he was not so certain. The wings of the stone dragons cast great black shadows in the light from the nightfire. He tried to tell himself that they were no more than carvings, cold and lifeless. *This was their place, once. A place of dragons and dragonlords, the seat of House Targaryen.* The Targaryens were the blood of old Valyria . . .

The wind sighed through the chamber, and in the hearth the flames gusted and swirled. He listened to the logs crackle and spit. When Davos left the window his shadow went before him, tall and thin, and fell across the Painted Table like a sword. And there he stood for a long time, waiting. He heard their boots on the stone steps as they ascended. The king's voice went before him. ". . . is not three," he was saying.

"Three is three," came Melisandre's answer. "I swear to you, Your Grace, I saw him die and heard his mother's wail."

"In the nightfire." Stannis and Melisandre came through the door together. "The flames are full of tricks. What is, what will be, what may be. You cannot tell me for a certainty . . ."

"Your Grace." Davos stepped forward. "Lady Melisandre saw it true. Your nephew Joffrey is dead."

If the king was surprised to find him at the Painted Table, he gave no sign. "Lord Davos," he said. "He was not my nephew. Though for years I believed he was."

"He choked on a morsel of food at his wedding feast," Davos said. "It may be that he was poisoned."

"He is the third," said Melisandre.

"I can count, woman." Stannis walked along the table, past Oldtown and the Arbor, up toward the Shield Islands and the mouth of the Mander. "Weddings have become more perilous than battles, it would seem. Who was the poisoner? Is it known?"

"His uncle, it's said. The Imp."

Stannis ground his teeth. "A dangerous man. I learned that on the Blackwater. How do you come by this report?"

"The Lyseni still trade at King's Landing. Salladhor Saan has no reason to lie to me."

"I suppose not." The king ran his fingers across the table. "Joffrey . . . I remember once, this kitchen cat . . . the cooks were wont to feed her scraps and fish heads. One told the boy that she had kittens in her belly, thinking he might want one. Joffrey opened up the poor thing with a dagger to see if it were true. When he found the kittens, he brought them to show to his father. Robert hit the boy so hard I thought he'd killed him." The king took off his crown and placed it on the table. "Dwarf or leech, this killer served the kingdom well. They *must* send for me now."

"They will not," said Melisandre. "Joffrey has a brother."

"Tommen." The king said the name grudgingly.

"They will crown Tommen, and rule in his name."

Stannis made a fist. "Tommen is gentler than Joffrey, but born of the same incest. Another monster in the making. Another leech upon the land. Westeros needs a man's hand, not a child's."

Melisandre moved closer. "Save them, sire. Let me wake the stone dragons. Three is three. Give me the boy."

"Edric Storm," Davos said.

Stannis rounded on him in a cold fury. "*I know his name*. Spare me your reproaches. I like this no more than you do, but my duty is to the realm. My duty . . ." He turned back to Melisandre. "You swear there is no other way? Swear it on your life, for I promise, you shall die by inches if you lie."

"You are he who must stand against the Other. The one whose coming was prophesied five thousand years ago. The red comet was your herald. You are the prince that was promised, and if you fail the world fails with you." Melisandre went to him, her red lips parted, her ruby throbbing. "Give me this boy," she whispered, "and I will give you your kingdom."

"He can't," said Davos. "Edric Storm is gone."

"Gone?" Stannis turned. "What do you mean, *gone?*"

"He is aboard a Lyseni galley, safely out to sea." Davos watched Melisandre's pale, heart-shaped face. He saw the flicker of dismay there, the sudden uncertainty. *She did not see it!*

The king's eyes were dark blue bruises in the hollows of his face. "The bastard was taken from Dragonstone without my leave? A galley, you say? If that Lysene pirate thinks to use the boy to squeeze gold from me –"

"This is your Hand's work, sire." Melisandre gave Davos a knowing look. "You will bring him back, my lord. You will."

"The boy is out of my reach," said Davos. "And out of your reach as well, my lady."

Her red eyes made him squirm. "I should have left you to the dark, ser. Do you know what you have done?"

"My duty."

"Some might call it treason." Stannis went to the window to stare out into the night. *Is he looking for the ship?* "I raised you up from dirt, Davos." He sounded more tired than angry. "Was loyalty too much to hope for?"

"Four of my sons died for you on the Blackwater. I might have died myself. You have my loyalty, always." Davos Seaworth had thought long and hard about the words he said next; he knew his life depended on them. "Your Grace, you made me swear to give you honest counsel and swift obedience, to defend your realm against your foes, to *protect your people*. Is not Edric Storm one of your people? One of those I swore to protect? I kept my oath. How could that be treason?"

Stannis ground his teeth again. "I never asked for this crown. Gold is cold and heavy on the head, but so long as I *am* the king, I have a duty . . . If I must sacrifice one child to the flames to save a million from the dark . . . *Sacrifice* . . . is never easy, Davos. Or it is no true sacrifice. Tell him, my lady."

Melisandre said, "Azor Ahai tempered Lightbringer with the heart's blood of his own beloved wife. If a man with a thousand cows gives one to god, that is nothing. But a man who offers the only cow he owns . . ."

"She talks of cows," Davos told the king. "I am speaking of a boy, your daughter's friend, your brother's son."

"A king's son, with the power of kingsblood in his veins." Melisandre's ruby glowed like a red star at her throat. "Do you think you've saved this boy, Onion Knight? When the long night falls, Edric Storm shall die with the rest, wherever he is hidden. Your own sons as well. Darkness and cold will cover the earth. You meddle in matters you do not understand."

"There's much I don't understand," Davos admitted. "I have never pretended elsewise. I know the seas and rivers, the shapes of the coasts, where the rocks and shoals lie. I know hidden coves where a boat can land unseen. And I know that a king protects his people, or he is no king at all."

Stannis's face darkened. "Do you mock me to my face? Must I learn a king's duty from an onion smuggler?"

Davos knelt. "If I have offended, take my head. I'll die as I lived, your loyal man. But hear me first. Hear me for the sake of the onions I brought you, and the fingers you took."

Stannis slid Lightbringer from its scabbard. Its glow filled the chamber. "Say what you will, but say it quickly." The muscles in the king's neck stood out like cords.

Davos fumbled inside his cloak and drew out the crinkled sheet of parchment. It seemed a thin and flimsy thing, yet it was all the shield he had. "A King's Hand should be able to read and write. Maester Pylos has been teaching me." He smoothed the letter flat upon his knee and began to read by the light of the magic sword.

JON

He dreamt he was back in Winterfell, limping past the stone kings on their thrones. Their grey granite eyes turned to follow him as he passed, and their grey granite fingers tightened on the hilts of the rusted swords upon their laps. *You are no Stark*, he could hear them mutter, in heavy granite voices. *There is no place for you here. Go away.* He walked deeper into the darkness. "Father?" he called. "Bran? Rickon?" No one answered. A chill wind was blowing on his neck. "Uncle?" he called. "Uncle Benjen? Father? Please, Father, help me." Up above he heard drums. *They are feasting in the Great Hall, but I am not welcome there. I am no Stark, and this is not my place.* His crutch slipped and he fell to his knees. The crypts were growing darker. *A light has gone out somewhere.* "Ygritte?" he whispered. "Forgive me. Please." But it was only a direwolf, grey and ghastly, spotted with blood, his golden eyes shining sadly through the dark . . .

The cell was dark, the bed hard beneath him. His own bed, he remembered, his own bed in his steward's cell beneath the Old Bear's chambers. By rights it should have brought him sweeter dreams. Even beneath the furs, he was cold. Ghost had shared his cell before the ranging, warming it against the chill of night. And in the wild, Ygritte had slept beside him. *Both gone now.* He had burned Ygritte himself, as he knew she would have wanted, and Ghost . . . *Where are you?* Was *he* dead as well, was that what his dream had meant, the bloody wolf in the crypts? But the wolf in the dream had been grey, not white. *Grey, like Bran's wolf.* Had the Thenns hunted him down and killed him after Queenscrown? If so, Bran was lost to him for good and all.

Jon was trying to make sense of that when the horn blew.

The Horn of Winter, he thought, still confused from sleep. But Mance never found Joramun's horn, so that couldn't be. A second blast followed, as long and deep as the first. Jon had to get up and go to the Wall, he knew, but it was so hard . . .

He shoved aside his furs and sat. The pain in his leg seemed duller, nothing he could not stand. He had slept in his breeches and tunic and smallclothes, for the added warmth, so he had only to pull on his boots and don leather and mail and cloak. The horn blew again, two long blasts, so he slung Longclaw over one shoulder, found his crutch, and hobbled down the steps.

It was the black of night outside, bitter cold and overcast. His brothers were spilling out of towers and keeps, buckling their swordbelts and walking toward the Wall. Jon looked for Pyp and Grenn, but could not find them. Perhaps one of them was the sentry blowing the horn. *It is Mance*, he thought. *He has come at last.* That was good. *We will fight a battle, and then we'll rest. Alive or dead, we'll rest.*

Where the stair had been, only an immense tangle of charred wood and broken ice remained below the Wall. The winch raised them up now, but the cage was only big enough for ten men at a time, and it was already on its way up by the time Jon arrived. He would need to wait for its return. Others waited with him; Satin, Mully, Spare Boot, Kegs, big blond Hareth with his buck teeth. Everyone called him Horse. He had been a stablehand in Mole's Town, one of the few moles who had stayed at Castle Black. The rest had run back to their fields and hovels, or their beds in the underground brothel. Horse wanted to take the black, though, the great buck-toothed fool. Zei remained as well, the whore who'd proved so handy with a crossbow, and Noye had kept three orphan boys whose father had died on the steps. They were young – nine and eight and five – but no one else seemed to want them.

As they waited for the cage to come back, Clydas brought them cups of hot mulled wine, while Three-Finger Hobb passed out chunks of black bread. Jon took a heel from him and gnawed on it.

"Is it Mance Rayder?" Satin asked anxiously.

"We can hope so." There were worse things than wildlings in the dark. Jon remembered the words the wildling king had spoken on the Fist of the First Men, as they stood amidst that pink snow. *When the dead walk, walls and stakes and swords mean nothing. You cannot fight the dead, Jon Snow. No man knows that half so well as me.* Just thinking of it made the wind seem a little colder.

Finally the cage came clanking back down, swaying at the end of the long chain, and they crowded in silently and shut the door.

Mully yanked the bell rope three times. A moment later they began to rise, by fits and starts at first, then more smoothly. No one spoke. At the top the cage swung sideways and they clambered out one by one. Horse gave Jon a hand down onto the ice. The cold hit him in the teeth like a fist.

A line of fires burned along the top of the Wall, contained in iron baskets on poles taller than a man. The cold knife of the wind stirred and swirled the flames, so the lurid orange light was always shifting. Bundles of quarrels, arrows, spears, and scorpion bolts stood ready on every hand. Rocks were piled ten feet high, big wooden barrels of pitch and lamp oil lined up beside them. Bowen Marsh had left Castle Black well supplied in everything save men. The wind was whipping at the black cloaks of the scarecrow sentinels who stood along the ramparts, spears in hand. "I hope it wasn't one of them who blew the horn," Jon said to Donal Noye when he limped up beside him.

"Did you hear that?" Noye asked.

There was the wind, and horses, and something else. "A mammoth," Jon said. "That was a mammoth."

The armorer's breath was frosting as it blew from his broad, flat nose. North of the Wall was a sea of darkness that seemed to stretch forever. Jon could make out the faint red glimmer of distant fires moving through the wood. It was Mance, certain as sunrise. The Others did not light torches.

"How do we fight them if we can't see them?" Horse asked.

Donal Noye turned toward the two great trebuchets that Bowen Marsh had restored to working order. "Give me *light!*" he roared.

Barrels of pitch were loaded hastily into the slings and set afire with a torch. The wind fanned the flames to a brisk red fury. "*NOW!*" Noye bellowed. The counterweights plunged downward, the throwing arms rose to *thud* against the padded crossbars. The burning pitch went tumbling through the darkness, casting an eerie flickering light upon the ground below. Jon caught a glimpse of mammoths moving ponderously through the half-light, and just as quickly lost them again. *A dozen, maybe more.* The barrels struck the earth and burst. They heard a deep bass trumpeting, and a giant roared something in the Old Tongue, his voice an ancient thunder that sent shivers up Jon's spine.

"*Again!*" Noye shouted, and the trebuchets were loaded once more. Two more barrels of burning pitch went crackling through the gloom to come crashing down amongst the foe. This time one of them struck a dead tree, enveloping it in flame. *Not a dozen mammoths*, Jon saw, *a hundred.*

He stepped to the edge of the precipice. *Careful*, he reminded himself, *it is a long way down.* Red Alyn sounded his sentry's horn once more, *Aaaaahooooooooooooooooooooooooooo, aaaaahoooooooooooooooooooooo.* And now the wildlings answered, not with one horn but with a dozen, and with drums and pipes as well. *We are come,* they seemed to say, *we are come to break your Wall, to take your lands and steal your daughters.* The wind howled, the trebuchets creaked and thumped, the barrels flew. Behind the giants and the mammoths, Jon saw men advancing on the Wall with bows and axes. Were there twenty or twenty thousand? In the dark there was no way to tell. *This is a battle of blind men, but Mance has a few thousand more of them than we do.*

"The gate!" Pyp cried out. "They're at the *GATE!*"

The Wall was too big to be stormed by any conventional means; too high for ladders or siege towers, too thick for battering rams. No catapult could throw a stone large enough to breach it, and if you tried to set it on fire, the icemelt would quench the flames. You could climb over, as the raiders did near Greyguard, but only if you were strong and fit and sure-handed, and even then you might end up like Jarl, impaled on a tree. *They must take the gate, or they cannot pass.*

But the gate was a crooked tunnel through the ice, smaller than any castle gate in the Seven Kingdoms, so narrow that rangers must lead their garrons through single file. Three iron grates closed the inner passage, each locked and chained and protected by a murder hole. The outer door was old oak, nine inches thick and studded with iron, not easy to break through. *But Mance has mammoths,* he reminded himself, *and giants as well.*

"Must be cold down there," said Noye. "What say we warm them up, lads?" A dozen jars of lamp oil had been lined up on the precipice. Pyp ran down the line with a torch, setting them alight. Owen the Oaf followed, shoving them over the edge one by one. Tongues of pale yellow fire swirled around the jars as they plunged downward. When the last was gone, Grenn kicked loose the chocks on a barrel of pitch and sent it rumbling and rolling over the edge as well. The sounds below changed to shouts and screams, sweet music to their ears.

Yet still the drums beat on, the trebuchets shuddered and thumped, and the sound of skinpipes came wafting through the night like the songs of strange fierce birds. Septon Cellador began to sing as well, his voice tremulous and thick with wine.

> *Gentle Mother, font of mercy,*
> *save our sons from war, we pray,*
> *stay the swords and stay the arrows,*
> *let them know . . .*

Donal Noye rounded on him. "Any man here stays his sword, I'll chuck his puckered arse right off this Wall . . . starting with you, Septon. *Archers!* Do we have any bloody archers?"

"Here," said Satin.

"And here," said Mully. "But how can I find a target? It's black as the inside of a pig's belly. Where are they?"

Noye pointed north. "Loose enough arrows, might be you'll find a few. At least you'll make them fretful." He looked around the ring of firelit faces. "I need two bows and two spears to help me hold the tunnel if they break the gate." More than ten stepped forward, and the smith picked his four. "Jon, you have the Wall till I return."

For a moment Jon thought he had misheard. It had sounded as if Noye were leaving him in command. "My lord?"

"*Lord?* I'm a blacksmith. I said, the Wall is yours."

There are older men, Jon wanted to say, *better men. I am still as green as summer grass. I'm wounded, and I stand accused of desertion.* His mouth had gone bone dry. "Aye," he managed.

Afterward it would seem to Jon Snow as if he'd dreamt that night. Side by side with the straw soldiers, with longbows or crossbows clutched in half-frozen hands, his archers launched a hundred flights of arrows against men they never saw. From time to time a wildling arrow came flying back in answer. He sent men to the smaller catapults and filled the air with jagged rocks the size of a giant's fist, but the darkness swallowed them as a man might swallow a handful of nuts. Mammoths trumpeted in the gloom, strange voices called out in stranger tongues, and Septon Cellador prayed so loudly and drunkenly for the dawn to come that Jon was tempted to chuck him over the edge himself. They heard a mammoth dying at their feet and saw another lurch burning through the woods, trampling down men and trees alike. The wind blew cold and colder. Hobb rode up the chain with cups of onion broth, and Owen and Clydas served them to the archers where they stood, so they could gulp them down between arrows. Zei took a place among them with her crossbow. Hours of repeated jars and shocks knocked something loose on the right-hand trebuchet, and its counterweight came crashing free, suddenly and catastrophically, wrenching the throwing arm sideways with a splintering crash. The left-hand trebuchet kept throwing, but the wildlings had quickly learned to shun the place where its loads were landing.

We should have twenty trebuchets, not two, and they should be mounted on sledges and turntables so we could move them. It was a futile thought. He might as well wish for another thousand men, and maybe a dragon or three.

Donal Noye did not return, nor any of them who'd gone down with him to hold that black cold tunnel. *The Wall is mine*, Jon reminded himself whenever he felt his strength flagging. He had taken up a long-bow himself, and his fingers felt crabbed and stiff, half-frozen. His fever was back as well, and his leg would tremble uncontrollably, sending a white-hot knife of pain right through him. *One more arrow, and I'll rest*, he told himself, half a hundred times. *Just one more.* Whenever his quiver was empty, one of the orphaned moles would bring him another. *One more quiver, and I'm done.* It couldn't be long until the dawn.

When morning came, none of them quite realized it at first. The world was still dark, but the black had turned to grey and shapes were beginning to emerge half-seen from the gloom. Jon lowered his bow to stare at the mass of heavy clouds that covered the eastern sky. He could see a glow behind them, but perhaps he was only dreaming. He notched another arrow.

Then the rising sun broke through to send pale lances of light across the battleground. Jon found himself holding his breath as he looked out over the half-mile swath of cleared land that lay between the Wall and the edge of the forest. In half a night they had turned it into a wasteland of blackened grass, bubbling pitch, shattered stone, and corpses. The carcass of the burned mammoth was already drawing crows. There were giants dead on the ground as well, but behind them . . .

Someone moaned to his left, and he heard Septon Cellador say, "Mother have mercy, oh. Oh, oh, oh, *Mother have mercy*."

Beneath the trees were all the wildlings in the world; raiders and giants, wargs and skinchangers, mountain men, salt sea sailors, ice river canni-bals, cave dwellers with dyed faces, dog chariots from the Frozen Shore, Hornfoot men with their soles like boiled leather, all the queer wild folk Mance had gathered to break the Wall. *This is not your land*, Jon wanted to shout at them. *There is no place for you here. Go away.* He could hear Tormund Giantsbane laughing at that. "You know nothing, Jon Snow," Ygritte would have said. He flexed his sword hand, opening and closing the fingers, though he knew full well that swords would not come into it up here.

He was chilled and feverish, and suddenly the weight of the longbow was too much. The battle with the Magnar had been nothing, he realized, and the night fight less than nothing, only a probe, a dagger in the dark to try and catch them unprepared. The real battle was only now beginning.

"I never knew there would be so *many*," Satin said.

Jon had. He had seen them before, but not like this, not drawn up in battle array. On the march the wildling column had sprawled over long leagues like some enormous worm, but you never saw all of it at once. But now . . .

"Here they come," someone said in a hoarse voice.

Mammoths centered the wildling line, he saw, a hundred or more with giants on their backs clutching mauls and huge stone axes. More giants loped beside them, pushing along a tree trunk on great wooden wheels, its end sharpened to a point. *A ram*, he thought bleakly. If the gate still stood below, a few kisses from that thing would soon turn it into splinters. On either side of the giants came a wave of horsemen in boiled leather harness with fire-hardened lances, a mass of running archers, hundreds of foot with spears, slings, clubs, and leathern shields. The bone chariots from the Frozen Shore clattered forward on the flanks, bouncing over rocks and roots behind teams of huge white dogs. *The fury of the wild*, Jon thought as he listened to the skirl of skins, to the dogs barking and baying, the mammoths trumpeting, the free folk whistling and screaming, the giants roaring in the Old Tongue. Their drums echoed off the ice like rolling thunder.

He could feel the despair all around him. "There must be a hundred thousand," Satin wailed. "How can we stop so many?"

"The Wall will stop them," Jon heard himself say. He turned and said it again, louder. "The *Wall* will stop them. *The Wall defends itself.*" Hollow words, but he needed to say them, almost as much as his brothers needed to hear them. "Mance wants to unman us with his numbers. Does he think we're *stupid?*" He was shouting now, his leg forgotten, and every man was listening. "The chariots, the horsemen, all those fools on foot . . . what are they going to do to us up here? Any of you ever see a mammoth climb a wall?" He laughed, and Pyp and Owen and half a dozen more laughed with him. "They're *nothing*, they're less use than our straw brothers here, they can't reach us, they can't hurt us, and they don't frighten us, do they?"

"*NO!*" Grenn shouted.

"They're down there and we're up here," Jon said, "and so long as we hold the gate they cannot pass. *They cannot pass!*" They were all shouting then, roaring his own words back at him, waving swords and longbows in the air as their cheeks flushed red. Jon saw Kegs standing there with a warhorn slung beneath his arm. "Brother," he told him, "sound for battle."

Grinning, Kegs lifted the horn to his lips, and blew the two long blasts that meant *wildlings*. Other horns took up the call until the Wall itself seemed to shudder, and the echo of those great deep-throated moans drowned all other sound.

"Archers," Jon said when the horns had died away, "you'll aim for the giants with that ram, every bloody one of you. Loose *at my command*, not before. *THE GIANTS AND THE RAM.* I want arrows raining on them with every step, but we'll wait till they're in range. Any man who wastes an arrow will need to climb down and fetch it back, do you hear me?"

"I do," shouted Owen the Oaf. "I hear you, Lord Snow."

Jon laughed, laughed like a drunk or a madman, and his men laughed with him. The chariots and the racing horsemen on the flanks were well ahead of the center now, he saw. The wildlings had not crossed a third of the half mile, yet their battle line was dissolving. "Load the trebuchet with caltrops," Jon said. "Owen, Kegs, angle the catapults toward the center. Scorpions, load with fire spears and loose at my command." He pointed at the Mole's Town boys. "You, you, and you, stand by with torches."

The wildling archers shot as they advanced; they would dash forward, stop, loose, then run another ten yards. There were so many that the air was constantly full of arrows, all falling woefully short. *A waste*, Jon thought. *Their want of discipline is showing.* The smaller horn-and-wood bows of the free folk were outranged by the great yew longbows of the Night's Watch, and the wildlings were trying to shoot at men seven hundred feet above them. *"Let them shoot,"* Jon said. "Wait. Hold." Their cloaks were flapping behind them. "The wind is in our faces, it will cost us range. Wait." *Closer, closer.* The skins wailed, the drums thundered, the wildling arrows fluttered and fell.

"DRAW." Jon lifted his own bow and pulled the arrow to his ear. Satin did the same, and Grenn, Owen the Oaf, Spare Boot, Black Jack Bulwer, Arron and Emrick. Zei hoisted her crossbow to her shoulder. Jon was watching the ram come on and on, the mammoths and giants lumbering forward on either side. They were so small he could have crushed them all in one hand, it seemed. *If only my hand was big enough.* Through the killing ground they came. A hundred crows rose from the carcass of the dead mammoth as the wildlings thundered past to either side of them. Closer and closer, until . . .

"LOOSE!"

The black arrows hissed downward, like snakes on feathered wings. Jon did not wait to see where they struck. He reached for a second arrow as soon as the first left his bow. *"NOTCH. DRAW. LOOSE."* As soon as the arrow flew he found another. *"NOTCH. DRAW. LOOSE."* Again, and then again. Jon shouted for the trebuchet, and heard the creak and heavy *thud* as a hundred spiked steel caltrops went spinning through the air. *"Catapults,"* he called, *"scorpions. Bowmen, loose at will."* Wildling arrows were striking the Wall now, a hundred feet below them. A second giant spun and staggered. *Notch, draw, loose.* A mammoth veered into another beside it, spilling giants on the ground. *Notch, draw, loose.* The ram was down and done, he saw, the giants who'd pushed it dead or dying. *"Fire arrows,"* he shouted. "I want that ram burning." The screams of wounded mammoths and the booming cries of giants mingled with the drums and pipes to make an awful music, yet still his archers drew and loosed, as if they'd all gone as deaf as dead Dick Follard. They might be the dregs of the order, but they were men of the Night's Watch, or near enough as made no matter. *That's why they shall not pass.*

One of the mammoths was running berserk, smashing wildlings with his trunk and crushing archers underfoot. Jon pulled back his bow once more, and launched another arrow at the beast's shaggy back to urge him on. To east and west, the flanks of the wildling host had reached the Wall unopposed. The chariots drew in or turned while the horsemen milled aimlessly beneath the looming cliff of ice. *"At the gate!"* a shout came. Spare Boot, maybe. *"Mammoth at the gate!"*

"Fire," Jon barked. "Grenn, Pyp."

Grenn thrust his bow aside, wrestled a barrel of oil onto its side, and rolled it to the edge of the Wall, where Pyp hammered out the plug that sealed it, stuffed in a twist of cloth, and set it alight with a torch. They shoved it over together. A hundred feet below it struck the Wall and burst, filling the air with shattered staves and burning oil. Grenn was rolling a second barrel to the precipice by then, and Kegs had one as well. Pyp lit them both. *"Got him!"* Satin shouted, his head sticking out so far that Jon was certain he was about to fall. *"Got him, got him, GOT him!"* He could hear the roar of fire. A flaming giant lurched into view, stumbling and rolling on the ground.

Then suddenly the mammoths were fleeing, running from the smoke and flames and smashing into those behind them in their terror. Those went backward too, the giants and wildlings behind them scrambling to get out of their way. In half a heartbeat the whole center was collapsing. The horsemen on the flanks saw themselves being abandoned and decided to fall back as well, not one so much as blooded. Even the chariots rumbled off, having done nothing but look fearsome and make a lot of noise. *When they break, they break hard*, Jon Snow thought as he watched them reel away. The drums had all gone silent. *How do you like that music, Mance? How do you like the taste of the Dornishman's wife?* "Do we have anyone hurt?" he asked.

"The bloody buggers got my leg." Spare Boot plucked the arrow out and waved it above his head. "The wooden one!"

A ragged cheer went up. Zei grabbed Owen by the hands, spun him around in a circle, and gave him a long wet kiss right there for all to see. She tried to kiss Jon too, but he held her by the shoulder and pushed her gently but firmly away. "No," he said. *I am done with kissing.* Suddenly he was too weary to stand, and his leg was agony from knee to groin. He fumbled for his crutch. "Pyp, help me to the cage. Grenn, you have the Wall."

"Me?" said Grenn. *"Him?"* said Pyp. It was hard to tell which of them was more horrified. "But," Grenn stammered, "b-but what do I do if the wildlings attack again?"

"Stop them," Jon told him.

As they rode down in the cage, Pyp took off his helm and wiped his brow. "Frozen sweat. Is there anything as disgusting as frozen sweat?" He laughed. "Gods, I don't think I have ever been so hungry. I could eat an aurochs whole, I swear it. Do you think Hobb will cook up Grenn for us?" When he saw Jon's face, his smile died. "What's wrong? Is it your leg?"

"My leg," Jon agreed. Even the words were an effort.

"Not the battle, though? We won the battle."

"Ask me when I've seen the gate," Jon said grimly. *I want a fire, a hot meal, a warm bed, and something to make my leg stop hurting*, he told himself. But first he had to check the tunnel and find what had become of Donal Noye.

After the battle with the Thenns it had taken them almost a day to clear the ice and broken beams away from the inner gate. Spotted Pate and Kegs and some of the other builders had argued heatedly that they ought just leave the debris there, another obstacle for Mance. That would have meant abandoning the defense of the tunnel, though, and Noye was having none of it. With men in the murder holes and archers and spears behind each inner grate, a few determined brothers could hold off a hundred times as many wildlings and clog the way with corpses. He did not mean to give Mance Rayder free passage through the ice. So with pick and spade and ropes, they had moved the broken steps aside and dug back down to the gate.

Jon waited by the cold iron bars while Pyp went to Maester Aemon for the spare key. Surprisingly, the maester himself returned with him, and Clydas with a lantern. "Come see me when we are done," the old man told Jon while Pyp was fumbling with the chains. "I need to change your dressing and apply a fresh poultice, and you will want some more dreamwine for the pain."

Jon nodded weakly. The door swung open. Pyp led them in, followed by Clydas and the lantern. It was all Jon could do to keep up with Maester Aemon. The ice pressed close around them, and he could feel the cold seeping into his bones, the weight of the Wall above his head. It felt like walking down the gullet of an ice dragon. The tunnel took a twist, and then another. Pyp unlocked a second iron gate. They walked farther, turned again, and saw light ahead, faint and pale through the ice. *That's bad*, Jon knew at once. *That's very bad.*

Then Pyp said, "There's blood on the floor."

The last twenty feet of the tunnel was where they'd fought and died. The outer door of studded oak had been hacked and broken and finally torn off its hinges, and one of the giants had crawled in through the splinters. The lantern bathed the grisly scene in a sullen reddish light. Pyp turned aside to retch, and Jon found himself envying Maester Aemon his blindness.

Noye and his men had been waiting within, behind a gate of heavy iron bars like the two Pyp had just unlocked. The two crossbows had gotten off a dozen quarrels as the giant struggled toward them. Then the spearmen must have come to the fore, stabbing through the bars. Still the giant found the strength to reach through, twist the head off Spotted Pate, seize the iron gate, and wrench the bars apart. Links of broken chain lay strewn across the floor. *One giant. All this was the work of one giant.*

"Are they all dead?" Maester Aemon asked softly.

"Yes. Donal was the last." Noye's sword was sunk deep in the giant's throat, halfway to the hilt. The armorer had always seemed such a big man to Jon, but locked in the giant's massive arms he looked almost like a child. "The giant crushed his spine. I don't know who died first." He took the lantern and moved forward for a better look. "Mag." *I am the last of the giants.* He could feel the sadness there, but he had no time for sadness. "It was Mag the Mighty. The king of the giants."

He needed sun then. It was too cold and dark inside the tunnel, and the stench of blood and death was suffocating. Jon gave the lantern back to Clydas, squeezed around the bodies and through the twisted bars, and walked toward the daylight to see what lay beyond the splintered door.

The huge carcass of a dead mammoth partially blocked the way. One of the beast's tusks snagged his cloak and tore it as he edged past. Three more giants lay outside, half buried beneath stone and slush and hardened pitch. He could see where the fire had melted the Wall, where great sheets of ice had come sloughing off in the heat to shatter on the blackened ground. He looked up at where they'd come from. *When you stand here it seems immense, as if it were about to crush you.*

Jon went back inside to where the others waited. "We need to repair the outer gate as best we can and then block up this section of the tunnel. Rubble, chunks of ice, anything. All the way to the second gate, if we can. Ser Wynton will need to take command, he's the last knight left, but he needs to move *now*, the giants will be back before we know it. We have to tell him –"

"Tell him what you will," said Maester Aemon, gently. "He will smile, nod, and forget. Thirty years ago Ser Wynton Stout came within a dozen votes of being Lord Commander. He would have made a fine one. Ten years ago he would still have been capable. No longer. You know that as well as Donal did, Jon."

It was true. "You give the order, then," Jon told the maester. "You have been on the Wall your whole life, the men will follow you. We have to close the gate."

"I am a maester chained and sworn. My order serves, Jon. We give counsel, not commands."

"Someone must –"

"You. You must lead."

"No."

"Yes, Jon. It need not be for long. Only until such time as the garrison returns. Donal chose you, and Qhorin Halfhand before him. Lord Commander Mormont made you his steward. You are a son of Winterfell, a nephew of Benjen Stark. It must be you or no one. The Wall is yours, Jon Snow."

ARYA

She could feel the hole inside her every morning when she woke. It wasn't hunger, though sometimes there was that too. It was a hollow place, an emptiness where her heart had been, where her brothers had lived, and her parents. Her head hurt too. Not as bad as it had at first, but still pretty bad. Arya was used to that, though, and at least the lump was going down. But the hole inside her stayed the same. *The hole will never feel any better*, she told herself when she went to sleep.

Some mornings Arya did not want to wake at all. She would huddle beneath her cloak with her eyes squeezed shut and try to will herself back to sleep. If the Hound would only have left her alone, she would have slept all day and all night.

And dreamed. That was the best part, the dreaming. She dreamed of wolves most every night. A great pack of wolves, with her at the head. She was bigger than any of them, stronger, swifter, faster. She could outrun horses and outfight lions. When she bared her teeth even men would run from her, her belly was never empty long, and her fur kept her warm even when the wind was blowing cold. And her brothers and sisters were with her, many and more of them, fierce and terrible and *hers*. They would never leave her.

But if her nights were full of wolves, her days belonged to the dog. Sandor Clegane made her get up every morning, whether she wanted to or not. He would curse at her in his raspy voice, or yank her to her feet and shake her. Once he dumped a helm full of cold water all over her head. She bounced up sputtering and shivering and tried to kick him, but he only laughed. "Dry off and feed the bloody horses," he told her, and she did.

They had two now, Stranger and a sorrel palfrey mare Arya had named Craven, because Sandor said she'd likely run off from the Twins the same as them. They'd found her wandering riderless through a field the morning after the slaughter. She was a good enough horse, but Arya could not love a coward. *Stranger would have fought.* Still, she tended the mare as best she knew. It was better than riding double with the Hound. And Craven might have been a coward, but she was young and strong as well. Arya thought that she might be able to outrun Stranger, if it came to it.

The Hound no longer watched her as closely as he had. Sometimes he did not seem to care whether she stayed or went, and he no longer bound her up in a cloak at night. *One night I'll kill him in his sleep,* she told herself, but she never did. *One day I'll ride away on Craven, and he won't be able to catch me,* she thought, but she never did that either. Where would she go? Winterfell was gone. Her grandfather's brother was at Riverrun, but he didn't know her, no more than she knew him. Maybe Lady Smallwood would take her in at Acorn Hall, but maybe she wouldn't. Besides, Arya wasn't even sure she could *find* Acorn Hall again. Sometimes she thought she might go back to Sharna's inn, if the floods hadn't washed it away. She could stay with Hot Pie, or maybe Lord Beric would find her there. Anguy would teach her to use a bow, and she could ride with Gendry and be an outlaw, like Wenda the White Fawn in the songs.

But that was just stupid, like something Sansa might dream. Hot Pie and Gendry had left her just as soon as they could, and Lord Beric and the outlaws only wanted to ransom her, just like the Hound. None of them wanted her around. *They were never my pack, not even Hot Pie and Gendry. I was stupid to think so, just a stupid little girl, and no wolf at all.*

So she stayed with the Hound. They rode every day, never sleeping twice in the same place, avoiding towns and villages and castles as best they could. Once she asked Sandor Clegane where they were going. "Away," he said. "That's all you need to know. You're not worth spit to me now, and I don't want to hear your whining. I should have let you run into that bloody castle."

"You should have," she agreed, thinking of her mother.

"You'd be dead if I had. You ought to thank me. You ought to sing me a pretty little song, the way your sister did."

"Did you hit her with an axe too?"

"I hit you with the *flat* of the axe, you stupid little bitch. If I'd hit you with the blade there'd still be chunks of your head floating down the Green Fork. Now shut your bloody mouth. If I had any sense I'd give you to the silent sisters. They cut the tongues out of girls who talk too much."

That wasn't fair of him to say. Aside from that one time, Arya hardly talked at all. Whole days passed when neither of them said anything. She was too empty to talk, and the Hound was too angry. She could feel the fury in him; she could see it on his face, the way his mouth would tighten and twist, the looks he gave her. Whenever he took his axe to chop some wood for a fire, he would slide into a cold rage, hacking savagely at the tree or the deadfall or the broken limb, until they had twenty times as much kindling and firewood as they'd needed. Sometimes he would be so sore and tired afterward that he would lie down and go right to sleep without even lighting a fire. Arya hated it when that happened, and hated him too. Those were the nights when she stared the longest at the axe. *It looks awfully heavy, but I bet I could swing it.* She wouldn't hit him with the flat, either.

Sometimes in their wanderings they glimpsed other people; farmers in their fields, swineherds with their pigs, a milkmaid leading a cow, a squire carrying a message down a rutted road. She never wanted to speak to them either. It was as if they lived in some distant land and spoke a queer alien tongue; they had nothing to do with her, or her with them.

Besides, it wasn't safe to be seen. From time to time columns of horsemen passed down the winding farm roads, the twin towers of Frey flying before them. "Hunting for stray northmen," the Hound said when they had passed. "Any time you hear hooves, get your head down fast, it's not like to be a friend."

One day, in an earthen hollow made by the roots of a fallen oak, they came face to face with another survivor of the Twins. The badge on his breast showed a pink maiden dancing in a swirl of silk, and he told them he was Ser Marq Piper's man; a bowman, though he'd lost his bow. His left shoulder was all twisted and swollen where it met his arm; a blow from a mace, he said, it had broken his shoulder and smashed his chainmail deep into his flesh. "A northman, it was," he wept. "His badge was a bloody man, and he saw mine and made a jape, red man and pink maiden, maybe they should get together. I drank to his Lord Bolton, he drank to Ser Marq, and we drank together to Lord Edmure and Lady Roslin and the King in the North. And then he killed me." His eyes were fever bright when he said that, and Arya could tell that it was true. His shoulder was swollen grotesquely, and pus and blood had stained his whole left side. There was a stink to him too. *He smells like a corpse.* The man begged them for a drink of wine.

"If I'd had any wine, I'd have drunk it myself," the Hound told him. "I can give you water, and the gift of mercy."

The archer looked at him a long while before he said, "You're Joffrey's dog."

"My own dog now. Do you want the water?"

"Aye." The man swallowed. "And the mercy. Please."

They had passed a small pond a short ways back. Sandor gave Arya his helm and told her to fill it, so she trudged back to the water's edge. Mud squished over the toe of her boots. She used the dog's head as a pail. Water ran out through the eyeholes, but the bottom of the helm still held a lot.

When she came back, the archer turned his face up and she poured the water into his mouth. He gulped it down as fast as she could pour, and what he couldn't gulp ran down his cheeks into the brown blood that crusted his whiskers, until pale pink tears dangled from his beard. When the water was gone he clutched the helm and licked the steel. "Good," he said. "I wish it was wine, though. I wanted wine."

"Me too." The Hound eased his dagger into the man's chest almost tenderly, the weight of his body driving the point through his surcoat, ringmail, and the quilting beneath. As he slid the blade back out and wiped it on the dead man, he looked at Arya. "That's where the heart is, girl. That's how you kill a man."

That's one way. "Will we bury him?"

"Why?" Sandor said. "He don't care, and we've got no spade. Leave him for the wolves and wild dogs. Your brothers and mine." He gave her a hard look. "First we rob him, though."

There were two silver stags in the archer's purse, and almost thirty coppers. His dagger had a pretty pink stone in the hilt. The Hound hefted the knife in his hand, then flipped it toward Arya. She caught it by the hilt, slid it through her belt, and felt a little better. It wasn't Needle, but it was steel. The dead man had a quiver of arrows too, but arrows weren't much good without a bow. His boots were too big for Arya and too small for the Hound, so those they left. She took his kettle helm as well, even though it came down almost past her nose, so she had to tilt it back to see. "He must have had a horse as well, or he wouldn't have got away," Clegane said, peering about, "but it's bloody well gone, I'd say. No telling how long he's been here."

By the time they found themselves in the foothills of the Mountains of the Moon, the rains had mostly stopped. Arya could see the sun and moon and stars, and it seemed to her that they were heading eastward. "Where are we going?" she asked again.

This time the Hound answered her. "You have an aunt in the Eyrie. Might be she'll want to ransom your scrawny arse, though the gods know why. Once we find the high road, we can follow it all the way to the Bloody Gate."

Aunt Lysa. The thought left Arya feeling empty. It was her mother she wanted, not her mother's sister. She didn't know her mother's sister any more than she knew her great uncle Blackfish. *We should have gone into the castle.* They didn't really *know* that her mother was dead, or Robb either. It wasn't like they'd seen them die or anything. Maybe Lord Frey had just taken them captive. Maybe they were chained up in his dungeon, or maybe the Freys were taking them to King's Landing so Joffrey could chop their heads off. They didn't *know.* "We should go back," she suddenly decided. "We should go back to the Twins and get my mother. She can't be dead. We have to help her."

"I thought your sister was the one with a head full of songs," the Hound growled. "Frey might have kept your mother alive to ransom, that's true. But there's no way in seven hells I'm going to pluck her out of his castle all by my bloody self."

"Not by yourself. I'd come too."

He made a sound that was almost a laugh. "*That* will scare the piss out of the old man."

"You're just afraid to die!" she said scornfully.

Now Clegane *did* laugh. "Death don't scare me. Only fire. Now be quiet, or I'll cut your tongue out myself and save the silent sisters the bother. It's the Vale for us."

Arya didn't think he'd *really* cut her tongue out; he was just saying that the way Pinkeye used to say he'd beat her bloody. All the same, she wasn't going to try him. Sandor Clegane was no Pinkeye. Pinkeye didn't cut people in half or hit them with axes. Not even with the flat of axes.

That night she went to sleep thinking of her mother, and wondering if she should kill the Hound in his sleep and rescue Lady Catelyn herself. When she closed her eyes she saw her mother's face against the back of her eyelids. *She's so close I could almost smell her . . .*

. . . and then she *could* smell her. The scent was faint beneath the other smells, beneath moss and mud and water, and the stench of rotting reeds and rotting men. She padded slowly through the soft ground to the river's edge, lapped up a drink, the lifted her head to sniff. The sky was grey and thick with cloud, the river green and full of floating things. Dead men clogged the shallows, some still moving as the water pushed them, others washed up on the banks. Her brothers and sisters swarmed around them, tearing at the rich ripe flesh.

The crows were there too, screaming at the wolves and filling the air with feathers. Their blood was hotter, and one of her sisters had snapped at one as it took flight and caught it by the wing. It made her want a crow herself. She wanted to taste the blood, to hear the bones crunch between her teeth, to fill her belly with warm flesh instead of cold. She was hungry and the meat was all around, but she knew she could not eat.

The scent was stronger now. She pricked her ears up and listened to the grumbles of her pack, the shriek of angry crows, the whirr of wings and sound of running water. Somewhere far off she could hear horses and the calls of living men, but they were not what mattered. Only the scent mattered. She sniffed the air again. There it was, and now she saw it too, something pale and white drifting down the river, turning where it brushed against a snag. The reeds bowed down before it.

She splashed noisily through the shallows and threw herself into the deeper water, her legs churning. The current was strong but she was stronger. She swam, following her nose. The river smells were rich and wet, but those were not the smells that pulled her. She paddled after the sharp red whisper of cold blood, the sweet cloying stench of death. She chased them as she had often chased a red deer through the trees, and in the end she ran them down, and her jaw closed around a pale white arm. She shook it to make it move, but there was only death and blood in her mouth. By now she was tiring, and it was all she could do to pull the body back to shore. As she dragged it up the muddy bank, one of her little brothers came prowling, his tongue lolling from his mouth. She had to snarl to drive him off, or else he would have fed. Only then did she stop to shake the water from her fur. The white thing lay facedown in the mud, her dead flesh wrinkled and pale, cold blood trickling from her throat. *Rise*, she thought. *Rise and eat and run with us.*

The sound of horses turned her head. *Men*. They were coming from downwind, so she had not smelled them, but now they were almost here. Men on horses, with flapping black and yellow and pink wings and long shiny claws in hand. Some of her younger brothers bared their teeth to defend the food they'd found, but she snapped at them until they scattered. That was the way of the wild. Deer and hares and crows fled before wolves, and wolves fled from men. She abandoned the cold white prize in the mud where she had dragged it, and ran, and felt no shame.

When morning came, the Hound did not need to shout at Arya or shake her awake. She had woken before him for a change, and even watered the horses. They broke their fast in silence, until Sandor said, "This thing about your mother . . ."

"It doesn't matter," Arya said in a dull voice. "I know she's dead. I saw her in a dream."

The Hound looked at her a long time, then nodded. No more was said of it. They rode on toward the mountains.

In the higher hills, they came upon a tiny isolated village surrounded by grey-green sentinels and tall blue soldier pines, and Clegane decided to risk going in. "We need food," he said, "and a roof over our heads. They're not like to know what happened at the Twins, and with any luck they won't know me."

The villagers were building a wooden palisade around their homes, and when they saw the breadth of the Hound's shoulders they offered them food and shelter and even coin for work. "If there's wine as well, I'll do it," he growled at them. In the end, he settled for ale, and drank himself to sleep each night.

His dream of selling Arya to Lady Arryn died there in the hills, though. "There's frost above us and snow in the high passes," the village elder said. "If you don't freeze or starve, the shadowcats will get you, or the cave bears. There's the clans as well. The Burned Men are fearless since Timett One-Eye came back from the war. And half a year ago, Gunthor son of Gurn led the Stone Crows down on a village not eight miles from here. They took every woman and every scrap of grain, and killed half the men. They have *steel* now, good swords and mail hauberks, and they watch the high road – the Stone Crows, the Milk Snakes, the Sons of the Mist, all of them. Might be you'd take a few with you, but in the end they'd kill you and make off with your daughter."

I'm not his daughter, Arya might have shouted, if she hadn't felt so tired. She was no one's daughter now. She was no one. Not Arya, not Weasel, not Nan nor Arry nor Squab, not even Lumpyhead. She was only some girl who ran with a dog by day, and dreamed of wolves by night.

It was quiet in the village. They had beds stuffed with straw and not too many lice, the food was plain but filling, and the air smelled of pines. All the same, Arya soon decided that she hated it. The villagers were cowards. None of them would even look at the Hound's face, at least not for long. Some of the women tried to put her in a dress and make her do needlework, but they weren't Lady Smallwood and she was having none of it. And there was one girl who took to following her, the village elder's daughter. She was of an age with Arya, but just a *child*; she cried if she skinned a knee, and carried a stupid cloth doll with her everywhere she went. The doll was made up to look like a man-at-arms, sort of, so the girl called him Ser Soldier and bragged how he kept her safe. "Go away," Arya told her half a hundred times. "Just leave me be." She wouldn't, though, so finally Arya took the doll away from her, ripped it open, and pulled the rag stuffing out of its belly with a finger. "Now he *really* looks like a soldier!" she said, before she threw the doll in a brook. After that the girl stopped pestering her, and Arya spent her days grooming Craven and Stranger or walking in the woods. Sometimes she would find a stick and practice her needlework, but then she would remember what had happened at the Twins and smash it against a tree until it broke.

"Might be we should stay here awhile," the Hound told her, after a fortnight. He was drunk on ale, but more brooding than sleepy. "We'd never reach the Eyrie, and the Freys will still be hunting survivors in the riverlands. Sounds like they need swords here, with these clansmen raiding. We can rest up, maybe find a way to get a letter to your aunt." Arya's face darkened when she heard that. She didn't want to stay, but there was nowhere to go, either. The next morning, when the Hound went off to chop down trees and haul logs, she crawled back into bed.

But when the work was done and the tall wooden palisade was finished, the village elder made it plain that there was no place for them. "Come winter, we will be hard pressed to feed our own," he explained. "And you . . . a man like you brings blood with him."

Sandor's mouth tightened. "So you do know who I am."

"Aye. We don't get travelers here, that's so, but we go to market, and to fairs. We know about King Joffrey's dog."

"When these Stone Crows come calling, you might be glad to have a dog."

"Might be." The man hesitated, then gathered up his courage. "But they say you lost your belly for fighting at the Blackwater. They say – "

"I know what they say." Sandor's voice sounded like two woodsaws grinding together. "Pay me, and we'll be gone."

When they left, the Hound had a pouch full of coppers, a skin of sour ale, and a new sword. It was a very old sword, if truth be told, though new to him. He swapped its owner the longaxe he'd taken at the Twins, the one he'd used to raise the lump on Arya's head. The ale was gone in less than a day, but Clegane sharpened the sword every night, cursing the man he'd swapped with for every nick and spot of rust. *If he lost his belly for fighting, why does he care if his sword is sharp?* It was not a question Arya dared ask him, but she thought on it a lot. Was that why he'd run from the Twins and carried her off?

Back in the riverlands, they found that the rains had ebbed away, and the flood waters had begun to recede. The Hound turned south, back toward the Trident. "We'll make for Riverrun," he told Arya as they roasted a hare he'd killed. "Maybe the Blackfish wants to buy himself a she-wolf."

"He doesn't know me. He won't even know I'm really me." Arya was tired of making for Riverrun. She had been making for Riverrun for years, it seemed, without ever getting there. Every time she made for Riverrun, she ended up someplace worse. "He won't give you any ransom. He'll probably just hang you."

"He's free to try." He turned the spit.

He doesn't talk like he's lost his belly for fighting. "I know where we could go," Arya said. She still had one brother left. *Jon will want me, even if no one else does. He'll call me "little sister" and muss my hair.* It was a long way, though, and she didn't think she could get there by herself. She hadn't even been able to reach Riverrun. "We could go to the Wall."

Sandor's laugh was half a growl. "The little wolf bitch wants to join the Night's Watch, does she?"

"My brother's on the Wall," she said stubbornly.

His mouth gave a twitch. "The Wall's a thousand leagues from here. We'd need to fight through the bloody Freys just to reach the Neck. There's lizard lions in those swamps that eat wolves every day for breakfast. And if we did reach the north with our skins intact, there's ironborn in half the castles, and thousands of bloody buggering northmen as well."

"Are you scared of them?" she asked. "Have you lost your belly for fighting?"

For a moment she thought he was going to hit her. By then the hare was brown, though, skin crackling and grease popping as it dripped down into the cookfire. Sandor took it off the stick, ripped it apart with his big hands, and tossed half of it into Arya's lap. "There's nothing wrong with my belly," he said as he pulled off a leg, "but I don't give a rat's arse for you *or* your brother. I have a brother too."

TYRION

"**T**yrion," Ser Kevan Lannister said wearily, "if you are indeed innocent of Joffrey's death, you should have no difficulty proving it at trial."

Tyrion turned from the window. "Who is to judge me?"

"Justice belongs to the throne. The king is dead, but your father remains Hand. Since it is his own son who stands accused and his grandson who was the victim, he has asked Lord Tyrell and Prince Oberyn to sit in judgment with him."

Tyrion was scarcely reassured. Mace Tyrell had been Joffrey's goodfather, however briefly, and the Red Viper was . . . well, a snake. "Will I be allowed to demand trial by battle?"

"I would not advise that."

"Why not?" It had saved him in the Vale, why not here? "Answer me, Uncle. Will I be allowed a trial by battle, and a champion to prove my innocence?"

"Certainly, if such is your wish. However, you had best know that your sister means to name Ser Gregor Clegane as *her* champion, in the event of such a trial."

The bitch checks my moves before I make them. A pity she didn't choose a Kettleblack. Bronn would make short work of any of the three brothers, but the Mountain That Rides was a kettle of a different color. "I shall need to sleep on this." *I need to speak with Bronn, and soon.* He didn't want to think about what this was like to cost him. Bronn had a lofty notion of what his skin was worth. "Does Cersei have witnesses against me?"

"More every day."

"Then I must have witnesses of my own."

"Tell me who you would have, and Ser Addam will send the Watch to bring them to the trial."

"I would sooner find them myself."

"You stand accused of regicide and kinslaying. Do you truly imagine you will be allowed to come and go as you please?" Ser Kevan waved at the table. "You have quill, ink, and parchment. Write the names of such witnesses as you require, and I shall do all in my power to produce them, you have my word as a Lannister. But you shall not leave this tower, except to go to trial."

Tyrion would not demean himself by begging. "Will you permit my squire to come and go? The boy Podrick Payne?"

"Certainly, if that is your wish. I shall send him to you."

"Do so. Sooner would be better than later, and now would be better than sooner." He waddled to the writing table. But when he heard the door open, he turned back and said, "Uncle?"

Ser Kevan paused. "Yes?"

"I did not do this."

"I wish I could believe that, Tyrion."

When the door closed, Tyrion Lannister pulled himself up into the chair, sharpened a quill, and pulled a blank parchment. *Who will speak for me?* He dipped his quill in the inkpot.

The sheet was still maiden when Podrick Payne appeared, sometime later. "My lord," the boy said.

Tyrion put down the quill. "Find Bronn and bring him at once. Tell him there's gold in it, more gold than he's ever dreamt of, and see that you don't return without him."

"Yes, my lord. I mean, no. I won't. Return." He went.

He had not returned by sunset, nor by moonrise. Tyrion fell asleep in the window seat to wake stiff and sore at dawn. A serving man brought porridge and apples to break his fast, with a horn of ale. He ate at the table, the blank parchment before him. An hour later, the serving man returned for the bowl. "Have you seen my squire?" Tyrion asked him. The man shook his head.

Sighing, he turned back to the table, and dipped the quill again. *Sansa,* he wrote upon the parchment. He sat staring at the name, his teeth clenched so hard they hurt.

Assuming Joffrey had not simply choked to death on a bit of food, which even Tyrion found hard to swallow, Sansa must have poisoned him. *Joff practically put his cup down in her lap, and he'd given her ample reason.* Any doubts Tyrion might have had vanished when his wife did. *One flesh, one heart, one soul.* His mouth twisted. *She wasted no time proving how much those vows meant to her, did she? Well, what did you expect, dwarf?*

And yet ... where would Sansa have gotten poison? He could not believe the girl had acted alone in this. *Do I really want to find her?* Would the judges believe that Tyrion's child bride had poisoned a king without her husband's knowledge? *I wouldn't.* Cersei would insist that they had done the deed together.

Even so, he gave the parchment to his uncle the next day. Ser Kevan frowned at it. "Lady Sansa is your only witness?"

"I will think of others in time."

"Best think of them now. The judges mean to begin the trial three days hence."

"That's too soon. You have me shut up here under guard, how am I to find witnesses to my innocence?"

"Your sister's had no difficulty finding witnesses to your guilt." Ser Kevan rolled up the parchment. "Ser Addam has men hunting for your wife. Varys has offered a hundred stags for word of her whereabouts, and a hundred dragons for the girl herself. If the girl can be found she will be found, and I shall bring her to you. I see no harm in husband and wife sharing the same cell and giving comfort to one another."

"You are too kind. Have you seen my squire?"

"I sent him to you yesterday. Did he not come?"

"He came," Tyrion admitted, "and then he went."

"I shall send him to you again."

But it was the next morning before Podrick Payne returned. He stepped inside the room hesitantly, with fear written all over his face. Bronn came in behind him. The sellsword knight wore a jerkin studded with silver and a heavy riding cloak, with a pair of fine-tooled leather gloves thrust through his swordbelt.

One look at Bronn's face gave Tyrion a queasy feeling in the pit of his stomach. "It took you long enough."

"The boy begged, or I wouldn't have come at all. I am expected at Castle Stokeworth for supper."

"Stokeworth?" Tyrion hopped from the bed. "And pray, what is there for you in Stokeworth?"

"A bride." Bronn smiled like a wolf contemplating a lost lamb. "I'm to wed Lollys the day after next."

"Lollys." *Perfect, bloody perfect.* Lady Tanda's lackwit daughter gets a knightly husband and a father of sorts for the bastard in her belly, and Ser Bronn of the Blackwater climbs another rung. It had Cersei's stinking fingers all over it. "My bitch sister has sold you a lame horse. The girl's dim-witted."

"If I wanted wits, I'd marry you."

"Lollys is big with another man's child."

"And when she pops him out, I'll get her big with mine."

"She's not even heir to Stokeworth," Tyrion pointed out. "She has an elder sister. Falyse. A *married* sister."

"Married ten years, and still barren," said Bronn. "Her lord husband shuns her bed. It's said he prefers virgins."

"He could prefer goats and it wouldn't matter. The lands will still pass to his wife when Lady Tanda dies."

"Unless Falyse should die before her mother."

Tyrion wondered whether Cersei had any notion of the sort of serpent she'd given Lady Tanda to suckle. *And if she does, would she care?* "Why are you here, then?"

Bronn shrugged. "You once told me that if anyone ever asked me to sell you out, you'd double the price."

Yes. "Is it two wives you want, or two castles?"

"One of each would serve. But if you want me to kill Gregor Clegane for you, it had best be a damned *big* castle."

The Seven Kingdoms were full of highborn maidens, but even the oldest, poorest, and ugliest spinster in the realm would balk at wedding such lowborn scum as Bronn. *Unless she was soft of body and soft of head, with a fatherless child in her belly from having been raped half a hundred times.* Lady Tanda had been so desperate to find a husband for Lollys that she had even pursued Tyrion for a time, and that had been *before* half of King's Landing enjoyed her. No doubt Cersei had sweetened the offer somehow, and Bronn *was* a knight now, which made him a suitable match for a younger daughter of a minor house.

"I find myself woefully short of both castles and highborn maidens at the moment," Tyrion admitted. "But I can offer you gold and gratitude, as before."

"I have gold. What can I buy with gratitude?"

"You might be surprised. A Lannister pays his debts."

"Your sister is a Lannister too."

"My lady wife is heir to Winterfell. Should I emerge from this with my head still on my shoulders, I may one day rule the north in her name. I could carve you out a big piece of it."

"If and when and might be," said Bronn. "And it's bloody cold up there. Lollys is soft, warm, and close. I could be poking her two nights hence."

"Not a prospect I would relish."

"Is that so?" Bronn grinned. "Admit it, Imp. Given a choice between fucking Lollys and fighting the Mountain, you'd have your breeches down and cock up before a man could blink."

He knows me too bloody well. Tyrion tried a different tack. "I'd heard that Ser Gregor was wounded on the Red Fork, and again at Duskendale. The wounds are bound to slow him."

Bronn looked annoyed. "He was never fast. Only freakish big and freakish strong. I'll grant you, he's quicker than you'd expect for a man that size. He has a monstrous long reach, and doesn't seem to feel blows the way a normal man would."

"Does he frighten you so much?" asked Tyrion, hoping to provoke him.

"If he didn't frighten me, I'd be a bloody fool." Bronn gave a shrug. "Might be I could take him. Dance around him until he was so tired of hacking at me that he couldn't lift his sword. Get him off his feet somehow. When they're flat on their backs it don't matter how tall they are. Even so, it's chancy. One misstep and I'm dead. Why should I risk it? I like you well enough, ugly little whoreson that you are . . . but if I fight your battle, I lose either way. Either the Mountain spills my guts, or I kill him and lose Stokeworth. I sell my sword, I don't give it away. I'm not your bloody brother."

"No," said Tyrion sadly. "You're not." He waved a hand. "Begone, then. Run to Stokeworth and Lady Lollys. May you find more joy in your marriage bed than I ever found in mine."

Bronn hesitated at the door. "What will you do, Imp?"

"Kill Gregor myself. Won't *that* make for a jolly song?"

"I hope I hear them sing it." Bronn grinned one last time, and walked out of the door, the castle, and his life.

Pod shuffled his feet. "I'm sorry."

"Why? Is it your fault that Bronn's an insolent black-hearted rogue? He's always been an insolent black-hearted rogue. That's what I liked about him." Tyrion poured himself a cup of wine and took it to the window seat. Outside the day was grey and rainy, but the prospect was still more cheerful than his. He could send Podrick Payne questing after Shagga, he supposed, but there were so many hiding places in the deep of the kingswood that outlaws often evaded capture for decades. *And Pod sometimes has difficulty finding the kitchens when I send him down for cheese.* Timett son of Timett would likely be back in the Mountains of the Moon by now. And despite what he'd told Bronn, going up against Ser Gregor Clegane in his own person would be a bigger farce than Joffrey's jousting dwarfs. He did not intend to die with gales of laughter ringing in his ears. *So much for trial by combat.*

Ser Kevan paid him another call later that day, and again the day after. Sansa had not been found, his uncle informed him politely. Nor the fool Ser Dontos, who'd vanished the same night. Did Tyrion have any more witnesses he wished to summon? He did not. *How do I bloody well prove I didn't poison the wine, when a thousand people saw me fill Joff's cup?*

He did not sleep at all that night.

Instead he lay in the dark, staring up at the canopy and counting his ghosts. He saw Tysha smiling as she kissed him, saw Sansa naked and shivering in fear. He saw Joffrey clawing his throat, the blood running down his neck as his face turned black. He saw Cersei's eyes, Bronn's wolfish smile, Shae's wicked grin. Even thought of Shae could not arouse him. He fondled himself, thinking that perhaps if he woke his cock and satisfied it, he might rest more easily afterward, but it was no good.

And then it was dawn, and time for his trial to begin.

It was not Ser Kevan who came for him that morning, but Ser Addam Marbrand with a dozen gold cloaks. Tyrion had broken his fast on boiled eggs, burned bacon, and fried bread, and dressed in his finest. "Ser Addam," he said. "I had thought my father might send the Kingsguard to escort me to trial. I am still a member of the royal family, am I not?"

"You are, my lord, but I fear that most of the Kingsguard stand witness against you. Lord Tywin felt it would not be proper for them to serve as your guards."

"Gods forbid we do anything *improper*. Please, lead on."

He was to be tried in the throne room, where Joffrey had died. As Ser Addam marched him through the towering bronze doors and down the long carpet, he felt the eyes upon him. Hundreds had crowded in to see him judged. At least he hoped that was why they had come. *For all I know, they're all witnesses against me.* He spied Queen Margaery up in the gallery, pale and beautiful in her mourning. *Twice wed and twice widowed, and only sixteen.* Her mother stood tall to one side of her, her grandmother small on the other, with her ladies in waiting and her father's household knights packing the rest of the gallery.

The dais still stood beneath the empty Iron Throne, though all but one table had been removed. Behind it sat stout Lord Mace Tyrell in a gold mantle over green, and slender Prince Oberyn Martell in flowing robes of striped orange, yellow, and scarlet. Lord Tywin Lannister sat between them. *Perhaps there's hope for me yet.* The Dornishman and the Highgardener despised each other. *If I can find a way to use that . . .*

The High Septon began with a prayer, asking the Father Above to guide them to justice. When he was done the father below leaned forward to say, "Tyrion, did you kill King Joffrey?"

He would not waste a heartbeat. "No."

"Well, that's a relief," said Oberyn Martell dryly.

"Did Sansa Stark do it, then?" Lord Tyrell demanded.

I would have, if I'd been her. Yet wherever Sansa was and whatever her part in this might have been, she remained his wife. He had wrapped the cloak of his protection about her shoulders, though he'd had to stand on a fool's back to do it. "The gods killed Joffrey. He choked on his pigeon pie."

Lord Tyrell reddened. "You would blame the bakers?"

"Them, or the pigeons. Just leave me out of it." Tyrion heard nervous laughter, and knew he'd made a mistake. *Guard your tongue, you little fool, before it digs your grave.*

"There are witnesses against you," Lord Tywin said. "We shall hear them first. Then you may present your own witnesses. You are to speak only with our leave."

There was naught that Tyrion could do but nod.

Ser Addam had told it true; the first man ushered in was Ser Balon Swann of the Kingsguard. "Lord Hand," he began, after the High Septon had sworn him to speak only truth, "I had the honor to fight beside your son on the bridge of ships. He is a brave man for all his size, and I will not believe he did this thing."

A murmur went through the hall, and Tyrion wondered what mad game Cersei was playing. *Why offer a witness that believes me innocent?* He soon learned. Ser Balon spoke reluctantly of how he had pulled Tyrion away from Joffrey on the day of the riot. "He did strike His Grace, that's so. It was a fit of wroth, no more. A summer storm. The mob near killed us all."

"In the days of the Targaryens, a man who struck one of the blood royal would lose the hand he struck him with," observed the Red Viper of Dorne. "Did the dwarf regrow his little hand, or did you White Swords forget your duty?"

"He was of the blood royal himself," Ser Balon answered. "And the King's Hand beside."

"No," Lord Tywin said. "He was *acting* Hand, in my stead."

Ser Meryn Trant was pleased to expand on Ser Balon's account, when he took his place as witness. "He knocked the king to the ground and began kicking him. He shouted that it was unjust that His Grace had escaped unharmed from the mobs."

Tyrion began to grasp his sister's plan. *She began with a man known to be honest, and milked him for all he would give. Every witness to follow will tell a worse tale, until I seem as bad as Maegor the Cruel and Aerys the Mad together, with a pinch of Aegon the Unworthy for spice.*

Ser Meryn went on to relate how Tyrion had stopped Joffrey's chastisement of Sansa Stark. "The dwarf asked His Grace if he knew what had happened to Aerys Targaryen. When Ser Boros spoke up in defense of the king, the Imp threatened to have him killed."

Blount himself came next, to echo *that* sorry tale. Whatever mislike Ser Boros might harbor toward Cersei for dismissing him from the Kingsguard, he said the words she wanted all the same.

Tyrion could no longer hold his tongue. "Tell the judges what Joffrey was *doing*, why don't you?"

The big jowly man glared at him. "You told your savages to kill me if I opened my mouth, that's what I'll tell them."

"Tyrion," Lord Tywin said. "You are to speak only when we call upon you. Take this for a warning."

Tyrion subsided, seething.

The Kettleblacks came next, all three of them in turn. Osney and Osfryd told the tale of his supper with Cersei before the Battle of the Blackwater, and of the threats he'd made.

"He told Her Grace that he meant to do her harm," said Ser Osfryd. "To hurt her." His brother Osney elaborated. "He said he would wait for a day when she was happy, and make her joy turn to ashes in her mouth." Neither mentioned Alayaya.

Ser Osmund Kettleblack, a vision of chivalry in immaculate scale armor and white wool cloak, swore that King Joffrey had long known that his uncle Tyrion meant to murder him. "It was the day they gave me the white cloak, my lords," he told the judges. "That brave boy said to me, 'Good Ser Osmund, guard me well, for my uncle loves me not. He means to be king in my place.'"

That was more than Tyrion could stomach. *"Liar!"* He took two steps forward before the gold cloaks dragged him back.

Lord Tywin frowned. "Must we have you chained hand and foot like a common brigand?"

Tyrion gnashed his teeth. *A second mistake, fool, fool, fool of a dwarf. Keep your calm or you're doomed.* "No. I beg your pardons, my lords. His lies angered me."

"His truths, you mean," said Cersei. "Father, I beg you to put him in fetters, for your own protection. You see how he is."

"I see he's a dwarf," said Prince Oberyn. "The day I fear a dwarf's wrath is the day I drown myself in a cask of red."

"We need no fetters." Lord Tywin glanced at the windows, and rose. "The hour grows late. We shall resume on the morrow."

That night, alone in his tower cell with a blank parchment and a cup of wine, Tyrion found himself thinking of his wife. Not Sansa; his *first* wife, Tysha. *The whore wife, not the wolf wife.* Her love for him had been pretense, and yet he had believed, and found joy in that belief. *Give me sweet lies, and keep your bitter truths.* He drank his wine and thought of Shae. Later, when Ser Kevan paid his nightly visit, Tyrion asked for Varys.

"You believe the eunuch will speak in your defense?"

"I won't know until I have talked with him. Send him here, Uncle, if you would be so good."

"As you wish."

Maesters Ballabar and Frenken opened the second day of trial. They had opened King Joffrey's noble corpse as well, they swore, and found no morsel of pigeon pie nor any other food lodged in the royal throat. "It was poison that killed him, my lords," said Ballabar, as Frenken nodded gravely.

Then they brought forth Grand Maester Pycelle, leaning heavily on a twisted cane and shaking as he walked, a few white hairs sprouting from his long chicken's neck. He had grown too frail to stand, so the judges permitted a chair to be brought in for him, and a table as well. On the table were laid a number of small jars. Pycelle was pleased to put a name to each.

"Greycap," he said in a quavery voice, "from the toadstool. Nightshade, sweetsleep, demon's dance. This is blindeye. Widow's blood, this one is called, for the color. A cruel potion. It shuts down a man's bladder and bowels, until he drowns in his own poisons. This wolfsbane, here basilisk venom, and this one the tears of Lys. Yes. I know them all. The Imp Tyrion Lannister stole them from my chambers, when he had me falsely imprisoned."

"*Pycelle*," Tyrion called out, risking his father's wrath, "could any of these poisons choke off a man's breath?"

"No. For that, you must turn to a rarer poison. When I was a boy at the Citadel, my teachers named it simply *the strangler*."

"But this rare poison was not found, was it?"

"No, my lord." Pycelle blinked at him. "You used it all to kill the noblest child the gods ever put on this good earth."

Tyrion's anger overwhelmed his sense. "Joffrey was cruel and stupid, but I did not kill him. Have my head off if you like, I had no hand in my nephew's death."

"*Silence!*" Lord Tywin said. "I have told you thrice. The next time, you shall be gagged and chained."

After Pycelle came the procession, endless and wearisome. Lords and ladies and noble knights, highborn and humble alike, they had all been present at the wedding feast, had all seen Joffrey choke, his face turning as black as a Dornish plum. Lord Redwyne, Lord Celtigar, and Ser Flement Brax had heard Tyrion threaten the king; two serving men, a juggler, Lord Gyles, Ser Hobber Redwyne, and Ser Philip Foote had observed him fill the wedding chalice; Lady Merryweather swore that she had seen the dwarf drop something into the king's wine while Joff and Margaery were cutting the pie; old Estermont, young Peckledon, the singer Galyeon of Cuy, and the squires Morros and Jothos Slynt told how Tyrion had picked up the chalice as Joff was dying and poured out the last of the poisoned wine onto the floor.

When did I make so many enemies? Lady Merryweather was all but a stranger. Tyrion wondered if she was blind or bought. At least Galyeon of Cuy had not set his account to music, or else there might have been seventy-seven bloody verses to it.

When his uncle called that night after supper, his manner was cold and distant. *He thinks I did it too.* "Do you have witnesses for us?" Ser Kevan asked him.

"Not as such, no. Unless you've found my wife."

His uncle shook his head. "It would seem the trial is going very badly for you."

"Oh, do you think so? I hadn't noticed." Tyrion fingered his scar. "Varys has not come."

"Nor will he. On the morrow he testifies against you."

Lovely. "I see." He shifted in his seat. "I am curious. You were always a fair man, Uncle. What convinced you?"

"Why steal Pycelle's poisons, if not to use them?" Ser Kevan said bluntly. "And Lady Merryweather saw –"

"– *nothing!* There was nothing to see. But how do I prove that? How do I prove *anything*, penned up here?"

"Perhaps the time has come for you to confess."

Even through the thick stone walls of the Red Keep, Tyrion could hear the steady wash of rain. "Say that again, Uncle? I could swear you urged me to confess."

"If you were to admit your guilt before the throne and repent of your crime, your father would withhold the sword. You would be permitted to take the black."

Tyrion laughed in his face. "Those were the same terms Cersei offered Eddard Stark. We all know how *that* ended."

"Your father had no part in that."

That much was true, at least. "Castle Black teems with murderers, thieves and rapists," Tyrion said, "but I don't recall meeting many regicides while I was there. You expect me to believe that if I admit to being a kinslayer and kingslayer, my father will simply nod, forgive me, and pack me off to the Wall with some warm woolen smallclothes." He hooted rudely.

"Naught was said of forgiveness," Ser Kevan said sternly. "A confession would put this matter to rest. It is for that reason your father sends me with this offer."

"Thank him kindly for me, Uncle," said Tyrion, "but tell him I am not presently in a confessing mood."

"Were I you, I'd change my mood. Your sister wants your head, and Lord Tyrell at least is inclined to give it to her."

"So one of my judges has already condemned me, without hearing a word in my defense?" It was no more than he expected. "Will I still be allowed to speak and present witnesses?"

"You *have* no witnesses," his uncle reminded him. "Tyrion, if you are guilty of this enormity, the Wall is a kinder fate than you deserve. And if you are blameless . . . there is fighting in the north, I know, but even so it will be a safer place for you than King's Landing, whatever the outcome of this trial. The mob is convinced of your guilt. Were you so foolish as to venture out into the streets, they would tear you limb from limb."

"I can see how much that prospect upsets you."

"You are my brother's son."

"You might remind *him* of that."

"Do you think he would allow you to take the black if you were not his own blood, and Joanna's? Tywin seems a hard man to you, I know, but he is no harder than he's had to be. Our own father was gentle and amiable, but so weak his bannermen mocked him in their cups. Some saw fit to defy him openly. Other lords borrowed our gold and never troubled to repay it. At court they japed of toothless lions. Even his mistress stole from him. A woman scarcely one step above a whore, and she helped herself to my mother's jewels! It fell to Tywin to restore House Lannister to its proper place. Just as it fell to him to rule this realm, when he was no more than twenty. He bore that heavy burden for *twenty years*, and all it earned him was a mad king's envy. Instead of the honor he deserved, he was made to suffer slights beyond count, yet he gave the Seven Kingdoms peace, plenty, and justice. He is a just man. You would be wise to trust him."

Tyrion blinked in astonishment. Ser Kevan had always been solid, stolid, pragmatic; he had never heard him speak with such fervor before. "You love him."

"He is my brother."

"I . . . I will think on what you've said."

"Think carefully, then. And quickly."

He thought of little else that night, but come morning was no closer to deciding if his father could be trusted. A servant brought him porridge and honey to break his fast, but all he could taste was bile at the thought of confession. *They will call me kinslayer till the end of my days. For a thousand years or more, if I am remembered at all, it will be as the monstrous dwarf who poisoned his young nephew at his wedding feast.* The thought made him so bloody angry that he flung the bowl and spoon across the room and left a smear of porridge on the wall. Ser Addam Marbrand looked at it curiously when he came to escort Tyrion to trial, but had the good grace not to inquire.

"Lord Varys," the herald said, "master of whisperers."

Powdered, primped, and smelling of rosewater, the Spider rubbed his hands one over the other all the time he spoke. *Washing my life away,*

Tyrion thought, as he listened to the eunuch's mournful account of how the Imp had schemed to part Joffrey from the Hound's protection and spoken with Bronn of the benefits of having Tommen as king. *Half-truths are worth more than outright lies.* And unlike the others, Varys had documents; parchments painstakingly filled with notes, details, dates, whole conversations. So much material that its recitation took all day, and so much of it damning. Varys confirmed Tyrion's midnight visit to Grand Maester Pycelle's chambers and the theft of his poisons and potions, confirmed the threat he'd made to Cersei the night of their supper, confirmed every bloody thing but the poisoning itself. When Prince Oberyn asked him how he could possibly know all this, not having been present at any of these events, the eunuch only giggled and said, "My little birds told me. Knowing is their purpose, and mine."

How do I question a little bird? thought Tyrion. *I should have had the eunuch's head off my first day in King's Landing. Damn him. And damn me for whatever trust I put in him.*

"Have we heard it all?" Lord Tywin asked his daughter as Varys left the hall.

"Almost," said Cersei. "I beg your leave to bring one final witness before you, on the morrow."

"As you wish," Lord Tywin said.

Oh, good, thought Tyrion savagely. *After this farce of a trial, execution will almost come as a relief.*

That night, as he sat by his window drinking, he heard voices outside his door. *Ser Kevan, come for my answer,* he thought at once, but it was not his uncle who entered.

Tyrion rose to give Prince Oberyn a mocking bow. "Are judges permitted to visit the accused?"

"Princes are permitted to go where they will. Or so I told your guards." The Red Viper took a seat.

"My father will be displeased with you."

"The happiness of Tywin Lannister has never been high on my list of concerns. Is it Dornish wine you're drinking?"

"From the Arbor."

Oberyn made a face. "Red water. Did you poison him?"

"No. Did you?"

The prince smiled. "Do all dwarfs have tongues like yours? Someone is going to cut it out one of these days."

"You are not the first to tell me that. Perhaps I should cut it out myself, it seems to make no end of trouble."

"So I've seen. I think I may drink some of Lord Redwyne's grape juice after all."

"As you like." Tyrion served him a cup.

The man took a sip, sloshed it about in his mouth, and swallowed. "It will serve, for the moment. I will send you up some strong Dornish wine on the morrow." He took another sip. "I have turned up that golden-haired whore I was hoping for."

"So you found Chataya's?"

"At Chataya's I bedded the black-skinned girl. Alayaya, I believe she is called. Exquisite, despite the stripes on her back. But the whore I referred to is your sister."

"Has she seduced you yet?" Tyrion asked, unsurprised.

Oberyn laughed aloud. "No, but she will if I meet her price. The queen has even hinted at marriage. Her Grace needs another husband, and who better than a prince of Dorne? Ellaria believes I should accept. Just the thought of Cersei in our bed makes her wet, the randy wench. And we should not even need to pay the dwarf's penny. All your sister requires from me is one head, somewhat overlarge and missing a nose."

"And?" said Tyrion, waiting.

By way of answer Prince Oberyn swirled his wine, and said, "When the Young Dragon conquered Dorne so long ago, he left the Lord of Highgarden to rule us after the Submission of Sunspear. This Tyrell moved with his tail from keep to keep, chasing rebels and making certain that our knees stayed bent. He would arrive in force, take a castle for his own, stay a moon's turn, and ride on to the next castle. It was his custom to turn the lords out of their own chambers and take their beds for himself. One night he found himself beneath a heavy velvet canopy. A sash hung down near the pillows, should he wish to summon a wench. He had a taste for Dornish women, this Lord Tyrell, and who can blame him? So he pulled upon the sash, and when he did the canopy above him split open, and a hundred red scorpions fell down upon his head. His death lit a fire that soon swept across Dorne, undoing all the Young Dragon's victories in a fortnight. The kneeling men stood up, and we were free again."

"I know the tale," said Tyrion. "What of it?"

"Just this. If I should ever find a sash beside my own bed, and pull on it, I would sooner have the scorpions fall upon me than the queen in all her naked beauty."

Tyrion grinned. "We have that much in common, then."

"To be sure, I have much to thank your sister for. If not for her accusation at the feast, it might well be you judging me instead of me judging you." The prince's eyes were dark with amusement. "Who knows more of poison than the Red Viper of Dorne, after all? Who has better reason to want to keep the Tyrells far from the crown? And with Joffrey in his grave, by *Dornish* law the Iron Throne should pass next to his sister Myrcella, who as it happens is betrothed to mine own nephew, thanks to you."

"Dornish law does not apply." Tyrion had been so ensnared in his own troubles that he'd never stopped to consider the succession. "My father will crown Tommen, count on that."

"He may indeed crown Tommen, here in King's Landing. Which is not to say that my brother may not crown Myrcella, down in Sunspear. Will your father make war on your niece on behalf of your nephew? Will your sister?" He gave a shrug. "Perhaps I should marry Queen Cersei after all, on the condition that she support her daughter over her son. Do you think she would?"

Never, Tyrion wanted to say, but the word caught in his throat. Cersei always resented being excluded from power on account of her sex. *If Dornish law applied in the west, she would be the heir to Casterly Rock in her own right.* She and Jaime were twins, but Cersei had come first into the world, and that was all it took. By championing Myrcella's cause she would be championing her own. "I do not know how my sister would choose, between Tommen and Myrcella," he admitted. "It makes no matter. My father will never give her that choice."

"Your father," said Prince Oberyn, "may not live forever."

Something about the way he said it made the hairs on the back of Tyrion's neck bristle. Suddenly he was mindful of Elia again, and all that Oberyn had said as they crossed the field of ashes. *He wants the head that spoke the words, not just the hand that swung the sword.* "It is not wise to speak such treasons in the Red Keep, my prince. The little birds are listening."

"Let them. Is it treason to say a man is mortal? *Valar morghulis* was how they said it in Valyria of old. *All men must die.* And the Doom came and proved it true." The Dornishman went to the window to gaze out into the night. "It is being said that you have no witnesses for us."

"I was hoping one look at this sweet face of mine would be enough to persuade you all of my innocence."

"You are mistaken, my lord. The Fat Flower of Highgarden is quite convinced of your guilt, and determined to see you die. His precious Margaery was drinking from that chalice too, as he has reminded us half a hundred times."

"And you?" said Tyrion.

"Men are seldom as they appear. You look so very guilty that I am convinced of your innocence. Still, you will likely be condemned. Justice is in short supply this side of the mountains. There has been none for Elia, Aegon, or Rhaenys. Why should there be any for you? Perhaps Joffrey's real killer was eaten by a bear. That seems to happen quite often in King's Landing. Oh, wait, the bear was at Harrenhal, now I remember."

"Is that the game we are playing?" Tyrion rubbed at his scarred nose. He had nothing to lose by telling Oberyn the truth. "There *was* a bear at Harrenhal, and it did kill Ser Amory Lorch."

"How sad for him," said the Red Viper. "And for you. Do all noseless men lie so badly, I wonder?"

"I am not lying. Ser Amory dragged Princess Rhaenys out from under her father's bed and stabbed her to death. He had some men-at-arms with him, but I do not know their names." He leaned forward. "It was Ser Gregor Clegane who smashed Prince Aegon's head against a wall and raped your sister Elia with his blood and brains still on his hands."

"What is this, now? Truth, from a Lannister?" Oberyn smiled coldly. "Your father gave the commands, yes?"

"No." He spoke the lie without hesitation, and never stopped to ask himself why he should.

The Dornishman raised one thin black eyebrow. "Such a dutiful son. And such a very feeble lie. It was Lord Tywin who presented my sister's children to King Robert all wrapped up in crimson Lannister cloaks."

"Perhaps you ought to have this discussion with my father. He was there. I was at the Rock, and still so young that I thought the thing between my legs was only good for pissing."

"Yes, but you are here now, and in some difficulty, I would say. Your innocence may be as plain as the scar on your face, but it will not save you. No more than your father will." The Dornish prince smiled. "But I might."

"You?" Tyrion studied him. "You are one judge in three. How could you save me?"

"Not as your judge. As your champion."

JAIME

A white book sat on a white table in a white room.

The room was round, its walls of whitewashed stone hung with white woolen tapestries. It formed the first floor of White Sword Tower, a slender structure of four stories built into an angle of the castle wall overlooking the bay. The undercroft held arms and armor, the second and third floors the small spare sleeping cells of the six brothers of the Kingsguard.

One of those cells had been his for eighteen years, but this morning he had moved his things to the topmost floor, which was given over entirely to the Lord Commander's apartments. Those rooms were spare as well, though spacious; and they were above the outer walls, which meant he would have a view of the sea. *I will like that,* he thought. *The view, and all the rest.*

As pale as the room, Jaime sat by the book in his Kingsguard whites, waiting for his Sworn Brothers. A longsword hung from his hip. *From the wrong hip.* Before he had always worn his sword on his left, and drawn it across his body when he unsheathed. He had shifted it to his right hip this morning, so as to be able to draw it with his left hand in the same manner, but the weight of it felt strange there, and when he had tried to pull the blade from the scabbard the whole motion seemed clumsy and unnatural. His clothing fit badly as well. He had donned the winter raiment of the Kingsguard, a tunic and breeches of bleached white wool and a heavy white cloak, but it all seemed to hang loose on him.

Jaime had spent his days at his brother's trial, standing well to the back of the hall. Either Tyrion never saw him there or he did not know him, but that was no surprise. Half the court no longer seemed to know him. *I am a stranger in my own House.* His son was dead, his father had disowned him, and his sister ... she had not allowed him to be alone with her once, after that first day in the royal sept where Joffrey lay amongst the candles. Even when they bore him across the city to his tomb in the Great Sept of Baelor, Cersei kept a careful distance.

He looked about the Round Room once more. White wool hangings covered the walls, and there was a white shield and two crossed longswords mounted above the hearth. The chair behind the table was old black oak, with cushions of blanched cowhide, the leather worn thin. *Worn by the bony arse of Barristan the Bold and Ser Gerold Hightower before him, by Prince Aemon the Dragonknight, Ser Ryam Redwyne, and the Demon of Darry, by Ser Duncan the Tall and the Pale Griffin Alyn Connington.* How could the Kingslayer belong in such exalted company?

Yet here he was.

The table itself was old weirwood, pale as bone, carved in the shape of a huge shield supported by three white stallions. By tradition the Lord Commander sat at the top of the shield, and the brothers three to a side, on the rare occasions when all seven were assembled. The book that rested by his elbow was massive; two feet tall and a foot and a half wide, a thousand pages thick, fine white vellum bound between covers of bleached white leather with gold hinges and fastenings. *The Book of the Brothers* was its formal name, but more often it was simply called the White Book.

Within the White Book was the history of the Kingsguard. Every knight who'd ever served had a page, to record his name and deeds for all time. On the top left-hand corner of each page was drawn the shield the man had carried at the time he was chosen, inked in rich colors. Down in the bottom right corner was the shield of the Kingsguard; snow-white, empty, pure. The upper shields were all different; the lower shields were all the same. In the space between were written the facts of each man's life and service. The heraldic drawings and illuminations were done by septons sent from the Great Sept of Baelor three times a year, but it was the duty of the Lord Commander to keep the entries up to date.

My duty, now. Once he learned to write with his left hand, that is. The White Book was well behind. The deaths of Ser Mandon Moore and Ser Preston Greenfield needed to be entered, and the brief bloody Kingsguard service of Sandor Clegane as well. New pages must be started for Ser Balon Swann, Ser Osmund Kettleblack, and the Knight of Flowers. *I will need to summon a septon to draw their shields.*

Ser Barristan Selmy had preceded Jaime as Lord Commander. The shield atop his page showed the arms of House Selmy: three stalks of wheat, yellow, on a brown field. Jaime was amused, though unsurprised, to find that Ser Barristan had taken the time to record his own dismissal before leaving the castle.

Ser Barristan of House Selmy. Firstborn son of Ser Lyonel Selmy of Harvest Hall. Served as squire to Ser Manfred Swann. Named "the Bold" in his 10th year, when he donned borrowed armor to appear as a mystery knight in the tourney at Blackhaven, where he was defeated and unmasked by Duncan, Prince of Dragonflies. Knighted in his 16th year by King Aegon V Targaryen, after performing great feats of prowess as a mystery knight in the winter tourney at King's Landing, defeating Prince Duncan the Small and Ser Duncan the Tall, Lord Commander of the Kingsguard. Slew Maelys the Monstrous, last of the Blackfyre Pretenders, in single combat during the War of the Ninepenny Kings. Defeated Lormelle Long Lance and Cedrik Storm, the Bastard of Bronzegate. Named to the Kingsguard in his 23rd year, by Lord Commander Ser Gerold Hightower. Defended the passage against all challengers in the tourney of the Silver Bridge. Victor in the mêlée at Maidenpool. Brought King Aerys II to safety during the Defiance of Duskendale, despite an arrow wound in the chest. Avenged the murder of his Sworn Brother, Ser Gwayne Gaunt. Rescued Lady Jeyne Swann and her septa from the Kingswood Brotherhood, defeating Simon Toyne and the Smiling Knight, and slaying the former. In the Oldtown tourney, defeated and unmasked the mystery knight Blackshield, revealing him as the Bastard of Uplands. Sole champion of Lord Steffon's tourney at Storm's End, whereat he unhorsed Lord Robert Baratheon, Prince Oberyn Martell, Lord Leyton Hightower, Lord Jon Connington, Lord Jason Mallister, and Prince Rhaegar Targaryen. Wounded by arrow, spear, and sword at the Battle of the Trident whilst fighting beside his Sworn Brothers and Rhaegar Prince of Dragonstone. Pardoned, and named Lord Commander of the Kingsguard, by King Robert I Baratheon. Served in the honor guard that brought Lady Cersei of House Lannister to King's Landing to wed King Robert. Led the attack on Old Wyk during Balon Greyjoy's Rebellion. Champion of the tourney at King's Landing, in his 57th year. Dismissed from service by King Joffrey I Baratheon in his 61st year, for reasons of advanced age.

The earlier part of Ser Barristan's storied career had been entered by Ser Gerold Hightower in a big forceful hand. Selmy's own smaller and more elegant writing took over with the account of his wounding on the Trident.

Jaime's own page was scant by comparison.

Ser Jaime of House Lannister. Firstborn son of Lord Tywin and Lady Joanna of Casterly Rock. Served against the Kingswood Brotherhood as squire to Lord Sumner Crakehall. Knighted in his 15th year by Ser Arthur Dayne of the Kingsguard, for valor in the field. Chosen for the Kingsguard in his 15th year by King Aerys II Targaryen. During the Sack of King's Landing, slew King Aerys II at the foot of the Iron Throne. Thereafter known as the "Kingslayer." Pardoned for his crime by King Robert I Baratheon. Served in the honor guard that brought his sister the Lady Cersei Lannister to King's Landing to wed King Robert. Champion in the tourney held at King's Landing on the occasion of their wedding.

Summed up like that, his life seemed a rather scant and mingy thing. Ser Barristan could have recorded a few of his other tourney victories, at least. And Ser Gerold might have written a few more words about the deeds he'd performed when Ser Arthur Dayne broke the Kingswood Brotherhood. He *had* saved Lord Sumner's life as Big Belly Ben was about to smash his head in, though the outlaw had escaped him. And he'd held his own against the Smiling Knight, though it was Ser Arthur who slew him. *What a fight that was, and what a foe.* The Smiling Knight was a madman, cruelty and chivalry all jumbled up together, but he did not know the meaning of fear. *And Dayne, with Dawn in hand . . .* The outlaw's longsword had so many notches by the end that Ser Arthur had stopped to let him fetch a new one. "It's that white sword of yours I want," the robber knight told him as they resumed, though he was bleeding from a dozen wounds by then. "Then you shall have it, ser," the Sword of the Morning replied, and made an end of it.

The world was simpler in those days, Jaime thought, *and men as well as swords were made of finer steel.* Or was it only that he had been fifteen? They were all in their graves now, the Sword of the Morning and the Smiling Knight, the White Bull and Prince Lewyn, Ser Oswell Whent with his black humor, earnest Jon Darry, Simon Toyne and his Kingswood Brotherhood, bluff old Sumner Crakehall. *And me, that boy I was . . . when did he die, I wonder? When I donned the white cloak? When I opened Aerys's throat?* That boy had wanted to be Ser Arthur Dayne, but someplace along the way he had become the Smiling Knight instead.

When he heard the door open, he closed the White Book and stood to receive his Sworn Brothers. Ser Osmund Kettleblack was the first to arrive. He gave Jaime a grin, as if they were old brothers-in-arms. "Ser Jaime," he said, "had you looked like this t'other night, I'd have known you at once."

"Would you indeed?" Jaime doubted that. The servants had bathed him, shaved him, and washed and brushed his hair. When he looked in a glass, he no longer saw the man who had crossed the riverlands with

Brienne . . . but he did not see himself either. His face was thin and hollow, and he had lines under his eyes. *I look like some old man.* "Stand by your seat, ser."

Kettleblack complied. The other Sworn Brothers filed in one by one. "Sers," Jaime said in a formal tone when all five had assembled, "who guards the king?"

"My brothers Ser Osney and Ser Osfryd," Ser Osmund replied.

"And my brother Ser Garlan," said the Knight of Flowers.

"Will they keep him safe?"

"They will, my lord."

"Be seated, then." The words were ritual. Before the seven could meet in session, the king's safety must be assured.

Ser Boros and Ser Meryn sat to his right, leaving an empty chair between them for Ser Arys Oakheart, off in Dorne. Ser Osmund, Ser Balon, and Ser Loras took the seats to his left. *The old and the new.* Jaime wondered if that meant anything. There had been times during its history where the Kingsguard had been divided against itself, most notably and bitterly during the Dance of the Dragons. Was that something he needed to fear as well?

It seemed queer to him to sit in the Lord Commander's seat where Barristan the Bold had sat for so many years. *And even queerer to sit here crippled.* Nonetheless, it was his seat, and this was his Kingsguard now. *Tommen's seven.*

Jaime had served with Meryn Trant and Boros Blount for years; adequate fighters, but Trant was sly and cruel, and Blount a bag of growly air. Ser Balon Swann was better suited to his cloak, and of course the Knight of Flowers was supposedly all a knight should be. The fifth man was a stranger to him, this Osmund Kettleblack.

He wondered what Ser Arthur Dayne would have to say of this lot. *"How is it that the Kingsguard has fallen so low,"* most like. *"It was my doing,"* I would have to answer. *"I opened the door, and did nothing when the vermin began to crawl inside."*

"The king is dead," Jaime began. "My sister's son, a boy of thirteen, murdered at his own wedding feast in his own hall. All five of you were present. All five of you were *protecting* him. And yet he's dead." He waited to see what they would say to that, but none of them so much as cleared a throat. *The Tyrell boy is angry, and Balon Swann's ashamed*, he judged. From the other three Jaime sensed only indifference. "Did my brother do this thing?" he asked them bluntly. "Did Tyrion poison my nephew?"

Ser Balon shifted uncomfortably in his seat. Ser Boros made a fist. Ser Osmund gave a lazy shrug. It was Meryn Trant who finally answered. "He filled Joffrey's cup with wine. That must have been when he slipped the poison in."

"You are certain it was the *wine* that was poisoned?"

"What else?" said Ser Boros Blount. "The Imp emptied the dregs on the floor. Why, but to spill the wine that might have proved him guilty?"

"He knew the wine was poisoned," said Ser Meryn.

Ser Balon Swann frowned. "The Imp was not alone on the dais. Far from it. That late in the feast, we had people standing and moving about, changing places, slipping off to the privy, servants were coming and going . . . the king and queen had just opened the wedding pie, every eye was on them or those thrice-damned doves. No one was watching the wine cup."

"Who else was on the dais?" asked Jaime.

Ser Meryn answered. "The king's family, the bride's family, Grand Maester Pycelle, the High Septon . . ."

"There's your poisoner," suggested Ser Oswald Kettleblack with a sly grin. "Too holy by half, that old man. Never liked the look o' him, myself." He laughed.

"No," the Knight of Flowers said, unamused. "Sansa Stark was the poisoner. You all forget, my sister was drinking from that chalice as well. Sansa Stark was the only person in the hall who had reason to want Margaery dead, as well as the king. By poisoning the wedding cup, she could hope to kill both of them. And why did she run afterward, unless she was guilty?"

The boy makes sense. Tyrion might yet be innocent. No one was any closer to finding the girl, however. Perhaps Jaime should look into that himself. For a start, it would be good to know how she had gotten out of the castle. *Varys may have a notion or two about that.* No one knew the Red Keep better than the eunuch.

That could wait, however. Just now Jaime had more immediate concerns. *You say you are the Lord Commander of the Kingsguard*, his father had said. *Go do your duty.* These five were not the brothers he would have chosen, but they were the brothers he had; the time had come to take them in hand.

"Whoever did it," he told them, "Joffrey is dead, and the Iron Throne belongs to Tommen now. I mean for him to sit on it until his hair turns white and his teeth fall out. And not from poison." Jaime turned to Ser Boros Blount. The man had grown stout in recent years, though he was big-boned enough to carry it. "Ser Boros, you look like a man who enjoys his food. Henceforth you'll taste everything Tommen eats or drinks."

Ser Osmund Kettleblack laughed aloud and the Knight of Flowers smiled, but Ser Boros turned a deep beet red. "I am no food taster! I am a knight of the Kingsguard!"

"Sad to say, you are." Cersei should never have stripped the man of his white cloak. But their father had only compounded the shame by restoring it. "My sister has told me how readily you yielded my nephew to Tyrion's sellswords. You will find carrots and pease less threatening, I hope. When your Sworn Brothers are training in the yard with sword and shield, you may train with spoon and trencher. Tommen loves applecakes. Try not to let any sellswords make off with them."

"You speak to me thus? *You?*"

"You should have died before you let Tommen be taken."

"As you died protecting Aerys, ser?" Ser Boros lurched to his feet, and clasped the hilt of his sword. "I *won't* . . . I won't suffer this. You should be the food taster, it seems to me. What else is a cripple good for?"

Jaime smiled. "I agree. I am as unfit to guard the king as you are. So draw that sword you're fondling, and we shall see how your two hands fare against my one. At the end one of us will be dead, and the Kingsguard will be improved." He rose. "Or, if you prefer, you may return to your duties."

"*Bah!*" Ser Boros hawked up a glob of green phlegm, spat it at Jaime's feet, and walked out, his sword still in its sheath.

The man is craven, and a good thing. Though fat, aging, and never more than ordinary, Ser Boros could still have hacked him into bloody pieces. *But Boros does not know that, and neither must the rest. They feared the man I was; the man I am they'd pity.*

Jaime seated himself again and turned to Kettleblack. "Ser Osmund. I do not know you. I find that curious. I've fought in tourneys, mêlées, and battles throughout the Seven Kingdoms. I know of every hedge knight, freerider, and upjumped squire of any skill who has ever presumed to break a lance in the lists. So how is it that I have never heard of you, Ser Osmund?"

"That I couldn't say, my lord." He had a great wide smile on his face, did Ser Osmund, as if he and Jaime were old comrades in arms playing some jolly little game. "I'm a soldier, though, not no tourney knight."

"Where had you served, before my sister found you?"

"Here and there, my lord."

"I have been to Oldtown in the south and Winterfell in the north. I have been to Lannisport in the west, and King's Landing in the east. But I have never been to Here. Nor There." For want of a finger, Jaime pointed his stump at Ser Osmund's beak of a nose. "I will ask once more. *Where have you served?*"

"In the Stepstones. Some in the Disputed Lands. There's always fighting there. I rode with the Gallant Men. We fought for Lys, and some for Tyrosh."

You fought for anyone who would pay you. "How did you come by your knighthood?"

"On a battlefield."

"Who knighted you?"

"Ser Robert . . . Stone. He's dead now, my lord."

"To be sure." Ser Robert Stone might have been some bastard from the Vale, he supposed, selling his sword in the Disputed Lands. On the other hand, he might be no more than a name Ser Osmund cobbled together from a dead king and a castle wall. *What was Cersei thinking when she gave this one a white cloak?*

At least Kettleblack would likely know how to use a sword and shield. Sellswords were seldom the most honorable of men, but they had to have a certain skill at arms to stay alive. "Very well, ser," Jaime said. "You may go."

The man's grin returned. He left swaggering.

"Ser Meryn." Jaime smiled at the sour knight with the rust-red hair and the pouches under his eyes. "I have heard it said that Joffrey made use of you to chastise Sansa Stark." He turned the White Book around one-handed. "Here, show me where it is in our vows that we swear to beat women and children."

"I did as His Grace commanded me. We are sworn to obey."

"Henceforth you will temper that obedience. My sister is Queen Regent. My father is the King's Hand. I am Lord Commander of the Kingsguard. Obey us. None other."

Ser Meryn got a stubborn look on his face. "Are you telling us not to obey the king?"

"The king is eight. Our first duty is to *protect* him, which includes protecting him from himself. Use that ugly thing you keep inside your helm. If Tommen wants you to saddle his horse, obey him. If he tells you to kill his horse, come to me."

"Aye. As you command, my lord."

"Dismissed." As he left, Jaime turned to Ser Balon Swann. "Ser Balon, I have watched you tilt many a time, and fought with and against you in mêlées. I'm told you proved your valor a hundred times over during the Battle of the Blackwater. The Kingsguard is honored by your presence."

"The honor's mine, my lord." Ser Balon sounded wary.

"There is only one question I would put to you. You served us loyally, it's true . . . but Varys tells me that your brother rode with Renly and then Stannis, whilst your lord father chose not to call his banners at all and remained behind the walls of Stonehelm all through the fighting."

"My father is an old man, my lord. Well past forty. His fighting days are done."

"And your brother?"

"Donnel was wounded in the battle and yielded to Ser Elwood Harte. He was ransomed afterward and pledged his fealty to King Joffrey, as did many other captives."

"So he did," said Jaime. "Even so . . . Renly, Stannis, Joffrey, Tommen . . . how did he come to omit Balon Greyjoy and Robb Stark? He might have been the first knight in the realm to swear fealty to all six kings."

Ser Balon's unease was plain. "Donnel erred, but he is Tommen's man now. You have my word."

"It's not Ser Donnel the Constant who concerns me. It's you." Jaime leaned forward. "What will you do if brave Ser Donnel gives his sword to yet another usurper, and one day comes storming into the throne room? And there you stand all in white, between your king and your blood. What will you do?"

"I . . . my lord, that will never happen."

"It happened to me," Jaime said.

Swann wiped his brow with the sleeve of his white tunic.

"You have no answer?"

"My lord." Ser Balon drew himself up. "On my sword, on my honor, on my father's name, I swear . . . I shall not do as you did."

Jaime laughed. "Good. Return to your duties . . . and tell Ser Donnel to add a weathervane to his shield."

And then he was alone with the Knight of Flowers.

Slim as a sword, lithe and fit, Ser Loras Tyrell wore a snowy linen tunic and white wool breeches, with a gold belt around his waist and a gold rose clasping his fine silk cloak. His hair was a soft brown tumble, and his eyes were brown as well, and bright with insolence. *He thinks this is a tourney, and his tilt has just been called.* "Seventeen and a knight of the Kingsguard," said Jaime. "You must be proud. Prince Aemon the Dragonknight was seventeen when he was named. Did you know that?"

"Yes, my lord."

"And did you know that I was *fifteen?*"

"That as well, my lord." He smiled.

Jaime hated that smile. "I was better than you, Ser Loras. I was bigger, I was stronger, and I was quicker."

"And now you're older," the boy said. "My lord."

He had to laugh. *This is too absurd. Tyrion would mock me unmercifully if he could hear me now, comparing cocks with this green boy.* "Older and wiser, ser. You should learn from me."

"As you learned from Ser Boros and Ser Meryn?"

That arrow hit too close to the mark. "I learned from the White Bull and Barristan the Bold," Jaime snapped. "I learned from Ser Arthur Dayne, the Sword of the Morning, who could have slain all five of you with his left hand while he was taking with a piss with the right. I learned from Prince Lewyn of Dorne and Ser Oswell Whent and Ser Jonothor Darry, good men every one."

"Dead men, every one."

He's me, Jaime realized suddenly. *I am speaking to myself, as I was, all cocksure arrogance and empty chivalry. This is what it does to you, to be too good too young.*

As in a swordfight, sometimes it is best to try a different stroke. "It's said you fought magnificently in the battle . . . almost as well as Lord Renly's ghost beside you. A Sworn Brother has no secrets from his Lord Commander. Tell me, ser. Who was wearing Renly's armor?"

For a moment Loras Tyrell looked as though he might refuse, but in the end he remembered his vows. "My brother," he said sullenly. "Renly was taller than me, and broader in the chest. His armor was too loose on me, but it suited Garlan well."

"Was the masquerade your notion, or his?"

"Lord Littlefinger suggested it. He said it would frighten Stannis's ignorant men-at-arms."

"And so it did." *And some knights and lordlings too.* "Well, you gave the singers something to make rhymes about, I suppose that's not to be despised. What did you do with Renly?"

"I buried him with mine own hands, in a place he showed me once when I was a squire at Storm's End. No one shall ever find him there to disturb his rest." He looked at Jaime defiantly. "I will defend King Tommen with all my strength, I swear it. I will give my life for his if need be. But I will never betray Renly, by word or deed. He was the king that should have been. He was the best of them."

The best dressed perhaps, Jaime thought, but for once he did not say it. The arrogance had gone out of Ser Loras the moment he began to speak of Renly. *He answered truly. He is proud and reckless and full of piss, but he is not false. Not yet.* "As you say. One more thing, and you may return to your duties."

"Yes, my lord?"

"I still have Brienne of Tarth in a tower cell."

The boy's mouth hardened. "A black cell would be better."

"You are certain that's what she deserves?"

"She deserves death. I told Renly that a woman had no place in the Rainbow Guard. She won the mêlée with a trick."

"I seem to recall another knight who was fond of tricks. He once rode a mare in heat against a foe mounted on a bad-tempered stallion. What sort of trickery did Brienne use?"

Ser Loras flushed. "She leapt . . . it makes no matter. She won, I grant her that. His Grace put a rainbow cloak around her shoulders. And she killed him. Or let him die."

"A large difference there." *The difference between my crime and the shame of Boros Blount.*

"She had sworn to protect him. Ser Emmon Cuy, Ser Robar Royce, Ser Parmen Crane, they'd sworn as well. How could anyone have hurt him, with her inside his tent and the others just outside? Unless they were part of it."

"There were five of you at the wedding feast," Jaime pointed out. "How could Joffrey die? Unless you were part of it?"

Ser Loras drew himself up stiffly. "There was nothing we could have done."

"The wench says the same. She grieves for Renly as you do. I promise you, I never grieve for Aerys. Brienne's ugly, and pighead stubborn. But she lacks the wits to be a liar, and she is loyal past the point of sense. She swore an oath to bring me to King's Landing, and here I sit. This hand I lost . . . well, that was my doing as much as hers. Considering all she did to protect me, I have no doubt that she would have fought for Renly, had there been a foe to fight. But a shadow?" Jaime shook his head. "Draw your sword, Ser Loras. Show me how *you'd* fight a shadow. I should like to see that."

Ser Loras made no move to rise. "She fled," he said. "She and Catelyn Stark, they left him in his blood and ran. Why would they, if it was not their work?" He stared at the table. "Renly gave me the van. Otherwise it would have been me helping him don his armor. He often entrusted that task to me. We had . . . we had prayed together that night. I left him with her. Ser Parmen and Ser Emmon were guarding the tent, and Ser Robar Royce was there as well. Ser Emmon swore Brienne had . . . although . . ."

"Yes?" Jaime prompted, sensing a doubt.

"The gorget was cut through. One clean stroke, through a steel gorget. Renly's armor was the best, the finest steel. How could she do that? I tried myself, and it was not possible. She's freakish strong for a woman, but even the Mountain would have needed a heavy axe. And why armor him and *then* cut his throat?" He gave Jaime a confused look. "If not her, though . . . how could it be a *shadow?*"

"Ask her." Jaime came to a decision. "Go to her cell. Ask your questions and hear her answers. If you are still convinced that she murdered Lord Renly, I will see that she answers for it. The choice will be yours. Accuse her, or release her. All I ask is that you judge her fairly, on your honor as a knight."

Ser Loras stood. "I shall. On my honor."

"We are done, then."

The younger man started for the door. But there he turned back. "Renly thought she was absurd. A woman dressed in man's mail, pretending to be a knight."

"If he'd ever seen her in pink satin and Myrish lace, he would not have complained."

"I asked him why he kept her close, if he thought her so grotesque. He said that all his other knights wanted things of him, castles or honors or riches, but all that Brienne wanted was to die for him. When I saw him all bloody, with her fled and the three of them unharmed . . . if she's innocent, then Robar and Emmon . . ." He could not seem to say the words.

Jaime had not stopped to consider that aspect of it. "I would have done the same, ser." The lie came easy, but Ser Loras seemed grateful for it.

When he was gone, the Lord Commander sat alone in the white room, wondering. The Knight of Flowers had been so mad with grief for Renly that he had cut down two of his own Sworn Brothers, but it had never occurred to Jaime to do the same with the five who had failed Joffrey. *He was my son, my secret son . . . What am I, if I do not lift the hand I have left to avenge mine own blood and seed?* He ought to kill Ser Boros at least, just to be rid of him.

He looked at his stump and grimaced. *I must do something about that.* If the late Ser Jacelyn Bywater could wear an iron hand, he should have a gold one. *Cersei might like that. A golden hand to stroke her golden hair, and hold her hard against me.*

His hand could wait, though. There were other things to tend to first. There were other debts to pay.

SANSA

The ladder to the forecastle was steep and splintery, so Sansa accepted a hand up from Lothor Brune. *Ser Lothor*, she had to remind herself; the man had been knighted for his valor in the Battle of the Blackwater. Though no proper knight would wear those patched brown breeches and scuffed boots, nor that cracked and water-stained leather jerkin. A square-faced stocky man with a squashed nose and a mat of nappy grey hair, Brune spoke seldom. *He is stronger than he looks, though.* She could tell by the ease with which he lifted her, as if she weighed nothing at all.

Off the bow of the *Merling King* stretched a bare and stony strand, windswept, treeless, and uninviting. Even so, it made a welcome sight. They had been a long while clawing their way back on course. The last storm had swept them out of sight of land, and sent such waves crashing over the sides of the galley that Sansa had been certain they were all going to drown. Two men had been swept overboard, she had heard old Oswell saying, and another had fallen from the mast and broken his neck.

She had seldom ventured out on deck herself. Her little cabin was dank and cold, but Sansa had been sick for most of the voyage . . . sick with terror, sick with fever, or seasick . . . she could keep nothing down, and even sleep came hard. Whenever she closed her eyes she saw Joffrey tearing at his collar, clawing at the soft skin of his throat, dying with flakes of pie crust on his lips and wine stains on his doublet. And the wind keening in the lines reminded her of the terrible thin sucking sound he'd made as he fought to draw in air. Sometimes she dreamed of Tyrion as well. "He did nothing," she told Littlefinger once, when he paid a visit to her cabin to see if she were feeling any better.

"He did not kill Joffrey, true, but the dwarf's hands are far from clean. He had a wife before you, did you know that?"

"He told me."

"And did he tell you that when he grew bored with her, he made a gift of her to his father's guardsmen? He might have done the same to you, in time. Shed no tears for the Imp, my lady."

The wind ran salty fingers through her hair, and Sansa shivered. Even this close to shore, the rolling of the ship made her tummy queasy. She desperately needed a bath and a change of clothes. *I must look as haggard as a corpse, and smell of vomit.*

Lord Petyr came up beside her, cheerful as ever. "Good morrow. The salt air is bracing, don't you think? It always sharpens my appetite." He put a sympathetic arm about her shoulders. "Are you quite well? You look so pale."

"It's only my tummy. The seasickness."

"A little wine will be good for that. We'll get you a cup, as soon as we're ashore." Petyr pointed to where an old flint tower stood outlined against a bleak grey sky, the breakers crashing on the rocks beneath it. "Cheerful, is it not? I fear there's no safe anchorage here. We'll put ashore in a boat."

"Here?" She did not want to go ashore here. The Fingers were a dismal place, she'd heard, and there was something forlorn and desolate about the little tower. "Couldn't I stay on the ship until we make sail for White Harbor?"

"From here the *King* turns east for Braavos. Without us."

"But . . . my lord, you said . . . you said we were sailing home."

"And there it stands, miserable as it is. My ancestral home. It has no name, I fear. A great lord's seat ought to have a name, wouldn't you agree? Winterfell, the Eyrie, Riverrun, those are *castles*. Lord of Harrenhal now, that has a sweet ring to it, but what was I before? Lord of Sheepshit and Master of the Drearfort? It lacks a certain something." His grey-green eyes regarded her innocently. "You look distraught. Did you think we were making for Winterfell, sweetling? Winterfell has been taken, burned, and sacked. All those you knew and loved are dead. What northmen who have not fallen to the ironmen are warring amongst themselves. Even the Wall is under attack. Winterfell was the home of your childhood, Sansa, but you are no longer a child. You're a woman grown, and you need to make your own home."

"But not here," she said, dismayed. "It looks so . . ."

". . . small and bleak and mean? It's all that, and less. The Fingers are a lovely place, if you happen to be a stone. But have no fear, we shan't stay more than a fortnight. I expect your aunt is already riding to meet us." He smiled. "The Lady Lysa and I are to be wed."

"Wed?" Sansa was stunned. "You and my aunt?"

"The Lord of Harrenhal and the Lady of the Eyrie."

You said it was my mother you loved. But of course Lady Catelyn was dead, so even if she had loved Petyr secretly and given him her maidenhood, it made no matter now.

"So silent, my lady?" said Petyr. "I was certain you would wish to give me your blessing. It is a rare thing for a boy born heir to stones and sheep pellets to wed the daughter of Hoster Tully and the widow of Jon Arryn."

"I . . . I pray you will have long years together, and many children, and be very happy in one another." It had been years since Sansa last saw her mother's sister. *She will be kind to me for my mother's sake, surely. She's my own blood.* And the Vale of Arryn was beautiful, all the songs said so. Perhaps it would not be so terrible to stay here for a time.

Lothor and old Oswell rowed them ashore. Sansa huddled in the bow under her cloak with the hood drawn up against the wind, wondering what awaited her. Servants emerged from the tower to meet them; a thin old woman and a fat middle-aged one, two ancient white-haired men, and a girl of two or three with a sty on one eye. When they recognized Lord Petyr they knelt on the rocks. "My household," he said. "I don't know the child. Another of Kella's bastards, I suppose. She pops one out every few years."

The two old men waded out up to their thighs to lift Sansa from the boat so she would not get her skirts wet. Oswell and Lothor splashed their way ashore, as did Littlefinger himself. He gave the old woman a kiss on the cheek and grinned at the younger one. "Who fathered this one, Kella?"

The fat woman laughed. "I can't rightly say, m'lord. I'm not one for telling them no."

"And all the local lads are grateful, I am quite sure."

"It is good to have you home, my lord," said one old man. He looked to be at least eighty, but he wore a studded brigantine and a longsword at his side. "How long will you be in residence?"

"As short a time as possible, Bryen, have no fear. Is the place habitable just now, would you say?"

"If we knew you was coming we would have laid down fresh rushes, m'lord," said the crone. "There's a dung fire burning."

"Nothing says *home* like the smell of burning dung." Petyr turned to Sansa. "Grisel was my wet nurse, but she keeps my castle now. Umfred's my steward, and Bryen – didn't I name you captain of the guard the last time I was here?"

"You did, my lord. You said you'd be getting some more men too, but you never did. Me and the dogs stand all the watches."

"And very well, I'm sure. No one has made off with any of my rocks or sheep pellets, I see that plainly." Petyr gestured toward the fat woman. "Kella minds my vast herds. How many sheep do I have at present, Kella?"

She had to think a moment. "Three and twenty, m'lord. There was nine and twenty, but Bryen's dogs killed one and we butchered some others and salted down the meat."

"Ah, cold salt mutton. I *must* be home. When I break my fast on gulls' eggs and seaweed soup, I'll be certain of it."

"If you like, m'lord," said the old woman Grisel.

Lord Petyr made a face. "Come, let's see if my hall is as dreary as I recall." He led them up the strand over rocks slick with rotting seaweed. A handful of sheep were wandering about the base of the flint tower, grazing on the thin grass that grew between the sheepfold and thatched stable. Sansa had to step carefully; there were pellets everywhere.

Within, the tower seemed even smaller. An open stone stair wound round the inside wall, from undercroft to roof. Each floor was but a single room. The servants lived and slept in the kitchen at ground level, sharing the space with a huge brindled mastiff and a half-dozen sheep-dogs. Above that was a modest hall, and higher still the bedchamber. There were no windows, but arrowslits were embedded in the outer wall at intervals along the curve of the stair. Above the hearth hung a broken longsword and a battered oaken shield, its paint cracked and flaking.

The device painted on the shield was one Sansa did not know; a grey stone head with fiery eyes, upon a light green field. "My grandfather's shield," Petyr explained when he saw her gazing at it. "His own father was born in Braavos and came to the Vale as a sellsword in the hire of Lord Corbray, so my grandfather took the head of the Titan as his sigil when he was knighted."

"It's very fierce," said Sansa.

"Rather too fierce, for an amiable fellow like me," said Petyr. "I much prefer my mockingbird."

Oswell made two more trips out to the *Merling King* to offload provisions. Among the loads he brought ashore were several casks of wine. Petyr poured Sansa a cup, as promised. "Here, my lady, that should help your tummy, I would hope."

Having solid ground beneath her feet had helped already, but Sansa dutifully lifted the goblet with both hands and took a sip. The wine was very fine; an Arbor vintage, she thought. It tasted of oak and fruit and hot summer nights, the flavors blossoming in her mouth like flowers opening to the sun. She only prayed that she could keep it down. Lord Petyr was being so kind, she did not want to spoil it all by retching on him.

He was studying her over his own goblet, his bright grey-green eyes full of . . . was it amusement? Or something else? Sansa was not certain. "Grisel," he called to the old woman, "bring some food up. Nothing too heavy, my lady has a tender tummy. Some fruit might serve, perhaps. Oswell's brought some oranges and pomegranates from the *King*."

"Yes, m'lord."

"Might I have a hot bath as well?" asked Sansa.

"I'll have Kella draw some water, m'lady."

Sansa took another sip of wine and tried to think of some polite conversation, but Lord Petyr saved her the effort. When Grisel and the other servants had gone, he said, "Lysa will not come alone. Before she arrives, we must be clear on who you are."

"Who I . . . I don't understand."

"Varys has informers everywhere. If Sansa Stark should be seen in the Vale, the eunuch will know within a moon's turn, and that would create unfortunate . . . complications. It is not safe to be a Stark just now. So we shall tell Lysa's people that you are my natural daughter."

"Natural?" Sansa was aghast. "You mean, a bastard?"

"Well, you can scarcely be my trueborn daughter. I've never taken a wife, that's well known. What should you be called?"

"I . . . I could call myself after my mother . . ."

"Catelyn? A bit too obvious . . . but after *my* mother, that would serve. Alayne. Do you like it?"

"Alayne is pretty." Sansa hoped she would remember. "But couldn't I be the trueborn daughter of some knight in your service? Perhaps he died gallantly in the battle, and . . ."

"I have no gallant knights in my service, Alayne. Such a tale would draw unwanted questions as a corpse draws crows. It is rude to pry into the origins of a man's natural children, however." He cocked his head. "So, who are you?"

"Alayne . . . Stone, would it be?" When he nodded, she said, "But who is my mother?"

"Kella?"

"Please no," she said, mortified.

"I was teasing. Your mother was a gentlewoman of Braavos, daughter of a merchant prince. We met in Gulltown when I had charge of the port. She died giving you birth, and entrusted you to the Faith. I have some devotional books you can look over. Learn to quote from them. Nothing discourages unwanted questions as much as a flow of pious bleating. In any case, at your flowering you decided you did not wish to be a septa and wrote to me. That was the first I knew of your existence." He fingered his beard. "Do you think you can remember all that?"

"I hope. It will be like playing a game, won't it?"

"Are you fond of games, Alayne?"

The new name would take some getting used to. "Games? I . . . I suppose it would depend . . ."

Grisel reappeared before he could say more, balancing a large platter. She set it down between them. There were apples and pears and pomegranates, some sad-looking grapes, a huge blood orange. The old woman had brought a round of bread as well, and a crock of butter. Petyr cut a pomegranate in two with his dagger, offering half to Sansa. "You should try and eat, my lady."

"Thank you, my lord." Pomegranate seeds were so messy; Sansa chose a pear instead, and took a small delicate bite. It was very ripe. The juice ran down her chin.

Lord Petyr loosened a seed with the point of his dagger. "You must miss your father terribly, I know. Lord Eddard was a brave man, honest and loyal . . . but quite a hopeless player." He brought the seed to his mouth with the knife. "In King's Landing, there are two sorts of people. The players and the pieces."

"And I was a piece?" She dreaded the answer.

"Yes, but don't let that trouble you. You're still half a child. Every man's a piece to start with, and every maid as well. Even some who think they are players." He ate another seed. "Cersei, for one. She thinks herself sly, but in truth she is utterly predictable. Her strength rests on her beauty, birth, and riches. Only the first of those is truly her own, and it will soon desert her. I pity her then. She wants power, but has no notion what to do with it when she gets it. Everyone wants something, Alayne. And when you know what a man wants you know who he is, and how to move him."

"As you moved Ser Dontos to poison Joffrey?" It *had* to have been Dontos, she had concluded.

Littlefinger laughed. "Ser Dontos the Red was a skin of wine with legs. He could never have been trusted with a task of such enormity. He would have bungled it or betrayed me. No, all Dontos had to do was lead you from the castle . . . and make certain you wore your silver hair net."

The black amethysts. "But . . . if not Dontos, who? Do you have other . . . pieces?"

"You could turn King's Landing upside down and not find a single man with a mockingbird sewn over his heart, but that does not mean I am friendless." Petyr went to the steps. "Oswell, come up here and let the Lady Sansa have a look at you."

The old man appeared a few moments later, grinning and bowing. Sansa eyed him uncertainly. "What am I supposed to see?"

"Do you know him?" asked Petyr.

"No."

"Look closer."

She studied the old man's lined windburnt face, hook nose, white hair, and huge knuckly hands. There *was* something familiar about him, yet Sansa had to shake her head. "I don't. I never saw Oswell before I got into his boat, I'm certain."

Oswell grinned, showing a mouth of crooked teeth. "No, but m'lady might of met my three sons."

It was the "three sons," and that smile too. "*Kettleblack!*" Sansa's eyes went wide. "You're a Kettleblack!"

"Aye, m'lady, as it please you."

"She's beside herself with joy." Lord Petyr dismissed him with a wave, and returned to the pomegranate again as Oswell shuffled down the steps. "Tell me, Alayne – which is more dangerous, the dagger brandished by an enemy, or the hidden one pressed to your back by someone you never even see?"

"The hidden dagger."

"There's a clever girl." He smiled, his thin lips bright red from the pomegranate seeds. "When the Imp sent off her guards, the queen had Ser Lancel hire sellswords for her. Lancel found her the Kettleblacks, which delighted your little lord husband, since the lads were in his pay through his man Bronn." He chuckled. "But it was me who told Oswell to get his sons to King's Landing when I learned that Bronn was looking for swords. Three hidden daggers, Alayne, now perfectly placed."

"So one of the Kettleblacks put the poison in Joff's cup?" Ser Osmund had been near the king all night, she remembered.

"Did I say that?" Lord Petyr cut the blood orange in two with his dagger and offered half to Sansa. "The lads are far too treacherous to be part of any such scheme . . . and Osmund has become especially unreliable since he joined the Kingsguard. That white cloak does things to a man, I find. Even a man like him." He tilted his chin back and squeezed the blood orange, so the juice ran down into his mouth. "I love the juice but I loathe the sticky fingers," he complained, wiping his hands. "Clean hands, Sansa. Whatever you do, make certain your hands are clean."

Sansa spooned up some juice from her own orange. "But if it wasn't the Kettleblacks and it wasn't Ser Dontos . . . you weren't even in the city, and it couldn't have been Tyrion . . ."

"No more guesses, sweetling?"

She shook her head. "I don't . . ."

Petyr smiled. "I will wager you that at some point during the evening someone told you that your hair net was crooked and straightened it for you."

Sansa raised a hand to her mouth. "You cannot mean . . . she wanted to take me to Highgarden, to marry me to her grandson . . ."

"Gentle, pious, good-hearted Willas Tyrell. Be grateful you were spared, he would have bored you spitless. The old woman is not boring, though, I'll grant her that. A fearsome old harridan, and not near as frail as she pretends. When I came to Highgarden to dicker for Margaery's hand, she let her lord son bluster while she asked pointed questions about Joffrey's nature. I praised him to the skies, to be sure . . . whilst my men spread disturbing tales amongst Lord Tyrell's servants. That is how the game is played.

"I also planted the notion of Ser Loras taking the white. Not that I *suggested* it, that would have been too crude. But men in my party supplied grisly tales about how the mob had killed Ser Preston Greenfield and raped the Lady Lollys, and slipped a few silvers to Lord Tyrell's army of singers to sing of Ryam Redwyne, Serwyn of the Mirror Shield, and Prince Aemon the Dragonknight. A harp can be as dangerous as a sword, in the right hands.

"Mace Tyrell actually thought it was his own idea to make Ser Loras's inclusion in the Kingsguard part of the marriage contract. Who better to protect his daughter than her splendid knightly brother? And it relieved him of the difficult task of trying to find lands and a bride for a third son, never easy, and doubly difficult in Ser Loras's case.

"Be that as it may. Lady Olenna was not about to let Joff harm her precious darling granddaughter, but unlike her son she also realized that under all his flowers and finery, Ser Loras is as hot-tempered as Jaime Lannister. Toss Joffrey, Margaery, and Loras in a pot, and you've got the makings for kingslayer stew. The old woman understood something else as well. Her son was determined to make Margaery a queen, and for that he needed a king . . . but he did not need *Joffrey*. We shall have another wedding soon, wait and see. Margaery will marry Tommen. She'll keep her queenly crown and her maidenhead, neither of which she especially wants, but what does that matter? The great western alliance will be preserved . . . for a time, at least."

Margaery and Tommen. Sansa did not know what to say. She had liked Margaery Tyrell, and her small sharp grandmother as well. She thought wistfully of Highgarden with its courtyards and musicians, and the pleasure barges on the Mander; a far cry from this bleak shore. *At least I am safe here. Joffrey is dead, he cannot hurt me anymore, and I am only a bastard girl now. Alayne Stone has no husband and no claim.* And her aunt would soon be here as well. The long nightmare of King's Landing was behind her, and her mockery of a marriage as well. She could make herself a new home here, just as Petyr said.

It was eight long days until Lysa Arryn arrived. On five of them it rained, while Sansa sat bored and restless by the fire, beside the old blind dog. He was too sick and toothless to walk guard with Bryen anymore, and mostly all he did was sleep, but when she patted him he whined and licked her hand, and after that they were fast friends. When the rains let up, Petyr walked with her around his holdings, which took less than half a day. He owned a lot of rocks, just as he had said. There was one place where the tide came jetting up out of a blowhole to shoot thirty feet into the air, and another where someone had chiseled the seven-pointed star of the new gods upon a boulder. Petyr said that marked one of the places the Andals had landed, when they came across the sea to wrest the Vale from the First Men.

Farther inland a dozen families lived in huts of piled stone beside a peat bog. "Mine own smallfolk," Petyr said, though only the oldest seemed to know him. There was a hermit's cave on his land as well, but no hermit. "He's dead now, but when I was a boy my father took me to see him. The man had not washed in forty years, so you can imagine how he smelled, but supposedly he had the gift of prophecy. He groped me a bit and said I would be a great man, and for that my father gave him a skin of wine." Petyr snorted. "I would have told him the same thing for half a cup."

Finally, on a grey windy afternoon, Bryen came running back to the tower with his dogs barking at his heels, to announce that riders were approaching from the southwest. "Lysa," Lord Petyr said. "Come, Alayne, let us greet her."

They put on their cloaks and waited outside. The riders numbered no more than a score; a very modest escort, for the Lady of the Eyrie. Three maids rode with her, and a dozen household knights in mail and plate. She brought a septon as well, and a handsome singer with a wisp of a mustache and long sandy curls.

Could that be my aunt? Lady Lysa was two years younger than Mother, but this woman looked ten years older. Thick auburn tresses fell down past her waist, but beneath the costly velvet gown and jeweled bodice her body sagged and bulged. Her face was pink and painted, her breasts heavy, her limbs thick. She was taller than Littlefinger, and heavier; nor did she show any grace in the clumsy way she climbed down off her horse.

Petyr knelt to kiss her fingers. "The king's small council commanded me to woo and win you, my lady. Do you think you might have me for your lord and husband?"

Lady Lysa pooched her lips and pulled him up to plant a kiss upon his cheek. "Oh, mayhaps I could be persuaded." She giggled. "Have you brought gifts to melt my heart?"

"The king's peace."

"Oh, poo to the peace, what else have you brought me?"

"My daughter." Littlefinger beckoned Sansa forward with a hand. "My lady, allow me to present you Alayne Stone."

Lysa Arryn did not seem greatly pleased to see her. Sansa did a deep curtsy, her head bowed. "A bastard?" she heard her aunt say. "Petyr, have you been wicked? Who was her mother?"

"The wench is dead. I'd hoped to take Alayne to the Eyrie."

"What am I to do with her there?"

"I have a few notions," said Lord Petyr. "But just now I am more interested in what I might do with you, my lady."

All the sternness melted off her aunt's round pink face, and for a moment Sansa thought Lysa Arryn was about to cry. "Sweet Petyr, I've missed you so, you don't know, you can't know. Yohn Royce has been stirring up all sorts of trouble, demanding that I call my banners and go to war. And the others all swarm around me, Hunter and Corbray and that *dreadful* Nestor Royce, all wanting to wed me and take my son to ward, but none of them truly love me. Only you, Petyr. I've dreamed of you so long."

"And I of you, my lady." He slid an arm around behind her and kissed her on the neck. "How soon can we be wed?"

"Now," said Lady Lysa, sighing. "I've brought my own septon, and a singer, and mead for the wedding feast."

"Here?" That did not please him. "I'd sooner wed you at the Eyrie, with your whole court in attendance."

"Poo to my court. I have waited so long, I could not bear to wait another moment." She put her arms around him. "I want to share your bed tonight, my sweet. I want us to make another child, a brother for Robert or a sweet little daughter."

"I dream of that as well, sweetling. Yet there is much to be gained from a great public wedding, with all the Vale –"

"No." She stamped a foot. "I want you now, this very night. And I must warn you, after all these years of silence and whisperings, I mean to *scream* when you love me. I am going to scream so loud they'll hear me in the Eyrie!"

"Perhaps I could bed you now, and wed you later?"

The Lady Lysa giggled like a girl. "Oh, Petyr Baelish, you are so *wicked*. No, I say no, I am the Lady of the Eyrie, and I command you to wed me this very moment!"

Petyr gave a shrug. "As my lady commands, then. I am helpless before you, as ever."

They said their vows within the hour, standing beneath a sky-blue canopy as the sun sank in the west. Afterward trestle tables were set up beneath the small flint tower, and they feasted on quail, venison, and roast boar, washing it down with a fine light mead. Torches were lit as dusk crept in. Lysa's singer played "The Vow Unspoken" and "Seasons of My Love" and "Two Hearts That Beat as One." Several younger knights even asked Sansa to dance. Her aunt danced as well, her skirts whirling when Petyr spun her in his arms. Mead and marriage had taken years off Lady Lysa. She laughed at everything so long as she held her husband's hand, and her eyes seemed to glow whenever she looked at him.

When it was time for the bedding, her knights carried her up to the tower, stripping her as they went and shouting bawdy jests. *Tyrion spared me that*, Sansa remembered. It would not have been so bad being undressed for a man she loved, by friends who loved them both. *By Joffrey, though . . .* She shuddered.

Her aunt had brought only three ladies with her, so they pressed Sansa to help them undress Lord Petyr and march him up to his marriage bed. He submitted with good grace and a wicked tongue, giving as good as he got. By the time they had gotten him into the tower and out of his clothes, the other women were flushed, with laces unlaced, kirtles crooked, and skirts in disarray. But Littlefinger only smiled at Sansa as they marched him up to the bedchamber where his lady wife was waiting.

Lady Lysa and Lord Petyr had the third-story bedchamber to themselves, but the tower was small . . . and true to her word, her aunt screamed. It had begun to rain outside, driving the feasters into the hall one floor below, so they heard most every word. "Petyr," her aunt moaned. "Oh, Petyr, Petyr, sweet *Petyr*, oh oh oh. There, Petyr, there. That's where you belong." Lady Lysa's singer launched into a bawdy version of "Milady's Supper," but even his singing and playing could not drown out Lysa's cries. "Make me a baby, Petyr," she screamed, "make me another sweet little baby. Oh, Petyr, my precious, my precious, *PEEEEEETYR!*" Her last shriek was so loud that it set the dogs to barking, and two of her aunt's ladies could scarce contain their mirth.

Sansa went down the steps and out into the night. A light rain was falling on the remains of the feast, but the air smelled fresh and clean. The memory of her own wedding night with Tyrion was much with her. *In the dark, I am the Knight of Flowers*, he had said. *I could be good to you.* But that was only another Lannister lie. *A dog can smell a lie, you know*, the Hound had told her once. She could almost hear the rough rasp of his voice. *Look around you, and take a good whiff. They're all liars here, and every one better than you.* She wondered what had become of Sandor Clegane. Did he know that they'd killed Joffrey? Would he care? He had been the prince's sworn shield for years.

She stayed outside for a long time. When at last she sought her own bed, wet and chilled, only the dim glow of a peat fire lit the darkened hall. There was no sound from above. The young singer sat in a corner, playing a slow song to himself. One of her aunt's maids was kissing a knight in Lord Petyr's chair, their hands busy beneath each other's clothing. Several men had drunk themselves to sleep, and one was in the privy, being noisily sick. Sansa found Bryen's old blind dog in her little alcove beneath the steps, and lay down next to him. He woke and licked her face. "You sad old hound," she said, ruffling his fur.

"Alayne." Her aunt's singer stood over her. "Sweet Alayne. I am Marillion. I saw you come in from the rain. The night is chill and wet. Let me warm you."

The old dog raised his head and growled, but the singer gave him a cuff and sent him slinking off, whimpering.

"Marillion?" she said, uncertain. "You are . . . kind to think of me, but . . . pray forgive me. I am very tired."

"And very beautiful. All night I have been making songs for you in my head. A lay for your eyes, a ballad for your lips, a duet to your breasts. I will not sing them, though. They were poor things, unworthy of such beauty." He sat on her bed and put his hand on her leg. "Let me sing to you with my body instead."

She caught a whiff of his breath. "You're drunk."

"I never get drunk. Mead only makes me merry. I am on fire." His hand slipped up to her thigh. "And you as well."

"Unhand me. You forget yourself."

"Mercy. I have been singing love songs for hours. My blood is stirred. And yours, I know . . . there's no wench half so lusty as one bastard born. Are you wet for me?"

"I'm a *maiden*," she protested.

"Truly? Oh, Alayne, Alayne, my fair maid, give me the gift of your innocence. You will thank the gods you did. I'll have you singing louder than the Lady Lysa."

Sansa jerked away from him, frightened. "If you don't leave me, my au – my *father* will hang you. Lord Petyr."

"Littlefinger?" He chuckled. "Lady Lysa loves me well, and I am Lord Robert's favorite. If your father offends me, I will destroy him with a verse." He put a hand on her breast, and squeezed. "Let's get you out of these wet clothes. You wouldn't want them ripped, I know. Come, sweet lady, heed your heart –"

Sansa heard the soft sound of steel on leather. "Singer," a rough voice said, "best go, if you want to sing again." The light was dim, but she saw a faint glimmer of a blade.

The singer saw it too. "Find your own wench –" The knife flashed, and he cried out. "You *cut* me!"

"I'll do worse, if you don't go."

And quick as that, Marillion was gone. The other remained, looming over Sansa in the darkness. "Lord Petyr said watch out for you." It was Lothor Brune's voice, she realized. *Not the Hound's, no, how could it be? Of course it had to be Lothor . . .*

That night Sansa scarcely slept at all, but tossed and turned just as she had aboard the *Merling King*. She dreamt of Joffrey dying, but as he clawed at his throat and the blood ran down across his fingers she saw with horror that it was her brother Robb. And she dreamed of her wedding night too, of Tyrion's eyes devouring her as she undressed. Only then he was bigger than Tyrion had any right to be, and when he climbed into the bed his face was scarred only on one side. "*I'll have a song from you,*" he rasped, and Sansa woke and found the old blind dog beside her once again. "I wish that you were Lady," she said.

Come the morning, Grisel climbed up to the bedchamber to serve the lord and lady a tray of morning bread, with butter, honey, fruit, and cream. She returned to say that Alayne was wanted. Sansa was still drowsy from sleep. It took her a moment to remember that *she* was Alayne.

Lady Lysa was still abed, but Lord Petyr was up and dressed. "Your aunt wishes to speak with you," he told Sansa, as he pulled on a boot. "I've told her who you are."

Gods be good. "I . . . I thank you, my lord."

Petyr yanked on the other boot. "I've had about as much home as I can stomach. We'll leave for the Eyrie this afternoon." He kissed his lady wife and licked a smear of honey off her lips, then headed down the steps.

Sansa stood by the foot of the bed while her aunt ate a pear and studied her. "I see it now," the Lady Lysa said, as she set the core aside. "You look so much like Catelyn."

"It's kind of you to say so."

"It was not meant as flattery. If truth be told, you look too much like Catelyn. Something must be done. We shall darken your hair before we bring you back to the Eyrie, I think."

Darken my hair? "If it please you, Aunt Lysa."

"You must not call me that. No word of your presence here must be allowed to reach King's Landing. I do not mean to have my son endangered." She nibbled the corner of a honeycomb. "I have kept the Vale out of this war. Our harvest has been plentiful, the mountains protect us, and the Eyrie is impregnable. Even so, it would not do to draw Lord Tywin's wroth down upon us." Lysa set the comb down and licked honey from her fingers. "You were wed to Tyrion Lannister, Petyr says. That vile *dwarf*."

"They made me marry him. I never wanted it."

"No more than I did," her aunt said. "Jon Arryn was no dwarf, but he was *old*. You may not think so to see me now, but on the day we wed I was so lovely I put your mother to shame. But all Jon desired was my father's swords, to aid his darling boys. I should have refused him, but he was such an old man, how long could he live? Half his teeth were gone, and his breath smelled like bad cheese. I cannot abide a man with foul breath. Petyr's breath is always fresh . . . he was the first man I ever kissed, you know. My father said he was too lowborn, but *I* knew how high he'd rise. Jon gave him the customs for Gulltown to please me, but when he increased the incomes tenfold my lord husband saw how clever he was and gave him other appointments, even brought him to King's Landing to be master of coin. That was hard, to see him every day and still be wed to that old cold man. Jon did his *duty* in the bedchamber, but he could no more give me pleasure than he could give me children. His seed was old and weak. All my babies died but Robert, three girls and two boys. All my sweet little babies dead, and that old man just went on and on with his stinking breath. So you see, I have suffered too." Lady Lysa sniffed. "You do know that your poor mother is dead?"

"Tyrion told me," said Sansa. "He said the Freys murdered her at The Twins, with Robb."

Tears welled suddenly in Lady Lysa's eyes. "We are women alone now, you and I. Are you afraid, child? Be brave. I would never turn away Cat's daughter. We are bound by blood." She beckoned Sansa closer. "You may come kiss my cheek, Alayne."

Dutifully she approached and knelt beside the bed. Her aunt was drenched in sweet scent, though under that was a sour milky smell. Her cheek tasted of paint and powder.

As Sansa stepped back, Lady Lysa caught her wrist. "Now tell me," she said sharply. "Are you with child? The truth now, I will know if you lie."

"No," she said, startled by the question.

"You *are* a woman flowered, are you not?"

"Yes." Sansa knew the truth of her flowering could not be long hidden in the Eyrie. "Tyrion didn't . . . he never . . ." She could feel the blush creeping up her cheeks. "I am still a maid."

"Was the dwarf incapable?"

"No. He was only . . . he was . . ." *Kind?* She could not say that, not here, not to this aunt who hated him so. "He . . . he had whores, my lady. He told me so."

"Whores." Lysa released her wrist. "Of course he did. What woman would bed such a creature, but for gold? I should have killed the Imp when he was in my power, but he tricked me. He is full of low cunning, that one. His sellsword slew my good Ser Vardis Egen. Catelyn should not have brought him here, I told her that. She made off with our uncle too. That was wrong of her. The Blackfish was my Knight of the Gate, and since he left us the mountain clans are growing very bold. Petyr will soon set all that to rights, though. I shall make him Lord Protector of the Vale." Her aunt smiled for the first time, almost warmly. "He may not look as tall or strong as some, but he is worth more than all of them. Trust in him and do as he says."

"I shall, Aunt . . . my lady."

Lady Lysa seemed pleased by that. "I knew that boy Joffrey. He used to call my Robert cruel names, and once he slapped him with a wooden sword. A man will tell you poison is dishonorable, but a woman's honor is different. The Mother shaped us to protect our children, and our only dishonor is in failure. You'll know that, when you have a child."

"A child?" said Sansa, uncertainly.

Lysa waved a hand negligently. "Not for many years. You are too young to be a mother. One day you shall want children, though. Just as you will want to marry."

"I . . . I *am* married, my lady."

"Yes, but soon a widow. Be glad the Imp preferred his whores. It would not be fitting for my son to take that *dwarf's* leavings, but as he never touched you . . . How would you like to marry your cousin, the Lord Robert?"

The thought made Sansa weary. All she knew of Robert Arryn was that he was a little boy, and sickly. *It is not me she wants her son to marry, it is my claim. No one will ever marry me for love.* But lying came easy to her now. "I . . . can scarcely wait to meet him, my lady. But he is still a child, is he not?"

"He is eight. And not robust. But such a good boy, so bright and clever. He will be a great man, Alayne. *The seed is strong,* my lord husband said before he died. His last words. The gods sometimes let us glimpse the future as we lay dying. I see no reason why you should not be wed as soon as we know that your Lannister husband is dead. A secret wedding, to be sure. The Lord of the Eyrie could scarcely be thought to have married a bastard, that would not be fitting. The ravens should bring us the word from King's Landing once the Imp's head rolls. You and Robert can be wed the next day, won't that be joyous? It will be good for him to have a little companion. He played with Vardis Egen's boy when we first returned to the Eyrie, and my steward's sons as well, but they were much too rough and I had no choice but to send them away. Do you read well, Alayne?"

"Septa Mordane was good enough to say so."

"Robert has weak eyes, but he loves to be read to," Lady Lysa confided. "He likes stories about animals the best. Do you know the little song about the chicken who dressed as a fox? I sing him that all the time, he never grows tired of it. And he likes to play hopfrog and spin-the-sword and come-into-my-castle, but you must always let him win. That's only proper, don't you think? He is the Lord of the Eyrie, after all, you must never forget that. You are well born, and the Starks of Winterfell were always proud, but Winterfell has fallen and you are really just a beggar now, so put that pride aside. Gratitude will better become you, in your present circumstances. Yes, and obedience. My son will have a grateful and obedient wife."

JON

Day and night the axes rang.

Jon could not remember the last time he had slept. When he closed his eyes he dreamed of fighting; when he woke he fought. Even in the King's Tower he could hear the ceaseless *thunk* of bronze and flint and stolen steel biting into wood, and it was louder when he tried to rest in the warming shed atop the Wall. Mance had sledgehammers at work as well, and long saws with teeth of bone and flint. Once, as he was drifting off into an exhausted sleep, there came a great cracking from the haunted forest, and a sentinel tree came crashing down in a cloud of dirt and needles.

He was awake when Owen came to him, lying restless under a pile of furs on the floor of the warming shed. "Lord Snow," said Owen, shaking his shoulder, "the dawn." He gave Jon a hand to help pull him back onto his feet. Others were waking as well, jostling one another as they pulled on their boots and buckled their swordbelts in the close confines of the shed. No one spoke. They were all too tired for talk. Few of them ever left the Wall these days. It took too long to ride up and down in the cage. Castle Black had been abandoned to Maester Aemon, Ser Wynton Stout, and a few others too old or ill to fight.

"I had a dream that the king had come," Owen said happily. "Maester Aemon sent a raven, and King Robert came with all his strength. I dreamed I saw his golden banners."

Jon made himself smile. "That would be a welcome sight to see, Owen." Ignoring the twinge of pain in his leg, he swept a black fur cloak about his shoulders, gathered up his crutch, and went out onto the Wall to face another day.

A gust of wind sent icy tendrils wending through his long brown hair. Half a mile north, the wildling encampments were stirring, their camp-fires sending up smoky fingers to scratch against the pale dawn sky. Along the edge of the forest they had raised their tents of hide and fur, even a crude longhall of logs and woven branches; there were horselines to the east, mammoths to the west, and men everywhere, sharpening their swords, putting points on crude spears, donning makeshift armor of hide and horn and bone. For every man that he could see, Jon knew there were a score unseen in the wood. The brush gave them some shelter from the elements and hid them from the eyes of the hated crows.

Already their archers were stealing forward, pushing their rolling mantlets. "Here come our breakfast arrows," Pyp announced cheerfully, as he did every morning. *It's good that he can make a jape of it*, Jon thought. *Someone has to.* Three days ago, one of those breakfast arrows had caught Red Alyn of the Rosewood in the leg. You could still see his body at the foot of the Wall, if you cared to lean out far enough. Jon had to think that it was better for them to smile at Pyp's jest than to brood over Alyn's corpse.

The mantlets were slanting wooden shields, wide enough for five of the free folk to hide behind. The archers pushed them close, then knelt behind them to loose their arrows through slits in the wood. The first time the wildlings rolled them out, Jon had called for fire arrows and set a half-dozen ablaze, but after that Mance started covering them with raw hides. All the fire arrows in the world couldn't make them catch now. The brothers had even started wagering as to which of the straw sentinels would collect the most arrows before they were done. Dolorous Edd was leading with four, but Othell Yarwyck, Tumberjon, and Watt of Long Lake had three apiece. It was Pyp who'd started naming the scarecrows after their missing brothers, too. "It makes it seem as if there's more of us," he said.

"More of us with arrows in our bellies," Grenn complained, but the custom did seem to give his brothers heart, so Jon let the names stand and the wagering continue.

On the edge of the Wall an ornate brass Myrish eye stood on three spindly legs. Maester Aemon had once used it to peer at the stars, before his own eyes had failed him. Jon swung the tube down to have a look at the foe. Even at this distance there was no mistaking Mance Rayder's huge white tent, sewn together from the pelts of snow bears. The Myrish lenses brought the wildlings close enough for him to make out faces. Of Mance himself he saw no sign this morning, but his woman Dalla was outside tending the fire, while her sister Val milked a she-goat beside the tent. Dalla looked so big it was a wonder she could move. *The child must be coming very soon*, Jon thought. He swiveled the eye east and searched amongst the tents and trees till he found the turtle. *That will be coming very soon as well.* The wildlings had skinned one of the dead mammoths during the night, and they were lashing the raw bloody hide over the turtle's roof, one more layer on top of the sheepskins and pelts. The turtle had a rounded top and eight huge wheels, and under the hides was a stout wooden frame. When the wildlings had begun knocking it together, Satin thought they were building a ship. *Not far wrong.* The turtle was a hull turned upside down and opened fore and aft; a longhall on wheels.

"It's done, isn't it?" asked Grenn.

"Near enough." Jon shoved away the eye. "It will come today, most like. Did you fill the barrels?"

"Every one. They froze hard during the night, Pyp checked."

Grenn had changed a great deal from the big, clumsy, red-necked boy Jon had first befriended. He had grown half a foot, his chest and shoulders had thickened, and he had not cut his hair nor trimmed his beard since the Fist of the First Men. It made him look as huge and shaggy as an aurochs, the mocking name that Ser Alliser Thorne had hung on him during training. He looked weary now, though. When Jon said as much, he nodded. "I heard their axes all night. Couldn't sleep for all the chopping."

"Then go sleep now."

"I don't need –"

"You do. I want you rested. Go on, I'm not going to let you sleep through the fight." He made himself smile. "You're the only one who can move those bloody barrels."

Grenn went off muttering, and Jon returned to the far eye, searching the wildling camp. From time to time an arrow would sail past overhead, but he had learned to ignore those. The range was long and the angle was bad, the chances of being hit were small. He still saw no sign of Mance Rayder in the camp, but he spied Tormund Giantsbane and two of his sons around the turtle. The sons were struggling with the mammoth hide while Tormund gnawed on the roast leg of a goat and bellowed orders. Elsewhere he found the wildling skinchanger, Varamyr Sixskins, walking through the trees with his shadowcat dogging his heels.

When he heard the rattle of the winch chains and the iron groan of the cage door opening, he knew it would be Hobb bringing their breakfast as he did every morning. The sight of Mance's turtle had robbed Jon of his appetite. Their oil was all but gone, and the last barrel of pitch had been rolled off the Wall two nights ago. They would soon run short of arrows as well, and there were no fletchers making more. And the night before last, a raven had come from the west, from Ser Denys Mallister. Bowen Marsh had chased the wildlings all the way to the Shadow Tower, it seemed, and then farther, down into the gloom of the Gorge. At the Bridge of Skulls he had met the Weeper and three hundred wildlings and won a bloody battle. But the victory had been a costly one. More than a hundred brothers slain, among them Ser Endrew Tarth and Ser Aladale Wynch. The Old Pomegranate himself had been carried back to the Shadow Tower sorely wounded. Maester Mullin was tending him, but it would be some time before he was fit to return to Castle Black.

When he had read that, Jon had dispatched Zei to Mole's Town on their best horse to plead with the villagers to help man the Wall. She never returned. When he sent Mully after her, he came back to report the whole village deserted, even the brothel. Most likely Zei had followed them, straight down the kingsroad. *Maybe we should all do the same,* Jon reflected glumly.

He made himself eat, hungry or no. Bad enough he could not sleep, he could not go on without food as well. *Besides, this might be my last meal. It might be the last meal for all of us.* So it was that Jon had a belly full of bread, bacon, onions, and cheese when he heard Horse shout, *"IT'S COMING!"*

No one needed to ask what "it" was. Nor did Jon need the maester's Myrish eye to see it creeping out from amongst the tents and trees. "It doesn't really look much like a turtle," Satin commented. "Turtles don't have fur."

"Most of them don't have wheels either," said Pyp.

"Sound the warhorn," Jon commanded, and Kegs blew two long blasts, to wake Grenn and the other sleepers who'd had the watch during the night. If the wildlings were coming, the Wall would need every man. *Gods know, we have few enough.* Jon looked at Pyp and Kegs and Satin, Horse and Owen the Oaf, Tim Tangletongue, Mully, Spare Boot, and the rest, and tried to imagine them going belly to belly and blade to blade against a hundred screaming wildlings in the freezing darkness of that tunnel, with only a few iron bars between them. That was what it would come down to, unless they could stop the turtle before the gate was breached.

"It's big," Horse said.

Pyp smacked his lips. "Think of all the soup it will make." The jape was stillborn. Even Pyp sounded tired. *He looks half dead,* thought Jon, *but so do we all.* The King-beyond-the-Wall had so many men that he could throw fresh attackers at them every time, but the same handful of black brothers had to meet every assault, and it had worn them ragged.

The men beneath the wood and hides would be pulling hard, Jon knew, putting their shoulders into it, straining to keep the wheels turning, but once the turtle was flush against the gate they would exchange their ropes for axes. At least Mance was not sending his mammoths today. Jon was glad of that. Their awesome strength was wasted on the Wall, and their size only made them easy targets. The last had been a day and a half in the dying, its mournful trumpetings terrible to hear.

The turtle crept slowly through stones and stumps and brush. The earlier attacks had cost the free folk a hundred lives or more. Most still lay where they had fallen. In the lulls the crows would come and pay them court, but now the birds fled screeching. They liked the look of that turtle no more than he did.

Satin, Horse, and the others were looking to him, Jon knew, waiting for his orders. He was so tired, he hardly knew any more. *The Wall is mine*, he reminded himself. "Owen, Horse, to the catapults. Kegs, you and Spare Boot on the scorpions. The rest of you string your bows. Fire arrows. Let's see if we can burn it." It was likely to be a futile gesture, Jon knew, but it had to be better than standing helpless.

Cumbersome and slow-moving, the turtle made for an easy shot, and his archers and crossbowmen soon turned it into a lumbering wooden hedgehog . . . but the wet hides protected it, just as they had the mantlets, and the flaming arrows guttered out almost as soon as they struck. Jon cursed under his breath. "Scorpions," he commanded. "Catapults."

The scorpions bolts punched deep into the pelts, but did no more damage than the fire arrows. The rocks went bouncing off the turtle's roof, leaving dimples in the thick layers of hides. A stone from one of the trebuchets might have crushed it, but the one machine was still broken, and the wildlings had gone wide around the area where the other dropped its loads.

"Jon, it's still coming," said Owen the Oaf.

He could see that for himself. Inch by inch, yard by yard, the turtle crept closer, rolling, rumbling and rocking as it crossed the killing ground. Once the wildlings got it flush against the Wall, it would give them all the shelter they needed while their axes crashed through the hastily-repaired outer gates. Inside, under the ice, they would clear the loose rubble from the tunnel in a matter of hours, and then there would be nothing to stop them but two iron gates, a few half-frozen corpses, and whatever brothers Jon cared to throw in their path, to fight and die down in the dark.

To his left, the catapult made a *thunk* and filled the air with spinning stones. They plonked down on the turtle like hail, and caromed harmlessly aside. The wildling archers were still loosing arrows from behind their mantlets. One thudded into the face of a straw man, and Pyp said, "Four for Watt of Long Lake! We have a tie!" The next shaft whistled past his own ear, however. "*Fie!*" he shouted down. "I'm not in the tourney!"

"The hides won't burn," Jon said, as much to himself as to the others. Their only hope was to try and crush the turtle when it reached the Wall. For that, they needed boulders. No matter how stoutly built the turtle was, a huge chunk of rock crashing straight down on top of it from seven hundred feet was bound to do some damage. "Grenn, Owen, Kegs, it's time."

Alongside the warming shed a dozen stout oaken barrels were lined up in a row. They were full of crushed rock; the gravel that the black brothers customarily spread on the footpaths to give themselves better footing atop the Wall. Yesterday, after he'd seen the free folk covering the turtle with sheepskins, Jon told Grenn to pour water into the barrels, as much as they would take. The water would seep down through the crushed stone, and overnight the whole thing would freeze solid. It was the nearest thing to a boulder they were going to get.

"Why do we need to freeze it?" Grenn had asked him. "Why don't we just roll the barrels off the way they are?"

Jon answered, "If they crash against the Wall on the way down they'll burst, and loose gravel will spray everywhere. We don't want to rain pebbles on the whoresons."

He put his shoulder to the one barrel with Grenn, while Kegs and Owen were wrestling with another. Together they rocked it back and forth to break the grip of the ice that had formed around its bottom. "The bugger weighs a ton," said Grenn.

"Tip it over and roll it," Jon said. "Careful, if it rolls over your foot you'll end up like Spare Boot."

Once the barrel was on its side, Jon grabbed a torch and waved it above the surface of the Wall, back and forth, just enough to melt the ice a little. The thin film of water helped the barrel roll more easily. Too easily, in fact; they almost lost it. But finally, with four of them pooling their efforts, they rolled their boulder to the edge and stood it up again.

They had four of the big oak barrels lined up above the gate by the time Pyp shouted, "There's a turtle at our door!" Jon braced his injured leg and leaned out for a look. *Hoardings, Marsh should have built hoardings.* So many things they should have done. The wildlings were dragging the dead giants away from the gate. Horse and Mully were dropping rocks down on them, and Jon thought he saw one man go down, but the stones were too small to have any effect on the turtle itself. He wondered what the free folk would do about the dead mammoth in the path, but then he saw. The turtle was almost as wide as a longhall, so they simply pushed it *over* the carcass. His leg twitched, but Horse caught his arm and drew him back to safety. "You shouldn't lean out like that," the boy said.

"We should have built hoardings." Jon thought he could hear the crash of axes on wood, but that was probably just fear ringing in his ears. He looked to Grenn. "Do it."

Grenn got behind a barrel, put his shoulder against it, grunted, and began to push. Owen and Mully moved to help him. They shoved the barrel out a foot, and then another. And suddenly it was gone.

They heard the *thump* as it struck the Wall on the way down, and then, much louder, the crash and *crack* of splintering wood, followed by shouts and screams. Satin whooped and Owen the Oaf danced in circles, while Pyp leaned out and called, "The turtle was stuffed full of rabbits! Look at them hop away!"

"*Again*," Jon barked, and Grenn and Kegs slammed their shoulders against the next barrel, and sent it tottering out into empty air.

By the time they were done, the front of Mance's turtle was a crushed and splintered ruin, and wildlings were spilling out the other end and scrambling for their camp. Satin scooped up his crossbow and sent a few quarrels after them as they ran, to see them off the faster. Grenn was grinning through his beard, Pyp was making japes, and none of them would die today.

On the morrow, though . . . Jon glanced toward the shed. Eight barrels of gravel remained where twelve had stood a few moments before. He realized how tired he was then, and how much his wound was hurting. *I need to sleep. A few hours, at least.* He could go to Maester Aemon for some dreamwine, that would help. "I am going down to the King's Tower," he told them. "Call me if Mance gets up to anything. Pyp, you have the Wall."

"Me?" said Pyp.

"Him?" said Grenn.

Smiling, he left them to it and rode down in the cage.

A cup of dreamwine *did* help, as it happened. No sooner had he stretched out on the narrow bed in his cell than sleep took him. His dreams were strange and formless, full of strange voices, shouts and cries, and the sound of a warhorn, blowing low and loud, a single deep booming note that lingered in the air.

When he awoke the sky was black outside the arrow slit that served him for a window, and four men he did not know were standing over him. One held a lantern. "Jon Snow," the tallest of them said brusquely, "pull on your boots and come with us."

His first groggy thought was that somehow the Wall had fallen whilst he slept, that Mance Rayder had sent more giants or another turtle and broken through the gate. But when he rubbed his eyes he saw that the strangers were all in black. *They're men of the Night's Watch*, Jon realized. "Come where? Who are you?"

The tall man gestured, and two of the others pulled Jon from the bed. With the lantern leading the way they marched him from his cell and up a half turn of stair, to the Old Bear's solar. He saw Maester Aemon standing by the fire, his hands folded around the head of a blackthorn cane. Septon Cellador was half drunk as usual, and Ser Wynton Stout was asleep in a window seat. The other brothers were strangers to him. All but one.

Immaculate in his fur-trimmed cloak and polished boots, Ser Alliser

Thorne turned to say, "Here's the turncloak now, my lord. Ned Stark's bastard, of Winterfell."

"I'm no turncloak, Thorne," Jon said coldly.

"We shall see." In the leather chair behind the table where the Old Bear wrote his letters sat a big, broad, jowly man Jon did not know. "Yes, we shall see," he said again. "You will not deny that you are Jon Snow, I hope? Stark's bastard?"

"*Lord* Snow, he likes to call himself." Ser Alliser was a spare, slim man, compact and sinewy, and just now his flinty eyes were dark with amusement.

"You're the one who named me Lord Snow," said Jon. Ser Alliser had been fond of naming the boys he trained, during his time as Castle Black's master-at-arms. The Old Bear had sent Thorne to Eastwatch-by-the-Sea. *These others must be Eastwatch men. The bird reached Cotter Pyke and he's sent us help.* "How many men have you brought?" he asked the man behind the table.

"It's me who'll ask the questions," the jowly man replied. "You've been charged with oathbreaking, cowardice, and desertion, Jon Snow. Do you deny that you abandoned your brothers to die on the Fist of the First Men and joined the wildling Mance Rayder, this self-styled King-beyond-the-Wall?"

"*Abandoned . . . ?*" Jon almost choked on the word.

Maester Aemon spoke up then. "My lord, Donal Noye and I discussed these issues when Jon Snow first returned to us, and were satisfied by Jon's explanations."

"Well, *I* am not satisfied, Maester," said the jowly man. "I will hear these *explanations* for myself. Yes I will!"

Jon swallowed his anger. "I abandoned no one. I left the Fist with Qhorin Halfhand to scout the Skirling Pass. I joined the wildlings under orders. The Halfhand feared that Mance might have found the Horn of Winter . . ."

"The Horn of Winter?" Ser Alliser chuckled. "Were you commanded to count their snarks as well, Lord Snow?"

"No, but I counted their *giants* as best I could."

"*Ser*," snapped the jowly man. "You will address Ser Alliser as *ser*, and myself as *m'lord*. I am Janos Slynt, Lord of Harrenhal, and commander here at Castle Black until such time as Bowen Marsh returns with his garrison. You will grant us our courtesies, yes. I will not suffer to hear an anointed knight like the good Ser Alliser mocked by a traitor's bastard." He raised a hand and pointed a meaty finger at Jon's face. "Do you deny that you took a wildling woman into your bed?"

"No." Jon's grief over Ygritte was too fresh for him to deny her now. "No, my lord."

"I suppose it was also the Halfhand who commanded you to fuck this unwashed whore?" Ser Alliser asked with a smirk.

"*Ser*. She was no whore, *ser*. The Halfhand told me not to balk, whatever the wildlings asked of me, but . . . I will not deny that I went beyond what I had to do, that I . . . cared for her."

"You admit to being an oathbreaker, then," said Janos Slynt.

Half the men at Castle Black visited Mole's Town from time to time to dig for buried treasures in the brothel, Jon knew, but he would not dishonor Ygritte by equating her with the Mole's Town whores. "I broke my vows with a woman. I admit that. Yes."

"Yes, *m'lord!*" When Slynt scowled, his jowls quivered. He was as broad as the Old Bear had been, and no doubt would be as bald if he lived to Mormont's age. Half his hair was gone already, though he could not have been more than forty.

"Yes, my lord," Jon said. "I rode with the wildlings and ate with them, as the Halfhand commanded me, and I shared my furs with Ygritte. But I swear to you, I never turned my cloak. I escaped the Magnar as soon as I could, and never took up arms against my brothers or the realm."

Lord Slynt's small eyes studied him. "Ser Glendon," he commanded, "bring in the other prisoner."

Ser Glendon was the tall man who had dragged Jon from his bed. Four other men went with him when he left the room, but they were back soon enough with a captive, a small, sallow, battered man fettered hand and foot. He had a single eyebrow, a widow's peak, and a mustache that looked like a smear of dirt on his upper lip, but his face was swollen and mottled with bruises, and most of his front teeth had been knocked out.

The Eastwatch men threw the captive roughly to the floor. Lord Slynt frowned down at him. "Is this the one you spoke of?"

The captive blinked yellow eyes. "Aye." Not until that instant did Jon recognize Rattleshirt. *He is a different man without his armor*, he thought. "Aye," the wildling repeated, "he's the craven killed the Halfhand. Up in the Frostfangs, it were, after we hunted down t'other crows and killed them, every one. We would have done for this one too, only he begged f' his worthless life, offered t' join us if we'd have him. The Halfhand swore he'd see the craven dead first, but the wolf ripped Qhorin half t' pieces and this one opened his throat." He gave Jon a cracktooth smile then, and spat blood on his foot.

"Well?" Janos Slynt demanded of Jon harshly. "Do you deny it? Or will you claim Qhorin commanded you to kill him?"

"He told me . . ." The words came hard. "He told me to do *whatever* they asked of me."

Slynt looked about the solar, at the other Eastwatch men. "Does this boy think I fell off a turnip wagon onto my head?"

"Your lies won't save you now, Lord Snow," warned Ser Alliser Thorne. "We'll have the truth from you, bastard."

"I've told you the truth. Our garrons were failing, and Rattleshirt was close behind us. Qhorin told me to pretend to join the wildlings. '*You must not balk, whatever is asked of you,*' he said. He knew they would make me kill him. Rattleshirt was going to kill him anyway, he knew that too."

"So now you claim the great Qhorin Halfhand feared *this* creature?" Slynt looked at Rattleshirt, and snorted.

"All men fear the Lord o' Bones," the wildling grumbled. Ser Glendon kicked him, and he lapsed back into silence.

"I never said that," Jon insisted.

Slynt slammed a fist on the table. "I heard you! Ser Alliser had your measure true enough, it seems. You lie through your bastard's teeth. Well, I will not suffer it. I will not! You might have fooled this crippled *blacksmith*, but not Janos Slynt! Oh, no. Janos Slynt does not swallow lies so easily. Did you think my skull was stuffed with cabbage?"

"I don't know what your skull is stuffed with. My lord."

"Lord Snow is nothing if not arrogant," said Ser Alliser. "He murdered Qhorin just as his fellow turncloaks did Lord Mormont. It would not surprise me to learn that it was all part of the same fell plot. Benjen Stark may well have a hand in all this as well. For all we know, he is sitting in Mance Rayder's tent even now. You know these Starks, my lord."

"I do," said Janos Slynt. "I know them too well."

Jon peeled off his glove and showed them his burned hand. "I burned my hand defending Lord Mormont from a wight. And my uncle was a man of honor. He would never have betrayed his vows."

"No more than you?" mocked Ser Alliser.

Septon Cellador cleared his throat. "Lord Slynt," he said, "this boy refused to swear his vows properly in the sept, but went beyond the Wall to say his words before a heart tree. His father's gods, he said, but they are wildling gods as well."

"They are the gods of the north, Septon." Maester Aemon was courteous, but firm. "My lords, when Donal Noye was slain, it was this young man Jon Snow who took the Wall and held it, against all the fury of the north. He has proved himself valiant, loyal, and resourceful. Were it not for him, you would have found Mance Rayder sitting here when you arrived, Lord Slynt. You are doing him a great wrong. Jon Snow was Lord Mormont's own steward and squire. He was chosen for that duty because the Lord Commander saw much promise in him. As do I."

"Promise?" said Slynt. "Well, promise may turn false. Qhorin Halfhand's blood is on his hands. Mormont trusted him, you say, but what of that? I know what it is to be betrayed by men you trusted. Oh, yes.

And I know the ways of wolves as well." He pointed at Jon's face. "Your father died a traitor."

"My father was murdered." Jon was past caring what they did to him, but he would not suffer any more lies about his father.

Slynt purpled. "Murder? You insolent pup. King Robert was not even cold when Lord Eddard moved against his son." He rose to his feet; a shorter man than Mormont, but thick about the chest and arms, with a gut to match. A small gold spear tipped with red enamel pinned his cloak at the shoulder. "Your father died by the sword, but he was highborn, a King's Hand. For you, a noose will serve. Ser Alliser, take this turncloak to an ice cell."

"My lord is wise." Ser Alliser seized Jon by the arm.

Jon yanked away and grabbed the knight by the throat with such ferocity that he lifted him off the floor. He would have throttled him if the Eastwatch men had not pulled him off. Thorne staggered back, rubbing the marks Jon's fingers had left on his neck. "You see for yourselves, brothers. The boy is a wildling."

TYRION

W hen dawn broke, he found he could not face the thought of food. *By evenfall I may stand condemned.* His belly was acid with bile, and his nose itched. Tyrion scratched at it with the point of his knife. *One last witness to endure, then my turn.* But what to do? Deny everything? Accuse Sansa and Ser Dontos? Confess, in the hope of spending the rest of his days on the Wall? Let the dice fly and pray the Red Viper could defeat Ser Gregor Clegane?

Tyrion stabbed listlessly at a greasy grey sausage, wishing it were his sister. *It is bloody cold on the Wall, but at least I would be shut of Cersei.* He did not think he would make much of a ranger, but the Night's Watch needed clever men as well as strong ones. Lord Commander Mormont had said as much, when Tyrion had visited Castle Black. *There are those inconvenient vows, though.* It would mean the end of his marriage and whatever claim he might ever have made for Casterly Rock, but he did not seem destined to enjoy either in any case. And he seemed to recall that there was a brothel in a nearby village.

It was not a life he'd ever dreamed of, but it was life. And all he had to do to earn it was trust in his father, stand up on his little stunted legs, and say, "Yes, I did it, I confess." That was the part that tied his bowels in knots. He almost wished he *had* done it, since it seemed he must suffer for it anyway.

"My lord?" said Podrick Payne. "They're here, my lord. Ser Addam. And the gold cloaks. They wait without."

"Pod, tell me true . . . do you think I did it?"

The boy hesitated. When he tried to speak, all he managed to produce was a weak sputter.

I am doomed. Tyrion sighed. "No need to answer. You've been a good squire to me. Better than I deserved. Whatever happens, I thank you for your leal service."

Ser Addam Marbrand waited at the door with six gold cloaks. He had nothing to say this morning, it seemed. *Another good man who thinks me a kinslayer.* Tyrion summoned all the dignity he could find and waddled down the steps. He could feel them all watching him as he crossed the yard; the guards on the walls, the grooms by the stables, the scullions and washerwomen and serving girls. Inside the throne room, knights and lordlings moved aside to let them through, and whispered to their ladies.

No sooner had Tyrion taken his place before the judges than another group of gold cloaks led in Shae.

A cold hand tightened round his heart. *Varys betrayed her*, he thought. Then he remembered. *No. I betrayed her myself. I should have left her with Lollys. Of course they'd question Sansa's maids, I'd do the same.* Tyrion rubbed at the slick scar where his nose had been, wondering why Cersei had bothered. *Shae knows nothing that can hurt me.*

"They plotted it together," she said, this girl he'd loved. "The Imp and Lady Sansa plotted it after the Young Wolf died. Sansa wanted revenge for her brother and Tyrion meant to have the throne. He was going to kill his sister next, and then his own lord father, so he could be Hand for Prince Tommen. But after a year or so, before Tommen got too old, he would have killed him too, so as to take the crown for his own head."

"How could you know all this?" demanded Prince Oberyn. "Why would the Imp divulge such plans to his wife's maid?"

"I overheard some, m'lord," said Shae, "and m'lady let things slip too. But most I had from his own lips. I wasn't only Lady Sansa's maid. I was his whore, all the time he was here in King's Landing. On the morning of the wedding, he dragged me down where they keep the dragon skulls and fucked me there with the monsters all around. And when I cried, he said I ought to be more grateful, that it wasn't every girl who got to be the king's whore. That was when he told me how he meant to be king. He said that poor boy Joffrey would never know his bride the way he was knowing me." She started sobbing then. "I never meant to be a whore, m'lords. I was to be married. A squire, he was, and a good brave boy, gentle born. But the Imp saw me at the Green Fork and put the boy I meant to marry in the front rank of the van, and after he was killed he sent his wildlings to bring me to his tent. Shagga, the big one, and Timett with the burned eye. He said if I didn't pleasure him, he'd give me to them, so I did. Then he brought me to the city, so I'd be close when he wanted me. He made me do such shameful things . . ."

Prince Oberyn looked curious. "What sorts of things?"

"*Unspeakable* things." As the tears rolled slowly down that pretty face, no doubt every man in the hall wanted to take Shae in his arms and comfort her. "With my mouth and . . . other parts, m'lord. All my parts. He used me every way there was, and . . . he used to make me tell him how big he was. *My giant*, I had to call him, *my giant of Lannister.*"

Oswald Kettleblack was the first to laugh. Boros and Meryn joined in, then Cersei, Ser Loras, and more lords and ladies than he could count. The sudden gale of mirth made the rafters ring and shook the Iron Throne. "It's true," Shae protested. "My giant of Lannister." The laughter swelled twice as loud. Their mouths were twisted in merriment, their bellies shook. Some laughed so hard that snot flew from their nostrils.

I saved you all, Tyrion thought. *I saved this vile city and all your worthless lives.* There were hundreds in the throne room, every one of them laughing but his father. Or so it seemed. Even the Red Viper chortled, and Mace Tyrell looked like to bust a gut, but Lord Tywin Lannister sat between them as if made of stone, his fingers steepled beneath his chin.

Tyrion pushed forward. "*MY LORDS!*" he shouted. He had to shout, to have any hope of being heard.

His father raised a hand. Bit by bit, the hall grew silent.

"Get this lying whore out of my sight," said Tyrion, "and I will give you your confession."

Lord Tywin nodded, gestured. Shae looked half in terror as the gold cloaks formed up around her. Her eyes met Tyrion's as they marched her from the wall. Was it shame he saw there, or fear? He wondered what Cersei had promised her. *You will get the gold or jewels, whatever it was you asked for,* he thought as he watched her back recede, *but before the moon has turned she'll have you entertaining the gold cloaks in their barracks.*

Tyrion stared up at his father's hard green eyes with their flecks of cold bright gold. "Guilty," he said, "so guilty. Is that what you wanted to hear?"

Lord Tywin said nothing. Mace Tyrell nodded. Prince Oberyn looked mildly disappointed. "You admit you poisoned the king?"

"Nothing of the sort," said Tyrion. "Of Joffrey's death I am innocent. I am guilty of a more monstrous crime." He took a step toward his father. "I was born. I lived. I am guilty of being a dwarf, I confess it. And no matter how many times my good father forgave me, I have persisted in my infamy."

"This is folly, Tyrion," declared Lord Tywin. "Speak to the matter at hand. You are not on trial for being a dwarf."

"That is where you err, my lord. I have been on trial for being a dwarf my entire life."

"Have you nothing to say in your defense?"

"Nothing but this: I did not do it. Yet now I wish I had." He turned to face the hall, that sea of pale faces. "I wish I had enough poison for you all. You make me sorry that I am not the monster you would have me be, yet there it is. I am innocent, but I will get no justice here. You leave me no choice but to appeal to the gods. I demand trial by battle."

"Have you taken leave of your wits?" his father said.

"No, I've found them. *I demand trial by battle!*"

His sweet sister could not have been more pleased. "He has that right, my lords," she reminded the judges. "Let the gods judge. Ser Gregor Clegane will stand for Joffrey. He returned to the city the night before last, to put his sword at my service."

Lord Tywin's face was so dark that for half a heartbeat Tyrion wondered if he'd drunk some poisoned wine as well. He slammed his fist down on the table, too angry to speak. It was Mace Tyrell who turned to Tyrion and asked the question. "Do you have a champion to defend your innocence?"

"He does, my lord." Prince Oberyn of Dorne rose to his feet. "The dwarf has quite convinced me."

The uproar was deafening. Tyrion took especial pleasure in the sudden doubt he glimpsed in Cersei's eyes. It took a hundred gold cloaks pounding the butts of their spears against the floor to quiet the throne room again. By then Lord Tywin Lannister had recovered himself. "Let the issue be decided on the morrow," he declared in iron tones. "I wash my hands of it." He gave his dwarf son a cold angry look, then strode from the hall, out the king's door behind the Iron Throne, his brother Kevan at his side.

Later, back in his tower cell, Tyrion poured himself a cup of wine and sent Podrick Payne off for cheese, bread, and olives. He doubted whether he could keep down anything heavier just now. *Did you think I would go meekly, Father?* he asked the shadow his candles etched upon the wall. *I have too much of you in me for that.* He felt strangely at peace, now that he had snatched the power of life and death from his father's hands and placed it in the hands of the gods. *Assuming there are gods, and they give a mummer's fart. If not, then I'm in Dornish hands.* No matter what happened, Tyrion had the satisfaction of knowing that he'd kicked Lord Tywin's plans to splinters. If Prince Oberyn won, it would further inflame Highgarden against the Dornish; Mace Tyrell would see the man who crippled his son helping the dwarf who almost poisoned his daughter to escape his rightful punishment. And if the Mountain triumphed, Doran Martell might well demand to know why his brother had been served with death instead of the justice Tyrion had promised him. Dorne might crown Myrcella after all.

It was almost worth dying to know all the trouble he'd made. *Will you come to see the end, Shae? Will you stand there with the rest, watching as Ser Ilyn lops my ugly head off? Will you miss your giant of Lannister when he's dead?* He drained his wine, flung the cup aside, and sang lustily.

> *He rode through the streets of the city,*
>   *down from his hill on high,*
> *O'er the wynds and the steps and the cobbles,*
>   *he rode to a woman's sigh.*
> *For she was his secret treasure,*
>   *she was his shame and his bliss.*
> *And a chain and a keep are nothing,*
>   *compared to a woman's kiss.*

Ser Kevan did not visit him that night. He was probably with Lord Tywin, trying to placate the Tyrells. *I have seen the last of that uncle, I fear.* He poured another cup of wine. A pity he'd had Symon Silver Tongue killed before learning all the words of that song. It wasn't a bad song, if truth be told. Especially compared to the ones that would be written about him henceforth. *"For hands of gold are always cold, but a woman's hands are warm,"* he sang. Perhaps he should write the other verses himself. If he lived so long.

That night, surprisingly, Tyrion Lannister slept long and deep. He rose at first light, well rested and with a hearty appetite, and broke his fast on fried bread, blood sausage, applecakes, and a double helping of eggs cooked with onions and fiery Dornish peppers. Then he begged leave of his guards to attend his champion. Ser Addam gave his consent.

Tyrion found Prince Oberyn drinking a cup of red wine as he donned his armor. He was attended by four of his younger Dornish lordlings. "Good morrow to you, my lord," the prince said. "Will you take a cup of wine?"

"Should you be drinking before battle?"

"I always drink before battle."

"That could get you killed. Worse, it could get *me* killed."

Prince Oberyn laughed. "The gods defend the innocent. You *are* innocent, I trust?"

"Only of killing Joffrey," Tyrion admitted. "I do hope you know what you are about to face. Gregor Clegane is –"

"– large? So I have heard."

"He is almost eight feet tall and must weigh thirty stone, all of it muscle. He fights with a two-handed greatsword, but needs only one hand to wield it. He has been known to cut men in half with a single blow. His armor is so heavy that no lesser man could bear the weight, let alone move in it."

Prince Oberyn was unimpressed. "I have killed large men before. The trick is to get them off their feet. Once they go down, they're dead." The Dornishman sounded so blithely confident that Tyrion felt almost reassured, until he turned and said, "Daemon, my spear!" Ser Daemon tossed it to him, and the Red Viper snatched it from the air.

"You mean to face the Mountain with a *spear?*" That made Tyrion uneasy all over again. In battle, ranks of massed spears made for a formidable front, but single combat against a skilled swordsman was a very different matter.

"We are fond of spears in Dorne. Besides, it is the only way to counter his reach. Have a look, Lord Imp, but see you do not touch." The spear was turned ash eight feet long, the shaft smooth, thick, and heavy. The last two feet of that was steel: a slender leaf-shaped spearhead narrowing to a wicked spike. The edges looked sharp enough to shave with. When Oberyn spun the haft between the palms of his hand, they glistened black. *Oil? Or poison?* Tyrion decided that he would sooner not know. "I hope you are good with that," he said doubtfully.

"You will have no cause for complaint. Though Ser Gregor may. However thick his plate, there will be gaps at the joints. Inside the elbow and knee, beneath the arms ... I will find a place to tickle him, I promise you." He set the spear aside. "It is said that a Lannister always pays his debts. Perhaps you will return to Sunspear with me when the day's bloodletting is done. My brother Doran would be most pleased to meet the rightful heir to Casterly Rock ... especially if he brought his lovely wife, the Lady of Winterfell."

Does the snake think I have Sansa squirreled away somewhere, like a nut I'm hoarding for winter? If so, Tyrion was not about to disabuse him. "A trip to Dorne might be very pleasant, now that I reflect on it."

"Plan on a lengthy visit." Prince Oberyn sipped his wine. "You and Doran have many matters of mutual interest to discuss. Music, trade, history, wine, the dwarf's penny ... the laws of inheritance and succession. No doubt an uncle's counsel would be of benefit to Queen Myrcella in the trying times ahead."

If Varys had his little birds listening, Oberyn was giving them a ripe earful. "I believe I will have that cup of wine," said Tyrion. *Queen Myrcella?* It would have been more tempting if only he did have Sansa tucked beneath his cloak. *If she declared for Myrcella over Tommen, would the north follow?* What the Red Viper was hinting at was treason. Could Tyrion truly take up arms against Tommen, against his own father? *Cersei would spit blood.* It might be worth it for that alone.

"Do you recall the tale I told you of our first meeting, Imp?" Prince

Oberyn asked, as the Bastard of Godsgrace knelt before him to fasten his greaves. "It was not for your tail alone that my sister and I came to Casterly Rock. We were on a quest of sorts. A quest that took us to Starfall, the Arbor, Oldtown, the Shield Islands, Crakehall, and finally Casterly Rock ... but our true destination was marriage. Doran was betrothed to Lady Mellario of Norvos, so he had been left behind as castellan of Sunspear. My sister and I were yet unpromised.

"Elia found it all exciting. She was of that age, and her delicate health had never permitted her much travel. I preferred to amuse myself by mocking my sister's suitors. There was Little Lord Lazyeye, Squire Squishlips, one I named the Whale That Walks, that sort of thing. The only one who was even halfway presentable was young Baelor Hightower. A pretty lad, and my sister was half in love with him until he had the misfortune to fart once in our presence. I promptly named him Baelor Breakwind, and after that Elia couldn't look at him without laughing. I was a monstrous young fellow, someone should have sliced out my vile tongue."

Yes, Tyrion agreed silently. Baelor Hightower was no longer young, but he remained Lord Leyton's heir; wealthy, handsome, and a knight of splendid repute. *Baelor Brightsmile,* they called him now. Had Elia wed him in place of Rhaegar Targaryen, she might be in Oldtown with her children growing tall around her. He wondered how many lives had been snuffed out by that fart.

"Lannisport was the end of our voyage," Prince Oberyn went on, as Ser Arron Qorgyle helped him into a padded leather tunic and began lacing it up the back. "Were you aware that our mothers knew each other of old?"

"They had been at court together as girls, I seem to recall. Companions to Princess Rhaella?"

"Just so. It was my belief that the mothers had cooked up this plot between them. Squire Squishlips and his ilk and the various pimply young maidens who'd been paraded before me were the almonds before the feast, meant only to whet our appetites. The main course was to be served at Casterly Rock."

"Cersei and Jaime."

"Such a clever dwarf. Elia and I were older, to be sure. Your brother and sister could not have been more than eight or nine. Still, a difference of five or six years is little enough. And there was an empty cabin on our ship, a very nice cabin, such as might be kept for a person of high birth. As if it were intended that we take someone back to Sunspear. A young page, perhaps. Or a companion for Elia. Your lady mother meant to betroth Jaime to my sister, or Cersei to me. Perhaps both."

"Perhaps," said Tyrion, "but my father –"

"– ruled the Seven Kingdoms, but was ruled at home by his lady wife, or so *my* mother always said." Prince Oberyn raised his arms, so Lord Dagos Manwoody and the Bastard of Godsgrace could slip a chainmail byrnie down over his head. "At Oldtown we learned of your mother's death, and the monstrous child she had borne. We might have turned back there, but my mother chose to sail on. I told you of the welcome we found at Casterly Rock.

"What I did not tell you was that my mother waited as long as was decent, and then broached your father about our purpose. Years later, on her deathbed, she told me that Lord Tywin had refused us brusquely. His daughter was meant for Prince Rhaegar, he informed her. And when she asked for Jaime, to espouse Elia, he offered her you instead."

"Which offer she took for an outrage."

"It *was*. Even you can see that, surely?"

"Oh, surely." *It all goes back and back,* Tyrion thought, *to our mothers and fathers and theirs before them. We are puppets dancing on the strings of those who came before us, and one day our own children will take up our strings and dance on in our steads.* "Well, Prince Rhaegar married Elia of Dorne, not Cersei Lannister of Casterly Rock. So it would seem your mother won that tilt."

"She thought so," Prince Oberyn agreed, "but your father is not a man to forget such slights. He taught that lesson to Lord and Lady Tarbeck once, and to the Reynes of Castamere. And at King's Landing, he taught it to my sister. My helm, Dagos." Manwoody handed it to him; a high golden helm with a copper disk mounted on the brow, the sun of Dorne. The visor had been removed, Tyrion saw. "Elia and her children have waited long for justice." Prince Oberyn pulled on soft red leather gloves, and took up his spear again. "But this day they shall have it."

The outer ward had been chosen for the combat. Tyrion had to skip and run to keep up with Prince Oberyn's long strides. *The snake is eager,* he thought. *Let us hope he is venomous as well.* The day was grey and windy. The sun was struggling to break through the clouds, but Tyrion could no more have said who was going to win that fight than the one on which his life depended.

It looked as though a thousand people had come to see if he would live or die. They lined the castle wallwalks and elbowed one another on the steps of keeps and towers. They watched from the stable doors, from windows and bridges, from balconies and roofs. And the yard was packed with them, so many that the gold cloaks and the knights of the Kingsguard had to shove them back to make enough room for the fight. Some had dragged out chairs to watch more comfortably, while others perched on barrels. *We should have done this in the Dragonpit,* Tyrion thought sourly. *We could have charged a penny a head and paid for Joffrey's wedding and funeral both.* Some of the onlookers even had small children sitting on their shoulders, to get a better view. They shouted and pointed at the sight of Tyrion.

Cersei seemed half a child herself beside Ser Gregor. In his armor, the Mountain looked bigger than any man had any right to be. Beneath a long yellow surcoat bearing the three black dogs of Clegane, he wore heavy plate over chainmail, dull grey steel dinted and scarred in battle. Beneath that would be boiled leather and a layer of quilting. A flat-topped greathelm was bolted to his gorget, with breaths around the mouth and nose and a narrow slit for vision. The crest atop it was a stone fist.

If Ser Gregor was suffering from wounds, Tyrion could see no sign of it from across the yard. *He looks as though he was chiseled out of rock, standing there.* His greatsword was planted in the ground before him, six feet of scarred metal. Ser Gregor's huge hands, clad in gauntlets of lobstered steel, clasped the crosshilt to either side of the grip. Even Prince Oberyn's paramour paled at the sight of him. "You are going to fight *that?*" Ellaria Sand said in a hushed voice.

"I am going to kill that," her lover replied carelessly.

Tyrion had his own doubts, now that they stood on the brink. When he looked at Prince Oberyn, he found himself wishing he had Bronn defending him ... or even better, Jaime. The Red Viper was lightly armored; greaves, vambraces, gorget, spaulder, steel codpiece. Elsewise Oberyn was clad in supple leather and flowing silks. Over his byrnie he wore his scales of gleaming copper, but mail and scale together would not give him a quarter the protection of Gregor's heavy plate. With its visor removed, the prince's helm was effectively no better than a half-helm, lacking even a nasal. His round steel shield was brightly polished, and showed the sun-and-spear in red gold, yellow gold, white gold, and copper.

Dance around him until he's so tired he can hardly lift his arm, then put him on his back. The Red Viper seemed to have the same notion as Bronn. But the sellsword had been blunt about the risks of such tactics. *I hope to seven hells that you know what you are doing, snake.*

A platform had been erected beside the Tower of the Hand, halfway between the two champions. That was where Lord Tywin sat with his brother Ser Kevan. King Tommen was not in evidence; for that, at least, Tyrion was grateful.

Lord Tywin glanced briefly at his dwarf son, then lifted his hand. A dozen trumpeters blew a fanfare to quiet the crowd. The High Septon shuffled forward in his tall crystal crown, and prayed that the Father Above would help them in this judgment, and that the Warrior would lend his strength to the arm of the man whose cause was just. *That would be me*, Tyrion almost shouted, but they would only laugh, and he was sick unto death of laughter.

Ser Osmund Kettleblack brought Clegane his shield, a massive thing of heavy oak rimmed in black iron. As the Mountain slid his left arm through the straps, Tyrion saw that the hounds of Clegane had been painted over. This morning Ser Gregor bore the seven-pointed star the Andals had brought to Westeros when they crossed the narrow sea to overwhelm the First Men and their gods. *Very pious of you, Cersei, but I doubt the gods will be impressed.*

There were fifty yards between them. Prince Oberyn advanced quickly, Ser Gregor more ominously. *The ground does not shake when he walks*, Tyrion told himself. *That is only my heart fluttering.* When the two men were ten yards apart, the Red Viper stopped and called out, "Have they told you who I am?"

Ser Gregor grunted through his breaths. "Some dead man." He came on, inexorable.

The Dornishman slid sideways. "I am Oberyn Martell, a prince of Dorne," he said, as the Mountain turned to keep him in sight. "Princess Elia was my sister."

"Who?" asked Gregor Clegane.

Oberyn's long spear jabbed, but Ser Gregor took the point on his shield, shoved it aside, and bulled back at the prince, his great sword flashing. The Dornishman spun away untouched. The spear darted forward. Clegane slashed at it, Martell snapped it back, then thrust again. Metal screamed on metal as the spearhead slid off the Mountain's chest, slicing through the surcoat and leaving a long bright scratch on the steel beneath. "Elia Martell, Princess of Dorne," the Red Viper hissed. "You raped her. You murdered her. You killed her children."

Ser Gregor grunted. He made a ponderous charge to hack at the Dornishman's head. Prince Oberyn avoided him easily. "You raped her. You murdered her. You killed her children."

"Did you come to talk or to fight?"

"I came to hear you confess." The Red Viper landed a quick thrust on the Mountain's belly, to no effect. Gregor cut at him, and missed. The long spear lanced in above his sword. Like a serpent's tongue it flickered in and out, feinting low and landing high, jabbing at groin, shield, eyes. *The Mountain makes for a big target, at the least*, Tyrion thought. Prince Oberyn could scarcely miss, though none of his blows was penetrating Ser Gregor's heavy plate. The Dornishman kept circling, jabbing, then darting back again, forcing the bigger man to turn and turn again. *Clegane is losing sight of him.* The Mountain's helm had a narrow eyeslit, severely limiting his vision. Oberyn was making good use of that, and the length of his spear, and his quickness.

It went on that way for what seemed a long time. Back and forth they moved across the yard, and round and round in spirals, Ser Gregor slashing at the air while Oberyn's spear struck at arm, and leg, twice at his temple. Gregor's big wooden shield took its share of hits as well, until a dog's head peeped out from under the star, and elsewhere the raw oak showed through. Clegane would grunt from time to time, and once Tyrion heard him mutter a curse, but otherwise he fought in a sullen silence.

Not Oberyn Martell. "You raped her," he called, feinting. "You murdered her," he said, dodging a looping cut from Gregor's greatsword. "You killed her children," he shouted, slamming the spearpoint into the giant's throat, only to have it glance off the thick steel gorget with a screech.

"Oberyn is toying with him," said Ellaria Sand.

That is fool's play, thought Tyrion. "The Mountain is too bloody big to be any man's toy."

All around the yard, the throng of spectators was creeping in toward the two combatants, edging forward inch by inch to get a better view. The Kingsguard tried to keep them back, shoving at the gawkers forcefully with their big white shields, but there were hundreds of gawkers and only six of the men in white armor.

"You raped her." Prince Oberyn parried a savage cut with his spearhead. "You murdered her." He sent the spearpoint at Clegane's eyes, so fast the huge man flinched back. "You killed her children." The spear flickered sideways and down, scraping against the Mountain's breastplate. "You raped her. You murdered her. You killed her children." The spear was two feet longer than Ser Gregor's sword, more than enough to keep him at an awkward distance. He hacked at the shaft whenever Oberyn lunged at him, trying to lop off the spearhead, but he might as well have been trying to hack the wings off a fly. "You raped her. You murdered her. You killed her children." Gregor tried to bull rush, but Oberyn skipped aside and circled round his back. "You raped her. You murdered her. You killed her children."

"Be quiet." Ser Gregor seemed to be moving a little slower, and his greatsword no longer rose quite so high as it had when the contest began. "Shut your bloody mouth."

"You raped her," the prince said, moving to the right.

"*Enough!*" Ser Gregor took two long strides and brought his sword down at Oberyn's head, but the Dornishman backstepped once more. "You murdered her," he said.

"*SHUT UP!*" Gregor charged headlong, right at the point of the spear, which slammed into his right breast then slid aside with a hideous steel shriek. Suddenly the Mountain was close enough to strike, his huge sword flashing in a steel blur. The crowd was screaming as well. Oberyn slipped the first blow and let go of the spear, useless now that Ser Gregor was inside it. The second cut the Dornishman caught on his shield. Metal met metal with an ear-splitting clang, sending the Red Viper reeling. Ser Gregor followed, bellowing. *He doesn't use words, he just roars like an animal*, Tyrion thought. Oberyn's retreat became a headlong backward flight mere inches ahead of the greatsword as it slashed at his chest, his arms, his head.

The stable was behind him. Spectators screamed and shoved at each other to get out of the way. One stumbled into Oberyn's back. Ser Gregor hacked down with all his savage strength. The Red Viper threw himself sideways, rolling. The luckless stableboy behind him was not so quick. As his arm rose to protect his face, Gregor's sword took it off between elbow and shoulder. *"Shut UP!"* the Mountain howled at the stableboy's scream, and this time he swung the blade sideways, sending the top half of the lad's head across the yard in a spray of blood and brains. Hundreds of spectators suddenly seemed to lose all interest in the guilt or innocence of Tyrion Lannister, judging by the way they pushed and shoved at each other to escape the yard.

But the Red Viper of Dorne was back on his feet, his long spear in hand. "Elia," he called at Ser Gregor. "You raped her. You murdered her. You killed her children. Now say her name."

The Mountain whirled. Helm, shield, sword, surcoat; he was spattered with gore from head to heels. "You talk too much," he grumbled. "You make my head hurt."

"I will hear you say it. She was Elia of Dorne."

The Mountain snorted contemptuously, and came on . . . and in that moment, the sun broke through the low clouds that had hidden the sky since dawn.

The sun of Dorne, Tyrion told himself, but it was Gregor Clegane who moved first to put the sun at his back. *This is a dim and brutal man, but he has a warrior's instincts.*

The Red Viper crouched, squinting, and sent his spear darting forward again. Ser Gregor hacked at it, but the thrust had only been a feint. Off balance, he stumbled forward a step.

Prince Oberyn tilted his dinted metal shield. A shaft of sunlight blazed blindingly off polished gold and copper, into the narrow slit of his foe's helm. Clegane lifted his own shield against the glare. Prince Oberyn's spear flashed like lightning and found the gap in the heavy plate, the joint under the arm. The point punched through mail and boiled leather. Gregor gave a choked grunt as the Dornishman twisted his spear and yanked it free. "Elia. Say it! Elia of Dorne!" He was circling, spear poised for another thrust. *"Say it!"*

Tyrion had his own prayer. *Fall down and die*, was how it went. *Damn you, fall down and die!* The blood trickling from the Mountain's armpit was his own now, and he must be bleeding even more heavily inside the breastplate. When he tried to take a step, one knee buckled. Tyrion thought he was going down.

Prince Oberyn had circled behind him. *"ELIA OF DORNE!"* he shouted. Ser Gregor started to turn, but too slow and too late. The spear-head went through the back of the knee this time, through the layers of chain and leather between the plates on thigh and calf. The Mountain reeled, swayed, then collapsed face first on the ground. His huge sword went flying from his hand. Slowly, ponderously, he rolled onto his back.

The Dornishman flung away his ruined shield, grasped the spear in both hands, and sauntered away. Behind him the Mountain let out a groan, and pushed himself onto an elbow. Oberyn whirled cat-quick, and *ran* at his fallen foe. *"EEEEELLLLLLIIIIIAAAAA!"* he screamed, as he drove the spear down with the whole weight of his body behind it. The *crack* of the ashwood shaft snapping was almost as sweet a sound as Cersei's wail of fury, and for an instant Prince Oberyn had wings. *The snake has vaulted over the Mountain.* Four feet of broken spear jutted from Clegane's belly as Prince Oberyn rolled, rose, and dusted himself off. He tossed aside the splintered spear and claimed his foe's greatsword. "If you die before you say her name, ser, I will hunt you through all seven hells," he promised.

Ser Gregor tried to rise. The broken spear had gone through him, and was pinning him to the ground. He wrapped both hands about the shaft, grunting, but could not pull it out. Beneath him was a spreading pool of red. "I am feeling more innocent by the instant," Tyrion told Ellaria Sand beside him.

Prince Oberyn moved closer. *"Say the name!"* He put a foot on the Mountain's chest and raised the greatsword with both hands. Whether he intended to hack off Gregor's head or shove the point through his eyeslit was something Tyrion would never know.

Clegane's hand shot up and grabbed the Dornishman behind the knee. The Red Viper brought down the greatsword in a wild slash, but he was off-balance, and the edge did no more than put another dent in the Mountain's vambrace. Then the sword was forgotten as Gregor's hand tightened and twisted, yanking the Dornishman down on top of him. They wrestled in the dust and blood, the broken spear wobbling back and forth. Tyrion saw with horror that the Mountain had wrapped one huge arm around the prince, drawing him tight against his chest, like a lover.

"Elia of Dorne," they all heard Ser Gregor say, when they were close enough to kiss. His deep voice boomed within the helm. "I killed her screaming whelp." He thrust his free hand into Oberyn's unprotected face, pushing steel fingers into his eyes. *"Then* I raped her." Clegane slammed his fist into the Dornishman's mouth, making splinters of his teeth. "Then I smashed her fucking head in. Like this." As he drew back his huge fist, the blood on his gauntlet seemed to smoke in the cold dawn air. There was a sickening *crunch*. Ellaria Sand wailed in terror, and Tyrion's breakfast came boiling back up. He found himself on his knees retching bacon and sausage and applecakes, and that double helping of fried eggs cooked up with onions and fiery Dornish peppers.

He never heard his father speak the words that condemned him. Perhaps no words were necessary. *I put my life in the Red Viper's hands, and he dropped it.* When he remembered, too late, that snakes had no hands, Tyrion began to laugh hysterically.

He was halfway down the serpentine steps before he realized that the gold cloaks were not taking him back to his tower room. "I've been consigned to the black cells," he said. They did not bother to answer. *Why waste your breath on the dead?*

DAENERYS

Dany broke her fast under the persimmon tree that grew in the terrace garden, watching her dragons chase each other about the apex of the Great Pyramid where the huge bronze harpy once stood. Meereen had a score of lesser pyramids, but none stood even half as tall. From here she could see the whole city: the narrow twisty alleys and wide brick streets, the temples and granaries, hovels and palaces, brothels and baths, gardens and fountains, the great red circles of the fighting pits. And beyond the walls was the pewter sea, the winding Skahazadhan, the dry brown hills, burnt orchards, and blackened fields. Up here in her garden Dany sometimes felt like a god, living atop the highest mountain in the world.

Do all gods feel so lonely? Some must, surely. Missandei had told her of the Lord of Harmony, worshiped by the Peaceful People of Naath; he was the only true god, her little scribe said, the god who always was and always would be, who made the moon and stars and earth, and all the creatures that dwelt upon them. *Poor Lord of Harmony.* Dany pitied him. It must be terrible to be alone for all time, attended by hordes of butterfly women you could make or unmake at a word. Westeros had seven gods at least, though Viserys had told her that some septons said the seven were only aspects of a single god, seven facets of a single crystal. That was just confusing. The red priests believed in two gods, she had heard, but two who were eternally at war. Dany liked that even less. She would not want to be eternally at war.

Missandei served her duck eggs and dog sausage, and half a cup of sweetened wine mixed with the juice of a lime. The honey drew flies, but a scented candle drove them off. The flies were not so troublesome up here as they were in the rest of her city, she had found, something else she liked about the pyramid. "I must remember to do something about the flies," Dany said. "Are there many flies on Naath, Missandei?"

"On Naath there are butterflies," the scribe responded in the Common Tongue. "More wine?"

"No. I must hold court soon." Dany had grown very fond of Missandei. The little scribe with the big golden eyes was wise beyond her years. *She is brave as well. She had to be, to survive the life she's lived.* One day she hoped to see this fabled isle of Naath. Missandei said the Peaceful People made music instead of war. They did not kill, not even animals; they ate only fruit and never flesh. The butterfly spirits sacred to their Lord of Harmony protected their isle against those who would do them harm. Many conquerors had sailed on Naath to blood their swords, only to sicken and die. *The butterflies do not help them when the slave ships come raiding, though.* "I am going to take you home one day, Missandei," Dany promised. *If I had made the same promise to Jorah, would he still have sold me?* "I swear it."

"This one is content to stay with you, Your Grace. Naath will be there, always. You are good to this –, to me."

"And you to me." Dany took the girl by the hand. "Come help me dress."

Jhiqui helped Missandei bathe her while Irri was laying out her clothes. Today she wore a robe of purple samite and a silver sash, and on her head the three-headed dragon crown the Tourmaline Brotherhood had given her in Qarth. Her slippers were silver as well, with heels so high that she was always half afraid she was about to topple over. When she was dressed, Missandei brought her a polished silver glass so she could see how she looked. Dany stared at herself in silence. *Is this the face of a conqueror?* So far as she could tell, she still looked like a little girl.

No one was calling her Daenerys the Conqueror yet, but perhaps they would. Aegon the Conqueror had won Westeros with three dragons, but she had taken Meereen with sewer rats and a wooden cock, in less than a day. *Poor Groleo.* He still grieved for his ship, she knew. If a war galley could ram another ship, why not a gate? That had been her thought when she commanded the captains to drive their ships ashore. Their masts had become her battering rams, and swarms of freedmen had torn their hulls apart to build mantlets, turtles, catapults, and ladders. The sellswords had given each ram a bawdy name, and it had been the mainmast of *Meraxes* – formerly *Joso's Prank* – that had broken the eastern gate. Joso's Cock, they called it. The fighting had raged bitter and bloody for most of a day and well into the night before the wood began to splinter and *Meraxes'* iron figurehead, a laughing jester's face, came crashing through.

Dany had wanted to lead the attack herself, but to a man her captains said that would be madness, and her captains never agreed on anything. Instead she remained in the rear, sitting atop her silver in a long shirt of mail. She *heard* the city fall from half a league away, though, when the defenders' shouts of defiance changed to cries of fear. Her dragons had roared as one in that moment, filling the night with flame. *The slaves are rising*, she knew at once. *My sewer rats have gnawed off their chains.*

When the last resistance had been crushed by the Unsullied and the sack had run its course, Dany entered her city. The dead were heaped so high before the broken gate that it took her freedmen near an hour to make a path for her silver. Joso's Cock and the great wooden turtle that had protected it, covered with horsehides, lay abandoned within. She rode past burned buildings and broken windows, through brick streets where the gutters were choked with the stiff and swollen dead. Cheering slaves lifted bloodstained hands to her as she went by, and called her "Mother."

In the plaza before the Great Pyramid, the Meereenese huddled forlorn. The Great Masters had looked anything but great in the morning light. Stripped of their jewels and their fringed *tokar*s, they were contemptible; a herd of old men with shriveled balls and spotted skin and young men with ridiculous hair. Their women were either soft and fleshy or as dry as old sticks, their face paint streaked by tears. "I want your leaders," Dany told them. "Give them up, and the rest of you shall be spared."

"How many?" one old woman had asked, sobbing. "How many must you have to spare us?"

"One hundred and sixty-three," she answered.

She had them nailed to wooden posts around the plaza, each man pointing at the next. The anger was fierce and hot inside her when she gave the command; it made her feel like an avenging dragon. But later, when she passed the men dying on the posts, when she heard their moans and smelled their bowels and blood . . .

Dany put the glass aside, frowning. *It was just. It was. I did it for the children.*

Her audience chamber was on the level below, an echoing high-ceilinged room with walls of purple marble. It was a chilly place for all its grandeur. There had been a throne there, a fantastic thing of carved and gilded wood in the shape of a savage harpy. She had taken one long look and commanded it be broken up for firewood. "I will not sit in the harpy's lap," she told them. Instead she sat upon a simple ebony bench. It served, though she had heard the Meereenese muttering that it did not befit a queen.

Her bloodriders were waiting for her. Silver bells tinkled in their oiled braids, and they wore the gold and jewels of dead men. Meereen had been rich beyond imagining. Even her sellswords seemed sated, at least for now. Across the room, Grey Worm wore the plain uniform of the Unsullied, his spiked bronze cap beneath one arm. These at least she could rely on, or so she hoped ... and Brown Ben Plumm as well, solid Ben with his grey-white hair and weathered face, so beloved of her dragons. And Daario beside him, glittering in gold. Daario and Ben Plumm, Grey Worm, Irri, Jhiqui, Missandei ... as she looked at them Dany found herself wondering which of them would betray her next.

The dragon has three heads. There are two men in the world who I can trust, if I can find them. I will not be alone then. We will be three against the world, like Aegon and his sisters.

"Was the night as quiet as it seemed?" Dany asked.

"It seems it was, Your Grace," said Brown Ben Plumm.

She was pleased. Meereen had been sacked savagely, as new-fallen cities always were, but Dany was determined that should end now that the city was hers. She had decreed that murderers were to be hanged, that looters were to lose a hand, and rapists their manhood. Eight killers swung from the walls, and the Unsullied had filled a bushel basket with bloody hands and soft red worms, but Meereen was calm again. *But for how long?*

A fly buzzed her head. Dany waved it off, irritated, but it returned almost at once. "There are too many flies in this city."

Ben Plumm gave a bark of laughter. "There were flies in my ale this morning. I swallowed one of them."

"Flies are the dead man's revenge." Daario smiled, and stroked the center prong of his beard. "Corpses breed maggots, and maggots breed flies."

"We will rid ourselves of the corpses, then. Starting with those in the plaza below. Grey Worm, will you see to it?"

"The queen commands, these ones obey."

"Best bring sacks as well as shovels, Worm," Brown Ben counseled. "Well past ripe, those ones. Falling off those poles in bits and pieces, and crawling with ..."

"He knows. So do I." Dany remembered the horror she had felt when she had seen the Plaza of Punishment in Astapor. *I made a horror just as great, but surely they deserved it. Harsh justice is still justice.*

"Your Grace," said Missandei, "Ghiscari inter their honored dead in crypts below their manses. If you would boil the bones clean and return them to their kin, it would be a kindness."

The widows will curse me all the same. "Let it be done." Dany beckoned to Daario. "How many seek audience this morning?"

"Two have presented themselves to bask in your radiance."

Daario had plundered himself a whole new wardrobe in Meereen, and to match it he had redyed his trident beard and curly hair a deep rich purple. It made his eyes look almost purple too, as if he were some lost Valyrian. "They arrived in the night on the *Indigo Star*, a trading galley out of Qarth."

A slaver, you mean. Dany frowned. "Who are they?"

"The *Star*'s master and one who claims to speak for Astapor."

"I will see the envoy first."

He proved to be a pale ferret-faced man with ropes of pearls and spun gold hanging heavy about his neck. "Your Worship!" he cried. "My name is Ghael. I bring greetings to the Mother of Dragons from King Cleon of Astapor, Cleon the Great."

Dany stiffened. "I left a council to rule Astapor. A healer, a scholar, and a priest."

"Your Worship, those sly rogues betrayed your trust. It was revealed that they were scheming to restore the Good Masters to power and the people to chains. Great Cleon exposed their plots and hacked their heads off with a cleaver, and the grateful folk of Astapor have crowned him for his valor."

"Noble Ghael," said Missandei, in the dialect of Astapor, "is this the same Cleon once owned by Grazdan mo Ullhor?"

Her voice was guileless, yet the question plainly made the envoy anxious. "The same," he admitted. "A great man."

Missandei leaned close to Dany. "He was a butcher in Grazdan's kitchen," the girl whispered in her ear. "It was said he could slaughter a pig faster than any man in Astapor."

I have given Astapor a butcher king. Dany felt ill, but she knew she must not let the envoy see it. "I will pray that King Cleon rules well and wisely. What would he have of me?"

Ghael rubbed his mouth. "Perhaps we should speak more privily, Your Grace?"

"I have no secrets from my captains and commanders."

"As you wish. Great Cleon bids me declare his devotion to the Mother of Dragons. Your enemies are his enemies, he says, and chief among them are the Wise Masters of Yunkai. He proposes a pact between Astapor and Meereen, against the Yunkai'i."

"I swore no harm would come to Yunkai if they released their slaves," said Dany.

"These Yunkish dogs cannot be trusted, Your Worship. Even now they plot against you. New levies have been raised and can be seen drilling outside the city walls, warships are being built, envoys have been sent to New Ghis and Volantis in the west, to make alliances and hire sellswords. They have even dispatched riders to Vaes Dothrak to bring a *khalasar* down upon you. Great Cleon bid me tell you not to be afraid.

Astapor remembers. Astapor will not forsake you. To prove his faith, Great Cleon offers to seal your alliance with a marriage."

"A marriage? To me?"

Ghael smiled. His teeth were brown and rotten. "Great Cleon will give you many strong sons."

Dany found herself bereft of words, but little Missandei came to her rescue. "Did his first wife give him sons?"

The envoy looked at her unhappily. "Great Cleon has three daughters by his first wife. Two of his newer wives are with child. But he means to put all of them aside if the Mother of Dragons will consent to wed him."

"How noble of him," said Dany. "I will consider all you've said, my lord." She gave orders that Ghael be given chambers for the night, somewhere lower in the pyramid.

All my victories turn to dross in my hands, she thought. *Whatever I do, all I make is death and horror.* When word of what had befallen Astapor reached the streets, as it surely would, tens of thousands of newly freed Meereenese slaves would doubtless decide to follow her when she went west, for fear of what awaited them if they stayed . . . yet it might well be that worse would await them on the march. Even if she emptied every granary in the city and left Meereen to starve, how could she feed so many? The way before her was fraught with hardship, bloodshed, and danger. Ser Jorah had warned her of that. He'd warned her of so many things . . . he'd . . . *No, I will not think of Jorah Mormont. Let him keep a little longer.* "I shall see this trader captain," she announced. Perhaps he would have some better tidings.

That proved to be a forlorn hope. The master of the *Indigo Star* was Qartheen, so he wept copiously when asked about Astapor. "The city bleeds. Dead men rot unburied in the streets, each pyramid is an armed camp, and the markets have neither food nor slaves for sale. And the poor children! King Cleaver's thugs have seized every highborn boy in Astapor to make new Unsullied for the trade, though it will be years before they are trained."

The thing that surprised Dany most was how unsurprised she was. She found herself remembering Eroeh, the Lhazarene girl she had once tried to protect, and what had happened to her. *It will be the same in Meereen once I march*, she thought. The slaves from the fighting pits, bred and trained to slaughter, were already proving themselves unruly and quarrelsome. They seemed to think they owned the city now, and every man and woman in it. Two of them had been among the eight she'd hanged. *There is no more I can do*, she told herself. "What do you want of me, Captain?"

"Slaves," he said. "My holds are full to bursting with ivory, ambergris, zorse hides, and other fine goods. I would trade them here for slaves, to sell in Lys and Volantis."

"We have no slaves for sale," said Dany.

"My queen?" Daario stepped forward. "The riverside is full of Meereenese, begging leave to be allowed to sell themselves to this Qartheen. They are thicker than the flies."

Dany was shocked. "They *want* to be slaves?"

"The ones who come are well spoken and gently born, sweet queen. Such slaves are prized. In the Free Cities they will be tutors, scribes, bed slaves, even healers and priests. They will sleep in soft beds, eat rich foods, and dwell in manses. Here they have lost all, and live in fear and squalor."

"I see." Perhaps it was not so shocking, if these tales of Astapor were true. Dany thought a moment. "Any man who wishes to sell *himself* into slavery may do so. Or woman." She raised a hand. "But they may not sell their children, nor a man his wife."

"In Astapor the city took a tenth part of the price, each time a slave changed hands," Missandei told her.

"We'll do the same," Dany decided. Wars were won with gold as much as swords. "A tenth part. In gold or silver coin, or ivory. Meereen has no need of saffron, cloves, or zorse hides."

"It shall be done as you command, glorious queen," said Daario. "My Stormcrows will collect your tenth."

If the Stormcrows saw to the collections at least half the gold would somehow go astray, Dany knew. But the Second Sons were just as bad, and the Unsullied were as unlettered as they were incorruptible. "Records must be kept," she said. "Seek among the freedmen for men who can read, write, and do sums."

His business done, the captain of the *Indigo Star* bowed and took his leave. Dany shifted uncomfortably on the ebony bench. She dreaded what must come next, yet she knew she had put it off too long already. Yunkai and Astapor, threats of war, marriage proposals, the march west looming over all . . . *I need my knights. I need their swords, and I need their counsel.* Yet the thought of seeing Jorah Mormont again made her feel as if she'd swallowed a spoonful of flies; angry, agitated, sick. She could almost feel them buzzing round her belly. *I am the blood of the dragon. I must be strong. I must have fire in my eyes when I face them, not tears.* "Tell Belwas to bring my knights," Dany commanded, before she could change her mind. "My good knights."

Strong Belwas was puffing from the climb when he marched them through the doors, one meaty hand wrapped tight around each man's arm. Ser Barristan walked with his head held high, but Ser Jorah stared at the marble floor as he approached. *The one is proud, the other guilty.*

The old man had shaved off his white beard. He looked ten years younger without it. But her balding bear looked older than he had. They halted before the bench. Strong Belwas stepped back and stood with his arms crossed across his scarred chest. Ser Jorah cleared his throat. "*Khaleesi . . .*"

She had missed his voice so much, but she had to be stern. "Be quiet. I will tell you when to speak." She stood. "When I sent you down into the sewers, part of me hoped I'd seen the last of you. It seemed a fitting end for liars, to drown in slavers' filth. I thought the gods would deal with you, but instead you returned to me. My gallant knights of Westeros, an informer and a turncloak. My brother would have hanged you both." Viserys would have, anyway. She did not know what Rhaegar would have done. "I will admit you helped win me this city . . ."

Ser Jorah's mouth tightened. "We won you this city. We sewer rats."

"Be quiet," she said again . . . though there *was* truth to what he said. While Joso's Cock and the other rams were battering the city gates and her archers were firing flights of flaming arrows over the walls, Dany had sent two hundred men along the river under cover of darkness to fire the hulks in the harbor. But that was only to hide their true purpose. As the flaming ships drew the eyes of the defenders on the walls, a few half-mad swimmers found the sewer mouths and pried loose a rusted iron grating. Ser Jorah, Ser Barristan, Strong Belwas, and twenty brave fools slipped beneath the brown water and up the brick tunnel, a mixed force of sellswords, Unsullied, and freedmen. Dany had told them to choose only men who had no families . . . and preferably no sense of smell.

They had been lucky as well as brave. It had been a moon's turn since the last good rain, and the sewers were only thigh-high. The oilcloth they'd wrapped around their torches kept them dry, so they had light. A few of the freedmen were frightened of the huge rats until Strong Belwas caught one and bit it in two. One man was killed by a great pale lizard that reared up out of the dark water to drag him off by the leg, but when next ripples were spied Ser Jorah butchered the beast with his blade. They took some wrong turnings, but once they found the surface Strong Belwas led them to the nearest fighting pit, where they surprised a few guards and struck the chains off the slaves. Within an hour, half the fighting slaves in Meereen had risen.

"You *helped* win this city," she repeated stubbornly. "And you have served me well in the past. Ser Barristan saved me from the Titan's Bastard, and from the Sorrowful Man in Qarth. Ser Jorah saved me from the poisoner in Vaes Dothrak, and again from Drogo's bloodriders after my sun-and-stars had died." So many people wanted her dead, sometimes she lost count. "And yet you lied, deceived me, betrayed me." She turned to Ser Barristan. "You protected my father for many years, fought beside my brother on the Trident, but you abandoned Viserys in his exile and bent your knee to the Usurper instead. Why? And tell it *true*."

"Some truths are hard to hear. Robert was a . . . a good knight . . . chivalrous, brave . . . he spared my life, and the lives of many others . . . Prince Viserys was only a boy, it would have been years before he was fit to rule, and . . . forgive me, my queen, but you asked for truth . . . even as a child, your brother Viserys oft seemed to be his father's son, in ways that Rhaegar never did."

"His father's son?" Dany frowned. "What does that mean?"

The old knight did not blink. "Your father is called 'the Mad King' in Westeros. Has no one ever told you?"

"Viserys did." *The Mad King.* "The *Usurper* called him that, the Usurper and his dogs." *The Mad King.* "It was a lie."

"Why ask for truth," Ser Barristan said softly, "if you close your ears to it?" He hesitated, then continued. "I told you before that I used a false name so the Lannisters would not know that I'd joined you. That was less than half of it, Your Grace. The truth is, I wanted to watch you for a time before pledging you my sword. To make certain that you were not . . ."

". . . my father's daughter?" If she was not her father's daughter, who was she?

". . . mad," he finished. "But I see no taint in you."

"*Taint?*" Dany bristled.

"I am no maester to quote history at you, Your Grace. Swords have been my life, not books. But every child knows that the Targaryens have always danced too close to madness. Your father was not the first. King Jaehaerys once told me that madness and greatness are two sides of the same coin. Every time a new Targaryen is born, he said, the gods toss the coin in the air and the world holds its breath to see how it will land."

Jaehaerys. This old man knew my grandfather. The thought gave her pause. Most of what she knew of Westeros had come from her brother, and the rest from Ser Jorah. Ser Barristan would have forgotten more than the two of them had ever known. *This man can tell me what I came from.* "So I am a coin in the hands of some god, is that what you are saying, ser?"

"No," Ser Barristan replied. "You are the trueborn heir of Westeros. To the end of my days I shall remain your faithful knight, should you find me worthy to bear a sword again. If not, I am content to serve Strong Belwas as his squire."

"What if I decide you're only worthy to be my fool?" Dany asked scornfully. "Or perhaps my cook?"

"I would be honored, Your Grace," Selmy said with quiet dignity. "I can bake apples and boil beef as well as any man, and I've roasted many a duck over a campfire. I hope you like them greasy, with charred skin and bloody bones."

That made her smile. "I'd have to be mad to eat such fare. Ben Plumm, come give Ser Barristan your longsword."

But Whitebeard would not take it. "I flung my sword at Joffrey's feet and have not touched one since. Only from the hand of my queen will I accept a sword again."

"As you wish." Dany took the sword from Brown Ben and offered it hilt first. The old man took it reverently. "Now kneel," she told him, "and swear it to my service."

He went to one knee and lay the blade before her as he said the words. Dany scarcely heard them. *He was the easy one*, she thought. *The other will be harder.* When Ser Barristan was done, she turned to Jorah Mormont. "And now you, ser. Tell me true."

The big man's neck was red; whether from anger or shame she did not know. "I have tried to tell you true, half a hundred times. I told you Arstan was more than he seemed. I warned you that Xaro and Pyat Pree were not to be trusted. I warned you –"

"You warned me against everyone except yourself." His insolence angered her. *He should be humbler. He should beg for my forgiveness.* "Trust no one but Jorah Mormont, you said . . . and all the time you were the Spider's creature!"

"I am no man's *creature*. I took the eunuch's gold, yes. I learned some ciphers and wrote some letters, but that was all –"

"*All?* You spied on me and sold me to my enemies!"

"For a time." He said it grudgingly. "I stopped."

"When? When did you stop?"

"I made one report from Qarth, but –"

"From *Qarth?*" Dany had been hoping it had ended much earlier. "What did you write from Qarth? That you were my man now, that you wanted no more of their schemes?" Ser Jorah could not meet her eyes. "When Khal Drogo died, you asked me to go with you to Yi Ti and the Jade Sea. Was that your wish or Robert's?"

"That was to protect you," he insisted. "To keep you away from them. I knew what snakes they were . . . ."

"*Snakes?* And what are you, ser?" Something unspeakable occurred to her. "You told them I was carrying Drogo's child . . . ."

"*Khaleesi* . . ."

"Do not think to deny it, ser," Ser Barristan said sharply. "I was there when the eunuch told the council, and Robert decreed that Her Grace and her child must die. You were the source, ser. There was even talk that you might do the deed, for a pardon."

"A lie." Ser Jorah's face darkened. "I would never . . . Daenerys, it was me who *stopped* you from drinking the wine."

"Yes. And how was it you knew the wine was poisoned?"

"I . . . I but suspected . . . the caravan brought a letter from Varys, he warned me there would be attempts. He wanted you watched, yes, but not harmed." He went to his knees. "If I had not told them someone else would have. You *know* that."

"I know you betrayed me." She touched her belly, where her son Rhaego had perished. "I know a poisoner tried to kill my son, because of you. That's what I *know*."

"No . . . no." He shook his head. "I never meant . . . forgive me. You have to forgive me."

"*Have* to?" It was too late. *He should have begun by begging forgiveness.* She could not pardon him as she'd intended. She had dragged the wineseller behind her horse until there was nothing left of him. Didn't the man who brought him deserve the same? *This is Jorah, my fierce bear, the right arm that never failed me. I would be dead without him, but . . .* "I can't forgive you," she said. "I can't."

"You forgave the old man . . ."

"He lied to me about his name. You sold my secrets to the men who killed my father and stole my brother's throne."

"I protected you. I fought for you. Killed for you."

Kissed me, she thought, *betrayed me.*

"I went down into the sewers like a rat. For you."

It might have been kinder if you'd died there. Dany said nothing. There was nothing to say.

"Daenerys," he said, "I have loved you."

And there it was. *Three treasons will you know. Once for blood and once for gold and once for love.* "The gods do nothing without a purpose, they say. You did not die in battle, so it must be they still have some use for you. But I don't. I will not have you near me. You are banished, ser. Go back to your masters in King's Landing and collect your pardon, if you can. Or to Astapor. No doubt the butcher king needs knights."

"No." He reached for her. "Daenerys, please, hear me . . ."

She slapped his hand away. "Do not ever presume to touch me again, or to speak my name. You have until dawn to collect your things and leave this city. If you're found in Meereen past break of day, I will have Strong Belwas twist your head off. I will. Believe that." She turned her back on him, her skirts swirling. *I cannot bear to see his face.* "Remove this liar from my sight," she commanded. *I must not weep. I must not. If I weep I will forgive him.* Strong Belwas seized Ser Jorah by the arm and dragged him out. When Dany glanced back, the knight was walking as if drunk, stumbling and slow. She looked away until she heard the doors open and close. Then she sank back onto the ebony bench. *He's gone, then. My father and my mother, my brothers, Ser Willem Darry, Drogo who was my sun-and-stars, his son who died inside me, and now Ser Jorah . . .*

"The queen has a good heart," Daario purred through his deep purple whiskers, "but that one is more dangerous than all the Oznaks and Meros rolled up in one." His strong hands caressed the hilts of his matched blades, those wanton golden women. "You need not even say the word, my radiance. Only give the tiniest nod, and your Daario shall fetch you back his ugly head."

"Leave him be. The scales are balanced now. Let him go home." Dany pictured Jorah moving amongst old gnarled oaks and tall pines, past flowering thornbushes, grey stones bearded with moss, and little creeks running icy down steep hillsides. She saw him entering a hall built of huge logs, where dogs slept by the hearth and the smell of meat and mead hung thick in the smoky air. "We are done for now," she told her captains.

It was all she could do not to run back up the wide marble stairs. Irri helped her slip from her court clothes and into more comfortable garb; baggy woolen breeches, a loose felted tunic, a painted Dothraki vest. "You are trembling, *Khaleesi*," the girl said as she knelt to lace up Dany's sandals.

"I'm cold," Dany lied. "Bring me the book I was reading last night." She wanted to lose herself in the words, in other times and other places. The fat leather-bound volume was full of songs and stories from the Seven Kingdoms. Children's stories, if truth be told; too simple and fanciful to be true history. All the heroes were tall and handsome, and you could tell the traitors by their shifty eyes. Yet she loved them all the same. Last night she had been reading of the three princesses in the red tower, locked away by the king for the crime of being beautiful.

When her handmaid brought the book, Dany had no trouble finding the page where she had left off, but it was no good. She found herself reading the same passage half a dozen times. *Ser Jorah gave me this book as a bride's gift, the day I wed Khal Drogo. But Daario is right, I shouldn't have banished him. I should have kept him, or I should have killed him.* She played at being a queen, yet sometimes she still felt like a scared little girl. *Viserys always said what a dolt I was. Was he truly mad?* She closed the book. She could still recall Ser Jorah, if she wished. Or send Daario to kill him.

Dany fled from the choice, out onto the terrace. She found Rhaegal asleep beside the pool, a green and bronze coil basking in the sun. Drogon was perched up atop the pyramid, in the place where the huge bronze harpy had stood before she had commanded it to be pulled down. He spread his wings and roared when he spied her. There was no sign of Viserion, but when she went to the parapet and scanned the horizon she saw pale wings in the far distance, sweeping above the river. *He is hunting. They grow bolder every day.* Yet it still made her anxious when they flew too far away. *One day one of them may not return,* she thought.

"Your Grace?"

She turned to find Ser Barristan behind her. "What more would you have of me, ser? I spared you, I took you into my service, now give me some peace."

"Forgive me, Your Grace. It was only . . . now that you know who I am . . ." The old man hesitated. "A knight of the Kingsguard is in the king's presence day and night. For that reason, our vows require us to protect his secrets as we would his life. But your father's secrets by rights belong to you now, along with his throne, and . . . I thought perhaps you might have questions for me."

Questions? She had a hundred questions, a thousand, ten thousand. Why couldn't she think of one? "Was my father truly mad?" she blurted out. *Why do I ask that?* "Viserys said this talk of madness was a ploy of the Usurper's . . ."

"Viserys was a child, and the queen sheltered him as much as she could. Your father always had a little madness in him, I now believe. Yet he was charming and generous as well, so his lapses were forgiven. His reign began with such promise . . . but as the years passed, the lapses grew more frequent, until . . ."

Dany stopped him. "Do I want to hear this now?"

Ser Barristan considered a moment. "Perhaps not. Not now."

"Not now," she agreed. "One day. One day you must tell me all. The good and the bad. There is *some* good to be said of my father, surely?"

"There is, Your Grace. Of him, and those who came before him. Your grandfather Jaehaerys and his brother, their father Aegon, your mother . . . and Rhaegar. Him most of all."

"I wish I could have known him." Her voice was wistful.

"I wish he could have known you," the old knight said. "When you are ready, I will tell you all."

Dany kissed him on the cheek and sent him on his way.

That night her handmaids brought her lamb, with a salad of raisins and carrots soaked in wine, and a hot flaky bread dripping with honey. She could eat none of it. *Did Rhaegar ever grow so weary?* she wondered. *Did Aegon, after his conquest?*

Later, when the time came for sleep, Dany took Irri into bed with her, for the first time since the ship. But even as she shuddered in release and wound her fingers through her handmaid's thick black hair, she pretended it was Drogo holding her . . . only somehow his face kept turning into Daario's. *If I want Daario I need only say so.* She lay with Irri's legs entangled in her own. *His eyes looked almost purple today . . .*

Dany's dreams were dark that night, and she woke three times from half-remembered nightmares. After the third time she was too restless to return to sleep. Moonlight streamed through the slanting windows, silvering the marble floors. A cool breeze was blowing through the open terrace doors. Irri slept soundly beside her, her lips slightly parted, one dark brown nipple peeping out above the sleeping silks. For a moment Dany was tempted, but it was Drogo she wanted, or perhaps Daario. Not Irri. The maid was sweet and skillful, but all her kisses tasted of duty.

She rose, leaving Irri asleep in the moonlight. Jhiqui and Missandei slept in their own beds. Dany slipped on a robe and padded barefoot across the marble floor, out onto the terrace. The air was chilly, but she liked the feel of grass between her toes and the sound of the leaves whispering to one another. Wind ripples chased each other across the surface of the little bathing pool and made the moon's reflection dance and shimmer.

She leaned against a low brick parapet to look down upon the city. Meereen was sleeping too. *Lost in dreams of kinder days, perhaps.* Night covered the streets like a black blanket, hiding the corpses and the grey rats that came up from the sewers to feast on them, the swarms of stinging flies. Distant torches glimmered red and yellow where her sentries walked their rounds, and here and there she saw the faint glow of lanterns bobbing down an alley. Perhaps one was Ser Jorah, leading his horse slowly toward the gate. *Farewell, old bear. Farewell, betrayer.*

She was Daenerys Stormborn, the Unburnt, *khaleesi* and queen, Mother of Dragons, slayer of warlocks, breaker of chains, and there was no one in the world that she could trust.

"Your Grace?" Missandei stood at her elbow wrapped in a bedrobe, wooden sandals on her feet. "I woke, and saw that you were gone. Did you sleep well? What are you looking at?"

"My city," said Dany. "I was looking for a house with a red door, but by night all the doors are black."

"A red door?" Missandei was puzzled. "What house is this?"

"No house. It does not matter." Dany took the younger girl by the hand. "Never lie to me, Missandei. Never betray me."

"I never would," Missandei promised. "Look, dawn comes."

The sky had turned a cobalt blue from the horizon to the zenith, and behind the line of low hills to the east a glow could be seen, pale gold and oyster pink. Dany held Missandei's hand as they watched the sun come up. All the grey bricks became red and yellow and blue and green and orange. The scarlet sands of the fighting pits transformed them into bleeding sores before her eyes. Elsewhere the golden dome of the Temple of the Graces blazed bright, and bronze stars winked along the walls where the light of the rising sun touched the spikes on the helms of the Unsullied. On the terrace, a few flies stirred sluggishly. A bird began to chirp in the persimmon tree, and then two more. Dany cocked her head to hear their song, but it was not long before the sounds of the waking city drowned them out.

The sounds of my city.

That morning she summoned her captains and commanders to the garden, rather than descending to the audience chamber. "Aegon the Conqueror brought fire and blood to Westeros, but afterward he gave them peace, prosperity, and justice. But all I have brought to Slaver's Bay is death and ruin. I have been more *khal* than queen, smashing and plundering, then moving on."

"There is nothing to stay for," said Brown Ben Plumm.

"Your Grace, the slavers brought their doom on themselves," said Daario Naharis.

"You have brought freedom as well," Missandei pointed out.

"Freedom to starve?" asked Dany sharply. "Freedom to die? Am I a dragon, or a harpy?" *Am I mad? Do I have the taint?*

"A dragon," Ser Barristan said with certainty. "Meereen is not Westeros, Your Grace."

"But how can I rule seven kingdoms if I cannot rule a single city?" He had no answer to that. Dany turned away from them, to gaze out over the city once again. "My children need time to heal and learn. My dragons need time to grow and test their wings. And I need the same. I will not let this city go the way of Astapor. I will not let the harpy of Yunkai chain up those I've freed all over again." She turned back to look at their faces. "I will not march."

"What will you do then, *Khaleesi*?" asked Rakharo.

"Stay," she said. "Rule. And be a queen."

JAIME

The king sat at the head of the table, a stack of cushions under his arse, signing each document as it was presented to him.

"Only a few more, Your Grace," Ser Kevan Lannister assured him. "This is a bill of attainder against Lord Edmure Tully, stripping him of Riverrun and all its lands and incomes, for rebelling against his lawful king. This is a similar attainder, against his uncle Ser Brynden Tully, the Blackfish." Tommen signed them one after the other, dipping the quill carefully and writing his name in a broad childish hand.

Jaime watched from the foot of the table, thinking of all those lords who aspired to a seat on the king's small council. *They can bloody well have mine.* If this was power, why did it taste like tedium? He did not feel especially powerful, watching Tommen dip his quill in the inkpot again. He felt bored.

And sore. Every muscle in his body ached, and his ribs and shoulders were bruised from the battering they'd gotten, courtesy of Ser Addam Marbrand. Just thinking of it made him wince. He could only hope the man would keep his mouth shut. Jaime had known Marbrand since he was a boy, serving as a page at Casterly Rock; he trusted him as much as he trusted anyone. Enough to ask him to take up shields and tourney swords. He had wanted to know if he could fight with his left hand.

And now I do. The knowledge was more painful than the beating that Ser Addam had given him, and the beating was so bad he could hardly dress himself this morning. If they had been fighting in earnest, Jaime would have died two dozen deaths. It seemed so simple, changing hands. It wasn't. Every instinct he had was wrong. He had to *think* about everything, where once he'd just moved. And while he was thinking, Marbrand was thumping him. His left hand couldn't even seem to *hold* a longsword properly; Ser Addam had disarmed him thrice, sending his blade spinning.

"This grants said lands, incomes, and castle to Ser Emmon Frey and his lady wife, Lady Genna." Ser Kevan presented another sheaf of parchments to the king. Tommen dipped and signed. "This is a decree of legitimacy for a natural son of Lord Roose Bolton of the Dreadfort. And this names Lord Bolton your Warden of the North." Tommen dipped, signed, dipped, signed. "This grants Ser Rolph Spicer title to the castle Castamere and raises him to the rank of lord." Tommen scrawled his name.

I should have gone to Ser Ilyn Payne, Jaime reflected. The King's Justice was not a friend as Marbrand was, and might well have beat him bloody . . . but without a tongue, he was not like to boast of it afterward. All it would take would be one chance remark by Ser Addam in his cups, and the whole world would soon know how useless he'd become. *Lord Commander of the Kingsguard.* It was a cruel jape, that . . . though not quite so cruel as the gift his father had sent him.

"This is your royal pardon for Lord Gawen Westerling, his lady wife, and his daughter Jeyne, welcoming them back into the king's peace," Ser Kevan said. "This is a pardon for Lord Jonos Bracken of Stone Hedge. This is a pardon for Lord Vance. This for Lord Goodbrook. This for Lord Mooton of Maidenpool."

Jaime pushed himself to his feet. "You seem to have these matters well in hand, Uncle. I shall leave His Grace to you."

"As you wish." Ser Kevan rose as well. "Jaime, you should go to your father. This breach between you –"

" – is his doing. Nor will he mend it by sending me mocking gifts. Tell him that, if you can pry him away from the Tyrells long enough."

His uncle looked distressed. "The gift was heartfelt. We thought that it might encourage you –"

" – to grow a new hand?" Jaime turned to Tommen. Though he had Joffrey's golden curls and green eyes, the new king shared little else with his late brother. He inclined to plumpness, his face was pink and round, and he even liked to read. *He is still shy of nine, this son of mine. The boy is not the man.* It would be seven years before Tommen was ruling in his own right. Until then the realm would remain firmly in the hands of his lord grandfather. "Sire," he asked, "do I have your leave to go?"

"As you like, Ser Uncle." Tommen looked back to Ser Kevan. "Can I seal them now, Great-Uncle?" Pressing his royal seal into the hot wax was his favorite part of being king, so far.

Jaime strode from the council chamber. Outside the door he found Ser

Meryn Trant standing stiff at guard in white scale armor and snowy cloak. *If this one should learn how feeble I am, or Kettleblack or Blount should hear of it* . . . "Remain here until His Grace is done," he said, "then escort him back to Maegor's."

Trant inclined his head. "As you say, my lord."

The outer ward was crowded and noisy that morning. Jaime made for the stables, where a large group of men were saddling their horses. "Steelshanks!" he called. "Are you off, then?"

"As soon as m'lady is mounted," said Steelshanks Walton. "My lord of Bolton expects us. Here she is now."

A groom led a fine grey mare out the stable door. On her back was mounted a skinny hollow-eyed girl wrapped in a heavy cloak. Grey, it was, like the dress beneath it, and trimmed with white satin. The clasp that pinned it to her breast was wrought in the shape of a wolf's head with slitted opal eyes. The girl's long brown hair blew wild in the wind. She had a pretty face, he thought, but her eyes were sad and wary.

When she saw him, she inclined her head. "Ser Jaime," she said in a thin anxious voice. "You are kind to see me off."

Jaime studied her closely. "You know me, then?"

She bit her lip. "You may not recall, my lord, as I was littler then . . . but I had the honor to meet you at Winterfell when King Robert came to visit my father Lord Eddard." She lowered her big brown eyes and mumbled, "I'm Arya Stark."

Jaime had never paid much attention to Arya Stark, but it seemed to him that this girl was older. "I understand you're to be married."

"I am to wed Lord Bolton's son, Ramsay. He used to be a Snow, but His Grace has made him a Bolton. They say he's very brave. I am so happy."

Then why do you sound so frightened? "I wish you joy, my lady." Jaime turned back to Steelshanks. "You have the coin you were promised?"

"Aye, and we've shared it out. You have my thanks." The northman grinned. "A Lannister always pays his debts."

"Always," said Jaime, with a last glance at the girl. He wondered if there was much resemblance. Not that it mattered. The real Arya Stark was buried in some unmarked grave in Flea Bottom in all likelihood. With her brothers dead, and both parents, who would dare name this one a fraud? "Good speed," he told Steelshanks. Nage raised his peace banner, and the northmen formed a column as ragged as their fur cloaks and trotted out the castle gate. The thin girl on the grey mare looked small and forlorn in their midst.

A few of the horses still shied away from the dark splotch on the hard-packed ground where the earth had drunk the life's blood of the stableboy Gregor Clegane had killed so clumsily. The sight of it made

Jaime angry all over again. He had told his Kingsguard to keep the crowd out of the way, but that oaf Ser Boros had let himself be distracted by the duel. The fool boy himself shared some of the blame, to be sure; the dead Dornishman as well. And Clegane most of all. The blow that took the boy's arm off had been mischance, but that second cut . . .

Well, Gregor is paying for it now. Grand Maester Pycelle was tending to the man's wounds, but the howls heard ringing from the maester's chambers suggested that the healing was not going as well as it might. "The flesh mortifies and the wounds ooze pus," Pycelle told the council. "Even maggots will not touch such foulness. His convulsions are so violent that I have had to gag him to prevent him from biting off his tongue. I have cut away as much tissue as I dare, and treated the rot with boiling wine and bread mold, to no avail. The veins in his arm are turning black. When I leeched him, all the leeches died. My lords, I must know what malignant substance Prince Oberyn used on his spear. Let us detain these other Dornishmen until they are more forthcoming."

Lord Tywin had refused him. "There will be trouble enough with Sunspear over Prince Oberyn's death. I do not mean to make matters worse by holding his companions captive."

"Then I fear Ser Gregor may die."

"Undoubtedly. I swore as much in the letter I sent to Prince Doran with his brother's body. But it must be seen to be the sword of the King's Justice that slays him, not a poisoned spear. Heal him."

Grand Maester Pycelle blinked in dismay. "My lord –"

"*Heal him,*" Lord Tywin said again, vexed. "You are aware that Lord Varys has sent fishermen into the waters around Dragonstone. They report that only a token force remains to defend the island. The Lyseni are gone from the bay, and the great part of Lord Stannis's strength with them."

"Well and good," announced Pycelle. "Let Stannis rot in Lys, I say. We are well rid of the man and his ambitions."

"Did you turn into an utter fool when Tyrion shaved your beard? This is *Stannis Baratheon.* The man will fight to the bitter end and then some. If he is gone, it can only mean he intends to resume the war. Most likely he will land at Storm's End and try and rouse the storm lords. If so, he's finished. But a bolder man might roll the dice for Dorne. If he should win Sunspear to his cause, he might prolong this war for years. So we will *not* offend the Martells any further, for *any* reason. The Dornishmen are free to go, and you *will* heal Ser Gregor."

And so the Mountain screamed, day and night. Lord Tywin Lannister could cow even the Stranger, it would seem.

As Jaime climbed the winding steps of White Sword Tower, he could hear Ser Boros snoring in his cell. Ser Balon's door was shut as well; he had the king tonight, and would sleep all day. Aside from Blount's snores, the tower was very quiet. That suited Jaime well enough. *I ought to rest myself.* Last night, after his dance with Ser Addam, he'd been too sore to sleep.

But when he stepped into his bedchamber, he found his sister waiting for him.

She stood beside the open window, looking over the curtain walls and out to sea. The bay wind swirled around her, flattening her gown against her body in a way that quickened Jaime's pulse. It was white, that gown, like the hangings on the wall and the draperies on his bed. Swirls of tiny emeralds brightened the ends of her wide sleeves and spiraled down her bodice. Larger emeralds were set in the golden spiderweb that bound her golden hair. The gown was cut low, to bare her shoulders and the tops of her breasts. *She is so beautiful.* He wanted nothing more than to take her in his arms.

"Cersei." He closed the door softly. "Why are you here?"

"Where else could I go?" When she turned to him there were tears in her eyes. "Father's made it clear that I am no longer wanted on the council. Jaime, won't you talk to him?"

Jaime took off his cloak and hung it from a peg on the wall. "I talk to Lord Tywin every day."

"*Must* you be so stubborn? All he wants . . ."

". . . is to force me from the Kingsguard and send me back to Casterly Rock."

"That need not be so terrible. He is sending me back to Casterly Rock as well. He wants me far away, so he'll have a free hand with Tommen. Tommen is *my* son, not his!"

"Tommen is the king."

"He is a boy! A frightened little boy who saw his brother *murdered* at his own wedding. And now they are telling him that *he* must marry. The girl is twice his age and twice a widow!"

He eased himself into a chair, trying to ignore the ache of bruised muscles. "The Tyrells are insisting. I see no harm in it. Tommen's been lonely since Myrcella went to Dorne. He likes having Margaery and her ladies about. Let them wed."

"He is your son . . ."

"He is my seed. He's never called me Father. No more than Joffrey ever did. You warned me a thousand times never to show any undue interest in them."

"To keep them safe! You as well. How would it have looked if my brother had played the father to the king's children? Even Robert might have grown suspicious."

"Well, he's beyond suspicion now." Robert's death still left a bitter taste in Jaime's mouth. *It should have been me who killed him, not Cersei.* "I only wished he'd died at my hands." *When I still had two of them.* "If I'd let kingslaying become a habit, as he liked to say, I could have taken you as my wife for all the world to see. I'm not ashamed of loving you, only of the things I've done to hide it. That boy at Winterfell . . ."

"Did I tell you to throw him out the window? If you'd gone hunting as I begged you, nothing would have happened. But no, you had to have me, you could not wait until we returned to the city."

"I'd waited long enough. I hated watching Robert stumble to your bed every night, always wondering if maybe this night he'd decide to claim his rights as husband." Jaime suddenly remembered something else that troubled him about Winterfell. "At Riverrun, Catelyn Stark seemed convinced I'd sent some footpad to slit her son's throat. That I'd given him a dagger."

"That," she said scornfully. "Tyrion asked me about that."

"There *was* a dagger. The scars on Lady Catelyn's hands were real enough, she showed them to me. Did you . . . ?"

"Oh, don't be absurd." Cersei closed the window. "Yes, I hoped the boy would die. So did you. Even *Robert* thought that would have been for the best. 'We kill our horses when they break a leg, and our dogs when they go blind, but we are too weak to give the same mercy to crippled children,' he told me. He was blind himself at the time, from drink."

Robert? Jaime had guarded the king long enough to know that Robert Baratheon said things in his cups that he would have denied angrily the next day. "Were you alone when Robert said this?"

"You don't think he said it to Ned Stark, I hope? Of course we were alone. Us and the children." Cersei removed her hairnet and draped it over a bedpost, then shook out her golden curls. "Perhaps Myrcella sent this man with the dagger, do you think so?"

It was meant as mockery, but she'd cut right to the heart of it, Jaime saw at once. "Not Myrcella. Joffrey."

Cersei frowned. "Joffrey had no love for Robb Stark, but the younger boy was nothing to him. He was only a child himself."

"A child hungry for a pat on the head from that sot you let him believe was his father." He had an uncomfortable thought. "Tyrion almost died because of this bloody dagger. If he knew the whole thing was Joffrey's work, that might be why . . ."

"I don't care *why*," Cersei said. "He can take his reasons down to hell with him. If you had seen how Joff died . . . he *fought*, Jaime, he fought for every breath, but it was as if some malign spirit had its hands about his throat. He had such terror in his eyes . . . When he was little, he'd run to me when he was scared or hurt and I would protect him. But that night there was nothing I could do. Tyrion murdered him in front of me, and *there was nothing I could do."* Cersei sank to her knees before his chair and took Jaime's good hand between both of hers. "Joff is dead and Myrcella's in Dorne. Tommen's all I have left. You mustn't let Father take him from me. Jaime, please."

"Lord Tywin has not asked for my approval. I can talk to him, but he will not listen . . ."

"He will if you agree to leave the Kingsguard."

"I'm not leaving the Kingsguard."

His sister fought back tears. "Jaime, you're my shining knight. You cannot abandon me when I need you most! He is stealing my son, sending me away . . . and unless you stop him, Father is going to force me to wed again!"

Jaime should not have been surprised, but he was. The words were a blow to his gut harder than any that Ser Addam Marbrand had dealt him. "Who?"

"Does it matter? Some lord or other. Someone Father thinks he needs. I don't care. I will not have another husband. You are the only man I want in my bed, ever again."

"Then *tell* him that!"

She pulled her hands away. "You are talking madness again. Would you have us ripped apart, as Mother did that time she caught us playing? Tommen would lose the throne, Myrcella her marriage . . . I *want* to be your wife, we belong to each other, but it can never be, Jaime. We are brother and sister."

"The Targaryens . . ."

"We are not Targaryens!"

"Quiet," he said, scornfully. "So loud, you'll wake my Sworn Brothers. We can't have that, now, can we? People might learn that you had come to see me."

"Jaime," she sobbed, "don't you think *I* want it as much as you do? It makes no matter who they wed me to, I want you at my side, I want you in my bed, I want you inside me. Nothing has changed between us. Let me prove it to you." She pushed up his tunic and began to fumble with the laces of his breeches.

Jaime felt himself responding. "No," he said, "not here." They had never done it in White Sword Tower, much less in the Lord Commander's chambers. "Cersei, this is not the place."

"You took me in the sept. This is no different." She drew out his cock and bent her head over it.

Jaime pushed her away with the stump of his right hand. *"No.* Not here, I said." He forced himself to stand.

For an instant he could see confusion in her bright green eyes, and fear as well. Then rage replaced it. Cersei gathered herself together, got to her feet, straightened her skirts. "Was it your hand they hacked off in Harrenhal, or your manhood?" As she shook her head, her hair tumbled around her bare white shoulders. "I was a fool to come. You lacked the courage to avenge Joffrey, why would I think that you'd protect Tommen? Tell me, if the Imp had killed all three of your children, would *that* have made you wroth?"

"Tyrion is not going to harm Tommen or Myrcella. I am still not certain he killed Joffrey."

Her mouth twisted in anger. "How can you *say* that? After all his threats –"

"Threats mean nothing. He swears he did not do it."

"Oh, he *swears*, is that it? And dwarfs don't lie, is that what you think?"

"Not to me. No more than you would."

"You great golden fool. He's lied to you a thousand times, and so have I." She bound up her hair again, and scooped up the hairnet from the bedpost where she'd hung it. "Think what you will. The little monster is in a black cell, and soon Ser Ilyn will have his head off. Perhaps you'd like it for a keepsake." She glanced at the pillow. "He can watch over you as you sleep alone in that cold white bed. Until his eyes rot out, that is."

"You had best go, Cersei. You're making me angry."

"Oh, an angry cripple. How terrifying." She laughed. "A pity Lord Tywin Lannister never had a son. I could have been the heir he wanted, but I lacked the cock. And speaking of such, best tuck yours away, brother. It looks rather sad and small, hanging from your breeches like that."

When she was gone Jaime took her advice, fumbling one-handed at his laces. He felt a bone-deep ache in his phantom fingers. *I've lost a hand, a father, a son, a sister, and a lover, and soon enough I will lose a brother. And yet they keep telling me House Lannister won this war.*

Jaime donned his cloak and went downstairs, where he found Ser Boros Blount having a cup of wine in the common room. "When you're done with your drink, tell Ser Loras I'm ready to see her."

Ser Boros was too much of a coward to do much more than glower. "You are ready to see who?"

"Just tell Loras."

"Aye." Ser Boros drained his cup. "Aye, Lord Commander."

He took his own good time about it, though, or else the Knight of Flowers proved hard to find. Several hours had passed by the time they arrived, the slim handsome youth and the big ugly maid. Jaime was sitting alone in the round room, leafing idly through the White Book. "Lord

Commander," Ser Loras said, "you wished to see the Maid of Tarth?"

"I did." Jaime waved them closer with his left hand. "You have talked with her, I take it?"

"As you commanded, my lord."

"And?"

The lad tensed. "I . . . it may be it happened as she says, ser. That it was Stannis. I cannot be certain."

"Varys tells me that the castellan of Storm's End perished strangely as well," said Jaime.

"Ser Cortnay Penrose," said Brienne sadly. "A good man."

"A stubborn man. One day he stood square in the way of the King of Dragonstone. The next he leapt from a tower." Jaime stood. "Ser Loras, we will talk more of this later. You may leave Brienne with me."

The wench looked as ugly and awkward as ever, he decided when Tyrell left them. Someone had dressed her in woman's clothes again, but this dress fit much better than that hideous pink rag the goat had made her wear. "Blue is a good color on you, my lady," Jaime observed. "It goes well with your eyes." *She does have astonishing eyes.*

Brienne glanced down at herself, flustered. "Septa Donyse padded out the bodice, to give it that shape. She said you sent her to me." She lingered by the door, as if she meant to flee at any second. "You look . . ."

"Different?" He managed a half-smile. "More meat on the ribs and fewer lice in my hair, that's all. The stump's the same. Close the door and come here."

She did as he bid her. "The white cloak . . ."

". . . is new, but I'm sure I'll soil it soon enough."

"That wasn't . . . I was about to say that it becomes you."

She came closer, hesitant. "Jaime, did you mean what you told Ser Loras? About . . . about King Renly, and the shadow?"

Jaime shrugged. "I would have killed Renly myself if we'd met in battle, what do I care who cut his throat?"

"You said I had honor . . ."

"I'm the bloody Kingslayer, remember? When I say you have honor, that's like a whore vouchsafing your maidenhood." He leaned back and looked up at her. "Steelshanks is on his way back north, to deliver Arya Stark to Roose Bolton."

"You gave her to *him?*" she cried, dismayed. "You swore an oath to Lady Catelyn . . ."

"With a sword at my throat, but never mind. Lady Catelyn's dead. I could not give her back her daughters even if I had them. And the girl my father sent with Steelshanks was not Arya Stark."

"*Not* Arya Stark?"

"You heard me. My lord father found some skinny northern girl more or less the same age with more or less the same coloring. He dressed her up in white and grey, gave her a silver wolf to pin her cloak, and sent her off to wed Bolton's bastard." He lifted his stump to point at her. "I wanted to tell you that before you went galloping off to rescue her and got yourself killed for no good purpose. You're not half bad with a sword, but you're not good enough to take on two hundred men by yourself."

Brienne shook her head. "When Lord Bolton learns that your father paid him with false coin . . ."

"Oh, he knows. *Lannisters lie,* remember? It makes no matter, this girl serves his purpose just as well. Who is going to say that she *isn't* Arya Stark? Everyone the girl was close to is dead except for her sister, who has disappeared."

"Why would you tell me all this, if it's true? You are betraying your father's secrets."

The Hand's secrets, he thought. *I no longer have a father.* "I pay my debts like every good little lion. I did promise Lady Stark her daughters . . . and one of them is still alive. My brother may know where she is, but if so he isn't saying. Cersei is convinced that Sansa helped him murder Joffrey."

The wench's mouth got stubborn. "I will not believe that gentle girl a poisoner. Lady Catelyn said that she had a loving heart. It was your brother. There was a trial, Ser Loras said."

"Two trials, actually. Words and swords both failed him. A bloody mess. Did you watch from your window?"

"My cell faces the sea. I heard the shouting, though."

"Prince Oberyn of Dorne is dead, Ser Gregor Clegane lies dying, and Tyrion stands condemned before the eyes of gods and men. They're keeping him in a black cell till they kill him."

Brienne looked at him. "You do not believe he did it."

Jaime gave her a hard smile. "See, wench? We know each other too well. Tyrion's wanted to be me since he took his first step, but he'd never follow me in kingslaying. Sansa Stark killed Joffrey. My brother's kept silent to protect her. He gets these fits of gallantry from time to time. The last one cost him a nose. This time it will mean his head."

"No," Brienne said. "It was not my lady's daughter. It could not have been her."

"There's the stubborn stupid wench that I remember."

She reddened. "My name is . . ."

"Brienne of Tarth." Jaime sighed. "I have a gift for you." He reached down under the Lord Commander's chair and brought it out, wrapped in folds of crimson velvet.

Brienne approached as if the bundle was like to bite her, reached out a huge freckled hand, and flipped back a fold of cloth. Rubies glimmered in the light. She picked the treasure up gingerly, curled her fingers around the leather grip, and slowly slid the sword free of its scabbard. Blood and black the ripples shone. A finger of reflected light ran red along the edge. "Is this Valyrian steel? I have never seen such colors."

"Nor I. There was a time that I would have given my right hand to wield a sword like that. Now it appears I have, so the blade is wasted on me. Take it." Before she could think to refuse, he went on. "A sword so fine must bear a name. It would please me if you would call this one Oathkeeper. One more thing. The blade comes with a price."

Her face darkened. "I told you, I will never serve . . ."

". . . such foul creatures as us. Yes, I recall. Hear me out, Brienne. Both of us swore oaths concerning Sansa Stark. Cersei means to see that the girl is found and killed, wherever she has gone to ground . . ."

Brienne's homely face twisted in fury. "If you believe that I would harm my lady's daughter for a *sword*, you –"

"*Just listen*," he snapped, angered by her assumption. "I want you to find Sansa first, and get her somewhere safe. How else are the two of us going to make good our stupid vows to your precious dead Lady Catelyn?"

The wench blinked. "I . . . I thought . . ."

"I know what you *thought*." Suddenly Jaime was sick of the sight of her. *She bleats like a bloody sheep.* "When Ned Stark died, his greatsword was given to the King's Justice," he told her. "But my father felt that such a fine blade was wasted on a mere headsman. He gave Ser Ilyn a new sword, and had Ice melted down and reforged. There was enough metal for two new blades. You're holding one. So you'll be defending Ned Stark's daughter with Ned Stark's own steel, if that makes any difference to you."

"Ser, I . . . I owe you an apolo . . ."

He cut her off. "Take the bloody sword and go, before I change my mind. There's a bay mare in the stables, as homely as you are but somewhat better trained. Chase after Steelshanks, search for Sansa, or ride home to your isle of sapphires, it's naught to me. I don't want to look at you anymore."

"Jaime . . ."

"*Kingslayer*," he reminded her. "Best use that sword to clean the wax out of your ears, wench. We're done."

Stubbornly, she persisted. "Joffrey was your . . ."

"My king. Leave it at that."

"You say Sansa killed him. Why protect her?"

Because Joff was no more to me than a squirt of seed in Cersei's cunt. And because he deserved to die. "I have made kings and unmade them. Sansa Stark is my last chance for honor." Jaime smiled thinly. "Besides, kingslayers should band together. Are you ever going to go?"

Her big hand wrapped tight around Oathkeeper. "I will. And I will find

the girl and keep her safe. For her lady mother's sake. And for yours."
She bowed stiffly, whirled, and went.

Jaime sat alone at the table while the shadows crept across the room.
As dusk began to settle, he lit a candle and opened the White Book to
his own page. Quill and ink he found in a drawer. Beneath the last line
Ser Barristan had entered, he wrote in an awkward hand that might have
done credit to a six-year-old being taught his first letters by a maester:

*Defeated in the Whispering Wood by the Young Wolf Robb Stark
during the War of the Five Kings. Held captive at Riverrun and ransomed
for a promise unfulfilled. Captured again by the Brave Companions, and
maimed at the word of Vargo Hoat their captain, losing his sword hand
to the blade of Zollo the Fat. Returned safely to King's Landing by
Brienne, the Maid of Tarth.*

When he was done, more than three-quarters of his page still remained
to be filled between the gold lion on the crimson shield on top and the
blank white shield at the bottom. Ser Gerold Hightower had begun his
history, and Ser Barristan Selmy had continued it, but the rest Jaime
Lannister would need to write for himself. He could write whatever he
chose, henceforth.

Whatever he chose . . .

JON

The wind was blowing wild from the east, so strong the heavy cage would rock whenever a gust got it in its teeth. It skirled along the Wall, shivering off the ice, making Jon's cloak flap against the bars. The sky was slate grey, the sun no more than a faint patch of brightness behind the clouds. Across the killing ground, he could see the glimmer of a thousand campfires burning, but their lights seemed small and powerless against such gloom and cold.

A grim day. Jon Snow wrapped gloved hands around the bars and held tight as the wind hammered at the cage once more. When he looked straight down past his feet, the ground was lost in shadow, as if he were being lowered into some bottomless pit. *Well, death is a bottomless pit of sorts*, he reflected, *and when this day's work is done my name will be shadowed forever.*

Bastard children were born from lust and lies, men said; their nature was wanton and treacherous. Once Jon had meant to prove them wrong, to show his lord father that he could be as good and true a son as Robb. *I made a botch of that.* Robb had become a hero king; if Jon was remembered at all, it would be as a turncloak, an oathbreaker, and a murderer. He was glad that Lord Eddard was not alive to see his shame.

I should have stayed in that cave with Ygritte. If there was a life beyond this one, he hoped to tell her that. *She will claw my face the way the eagle did, and curse me for a coward, but I'll tell her all the same.* He flexed his sword hand, as Maester Aemon had taught him. The habit had become part of him, and he would need his fingers to be limber to have even half a chance of murdering Mance Rayder.

They had pulled him out this morning, after four days in the ice, locked up in a cell five by five by five, too low for him to stand, too tight for him to stretch out on his back. The stewards had long ago discovered that food and meat kept longer in the icy storerooms carved from the base of the Wall . . . but prisoners did not. "You will die in here, Lord Snow," Ser Alliser had said just before he closed the heavy wooden door, and Jon had believed it. But this morning they had come and pulled him out again, and marched him cramped and shivering back to the King's Tower, to stand before jowly Janos Slynt once more

"That old maester says I cannot hang you," Slynt declared. "He has written Cotter Pyke, and even had the bloody gall to show me the letter. He says you are no turncloak."

"Aemon's lived too long, my lord," Ser Alliser assured him. "His wits have gone dark as his eyes."

"Aye," Slynt said. "A blind man with a chain about his neck, who does he think he is?"

Aemon Targaryen, Jon thought, *a king's son and a king's brother and a king who might have been.* But he said nothing.

"Still," Slynt said, "I will not have it said that Janos Slynt hanged a man unjustly. I will not. I have decided to give you one last chance to prove you are as loyal as you claim, Lord Snow. One last chance to do your duty, yes!" He stood. "Mance Rayder wants to parley with us. He knows he has no chance now that Janos Slynt has come, so he wants to talk, this King-beyond-the-Wall. But the man is craven, and will not come to us. No doubt he knows I'd hang him. Hang him by his feet from the top of the Wall, on a rope two hundred feet long! But he will not come. He asks that we send an envoy to him."

"We're sending you, Lord Snow." Ser Alliser smiled.

"Me." Jon's voice was flat. "Why me?"

"You rode with these wildlings," said Thorne. "Mance Rayder knows you. He will be more inclined to trust you."

That was so wrong Jon might have laughed. "You've got it backward. Mance suspected me from the first. If I show up in his camp wearing a black cloak again and speaking for the Night's Watch, he'll know that I betrayed him."

"He asked for an envoy, we are sending one," said Slynt. "If you are too craven to face this turncloak king, we can return you to your ice cell. This time without the furs, I think. Yes."

"No need for that, my lord," said Ser Alliser. "Lord Snow will do as we ask. He wants to show us that he is no turncloak. He wants to prove himself a loyal man of the Night's Watch."

Thorne was much the more clever of the two, Jon realized; this had his stink all over it. He was trapped. "I'll go," he said in a clipped, curt voice.

"*M'lord*," Janos Slynt reminded him. "You'll address me – "

"I'll go, *my lord*. But you are making a mistake, *my lord*. You are sending the wrong man, *my lord*. Just the sight of me is going to anger Mance. *My lord* would have a better chance of reaching terms if he sent – "

"Terms?" Ser Alliser chuckled.

"Janos Slynt does not make terms with lawless savages, Lord Snow. No, he does not."

"We're not sending you to *talk* with Mance Rayder," Ser Alliser said. "We're sending you to kill him."

The wind whistled through the bars, and Jon Snow shivered. His leg was throbbing, and his head. He was not fit to kill a kitten, yet here he was. *The trap had teeth.* With Maester Aemon insisting on Jon's innocence, Lord Janos had not dared to leave him in the ice to die. This was better. "Our honor means no more than our lives, so long as the realm is safe," Qhorin Halfhand had said in the Frostfangs. He must remember that. Whether he slew Mance or only tried and failed, the free folk would kill him. Even desertion was impossible, if he'd been so inclined; to Mance he was a proven liar and betrayer.

When the cage jerked to a halt, Jon swung down onto the ground and rattled Longclaw's hilt to loosen the bastard blade in its scabbard. The gate was a few yards to his left, still blocked by the splintered ruins of the turtle, the carcass of a mammoth ripening within. There were other corpses too, strewn amidst broken barrels, hardened pitch, and patches of burnt grass, all shadowed by the Wall. Jon had no wish to linger here. He started walking toward the wildling camp, past the body of a dead giant whose head had been crushed by a stone. A raven was pulling out bits of brain from the giant's shattered skull. It looked up as he walked by. "*Snow*," it screamed at him. "*Snow, snow.*" Then it opened its wings and flew away.

No sooner had he started out than a lone rider emerged from the wildling camp and came toward him. He wondered if Mance was coming out to parley in no-man's-land. *That might make it easier, though nothing will make it easy.* But as the distance between them diminished Jon saw that the horseman was short and broad, with gold rings glinting on thick arms and a white beard spreading out across his massive chest.

"*Har!*" Tormund boomed when they came together. "Jon Snow the crow. I feared we'd seen the last o' you."

"I never knew you feared anything, Tormund."

That made the wildling grin. "Well said, lad. I see your cloak is black. Mance won't like that. If you've come to change sides again, best climb back on that Wall o' yours."

"They've sent me to treat with the King-beyond-the-Wall."

"Treat?" Tormund laughed. "Now there's a word. Har! Mance wants to talk, that's true enough. Can't say he'd want to talk with *you*, though."

"I'm the one they've sent."

"I see that. Best come along, then. You want to ride?"

"I can walk."

"You fought us hard here." Tormund turned his garron back toward the wildling camp. "You and your brothers. I give you that. Two hundred dead, and a dozen giants. Mag himself went in that gate o' yours and never did come out."

"He died on the sword of a brave man named Donal Noye."

"Aye? Some great lord was he, this Donal Noye? One of your shiny knights in their steel smallclothes?"

"A blacksmith. He only had one arm."

"A one-armed smith slew Mag the Mighty? Har! That must o' been a fight to see. Mance will make a song of it, see if he don't." Tormund took a waterskin off his saddle and pulled the cork. "This will warm us some. To Donal Noye, and Mag the Mighty." He took a swig, and handed it down to Jon.

"To Donal Noye, and Mag the Mighty." The skin was full of mead, but a mead so potent that it made Jon's eyes water and sent tendrils of fire snaking through his chest. After the ice cell and the cold ride down in the cage, the warmth was welcome.

Tormund took the skin back and downed another swig, then wiped his mouth. "The Magnar of Thenn swore t'us that he'd have the gate wide open, so all we'd need to do was stroll through singing. He was going to bring the whole Wall down."

"He brought down part," Jon said. "On his head."

"Har!" said Tormund. "Well, I never had much use for Styr. When a man's got no beard nor hair nor ears, you can't get a good grip on him when you fight." He kept his horse at a slow walk so Jon could limp beside him. "What happened to that leg?"

"An arrow. One of Ygritte's, I think."

"That's a woman for you. One day she's kissing you, the next she's filling you with arrows."

"She's dead."

"Aye?" Tormund gave a sad shake of the head. "A waste. If I'd been ten years younger, I'd have stolen her meself. That hair she had. Well, the hottest fires burn out quickest." He lifted the skin of mead. "To Ygritte, kissed by fire!" He drank deep.

"To Ygritte, kissed by fire," Jon repeated when Tormund handed him back the skin. He drank even deeper.

"Was it you killed her?"

"My brother." Jon had never learned which one, and hoped he never would.

"You bloody crows." Tormund's tone was gruff, yet strangely gentle.

"That Longspear stole me daughter. Munda, me little autumn apple. Took her right out o' my tent with all four o' her brothers about. Toregg slept through it, the great lout, and Torwynd . . . well, Torwynd the Tame, that says all that needs saying, don't it? The young ones gave the lad a fight, though."

"And Munda?" asked Jon.

"She's my own blood," said Tormund proudly. "She broke his lip for him and bit one ear half off, and I hear he's got so many scratches on his back he can't wear a cloak. She likes him well enough, though. And why not? He don't fight with no spear, you know. Never has. So where do you think he got that name? *Har!*"

Jon had to laugh. Even now, even here. Ygritte had been fond of Longspear Ryk. He hoped he found some joy with Tormund's Munda. Someone needed to find some joy somewhere.

"You know nothing, Jon Snow," Ygritte would have told him. *I know that I am going to die*, he thought. *I know that much, at least.* "All men die," he could almost hear her say, "and women too, and every beast that flies or swims or runs. It's not the *when* o' dying that matters, it's the *how* of it, Jon Snow." *Easy for you to say*, he thought back. *You died brave in battle, storming the castle of a foe. I'm going to die a turncloak and a killer.* Nor would his death be quick, unless it came on the end of Mance's sword.

Soon they were among the tents. It was the usual wildling camp; a sprawling jumble of cookfires and piss pits, children and goats wandering freely, sheep bleating among the trees, horse hides pegged up to dry. There was no plan to it, no order, no defenses. But there were men and women and animals everywhere.

Many ignored him, but for every one who went about his business there were ten who stopped to stare; children squatting by the fires, old women in dog carts, cave dwellers with painted faces, raiders with claws and snakes and severed heads painted on their shields, all turned to have a look. Jon saw spearwives too, their long hair streaming in the piney wind that sighed between the trees.

There were no true hills here, but Mance Rayder's white fur tent had been raised on a spot of high stony ground right on the edge of the trees. The King-beyond-the-Wall was waiting outside, his ragged red-and-black cloak blowing in the wind. Harma Dogshead was with him, Jon saw, back from her raids and feints along the Wall, and Varamyr Sixskins as well, attended by his shadowcat and two lean grey wolves.

When they saw who the Watch had sent, Harma turned her head and spat, and one of Varamyr's wolves bared its teeth and growled. "You must be very brave or very stupid, Jon Snow," Mance Rayder said, "to come back to us wearing a black cloak."

"What else would a man of the Night's Watch wear?"

"Kill him," urged Harma. "Send his body back up in that cage o' theirs and tell them to send us someone else. I'll keep his head for my standard. A turncloak's worse than a dog."

"I warned you he was false." Varamyr's tone was mild, but his shadow-cat was staring at Jon hungrily through slitted grey eyes. "I never did like the smell o' him."

"Pull in your claws, beastling." Tormund Giantsbane swung down off his horse. "The lad's here to hear. You lay a paw on him, might be I'll take me that shadowskin cloak I been wanting."

"Tormund Crowlover," Harma sneered. "You are a great sack o' wind, old man."

The skinchanger was grey-faced, round-shouldered, and bald, a mouse of a man with a wolfling's eyes. "Once a horse is broken to the saddle, any man can mount him," he said in a soft voice. "Once a beast's been joined to a man, any skinchanger can slip inside and ride him. Orell was withering inside his feathers, so I took the eagle for my own. But the joining works both ways, warg. Orell lives inside me now, whispering how much he hates you. And I can soar above the Wall, and see with eagle eyes."

"So we know," said Mance. "We know how few you were, when you stopped the turtle. We know how many came from Eastwatch. We know how your supplies have dwindled. Pitch, oil, arrows, spears. Even your stair is gone, and that cage can only lift so many. We know. And now you know we know." He opened the flap of the tent. "Come inside. The rest of you, wait here."

"What, even me?" said Tormund.

"*Particularly* you. Always."

It was warm within. A small fire burned beneath the smoke holes, and a brazier smouldered near the pile of furs where Dalla lay, pale and sweating. Her sister was holding her hand. *Val*, Jon remembered. "I was sorry when Jarl fell," he told her.

Val looked at him with pale grey eyes. "He always climbed too fast." She was as fair as he'd remembered, slender, full-breasted, graceful even at rest, with high sharp cheekbones and a thick braid of honey-colored hair that fell to her waist.

"Dalla's time is near," Mance explained. "She and Val will stay. They know what I mean to say."

Jon kept his face as still as ice. *Foul enough to slay a man in his own tent under truce. Must I murder him in front of his wife as their child is being born?* He closed the fingers of his sword hand. Mance was not wearing armor, but his own sword was sheathed on his left hip. And there were other weapons in the tent, daggers and dirks, a bow and a

quiver of arrows, a bronze-headed spear lying beside that big black . . .
. . . horn.

Jon sucked in his breath.

A warhorn, a bloody great warhorn.

"Yes," Mance said. "The Horn of Winter, that Joramun once blew to wake giants from the earth."

The horn was huge, eight feet along the curve and so wide at the mouth that he could have put his arm inside up to the elbow. *If this came from an aurochs, it was the biggest that ever lived.* At first he thought the bands around it were bronze, but when he moved closer he realized they were gold. *Old gold, more brown than yellow, and graven with runes.*

"Ygritte said you never found the horn."

"Did you think only crows could lie? I liked you well enough, for a bastard . . . but I never trusted you. A man needs to earn my trust."

Jon faced him. "If you've had the Horn of Joramun all along, why haven't you used it? Why bother building turtles and sending Thenns to kill us in our beds? If this horn is all the songs say, why not just sound it and be done?"

It was Dalla who answered him, Dalla great with child, lying on her pile of furs beside the brazier. "We free folk know things you kneelers have forgotten. Sometimes the short road is not the safest, Jon Snow. The Horned Lord once said that sorcery is a sword without a hilt. There is no safe way to grasp it."

Mance ran a hand along the curve of the great horn. "No man goes hunting with only one arrow in his quiver," he said. "I had hoped that Styr and Jarl would take your brothers unawares, and open the gate for us. I drew your garrison away with feints and raids and secondary attacks. Bowen Marsh swallowed that lure as I knew he would, but your band of cripples and orphans proved to be more stubborn than anticipated. Don't think you've stopped us, though. The truth is, you are too few and we are too many. I could continue the attack here and still send ten thousand men to cross the Bay of Seals on rafts and take Eastwatch from the rear. I could storm the Shadow Tower too, I know the approaches as well as any man alive. I could send men and mammoths to dig out the gates at the castles you've abandoned, all of them at once."

"Why don't you, then?" Jon could have drawn Longclaw then, but he wanted to hear what the wildling had to say.

"Blood," said Mance Rayder. "I'd win in the end, yes, but you'd bleed me, and my people have bled enough."

"Your losses haven't been that heavy."

"Not at your hands." Mance studied Jon's face. "You saw the Fist of the First Men. You know what happened there. You know what we are facing."

"The Others . . ."

"They grow stronger as the days grow shorter and the nights colder. First they kill you, then they send your dead against you. The giants have not been able to stand against them, nor the Thenns, the ice river clans, the Hornfoots."

"Nor you?"

"Nor me." There was anger in that admission, and bitterness too deep for words. "Raymun Redbeard, Bael the Bard, Gendel and Gorne, the Horned Lord, they all came south to conquer, but I've come with my tail between my legs to hide behind your Wall." He touched the horn again. "If I sound the Horn of Winter, the Wall will fall. Or so the songs would have me believe. There are those among my people who want nothing more . . ."

"But once the Wall is fallen," Dalla said, *"what will stop the Others?"*

Mance gave her a fond smile. "It's a wise woman I've found. A true queen." He turned back to Jon. "Go back and tell them to open their gate and let us pass. If they do, I will give them the horn, and the Wall will stand until the end of days."

Open the gate and let them pass. Easy to say, but what must follow? Giants camping in the ruins of Winterfell? Cannibals in the wolfswood, chariots sweeping across the barrowlands, free folk stealing the daughters of shipwrights and silversmiths from White Harbor and fishwives off the Stony Shore? "Are you a true king?" Jon asked suddenly.

"I've never had a crown on my head or sat my arse on a bloody throne, if that's what you're asking," Mance replied. "My birth is as low as a man's can get, no septon's ever smeared my head with oils, I don't own any castles, and my queen wears furs and amber, not silk and sapphires. I am my own champion, my own fool, and my own harpist. You don't become King-beyond-the-Wall because your father was. The free folk won't follow a name, and they don't care which brother was born first. They follow fighters. When I left the Shadow Tower there were five men making noises about how they might be the stuff of kings. Tormund was one, the Magnar another. The other three I slew, when they made it plain they'd sooner fight than follow."

"You can kill your enemies," Jon said bluntly, "but can you rule your friends? If we let your people pass, are you strong enough to make them keep the king's peace and obey the laws?"

"Whose laws? The laws of Winterfell and King's Landing?" Mance laughed. "When we want laws we'll make our own. You can keep your king's justice too, and your king's taxes. I'm offering you the horn, not our freedom. We will not kneel to you."

"What if we refuse the offer?" Jon had no doubt that they would. The Old Bear might at least have listened, though he would have balked at the notion of letting thirty or forty thousand wildlings loose on the Seven Kingdoms. But Alliser Thorne and Janos Slynt would dismiss the notion out of hand.

"If you refuse," Mance Rayder said, "Tormund Giantsbane will sound the Horn of Winter three days hence, at dawn."

He could carry the message back to Castle Black and tell them of the horn, but if he left Mance still alive Lord Janos and Ser Alliser would seize on that as proof that he was a turncloak. A thousand thoughts flickered through Jon's head. *If I can destroy the horn, smash it here and now* . . . but before he could begin to think that through, he heard the low moan of some other horn, made faint by the tent's hide walls. Mance heard it too. Frowning, he went to the door. Jon followed.

The warhorn was louder outside. Its call had stirred the wildling camp. Three Hornfoot men jogged past, carrying long spears. Horses were whinnying and snorting, giants roaring in the Old Tongue, and even the mammoths were restless.

"Outrider's horn," Tormund told Mance.

"Something's coming." Varamyr sat crosslegged on the half-frozen ground, his wolves circled restlessly around him. A shadow swept over him, and Jon looked up to see the eagle's blue-grey wings. "Coming, from the east."

When the dead walk, walls and stakes and swords mean nothing, he remembered. *You cannot fight the dead, Jon Snow. No man knows that half so well as me.*

Harma scowled. "East? The wights should be behind us."

"East," the skinchanger repeated. "*Something's coming.*"

"The Others?" Jon asked.

Mance shook his head. "The Others never come when the sun is up." Chariots were rattling across the killing ground, jammed with riders waving spears of sharpened bone. The king groaned. "Where the bloody hell do they think they're going? Quenn, get those fools back where they belong. Someone bring my horse. The mare, not the stallion. I'll want my armor too." Mance glanced suspiciously at the Wall. Atop the icy parapets, the straw soldiers stood collecting arrows, but there was no sign of any other activity. "Harma, mount up your raiders. Tormund, find your sons and give me a triple line of spears."

"Aye," said Tormund, striding off.

The mousy little skinchanger closed his eyes and said, "I see them. They're coming along the streams and game trails . . ."

"Who?"

"Men. Men on horses. Men in steel and men in black."

"Crows." Mance made the word a curse. He turned on Jon. "Did my old brothers think they'd catch me with my breeches down if they attacked while we were talking?"

"If they planned an attack they never told me about it." Jon did not believe it. Lord Janos lacked the men to attack the wildling camp. Besides, he was on the wrong side of the Wall, and the gate was sealed with rubble. *He had a different sort of treachery in mind, this can't be his work.*

"If you're lying to me again, you won't be leaving here alive," Mance warned. His guards brought him his horse and armor. Elsewhere around the camp, Jon saw people running at cross purposes, some men forming up as if to storm the Wall while others slipped into the woods, women driving dog carts east, mammoths wandering west. He reached back over his shoulder and drew Longclaw just as a thin line of rangers emerged from the fringes of the wood three hundred yards away. They wore black mail, black halfhelms, and black cloaks. Half-armored, Mance drew his sword. "You knew nothing of this, did you?" he said to Jon, coldly.

Slow as honey on a cold morning, the rangers swept down on the wildling camp, picking their way through clumps of gorse and stands of trees, over roots and rocks. Wildlings flew to meet them, shouting war cries and waving clubs and bronze swords and axes made of flint, galloping headlong at their ancient enemies. *A shout, a slash, and a fine brave death*, Jon had heard brothers say of the free folk's way of fighting.

"Believe what you will," Jon told the King-beyond-the-Wall, "but I knew nothing of any attack."

Harma thundered past before Mance could reply, riding at the head of thirty raiders. Her standard went before her; a dead dog impaled on a spear, raining blood at every stride. Mance watched as she smashed into the rangers. "Might be you're telling it true," he said. "Those look like Eastwatch men. Sailors on horses. Cotter Pyke always had more guts than sense. He took the Lord of Bones at Long Barrow, he might have thought to do the same with me. If so, he's a fool. He doesn't have the men, he –"

"*Mance!*" the shout came. It was a scout, bursting from the trees on a lathered horse. "*Mance*, there's more, they're all around us, iron men, *iron*, a *host* of iron men."

Cursing, Mance swung up into the saddle. "Varamyr, stay and see that no harm comes to Dalla." The King-beyond-the-Wall pointed his sword at Jon. "And keep a few extra eyes on this crow. If he runs, rip out his throat."

"Aye, I'll do that." The skinchanger was a head shorter than Jon, slumped and soft, but that shadowcat could disembowel him with one paw. "They're coming from the north too," Varamyr told Mance. "You best go."

Mance donned his helm with its raven wings. His men were mounted up as well. "Arrowhead," Mance snapped, "to me, form wedge." Yet when he slammed his heels into the mare and flew across the field at the rangers, the men who raced to catch him lost all semblance of formation.

Jon took a step toward the tent, thinking of the Horn of Winter, but the shadowcat blocked him, tail lashing. The beast's nostrils flared, and slaver ran from his curved front teeth. *He smells my fear.* He missed Ghost more than ever then. The two wolves were behind him, growling.

"Banners," he heard Varamyr murmur, "I see golden banners, oh . . ." A mammoth lumbered by, trumpeting, a half-dozen bowmen in the wooden tower on its back. "The king . . . no . . ."

Then the skinchanger threw back his head and *screamed.*

The sound was shocking, ear-piercing, thick with agony. Varamyr fell, writhing, and the 'cat was screaming too . . . and high, high in the eastern sky, against the wall of cloud, Jon saw the eagle *burning.* For a heartbeat it flamed brighter than a star, wreathed in red and gold and orange, its wings beating wildly at the air as if it could fly from the pain. Higher it flew, and higher, and higher still.

The scream brought Val out of the tent, white-faced. "What is it, what's happened?" Varamyr's wolves were fighting each other, and the shadowcat had raced off into the trees, but the man was still twisting on the ground. "What's wrong with him?" Val demanded, horrified. "Where's Mance?"

"There." Jon pointed. "Gone to fight." The king led his ragged wedge into a knot of rangers, his sword flashing.

"Gone? He can't be gone, not now. It's started."

"The battle?" He watched the rangers scatter before Harma's bloody dog's head. The raiders screamed and hacked and chased the men in black back into the trees. But there were more men coming from the wood, a column of horse. *Knights on heavy horse,* Jon saw. Harma had to regroup and wheel to meet them, but half of her men had raced too far ahead.

"The *birth!*" Val was shouting at him.

Trumpets were blowing all around, loud and brazen. *The wildlings have no trumpets, only warhorns.* They knew that as well as he did; the sound sent free folk running in confusion, some toward the fighting, others away. A mammoth was stomping through a flock of sheep that three men were trying to herd off west. The drums were beating as the wildlings ran to form squares and lines, but they were too late, too disorganized, too slow. The enemy was emerging from the forest, from the east, the northeast, the north; three great columns of heavy horse, all dark glinting steel and bright wool surcoats. Not the men of Eastwatch, those had been no more than a line of scouts. An army. *The king!* Jon was as confused as the wildlings. Could Robb have returned? Had the boy on the Iron Throne finally bestirred himself? "You best get back inside the tent," he told Val.

Across the field one column had washed over Harma Dogshead. Another smashed into the flank of Tormund's spearmen as he and his sons desperately tried to turn them. The giants were climbing onto their mammoths, though, and the knights on their barded horses did not like that at all; he could see how the coursers and destriers screamed and scattered at the sight of those lumbering mountains. But there was fear on the wildling side as well, hundreds of women and children rushing away from the battle, some of them blundering right under the hooves of garrons. He saw an old woman's dog cart veer into the path of three chariots, to send them crashing into each other.

"Gods," Val whispered, "gods, why are they doing this?"

"Go inside the tent and stay with Dalla. It's not safe out here." It wouldn't be a great deal safer inside, but she didn't need to hear that.

"I need to find the midwife," Val said.

"You're the midwife. I'll stay here until Mance comes back." He had lost sight of Mance but now he found him again, cutting his way through a knot of mounted men. The mammoths had shattered the center column, but the other two were closing like pincers. On the eastern edge of the camps, some archers were loosing fire arrows at the tents. He saw a mammoth pluck a knight from his saddle and fling him forty feet with a flick of its trunk. Wildlings streamed past, women and children running from the battle, some with men hurrying them along. A few of them gave Jon dark looks but Longclaw was in his hand, and no one troubled him. Even Varamyr fled, crawling off on his hands and knees.

More and more men were pouring from the trees, not only knights now but freeriders and mounted bowmen and men-at-arms in jacks and kettle helms, dozens of men, hundreds of men. A blaze of banners flew above them. The wind was whipping them too wildly for Jon to see the sigils, but he glimpsed a seahorse, a field of birds, a ring of flowers. And yellow, so much yellow, yellow banners with a red device, whose arms were those?

East and north and northeast, he saw bands of wildlings trying to stand and fight, but the attackers rode right over them. The free folk still had the numbers, but the attackers had steel armor and heavy horses. In the thickest part of the fray, Jon saw Mance standing tall in his stirrups. His red-and-black cloak and raven-winged helm made him easy to pick out. He had his sword raised and men were rallying to him when a wedge of knights smashed into them with lance and sword and longaxe. Mance's mare went up on her hind legs, kicking, and a spear took her through the breast. Then the steel tide washed over him.

It's done, Jon thought, *they're breaking.* The wildlings were running, throwing down their weapons, Hornfoot men and cave dwellers and

Thenns in bronze scales, they were running. Mance was gone, someone was waving Harma's head on a pole, Tormund's lines had broken. Only the giants on their mammoths were holding, hairy islands in a red steel sea. The fires were leaping from tent to tent and some of the tall pines were going up as well. And through the smoke another wedge of armored riders came, on barded horses. Floating above them were the largest banners yet, royal standards as big as sheets; a yellow one with long pointed tongues that showed a flaming heart, and another like a sheet of beaten gold, with a black stag prancing and rippling in the wind.

Robert, Jon thought for one mad moment, remembering poor Owen, but when the trumpets blew again and the knights charged, the name they cried was *"Stannis! Stannis! STANNIS!"*

Jon turned away, and went inside the tent.

ARYA

Outside the inn on a weathered gibbet, a woman's bones were twisting and rattling at every gust of wind.

I know this inn. There hadn't been a gibbet outside the door when she had slept here with her sister Sansa under the watchful eye of Septa Mordane, though. "We don't want to go in," Arya decided suddenly, "there might be ghosts."

"You know how long it's been since I had a cup of wine?" Sandor swung down from the saddle. "Besides, we need to learn who holds the ruby ford. Stay with the horses if you want, it's no hair off my arse."

"What if they know you?" Sandor no longer troubled to hide his face. He no longer seemed to care who knew him. "They might want to take you captive."

"Let them try." He loosened his longsword in its scabbard, and pushed through the door.

Arya would never have a better chance to escape. She could ride off on Craven and take Stranger too. She chewed her lip. Then she led the horses to the stables, and went in after him.

They know him. The silence told her that. But that wasn't the worst thing. She knew them too. Not the skinny innkeep, nor the women, nor the fieldhands by the hearth. But the others. The soldiers. She knew the soldiers.

"Looking for your brother, Sandor?" Polliver's hand was down the bodice of the girl on his lap, but now he slid it out.

"Looking for a cup of wine. Innkeep, a flagon of red." Clegane threw a handful of coppers on the floor.

"I don't want no trouble, ser," the innkeep said.

"Then don't call me *ser*." His mouth twitched. "Are you deaf, fool? I ordered wine." As the man ran off, Clegane shouted after him, "*Two cups!* The girl's thirsty too!"

There are only three, Arya thought. Polliver gave her a fleeting glance and the boy beside him never looked at her at all, but the third one gazed long and hard. He was a man of middling height and build, with a face so ordinary that it was hard to say how old he was. *The Tickler. The Tickler and Polliver both.* The boy was a squire, judging by his age and dress. He had a big white pimple on one side of his nose, and some red ones on his forehead. "Is this the lost puppy Ser Gregor spoke of?" he asked the Tickler. "The one who piddled in the rushes and ran off?"

The Tickler put a warning hand on the boy's arm, and gave a short sharp shake of his head. Arya read that plain enough.

The squire didn't, or else he didn't care. "Ser said his puppy brother tucked his tail between his legs when the battle got too warm at King's Landing. He said he ran off whimpering." He gave the Hound a stupid mocking grin.

Clegane studied the boy and never said a word. Polliver shoved the girl off his lap and got to his feet. "The lad's drunk," he said. The man-at-arms was almost as tall as the Hound, though not so heavily muscled. A spade-shaped beard covered his jaws and jowls, thick and black and neatly trimmed, but his head was more bald than not. "He can't hold his wine, is all."

"Then he shouldn't drink."

"The puppy doesn't scare . . ." the boy began, till the Tickler casually twisted his ear between thumb and forefinger. The words became a squeal of pain.

The innkeep came scurrying back with two stone cups and a flagon on a pewter platter. Sandor lifted the flagon to his mouth. Arya could see the muscles in his neck working as he gulped. When he slammed it back down on the table, half the wine was gone. "Now you can pour. Best pick up those coppers too, it's the only coin you're like to see today."

"We'll pay when we're done drinking," said Polliver.

"When you're done drinking you'll tickle the innkeep to see where he keeps his gold. The way you always do."

The innkeep suddenly remembered something in the kitchen. The locals were leaving too, and the girls were gone. The only sound in the common room was the faint crackling of the fire in the hearth. *We should go too*, Arya knew.

"If you're looking for Ser, you come too late," Polliver said. "He was at Harrenhal, but now he's not. The queen sent for him." He wore three blades on his belt, Arya saw; a longsword on his left hip, and on his right a dagger and a slimmer blade, too long to be a dirk and too short to be a sword. "King Joffrey's dead, you know," he added. "Poisoned at his own wedding feast."

Arya edged farther into the room. *Joffrey's dead.* She could almost see him, with his blond curls and his mean smile and his fat soft lips. *Joffrey's dead!* She knew it ought to make her happy, but somehow she still felt empty inside. Joffrey was dead, but if Robb was dead too, what did it matter?

"So much for my brave brothers of the Kingsguard." The Hound gave a snort of contempt. "Who killed him?"

"The Imp, it's thought. Him and his little wife."

"What wife?"

"I forgot, you've been hiding under a rock. The northern girl. Winterfell's daughter. We heard she killed the king with a spell, and afterward changed into a wolf with big leather wings like a bat, and flew out a tower window. But she left the dwarf behind and Cersei means to have his head."

That's stupid, Arya thought. *Sansa only knows songs, not spells, and she'd never marry the Imp.*

The Hound sat on the bench closest the door. His mouth twitched, but only the burned side. "She ought to dip him in wildfire and cook him. Or tickle him till the moon turns black." He raised his wine cup and drained it straightaway.

He's one of them, Arya thought when she saw that. She bit her lip so hard she tasted blood. *He's just like they are. I should kill him when he sleeps.*

"So Gregor took Harrenhal?" Sandor said.

"Didn't require much taking," said Polliver. "The sellswords fled as soon as they knew we were coming, all but a few. One of the cooks opened a postern gate for us, to get back at Hoat for cutting off his foot." He chuckled. "We kept him to cook for us, a couple wenches to warm our beds, and put all the rest to the sword."

"*All* the rest?" Arya blurted out.

"Well, Ser kept Hoat to pass the time."

Sandor said, "The Blackfish is still in Riverrun?"

"Not for long," said Polliver. "He's under siege. Old Frey's going to hang Edmure Tully unless he yields the castle. The only real fighting's around Raventree. Blackwoods and Brackens. The Brackens are ours now."

The Hound poured a cup of wine for Arya and another for himself, and drank it down while staring at the hearthfire. "The little bird flew away, did she? Well, bloody good for her. She shit on the Imp's head and flew off."

"They'll find her," said Polliver. "If it takes half the gold in Casterly Rock."

"A pretty girl, I hear," said the Tickler. "Honey sweet." He smacked his lips and smiled.

"And courteous," the Hound agreed. "A proper little lady. Not like her bloody sister."

"They found her too," said Polliver. "The sister. She's for Bolton's bastard, I hear."

Arya sipped her wine so they could not see her mouth. She didn't understand what Polliver was talking about. *Sansa has no other sister.* Sandor Clegane laughed aloud.

"What's so bloody funny?" asked Polliver.

The Hound never flicked an eye at Arya. "If I'd wanted you to know, I'd have told you. Are there ships at Saltpans?"

"Saltpans? How should I know? The traders are back at Maidenpool, I heard. Randyll Tarly took the castle and locked Mooton in a tower cell. I haven't heard shit about Saltpans."

The Tickler leaned forward. "Would you put to sea without bidding farewell to your brother?" It gave Arya chills to hear him ask a question. "Ser would sooner you returned to Harrenhal with us, Sandor. I bet he would. Or King's Landing . . ."

"Bugger that. Bugger him. Bugger you."

The Tickler shrugged, straightened, and reached a hand behind his head to rub the back of his neck. Everything seemed to happen at once then; Sandor lurched to his feet, Polliver drew his longsword, and the Tickler's hand whipped around in a blur to send something silver flashing across the common room. If the Hound had not been moving, the knife might have cored the apple of his throat; instead it only grazed his ribs, and wound up quivering in the wall near the door. He laughed then, a laugh as cold and hollow as if it had come from the bottom of a deep well. "I was hoping you'd do something stupid." His sword slid from its scabbard just in time to knock aside Polliver's first cut.

Arya took a step backward as the long steel song began. The Tickler came off the bench with a shortsword in one hand and a dagger in the other. Even the chunky brown-haired squire was up, fumbling for his swordhilt. She snatched her wine cup off the table and threw it at his face. Her aim was better than it had been at the Twins. The cup hit him right on his big white pimple and he went down hard on his tail.

Polliver was a grim, methodical fighter, and he pressed Sandor steadily backward, his heavy longsword moving with brutal precision. The Hound's own cuts were sloppier, his parries rushed, his feet slow and clumsy. *He's drunk*, Arya realized with dismay. *He drank too much too fast, with no food in his belly.* And the Tickler was sliding around the wall to get behind him. She grabbed the second wine cup and flung it at him, but he was quicker than the squire had been and ducked his head in time. The look he gave her then was cold with promise. *Is there gold hidden in the village?* she could hear him ask. The stupid squire was clutching the edge of a table and pulling himself to his knees. Arya could taste the beginnings of panic in the back of her throat. *Fear cuts deeper than swords. Fears cuts deeper . . .*

Sandor gave a grunt of pain. The burned side of his face ran red from temple to cheek, and the stub of his ear was gone. That seemed to make him angry. He drove back Polliver with a furious attack, hammering at him with the old nicked longsword he had swapped for in the hills. The bearded man gave way, but none of the cuts so much as touched him. And then the Tickler leapt over a bench quick as a snake, and slashed at the back of the Hound's neck with the edge of his short sword.

They're killing him. Arya had no more cups, but there was something better to throw. She drew the dagger they'd robbed off the dying archer and tried to fling it at the Tickler the way he'd done. It wasn't the same as throwing a rock or a crabapple, though. The knife wobbled, and hit him in the arm hilt first. *He never even felt it.* He was too intent on Clegane.

As he stabbed, Clegane twisted violently aside, winning himself half a heartbeat's respite. Blood ran down his face and from the gash in his neck. Both of the Mountain's men came after him hard, Polliver hacking at his head and shoulders while the Tickler darted in to stab at back and belly. The heavy stone flagon was still on the table. Arya grabbed it with two hands, but as she lifted it someone grabbed her arm. The flagon slipped from her fingers and crashed to the floor. Wrenched around, she found herself nose to nose with the squire. *You stupid, you forgot all about him.* His big white pimple had burst, she saw.

"Are you the puppy's puppy?" He had his sword in his right hand and her arm in his left, but her own hands were free, so she jerked his knife from its sheath and sheathed it again in his belly, twisting. He wasn't wearing mail or even boiled leather, so it went right in, the same way Needle had when she killed the stableboy at King's Landing. The squire's eyes got big and he let go of her arm. Arya spun to the door and wrenched the Tickler's knife from the wall.

Polliver and the Tickler had driven the Hound into a corner behind a bench, and one of them had given him an ugly red gash on his upper thigh to go with his other wounds. Sandor was leaning against the wall, bleeding and breathing noisily. He looked as though he could barely stand, let alone fight. "Throw down the sword, and we'll take you back to Harrenhal," Polliver told him.

"So Gregor can finish me himself?"

The Tickler said, "Maybe he'll give you to me."

"If you want me, come get me." Sandor pushed away from the wall and stood in a half-crouch behind the bench, his sword held across his body.

"You think we won't?" said Polliver. "You're drunk."

"Might be," said the Hound, "but you're dead." His foot lashed out and caught the bench, driving it hard into Polliver's shins. Somehow the bearded man kept his feet, but the Hound ducked under his wild slash and brought his own sword up in a vicious backhand cut. Blood spattered on the ceiling and walls. The blade caught in the middle of Polliver's face, and when the Hound wrenched it loose half his head came with it.

The Tickler backed away. Arya could smell his fear. The shortsword in his hand suddenly seemed almost a toy against the long blade the Hound was holding, and he wasn't armored either. He moved swiftly, light on his feet, never taking his eyes off Sandor Clegane. It was the easiest thing in the world for Arya to step up behind him and stab him.

"Is there gold hidden in the village?" she shouted as she drove the blade up through his back. "Is there silver? Gems?" She stabbed twice more. "Is there food? Where is Lord Beric?" She was on top of him by then, still stabbing. "Where did he go? How many men were with him? How many knights? How many bowmen? How many, how many, how many, how many, how many, how many? Is there *gold* in the village?"

Her hands were red and sticky when Sandor dragged her off him. "Enough," was all he said. He was bleeding like a butchered pig himself, and dragging one leg when he walked.

"There's one more," Arya reminded him.

The squire had pulled the knife out of his belly and was trying to stop the blood with his hands. When the Hound yanked him upright, he screamed and started to blubber like a baby. "Mercy," he wept, "please. Don't kill me. Mother have mercy."

"Do I look like your bloody mother?" The Hound looked like nothing human. "You killed this one too," he told Arya. "Pricked him in his bowels, that's the end of him. He'll be a long time dying, though."

The boy didn't seemed to hear him. "I came for the girls," he whimpered. ". . . make me a man, Polly said . . . oh, gods, please, take me to a castle . . . a maester, take me to a maester, my father's got gold . . . it was only for the girls . . . mercy, ser."

The Hound gave him a crack across the face that made him scream again. "Don't call me ser." He turned back to Arya. "This one is yours, she-wolf. You do it."

She knew what he meant. Arya went to Polliver and knelt in his blood long enough to undo his swordbelt. Hanging beside his dagger was a slimmer blade, too long to be a dirk, too short to be a man's sword . . . but it felt just right in her hand.

"You remember where the heart is?" the Hound asked.

She nodded. The squire rolled his eyes. "Mercy."

Needle slipped between his ribs and gave it to him.

"Good." Sandor's voice was thick with pain. "If these three were whoring here, Gregor must hold the ford as well as Harrenhal. More of his pets could ride up any moment, and we've killed enough of the bloody buggers for one day."

"Where will we go?" she asked.

"Saltpans." He put a big hand on her shoulder to keep from falling. "Get some wine, she-wolf. And take whatever coin they have as well, we'll need it. If there's ships at Saltpans, we can reach the Vale by sea." His mouth twitched at her, as more blood ran down from where his ear had been. "Maybe Lady Lysa will marry you to her little Robert. *There's* a match I'd like to see." He started to laugh, then groaned instead.

When the time came to leave, he needed Arya's help to get back up on Stranger. He had tied a strip of cloth about his neck and another around his thigh, and taken the squire's cloak off its peg by the door. The cloak was green, with a green arrow on a white bend, but when the Hound wadded it up and pressed it to his ear it soon turned red. Arya was afraid he would collapse the moment they set out, but somehow he stayed in the saddle.

They could not risk meeting whoever held the ruby ford, so instead of following the kingsroad they angled south by east, through weedy fields, woods, and marshes. It was hours before they reached the banks of the Trident. The river had returned meekly to its accustomed channel, Arya saw, all its wet brown rage vanished with the rains. *It's tired too*, she thought.

Close by the water's edge, they found some willows rising from a jumble of weathered rocks. Together the rocks and trees formed a sort of natural fort where they could hide from both river and trail. "Here will do," the Hound said. "Water the horses and gather some deadwood for a fire." When he dismounted, he had to catch himself on a tree limb to keep from falling.

"Won't the smoke be seen?"

"Anyone wants to find us, all they need to do is follow my blood. Water and wood. But bring me that wineskin first."

When he got the fire going, Sandor propped up his helm in the flames, emptied half the wineskin into it, and collapsed back against a jut of moss-covered stone as if he never meant to rise again. He made Arya wash out the squire's cloak and cut it into strips. Those went into his helm as well. "If I had more wine, I'd drink till I was dead to the world. Maybe I ought to send you back to that bloody inn for another skin or three."

"No," Arya said. *He wouldn't, would he? If he does, I'll just leave him and ride off.*

Sandor laughed at the fear on her face. "A jest, wolf girl. A bloody jest. Find me a stick, about so long and not too big around. And wash the mud off it. I hate the taste of mud."

He didn't like the first two sticks she brought him. By the time she found one that suited him, the flames had scorched his dog's snout black all the way to the eyes. Inside the wine was boiling madly. "Get the cup from my bedroll and dip it half full," he told her. "Be careful. You knock the damn thing over, I *will* send you back for more. Take the wine and pour it on my wounds. Think you can do that?" Arya nodded. "Then what are you waiting for?" he growled.

Her knuckles brushed the steel the first time she filled the cup, burning her so badly she got blisters. Arya had to bite her lip to keep from screaming. The Hound used the stick for the same purpose, clamping it between his teeth as she poured. She did the gash in his thigh first, then the shallower cut on the back of his neck. Sandor coiled his right hand into a fist and beat against the ground when she did his leg. When it came to his neck, he bit the stick so hard it broke, and she had to find him a new one. She could see the terror in his eyes. "Turn your head." She trickled the wine down over the raw red flesh where his ear had been, and fingers of brown blood and red wine crept over his jaw. He *did* scream then, despite the stick. Then he passed out from the pain.

Arya figured the rest out by herself. She fished the strips they'd made of the squire's cloak out of the bottom of the helm and used them to bind the cuts. When she came to his ear, she had to wrap up half his head to stop the bleeding. By then dusk was settling over the Trident. She let the horses graze, then hobbled them for the night and made herself as comfortable as she could in a niche between two rocks. The fire burned a while and died. Arya watched the moon through the branches overhead.

"Ser Gregor the Mountain," she said softly. "Dunsen, Raff the Sweetling, Ser Ilyn, Ser Meryn, Queen Cersei." It made her feel queer to leave out Polliver and the Tickler. And Joffrey too. She was glad he was dead, but she wished she could have been there to see him die, or maybe kill him herself. *Polliver said that Sansa killed him, and the Imp.* Could that be true? The Imp was a Lannister, and Sansa ... *I wish I could change into a wolf and grow wings and fly away.*

If Sansa was gone too, there were no more Starks but her. Jon was on the Wall a thousand leagues away, but he was a Snow, and these different aunts and uncles the Hound wanted to sell her to, they weren't Starks either. They weren't *wolves.*

Sandor moaned, and she rolled onto her side to look at him. She had left his name out too, she realized. Why had she done that? She tried to think of Mycah, but it was hard to remember what he'd looked like. She hadn't known him long. *All he ever did was play at swords with me.* "The Hound," she whispered, and, "*Valar morghulis.*" Maybe he'd be dead by morning . . .

But when the pale dawn light came filtering through the trees, it was him who woke her with the toe of his boot. She had dreamed she was a wolf again, chasing a riderless horse up a hill with a pack behind her, but his foot brought her back just as they were closing for the kill.

The Hound was still weak, every movement slow and clumsy. He slumped in the saddle, and sweated, and his ear began to bleed through the bandage. He needed all his strength just to keep from falling off Stranger. Had the Mountain's men come hunting them, she doubted if he would even be able to lift a sword. Arya glanced over her shoulder, but there was nothing behind them but a crow flitting from tree to tree. The only sound was the river.

Long before noon, Sandor Clegane was reeling. There were hours of daylight still remaining when he called a halt. "I need to rest," was all he said. This time when he dismounted he *did* fall. Instead of trying to get back up he crawled weakly under a tree, and leaned up against the trunk. "Bloody hell," he cursed. "Bloody hell." When he saw Arya staring at him, he said, "I'd skin you alive for a cup of wine, girl."

She brought him water instead. He drank a little of it, complained that it tasted of mud, and slid into a noisy fevered sleep. When she touched him, his skin was burning up. Arya sniffed at his bandages the way Maester Luwin had done sometimes when treating her cut or scrape. His face had bled the worst, but it was the wound on his thigh that smelled funny to her.

She wondered how far this Saltpans was, and whether she could find it by herself. *I wouldn't have to kill him. If I just rode off and left him, he'd die all by himself. He'll die of fever, and lie there beneath that tree until the end of days.* But maybe it would be better if she killed him herself. She had killed the squire at the inn and he hadn't done anything except grab her arm. The Hound had killed Mycah. *Mycah and more. I bet he's killed a hundred Mycahs.* He probably would have killed her too, if not for the ransom.

Needle glinted as she drew it. Polliver had kept it nice and sharp, at least. She turned her body sideways in a water dancer's stance without even thinking about it. Dead leaves crunched beneath her feet. *Quick as a snake*, she thought. *Smooth as summer silk.*

His eyes opened. "You remember where the heart is?" he asked in a hoarse whisper.

As still as stone she stood. "I . . . I was only . . ."

"*Don't lie*," he growled. "I hate liars. I hate gutless frauds even worse.

Go on, do it." When Arya did not move, he said, "I killed your butcher's boy. I cut him near in half, and laughed about it after." He made a queer sound, and it took her a moment to realize he was sobbing. "And the little bird, your pretty sister, I stood there in my white cloak and let them beat her. I *took* the bloody song, she never gave it. I meant to take her too. I should have. I should have fucked her bloody and ripped her heart out before leaving her for that dwarf." A spasm of pain twisted his face. "Do you mean to make me beg, bitch? *Do it!* The gift of mercy . . . avenge your little Michael . . ."

"*Mycah.*" Arya stepped away from him. "You don't deserve the gift of mercy."

The Hound watched her saddle Craven through eyes bright with fever. Not once did he attempt to rise and stop her. But when she mounted, he said, "A real wolf would finish a wounded animal."

Maybe some real wolves will find you, Arya thought. *Maybe they'll smell you when the sun goes down.* Then he would learn what wolves did to dogs. "You shouldn't have hit me with an axe," she said. "You should have saved my mother." She turned her horse and rode away from him, and never looked back once.

On a bright morning six days later, she came to a place where the Trident began to widen out and the air smelled more of salt than trees. She stayed close to the water, passing fields and farms, and a little after midday a town appeared before her. *Saltpans*, she hoped. A small castle dominated the town; no more than a holdfast, really, a single tall square keep with a bailey and a curtain wall. Most of the shops and inns and alehouses around the harbor had been plundered or burned, though some looked still inhabited. But the port was there, and eastward spread the Bay of Crabs, its waters shimmering blue and green in the sun.

And there were ships.

Three, thought Arya, *there are three.* Two were only river galleys, shallow draft boats made to ply the waters of the Trident. The third was bigger, a salt sea trader with two banks of oars, a gilded prow, and three tall masts with furled purple sails. Her hull was painted purple too. Arya rode Craven down to the docks to get a better look. Strangers are not so strange in a port as they are in little villages, and no one seemed to care who she was or why she was here.

I need silver. The realization made her bite her lip. They had found a stag and a dozen coppers on Polliver, eight silvers on the pimply squire she'd killed, and only a couple of pennies in the Tickler's purse. But the Hound had told her to pull off his boots and slice open his blood-drenched clothes, and she'd turned up a stag in each toe, and three golden dragons sewn in the lining of his jerkin. Sandor had kept it all, though. *That wasn't fair. It was mine as much as his.* If she had given him the gift of mercy . . . she hadn't, though. She couldn't go back, no more than she could beg for help. *Begging for help never gets you any.* She would have to sell Craven, and hope she brought enough.

The stable had been burnt, she learned from a boy by the docks, but the woman who'd owned it was still trading behind the sept. Arya found her easily; a big, robust woman with a good horsey smell to her. She liked Craven at first look, asked Arya how she'd come by her, and grinned at her answer. "She's a well-bred horse, that's plain enough, and I don't doubt she belonged to a knight, sweetling," she said. "But the knight wasn't no dead brother o' yours. I been dealing with the castle there many a year, so I know what gentleborn folk is like. This mare is well-bred, but you're not." She poked a finger at Arya's chest. "Found her or stole her, never mind which, that's how it was. Only way a scruffy little thing like you comes to ride a palfrey."

Arya bit her lip. "Does that mean you won't buy her?"

The woman chuckled. "It means you'll take what I give you, sweetling. Else we go down to the castle, and maybe you get nothing. Or even hanged, for stealing some good knight's horse."

A half-dozen other Saltpans folks were around, going about their business, so Arya knew she couldn't kill the woman. Instead she had to bite her lip and let herself be cheated. The purse she got was pitifully flat, and when she asked for more for the saddle and bridle and blanket, the woman just laughed at her.

She would never have cheated the Hound, she thought during the long walk back to the docks. The distance seemed to have grown by miles since she'd ridden it.

The purple galley was still there. If the ship had sailed while she was being robbed, that would have been too much to bear. A cask of mead was being rolled up the plank when she arrived. When she tried to follow, a sailor up on deck shouted down at her in a tongue she did not know. "I want to see the captain," Arya told him. He only shouted louder. But the commotion drew the attention of a stout grey-haired man in a coat of purple wool, and he spoke the Common Tongue. "I am captain here," he said. "What is your wish? Be quick, child, we have a tide to catch."

"I want to go north, to the Wall. Here, I can pay." She gave him the purse. "The Night's Watch has a castle on the sea."

"Eastwatch." The captain spilled out the silver onto his palm and frowned. "Is this all you have?"

It is not enough, Arya knew without being told. She could see it on his face. "I wouldn't need a cabin or anything," she said. "I could sleep down in the hold, or . . ."

"Take her on as cabin girl," said a passing oarsman, a bolt of wool over one shoulder. "She can sleep with me."

"Mind your tongue," the captain snapped.

"I could work," said Arya. "I could scrub the decks. I scrubbed a castle steps once. Or I could row . . ."

"No," he said, "you couldn't." He gave her back her coins. "It would make no difference if you could, child. The north has nothing for us. Ice and war and pirates. We saw a dozen pirate ships making north as we rounded Crackclaw Point, and I have no wish to meet them again. From here we bend our oars for home, and I suggest you do the same."

I have no home, Arya thought. *I have no pack. And now I don't even have a horse.*

The captain was turning away when she said, "What ship is this, my lord?"

He paused long enough to give her a weary smile. "This is the galleas *Titan's Daughter*, of the Free City of Braavos."

"Wait," Arya said suddenly. "I have something else." She had stuffed it down inside her smallclothes to keep it safe, so she had to dig deep to find it, while the oarsmen laughed and the captain lingered with obvious impatience. "One more silver will make no difference, child," he finally said.

"It's not silver." Her fingers closed on it. "It's iron. Here." She pressed it into his hand, the small black iron coin that Jaqen H'ghar had given her, so worn the man whose head it bore had no features. *It's probably worthless, but . . .*

The captain turned it over and blinked at it, then looked at her again. "This . . . how . . . ?"

Jaqen said to say the words too. Arya crossed her arms against her chest. "*Valar morghulis*," she said, as loud as if she'd known what it meant.

"*Valar dohaeris*," he replied, touching his brow with two fingers. "Of *course* you shall have a cabin."

SAMWELL

"He sucks harder than mine." Gilly stroked the babe's head as she held him to her nipple.

"He's hungry," said the blonde woman Val, the one the black brothers called the wildling princess. "He's lived on goats' milk up to now, and potions from that blind maester."

The boy did not have a name yet, no more than Gilly's did. That was the wildling way. Not even Mance Rayder's son would get a name till his third year, it would seem, though Sam had heard the brothers calling him "the little prince" and "born-in-battle."

He watched the child nurse at Gilly's breast, and then he watched Jon watch. *Jon is smiling.* A sad smile, still, but definitely a smile of sorts. Sam was glad to see it. *It is the first time I've seen him smile since I got back.*

They had walked from the Nightfort to Deep Lake, and from Deep Lake to Queensgate, following a narrow track from one castle to the next, never out of sight of the Wall. A day and a half from Castle Black, as they trudged along on callused feet, Gilly heard horses behind them, and turned to see a column of black riders coming from the west. "My brothers," Sam assured her. "No one uses this road but the Night's Watch." It had turned out to be Ser Denys Mallister from the Shadow Tower, along with the wounded Bowen Marsh and the survivors from the fight at the Bridge of Skulls. When Sam saw Dywen, Giant, and Dolorous Edd Tollett, he broke down and wept.

It was from them that he learned about the battle beneath the Wall. "Stannis landed his knights at Eastwatch, and Cotter Pyke led him along the ranger's roads, to take the wildlings unawares," Giant told him. "He smashed them. Mance Rayder was taken captive, a thousand of his best slain, including Harma Dogshead. The rest scattered like leaves before a storm, we heard." *The gods are good*, Sam thought. If he had not gotten lost as he made his way south from Craster's Keep, he and Gilly might have walked right into the battle . . . or into Mance Rayder's camp, at the very least. That might have been well enough for Gilly and the boy, but not for him. Sam had heard all the stories about what wildlings did with captured crows. He shuddered.

Nothing that his brothers told him prepared him for what he found at Castle Black, however. The common hall had burned to the ground and the great wooden stair was a mound of broken ice and scorched timbers. Donal Noye was dead, along with Rast, Deaf Dick, Red Alyn, and so many more, yet the castle was more crowded than Sam had ever seen; not with black brothers, but with the king's soldiers, more than a thousand of them. There was a king in the King's Tower for the first time in living memory, and banners flew from the Lance, Hardin's Tower, the Grey Keep, the Shieldhall, and other buildings that had stood empty and abandoned for long years. "The big one, the gold with the black stag, that's the royal standard of House Baratheon," he told Gilly, who had never seen banners before. "The fox-and-flowers is House Florent. The turtle is Estermont, the swordfish is Bar Emmon, and the crossed trumpets are for Wensington."

"They're all bright as flowers." Gilly pointed. "I like those yellow ones, with the fire. Look, and some of the fighters have the same thing on their blouses."

"A fiery heart. I don't know whose sigil that is."

He found out soon enough. "*Queen's men*," Pyp told him – after he let out a whoop, and shouted, "Run and bar the doors, lads, it's Sam the Slayer come back from the grave," while Grenn was hugging Sam so hard he thought his ribs might break – "but best you don't go asking where the queen is. Stannis left her at Eastwatch, with their daughter and his fleet. He brought no woman but the red one."

"The red one?" said Sam uncertainly.

"Melisandre of Asshai," said Grenn. "The king's sorceress. They say she burned a man alive at Dragonstone so Stannis would have favorable winds for his voyage north. She rode beside him in the battle too, and gave him his magic sword. Lightbringer, they call it. Wait till you see it. It glows like it had a piece of sun inside it." He looked at Sam again and grinned a big helpless stupid grin. "I still can't believe you're here."

Jon Snow had smiled to see him too, but it was a tired smile, like the one he wore now. "You made it back after all," he said. "And brought Gilly out as well. You've done well, Sam."

Jon had done more than well himself, to hear Grenn tell it. Yet even capturing the Horn of Winter and a wildling prince had not been enough for Ser Alliser Thorne and his friends, who still named him turncloak. Though Maester Aemon said his wound was healing well, Jon bore other scars, deeper than the ones around his eye. *He grieves for his wildling girl, and for his brothers.*

"It's strange," he said to Sam. "Craster had no love for Mance, nor Mance for Craster, but now Craster's daughter is feeding Mance's son."

"I have the milk," Gilly said, her voice soft and shy. "Mine takes only a little. He's not so greedy as this one."

The wildling woman Val turned to face them. "I've heard the queen's men saying that the red woman means to give Mance to the fire, as soon as he is strong enough."

Jon gave her a weary look. "Mance is a deserter from the Night's Watch. The penalty for that is death. If the Watch had taken him, he would have been hanged by now, but he's the king's captive, and no one knows the king's mind but the red woman."

"I want to see him," Val said. "I want to show him his son. He deserves that much, before you kill him."

Sam tried to explain. "No one is permitted to see him but Maester Aemon, my lady."

"If it were in my power, Mance could hold his son." Jon's smile was gone. "I'm sorry, Val." He turned away. "Sam and I have duties to return to. Well, Sam does, anyway. We'll ask about your seeing Mance. That's all I can promise."

Sam lingered long enough to give Gilly's hand a squeeze and promise to return again after supper. Then he hurried after. There were guards outside the door, queen's men with spears. Jon was halfway down the steps, but he waited when he heard Sam puffing after him. "You're more than fond of Gilly, aren't you?"

Sam reddened. "Gilly's good. She's good and kind." He was glad that his long nightmare was done, glad to be back with his brothers at Castle Black . . . but some nights, alone in his cell, he thought of how warm Gilly had been when they'd curled up beneath the furs with the babe between them. "She . . . she made me braver, Jon. Not *brave*, but . . . braver."

"You know you cannot keep her," Jon said gently, "no more than I could stay with Ygritte. You said the words, Sam, the same as I did. The same as all of us."

"I know. Gilly said she'd be a wife to me, but . . . I told her about the words, and what they meant. I don't know if that made her sad or glad, but I told her." He swallowed nervously and said, "Jon, could there be honor in a lie, if it were told for a . . . a good purpose?"

"It would depend on the lie and the purpose, I suppose." Jon looked at Sam. "I wouldn't advise it. You're not made to lie, Sam. You blush and squeak and stammer."

"I do," said Sam, "but I could lie in a letter. I'm better with a quill in hand. I had a . . . a thought. When things are more settled here, I thought maybe the best thing for Gilly . . . I thought I might send her to Horn Hill. To my mother and sisters and my . . . my f-f-father. If Gilly were to say the babe was m-mine . . ." He was blushing again. "My mother would want him, I know. She would find some place for Gilly, some kind of service, it wouldn't be as hard as serving Craster. And Lord R-Randyll, he . . . he would never *say* so, but he might be pleased to believe I got a bastard on some wildling girl. At least it would prove I was man enough to lie with a woman and father a child. He told me once that I was sure to die a maiden, that no woman would ever . . . you know . . . Jon, if I did this, wrote this lie . . . would that be a good thing? The life the boy would have . . ."

"Growing up a bastard in his grandfather's castle?" Jon shrugged. "That depends in great part on your father, and what sort of boy this is. If he takes after you . . ."

"He won't. Craster's his real father. You saw him, he was hard as an old tree stump, and Gilly is stronger than she looks."

"If the boy shows any skill with sword or lance, he should have a place with your father's household guard at the least," Jon said. "It's not unknown for bastards to be trained as squires and raised to knighthood. But you'd best be sure Gilly can play this game convincingly. From what you've told me of Lord Randyll, I doubt he would take kindly to being deceived."

More guards were posted on the steps outside the tower. These were king's men, though; Sam had quickly learned the difference. The king's men were as earthy and impious as any other soldiers, but the queen's men were fervid in their devotion to Melisandre of Asshai and her Lord of Light. "Are you going to the practice yard again?" Sam asked as they crossed the yard. "Is it wise to train so hard before your leg's done healing?"

Jon shrugged. "What else is there for me to do? Marsh has removed me from duty, for fear that I'm still a turncloak."

"It's only a few who believe that," Sam assured him. "Ser Alliser and his friends. Most of the brothers know better. King Stannis knows as well, I'll wager. You brought him the Horn of Winter and captured Mance Rayder's son."

"All I did was protect Val and the babe against looters when the wild-lings fled, and keep them there until the rangers found us. I never *captured* anyone. King Stannis keeps his men well in hand, that's plain. He lets them plunder some, but I've only heard of three wildling women being raped, and the men who did it have all been gelded. I suppose I should have been killing the free folk as they ran. Ser Alliser has been putting it about that the only time I bared my sword was to defend our foes. I failed to kill Mance Rayder because I was in league with him, he says."

"That's only Ser Alliser," said Sam. "Everyone knows the sort of man he is." With his noble birth, his knighthood, and his long years in the Watch, Ser Alliser Thorne might have been a strong challenger for the Lord Commander's title, but almost all the men he'd trained during his years as master-at-arms despised him. His name had been offered, of course, but after running a weak sixth on the first day and actually *losing* votes on the second, Thorne had withdrawn to support Lord Janos Slynt.

"What everyone knows is that Ser Alliser is a knight from a noble line, and trueborn, while I'm the bastard who killed Qhorin Halfhand and bedded with a spearwife. The *warg*, I've heard them call me. How can I be a warg without a wolf, I ask you?" His mouth twisted. "I don't even dream of Ghost anymore. All my dreams are of the crypts, of the stone kings on their thrones. Sometimes I hear Robb's voice, and my father's, as if they were at a feast. But there's a wall between us, and I know that no place has been set for me."

The living have no place at the feasts of the dead. It tore the heart from Sam to hold his silence then. *Bran's not dead, Jon,* he wanted to stay. *He's with friends, and they're going north on a giant elk to find a three-eyed crow in the depths of the haunted forest.* It sounded so mad that there were times Sam Tarly thought he must have dreamt it all, conjured it whole from fever and fear and hunger . . . but he would have blurted it out anyway, if he had not given his word.

Three times he had sworn to keep the secret; once to Bran himself, once to that strange boy Jojen Reed, and last of all to Coldhands. "The world believes the boy is dead," his rescuer had said as they parted. "Let his bones lie undisturbed. We want no seekers coming after us. Swear it, Samwell of the Night's Watch. Swear it for the life you owe me."

Miserable, Sam shifted his weight and said, "Lord Janos will never be chosen Lord Commander." It was the best comfort he had to offer Jon, the only comfort. "That won't happen."

"Sam, you're a sweet fool. Open your eyes. It's been happening for days." Jon pushed his hair back out of his eyes and said, "I may know nothing, but I know that. Now pray excuse me, I need to hit someone very hard with a sword."

There was naught that Sam could do but watch him stride off toward the armory and the practice yard. That was where Jon Snow spent most of his waking hours. With Ser Endrew dead and Ser Alliser disinterested,

Castle Black had no master-at-arms, so Jon had taken it on himself to work with some of the rawer recruits; Satin, Horse, Hop-Robin with his clubfoot, Arron and Emrick. And when they had duties, he would train alone for hours with sword and shield and spear, or match himself against anyone who cared to take him on.

Sam, you're a sweet fool, he could hear Jon saying, all the way back to the maester's keep. *Open your eyes. It's been happening for days.* Could he be right? A man needed the votes of two-thirds of the Sworn Brothers to become the Lord Commander of the Night's Watch, and after nine days and nine votes no one was even close to that. Lord Janos *had* been gaining, true, creeping up past first Bowen Marsh and then Othell Yarwyck, but he was still well behind Ser Denys Mallister of the Shadow Tower and Cotter Pyke of Eastwatch-by-the-Sea. *One of them will be the new Lord Commander, surely*, Sam told himself.

Stannis had posted guards outside the maester's door too. Within, the rooms were hot and crowded with the wounded from the battle; black brothers, king's men, and queen's men, all three. Clydas was shuffling amongst them with flagons of goats' milk and dreamwine, but Maester Aemon had not yet returned from his morning call on Mance Rayder. Sam hung his cloak upon a peg and went to lend a hand. But even as he fetched and poured and changed dressings, Jon's words nagged at him. *Sam, you're a sweet fool. Open your eyes. It's been happening for days.*

It was a good hour before he could excuse himself to feed the ravens. On the way up to the rookery, he stopped to check the tally he had made of last night's count. At the start of the choosing, more than thirty names had been offered, but most had withdrawn once it became clear they could not win. Seven remained as of last night. Ser Denys Mallister had collected two hundred and thirteen tokens, Cotter Pyke one hundred and eighty-seven, Lord Slynt seventy-four, Othell Yarwyck sixty, Bowen Marsh forty-nine, Three-Finger Hobb five, and Dolorous Edd Tollett one. *Pyp and his stupid japes.* Sam shuffled through the earlier counts. Ser Denys, Cotter Pyke, and Bowen Marsh had all been falling since the third day, Othell Yarwyck since the sixth. Only Lord Janos Slynt was climbing, day after day after day.

He could hear the birds *quorking* in the rookery, so he put the papers away and climbed the steps to feed them. Three more ravens had come in, he saw with pleasure. *"Snow,"* they cried at him. *"Snow, snow, snow."* He had taught them that. Even with the newcomers, the ravenry seemed dismally empty. Few of the birds that Aemon had sent off had returned as yet. *One reached Stannis, though. One found Dragonstone, and a king who still cared.* A thousand leagues south, Sam knew, his father had joined House Tarly to the cause of the boy on the Iron Throne, but neither King Joffrey nor little King Tommen had bestirred himself when the Watch cried out for help. *What good is a king who will not defend his realm?* he thought angrily, remembering the night on the Fist of the First Men and the terrible trek to Craster's Keep through darkness, fear, and falling snow. The queen's men made him uneasy, it was true, but at least they had *come.*

That night at supper Sam looked for Jon Snow, but did not see him anywhere in the cavernous stone vault where the brothers now took their meals. He finally took a place on the bench near his other friends. Pyp was telling Dolorous Edd about the contest they'd had to see which of the straw soldiers could collect the most wildling arrows. "You were leading most of the way, but Watt of Long Lake got three in the last day and passed you."

"I never win anything," Dolorous Edd complained. "The gods always smiled on Watt, though. When the wildlings knocked him off the Bridge of Skulls, somehow he landed in a nice deep pool of water. How lucky was that, missing all those rocks?"

"Was it a long fall?" Grenn wanted to know. "Did landing in the pool of water save his life?"

"No," said Dolorous Edd. "He was dead already, from that axe in his head. Still, it was pretty lucky, missing the rocks."

Three-Finger Hobb had promised the brothers roast haunch of mammoth that night, maybe in hopes of cadging a few more votes. *If that was his notion, he should have found a younger mammoth*, Sam thought, as he pulled a string of gristle out from between his teeth. Sighing, he pushed the food away.

There would be another vote shortly, and the tensions in the air were thicker than the smoke. Cotter Pyke sat by the fire, surrounded by rangers from Eastwatch. Ser Denys Mallister was near the door with a smaller group of Shadow Tower men. *Janos Slynt has the best place*, Sam realized, *halfway between the flames and the drafts.* He was alarmed to see Bowen Marsh beside him, wan-faced and haggard, his head still wrapped in linen, but listening to all that Lord Janos had to say. When he pointed that out to his friends, Pyp said, "And look down there, that's Ser Alliser whispering with Othell Yarwyck."

After the meal Maester Aemon rose to ask if any of the brothers wished to speak before they cast their tokens. Dolorous Edd got up, stone-faced and glum as ever. "I just want to say to whoever is voting for me that I would certainly make an awful Lord Commander. But so would all these others." He was followed by Bowen Marsh, who stood with one hand on Lord Slynt's shoulder. "Brothers and friends, I am asking that my name be withdrawn from this choosing. My wound still troubles me, and the task is too large for me, I fear ... but not for Lord Janos here, who commanded the gold cloaks of King's Landing for many years. Let us all give him our support."

Sam heard angry mutters from Cotter Pyke's end of the room, and Ser Denys looked at one of his companions and shook his head. *It is too late, the damage is done.* He wondered where Jon was, and why he had stayed away.

Most of the brothers were unlettered, so by tradition the choosing was done by dropping tokens into a big potbellied iron kettle that Three-Finger Hobb and Owen the Oaf had dragged over from the kitchens. The barrels of tokens were off in a corner behind a heavy drape, so the voters could make their choice unseen. You were allowed to have a friend cast your token if you had duty, so some men took two tokens, three, or four, and Ser Denys and Cotter Pyke voted for the garrisons they had left behind.

When the hall was finally empty, save for them, Sam and Clydas upended the kettle in front of Maester Aemon. A cascade of seashells, stones, and copper pennies covered the table. Aemon's wrinkled hands sorted with surprising speed, moving the shells here, the stones there, the pennies to one side, the occasional arrowhead, nail, and acorn off to themselves. Sam and Clydas counted the piles, each of them keeping his own tally.

Tonight it was Sam's turn to give his results first. "Two hundred and three for Ser Denys Mallister," he said. "One hundred and sixty-nine for Cotter Pyke. One hundred and thirty-seven for Lord Janos Slynt, seventy-two for Othell Yarwyck, five for Three-Finger Hobb, and two for Dolorous Edd."

"I had one hundred and sixty-eight for Pyke," Clydas said. "We are two votes short by my count, and one by Sam's."

"Sam's count is correct," said Maester Aemon. "Jon Snow did not cast a token. It makes no matter. No one is close."

Sam was more relieved than disappointed. Even with Bowen Marsh's support, Lord Janos was still only third. "Who are these five who keep voting for Three-Finger Hobb?" he wondered.

"Brothers who want him out of the kitchens?" said Clydas.

"Ser Denys is down ten votes since yesterday," Sam pointed out. "And Cotter Pyke is down almost twenty. That's not good."

"Not good for their hopes of becoming Lord Commander, certainly," said Maester Aemon. "Yet it may be good for the Night's Watch, in the end. That is not for us to say. Ten days is not unduly long. There was once a choosing that lasted near two years, some seven hundred votes. The brothers will come to a decision in their own time."

Yes, Sam thought, *but what decision?*

Later, over cups of watered wine in the privacy of Pyp's cell, Sam's tongue loosened and he found himself thinking aloud. "Cotter Pyke and

Ser Denys Mallister have been losing ground, but between them they still have almost two-thirds," he told Pyp and Grenn. "Either one would be fine as Lord Commander. Someone needs to convince one of them to withdraw and support the other."

"Someone?" said Grenn, doubtfully. "What someone?"

"Grenn is so dumb he thinks *someone* might be him," said Pyp. "Maybe when someone is done with Pyke and Mallister, he should convince King Stannis to marry Queen Cersei too."

"King Stannis is married," Grenn objected.

"What am I going to do with him, Sam?" sighed Pyp.

"Cotter Pyke and Ser Denys don't like each other much," Grenn argued stubbornly. "They fight about *everything*."

"Yes, but only because they have different ideas about what's best for the Watch," said Sam. "If we explained –"

"*We?*" said Pyp. "How did *someone* change to *we?* I'm the mummer's monkey, remember? And Grenn is, well, *Grenn*." He smiled at Sam, and wiggled his ears. "You, now . . . you're a lord's son, and the maester's steward . . ."

"And Sam the Slayer," said Grenn. "You slew an Other."

"It was the *dragonglass* that killed it," Sam told him for the hundredth time.

"A lord's son, the maester's steward, and Sam the Slayer," Pyp mused. "*You* could talk to them, might be . . ."

"I could," said Sam, sounding as gloomy as Dolorous Edd, "if I wasn't too craven to face them."

JON

Jon prowled around Satin in a slow circle, sword in hand, forcing him to turn. "Get your shield up," he said.

"It's too heavy," the Oldtown boy complained.

"It's as heavy as it needs to be to stop a sword," Jon said. "Now get it up." He stepped forward, slashing. Satin jerked the shield up in time to catch the sword on its rim, and swung his own blade at Jon's ribs. "Good," Jon said, when he felt the impact on his own shield. "That was good. But you need to put your body into it. Get your weight behind the steel and you'll do more damage than with arm strength alone. Come, try it again, drive at me, but keep the shield up or I'll ring your head like a bell . . ."

Instead Satin took a step backward and raised his visor. "Jon," he said, in an anxious voice.

When he turned, she was standing behind him, with half a dozen queen's men around her. *Small wonder the yard grew so quiet.* He had glimpsed Melisandre at her nightfires, and coming and going about the castle, but never so close. *She's beautiful*, he thought . . . but there was something more than a little unsettling about red eyes. "My lady."

"The king would speak with you, Jon Snow."

Jon thrust the practice sword into the earth. "Might I be allowed to change? I am in no fit state to stand before a king."

"We shall await you atop the Wall," said Melisandre. *We*, Jon heard, *not he. It's as they say. This is his true queen, not the one he left at Eastwatch.*

He hung his mail and plate inside the armory, returned to his own cell, discarded his sweat-stained clothes, and donned a fresh set of blacks. It would be cold and windy in the cage, he knew, and colder and windier still on top of the ice, so he chose a heavy hooded cloak. Last of all he collected Longclaw, and slung the bastard sword across his back.

Melisandre was waiting for him at the base of the Wall. She had sent her queen's men away. "What does His Grace want of me?" Jon asked her as they entered the cage.

"All you have to give, Jon Snow. He is a king."

He shut the door and pulled the bell cord. The winch began to turn. They rose. The day was bright and the Wall was weeping, long fingers of water trickling down its face and glinting in the sun. In the close confines of the iron cage, he was acutely aware of the red woman's presence. *She even smells red.* The scent reminded him of Mikken's forge, of the way iron smelled when red-hot; the scent was smoke and blood. *Kissed by fire,* he thought, remembering Ygritte. The wind got in amongst Melisandre's long red robes and sent them flapping against Jon's legs as he stood beside her. "You are not cold, my lady?" he asked her.

She laughed. "Never." The ruby at her throat seemed to pulse, in time with the beating of her heart. "The Lord's fire lives within me, Jon Snow. Feel." She put her hand on his cheek, and held it there while he felt how warm she was. "That is how life should feel," she told him. "Only death is cold."

They found Stannis Baratheon standing alone at the edge of the Wall, brooding over the field where he had won his battle, and the great green forest beyond. He was dressed in the same black breeches, tunic, and boots that a brother of the Night's Watch might wear. Only his cloak set him apart; a heavy golden cloak trimmed in black fur, and pinned with a brooch in the shape of a flaming heart. "I have brought you the Bastard of Winterfell, Your Grace," said Melisandre.

Stannis turned to study him. Beneath his heavy brow were eyes like bottomless blue pools. His hollow cheeks and strong jaw were covered with a short-cropped blue-black beard that did little to conceal the gauntness of his face, and his teeth were clenched. His neck and shoulders were clenched as well, and his right hand. Jon found himself remembering something Donal Noye once said about the Baratheon brothers. *Robert was the true steel. Stannis is pure iron, black and hard and strong, but brittle, the way iron gets. He'll break before he bends.* Uneasily, he knelt, wondering why this brittle king had need of him.

"Rise. I have heard much and more of you, Lord Snow."

"I am no lord, sire." Jon rose. "I know what you have heard. That I am a turncloak, and craven. That I slew my brother Qhorin Halfhand so the wildlings would spare my life. That I rode with Mance Rayder, and took a wildling wife."

"Aye. All that, and more. You are a warg too, they say, a skinchanger who walks at night as a wolf." King Stannis had a hard smile. "How much of it is true?"

"I had a direwolf, Ghost. I left him when I climbed the Wall near Greyguard, and have not seen him since. Qhorin Halfhand commanded me to join the wildlings. He knew they would make me kill him to prove myself, and told me to do whatever they asked of me. The woman was named Ygritte. I broke my vows with her, but I swear to you on my father's name that I never turned my cloak."

"I believe you," the king said.

That startled him. "Why?"

Stannis snorted. "I know Janos Slynt. And I knew Ned Stark as well. Your father was no friend of mine, but only a fool would doubt his honor or his honesty. You have his look." A big man, Stannis Baratheon towered over Jon, but he was so gaunt that he looked ten years older than he was. "I know more than you might think, Jon Snow. I know it was you who found the dragonglass dagger that Randyll Tarly's son used to slay the Other."

"Ghost found it. The blade was wrapped in a ranger's cloak and buried beneath the Fist of the First Men. There were other blades as well . . . spearheads, arrowheads, all dragonglass."

"I know you held the gate here," King Stannis said. "If not, I would have come too late."

"Donal Noye held the gate. He died below in the tunnel, fighting the king of the giants."

Stannis grimaced. "Noye made my first sword for me, and Robert's warhammer as well. Had the god seen fit to spare him, he would have made a better Lord Commander for your order than any of these fools who are squabbling over it now."

"Cotter Pyke and Ser Denys Mallister are no fools, sire," Jon said. "They're good men, and capable. Othell Yarwyck as well, in his own way. Lord Mormont trusted each of them."

"Your Lord Mormont trusted too easily. Else he would not have died as he did. But we were speaking of you. I have not forgotten that it was you who brought us this magic horn, and captured Mance Rayder's wife and son."

"Dalla died." Jon was saddened by that still. "Val is her sister. She and the babe did not require much capturing, Your Grace. You had put the wildlings to flight, and the skinchanger Mance had left to guard his queen went mad when the eagle burned." Jon looked at Melisandre. "Some say that was your doing."

She smiled, her long copper hair tumbling across her face. "The Lord of Light has fiery talons, Jon Snow."

Jon nodded, and turned back to the king. "Your Grace, you spoke of Val. She has asked to see Mance Rayder, to bring his son to him. It would be a . . . a kindness."

"The man is a deserter from your order. Your brothers are all insisting on his death. Why should I do him a kindness?"

Jon had no answer for that. "If not for him, for Val. For her sister's sake, the child's mother."

"You are fond of this Val?"

"I scarcely know her."

"They tell me she is comely."

"Very," Jon admitted.

"Beauty can be treacherous. My brother learned that lesson from Cersei Lannister. She murdered him, do not doubt it. Your father and Jon Arryn as well." He scowled. "You rode with these wildlings. Is there any honor in them, do you think?"

"Yes," Jon said, "but their own sort of honor, sire."

"In Mance Rayder?"

"Yes. I think so."

"In the Lord of Bones?"

Jon hesitated. "Rattleshirt, we called him. Treacherous and blood-thirsty. If there's honor in him, he hides it down beneath his suit of bones."

"And this other man, this Tormund of the many names who eluded us after the battle? Answer me truly."

"Tormund Giantsbane seemed to me the sort of man who would make a good friend and a bad enemy, Your Grace."

Stannis gave a curt nod. "Your father was a man of honor. He was no friend to me, but I saw his worth. Your brother was a rebel and a traitor who meant to steal half my kingdom, but no man can question his courage. What of you?"

Does he want me to say I love him? Jon's voice was stiff and formal as he said, "I am a man of the Night's Watch."

"Words. Words are wind. Why do you think I abandoned Dragonstone and sailed to the Wall, Lord Snow?"

"I am no lord, sire. You came because we sent for you, I hope. Though I could not say why you took so long about it."

Surprisingly, Stannis smiled at that. "You're bold enough to be a Stark. Yes, I should have come sooner. If not for my Hand, I might not have come at all. Lord Seaworth is a man of humble birth, but he reminded me of my duty, when all I could think of was my rights. I had the cart before the horse, Davos said. I was trying to win the throne to save the kingdom, when I should have been trying to save the kingdom to win the throne." Stannis pointed north. "There is where I'll find the foe that I was born to fight."

"His name may not be spoken," Melisandre added softly. "He is the God of Night and Terror, Jon Snow, and these shapes in the snow are his creatures."

"They tell me that you slew one of these walking corpses to save Lord Mormont's life," Stannis said. "It may be that this is your war as well, Lord Snow. If you will give me your help."

"My sword is pledged to the Night's Watch, Your Grace," Jon Snow answered carefully.

That did not please the king. Stannis ground his teeth and said, "I need more than a sword from you."

Jon was lost. "My lord?"

"I need the north."

The north. "I . . . my brother Robb was King in the North . . ."

"Your brother was the rightful Lord of Winterfell. If he had stayed home and done his duty, instead of crowning himself and riding off to conquer the riverlands, he might be alive today. Be that as it may. You are not Robb, no more than I am Robert."

The harsh words had blown away whatever sympathy Jon might have had for Stannis. "I loved my brother," he said.

"And I mine. Yet they were what they were, and so are we. I am the only true king in Westeros, north or south. And you are Ned Stark's bastard." Stannis studied him with those dark blue eyes. "Tywin Lannister has named Roose Bolton his Warden of the North, to reward him for betraying your brother. The ironmen are fighting amongst themselves since Balon Greyjoy's death, yet they still hold Moat Cailin, Deepwood Motte, Torrhen's Square, and most of the Stony Shore. Your father's lands are bleeding, and I have neither the strength nor the time to stanch the wounds. What is needed is a Lord of Winterfell. A *loyal* Lord of Winterfell."

He is looking at me, Jon thought, stunned. "Winterfell is no more. Theon Greyjoy put it to the torch."

"Granite does not burn easily," Stannis said. "The castle can be rebuilt, in time. It's not the walls that make a lord, it's the man. Your northmen do not know me, have no reason to love me, yet I will need their strength in the battles yet to come. I need a son of Eddard Stark to win them to my banner."

He would make me Lord of Winterfell. The wind was gusting, and Jon felt so light-headed he was half afraid it would blow him off the Wall. "Your Grace," he said, "you forget. I am a Snow, not a Stark."

"It's you who are forgetting," King Stannis replied.

Melisandre put a warm hand on Jon's arm. "A king can remove the taint of bastardy with a stroke, Lord Snow."

Lord Snow. Ser Alliser Thorne had named him that, to mock his bastard birth. Many of his brothers had taken to using it as well, some with affection, others to wound. But suddenly it had a different sound to it in Jon's ears. It sounded . . . real. "Yes," he said, hesitantly, "kings have legitimized bastards before, but . . . I am still a brother of the Night's Watch. I knelt before a heart tree and swore to hold no lands and father no children."

"Jon." Melisandre was so close he could feel the warmth of her breath. "R'hllor is the only true god. A vow sworn to a tree has no more power than one sworn to your shoes. Open your heart and let the light of the Lord come in. Burn these weirwoods, and accept Winterfell as a gift of the Lord of Light."

When Jon had been very young, too young to understand what it meant to be a bastard, he used to dream that one day Winterfell might be his. Later, when he was older, he had been ashamed of those dreams. Winterfell would go to Robb and then his sons, or to Bran or Rickon should Robb die childless. And after them came Sansa and Arya. Even to dream otherwise seemed disloyal, as if he were betraying them in his heart, wishing for their deaths. *I never wanted this,* he thought as he stood before the blue-eyed king and the red woman. *I loved Robb, loved all of them . . . I never wanted any harm to come to any of them, but it did. And now there's only me.* All he had to do was say the word, and he would be Jon Stark, and nevermore a Snow. All he had to do was pledge this king his fealty, and Winterfell was his. All he had to do . . .

. . . was forswear his vows again.

And this time it would not be a ruse. To claim his father's castle, he must turn against his father's gods.

King Stannis gazed off north again, his gold cloak streaming from his shoulders. "It may be that I am mistaken in you, Jon Snow. We both know the things that are said of bastards. You may lack your father's honor, or your brother's skill in arms. But you are the weapon the Lord has given me. I have found you here, as you found the cache of dragonglass beneath the Fist, and I mean to make use of you. Even Azor Ahai did not win his war alone. I killed a thousand wildlings, took another thousand captive, and scattered the rest, but we both know they will return. Melisandre has seen that in her fires. This Tormund Thunderfist is likely re-forming them even now, and planning some new assault. And the more we bleed each other, the weaker we shall all be when the real enemy falls upon us."

Jon had come to that same realization. "As you say, Your Grace." He wondered where this king was going.

"Whilst your brothers have been struggling to decide who shall lead them, I have been speaking with this Mance Rayder." He ground his teeth. "A stubborn man, that one, and prideful. He will leave me no choice but to give him to the flames. But we took other captives as well, other leaders. The one who calls himself the Lord of Bones, some of their clan chiefs, the new Magnar of Thenn. Your brothers will not like it, no more than your father's lords, but I mean to allow the wildlings through the Wall ... those who will swear me their fealty, pledge to keep the king's peace and the king's laws, and take the Lord of Light as their god. Even the giants, if those great knees of theirs can bend. I will settle them on the Gift, once I have wrested it away from your new Lord Commander. When the cold winds rise, we shall live or die together. It is time we made alliance against our common foe." He looked at Jon. "Would you agree?"

"My father dreamed of resettling the Gift," Jon admitted. "He and my uncle Benjen used to talk of it." *He never thought of settling it with wildlings, though ... but he never rode with wildlings, either.* He did not fool himself; the free folk would make for unruly subjects and dangerous neighbors. Yet when he weighed Ygritte's red hair against the cold blue eyes of the wights, the choice was easy. "I agree."

"Good," King Stannis said, "for the surest way to seal a new alliance is with a marriage. I mean to wed my Lord of Winterfell to this wildling princess."

Perhaps Jon had ridden with the free folk too long; he could not help but laugh. "Your Grace," he said, "captive or no, if you think you can just *give* Val to me, I fear you have a deal to learn about wildling women. Whoever weds her had best be prepared to climb in her tower window and carry her off at swordpoint ..."

"*Whoever?*" Stannis gave him a measuring look. "Does this mean you will not wed the girl? I warn you, she is part of the price you must pay, if you want your father's name and your father's castle. This match is necessary, to help assure the loyalty of our new subjects. Are you refusing me, Jon Snow?"

"No," Jon said, too quickly. It was Winterfell the king was speaking of, and Winterfell was not to be lightly refused. "I mean ... this has all come very suddenly, Your Grace. Might I beg you for some time to consider?"

"As you wish. But consider quickly. I am not a patient man, as your black brothers are about to discover." Stannis put a thin, fleshless hand on Jon's shoulder. "Say nothing of what we've discussed here today. To anyone. But when you return, you need only bend your knee, lay your sword at my feet, and pledge yourself to my service, and you shall rise again as Jon Stark, the Lord of Winterfell."

TYRION

When he heard noises through the thick wooden door of his cell, Tyrion Lannister prepared to die.

Past time, he thought. *Come on, come on, make an end to it.* He pushed himself to his feet. His legs were asleep from being folded under him. He bent down and rubbed the knives from them. *I will not go stumbling and waddling to the headsman's block.*

He wondered whether they would kill him down here in the dark or drag him through the city so Ser Ilyn Payne could lop his head off. After his mummer's farce of a trial, his sweet sister and loving father might prefer to dispose of him quietly, rather than risk a public execution. *I could tell the mob a few choice things, if they let me speak.* But would they be that foolish?

As the keys rattled and the door to his cell pushed inward, creaking, Tyrion pressed back against the dampness of the wall, wishing for a weapon. *I can still bite and kick. I'll die with the taste of blood in my mouth, that's something.* He wished he'd been able to think of some rousing last words. "Bugger you all" was not like to earn him much of a place in the histories.

Torchlight fell across his face. He shielded his eyes with a hand. "*Come on, are you frightened of a dwarf? Do it, you son of a poxy whore.*" His voice had grown hoarse from disuse.

"Is that any way to speak about our lady mother?" The man moved forward, a torch in his left hand. "This is even more ghastly than my cell at Riverrun, though not quite so dank."

For a moment Tyrion could not breathe. "You?"

"Well, most of me." Jaime was gaunt, his hair hacked short. "I left a hand at Harrenhal. Bringing the Brave Companions across the narrow sea was not one of Father's better notions." He lifted his arm, and Tyrion saw the stump.

A bark of hysterical laughter burst from his lips. "Oh, gods," he said. "Jaime, I am so sorry, but . . . gods be good, look at the two of us. Handless and Noseless, the Lannister boys."

"There were days when my hand smelled so bad I wished I was noseless." Jaime lowered the torch, so the light bathed his brother's face. "An impressive scar."

Tyrion turned away from the glare. "They made me fight a battle without my big brother to protect me."

"I heard tell you almost burned the city down."

"A filthy lie. I only burned the river." Abruptly, Tyrion remembered where he was, and why. "Are you here to kill me?"

"Now that's ungrateful. Perhaps I should leave you here to rot if you're going to be so discourteous."

"Rotting is not the fate Cersei has in mind for me."

"Well no, if truth be told. You're to be beheaded on the morrow, out on the old tourney grounds."

Tyrion laughed again. "Will there be food? You'll have to help me with my last words, my wits have been running about like a rat in a root cellar."

"You won't need last words. I'm rescuing you." Jaime's voice was strangely solemn.

"Who said I required rescue?"

"You know, I'd almost forgotten what an annoying little man you are. Now that you've reminded me, I do believe I'll let Cersei cut your head off after all."

"Oh no you won't." He waddled out of the cell. "Is it day or night up above? I've lost all sense of time."

"Three hours past midnight. The city sleeps." Jaime slid the torch back into its sconce, on the wall between the cells.

The corridor was so poorly lit that Tyrion almost stumbled on the turnkey, sprawled across the cold stone floor. He prodded him with a toe. "Is he dead?"

"Asleep. The other three as well. The eunuch dosed their wine with sweetsleep, but not enough to kill them. Or so he swears. He is waiting back at the stair, dressed up in a septon's robe. You're going down into the sewers, and from there to the river. A galley is waiting in the bay. Varys has agents in the Free Cities who will see that you do not lack for funds . . . but try not to be conspicuous. Cersei will send men after you, I have no doubt. You might do well to take another name."

"Another name? Oh, certainly. And when the Faceless Men come to kill me, I'll say, 'No, you have the wrong man, I'm a *different* dwarf with a hideous facial scar.'" Both Lannisters laughed at the absurdity of it all. Then Jaime went to one knee and kissed him quickly once on each cheek, his lips brushing against the puckered ribbon of scar tissue.

"Thank you, Brother," Tyrion said. "For my life."

"It was . . . a debt I owed you." Jaime's voice was strange.

"A debt?" He cocked his head. "I do not understand."

"Good. Some doors are best left closed."

"Oh, dear," said Tyrion. "Is there something grim and ugly behind it? Could it be that someone said something *cruel* about me once? I'll try not to weep. Tell me."

"Tyrion . . ."

Jaime is afraid. "Tell me," Tyrion said again.

His brother looked away. "Tysha," he said softly.

"Tysha?" His stomach tightened. "What of her?"

"She was no whore. I never bought her for you. That was a lie that Father commanded me to tell. Tysha was . . . she was what she seemed to be. A crofter's daughter, chance met on the road."

Tyrion could hear the faint sound of his own breath whistling hollowly through the scar of his nose. Jaime could not meet his eyes. *Tysha.* He tried to remember what she had looked like. *A girl, she was only a girl, no older than Sansa.* "My wife," he croaked. "She wed me."

"For your gold, Father said. She was lowborn, you were a Lannister of Casterly Rock. All she wanted was the gold, which made her no different from a whore, so . . . so it would not be a lie, not truly, and . . . he said that you required a sharp lesson. That you would learn from it, and thank me later . . ."

"*Thank* you?" Tyrion's voice was choked. "He gave her to his guards. A barracks full of guards. He made me . . . watch." *Aye, and more than watch. I took her too . . . my wife . . .*

"I never knew he would do that. You must believe me."

"Oh, *must* I?" Tyrion snarled. "Why should I believe you about anything, ever? She was my *wife!*"

"Tyrion –"

He hit him. It was a slap, backhanded, but he put all his strength into it, all his fear, all his rage, all his pain. Jaime was squatting, unbalanced. The blow sent him tumbling backward to the floor. "I . . . I suppose I earned that."

"Oh, you've earned more than that, Jaime. You and my sweet sister and our loving father, yes, I can't begin to tell you what you've earned. But you'll have it, that I swear to you. A Lannister always pays his debts." Tyrion waddled away, almost stumbling over the turnkey again in his haste. Before he had gone a dozen yards, he bumped up against an iron gate that closed the passage. *Oh, gods*. It was all he could do not to scream.

Jaime came up behind him. "I have the gaoler's keys."

"Then use them." Tyrion stepped aside.

Jaime unlocked the gate, pushed it open, and stepped through. He looked back over his shoulder. "Are you coming?"

"Not with you." Tyrion stepped through. "Give me the keys and go. I will find Varys on my own." He cocked his head and stared up at his brother with his mismatched eyes. "Jaime, can you fight left-handed?"

"Rather less well than you," Jaime said bitterly.

"Good. Then we will be well matched if we should ever meet again. The cripple and the dwarf."

Jaime handed him the ring of keys. "I gave you the truth. You owe me the same. Did you do it? Did you kill him?"

The question was another knife, twisting in his guts. "Are you sure you want to know?" asked Tyrion. "Joffrey would have been a worse king than Aerys ever was. He stole his father's dagger and gave it to a footpad to slit the throat of Brandon Stark, did you know that?"

"I . . . I thought he might have."

"Well, a son takes after his father. Joff would have killed me as well, once he came into his power. For the crime of being short and ugly, of which I am so conspicuously guilty."

"You have not answered my question."

"You poor stupid blind crippled fool. Must I spell every little thing out for you? Very well. Cersei is a lying whore, she's been fucking Lancel and Osmund Kettleblack and probably Moon Boy for all I know. And I am the monster they all say I am. Yes, I killed your vile son." He made himself grin. It must have been a hideous sight to see, there in the torchlit gloom.

Jaime turned without a word and walked away.

Tyrion watched him go, striding on his long strong legs, and part of him wanted to call out, to tell him that it wasn't true, to beg for his forgiveness. But then he thought of Tysha, and he held his silence. He listened to the receding footsteps until he could hear them no longer, then waddled off to look for Varys.

The eunuch was lurking in the dark of a twisting turnpike stair, garbed in a moth-eaten brown robe with a hood that hid the paleness of his face. "You were so long, I feared that something had gone amiss," he said when he saw Tyrion.

"Oh, no," Tyrion assured him, in poisonous tones. "What could *possibly* have gone amiss?" He twisted his head back to stare up. "I sent for you during my trial."

"I could not come. The queen had me watched, night and day. I dared not help you."

"You're helping me now."

"Am I? Ah." Varys giggled. It seemed strangely out of place in this place of cold stone and echoing darkness. "Your brother can be most persuasive."

"Varys, you are as cold and slimy as a slug, has anyone ever told you? You did your best to kill me. Perhaps I ought to return the favor."

The eunuch sighed. "The faithful dog is kicked, and no matter how the spider weaves, he is never loved. But if you slay me here, I fear for you, my lord. You may never find your way back to daylight." His eyes glittered in the shifting torchlight, dark and wet. "These tunnels are full of traps for the unwary."

Tyrion snorted. "Unwary? I'm the wariest man who ever lived, you helped see to that." He rubbed at his nose. "So tell me, wizard, where is my innocent maiden wife?"

"I have found no trace of Lady Sansa in King's Landing, sad to say. Nor of Ser Dontos Hollard, who by rights should have turned up somewhere drunk by now. They were seen together on the serpentine steps the night she vanished. After that, nothing. There was much confusion that night. My little birds are silent." Varys gave a gentle tug at the dwarf's sleeve and pulled him into the stair. "My lord, we must away. Your path is down."

That's no lie, at least. Tyrion waddled along in the eunuch's wake, his heels scraping against the rough stone as they descended. It was very cold within the stairwell, a damp bone-chilling cold that set him to shivering at once. "What part of the dungeons are these?" he asked.

"Maegor the Cruel decreed four levels of dungeons for his castle," Varys replied. "On the upper level, there are large cells where common criminals may be confined together. They have narrow windows set high in the walls. The second level has the smaller cells where highborn captives are held. They have no windows, but torches in the halls cast light through the bars. On the third level the cells are smaller and the doors are wood. The black cells, men call them. That was where you were kept, and Eddard Stark before you. But there is a level lower still. Once a man is taken down to the fourth level, he never sees the sun again, nor hears a human voice, nor breathes a breath free of agonizing pain. Maegor had the cells on the fourth level built for torment." They had reached the bottom of the steps. An unlighted door opened before them. "This is the fourth level. Give me your hand, my lord. It is safer to walk in darkness here. There are things you would not wish to see."

Tyrion hung back a moment. Varys had already betrayed him once. Who knew what game the eunuch was playing? And what better place to murder a man than down in the darkness, in a place that no one knew existed? His body might never be found.

On the other hand, what choice did he have? To go back up the steps and walk out the main gate? No, that would not serve.

Jaime would not be afraid, he thought, before he remembered what Jaime had done to him. He took the eunuch by the hand and let himself be led through the black, following the soft scrape of leather on stone. Varys walked quickly, from time to time whispering, "Careful, there are three steps ahead," or, "The tunnel slopes downward here, my lord." *I arrived here a King's Hand, riding through the gates at the head of my own sworn men,* Tyrion reflected, *and I leave like a rat scuttling through the dark, holding hands with a spider.*

A light appeared ahead of them, too dim to be daylight, and grew as they hurried toward it. After a while he could see it was an arched doorway, closed off by another iron gate. Varys produced a key. They stepped through into a small round chamber. Five other doors opened off the room, each barred in iron. There was an opening in the ceiling as well, and a series of rungs set in the wall below, leading upward. An ornate brazier stood to one side, fashioned in the shape of a dragon's head. The coals in the beast's yawning mouth had burnt down to embers, but they still glowed with a sullen orange light. Dim as it was, the light was welcome after the blackness of the tunnel.

The juncture was otherwise empty, but on the floor was a mosaic of a three-headed dragon wrought in red and black tiles. Something niggled at Tyrion for a moment. Then it came to him. *This is the place Shae told me of, when Varys first led her to my bed.* "We are below the Tower of the Hand."

"Yes." Frozen hinges screamed in protest as Varys pulled open a long-closed door. Flakes of rust drifted to the floor. "This will take us out to the river."

Tyrion walked slowly to the ladder, ran his hand across the lowest rung. "This will take me up to my bedchamber."

"Your lord father's bedchamber now."

He looked up the shaft. "How far must I climb?"

"My lord, you are too weak for such follies, and there is besides no time. We must go."

"I have business above. How far?"

"Two hundred and thirty rungs, but whatever you intend –"

"Two hundred and thirty rungs, and then?"

"The tunnel to the left, but hear me –"

"How far along to the bedchamber?" Tyrion lifted a foot to the lowest rung of the ladder.

"No more than sixty feet. Keep one hand on the wall as you go. You will feel the doors. The bedchamber is the third." He sighed. "This is folly, my lord. Your brother has given you your life back. Would you cast it away, and mine with it?"

"Varys, the only thing I value less than my life just now is yours. Wait for me here." He turned his back on the eunuch and began to climb, counting silently as he went.

Rung by rung, he ascended into darkness. At first he could see the dim outline of each rung as he grasped it, and the rough grey texture of the stone behind, but as he climbed the black grew thicker. *Thirteen fourteen fifteen sixteen.* By thirty, his arms trembled with the strain of pulling. He paused a moment to catch his breath and glanced down. A circle of faint light shone far below, half obscured by his own feet. Tyrion resumed his ascent. *Thirty-nine forty forty-one.* By fifty, his legs burned. The ladder was endless, numbing. *Sixty-eight sixty-nine seventy.* By eighty, his back was a dull agony. Yet still he climbed. He could not have said why. *One thirteen one fourteen one fifteen.*

At two hundred and thirty, the shaft was black as pitch, but he could *feel* the warm air flowing from the tunnel to his left, like the breath of some great beast. He poked about awkwardly with a foot and edged off the ladder. The tunnel was even more cramped than the shaft. Any man of normal size would have had to crawl on hands and knees, but Tyrion was short enough to walk upright. *At last, a place made for dwarfs.* His boots scuffed softly against the stone. He walked slowly, counting steps, feeling for gaps in the walls. Soon he began to hear voices, muffled and indistinct at first, then clearer. He listened more closely. Two of his father's guardsmen were joking about the Imp's whore, saying how sweet it would be to fuck her, and how bad she must want a real cock in place of the dwarf's stunted little thing. "Most like it's got a crook in it," said Lum. That led him into a discussion of how Tyrion would die on the morrow. "He'll weep like a woman and beg for mercy, you'll see," Lum insisted. Lester figured he'd face the axe brave as a lion, being a Lannister, and he was willing to bet his new boots on it. "Ah, shit in your boots," said Lum, "you know they'd never fit these feet o'mine. Tell you what, if I win you can scour my bloody mail for a fortnight."

For the space of a few feet, Tyrion could hear every word of their haggling, but when he moved on, the voices faded quickly. *Small wonder Varys did not want me to climb the bloody ladder,* Tyrion thought, smiling in the dark. *Little birds indeed.*

He came to the third door and fumbled about for a long time before his fingers brushed a small iron hook set between two stones. When he pulled down on it, there was a soft rumble that sounded loud as an avalanche in the stillness, and a square of dull orange light opened a foot to his left.

The hearth! He almost laughed. The fireplace was full of hot ash, and a black log with a hot orange heart burning within. He edged past gingerly, taking quick steps so as not to burn his boots, the warm cinders crunching softly under his heels. When he found himself in what had once been his bedchamber, he stood a long moment, breathing the silence. Had his father heard? Would he reach for his sword, raise the hue and cry?

"M'lord?" a woman's voice called.

That might have hurt me once, when I still felt pain. The first step was the hardest. When he reached the bed Tyrion pulled the draperies aside and there she was, turning toward him with a sleepy smile on her lips. It died when she saw him. She pulled the blankets up to her chin, as if that would protect her.

"Were you expecting someone taller, sweetling?"

Big wet tears filled her eyes. "I never meant those things I said, the queen made me. *Please.* Your father frightens me so." She sat up, letting the blanket slide down to her lap. Beneath it she was naked, but for the chain about her throat. A chain of linked golden hands, each holding the next.

"My lady Shae," Tyrion said softly. "All the time I sat in the black cell waiting to die, I kept remembering how beautiful you were. In silk or roughspun or nothing at all . . ."

"M'lord will be back soon. You should go, or . . . did you come to take me away?"

"Did you ever like it?" He cupped her cheek, remembering all the times he had done this before. All the times he'd slid his hands around her waist, squeezed her small firm breasts, stroked her short dark hair, touched her lips, her cheeks, her ears. All the times he had opened her with a finger to probe her secret sweetness and make her moan. "Did you ever like my touch?"

"More than anything," she said, "my giant of Lannister."

That was the worst thing you could have said, sweetling.

Tyrion slid a hand under his father's chain, and twisted. The links tightened, digging into her neck. "For hands of gold are always cold, but a woman's hands are warm," he said. He gave cold hands another twist as the warm ones beat away his tears.

Afterward he found Lord Tywin's dagger on the bedside table and shoved it through his belt. A lion-headed mace, a poleaxe, and a crossbow had been hung on the walls. The poleaxe would be clumsy to wield inside a castle, and the mace was too high to reach, but a large wood-and-iron chest had been placed against the wall directly under the crossbow. He climbed up, pulled down the bow and a leather quiver packed with quarrels, jammed a foot into the stirrup, and pushed down until the bowstring cocked. Then he slipped a bolt into the notch.

Jaime had lectured him more than once on the drawbacks of crossbows. If Lum and Lester emerged from wherever they were talking, he'd never have time to reload, but at least he'd take one down to hell with him. Lum, if he had a choice. *You'll have to clean your own mail, Lum. You lose.*

Waddling to the door, he listened a moment, then eased it open slowly. A lamp burned in a stone niche, casting wan yellow light over the empty hallway. Only the flame was moving. Tyrion slid out, holding the crossbow down against his leg.

He found his father where he knew he'd find him, seated in the dimness of the privy tower, bedrobe hiked up around his hips. At the sound of steps, Lord Tywin raised his eyes.

Tyrion gave him a mocking half bow. "My lord."

"Tyrion." If he was afraid, Tywin Lannister gave no hint of it. "Who released you from your cell?"

"I'd love to tell you, but I swore a holy oath."

"The eunuch," his father decided. "I'll have his head for this. Is that my crossbow? Put it down."

"Will you punish me if I refuse, Father?"

"This escape is folly. You are not to be killed, if that is what you fear. It's still my intent to send you to the Wall, but I could not do it without Lord Tyrell's consent. Put down the crossbow and we will go back to my chambers and talk of it."

"We can talk here just as well. Perhaps I don't choose to go to the Wall, Father. It's bloody cold up there, and I believe I've had enough coldness from you. So just tell me something, and I'll be on my way. One simple question, you owe me that much."

"I owe you nothing."

"You've given me less than that, all my life, but you'll give me this. What did you do with Tysha?"

"Tysha?"

He does not even remember her name. "The girl I married."

"Oh, yes. Your first whore."

Tyrion took aim at his father's chest. "The next time you say that word, I'll kill you."

"You do not have the courage."

"Shall we find out? It's a short word, and it seems to come so easily to your lips." Tyrion gestured impatiently with the bow. "Tysha. What did you do with her, after my little lesson?"

"I don't recall."

"Try harder. Did you have her killed?"

His father pursed his lips. "There was no reason for that, she'd learned her place . . . and had been well paid for her day's work, I seem to recall. I suppose the steward sent her on her way. I never thought to inquire."

"On her way *where?*"

"Wherever whores go."

Tyrion's finger clenched. The crossbow *whanged* just as Lord Tywin started to rise. The bolt slammed into him above the groin and he sat back down with a grunt. The quarrel had sunk deep, right to the fletching. Blood seeped out around the shaft, dripping down into his pubic hair and over his bare thighs. "You shot me," he said incredulously, his eyes glassy with shock.

"You always were quick to grasp a situation, my lord," Tyrion said. "That must be why you're the Hand of the King."

"You . . . you are no . . . no son of mine."

"Now that's where you're wrong, Father. Why, I believe I'm you writ small. Do me a kindness now, and die quickly. I have a ship to catch."

For once, his father did what Tyrion asked him. The proof was the sudden stench, as his bowels loosened in the moment of death. *Well, he was in the right place for it,* Tyrion thought. But the stink that filled the privy gave ample evidence that the oft-repeated jape about his father was just another lie.

Lord Tywin Lannister did not, in the end, shit gold.

SAMWELL

The king was angry. Sam saw that at once.

As the black brothers entered one by one and knelt before him, Stannis shoved away his breakfast of hardbread, salt beef, and boiled eggs, and eyed them coldly. Beside him, the red woman Melisandre looked as if she found the scene amusing.

I have no place here, Sam thought anxiously, when her red eyes fell upon him. *Someone had to help Maester Aemon up the steps. Don't look at me, I'm just the maester's steward.* The others were contenders for the Old Bear's command, all but Bowen Marsh, who had withdrawn from the contest but remained castellan and Lord Steward. Sam did not understand why Melisandre should seem so interested in *him*.

King Stannis kept the black brothers on their knees for an extraordinarily long time. "Rise," he said at last. Sam gave Maester Aemon his shoulder to help him back up.

The sound of Lord Janos Slynt clearing his throat broke the strained silence. "Your Grace, let me say how pleased we are to be summoned here. When I saw your banners from the Wall, I knew the realm was saved. 'There comes a man who ne'er forgets his duty,' I said to good Ser Alliser. 'A *strong* man, and a true king.' May I congratulate you on your victory over the savages? The singers will make much of it, I know –"

"The singers may do as they like," Stannis snapped. "Spare me your fawning, Janos, it will not serve you." He rose to his feet and frowned at them all. "Lady Melisandre tells me that you have not yet chosen a Lord Commander. I am displeased. How much longer must this folly last?"

"Sire," said Bowen Marsh in a defensive tone, "no one has achieved two-thirds of the vote yet. It has only been ten days."

"Nine days too long. I have captives to dispose of, a realm to order, a war to fight. Choices must be made, decisions that involve the Wall and the Night's Watch. By rights your Lord Commander should have a voice in those decisions."

"He should, yes," said Janos Slynt. "But it must be said. We brothers are only simple soldiers. Soldiers, yes! And Your Grace will know that soldiers are most comfortable taking orders. They would benefit from your royal guidance, it seems to me. For the good of the realm. To help them choose wisely."

The suggestion outraged some of the others. "Do you want the king to wipe our arses for us too?" said Cotter Pyke angrily. "The choice of a Lord Commander belongs to the Sworn Brothers, and to them alone," insisted Ser Denys Mallister. "If they choose wisely they won't be choosing me," moaned Dolorous Edd. Maester Aemon, calm as always, said, "Your Grace, the Night's Watch has been choosing its own leader since Brandon the Builder raised the Wall. Through Jeor Mormont we have had nine hundred and ninety-seven Lords Commander in unbroken succession, each chosen by the men he would lead, a tradition many thousands of years old."

Stannis ground his teeth. "It is not my wish to tamper with your rights and traditions. As to *royal guidance*, Janos, if you mean that I ought to tell your brothers to choose you, have the courage to say so."

That took Lord Janos aback. He smiled uncertainly and began to sweat, but Bowen Marsh beside him said, "Who better to command the black cloaks than a man who once commanded the gold, sire?"

"Any of you, I would think. Even the cook." The look the king gave Slynt was cold. "Janos was hardly the first gold cloak ever to take a bribe, I grant you, but he may have been the first commander to fatten his purse by selling places and promotions. By the end he must have had half the officers in the City Watch paying him part of their wages. Isn't that so, Janos?"

Slynt's neck was purpling. "Lies, all lies! A strong man makes enemies, Your Grace knows that, they whisper lies behind your back. Naught was ever proven, not a man came forward . . ."

"Two men who were prepared to come forward died suddenly on their rounds." Stannis narrowed his eyes. "Do not trifle with me, my lord. I saw the proof Jon Arryn laid before the small council. If I had been king you would have lost more than your office, I promise you, but Robert shrugged away your little lapses. 'They all steal,' I recall him saying. 'Better a thief we know than one we don't, the next man might be worse.' Lord Petyr's words in my brother's mouth, I'll warrant. Littlefinger had a nose for gold, and I'm certain he arranged matters so the crown profited as much from your corruption as you did yourself."

Lord Slynt's jowls were quivering, but before he could frame a further protest Maester Aemon said, "Your Grace, by law a man's past crimes and transgressions are wiped clean when he says his words and becomes a Sworn Brother of the Night's Watch."

"I am aware of that. If it happens that Lord Janos here is the best the Night's Watch can offer, I shall grit my teeth and choke him down. It is naught to me which man of you is chosen, so long as you *make a choice*. We have a war to fight."

"Your Grace," said Ser Denys Mallister, in tones of wary courtesy. "If you are speaking of the wildlings . . ."

"I am not. And you know that, ser."

"And you must know that whilst we are thankful for the aid you rendered us against Mance Rayder, we can offer you no help in your contest for the throne. The Night's Watch takes no part in the wars of the Seven Kingdoms. For eight thousand years –"

"I know your history, Ser Denys," the king said brusquely. "I give you my word, I shall not ask you to lift your swords against any of the rebels and usurpers who plague me. I do expect that you will continue to defend the Wall as you always have."

"We'll defend the Wall to the last man," said Cotter Pyke.

"Probably me," said Dolorous Edd, in a resigned tone.

Stannis crossed his arms. "I shall require a few other things from you as well. Things that you may not be so quick to give. I want your castles. And I want the Gift."

Those blunt words burst among the black brothers like a pot of wildfire tossed onto a brazier. Marsh, Mallister, and Pyke all tried to speak at once. King Stannis let them talk. When they were done, he said, "I have three times the men you do. I can take the lands if I wish, but I would prefer to do this legally, with your consent."

"The Gift was given to the Night's Watch in perpetuity, Your Grace," Bowen Marsh insisted.

"Which means it cannot be lawfully seized, attainted, or taken from you. But what was given once can be given again."

"What will you do with the Gift?" demanded Cotter Pyke.

"Make better use of it than you have. As to the castles, Eastwatch, Castle Black, and the Shadow Tower shall remain yours. Garrison them as you always have, but I must take the others for *my* garrisons if we are to hold the Wall."

"You do not have the men," objected Bowen Marsh.

"Some of the abandoned castles are scarce more than ruins," said Othell Yarwyck, the First Builder.

"Ruins can be rebuilt."

"Rebuilt?" Yarwyck said. "But who will do the work?"

"That is my concern. I shall require a list from you, detailing the present state of every castle and what might be required to restore it. I mean to have them all garrisoned again within the year, and nightfires burning before their gates."

"Nightfires?" Bowen Marsh gave Melisandre an uncertain look. "We're to light nightfires now?"

"You are." The woman rose in a swirl of scarlet silk, her long copper-bright hair tumbling about her shoulders. "Swords alone cannot hold this darkness back. Only the light of the Lord can do that. Make no mistake, good sers and valiant brothers, the war we've come to fight is no petty squabble over lands and honors. Ours is a war for life itself, and should we fail the world dies with us."

The officers did not know how to take that, Sam could see. Bowen Marsh and Othell Yarwyck exchanged a doubtful look, Janos Slynt was fuming, and Three-Finger Hobb looked as though he would sooner be back chopping carrots. But all of them seemed surprised to hear Maester Aemon murmur, "It is the war for the dawn you speak of, my lady. But where is the prince that was promised?"

"He stands before you," Melisandre declared, "though you do not have the eyes to see. Stannis Baratheon is Azor Ahai come again, the warrior of fire. In him the prophecies are fulfilled. The red comet blazed across the sky to herald his coming, and he bears Lightbringer, the red sword of heroes."

Her words seemed to make the king desperately uncomfortable, Sam saw. Stannis ground his teeth, and said, "You called and I came, my lords. Now you must live with me, or die with me. Best get used to that." He made a brusque gesture. "That's all. Maester, stay a moment. And you, Tarly. The rest of you may go."

Me? Sam thought, stricken, as his brothers were bowing and making their way out. *What does he want with me?*

"You are the one that killed the creature in the snow," King Stannis said, when only the four of them remained.

"Sam the Slayer." Melisandre smiled.

Sam felt his face turning red. "No, my lady. Your Grace. I mean, I am, yes. I'm Samwell Tarly, yes."

"Your father is an able soldier," King Stannis said. "He defeated my brother once, at Ashford. Mace Tyrell has been pleased to claim the honors for that victory, but Lord Randyll had decided matters before Tyrell ever found the battlefield. He slew Lord Cafferen with that great Valyrian sword of his and sent his head to Aerys." The king rubbed his jaw with a finger. "You are not the sort of son I would expect such a man to have."

"I . . . I am not the sort of son he wanted, sire."

"If you had not taken the black, you would make a useful hostage," Stannis mused.

"He has taken the black, sire," Maester Aemon pointed out.

"I am well aware of that," the king said. "I am aware of more than you know, Aemon Targaryen."

The old man inclined his head. "I am only Aemon, sire. We give up our House names when we forge our maester's chains."

The king gave that a curt nod, as if to say he knew and did not care. "You slew this creature with an obsidian dagger, I am told," he said to Sam.

"Y-yes, Your Grace. Jon Snow gave it to me."

"Dragonglass." The red woman's laugh was music. "*Frozen fire*, in the tongue of old Valyria. Small wonder it is anathema to these cold children of the Other."

"On Dragonstone, where I had my seat, there is much of this obsidian to be seen in the old tunnels beneath the mountain," the king told Sam. "Chunks of it, boulders, ledges. The great part of it was black, as I recall, but there was some green as well, some red, even purple. I have sent word to Ser Rolland my castellan to begin mining it. I will not hold Dragonstone for very much longer, I fear, but perhaps the Lord of Light shall grant us enough *frozen fire* to arm ourselves against these creatures, before the castle falls."

Sam cleared his throat. "S-sire. The dagger . . . the dragonglass only shattered when I tried to stab a wight."

Melisandre smiled. "Necromancy animates these wights, yet they are still only dead flesh. Steel and fire will serve for them. The ones you call the Others are something more."

"Demons made of snow and ice and cold," said Stannis Baratheon. "The ancient enemy. The only enemy that matters." He considered Sam again. "I am told that you and this wildling girl passed beneath the Wall, through some magic gate."

"The B-black Gate," Sam stammered. "Below the Nightfort."

"The Nightfort is the largest and oldest of the castles on the Wall," the king said. "That is where I intend to make my seat, whilst I fight this war. You will show me this gate."

"I," said Sam, "I w-will, if . . ." *If it is still there. If it will open for a man not of the black. If . . .*

"You will," snapped Stannis. "I shall tell you when."

Maester Aemon smiled. "Your Grace," he said, "before we go, I wonder if you would do us the great honor of showing us this wondrous blade we have all heard so very much of."

"You want to see Lightbringer? A *blind* man?"

"Sam shall be my eyes."

The king frowned. "Everyone else has seen the thing, why not a blind man?" His swordbelt and scabbard hung from a peg near the hearth. He took the belt down and drew the longsword out. Steel scraped against wood and leather, and radiance filled the solar; shimmering, shifting, a dance of gold and orange and red light, all the bright colors of fire.

"Tell me, Samwell." Maester Aemon touched his arm.

"It *glows*," said Sam, in a hushed voice. "As if it were on fire. There are no flames, but the steel is yellow and red and orange, all flashing and glimmering, like sunshine on water, but prettier. I wish you could see it, Maester."

"I see it now, Sam. A sword full of sunlight. So lovely to behold." The old man bowed stiffly. "Your Grace. My lady. This was most kind of you."

When King Stannis sheathed the shining sword, the room seemed to grow very dark, despite the sunlight streaming through the window. "Very well, you've seen it. You may return to your duties now. And remember what I said. Your brothers will chose a Lord Commander tonight, or I shall make them wish they had."

Maester Aemon was lost in thought as Sam helped him down the narrow turnpike stair. But as they were crossing the yard, he said, "I felt no heat. Did you, Sam?"

"Heat? From the sword?" He thought back. "The air around it was shimmering, the way it does above a hot brazier."

"Yet you *felt* no heat, did you? And the scabbard that held this sword, it is wood and leather, yes? I heard the sound when His Grace drew out the blade. Was the leather scorched, Sam? Did the wood seem burnt or blackened?"

"No," Sam admitted. "Not that I could see."

Maester Aemon nodded. Back in his own chambers, he asked Sam to set a fire and help him to his chair beside the hearth. "It is hard to be so old," he sighed as he settled onto the cushion. "And harder still to be so blind. I miss the sun. And books. I miss books most of all." Aemon waved a hand. "I shall have no more need of you till the choosing."

"The choosing . . . Maester, isn't there something you could do? What the king said of Lord Janos . . ."

"I recall," Maester Aemon said, "but Sam, I am a maester, chained and sworn. My duty is to counsel the Lord Commander, whoever he might be. It would not be proper for me to be seen to favor one contender over another."

"I'm not a maester," said Sam. "Could *I* do something?"

Aemon turned his blind white eyes toward Sam's face, and smiled softly. "Why, I don't know, Samwell. Could you?"

I could, Sam thought. *I have to*. He had to do it right away, too. If he hesitated he was certain to lose his courage. *I am a man of the Night's Watch*, he reminded himself as he hurried across the yard. *I am. I can do this.* There had been a time when he had quaked and squeaked if Lord Mormont so much as looked at him, but that was the old Sam, before the Fist of the First Men and Craster's Keep, before the wights and Coldhands and the Other on his dead horse. He was braver now. *Gilly made me braver*, he'd told Jon. It was true. It had to be true.

Cotter Pyke was the scarier of the two commanders, so Sam went to him first, while his courage was still hot. He found him in the old Shieldhall, dicing with three of his Eastwatch men and a red-headed sergeant who had come from Dragonstone with Stannis.

When Sam begged leave to speak with him, though, Pyke barked an order, and the others took the dice and coins and left them.

No man would ever call Cotter Pyke handsome, though the body under his studded brigantine and roughspun breeches was lean and hard and wiry strong. His eyes were small and close-set, his nose broken, his widow's peak as sharply pointed as the head of a spear. The pox had ravaged his face badly, and the beard he'd grown to hide the scars was thin and scraggly.

"Sam the Slayer!" he said, by way of greeting. "Are you sure you stabbed an Other, and not some child's snow knight?"

This isn't starting well. "It was the dragonglass that killed it, my lord," Sam explained feebly.

"Aye, no doubt. Well, out with it, Slayer. Did the maester send you to me?"

"The maester?" Sam swallowed. "I . . . I just left him, my lord." That wasn't truly a lie, but if Pyke chose to read it wrong, it might make him more inclined to listen. Sam took a deep breath and launched into his plea.

Pyke cut him off before he'd said twenty words. "You want me to kneel down and kiss the hem of Mallister's pretty cloak, is that it? I might have known. You lordlings all flock like sheep. Well, tell Aemon that he's wasted your breath and my time. If anyone withdraws it should be Mallister. The man's too bloody *old* for the job, maybe you ought to go tell him that. We choose him, and we're like to be back here in a year, choosing someone else."

"He's old," Sam agreed, "but he's well ex-experienced."

"At sitting in his tower and fussing over maps, maybe. What does he plan to do, write letters to the wights? He's a knight, well and good, but he's not a *fighter*, and I don't give a kettle of piss who he unhorsed in some fool tourney fifty years ago. The Halfhand fought all his battles, even an old blind man should see that. And we need a fighter more than ever with this bloody king on top of us. Today it's ruins and empty fields, well and good, but what will *His Grace* want come the morrow? You think *Mallister* has the belly to stand up to Stannis Baratheon and that red bitch?" He laughed. "I don't."

"You won't support him, then?" said Sam, dismayed.

"Are you Sam the Slayer or Deaf Dick? No, I won't support him." Pyke jabbed a finger at his face. "Understand this, boy. I don't *want* the bloody job, and never did. I fight best with a deck beneath me, not a horse, and Castle Black is too far from the sea. But I'll be buggered with a red-hot sword before I turn the Night's Watch over to that preening eagle from the Shadow Tower. And you can run back to the old man and tell him I said so, if he asks." He stood. "Get out of my sight."

It took all the courage Sam had left in him to say, "W-what if there was someone else? Could you s-support someone else?"

"Who? Bowen Marsh? The man counts spoons. Othell's a follower, does what he's told and does it well, but no more'n that. Slynt . . . well, his men like him, I'll grant you, and it would almost be worth it to stick him down the royal craw and see if Stannis gagged, but no. There's too much of King's Landing in that one. A toad grows wings and thinks he's a bloody dragon." Pyke laughed. "Who does that leave, Hobb? We could pick him, I suppose, only then who's going to boil your mutton, Slayer? You look like a man who likes his bloody mutton."

There was nothing more to say. Defeated, Sam could only stammer out his thanks and take his leave. *I will do better with Ser Denys*, he tried to tell himself as he walked through the castle. Ser Denys was a knight, highborn and well-spoken, and he had treated Sam most courteously when he'd found him and Gilly on the road. *Ser Denys will listen to me, he has to.*

The commander of the Shadow Tower had been born beneath the Booming Tower of Seagard, and looked every inch a Mallister. Sable trimmed his collar and accented the sleeves of his black velvet doublet. A silver eagle fastened its claws in the gathered folds of his cloak. His beard was white as snow, his hair was largely gone, and his face was deeply lined, it was true. Yet he still had grace in his movements and teeth in his mouth, and the years had dimmed neither his blue-grey eyes nor his courtesy.

"My lord of Tarly," he said, when his steward brought Sam to him in the Lance, where the Shadow Tower men were staying. "I am pleased to see that you've recovered from your ordeal. Might I offer you a cup of wine? Your lady mother is a Florent, I recall. One day I must tell you about the time I unhorsed both of your grandfathers in the same tourney. Not today, though, I know we have more pressing concerns. You come from Maester Aemon, to be sure. Does he have counsel to offer me?"

Sam took a sip of wine, and chose his words with care. "A maester chained and sworn . . . it would not be proper for him to be seen as having influenced the choice of Lord Commander . . ."

The old knight smiled. "Which is why he has not come to me himself. Yes, I quite understand, Samwell. Aemon and I are both old men, and wise in such matters. Say what you came to say."

The wine was sweet, and Ser Denys listened to Sam's plea with grave courtesy, unlike Cotter Pyke. But when he was done, the old knight shook his head. "I agree that it would be a dark day in our history if a king were to name our Lord Commander. This king especially. He is not like to keep his crown for long. But truly, Samwell, it ought to be Pyke who withdraws. I have more support than he does, and I am better suited to the office."

"You are," Sam agreed, "but Cotter Pyke might serve. It's said he has oft proved himself in battle." He did not mean to offend Ser Denys by praising his rival, but how else could he convince him to withdraw?

"Many of my brothers have proved themselves in battle. It is not enough. Some matters cannot be settled with a battleaxe. Maester Aemon will understand that, though Cotter Pyke does not. The Lord Commander of the Night's Watch is a *lord*, first and foremost. He must be able to treat with other lords . . . and with kings as well. He must be a man worthy of respect." Ser Denys leaned forward. "We are the sons of great lords, you and I. We know the importance of birth, blood, and that early training that can ne'er be replaced. I was a squire at twelve, a knight at eighteen, a champion at two-and-twenty. I have been the commander at the Shadow Tower for thirty-three years. Blood, birth, and training have fitted me to deal with kings. Pyke . . . well, did you hear him this morning, asking if His Grace would wipe his bottom? Samwell, it is not my habit to speak unkindly of my brothers, but let us be frank . . . the ironborn are a race of pirates and thieves, and Cotter Pyke was raping and murdering when he was still half a boy. Maester Harmune reads and writes his letters, and has for years. No, loath as I am to disappoint Maester Aemon, I could not in honor stand aside for Pyke of Eastwatch."

This time Sam was ready. "Might you for someone else? If it was someone more suitable?"

Ser Denys considered a moment. "I have never desired the honor for its own sake. At the last choosing, I stepped aside gratefully when Lord Mormont's name was offered, just as I had for Lord Qorgyle at the choosing before that. So long as the Night's Watch remains in good hands, I am content. But Bowen Marsh is not equal to the task, no more than Othell Yarwyck. And this so-called Lord of Harrenhal is a butcher's whelp upjumped by the Lannisters. Small wonder he is venal and corrupt."

"There's another man," Sam blurted out. "Lord Commander Mormont trusted him. So did Donal Noye and Qhorin Halfhand. Though he's not as highly born as you, he comes from old blood. He was castle-born and castle-raised, and he learned sword and lance from a knight and letters from a maester of the Citadel. His father was a lord, and his brother a king."

Ser Denys stroked his long white beard. "Mayhaps," he said, after a long moment. "He is very young, but . . . mayhaps. He might serve, I grant you, though I would be more suitable. I have no doubt of that. I would be the wiser choice."

Jon said there could be honor in a lie, if it were told for the right reason. Sam said, "If we do not choose a Lord Commander tonight, King Stannis means to name Cotter Pyke. He said as much to Maester Aemon this morning, after all of you had left."

"I see." Ser Denys rose. "I must think on this. Thank you, Samwell. And give my thanks to Maester Aemon as well."

Sam was trembling by the time he left the Lance. *What have I done?* he thought. *What have I said?* If they caught him in his lie, they would *. . . what? Send me to the Wall? Rip my entrails out? Turn me into a wight?* Suddenly it all seemed absurd. How could he be so frightened of Cotter Pyke and Ser Denys Mallister, when he had seen a raven eating Small Paul's face?

Pyke was not pleased by his return. "You again? Make it quick, you are starting to annoy me."

"I only need a moment more," Sam promised. "You won't withdraw for Ser Denys, you said, but you might for someone else."

"Who is it this time, Slayer? You?"

"No. A fighter. Donal Noye gave him the Wall when the wildlings came, and he was the Old Bear's squire. The only thing is, he's bastard-born."

Cotter Pyke laughed. "Bloody hell. That would shove a spear up Mallister's arse, wouldn't it? Might be worth it just for that. How bad could the boy be?" He snorted. "I'd be better, though. I'm what's needed, any fool can see that."

"Any fool," Sam agreed, "even me. But . . . well, I shouldn't be telling you, but . . . King Stannis means to force Ser Denys on us, if we do not choose a man tonight. I heard him tell Maester Aemon that, after the rest of you were sent away."

JON

Iron Emmett was a long, lanky young ranger whose endurance, strength, and swordsmanship were the pride of Eastwatch. Jon always came away from their sessions stiff and sore, and woke the next day covered with bruises, which was just the way he wanted it. He would never get any better going up against the likes of Satin and Horse, or even Grenn.

Most days he gave as good as he got, Jon liked to think, but not today. He had hardly slept last night, and after an hour of restless tossing he had given up even the attempt, dressed, and walked the top of the Wall till the sun came up, wrestling with Stannis Baratheon's offer. The lack of sleep was catching up with him now, and Emmett was hammering him mercilessly across the yard, driving him back on his heels with one long looping cut after another, and slamming him with his shield from time to time for good measure. Jon's arm had gone numb from the shock of impact, and the edgeless practice sword seemed to be growing heavier with every passing moment.

He was almost ready to lower his blade and call a halt when Emmett feinted low and came in over his shield with a savage forehand slash that caught Jon on the temple. He staggered, his helm and head both ringing from the force of the blow. For half a heartbeat the world beyond his eyeslit was a blur.

And then the years were gone, and he was back at Winterfell once more, wearing a quilted leather coat in place of mail and plate. His sword was made of wood, and it was Robb who stood facing him, not Iron Emmett.

Every morning they had trained together, since they were big enough to walk; Snow and Stark, spinning and slashing about the wards of Winterfell, shouting and laughing, sometimes crying when there was no one else to see. They were not little boys when they fought, but knights and mighty heroes. "I'm Prince Aemon the Dragonknight," Jon would call out, and Robb would shout back, "Well, I'm Florian the Fool." Or Robb would say, "I'm the Young Dragon," and Jon would reply, "I'm Ser Ryam Redwyne."

That morning he called it first. "I'm Lord of Winterfell!" he cried, as he had a hundred times before. Only this time, *this* time, Robb had answered, "You can't be Lord of Winterfell, you're bastard-born. My lady mother says you can't ever be the Lord of Winterfell."

I thought I had forgotten that. Jon could taste blood in his mouth, from the blow he'd taken.

In the end Halder and Horse had to pull him away from Iron Emmett, one man on either arm. The ranger sat on the ground dazed, his shield half in splinters, the visor of his helm knocked askew, and his sword six yards away. "Jon, enough," Halder was shouting, "he's down, you disarmed him. *Enough!*"

No. Not enough. Never enough. Jon let his sword drop. "I'm sorry," he muttered. "Emmett, are you hurt?"

Iron Emmett pulled his battered helm off. "Was there some part of *yield* you could not comprehend, Lord Snow?" It was said amiably, though. Emmett was an amiable man, and he loved the song of swords. "Warrior defend me," he groaned, "now I know how Qhorin Halfhand must have felt."

That was too much. Jon wrenched free of his friends and retreated to the armory, alone. His ears were still ringing from the blow Emmett had dealt him. He sat on the bench and buried his head in his hands. *Why am I so angry?* he asked himself, but it was a stupid question. *Lord of Winterfell. I could be the Lord of Winterfell. My father's heir.*

It was not Lord Eddard's face he saw floating before him, though; it was Lady Catelyn's. With her deep blue eyes and hard cold mouth, she looked a bit like Stannis. *Iron,* he thought, *but brittle.* She was looking at him the way she used to look at him at Winterfell, whenever he had bested Robb at swords or sums or most anything. *Who are you?* that look had always seemed to say. *This is not your place. Why are you here?*

His friends were still out in the practice yard, but Jon was in no fit state to face them. He left the armory by the back, descending a steep flight of stone steps to the wormways, the tunnels that linked the castle's keeps and towers below the earth. It was short walk to the bathhouse, where he took a cold plunge to wash the sweat off and soaked in a hot stone tub. The warmth took some of the ache from his muscles and made him think of Winterfell's muddy pools, steaming and bubbling in the godswood. *Winterfell*, he thought. *Theon left it burned and broken, but I could restore it.* Surely his father would have wanted that, and Robb as well. They would never have wanted the castle left in ruins.

You can't be the Lord of Winterfell, you're bastard-born, he heard Robb say again. And the stone kings were growling at him with granite tongues. *You do not belong here. This is not your place.* When Jon closed his eyes he saw the heart tree, with its pale limbs, red leaves, and solemn face. The weirwood was the heart of Winterfell, Lord Eddard always said ... but to save the castle Jon would have to tear that heart up by its ancient roots, and feed it to the red woman's hungry fire god. *I have no right*, he thought. *Winterfell belongs to the old gods.*

The sound of voices echoing off the vaulted ceiling brought him back to Castle Black. "I don't know," a man was saying, in a voice thick with doubts. "Maybe if I knew the man better ... Lord Stannis didn't have much good to say of him, I'll tell you that."

"When has Stannis Baratheon ever had much good to say of anyone?" Ser Alliser's flinty voice was unmistakable. "If we let Stannis choose our Lord Commander, we become his bannermen in all but name. Tywin Lannister is not like to forget that, and you know it will be Lord Tywin who wins in the end. He's already beaten Stannis once, on the Blackwater."

"Lord Tywin favors Slynt," said Bowen Marsh, in a fretful, anxious voice. "I can show you his letter, Othell. 'Our faithful friend and servant,' he called him."

Jon Snow sat up suddenly, and the three men froze at the sound of the slosh. "My lords," he said with cold courtesy.

"What are you doing here, bastard?" Thorne asked.

"Bathing. But don't let me spoil your plotting." Jon climbed from the water, dried, dressed, and left them to conspire.

Outside, he found he had no idea where he was going. He walked past the shell of the Lord Commander's Tower, where once he'd saved the Old Bear from a dead man; past the spot where Ygritte had died with that sad smile on her face; past the King's Tower where he and Satin and Deaf Dick Follard had waited for the Magnar and his Thenns; past the heaped and charred remains of the great wooden stair. The inner gate was open, so Jon went down the tunnel, through the Wall. He could feel the cold around him, the weight of all the ice above his head. He walked past the place where Donal Noye and Mag the Mighty had fought and died together, through the new outer gate, and back into the pale cold sunlight.

Only then did he permit himself to stop, to take a breath, to think. Othell Yarwyck was not a man of strong convictions, except when it came to wood and stone and mortar. The Old Bear had known that. *Thorne and Marsh will sway him, Yarwyck will support Lord Janos, and Lord Janos will be chosen Lord Commander. And what does that leave me, if not Winterfell?*

A wind swirled against the Wall, tugging at his cloak. He could feel the cold coming off the ice the way heat comes off a fire. Jon pulled up his hood and began to walk again. The afternoon was growing old, and the sun was low in the west. A hundred yards away was the camp where King Stannis had confined his wildling captives within a ring of ditches, sharpened stakes, and high wooden fences. To his left were three great firepits, where the victors had burned the bodies of all the free folk to die beneath the Wall, huge pelted giants and little Hornfoot men alike. The killing ground was still a desolation of scorched weeds and hardened pitch, but Mance's people had left traces of themselves everywhere; a torn hide that might have been part of a tent, a giant's maul, the wheel of a chariot, a broken spear, a pile of mammoth dung. On the edge of the haunted forest, where the tents had been, Jon found an oakwood stump and sat.

Ygritte wanted me to be a wildling. Stannis wants me to be the Lord of Winterfell. But what do I want? The sun crept down the sky to dip behind the Wall where it curved through the western hills. Jon watched as that towering expanse of ice took on the reds and pinks of sunset. *Would I sooner be hanged for a turncloak by Lord Janos, or forswear my vows, marry Val, and become the Lord of Winterfell?* It seemed an easy choice when he thought of it in those terms ... though if Ygritte had still been alive, it might have been even easier. Val was a stranger to him. She was not hard on the eyes, certainly, and she had been sister to Mance Rayder's queen, but still ...

I would need to steal her if I wanted her love, but she might give me children. I might someday hold a son of my own blood in my arms. A son was something Jon Snow had never dared dream of, since he decided to live his life on the Wall. *I could name him Robb. Val would want to keep her sister's son, but we could foster him at Winterfell, and Gilly's boy as well. Sam would never need to tell his lie. We'd find a place for Gilly too, and Sam could come visit her once a year or so. Mance's son and Craster's would grow up brothers, as I once did with Robb.*

He wanted it, Jon knew then. He wanted it as much as he had ever wanted anything. *I have always wanted it,* he thought, guiltily. *May the gods forgive me.* It was a hunger inside him, sharp as a dragonglass blade. A hunger ... he could feel it. It was food he needed, prey, a red deer that stank of fear or a great elk proud and defiant. He needed to kill and fill his belly with fresh meat and hot dark blood. His mouth began to water with the thought.

It was a long moment before he understood what was happening. When
he did, he bolted to his feet. *"Ghost!"* He turned toward the wood, and
there he came, padding silently out of the green dusk, the breath coming
warm and white from his open jaws. *"Ghost!"* he shouted, and the direwolf broke into a run. He was leaner than he had been, but bigger as
well, and the only sound he made was the soft crunch of dead leaves
beneath his paws. When he reached Jon he leapt, and they wrestled amidst
brown grass and long shadows as the stars came out above them. "Gods,
wolf, where have you *been*?" Jon said when Ghost stopped worrying at
his forearm. "I thought you'd died on me, like Robb and Ygritte and all
the rest. I've had no sense of you, not since I climbed the Wall, not even
in dreams." The direwolf had no answer, but he licked Jon's face with a
tongue like a wet rasp, and his eyes caught the last light and shone like
two great red suns.

Red eyes, Jon realized, *but not like Melisandre's.* He had a weirwood's
eyes. *Red eyes, red mouth, white fur. Blood and bone, like a heart tree.
He belongs to the old gods, this one.* And he alone of all the direwolves
was white. Six pups they'd found in the late summer snows, him and
Robb; five that were grey and black and brown, for the five Starks, and
one white, as white as Snow.

He had his answer then.

Beneath the Wall, the queen's men were kindling their nightfire. He
saw Melisandre emerge from the tunnel with the king beside her, to lead
the prayers she believed would keep the dark away. "Come, Ghost," Jon
told the wolf. "With me. You're hungry, I know. I could feel it." They
ran together for the gate, circling wide around the nightfire, where reaching flames clawed at the black belly of the night.

The king's men were much in evidence in the yards of Castle Black.
They stopped as Jon went by, and gaped at him. None of them had ever
seen a direwolf before, he realized, and Ghost was twice as large as the
common wolves that prowled their southron greenwoods. As he walked
toward the armory, Jon chanced to look up and saw Val standing in her
tower window. *I'm sorry*, he thought. *I'm not the man to steal you out
of there.*

In the practice yard he came upon a dozen king's men with torches
and long spears in their hands. Their sergeant looked at Ghost and
scowled, and a couple of his men lowered their spears until the knight
who led them said, "Move aside and let them pass." To Jon he said,
"You're late for your supper."

"Then get out of my way, ser," Jon replied, and he did.

He could hear the noise even before he reached the bottom of the
steps; raised voices, curses, someone pounding on a table. Jon stepped
into the vault all but unnoticed. His brothers crowded the benches and

the tables, but more were standing and shouting than were sitting, and no one was eating. There was no food. *What's happening here?* Lord Janos Slynt was bellowing about turncloaks and treason, Iron Emmett stood on a table with a naked sword in his fist, Three-Finger Hobb was cursing a ranger from the Shadow Tower . . . some Eastwatch man slammed his fist onto the table again and again, demanding quiet, but all that did was add to the din echoing off the vaulted ceiling.

Pyp was the first to see Jon. He grinned at the sight of Ghost, put two fingers in his mouth, and whistled as only a mummer's boy could whistle. The shrill sound cut through the clamor like a sword. As Jon walked toward the tables, more of the brothers took note, and fell quiet. A hush spread across the cellar, until the only sounds were Jon's heels clicking on the stone floor, and the soft crackle of the logs in the hearth.

Ser Alliser Thorne shattered the silence. "The turncloak graces us with his presence at last."

Lord Janos was red-faced and quivering. "The *beast*," he gasped. "Look! The beast that tore the life from Halfhand. A warg walks among us, brothers. A *WARG!* This . . . this *creature* is not fit to lead us! This *beastling* is not fit to live!"

Ghost bared his teeth, but Jon put a hand on his head. "My lord," he said, "will you tell me what's happened here?"

Maester Aemon answered, from the far end of the hall. "Your name has been put forth as Lord Commander, Jon."

That was so absurd Jon had to smile. "By who?" he said, looking for his friends. This had to be one of Pyp's japes, surely. But Pyp shrugged at him, and Grenn shook his head. It was Dolorous Edd Tollett who stood. "By me. Aye, it's a terrible cruel thing to do to a friend, but better you than me."

Lord Janos started sputtering again. "This, this is an outrage. We ought to hang this *boy*. Yes! Hang him, I say, hang him for a turncloak and a warg, along with his friend Mance Rayder. Lord *Commander?* I will not have it, I will not suffer it!"

Cotter Pyke stood up. "*You* won't suffer it? Might be you had those gold cloaks trained to lick your bloody arse, but you're wearing a black cloak now."

"Any brother may offer any name for our consideration, so long as the man has said his vows," Ser Denys Mallister said. "Tollett is well within his rights, my lord."

A dozen men started to talk at once, each trying to drown out the others, and before long half the hall was shouting once more. This time it was Ser Alliser Thorne who leapt up on the table, and raised his hands for quiet. "*Brothers!*" he cried, "this gains us naught. I say we vote. This *king* who has taken the King's Tower has posted men at all the doors to see that we do not eat nor leave till we have made a choice. So be it! We will choose, and choose again, all night if need be, until we have our lord . . . but before we cast our tokens, I believe our First Builder has something to say to us."

Othell Yarwyck stood up slowly, frowning. The big builder rubbed his long lantern jaw and said, "Well, I'm pulling my name out. If you wanted me, you had ten chances to choose me, and you didn't. Not enough of you, anyway. I was going to say that those who were casting a token for me ought to choose Lord Janos . . ."

Ser Alliser nodded. "Lord Slynt is the best possible –"

"I wasn't *done*, Alliser," Yarwyck complained. "Lord Slynt commanded the City Watch in King's Landing, we all know, and he was Lord of Harrenhal . . ."

"He's never *seen* Harrenhal," Cotter Pyke shouted out.

"Well, that's so," said Yarwyck. "Anyway, now that I'm standing here, I don't recall why I thought Slynt would be such a good choice. That would be sort of kicking King Stannis in the mouth, and I don't see how that serves us. Might be Snow would be better. He's been longer on the Wall, he's Ben Stark's nephew, and he served the Old Bear as squire." Yarwyck shrugged. "Pick who you want, just so it's not me." He sat down.

Janos Slynt had turned from red to purple, Jon saw, but Ser Alliser Thorne had gone pale. The Eastwatch man was pounding his fist on the table again, but now he was shouting for the kettle. Some of his friends took up the cry. "*Kettle!*" they roared, as one. "*Kettle, kettle, KETTLE!*"

The kettle was in the corner by the hearth, a big black potbellied thing with two huge handles and a heavy lid. Maester Aemon said a word to Sam and Clydas and they went and grabbed the handles and dragged the kettle over to the table. A few of the brothers were already queueing up by the token barrels as Clydas took the lid off and almost dropped it on his foot. With a raucous scream and a clap of wings, a huge raven burst out of the kettle. It flapped upward, seeking the rafters perhaps, or a window to make its escape, but there were no rafters in the vault, nor windows either. The raven was trapped. Cawing loudly, it circled the hall, once, twice, three times. And Jon heard Samwell Tarly shout, "I know that bird! That's Lord Mormont's raven!"

The raven landed on the table nearest Jon. "*Snow,*" it cawed. It was an old bird, dirty and bedraggled. "*Snow,*" it said again, "*Snow, snow, snow.*" It walked to the end of the table, spread its wings again, and flew to Jon's shoulder.

Lord Janos Slynt sat down so heavily he made a *thump*, but Ser Alliser filled the vault with mocking laughter. "Ser Piggy thinks we're all fools, brothers," he said. "He's taught the bird this little trick. They all say *snow*, go up to the rookery and hear for yourselves. Mormont's bird had more words than that."

The raven cocked its head and looked at Jon. "*Corn?*" it said hopefully. When it got neither corn nor answer, it *quork*ed and muttered, "*Kettle? Kettle? Kettle?*"

The rest was arrowheads, a torrent of arrowheads, a flood of arrowheads, arrowheads enough to drown the last few stones and shells, and all the copper pennies too.

When the count was done, Jon found himself surrounded. Some clapped him on the back, whilst others bent the knee to him as if he were a lord in truth. Satin, Owen the Oaf, Halder, Toad, Spare Boot, Giant, Mully, Ulmer of the Kingswood, Sweet Donnel Hill, and half a hundred more pressed around him. Dywen clacked his wooden teeth and said, "Gods be good, our Lord Commander's still in swaddling clothes." Iron Emmett said, "I hope this don't mean I can't beat the bloody piss out of you next time we train, my lord." Three-Finger Hobb wanted to know if he'd still be eating with the men, or if he'd want his meals sent up to his solar. Even Bowen Marsh came up to say he would be glad to continue as Lord Steward if that was Lord Snow's wish.

"Lord Snow," said Cotter Pyke, "if you muck this up, I'm going to rip your liver out and eat it raw with onions."

Ser Denys Mallister was more courteous. "It was a hard thing young Samwell asked of me," the old knight confessed. "When Lord Qorgyle was chosen, I told myself, 'No matter, he has been longer on the Wall than you have, your time will come.' When it was Lord Mormont, I thought, 'He is strong and fierce, but he is old, your time may yet come.' But you are half a boy, Lord Snow, and now I must return to the Shadow Tower knowing that my time will never come." He smiled a tired smile. "Do not make me die regretful. Your uncle was a great man. Your lord father and his father as well. I shall expect full as much of you."

"Aye," said Cotter Pyke. "And you can start by telling those king's men that it's done, and we want our bloody supper."

"*Supper*," screamed the raven. "*Supper, supper.*"

The king's men cleared the door when they told them of the choosing, and Three-Finger Hobb and half a dozen helpers went trotting off to the kitchen to fetch the food. Jon did not wait to eat. He walked across the castle, wondering if he were dreaming, with the raven on his shoulder and Ghost at his heels. Pyp, Grenn, and Sam trailed after him, chattering, but he hardly heard a word until Grenn whispered, "*Sam* did it," and Pyp said, "Sam *did* it!" Pyp had brought a wineskin with him, and he took a long drink and chanted, "Sam, Sam, Sam the wizard, Sam the wonder, Sam Sam the marvel man, he did it. But when did you hide the raven in the kettle, Sam, and how in seven hells could you be certain it would fly to Jon? It would have mucked up everything if the bird had decided to perch on Janos Slynt's fat head."

"I had nothing to do with the bird," Sam insisted. "When it flew out of the kettle I almost wet myself."

Jon laughed, half amazed that he still remembered how. "You're all a bunch of mad fools, do you know that?"

"Us?" said Pyp. "You call *us* fools? We're not the ones who got chosen as the nine-hundredth-and-ninety-eighth Lord Commander of the Night's Watch. You best have some wine, Lord Jon. I think you're going to need a *lot* of wine."

So Jon Snow took the wineskin from his hand and had a swallow. But only one. The Wall was his, the night was dark, and he had a king to face.

SANSA

She awoke all at once, every nerve atingle. For a moment she did not remember where she was. She had dreamt that she was little, still sharing a bedchamber with her sister Arya. But it was her maid she heard tossing in sleep, not her sister, and this was not Winterfell, but the Eyrie. *And I am Alayne Stone, a bastard girl.* The room was cold and black, though she was warm beneath the blankets. Dawn had not yet come. Sometimes she dreamed of Ser Ilyn Payne and woke with her heart thumping, but this dream had not been like that. *Home. It was a dream of home.*

The Eyrie was no home. It was no bigger than Maegor's Holdfast, and outside its sheer white walls was only the mountain and the long treacherous descent past Sky and Snow and Stone to the Gates of the Moon on the valley floor. There was no place to go and little to do. The older servants said these halls rang with laughter when her father and Robert Baratheon had been Jon Arryn's wards, but those days were many years gone. Her aunt kept a small household, and seldom permitted any guests to ascend past the Gates of the Moon. Aside from her aged maid, Sansa's only companion was the Lord Robert, eight going on three.

And Marillion. There is always Marillion. When he played for them at supper, the young singer often seemed to be singing directly at her. Her aunt was far from pleased. Lady Lysa doted on Marillion, and had banished two serving girls and even a page for telling lies about him.

Lysa was as lonely as she was. Her new husband seemed to spend more time at the foot of the mountain than he did atop it. He was gone now, had been gone the past four days, meeting with the Corbrays. From bits and pieces of overheard conversations Sansa knew that Jon Arryn's bannermen resented Lysa's marriage and begrudged Petyr his authority as Lord Protector of the Vale. The senior branch of House Royce was close to open revolt over her aunt's failure to aid Robb in his war, and the Waynwoods, Redforts, Belmores, and Templetons were giving them every support. The mountain clans were being troublesome as well, and old Lord Hunter had died so suddenly that his two younger sons were accusing their elder brother of having murdered him. The Vale of Arryn might have been spared the worst of the war, but it was hardly the idyllic place that Lady Lysa had made it out to be.

I am not going back to sleep, Sansa realized. *My head is all a tumult.* She pushed her pillow away reluctantly, threw back the blankets, went to her window, and opened the shutters.

Snow was falling on the Eyrie.

Outside the flakes drifted down as soft and silent as memory. *Was this what woke me?* Already the snowfall lay thick upon the garden below, blanketing the grass, dusting the shrubs and statues with white and weighing down the branches of the trees. The sight took Sansa back to cold nights long ago, in the long summer of her childhood.

She had last seen snow the day she'd left Winterfell. *That was a lighter fall than this*, she remembered. *Robb had melting flakes in his hair when he hugged me, and the snowball Arya tried to make kept coming apart in her hands.* It hurt to remember how happy she had been that morning. Hullen had helped her mount, and she'd ridden out with the snowflakes swirling around her, off to see the great wide world. *I thought my song was beginning that day, but it was almost done.*

Sansa left the shutters open as she dressed. It would be cold, she knew, though the Eyrie's towers encircled the garden and protected it from the worst of the mountain winds. She donned silken smallclothes and a linen shift, and over that a warm dress of blue lambswool. Two pairs of hose for her legs, boots that laced up to her knees, heavy leather gloves, and finally a hooded cloak of soft white fox fur.

Her maid rolled herself more tightly in her blanket as the snow began to drift in the window. Sansa eased open the door, and made her way down the winding stair. When she opened the door to the garden, it was so lovely that she held her breath, unwilling to disturb such perfect beauty. The snow drifted down and down, all in ghostly silence, and lay thick and unbroken on the ground. All color had fled the world outside. It was a place of whites and blacks and greys. White towers and white snow and white statues, black shadows and black trees, the dark grey sky above. *A pure world*, Sansa thought. *I do not belong here.*

Yet she stepped out all the same. Her boots tore ankle-deep holes into the smooth white surface of the snow, yet made no sound. Sansa drifted past frosted shrubs and thin dark trees, and wondered if she were still dreaming. Drifting snowflakes brushed her face as light as lover's kisses, and melted on her cheeks. At the center of the garden, beside the statue of the weeping woman that lay broken and half-buried on the ground, she turned her face up to the sky and closed her eyes. She could feel the snow on her lashes, taste it on her lips. It was the taste of Winterfell. The taste of innocence. The taste of dreams.

When Sansa opened her eyes again, she was on her knees. She did not remember falling. It seemed to her that the sky was a lighter shade of grey. *Dawn*, she thought. *Another day. Another new day*. It was the old days she hungered for. Prayed for. But who could she pray to? The garden had been meant for a godswood once, she knew, but the soil was too thin and stony for a weirwood to take root. *A godswood without gods, as empty as me.*

She scooped up a handful of snow and squeezed it between her fingers. Heavy and wet, the snow packed easily. Sansa began to make snowballs, shaping and smoothing them until they were round and white and perfect. She remembered a summer's snow in Winterfell when Arya and Bran had ambushed her as she emerged from the keep one morning. They'd each had a dozen snowballs to hand, and she'd had none. Bran had been perched on the roof of the covered bridge, out of reach, but Sansa had chased Arya through the stables and around the kitchen until both of them were breathless. She might even have caught her, but she'd slipped on some ice. Her sister came back to see if she was hurt. When she said she wasn't, Arya hit her in the face with another snowball, but Sansa grabbed her leg and pulled her down and was rubbing snow in her hair when Jory came along and pulled them apart, laughing.

What do I want with snowballs? She looked at her sad little arsenal. *There's no one to throw them at.* She let the one she was making drop from her hand. *I could build a snow knight instead*, she thought. *Or even . . .*

She pushed two of her snowballs together, added a third, packed more snow in around them, and patted the whole thing into the shape of a cylinder. When it was done, she stood it on end and used the tip of her little finger to poke holes in it for windows. The crenellations around the top took a little more care, but when they were done she had a tower. *I need some walls now*, Sansa thought, *and then a keep*. She set to work.

The snow fell and the castle rose. Two walls ankle-high, the inner taller than the outer. Towers and turrets, keeps and stairs, a round kitchen, a square armory, the stables along the inside of the west wall. It was only a castle when she began, but before very long Sansa knew it was Winterfell. She found twigs and fallen branches beneath the snow and broke off the ends to make the trees for the godswood. For the gravestones in the lichyard she used bits of bark. Soon her gloves and her boots were crusty white, her hands were tingling, and her feet were soaked and cold, but she did not care. The castle was all that mattered. Some things were hard to remember, but most came back to her easily, as if she had been there only yesterday. The Library Tower, with the steep stonework stair twisting about its exterior. The gatehouse, two huge bulwarks, the arched gate between them, crenellations all along the top . . .

And all the while the snow kept falling, piling up in drifts around her buildings as fast as she raised them. She was patting down the pitched roof of the Great Hall when she heard a voice, and looked up to see her maid calling from her window. Was my lady well? Did she wish to break her fast? Sansa shook her head, and went back to shaping snow, adding a chimney to one end of the Great Hall, where the hearth would stand inside.

Dawn stole into her garden like a thief. The grey of the sky grew lighter still, and the trees and shrubs turned a dark green beneath their stoles of snow. A few servants came out and watched her for a time, but she paid them no mind and they soon went back inside where it was warmer. Sansa saw Lady Lysa gazing down from her balcony, wrapped up in a blue velvet robe trimmed with fox fur, but when she looked again her aunt was gone. Maester Colemon popped out of the rookery and peered down for a while, skinny and shivering but curious.

Her bridges kept falling down. There was a covered bridge between the armory and the main keep, and another that went from the fourth floor of the bell tower to the second floor of the rookery, but no matter how carefully she shaped them, they would not hold together. The third time one collapsed on her, she cursed aloud and sat back in helpless frustration.

"Pack the snow around a stick, Sansa."

She did not know how long he had been watching her, or when he had returned from the Vale. "A stick?" she asked.

"That will give it strength enough to stand, I'd think," Petyr said. "May I come into your castle, my lady?"

Sansa was wary. "Don't break it. Be . . ."

". . . gentle?" He smiled. "Winterfell has withstood fiercer enemies than me. It *is* Winterfell, is it not?"

"Yes," Sansa admitted.

He walked along outside the walls. "I used to dream of it, in those years after Cat went north with Eddard Stark. In my dreams it was ever a dark place, and cold."

"No. It was always warm, even when it snowed. Water from the hot springs is piped through the walls to warm them, and inside the glass gardens it was always like the hottest day of summer." She stood, towering over the great white castle. "I can't think how to do the glass roof over the gardens."

Littlefinger stroked his chin, where his beard had been before Lysa had asked him to shave it off. "The glass was locked in frames, no? Twigs are your answer. Peel them and cross them and use bark to tie them together into frames. I'll show you." He moved through the garden, gathering up twigs and sticks and shaking the snow from them. When he had enough, he stepped over both walls with a single long stride and squatted on his heels in the middle of the yard. Sansa came closer to watch what he was doing. His hands were deft and sure, and before long he had a crisscrossing latticework of twigs, very like the one that roofed the glass gardens of Winterfell. "We will need to imagine the glass, to be sure," he said when he gave it to her.

"This is just right," she said.

He touched her face. "And so is that."

Sansa did not understand. "And so is what?"

"Your smile, my lady. Shall I make another for you?"

"If you would."

"Nothing could please me more."

She raised the walls of the glass gardens while Littlefinger roofed them over, and when they were done with that he helped her extend the walls and build the guardshall. When she used sticks for the covered bridges, they stood, just as he had said they would. The First Keep was simple enough, an old round drum tower, but Sansa was stymied again when it came to putting the gargoyles around the top. Again he had the answer. "It's been snowing on your castle, my lady," he pointed out. "What do the gargoyles look like when they're covered with snow?"

Sansa closed her eyes to see them in memory. "They're just white lumps."

"Well, then. Gargoyles are hard, but white lumps should be easy." And they were.

The Broken Tower was easier still. They made a tall tower together, kneeling side by side to roll it smooth, and when they'd raised it Sansa stuck her fingers through the top, grabbed a handful of snow, and flung it full in his face. Petyr yelped, as the snow slid down under his collar. "That was unchivalrously done, my lady."

"As was bringing me here, when you swore to take me home."

She wondered where this courage had come from, to speak to him so frankly. *From Winterfell*, she thought. *I am stronger within the walls of Winterfell.*

His face grew serious. "Yes, I played you false in that . . . and in one other thing as well."

Sansa's stomach was aflutter. "What other thing?"

"I told you that nothing could please me more than to help you with your castle. I fear that was a lie as well. Something else would please me more." He stepped closer. "This."

Sansa tried to step back, but he pulled her into his arms and suddenly he was kissing her. Feebly, she tried to squirm, but only succeeded in pressing herself more tightly against him. His mouth was on hers, swallowing her words. He tasted of mint. For half a heartbeat she yielded to his kiss ... before she turned her face away and wrenched free. "What are you *doing?*"

Petyr straightened his cloak. "Kissing a snow maid."

"You're supposed to kiss *her.*" Sansa glanced up at Lysa's balcony, but it was empty now. "Your lady wife."

"I do. Lysa has no cause for complaint." He smiled. "I wish you could see yourself, my lady. You are so beautiful. You're crusted over with snow like some little bear cub, but your face is flushed and you can scarcely breathe. How long have you been out here? You must be very cold. Let me warm you, Sansa. Take off those gloves, give me your hands."

"I won't." He sounded almost like Marillion, the night he'd gotten so drunk at the wedding. Only this time Lothor Brune would not appear to save her; Ser Lothor was Petyr's man. "You shouldn't kiss me. I might have been your own daughter ..."

"Might have been," he admitted, with a rueful smile. "But you're not, are you? You are Eddard Stark's daughter, and Cat's. But I think you might be even more beautiful than your mother was, when she was your age."

"Petyr, please." Her voice sounded so weak. "Please ..."

"A *castle!*"

The voice was loud, shrill, and childish. Littlefinger turned away from her. "Lord Robert." He sketched a bow. "Should you be out in the snow without your gloves?"

"Did you make the snow castle, Lord Littlefinger?"

"Alayne did most of it, my lord."

Sansa said, "It's meant to be Winterfell."

"Winterfell?" Robert was small for eight, a stick of a boy with splotchy skin and eyes that were always runny. Under one arm he clutched the threadbare cloth doll he carried everywhere.

"Winterfell is the seat of House Stark," Sansa told her husband-to-be. "The great castle of the north."

"It's not so great." The boy knelt before the gatehouse. "Look, here comes a giant to knock it down." He stood his doll in the snow and moved it jerkily. "*Tromp tromp I'm a giant, I'm a giant,*" he chanted. "*Ho ho ho, open your gates or I'll mash them and smash them.*" Swinging the doll by the legs, he knocked the top off one gatehouse tower and then the other.

It was more than Sansa could stand. "Robert, *stop that.*" Instead he swung the doll again, and a foot of wall exploded. She grabbed for his hand but she caught the doll instead. There was a loud ripping sound as the thin cloth tore. Suddenly she had the doll's head, Robert had the legs and body, and the rag-and-sawdust stuffing was spilling in the snow.

Lord Robert's mouth trembled. "You *killllllllled* him," he wailed. Then he began to shake. It started with no more than a little shivering, but within a few short heartbeats he had collapsed across the castle, his limbs flailing about violently. White towers and snowy bridges shattered and fell on all sides. Sansa stood horrified, but Petyr Baelish seized her cousin's wrists and shouted for the maester.

Guards and serving girls arrived within instants to help restrain the boy, Maester Colemon a short time later. Robert Arryn's shaking sickness was nothing new to the people of the Eyrie, and Lady Lysa had trained them all to come rushing at the boy's first cry. The maester held the little lord's head and gave him half a cup of dreamwine, murmuring soothing words. Slowly the violence of the fit seemed to ebb away, till nothing remained but a small shaking of the hands. "Help him to my chambers," Colemon told the guards. "A leeching will help calm him."

"It was my fault." Sansa showed them the doll's head. "I ripped his doll in two. I never meant to, but . . ."

"His lordship was destroying the castle," said Petyr.

"A giant," the boy whispered, weeping. "It wasn't me, it was a giant hurt the castle. She *killed* him! I hate her! She's a bastard and I *hate* her! I don't *want* to be leeched!"

"My lord, your blood needs thinning," said Maester Colemon. "It is the bad blood that makes you angry, and the rage that brings on the shaking. Come now."

They led the boy away. *My lord husband*, Sansa thought, as she contemplated the ruins of Winterfell. The snow had stopped, and it was colder than before. She wondered if Lord Robert would shake all through their wedding. *At least Joffrey was sound of body.* A mad rage seized hold of her. She picked up a broken branch and smashed the torn doll's head down on top of it, then pushed it down atop the shattered gatehouse of her snow castle. The servants looked aghast, but when Littlefinger saw what she'd done he laughed. "If the tales be true, that's not the first giant to end up with his head on Winterfell's walls."

"Those are only stories," she said, and left him there.

Back in her bedchamber, Sansa took off her cloak and her wet boots and sat beside the fire. She had no doubt that she would be made to answer for Lord Robert's fit. *Perhaps Lady Lysa will send me away.* Her aunt was quick to banish anyone who displeased her, and nothing displeased her quite so much as people she suspected of mistreating her son.

Sansa would have welcomed banishment. The Gates of the Moon was much larger than the Eyrie, and livelier as well. Lord Nestor Royce seemed gruff and stern, but his daughter Myranda kept his castle for him, and everyone said how frolicsome she was. Even Sansa's supposed bastardy might not count too much against her below. One of King Robert's baseborn daughters was in service to Lord Nestor, and she and the Lady Myranda were said to be fast friends, as close as sisters.

I will tell my aunt that I don't want to marry Robert. Not even the High Septon himself could declare a woman married if she refused to say the vows. She wasn't a beggar, no matter what her aunt said. She was thirteen, a woman flowered and wed, the heir to Winterfell. Sansa felt sorry for her little cousin sometimes, but she could not imagine ever wanting to be his wife. *I would sooner be married to Tyrion again.* If Lady Lysa knew that, surely she'd send her away . . . away from Robert's pouts and shakes and runny eyes, away from Marillion's lingering looks, away from Petyr's kisses. *I will tell her. I will!*

It was late that afternoon when Lady Lysa summoned her. Sansa had been marshaling her courage all day, but no sooner did Marillion appear at her door than all her doubts returned. "Lady Lysa requires your presence in the High Hall." The singer's eyes undressed her as he spoke, but she was used to that.

Marillion was comely, there was no denying it; boyish and slender, with smooth skin, sandy hair, a charming smile. But he had made himself well hated in the Vale, by everyone but her aunt and little Lord Robert. To hear the servants talk, Sansa was not the first maid to suffer his advances, and the others had not had Lothor Brune to defend them. But Lady Lysa would hear no complaints against him. Since coming to the Eyrie, the singer had become her favorite. He sang Lord Robert to sleep every night, and tweaked the noses of Lady Lysa's suitors with verses that made mock of their foibles. Her aunt had showered him with gold and gifts; costly clothes, a gold arm ring, a belt studded with moonstones, a fine horse. She had even given him her late husband's favorite falcon. It all served to make Marillion unfailingly courteous in Lady Lysa's presence, and unfailingly arrogant outside it.

"Thank you," Sansa told him stiffly. "I know the way."

He would not leave. "My lady said to bring you."

Bring me? She did not like the sound of that. "Are you a guardsman now?" Littlefinger had dismissed the Eyrie's captain of guards and put Ser Lothor Brune in his place.

"Do you require guarding?" Marillion said lightly. "I am composing a new song, you should know. A song so sweet and sad it will melt even your frozen heart. 'The Roadside Rose,' I mean to call it. About a baseborn girl so beautiful she bewitched every man who laid eyes upon her."

I am a Stark of Winterfell, she longed to tell him. Instead she nodded, and let him escort her down the tower steps and along a bridge. The High Hall had been closed as long as she'd been at the Eyrie. Sansa wondered why her aunt had opened it. Normally she preferred the comfort of her solar, or the cozy warmth of Lord Arryn's audience chamber with its view of the waterfall.

Two guards in sky-blue cloaks flanked the carved wooden doors of the High Hall, spears in hand. "No one is to enter so long as Alayne is with Lady Lysa," Marillion told them.

"Aye." The men let them pass, then crossed their spears. Marillion swung the doors shut and barred them with a third spear, longer and thicker than those the guards had borne.

Sansa felt a prickle of unease. "Why did you do that?"

"My lady awaits you."

She looked about uncertainly. Lady Lysa sat on the dais in a high-backed chair of carved weirwood, alone. To her right was a second chair, taller than her own, with a stack of blue cushions piled on the seat, but Lord Robert was not in it. Sansa hoped he'd recovered. Marillion was not like to tell her, though.

Sansa walked down the blue silk carpet between rows of fluted pillars slim as lances. The floors and walls of the High Hall were made of milk-white marble veined with blue. Shafts of pale daylight slanted down through narrow arched windows along the eastern wall. Between the windows were torches, mounted in high iron sconces, but none of them was lit. Her footsteps fell softly on the carpet. Outside the wind blew cold and lonely.

Amidst so much white marble even the sunlight looked chilly, some-how . . . though not half so chilly as her aunt. Lady Lysa had dressed in a gown of cream-colored velvet and a necklace of sapphires and moon-stones. Her auburn hair had been done up in a thick braid, and fell across one shoulder. She sat in the high seat watching her niece approach, her face red and puffy beneath the paint and powder. On the wall behind her hung a huge banner, the moon-and-falcon of House Arryn in cream and blue.

Sansa stopped before the dais, and curtsied. "My lady. You sent for me." She could still hear the sound of the wind, and the soft chords Marillion was playing at the foot of the hall.

"I saw what you did," the Lady Lysa said.

Sansa smoothed down the folds of her skirt. "I trust Lord Robert is better? I never meant to rip his doll. He was smashing my snow castle, I only . . ."

"Will you play the coy deceiver with me?" her aunt said. "I was not speaking of Robert's doll. I *saw* you kissing him."

The High Hall seemed to grow a little colder. The walls and floor and columns might have turned to ice. "He kissed me."

Lysa's nostrils flared. "And why would he do that? He has a wife who loves him. A woman grown, not a little girl. He has no need for the likes of you. Confess, child. You threw yourself at him. That was the way of it."

Sansa took a step backward. "That's not true."

"Where are you going? Are you afraid? Such wanton behavior must be punished, but I will not be hard on you. We keep a whipping boy for Robert, as is the custom in the Free Cities. His health is too delicate for him to bear the rod himself. I shall find some common girl to take your whipping, but first you must own up to what you've done. I cannot abide a liar, Alayne."

"I was building a snow castle," Sansa said. "Lord Petyr was helping me, and then he kissed me. That's what you saw."

"Have you no honor?" her aunt said sharply. "Or do you take me for a fool? You do, don't you? You take me for a fool. Yes, I see that now. I am not a fool. You think you can have any man you want because you're young and beautiful. Don't think I haven't seen the looks you give Marillion. I know everything that happens in the Eyrie, little lady. And I have known your like before, too. But you are mistaken if you think big eyes and strumpet's smiles will win you Petyr. He is mine." She rose to her feet. "They all tried to take him from me. My lord father, my husband, your mother . . . Catelyn most of all. She liked to kiss my Petyr too, oh yes she did."

Sansa retreated another step. "My mother?"

"Yes, your mother, your precious mother, my own sweet sister Catelyn. Don't you think to play the innocent with me, you vile little liar. All those years in Riverrun, she played with Petyr as if he were her little toy. She teased him with smiles and soft words and wanton looks, and made his nights a torment."

"No." *My mother is dead,* she wanted to shriek. *She was your own sister, and she's dead.* "She didn't. She wouldn't."

"How would you know? Were you there?" Lysa descended from the high seat, her skirts swirling. "Did you come with Lord Bracken and Lord Blackwood, the time they visited to lay their feud before my father? Lord Bracken's singer played for us, and Catelyn danced six dances with Petyr that night, *six,* I counted. When the lords began to argue my father took them up to his audience chamber, so there was no one to stop us drinking. Edmure got drunk, young as he was . . . and Petyr tried to kiss your mother, only she pushed him away. She *laughed* at him. He looked so wounded I thought my heart would burst, and afterward he drank until he passed out at the table. Uncle Brynden carried him up to bed before my father could find him like that. But you remember none of it, do you?" She looked down angrily. *"Do you?"*

Is she drunk, or mad? "I was not born, my lady."

"You were not born. But I was, so do not presume to tell what is true. I *know* what is true. You kissed him!"

"He kissed me," Sansa insisted again. "I never wanted –"

"Be quiet, I haven't given you leave to speak. You enticed him, just as your mother did that night in Riverrun, with her smiles and her dancing. You think I could forget? That was the night I stole up to his bed to give him comfort. I bled, but it was the sweetest hurt. He told me he loved me then, but he called me *Cat*, just before he fell back to sleep. Even so, I stayed with him until the sky began to lighten. Your mother did not deserve him. She would not even give him her favor to wear when he fought Brandon Stark. *I* would have given him my favor. I gave him everything. He is mine now. Not Catelyn's and not yours."

All of Sansa's resolve had withered in the face of her aunt's onslaught. Lysa Arryn was frightening her as much as Queen Cersei ever had. "He's yours, my lady," she said, trying to sound meek and contrite. "May I have your leave to go?"

"You may not." Her aunt's breath smelled of wine. "If you were anyone else, I would banish you. Send you down to Lord Nestor at the Gates of the Moon, or back to the Fingers. How would you like to spend your life on that bleak shore, surrounded by slatterns and sheep pellets? That was what my father meant for Petyr. Everyone thought it was because of that stupid duel with Brandon Stark, but that wasn't so. Father said I ought to thank the gods that so great a lord as Jon Arryn was willing to take me soiled, but I knew it was only for the swords. I had to marry Jon, or my father would have turned me out as he did his brother, but it was Petyr I was meant for. I am telling you all this so you will understand how much we love each other, how long we have suffered and dreamed of one another. We made a baby together, a precious little baby." Lysa put her hands flat against her belly, as if the child was still there. "When they stole him from me, I made a promise to myself that I would never let it happen again. Jon wished to send my sweet Robert to Dragonstone, and that sot of a king would have given him to Cersei Lannister, but I never let them . . . no more than I'll let you steal my Petyr Littlefinger. Do you hear me, Alayne or Sansa or whatever you call yourself? Do you hear what I am telling you?"

"Yes. I swear, I won't ever kiss him again, or . . . or entice him." Sansa thought that was what her aunt wanted to hear.

"So you admit it now? It was you, just as I thought. You are as wanton as your mother." Lysa grabbed her by the wrist. "Come with me now. There is something I want to show you."

"You're hurting me." Sansa squirmed. "Please, Aunt Lysa, I haven't done anything. I swear it."

Her aunt ignored her protests. "*Marillion!*" she shouted. "I need you, Marillion! I *need* you!"

The singer had remained discreetly in the rear of the hall, but at Lady Arryn's shout he came at once. "My lady?"

"Play us a song. Play 'The False and the Fair.'"

Marillion's fingers brushed the strings. "*The lord he came a-riding upon a rainy day, hey-nonny, hey-nonny, hey-nonny-hey . . .*"

Lady Lysa pulled at Sansa's arm. It was either walk or be dragged, so she chose to walk, halfway down the hall and between a pair of pillars, to a white weirwood door set in the marble wall. The door was firmly closed, with three heavy bronze bars to hold it in place, but Sansa could hear the wind outside worrying at its edges. When she saw the crescent moon carved in the wood, she planted her feet. "The Moon Door." She tried to yank free. "Why are you showing me the Moon Door?"

"You squeak like a mouse now, but you were bold enough in the garden, weren't you? You were bold enough in the snow."

"*The lady sat a-sewing upon a rainy day,*" Marillion sang. "*Hey-nonny, hey-nonny, hey-nonny-hey.*"

"Open the door," Lysa commanded. "*Open* it, I say. You will do it, or I'll send for my guards." She shoved Sansa forward. "Your mother was brave, at least. Lift off the bars."

If I do as she says, she will let me go. Sansa grabbed one of the bronze bars, yanked it loose, and tossed it down. The second bar clattered to the marble, then the third. She had barely touched the latch when the heavy wooden door *flew* inward and slammed back against the wall with a bang. Snow had piled up around the frame, and it all came blowing in at them, borne on a blast of cold air that left Sansa shivering. She tried to step backward, but her aunt was behind her. Lysa seized her by the wrist and put her other hand between her shoulder blades, propelling her forcefully toward the open door.

Beyond was white sky, falling snow, and nothing else.

"Look down," said Lady Lysa. "Look *down*."

She tried to wrench free, but her aunt's fingers were digging into her arm like claws. Lysa gave her another shove, and Sansa shrieked. Her left foot broke through a crust of snow and knocked it loose. There was nothing in front of her but empty air, and a waycastle six hundred feet below clinging to the side of the mountain. "Don't!" Sansa screamed. "You're scaring me!" Behind her, Marillion was still playing his woodharp and singing, "*Hey-nonny, hey-nonny, hey-nonny-hey.*"

"Do you still want my leave to go? Do you?"

"No." Sansa planted her feet and tried to squirm backward, but her

aunt did not budge. "Not this way. Please . . ." She put a hand up, her
fingers scrabbling at the doorframe, but she could not get a grip, and
her feet were sliding on the wet marble floor. Lady Lysa pressed her
forward inexorably. Her aunt outweighed her by three stone. "*The lady
lay a-kissing, upon a mound of hay,*" Marillion was singing. Sansa twisted
sideways, hysterical with fear, and one foot slipped out over the void.
She screamed. "*Hey-nonny, hey-nonny, hey-nonny-hey.*" The wind
flapped her skirts up and bit at her bare legs with cold teeth. She could
feel snowflakes melting on her cheeks. Sansa flailed, found Lysa's thick
auburn braid, and clutched it tight. "My hair!" her aunt shrieked. "*Let
go of my hair!*" She was shaking, sobbing. They teetered on the edge. Far
off, she heard the guards pounding on the door with their spears,
demanding to be let in. Marillion broke off his song.

"*Lysa!* What's the meaning of this?" The shout cut through the sobs
and heavy breathing. Footsteps echoed down the High Hall. "Get *back*
from there! Lysa, what are you doing?" The guards were still beating at
the door; Littlefinger had come in the back way, through the lords'
entrance behind the dais.

As Lysa turned, her grip loosened enough for Sansa to rip free. She
stumbled to her knees, where Petyr Baelish saw her. He stopped suddenly.
"Alayne. What is the trouble here?"

"*Her.*" Lady Lysa grabbed a handful of Sansa's hair. "*She's* the trouble.
She *kissed* you."

"Tell her," Sansa begged. "Tell her we were just building a castle . . ."

"*Be quiet!*" her aunt screamed. "I never gave you leave to speak. No
one cares about your castle."

"She's a child, Lysa. Cat's daughter. What did you think you were
doing?"

"I was going to marry her to *Robert!* She has no gratitude. No . . . no
decency. You are not hers to kiss. *Not hers!* I was teaching her a lesson,
that was all."

"I see." He stroked his chin. "I think she understands now. Isn't that
so, Alayne?"

"Yes," sobbed Sansa. "I understand."

"I don't want her here." Her aunt's eyes were shiny with tears. "Why
did you bring her to the Vale, Petyr? This isn't her place. She doesn't
belong here."

"We'll send her away, then. Back to King's Landing, if you like." He
took a step toward them. "Let her up, now. Let her away from the door."

"*NO!*" Lysa gave Sansa's head another wrench. Snow eddied around
them, making their skirts snap noisily. "You can't want her. You *can't.*
She's a stupid empty-headed little girl. She doesn't love you the way I
have. I've always loved you. I've proved it, haven't I?" Tears ran down

her aunt's puffy red face. "I gave you my maiden's gift. I would have given you a son too, but they murdered him with moon tea, with tansy and mint and wormwood, a spoon of honey and a drop of pennyroyal. It wasn't me, I never *knew*, I only drank what Father gave me . . ."

"That's past and done, Lysa. Lord Hoster's dead, and his old maester as well." Littlefinger moved closer. "Have you been at the wine again? You ought not to talk so much. We don't want Alayne to know more than she should, do we? Or Marillion?"

Lady Lysa ignored that. "Cat never gave you anything. It was me who got you your first post, who made Jon bring you to court so we could be close to one another. You promised me you would never forget that."

"Nor have I. We're together, just as you always wanted, just as we always planned. Just let go of Sansa's hair . . ."

"I won't! I saw you kissing in the snow. She's just like her mother. Catelyn kissed you in the godswood, but she never *meant* it, she never wanted you. Why did you love her best? It was me, it was always *meeee!*"

"I know, love." He took another step. "And I am here. All you need to do is take my hand, come on." He held it out to her. "There's no cause for all these tears."

"Tears, tears, *tears*," she sobbed hysterically. "No need for tears . . . but that's not what you said in King's Landing. You told me to put the tears in Jon's wine, and I did. For Robert, and for *us!* And I wrote Catelyn and told her the Lannisters had killed my lord husband, just as you said. That was so clever . . . you were always clever, I told Father that, I said Petyr's so clever, he'll rise high, he will, he *will*, and he's sweet and gentle and I have his little baby in my belly . . . Why did you kiss her? *Why?* We're together now, we're together after so long, so very long, why would you want to kiss *herrrrr?*"

"Lysa," Petyr sighed, "after all the storms we've suffered, you should trust me better. I swear, I shall never leave your side again, for as long as we both shall live."

"Truly?" she asked, weeping. "Oh, *truly?*"

"Truly. Now unhand the girl and come give me a kiss."

Lysa threw herself into Littlefinger's arms, sobbing. As they hugged, Sansa crawled from the Moon Door on hands and knees and wrapped her arms around the nearest pillar. She could feel her heart pounding. There was snow in her hair and her right shoe was missing. *It must have fallen.* She shuddered, and hugged the pillar tighter.

Littlefinger let Lysa sob against his chest for a moment, then put his hands on her arms and kissed her lightly. "My sweet silly jealous wife," he said, chuckling. "I've only loved one woman, I promise you."

Lysa Arryn smiled tremulously. "Only one? Oh, Petyr, do you swear it? Only one?"

"Only Cat." He gave her a short, sharp shove.

Lysa stumbled backward, her feet slipping on the wet marble. And then she was gone. She never screamed. For the longest time there was no sound but the wind.

Marillion gasped, "You . . . you . . ."

The guards were shouting outside the door, pounding with the butts of their heavy spears. Lord Petyr pulled Sansa to her feet. "You're not hurt?" When she shook her head, he said, "Run let my guards in, then. Quick now, there's no time to lose. This singer's killed my lady wife."

EPILOGUE

The road up to Oldstones went twice around the hill before reaching the summit. Overgrown and stony, it would have been slow going even in the best of times, and last night's snow had left it muddy as well. *Snow in autumn in the riverlands, it's unnatural*, Merrett thought gloomily. It had not been much of a snow, true; just enough to blanket the ground for a night. Most of it had started melting away as soon as the sun came up. Still, Merrett took it for a bad omen. Between rains, floods, fire, and war, they had lost two harvests and a good part of a third. An early winter would mean famine all across the riverlands. A great many people would go hungry, and some of them would starve. Merrett only hoped he wouldn't be one of them. *I may, though. With my luck, I just may. I never did have any luck.*

Beneath the castle ruins, the lower slopes of the hill were so thickly forested that half a hundred outlaws could well have been lurking there. *They could be watching me even now.* Merrett glanced about, and saw nothing but gorse, bracken, thistle, sedge, and blackberry bushes between the pines and grey-green sentinels. Elsewhere skeletal elm and ash and scrub oaks choked the ground like weeds. He saw no outlaws, but that meant little. Outlaws were better at hiding than honest men.

Merrett hated the woods, if truth be told, and he hated outlaws even more. "Outlaws stole my life," he had been known to complain when in his cups. He was too often in his cups, his father said, often and loudly. *Too true*, he thought ruefully. You needed some sort of distinction in the Twins, else they were liable to forget you were alive, but a reputation as the biggest drinker in the castle had done little to enhance his prospects, he'd found. *I once hoped to be the greatest knight who ever couched a lance. The gods took that away from me. Why shouldn't I have a cup of wine from time to time? It helps my headaches. Besides, my wife is a shrew, my father despises me, my children are worthless. What do I have to stay sober for?*

He was sober now, though. Well, he'd had two horns of ale when he broke his fast, and a small cup of red when he set out, but that was just to keep his head from pounding. Merrett could feel the headache building behind his eyes, and he knew that if he gave it half a chance he would soon feel as if he had a thunderstorm raging between his ears. Sometimes his headaches got so bad that it even hurt too much to weep. Then all he could do was rest on his bed in a dark room with a damp cloth over his eyes, and curse his luck and the nameless outlaw who had done this to him.

Just thinking about it made him anxious. He could no wise afford a headache now. *If I bring Petyr back home safely, all my luck will change.* He had the gold, all he needed to do was climb to the top of Oldstones, meet the bloody outlaws in the ruined castle, and make the exchange. A simple ransom. Even he could not muck it up . . . unless he got a headache, one so bad that it left him unable to ride. He was supposed to be at the ruins by sunset, not weeping in a huddle at the side of the road. Merrett rubbed two fingers against his temple. *Once more around the hill, and there I am.* When the message had come in and he had stepped forward to offer to carry the ransom, his father had squinted down and said, "*You*, Merrett?" and started laughing through his nose, that hideous *heh heh heh* laugh of his. Merrett practically had to beg before they'd give him the bloody bag of gold.

Something moved in the underbrush along the side of the road. Merrett reined up hard and reached for his sword, but it was only a squirrel. "Stupid," he told himself, shoving the sword back in its scabbard without ever having gotten it out. "Outlaws don't have tails. Bloody hell, Merrett, get hold of yourself." His heart was thumping in his chest as if he were some green boy on his first campaign. *As if this were the kingswood and it was the old Brotherhood I was going to face, not the lightning lord's sorry lot of brigands.* For a moment he was tempted to trot right back down the hill and find the nearest alehouse. That bag of gold would buy a lot of ale, enough for him to forget all about Petyr Pimple. *Let them hang him, he brought this on himself. It's no more than he deserves, wandering off with some bloody camp follower like a stag in rut.*

His head had begun to pound; soft now, but he knew it would get worse. Merrett rubbed the bridge of his nose. He really had no right to think so ill of Petyr. *I did the same myself when I was his age.* In his case all it got him was a pox, but still, he shouldn't condemn. Whores

did have charms, especially if you had a face like Petyr's. The poor lad
had a wife, to be sure, but she was half the problem. Not only was she
twice his age, but she was bedding his brother Walder too, if the talk was
true. There was always lots of talk around the Twins, and only a little
was ever true, but in this case Merrett believed it. Black Walder was a
man who took what he wanted, even his brother's wife. He'd had Edwyn's
wife too, that was common knowledge, Fair Walda had been known to
slip into his bed from time to time, and some even said he'd known the
seventh Lady Frey a deal better than he should have. Small wonder he
refused to marry. Why buy a cow when there were udders all around
begging to be milked?

Cursing under his breath, Merrett jammed his heels into his horse's
flanks and rode on up the hill. As tempting as it was to drink the gold
away, he knew that if he didn't come back with Petyr Pimple, he had as
well not come back at all.

Lord Walder would soon turn two-and-ninety. His ears had started to
go, his eyes were almost gone, and his gout was so bad that he had to be
carried everywhere. He could not possibly last much longer, all his sons
agreed. *And when he goes, everything will change, and not for the better.*
His father was querulous and stubborn, with an iron will and a wasp's
tongue, but he did believe in taking care of his own. *All* of his own, even
the ones who had displeased and disappointed him. *Even the ones whose
names he can't remember.* Once he was gone, though . . .

When Ser Stevron had been heir, that was one thing. The old man had
been grooming Stevron for sixty years, and had pounded it into his head
that blood was blood. But Stevron had died whilst campaigning with the
Young Wolf in the west – "of waiting, no doubt," Lame Lothar had
quipped when the raven brought them the news – and his sons and
grandsons were a different sort of Frey. Stevron's son Ser Ryman stood
to inherit now; a thick-witted, stubborn, greedy man. And after Ryman
came his own sons, Edwyn and Black Walder, who were even worse.
"Fortunately," Lame Lothar once said, "they hate each other even more
than they hate us."

Merrett wasn't certain that was fortunate at all, and for that matter
Lothar himself might be more dangerous than either of them. Lord Walder
had ordered the slaughter of the Starks at Roslin's wedding, but it had
been Lame Lothar who had plotted it out with Roose Bolton, all the way
down to which songs would be played. Lothar was a very amusing fellow
to get drunk with, but Merrett would never be so foolish as to turn his
back on him. In the Twins, you learned early that only full blood siblings
could be trusted, and them not very far.

It was like to be every son for himself when the old man died, and
every daughter as well. The new Lord of the Crossing would doubtless

keep on *some* of his uncles, nephews, and cousins at the Twins, the ones he happened to like or trust, or more likely the ones he thought would prove useful to him. *The rest of us he'll shove out to fend for ourselves.*

The prospect worried Merrett more than words could say. He would be forty in less than three years, too old to take up the life of a hedge knight . . . even if he'd *been* a knight, which as it happened he wasn't. He had no land, no wealth of his own. He owned the clothes on his back but not much else, not even the horse he was riding. He wasn't clever enough to be a maester, pious enough to be a septon, or savage enough to be a sellsword. *The gods gave me no gift but birth, and they stinted me there.* What good was it to be the son of a rich and powerful House if you were the *ninth* son? When you took grandsons and great-grandsons into account, Merrett stood a better chance of being chosen High Septon than he did of inheriting the Twins.

I have no luck, he thought bitterly. *I have never had any bloody luck.* He was a big man, broad around the chest and shoulders if only of middling height. In the last ten years he had grown soft and fleshy, he knew, but when he'd been younger Merrett had been almost as robust as Ser Hosteen, his eldest full brother, who was commonly regarded as the strongest of Lord Walder Frey's brood. As a boy he'd been packed off to Crakehall to serve his mother's family as a page. When old Lord Sumner had made him a squire, everyone had assumed he would be Ser Merrett in no more than a few years, but the outlaws of the Kingswood Brotherhood had pissed on those plans. While his fellow squire Jaime Lannister was covering himself in glory, Merrett had first caught the pox from a camp follower, then managed to get captured by a *woman*, the one called the White Fawn. Lord Sumner had ransomed him back from the outlaws, but in the very next fight he'd been felled by a blow from a mace that had broken his helm and left him insensible for a fortnight. Everyone gave him up for dead, they told him later.

Merrett hadn't died, but his fighting days were done. Even the lightest blow to his head brought on blinding pain and reduced him to tears. Under these circumstances knighthood was out of the question, Lord Sumner told him, not unkindly. He was sent back to the Twins to face Lord Walder's poisonous disdain.

After that, Merrett's luck had only grown worse. His father had managed to make a good marriage for him, somehow; he wed one of Lord Darry's daughters, back when the Darrys stood high in King Aerys's favor. But it seemed as if he no sooner had deflowered his bride than Aerys lost his throne. Unlike the Freys, the Darrys had been prominent Targaryen loyalists, which cost them half their lands, most of their wealth, and almost all their power. As for his lady wife, she found him a great disappointment from the first, and insisted on popping out nothing but girls for years; three live ones, a stillbirth, and one that died in infancy before she finally produced a son. His eldest daughter had turned out to be a slut, his second a glutton. When Ami was caught in the stables with no fewer than *three* grooms, he'd been forced to marry her off to a bloody *hedge knight*. That situation could not possibly get any worse, he'd thought . . . until Ser Pate decided he could win renown by defeating Ser Gregor Clegane. Ami had come running back a widow, to Merrett's dismay and the undoubted delight of every stablehand in the Twins.

Merrett had dared to hope that his luck was finally changing when Roose Bolton chose to wed *his* Walda instead of one of her slimmer, comelier cousins. The Bolton alliance was important for House Frey and his daughter had helped secure it; he thought that must surely count for something. The old man had soon disabused him. "He picked her because she's *fat*," Lord Walder said. "You think Bolton gave a mummer's fart that she was your whelp? Think he sat about thinking, '*Heh*, Merrett Muttonhead, that's the very man I need for a good-father'? Your Walda's a sow in silk, that's why he picked her, and I'm not like to thank you for it. We'd have had the same alliance at half the price if your little porkling put down her spoon from time to time."

The final humiliation had been delivered with a smile, when Lame Lothar had summoned him to discuss his role in Roslin's wedding. "We must each play our part, according to our gifts," his half-brother told him. "You shall have one task and one task only, Merrett, but I believe you are well suited to it. I want you to see to it that Greatjon Umber is so bloody drunk that he can hardly stand, let alone fight."

And even that I failed at. He'd cozened the huge northman into drinking enough wine to kill any three normal men, yet after Roslin had been bedded the Greatjon still managed to snatch the sword of the first man to accost him and break his arm in the snatching. It had taken eight of them to get him into chains, and the effort had left two men wounded, one dead, and poor old Ser Leslyn Haigh short half a ear. When he couldn't fight with his hands any longer, Umber had fought with his teeth.

Merrett paused a moment and closed his eyes. His head was throbbing like that bloody drum they'd played at the wedding, and for a moment it was all he could do to stay in the saddle. *I have to go on*, he told himself. If he could bring back Petyr Pimple, surely it would put him in Ser Ryman's good graces. Petyr might be a whisker on the hapless side, but he wasn't as cold as Edwyn, nor as hot as Black Walder. *The boy will be grateful for my part, and his father will see that I'm loyal, a man worth having about.*

But only if he was there by sunset with the gold. Merrett glanced at the sky. *Right on time.* He needed something to steady his hands. He pulled up the waterskin hung from his saddle, uncorked it, and took a long swallow. The wine was thick and sweet, so dark it was almost black, but gods it tasted good.

The curtain wall of Oldstones had once encircled the brow of the hill like the crown on a king's head. Only the foundation remained, and a few waist-high piles of crumbling stone spotted with lichen. Merrett rode along the line of the wall until he came to the place where the gatehouse would have stood. The ruins were more extensive here, and he had to dismount to lead his palfrey through them. In the west, the sun had vanished behind a bank of low clouds. Gorse and bracken covered the slopes, and once inside the vanished walls the weeds were chest high. Merrett loosened his sword in its scabbard and looked about warily, but saw no outlaws. *Could I have come on the wrong day?* He stopped and rubbed his temples with his thumbs, but that did nothing to ease the pressure behind his eyes. *Seven bloody hells . . .*

From somewhere deep within the castle, faint music came drifting through the trees.

Merrett found himself shivering, despite his cloak. He pulled open his waterskin and had another drink of wine. *I could just get back on my horse, ride to Oldtown, and drink the gold away. No good ever came from dealing with outlaws.* That vile little bitch Wenda had burned a fawn into the cheek of his arse while she had him captive. No wonder his wife despised him. *I have to go through with this. Petyr Pimple might be Lord of the Crossing one day, Edwyn has no sons and Black Walder's only got bastards. Petyr will remember who came to get him.* He took another swallow, corked the skin up, and led his palfrey through broken stones, gorse, and thin wind-whipped trees, following the sounds to what had been the castle ward.

Fallen leaves lay thick upon the ground, like soldiers after some great slaughter. A man in patched, faded greens was sitting crosslegged atop a weathered stone sepulcher, fingering the strings of a woodharp. The music was soft and sad. Merrett knew the song. *High in the halls of the kings who are gone, Jenny would dance with her ghosts . . .*

"Get off there," Merrett said. "You're sitting on a king."

"Old Tristifer don't mind my bony arse. The Hammer of Justice, they called him. Been a long while since he heard any new songs." The outlaw hopped down. Trim and slim, he had a narrow face and foxy features, but his mouth was so wide that his smile seemed to touch his ears. A few strands of thin brown hair were blowing across his brow. He pushed them back with his free hand and said, "Do you remember me, my lord?"

"No." Merrett frowned. "Why would I?"

"I sang at your daughter's wedding. And passing well, I thought. That Pate she married was a cousin. We're all cousins in Sevenstreams. Didn't stop him from turning niggard when it was time to pay me." He shrugged. "Why is it your lord father never has me play at the Twins? Don't I make enough noise for his lordship? He likes it loud, I have been hearing."

"You bring the gold?" asked a harsher voice, behind him.

Merrett's throat was dry. *Bloody outlaws, always hiding in the bushes.* It had been the same in the kingswood. You'd think you'd caught five of them, and ten more would spring from nowhere.

When he turned, they were all around him; an ill-favored gaggle of leathery old men and smooth-cheeked lads younger than Petyr Pimple, the lot of them clad in roughspun rags, boiled leather, and bits of dead men's armor. There was one woman with them, bundled up in a hooded cloak three times too big for her. Merrett was too flustered to count them, but there seemed to be a dozen at the least, maybe a score.

"I asked a question." The speaker was a big bearded man with crooked green teeth and a broken nose; taller than Merrett, though not so heavy in the belly. A halfhelm covered his head, a patched yellow cloak his broad shoulders. "Where's our gold?"

"In my saddlebag. A hundred golden dragons." Merrett cleared his throat. "You'll get it when I see that Petyr –"

A squat one-eyed outlaw strode forward before he could finish, reached into the saddlebag bold as you please, and found the sack. Merrett started to grab him, then thought better of it. The outlaw opened the drawstring, removed a coin, and bit it. "Tastes right." He hefted the sack. "Feels right too."

They're going to take the gold and keep Petyr too, Merrett thought in sudden panic. "That's the whole ransom. All you asked for." His palms were sweating. He wiped them on his breeches. "Which one of you is Beric Dondarrion?" Dondarrion had been a lord before he turned outlaw, he might still be a man of honor.

"Why, that would be me," said the one-eyed man.

"You're a bloody liar, Jack," said the big bearded man in the yellow cloak. "It's my turn to be Lord Beric."

"Does that mean I have to be Thoros?" The singer laughed. "My lord, sad to say, Lord Beric was needed elsewhere. The times are troubled, and there are many battles to fight. But we'll sort you out just as he would, have no fear."

Merrett had plenty of fear. His head was pounding too. Much more of this and he'd be sobbing. "You have your gold," he said. "Give me my nephew, and I'll be gone." Petyr was actually more a great half-nephew, but there was no need to go into that.

"He's in the godswood," said the man in the yellow cloak. "We'll take you to him. Notch, you hold his horse."

Merrett handed over the bridle reluctantly. He did not see what other choice he had. "My water skin," he heard himself say. "A swallow of wine, to settle my – "

"We don't drink with your sort," yellow cloak said curtly. "It's this way. Follow me."

Leaves crunched beneath their heels, and every step sent a spike of pain through Merrett's temple. They walked in silence, the wind gusting around them. The last light of the setting sun was in his eyes as he clambered over the mossy hummocks that were all that remained of the keep. Behind was the godswood.

Petyr Pimple was hanging from the limb of an oak, a noose tight around his long thin neck. His eyes bulged from a black face, staring down at Merrett accusingly. *You came too late*, they seemed to say. But he hadn't. He *hadn't!* He had come when they told him. "You killed him," he croaked.

"Sharp as a blade, this one," said the one-eyed man.

An aurochs was thundering through Merrett's head. *Mother have mercy*, he thought. "I brought the gold."

"That was good of you," said the singer amiably. "We'll see that it's put to good use."

Merrett turned away from Petyr. He could taste the bile in the back of his throat. "You . . . you had no right."

"We had a rope," said yellow cloak. "That's right enough."

Two of the outlaws seized Merrett's arms and bound them tight behind his back. He was too deep in shock to struggle. "No," was all he could manage. "I only came to ransom Petyr. You said if you had the gold by sunset he wouldn't be harmed . . ."

"Well," said the singer, "you've got us there, my lord. That was a lie of sorts, as it happens."

The one-eyed outlaw came forward with a long coil of hempen rope. He looped one end around Merrett's neck, pulled it tight, and tied a hard knot under his ear. The other end he threw over the limb of the oak. The big man in the yellow cloak caught it.

"What are you doing?" Merrett knew how stupid that sounded, but he could not believe what was happening, even then. "You'd never dare hang a Frey."

Yellow cloak laughed. "That other one, the pimply boy, he said the same thing."

He doesn't mean it. He cannot mean it. "My father will pay you. I'm worth a good ransom, more than Petyr, twice as much."

The singer sighed. "Lord Walder might be half-blind and gouty, but he's not so stupid as to snap at the same bait twice. Next time he'll send a hundred swords instead of a hundred dragons, I fear."

"He will!" Merrett tried to sound stern, but his voice betrayed him. "He'll send a thousand swords, and kill you all."

"He has to catch us first." The singer glanced up at poor Petyr. "And he can't hang us twice, now can he?" He drew a melancholy air from the strings of his woodharp. "Here now, don't soil yourself. All you need to do is answer me a question, and I'll tell them to let you go."

Merrett would tell them anything if it meant his life. "What do you want to know? I'll tell you true, I swear it."

The outlaw gave him an encouraging smile. "Well, as it happens, we're looking for a dog that ran away."

"A dog?" Merrett was lost. "What kind of dog?"

"He answers to the name Sandor Clegane. Thoros says he was making for the Twins. We found the ferrymen who took him across the Trident, and the poor sod he robbed on the kingsroad. Did you see him at the wedding, perchance?"

"The Red Wedding?" Merrett's skull felt as if it were about to split, but he did his best to recall. There had been so much confusion, but surely someone would have mentioned Joffrey's dog sniffing round the Twins. "He wasn't in the castle. Not at the main feast . . . he might have been at the bastard feast, or in the camps, but . . . no, someone would have said . . ."

"He would have had a child with him," said the singer. "A skinny girl, about ten. Or perhaps a boy the same age."

"I don't think so," said Merrett. "Not that I knew."

"No? Ah, that's a pity. Well, up you go."

"*No,*" Merrett squealed loudly. "No, *don't,* I gave you your answer, you said you'd let me go."

"Seems to me that what I said was I'd *tell* them to let you go." The singer looked at yellow cloak. "Lem, let him go."

"Go bugger yourself," the big outlaw replied brusquely.

The singer gave Merrett a helpless shrug and began to play, "The Day They Hanged Black Robin."

"*Please.*" The last of Merrett's courage was running down his leg. "I've done you no harm. I brought the gold, the way you said. I answered your question. I have *children.*"

"That Young Wolf never will," said the one-eyed outlaw.

Merrett could hardly think for the pounding in his head. "He shamed us, the whole realm was laughing, we had to cleanse the stain on our honor." His father had said all that and more.

"Maybe so. What do a bunch o' bloody peasants know about a lord's honor?" Yellow cloak wrapped the end of the rope around his hand three times. "We know some about murder, though."

"Not murder." His voice was shrill. "It was vengeance, we had a right to our vengeance. It was *war.* Aegon, we called him Jinglebell, a poor lackwit never hurt anyone, Lady Stark cut his throat. We lost half a hundred men in the camps. Ser Garse Goodbrook, Kyra's husband, and Ser Tytos, Jared's son . . . someone smashed his head in with an axe . . . Stark's direwolf killed four of our wolfhounds and tore the kennelmaster's arm off his shoulder, even after we'd filled him full of quarrels . . ."

"So you sewed his head on Robb Stark's neck after both o' them were dead," said yellow cloak.

"My father did that. All I did was drink. You wouldn't kill a man for drinking." Merrett remembered something then, something that might be the saving of him. "They say Lord Beric always gives a man a trial, that he won't kill a man unless something's proved against him. You can't prove anything against me. The Red Wedding was my father's work, and Ryman's and Lord Bolton's. Lothar rigged the tents to collapse and put the crossbowmen in the gallery with the musicians, Bastard Walder led the attack on the camps . . . they're the ones you want, not me, I only drank some wine . . . *you have no witness.*"

"As it happens, you're wrong there." The singer turned to the hooded woman. "Milady?"

The outlaws parted as she came forward, saying no word. When she lowered her hood, something tightened inside Merrett's chest, and for a moment he could not breathe. *No. No, I saw her die. She was dead for a day and night before they stripped her naked and threw her body in the river. Raymund opened her throat from ear to ear. She was dead.*

Her cloak and collar hid the gash his brother's blade had made, but her face was even worse than he remembered. The flesh had gone pudding soft in the water and turned the color of curdled milk. Half her hair was gone and the rest had turned as white and brittle as a crone's. Beneath her ravaged scalp, her face was shredded skin and black blood where she had raked herself with her nails. But her eyes were the most terrible thing. Her eyes saw him, and they hated.

"She don't speak," said the big man in the yellow cloak. "You bloody bastards cut her throat too deep for that. But she remembers." He turned to the dead woman and said, "What do you say, m'lady? Was he part of it?"

Lady Catelyn's eyes never left him. She nodded.

Merrett Frey opened his mouth to plead, but the noose choked off his words. His feet left the ground, the rope cutting deep into the soft flesh beneath his chin. Up into the air he jerked, kicking and twisting, up and up and up.

APPENDIX

THE KINGS AND THEIR COURTS

THE KING ON THE IRON THRONE

JOFFREY BARATHEON, the First of His Name, a boy of thirteen years, the eldest son of King Robert I Baratheon and Queen Cersei of House Lannister,

— his mother, QUEEN CERSEI, of House Lannister, Queen Regent and Protector of the Realm,
  — Cersei's sworn swords:
    — SER OSFRYD KETTLEBLACK, younger brother to Ser Osmund Kettleblack of the Kingsguard,
    — SER OSNEY KETTLEBLACK, youngest brother of Ser Osmund and Ser Osfryd,
— his sister, PRINCESS MYRCELLA, a girl of nine, a ward of Prince Doran Martell at Sunspear,
— his brother, PRINCE TOMMEN, a boy of eight, next heir to the Iron Throne,
— his grandfather, TYWIN LANNISTER, Lord of Casterly Rock, Warden of the West, and Hand of the King,
— his uncles and cousins, paternal,
  — his father's brother, STANNIS BARATHEON, rebel Lord of Dragonstone, styling himself King Stannis the First,
    — Stannis's daughter, SHIREEN, a girl of eleven,
  — his father's brother, {RENLY BARATHEON}, rebel Lord of Storm's End, murdered in the midst of his army,
  — his grandmother's brother, SER ELDON ESTERMONT,
    — Ser Eldon's son, SER AEMON ESTERMONT,
      — Ser Aemon's son, SER ALYN ESTERMONT,
— his uncles and cousins, maternal,

— his mother's brother, SER JAIME LANNISTER, called THE KINGSLAYER, a captive at Riverrun,
— his mother's brother, TYRION LANNISTER, called THE IMP, a dwarf, wounded in the Battle of the Blackwater,
  — Tyrion's squire, PODRICK PAYNE,
  — Tyrion's captain of guards, SER BRONN OF THE BLACK-WATER, a former sellsword,
  — Tyrion's concubine, SHAE, a camp follower now serving as bedmaid to Lollys Stokeworth,
— his grandfather's brother, SER KEVAN LANNISTER,
  — Ser Kevan's son, SER LANCEL LANNISTER, formerly squire to King Robert, wounded in the Battle of the Black-water, near death,
— his grandfather's brother, {TYGETT LANNISTER}, died of a pox,
  — Tygett's son, TYREK LANNISTER, a squire, missing since the great riot,
    — Tyrek's infant wife, LADY ERMESANDE HAYFORD,
— his baseborn siblings, King Robert's bastards:
  — MYA STONE, a maid of nineteen, in the service of Lord Nestor Royce, of the Gates of the Moon,
  — GENDRY, an apprentice smith, a fugitive in the riverlands and ignorant of his heritage,
  — EDRIC STORM, King Robert's only acknowledged bastard son, a ward of his uncle Stannis on Dragonstone,

— his Kingsguard:
  — SER JAIME LANNISTER, Lord Commander,
  — SER MERYN TRANT,
  — SER BALON SWANN,
  — SER OSMUND KETTLEBLACK,
  — SER LORAS TYRELL, the Knight of Flowers,
  — SER ARYS OAKHEART,

— his small council:
  — LORD TYWIN LANNISTER, Hand of the King,
  — SER KEVAN LANNISTER, master of laws,
  — LORD PETYR BAELISH, called LITTLEFINGER, master of coin,
  — VARYS, a eunuch, called THE SPIDER, master of whisperers,
  — LORD MACE TYRELL, master of ships,
  — GRAND MAESTER PYCELLE,

— his court and retainers:
- — SER ILYN PAYNE, the King's Justice, a headsman,
- — LORD HALLYNE THE PYROMANCER, a Wisdom of the Guild of Alchemists,
- — MOON BOY, a jester and fool,
- — ORMOND OF OLDTOWN, the royal harper and bard,
- — DONTOS HOLLARD, a fool and a drunkard, formerly a knight called SER DONTOS THE RED,
- — JALABHAR XHO, Prince of the Red Flower Vale, an exile from the Summer Isles,
- — LADY TANDA STOKEWORTH,
  - — her daughter, FALYSE, wed to Ser Balman Byrch,
  - — her daughter, LOLLYS, thirty-four, unwed, and soft of wits, with child after being raped,
  - — her healer and counselor, MAESTER FRENKEN,
- — LORD GYLES ROSBY, a sickly old man,
- — SER TALLAD, a promising young knight,
- — LORD MORROS SLYNT, a squire, eldest son of the former Commander of the City Watch,
  - — JOTHOS SLYNT, his younger brother, a squire,
  - — DANOS SLYNT, younger still, a page,
- — SER BOROS BLOUNT, a former knight of the Kingsguard, dismissed for cowardice by Queen Cersei,
- — JOSMYN PECKLEDON, a squire, and a hero of the Battle of the Blackwater,
- — SER PHILIP FOOTE, made Lord of the Marches for his valor during the Battle of the Blackwater,
- — SER LOTHOR BRUNE, named LOTHOR APPLE-EATER for his deeds during the Battle of the Blackwater, a former freerider in service to Lord Baelish,

— other lords and knights at King's Landing:
- — MATHIS ROWAN, Lord of Goldengrove,
- — PAXTER REDWYNE, Lord of the Arbor,
  - — Lord Paxter's twin sons, SER HORAS and SER HOBBER, mocked as HORROR and SLOBBER,
  - — Lord Redwyne's healer, MAESTER BALLABAR,
- — ARDRIAN CELTIGAR, the Lord of Claw Isle,
- — LORD ALESANDER STAEDMON, called PENNYLOVER,
- — SER BONIFER HASTY, called THE GOOD, a famed knight,
- — SER DONNEL SWANN, heir to Stonehelm,
- — SER RONNET CONNINGTON, called RED RONNET, the Knight of Griffin's Roost,
- — AURANE WATERS, the Bastard of Driftmark,

— SER DERMOT OF THE RAINWOOD, a famed knight,
— SER TIMON SCRAPESWORD, a famed knight,

— the people of King's Landing:
  — the City Watch (the "gold cloaks"),
    — {SER JACELYN BYWATER, called IRONHAND}, Commander of the City Watch, slain by his own men during the Battle of the Blackwater,
    — SER ADDAM MARBRAND, Commander of the City Watch, Ser Jacelyn's successor,
  — CHATAYA, owner of an expensive brothel,
  — ALAYAYA, her daughter,
  — DANCY, MAREI, JAYDE, Chataya's girls,
  — TOBHO MOTT, a master armorer,
  — IRONBELLY, a blacksmith,
  — HAMISH THE HARPER, a famed singer,
  — COLLIO QUAYNIS, a Tyroshi singer,
  — BETHANY FAIR-FINGERS, a woman singer,
  — ALARIC OF EYSEN, a singer, far-traveled,
  — GALYEON OF CUY, a singer notorious for the length of his songs,
  — SYMON SILVER TONGUE, a singer.

King Joffrey's banner shows the crowned stag of Baratheon, black on gold, and the lion of Lannister, gold on crimson, combatant.

THE KING IN THE NORTH
THE KING OF THE TRIDENT

ROBB STARK, Lord of Winterfell, King in the North, and King of the Trident, the eldest son of Eddark Stark, Lord of Winterfell, and Lady Catelyn of House Tully,
— his direwolf, GREY WIND,
— his mother, LADY CATELYN, of House Tully, widow of Lord Eddard Stark,
— his siblings:
— his sister, PRINCESS SANSA, a maid of twelve, a captive in King's Landing,
— Sansa's direwolf, {LADY}, killed at Castle Darry,
— his sister, PRINCESS ARYA, a girl of ten, missing and presumed dead,
— Arya's direwolf, NYMERIA, lost near the Trident,
— his brother, PRINCE BRANDON, called BRAN, heir to the north, a boy of nine, believed dead,
— Bran's direwolf, SUMMER,
— Bran companions and protectors:
— MEERA REED, a maid of sixteen, daughter of Lord Howland Reed of Greywater Watch,
— JOJEN REED, her brother, thirteen,
— HODOR, a simpleminded stableboy, seven feet tall,
— his brother, PRINCE RICKON, a boy of four, believed dead,
— Rickon's direwolf, SHAGGYDOG,
— Rickon's companion and protector:

— OSHA, a wildling captive who served as a scullion at Winterfell,
— his half-brother, JON SNOW, a Sworn Brother of the Night's Watch,
  — Jon's direwolf, GHOST,

— his uncles and aunts, paternal:
  — his father's elder brother, {BRANDON STARK}, slain at the command of King Aerys II Targaryen,
  — his father's sister, {LYANNA STARK}, died in the Mountains of Dorne during Robert's Rebellion,
  — his father's younger brother, BENJEN STARK, a man of the Night's Watch, lost beyond the Wall,
— his uncles, aunts, and cousins, maternal:
  — his mother's younger sister, LYSA ARRYN, Lady of the Eyrie and widow of Lord Jon Arryn,
    — their son, ROBERT ARRYN, Lord of the Eyrie,
  — his mother's younger brother, SER EDMURE TULLY, heir to Riverrun,
  — his grandfather's brother, SER BRYNDEN TULLY, called THE BLACKFISH,
— his sworn swords and companions:
  — his squire, OLYVAR FREY,
  — SER WENDEL MANDERLY, second son to the Lord of White Harbor,
  — PATREK MALLISTER, heir to Seagard,
  — DACEY MORMONT, eldest daughter of Lady Maege Mormont and heir to Bear Island,
  — JON UMBER, called THE SMALLJON, heir to Last Hearth,
  — DONNEL LOCKE, OWEN NORREY, ROBIN FLINT, northmen,

— his lords bannermen, captains and commanders:
— (with Robb's army in the Westerlands)
  — SER BRYNDEN TULLY, the BLACKFISH, commanding the scouts and outriders,
  — JON UMBER, called THE GREATJON, commanding the van,
  — RICKARD KARSTARK, Lord of Karhold,
  — GALBART GLOVER, Master of Deepwood Motte,
  — MAEGE MORMONT, Lady of Bear Island,
  — {SER STEVRON FREY}, eldest son of Lord Walder Frey and heir to the Twins, died at Oxcross,
    — Ser Stevron's eldest son, SER RYMAN FREY,

— Ser Ryman's son, BLACK WALDER FREY,

— MARTYN RIVERS, a bastard son of Lord Walder Frey,

— (with Roose Bolton's host at Harrengal),
   — ROOSE BOLTON, Lord of the Dreadfort,
   — SER AENYS FREY, SER JARED FREY, SER HOSTEEN FREY, SER DANWELL FREY
      — their bastard half-brother, RONEL RIVERS,
   — SER WYLIS MANDERLY, heir to White Harbor,
      — SER KYLE CONDON, a knight in his service,
   — RONNEL STOUT,
   — VARGO HOAT of the Free City of Qohor, captain of a sellsword company, the Brave Companions,
      — his lieutenant, URSWYCK called THE FAITHFUL,
      — his lieutenant, SEPTON UTT,
      — TIMEON OF DORNE, RORGE, IGGO, FAT ZOLLO, BITER, TOGG JOTH of Ibben, PYG, THREE TOES, his men,
      — QYBURN, a chainless maester and sometime necromancer, his healer,

— (with the northern army attacking Duskendale)
   — ROBETT GLOVER, of Deepwood Motte,
   — SER HELMAN TALLHART, of Torrhen's Square,
   — HARRION KARSTARK, sole surviving son of Lord Rickard Karstark, and heir to Karhold,

— (traveling north with Lord Eddard's bones)
   — HALLIS MOLLEN, captain of guards for Winterfell,
      — JACKS, QUENT, SHADD, guardsmen,

— his lord bannermen and castellans, in the north:
   — WYMAN MANDERLY, Lord of White Harbor,
   — HOWLAND REED, Lord of Greywater Watch, a crannogman,
   — MORS UMBER, called CROWFOOD, and HOTHER UMBER, called WHORESBANE, uncles to Greatjon Umber, joint castellans at the Last Hearth,
   — LYESSA FLINT, Lady of Widow's Watch,
   — ONDREW LOCKE, Lord of Oldcastle, an old man,
   — {CLEY CERWYN}, Lord of Cerwyn, a boy of fourteen, killed in battle at Winterfell,
      — his sister, JONELLE CERWYN, a maid of two-and-thirty, now the Lady of Cerwyn,

— {LEOBALD TALLHART}, younger brother to Ser Helman, castellan at Torrhen's Square, killed in battle at Winterfell,
   — Leobald's wife, BERENA of House Hornwood,
   — Leobald's son, BRANDON, a boy of fourteen,
   — Leobald's son, BEREN, a boy of ten,
   — Ser Helman's son, {BENFRED}, killed by ironmen on the Stony Shore,
   — Ser Helman's daughter, EDDARA, a girl of nine, heir to Torrhen's Square,
— LADY SYBELLE, wife to Robett Glover, a captive of Asha Greyjoy at Deepwood Motte,
   — Robett's son, GAWEN, three, rightful heir to Deepwood Motte, a captive of Asha Greyjoy,
   — Robett's daughter, ERENA, a babe of one, a captive of Asha Greyjoy at Deepwood Motte,
   — LARENCE SNOW, a bastard son of Lord Hornwood, and ward of Galbart Glover, thirteen, a captive of Asha Greyjoy at Deepwood Motte.

The banner of the King in the North remains as it has for thousands of years: the grey direwolf of the Starks of Winterfell, running across an ice-white field.

THE KING IN THE NARROW SEA

STANNIS BARATHEON, the First of His Name, second son of Lord
  Steffon Baratheon and Lady Cassana of House Estermont, formerly
  Lord of Dragonstone,
— his wife, QUEEN SELYSE of House Florent,
  — PRINCESS SHIREEN, their daughter, a girl of eleven,
    — PATCHFACE, her lackwit fool,
— his baseborn nephew, EDRIC STORM, a boy of twelve, bastard
  son of King Robert by Delena Florent,
— his squires, DEVAN SEAWORTH and BRYEN FARRING,
— his court and retainers:
  — LORD ALESTER FLORENT, Lord of Brightwater Keep and
    Hand of the King, the queen's uncle,
  — SER AXELL FLORENT, castellan of Dragonstone and leader
    of the queen's men, the queen's uncle,
  — LADY MELISANDRE OF ASSHAI, called THE RED
    WOMAN, priestess of R'hllor, the Lord of Light and God of
    Flame and Shadow,
  — MAESTER PYLOS, healer, tutor, counselor,
  — SER DAVOS SEAWORTH, called THE ONION KNIGHT and
    sometimes SHORTHAND, once a smuggler,
    — Davos's wife, LADY MARYA, a carpenter's daughter,
      — their seven sons:
        — {DALE}, lost on the Blackwater,
        — {ALLARD}, lost on the Blackwater,
        — {MATTHOS}, lost on the Blackwater,
        — {MARIC}, lost on the Blackwater,
        — DEVAN, squire to King Stannis,

— STANNIS, a boy of nine years,
— STEFFON, a boy of six years,
— SALLADHOR SAAN, of the Free City of Lys, styling himself Prince of the Narrow Sea and Lord of Blackwater Bay, master of the *Valyrian* and a fleet of sister galleys,
— MEIZO MAHR, a eunuch in his hire,
— KHORANE SATHMANTES, captain of his galley *Shayala's Dance*,
— "PORRIDGE" and "LAMPREY," two gaolers,

— his lords bannermen,
— MONTERYS VELARYON, Lord of the Tides and Master of Driftmark, a boy of six,
— DURAM BAR EMMON, Lord of Sharp Point, a boy of fifteen years,
— SER GILBERT FARRING, castellan of Storm's End,
— LORD ELWOOD MEADOWS, Ser Gilbert's second,
— MAESTER JURNE, Ser Gilbert's counselor and healer,
— LORD LUCOS CHYTTERING, called LITTLE LUCOS, a youth of sixteen,
— LESTER MORRIGEN, Lord of Crows Nest,

— his knights and sworn swords,
— SER LOMAS ESTERMONT, the king's maternal uncle,
— his son, SER ANDREW ESTERMONT,
— SER ROLLAND STORM, called THE BASTARD OF NIGHTSONG, a baseborn son of the late Lord Bryen Caron,
— SER PARMEN CRANE, called PARMEN THE PURPLE, held captive at Highgarden,
— SER ERREN FLORENT, younger brother to Queen Selyse, held captive at Highgarden,
— SER GERALD GOWER,
— SER TRISTON OF TALLY HILL, formerly in service to Lord Guncer Sunglass,
— LEWYS, called THE FISHWIFE,
— OMER BLACKBERRY.

King Stannis has taken for his banner the fiery heart of the Lord of Light: a red heart surrounded by orange flames upon a yellow field. Within the heart is the crowned stag of House Baratheon, in black.

THE QUEEN ACROSS THE WATER

DAENERYS TARGARYEN, the First of Her Name, *Khaleesi* of the
Dothraki, called DAENERYS STORMBORN, the UNBURNT,
MOTHER OF DRAGONS, sole surviving heir of Aerys II Targaryen,
widow of Khal Drogo of the Dothraki,
— her growing dragons, DROGON, VISERION, RHAEGAL,
— her Queensguard:
— SER JORAH MORMONT, formerly Lord of Bear Island, exiled
for slaving,
— JHOGO, *ko* and bloodrider, the whip,
— AGGO, *ko* and bloodrider, the bow,
— RAKHARO, *ko* and bloodrider, the *arakh*,
— STRONG BELWAS, a former eunuch slave from the fighting
pits of Meereen,
— his aged squire, ARSTAN called WHITEBEARD, a man
of Westeros,
— her handmaids:
— IRRI, a Dothraki girl, fifteen,
— JHIQUI, a Dothraki girl, fourteen,
— GROLEO, captain of the great cog *Balerion*, a Pentoshi seafarer
in the hire of Illyrio Mopatis,

— her late kin:
— {RHAEGAR}, her brother, Prince of Dragonstone and heir to
the Iron Throne, slain by Robert Baratheon on the Trident,
— {RHAENYS}, Rhaegar's daughter by Elia of Dorne, murdered during the Sack of King's Landing,

— {AEGON}, Rhaegar's son by Elia of Dorne, murdered during the Sack of King's Landing,
— {VISERYS}, her brother, styling himself King Viserys, the Third of His Name, called THE BEGGAR KING, slain in Vaes Dothrak by Khal Drogo,
— {DROGO}, her husband, a great *khal* of the Dothraki, never defeated in battle, died of a wound,
   — {RHAEGO}, her stillborn son by Khal Drogo, slain in the womb by Mirri Maz Duur,

— her known enemies:
— KHAL PONO, once *ko* to Drogo,
— KHAL JHAQO, once *ko* to Drogo,
   — MAGGO, his bloodrider,
— THE UNDYING OF QARTH, a band of warlocks,
   — PYAT PREE, a Qartheen warlock,
— THE SORROWFUL MEN, a guild of Qartheen assassins,

— her uncertain allies, past and present:
— XARO XHOAN DAXOS, a merchant prince of Qarth,
— QUAITHE, a masked shadowbinder from Asshai,
— ILLYRIO MOPATIS, a magister of the Free City of Pentos, who brokered her marriage to Khal Drogo,

— in Astapor:
— KRAZNYS MO NAKLOZ, a wealthy slave trader,
   — his slave, MISSANDEI, a girl of ten, of the Peaceful People of Naath,
— GRAZDAN MO ULLHOR, an old slave trader, very rich,
   — his slave, CLEON, a butcher and cook,
— GREY WORM, an eunuch of the Unsullied,

— in Yunkai:
— GRAZDAN MO ERAZ, envoy and nobleman,
— MERO OF BRAAVOS, called THE TITAN'S BASTARD, captain of the Second Sons, a free company,
   — BROWN BEN PLUMM, a sergeant in the Second Sons, a sellsword of dubious descent,
— PRENDAHL NA GHEZN, a Ghiscari sellsword, captain of the Stormcrows, a free company,
— SALLOR THE BALD, a Qartheen sellsword, captain of the Stormcrows,

    — DAARIO NAHARIS, a flamboyant Tyroshi sellsword, captain of the Stormcrows,

— in Meereen:
  — OZNAK ZO PAHL, a hero of the city.

The banner of Daenerys Targaryen is the banner of Aegon the Conqueror and the dynasty he established: a three-headed dragon, red on black.

KING OF THE ISLES
AND THE NORTH

BALON GREYJOY, the Ninth of His Name Since the Grey King, styling himself King of the Iron Islands and the North, King of Salt and Rock, Son of the Sea Wind, and Lord Reaper of Pyke,
— his wife, QUEEN ALANNYS, of House Harlaw,
— their children:
— {RODRIK}, their eldest son, slain at Seagard during Greyjoy's Rebellion,
— {MARON}, their second son, slain at Pyke during Greyjoy's Rebellion,
— ASHA, their daughter, captain of the *Black Wind* and conqueror of Deepwood Motte,
— THEON, their youngest son, captain of the *Sea Bitch* and briefly Prince of Winterfell,
— Theon's squire, WEX PYKE, bastard son of Lord Botley's half-brother, a mute lad of twelve,
— Theon's crew, the men of the *Sea Bitch*:
— URZEN, MARON BOTLEY called FISHWHISKERS, STYGG, GEVIN HARLAW, CADWYLE,

— his brothers:
— EURON, called Crow's Eye, captain of the *Silence*, a notorious outlaw, pirate, and raider,
— VICTARION, Lord Captain of the Iron Fleet, master of the *Iron Victory*,
— AERON, called DAMPHAIR, a priest of the Drowned God,

— his household on Pyke:
  — MAESTER WENDAMYR, healer and counselor,
  — HELYA, keeper of the castle,
— his warriors and sworn swords:
  — DAGMER called CLEFTJAW, captain of *Foamdrinker*,
  — BLUETOOTH, a longship captain,
  — ULLER, SKYTE, oarsmen and warriors,
  — ANDRIK THE UNSMILING, a giant of a man,
  — QARL, called QARL THE MAID, beardless but deadly,

— people of Lordsport:
  — OTTER GIMPKNEE, innkeeper and whoremonger,
  — SIGRIN, a shipwright,

— his lords bannermen:
  — SAWANE BOTLEY, Lord of Lordsport, on Pyke,
  — LORD WYNCH, of Iron Holt, on Pyke,
  — STONEHOUSE, DRUMM, and GOODBROTHER of Old Wyk,
  — LORD GOODBROTHER, SPARR, LORD MERLYN, and LORD FARWYND of Great Wyk,
  — LORD HARLAW, of Harlaw,
  — VOLMARK, MYRE, STONETREE, and KENNING, of Harlaw,
  — ORKWOOD and TAWNEY of Orkmont,
  — LORD BLACKTYDE of Blacktyde,
  — LORD SALTCLIFFE and LORD SUNDERLY of Saltcliffe.

OTHER HOUSES GREAT
AND SMALL

HOUSE ARRYN

The Arryns are descended from the Kings of Mountain and Vale, one of the oldest and purest lines of Andal nobility. House Arryn has taken no part in the War of the Five Kings, holding back its strength to protect the Vale of Arryn. The Arryn sigil is the moon-and-falcon, white, upon a sky-blue field. The Arryn words are *As High As Honor*.

ROBERT ARRYN, Lord of the Eyrie, Defender of the Vale, Warden of the East, a sickly boy of eight years,
— his mother, LADY LYSA, of House Tully, third wife and widow of Lord Jon Arryn, and sister to Catelyn Stark,
— their household:
— MARILLION, a handsome young singer, much favored by Lady Lysa,
— MAESTER COLEMON, counselor, healer, and tutor,
— SER MARWYN BELMORE, captain of guards,
— MORD, a brutal gaoler,

— his lords bannermen, knights, and retainers:
— LORD NESTOR ROYCE, High Steward of the Vale and castellan of the Gates of the Moon, of the junior branch of House Royce,
— Lord Nestor's son, SER ALBAR,
— Lord Nestor's daughter, MYRANDA,
— MYA STONE, a bastard girl in his service, natural daughter of King Robert I Baratheon,
— LORD YOHN ROYCE, called BRONZE YOHN, Lord of Runestone, of the senior branch of House Royce, cousin to Lord Nestor,

— Lord Yohn's eldest son, SER ANDAR,

— Lord Yohn's second son, {SER ROBAR}, a knight of Renly
Baratheon's Rainbow Guard, slain at Storm's End by Ser
Loras Tyrell,

— Lord Yohn's youngest son, {SER WAYMAR}, a man of the
Night's Watch, lost beyond the Wall,

— SER LYN CORBRAY, a suitor to Lady Lysa,

    — MYCHEL REDFORT, his squire,

— LADY ANYA WAYNWOOD,

    — Lady Anya's eldest son and heir, SER MORTON, a
suitor to Lady Lysa,

    — Lady Anya's second son, SER DONNEL, the Knight of
the Gate,

— EON HUNTER, Lord of Longbow Hall, an old man, and a
suitor to Lady Lysa,

— HORTON REDFORT, Lord of Redfort.

HOUSE FLORENT

The Florents of Brightwater Keep are Tyrell bannermen, despite a superior claim to Highgarden by virtue of a blood tie to House Gardener, the old Kings of the Reach. At the outbreak of the War of the Five Kings, Lord Alester Florent followed the Tyrells in declaring for King Renly, but his brother Ser Axell chose King Stannis, whom he had served for years as castellan of Dragonstone. Their niece Selyse was and is King Stannis's queen. When Renly died at Storm's End, the Florents went over to Stannis with all their strength, the first of Renly's bannermen to do so. The sigil of House Florent shows a fox head in a circle of flowers.

ALESTER FLORENT, Lord of Brightwater,
— his wife, LADY MELARA, of House Crane,
— their children:
  — ALEKYNE, heir to Brightwater,
  — MELESSA, wed to Lord Randyll Tarly,
  — RHEA, wed to Lord Leyton Hightower,
— his siblings:
  — SER AXELL, castellan of Dragonstone,
  — {SER RYAM}, died in a fall from a horse,
    — Ser Ryam's daughter, QUEEN SELYSE, wed to King Stannis Baratheon,
    — Ser Ryam's son, {SER IMRY}, commanding Stannis Baratheon's fleet on the Blackwater, lost with the *Fury*,
    — Ser Ryam's second son, SER ERREN, held captive at Highgarden,
  — SER COLIN,
    — Ser Colin's daughter, DELENA, wed to SER HOSMAN NORCROSS,

— Delena's son, EDRIC STORM, a bastard of King Robert
I Baratheon, twelve years of age,
— Delena's son, ALESTER NORCROSS, eight,
— Delena's son, RENLY NORCROSS, a boy of two,
— Ser Colin's son, MAESTER OMER, in service at Old Oak,
— Ser Colin's son, MERRELL, a squire on the Arbor,
— his sister, RYLENE, wed to Ser Rycherd Crane.

HOUSE FREY

Powerful, wealthy, and numerous, the Freys are bannermen to House Tully, but they have not always been diligent in their duty. When Robert Baratheon met Rhaegar Targaryen on the Trident, the Freys did not arrive until the battle was done, and thereafter Lord Hoster Tully always called Lord Walder "the Late Lord Frey." It is also said of Walder Frey that he is the only lord in the Seven Kingdoms who could field an army out of his breeches.

At the onset of the War of the Five Kings, Robb Stark won Lord Walder's allegiance by pledging to wed one of his daughters or granddaughters. Two of Lord Walder's grandsons were sent to Winterfell to be fostered.

WALDER FREY, Lord of the Crossing,
— by his first wife, {LADY PERRA, of House Royce}:
— {SER STEVRON}, their eldest son, died after the Battle of Oxcross,
— m. {Corenna Swann, died of a wasting illness},
— Stevron's eldest son, SER RYMAN, heir to the Twins,
— Ryman's son, EDWYN, wed to Janyce Hunter,
— Edwyn's daughter, WALDA, a girl of eight,
— Ryman's son, WALDER, called BLACK WALDER,
— Ryman's son, PETYR, called PETYR PIMPLE,
— m. Mylenda Caron,
— Petyr's daughter, PERRA, a girl of five,
— m. {Jeyne Lydden, died in a fall from a horse},
— Stevron's son, AEGON, a halfwit called JINGLEBELL,
— Stevron's daughter, {MAEGELLE, died in childbed}, m. Ser Dafyn Vance,
— Maegelle's daughter, MARIANNE, a maiden,

— Maegelle's son, WALDER VANCE, a squire,
— Maegelle's son, PATREK VANCE,
— m. {Marsella Waynwood, died in childbed},
— Stevron's son, WALTON, m. Deana Hardyng,
  — Walton's son, STEFFON, called THE SWEET,
  — Walton's daughter, WALDA, called FAIR WALDA,
  — Walton's son, BRYAN, a squire,
— SER EMMON, m. Genna of House Lannister,
  — Emmon's son, SER CLEOS, m. Jeyne Darry,
    — Cleos's son, TYWIN, a squire of eleven,
    — Cleos's son, WILLEM, a page at Ashemark, nine,
  — Emmon's son, SER LYONEL, m. Melesa Crakehall,
  — Emmon's son, TION, a captive at Riverrun,
  — Emmon's son, WALDER, called RED WALDER, fourteen,
    a squire at Casterly Rock,
— SER AENYS, m. {Tyana Wylde, died in childbed},
  — Aenys's son, AEGON BLOODBORN, an outlaw,
  — Aenys's son, RHAEGAR, m. Jeyne Beesbury,
    — Rhaegar's son, ROBERT, a boy of thirteen,
    — Rhaegar's daughter, WALDA, a girl of ten, called
      WHITE WALDA,
    — Rhaegar's son, JONOS, a boy of eight,
— PERRIANE, m. Ser Leslyn Haigh,
  — Perriane's son, SER HARYS HAIGH,
    — Harys's son, WALDER HAIGH, a boy of four,
  — Perriane's son, SER DONNEL HAIGH,
  — Perriane's son, ALYN HAIGH, a squire,

— by his second wife, {LADY CYRENNA, of House Swann}:
— SER JARED, their eldest son, m. {Alys Frey},
  — Jared's son, SER TYTOS, m. Zhoe Blanetree,
    — Tytos's daughter, ZIA, a maid of fourteen,
    — Tytos's son, ZACHERY, a boy of twelve, training at
      the Sept of Oldtown,
  — Jared's daughter, KYRA, m. Ser Garse Goodbrook,
    — Kyra's son, WALDER GOODBROOK, a boy of nine,
    — Kyra's daughter, JEYNE GOODBROOK, six,
— SEPTON LUCEON, in service at the Great Sept of Baelor in
  King's Landing,

— by his third wife, {LADY AMAREI of House Crakehall}:
— SER HOSTEEN, their eldest son, m. Bellena Hawick,
  — Hosteen's son, SER ARWOOD, m. Ryella Royce,

— Arwood's daughter, RYELLA, a girl of five,

— Arwood's twin sons, ANDROW and ALYN, three,

— LADY LYTHENE, m. Lord Lucias Vypren,

   — Lythene's daughter, ELYANA, m. Ser Jon Wylde,

      — Elyana's son, RICKARD WYLDE, four,

   — Lythene's son, SER DAMON VYPREN,

— SYMOND, m. Betharios of Braavos,

   — Symond's son, ALESANDER, a singer,

   — Symond's daughter, ALYX, a maid of seventeen,

   — Symond's son, BRADAMAR, a boy of ten, fostered on Braavos as a ward of Oro Tendyris, a merchant of that city,

— SER DANWELL, m. Wynafrei Whent,

   — {many stillbirths and miscarriages},

— MERRETT, m. Mariya Darry,

   — Merrett's daughter, AMEREI, called AMI, a widow of sixteen, m. {Ser Pate of the Blue Fork},

   — Merrett's daughter, WALDA, called FAT WALDA, a wife of fifteen years, m. Lord Roose Bolton,

   — Merrett's daughter, MARISSA, a maid of thirteen,

   — Merrett's son, WALDER, called LITTLE WALDER, a boy of seven, taken captive at Winterfell while a ward of Lady Catelyn Stark,

— {SER GEREMY, drowned}, m. Carolei Waynwood,

   — Geremy's son, SANDOR, a boy of twelve, a squire to Ser Donnel Waynwood,

   — Geremy's daughter, CYNTHEA, a girl of nine, a ward of Lady Anya Waynwood,

— SER RAYMUND, m. Beony Beesbury,

   — Raymund's son, ROBERT, sixteen, in training at the Citadel in Oldtown,

   — Raymund's son, MALWYN, fifteen, apprenticed to an alchemist in Lys,

   — Raymund's twin daughters, SERRA and SARRA, maiden girls of fourteen,

   — Raymund's daughter, CERSEI, six, called LITTLE BEE,

— by his fourth wife, {LADY ALYSSA, of House Blackwood}:

— LOTHAR, their eldest son, called LAME LOTHAR, m. Leonella Lefford,

   — Lothar's daughter, TYSANE, a girl of seven,

   — Lothar's daughter, WALDA, a girl of four,

   — Lothar's daughter, EMBERLEI, a girl of two,

— SER JAMMOS, m. Sallei Paege,
  — Jammos's son, WALDER, called BIG WALDER, a boy of
  eight, taken captive at Winterfell while a ward of Lady
  Catelyn Stark,
  — Jammos's twin sons, DICKON and MATHIS, five,
— SER WHALEN, m. Sylwa Paege,
  — Whalen's son, HOSTER, a boy of twelve, a squire to Ser
  Damon Paege,
  — Whalen's daughter, MERIANNE, called MERRY, a girl of
  eleven,
— LADY MORYA, m. Ser Flement Brax,
  — Morya's son, ROBERT BRAX, nine, fostered at Casterly
  Rock as a page,
  — Morya's son, WALDER BRAX, a boy of six,
  — Morya's son, JON BRAX, a babe of three,
— TYTA, called TYTA THE MAID, a maid of twenty-nine,

— by his fifth wife, {LADY SARYA of House Whent}:
— no progeny,

— by his sixth wife, {LADY BETHANY of House Rosby}:
— SER PERWYN, their eldest son,
— SER BENFREY, m. Jyanna Frey, a cousin,
  — Benfrey's daughter, DELLA, called DEAF DELLA, a girl
  of three,
  — Benfrey's son, OSMUND, a boy of two,
— MAESTER WILLAMEN, in service at Longbow Hall,
— OLYVAR, squire to Robb Stark,
— ROSLIN, a maid of sixteen,

— by his seventh wife, {LADY ANNARA of House Farring}:
— ARWYN, a maid of fourteen,
— WENDEL, their eldest son, a boy of thirteen, fostered at Sea-
  gard as a page,
— COLMAR, promised to the Faith, eleven,
— WALTYR, called TYR, a boy of ten,
— ELMAR, formerly betrothed to Arya Stark, a boy of nine,
— SHIREI, a girl of six,

— his eighth wife, LADY JOYEUSE of House Erenford,
— no progeny as yet,

— Lord Walder's natural children, by sundry mothers,

— WALDER RIVERS, called BASTARD WALDER,
  — Bastard Walder's son, SER AEMON RIVERS,
  — Bastard Walder's daughter, WALDA RIVERS,
— MAESTER MELWYS, in service at Rosby,
— JEYNE RIVERS, MARTYN RIVERS, RYGER RIVERS, RONEL RIVERS, MELLARA RIVERS, others.

HOUSE LANNISTER

The Lannisters of Casterly Rock remain the principal support of King Joffrey's claim to the Iron Throne. They boast of descent from Lann the Clever, the legendary trickster of the Age of Heroes. The gold of Casterly Rock and the Golden Tooth has made them the wealthiest of the Great Houses. The Lannister sigil is a golden lion upon a crimson field. Their words are *Hear Me Roar!*

TYWIN LANNISTER, Lord of Casterly Rock, Warden of the West, Shield of Lannisport, and Hand of the King,
— his son, SER JAIME, called THE KINGSLAYER, a twin to Queen Cersei, Lord Commander of the Kingsguard, and Warden of the East, a captive at Riverrun,
— his daughter, QUEEN CERSEI, twin to Jaime, widow of King Robert I Baratheon, Queen Regent for her son Joffrey,
— her son, KING JOFFREY BARATHEON, a boy of thirteen,
— her daughter, PRINCESS MYRCELLA BARATHEON, a girl of nine, a ward of Prince Doran Martell in Dorne,
— her son, PRINCE TOMMEN BARATHEON, a boy of eight, heir to the Iron Throne,
— his dwarf son, TYRION, called THE IMP, called HALFMAN, wounded and scarred on the Blackwater,

— his siblings:
— SER KEVAN, Lord Tywin's eldest brother,
— Ser Kevan's wife, DORNA, of House Swyft,
— their son, SER LANCEL, formerly a squire to King Robert, wounded and near death,

— their son, WILLEM, twin to Martyn, a squire, captive at Riverrun,
— their son, MARTYN, twin to Willem, a squire, a captive with Robb Stark,
— their daughter, JANEI, a girl of two,
— GENNA, his sister, wed to Ser Emmon Frey,
— their son, SER CLEOS FREY, a captive at Riverrun,
— their son, SER LYONEL,
— their son, TION FREY, a squire, captive at Riverrun,
— their son, WALDER, called RED WALDER, a squire at Casterly Rock,
— {SER TYGETT}, his second brother, died of a pox,
— Tygett's widow, DARLESSA, of House Marbrand,
— their son, TYREK, squire to the king, missing,
— {GERION}, his youngest brother, lost at sea,
— Gerion's bastard daughter, JOY, eleven,

— his cousin, {SER STAFFORD LANNISTER}, brother to the late Lady Joanna, slain at Oxcross,
— Ser Stafford's daughters, CERENNA and MYRIELLE,
— Ser Stafford's son, SER DAVEN,
— his cousins:
— SER DAMION LANNISTER, m. Lady Shiera Crakehall,
— his son, SER LUCION,
— his daughter, LANNA, m. Lord Antario Jast,
— MARGOT, m. Lord Titus Peake,

— his household:
— MAESTER CREYLEN, healer, tutor, and counselor,
— VYLARR, captain-of-guards,
— LUM and RED LESTER, guardsmen,
— WHITESMILE WAT, a singer,
— SER BENEDICT BROOM, master-at-arms,

— his lords bannermen:
— DAMON MARBRAND, Lord of Ashemark,
— SER ADDAM MARBRAND, his son and heir,
— ROLAND CRAKEHALL, Lord of Crakehall,
— his brother, {SER BURTON CRAKEHALL}, killed by Lord Beric Dondarrion and his outlaws,
— his son and heir, SER TYBOLT CRAKEHALL,
— his second son, SER LYLE CRAKEHALL, called STRONGBOAR, a captive at Pinkmaiden Castle,

— his youngest son, SER MERLON CRAKEHALL,
— {ANDROS BRAX}, Lord of Hornvale, drowned during the Battle of the Camps,
— his brother, {SER RUPERT BRAX}, slain at Oxcross,
— his eldest son, SER TYTOS BRAX, now Lord of Hornvale, a captive at the Twins,
— his second son, {SER ROBERT BRAX}, slain at the Battle of the Fords,
— his third son, SER FLEMENT BRAX, now heir,
— {LORD LEO LEFFORD}, drowned at the Stone Mill,
— REGENARD ESTREN, Lord of Wyndhall, a captive at the Twins,
— GAWEN WESTERLING, Lord of the Crag, a captive at Seagard,
— his wife, LADY SYBELL, of House Spicer,
— her brother, SER ROLPH SPICER,
— her cousin, SER SAMWELL SPICER,
— their children:
— SER RAYNALD WESTERLING,
— JEYNE, a maid of sixteen years,
— ELEYNA, a girl of twelve,
— ROLLAM, a boy of nine,
— LEWYS LYDDEN, Lord of the Deep Den,
— LORD ANTARIO JAST, a captive at Pinkmaiden Castle,
— LORD PHILIP PLUMM,
— his sons, SER DENNIS PLUMM, SER PETER PLUMM, and SER HARWYN PLUMM, called HARDSTONE,
— QUENTEN BANEFORT, Lord of Banefort, a captive of Lord Jonos Bracken,
— his knights and captains:
— SER HARYS SWYFT, good-father to Ser Kevan Lannister,
— Ser Harys's son, SER STEFFON SWYFT,
— Ser Steffon's daughter, JOANNA,
— Ser Harys's daughter, SHIERLE, m. Ser Melwyn Sarsfield,
— SER FORLEY PRESTER,
— SER GARTH GREENFIELD, a captive at Raventree Hall,
— SER LYMOND VIKARY, a captive at Wayfarer's Rest,
— LORD SELMOND STACKSPEAR,
— his son, SER STEFFON STACKSPEAR,
— his younger son, SER ALYN STACKSPEAR,
— TERRENCE KENNING, Lord of Kayce,
— SER KENNOS OF KAYCE, a knight in his service,
— SER GREGOR CLEGANE, the Mountain That Rides,

— POLLIVER, CHISWYCK, RAFF THE SWEETLING, DUNSEN, and THE TICKLER, soldiers in his service,
— {SER AMORY LORCH}, fed to a bear by Vargo Hoat after the fall of Harrenhal.

HOUSE MARTELL

Dorne was the last of the Seven Kingdoms to swear fealty to the Iron Throne. Blood, custom, and history all set the Dornishmen apart from the other kingdoms. At the outbreak of the War of the Five Kings, Dorne took no part. With the betrothal of Myrcella Baratheon to Prince Trystane, Sunspear declared its support for King Joffrey and called its banners. The Martell banner is a red sun pierced by a golden spear. Their words are *Unbowed, Unbent, Unbroken.*

DORAN NYMEROS MARTELL, Lord of Sunspear, Prince of Dorne,
— his wife, MELLARIO, of the Free City of Norvos,
— their children:
— PRINCESS ARIANNE, their eldest daughter, heir to Sunspear,
— PRINCE QUENTYN, their elder son,
— PRINCE TRYSTANE, their younger son, betrothed to Myrcella Baratheon,
— his siblings:
— his sister, {PRINCESS ELIA}, wife of Prince Rhaegar Targaryen, slain during the Sack of King's Landing,
— their children:
— {PRINCESS RHAENYS}, a young girl, slain during the Sack of King's Landing,
— {PRINCE AEGON}, a babe, slain during the Sack of King's Landing,
— his brother, PRINCE OBERYN, called THE RED VIPER,
— Prince Oberyn's paramour, ELLARIA SAND,
— Prince Oberyn's bastard daughters, OBARA, NYMERIA,

TYENE, SARELLA, ELIA, OBELLA, DOREA, LOREZA, called THE SAND SNAKES,

— Prince Oberyn's companions:
— HARMEN ULLER, Lord of Hellholt,
— Harmen's brother, SER ULWYCK ULLER,
— SER RYON ALLYRION,
— Ser Ryon's natural son, SER DAEMON SAND, the Bastard of Godsgrace,
— DAGOS MANWOODY, Lord of Kingsgrave,
— Dagos's sons, MORS and DICKON,
— Dagos's brother, SER MYLES MANWOODY,
— SER ARRON QORGYLE,
— SER DEZIEL DALT, the Knight of Lemonwood,
— MYRIA JORDAYNE, heir to the Tor,
— LARRA BLACKMONT, Lady of Blackmont,
— her daughter, JYNESSA BLACKMONT,
— her son, PERROS BLACKMONT, a squire,
— his household:
— AREO HOTAH, a Norvoshi sellsword, captain of guards,
— MAESTER CALEOTTE, counselor, healer, and tutor,
— his lords bannermen:
— HARMEN ULLER, Lord of Hellholt,
— EDRIC DAYNE, Lord of Starfall,
— DELONNE ALLYRION, Lady of Godsgrace,
— DAGOS MANWOODY, Lord of Kingsgrave,
— LARRA BLACKMONT, Lady of Blackmont,
— TREMOND GARGALEN, Lord of Salt Shore,
— ANDERS YRONWOOD, Lord of Yronwood,
— NYMELLA TOLAND.

HOUSE TULLY

Lord Edmyn Tully of Riverrun was one of the first of the river lords to swear fealty to Aegon the Conqueror. The victorious Aegon rewarded him by raising House Tully to dominion over all the lands of the Trident. The Tully sigil is a leaping trout, silver, on a field of rippling blue and red. The Tully words are *Family, Duty, Honor*.

HOSTER TULLY, Lord of Riverrun,
— his wife, {LADY MINISA, of House Whent}, died in childbed,
— their children:
— CATELYN, widow of Lord Eddard Stark of Winterfell,
— her eldest son, ROBB STARK, Lord of Winterfell, King in the North, and King of the Trident,
— her daughter, SANSA STARK, a maid of twelve, captive at King's Landing,
— her daughter, ARYA STARK, ten, missing for a year,
— her son, BRANDON STARK, eight, believed dead,
— her son, RICKON STARK, four, believed dead,
— LYSA, widow of Lord Jon Arryn of the Eyrie,
— her son, ROBERT, Lord of the Eyrie and Defender of the Vale, a sickly boy of seven years,
— SER EDMURE, his only son, heir to Riverrun,
— Ser Edmure's friends and companions:
— SER MARQ PIPER, heir to Pinkmaiden,
— LORD LYMOND GOODBROOK,
— SER RONALD VANCE, called THE BAD, and his brothers, SER HUGO, SER ELLERY, and KIRTH,
— PATREK MALLISTER, LUCAS BLACKWOOD, SER

  PERWYN FREY, TRISTAN RYGER, SER ROBERT
  PAEGE,
— his brother, SER BRYNDEN, called The Blackfish,
— his household:
 — MAESTER VYMAN, counselor, healer, and tutor,
 — SER DESMOND GRELL, master-at-arms,
 — SER ROBIN RYGER, captain of the guard,
  — LONG LEW, ELWOOD, DELP, guardsmen,
 — UTHERYDES WAYN, steward of Riverrun,
 — RYMUND THE RHYMER, a singer,
— his lords bannermen:
 — JONOS BRACKEN, Lord of the Stone Hedge,
 — JASON MALLISTER, Lord of Seagard,
 — WALDER FREY, Lord of the Crossing,
 — CLEMENT PIPER, Lord of Pinkmaiden Castle,
 — KARYL VANCE, Lord of Wayfarer's Rest,
 — NORBERT VANCE, Lord of Atranta,
 — THEOMAR SMALLWOOD, Lord of Acorn Hall,
  — his wife, LADY RAVELLA, of House Swann,
  — their daughter, CARELLEN,
 — WILLIAM MOOTON, Lord of Maidenpool,
 — SHELLA WHENT, dispossessed Lady of Harrenhal,
 — SER HALMON PAEGE.
 — TYTOS BLACKWOOD, Lord of Raventree

HOUSE TYRELL

The Tyrells rose to power as stewards to the Kings of the Reach, whose domain included the fertile plains of the southwest from the Dornish marches and Blackwater Rush to the shores of the Sunset Sea. Through the female line, they claim descent from Garth Greenhand, gardener king of the First Men, who wore a crown of vines and flowers and made the land bloom. When Mern IX, last king of House Gardener, was slain on the Field of Fire, his steward Harlen Tyrell surrendered Highgarden to Aegon the Conqueror. Aegon granted him the castle and dominion over the Reach. The Tyrell sigil is a golden rose on a grass-green field. Their words are *Growing Strong*.

Lord Mace Tyrell declared his support for Renly Baratheon at the onset of the War of the Five Kings, and gave him the hand of his daughter Margaery. Upon Renly's death, Highgarden made alliance with House Lannister, and Margaery was betrothed to King Joffrey.

MACE TYRELL, Lord of Highgarden, Warden of the South, Defender of the Marches, and High Marshall of the Reach,
— his wife, LADY ALERIE, of House Hightower of Oldtown,
— their children:
— WILLAS, their eldest son, heir to Highgarden,
— SER GARLAN, called THE GALLANT, their second son,
— his wife, LADY LEONETTE of House Fossoway,
— SER LORAS, the Knight of Flowers, their youngest son, a Sworn Brother of the Kingsguard,
— MARGAERY, their daughter, a widow of fifteen years, betrothed to King Joffrey I Baratheon,
— Margaery's companions and ladies-in-waiting:
— her cousins, MEGGA, ALLA, and ELINOR TYRELL,

   — Elinor's betrothed, ALYN AMBROSE, squire,

   — LADY ALYSANNE BULWER, a girl of eight,

   — MEREDYTH CRANE, called MERRY,

   — TAENA OF MYR, wife to LORD ORTON MERRY-
     WEATHER,

   — LADY ALYCE GRACEFORD,

   — SEPTA NYSTERICA, a sister of the Faith,

— his widowed mother, LADY OLENNA of House Redwyne, called
the Queen of Thorns,

   — Lady Olenna's guardsmen, ARRYK and ERRYK, called LEFT
   and RIGHT,

— his sisters:

   — LADY MINA, wed to Paxter Redwyne, Lord of the Arbor,

   — their children:

     — SER HORAS REDWYNE, twin to Hobber, mocked as
      HORROR,

     — SER HOBBER REDWYNE, twin to Horas, mocked as
      SLOBBER,

     — DESMERA REDWYNE, a maid of sixteen,

   — LADY JANNA, wed to Ser Jon Fossoway,

— his uncles and cousins:

   — his father's brother, GARTH, called THE GROSS, Lord Seneschal of Highgarden,

     — Garth's bastard sons, GARSE and GARRETT FLOWERS,

   — his father's brother, SER MORYN, Lord Commander of the
   City Watch of Oldtown,

     — Moryn's son, {SER LUTHOR}, m. Lady Elyn Norridge,

      — Luthor's son, SER THEODORE, m. Lady Lia Serry,

       — Theodore's daughter, ELINOR,

       — Theodore's son, LUTHOR, a squire,

      — Luthor's son, MAESTER MEDWICK,

      — Luthor's daughter, OLENE, m. Ser Leo Blackbar,

     — Moryn's son, LEO, called LEO THE LAZY,

   — his father's brother, MAESTER GORMON, a scholar of the
   Citadel,

   — his cousin, {SER QUENTIN}, died at Ashford,

     — Quentin's son, SER OLYMER, m. Lady Lysa Meadows,

      — Olymer's sons, RAYMUND and RICKARD,

      — Olymer's daughter, MEGGA,

   — his cousin, MAESTER NORMUND, in service at
   Blackcrown,

   — his cousin, {SER VICTOR}, slain by the Smiling Knight of the
   Kingswood Brotherhood,

— Victor's daughter, VICTARIA, m. {Lord Jon Bulwer}, died of a summer fever,
— their daughter, LADY ALYSANNE BULWER, eight,
— Victor's son, SER LEO, m. Lady Alys Beesbury,
— Leo's daughters, ALLA and LEONA,
— Leo's sons, LYONEL, LUCAS, and LORENT,

— his household at Highgarden:
— MAESTER LOMYS, counselor, healer, and tutor,
— IGON VYRWEL, captain of the guard,
— SER VORTIMER CRANE, master-at-arms,
— BUTTERBUMPS, fool and jester, hugely fat,

— his lords bannermen:
— RANDYLL TARLY, Lord of Horn Hill,
— PAXTER REDWYNE, Lord of the Arbor,
— ARWYN OAKHEART, Lady of Old Oak,
— MATHIS ROWAN, Lord of Goldengrove,
— ALESTER FLORENT, Lord of Brightwater Keep, a rebel in support of Stannis Baratheon,
— LEYTON HIGHTOWER, Voice of Oldtown, Lord of the Port,
— ORTON MERRYWEATHER, Lord of Longtable,
— LORD ARTHUR AMBROSE,
— his knights and sworn swords:
— SER MARK MULLENDORE, crippled during the Battle of the Blackwater,
— SER JON FOSSOWAY, of the green-apple Fossoways,
— SER TANTON FOSSOWAY, of the red-apple Fossoways.

REBELS, ROGUES, AND SWORN BROTHERS

THE SWORN BROTHERS OF THE NIGHT'S WATCH

(ranging Beyond the Wall)

JEOR MORMONT, called THE OLD BEAR, Lord Commander of the Night's Watch,
- — JON SNOW, the Bastard of Winterfell, his steward and squire, lost while scouting the Skirling Pass,
  - — GHOST, his direwolf, white and silent,
  - — EDDISON TOLLETT, called DOLOROUS EDD, his squire,
- — THOREN SMALLWOOD, commanding the rangers,
  - — DYWEN, DIRK, SOFTFOOT, GRENN, BEDWYCK called GIANT, OLLO LOPHAND, GRUBBS, BERNARR called BROWN BERNARR, another BERNARR called BLACK BERNARR, TIM STONE, ULMER OF KINGSWOOD, GARTH called GREYFEATHER, GARTH OF GREENA-WAY, GARTH OF OLDTOWN, ALAN OF ROSBY, RON-NEL HARCLAY, AETHAN, RYLES, MAWNEY, rangers,
- — JARMEN BUCKWELL, commanding the scouts,
  - — BANNEN, KEDGE WHITEYE, TUMBERJON, FORNIO, GOADY, rangers and scouts,
- — SER OTTYN WYTHERS, commanding the rearguard,
- — SER MALADOR LOCKE, commanding the baggage,
  - — DONNEL HILL, called SWEET DONNEL, his squire and steward,
  - — HAKE, a steward and cook,
  - — CHETT, an ugly steward, keeper of hounds,

— SAMWELL TARLY, a fat steward, keeper of ravens, mocked as SER PIGGY,

— LARK called THE SISTERMAN, his cousin ROLLEY OF SISTERTON, CLUBFOOT KARL, MASLYN, SMALL PAUL, SAWWOOD, LEFT HAND LEW, ORPHAN OSS, MUTTERING BILL, stewards,

— {QHORIN HALFHAND}, commanding the rangers from the Shadow Tower, slain in the Skirling Pass,

— {SQUIRE DALBRIDGE, EGGEN}, rangers, slain in the Skirling Pass,

— STONESNAKE, a ranger and mountaineer, lost afoot in Skirling Pass,

— BLANE, Qhorin Halfhand's second, commanding the Shadow Tower men on the Fist of the First Men,

— SER BYAM FLINT,

(at Castle Black)
BOWEN MARSH, Lord Steward and castellan,

— MAESTER AEMON (TARGARYEN), healer and counselor, a blind man, one hundred years old,

— his steward, CLYDAS,

— BENJEN STARK, First Ranger, missing, feared dead,

— SER WYNTON STOUT, eighty years a ranger,

— SER ALADALE WYNCH, PYPAR, DEAF DICK FOLLARD, HAIRY HAL, BLACK JACK BULWER, ELRON, MATTHAR, rangers,

— OTHELL YARWYCK, First Builder,

— SPARE BOOT, YOUNG HENLY, HALDER, ALBETT, KEGS, SPOTTED PATE OF MAIDENPOOL, builders,

— DONAL NOYE, armorer, smith, and steward, one-armed,

— THREE-FINGER HOBB, steward and chief cook,

— TIM TANGLETONGUE, EASY, MULLY, OLD HENLY, CUGEN, RED ALYN OF THE ROSEWOOD, JEREN, stewards,

— SEPTON CELLADOR, a drunken devout,

— SER ENDREW TARTH, master-at-arms,

— RAST, ARRON, EMRICK, SATIN, HOP-ROBIN, recruits in training,

— CONWY, GUEREN, recruiters and collectors,

(at Eastwatch-by-the-Sea)
COTTER PYKE, Commander Eastwatch,

— MAESTER HARMUNE, healer and counselor,

— SER ALLISER THORNE, master-at-arms,
— JANOS SLYNT, former commander of the City Watch of King's Landing, briefly Lord of Harrenhal,
— SER GLENDON HEWETT,
— DAREON, steward and singer,
— IRON EMMETT, a ranger famed for his strength,

(at Shadow Tower)
SER DENYS MALLISTER, Commander, Shadow Tower
— his steward and squire, WALLACE MASSEY,
— MAESTER MULLIN, healer and counselor.

THE BROTHERHOOD WITHOUT BANNERS
AN OUTLAW FELLOWSHIP

BERIC DONDARRION, Lord of Blackhaven, called THE LIGHTNING
LORD, oft reported dead,
— his right hand, THOROS OF MYR, a red priest,
— his squire, EDRIC DAYNE, Lord of Starfall, twelve,
— his followers:
— LEM, called LEM LEMONCLOAK, a one-time soldier,
— HARWIN, son of Hullen, formerly in service to Lord Eddard
Stark at Winterfell,
— GREENBEARD, a Tyroshi sellsword,
— TOM OF SEVENSTREAMS, a singer of dubious report, called
TOM SEVENSTRINGS and TOM O' SEVENS,
— ANGUY THE ARCHER, a bowman from the Dornish
Marches,
— JACK-BE-LUCKY, a wanted man, short an eye,
— THE MAD HUNTSMAN, of Stoney Sept,
— KYLE, NOTCH, DENNETT, longbowmen,
— MERRIT O' MOONTOWN, WATTY THE MILLER, LIKELY
LUKE, MUDGE, BEARDLESS DICK, outlaws in his band,

— at the Inn of the Kneeling Man:
— SHARNA, the innkeep, a cook and midwife,
— her husband, called HUSBAND,
— BOY, an orphan of the war,

— at the Peach, a brothel in Stoney Sept:
   — TANSY, the red-haired proprietor,
      — ALYCE, CASS, LANNA, JYZENE, HELLY, BELLA, some
      of her peaches,

— at Acorn Hall, the seat of House Smallwood:
   — LADY RAVELLA, formerly of House Swann, wife to Lord
   Theomar Smallwood,

— here and there and elsewhere:
   — LORD LYMOND LYCHESTER, an old man of wandering
   wit, who once held Ser Maynard at the bridge,
      — his young caretaker, MAESTER ROONE,
   — the ghost of High Heart,
   — the Lady of the Leaves,
   — the septon at Sallydance.

the WILDLINGS, or the FREE FOLK

MANCE RAYDER, King-beyond-the-Wall,
— DALLA, his pregnant wife,
— VAL, her younger sister,

— his chiefs and captains:
— HARMA, called DOGSHEAD, commanding his van,
— THE LORD OF BONES, mocked as RATTLESHIRT, leader of a war band,
— YGRITTE, a young spearwife, a member of his band,
— RYK, called LONGSPEAR, a member of his band,
— RAGWYLE, LENYL, members of his band,
— his captive, JON SNOW, the crow-come-over,
— GHOST, Jon's direwolf, white and silent,
— STYR, Magnar of Thenn,
— JARL, a young raider, Val's lover,
— GRIGG THE GOAT, ERROK, QUORT, BODGER, DEL, BIG BOIL, HEMPEN DAN, HENK THE HELM, LENN, TOEFINGER, STONE THUMBS, raiders,
— TORMUND, Mead-King of Ruddy Hall, called GIANTS-BANE, TALL-TALKER, HORN-BLOWER, and BREAKER OF ICE, also THUNDERFIST, HUSBAND TO BEARS, SPEAKER TO GODS, and FATHER OF HOSTS, leader of a war band,
— his sons, TOREGG THE TALL, TORWYRD THE TAME, DORMUND, and DRYN, his daughter MUNDA,

— {ORELL, called ORELL THE EAGLE}, a skinchanger slain by Jon Snow in the Skirling Pass,

— MAG MAR TUN DOH WEG, called MAG THE MIGHTY, of the giants,

— VARAMYR called SIXSKINS, a skinchanger, master of three wolves, a shadowcat, and a snow bear,

— THE WEEPER, a raider and leader of a war band,

— {ALFYN CROWKILLER}, a raider, slain by Qhorin Halfhand of the Night's Watch,

CRASTER, of Craster's Keep, who kneels to none,

— GILLY, his daughter and wife, great with child,

— DYAH, FERNY, NELLA, three of his nineteen wives.

ACKNOWLEDGMENTS

If the bricks aren't well made, the wall falls down.

This is an awfully big wall I'm building here, so I need a lot of bricks. Fortunately, I know a lot of brickmakers, and all sorts of other useful folks as well.

Thanks and appreciation, once more, to those good friends who so kindly lent me their expertise (and in some cases, even their *books*) so my bricks would be nice and solid – to my Archmaester Sage Walker, to First Builder Carl Keim, to Melinda Snodgrass my master of horse.

And as ever, to Parris.

ABOUT THE AUTHOR

GEORGE R. R. MARTIN sold his first story in 1971 and hasn't stopped. As a writer-producer, he worked on *The Twilight Zone, Beauty and the Beast,* and various feature films and pilots that were never made. In the mid '90s he returned to prose and began work on A Song of Ice and Fire. He has been in the Seven Kingdoms ever since. He lives with the lovely Parris in Santa Fe, New Mexico.

Also by
GEORGE R. R. MARTIN

Novels

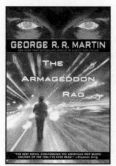

The
Armageddon Rag

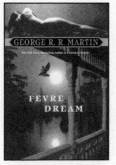

Fevre Dream

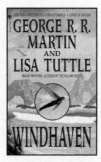

Windhaven

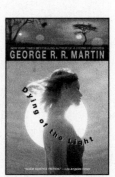

Dying of the Light

Short Stories

Dreamsongs:
Volume I

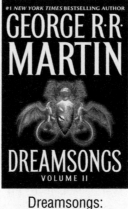

Dreamsongs:
Volume II

Also available in Audio and eBook
THE RANDOM HOUSE PUBLISHING GROUP
www.GeorgeRRMartin.com

Now, here's a special preview of
the next book in

George R. R. Martin's

landmark series

A FEAST FOR CROWS

the riveting sequel to
A GAME OF THRONES
A CLASH OF KINGS
and
A STORM OF SWORDS

Available now

CERSEI

A cold rain fell from a slate grey sky, turning the walls·and ramparts of the Red Keep dark as blood. The queen held the king's hand and led him firmly across the muddy yard to where her litter waited with its escort. "Uncle Jaime said I could ride my horse and throw pennies to the smallfolk," the boy objected.

"Do you want to catch a chill?" Tommen had never been as robust as Joffrey. "Your lord grandfather would want you to look a proper king at his wake. We cannot appear at the Great Sept wet and bedraggled." *Bad enough I must wear mourning again.* Black had never been a happy color on her. With her fair skin, it made her look half a corpse herself. Cersei had risen an hour before dawn to bathe and fix her hair, and she did not intend to let the rain destroy her efforts.

Inside the litter, Tommen settled back against his pillows and peered out at the falling rain. "The gods are weeping for grandfather. Lady Jocelyn says the raindrops are their tears."

"Jocelyn Swyft is a fool. If the gods could weep, they would have wept for your brother. Rain is rain. Close the curtain before you let any more in. That mantle is sable, would you have it soaked?"

Tommen did as he was bid. She was glad of that, yet his meekness troubled her as well. A king had to be strong. *Joffrey would have argued with me. He was never easy to cow.* "You should not slump so," she told Tommen, just to see. "Sit like a king. Put your shoulders back, and straighten your crown. Would you have it falling off of your head in front of all your lords?"

"No, Mother." The boy sat straight and reached up to fix the crown. Joff's crown was too big for him. Tommen had always been inclined to plumpness, but his face seemed thinner now. *Is he eating well?* She must remember to ask the steward. She could not risk Tommen growing ill, not with Myrcella in the hands of the Dornishmen. *He will grow into Joff's crown in time.* But until he did, a smaller one might be needed, one that did not threaten to swallow his head. She would take it up with the goldsmiths.

The litter made its slow way down Aegon's High Hill. Two Kingsguard went before them, white knights on white horses with their cloaks hanging sodden from their shoulders. Behind came fifty Lannister guardsmen in gold and crimson.

Tommen peered through the drapes at the empty streets. "I thought there would be more people. When Father died all the people came out and watched us go by."

"This rain has driven them inside." The Kingslanders had never loved Lord Tywin, not even before the Sack. *He never wanted love, though. Only respect, and all the honors due him. 'You cannot eat love, nor buy a horse with it, nor warm your halls on a cold night,' she heard him tell Jaime once, when her brother had been as young as Tommen.*

At the Great Sept of Baelor, that magnificence in marble atop Visenya's Hill, the little knot of mourners were outnumbered by the gold cloaks that Ser Addam Marbrand had drawn up across the plaza. *More will turn out later,* the queen told herself as Ser Meryn Trant helped her from the litter. Only the highborn and their retinues were to be admitted to the morning service; there would be another in the afternoon for the commons, and the evening prayers were open to all. Cersei would need to return for that, so that the smallfolk might see her mourn. Certain things were expected of her. *The mob must have its show.* It was a nuisance, though. She had offices to fill, letters to write, a war to win, a realm to rule.

The High Septon met them at the top of the steps. A bent old man with a wispy grey beard, he was so stooped by the weight of his ornate embroidered robes that his eyes were on a level with the queen's breasts . . . though his crown, an airy confection of cut crystal and spun gold, added a good foot and a half to his height. Lord Tywin had given him that crown to replace the one that was lost when the mob killed the previous High Septon. They had pulled the fat fool from his litter and torn him apart, the day Myrcella sailed for Dorne. *That one was a great glutton, and biddable. This one . . .* This High Septon was of Tyrion's making, Cersei recalled suddenly. It was a disquieting thought.

The old man's spotted hand looked like a chicken claw as it poked from a sleeve encrusted with golden scrollwork and small crystals. Cersei knelt on the wet marble and kissed his fingers, and bid Tommen to do the same. *What does he know of me? How much did the dwarf tell him?* The High Septon smiled as he helped her back to her feet and escorted her inside, but was it a threatening smile full of unspoken knowledge, or just some vacuous twitch of an old man's wrinkled lips? She found it impossible to tell.

She held Tommen's hand as they made their way through the Hall of Lamps beneath globes of leaded glass. Trant and Kettleblack flanked them, water dripping from their wet cloaks to puddle on the floor. The High Septon walked slowly, leaning on a weirwood staff topped by an crystal orb. Seven of the Most Devout attended him, shimmering in cloth-of-silver. Tommen followed, dressed in cloth-of-gold beneath his sable mantle. The queen wore an old gown of black velvet lined with ermine. There'd been no time to have a new one made, and she could not wear the same dress she had worn for Joffrey, nor the one she'd buried Robert in.

At least I will not be expected to don mourning for Tyrion. I shall dress in crimson silk and cloth-of-gold for that, and wear rubies in my hair. The man who brought her the dwarf's head would be raised to lordship, no matter how mean and low his birth or station. Pycelle's ravens were carrying her promise to every part of the Seven Kingdoms even now, and soon enough word would cross the narrow sea to the Nine Free Cities and the lands beyond. *Let the Imp run to the ends of the earth, he will not escape me.*

They stepped through the inner doors together, into the cavernous heart of the Great Sept, and began their slow progress down a wide aisle, one of seven that met beneath the dome. To right and left, highborn mourners sank at their passing. Many of her father's bannermen were here, and knights who had fought beside Lord Tywin in half a hundred battles. The sight of them made her feel more confident. *I am not without friends.*

Under the lofty dome of glass and gold and crystal, Lord Tywin Lannister's body rested upon a stepped marble bier. At its head Jaime stood at vigil, his one good hand curled about the hilt of a tall golden greatsword whose point rested on the floor. The hooded cloak he wore was as white as freshly fallen snow, and the scales of his long hauberk were mother-of-pearl chased with gold. *Lord Tywin would have wanted him in Lannister gold and crimson,* she thought when she saw his garb. *It always angered him to see Jaime all in white.* Her brother was growing his beard again as well. The stubble covered his jaw and cheeks, and gave him a rough, uncouth look. *He might at least have waited till Father's bones were interred beneath the Rock.*

Cersei led the king up three short steps to kneel beside the body. Tommen's eyes were filled with tears. "Weep quietly," she told him, leaning close. "You are a king, not a squalling child. Your lords are watching you." The boy swiped the tears away with the back of his hand. He had her eyes, emerald green, as large and bright as Jaime's eyes had been when he was Tommen's age. Her brother had been such a *pretty* boy . . . but fierce as Joffrey, a lion cub in truth. The queen put her arm around Tommen and kissed his golden curls. *He will need me to teach him how to rule, and keep him safe from his enemies.* Some of them stood around them even now, pretending to be friends.

The silent sisters had armored Lord Tywin as if to fight some final battle. He wore his finest plate, heavy steel enameled a deep, dark crimson, with gold inlay on his gauntlets, greaves, and breastplate. His rondels were golden sunbursts; a golden lioness crouched upon each shoulder; a maned lion crested the greathelm beside his head. Upon his chest lay a longsword in a gilded scabbard studded with rubies, his hands folded about its hilt in gloves of gilded mail. *Even in death his face is noble,* she thought, *although the mouth* . . . The corners of her father's lips curved upward ever so slightly, giving him a look of vague bemusement. *That should not be.* She blamed Pycelle; she should have told the silent sisters that Lord Tywin Lannister never smiled. *The man is as useless as nipples on a breastplate.* Cersei resolved once more to demand a replacement of the Citadel.

That odd half-smile made Lord Tywin seem less fearful, somehow. That, and the fact that his eyes were closed. Her father's eyes had always been unsettling; pale green, almost luminous, and flecked with gold. His eyes could see inside you, could see how weak and worthless and ugly you were down deep. *When he looked at you, you knew.*

Unbidden, a memory came back to her, of the feast King Aerys had thrown to welcome her when first she'd come to court, a girl as green as summer grass. When old Merryweather the master of coin said something about raising the duty on wine, Lord Rykker boomed out, "If the crown wants for gold, His Grace can keep Lord Tywin on his chamberpot." The king and his lickspittles laughed loudly, whilst Father stared at Rykker over his wine cup. Long after the merriment had died that gaze lingered. Rykker turned away, turned back, met Father's eyes and then ignored them, drank a tankard of ale, and finally bolted to his feet and stalked off red-faced, defeated by a pair of unflinching eyes.

His eyes are closed forever now, she thought, *but my eyes are green as well. It is my look they will flinch from now, my frown that they must fear. I am a lion too.*

It was gloomy within the sept, with the sky so grey outside. If the rain ever stopped, the sun would slant down through the hanging crystals to drape the corpse from head to heel in rainbows. The Lord of Casterly Rock deserved rainbows, Cersei thought. He had been a great man. *I shall be greater, though. A thousand years from now, when the maesters write about this time, you shall be remembered only as Queen Cersei's sire.*

"Mother." Tommen tugged her sleeve. "What smells so bad?"

My lord father. "Death." She could smell it too; a faint whisper of decay that made her want to wrinkle her nose. Cersei paid it no mind. The seven septons in the silver robes stood behind the bier, beseeching the Father Above to judge Lord Tywin justly. When they were done, seventy-seven septas gathered beneath the statue of the Mother and began to sing to her for mercy. Tommen was fidgeting by then, and even the queen's knees had begun to ache. She glanced up at Jaime. Her twin stood there as if he had been carved from stone, and would not meet her eyes.

On the benches behind him her uncle Kevan knelt with his thick shoulders slumped, his son beside him. *Lancel looks worse than Father.* Only seventeen, her cousin might have passed for seventy: grey-faced, gaunt, with hollow cheeks, sunken eyes, and hair as white and brittle as chalk. *How can Lancel be among the living when Tywin Lannister is dead? Have the gods taken leave of their wits?*

Lord Gyles was coughing more than usual, and covering his nose with a square of red silk. *He can smell it too.* Grand Maester Pycelle had his eyes closed. *Asleep again,* she decided.

To the right of the bier were the Tyrells, the Lord of Highgarden foremost amongst them, flanked by his hideous mother and vacuous wife, his son Garlan and his daughter Margaery. *Queen Margaery,* she reminded herself; Joff's widow and Tommen's future wife. Twice wedded and never bedded, they said, but Cersei had her own suspicions. Margaery looked very much like her brother, the Knight of Flowers. The queen wondered if they had other things as common as well. *Our little rose has a good many ladies waiting attendance on her, night and day.* They stood behind her now, almost a dozen of them. Cersei studied their faces, wondering which of them might have the loosest tongue. *Who is the most fearful, the most wanton, the hungriest for favor?* She really must find out.

It was a relief when the singing ended. The smell coming off her father's corpse seemed to have grown stronger. Most of the mourners had the decency to pretend that nothing was amiss, but Cersei saw some of Margaery's ladies wrinkling their little Tyrell noses. As she and Tommen were walking back down the aisle the queen thought she heard someone mutter "privy" and chortle, but when she turned her head to see who had spoken a sea of solemn faces gazed at her blankly. *They would never have dared make japes about him when he was still alive. He would have turned their bowels to water with a look.*

Back out in the Hall of Lamps, the mourners were buzzing thick as flies. The Redwyne twins kissed her hand, and their father her cheek. Hallyne the Pyromancer promised that a flaming hand would burn in the sky above the city on the day her father's bones went west. Lord Gyles announced that he had hired a master stonecarver to make a mighty statue of Lord Tywin, to stand eternal vigil beside the Lion Gate. Ser Lyman Turnberry appeared with a patch over his right eye, swearing that he would wear it until he could bring her the head of her dwarf brother.

"You are too kind." Cersei kissed his cheek and moved away quickly, looking for Tommen. He was easy enough to find, with two Kingsguard beside him in white armor, but to her annoyance she saw that he had fallen into the clutches of Margaery Tyrell and her grandmother. The Queen of Thorns was almost of a height with Tommen, and for an instant Cersei took her for another child.

Before she could rescue him, the press brought her face-to-face with her uncle. When the queen reminded him of their meeting later, Ser

Kevan gave a weary nod, and begged leave to withdraw. But Lancel lingered behind, the very picture of a man with one foot in the grave. *But is he climbing in or climbing out?*

Cersei forced herself to smile. "Lancel, I am happy to see you looking so much stronger. Maester Ballabar brought us such dire reports, we feared for your life. But I would have thought you on your way to Darry by now, to take up your lordship." Her father had made Lancel a lord after the Battle of the Blackwater, as a sop to his brother Kevan.

"My father will ride with me to Darry when he escorts Lord Tywin's bones back to Casterly Rock." Her cousin's voice was as wispy as the mustache on his upper lip. Though his hair had gone white, his mustache fuzz remained a sandy color. Cersei had often gazed up at it while the boy was inside her, pumping dutifully away. *It looks like a smudge of dirt on his lip.* She used to threaten to scrub it off with a little spit. "The riverlands have need of a strong hand," Lancel added.

A pity that they're getting such a feeble one, she wanted to say. Instead she smiled. "And you are to be wed as well."

A gloomy look passed across the young knight's ravaged face. "A Frey girl, and not of my choosing. She is not even maiden. A widow, of Darry blood. My father says that will help me with the peasants, but the peasants are all dead." He reached for her hand, looking as if he might burst into tears. "It is cruel, Cersei. Your Grace knows that I love—"

"—House Lannister," she finished for him. "No one can doubt that, Lancel. May your wife give you strong sons." *Best not let her father host the wedding, though.* "I know you will do many noble deeds in Darry."

Lancel nodded, plainly miserable. "When it seemed that I might die, my father brought the High Septon to pray for me. He is a good man, Cersei. He says the Mother spared me for some holy purpose, so I might atone for my sins." His eyes were wet and shiny, a child's eyes in an old man's face.

Cersei wondered how he intended to atone for her. *Mine own blood,* she thought, disgusted. Was she the only lion left alive? *Knighting him was a mistake, and bedding him a bigger one.* Lancel was a weak reed, and she liked this newfound piety of his not at all; he had been much more amusing when he was trying to be Jaime. *What has this mewling fool told the High Septon? And what will he tell his little Frey when they lay together in the dark?* If he wished to boast of bedding a queen, well, men were always lying about women. She would put it down as the braggadocio of a callow boy smitten by unrequited love. *But if he sings of Robert and the strongwine . . .* "Atonement is best achieved through prayer," Cersei told her cousin pointedly. "*Silent* prayer." She left him to think about that, and girded herself to face the Tyrell host.

Margaery embraced her like a sister, which the queen found presumptuous, but this was not the place to reproach her. Lady Alerie and the cousins contented themselves with kissing fingers. Lady Graceford, who was large with child, asked the queen's leave to name it Tywin if it were a boy, or Lanna if it were a girl. *Lickspittles like you will drown the realm in Tywins,* she reflected, but she graciously gave consent, feigning delight.

Lady Merryweather was the only one who truly pleased her. "Your Grace," she said, in her sultry Myrish tones, "I have sent word to my friends across the narrow sea, asking them to seize the Imp at once should he show his ugly face in the Free Cities."

"Do you have many friends across the water?"

"In Myr, many. In Lys as well, and Tyrosh. Men of power."

Cersei could well believe it. The Myrish woman was too beautiful by half; long-legged and full-breasted, with smooth olive skin, ripe lips, huge dark eyes, and thick black hair that always looked as if she'd just come from bed. *She even smells like sin, like some exotic lotus.* "Lord Merryweather and I wish only to serve Your Grace and the little king," the woman said, with a look that was as pregnant as Lady Graceford.

This one is ambitious, and her lord is proud but poor. "We must speak again, my lady. Taena, is it? You are most kind. I know that we shall be great friends."

And then the Lord of Highgarden himself fell upon her.

Mace Tyrell was no more than ten years older than Cersei, yet she thought of him as her father's age, not her own. He was not quite so tall as Lord Tywin had been, but elsewise he was bigger, with a thick chest and a gut that had grown even thicker. His hair was chestnut colored and his eyes looked a bit like chestnuts too, but there were specks of white and grey in his beard. His face was often red. "Lord Tywin was a great man, and will be greatly missed," he declared ponderously after he had kissed both her cheeks. "No man alive is fit to don his armor, that is plain. We all grieve for him."

"My lord is good to say so."

"If there is aught that I might do to serve in this dark hour, Your Grace need only ask."

If you want to be Hand, my lord, at least have the courage to say it plainly. The queen smiled at him warmly. *Let him read into that as much as he likes.* "His Grace will be heartened to hear it . . . though surely you are needed in the Reach."

"My son Willas is an able lad," the man replied, refusing to take her pefectly good hint. "His leg may be twisted but he has no want of wits. And Garlan will soon take Brightwater. Between them the Reach will be in good hands, if it happens that I am needed elsewhere. The governance of the realm must come first, Lord Tywin often said. And I am pleased to bring Your Grace good tidings in that regard. My uncle Garth has agreed to serve as master of coin, as your lord father wished. He is making his way to Oldtown to take ship. His sons will accompany him. Lord Tywin mentioned something about finding places for the two of them as well. Perhaps in the City Watch."

The queen's smile had frozen so hard she feared her teeth might crack.

Garth the Gross on the small council and his two bastards in the gold cloaks. Do the Tyrells think I will just serve the realm up to them on a gilded platter? The arrogance of it took her breath away.

"Garth has served me well as Lord Seneschal, as he served my father before me," Tyrell was going on. "Littlefinger had a nose for gold, I grant you, but Garth—"

"My lord," Cersei broke in, "I fear there has been some misunderstanding. I have asked Lord Gyles Rosby to serve as our new master of coin, and he has done me the honor of accepting."

Mace gaped at her. "Rosby? That . . . *cougher*? But . . . the matter was agreed, Your Grace. Garth is on his way to Oldtown."

"Best send a raven to Lord Hightower and ask him to make certain your uncle does not take ship. We would hate for Garth to brave an autumn sea for nought." She smiled pleasantly.

A flush crept up Lord Tyrell's thick neck and spread across his cheeks. "This . . . your lord father assured me . . ."

His mother appeared beside him, and slid her arm through his own. "It would seem that Lord Tywin did not share his plans with our regent, I can't *imagine* why. Still, there 'tis, no use hectoring Her Grace. She is quite right, you must write Lord Leyton before Garth boards a ship. You know the sea will sicken him, and make his farting worse." She gave Cersei a toothless smile. "Your council chambers will smell sweeter with Lord Gyles, though I daresay that coughing would drive me to distraction. We all adore dear old Uncle Garth, but the man is flatulent, that cannot be gainsaid. I do abhor foul smells." Her wrinkled face wrinkled up even more. "I caught a whiff of something unpleasant in the holy sept, in truth. Mayhaps you smelled it too?"

"No," Cersei said coldly. "A scent, you say?"

"More like a stink."

"Perhaps you miss your autumn roses. We have kept you here too long." The sooner she rid the court of Lady Olenna the better. Lord Tyrell would doubtless send off a goodly number of his soldiers to see his mother safely home.

"I do long for the fragrances of Highgarden, I confess it," said the old lady, "but of course I can not leave until I have seen my sweet Margaery wed to your precious little Tommen."

"I await that day eagerly as well," Lord Tyrell put in, too loudly. "Lord Tywin and I were on the very point of setting a date, as it happens. Perhaps you and I might take up that discussion, Your Grace."

"Soon."

"Soon will serve," said Lady Olenna, with a sniff. "Now come along, Mace, let Her Grace get on with her . . . grief."

I will see you dead, old woman, Cersei promised herself as the Queen of Thorns tottered off to her towering guardsmen, a pair of seven footers she called Left and Right. *We'll see how sweet a corpse you make.*

She went in search of Tommen again, rescued him from Margaery and her cousins, and made for the doors. Outside, the rain had finally stopped. The autumn air smelled sweet and fresh. Tommen started to take his crown off.

"Put that back on," Cersei commanded him.

"It makes my neck hurt," he said, but he did as he was bid. "Will I be married soon? Margaery says that as soon we're wed we can go to Highgarden."

"You are not going to Highgarden, but you can ride back to the castle." Cersei beckoned to Ser Meryn Trant. "Bring His Grace a mount, and ask Lord Gyles if he would do me the honor of sharing my litter." Things were moving more quickly than she had anticipated; there was no time to be squandered.

Tommen was happy at the prospect of a ride, and of course Lord Gyles was honored by her invitation . . . though when she asked him to be her master of coin, he began coughing so violently that she feared he might die right then and there. But the Mother was merciful, and Gyles eventually recover sufficiently to accept, and even began coughing out the names of men he wanted to replace, customs officers and wool factors appointed by Littlefinger, even one of the keepers of the keys.

"Name the cow what you will, so long as the milk flows. And should the question arise, you joined the council yesterday."

"Yester—" A fit of coughing bent him over. "Yesterday. To be sure." Lord Gyles coughed into a square of red silk, as if to hide the blood in his spittle. Cersei pretended not to notice. She did not think that he would be her master of coin for very long. *When he dies I will find someone else.* Perhaps she would recall Littlefinger. The queen could not imagine that Petyr Baelish would be allowed to remain Lord Protector of the Vale for very long, with Lysa Arryn dead. The Vale lords were already stirring, if what Pycelle said was true. *They will take that wretched boy away from him, and he will come crawling back.*

"Your, *kaf,* Grace?" Lord Gyles dabbed his mouth. "Might I, *kaf,* ask, *kaf kaf,* who will be, *kaf,* the King's Hand?"

"My uncle," she replied absently.

It was a relief to see the gates of the Red Keep looming large before her. She gave Tommen over to the charge of his squires, and retired gratefully to her own chambers to rest.

No sooner had she eased off her shoes than Jocelyn entered timidly to say that Qyburn was without and craved audience. "Send him in," the queen commanded. *A ruler gets no rest.*

Qyburn was old, but his hair still had more ash than snow in it, and the laugh lines around his mouth made him look like some little girl's favorite grandfather. *A rather shabby grandfather, though.* The collar of his robe was frayed, and one sleeve had been torn and badly sewn. "Your Grace," he began, "I have examined Ser Gregor Clegane, as you commanded. The poison on the Viper's spear was manticore venom from the east, I would stake my life on that."

"Pycelle says no. He told my lord father that manticore venom kills the instant it reaches the heart."

"And so it does. But this venom has been *thickened* somehow so as to draw out the Mountain's dying."

"Thickened? Thickened *how*? With some other substance?"

"It may be as Your Grace suggests, though in most cases adulterating a poison only lessens its potency. It may be that the cause is . . . less natural, let us say. A spell, I think."

Is this one as big a fool as Pycelle? "So are you telling me that the Mountain is dying of some black *sorcery*?"

Qyburn ignored the mockery in her voice. "He is dying of the venom, but slowly, and in exquisite agony. My efforts to ease his pain have proved as fruitless as Pycelle's. Ser Gregor is overly accustomed to the poppy, I fear. His squire tells me that he is plagued by blinding headaches and oft quaffs the milk of the poppy as lesser men quaff ale. Be that as it may, his veins have turned black from head to heel, his water is clouded with pus, and the venom has eaten a hole in his side as large as my fist. It is a wonder that the man is still alive, if truth be told."

"His size," the queen suggested, frowning. "Gregor is a very large man. Also a very stupid one. Too stupid to know when he should die, it seems." She held out her cup, and Senelle filled it once again. "The Dornishmen want his head, and his screaming frightens Tommen. It has even been known to wake me of a night. I would say it is past time we summoned Ilyn Payn."

"Your Grace," said Qyburn, "mayhaps I might move Ser Gregor to the dungeons? His screams will not disturb you there, and I will be able to tend to him more freely."

"Tend to him?" She laughed. "Let Ser Ilyn tend to him."

"If that is Your Grace's wish," Qyburn said, "but this poison . . . it would be useful to know more about it, would it not? Send a knight to slay a knight and an archer to kill an archer, the smallfolk often say. To combat the black arts . . ." He did not finish the thought, but only smiled at her.

He is not Pycelle, that much is plain. The queen weighed him, wondering. "Why did the Citadel take your chain? Tell me true, I warn you. I will have your tongue if you lie to me."

"The archmaesters are cravens at heart. The grey sheep, Marwyn calls them. I was as skilled a healer as Ebrose, but aspired to surpass him. For hundreds of years the men of the Citadel have opened the bodies of the dead, to study the nature of life. I wished to understand the nature of death, so I opened the bodies of the living. For that crime the grey sheep shamed me and forced me into exile . . . but even now I know more of life and death than any man in Oldtown."

"Do you?" She smiled. "Very well. The Mountain is yours. Do what you will with him, but confine your studies to the black cells. When he dies, bring me his head. My father promised it to Dorne. Prince Doran would no doubt prefer to kill Gregor himself, but we all must suffer disappointments in this life."

"Very good, Your Grace." Qyburn cleared his throat. "I am am not so well provided as Pycelle, however. I must needs equip myself with certain . . ."

"I shall instruct Lord Gyles to provide you with gold sufficient for your needs. Buy yourself some new robes as well. You look as though you've wandered up from Flea Bottom. Now go."

He bowed, and went.

Her uncle arrived promptly at sunset, wearing a quilted doublet of charcoal-colored wool as somber as his face. Like all the Lannisters, Ser Kevan was fair-skinned and blond, though at five-and-fifty he had lost most of his hair. No one would ever call him comely. Thick of waist, round of shoulder, with a square jutting chin that his close-cropped yellow beard did little to conceal, he reminded her of some old mastiff . . . but a faithful old mastiff was the very thing that she required.

They ate a simple supper of beets and bread and bloody beef with a flagon of Dornish red to wash it all down. Ser Kevan ate slowly and said little, and scarcely touched his wine cup. *He broods too much on Father,* the queen decided. *He needs to be put to work to get beyond his grief.*

She said as much, when the last of the food had been cleared away and the servants had departed. "I know how much my father relied on you, Uncle. Now I must do the same."

"You need a Hand," he said, "and Jaime has refused you."

He is blunt. Very well. She glanced away. "Jaime . . . I felt so lost with Father dead, I scarce knew what I was saying. Jaime is gallant, but a bit of a fool, let us be frank. Tommen needs a more seasoned man. Someone older . . ."

"Mace Tyrell is older."

Her nostrils flared. "Never." Cersei pushed a lock of hair off her brow. "The Tyrells overreach themselves."

"You would be a fool to make Mace Tyrell your Hand," Ser Kevan warned, "but a bigger fool to make him your foe. I've heard what happened in the Hall of Lamps. Mace should have known better than to broach such matters in public, but even so, you were unwise to shame him in front of half the Reach."

"It was that, or kiss his hand and welcome another Tyrell to the small council." His reproach annoyed her. "Rosby will be more than adequate as master of coin. You've seen his horses, and that litter of his. A man that rich should have no problem finding gold. As for the Hand . . . who better to finish my father's work than the brother who shared his counsels?"

"Every man needs someone he can trust. Tywin had me, and once your mother."

"He loved her very much." Cersei refused to think about the dead whore in his bed. "I know they are together now."

"So I pray." Ser Kevan studied her face for a long moment before he replied. "You ask much of me, Cersei."

"No more than my father did."

"I am tired." Her uncle reached for his wine cup and took a swallow. "I have a wife I have not seen in two years, a dead son whose tomb I have yet to visit, another son who might have died as well. And Lancel must needs establish himself in Darry. There are outlaws stabling their horses in his great hall. Castle Darry must be made strong again, its lands protected, its burned fields ploughed and planted anew. He needs my help."

"As does Tommen." Cersei had not expected Kevan to require coaxing. *He never played coy with Father.* "The realm needs you."

"The realm. Aye. And House Lannister." He sipped his wine again. "Very well. I will remain and serve His Grace . . ."

"Very good," she started to say, but Ser Kevan raised his voice and bulled right over her.

". . . so long as you name me regent as well as Hand, and take yourself back to Casterly Rock."

For half a heartbeat Cersei could only stare at him. *What did he say?* "*I* am the regent," she reminded him.

"You were. Your father did not intend that you continue in that role. He told me of his plans to send you back to the Rock and find a new husband for you."

Cersei could feel her anger rising. "He spoke of such, yes. And I told him it was not my wish to wed again."

Her uncle was unmoved. "There are good reasons why you should, but if you are resolved against another marriage I will not force it on you. As to the other, though . . . you are the Lady of Casterly Rock now. Your place is there."

How dare you? she wanted to scream. Instead she said, "I am also the Queen Regent. My place is with my son."

"Your father thought not."

"My father is dead."

"To my grief, and the woe of all the realm. Open your eyes and look about you, Cersei. The kingdom is in ruins. Tywin might have been able to set matters aright, but . . ."

"*I* shall set matters aright!" That sounded shrill. Cersei softened her tone. "With your help, Uncle. If you will serve me as faithfully as you served my father—"

"You are not your father." His voice was hard. "Tywin regarded Jaime as his rightful heir."

"*Jaime* . . . Jaime has taken vows. The Kingsguard serve for life. Jaime never thinks, he laughs at everything and everyone and says whatever comes into his head. Jaime is a handsome fool."

"And yet he was your first choice to be the King's Hand. What does that make you, Cersei?"

"I told you, I was sick with grief, I did not think—"

"No," Ser Kevan agreed, "which is why you should return to Casterly Rock, and leave the king with those who do."

The king is my son!" Cersei rose to her feet.

"Aye," her uncle said, "and from what I saw of Joffrey, you are as unfit as a mother as you are as a ruler."

She threw the contents of her wine cup full in his face.

Ser Kevan rose with a ponderous dignity. "Your Grace." Wine trickled down his cheeks and dripped from his close-cropped beard. "With your leave, might I withdraw?"

"By what right do you presume to give *me* terms? You are no more than one of my father's household knights."

"I hold no lands, that is true. But I have certain incomes, and chests of coin set aside. My own father forgot none of his children when he died, and Tywin knew how to reward good service. I feed two hundred knights and can double that number if need be. There are freeriders who will follow my banner, and I have the gold to hire sellswords. You would be wise not to take me lightly, Your Grace . . . and wiser still not to make of me a foe."

"Are you *threatening* me?"

"Say rather than I am counseling you."

"I should throw you in a black cell."

"No. You should yield the regency to me. As you will not, however, then name me your castellan for Casterly Rock, and make either Mathis Rowan or Randyll Tarly the Hand of the King."

Tyrell bannermen, both of them. The suggestion left her speechless. *Is he bought?* she wondered. *Has he taken Tyrell gold to betray House Lannister?*

"Mathis Rowan is sensible, prudent, well-liked," her uncle went on, oblivious. "Randyll Tarly is the finest soldier in the realm. A poor Hand for peacetime, but with Tywin dead there's no better man to finish this war. Lord Tyrell cannot openly take offense if you choose one of his own bannermen as Hand. Both Tarly and Towan are able men . . . and *loyal.* Name either one, and you make him yours. You will strengthen yourself and weaken Highgarden at the same time, yet Mace will likely thank you for it." He gave a shrug. "That is my counsel, take it or no. You may make Moon Boy your Hand for all I care. My brother is dead, woman. I am going to take him home."

Traitor, she thought. *Turncloak.* She wondered how much Mace Tyrell had given him. "You would abandon your king when he needs you most," she told him. "You would abandon Tommen."

"Tommen has his mother." Ser Kevan's green eyes met her own, unblinking. A last drop of wine trembled wet and red beneath his chin, and finally fell. "Aye," he added softly, after a pause, "and his father too, I think."